THE
STORY

LOVE, LOSS
& THE LIVES OF
WOMEN

THE
STORY

LOVE, LOSS
& THE LIVES OF
WOMEN

100 GREAT SHORT
STORIES CHOSEN BY

VICTORIA
HISLOP

First published in the UK in 2013 by Head of Zeus Ltd
This paperback edition first published in 2017 by Head of Zeus Ltd

9 7 5 3 1 2 4 6 8

A CIP catalogue record for this book is available from the British Library.

ISBN (TPB): 9781786691460
ISBN (E): 9781781853603

Printed and bound by CPI Books GmbH, in Leck, Germany

Typeset by Ellipsis Digital Limited, Glasgow

Head of Zeus Ltd
First Floor East
5–8 Hardwick Street
London EC1R 4RG

WWW.HEADOFZEUS.COM

THE
STORY

LOVE, LOSS
& THE LIVES OF
WOMEN

CONTENTS

LOSS

THE LIVES OF WOMEN

INTRODUCTION

While gathering the short stories for this anthology, I have read some of the most brilliant and profound pieces of writing that I have ever come across.

The authors in this anthology range from a Nobel Prize winner, Doris Lessing, to the acknowledged queen of short stories, Alice Munro. There are Man Booker winners, Costa winners and Pulitzer winners. A few were born in the 19th century but the majority are more modern. Several of them are as yet unknown, others are household names, like Virginia Woolf. Many of the most vivid and passionate storytellers are young. And without doubt many of the most powerfully original are contemporary writers.

Apart from the writers all being female, the other guiding factor in the selection is that the stories have been written in English. The stories are varied and I am sure that no single reader will like them all. Perhaps I enjoyed certain stories because they meant something very personal to me. Others I think would be admired by any reader.

I discovered that it is possible for a short story (unlike a novel) to attain something close to perfection. Its brevity can mean that an author has the chance to produce a series of almost perfectly formed sentences, where every carefully chosen word contributes to its meaning. Occasionally the result is flawless, something a novel can never be.

Readers are allowed to be impatient with short stories. My own patience limit for a novel which I am not hugely enjoying may be three or four chapters. If it has not engaged me by then, it has lost me and is returned to the library or taken to a charity shop. With a short story, three or four pages are the maximum I allow (sometimes they are only five or six pages long in any case). A short story can entice us in without preamble or background information, and for that reason it has no excuse. It must not bore us even for a second.

If a short story has no excuse for being dull, it has even less reason to be bland. As I selected the stories for this anthology, I found myself reading stories that made me laugh out loud, gasp and often weep. If a story did not arouse a strong response in me, then I did not select it. Even if it is elegaic or whimsical, it must still stir something deep in the pit of the stomach or make the heart race.

Some stories had such a strong effect on me that I had to put a collection down and do something different with the rest of my day. I could read nothing else. I needed to ponder it, or possibly read it for a second time. Muriel Spark's 'The First Year of My Life' dazzled me with its brilliance. That was a day when I didn't need to do anything other than reflect on her wisdom. For different reasons, Alice Munro's 'Miles City Montana' rendered me incapable of continuing to read. She moves seamlessly from a description of a drowned boy's funeral to an incident on a family outing where we believe that one of the children will drown. Even the relief I felt at the story's relatively happy conclusion was not enough to lift my mood.

Quite often an anthology is named after the author's favourite short story, and if that were the case I would read the eponymous story first. More often, there is no particular entry point into an anthology (unless you are happy to read them in the order they appear, something I usually resisted) and in that case, there was no better guide than simply whether the title intrigued me. Who, for example, would not go straight to a story entitled 'How I Finally Lost My Heart' (Doris Lessing), 'A Weight Problem' (Elspeth Davie), 'How Did I Get Away with Killing One of the Biggest Lawyers in the State? It Was Easy.' (Alice Walker) or even the intriguingly named: 'The Life You Save May Be Your Own' (Flannery O'Connor)?

A short story can be more surreal than many readers might tolerate with a novel and, perhaps, less grounded in reality. Succinctness sometimes allows a writer to explore ideas that may not sustain over a greater length. An example of this is Nicola Barker's 'Inside Information', a shiningly original story told through the voice of an unborn child who is considering the suitability of its soon-to-be mother. Personally, I love the slightly quirky in a short story, but I would probably not be so patient if I had to listen to the voice of a foetus over three hundred pages.

I think the short story can give a writer the opportunity to experiment and to try a style or a voice that they would not use in the novel form, so there is often an element of freshness and surprise for the reader – and perhaps for the writer too.

For me, the stories that make the greatest impact are those that are the most emotional. On a few occasions, when I was reading in the library, I noted curious glances from my neighbours. They gave me sympathetic looks, but tactfully chose to ignore my tears, the context probably reassuring them that I was weeping over the fate of a fictional character rather than some personal catastrophe. Perhaps a few hours later, I would be shaking with suppressed laughter. I think I must have been a very annoying person with whom to share a desk.

I have divided the stories into three categories – Love, Loss and The Lives of Women – but these titles are loose.

Love is, of course, a central preoccupation of literature, but a love story is so often a story of loss, or indeed a story of life. Many of these stories take an amusing and sardonic look at love, so the division, though slightly artificial, is designed to give a reader the chance to read according to her or his mood. Many of them could appear under more than one heading and, I will admit, some stories could probably fit happily into all three categories.

LOVE

Love appears here in all its guises and disguises. As Yiyun Li describes in 'Love in the Marketplace': 'A romance is more than a love story with a man.'

Perhaps maternal love is the most visceral of all loves. At least it felt so the first time I read the phenomenal 'My Son the Hero' by Clare Boylan. 'Reach' by Rachel Seiffert and 'The Turtle' by Roshi Fernando also powerfully evoke the strength of a mother's love, and 'Even Pretty Eyes Commit Crimes' by M. J. Hyland touches beautifully on the love between father and son.

In this section there is the painful poignancy of romantic love in Margaret Drabble's 'Faithful Lovers', love that is more like madness in 'Master' by Angela Carter and love that is unrecognised until it is too late in 'The Man from Mars' by Margaret Atwood. There is love that for some reason is not meant to be. Chimamanda Ngozi Adichie writes about this in 'The Thing Around your Neck'. There is love as infatuation, short-lived and potentially destructive, in Jennifer Egan's 'The Watch Trick', and the making of love, sometimes kinkily, as in Anne Enright's 'Revenge'.

Many readers will know the experience of being haunted by an ex, and Alison Lurie writes vividly about the effect of lost or past loves in her characters' lives ('In the Shadow' and also the even more extraordinary 'Ilse's House').

LOSS

Many of the stories in Loss are tragic, some are shocking. All of them are emotional.

From Katherine Mansfield's almost unbearably poignant 'The Canary', which is written with a feather-light touch, to Alice Munro's 'Gravel', which is blunt to the point of brutality, I think few of these stories will leave readers cold.

There are lost lives, lost loves, lost innocence, a lost mother (Colette Paul's 'Renaissance'), lost breasts (Ellen Gilchrist's 'Indignities'), loss of hearing (Helen Simpson's 'Sorry?') and even a lost leopard (Anna Kavan's extraordinary 'A Visit').

'The First Year of My Life' by Muriel Spark takes the idea that babies are born omniscient and gradually lose their power and their knowledge. In this story, a baby is born in 1913, 'in the very worst year that the world had ever seen so far', and watches, dismayed, unsmiling, sardonic: 'My teeth were coming through very nicely in my opinion, and well worth all the trouble I was put to in bringing them forth. I weighed twenty pounds. On all the world's fighting fronts the men killed in action or dead of wounds numbered 8,538,315 and the warriors wounded and maimed were 21,219,452. With these figures in mind I sat up in my high chair and banged my spoon on the table.'

It is a profound story – a curious companion piece to others in the anthology in which the story is also told by a wise, all-knowing baby: Nicola Barker's masterful 'Inside Information' and Ali Smith's 'The Child' (in The Lives of Women) are especially engaging and fresh.

Carol Shields' 'Fragility', with its hinterland story of a disabled child and a couple's lost happiness, shares much of the pathos of Yiyun Li's 'After a Life', in which a dying child lies incarcerated in a small apartment. Both stories are agonising to read. Lorrie Moore's 'Agnes of Iowa' is similarly tragic but even more open-ended, with a couple doomed to live in perpetuity with their woes.

Susan Hill's 'Father, Father', a story of two daughters 'losing' their father to a second wife, their step-mother, is insightful and real, a common situation faultlessly described.

THE LIVES OF WOMEN

Life provides infinite shades of light and dark and in this section there are many curious tales and unusual settings. There is a handful of stories that made me ask: What on earth gave her this idea? Where did this come from? One example is 'The Axe' by Penelope Fitzgerald.

It is a chilling horror story that takes place in the deceptively banal environment of an office and describes what happens when a man finds his job has been 'axed'. The narrator leaves us, as she should in such a story, with our hairs standing on end.

There is plenty of humour in this section and this is often provided by an unexpected or rather marvellous twist. 'How Did I Get Away with Killing One of the Biggest Lawyers in the State? It Was Easy.' by Alice Walker is flawless. And Penelope Lively's 'Corruption' is too, with the most brilliant visual image perhaps of any story – where a judge, involved in a pornography trial, takes some of his 'research papers' on holiday. A gust of wind sends copies of the offending magazines flying around the beach to be gathered by innocent children and even a woman who, until this moment, has been flirting with the judge. It is brilliantly comic. I felt I was watching the action unfold scene by scene, just as if I was watching a film.

There is a mildly pornographic element too in A. M. Homes' darkly comic 'A Real Doll'. It's almost about love, but more to do with sex. A boy uses his sister's Barbie as a sex toy and all sorts of jealousies ensue (Ken has an opinion, naturally). It's funny, outrageous and totally original.

Alison Lurie's 'Fat People' is once again funny, dark and unique. One could say it is about dieting, but that would only be one per cent of it. But, for me, Nicola Barker is the wittiest and often the most original. I chose three of her stories but had to restrain myself from selecting so many more. In 'G-String', her powers of description had me laughing out loud: 'It felt like her G-string was making headway from between her buttocks up into her throat... now she knew how a horse felt when offered a new bit and bridle for the first time.' Most women will know how accurate this is. Needless to say, this is a hilarious tale right to the very end, where the woman ends up 'knickerless... a truly modern female'.

Ali Smith's 'The Child' is also comic and surreal. A baby with the voice of an adult is placed in a woman's supermarket trolley. It's the reverse of a baby-snatching drama, and is both farcical and strangely daring. It was one of my favourites, and visits to the supermarket have not been the same since...

Elspeth Davie's 'Change of Face' about a street artist is haunting as is her story 'A Weight Problem'. The situations she describes seem to have been magicked from thin air.

Other stories are slightly more shocking: a death may take place, but the 'loss' is not, in itself, a focal point. It is perhaps more to do with learning. Margaret Atwood's very clever story, 'Betty', is about this. Over a small number of pages, one gets a strong sense of the narrator's identity, her stages of growing up and how she reinterprets the past in the light of her age and experience. It is full of wisdom.

Helen Simpson's story 'Ahead of the Pack' is brief but brilliant. The central notion is that we should have a quota of carbon points each day (in the same way that people on diets allow themselves a certain number of calories). It is such a clever idea that I wondered if it should not become a reality. What better way to ensure that we do not get 'in terms of [our] planetary profile... an absolutely vast arse'.

I happily included the slightly self-referential 'A Society' by Virginia Woolf, where the character of Poll is left a fortune by her father on condition that she reads all the books in the London Library. She declares them 'for the most part unutterably bad!' Having done most of my research for this anthology there, I can confirm that Poll is wrong.

I have had interesting discussions about whether there is a female 'voice' and whether women write differently from men. I believe there are some quintessentially feminine writers – and some whose writing provides no clues as to their identity. Angela Carter's 'The Bloody Chamber', for example, is neither masculine nor feminine. It is simply one of the most powerful, imaginative and sensual pieces of writing that I have ever come across. If I did not have

the knowledge, I would certainly not be able to identify that A. M. Homes' stories are from a woman's pen. Her male protagonists are totally convincing and their 'voices' provocative and disturbing.

Some stories are so vivid that it is hard to imagine them as anything other than autobiography – even when the writer is female and the narrator is male. 'Before He Left the Family' by Carrie Tiffany is a very matter-of-fact, no-blame narration of parental separation, but in subtle ways leaves the reader with little doubt over the effect this had on the sons. It is masterful storytelling. The male voice is very real.

I believe that many of the writers in this volume have the ability to leave their gender behind in their writing, whether through deliberately disguising themselves behind a male narrator, or adopting a masculine sensibility. Once again, this is something that would be more difficult to sustain over the duration of an entire novel.

Short stories seem ideally suited to how many of us are reading now. They are perfect to read on an iPad, even on a phone. They can last as long as a short bus or train journey. They are complete in themselves – though from time to time they leave us hanging in mid-air with some kind of twist or ambiguity, as if this story we have in our hands is merely a beginning.

This is a very personal selection of my favourite stories. There will definitely be omissions (some of them accidental, some of them deliberate). Many of these writers were suggested by friends and colleagues. It seems that everyone has a favourite writer of short stories – and whenever I mentioned to people what I was doing they all insisted that I must read one author or another. I always followed up on recommendations, but I did not always find that I shared their taste.

It's been a glorious adventure putting this book together. I hope readers will share some of my excitement and enthusiasm and use it as a starting point for their own explorations into this extraordinary genre.

Victoria Hislop
September 2013

LOVE

A MARRIED MAN'S STORY

Katherine Mansfield

Katherine Mansfield (1888–1923) was born in Wellington, New Zealand.
After moving to England at nineteen, Mansfield secured her reputation
as a writer with the story collection *Bliss*, published in 1920. She reached
the height of her powers with her 1922 collection *The Garden Party*. Her
last five years were shadowed by tuberculosis; she died from the disease
at the age of thirty-four.

It is evening. Supper is over. We have left the small, cold dining room; we have
come back to the sitting room where there is a fire. All is as usual. I am sitting
at my writing table which is placed across a corner so that I am behind it,
as it were, and facing the room. The lamp with the green shade is alight; I have
before me two large books of reference, both open, a pile of papers. ... All the
paraphernalia, in fact, of an extremely occupied man. My wife, with our little
boy on her lap, is in a low chair before the fire. She is about to put him to bed
before she clears away the dishes and piles them up in the kitchen for the servant
girl to-morrow morning. But the warmth, the quiet, and the sleepy baby have
made her dreamy. One of his red woollen boots is off; one is on. She sits, bent
forward, clasping the little bare foot, staring into the glow, and as the fire quickens,
falls, flares again, her shadow – an immense *Mother and Child* – is here and gone
again upon the wall. ...

Outside it is raining. I like to think of that cold drenched window behind the
blind, and beyond, the dark bushes in the garden, their broad leaves bright with
rain, and beyond the fence, the gleaming road with the two hoarse little gutters
singing against each other, and the wavering reflections of the lamps, like fishes'
tails. ... While I am here, I am there, lifting my face to the dim sky, and it seems
to me it must be raining all over the world – that the whole earth is drenched,
is sounding with a soft quick patter or hard steady drumming, or gurgling and
something that is like sobbing and laughing mingled together, and that light
playful splashing that is of water falling into still lakes and flowing rivers. And
all at one and the same moment I am arriving in a strange city, slipping under
the hood of the cab while the driver whips the cover off the breathing horse,
running from shelter to shelter, dodging someone, swerving by someone else. I
am conscious of tall houses, their doors and shutters sealed against the night,
of dripping balconies and sodden flower pots, I am brushing through deserted
gardens and peering into moist smelling summer-houses (you know how soft
and almost crumbling the wood of a summer-house is in the rain), I am standing
on the dark quayside, giving my ticket into the wet red hand of the old sailor in

an oilskin – How strong the sea smells! How loudly those tied-up boats knock against one another! I am crossing the wet stackyard, hooded in an old sack, carrying a lantern, while the house-dog, like a soaking doormat, springs, shakes himself over me. And now I am walking along a deserted road – it is impossible to miss the puddles and the trees are stirring – stirring. ...

But one could go on with such a catalogue for ever – on and on – until one lifted the single arum lily leaf and discovered the tiny snails clinging, until one counted ... and what then? Aren't those just the signs, the traces of my feeling? The bright green streaks made by someone who walks over the dewy grass? Not the feeling itself. And as I think that, a mournful glorious voice begins to sing in my bosom. Yes, perhaps that is nearer what I mean. What a voice! What power! What velvety softness! Marvellous!

Suddenly my wife turns round quickly. She knows – how long has she known? – that I am not 'working'! It is strange that with her full, open gaze, she should smile so timidly – and that she should say in such a hesitating voice: 'What are you thinking?'

I smile and draw two fingers across my forehead in the way I have. 'Nothing,' I answer softly.

At that she stirs, and still trying not to make it sound important, she says: 'Oh, but you must have been thinking of something!'

Then I really meet her gaze, meet it fully, and I fancy her face quivers. Will she never grow accustomed to these simple – one might say – everyday little lies? Will she never learn not to expose herself – or to build up defences?

'Truly, I was thinking of nothing!'

There! I seem to see it dart at her. She turns away, pulls the other red sock off the baby – sits him up, and begins to unbutton him behind. I wonder if that little soft rolling bundle sees anything, feels anything? Now she turns him over on her knee, and in this light, his soft arms and legs waving, he is extraordinarily like a young crab. A queer thing is I can't connect him with my wife and myself; I've never accepted him as ours. Each time when I come into the hall and see the perambulator, I catch myself thinking: 'H'm, someone has brought a baby.' Or, when his crying wakes me at night, I feel inclined to blame my wife for having brought the baby in from outside. The truth is, that though one might suspect her of strong maternal feelings, my wife doesn't seem to me the type of woman who bears children in her own body. There's an immense difference! Where is that ... animal ease and playfulness, that quick kissing and cuddling one has been taught to expect of young mothers? She hasn't a sign of it. I believe that when she ties its bonnet she feels like an aunt and not a mother. But of course I may be wrong; she may be passionately devoted. ... I don't think so. At any rate, isn't it a trifle indecent to feel like this about one's own wife? Indecent or not, one has these feelings. And one other thing. How can I reasonably expect my wife, *a broken-hearted woman*, to spend her time tossing the baby? But that is beside the mark. She never even began to toss when her heart was whole.

And now she has carried the baby to bed. I hear her soft deliberate steps moving between the dining room and the kitchen, there and back again, to the tune of the clattering dishes. And now all is quiet. What is happening now? Oh, I know just as surely as if I'd gone to see – she is standing in the middle of the kitchen, facing the rainy window. Her head is bent, with one finger she is tracing something – nothing – on the table. It is cold in the kitchen; the gas jumps; the tap drips; it's a forlorn picture. And nobody is going to come behind her, to take her in his arms, to kiss her soft hair, to lead her to the fire and to rub her hands warm again. Nobody is going to call her or to wonder what she is doing out there. And she knows it. And yet, being a woman, deep down, deep down, she really does expect the miracle to happen; she really could embrace that dark, dark deceit, rather than live – like this.

To live like this ... I write those words, very carefully, very beautifully. For some reason I feel inclined to sign them, or to write underneath – Trying a New Pen. But seriously, isn't it staggering to think what may be contained in one innocent-looking little phrase? It tempts me – it tempts me terribly. Scene. The supper-table. My wife has just handed me my tea. I stir it, lift the spoon, idly chase and then carefully capture a speck of tea-leaf, and having brought it ashore, I murmur, quite gently, 'How long shall we continue to live – like – this?' And immediately there is that famous 'blinding flash and deafening roar. Huge pieces of débris (I must say I like débris) are flung into the air ... and when the dark clouds of smoke have drifted away ... ' But this will never happen; I shall never know it. It will be found upon me 'intact' as they say. 'Open my heart and you will see ... '

Why? Ah, there you have me! There is the most difficult question of all to answer. Why do people stay together? Putting aside 'for the sake of the children', and 'the habit of years' and 'economic reasons' as lawyers' nonsense – it's not much more – if one really does try to find out why it is that people don't leave each other, one discovers a mystery. It is because they can't; they are bound. And nobody on earth knows what are the bands that bind them except those two. Am I being obscure? Well, the thing itself isn't so frightfully crystal clear, is it? Let me put it like this. Supposing you are taken, absolutely, first into his confidence and then into hers. Supposing you know all there is to know about the situation. And having given it not only your deepest sympathy but your most honest impartial criticism, you declare, very calmly (but not without the slightest suggestion of re-lish – for there is – I swear there is – in the very best of us – something that leaps up and cries 'A-ahh!' for joy at the thought of destroying), 'Well, my opinion is that you two people ought to part. You'll do no earthly good together. Indeed, it seems to me, it's the duty of either to set the other free.' What happens then? He – and she – agree. It is their conviction too. You are only saying what they have been thinking all last night. And away they go to act on your advice, immediately ... And the next time you hear of them they are still together. You see – you've reckoned without the unknown quantity – which is their secret relation to each other – and that they can't disclose even if they want to. Thus far you may tell and no further. Oh, don't misunderstand me! It need not necessarily have anything to do with their sleeping together ... But this brings me to a thought I've often half entertained. Which is, that human beings, as we know them, don't choose each other at all. It is the owner, the second self inhabiting them, who makes the choice for his own particular purposes, and – this may sound absurdly far-fetched – it's the second self in the other which responds. Dimly – dimly – or so it has seemed to me – we realise this, at any rate to the extent that we realise the hopelessness of trying to escape. So that, what it all amounts to is – if the impermanent selves of my wife and me are happy – *tant mieux pour nous* – if miserable – *tant pis*. ... But I don't know, I don't know. And it may be that it's something entirely individual in me – this sensation (yes, it is even a sensation) of how extraordinarily *shell-like* we are as we are – little creatures, peering out of the sentry-box at the gate, ogling through our glass case at the entry, wan little servants, who never can say for certain, even, if the master is out or in ...

The door opens ... My wife. She says: 'I am going to bed.'

And I look up vaguely, and vaguely say: 'You are going to bed.'

'Yes.' A tiny pause. 'Don't forget – will you? – to turn out the gas in the hall.'

And again I repeat: 'The gas in the hall.'

There was a time – the time before – when this habit of mine (it really has become a habit now – it wasn't one then) was one of our sweetest jokes together. It began, of course, when, on several occasions, I really was deeply engaged and I didn't hear. I emerged only to see her shaking her head and laughing at me, 'You haven't heard a word!'

'No. What did you say?'

Why should she think that so funny and charming? She did; it delighted her. 'Oh, my darling, it's so like you! It's so – so – .' And I knew she loved me for it – knew she positively looked forward to coming in and disturbing me, and so – as one does – I played up. I was guaranteed to be wrapped away every evening at 10.30 p.m. But now? For some reason I feel it would be crude to stop my performance. It's simplest to play on. But what is she waiting for to-night? Why doesn't she go? Why prolong this? She is going. No, her hand on the door-knob, she turns round again, and she says in the most curious, small, breathless voice, 'You're not cold?'

Oh, it's not fair to be as pathetic as that! That was simply damnable, I shudder all over before I manage to bring out a slow 'No-o,' while my left hand ruffles the reference pages.

She is gone; she will not come back again to-night. It is not only I who recognise that; the room changes, too. It relaxes, like an old actor. Slowly the mask is rubbed off; the look of strained attention changes to an air of heavy, sullen brooding. Every line, every fold breathes fatigue. The mirror is quenched; the ash whitens; only my shy lamp burns on ... But what a cynical indifference to me it all shows! Or should I perhaps be flattered? No, we understand each other. You know those stories of little children who are suckled by wolves and accepted by the tribe, and how for ever after they move freely among their fleet grey brothers? Something like that has happened to me. But wait – that about the wolves won't do. Curious!

Before I wrote it down, while it was still in my head, I was delighted with it. It seemed to express, and more, to suggest, just what I wanted to say. But written, I can smell the falseness immediately and the ... source of the smell is in that word fleet. Don't you agree? Fleet, grey brothers! 'Fleet.' A word I never use. When I wrote 'wolves' it skimmed across my mind like a shadow and I couldn't resist it. Tell me! Tell me! Why is it so difficult to write simply – and not only simply but *sotto voce*, if you know what I mean? That is how I long to write. No fine effects – no bravuras. But just the plain truth, as only a liar can tell it.

I light a cigarette, lean back, inhale deeply – and find myself wondering if my wife is asleep. Or is she lying in her cold bed, staring into the dark with those trustful, bewildered eyes? Her eyes are like the eyes of a cow being driven along a road. 'Why am I being driven – what harm have I done? But I really am not responsible for that look; it's her natural expression. One day, when she was turning out a cupboard, she found a little old photograph of herself, taken when she was a girl at school. In her confirmation dress, she explained. And there were the eyes, even then. I remember saying to her: 'Did you always look so sad?' Leaning over my shoulder, she laughed lightly. 'Do I look sad? I think it's just … me.' And she waited for me to say something about it. But I was marvelling at her courage at having shown it to me at all. It was a hideous photograph! And I wondered again if she realised how plain she was, and comforted herself with the idea that people who loved each other didn't criticise but accepted everything, or if she really rather liked her appearance and expected me to say something complimentary. Oh, that was base of me! How could I have forgotten all the countless times when I have known her turn away, avoid the light, press her face into my shoulders. And above all, how could I have forgotten the afternoon of our wedding day, when we sat on the green bench in the Botanical Gardens and listened to the band, how, in an interval between two pieces, she suddenly turned to me and said in the voice in which one says: 'Do you think the grass is damp?' or 'Do you think it's time for tea?' … 'Tell me – do you think physical beauty is so very important?' I don't like to think how often she rehearsed that question. And do you know what I answered? At that moment, as if at my command, there came a great gush of hard bright sound from the band. And I managed to shout above it – cheerfully – 'I didn't hear what you said.' Devilish! Wasn't it? Perhaps not wholly. She looked like the poor patient who hears the surgeon say, 'It will certainly be necessary to perform the operation – but not now!'

But all this conveys the impression that my wife and I were never really happy together. Not true! Not true! We were marvellously, radiantly happy. We were a model couple. If you had seen us together, any time, any place, if you had followed us, tracked us down, spied, taken us off our guard, you still would have been forced to confess, 'I have never seen a more ideally suited pair.' Until last autumn.

But really to explain what happened then I should have to go back and back, I should have to dwindle until my tiny hands clutched the bannisters, the stair-rail was higher than my head, and I peered through to watch my father padding softly up and down. There were coloured windows on the landings. As he came up, first his bald head was scarlet; then it was yellow. How frightened I was! And when they put me to bed, it was to dream that we were living inside one of my father's big coloured bottles. For he was a chemist. I was born nine years after my parents were married; I was an only child, and the effort to produce even me – small, withered bud I must have been – sapped all my mother's strength. She never left her room again. Bed, sofa, window, she moved between the three.

Well I can see her, on the window days, sitting, her cheek in her hand, staring out. Her room looked over the street. Opposite there was a wall plastered with advertisement for travelling shows and circuses and so on. I stand beside her, and we gaze at the slim lady in a red dress hitting a dark gentleman over the head with her parasol, or at the tiger peering through the jungle while the clown, close by, balances a bottle on his nose, or at a little golden-haired girl sitting on the knee of an old black man in a broad cotton hat ... She says nothing. On sofa days there is a flannel dressing-gown that I loathe, and a cushion that keeps on slipping off the hard sofa. I pick it up. It has flowers and writing sewn on. I ask what the writing says, and she whispers, 'Sweet Repose!' In bed her fingers plait, in tight little plaits, the fringe of the quilt, and her lips are thin. And that is all there is of my mother, except the last queer 'episode' that comes later ...

My father – curled up in the corner on the lid of a round box that held sponges, I stared at my father so long it's as though his image, cut off at the waist by the counter, has remained solid in my memory. Perfectly bald, polished head, shaped like a thin egg, creased creamy cheeks, little bags under the eyes, large pale ears like handles. His manner was discreet, sly, faintly amused and tinged with impudence. Long before I could appreciate it I knew the mixture ... I even used to copy him in my corner, bending forward, with a small reproduction of his faint sneer. In the evening his customers were, chiefly, young women; some of them came in every day for his famous five-penny pick-me-up. Their gaudy looks, their voices, their free ways, fascinated me. I longed to be my father, handing them across the counter the little glass of bluish stuff they tossed off so greedily. God knows what it was made of. Years after I drank some, just to see what it tasted like, and I felt as though someone had given me a terrific blow on the head; I felt stunned. One of those evenings I remember vividly. It was cold; it must have been autumn, for the flaring gas was lighted after my tea. I sat in my corner and my father was mixing something; the shop was empty. Suddenly the bell jangled and a young woman rushed in, crying so loud, sobbing so hard, that it didn't sound real. She wore a green cape trimmed with fur and a hat with cherries dangling. My father came from behind the screen. But she couldn't stop herself at first. She stood in the middle of the shop and wrung her hands, and moaned. I've never heard such crying since. Presently she managed to gasp out, 'Give me a pick-me-up.' Then she drew a long breath, trembled away from him and quavered: 'I've had *bad news*!' And in the flaring gaslight I saw the whole side of her face was puffed up and purple; her lip was cut, and her eyelid looked as though it was gummed fast over the wet eye. My father pushed the glass across the counter, and she took her purse out of her stocking and paid him. But she couldn't drink; clutching the glass, she stared in front of her as if she could not believe what she saw. Each time she put her head back the tears spurted out again. Finally she put the glass down. It was no use. Holding the cape with one hand, she ran in the same way out of the shop again. My father gave no sign. But long after she had gone I crouched in my corner, and when I think back it's as though I felt my whole body vibrating – 'So that's what it is outside,' I thought. 'That's what it's like out there.'

Do you remember your childhood? I am always coming across these marvellous accounts by writers who declare that they remember 'everything, everything'. I certainly don't. The dark stretches, the blanks, are much bigger than the bright glimpses. I seem to have spent most of my time like a plant in a cupboard. Now and again, when the sun shone, a careless hand thrust me out on to the window-sill, and a careless hand whipped me in again – and that was all. But what happened in the darkness – I wonder? Did one grow? Pale stem ... timid leaves ... white, reluctant bud. No wonder I was hated at school. Even the masters shrank from me. I somehow knew that my soft hesitating voice disgusted them. I knew, too, how they turned away from my shocked, staring eyes. I was small and thin, and I smelled of the shop; my nickname was Gregory Powder. School was a tin building stuck on the raw hillside. There were dark red streaks like blood in the oozing clay banks of the playground. I hide in the dark passage, where the coats hang, and am discovered there by one of the masters. 'What are you doing there in the dark?' His terrible voice kills me; I die before his eyes. I am standing in a ring of thrust-out heads; some are grinning, some look greedy, some are spitting. And it is always cold. Big crushed up clouds press across the sky; the rusty water in the school tank is frozen; the bell sounds numb. One day they put a dead bird in my overcoat pocket. I found it just when I reached home. Oh, what a strange flutter there was at my heart, when I drew out that terribly soft, cold little body, with the legs thin as pins and the claws wrung. I sat on the back door step in the yard and put the bird in my cap. The feathers round the neck looked wet and there was a tiny tuft just above the closed eyes that stood up too. How tightly the beak was shut; I could not see the mark where it was divided. I stretched out one wing and touched the soft, secret down underneath; I tried to make the claws curl round my little finger. But I didn't feel sorry for it – no! I wondered. The smoke from our kitchen chimney poured downwards, and flakes of soot floated – soft, light in the air. Through a big crack in the cement yard a poor-looking plant with dull reddish flowers had pushed its way. I looked at the dead bird again ... And that is the first time that I remember singing, rather ... listening to a silent voice inside a little cage that was me.

But what has all this to do with my married happiness? How can all this affect my wife and me? Why – to tell what happened last autumn – do I run all this way back into the Past? The Past – what is the Past? I might say the star-shaped flake of soot on a leaf of the poor-looking plant, and the bird lying on the quilted lining of my cap, and my father's pestle and my mother's cushion, belong to it. But that is not to say they are any less mine than they were when I looked upon them with my very eyes, and touched them with these fingers. No, they are more; they are a living part of me. Who am I, in fact, as I sit here at this table, but my own past? If I deny that, I am nothing. And if I were to try and divide my life into childhood, youth, early manhood and so on, it would be a kind of affectation; I should know I was doing it just because of the pleasantly important sensation it gives one to rule lines, and to use green ink for childhood, red for the next stage, and purple for the period of adolescence. For, one thing I have learnt, one thing I do believe is, Nothing Happens Suddenly. Yes, that is my religion, I suppose ...

My mother's death, for instance. Is it more distant from me to-day than it was then? It is just as close, as strange, as puzzling, and in spite of all the countless times I have recalled the circumstances, I know no more now than I did then whether I dreamed them or whether they really occurred. It happened when I was thirteen and I slept in a little strip of a room on what was called the Half Landing. One night I woke up with a start to see my mother, in her nightgown, without even the hated flannel dressing-gown, sitting on my bed. But the strange thing which frightened me was, she wasn't looking at me. Her head was bent; the short thin tail of hair lay between her shoulders; her hands were pressed between her knees, and my bed shook; she was shivering. It was the first time I had ever seen her out of her own room. I said, or I think I said, 'Is that you, mother?' And as she turned round I saw in the moonlight how queer she looked. Her face looked small – quite different. She looked like one of the boys at the school baths, who sits on a step, shivering just like that, and wants to go in and yet is frightened.

'Are you awake?' she said. Her eyes opened; I think she smiled. She leaned towards me. 'I've been poisoned,' she whispered. 'Your father's poisoned me.' And she nodded. Then, before I could say a word, she was gone, and I thought I heard the door shut. I sat quite still; I couldn't move. I think I expected something else to happen. For a long time I listened for something; there wasn't a sound. The candle was by my bed, but I was too frightened to stretch out my hand for the matches. But even while I wondered what I ought to do, even while my heart thumped – everything became confused. I lay down and pulled the blankets round me. I fell asleep, and the next morning my mother was found dead of failure of the heart.

Did that visit happen? Was it a dream? Why did she come to tell me? Or why, if she came, did she go away so quickly? And her expression – so joyous under the frightened look – was that real? I believed it fully the afternoon of the funeral, when I saw my father dressed up for his part, hat and all. That tall hat so gleaming black and round was like a cork covered with black sealing-wax, and the rest of my father was awfully like a bottle, with his face for the label – *Deadly Poison*. It flashed into my mind as I stood opposite him in the hall. And Deadly Poison, or old D.P., was my private name for him from that day.

Late, it grows late. I love the night. I love to feel the tide of darkness rising slowly and slowly washing, turning over and over, lifting, floating, all that lies strewn upon the dark beach, all that lies hid in rocky hollows. I love, I love this strange feeling of drifting – whither? After my mother's death I hated to go to bed. I used to sit on the window-sill, folded up, and watch the sky. It seemed to me the moon moved much faster than the sun. And one big, bright green star I chose for my own. My star! But I never thought of it beckoning to me or twinkling merrily for my sake. Cruel, indifferent, splendid – it burned in the airy night. No matter – it was mine! But growing close up against the window there was a creeper with small, bunched up pink and purple flowers. These did know me. These, when I touched them at night, welcomed my fingers; the little tendrils, so weak, so delicate, knew I would not hurt them. When the wind moved the leaves I felt I understood their shaking. When I came to the window, it seemed to me the flowers said among themselves, 'The boy is here.'

As the months passed, there was often a light in my father's room below. And

I heard voices and laughter. 'He's got some woman with him,' I thought. But it meant nothing to me. Then the gay voice, the sound of the laughter, gave me the idea it was one of the girls who used to come to the shop in the evenings – and gradually I began to imagine which girl it was. It was the dark one in the red coat and skirt, who once had given me a penny. A merry face stooped over me – warm breath tickled my neck – there were little beads of black on her long lashes, and when she opened her arms to kiss me, there came a marvellous wave of scent! Yes, that was the one. Time passed, and I forgot the moon and my green star and my shy creeper – I came to the window to wait for the light in my father's window, to listen for the laughing voice, until one night I dozed and I dreamed she came again – again she drew me to her, something soft, scented, warm and merry hung over me like a cloud. But when I tried to see, her eyes only mocked me, her red lips opened and she hissed, 'Little sneak! little sneak!' But not as if she were angry, as if she understood, and her smile somehow was like a rat ... hateful!

The night after, I lighted the candle and sat down at the table instead. By and by, as the flame steadied, there was a small lake of liquid wax, surrounded by a white, smooth wall. I took a pin and made little holes in this wall and then sealed them up faster than the wax could escape. After a time I fancied the candle flame joined in the game; it leapt up, quivered, wagged; it even seemed to laugh. But while I played with the candle and smiled and broke off the tiny white peaks of wax that rose above the wall and floated them on my lake, a feeling of awful dreariness fastened on me – yes, that is the word. It crept up from my knees to my thighs, into my arms; I ached all over with misery. And I felt so strangely that I couldn't move. Something bound me there by the table – I couldn't even let the pin drop that I held between my finger and thumb. For a moment I came to a stop, as it were.

Then the shrivelled case of the bud split and fell, the plant in the cupboard came into flower. 'Who am I?' I thought. 'What is all this?' And I looked at my room, at the broken bust of the man called Hahnemann on top of the cupboard, at my little bed with the pillow like an envelope. I saw it all, but not as I had seen before ... Everything lived, but everything. But that was not all. I was equally alive and – it's the only way I can express it – the barriers were down between us – I had come into my own world!

The barriers were down. I had been all my life a little outcast; but until that moment no one had 'accepted' me; I had lain in the cupboard – or the cave forlorn. But now – I was taken, I was accepted, claimed. I did not consciously turn away from the world of human beings; I had never known it; but I from that night did beyond words consciously turn towards my silent brothers ...

A TELEPHONE CALL

Dorothy Parker

Dorothy Parker (1893–1967) was an American critic, satirical poet, and short story writer. Best known for her wit and eye for 20th-century foibles, Parker wrote book reviews, poetry and short fiction for the fledgling magazine the *New Yorker*. She wrote the screenplay for the Hitchcock film *Saboteur*, but her involvement with Communism led to her being blacklisted in Hollywood.

Please, God, let him telephone me now. Dear God, let him call me now. I won't ask anything else of You, truly I won't. It isn't very much to ask. It would be so little to You, God, such a little, little thing. Only let him telephone now. Please, God. Please, please, please.

If I didn't think about it, maybe the telephone might ring. Sometimes it does that. If I could think of something else. If I could think of something else. Maybe if I counted five hundred by fives, it might ring by that time. I'll count slowly. I won't cheat. And if it rings when I get to three hundred, I won't stop; I won't answer it until I get to five hundred. Five, ten, fifteen, twenty, twenty-five, thirty, thirty-five, forty, forty-five, fifty … Oh, please ring. Please.

This is the last time I'll look at the clock. I will not look at it again. It's ten minutes past seven. He said he would telephone at five o'clock. "I'll call you at five, darling." I think that's where he said "darling." I'm almost sure he said it there. I know he called me "darling" twice, and the other time was when he said good-by. "Good-by, darling." He was busy, and he can't say much in the office, but he called me "darling" twice. He couldn't have minded my calling him up. I know you shouldn't keep telephoning them – I know they don't like that. When you do that they know you are thinking about them and wanting them, and that makes them hate you. But I hadn't talked to him in three days – not in three days. And all I did was ask him how he was; it was just the way anybody might have called him up. He couldn't have minded that. He couldn't have thought I was bothering him. "No, of course you're not." he said. And he said he'd telephone me. He didn't have to say that. I didn't ask him to, truly I didn't. I'm sure I didn't. I don't think he would say he'd telephone me, and then just never do it. Please don't let him do that God. Please don't.

"I'll call you at five, darling." "Good-by, darling." He was busy, and he was in a hurry, and there were people around him, but he called me "darling" twice. That's mine, that's mine. I have that, even if I never see him again. Oh, but that's so little. That isn't enough. Nothing's enough, if I never see him again. Please let me see him again, God. Please, I want him so much. I want him so much. I'll be good, God. I will try to be better, I will, if You will let me see him again. If You let him telephone me. Oh, let him telephone me now.

Ah, don't let my prayer seem too little to You, God. You sit up there, so white and old, with all the angels about You and the stars slipping by. And I come to You with a prayer about a telephone call. Ah, don't laugh, God. You see, You don't know how it feels. You're so safe, there on Your throne, with the blue swirling under You. Nothing can touch You; no one can twist Your heart in his hands. This is suffering, God, this is bad, bad suffering. Won't You help me? For Your Son's sake, help me. You said You would do whatever was asked of You in His name. Oh, God, in the name of Thine only beloved Son, Jesus Christ, our Lord, let him telephone me now.

I must stop this. I mustn't be this way. Look. Suppose a young man says he'll call a girl up, and then something happens, and he doesn't. That isn't so terrible, is it? Why, it's going on all over the world, right this minute. Oh, what do I care what's going on all over the world? Why can't that telephone ring? Why can't it, why can't it? Couldn't you ring? Ah, please, couldn't you? You damned, ugly, shiny thing. It would hurt you to ring, wouldn't it? Oh, that would hurt you. Damn you, I'll pull your filthy roots out of the wall, I'll smash your smug black face in little bits. Damn you to hell.

No, no, no. I must stop. I must think about something else. This is what I'll do. I'll put the clock in the other room. Then I can't look at it. If I do have to look at it then I'll have to walk into the bedroom, and that will be something to do. Maybe, before I look at it again, he will call me. I'll be so sweet to him, if he calls me. If he says he can't see me tonight, I'll say, "Why, that's all right, dear. Why, of course it's all right." I'll be the way I was when I first met him. Then maybe he'll like me again. I was always sweet, at first. Oh, it's so easy to be sweet to people before you love them.

I think he must still like me a little. He couldn't have called me "darling" twice today, if he didn't still like me a little. It isn't all gone, if he still likes me a little; even if it's only a little, little bit. You see, God, if You would just let him telephone me, I wouldn't have to ask You anything more. I would be sweet to him, I would be gay, I would be just the way I used to be, and then he would love me again. And then I would never have to ask You for anything more. Don't You see, God? So won't You please let him telephone me? Won't You please, please, please?

Are You punishing me, God, because I've been bad? Are You angry with me because I did that? Oh, but God, there are so many bad people – You could not be hard only to me. And it wasn't very bad; it couldn't have been bad. We didn't hurt anybody, God. Things are only bad when they hurt people. We didn't hurt one single soul; You know that. You know it wasn't bad, don't You, God? So won't You let him telephone me now?

If he doesn't telephone me, I'll know God is angry with me. I'll count five hundred by fives, and if he hasn't called me then, I will know God isn't going to help me, ever again. That will be the sign. Five, ten, fifteen, twenty, twenty-five, thirty, thirty-five, forty, forty-five, fifty, fifty-five … It was bad. I knew it was bad. All right, God, send me to hell. You think You're frightening me with Your hell, don't You? You think Your hell is worse than mine.

I mustn't. I mustn't do this. Suppose he's a little late calling me up – that's nothing to get hysterical about. Maybe he isn't going to call – maybe he's coming straight up here without telephoning. He'll be cross if he sees I have been crying. They don't like you to cry. He doesn't cry. I wish to God I could make him cry. I wish I could make him cry and tread the floor and feel his heart heavy and big and festering in him. I wish I could hurt him like hell.

He doesn't wish that about me. I don't think he even knows how he makes me feel. I wish he could know, without my telling him. They don't like you to tell them they've made you cry. They don't like you to tell them you're unhappy because of them. If you do, they think you're possessive and exacting. And then they hate you. They hate you whenever you say anything you really think. You always have to keep playing little games. Oh, I thought we didn't have to; I thought this was so big I could say whatever I meant. I guess you can't, ever. I guess there isn't ever anything big enough for that. Oh, if he would just telephone, I wouldn't tell him I had been sad about him. They hate sad people. I would be so sweet and so gay, he couldn't help but like me. If he would only telephone. If he would only telephpne.

Maybe that's what he is doing. Maybe he is coming on here without calling me up. Maybe he's on his way now. Something might have happened to him. No, nothing could ever happen to him. I can't picture anything happening to him. I never picture him run over. I never see him lying still and long and dead. I wish he were dead. That's a terrible wish. That's a lovely wish. If he were dead, he would be mine. If he were dead, I would never think of now and the last few weeks. I would remember only the lovely times. It would be all beautiful. I wish he were dead. I wish he were dead, dead, dead.

This is silly. It's silly to go wishing people were dead just because they don't call you up the very minute they said they would. Maybe the clock's fast; I don't know whether it's right. Maybe he's hardly late at all. Anything could have made him a little late. Maybe he had to stay at his office. Maybe he went home, to call me up from there, and somebody came in. He doesn't like to telephone me in front of people. Maybe he's worried, just a little, little bit about keeping me waiting. He might even hope that I would call him up. I could do that. I could telephone him.

I mustn't. I mustn't, I mustn't. Oh, God, please don't let me telephone him. Please keep me from doing that. I know, God, just as well as You do, that if he were worried about me, he'd telephone no matter where he was or how many people there were around him. Please make me know that God. I don't ask You to make it easy for me – You can't do that, for all that You could make a world. Only let me know it, God. Don't let me go on hoping. Don't let me say comforting things to myself. Please don't let me hope, dear God. Please don't.

I won't telephone him. I'll never telephone him again as long as I live. He'll rot in hell, before I'll call him up. You don't have to give me strength, God; I have it myself. If he wanted me, he could get me. He knows where I am. He knows I'm waiting here. He's so sure of me, so sure. I wonder why they hate you as soon as they are sure of you. I should think it would be so sweet to be sure.

It would be so easy to telephone him. Then I'd know. Maybe it wouldn't be a foolish thing to do. Maybe he wouldn't mind. Maybe he'd like it. Maybe he has been trying to get me. Sometimes people try and try to get you on the telephone, and they say the number doesn't answer. I'm not just saving that to help myself; that really happens. You know that really happens, God. Oh, God, keep me away from that telephone. Keep me away. Let me still have just a little bit of pride. I think I'm going to need it, God. I think it will be all I'll have.

Oh, what does pride matter, when I can't stand it if I don't talk to him? Pride like that is such a silly, shabby little thing. The real pride, the big pride, is in having no pride. I'm not saying that just because I want to call him. I am not. That's true, I know that's true. I will be big. I will be beyond little prides.

Please, God, keep me from telephoning him. Please, God.

I don't see what pride has to do with it. This is such a little thing, for me to be bringing in pride, for me to be making such a fuss about. I may have misunderstood him. Maybe he said for me to call him up, at five. "Call me at five, darling." He could have said that, perfectly well. It's so possible that I didn't hear him right. "Call me at five, darling." I'm almost sure that's what he said. God, don't let me talk this way to myself. Make me know, please make me know.

I'll think about something else. I'll just sit quietly. If I could sit still. If I could sit still. Maybe I could read. Oh, all the books are about people who love each other, truly and sweetly. What do they want to write about that for? Don't they know it isn't true? Don't they know it's a lie, it's a God damned lie? What do they have to tell about that for, when they know how it hurts? Damn them, damn them, damn them.

I won't. I'll be quiet. This is nothing to get excited about. Look. Suppose he were someone I didn't know very well. Suppose he were another girl. Then I'd just telephone and say, "Well, for goodness' sake, what happened to you?" That's what I'd do, and I'd never even think about it. Why can't I be casual and natural, just because I love him? I can be. Honestly. I can be. I'll call him up, and be so easy and pleasant. You see if I won't God. Oh, don't let me call him. Don't, don't, don't.

God, aren't You really going to let him call me? Are You sure, God? Couldn't You please relent? Couldn't You? I don't even ask You to let him telephone me this minute. God: only let him do it in a little while. I'll count five hundred by fives. I'll do it so slowly and so fairly. If he hasn't telephoned then, I'll call him. I will. Oh, please, dear God, dear kind God, my blessed Father in Heaven, let him call before then. Please. God. Please.

Five, ten, fifteen, twenty, twenty-five, thirty, thirty-five ...

A MAN AND TWO WOMEN

Doris Lessing

Doris Lessing (b. 1919) is a British novelist, poet, playwright, biographer and short story writer. In 2001, Lessing was awarded the David Cohen Prize for a lifetime's achievement in British Literature and she was ranked fifth on *The Times* list of the '50 Greatest British Writers Since 1945'. Lessing was awarded the 2007 Nobel Prize in Literature.

Stella's friends the Bradfords had taken a cheap cottage in Essex for the summer, and she was going down to visit them. She wanted to see them, but there was no doubt there was something of a letdown (and for them too) in the English cottage. Last summer Stella had been wandering with her husband around Italy; had seen the English couple at a cafe table, and found them sympathetic. They all liked each other, and the four went about for some weeks, sharing meals, hotels, trips. Back in London the friendship had not, as might have been expected, fallen off. Then Stella's husband departed abroad, as he often did, and Stella saw Jack and Dorothy by herself. There were a great many people she might have seen, but it was the Bradfords she saw most often, two or three times a week, at their flat or hers. They were at ease with each other. Why were they? Well, for one thing they were all artists – in different ways. Stella designed wallpapers and materials; she had a name for it.

The Bradfords were real artists. He painted, she drew. They had lived mostly out of England in cheap places around the Mediterranean. Both from the North of England, they had met at art school, married at twenty, had taken flight from England, then returned to it, needing it, then off again: and so on, for years, in the rhythm of so many of their kind, needing, hating, loving England. There had been seasons of real poverty, while they lived on pasta or bread or rice, and wine and fruit and sunshine, in Majorca, southern Spain, Italy, North Africa.

A French critic had seen Jack's work, and suddenly he was successful. His show in Paris, then one in London, made money, and now he charged in the hundreds where a year or so ago he charged ten or twenty guineas. This had deepened his contempt for the values of the markets. For a while Stella thought that this was the bond between the Bradfords and herself. They were so very much, as she was, of the new generation of artists (and poets and playwrights and novelists) who had one thing in common, a cool derision about the racket. They were so very unlike (they felt) the older generation with their Societies and their Lunches and their salons and their cliques: their atmosphere of connivance with the snobberies of success. Stella, too, had been successful by a fluke. Not that she did not consider herself talented; it was that others as talented were unfêted, and unbought. When she was with the Bradfords and other fellow spirits, they would talk about the racket, using each other as yardsticks or fellow consciences about how much to give in, what to give, how to use without being used, how to enjoy without becoming dependent on enjoyment.

Of course Dorothy Bradford was not able to talk in quite the same way, since she had not yet been "discovered"; she had not "broken through." A few people with discrimination bought her unusual delicate drawings, which had a strength that was hard to understand unless one knew Dorothy herself. But she was not at all, as Jack was, a great success. There was a strain here, in the marriage, nothing much; it was kept in check by their scorn for their arbitrary rewards of "the racket." But it was there, nevertheless.

Stella's husband had said: "Well, I can understand that, it's like me and you – you're creative, whatever that may mean, I'm just a bloody TV journalist." There was no bitterness in this. He was a good journalist, and besides he sometimes got the chance to make a good small film. All the same, there was that between him and Stella, just as there was between Jack and his wife.

After a time Stella saw something else in her kinship with the couple. It was that the Bradfords had a close bond, bred of having spent so many years together in foreign places, dependent on each other because of their poverty. It had been a real love marriage, one could see it by looking at them. It was now. And Stella's marriage was a real marriage. She understood she enjoyed being with the Bradfords because the two couples were equal in this. Both marriages were those of strong, passionate, talented individuals, they shared a battling quality that strengthened them, not weakened them.

The reason why it had taken Stella so long to understand this was that the Bradfords had made her think about her own marriage, which she was beginning to take for granted, sometimes even found exhausting. She had understood, through them, how lucky she was in her husband; how lucky they all were. No marital miseries; nothing of (what they saw so often in friends) one partner in a marriage victim to the other, resenting the other; no claiming of outsiders as sympathisers or allies in an unequal battle.

There had been a plan for these four people to go off again to Italy or Spain, but then Stella's husband departed, and Dorothy got pregnant. So there was the cottage in Essex instead, a bad second choice, but better, they all felt, to deal with a new baby on home ground, at least for the first year. Stella, telephoned by Jack (on Dorothy's particular insistence, he said), offered and received commiserations on its being only Essex and not Majorca or Italy. She also received sympathy because her husband had been expected back this weekend, but had wired to say he wouldn't be back for another month, probably – there was trouble in Venezuela. Stella wasn't really forlorn; she didn't mind living alone, since she was always supported by knowing her man would be back. Besides, if she herself were offered the chance of a month's "trouble" in Venezuela, she wouldn't hesitate, so it wasn't fair ... fairness characterised their relationship. All the same, it was nice that she could drop down (or up) to the Bradfords, people with whom she could always be herself, neither more nor less.

She left London at midday by train, armed with food unobtainable in Essex: salamis, cheeses, spices, wine. The sun shone, but it wasn't particularly warm.

She hoped there would be heating in the cottage, July or not.

The train was empty. The little station seemed stranded in a green nowhere. She got out, cumbered by bags full of food. A porter and a stationmaster examined, then came to succour her. She was a tallish, fair woman, rather ample; her soft hair, drawn back, escaped in tendrils, and she had great helpless-looking blue eyes. She wore a dress made in one of the materials she had designed. Enormous green leaves laid hands all over her body, and fluttered about her knees. She stood smiling, accustomed to men running to wait on her, enjoying them enjoying her. She walked with them to the barrier where Jack waited, appreciating the scene. He was a smallish man, compact, dark. He wore a blue-green summer shirt, and smoked a pipe and smiled, watching. The two men delivered her into the hands of the third, and departed, whistling, to their duties.

Jack and Stella kissed, then pressed their cheeks together.

"Food," he said, "food," relieving her of the parcels.

"What's it like here, shopping?"

"Vegetables all right, I suppose."

Jack was still northern in this: he seemed brusque, to strangers; he wasn't shy, he simply hadn't been brought up to enjoy words. Now he put his arm briefly around Stella's waist, and said: "Marvellous, Stell, marvellous." They walked on, pleased with each other. Stella had with Jack, her husband had with Dorothy, these moments, when they said to each other wordlessly: If I were not married to my husband, if you were not married to your wife, how delightful it would be to be married to you. These moments were not the least of the pleasures of this four-sided friendship.

"Are you liking it down here?"

"It's what we bargained for."

There was more than his usual shortness in this, and she glanced at him to find him frowning. They were walking to the car, parked under a tree.

"How's the baby?"

"Little bleeder never sleeps; he's wearing us out, but he's fine."

The baby was six weeks old. Having the baby was a definite achievement: getting it safely conceived and born had taken a couple of years. Dorothy, like most independent women, had had divided thoughts about a baby. Besides, she was over thirty and complained she was set in her ways. All this – the difficulties, Dorothy's hesitations – had added up to an atmosphere which Dorothy herself described as "like wondering if some damned horse is going to take the fence." Dorothy would talk, while she was pregnant, in a soft staccato voice: "Perhaps I don't really want a baby at all? Perhaps I'm not fitted to be a mother? Perhaps ... and if so ... and how ... ?"

She said: "Until recently Jack and I were always with people who took it for granted that getting pregnant was a disaster, and now suddenly all the people we know have young children and baby-sitters and ... perhaps ... if ..."

Jack said: "You'll feel better when it's born."

Once Stella had heard him say, after one of Dorothy's long troubled dialogues with herself: "Now that's enough, that's enough, Dorothy." He had silenced her, taking the responsibility.

They reached the car, got in. It was a secondhand job recently bought. "They" (being the Press, the enemy generally) "wait for us" (being artists or writers who have made money) "to buy flashy cars." They had discussed it, decided that *not* to buy an expensive car if they felt like it would be allowing themselves to be bullied; but bought a secondhand one after all. Jack wasn't going to give *them* so much satisfaction, apparently.

"Actually we could have walked," he said, as they shot down a narrow lane, "but with these groceries, it's just as well."

"If the baby's giving you a tough time, there can't be much time for cooking." Dorothy was a wonderful cook. But now again there was something in the air as he said: "Food's definitely not too good just now. You can cook supper, Stell, we could do with a good feed."

Now Dorothy hated anyone in her kitchen, except, for certain specified jobs, her husband; and this was surprising.

"The truth is, Dorothy's worn out," he went on, and now Stella understood he was warning her.

"Well, it is tiring," said Stella soothingly.

"You were like that?"

"Like that" was saying a good deal more than just worn out, or tired, and Stella understood that Jack was really uneasy. She said, plaintively humorous: "You two always expect me to remember things that happened a hundred years ago. Let me think. ..."

She had been married when she was eighteen, got pregnant at once. Her husband had left her. Soon she had married Philip, who also had a small child from a former marriage. These two children, her daughter, seventeen, his son, twenty, had grown up together.

She remembered herself at nineteen, alone, with a small baby. "Well, I was alone," she said. "That makes a difference. I remember I was exhausted. Yes, I was definitely irritable and unreasonable."

"Yes," said Jack, with a brief reluctant look at her.

"All right, don't worry," she said, replying aloud as she often did to things that Jack had not said aloud.

"Good," he said.

Stella thought of how she had seen Dorothy, in the hospital room, with the new baby. She had sat up in bed, in a pretty bed-jacket, the baby beside her in a basket. He was restless. Jack stood between basket and bed, one large hand on his son's stomach. "Now, you just shut up, little bleeder," he had said, as he grumbled. Then he had picked him up, as if he'd been doing it always, held him against his shoulder, and, as Dorothy held her arms out, had put the baby into them. "Want your mother, then? Don't blame you."

That scene, the ease of it, the way the two parents were together, had, for Stella, made nonsense of all the months of Dorothy's self-questioning. As for Dorothy, she had said, parodying the expected words but meaning them: "He's the most beautiful baby ever born. I can't imagine why I didn't have him before."

"There's the cottage," said Jack. Ahead of them was a small labourer's cottage, among full green trees, surrounded by green grass. It was painted white, had four sparkling windows. Next to it a long shed or structure that turned out to be a greenhouse.

"The man grew tomatoes," said Jack. "Fine studio now."

The car came to rest under another tree.

"Can I just drop in to the studio?"

"Help yourself." Stella walked into the long, glass-roofed shed. In London Jack and Dorothy shared a studio. They had shared huts, sheds, any suitable building, all around the Mediterranean. They always worked side by side. Dorothy's end was tidy, exquisite, Jack's lumbered with great canvases, and he worked in a clutter. Now Stella looked to see if this friendly arrangement continued, but as Jack came in behind her he said: "Dorothy's not set herself up yet. I miss her, I can tell you."

The greenhouse was still partly one: trestles with plants stood along the ends. It was lush and warm.

"As hot as hell when the sun's really going, it makes up. And Dorothy brings Paul in sometimes, so he can get used to a decent climate young."

Dorothy came in, at the far end, without the baby. She had recovered her figure. She was a small dark woman, with neat, delicate limbs. Her face was white, with scarlet rather irregular lips, and black glossy brows, a little crooked. So while she was not pretty, she was lively and dramatic-looking. She and Stella had their moments together, when they got pleasure from contrasting their differences, one woman so big and soft and blond, the other so dark and vivacious,

Dorothy came forward through shafts of sunlight, stopped, and said: "Stella, I'm glad you've come." Then forward again, to a few steps off, where she stood looking at them. "You two look good together," she said, frowning. There was something heavy and over-emphasised about both statements, and Stella said: "I was wondering what Jack had been up to."

"Very good, I think," said Dorothy, coming to look at the new canvas on the easel. It was of sunlit rocks, brown and smooth, with blue sky, blue water, and people swimming in spangles of light. When Jack was in the south, he painted pictures that his wife described as "dirt and grime and misery" – which was how they both described their joint childhood background. When he was in England he painted scenes like these.

"Like it? It's good, isn't it?" said Dorothy.

"Very much," said Stella. She always took pleasure from the contrast between Jack's outward self – the small, self-contained little man who could have vanished in a moment into a crowd of factory workers in, perhaps Manchester, and the sensuous bright pictures like these.

"And you?" asked Stella.

"Having a baby's killed everything creative in me – quite different from being pregnant," said Dorothy, but not complaining of it. She had worked like a demon while she was pregnant.

"Have a heart," said Jack, "he's only just got himself born."

"Well, I don't care," said Dorothy. "That's the funny thing, I *don't* care." She said this flat, indifferent. She seemed to be looking at them both again from a small troubled distance. "You two look good together," she said, and again there was the small jar.

"Well, how about some tea?" said Jack, and Dorothy said at once: "I made it when I heard the car. I thought better inside, it's not really hot in the sun." She led the way out of the greenhouse, her white linen dress dissolving in lozenges of yellow light from the glass panes above, so that Stella was reminded of the white limbs of Jack's swimmers disintegrating under sunlight in his new picture. The work of these two people was always reminding one of each other, or each other's work, and in all kinds of ways: they were so much married, so close.

The time it took to cross the space of rough grass to the door of the little house was enough to show Dorothy was right: it was really chilly in the sun. Inside two electric heaters made up for it. There had been two little rooms downstairs, but they had been knocked into one fine lowceilinged room, stone-floored, whitewashed. A tea table, covered with a purple checked cloth, stood waiting near a window where flowering bushes and trees showed through clean panes. Charming. They adjusted the heaters and arranged themselves so they could admire the English countryside through glass. Stella looked for the baby; Dorothy said: "In the pram at the back." Then she asked: "Did yours cry a lot?"

Stella laughed and said again: "I'll try to remember."

"We expect you to guide and direct, with all your experience," said Jack.

"As far as I can remember, she was a little demon for about three months, for no reason I could see, then suddenly she became civilised."

"Roll on the three months," said Jack.

"Six weeks to go," said Dorothy, handling teacups in a languid indifferent manner Stella found new in her.

"Finding it tough going?"

"I've never felt better in my life," said Dorothy at once, as if being accused.

"You look fine."

She looked a bit tired, nothing much; Stella couldn't see what reason there was for Jack to warn her. Unless he meant the languor, a look of self-absorption? Her vivacity, a friendly, aggressiveness that was the expression of her lively intelligence, was dimmed. She sat leaning back in a deep airchair, letting Jack manage things, smiling vaguely.

"I'll bring him in in a minute," she remarked, listening to the silence from the sunlit garden at the back.

"Leave him," said Jack. "He's quiet seldom, enough. Relax, woman, and have a cigarette."

He lit a cigarette for her, and she took it in the same vague way, and sat breathing out smoke, her eyes half-closed.

"Have you heard from Philip?" she asked, not from politeness, but with sudden insistence.

"Of course she has, she got a wire," said Jack.

"I want to know how she feels," said Dorothy. "How do you feel, Stell?" She was listening for the baby all the time.

"Feel about what?"

"About his not coming back."

"But he is coming back, it's only a month," said Stella, and heard, with surprise, that her voice sounded edgy.

"You see?" said Dorothy to Jack, meaning the words, not the edge on them.

At this evidence that she and Philip had been discussed, Stella felt, first, pleasure: because it was pleasurable to be understood by two such good friends; then she felt discomfort, remembering Jack's warning.

"See what?" she asked Dorothy, smiling.

"That's enough now," said Jack to his wife in a flash of stubborn anger, which continued the conversation that had taken place.

Dorothy took direction from her husband, and kept quiet a moment, then seemed impelled to continue: "I've been thinking it must be nice, having your husband go off, then come back. Do you realise Jack and I haven't been separated since we married? That's over ten years. Don't you think there's something awful in two grown people stuck together all the time like Siamese twins?" This ended in a wail of genuine appeal to Stella.

"No, I think it's marvellous."

"But you don't mind being alone so much?"

"It's not *so* much; it's two or three months in a year. Well of course I mind. But I enjoy being alone, really. But I'd enjoy it too if we were together all the time. I envy you two." Stella was surprised to find her eyes wet with self-pity because she had to be without her husband another month.

"And what does he think?" demanded Dorothy. "What does Philip think?"

Stella said: "Well, I think he likes getting away from time to time – yes. He likes intimacy, he enjoys it, but it doesn't come as easily to him as it does to me." She had never said this before because she had never thought about it. She was annoyed with herself that she had had to wait for Dorothy to prompt her. Yet she knew that getting annoyed was what she must not do, with the state Dorothy was in, whatever it was. She glanced at Jack for guidance, but he was determinedly busy on his pipe.

"Well, I'm like Philip," announced Dorothy. "Yes, I'd love it if Jack went off sometimes. I think I'm being stifled being shut up with Jack day and night, year in year out."

"Thanks," said Jack, short but good-humoured.

"No, but I mean it. There's something humiliating about two adult people never for one second out of each other's sight."

"Well," said Jack, "when Paul's a bit bigger, you buzz off for a month or so and you'll appreciate me when you get back."

"It's not that I don't appreciate you, it's not that at all," said Dorothy, insistent, almost strident, apparently fevered with restlessness. Her languor had quite gone, and her limbs jerked and moved. And now the baby, as if he had been prompted by his father's mentioning him, let out a cry. Jack got up, forestalling his wife, saying: "I'll get him."

Dorothy sat, listening for her husband's movements with the baby, until he came back, which he did, supporting the infant sprawled against his shoulder with a competent hand. He sat down, let his son slide on to his chest, and said: "There now, you shut up and leave us in peace a bit longer." The baby was looking up into his face with the astonished expression of the newly born, and Dorothy sat smiling at both of them. Stella understood that her restlessness, her repeated curtailed movements, meant that she longed – more, needed – to have the child in her arms, have its body against hers. And Jack seemed to feel this, because Stella could have sworn it was not a conscious decision that made him rise and slide the infant into his wife's arms. Her flesh, her needs, had spoken direct to him without words, and he had risen at once to give her what she wanted. This silent instinctive conversation between husband and wife made Stella miss her own husband violently, and with resentment against fate that kept them apart so often. She ached for Philip.

Meanwhile Dorothy, now the baby was sprawled softly against her chest, the small feet in her hand, seemed to have lapsed into good humour. And Stella, watching, remembered something she really had forgotten: the close, fierce physical tie between herself and her daughter when she had been a tiny baby. She saw this bond in the way Dorothy stroked the small head that trembled on its neck as the baby looked up into his mother's face. Why, she remembered it was like being in love, having a new baby. All kinds of forgotten or unused instincts woke in Stella. She lit a cigarette, took herself in hand; set herself to enjoy the other woman's love affair with her baby instead of envying her.

The sun, dropping into the trees, struck the windowpanes, and there was a dazzle and a flashing of yellow and white light into the room, particularly over Dorothy in her white dress and the baby. Again Stella was reminded of Jack's picture of the white-limbed swimmers in sun-dissolving water. Dorothy shielded the baby's eyes with her hand and remarked dreamily: "This is better than any man, isn't it, Stell? Isn't it better than any man?"

"Well – no," said Stella laughing. "No, not for long."

"If you say so, you should know … but I can't imagine ever … Tell me, Stell, does your Philip have affairs when he's away?"

"For God's sake!" said Jack, angry. But he checked himself.

"Yes, I am sure he does."

"Do you mind?" asked Dorothy, loving the baby's feet with her enclosing palm.

And now Stella was forced to remember, to think about having minded, minding, coming to terms, and the ways in which she now did not mind.

"I don't think about it," she said.

"Well, I don't think I'd mind," said Dorothy.

"Thanks for letting me know," said Jack, short despite himself. Then he made himself laugh.

"And you, do you have affairs while Philip's away?"

"Sometimes. Not really."

"Do you know, Jack was unfaithful to me this week," remarked Dorothy, smiling at the baby.

"That's *enough*," said Jack, really angry.

"No it isn't enough, it isn't. Because what's awful is, I don't care."

"Well why should you care, in the circumstances?" Jack turned to Stella. "There's a silly bitch Lady Edith lives across that field. She got all excited, real live artists living down her lane. Well Dorothy was lucky, she had an excuse in the baby, but I had to go to her silly party. Booze flowing in rivers, and the most incredible people – you know. If you read about them in a novel, you'd never believe … but I can't remember much after about twelve."

"Do you know what happened?" said Dorothy. "I was feeding the baby, it was terribly early. Jack sat straight up in bed and said: 'Jesus, Dorothy, I've just remembered, I screwed, that silly bitch Lady Edith on her brocade sofa.' "

Stella laughed. Jack let out a snort of laughter. Dorothy laughed, an unscrupulous chuckle of appreciation. Then she said seriously: "But that's the point, Stella – the thing is, I don't care a tuppenny damn."

"But why should you?" asked Stella.

"But it's the first time he ever has, and surely I should have minded?"

"Don't you be too sure of that," said Jack, energetically puffing his pipe. "Don't be too sure." But it was only for form's sake, and Dorothy knew it, and said: "Surely I should have cared, Stell?"

"No. You'd have cared if you and Jack weren't so marvellous together. Just as I'd care if Philip and I weren't. ..." Tears came running down her face. She let them. These were her good friends; and besides, instinct told her tears weren't a bad thing, with Dorothy in this mood. She said, sniffing: "When Philip gets home, we always have a flaming bloody row in the first day or two, about something unimportant, but what it's really about, and we know it, is that I'm jealous of any affair he's had and vice versa. Then we go to bed and make up." She wept, bitterly, thinking of this happiness, postponed for a month, to be succeeded by the delightful battle of their day-to-day living.

"Oh Stella," said Jack. "Stell ..." He got up, fished out a handkerchief, dabbed her eyes for her. "There, love, he'll be back soon."

"Yes, I know. It's just that you two are so good together and whenever I'm with you I miss Philip."

"Well, I suppose we're good together?" said Dorothy, sounding surprised. Jack, bending over Stella with his back to his wife, made a warning grimace, then stood up and turned, commanding the situation. "It's nearly six. You'd better feed Paul. Stella's going to cook supper."

"Is she? How nice," said Dorothy. "There's everything in the kitchen, Stella. How lovely to be looked after."

"I'll show you our mansion," said Jack.

Upstairs were two small white rooms. One was the bedroom, with their things and the baby's in it. The other was an overflow room, jammed with stuff. Jack picked up a large leather folder off the spare bed and said: "Look at these, Stell." He stood at the window, back to her, his thumb at work in his pipe bowl, looking into the garden. Stella sat on the bed, opened the folder and at once exclaimed: "When did she do these?"

"The last three months she was pregnant. Never seen anything like it, she just turned them out one after the other."

There were a couple of hundred pencil drawings, all of two bodies in every kind of balance, tension, relationship. The two bodies were Jack's and Dorothy's, mostly unclothed, but not all. The drawings startled, not only because they marked a real jump forward in Dorothy's achievement, but because of their bold sensuousness. They were a kind of chant, or exaltation about the marriage. The instinctive closeness, the harmony of Jack and Dorothy, visible in every movement they made towards or away from each other, visible even when they were not together, was celebrated here with a frank, calm triumph.

"Some of them are pretty strong," said Jack, the northern workingclass boy reviving in him for a moment's puritanism.

But Stella laughed, because the prudishness masked pride: some of the drawings were indecent.

In the last few of the series the woman's body was swollen in pregnancy. They showed her trust in her husband, whose body, commanding hers, stood or lay in positions of strength and confidence. In the very last Dorothy stood turned away from her husband, her two hands supporting her big belly, and Jack's hands were protective on her shoulders.

"They are marvellous," said Stella.

"They are, aren't they."

Stella looked, laughing, and with love, towards Jack; for she saw that his showing her the drawings was not only pride in his wife's talent, but that he was using this way of telling Stella not to take Dorothy's mood too seriously. And to cheer himself up. She said, impulsively: "Well that's all right then, isn't it?"

"What? Oh yes, I see what you mean, yes, I think it's all right."

"Do you know what?" said Stella, lowering her voice. "I think Dorothy's guilty because she feels unfaithful to you."

"*What?*"

"No, I mean, with the baby, and that's what it's all about."

He turned to face her, troubled, then slowly smiling. There was the same rich unscrupulous quality of appreciation in that smile as there had been in Dorothy's laugh over her husband and Lady Edith. "You think so?" They laughed together, irrepressibly and loudly.

"What's the joke?" shouted Dorothy.

"I'm laughing because your drawings are so good," shouted Stella.

"Yes, they are, aren't they?" But Dorothy's voice changed to flat incredulity: "The trouble is, I can't imagine how I ever did them, I can't imagine ever being able to do it again."

"Downstairs," said Jack to Stella, and they went down to find Dorothy nursing the baby. He nursed with his whole being, all of him in movement. He was wrestling with the breast, thumping Dorothy's plump pretty breast with his fists. Jack stood looking down at the two of them, grinning. Dorothy reminded Stella of a cat, half-closing her yellow eyes to stare over her kittens at work on her side, while she stretched out a paw where claws sheathed and unsheathed themselves, making a small rip-rip-rip on the carpet she lay on.

"You're a savage creature," said Stella, laughing.

Dorothy raised her small vivid face and smiled. "Yes, I am," she said, and looked at the two of them calm, and from a distance, over the head of her energetic baby.

Stella cooked supper in a stone kitchen, with a heater brought by Jack to make it tolerable. She used the good food she had brought with her, taking trouble. It took some time, then the three ate slowly over a big wooden table. The baby was not asleep. He grumbled for some minutes on a cushion on the floor, then his father held him briefly, before passing him over, as he had done earlier, in response to his mother's need to have him close.

"I'm supposed to let him cry," remarked Dorothy. "But why should he? If he were an Arab or an African baby he'd be plastered to my back."

"And very nice too," said Jack. "I think they come out too soon into the light of day; they should just stay inside for about eighteen months, much better all around."

"Have a heart," said Dorothy and Stella together, and they all laughed; but Dorothy added, quite serious: "Yes, I've been thinking so too."

This good nature lasted through the long meal. The light went cool and thin outside; and inside they let the summer dusk deepen, without lamps.

"I've got to go quite soon," said Stella, with regret.

"Oh, no, you've got to stay!" said Dorothy, strident. It was sudden, the return of the woman who made Jack and Dorothy tense themselves to take strain.

"We all thought Philip was coming. The children will be back tomorrow night, they've been on holiday."

"Then stay till tomorrow, I *want* you," said Dorothy, petulant.

"But I can't," said Stella.

"I never thought I'd want another woman around, cooking in my kitchen, looking after me, but I do," said Dorothy, apparently about to cry.

"Well, love, you'll have to put up with me," said Jack.

"Would you mind, Stell?"

"Mind *what*?" asked Stella, cautious.

"Do you find Jack attractive?"

"Very."

"Well I know you do. Jack, do you find Stella attractive?"

"Try me," said Jack, grinning; but at the same time signalling warnings to Stella.

"Well, then!" said Dorothy.

"A *ménage à trois*?" asked Stella, laughing. "And how about my Philip? Where does he fit in?"

"Well, if it comes to that, I wouldn't mind Philip myself," said Dorothy, knitting her sharp black brows and frowning.

"I don't blame you," said Stella, thinking of her handsome husband.

"Just for a month, till he comes back," said Dorothy. "I tell you what, we'll abandon this silly cottage, we must have been mad to stick ourselves away in England in the first place. The three of us'll just pack up and go off to Spain or Italy with the baby."

"And what else?" enquired Jack, good-natured at all costs, using his pipe as a safety valve.

"Yes, I've decided I approve of polygamy," announced Dorothy. She had opened her dress and the baby was nursing again, quietly this time, relaxed against her. She stroked his head, softly, softly, while her voice rose and insisted at the other two people: "I never understood it before, but I do now. I'll be the senior wife, and you two can look after me."

"Any other plans?" enquired Jack, angry now. "You just drop in from time to time to watch Stella and me have a go, is that it? Or are you going to tell us when we can go off and do it, give us your gracious permission?"

"Oh I don't care what you do, that's the point," said Dorothy, sighing, sounding forlorn, however.

Jack and Stella, careful not to look at each other, sat waiting.

"I read something in the newspaper yesterday, it struck me," said Dorothy, conversational. "A man and two women living together – here, in England. They are both his wives, they consider themselves his wives. The senior wife has a baby, and the younger wife sleeps with him – well, that's what it looked like, reading between the lines."

"You'd better stop reading between lines," said Jack. "It's not doing you any good."

"No, I'd like it," insisted Dorothy. "I think our marriages are silly. Africans and people like that, they know better, they've got some sense."

"I can just see you if I did make love to Stella," said Jack.

"Yes!" said Stella, with a short laugh, which, against her will, was resentful.

"But I wouldn't mind," said Dorothy, and burst into tears.

"Now, Dorothy, that's enough," said Jack. He got up, took the baby, whose sucking was mechanical now, and said: "Now listen, you're going right upstairs and you're going to sleep. This little stinker's full as a tick, he'll be asleep for hours, that's my bet."

"I don't feel sleepy," said Dorothy, sobbing.

"I'll give you a sleeping pill, then."

Then started a search for sleeping pills. None to be found.

"That's just like us," wailed Dorothy, "we don't even have a sleeping pill in the place. ... Stella, I wish you'd stay, I really do. Why can't you?"

"Stella's going in just a minute, I'm taking her to the station," said Jack. He poured some Scotch into a glass, handed it to his wife and said: "Now drink that, love, and let's have an end of it. I'm getting fed-up." He sounded fed-up.

Dorothy obediently drank the Scotch, got unsteadily from her chair and went slowly upstairs. "Don't let him cry," she demanded, as she disappeared.

"Oh you silly bitch!" he shouted after her. "When have I let him cry? Here, you hold on a minute," he said to Stella, handing her the baby. He ran upstairs.

Stella held the baby. This was almost for the first time, since she sensed how much another woman's holding her child made Dorothy's fierce new possessiveness uneasy. She looked down at the small, sleepy, red face and said softly: "Well, you're causing a lot of trouble, aren't you?"

Jack shouted from upstairs: "Come up a minute, Stell." She went up, with the baby. Dorothy was tucked up in bed, drowsy from the Scotch, the bedside light turned away from her. She looked at the baby, but Jack took it from Stella.

"Jack says I'm a silly bitch," said Dorothy, apologetic to Stella.

"Well, never mind, you'll feel different soon."

"I suppose so, if you say so. All right, I *am* going to sleep," said Dorothy, in a stubborn, sad little voice. She turned over, away from them. In the last flare of her hysteria she said: "Why don't you two walk to the station together? It's a lovely night."

"We're going to," said Jack, "don't worry."

She let out a weak giggle, but did not turn. Jack carefully deposited the now sleeping baby in the bed, about a foot from Dorothy. Who suddenly wriggled over until her small, defiant white back was in contact with the blanketed bundle that was her son.

Jack raised his eyebrows at Stella: but Stella was looking at mother and baby, the nerves of her memory filling her with sweet warmth. What right had this woman, who was in possession of such delight, to torment her husband, to torment her friend, as she had been doing – what right had she to rely on their decency as she did?

Surprised by these thoughts, she walked away downstairs, and stood at the door into the garden, her eyes shut, holding herself rigid against tears.

She felt a warmth on her bare arm – Jack's hand. She opened her eyes to see him bending towards her, concerned.

"It'd serve Dorothy right if I did drag you off into the bushes …"

"Wouldn't have to drag me," he said; and while the words had the measure of facetiousness the situation demanded, she felt his seriousness envelop them both in danger.

The warmth of his hand slid across her back, and she turned towards him under its pressure. They stood together, cheeks touching, scents of skin and hair mixing with the smells of warmed grass and leaves.

She thought: What is going to happen now will blow Dorothy and Jack and that baby sky-high; it's the end of my marriage; I'm going to blow everything to bits. There was almost uncontrollable pleasure in it.

She saw Dorothy, Jack, the baby, her husband, and two half-grown children, all dispersed, all spinning downwards through the sky like bits of debris after an explosion.

Jack's mouth was moving along her cheek towards her mouth, dissolving her whole self in delight. She saw, against closed lids, the bundled baby upstairs, and pulled back from the situation, exclaiming energetically: "Damn Dorothy, damn her, damn her, I'd like to kill her …"

And he, exploding into reaction, said in a low furious rage: "Damn you both! I'd like to wring both your bloody necks …"

Their faces were at a foot's distance from each other, their eyes staring hostility. She thought that if she had not the vision of the helpless baby they would now be in each other's arms – generating tenderness and desire like a couple of dynamos, she said to herself, trembling with dry anger.

"I'm going to miss my train if I don't go," she said.

"I'll get your coat," he said, and went in, leaving her defenceless against the emptiness of the garden.

When he came out, he slid the coat around her without touching her, and said: "Come on, I'll take you by car." He walked away in front of her to the car, and she followed meekly over rough lawn. It really was a lovely night.

HOW I FINALLY LOST MY HEART

Doris Lessing

Doris Lessing (b. 1919) is a British novelist, poet, playwright, biographer and short story writer. In 2001, Lessing was awarded the David Cohen Prize for a lifetime's achievement in British Literature and she was ranked fifth on *The Times* list of the '50 Greatest British Writers Since 1945'. Lessing was awarded the 2007 Nobel Prize in Literature.

It would be easy to say that I picked up a knife, slit open my side, took my heart out, and threw it away; but unfortunately it wasn't as easy as that. Not that I, like everyone else, had not often wanted to do it. No, it happened differently, and not as I expected.

It was just after I had had a lunch and a tea with two different men. My lunch partner I had lived with for (more or less) four and seven-twelfths years. When he left me for new pastures, I spent two years, or was it three, half-dead, and my heart was a stone, impossible to carry about, considering all the other things weighing on one. Then I slowly, and with difficulty, got free, because my heart cherished a thousand adhesions to my first love – though from another point of view he could be legitimately described as either my second *real* love (my father being the first) or my third (my brother intervening).

As the folk song has it:

> *I have loved but three men in my life,*
> *My father, my brother, and the man that*
> *took my life.*

But if one were going to look at the thing from outside, without insight, he could be seen as (perhaps, I forget) the thirteenth, but to do that means disregarding the inner emotional truth. For we all know that those affairs or entanglements one has between *serious* loves, though they may number dozens and stretch over years, *don't really count.*

This way of looking at things creates a number of unhappy people, for it is well known that what doesn't really count for me might very well count for you. But there is no way of getting over this difficulty, for a *serious* love is the most important business in life, or nearly so. At any rate, most of us are engaged in looking for it. Even when we are in fact being very serious indeed with one person we still have an eighth of an eye cocked in case some stranger unexpectedly encountered might turn out to be even more serious. We are all entirely in agreement that we are in the right to taste, test, sip and sample a thousand people on our way to the *real* one. It is not too much to say that in our circles tasting and sampling is probably the second most important activity, the first being earning money. Or to put it another way, if you are serious about this thing, you go on laying everybody that offers until something clicks and you're all set to go.

I have digressed from an earlier point: that I regarded this man I had lunch with (we call him A) as my first love, and still do, despite the Freudians, who insist on seeing my father as A and possibly my brother as B, making my (real) first love C. And despite, also, those who might ask: What about your two husbands and all those affairs?

What about them? I did not *really* love them, the way I loved A.

I had lunch with him. Then, quite by chance, I had tea with B. When I say B, here, I mean my *second* serious love, not my brother, or the little boys I was in love with between the ages of five and fifteen, if we are going to take fifteen (arbitrarily) as the point of no return ... which last phrase is in itself a pretty brave defiance of the secular arbiters.

In between A and B (my count) there were a good many affairs, or samples, but they didn't score. B and I *clicked*, we went off like a bomb, though not quite as simply as A and I had clicked, because my heart was bruised, sullen, and suspicious because of A's throwing me over. Also there were all those ligaments and adhesions binding me to A still to be loosened, one by one. However, for a time B and I got on like a house on fire, and then we came to grief. My heart was again a ton weight in my side.

If this were a stone in my side, a stone,
I could pluck it out and be free ...

Having lunch with A, then tea with B, two men who between them had consumed a decade of my precious years (I am not counting the test or trial affairs in between) and, it is fair to say, had balanced all the delight (plenty and intense) with misery (oh Lord, Lord) – moving from one to the other, in the course of an afternoon, conversing amiably about this and that, with meanwhile my heart giving no more than slight reminiscent tugs, the fish of memory at the end of a long slack line ...

To sum up, it was salutary.

Particularly as that evening I was expecting to meet C, or someone who might very well turn out to be C; though I don't want to give too much emphasis to C, the truth is I can hardly remember what he looked like, but one can't be expected to remember the unimportant ones one has sipped or tasted in between. But after all, he might have turned out to be C, we might have *clicked*, and I was in that state of mind (in which we all so often are) of thinking: He might turn out to be the one. (I use a woman's magazine phrase deliberately here, instead of saying, as I might: *Perhaps it will be serious.*)

So there I was (I want to get the details and atmosphere right) standing at a window looking into a street (Great Portland Street, as a matter of fact) and thinking that while I would not dream of regretting my affairs, or experiences, with A and B (it is better to have loved and lost than never to have loved at all), my anticipation of the heart because of spending an evening with a possible C had a certain unreality, because there was no doubt that both A and B had caused me unbelievable pain. Why, therefore, was I looking forward to C? I should rather be running away as fast as I could.

It suddenly occurred to me that I was looking at the whole phenomenon quite inaccurately. My (or perhaps I am permitted to say our?) way of looking at it is that one must search for an A, or a B, or a C or a D with a certain combination of desirable or sympathetic qualities so that one may click, or spontaneously combust: or to put it differently, one needs a person who, like a saucer of water, allows one to float off on him/her, like a transfer. But this wasn't so at all. Actually one carries with one a sort of burning spear stuck in one's side, that one waits for someone else to pull out; it is something painful, like a sore or a wound, that one cannot wait to share with someone else.

I saw myself quite plainly in a moment of truth: I was standing at a window (on the third floor) with A and B (to mention only the mountain peaks of my emotional experience) behind me, a rather attractive woman, if I may say so, with a mellowness that I would be the first to admit is the sad harbinger of age, but is attractive by definition, because it is a testament to the amount of sampling and sipping (I nearly wrote "simpling" and "sapping") I have done in my time ... There I stood, brushed, dressed, red-lipped, kohl-eyed, all waiting for an evening with a possible C. And at another window overlooking (I think I am right in saying) Margaret Street, stood C, brushed, washed, shaved, smiling: an attractive man (I think), and *he* was thinking: Perhaps she will turn out to be D (or A or 3 or ? or %, or whatever symbol he used). We stood, separated by space, certainly, in identical conditions of pleasant uncertainty and anticipation; and we both held our hearts in our hands, all pink and palpitating and ready for pleasure and pain, and we were about to throw these hearts in each other's face like snowballs, or cricket balls (How's that?) or, more accurately, like great bleeding wounds: "Take my wound." Because the last thing one ever thinks at such moments is that he (or she) will say: Take *my* wound, please remove the spear from *my* side. No, not at all; one simply expects to get rid of one's own.

I decided I must go to the telephone and say, C! – You know that joke about the joke-makers who don't trouble to tell each other jokes, but simply say Joke 1 or Joke 2, and everyone roars with laughter, or snickers, or giggles appropriately ... Actually one could reverse the game by guessing whether it was Joke C(b) or Joke A(d) according to what sort of laughter a person made to match the silent thought ... Well, C (I imagined myself saying), the analogy is for our instruction: Let's take the whole thing as read or said. Let's not lick each other's sores; let's keep our hearts to ourselves. Because just consider it, C, how utterly absurd – here we stand at our respective windows with our palpitating hearts in our hands ...

At this moment, dear reader, I was forced simply to put down the telephone with an apology. For I felt the fingers of my left hand push outwards around something rather large, light, and slippery – hard to describe this sensation, really. My hand is not large, and my heart was in a state of inflation after having had lunch with A, tea with B, and then looking forward to C ... Anyway, my fingers were stretching out rather desperately to encompass an unknown, largish, lightish object, and I said: Excuse me a minute, to C, looked down, and there was my heart, in my hand.

I had to end the conversation there.

For one thing, to find that one has achieved something so often longed for, so easily, is upsetting. It's not as if I had been trying. To get something one wants simply by accident – no, there's no pleasure in it, no feeling of achievement. So to find myself heart-whole, or, more accurately, heart-less, or at any rate, rid of the damned thing, and at such an awkward moment, in the middle of an imaginary telephone call with a man who might possibly turn out to be C – well, it was irritating rather than not.

For another thing, a heart, raw and bleeding and fresh from one's side is not the prettiest sight. I'm not going into that at all. I was appalled, and indeed embarrassed that *that* was what had been loving and beating away all those years, because if I'd had any idea at all – well, enough of that.

My problem was how to get rid of it.

Simple, you'll say, drop it into the waste bucket.

Well, let me tell you, that's what I tried to do. I took a good look at this object, nearly died with embarrassment, and walked over to the rubbish-can, where I tried to let it roll off my fingers. It wouldn't. It was stuck. There was my heart, a large red pulsing bleeding repulsive object, stuck to my fingers. What was I going to do? I sat down, lit a cigarette (with one hand, holding the matchbox between my knees), held my hand with the heart stuck on it over the side of the chair so that it could drip into a bucket, and considered.

> If this were a stone in my hand, a stone,
> I could throw it over a tree ...

When I had finished the cigarette, I carefully unwrapped some tin foil of the kind used to wrap food in when cooking, and I fitted a sort of cover around my heart. This was absolutely and urgently necessary. First, it was smarting badly. After all, it had spent some forty years protected by flesh and ribs, and the air was too much for it. Secondly, I couldn't have any Tom, Dick and Harry walking in and looking at it. Thirdly, I could not look at it for too long myself, it filled me with shame. The tin foil was effective, and indeed rather striking. It is quite pliable and now it seemed as if there were a stylised heart balanced on my palm, like a globe, in glittering, silvery substance. I almost felt I needed a sceptre in the other hand to balance it ... But the thing was, there is no other word for it, in bad taste. I then wrapped a scarf around hand and tin-foiled heart, and felt safer. Now it was a question of pretending to have hurt my hand until I could think of a way of getting rid of my heart altogether, short of amputating my hand.

Meanwhile I telephoned (really, not in imagination) C, who now would never be C. I could feel my heart, which was stuck so close to my fingers that I could feel every beat or tremor, give a gulp of resigned grief at the idea of this beautiful experience now never to be. I told him some idiotic lie about having 'flu. Well, he was all stiff and indignant, but concealing it urbanely, as I would have done, making a joke but allowing a tiny barb of sarcasm to rankle in the last well-chosen phrase. Then I sat down again to think out my whole situation.

There I sat.

What was I going to do?

There I sat.

I am going to have to skip about four days here, vital enough in all conscience, because I simply cannot go heartbeat by heartbeat through my memories. A pity, since I suppose this is what this story is about; but in brief: I drew the curtains, I took the telephone off the hook, I turned on the lights, I took the scarf off the glittering shape, then the tin foil; then I examined the heart. There were two-fifths of a century's experience to work through, and before I had even got through the first night, I was in a state hard to describe ...

> Or if I could pull the nerves from my skin
> A quick red net to drag through a sea for fish ...

By the end of the fourth day I was worn out. By no act of will, or intention, or desire, could I move that heart by a fraction – on the contrary, it was not only stuck to my fingers, like a sucked boiled sweet, but was actually growing to the flesh of my fingers and my palm.

I wrapped it up again in tin foil and scarf, and turned out the lights and pulled up the blinds and opened the curtains. It was about ten in the morning, an ordinary London day, neither hot nor cold nor clear nor clouded nor wet nor fine. And while the street is interesting, it is not exactly beautiful, so I wasn't looking at it so much as waiting for something to catch my attention while thinking of something else.

Suddenly I heard a tap-tap-tapping that got louder, sharp and clear, and I knew before I saw her that this was the sound of high heels on a pavement though it might just as well have been a hammer against stone. She walked fast opposite my window and her heels hit the pavement so hard that all the noises of the street seemed absorbed into that single tap-tap-clang-clang. As she reached the corner at Great Portland Street two London pigeons swooped diagonally from the sky very fast, as if they were bullets aimed to kill her; and then as they saw her they swooped up and off at an angle. Meanwhile she had turned the corner. All this has taken time to write down, but the thing happening took a couple of seconds: the woman's body hitting the pavement bang-bang through her heels then sharply turning the corner in a right angle; and the pigeons making another acute angle across hers and intersecting it in a fast swoop of displaced air. Nothing to all that, of course, nothing – she had gone off down the street, her heels tip-tapping, and the pigeons landed on my windowsill and began cooing. All gone, all vanished, the marvellous exact co-ordination of sound and movement, but it had happened, it had made me happy and exhilarated, I had no problems in this world, and I realised that the heart stuck to my fingers was quite loose. I couldn't get it off altogether, though I was tugging at it under the scarf and the tin foil, but almost.

I understood that sitting and analysing each movement or pulse or beat of my heart through forty years was a mistake. I was on the wrong track altogether: this was the way to attach my red, bitter, delighted heart to my flesh for ever and ever …

> *Ha! So you think I'm done! You think …*
> *Watch, I'll roll my heart in a mesh of rage*
> *And bounce it like a handball off*
> *Walls, faces, railings, umbrellas and pigeons' backs …*

No, all that was no good at all; it just made things worse. What I must do is to take myself by surprise, as it were, the way I was taken by surprise over the woman and the pigeons and the sharp sounds of heels and silk wings.

I put on my coat, held my lumpy scarfed arm across my chest, so that if anyone said: What have you done with your hand? I could say: I've banged my finger, in the door. Then I walked down into the street.

It wasn't easy to go among so many people, when I was worried that they were thinking: What has that woman done to her hand? because that made it hard to forget myself. And all the time it tingled and throbbed against my fingers, reminding me.

Now I was out, I didn't know what to do. Should I go and have lunch with someone? Or wander in the park? Or buy myself a dress? I decided to go to the Round Pond, and walk around it by myself. I was tired after four days and nights without sleep. I went down into the underground at Oxford Circus. Midday. Crowds of people. I felt self-conscious, but of course need not have worried. I swear you could walk naked down the street in London and no one would even turn round.

So I went down the escalator and looked at the faces coming up past me on the other side, as I always do; and wondered, as I always do, how strange it is that those people and I should meet by chance in such a way, and how odd that we would never see each other again, or, if we did, we wouldn't know it. And I went on to the crowded platform and looked at the faces as I always do, and got into the train, which was very full, and found a seat. It wasn't as bad as at rush hour, but all the seats were filled. I leaned back and closed my eyes, deciding to sleep a little, being so tired. I was just beginning to doze off when I heard a woman's voice muttering, or rather, declaiming:

> *"A gold cigarette case, well, that's a nice thing,*
> *isn't it, I must say, a gold case, yes …"*

There was something about this voice which made me open my eyes: on the other side of the compartment, about eight persons away, sat a youngish woman, wearing a cheap green cloth coat, gloveless hands, flat brown shoes, and lisle stockings. She must be rather poor – a woman dressed like this is a rare sight, these days. But it was her posture that struck me. She was sitting half-twisted in her seat, so that her head was turned over her left shoulder, and she was looking straight at the stomach of an elderly man next to her. But it was clear she was not seeing it: her young staring eyes were sightless, she was looking inwards.

She was so clearly alone, in the crowded compartment, that it was not as embarrassing as it might have been. I looked around, and people were smiling, or exchanging glances, or winking, or ignoring her, according to their natures, but she was oblivious of us all.

She suddenly aroused herself, turned so that she sat straight in her seat, and directed her voice and her gaze to the opposite seat:

> *"Well so that's what you think, you think that,*
> *you think that do you, well, you think I'm just going*
> *to wait at home for you, but you gave her a gold*
> *case and ..."*

And with a clockwork movement of her whole thin person, she turned her narrow pale-haired head sideways over her left shoulder, and resumed her stiff empty stare at the man's stomach. He was grinning uncomfortably. I leaned forward to look along the line of people in the row of seats I sat in, and the man opposite her, a young man, had exactly the same look of discomfort which he was determined to keep amused. So we all looked at her, the young, thin, pale woman in her private drama of misery, who was so completely unconscious of us that she spoke and thought out loud. And again, without particular warning or reason, in between stops, so it wasn't that she was disturbed from her dream by the train stopping at Bond Street, and then jumping forward again, she twisted her body frontways, and addressed the seat opposite her (the young man had got off, and a smart grey-curled matron had got in):

> *"Well I know about it now, don't I, and if you come*
> *in all smiling and pleased well then I know, don't*
> *I, you don't have to tell me, I know, and I've said*
> *to her, I've said, I know he gave you a gold cigarette*
> *case ..."*

At which point, with the same clockwork impulse, she stopped, or was checked, or simply ran out, and turned herself half around to stare at the stomach – the same stomach, for the middleaged man was still there. But we stopped at Marble Arch and he got out, giving the compartment, rather than the people in it, a tolerant half-smile which said: I am sure I can trust you to realise that this unfortunate woman is stark staring mad ...

His seat remained empty. No people got in at Marble Arch, and the two people standing waiting for seats did not want to sit by her to receive her stare.

We all sat, looking gently in front of us, pretending to ourselves and to each other that we didn't know the poor woman was mad and that in fact we ought to be doing something about it. I even wondered what I should say: Madam, you're mad – shall I escort you to your home? Or: Poor thing, don't go on like that, it doesn't do any good, you know – just leave him, that'll bring him to his senses …

And behold, after the interval that was regulated by her inner mechanism had elapsed, she turned back and said to the smart matron who received this statement of accusation with perfect self-command:

> *"Yes, I know! Oh yes! And what about my*
> *shoes, what about them, a golden cigarette*
> *case is what she got, the filthy bitch,*
> *a golden case …"*

Stop. Twist. Stare. At the empty seat by her.

Extraordinary. Because it was a frozen misery, how shall I put it? A passionless passion – we were seeing unhappiness embodied; we were looking at the essence of some private tragedy – rather, Tragedy. There was no emotion in it. She was like an actress doing Accusation, or Betrayed Love, or Infidelity, when she has only just learned her lines and is not bothering to do more than get them right.

And whether she sat in her half-twisted position, her unblinking eyes staring at the greenish, furry, ugly covering of the train seat, or sat straight, directing her accusation to the smart woman opposite, there was a frightening immobility about her – yes, that was why she frightened us. For it was clear that she might very well (if the inner machine ran down) stay silent, forever, in either twisted or straight position, or at any point between them – yes, we could all imagine her, frozen perpetually in some arbitrary pose. It was as if we watched the shell of some woman going through certain predetermined motions.

For *she* was simply not there. *What* was there, who she was, it was impossible to tell, though it was easy to imagine her thin, gentle little face breaking into a smile in total forgetfulness of what she was enacting now. She did not know she was in a train between Marble Arch and Queensway, nor that she was publicly accusing her husband or lover, nor that we were looking at her.

And we, looking at her, felt an embarrassment and shame that was not on her account at all …

Suddenly I felt, under the scarf and the tin foil, a lightening of my fingers, as my heart rolled loose.

I hastily took it off my palm, in case it decided to adhere there again, and I removed the scarf, leaving balanced on my knees a perfect stylised heart, like a silver heart on a Valentine card, though of course it was three-dimensional. This heart was not so much harmless, no that isn't the word, as artistic, but in very bad taste, as I said. I could see that the people in the train, now looking at me and the heart, and not at the poor madwoman, were pleased with it.

I got up, took the four or so paces to where she was, and laid the tin-foiled heart down on the seat so that it received her stare.

For a moment she did not react, then with a groan or a mutter of relieved and entirely theatrical grief, she leaned forward, picked up the glittering heart, and clutched it in her arms, hugging it and rocking it back and forth, even laying her cheek against it, while staring over its top at her husband as if to say: Look what I've got, I don't care about you and your cigarette case, I've got a silver heart.

I got up, since we were at Notting Hill Gate, and, followed by the pleased congratulatory nods and smiles of the people left behind, I went out onto the platform, up the escalators, into the street, and along to the park.

No heart. No heart at all. What bliss. What freedom ...

Hear that sound? That's laughter, yes.
That's me laughing, yes, that's me.

FAITHFUL LOVERS

Margaret Drabble

Margaret Drabble (b. 1939) is a British novelist, biographer and critic. Awarded a CBE in 1980, Drabble was promoted to Dame Commander of the Order of the British Empire in the 2008 Birthday Honours. In 2011, she was awarded the Golden PEN Award by English PEN for a lifetime's distinguished service to literature.

There must have been a moment at which she decided to go down the street and around the corner and into the café. For at one point she was walking quite idly, quite innocently, with no recollection or association in her head but the dimmest shadow of long-past knowledge, and within ten yards she had made up her mind that she would go and have her lunch in that place where they had had lunch together once a fortnight or so over that long and lovely year. It was the kind of place where nobody either of them knew would ever see them. At the same time, it was not impossibly inconvenient, not so very far from Holborn, where they both had good reason to be from time to time. They had felt safe there – as safe as they could ever feel – yet at the same time aware that they had not allowed themselves to be driven into grotesque precautions.

And now, after so long, after three years, she found herself there – and at lunchtime, too. She was hungry. There is nothing more to it than that, she said to herself. I happened to be near, and the fact that I wanted my lunch reminded me of this place, and moreover, there is nowhere else possible within a five-minute walk. She had done enough walking, she thought – from the Old Street tube station to the place where they had made her new tooth. She ran her tongue over the new front tooth, reassuringly, and was slightly ashamed by the immense relief that she felt at being once more presentable, no longer disfigured by that humiliating gap. She had always made much of caring little for her beauty, and was always disturbed by the accidents that brought her face to face with her own vanity – by the inconvenient pimple, by the unperceived smudge on the cheek, by the heavy cold. And that lost tooth had been something of a test case ever since she had had it knocked out, while still a child at school. Her dentist had made her the most elaborate and delicate bridge then, but the night before last she had fallen after a party and broken it. She had rung up her dentist in the morning, and he had promised her a temporary bridge to last her until he could make her a new one. When he had told her the name of the place she should go to collect the bridge, she had noticed in herself a small flicker of recollection. He went on explaining to her, obliging yet irritable. 'You've got that then, Mrs Harvey?

Eighty-two St Luke's Street? You go to Old Street Station, then turn right ...' And he had explained to her that she should express her gratitude to the man at the laboratory, in view of the shortness of the notice. And she had duly expressed it to the man when, ten minutes ago, he handed her the tooth.

Then she had come out and walked along this street. And as she paused at the café door, she knew that she had been thinking of him and of that other year all this time, that she could not very well have avoided the thought of him, among so much familiar scenery. There they had sat in the car and kissed, and endlessly discussed the impossibility of their kissing; there they had stood by that lamp-post, transfixed, unable to move. The pavement seemed still to bear the marks of their feet. And yet it was all so long ago, so thoroughly slaughtered and decayed. It was two years since she had cared, more than two years since she had suffered.

She was content, she was occupied, she had got her tooth back, everything was under control. And in a way it made her almost happy to be back in this place, to find how thoroughly dead it all was. She saw no ghosts of him here; for a year after their parting she had seen him on every street corner, in every passing car, in shapes of heads and hands and forms of movement, but now he was nowhere any more, not even here. For as long as she had imagined that she saw him, she had imagined that he had remembered. Those false ghosts had been in some way the projected shadows of his love; but now she knew that surely they had both forgotten.

She pushed open the door and went in. It looked the same. She went to the side of the room that they had always favoured, away from the door and the window, and sat at the corner table, where they had always sat when they could, with her back to the door. She sat there and looked down at the red-veined Formica tabletop, with its cluster of sugar bowl, salt and pepper, mustard and ketchup, and an ashtray. Then she looked up at the dark yellow ceiling, with its curiously useless trelliswork hung with plastic lemons and bananas, and then at the wall, papered in a strange, delicate, dirty flowered print. On the wall hung the only thing that was different. It was a calendar, a gift from the garage, and the picture showed an Alpine hut in snowy mountains, for all that the month was May. In their day the calendar had been one donated by a fruit-juice firm, and they had seen it through three seasons; she recalled the anguish with which she had seen its leaves turn, more relentless even than those leaves falling so ominously from real trees, and she recalled that at the time of their parting the calendar showed an appalling photograph of an autumn evening in a country garden, with an old couple sitting by their ivy-covered doorway.

They had both been merciless deliverers of ultimatums, the one upon the other. And she had selected in her own soul the month, and the day of that month, and had said, 'Look, on the twenty-third, that's it, and I mean it this time.' She wondered if he had known that this time it was for real. Because he had taken her at her word. It was the first time that she had not relented, nor he persisted; each other time they had parted forever, a telephone call had been enough to reunite them; each time she had left him, she had sat by the telephone biting her nails and waiting for it to ring. But this time it did not ring.

The menu, when it was brought to her, had not altered much. Though she never knew why she bothered to read menus, for she always ate the same lunch – a cheese omelette and chips. So she ordered her meal, and then sat back to wait. Usually, whenever left alone in a public place, she would read, and through habit she propped a book up against the sugar bowl and opened it. But she did not look at the words. Nor was she dwelling entirely upon the past, for a certain pleasurable anxiety about that evening's show was stealing most of her attention, and she found herself wondering whether she had adequately prepared her piece about interior decoration for the discussion programme she'd been asked to appear on, and whether David Rathbone, the producer, would offer to drive her home, and whether her hair would look all right. And most of all, she wondered if she ought to wear her grey skirt. She was not at all sure that it was not just a little bit too tight. If it wasn't, then it was perfect, for it was the kind of thing that she always looked marvellous in. Then she said to herself: The very fact that I'm *worrying* about it must mean that it must be too tight after all, or the thought of its being too tight wouldn't have crossed my mind, would it? And then she saw him.

What was really most shocking about it was the way they noticed each other simultaneously, without a chance of turning away or in any way managing the shock. Their eyes met, and they both jerked, beyond hope of dissimulation.

'Oh, God,' he said, after a second, and he stood there looking at her.

And she felt at such a loss, sitting there with her book propped up against the sugar bowl, and her head full of thoughts of skirts and false teeth, that she said, hurriedly, throwing away what might after all have been really quite a moment, 'Oh, Lord, oh, well, since you're there, do sit down.' And she moved up the wooden bench, closing up her book with a snap, averting her eyes, confused, unable to look.

And he sat down by her, and then said quite suddenly and intimately, as though perfectly at home with her after so many years of silence, 'Oh, Lord, my darling Viola, what a dreadful, dreadful surprise. I don't think I shall ever recover.'

'Oh, I don't know, Kenneth,' she said, as though she too had discovered exactly where she was. 'One gets over these things quite quickly. I feel better already, don't you?'

'Why, yes, I suppose I do,' he said. 'I feel better now that I'm sitting down. I thought I was going to faint, standing there and looking at you. Didn't you feel some sort of slight tremor?'

'It's hard to tell,' she said, 'when one's sitting down. It isn't a fair test. Even of tremors.'

'No,' he said, 'no.'

Then they were silent for a moment or two, and then she said, very precisely and carefully, offering her first generous signal of intended retreat, 'I suppose that what *is* odd, really, is that we haven't come across one another before.'

'Have you ever been back here before this?' he asked.

'No, never,' she said. 'Have you?'

'Yes,' he said. 'Yes, I have. And if you had been back, you might have seen me. I looked for you.'

'You're lying,' she said quickly, elated, looking at him for the first time since he had sat down by her, and then looking away again quickly, horrified by the dangerous proximity of his head.

'No, I'm not,' he said. 'I came here, and I looked for you. I was sure that you would come.'

'It's a safe lie,' she said, 'like all your lies. A lie I could never catch you out in. Unless I really had been here, looking for you, and simply hadn't wanted to admit it.'

'But,' he said with conviction, 'you weren't here at all. I came, but you didn't. You were faithless, weren't you, my darling?'

'Faithless?'

'You forgot me quicker than I forgot you, didn't you? How long did you remember me?'

'Oh, how can one say?' she said. 'After all, there are degrees of remembrance.'

'Tell me,' he said. 'What harm can it do to tell me now?'

She moved a little on the seat, away from him, but settling at the same time into a more comfortable pose of confidence, because she had been waiting for years to tell him.

'I suffered quite horribly,' she said. 'Really quite horribly. That's what you want to hear, isn't it?'

'Of course it is,' he said.

'Oh, I really did,' she said. 'I can't tell you. I cried all the time, for weeks. For at least a month. And whenever the phone rang, I started, I jumped, like a fool, as though I'd been shot. It was pathetic, it was ludicrous. Each time I answered and it wasn't you I would stand there listening, and they would go on talking, and sometimes I would say yes or no, as I waited for them to ring off. And when they did ring off I would sit down and I would cry. Is that what you want me to say?'

'I want to hear it,' he said, 'but it can't, it can't be true.'

'It's as true as that you came to this place to look for me,' she said.

'I did come,' he said.

'And I did weep,' she said.

'Did you ever try to ring me?' he asked then, unable to resist.

'No!' she said with some pride. 'No, not once. I'd said I wouldn't, and I didn't.'

'I rang you, once,' he said.

'You didn't,' she said, and became aware at that instant that her knees under the table were trembling.

'I did,' he said. 'It was just over a year ago, and we'd just got back from a party – about three in the morning it was – and I rang you.'

'Oh, God,' she said, 'oh, God. It's true, it's not a lie, because I remember it! Oliver went to answer it, and he came back saying no one was there. But I immediately thought of you. Oh, my darling, I can't tell you how I've had to stop myself from ringing you, how I've sat there by the phone and lifted the receiver and dialled the beginning of your number, and then stopped. Wasn't that good of me?'

'Oh,' he said, 'if you knew how I'd wanted you to ring.'

'I did write to you once,' she said. 'But I couldn't bring myself to post it. But I'll tell you what I did do: I typed out an envelope to you, and I put one of those circulars from that absurd poetry club of mine into it, and I sent it off to you, because I thought that at least it might create in you a passing thought of me. And I liked the thought of something from my house reaching your house. Though perhaps she threw it away before it even got to you.'

'I remember it,' he said. 'I did think of you. But I didn't think you sent it, because the postmark was Croydon.'

'Oh,' she said, weakly. 'You got it. Oh, Lord, how alarmingly faithful we have both been.'

'Did you expect us not to be? We swore that we would be. Oh, look, my darling, here's your lunch. Are you still eating cheese omelettes every day? Now, that really *is* what I call alarming consistency. And I haven't even ordered. What about some moussaka? I always used to like that; it was always rather nice, in its own disgusting way. One moussaka, please.'

After her first mouthful, she put down her fork and said reflectively, 'From my point of view, at least, the whole business was quite unnecessary. What I mean is, Oliver hadn't the faintest suspicion. Which, considering how ludicrously careless we were, is quite astonishing. We could have gone on forever, and he'd never have known. He was far too preoccupied with his own affairs.'

'You know,' he said, 'all those continual threats of separation, of ending it – that was really corrupt. I feel bad about it now, looking back. Don't you?'

'How do you mean, bad about it?' she said.

'I feel we ought to have been able to do better than that. Though, come to think of it, it was you that did nearly all the threatening. Every time I saw you, you said it was for the last time. Every time. And I must have seen you six days in every week for over a year. You can't have meant it each time.'

'I did mean it,' she said. 'Every time I said it. I must have meant it, because I finally did it, didn't I?'

'You mean *we* did it,' he said. 'You couldn't have done it without my help. If I'd rung you, if I'd written to you, it would have started all over again.'

'Do you really think so?' she said, sadly, without malice, without recrimination. 'Yes, I suppose you might be right. It takes two to part, just as it takes two to love.'

'It was corrupt,' he said, 'to make ourselves live under that perpetual threat.'

'Yes,' she said, 'but remember how lovely it was, how horribly lovely, each time that one relented. Each time one said, "I'll never see you again ... all right, I'll meet you tomorrow in the usual place at half-past one." It was lovely.'

'Lovely, but wicked,' he said.

'Oh, that sensation,' she said, 'that sensation of defeat. That was so lovely, every time, every time you touched me, every time I saw you. And I felt so sure, so entirely sure that what you felt was what I felt. Lord, we were so alike. And to think that when I first knew you I couldn't think of anything to say to you at all; I thought you came from another world, that we had nothing in common at all, nothing except, well, except you know what; I feel it would be dangerous even to mention it, even now. Oh, darling, what a disaster, our being so alike.'

'I liked it, though,' he said. 'I liked breaking up together. Better than having it done to one; better than doing it.'

'Yes, but more seriously incurable,' she said. And silence threatening to fall once more, she said quickly, 'Anyway, tell me what you're doing round here. I mean to say, one has to have some reason for coming to a place like this.'

'I told you,' he said. 'I was looking for you.'

'You *are* a liar,' she said, smiling, amazed that even here she could allow herself to be amused; indeed, could not prevent herself from smiling.

'What are you doing here, then?'

'Oh, I had a perfectly good reason,' she said. 'You know that false front tooth? Well, yesterday morning I broke it, and I've got to do a programme on television tonight, so I went to my dentist and he made me a temporary new bridge, and I had to come round here to the laboratory to pick it up.'

'Have you got it in?'

'Look,' she said, and turned to face him, smiling, lifting her upper lip.

'Well, that's convincing enough, I guess,' he said.

'You still haven't told me what you're doing here,' she said. 'I bet you haven't got as good a reason as me. Mine is entirely convincing, don't you think? I mean, where else could I have had lunch? I think my reason clears me entirely of suspicion of any kind, don't you?'

'Any suspicion of sentiment?'

'That's what I meant.'

He thought for a moment, and then said, 'I had to call on a man about my income tax. Look, here's his address.' And he got an envelope out of his pocket and showed her.

'Ah,' she said.

'I came here on purpose,' he said. 'To think of you. I could have had lunch at lots of places between London Wall and here.'

'You didn't come here because of me; you came here because it's the only place you could think of,' she said.

'It comes to the same thing,' he said.

'No, it doesn't,' she said firmly. She felt creeping upon her the familiar illusion of control, created as always before by a concentration upon trivialities; she reflected that their conversations had always followed the patterns of their times in bed, and that these idle points of contention were like those frivolous, delaying gestures in which she would turn aside, in which he would lie still and stare at the ceiling, not daring to touch her, thus merely deferring the inevitable. Thinking this, and able to live only in the deferment, for now there was no inevitable outcome that she could see, she said, eating her last chip, 'And how are your children?'

'They're fine,' he said, 'fine. Saul started grammar school. We were pleased about that. What about yours?'

'Oh, they're all right, too. I've had some dreadful nights with Laura recently. I must say I thought I was through with all that – I mean, the child's five now – but she says she can't sleep and has these dreadful nightmares, so she's been in my bed every night for the last fortnight. It's wearing me out. Then in the morning she just laughs. She doesn't kick; it's just that I can't sleep with anyone else in the bed.'

'What does Oliver say?' he asked, and she said, without thinking, 'Oh, I don't sleep with Oliver any more,' and wondered as she said it how she could have made such a mistake, and wondered how to get out of it. But fortunately at that instant his moussaka arrived, making it unnecessary to pursue the subject. Though once it had become unnecessary, she regretted the subject's disappearance; she thought of saying what was the truth itself – that she had slept with nobody since she had slept with him, that for three years she had slept alone, and that she was quite prepared to sleep alone forever. But she was not entirely sure that he would want to hear it, and she knew that such a remark, once made, could never be retracted, so she said nothing.

'It looks all right,' he said, staring at the moussaka. He took a mouthful and chewed it, and then he put his fork down and said, 'Oh, Lord, oh, Lord, what a Proustian experience. I can't believe it. I can't believe that I'm sitting here with you. It tastes of you, this stuff. Oh, God, it reminds me of you. You look so beautiful, you look so lovely, my darling. Oh, God, I loved you so much. Do you believe me – that I really loved you?'

'I haven't slept with anyone,' she said, 'since I last slept with you.'

'Oh, darling,' he said. And she could feel herself fainting and sighing away, drifting downward on that fatefully descending, eddying spiral, like Paolo and Francesca in hell, helpless, the mutually entwined drifting fall of all true lovers, unresisting. It was as though three years of solitude had been nothing but a pause, nothing but a long breath before this final acknowledgement of nature, damnation and destiny. She turned towards him and said, 'Oh, my darling, I love you. What can I do? I love you.' And he, with the same breath, said, 'I love you, all the time I love you, I want you,' and they kissed there, their faces already so close that they hardly had to move.

Like many romantics, they habitually connived with fate by remembering the names of restaurants and the streets they had once walked along as lovers. Those who forget forget, he said to her later, and those who do not forget will meet again.

MASTER

Angela Carter

Angela Carter (1940–1992) was a British novelist and journalist, known for her unique blend of feminism and magical realism. In 2008, *The Times* ranked her tenth in their list of the '50 Greatest British Writers Since 1945', and in 2012 her novel, *Nights at the Circus*, was selected as the best ever winner of the James Tait Black Memorial Prize.

After he discovered that his vocation was to kill animals, the pursuit of it took him far away from temperate weather until, in time, the insatiable suns of Africa eroded the pupils of his eyes, bleached his hair and tanned his skin until he no longer looked the thing he had been but its systematic negative; he became the white hunter, victim of an exile which is the imitation of death, a willed bereavement. He would emit a ravished gasp when he saw the final spasm of his prey. He did not kill for money but for love.

He had first exercised a propensity for savagery in the acrid lavatories of a minor English public school where he used to press the heads of the new boys into the ceramic bowl and then pull the flush upon them to drown their gurgling protests. After puberty, he turned his indefinable but exacerbated rage upon the pale, flinching bodies of young women whose flesh he lacerated with teeth, fingernails and sometimes his leather belt in the beds of cheap hotels near London's great rail termini (King's Cross, Victoria, Euston ...). But these pastel-coloured excesses, all the cool, rainy country of his birth could offer him, never satisfied him; his ferocity would attain the colouring of the fauves only when he took it to the torrid zones and there refined it until it could be distinguished from that of the beasts he slaughtered only by the element of self-consciousness it retained, for, if little of him now pertained to the human, the eyes of his self still watched him so that he was able to applaud his own depredations.

Although he decimated herds of giraffe and gazelle as they grazed in the savannahs until they learned to snuff their annihilation upon the wind as he approached, and dispatched heraldically plated hippopotami as they lolled up to their armpits in ooze, his rifle's particular argument lay with the silken indifference of the great cats, and, finally, he developed a speciality in the extermination of the printed beasts, leopards and lynxes, who carry ideograms of death in the clotted language pressed in brown ink upon their pelts by the fingertips of mute gods who do not acknowledge any divinity in humanity.

When he had sufficiently ravaged the cats of Africa, a country older by far than we are yet to whose innocence he had always felt superior, he decided to explore the nether regions of the New World, intending to kill the painted beast, the jaguar, and so arrived in the middle of a metaphor for desolation, the place where time runs back on itself, the moist, abandoned cleft of the world whose fructifying river is herself a savage woman, the Amazon. A green, irrevocable silence closed upon him in that serene kingdom of giant vegetables. Dismayed, he clung to the bottle as if it were a teat.

He travelled by jeep through an invariable terrain of architectonic vegetation where no wind lifted the fronds of palms as ponderous as if they had been sculpted out of viridian gravity at the beginning of time and then abandoned, whose trunks were so heavy they did not seem to rise into the air but, instead, drew the oppressive sky down upon the forest like a coverlid of burnished metal. These tree trunks bore an outcrop of plants, orchids, poisonous, iridescent blossoms and creepers the thickness of an arm with flowering mouths that stuck out viscous tongues to trap the flies that nourished them. Bright birds of unknown shapes infrequently darted past him and sometimes monkeys, chattering like the third form, leaped from branch to branch that did not move beneath them. But no motion nor sound did more than ripple the surface of the profound, inhuman introspection of the place so that, here, to kill became the only means that remained to him to confirm he himself was still alive, for he was not prone to introspection and had never found any consolation in nature. Slaughter was his only proclivity and his unique skill.

He came upon the Indians who lived among the lugubrious trees. They represented such a diversity of ethnic types they were like a living museum of man organised on a principle of regression for, the further inland he went, the more primitive they became, as if to demonstrate that evolution could be inverted. Some of the brown men had no other habitation than the sky and, like the flowers, ate insects; they would paint their bodies with the juice of leaves and berries and ornament their heads with diadems of feathers or the claws of eagles. Placid and decorative, the men and women would come softly twittering round his jeep, a mild curiosity illuminating the inward-turning, amber suns of their eyes, and he did not recognise that they were men although they distilled demented alcohol in stills of their own devising and he drank it, in order to people the inside of his head with familiar frenzy among so much that was strange.

His half-breed guide would often take one of the brown girls who guilelessly offered him her bare, pointed breasts and her veiled, limpid smile and, then and there, infect her with the clap to which he was a chronic martyr in the bushes at the rim of the clearing. Afterwards, licking his chops with remembered appetite, he would say to the hunter: 'Brown meat, brown meat.' In drunkenness one night, troubled by the prickings of a carnality that often visited him at the end of his day's work, the hunter bartered, for the spare tyre of his jeep, a pubescent girl as virgin as the forest that had borne her.

She wore a vestigial slip of red cotton twisted between her thighs and her long, sinuous back was upholstered in cut velvet, for it was whorled and ridged with the tribal markings incised on her when her menses began – raised designs like the contour map of an unknown place. The women of her tribe dipped their hairs in liquid mud and then wound their locks into long curls around sticks and let them dry in the sun until each one possessed a hairdo of rigid ringlets the consistency of baked, unglazed pottery, so she looked as if her head was surrounded by one of those spiked haloes allotted to famous sinners in Sunday-school picture books. Her eyes held the gentleness and the despair of those about to be dispossessed; she had the immovable smile of a cat, which is forced by physiology to smile whether it wants to or not.

The beliefs of her tribe had taught her to regard herself as a sentient abstraction, an intermediary between the ghosts and the fauna, so she looked at her purchaser's fever-shaking, skeletal person with scarcely curiosity, for he was to her no more yet no less surprising than any other gaunt manifestation of the forest. If she did not perceive him as a man, either, that was because her cosmogony admitted no essential difference between herself and the beasts and the spirits, it was so sophisticated. Her tribe never killed; they only ate roots. He taught her to eat the meat he roasted over his camp fire and, at first, she did not like it much but dutifully consumed it as though he were ordering her to partake of a sacrament for, when she saw how casually he killed the jaguar, she soon realised he was death itself. Then she began to look at him with wonder for she recognised immediately how death had glorified itself to become the principle of his life. But when he looked at her, he saw only a piece of curious flesh he had not paid much for.

He thrust his virility into her surprise and, once her wound had healed, used her to share his sleeping bag and carry his pelts. He told her her name would be Friday, which was the day he bought her; he taught her to say 'master' and then let her know that was to be his name. Her eyelids fluttered for, though she could move her lips and tongue and so reproduce the sounds he made, she did not understand them. And, daily, he slaughtered the jaguar. He sent away the guide for, now he had bought the girl, he did not need him; so the ambiguous couple went on together, while the girl's father made sandals from the rubber tyre to shoe his family's feet and they walked a little way into the twentieth century in them, but not far.

Among her tribe circulated the following picturesque folk-tale. The jaguar invited the anteater to a juggling contest in which they would use their eyes to play with, so they drew their eyes out of the sockets. When they had finished, the anteater threw his eyes up into the air and back they fell – plop! in place in his head; but when the jaguar imitated him, his eyes caught in the topmost branches of a tree and he could not reach them. So he became blind. Then the anteater asked the macaw to make new eyes out of water for the jaguar and, with these eyes, the jaguar found that it could see in the dark. So all turned out well for the jaguar, and she too, the girl who did not know her own name, could see in the dark. As they moved always more deeply into the forest, away from the little settlements, nightly he extorted his pleasure from her flesh and she would gaze over her shoulder at shapes of phantoms in the thickly susurrating undergrowth, phantoms – it seemed to her – of beasts he had slaughtered that day, for she had been born into the clan of the jaguar and, when his leather belt cut her shoulder, the magic water of which her eyes were made would piteously leak.

He could not reconcile himself to the rain forest, which oppressed and devastated him. He began to shake with malaria. He killed continually, stripped the pelts and left the corpses behind him for the vultures and the flies.

Then they came to a place where there were no more roads.

His heart leaped with ecstatic fear and longing when he saw how nothing but beasts inhabited the interior. He wanted to destroy them all, so that he would feel less lonely, and, in order to penetrate this absence with his annihilating presence, he left the jeep behind at a forgotten township where a green track ended and an ancient whisky priest sat all day in the ruins of a forsaken church brewing fire-water from wild bananas and keening the stations of the cross. Master loaded his brown mistress with his guns and the sleeping bag and the gourds filled with liquid fever. They left a wake of corpses behind them for the plants and the vultures to eat.

At night, after she lit the fire, he would first abuse her with the butt of his rifle about the shoulders and, after that, with his sex; then drink from a gourd and sleep. When she had wiped the tears from her face with the back of her hand, she was herself again, and, after they had been together a few weeks she seized the opportunity of solitude to examine his guns, the instruments of his passion and, perhaps, learn a little of Master's magic.

She squinted her eye to peer down the long barrel; she caressed the metal trigger; and, pointing the barrel carefully away from her as she had seen Master do, she softly squeezed it in imitation of his gestures to see if she, too, could provoke the same shattering exhalation. But, to her disappointment, she provoked nothing. She clicked her tongue against her teeth in irritation. Exploring further, however, she discovered the secret of the safety catch.

Ghosts came out of the jungle and sat at her feet, cocking their heads on one side to watch her. She greeted them with a friendly wave of her hand. The fire began to fail but she could see clearly through the sights of the rifle since her eyes were made of water and, raising it to her shoulder as she had seen Master do, she took aim at the disc of moon stuck to the sky beyond the ceiling of boughs above her, for she wanted to shoot the moon down since it was a bird in her scheme of things and, since he had taught her to eat meat, now she thought she must be death's apprentice.

He woke from sleep in a paroxysm of fear and saw her, dimly illuminated by the dying fire, naked but for the rag that covered her sex, with the rifle in her hand; it seemed to him her clay-covered head was about to turn into a nest of birds of prey. She laughed delightedly at the corpse of the sleeping bird her bullet had knocked down from the tree and the moonlight glimmered on her curiously pointed teeth. She believed the bird she shot down had been the moon and now, in the night sky, she saw only the ghost of the moon. Though they were lost, hopelessly lost, in the trackless forest, she knew quite well where she was; she was always at home in the ghost town.

Next day, he oversaw the beginnings of her career as a markswoman and watched her tumble down from the boughs of the forest representatives of all the furred and feathered beings it contained. She always gave the same delighted laugh to see them fall for she had never thought it would be so easy to populate her fireside with fresh ghosts. But she could not bring herself to kill the jaguar, since the jaguar was the emblem of her clan; with forceful gestures of her head and hands, she refused. But, after she learned to shoot, soon she became a better hunter than he although there was no method to her killing and they went banging away together indiscriminately through the dim, green undergrowth.

The descent of the banana spirit in the gourd marked the passage of time and they left a gross trail of carnage behind them. The spectacle of her massacres moved him and he mounted her in a frenzy, forcing apart her genital lips so roughly the crimson skin on the inside bruised and festered while the bites on her throat and shoulders oozed diseased pearls of pus that brought the blowflies buzzing about her in a cloud. Her screams were a universal language; even the monkeys understood she suffered when Master took his pleasure, yet he did not. As she grew more like him, so she began to resent him.

While he slept, she flexed her fingers in the darkness that concealed nothing from her and without surprise she discovered her fingernails were growing long, curved, hard and sharp. Now she could tear his back when he inflicted himself upon her and leave red runnels in his skin; yelping with delight, he only used her the more severely and, twisting her head with its pottery appendages this way and that in pained perplexity, she gouged the empty air with her claws.

They came to a spring of water and she plunged into it in order to wash herself but she sprang out again immediately because the touch of water aroused such an unpleasant sensation on her pelt. When she impatiently tossed her head to shake away the waterdrops, her clay ringlets melted altogether and trickled down her shoulders. She could no longer tolerate cooked meat but must tear it raw between her fingers off the bone before Master saw. She could no longer twist her scarlet tongue around the two syllables of his name, 'mas-tuh'; when she tried to speak, only a diffuse and rumbling purr shivered the muscles of her throat and she dug neat holes in the earth to bury her excrement, she had become so fastidious since she grew whiskers.

Madness and fever consumed him. When he killed the jaguar, he abandoned them in the forest with the stippled pelts still on them. To possess the clawed was in itself a kind of slaughter, and, tracking behind her, his eyes dazed with strangeness and liquor, he would watch the way the intermittent dentellation of the sun through the leaves mottled the ridged tribal markings down her back until it seemed the blotched areas of pigmentation were subtly mimicking the beasts who mimicked the patterns of the sun through the leaves and, if she had not walked upright on two legs, he would have shot her. As it was, he thrust her down into the undergrowth, amongst the orchids, and drove his other weapon into her soft, moist hole whilst he tore her throat with his teeth and she wept, until, one day, she found she was not able to cry any more.

The day the liquor ended, he was alone with fever. He reeled, screaming and shaking, in the clearing where she had abandoned his sleeping bag; she crouched among the lianas and crooned in a voice like soft thunder. Though it was daylight, the ghosts of innumerable jaguar crowded round to see what she would do. Their invisible nostrils twitched with the prescience of blood. The shoulder to which she raised the rifle now had the texture of plush.

His prey had shot the hunter, but now she could no longer hold the gun. Her brown and amber dappled sides rippled like water as she trotted across the clearing to worry the clothing of the corpse with her teeth. But soon she grew bored and bounded away.

Then only the flies crawling on his body were alive and he was far from home.

THE MAN FROM MARS

Margaret Atwood

Margaret Atwood (b. 1939) is a Canadian writer and environmental activist. She is amongst the most honoured authors of fiction in recent history. She is a winner of the Arthur C. Clarke Award and has been shortlisted for the Man Booker Prize five times, winning in 2000 for her novel *The Blind Assassin*. She is the author of more than fifty volumes of poetry, children's literature, fiction and non-fiction.

A long time ago Christine was walking through the park. She was still wearing her tennis dress; she hadn't had time to shower and change, and her hair was held back with an elastic band. Her chunky reddish face, exposed with no softening fringe, looked like a Russian peasant's, but without the elastic band the hair got in her eyes. The afternoon was too hot for April; the indoor courts had been steaming, her skin felt poached.

The sun had brought the old men out from wherever they spent the winter: she had read a story recently about one who lived for three years in a manhole. They sat weedishly on the benches or lay on the grass with their heads on squares of used newspaper. As she passed, their wrinkled toadstool faces drifted towards her, drawn by the movement of her body, then floated away again, uninterested.

The squirrels were out, too, foraging; two or three of them moved towards her in darts and pauses, eyes fixed on her expectantly, mouths with the ratlike receding chins open to show the yellowed front teeth. Christine walked faster, she had nothing to give them. People shouldn't feed them, she thought; it makes them anxious and they get mangy.

Halfway across the park she stopped to take off her cardigan. As she bent over to pick up her tennis racquet again someone touched her on her freshly bared arm. Christine seldom screamed; she straightened up suddenly, gripping the handle of her racquet. It was not one of the old men, however it was a dark-haired boy of twelve or so.

"Excuse me," he said, "I search for Economics Building. Is it there?" He motioned towards the west.

Christine looked at him more closely. She had been mistaken: he was not young, just short. He came a little above her shoulder, but then, she was above the average height; "statuesque," her mother called it when she was straining. He was also what was referred to in their family as "a person from another culture": oriental without a doubt, though perhaps not Chinese. Christine judged he must be a foreign student and gave him her official welcoming smile. In high school she had been president of the United Nations Club; that year her school had been picked to represent the Egyptian delegation at the Mock Assembly. It had been an unpopular assignment – nobody wanted to be the Arabs – but she had seen it through. She had made rather a good speech about the Palestinian refugees.

"Yes," she said, "that's it over there. The one with the flat roof See it?"

The man had been smiling nervously at her the whole time. He was wearing glasses with transparent plastic rims, through which his eyes bulged up at her as though through a goldfish bowl. He had not followed where she was pointing Instead he thrust towards her a small pad of green paper and a ball-point pen.

"You make map," he said.

Christine set down her tennis racquet and drew a careful map. "We are here," she said, pronouncing distinctly. "You go this way. The building is here." She indicated the route with a dotted line and an X. The man leaned close to her, watching the progress of the map attentively; he smelled of cooked cauliflower and an unfamiliar brand of hair grease. When she had finished Christine handed the paper and pen back to him with a terminal smile.

"Wait," the man said. He tore the piece of paper with the map off the pad, folded it carefully and put it in his jacket pocket; the jacket sleeves came down over his wrists and had threads at the edges. He began to write something; she noticed with a slight feeling of revulsion that his nails and the ends of his fingers were so badly bitten they seemed almost deformed. Several of his fingers were blue from the leaky ball-point.

"Here is my name," he said, holding the pad out to her.

Christine read an odd assemblage of Gs, Ys and Ns, neatly printed in block letters. "Thank you," she said.

"You now write *your* name," he said, extending the pen.

Christine hesitated. If this had been a person from her own culture she would have thought he was trying to pick her up. But then, people from her own culture never tried to pick her up; she was too big. The only one who had made the attempt was the Moroccan waiter at the beer parlour where they sometimes went after meetings, and he had been direct. He had just intercepted her on the way to the Ladies' Room and asked and she said no; that had been that. This man was not a waiter though, but a student; she didn't want to offend him. In his culture, whatever it was, this exchange of names on pieces of paper was probably a formal politeness, like saying thank you. She took the pen from him.

"That is a very pleasant name," he said. He folded the paper and placed it in his jacket with the map.

Christine felt she had done her duty. "Well goodbye," she said. "It was nice to have met you." She bent for her tennis racquet but he had already stooped and retrieved it and was holding it with both hands in front of him, like a captured banner.

"I carry this for you."

"Oh no, please. Don't bother, I am in a hurry," she said, articulating clearly. Deprived of her tennis racquet she felt weaponless. He started to saunter along the path; he was not nervous at all now, he seemed completely at ease.

"*Vous parlez français?*" he asked conversationally.

"*Oui un petit peu*," she said. "Not very well." How am I going to get my racquet away from him without being rude? she was wondering.

"*Mais vous avez un bel accent*." His eyes goggled at her through the glasses: was he being flirtatious? She was well aware that her accent was wretched.

"Look," she said, for the first time letting her impatience show, "I really have to go. Give me my racquet, please."

He quickened his pace but gave no sign of returning the racquet. "Where you are going?"

"Home," she said. "My house."

"I go with you now," he said hopefully.

"No," she said: she would have to be firm with him. She made a lunge and got a grip on her racquet; after a brief tug of war it came free.

"Goodbye," she said, turning away from his puzzled face and setting off at what she hoped was a discouraging jog-trot. It was like walking away from a growling dog: you shouldn't let on you were frightened. Why should she be frightened anyway? He was only half her size and she had the tennis racquet, there was nothing he could do to her.

Although she did not look back she could tell he was still following. Let there be a streetcar, she thought, and there was one, but it was far down the line, stuck behind a red light. He appeared at her side, breathing audibly, a moment after she reached the stop. She gazed ahead, rigid.

"You are my friend," he said tentatively.

Christine relented: he hadn't been trying to pick her up after all, he was a stranger, he just wanted to meet some of the local people; in his place she would have wanted the same thing.

"Yes," she said, doling him out a smile.

"That is good," he said. "My country is very far."

Christine couldn't think of an apt reply. "That's interesting," she said. "*Très interessant*." The streetcar was coming at last; she opened her purse and got out a ticket.

"I go with you now," he said. His hand clamped on her arm above the elbow.

"*You … stay … here*," Christine said, resisting the impulse to shout but pausing between each word as though for a deaf person. She detached his hand – his hold was quite feeble and could not compete with her tennis biceps – and leapt off the curb and up the streetcar steps, hearing with relief the doors grind shut behind her. Inside the car and a block away she permitted herself a glance out a side window. He was standing where she had left him; he seemed to be writing something on his little pad of paper.

When she reached home she had only time for a snack, and even then she was almost late for the Debating Society, The topic was, "Resolved: That War Is Obsolete." Her team took the affirmative and won.

Christine came out of her last examination feeling depressed. It was not the exam that depressed her but the fact that it was the last one: it meant the end of the school year. She dropped into the coffee shop as usual, then went home early because there didn't seem to be anything else to do.

"Is that you, dear?" her mother called from the living room. She must have heard the front door close. Christine went in and flopped on the sofa, disturbing the neat pattern of cushions.

"How was your exam, dear?" her mother asked.

"Fine," said Christine flatly. It had been fine; she had passed. She was not a brilliant student, she knew that, but she was conscientious. Her professors always wrote things like "A serious attempt" and "Well thought out but perhaps lacking in élan" on her term papers; they gave her Bs, the occasional B+. She was taking Political Science and Economics, and hoped for a job with the Government after she graduated; with her father's connections she had a good chance.

"That's nice."

Christine felt, resentfully, that her mother had only a hazy idea of what an exam was. She was arranging gladioli in a vase; she had rubber gloves on to protect her hands as she always did when engaged in what she called "housework." As far as Christine could tell her housework consisted of arranging flowers in vases: daffodils and tulips and hyacinths through gladioli, irises and roses, all the way to asters and mums. Sometimes she cooked, elegantly and with chafing-dishes, but she thought of it as a hobby. The girl did everything else. Christine thought it faintly sinful to have a girl. The only ones available now were either foreign or pregnant; their expressions usually suggested they were being taken advantage of somehow. But her mother asked what they would do otherwise; they'd either have to go into a Home or stay in their own countries, and Christine had to agree this was probably true. It was hard, anyway, to argue with her mother. She was so delicate, so preserved-looking, a harsh breath would scratch the finish.

"An interesting young man phoned today," her mother said. She had finished the gladioli and was taking off her rubber gloves. "He asked to speak with you and when I said you weren't in we had quite a little chat. You didn't tell me about him, dear." She put on the glasses which she wore on a decorative chain around her neck, a signal that she was in her modern, intelligent mood rather than her old-fashioned whimsical one.

"Did he leave his name?" Christine asked. She knew a lot of young men but they didn't often call her; they conducted their business with her in the coffee shop or after meetings.

"He's a person from another culture. He said he would call back later."

Christine had to think a moment. She was vaguely acquainted with several people from other cultures, Britain mostly; they belonged to the Debating Society.

"He's studying Philosophy in Montreal," her mother prompted. "He sounded French."

Christine began to remember the man in the park. "I don't think he's French, exactly," she said.

Her mother had taken off her glasses again and was poking absentmindedly at a bent gladiolus. "Well, he sounded French." She meditated, flowery sceptre in hand. "I think it would be nice if you had him to tea."

Christine's mother did her best. She had two other daughters, both of whom took after her. They were beautiful; one was well married already and the other would clearly have no trouble. Her friends consoled her about Christine by saying, "She's not fat, she's just big-bones, it's the father's side," and "Christine is so healthy." Her other daughters had never gotten involved in activities when they were at school, but since Christine could not possibly ever be beautiful even if she took off weight, it was just as well she was so athletic and political, it was a good thing she had interests. Christine's mother tried to encourage her interests whenever possible. Christine could tell when she was making an extra effort, there was a reproachful edge to her voice.

She knew her mother expected enthusiasm but she could not supply it. "I don't know, I'll have to see," she said dubiously.

"You look tired, darling," said her mother. "Perhaps you'd like a glass of milk."

Christine was in the bathtub when the phone rang. She was not prone to fantasy but when she was in the bathtub she often pretended she was a dolphin, a game left over from one of the girls who used to bathe her when she was small. Her mother was being bell-voiced and gracious in the hall; then there was a tap at the door.

"It's that nice young French student, Christine," her mother said.

"Tell him I'm in the bathtub," Christine said, louder than necessary. "He isn't French."

She could hear her mother frowning. "That wouldn't be very polite, Christine. I don't think he'd understand."

"Oh, all right," Christine said. She heaved herself out of the bathtub, swathed her pink bulk in a towel and splattered to the phone.

"Hello," she said gruffly. At a distance he was not pathetic, he was a nuisance. She could not imagine how he had tracked her down: most likely he went through the phone book, calling all the numbers with her last name until he hit on the right one.

"It is your friend."

"I know," she said. "How are you?"

"I am very fine." There was a long pause, during which Christine had a vicious urge to say, "Well goodbye then," and hang up; but she was aware of her mother poised figurine-like in her bedroom doorway. Then he said, "I hope you also are very fine."

"Yes," said Christine. She wasn't going to participate.

"I come to tea," he said.

This took Christine by surprise. "You do?"

"Your pleasant mother ask me. I come Thursday, four o'clock."

"Oh," Christine said, ungraciously.

"See you then," he said, with the conscious pride of one who has mastered a difficult idiom.

Christine set down the phone and went along the hall. Her mother was in her study, sitting innocently at her writing desk.

"Did you ask him to tea on Thursday?"

"Not exactly, dear," her mother said. "I did mention he might come round to tea sometime, though."

"Well, he's coming Thursday. Four o'clock."

"What's wrong with that?" her mother said serenely. "I think it's a very nice gesture for us to make. I do think you might try to be a little more co-operative." She was pleased with herself.

"Since you invited him," said Christine, "you can bloody well stick around and help me entertain him. I don't want to be left making nice gestures all by myself."

"Christine, *dear*," her mother said, above being shocked. "You ought to put on your dressing gown, you'll catch a chill."

After sulking for an hour Christine tried to think of the tea as a cross between an examination and an executive meeting: not enjoyable, certainly, but to be got through as tactfully as possible. And it was a nice gesture. When the cakes her mother had ordered arrived from The Patisserie on Thursday morning she began to feel slightly festive; she even resolved to put on a dress, a good one, instead of a skirt and blouse. After all, she had nothing against him, except the memory of the way he had grabbed her tennis racquet and then her arm. She suppressed a quick impossible vision of herself pursued around the living room, fending him off with thrown sofa cushions and vases of gladioli; nevertheless she told the girl they would have tea in the garden. It would be a treat for him, and there was more space outdoors.

She had suspected her mother would dodge the tea, would contrive to be going out just as he was arriving: that way she could size him up and then leave them alone together. She had done things like that to Christine before; the excuse this time was the Symphony Committee. Sure enough, her mother carefully mislaid her gloves and located them with a faked murmur of joy when the doorbell rang. Christine relished for weeks afterwards the image of her mother's dropped jaw and flawless recovery when he was introduced: he wasn't quite the foreign potentate her optimistic, veil-fragile mind had concocted.

He was prepared for celebration. He had slicked on so much hair cream that his head seemed to be covered with a tight black patent-leather cap, and he had cut the threads off his jacket sleeves. His orange tie was overpoweringly splendid. Christine noticed, however, as he shook her mother's suddenly braced white glove that the ball-point ink on his fingers was indelible. His face had broken out; possibly in anticipation of the delights in store for him he had a tiny camera slung over his shoulder and was smoking an exotic-smelling cigarette.

Christine led him through the cool flowery softly padded living room and out by the French doors into the garden. "You sit here," she said. "I will have the girl bring tea."

This girl was from the West Indies: Christine's parents had been enraptured with her when they were down at Christmas and had brought her back with them. Since that time she had become pregnant, but Christine's mother had not dismissed her. She said she was slightly disappointed but what could you expect, and she didn't see any real difference between a girl who was pregnant before you hired her and one who got that way afterwards. She prided herself on her tolerance; also there was a scarcity of girls. Strangely enough, the girl became progressively less easy to get along with. Either she did not share Christine's mother's view of her own generosity, or she felt she had gotten away with something and was therefore free to indulge in contempt. At first Christine had tried to treat her as an equal. "Don't call me 'Miss Christine,'" she had said with an imitation of light, comradely laughter. "What you want me to call you then?" the girl had said, scowling. They had begun to have brief, surly arguments in the kitchen, which Christine decided were like the arguments between one servant and another: her mother's attitude towards each of them was similar, they were not altogether satisfactory but they would have to do.

The cakes, glossy with icing, were set out on a plate and the teapot was standing ready; on the counter the electric kettle boiled. Christine headed for it, but the girl, till then sitting with her elbows on the kitchen table and watching her expressionlessly, made a dash and intercepted her. Christine waited until she had poured the water into the pot. Then, "I'll carry it out, Elvira," she said. She had just decided she didn't want the girl to see her visitor's orange tie; already, she knew, her position in the girl's eyes had suffered because no one had yet attempted to get *her* pregnant.

"What you think they pay me for, Miss Christine?" the girl said insolently. She swung towards the garden with the tray; Christine trailed her, feeling lumpish and awkward. The girl was at least as big as she was but in a different way.

"Thank you, Elvira," Christine said when the tray was in place. The girl departed without a word, casting a disdainful backward glance at the frayed jacket sleeves, the stained fingers. Christine was now determined to be especially kind to him.

"You are very rich," he said.

"No," Christine protested, shaking her head, "we're not." She had never thought of her family as rich; it was one of her father's sayings that nobody made any money with the Government.

"Yes," he repeated, "you are very rich." He sat back in his lawn chair, gazing about him as though dazed.

Christine set his cup of tea in front of him. She wasn't in the habit of paying much attention to the house or the garden; they were nothing special, far from being the largest on the street; other people took care of them. But now she looked where he was looking, seeing it all as though from a different height: the long expanses, the border flowers blazing in the early-summer sunlight, the flagged patio and walks, the high walls and the silence.

He came back to her face, sighing a little. "My English is not good," he said, "but I improve."

"You do," Christine said, nodding encouragement.

He took sips of his tea, quickly and tenderly, as though afraid of injuring the cup. "I like to stay here."

Christine passed him the cakes. He took only one, making a slight face as he ate it; but he had several more cups of tea while she finished the cakes. She managed to find out from him that he had come over on a church fellowship – she could not decode the denomination – and was studying Philosophy or Theology, or possibly both. She was feeling well disposed towards him: he had behaved himself, he had caused her no inconvenience.

The teapot was at last empty. He sat up straight in his chair, as though alerted by a soundless gong. "You look this way, please," he said. Christine saw that he had placed his miniature camera on the stone sundial her mother had shipped back from England two years before. He wanted to take her picture. She was flattered, and settled herself to pose, smiling evenly.

He took off his glasses and laid them beside his plate. For a moment she saw his myopic, unprotected eyes turned towards her, with something tremulous and confiding in them she wanted to close herself off from knowing about. Then he went over and did something to the camera, his back to her. The next instant he was crouched beside her, his arm around her waist as far as it could reach, his other hand covering her own hands which she had folded in her lap, his cheek jammed up against hers. She was too startled to move. The camera clicked.

He stood up at once and replaced his glasses, which glittered now with a sad triumph. "Thank you, miss," he said to her. "I go now." He slung the camera back over his shoulder, keeping his hand on it as though to hold the lid on and prevent escape. "I send to my family, they will like."

He was out the gate and gone before Christine had recovered; then she laughed. She had been afraid he would attack her, she could admit it now, and he had; but not in the usual way. He had raped, *rapeo, rapere, rapui, to seize and carry off*, not herself but her celluloid image, and incidentally that of the silver tea service, which glinted mockingly at her as the girl bore it away, carrying it regally, the insignia, the official jewels.

Christine spent the summer as she had for the past three years: she was the sailing instructress at an expensive all-girls camp near Algonquin Park. She had been a camper there, everything was familiar to her; she sailed almost better than she played tennis.

The second week she got a letter from him, postmarked Montreal and forwarded from her home address. It was printed in block letters on a piece of the green paper, two or three sentences. It began, "I hope you are well," then described the weather in monosyllables and ended, "I am fine." It was signed, "Your friend." Each week she got another of these letters, more or less identical. In one of them a colour print was enclosed: himself, slightly cross-eyed and grinning hilariously, even more spindly than she remembered him against her billowing draperies, flowers exploding around them like firecrackers, one of his hands an equivocal blur in her lap, the other out of sight; on her own face, astonishment and outrage, as though he was sticking her in the behind with his hidden thumb.

She answered the first letter, but after that the seniors were in training for the races. At the end of the summer, packing to go home, she threw all the letters away.

When she had been back for several weeks she received another of the green letters. This time there was a return address printed at the top which Christine noted with foreboding was in her own city. Every day she waited for the phone to ring; she was so certain his first attempt at contact would be a disembodied voice that when he came upon her abruptly in mid-campus she was unprepared.

"How are you?"

His smile was the same, but everything else about him had deteriorated. He was, if possible; thinner; his jacket sleeves had sprouted a lush new crop of threads, as though to conceal hands now so badly bitten they appeared to have been gnawed by rodents. His hair fell over his eyes, uncut, ungreased; his eyes in the hollowed face, a delicate triangle of skin stretched on bone, jumped behind his glasses like hooded fish. He had the end of a cigarette in the corner of his mouth, and as they walked he lit a new one from it.

"I'm fine," Christine said. She was thinking, I'm not going to get involved again, enough is enough, I've done my bit for internationalism. "How are you?"

"I live here now," he said. "Maybe I study Economics."

"That's nice." He didn't sound as though he was enrolled anywhere.

"I come to see you."

Christine didn't know whether he meant he had left Montreal in order to be near her or just wanted to visit her at her house as he had done in the spring; either way she refused to be implicated. They were outside the Political Science Building. "I have a class here," she said. "Goodbye." She was being callous, she realized that, but a quick chop was more merciful in the long run, that was what her beautiful sisters used to say.

Afterwards she decided it had been stupid of her to let him find out where her class was. Though a timetable was posted in each of the colleges; all he had to do was look her up and record her every probable movement in block letters on his green notepad. After that day he never left her alone.

Initially he waited outside the lecture rooms for her to come out. She said hello to him curtly at first and kept on going, but this didn't work; he followed her at a distance, smiling his changeless smile. Then she stopped speaking altogether and pretended to ignore him, but it made no difference, he followed her anyway. The fact that she was in some way afraid of him – or was it just embarrassment? – seemed only to encourage him. Her friends started to notice, asking her who he was and why he was tagging along behind her; she could hardly answer because she hardly knew.

As the weekdays passed and he showed no signs of letting up, she began to jog-trot between classes, finally to run. He was tireless, and had an amazing wind for one who smoked so heavily: he would speed along behind her, keeping the distance between them the same, as though he were a pull-toy attached to her by a string. She was aware of the ridiculous spectacle they must make, galloping across campus, something out of a cartoon short, a lumbering elephant stampeded by a smiling, emaciated mouse, both of them locked in the classic pattern of comic pursuit and flight; but she found that to race made her less nervous than to walk sedately, the skin on the back of her neck crawling with the feel of his eyes on it. At least she could use her muscles. She worked out routines, escapes: she would dash in the front door of the Ladies' Room in the coffee shop and out the backdoor, and he would lose the trail, until he discovered the other entrance. She would try to shake him by detours through baffling archways and corridors, but he seemed as familiar with the architectural mazes as she was herself. As a last refuge she could head for the women's dormitory and watch from safety as he was skidded to a halt by the receptionist's austere voice: men were not allowed past the entrance.

Lunch became difficult. She would be sitting, usually with other members of the Debating Society, just digging nicely into a sandwich, when he would appear suddenly as though he'd come up through an unseen manhole. She then had the choice of barging out through the crowded cafeteria, sandwich half-eaten, or finishing her lunch with him standing behind her chair, everyone at the table acutely aware of him, the conversation stilting and dwindling. Her friends learned to spot him from a distance; they posted lookouts. "Here he comes," they would whisper, helping her collect her belongings for the sprint they knew would follow.

Several times she got tired of running and turned to confront him. "What do you want?" she would ask, glowering belligerently down at him, almost clenching her fists; she felt like shaking him, hitting him.

"I wish to talk with you."

"Well, here I am," she would say. "What do you want to talk about?"

But he would say nothing; he would stand in front of her, shifting his feet, smiling perhaps apologetically (though she could never pinpoint the exact tone of that smile, chewed lips stretched apart over the nicotine-yellowed teeth, rising at the corners, flesh held stiffly in place for an invisible photographer), his eyes jerking from one part of her face to another as though he saw her in fragments.

Annoying and tedious though it was, his pursuit of her had an odd result: mysterious in itself, it rendered her equally mysterious. No one had ever found Christine mysterious before. To her parents she was a beefy heavyweight, a plodder, lacking in flair, ordinary as bread. To her sisters she was the plain one, treated with an indulgence they did not give to each other: they did not fear her as a rival. To her male friends she was the one who could be relied on. She was helpful and a hard worker, always good for a game of tennis with the athletes among them. They invited her along to drink beer with them so they could get into the cleaner, more desirable Ladies and Escorts side of the beer parlour, taking it for granted she would buy her share of the rounds. In moments of stress they confided to her their problems with women. There was nothing devious about her and nothing interesting.

Christine had always agreed with these estimates of herself. In childhood she had identified with the false bride or the ugly sister, whenever a story had begun, "Once there was a maiden as beautiful as she was good," she had known it wasn't her. That was just how it was, but it wasn't so bad. Her parents never expected her to be a brilliant social success and weren't overly disappointed when she wasn't. She was spared the manoeuvring and anxiety she witnessed among others her age, and she even had a kind of special position among men: she was an exception, she fitted none of the categories they commonly used when talking about girls; she wasn't a cock-teaser, a cold fish, an easy lay or a snarky bitch; she was an honorary person. She had grown to share their contempt for most women.

Now, however, there was something about her that could not be explained. A man was chasing her, a peculiar sort of man, granted, but still a man, and he was without doubt attracted to her, he couldn't leave her alone. Other men examined her more closely than they ever had, appraising her, trying to find out what it was those twitching bespectacled eyes saw in her. They started to ask her out, though they returned from these excursions with their curiosity unsatisfied, the secret of her charm still intact. Her opaque dumpling face, her solid bearshaped body became for them parts of a riddle no one could solve. Christine sensed this. In the bathtub she no longer imagined she was a dolphin; instead she imagined she was an elusive water-nixie; or sometimes, in moments of audacity, Marilyn Monroe. The daily chase was becoming a habit; she even looked forward to it. In addition to its other benefits she was losing weight.

All these weeks he had never phoned her or turned up at the house. He must have decided however that his tactics were not having the desired result, or perhaps he sensed she was becoming bored. The phone began to ring in the early morning or late at night when he could be sure she would be there. Sometimes he would simply breathe (she could recognize, or thought she could, the quality of his breathing), in which case she would hang up. Occasionally he would say again that he wanted to talk to her, but even when she gave him lots of time nothing else would follow. Then he extended his range: she would see him on her streetcar, smiling at her silently from a seat never closer than three away; she could feel him tracking her down her own street, though when she would break her resolve to pay no attention and would glance back he would be invisible or in the act of hiding behind a tree or hedge.

Among crowds of people and in daylight she had not really been afraid of him; she was stronger than he was and he had made no recent attempt to touch her. But the days were growing shorter and colder, it was almost November. Often she was arriving home in twilight or a darkness broken only by the feeble orange streetlamps. She brooded over the possibility of razors, knives, guns; by acquiring a weapon he could quickly turn the odds against her. She avoided wearing scarves, remembering the newspaper stories about girls who had been strangled by men. Putting on her nylons in the morning gave her a funny feeling. Her body seemed to have diminished, to have become smaller than his.

Was he deranged, was he a sex maniac? He seemed so harmless, yet it was that kind who often went berserk in the end. She pictured those ragged fingers at her throat; tearing at her clothes, though she could not think of herself as screaming. Parked cars, the shrubberies near her house, the driveways on either side of it, changed as she passed them from unnoticed background to sinister shadowed foreground, every detail distinct and harsh: they were places a man might crouch, leap out from. Yet every time she saw him in the clear light of morning or afternoon (for he still continued his old methods of pursuit), his aging jacket and jittery eyes convinced her that it was she herself who was the tormentor, the persecutor. She was in some sense responsible; from the folds and crevices of the body she had treated for so long as a reliable machine was emanating, against her will, some potent invisible odour, like a dog's in heat or a female moth's, that made him unable to stop following her.

Her mother, who had been too preoccupied with the unavoidable fall entertaining to pay much attention to the number of phone calls Christine was getting or to the hired girl's complaints of a man who hung up without speaking, announced that she was flying down to New York for the weekend; her father decided to go too; Christine panicked: she saw herself in the bathtub with her throat slit, the blood drooling out of her neck and running in a little spiral down the drain (for by this time she believed he could walk through walls, could be everywhere at once). The girl would do nothing to help; she might even stand in the bathroom door with her arms folded, watching. Christine arranged to spend the weekend at her married sister's.

When she arrived back Sunday evening she found the girl close to hysterics. She said that on Saturday she had gone to pull the curtains across the French doors at dusk and had found a strangely contorted face, a man's face, pressed against the glass, staring in at her from the garden. She claimed she had fainted and had almost had her baby a month too early right there on the living-room carpet. Then she had called the police. He was gone by the time they got there but she had recognized him from the afternoon of the tea; she had informed them he was a friend of Christine's.

They called Monday evening to investigate, two of them. They were very polite, they knew who Christine's father was. Her father greeted them heartily; her mother hovered, in the background, fidgeting with her porcelain hands, letting them see how frail and worried she was. She didn't like having them in the living room but they were necessary.

Christine had to admit he'd been following her around. She was relieved he'd been discovered, relieved also that she hadn't been the one to tell, though if he'd been a citizen of the country she would have called the police a long time ago. She insisted he was not dangerous, he had never hurt her.

"That kind don't hurt you," one of the policemen said. "They just kill you. You're lucky you aren't dead."

"Nut cases," the other one said.

Her mother volunteered that the thing about people from another culture was that you could never tell whether they were insane or not because their ways were so different. The policemen agreed with her, deferential but also condescending, as though she was a royal halfwit who had to be humoured.

"You know where he lives?" the first policeman asked. Christine had long ago torn up the letter with his address on it; she shook her head.

"We'll have to pick him up tomorrow then," he said. "Think you can keep him talking outside your class if he's waiting for you?"

After questioning her they held a murmured conversation with her father in the front hall. The girl, clearing away the coffee cups, said if they didn't lock him up she was leaving, she wasn't going to be scared half out of her skin like that again.

Next day when Christine came out of her Modem History lecture he was there, right on schedule. He seemed puzzled when she did not begin to run. She approached him, her heart thumping with treachery and the prospect of freedom. Her body was back to its usual size; she felt herself a giantess, self-controlled, invulnerable.

"How are you?" she asked, smiling brightly.

He looked at her with distrust.

"How have you been?" she ventured again. His own perennial smile faded; he took a step back from her.

"This the one?" said the policeman, popping out from behind a notice board like a Keystone Cop and laying a competent hand on the worn jacket shoulder. The other policeman lounged in the background; force would not be required.

"Don't *do* anything to him," she pleaded as they took him away. They nodded and grinned, respectful, scornful. He seemed to know perfectly well who they were and what they wanted.

The first policeman phoned that evening to make his report. Her father talked with him, jovial and managing. She herself was now out of the picture; she had been protected, her function was over.

"What did they *do* to him?" she asked anxiously as he came back into the living room. She was not sure what went on in police stations.

"They didn't do anything to him," he said, amused by her concern. "They could have booked him for Watching and Besetting, they wanted to know if I'd like to press charges. But it's not worth a court case: he's got a visa that says he's only allowed in the country as long as he studies in Montreal, so I told them to just ship him down there. If he turns up here again they'll deport him. They went around to his rooming house, his rent's two weeks overdue, the landlady said she was on the point of kicking him out. He seems happy enough to be getting his back rent paid and a free train ticket to Montreal." He paused. "They couldn't get anything out of him though."

"*Out* of him?" Christine asked.

"They tried to find out why he was doing it; following you, I mean." Her father's eyes swept her as though it was a riddle to him also. "They said when they asked him about that he just clammed up. Pretended he didn't understand English. He understood well enough, but he wasn't answering."

Christine thought this would be the end, but somehow between his arrest and the departure of the train he managed to elude his escort long enough for one more phone call.

"I see you again," he said. He didn't wait for her to hang up.

Now that he was no longer an embarrassing present reality, he could be talked about, he could become an amusing story. In fact, he was the only amusing story Christine had to tell, and telling it preserved both for herself and for others the aura of her strange allure. Her friends and the men who continued to ask her out speculated about his motives. One suggested he had wanted to marry her so he could remain in the country; another said that oriental men were fond of well-built women: "It's your Rubens quality."

Christine thought about him a lot. She had not been attracted to him, rather the reverse, but as an idea only he was a romantic figure, the one man who had found her irresistible; though she often wondered, inspecting her unchanged pink face and hefty body in her full-length mirror, just what it was about her that had done it. She avoided whenever it was proposed the theory of his insanity: it was only that there was more than one way of being sane.

But a new acquaintance, hearing the story for the first time, had a different explanation. "So he got you, too," he said laughing. "That has to be the same guy who was hanging around our day camp a year ago this summer. He followed all the girls like that, a short guy, Japanese or something, glasses, smiling all the time."

"Maybe it was another one," Christine said.

"There couldn't be two of them, everything fits. This was a pretty weird guy."

"What ... *kind* of girls did he follow?" Christine asked.

"Oh, just anyone who happened to be around. But if they paid any attention to him at first, if they were nice to him or anything, he was unshakeable. He was a bit of a pest, but harmless."

Christine ceased to tell her amusing story. She had been one among many, then. She went back to playing tennis, she had been neglecting her game.

A few months later the policeman who had been in charge of the case telephoned her again.

"Like you to know, miss, that fellow you were having the trouble with was sent back to his own country. Deported."

"What for?" Christine asked. "Did he try to come back here?" Maybe she had been special after all, maybe he had dared everything for her.

"Nothing like it," the policeman said. "He was up to the same tricks in Montreal but he really picked the wrong woman this time – a Mother Superior of a convent. They don't stand for things like that in Quebec – had him out of here before he knew what happened. I guess he'll be better off in his own place."

"How old was she?" Christine asked, after a silence.

"Oh, around sixty, I guess."

"Thank you very much for letting me know," Christine said in her best official manner. "It's such a relief." She wondered if the policeman had called to make fun of her.

She was almost crying when she put down the phone. What *had* he wanted from her then? A Mother Superior. Did she really look sixty, did she look like a mother? What did convents mean? Comfort, charity? Refuge? Was it that something had happened to him, some intolerable strain just from being in this country; her tennis dress and exposed legs too much for him, flesh and money seemingly available everywhere but withheld from him wherever he turned, the nun the symbol of some final distortion, the robe and veil reminiscent to his nearsighted eyes of the women of his homeland, the ones he was able to understand? But he was back in his own country, remote from her as another planet; she would never know.

He hadn't forgotten her though. In the spring she got a postcard with a foreign stamp and the familiar block-letter writing. On the front was a picture of a temple. He was fine, he hoped she was fine also, he was her friend. A month later another print of the picture he had taken in the garden arrived, in a sealed manila envelope otherwise empty.

Christine's aura of mystery soon faded; anyway, she herself no longer believed in it. Life became again what she had always expected. She graduated with mediocre grades and went into the Department of Health and Welfare; she did a good job, and was seldom discriminated against for being a woman because nobody thought of her as one. She could afford a pleasant-sized apartment, though she did not put much energy into decorating it. She played less and less tennis; what had been muscle with a light coating of fat turned gradually into fat with a thin substratum of muscle. She began to get headaches.

As the years were used up and the war began to fill the newspapers and magazines, she realized which Eastern country he had actually been from. She had known the name but it hadn't registered at the time, it was such a minor place; she could never keep them separate in her mind.

But though she tried, she couldn't remember the name of the city and the postcard was long gone – had he been from the North or the South, was he near the battle zone or safely far from it? Obsessively she bought magazines and pored over the available photographs, dead villagers, soldiers on the march, colour blowups of frightened or angry faces, spies being executed; she studied maps, she watched the late-night newscasts, the distant country and terrain becoming almost more familiar to her than her own. Once or twice she thought she could recognize him but it was no use, they all looked like him.

Finally she had to stop looking at the pictures. It bothered her too much, it was bad for her; she was beginning to have nightmares in which he was coming through the French doors of her mother's house in his shabby jacket, carrying a packsack and a rifle and a huge bouquet of richly coloured flowers. He was smiling in the same way but with blood streaked over his face, partly blotting out the features. She gave her television set away and took to reading nineteenth-century novels instead; Trollope and Galsworthy were her favourites. When, despite herself, she would think about him, she would tell herself that he had been crafty and agile-minded enough to survive, more or less, in her country, so surely he would be able to do it in his own, where he knew the language. She could not see him in the army, on either side; he wasn't the type, and to her knowledge he had not believed in any particular ideology. He would be something nondescript, something in the background, like herself perhaps he had become an interpreter.

THE BLOODY CHAMBER

Angela Carter

Angela Carter (1940–1992) was a British novelist and journalist, known for her unique blend of feminism and magical realism. In 2008, *The Times* ranked her tenth in their list of the '50 Greatest British Writers Since 1945', and in 2012 her novel, *Nights at the Circus*, was selected as the best ever winner of the James Tait Black Memorial Prize.

I remember how, that night, I lay awake in the wagon-lit in a tender, delicious ecstasy of excitement, my burning cheek pressed against the impeccable linen of the pillow and the pounding of my heart mimicking that of the great pistons ceaselessly thrusting the train that bore me through the night, away from Paris, away from girlhood, away from the white, enclosed quietude of my mother's apartment, into the unguessable country of marriage.

And I remember I tenderly imagined how, at this very moment, my mother would be moving slowly about the narrow bedroom I had left behind for ever, folding up and putting away all my little relics, the tumbled garments I would not need any more, the scores for which there had been no room in my trunks, the concert programmes I'd abandoned; she would linger over this torn ribbon and that faded photograph with all the half-joyous, half-sorrowful emotions of a woman on her daughter's wedding day. And, in the midst of my bridal triumph, I felt a pang of loss as if, when he put the gold band on my finger, I had, in some way, ceased to be her child in becoming his wife.

Are you sure, she'd said when they delivered the gigantic box that held the wedding dress he'd bought me, wrapped up in tissue paper and red ribbon like a Christmas gift of crystallized fruit. Are you sure you love him? There was a dress for her, too; black silk, with the dull, prismatic sheen of oil on water, finer than anything she'd worn since that adventurous girlhood in Indo-China, daughter of a rich tea planter. My eagle-featured, indomitable mother; what other student at the Conservatoire could boast that her mother had outfaced a junkful of Chinese pirates, nursed a village through a visitation of the plague, shot a man-eating tiger with her own hand and all before she was as old as I?

'Are you sure you love him?'

'I'm sure I want to marry him,' I said.

And would say no more. She sighed, as if it was with reluctance that she might at last banish the spectre of poverty from its habitual place at our meagre table. For my mother herself had gladly, scandalously, defiantly beggared herself for love; and, one fine day, her gallant soldier never returned from the wars, leaving his wife and child a legacy of tears that never quite dried, a cigar box full of medals and the antique service revolver that my mother, grown magnificently eccentric in hardship, kept always in her reticule, in case – how I teased her – she was surprised by footpads on her way home from the grocer's shop.

Now and then a starburst of lights spattered the drawn blinds as if the railway company had lit up all the stations through which we passed in celebration of the bride. My satin nightdress had just been shaken from its wrappings; it had slipped over my young girl's pointed breasts and shoulders, supple as a garment of heavy water, and now teasingly caressed me, egregious, insinuating, nudging between my thighs as I shifted restlessly in my narrow berth. His kiss, his kiss with tongue and teeth in it and a rasp of beard, had hinted to me, though with the same exquisite tact as this nightdress he'd given me, of the wedding night, which would be voluptuously deferred until we lay in his great ancestral bed in the sea-girt, pinnacled domain that lay, still, beyond the grasp of my imagination … that magic place, the fairy castle whose walls were made of foam, that legendary habitation in which he had been born. To which, one day, I might bear an heir. Our destination, my destiny.

Above the syncopated roar of the train, I could hear his even, steady breathing. Only the communicating door kept me from my husband and it stood open. If I rose up on my elbow, I could see the dark, leonine shape of his head and my nostrils caught a whiff of the opulent male scent of leather and spices that always accompanied him and sometimes, during his courtship, had been the only hint he gave me that he had come into my mother's sitting room, for, though he was a big man, he moved as softly as if all his shoes had soles of velvet, as if his footfall turned the carpet into snow.

He had loved to surprise me in my abstracted solitude at the piano. He would tell them not to announce him, then soundlessly open the door and softly creep up behind me with his bouquet of hot-house flowers or his box of marrons glacés, lay his offering upon the keys and clasp his hands over my eyes as I was lost in a Debussy prelude. But that perfume of spiced leather always betrayed him; after my first shock, I was forced always to mimic surprise, so that he would not be disappointed.

He was older than I. He was much older than I; there were streaks of pure silver in his dark mane. But his strange, heavy, almost waxen face was not lined by experience. Rather, experience seemed to have washed it perfectly smooth, like a stone on a beach whose fissures have been eroded by successive tides. And sometimes that face, in stillness when he listened to me playing, with the heavy eyelids folded over eyes that always disturbed me by their absolute absence of light, seemed to me like a mask, as if his real face, the face that truly reflected all the life he had led in the world before he met me, before, even, I was born, as though that face lay underneath this mask. Or else, elsewhere. As though he had laid by the face in which he had lived for so long in order to offer my youth a face unsigned by the years.

And, elsewhere, I might see him plain. Elsewhere. But, where?

In, perhaps, that castle to which the train now took us, that marvellous castle in which he had been born.

Even when he asked me to marry him, and I said: 'Yes,' still he did not lose that heavy, fleshy composure of his. I know it must seem a curious analogy, a man with a flower, but sometimes he seemed to me like a lily. Yes. A lily. Possessed of that strange, ominous calm of a sentient vegetable, like one of those cobra-headed, funereal lilies whose white sheaths are curled out of a flesh as thick and tensely yielding to the touch as vellum. When I said that I would marry him, not one muscle in his face stirred, but he let out a long, extinguished sigh. I thought: Oh! how he must want me! And it was as though the imponderable weight of his desire was a force I might not withstand, not by virtue of its violence but because of its very gravity.

He had the ring ready in a leather box lined with crimson velvet, a fire opal the size of a pigeon's egg set in a complicated circle of dark antique gold. My old nurse, who still lived with my mother and me, squinted at the ring askance; opals are bad luck, she said. But this opal had been his own mother's ring, and his grandmother's, and her mother's before that, given to an ancestor by Catherine de Medici ... every bride that came to the castle wore it, time out of mind. And did he give it to his other wives and have it back from them? asked the old woman rudely; yet she was a snob. She hid her incredulous joy at my marital coup – her little Marquise – behind a façade of fault-finding. But, here, she touched me. I shrugged and turned my back pettishly on her. I did not want to remember how he had loved other women before me, but the knowledge often teased me in the threadbare self-confidence of the small hours.

I was seventeen and knew nothing of the world; my Marquis had been married before, more than once, and I remained a little bemused that, after those others, he should now have chosen me. Indeed, was he not still in mourning for his last wife? Tsk, tsk, went my old nurse. And even my mother had been reluctant to see her girl whisked off by a man so recently bereaved. A Romanian countess, a lady of high fashion. Dead just three short months before I met him, a boating accident, at his home, in Brittany. They never found her body but I rummaged through the back copies of the society magazines my old nanny kept in a trunk under her bed and tracked down her photograph. The sharp muzzle of a pretty, witty, naughty monkey; such potent and bizarre charm, of a dark, bright, wild yet worldly thing whose natural habitat must have been some luxurious interior decorator's jungle filled with potted palms and tame, squawking parakeets.

Before that? *Her* face is common property; everyone painted her but the Redon engraving I liked best, *The Evening Star Walking on the Rim of Night*. To see her skeletal, enigmatic grace, you would never think she had been a barmaid in a café in Montmartre until Puvis de Chavannes saw her and had her expose her flat breasts and elongated thighs to his brush. And yet it was the absinthe doomed her, or so they said.

The first of all his ladies? That sumptuous diva; I had heard her sing Isolde, precociously musical child that I was, taken to the opera for a birthday treat. My first opera; I had heard her sing Isolde. With what white-hot passion had she burned from the stage! So that you could tell she would die young. We sat high up, halfway to heaven in the gods, yet she half-blinded me. And my father, still alive (oh, so long ago), took hold of my sticky little hand, to comfort me, in the last act, yet all I heard was the glory of her voice.

Married three times within my own brief lifetime to three different graces, now, as if to demonstrate the eclecticism of his taste, he had invited me to join this gallery of beautiful women, I, the poor widow's child with my mouse-coloured hair that still bore the kinks of the plaits from which it had so recently been freed, my bony hips, my nervous, pianist's fingers.

He was rich as Croesus. The night before our wedding – a simple affair, at the Mairie, because his countess was so recently gone – he took my mother and me, curious coincidence, to see *Tristan*. And, do you know, my heart swelled and ached so during the Liebestod that I thought I must truly love him. Yes. I did. On his arm, all eyes were upon me. The whispering crowd in the foyer parted like the Red Sea to let us through. My skin crisped at his touch.

How my circumstances had changed since the first time I heard those volup-tuous chords that carry such a charge of deathly passion in them! Now, we sat in a loge, in red velvet armchairs, and a braided, bewigged flunkey brought us a silver bucket of iced champagne in the interval. The froth spilled over the rim of my glass and drenched my hands, I thought: My cup runneth over. And I had on a Poiret dress. He had prevailed upon my reluctant mother to let him buy my trousseau; what would I have gone to him in, otherwise? Twice-darned under-wear, faded gingham, serge skirts, hand-me-downs. So, for the opera, I wore a sinuous shift of white muslin tied with a silk string under the breasts. And every-one stared at me. And at his wedding gift.

His wedding gift, clasped round my throat. A choker of rubies, two inches wide, like an extraordinarily precious slit throat.

After the Terror, in the early days of the Directory, the aristos who'd escaped the guillotine had an ironic fad of tying a red ribbon round their necks at just the point where the blade would have sliced it through, a red ribbon like the memory of a wound. And his grandmother, taken with the notion, had her ribbon made up in rubies; such a gesture of luxurious defiance! That night at the opera comes back to me even now ... the white dress; the frail child within it; and the flashing crimson jewels round her throat, bright as arterial blood.

I saw him watching me in the gilded mirrors with the assessing eye of a con-noisseur inspecting horseflesh, or even of a housewife in the market, inspecting cuts on the slab. I'd never seen, or else had never acknowledged, that regard of his before, the sheer carnal avarice of it; and it was strangely magnified by the monocle lodged in his left eye. When I saw him look at me with lust, I dropped my eyes but, in glancing away from him, I caught sight of myself in the mirror. And I saw myself, suddenly, as he saw me, my pale face, the way the muscles in my neck stuck out like thin wire. I saw how much that cruel necklace became me. And, for the first time in my innocent and confined life, I sensed in myself a potentiality for corruption that took my breath away.

The next day, we were married.

The train slowed, shuddered to a halt. Lights; clank of metal; a voice declaring the name of an unknown, never-to-be visited station; silence of the night; the rhythm of his breathing, that I should sleep with, now, for the rest of my life. And I could not sleep. I stealthily sat up, raised the blind a little and huddled against the cold window that misted over with the warmth of my breathing, gazing out at the dark platform towards those rectangles of domestic lamplight that prom-ised warmth, company, a supper of sausages hissing in a pan on the stove for the station master, his children tucked up in bed asleep in the brick house with the painted shutters ... all the paraphernalia of the everyday world from which I, with my stunning marriage, had exiled myself.

Into marriage, into exile; I sensed it, I knew it – that, henceforth, I would always be lonely. Yet that was part of the already familiar weight of the fire opal that glimmered like a gypsy's magic ball, so that I could not take my eyes off it when I played the piano. This ring, the bloody bandage of rubies, the wardrobe of clothes from Poiret and Worth, his scent of Russian leather – all had conspired to seduce me so utterly that I could not say I felt one single twinge of regret for the world of tartines and maman that now receded from me as if drawn away on a string, like a child's toy, as the train began to throb again as if in delighted anticipation of the distance it would take me.

The first grey streamers of the dawn now flew in the sky and an eldritch half-light seeped into the railway carriage. I heard no change in his breathing but my heightened, excited senses told me he was awake and gazing at me. A huge man, an enormous man, and his eyes, dark and motionless as those eyes the ancient Egyptians painted upon their sarcophagi, fixed upon me. I felt a certain tension in the pit of my stomach, to be so watched, in such silence. A match struck. He was igniting a Romeo y Julieta fat as a baby's arm.

'Soon,' he said in his resonant voice that was like the tolling of a bell and I felt, all at once, a sharp premonition of dread that lasted only as long as the match flared and I could see his white, broad face as if it were hovering, disembodied, above the sheets, illuminated from below like a grotesque carnival head. Then the flame died, the cigar glowed and filled the compartment with a remembered fragrance that made me think of my father, how he would hug me in a warm fug of Havana, when I was a little girl, before he kissed me and left me and died.

As soon as my husband handed me down from the high step of the train, I smelled the amniotic salinity of the ocean. It was November; the trees, stunted by the Atlantic gales, were bare and the lonely halt was deserted but for his leather-gaitered chauffeur waiting meekly beside the sleek black motor car. It was cold; I drew my furs about me, a wrap of white and black, broad stripes of ermine and sable, with a collar from which my head rose like the calyx of a wild-flower. (I swear to you, I had never been vain until I met him.) The bell clanged; the straining train leapt its leash and left us at that lonely wayside halt where only he and I had descended. Oh, the wonder of it; how all that might of iron and steam had paused only to suit his convenience. The richest man in France.

'Madame.'

The chauffeur eyed me; was he comparing me, invidiously, to the countess, the artist's model, the opera singer? I hid behind my furs as if they were a system of soft shields. My husband liked me to wear my opal over my kid glove, a showy, theatrical trick – but the moment the ironic chauffeur glimpsed its simmering flash he smiled, as though it was proof positive I was his master's wife. And we drove towards the widening dawn, that now streaked half the sky with a wintry bouquet of pink of roses, orange of tiger-lilies, as if my husband had ordered me a sky from a florist. The day broke around me like a cool dream.

Sea; sand; a sky that melts into the sea – a landscape of misty pastels with a look about it of being continuously on the point of melting. A landscape with all the deliquescent harmonies of Debussy, of the études I played for him, the reverie I'd been playing that afternoon in the salon of the princess where I'd first met him, among the teacups and the little cakes, I, the orphan, hired out of charity to give them their digestive of music.

And, ah! his castle. The faery solitude of the place; with its turrets of misty blue, its courtyard, its spiked gate, his castle that lay on the very bosom of the sea with seabirds mewing about its attics, the casements opening on to the green and purple, evanescent departures of the ocean, cut off by the tide from land for half a day ... that castle, at home neither on the land nor on the water, a mysterious, amphibious place, contravening the materiality of both earth and the waves, with the melancholy of a mermaiden who perches on her rock and waits, endlessly, for a lover who had drowned far away, long ago. That lovely, sad, sea-siren of a place!

The tide was low; at this hour, so early in the morning, the causeway rose up out of the sea. As the car turned on to the wet cobbles between the slow margins of water, he reached out for my hand that had his sultry, witchy ring on it, pressed my fingers, kissed my palm with extraordinary tenderness. His face was as still as ever I'd seen it, still as a pond iced thickly over, yet his lips, that always looked so strangely red and naked between the black fringes of his beard, now curved a little. He smiled; he welcomed his bride home.

No room, no corridor that did not rustle with the sound of the sea and all the ceilings, the walls on which his ancestors in the stern regalia of rank lined up with their dark eyes and white faces, were stippled with refracted light from the waves which were always in motion; that luminous, murmurous castle of which I was the châtelaine, I, the little music student whose mother had sold all her jewellery, even her wedding ring, to pay the fees at the Conservatoire.

First of all, there was the small ordeal of my initial interview with the housekeeper, who kept this extraordinary machine, this anchored, castellated ocean liner, in smooth running order no matter who stood on the bridge; how tenuous, I thought, might be my authority here! She had a bland, pale, impassive, dislikeable face beneath the impeccably starched white linen headdress of the region. Her greeting, correct but lifeless, chilled me; daydreaming, I dared presume too much on my status ... briefly wondered how I might install my old nurse, so much loved, however cosily incompetent, in her place. Ill-considered schemings! He told me this one had been his foster mother; was bound to his family in the utmost feudal complicity, 'as much part of the house as I am, my dear'. Now her thin lips offered me a proud little smile. She would be my ally as long as I was his. And with that, I must be content.

But, here, it would be easy to be content. In the turret suite he had given me for my very own, I could gaze out over the tumultuous Atlantic and imagine myself the Queen of the Sea. There was a Bechstein for me in the music room and, on the wall, another wedding present – an early Flemish primitive of Saint Cecilia at her celestial organ. In the prim charm of this saint, with her plump, sallow cheeks and crinkled brown hair, I saw myself as I could have wished to be. I warmed to a loving sensitivity I had not hitherto suspected in him. Then he led me up a delicate spiral staircase to my bedroom; before she discreetly vanished, the housekeeper set him chuckling with some, I dare say, lewd blessing for newlyweds in her native Breton. That I did not understand. That he, smiling, refused to interpret.

And there lay the grand, hereditary matrimonial bed, itself the size, almost, of my little room at home, with the gargoyles carved on its surfaces of ebony, vermilion lacquer, gold leaf; and its white gauze curtains, billowing in the sea breeze. Our bed. And surrounded by so many mirrors! Mirrors on all the walls, in stately frames of contorted gold, that reflected more white lilies than I'd ever seen in my life before. He'd filled the room with them, to greet the bride, the young bride. The young bride, who had become that multitude of girls I saw in the mirrors, identical in their chic navy blue tailor-mades, for travelling, madame, or walking. A maid had dealt with the furs. Henceforth, a maid would deal with everything.

'See,' he said, gesturing towards those elegant girls. 'I have acquired a whole harem for myself!'

I found that I was trembling. My breath came thickly. I could not meet his eye and turned my head away, out of pride, out of shyness, and watched a dozen husbands approach me in a dozen mirrors and slowly, methodically, teasingly, unfasten the buttons of my jacket and slip it from my shoulders. Enough! No; more! Off comes the skirt; and, next, the blouse of apricot linen that cost more than the dress I had for first communion. The play of the waves outside in the cold sun glittered on his monocle; his movements seemed to me deliberately coarse, vulgar. The blood rushed to my face again, and stayed there.

And yet, you see, I guessed it might be so – that we should have a formal disrobing of the bride, a ritual from the brothel. Sheltered as my life had been, how could I have failed, even in the world of prim bohemia in which I lived, to have heard hints of *his* world?

He stripped me, gourmand that he was, as if he were stripping the leaves off an artichoke – but do not imagine much finesse about it; this artichoke was no particular treat for the diner nor was he yet in any greedy haste. He approached his familiar treat with a weary appetite. And when nothing but my scarlet, palpitating core remained, I saw, in the mirror, the living image of an etching by Rops from the collection he had shown me when our engagement permitted us to be alone together … the child with her sticklike limbs, naked but for her button boots, her gloves, shielding her face with her hand as though her face were the last repository of her modesty; and the old, monocled lecher who examined her, limb by limb. He in his London tailoring; she, bare as a lamb chop. Most pornographic of all confrontations. And so my purchaser unwrapped his bargain. And, as at the opera, when I had first seen my flesh in his eyes, I was aghast to feel myself stirring.

At once he closed my legs like a book and I saw again the rare movement of his lips that meant he smiled.

Not yet. Later. Anticipation is the greater part of pleasure, my little love.

And I began to shudder, like a racehorse before a race, yet also with a kind of fear, for I felt both a strange, impersonal arousal at the thought of love and at the same time a repugnance I could not stifle for his white, heavy flesh that had too much in common with the armfuls of arum lilies that filled my bedroom in great glass jars, those undertakers' lilies with the heavy pollen that powders your fingers as if you had dipped them in turmeric. The lilies I always associate with him; that are white. And stain you.

This scene from a voluptuary's life was now abruptly terminated. It turns out he has business to attend to; his estates, his companies – even on your honeymoon? Even then, said the red lips that kissed me before he left me alone with my bewildered senses – a wet, silken brush from his beard; a hint of the pointed tip of the tongue. Disgruntled, I wrapped a négligé of antique lace around me to sip the little breakfast of hot chocolate the maid brought me; after that, since it was second nature to me, there was nowhere to go but the music room and soon I settled down at my piano.

Yet only a series of subtle discords flowed from beneath my fingers: out of tune ... only a little out of tune; but I'd been blessed with perfect pitch and could not bear to play any more. Sea breezes are bad for pianos; we shall need a resident piano-tuner on the premises if I'm to continue with my studies! I flung down the lid in a little fury of disappointment; what should I do now, how shall I pass the long, sea-lit hours until my husband beds me?

I shivered to think of *that*.

His library seemed the source of his habitual odour of Russian leather. Row upon row of calf-bound volumes, brown and olive, with gilt lettering on their spines, the octavo in brilliant scarlet morocco. A deep-buttoned leather sofa to recline on. A lectern, carved like a spread eagle, that held open upon it an edition of Huysmans's *Là-bas*, from some over-exquisite private press; it had been bound like a missal, in brass, with gems of coloured glass. The rugs on the floor, deep, pulsing blues of heaven and red of the heart's dearest blood, came from Isfahan and Bokhara; the dark panelling gleamed; there was the lulling music of the sea and a fire of apple logs. The flames flickered along the spines inside a glass-fronted case that held books still crisp and new. Eliphas Levy; the name meant nothing to me. I squinted at a title or two: *The Initiation, The Key of Mysteries, The Secret of Pandora's Box*, and yawned. Nothing, here, to detain a seventeen-year-old girl waiting for her first embrace. I should have liked, best of all, a novel in yellow paper; I wanted to curl up on the rug before the blazing fire, lose myself in a cheap novel, munch sticky liqueur chocolates. If I rang for them, a maid would bring me chocolates.

Nevertheless, I opened the doors of that bookcase idly to browse. And I think I knew, I knew by some tingling of the fingertips, even before I opened that slim volume with no title at all on the spine, what I should find inside it. When he showed me the Rops, newly bought, dearly prized, had he not hinted that he was a connoisseur of such things? Yet I had not bargained for this, the girl with tears hanging on her cheeks like stuck pearls, her cunt a split fig below the great globes of her buttocks on which the knotted tails of the cat were about to descend, while a man in a black mask fingered with his free hand his prick, that curved upwards like the scimitar he held. The picture had a caption: 'Reproof of curiosity'. My mother, with all the precision of her eccentricity, had told me what it was that lovers did; I was innocent but not naïve. *The Adventures of Eulalie at the Harem of the Grand Turk* had been printed, according to the flyleaf, in Amsterdam in 1748, a rare collector's piece. Had some ancestor brought it back himself from that northern city? Or had my husband bought it for himself, from one of those dusty little bookshops on the Left Bank where an old man peers at you through spectacles an inch thick, daring you to inspect his wares ... I turned the pages in the anticipation of fear; the print was rusty. Here was another steel engraving: 'Immolation of the wives of the Sultan'. I knew enough for what I saw in that book to make me gasp.

There was a pungent intensification of the odour of leather that suffused his library; his shadow fell across the massacre.

'My little nun has found the prayerbooks, has she?' he demanded, with a curious mixture of mockery and relish; then, seeing my painful, furious bewilderment, he laughed at me aloud, snatched the book from my hands and put it down on the sofa.

'Have the nasty pictures scared Baby? Baby mustn't play with grown-ups' toys until she's learned how to handle them, must she?'

Then he kissed me. And with, this time, no reticence. He kissed me and laid his hand imperatively upon my breast, beneath the sheath of ancient lace. I stumbled on the winding stair that led to the bedroom, to the carved, gilded bed on which he had been conceived. I stammered foolishly: We've not taken luncheon yet; and, besides, it is broad daylight ...

All the better to see you.

He made me put on my choker, the family heirloom of one woman who had escaped the blade. With trembling fingers, I fastened the thing about my neck. It was cold as ice and chilled me. He twined my hair into a rope and lifted it off my shoulders so that he could the better kiss the downy furrows below my ears; that made me shudder. And he kissed those blazing rubies, too. He kissed them before he kissed my mouth. Rapt, he intoned: 'Of her apparel she retains/Only her sonorous jewellery.'

A dozen husbands impaled a dozen brides while the mewing gulls swung on invisible trapezes in the empty air outside.

I was brought to my senses by the insistent shrilling of the telephone. He lay beside me, felled like an oak, breathing stertorously, as if he had been fighting with me. In the course of that one-sided struggle, I had seen his deathly composure shatter like a porcelain vase flung against a wall; I had heard him shriek and blaspheme at the orgasm; I had bled. And perhaps I had seen his face without its mask; and perhaps I had not. Yet I had been infinitely dishevelled by the loss of my virginity.

I gathered myself together, reached into the cloisonné cupboard beside the bed that concealed the telephone and addressed the mouthpiece. His agent in New York. Urgent.

I shook him awake and rolled over on my side, cradling my spent body in my arms. His voice buzzed like a hive of distant bees. My husband. My husband, who, with so much love, filled my bedroom with lilies until it looked like an embalming parlour. Those somnolent lilies, that wave their heavy heads, distributing their lush, insolent incense reminiscent of pampered flesh.

When he'd finished with the agent, he turned to me and stroked the ruby necklace that bit into my neck, but with such tenderness now, that I ceased flinching and he caressed my breasts. My dear one, my little love, my child, did it hurt her? He's so sorry for it, such impetuousness, he could not help himself; you see, he loves her so … and this lover's recitative of his brought my tears in a flood. I clung to him as though only the one who had inflicted the pain could comfort me for suffering it. For a while, he murmured to me in a voice I'd never heard before, a voice like the soft consolations of the sea. But then he unwound the tendrils of my hair from the buttons of his smoking jacket, kissed my cheek briskly and told me the agent from New York had called with such urgent business that he must leave as soon as the tide was low enough. Leave the castle? Leave France! And would be away for at least six weeks.

'But it is our honeymoon!'

A deal, an enterprise of hazard and chance involving several millions, lay in the balance, he said. He drew away from me into that wax-works stillness of his; I was only a little girl, I did not understand. And, he said unspoken to my wounded vanity, I have had too many honeymoons to find them in the least pressing commitments. I know quite well that this child I've bought with a handful of coloured stones and the pelts of dead beasts won't run away. But, after he'd called his Paris agent to book a passage for the States next day – just one tiny call, my little one – we should have time for dinner together.

And I had to be content with that.

A Mexican dish of pheasant with hazelnuts and chocolate; salad; white, voluptuous cheese; a sorbet of muscat grapes and Asti spumante. A celebration of Krug exploded festively. And then acrid black coffee in precious little cups so fine it shadowed the birds with which they were painted. I had Cointreau, he had cognac in the library, with the purple velvet curtains drawn against the night, where he took me to perch on his knee in a leather armchair beside the flickering log fire. He had made me change into that chaste little Poiret shift of white muslin; he seemed especially fond of it, my breasts showed through the flimsy stuff, he said, like little soft white doves that sleep, each one, with a pink eye open. But he would not let me take off my ruby choker, although it was growing very uncomfortable, nor fasten up my descending hair, the sign of a virginity so recently ruptured that still remained a wounded presence between us. He twined his fingers in my hair until I winced; I said, I remember, very little.

'The maid will have changed our sheets already,' he said. 'We do not hang the bloody sheets out of the window to prove to the whole of Brittany you are a virgin, not in these civilized times. But I should tell you it would have been the first time in all my married lives I could have shown my interested tenants such a flag.'

Then I realized, with a shock of surprise, how it must have been my innocence that captivated him – the silent music, he said, of my unknowingness, like *La Terrasse des audiences au clair de lune* played upon a piano with keys of ether. You must remember how ill at ease I was in that luxurious place, how unease had been my constant companion during the whole length of my courtship by this grave satyr who now gently martyrized my hair. To know that my naïvety gave him some pleasure made me take heart. Courage! I shall act the fine lady to the manner born one day, if only by virtue of default.

Then, slowly yet teasingly, as if he were giving a child a great, mysterious treat, he took out a bunch of keys from some interior hidey-hole in his jacket – key after key, a key, he said, for every lock in the house. Keys of all kinds – huge, ancient things of black iron; others slender, delicate, almost baroque; wafer-thin Yale keys for safes and boxes. And, during his absence, it was I who must take care of them all.

I eyed the heavy bunch with circumspection. Until that moment, I had not given a single thought to the practical aspects of marriage with a great house, great wealth, a great man, whose key ring was as crowded as that of a prison warder. Here were the clumsy and archaic keys for the dungeons, for dungeons we had in plenty although they had been converted to cellars for his wines; the dusty bottles inhabited in racks all those deep holes of pain in the rock on which the castle was built. These are the keys to the kitchens, this is the key to the picture gallery, a treasure house filled by five centuries of avid collectors – ah! he foresaw I would spend hours there.

He had amply indulged his taste for the Symbolists, he told me with a glint of greed. There was Moreau's great portrait of his first wife, the famous *Sacrificial Victim* with the imprint of the lacelike chains on her pellucid skin. Did I know the story of the painting of that picture? How, when she took off her clothes for him for the first time, she fresh from her bar in Montmartre, she had robed herself involuntarily in a blush that reddened her breasts, her shoulders, her arms, her whole body? He had thought of that story, of that dear girl, when first he had undressed me ... Ensor, the great Ensor, his monolithic canvas: *The Foolish Virgins*. Two or three late Gauguins, his special favourite the one of the tranced brown girl in the deserted house which was called: *Out of the Night We Come, Into the Night We Go*. And, besides the additions he had made himself, his marvellous inheritance of Watteaus, Poussins and a pair of very special Fragonards, commissioned for a licentious ancestor who, it was said, had posed for the master's brush himself with his own two daughters ... He broke off his catalogue of treasures abruptly.

Your thin white face, chérie; he said, as if he saw it for the first time. Your thin white face, with its promise of debauchery only a connoisseur could detect.

A log fell in the fire, instigating a shower of sparks; the opal on my finger spurted green flame. I felt as giddy as if I were on the edge of a precipice; I was afraid, not so much of him, of his monstrous presence, heavy as if he had been gifted at birth with more specific *gravity* than the rest of us, the presence that, even when I thought myself most in love with him, always subtly oppressed me ... No. I was not afraid of him; but of myself. I seemed reborn in his unreflective eyes, reborn in unfamiliar shapes. I hardly recognized myself from his descriptions of me and yet, and yet – might there not be a grain of beastly truth in them? And, in the red firelight, I blushed again, unnoticed, to think he might have chosen me because, in my innocence, he sensed a rare talent for corruption.

Here is the key to the china cabinet – don't laugh, my darling; there's a king's ransom in Sèvres in that closet, and a queen's ransom in Limoges. And a key to the locked, barred room where five generations of plate were kept.

Keys, keys, keys. He would trust me with the keys to his office, although I was only a baby; and the keys to his safes, where he kept the jewels I should wear, he promised me, when we returned to Paris. Such jewels! Why, I would be able to change my earrings and necklaces three times a day, just as the Empress

Josephine used to change her underwear. He doubted, he said, with that hollow, knocking sound that served him for a chuckle, I would be quite so interested in his share certificates although they, of course, were worth infinitely more.

Outside our firelit privacy, I could hear the sound of the tide drawing back from the pebbles of the foreshore; it was nearly time for him to leave me. One single key remained unaccounted for on the ring and he hesitated over it; for a moment, I thought he was going to unfasten it from its brothers, slip it back into his pocket and take it away with him.

'What is *that* key?' I demanded, for his chaffing had made me bold. 'The key to your heart? Give it me!'

He dangled the key tantalizingly above my head, out of reach of my straining fingers; those bare red lips of his cracked sidelong in a smile.

'Ah, no,' he said. 'Not the key to my heart. Rather, the key to my enfer.'

He left it on the ring, fastened the ring together, shook it musically, like a carillon. Then threw the keys in a jingling heap in my lap. I could feel the cold metal chilling my thighs through my thin muslin frock. He bent over me to drop a beard-masked kiss on my forehead.

'Every man must have one secret, even if only one, from his wife,' he said. 'Promise me this, my whey-faced piano-player; promise me you'll use all the keys on the ring except that last little one I showed you. Play with anything you find, jewels, silver plate; make toy boats of my share certificates, if it pleases you, and send them sailing off to America after me. All is yours, everywhere is open to you – except the lock that this single key fits. Yet all it is is the key to a little room at the foot of the west tower, behind the still-room, at the end of a dark little corridor full of horrid cobwebs that would get into your hair and frighten you if you ventured there. Oh, and you'd find it such a dull little room! But you must promise me, if you love me, to leave it well alone. It is only a private study, a hideaway, a "den", as the English say, where I can go, sometimes, on those infrequent yet inevitable occasions when the yoke of marriage seems to weigh too heavily on my shoulders. There I can go, you understand, to savour the rare pleasure of imagining myself wifeless.'

There was a little thin starlight in the courtyard as, wrapped in my furs, I saw him to his car. His last words were, that he had telephoned the mainland and taken a piano-tuner on to the staff; this man would arrive to take up his duties the next day. He pressed me to his vicuña breast, once, and then drove away.

I had drowsed away that afternoon and now I could not sleep. I lay tossing and turning in his ancestral bed until another daybreak discoloured the dozen mirrors that were iridescent with the reflections of the sea. The perfume of the lilies weighed on my senses; when I thought that, henceforth, I would always share these sheets with a man whose skin, as theirs did, contained that toad-like, clammy hint of moisture, I felt a vague desolation that within me, now my female wound had healed, there had awoken a certain queasy craving like the cravings of pregnant women for the taste of coal or chalk or tainted food, for the renewal of his caresses. Had he not hinted to me, in his flesh as in his speech and looks, of the thousand, thousand baroque intersections of flesh upon flesh? I lay in our wide bed accompanied by a sleepless companion, my dark newborn curiosity.

I lay in bed alone. And I longed for him. And he disgusted me.

Were there jewels enough in all his safes to recompense me for this predicament? Did all that castle hold enough riches to recompense me for the company of the libertine with whom I must share it? And what, precisely, was the nature of my desirous dread for this mysterious being who, to show his mastery over me, had abandoned me on my wedding night?

Then I sat straight up in bed, under the sardonic masks of the gargoyles carved above me, riven by a wild surmise. Might he have left me, not for Wall Street but for an importunate mistress tucked away God knows where who knew how to pleasure him far better than a girl whose fingers had been exercised, hitherto, only by the practice of scales and arpeggios? And, slowly, soothed, I sank back on to the heaping pillows; I acknowledged that the jealous scare I'd just given myself was not unmixed with a little tincture of relief.

At last I drifted into slumber, as daylight filled the room and chased bad dreams away. But the last thing I remembered, before I slept, was the tall jar of lilies beside the bed, how the thick glass distorted their fat stems so they looked like arms, dismembered arms, drifting drowned in greenish water.

Coffee and croissants to console this bridal, solitary waking. Delicious. Honey, too, in a section of comb on a glass saucer. The maid squeezed the aromatic juice from an orange into a chilled goblet while I watched her as I lay in the lazy, midday bed of the rich. Yet nothing, this morning, gave me more than a fleeting pleasure except to hear that the piano-tuner had been at work already. When the maid told me that, I sprang out of bed and pulled on my old serge skirt and flannel blouse, costume of a student, in which I felt far more at ease with myself than in any of my fine new clothes.

After my three hours of practice, I called the piano-tuner in, to thank him. He was blind, of course; but young, with a gentle mouth and grey eyes that fixed upon me although they could not see me. He was a blacksmith's son from the village across the causeway; a chorister in the church whom the good priest had taught a trade so that he could make a living. All most satisfactory. Yes. He thought he would be happy here. And if, he added shyly, he might sometimes be allowed to hear me play ... for, you see, he loved music. Yes. Of course, I said. Certainly. He seemed to know that I had smiled.

After I dismissed him, even though I'd woken so late, it was still barely time for my 'five o'clock'. The housekeeper, who, thoughtfully forewarned by my husband, had restrained herself from interrupting my music, now made me a solemn visitation with a lengthy menu for a late luncheon. When I told her I did not need it, she looked at me obliquely, along her nose. I understood at once that one of my principal functions as châtelaine was to provide work for the staff. But, all the same, I asserted myself and said I would wait until dinner-time, although I looked forward nervously to the solitary meal. Then I found I had to tell her what I would like to have prepared for me; my imagination, still that of a schoolgirl, ran riot. A fowl in cream – or should I anticipate Christmas with a varnished turkey? No; I have decided. Avocado and shrimp, lots of it, followed by no entrée at all. But surprise me for dessert with every ice-cream in the ice box. She noted all down but sniffed; I'd shocked her. Such tastes! Child that I was, I giggled when she left me.

But, now ... what shall I do, now?

I could have spent a happy hour unpacking the trunks that contained my trousseau but the maid had done that already, the dresses, the tailor-mades hung in the wardrobe in my dressing room, the hats on wooden heads to keep their shape, the shoes on wooden feet as if all these inanimate objects were imitating the appearance of life, to mock me. I did not like to linger in my overcrowded dressing room, nor in my lugubriously lily-scented bedroom. How shall I pass the time?

I shall take a bath in my own bathroom! And found the taps were little dolphins made of gold, with chips of turquoise for eyes. And there was a tank of goldfish, who swam in and out of moving fronds of weeds, as bored, I thought, as I was. How I wished he had not left me. How I wished it were possible to chat with, say, a maid; or, the piano-tuner ... but I knew already my new rank forbade overtures of friendship to the staff.

I had been hoping to defer the call as long as I could, so that I should have something to look forward to in the dead waste of time I foresaw before me, after my dinner was done with, but, at a quarter before seven, when darkness already surrounded the castle, I could contain myself no longer. I telephoned my mother. And astonished myself by bursting into tears when I heard her voice.

No, nothing was the matter. Mother, I have gold bath taps.

I said, gold bath taps!

No; I suppose that's nothing to cry about, Mother.

The line was bad, I could hardly make out her congratulations, her questions, her concern, but I was a little comforted when I put the receiver down.

Yet there still remained one whole hour to dinner and the whole, unimaginable desert of the rest of the evening.

The bunch of keys lay, where he had left them, on the rug before the library fire which had warmed their metal so that they no longer felt cold to the touch but warm, almost, as my own skin. How careless I was; a maid, tending the logs, eyed me reproachfully as if I'd set a trap for her as I picked up the clinking bundle of keys, the keys to the interior doors of this lovely prison of which I was both the inmate and the mistress and had scarcely seen. When I remembered that, I felt the exhilaration of the explorer.

Lights! More lights!

At the touch of a switch, the dreaming library was brilliantly illuminated. I ran crazily about the castle, switching on every light I could find – I ordered the servants to light up all their quarters, too, so the castle would shine like a seaborne birthday cake lit with a thousand candles, one for every year of its life, and everybody on shore would wonder at it. When everything was lit as brightly as the café in the Gare du Nord, the significance of the possessions implied by that bunch of keys no longer intimidated me, for I was determined, now, to search through them all for evidence of my husband's true nature.

His office first, evidently.

A mahogany desk half a mile wide, with an impeccable blotter and a bank of telephones. I allowed myself the luxury of opening the safe that contained the jewellery and delved sufficiently among the leather boxes to find out how my marriage had given me access to a jinn's treasury – parures, bracelets, rings ... While I was thus surrounded by diamonds, a maid knocked on the door and entered before I spoke; a subtle discourtesy. I would speak to my husband about it. She eyed my serge skirt superciliously; did madame plan to dress for dinner?

She made a moue of disdain when I laughed to hear that, she was far more the lady than I. But, imagine – to dress up in one of my Poiret extravaganzas, with the jewelled turban and aigrette on my head, roped with pearl to the navel, to sit down all alone in the baronial dining hall at the head of that massive board at which King Mark was reputed to have fed his knights ... I grew calmer under the cold eye of her disapproval.

I adopted the crisp inflections of an officer's daughter. No, I would not dress for dinner. Furthermore, I was not hungry enough for dinner itself. She must tell the housekeeper to cancel the dormitory feast I'd ordered. Could they leave me sandwiches and a flask of coffee in my music room? And would they all dismiss for the night?

Mais oui, madame.

I knew by her bereft intonation I had let them down again but I did not care; I was armed against them by the brilliance of his hoard. But I would not find his heart amongst the glittering stones; as soon as she had gone, I began a systematic search of the drawers of his desk.

All was in order, so I found nothing. Not a random doodle on an old envelope, nor the faded photograph of a woman. Only the files of business correspondence, the bills from the home farms, the invoices from tailors, the billets-doux from international financiers. Nothing. And this absence of the evidence of his real life began to impress me strangely; there must, I thought, be a great deal to conceal if he takes such pains to hide it.

His office was a singularly impersonal room, facing inwards, on to the courtyard, as though he wanted to turn his back on the siren sea in order to keep a clear head while he bankrupted a small businessman in Amsterdam or – I noticed with a thrill of distaste – engaged in some business in Laos that must, from certain cryptic references to his amateur botanist's enthusiasm for rare poppies, be to do with opium. Was he not rich enough to do without crime? Or was the crime itself his profit? And yet I saw enough to appreciate his zeal for secrecy.

Now I had ransacked his desk, I must spend a cool-headed quarter of an hour putting every last letter back where I had found it, and, as I covered the traces of my visit, by some chance, as I reached inside a little drawer that had stuck fast, I must have touched a hidden spring, for a secret drawer flew open within that drawer itself; and this secret drawer contained – at last! – a file marked: *Personal*.

I was alone, but for my reflection in the uncurtained window.

I had the brief notion that his heart, pressed flat as a flower, crimson and thin as tissue paper, lay in this file. It was a very thin one.

I could have wished, perhaps, I had not found that touching, ill-spelt note, on a paper napkin marked *La Coupole*, that began: 'My darling, I cannot wait for the moment when you may make me yours completely.' The diva had sent him a page of the score of *Tristan*, the Liebestod, with the single, cryptic word: 'Until ...' scrawled across it. But the strangest of all these love letters was a postcard with a view of a village graveyard, among mountains, where some black-coated ghoul enthusiastically dug at a grave; this little scene, executed with the lurid exuberance of Grand Guignol, was captioned: 'Typical Transylvanian Scene – Midnight, All Hallows.' And, on the other side, the message: 'On the occasion of this marriage to the descendant of Dracula – always remember, "the supreme and unique pleasure of love is the certainty that one is doing evil". Toutes amitiés, C.'

A joke. A joke in the worst possible taste; for had he not been married to a Romanian countess? And then I remembered her pretty, witty face, and her name – Carmilla. My most recent predecessor in this castle had been, it would seem, the most sophisticated.

I put away the file, sobered. Nothing in my life of family love and music had prepared me for these grown-up games and yet these were clues to his self that showed me, at least, how much he had been loved, even if they did not reveal any good reason for it. But I wanted to know still more; and, as I closed the office door and locked it, the means to discover more fell in my way.

Fell, indeed; and with the clatter of a dropped canteen of cutlery, for, as I turned the slick Yale lock, I contrived, somehow, to open up the key ring itself, so that all the keys tumbled loose on the floor. And the very first key I picked out of that pile was, as luck or ill fortune had it, the key to the room he had forbidden me, the room he would keep for his own so that he could go there when he wished to feel himself once more a bachelor.

I made my decision to explore it before I felt a faint resurgence of my ill-defined fear of his waxen stillness. Perhaps I half-imagined, then, that I might find his real self in his den, waiting there to see if indeed I had obeyed him; that he had sent a moving figure of himself to New York, the enigmatic, self-sustaining carapace of his public person, while the real man, whose face I had glimpsed in the storm of orgasm, occupied himself with pressing private business in the study at the foot of the west tower, behind the still-room. Yet, if that were so, it was imperative that I should find him, should know him; and I was too deluded by his apparent taste for me to think my disobedience might truly offend him.

I took the forbidden key from the heap and left the others lying there.

It was now very late and the castle was adrift, as far as it could go from the land, in the middle of the silent ocean where, at my orders, it floated, like a garland of light. And all silent, all still, but for the murmuring of the waves.

I felt no fear, no intimation of dread. Now I walked as firmly as I had done in my mother's house.

Not a narrow, dusty little passage at all; why had he lied to me? But an ill-lit one, certainly; the electricity, for some reason, did not extend here, so I retreated to the still-room and found a bundle of waxed tapers in a cupboard, stored there with matches to light the oak board at grand dinners. I put a match to my little taper and advanced with it in my hand, like a penitent, along the corridor hung with heavy, I think Venetian, tapestries. The flame picked out, here, the head of a man, there, the rich breast of a woman spilling through a rent in her dress – the Rape of the Sabines, perhaps? The naked swords and immolated horses suggested some grisly mythological subject. The corridor wound downwards; there was an almost imperceptible ramp to the thickly carpeted floor. The heavy hangings on the wall muffled my footsteps, even my breathing. For some reason, it grew very warm; the sweat sprang out in beads on my brow. I could no longer hear the sound of the sea.

A long, a winding corridor, as if I were in the viscera of the castle; and this corridor led to a door of worm-eaten oak, low, round-topped, barred with black iron.

And still I felt no fear, no raising of the hairs on the back of the neck, no prickling of the thumbs.

The key slid into the new lock as easily as a hot knife into butter.

No fear; but a hesitation, a holding of the spiritual breath.

If I had found some traces of his heart in a file marked: *Personal*, perhaps, here, in his subterranean privacy, I might find a little of his soul. It was the consciousness of the possibility of such a discovery, of its possible strangeness, that kept me for a moment motionless, before, in the foolhardiness of my already subtly tainted innocence, I turned the key and the door creaked slowly back.

'There is a striking resemblance between the act of love and the ministrations of a torturer,' opined my husband's favourite poet; I had learned something of the nature of that similarity on my marriage bed. And now my taper showed me the outlines of a rack. There was also a great wheel, like the ones I had seen in woodcuts of the martyrdoms of the saints, in my old nurse's little store of holy books. And – just one glimpse of it before my little flame caved in and I was left in absolute darkness – a metal figure, hinged at the side, which I knew to be spiked on the inside and to have the name: the Iron Maiden.

Absolute darkness. And, about me, the instruments of mutilation.

Until that moment, this spoiled child did not know she had inherited nerves and a will from the mother who had defied the yellow outlaws of Indo-China. My mother's spirit drove me on, into that dreadful place, in a cold ecstasy to know the very worst. I fumbled for the matches in my pocket; what a dim, lugubrious light they gave! And yet, enough, oh, more than enough, to see a room designed for desecration and some dark night of unimaginable lovers whose embraces were annihilation.

The walls of this stark torture chamber were the naked rock; they gleamed as if they were sweating with fright. At the four corners of the room were funerary urns, of great antiquity, Etruscan, perhaps, and, on three-legged ebony stands, the bowls of incense he had left burning which filled the room with a sacerdotal reek. Wheel, rack and Iron Maiden were, I saw, displayed as grandly as if they were items of statuary and I was almost consoled, then, and almost persuaded myself that I might have stumbled only upon a little museum of his perversity, that he had installed these monstrous items here only for contemplation.

Yet at the centre of the room lay a catafalque, a doomed, ominous bier of Renaissance workmanship, surrounded by long white candles and, at its foot, an armful of the same lilies with which he had filled my bedroom, stowed in a four-foot-high jar glazed with a sombre Chinese red. I scarcely dared examine this catafalque and its occupant more closely; yet I knew I must.

Each time I struck a match to light those candles round her bed, it seemed a garment of that innocence of mine for which he had lusted fell away from me.

The opera singer lay, quite naked, under a thin sheet of very rare and precious linen, such as the princes of Italy used to shroud those whom they had poisoned. I touched her, very gently, on the white breast; she was cool, he had embalmed her. On her throat I could see the blue imprint of his strangler's fingers. The cool, sad flame of the candles flickered on her white, closed eyelids. The worst thing was, the dead lips smiled.

Beyond the catafalque, in the middle of the shadows, a white, nacreous glimmer; as my eyes accustomed themselves to the gathering darkness, I at last – oh, horrors! – made out a skull; yes, a skull, so utterly denuded, now, of flesh, that it scarcely seemed possible the stark bone had once been richly upholstered with life. And this skull was strung up by a system of unseen cords, so that it appeared to hang, disembodied, in the still, heavy air, and it had been crowned with a wreath of white roses, and a veil of lace, the final image of his bride.

Yet the skull was still so beautiful, had shaped with its sheer planes so imperiously the face that had once existed above it, that I recognized her the moment I saw her; face of the evening star walking on the rim of night. One false step, oh, my poor, dear girl, next in the fated sisterhood of his wives; one false step and into the abyss of the dark you stumbled.

And where was she, the latest dead, the Romanian countess who might have thought her blood would survive his depredations? I knew she must be here, in the place that had wound me through the castle towards it on a spool of inexorability. But, at first, I could see no sign of her. Then, for some reason – perhaps some change of atmosphere wrought by my presence – the metal shell of the Iron Maiden emitted a ghostly twang; my feverish imagination might have guessed its occupant was trying to clamber out, though, even in the midst of my rising hysteria, I knew she must be dead to find a home there.

With trembling fingers, I prised open the front of the upright coffin, with its sculpted face caught in a rictus of pain. Then, overcome, I dropped the key I still held in my other hand. It dropped into the forming pool of her blood.

She was pierced, not by one but by a hundred spikes, this child of the land of the vampires who seemed so newly dead, so full of blood … oh God! how recently had he become a widower? How long had he kept her in this obscene cell? Had it been all the time he had courted me, in the clear light of Paris?

I closed the lid of her coffin very gently and burst into a tumult of sobbing that contained both pity for his other victims and also a dreadful anguish to know I, too, was one of them.

The candles flared, as if in a draught from a door to elsewhere. The light caught the fire opal on my hand so that it flashed, once, with a baleful light, as if to tell me the eye of God – his eye – was upon me. My first thought, when I saw the ring for which I had sold myself to this fate, was, how to escape it.

I retained sufficient presence of mind to snuff out the candles round the bier with my fingers, to gather up my taper, to look around, although shuddering, to ensure I had left behind me no traces of my visit.

I retrieved the key from the pool of blood, wrapped it in my handkerchief to keep my hands clean, and fled the room, slamming the door behind me.

It crashed to with a juddering reverberation, like the door of hell.

I could not take refuge in my bedroom, for that retained the memory of his presence trapped in the fathomless silvering of his mirrors. My music room seemed the safest place, although I looked at the picture of Saint Cecilia with a faint dread; what had been the nature of her martyrdom? My mind was in a tumult; schemes for flight jostled with one another … as soon as the tide receded from the causeway, I would make for the mainland – on foot, running, stumbling; I did not trust that leather-clad chauffeur, nor the well-behaved housekeeper, and I dared not take any of the pale, ghostly maids into my confidence, either, since they were his creatures, all. Once at the village, I would fling myself directly on the mercy of the gendarmerie.

But – could I trust them, either? His forefathers had ruled this coast for eight centuries, from this castle whose moat was the Atlantic. Might not the police, the advocates, even the judge, all be in his service, turning a common blind eye to his vices since he was milord whose word must be obeyed? Who, on this distant coast, would believe the white-faced girl from Paris who came running to them with a shuddering tale of blood, of fear, of the ogre murmuring in the shadows? Or, rather, they would immediately know it to be true. But were all honour-bound to let me carry it no further.

Assistance. My mother. I ran to the telephone; and the line, of course, was dead.

Dead as his wives.

A thick darkness, unlit by any star, still glazed the windows. Every lamp in my room burned, to keep the dark outside, yet it seemed still to encroach on me, to be present beside me but as if masked by my lights, the night like a permeable substance that could seep into my skin. I looked at the precious little clock made from hypocritically innocent flowers long ago, in Dresden; the hands had scarcely moved one single hour forward from when I first descended to that private slaughterhouse of his. Time was his servant, too; it would trap me, here, in a night that would last until he came back to me, like a black sun on a hopeless morning.

And yet the time might still be my friend; at that hour, that very hour, he set sail for New York.

To know that, in a few moments, my husband would have left France calmed my agitation a little. My reason told me I had nothing to fear; the tide that would take him away to the New World would let me out of the imprisonment of the castle. Surely I could easily evade the servants. Anybody can buy a ticket at a railway station. Yet I was still filled with unease. I opened the lid of the piano; perhaps I thought my own particular magic might help me, now, that I could create a pentacle out of music that would keep me from harm for, if my music had first ensnared him, then might it not also give me the power to free myself from him?

Mechanically, I began to play but my fingers were stiff and shaking. At first, I could manage nothing better than the exercises of Czerny but simply the act of playing soothed me and, for solace, for the sake of the harmonious rationality of its sublime mathematics, I searched among his scores until I found *The Well-Tempered Clavier*. I set myself the therapeutic task of playing all Bach's equations, every one, and, I told myself, if I played them all through without a single mistake – then the morning would find me once more a virgin.

Crash of a dropped stick.

His silver-headed cane! What else? Sly, cunning, he had returned; he was waiting for me outside the door!

I rose to my feet; fear gave me strength. I flung back my head defiantly.

'Come in!' My voice astonished me by its firmness, its clarity.

The door slowly, nervously opened and I saw, not the massive, irredeemable bulk of my husband but the slight, stooping figure of the piano-tuner, and he looked far more terrified of me than my mother's daughter would have been of the Devil himself. In the torture chamber, it seemed to me that I would never laugh again; now, helplessly, laugh I did, with relief, and, after a moment's hesitation, the boy's face softened and he smiled a little, almost in shame. Though they were blind, his eyes were singularly sweet.

'Forgive me,' said Jean-Yves. 'I know I've given you grounds for dismissing me, that I should be crouching outside your door at midnight ... but I heard you walking about, up and down – I sleep in a room at the foot of the west tower – and some intuition told me you could not sleep and might, perhaps, pass the insomniac hours at your piano. And I could not resist that. Besides, I stumbled over these –'

And he displayed the ring of keys I'd dropped outside my husband's office door, the ring from which one key was missing. I took them from him, looked round for a place to stow them, fixed on the piano stool as if to hide them would protect me. Still he stood smiling at me. How hard it was to make everyday conversation.

'It's perfect,' I said. 'The piano. Perfectly in tune.'

But he was full of the loquacity of embarrassment, as though I would only forgive him for his impudence if he explained the cause of it thoroughly.

'When I heard you play this afternoon, I thought I'd never heard such a touch. Such technique. A treat for me, to hear a virtuoso! So I crept up to your door now, humbly as a little dog might, madame, and put my ear to the keyhole and listened, and listened – until my stick fell to the floor through a momentary clumsiness of mine, and I was discovered.'

He had the most touchingly ingenuous smile.

'Perfectly in tune,' I repeated. To my surprise, now I had said it, I found I could not say anything else. I could only repeat: 'In tune ... perfect ... in tune,' over and over again. I saw a dawning surprise in his face. My head throbbed. To see him, in his lovely, blind humanity, seemed to hurt me very piercingly, somewhere inside my breast; his figure blurred, the room swayed about me. After the dreadful revelation of that bloody chamber, it was his tender look that made me faint.

When I recovered consciousness, I found I was lying in the piano-tuner's arms and he was tucking the satin cushion from the piano-stool under my head.

'You are in some great distress,' he said. 'No bride should suffer so much, so early in her marriage.'

His speech had the rhythms of the countryside, the rhythms of the tides.

'Any bride brought to this castle should come ready dressed in mourning, should bring a priest and a coffin with her,' I said.

'What's this?'

It was too late to keep silent; and if he, too, were one of my husband's creatures, then at least he had been kind to me. So I told him everything, the keys, the interdiction, my disobedience, the room, the rack, the skull, the corpses, the blood.

'I can scarcely believe it,' he said, wondering. 'That man ... so rich; so well born.'

'Here's proof,' I said and tumbled the fatal key out of my handkerchief on to the silken rug.

'Oh God,' he said. 'I can smell the blood.'

He took my hand; he pressed his arms about me. Although he was scarcely more than a boy, I felt a great strength flow into me from his touch.

'We whisper all manner of strange tales up and down the coast,' he said. 'There was a Marquis, once, who used to hunt young girls on the mainland; he hunted them with dogs, as though they were foxes. My grandfather had it from his grand-father, how the Marquis pulled a head out of his saddle bag and showed it to the blacksmith while the man was shoeing his horse. "A fine specimen of the genus, brunette, eh, Guillaume?" And it was the head of the blacksmith's wife.'

But, in these more democratic times, my husband must travel as far as Paris to do his hunting in the salons. Jean-Yves knew the moment I shuddered.

'Oh, madame! I thought all these were old wives' tales, chattering of fools, spooks to scare bad children into good behaviour! Yet how could you know, a stranger, that the old name for this place is the Castle of Murder?'

How could I know, indeed? Except that, in my heart, I'd always known its lord would be the death of me.

'Hark!' said my friend suddenly. 'The sea has changed key; it must be near morning, the tide is going down.'

He helped me up. I looked from the window, towards the mainland, along the causeway where the stones gleamed wetly in the thin light of the end of the night and, with an almost unimaginable horror, a horror the intensity of which I cannot transmit to you, I saw, in the distance, still far away yet drawing moment by moment inexorably nearer, the twin headlamps of his great black car, gouging tunnels through the shifting mist.

My husband had indeed returned; this time, it was no fancy.

'The key!' said Jean-Yves. 'It must go back on the ring, with the others. As though nothing had happened.'

But the key was still caked with wet blood and I ran to my bathroom and held it under the hot tap. Crimson water swirled down the basin but, as if the key itself were hurt, the bloody token stuck. The turquoise eyes of the dolphin taps winked at me derisively; they knew my husband had been too clever for me! I scrubbed the stain with my nail brush but still it would not budge. I thought how the car would be rolling silently towards the closed courtyard gate; the more I scrubbed the key, the more vivid grew the stain.

The bell in the gatehouse would jangle. The porter's drowsy son would push back the patchwork quilt, yawning, pull the shirt over his head, thrust his feet into his sabots ... slowly, slowly; open the door for your master as slowly as you can ...

And still the bloodstain mocked the fresh water that spilled from the mouth of the leering dolphin.

'You have no more time,' said Jean-Yves. 'He is here. I know it. I must stay with you.'

'You shall not!' I said. 'Go back to your room, now. Please.'

He hesitated. I put an edge of steel in my voice, for I knew I must meet my lord alone.

'Leave me!'

As soon as he had gone, I dealt with the keys and went to my bedroom. The causeway was empty; Jean-Yves was correct, my husband had already entered the castle. I pulled the curtains close, stripped off my clothes and pulled the bedcurtain around me as a pungent aroma of Russian leather assured me my husband was once again beside me.

'Dearest!'

With the most treacherous, lascivious tenderness, he kissed my eyes, and, mimicking the new bride newly wakened, I flung my arms around him, for on my seeming acquiescence depended my salvation.

'Da Silva of Rio outwitted me,' he said wryly. 'My New York agent telegraphed Le Havre and saved me a wasted journey. So we may resume our interrupted pleasures, my love.'

I did not believe one word of it. I knew I had behaved exactly according to his desires; had he not bought me so that I should do so? I had been tricked into my own betrayal to that illimitable darkness whose source I had been compelled to seek in his absence and, now that I had met that shadowed reality of his that came to life only in the presence of its own atrocities, I must pay the price of my new knowledge. The secret of Pandora's box; but he had given me the box, himself, knowing I must learn the secret. I had played a game in which every move was governed by a destiny as oppressive and omnipotent as himself, since that destiny was himself; and I had lost. Lost at that charade of innocence and vice in which he had engaged me. Lost, as the victim loses to the executioner.

His hand brushed my breast, beneath the sheet. I strained my nerves yet could not help but flinch from the intimate touch, for it made me think of the piercing embrace of the Iron Maiden and of his lost lovers in the vault. When he saw my reluctance, his eyes veiled over and yet his appetite did not diminish. His tongue ran over red lips already wet. Silent, mysterious, he moved away from me to draw off his jacket. He took the gold watch from his waistcoat and laid it on the dressing table, like a good bourgeois; scooped out his rattling loose change and now – oh God! – makes a great play of patting his pockets officiously, puzzled lips pursed, searching for something that has been mislaid. Then turns to me with a ghastly, a triumphant smile.

'But of course! I gave the keys to you!'

'Your keys? Why, of course. Here, they're under the pillow; wait a moment – what – Ah! No ... now, where can I have left them? I was whiling away the evening without you at the piano, I remember. Of course! The music room!'

Brusquely he flung my négligé of antique lace on the bed.

'Go and get them.'

'Now? This moment? Can't it wait until morning, my darling?'

I forced myself to be seductive. I saw myself, pale, pliant as a plant that begs to be trampled underfoot, a dozen vulnerable, appealing girls reflected in as many mirrors, and I saw how he almost failed to resist me. If he had come to me in bed, I would have strangled him, then.

But he half-snarled: 'No. It won't wait. Now.'

The unearthly light of dawn filled the room; had only one previous dawn broken upon me in that vile place? And there was nothing for it but to go and fetch the keys from the music stool and pray he would not examine them too closely, pray to God his eyes would fail him, that he might be struck blind.

When I came back into the bedroom carrying the bunch of keys that jangled at every step like a curious musical instrument, he was sitting on the bed in his immaculate shirtsleeves, his head sunk in his hands.

And it seemed to me he was in despair.

Strange. In spite of my fear of him, that made me whiter than my wrap, I felt there emanate from him, at that moment, a stench of absolute despair, rank and ghastly, as if the lilies that surrounded him had all at once begun to fester, or the Russian leather of his scent were reverting to the elements of flayed hide and excrement of which it was composed. The chthonic gravity of his presence exerted a tremendous pressure on the room, so that the blood pounded in my ears as if we had been precipitated to the bottom of the sea, beneath the waves that pounded against the shore.

I held my life in my hands amongst those keys and, in a moment, would place it between his well-manicured fingers. The evidence of that bloody chamber had showed me I could expect no mercy. Yet, when he raised his head and stared at me with his blind, shuttered eyes as though he did not recognize me, I felt a terrified pity for him, for this man who lived in such strange, secret places that, if I loved him enough to follow him, I should have to die.

The atrocious loneliness of that monster!

The monocle had fallen from his face. His curling mane was disordered, as if he had run his hands through it in his distraction. I saw how he had lost his impassivity and was now filled with suppressed excitement. The hand he stretched out for those counters in his game of love and death shook a little; the face that turned towards me contained a sombre delirium that seemed to me compounded of a ghastly, yes, shame but also of a terrible, guilty joy as he slowly ascertained how I had sinned.

That tell-tale stain had resolved itself into a mark the shape and brilliance of the heart on a playing card. He disengaged the key from the ring and looked at it for a while, solitary, brooding.

'It is the key that leads to the kingdom of the unimaginable,' he said. His voice was low and had in it the timbre of certain great cathedral organs that seem, when they are played, to be conversing with God.

I could not restrain a sob.

'Oh, my love, my little love who brought me a white gift of music,' he said, almost as if grieving. 'My little love, you'll never know how much I hate daylight!'

Then he sharply ordered: 'Kneel!'

I knelt before him and he pressed the key lightly to my forehead, held it there for a moment. I felt a faint tingling of the skin and, when I involuntarily glanced at myself in the mirror, I saw the heart-shaped stain had transferred itself to my forehead, to the space between the eyebrows, like the caste mark of a brahmin woman. Or the mark of Cain. And now the key gleamed as freshly as if it had just been cut. He clipped it back on the ring, emitting that same, heavy sigh as he had done when I said that I would marry him.

'My virgin of the arpeggios, prepare yourself for martyrdom.'

'What form shall it take?' I said.

'Decapitation,' he whispered, almost voluptuously. 'Go and bathe yourself; put on that white dress you wore to hear *Tristan* and the necklace that prefigures your end. And I shall take myself off to the armoury, my dear, to sharpen my great-grandfather's ceremonial sword.'

'The servants?'

'We shall have absolute privacy for our last rites; I have already dismissed them. If you look out of the window you can see them going to the mainland.'

It was now the full, pale light of morning; the weather was grey, indeterminate, the sea had an oily, sinister look, a gloomy day on which to die. Along the causeway I could see trooping every maid and scullion, every pot-boy and pan-scourer, valet, laundress and vassal who worked in that great house, most on foot, a few on bicycles. The faceless housekeeper trudged along with a great basket in which, I guessed, she'd stowed as much as she could ransack from the larder. The Marquis must have given the chauffeur leave to borrow the motor for the day, for it went last of all, at a stately pace, as though the procession were a cortège and the car already bore my coffin to the mainland for burial.

But I knew no good Breton earth would cover me, like a last, faithful lover; I had another fate.

'I have given them all a day's holiday, to celebrate our wedding,' he said. And smiled.

However hard I stared at the receding company, I could see no sign of Jean-Yves, our latest servant, hired but the preceding morning.

'Go, now. Bathe yourself; dress yourself. The lustratory ritual and the ceremonial robing; after that, the sacrifice. Wait in the music room until I telephone for you. No, my dear!' And he smiled, as I started, recalling the line was dead. 'One may call inside the castle just as much as one pleases; but, outside – never.'

I scrubbed my forehead with the nail brush as I had scrubbed the key but this red mark would not go away, either, no matter what I did, and I knew I should wear it until I died, though that would not be long. Then I went to my dressing room and put on that white muslin shift, costume of a victim of an auto-da-fé, he had bought me to listen to the Liebestod in. Twelve young women combed out twelve listless sheaves of brown hair in the mirrors; soon, there would be none. The mass of lilies that surrounded me exhaled, now, the odour of their withering. They looked like the trumpets of the angels of death.

On the dressing table, coiled like a snake about to strike, lay the ruby choker.

Already almost lifeless, cold at heart, I descended the spiral staircase to the music room but there I found I had not been abandoned.

'I can be of some comfort to you,' the boy said. 'Though not much use.'

We pushed the piano stool in front of the open window so that, for as long as I could, I would be able to smell the ancient, reconciling smell of the sea that, in time, will cleanse everything, scour the old bones white, wash away all the stains. The last little chambermaid had trotted along the causeway long ago and now the tide, fated as I, came tumbling in, the crisp wavelets splashing on the old stones.

'You do not deserve this,' he said.

'Who can say what I deserve or no?' I said. 'I've done nothing; but that may be sufficient reason for condemning me.'

'You disobeyed him,' he said. 'That is sufficient reason for him to punish you.'

'I only did what he knew I would.'

'Like Eve,' he said.

The telephone rang a shrill imperative. Let it ring. But my lover lifted me up and set me on my feet; I knew I must answer it. The receiver felt heavy as earth.

'The courtyard. Immediately.'

My lover kissed me, he took my hand. He would come with me if I would lead him. Courage. When I thought of courage, I thought of my mother. Then I saw a muscle in my lover's face quiver.

'Hoofbeats!' he said.

I cast one last, desperate glance from the window and, like a miracle, I saw a horse and rider galloping at a vertiginous speed along the causeway, though the waves crashed, now, high as the horse's fetlocks. A rider, her black skirts tucked up around her waist so she could ride hard and fast, a crazy, magnificent horse-woman in widow's weeds.

As the telephone rang again.

'Am I to wait all morning?'

Every moment, my mother drew nearer.

'She will be too late,' Jean-Yves said and yet he could not restrain a note of hope that, though it must be so, yet it might not be so.

The third, intransigent call.

'Shall I come up to heaven to fetch you down, Saint Cecilia? You wicked woman, do you wish me to compound my crimes by desecrating the marriage bed?'

So I must go to the courtyard where my husband waited in his London-tailored trousers and the shirt from Turnbull and Asser, beside the mounting block, with, in his hand, the sword which his great-grandfather had presented to the little corporal, in token of surrender to the Republic, before he shot himself. The heavy sword, unsheathed, grey as that November morning, sharp as child-birth, mortal.

When my husband saw my companion, he observed: 'Let the blind lead the blind, eh? But does even a youth as besotted as you are think she was truly blind to her own desires when she took my ring? Give it me back, whore.'

The fires in the opal had all died down. I gladly slipped it from my finger and, even in that dolorous place, my heart was lighter for the lack of it. My husband took it lovingly and lodged it on the tip of his little finger; it would go no further.

'It will serve me for a dozen more fiancées,' he said. 'To the block, woman. No – leave the boy; I shall deal with him later, utilizing a less exalted instrument than the one with which I do my wife the honour of her immolation, for do not fear that in death you will be divided.'

Slowly, slowly, one foot before the other, I crossed the cobbles. The longer I dawdled over my execution, the more time it gave the avenging angel to descend ...

'Don't loiter, girl! Do you think I shall lose appetite for the meal if you are so long about serving it? No; I shall grow hungrier, more ravenous with each moment, more cruel ... Run to me, run! I have a place prepared for your exquisite corpse in my display of flesh!'

He raised the sword and cut bright segments from the air with it, but still I lingered although my hopes, so recently raised, now began to flag. If she is not here by now, her horse must have stumbled on the causeway, have plunged into the sea ... One thing only made me glad; that my lover would not see me die.

My husband laid my branded forehead on the stone and, as he had done once before, twisted my hair into a rope and drew it away from my neck.

'Such a pretty neck,' he said with what seemed to be a genuine, retrospective tenderness. 'A neck like the stem of a young plant.'

I felt the silken bristle of his beard and the wet touch of his lips as he kissed my nape. And, once again, of my apparel I must retain only my gems; the sharp blade ripped my dress in two and it fell from me. A little green moss, growing in the crevices of the mounting block, would be the last thing I should see in all the world.

The whizz of that heavy sword.

And – a great battering and pounding at the gate, the jangling of the bell, the frenzied neighing of a horse! The unholy silence of the place shattered in an instant. The blade did *not* descend, the necklace did *not* sever, my head did *not* roll. For, for an instant, the beast wavered in his stroke, a sufficient split second of astonished indecision to let me spring upright and dart to the assistance of my lover as he struggled sightlessly with the great bolts that kept her out.

The Marquis stood transfixed, utterly dazed, at a loss. It must have been as if he had been watching his beloved *Tristan* for the twelfth, the thirteenth time and Tristan stirred, then leapt from his bier in the last act, announced in a jaunty aria interposed from Verdi that bygones were bygones, crying over spilt milk did nobody any good and, as for himself, he proposed to live happily ever after. The puppet master, open-mouthed, wide-eyed, impotent at the last, saw his dolls break free of their strings, abandon the rituals he had ordained for them since time began and start to live for themselves; the king, aghast, witnesses the revolt of his pawns.

You never saw such a wild thing as my mother, her hat seized by the winds and blown out to sea so that her hair was her white mane, her black lisle legs exposed to the thigh, her skirts tucked round her waist, one hand on the reins of the rearing horse while the other clasped my father's service revolver and, behind her, the breakers of the savage, indifferent sea, like the witnesses of a furious justice. And my husband stood stock-still, as if she had been Medusa, the sword still raised over his head as in those clockwork tableaux of Bluebeard that you see in glass cases at fairs.

And then it was as though a curious child pushed his centime into the slot and set all in motion. The heavy, bearded figure roared out aloud, braying with fury, and, wielding the honourable sword as if it were a matter of death or glory, charged us, all three.

On her eighteenth birthday, my mother had disposed of a man-eating tiger that had ravaged the villages in the hills north of Hanoi. Now, without a moment's hesitation, she raised my father's gun, took aim and put a single, irreproachable bullet through my husband's head.

*

We lead a quiet life, the three of us. I inherited, of course, enormous wealth but we have given most of it away to various charities. The castle is now a school for the blind, though I pray that the children who live there are not haunted by any sad ghosts looking for, crying for, the husband who will never return to the bloody chamber, the contents of which are buried or burned, the door sealed.

I felt I had a right to retain sufficient funds to start a little music school here, on the outskirts of Paris, and we do well enough. Sometimes we can even afford to go to the Opéra, though never to sit in a box, of course. We know we are the source of many whisperings and much gossip but the three of us know the truth of it and mere chatter can never harm us. I can only bless the – what shall I call it? – the *maternal telepathy* that sent my mother running headlong from the telephone to the station after I had called her, that night. I never heard you cry before, she said, by way of explanation. Not when you were happy. And who ever cried because of gold bath taps?

The night train, the one I had taken; she lay in her berth, sleepless as I had been. When she could not find a taxi at that lonely halt, she borrowed old Dobbin from a bemused farmer, for some internal urgency told her that she must reach me before the incoming tide sealed me away from her for ever. My poor old nurse, left scandalized at home – what? interrupt milord on his honeymoon? – she died soon after. She had taken so much secret pleasure in the fact that her little girl had become a marquise; and now here I was, scarcely a penny the richer, widowed at seventeen in the most dubious circumstances and busily engaged in setting up house with a piano-tuner. Poor thing, she passed away in a sorry state of disillusion! But I do believe my mother loves him as much as I do.

No paint nor powder, no matter how thick or white, can mask that red mark on my forehead; I am glad he cannot see it – not for fear of his revulsion, since I know he sees me clearly with his heart – but, because it spares my shame.

1944

Ellen Gilchrist

Ellen Gilchrist (b. 1935) is an American author and poet who studied
creative writing under Eudora Welty. Her 1981 collection of stories, *In
the Land of Dreamy Dreams*, received immense critical acclaim and, in
1984, she won the National Book Award for her collection of stories,
Victory Over Japan.

When I was eight years old I had a piano made of nine martini glasses.
I could have had a real piano if I had been able to pay the terrible
price, been able to put up with piano lessons, but the old German
spy who taught piano in the small town of Seymour, Indiana, was jealous of my
talent.

"Stop it! Stop it! Stop it!" she would scream in her guttural accent, hitting me
on the knuckles with the stick she kept for that purpose. "Stopping this crazy
business. Can't you ever listen? Can't you sit still a minute? Can't you settle
down?"

God knows I tried to settle down. But the mere sight of the magnificent black
upright, the feel of the piano stool against my plump bottom, the cold ivory
touch of the keys would send me into paroxysms of musical bliss, and I would
throw back my head and begin to pound out melodies in two octaves.

"Stop it," she would be screaming. "This is no music, this crazy banging business. Stop on my piano. Stop before I call your momma!"

I remember the day I quit for good. I got up from the piano stool, slammed
the cover down on the keys, told her my father would have her arrested, and
stalked out of the house without my hat and gloves. It was a cold November day,
and I walked home with gray skies all around me, shivering and brokenhearted,
certain the secret lives of musical instruments were closed to me forever.

So music might have disappeared from my life. With my formal training at
this sorry end I might have had to content myself with tap and ballet and public
speaking, but a muse looked down from heaven and took pity on me.

She arrived in the form of a glamorous war widow, was waiting for me at the
bar when I walked into the officers' club with my parents that Saturday night.

There she sat, wearing black taffeta, smoking long white cigarettes, sipping
her third very dry martini.

"Isn't that Doris Treadway at the bar?" my mother said. "I can't believe she's
going out in public."

"What would you like her to do," my father said, "stay home and go crazy?"

"Well, after all," my mother whispered. "It's only been a month."

"Do you *know* that lady?" I asked, wondering if she was a movie star. She looked exactly like a movie star.

"She works for your daddy, Honey," my mother said. "Her husband got killed in the Philippines."

"Go talk to her," my father said. "Go cheer her up. Go tell her who you are."

As soon as we ordered dinner I did just that. I walked across the room and took up the stool beside her at the bar. I breathed deeply of her cool perfume, listening to the rustling of her sleeves as she took a long sophisticated drag on her Camel.

"So you are Dudley's daughter," she said, smiling at me. I squirmed with delight beneath her approving gaze, enchanted by the dark timbre of her voice, the marvelous fuchsia of her lips and fingertips, the brooding glamor of her widowhood.

"I'm Rhoda," I said. "The baby-sitter quit so they brought me with them."

"Would you like a drink?" she asked. "Could I persuade you to join me?"

"Sure," I said. "Sure I'll join you."

She conferred with the bartender and waved to my parents who were watching us from across the room.

"Well, Rhoda," she said. "I've been hearing about you from your father."

"What did you hear?" I asked, getting worried.

"Well," she said, "the best thing I heard was that you locked yourself in a bathroom for six hours to keep from eating fruit cocktail."

"I hate fruit cocktail," I said. "It makes me sick. I wouldn't eat fruit cocktail for all the tea in China."

"I couldn't agree with you more," she said, picking up her stirrer and tapping it on her martini glass. "I think people who hate fruit cocktail should always stick together."

The stirrer made a lovely sound against the glass. The bartender returned, bringing a wineglass foil of bright pink liquid.

"Taste it," she said, "go ahead. He made it just for you."

I picked up the glass in two fingers and brought it delicately to my lips as I had seen her do.

"It's wonderful," I said, "what's in it?"

"Something special," she said. "It's called a Shirley Temple. So little girls can pretend they're drinking." She laughed out loud and began to tap the glass stirrer against the line of empty glasses in front of her.

"Why doesn't he move the empty glasses?" I asked.

"Because I'm playing them," she said. "Listen." She tapped out a little tune. "Now, listen to this," she said, adding small amounts of water to the glasses. She tapped them again with the stirrer, calling out the notes ina very high, very clear soprano voice. "Do, Re, Mi, Fa, So, ... Bartender," she called, "bring us more glasses."

In a minute she had arranged a keyboard with nine perfect notes.

"Here," she said, moving the glasses in front of me, handing me the stirrer, "you play it."

"What should I play," I said. "I don't know any music."

"Of course you know music," she said. "Everyone knows music. Play anything you like. Play whatever comes into your head."

I began to hit the glasses with the stirrer, gingerly at first, then with more aban-don. Soon I had something going that sounded marvelous.

"Is that by any chance the 'Air Corps Hymn' you're playing?" she said.

"Well ... yes it is," I said. "How could you tell?"

She began to sing along with me, singing the words in her perfect voice as I beat upon the glasses. "Off we go," she sang, "into the wild blue yonder, climbing high into the sky, dum, dum, dum. Down we dive spouting a flame from under, off with one hell-of-a-roar, roar, roar ..."

People crowded around our end of the bar, listening to us, applauding. We fin-ished with the air corps and started right in on the army. "Over hill, over dale, as we hit the dusty trail, and those caissons go marching along, dum, dum, dum ... In and out, hear them shout, counter march and right about, and those caissons go rolling along. For it's hie, hie, hee, in the field artilll-a-reeeee ..."

A man near me began playing the bass on a brandy glass. Another man drummed on the bar with a pair of ashtrays.

Doris broke into "Begin the Beguine." "When they begin the beguine," she sang, "it brings back a night of tropical splendor. It brings back die sound of music so te-en-de-rr. It brings back a memorreeeeee ever green."

A woman in a green dress began dancing, swaying to our rhythm. My martini glasses shone in the light from the bar. As I struck them one by one the notes floated around me like bright translucent boats.

This was music! Not the stale order of the book and the metronome, not the stick and the German. Music was this wildness rising from the dark taffeta of Doris's dress. This praise, this brilliance.

The soft delicious light, the smell of perfume and gin, the perfection of our artistry almost overwhelmed me, but I played bravely on.

Every now and then I would look up and see Doris smiling at me while she sang. Doris and I were one. And that too was the secret of music.

I do not know how long we played. Perhaps we played until my dinner was served. Perhaps we played for hours. Perhaps we are playing still.

"Oh, just let them begin the beguine, let them plaaaaay ... Let the fire that was once a flame remain an ember. Let it burn like the long lost desire I only remember. When they begin, when they begin, when they begi-i-i-i-in the begui-i-i-i-ine ..."

THE LOVER

Alice Walker

Alice Walker (b. 1944) is an American author, poet, feminist and activist. She is best known for the critically acclaimed novel *The Color Purple*, published in 1982, for which she won the National Book Award and the Pulitzer Prize. Walker's published works include seven novels, four collections of short stories, four children's books and volumes of essays and poetry.

Her husband had wanted a child and so she gave him one as a gift, because she liked her husband and admired him greatly. Still, it had taken a lot out of her, especially in the area of sexual response. She had never been particularly passionate with him, not even during the early years of their marriage; it was more a matter of being sexually comfortable. After the birth of the child she simply never thought of him sexually at all. She supposed their marriage was better than most, even so. He was a teacher at a University near their home in the Midwest and cared about his students – which endeared him to her, who had had so many uncaring teachers; and toward her own work, which was poetry (that she set very successfully to jazz), he showed the utmost understanding and respect.

She was away for two months at an artists' colony in New England and that is where she met Ellis, whom she immediately dubbed, once she had got over thinking he resembled (with his top lip slightly raised over his right eye-tooth when he smiled) a wolf, "The Lover." They met one evening before dinner as she was busy ignoring the pompous bullshit of a fellow black poet, a man many years older than she who had no concept of other people's impatience. He had been rambling on about himself for over an hour and she had at first respectfully listened because she was the kind of person whose adult behavior – in a situation like this – reflected her childhood instruction; and she was instructed as a child, to be polite.

She was always getting herself stuck in one-sided conversations of this sort because she was – the people who talked to her seemed to think – an excellent listener. She was, up to a point. She was genuinely interested in older artists in particular and would sit, entranced, as they spun out their tales of art and lust (the gossip, though old, was delicious!) of forty years ago.

But there had been only a few of these artists whose tales she had listened to until the end. For as soon as a note of bragging entered into the conversation – a famous name dropped here, an expensive Paris restaurant's menu dropped there, and especially the names of the old artist's neglected books and on what occasion the wretched creature had insulted this or that weasel of a white person – her mind began to turn about upon itself until it rolled out some of her own thoughts to take the place of the trash that was coming in.

And so it was on that evening before dinner. The old poet – whose work was exceedingly mediocre, and whose only attractions, as far as she was concerned, were his age and his rather bitter wit – fastened his black, bloodshot eyes upon her (in which she read desperation and a prayer of unstrenuous seduction) and held her to a close attention to his words. Except that she had perfected the trick – as had many of her contemporaries who hated to be rude and who, also, had a strong sense of self-preservation (because the old poet, though, she thought, approaching senility, was yet a powerful figure in black literary circles and thought nothing of using his considerable influence to thwart the careers of younger talents) – of keeping her face quite animated and turned full onto the speaker, while inside her head she could be trying out the shades of paint with which to improve the lighting of her house. In fact, so intense did her concentration appear, it seemed she read the speaker's lips.

Ellis, who would be her lover, had come into the room and sat down on a chair by the fire. For although it was the middle of summer, a fire was needed against the chilly New England evenings.

"Have you been waiting long?" he asked.

And it suddenly occurred to her that indeed she had.

"But of course," she answered absently, noting the crooked smile that reminded her of a snarling, though not disagreeable, wolf – and turned back just as the old poet jealously reached out his hand to draw her attention to the, for him, hilarious ending of his story. She laughed and slapped her knee, a gesture of such fraudulent folksiness that she was soon laughing in earnest. Catching Ellis's eye as she thus amused herself she noticed therein a particular gleam that she instantly recognized.

"My lover," she thought, noticing for the first time his head of blue-black curls, his eyes as brown as the Mississippi, his skin that was not as successfully tanned as it might have been but which would definitely do. He was thin and tall, with practically no hips in the beige twill jeans he wore.

At dinner they sat together, looking out at the blue New England mountains in the distance, as the sun left tracings of orange and pink against the pale blue sky. He had heard she'd won some sort of prize – a prestigious one – for her "jazzed-up" poetry, and the way he said it made her glance critically at his long fingers wrapped around his wine glass. She wondered if they would be as sensitive on her skin as they looked. She had never heard of him, though she did not say so, probably because he had already said it for her. He talked a good deal – easily and early – about himself, and she was quite relaxed – even entertained – in her listener's role.

He wondered what, *if anything*, younger poets like herself had to say, since he was of the opinion that not much was learned about life until the middle years. He was in his forties. Of course he didn't look it, but he was much older than she, he said, and the reason that he was not better known was because he could not find a publisher for his two novels (still, by the way, unpublished – in case she knew publishers) or for his poetry, which an acquaintance of his had compared to something or other by Montaigne.

"You're lovely," he said into the brief silence.

"And you seem bright," she automatically replied.

She had blocked him out since his mention of the two unpublished novels. By the time he began complaining about the preferential treatment publishers now gave minorities and women she was on the point of yawning or gazing idly about the room. But she did not do either for a very simple reason: when she had first seen him she had thought – after the wolf thing – "my lover," and had liked, deep down inside, the illicit sound of it. She had never had a lover; he would be her first. Afterwards, she would be truly a woman of her time. She also responded to his curly hair and slim, almost nonexistent hips, in a surprisingly passionate way.

She was a woman who, after many tribulations in her life, few of which she ever discussed even with close friends, had reached the point of being generally pleased with herself. This self-acceptance was expressed in her eyes, which were large, dark and clear and which, more often than not, seemed predisposed to smile. Though not tall, her carriage gave the illusion of height, as did her carefully selected tall sandals and her naturally tall hair, which stood in an elegant black afro with exactly seven strands of silver hair – of which she was very proud (she was just thirty-one) – shining across the top. She wore long richly colored skirts that – when she walked – parted without warning along the side, and exposed a flash of her creamy brown thigh, and legs that were curvaceous and strong. If she came late to the dining room and stood in the doorway a moment longer than necessary – looking about for a place to sit after she had her tray – for that moment the noise from the cutlery already in use was still.

What others minded at the Colony – whether too many frogs in the frog pond (which was used for swimming) or not enough wine with the veal (there was talk of cutting out wine with meals altogether, and thereby ending a fine old Colony tradition!) – she did not seem to mind. She seemed open, bright, occasionally preoccupied, but always ready with an appreciative ear, or at times a humorous, if outdated joke of her own (which she nevertheless told with gusto and found funny herself, because she would laugh and laugh at it, regardless of what her listeners did). She seemed never to strain over her work, and literally never complained about its progress – or lack thereof. It was as if she worked only for herself, for her own enjoyment (or salvation) and was – whether working or simply thinking of working – calm about it.

Even the distraction caused by the birth of her child was a price she was ultimately prepared to pay. She did not intend to have a second one, after all – that would be too stupid – and this one would, before she knew it, be grown up enough for boarding school.

Relishing her short freedom during the summer as much as she contemplated enjoyment of her longer future one, she threw herself headlong into the interim relationship with Ellis, a professional lover of mainly older women artists who came to the Colony every year to work and play.

A New York Jew of considerable charm, intellectual pettiness, and so vast and uncritical a love of all things European it struck one as an illness (and who hated Brooklyn – where he had grown up – his parents, Jewish culture, and all he had observed of black behavior in New York City), Ellis found the listening silence of "the dark woman," as he euphemistically called her, restorative – after his endless evenings with talkative women who wrote for *Esquire* and the *New York Times*. Such women made it possible for him to be included in the proper tennis sets and swimming parties at the Colony – in which he hoped to meet contacts who would help his career along – but they were also driven to examine each and every one of their own thoughts aloud. His must be the attentive ear, since they had already "made it" and were comfortable exposing their own charming foibles to him, while he, not having made it yet, could afford to expose nothing that might discourage their assistance in his behalf.

It amused and thrilled him to almost hear the "click" when his eyes met those of the jazz poet. "Sex," he thought. And, "rest."

Of course he mistook her intensity.

After sitting before her piano for hours, setting one of her poems to music, she would fling open her cabin door and wave to him as he walked by on his way to or from the lake. He was writing a novella about his former wife and composed it in longhand down at the lake ("So if I get fed up with it I can toss myself in," he joked) and then took it back to his studio with him to type. She would call to him, her hair and clothing very loose, and entice him into her cabin with promises of sympathy and half her lunch.

When they made love she was disappointed. He did not appear to believe in unhurried pleasure, and thought the things she suggested he might do to please her very awkward at the least. But it hardly mattered, since what mattered was the fact of having a lover. She liked snuggling up to him, liked kissing him along the sides of his face – his cheeks were just beginning to be a trifle flabby but would still be good for several years – and loved to write him silly letters – scorching with passion and promises of abandon – that made her seem head over heels in love. She enjoyed writing the letters because she enjoyed feeling to her full capacity and for as long as possible the excitement having a lover brought. It was the kind of excitement she'd felt years ago, in high school and perhaps twice in college (once when she'd fallen for a student and once when she was seduced – with her help and consent – by a teacher), and she recognized it as a feeling to be enjoyed for all it was worth. Her body felt on fire, her heart jumped in her breast, her pulse raced – she was aware, for the first time in years, of actually *needing* to make love.

He began to think he must fight her off, at least a little bit. She was too intense, he said. He did not have time for intense relationships, that's why he had finally accepted a divorce from his wife. He was also writing a great poem which he had begun in 1950 and which – now that he was at the Colony – he hoped to finish. She should concentrate on her own work if she expected to win any more prizes. She *wanted* to win more, didn't she?

She laughed at him, but would not tell him why. Instead she tried, very gently (while sitting on his lap with her bosom maternally opposite his face), to tell him he misunderstood. That she wanted nothing from him beyond the sensation of being in love itself. (His stare was at first blank, then cynical, at this.) As for her work, she did not do hers the way he apparently did his. Hers did not mean to her what he seemed to think it meant. It did not get in the way of her living, for example, and if it ever did, she felt sure she would remove it. Prizes were nice – especially if they brought one money (which one might then use to explore

Barbados! China! Mozambique!) – but they were not rewards she could count on. Her life, on the other hand, *was* a reward she could count on. (He became impatient with this explanation and a little angry.)

It was their first quarrel.

When he saw her again she had spent the weekend (which had been coming up) in nearby Boston. She looked cheerful, happy and relaxed. From her letters to him – which he had thought embarrassingly self-revealing and erotic, though flattering, of course, to him – he had assumed she was on the point of declaring her undying love and of wanting to run away with him. Instead, she had gone off for two days, without mentioning it to him. And she had gone, so she said, by herself!

She soothed him as best she could. Lied, which she hated more than anything, about her work. "It was going so *poorly*," she complained (and the words rang metallic in her mouth); "I just couldn't bear staying here doing nothing where working conditions are so *idyllic*!" He appeared somewhat mollified. Actually, her work was going fine and she had sent off to her publishers a completed book of poems and jazz arrangements – which was what she had come to the Colony to do. "Your work was going swimmingly down at the lake," she giggled. "I didn't wish to disturb you."

And yet it was clear he was disturbed.

So she did not tell him she had flown all the way home.

He was always questioning her now about her town, her house, her child, her husband. She found herself describing her husband as if to a prospective bride. She lingered over the wiry bronze of his hair, the evenness of his teeth, his black, black eyes, the thrilling timbre of his deep voice. It *was* an exceptionally fine voice, it seemed to her now, listening to Ellis's rather whining one. Though, on second thought, it was perhaps nothing special.

At night, after a rousing but unsatisfactory evening with Ellis, she dreamed of her husband making love to her on the kitchen floor at home, where the sunlight collected in a pool beneath the window, and lay in bed next day dreaming of all the faraway countries, daring adventures, passionate lovers still to be found.

RUE DE LILLE

Mavis Gallant

Mavis Gallant (b. 1922) is a Canadian author. She has written two novels as well as numerous collections of stories, and is often cited as one of the best living short story writers. She was elected Companion of the Order of Canada in 1993 and, in 1989, was made a Foreign Honorary Member of the American Academy of Arts and Letters. Her work regularly appears in the *New Yorker*, often debuting there before subsequently being published in a collection.

My second wife, Juliette, died in the apartment on Rue de Lille, where she had lived – at first alone, more or less, then with me – since the end of the war. All the rooms gave onto the ivy-hung well of a court, and were for that reason dark. We often talked about looking for a brighter flat, on a top floor with southern exposure and a wide terrace, but Parisians seldom move until they're driven to. "We know the worst of what we've got," we told each other. "It's better than a bad surprise."

"And what about your books?" Juliette would add. "It would take you months to get them packed, and in the new place you'd never get them sorted." I would see myself as Juliette saw me, crouched over a slanting, shaking stack of volumes piled on a strange floor, cursing and swearing as I tried to pry out a dictionary. "Just the same, I don't intend to die here," she also said.

I once knew someone who believed drowning might be easy, even pleasant, until he almost drowned by accident. Juliette's father was a colonel who expected to die in battle or to be shot by a German firing squad, but he died of typhus in a concentration camp. I had once, long ago, imagined for myself a clandestine burial with full honors after some Resistance feat, but all I got out of the war was a few fractures and a broken nose in a motorcycle accident.

Juliette had thirty-seven years of blacked-out winter mornings in Rue de Lille. She was a few days short of her sixtieth birthday when I found her stretched out on the floor of our bedroom, a hand slackened on a flashlight. She had been trying to see under a chest of drawers, and her heart stopped. (Later, I pulled the chest away from the wall and discovered a five-franc coin.) Her gray-and-dark hair, which had grown soft and wayward with age, was tied back with a narrow satin ribbon. She looked more girlish than at any time since I'd first met her. (She fell in love with me young.) She wore a pleated flannel skirt, a tailored blouse, and one of the thick cardigans with gilt buttons she used to knit while watching television. She had been trained to believe that to look or to listen quietly is to do nothing; she would hum along with music, to show she wasn't idle. She was

discreet, she was generous to a sensible degree, she was anything but conten-
tious. I often heard her remark, a trifle worriedly, that she was never bored. She
was faithful, if "faithful" means avoiding the acknowledged forms of trouble.
She was patient. I know she was good. Any devoted male friend, any lover, any
husband would have shown up beside her as selfish, irritable, even cruel. She
displayed so little of the ordinary kinds of jealousy, the plain marital do-you-
often-have-lunch-with-her? sort, that I once asked her if she had a piece missing.

"Whoever takes this place over," she said, when we spoke of moving, "will be
staggered by the size of the electricity bills." (Juliette paid them; I looked after a
number of other things.) We had to keep the lights turned on all day in winter.
The apartment was L-shaped, bent round two sides of a court, like a train making a sharp turn. From our studies, at opposite ends of the train, we could look
out and see the comforting glow of each other's working life, a lamp behind a
window. Juliette would be giving some American novel a staunch, steady translation; I might be getting into shape my five-hour television series, "Stendhal and
the Italian Experience," which was to win an award in Japan.

We were together for a duration of time I daren't measure against the expanse
of Juliette's life; it would give me the feeling that I had decamped to a height of
land, a survivor's eminence, so as to survey the point at which our lives crossed and
mingled and began to move in the same direction: a long, narrow reach of time in
the Rue de Lille. It must be the washy, indefinite colorations of blue that carpeted,
papered, and covered floors, walls, and furniture and shaded our lamps which cast
over that reach the tone of a short season. I am thinking of the patches of distant,
neutral blue that appear over Paris in late spring, when it is still wet and cold in
the street and tourists have come too early. The tourists shelter in doorways, trying
to read their soaked maps, perennially unprepared in their jeans and thin jackets.
Overhead, there are scrapings of a color that carries no threat and promises all.

That choice, Juliette's preference, I sometimes put down to her Calvinist so-
briety – call it a temperament – and sometimes to a refinement of her Huguenot
taste. When I was feeling tired or impatient, I complained that I had been consigned to a Protestant Heaven by an arbitrary traffic cop, and that I was better
suited to a pagan Hell. Again, as I looked round our dining-room table at the
calm, clever faces of old friends of Juliette's family, at their competent and un-
assuming wives, I saw what folly it might be to set such people against a background of buttercup yellow or apple green. The soft clicking of their upper-class
Protestant consonants made conversation distant and neutral, too. It was a voice
that had puzzled me the first time I'd heard it from Juliette. I had supposed, mistakenly, that she was trying it on for effect; but she was wholly natural.

The sixteenth-century map of Paris I bought for her birthday is still at the
framer's; I sent a check but never picked it up. I destroyed her private correspondence without reading it, and gave armfuls of clothes away to a Protestant
charity. To the personal notice of her death in *Le Monde* was attached a brief
mention of her father, a hero of the Resistance for whom suburban streets are
named; and of her career as a respected translator, responsible for having introduced postwar American literature to French readers; and of her husband, the
well-known radio and television interviewer and writer, who survived her.

Another person to survive her was my first wife. One night when Juliette and

I were drinking coffee in the little sitting room where she received her women friends, and where we watched television, Juliette said, again, "But how much of what she says does she believe? About her Catholicism, and all those fantasies running round in her head – that she is your true and only wife, that your marriage is registered in Heaven, that you and she will be together in another world?"

"Those are things people put in letters," I said. "They sit down alone and pour it out. It's sincere at that moment. I don't know why she would suddenly be insincere."

"After all the trouble she's made," said Juliette. She meant that for many years my wife would not let me divorce.

"She couldn't help that," I said.

"How do you know?"

"I don't know. It's what I think. I hardly knew her."

"You must have known *something*."

"I haven't seen her more than three or four times in the last thirty-odd years, since I started living with you."

"What do you mean?" said Juliette. "You saw her just once, with me. We had lunch. You backed off asking for the divorce."

"You can't ask for a divorce at lunch. It had to be done by mail."

"And since then she hasn't stopped writing," said Juliette. "Do you mean three or four times, or do you mean once?"

I said, "Once, probably. Probably just that once."

Viewing me at close range, as if I were a novel she had to translate, Juliette replied that one ought to be spared unexpected visions. Just now, it was as if three walls of the court outside had been bombed flat. Through a bright new gap she saw straight through to my first marriage. We – my first wife and I – postured in the distance, like characters in fiction.

I had recently taken part in a panel discussion, taped for television, on the theme "What Literature, for Which Readers, at Whose Price?" I turned away from Juliette and switched on the set, about ten minutes too early. Juliette put the empty cups and the coffeepot on a tray she had picked up in Milan, the summer I was researching the Stendhal, and carried the tray down the dim passage to the kitchen. I watched the tag end of the late news. It must have been during the spring of 1976. Because of the energy crisis, daylight saving had been established. Like any novelty, it was deeply upsetting. People said they could no longer digest their food or be nice to their children, and that they needed sedation to help them through the altered day. A doctor was interviewed; he advised a light diet and early bed until mind and body adjusted to the change.

I turned, smiling, to where Juliette should have been. My program came on then, and I watched myself making a few points before I got up and went to find her. She was in the kitchen, standing in the dark, clutching the edge of the sink. She did not move when I turned the light on. I put my arms around her, and we came back to her sitting room and watched the rest of the program together. She was knitting squares of wool to be sewn together to make a blanket; there was always, somewhere, a flood or an earthquake or a flow of refugees, and those who outlasted jeopardy had to be covered.

WORDS

Carol Shields

> Carol Shields (1935–2003) was an American-born Canadian writer. She is best known for her 1993 novel *The Stone Diaries,* which won the Pulitzer Prize as well as the Governor General's Award in Canada. Shields published ten novels, three collections of poetry and five collections of short stories.

When the world first started heating up, an international conference was held in Rome to discuss ways of dealing with the situation. Ian's small northern country – small in terms of population, that is, not in size – sent him to the meetings as a junior observer, and it was there he met Isobel, who was representing her country as full-fledged delegate. She wore a terrible green dress the first time he saw her, and rather clumsy shoes, but he could see that her neck was slender, her waist narrow and her legs long and brown. For so young a woman, she was astonishingly articulate; in fact, it was her voice more than anything else that he fell in love with – its hills and valleys and its pliant, easy-sided wit. It was a voice that could be distinguished in any gathering, being both sweet and husky and having an edging of contralto merriment that seemed to Ian as rare and fine as a border of gold leaf.

They played truant, missing half the study sessions, the two of them lingering instead over tall, cool drinks in the café they found on the Via Traflori. There, under a cheerful striped canopy, Isobel leaned across a little table and placed long, ribbony Spanish phrases into Ian's mouth, encouraging and praising him when he got them right. And he, in his somewhat stiff northern voice, gave back the English equivalents. table, chair, glass, cold, hot, money, street, people, mouth. In the evenings, walking in the gardens in front of the institute where the conference was being held, they turned to each other and promised with their eyes, and in two languages as well, to love each other forever.

The second International Conference was held ten years later. The situation had become grave. One could use the word *crisis* and not be embarrassed. Ian – by then married to Isobel, who was at home with the children – attended every session and he listened attentively to the position papers of various physicists, engineers, geographers and linguists from all parts of the world. It was a solemn but distinguished assembly; many eminent men and women took their places at the lectern, including the spidery old Scottish demographer who years earlier had made the first correlation between substrata temperatures and highly verbalized societies. In every case, these speakers presented their concerns with admirable brevity, each word weighted and frugally chosen, and not one of them exceeded the two-minute time limitation. For by now no one really doubted that it was the extravagance and proliferation of language that had caused the temperature of the earth's crust to rise, and in places – California, Japan, London – to crack open and form long ragged lakes of fire. The evidence was everywhere and it was incontrovertible: thermal maps, and measurements, sonar readings, caloric separations, a network of subterranean monitoring systems – all these had reinforced the integrity of the original Scottish theories.

But the delegates, sitting in the plenary session of the second International Conference, were still reluctant to take regulatory action. It was partly a case of heads-in-the-sand; it was – human nature being what it is – partly a matter of political advantage or commercial gain. There lingered, too, a somewhat surprising nostalgia for traditional liberties and for the old verbal order of the world. Discussion at the conference had gone around and around all week, pointless and wasteful, and it looked very much as though the final meeting would end in yet another welter of indecision and deferral. It was at that point that Ian, seated in the front row, rose and requested permission to speak.

He was granted a one-minute slot on the agenda. In fact, he spoke for several minutes, but his eloquence, his sincerity (and no doubt his strong, boyish appearance, his shaggy hair and his blue eyes) seemed to merit an exception. Certainly not one person sitting in that gathering had any wish to stop him.

It was unfortunate, tragic some thought, that a freak failure in the electronic system – only a plug accidentally pulled from its socket – prevented his exact words from being recorded, but those who were present remembered afterward how passionately he pleaded his love, for the planet. (In truth – though who could know this? – he was thinking chiefly of his love for Isobel and his two children.)

We are living in a fool's dream, he told his fellow delegates, and the time has come for us to wake. Voluntary restraints were no longer adequate to preserve the little earth, which was the only home we know. Halfway measures like the old three-hour *temps tranquilles* were next to useless since they were never, or almost never, enforced. The evening curfew-lingua was ridiculously lenient. Abuses of every sort abounded, particularly the use of highly percussive words or words that were redolent with emotional potency, even though it had been established that these two classes of words were particularly damaging to bedrock and shales. Multilingualism continued to flourish. Wasteful antiphonic structures were actually on the increase in the more heavily populated regions, as was the use of elaborate ceremonial metaphor. It was as though, by refusing to make linguistic sacrifices, the human race had willed its own destruction.

When he finished speaking, the applause was prolonged and powerful. It perhaps held an element of shame, too; this young man had found the courage to say at last what should have been said long before. One after another the delegates rose to their feet, and soon their clapping fell into a steady rhythmic beat that had the effect of holding Ian hostage on the platform. The chairman whispered into his ear, begging him for a few additional words.

He assented. He could not say no. And, in a fever that was remarkably similar to the fever he had suffered as a child during a severe case of measles, or like the fever of love he had succumbed to ten years earlier in Rome, he announced to the audience, holding up a hand for attention, that he would be the first to take a vow of complete silence for the sake of the planet that had fathered him.

Almost at once he regretted his words, but hubris kept him from recanting for the first twenty-four hours and, after that, a kind of stubbornness took over. Isobel met him at the airport with the words, "You went too far." Later, after a miserable, silent attempt at lovemaking, she said, "I'll never forgive you." His children, clamoring to hear about his moment of heroism, poked at him, at his face and chest and arms, as though he were inert. He tried to tell them with his eyes that he was still their father, that he still loved them.

"Leave him alone," Isobel said sharply. "He might as well be a stranger now. He's no different than anyone else."

She became loud and shrewish. When his silent followers arrived at their door – and in time there were thousands of them, each with the same blank face and gold armband – she admitted them with bad grace. She grew garrulous. She rambled on and on, bitter and blaming, sometimes incoherent, sometimes obscene, sometimes reverting to a coarse, primitive schoolyard Spanish, sometimes shouting to herself or cursing into the mirror or chanting oaths – anything to furnish the emptiness of the house with words. She became disoriented. The solid plaster of the walls fell away from her, melting into a drift of vapor. There seemed to be no shadows, no sense of dimension, no delicate separation between one object and another. Privately, she pleaded with her husband for an act of apostasy. Later she taunted him. "Show me you're still human," she would say. "Give me just one word." The word *betrayal* came frequently out of her wide mobile mouth, and so did the scornful epithet *martyr*.

But time passes and people forget. She forgot, finally, what it was that had betrayed her. Next she forgot her husband's name. Sometimes she forgot that she had a husband at all, for how could anything be said to exist, she asked herself loudly, hoarsely – even a husband, even one's self – if it didn't also exist in the shape of a word.

He worried that she might be arrested, but for some reason – his position probably – she was always let off with a warning. In their own house she ignored him, passing him on the stairs without a look, or crossing in front of him as though he were a stuffed chair. Often she disappeared for hours, venturing out alone into the heat of the night, and he began to suspect she had taken a lover.

The thought preyed on him, though, in fact he had long since forgotten the word for *wife* and also the word for *fidelity*. One night, when she left the house, he attempted to follow her, but clearly she was suspicious because she walked very quickly, looking back over her shoulder, making a series of unnecessary turns and choosing narrow old streets whose curbs were blackened by fire. Within minutes he lost sight of her; soon after that he was driven back by the heat.

The next night he tried again, and this time he saw her disappear into an ancient dilapidated braiding, the sort of enclosure, he remembered, where children had once gone to learn to read and write. Unexpectedly, he felt a flash of pity, what a sad place for a tryst. He waited briefly, then entered the building and went up a flight of smoldering stairs that seemed on the point of collapse. There he found a dim corridor, thick with smoke, and a single room at one end.

Through the door he heard a waterfall of voices. There must have been a dozen people inside, all of them talking. The talk seemed to be about poetry. Someone – a woman – was giving a lecture. There were interruptions, a discussion, some laughter. He heard his wife's voice, her old gilt-edged contralto, asking a question, and the sound of it made him draw in his breath so sharply that something hard, like a cinder or a particle of gravel, formed in his throat.

It stayed stubbornly lodged there all night. He found it painful to breathe, and even Isobel noticed how he thrashed about in bed, gasping wildly for air. In the morning she called a doctor, who could find nothing wrong, but she remained uneasy, and that evening she stayed home and made him cups of iced honey-and-lemon tea to ease his throat. He took her hand at one point and held it to his lips as though it might be possible to find the air he needed inside the crevices of her skin. By now the scraping in his throat had become terrible, a raw agonizing rasp like a dull knife sawing through limestone. She looked at his face, from which the healthy, blood-filled elasticity had gone, and felt herself brushed by a current of air, or what might have been the memory of a name.

He began to choke violently, and she heard something grotesque come out of his mouth, a sound that was only half-human, but that rode on a curious rhythmic wave that for some reason stirred her deeply. She imagined it to be the word *Isobel*. "Isobel?" she asked, trying to remember its meaning. He said it a second time, and this time the syllables were more clearly formed.

The light of terror came into his eyes, or perhaps the beginning of a new fever; she managed to calm him by stroking his arm. Then she called the children inside the house, locked the doors and windows against the unbearable heat, and they began, slowly, patiently, hands linked, at the beginning where they had begun before – with table, chair, bed, cool, else, other, sleep, face, mouth, breath, tongue.

REVENGE

Anne Enright

Anne Enright (b. 1962) is an Irish author, born in Dublin. She has published essays, short stories, a work of non-fiction and four novels. Her novel, *The Gathering,* won the 2007 Man Booker Prize.

I work for a firm which manufactures rubber gloves. There are many kinds of protective gloves, from the surgical and veterinary (arm-length) to industrial, gardening and domestic. They have in common a niceness. They all imply revulsion. You might not handle a dead mouse without a pair of rubber gloves, someone else might not handle a baby. I need not tell you that shops in Soho sell nuns' outfits made of rubber, that some grown men long for the rubber under-blanket of their infancies, that rubber might save the human race. Rubber is a morally, as well as a sexually, exciting material. It provides us all with an elastic amnesty, to piss the bed, to pick up dead things, to engage in sexual practices, to not touch whomsoever we please.

I work with and sell an everyday material, I answer everyday questions about expansion ratios, tearing, petrifaction, I moved from market research to quality control. I have snapped more elastic in my day etcetera etcetera.

My husband and I are the kind of people who put small ads in the personal columns looking for other couples who may be interested in some discreet fun. This provokes a few everyday questions: How do people *do* that? What do they say to each other? What do they *say* to the couples who answer? To which the answers are: Easily. Very little. 'We must see each other again sometime.'

When I was a child it was carpet I loved. I should have made a career in floor-coverings. There was a brown carpet in the dining room with specks of black that was my parents' pride and joy. 'Watch the carpet!' they would say, and I did. I spent all my time sitting on it, joining up the warm, black dots. Things mean a lot to me.

The stench of molten rubber gives me palpitations. It also gives me eczema and a bad cough. My husband finds the smell anaphrodisiac in the extreme. Not even the products excite him, because after seven years you don't know who you are touching, or not touching, anymore.

My husband is called Malachy and I used to like him a lot. He was unfaithful to me in that casual, 'look, it didn't mean anything' kind of way. I was of course bewildered, because that is how I was brought up. I am supposed to be bewildered. I am supposed to say, 'What *is* love anyway? What is sex?'

Once the fiction between two people snaps then anything goes, or so they say. But it wasn't my marriage I wanted to save, it was myself. My head, you see, is a balloon on a string, my insides are elastic. I have to keep the tension between what is outside and what is in, if I am not to deflate, or explode.

So it was more than a suburban solution that made me want to be unfaithful *with* my husband, rather than *against* him. It was more than a question of the mortgage. I had my needs too: a need to be held in, to be filled, a need for sensation. I wanted revenge and balance. I wanted an awfulness of my own. Of course it was also suburban. Do you really want to know our sexual grief? How we lose our grip, how we feel obliged *to wear* things, how we are supposed to look as if we mean it.

Malachy and I laugh in bed, that is how we get over the problem of conviction. We laugh at breakfast too, on a good day, and sometimes we laugh again at dinner. Honest enough laughter, I would say, if the two words were in the same language, which I doubt. Here is one of the conversations that led to the ad in the personals:

'I think we're still good in bed.' (LAUGH)
'I think we're great in bed.' (LAUGH)
'I think we should advertise.' (LAUGH)

Here is another:

'You know John Jo at work? Well his wife was thirty-one yesterday. I said, "What did you give her for her birthday then?" He said, "I gave her one for every year. Beats blowing out candles." Do you believe that?'(LAUGH)

You may ask when did the joking stop and the moment of truth arrive? As if you didn't know how lonely living with someone can be.

The actual piece of paper with the print on is of very little importance. John Jo composed the ad for a joke during a coffee-break at work. My husband tried to snatch it away from him. There was a chase.

There was a similar chase a week later when Malachy brought the magazine home to me. I shrieked. I rolled it up and belted him over the head. I ran after him with a cup full of water and drenched his shirt. There was a great feeling of relief, followed by some very honest sex. I said, 'I wonder what the letters will say?' I said, 'What kind of couples *do* that kind of thing? What kind of people *answer* ads like that?' I also said, 'God, how vile!'

Some of the letters had photos attached. 'This is my wife.' Nothing is incomprehensible, when you know that life is sad. I answered one for a joke. I said to Malachy, 'Guess who's coming to dinner?'

I started off with mackerel pate, mackerel being a scavenger fish, and good for the heart. I followed with veal osso buco, for reasons I need not elaborate, and finished with a spiced fig pudding with rum butter. Both the eggs I cracked had double yolks, which I found poignant.

I hoovered everything in sight of course. Our bedroom is stranger-proof. It is the kind of bedroom you could die in and not worry about the undertakers. The carpet is a little more interesting than beige, the spread is an ochre brown, die pattern on the curtains is expensive and unashamed. One wall is mirrored in a sanitary kind of way; with little handles for the wardrobe doors.

'Ding Dong,' said the doorbell. Malachy let them in. I heard the sound of coats being taken and drinks offered. I took off my apron, paused at the mirror and opened the kitchen door.

Her hair was over-worked, I thought – too much perm and too much gel. Her make-up was shiny, her eyes were small. All her intelligence was in her mouth, which gave an ironic twist as she said hello. It was a large mouth, sexy and selfish. Malachy was holding out a gin and tonic for her in a useless kind of way.

Her husband was concentrating on the ice in his glass. His suit was a green so dark it looked black – very discreet, I thought, and out of our league, with Malachy in his cheap polo and jeans. I didn't want to look at his face, nor he at mine. In the slight crash of our glances I saw he was worn before his time.

I think he was an alcoholic. He drank his way through the meal and was polite. There was a feeling that he was pulling back from viciousness. Malachy, on the other hand, was over-familiar. He and the wife laughed at bad jokes and their feet were confused under the table. The husband asked me about my job and I told him about the machine I have for testing rubber squares; how it pulls the rubber four different ways at high speed. I made it sound like a joke, or something. He laughed.

*

I realised myself a slow, physical excitement, a kind of pornographic panic. It felt like the house was full of balloons pressing gently against the ceiling. I looked at the husband.

'Is this your first time?'

'No,' he said.

'What kind of people *do* this kind of thing?' I asked, because I honestly didn't know.

'Well they usually don't feed us so well, or even at all.' I felt guilty. 'This is much more civilised,' he said. 'A lot of them would be well on before we arrive, I'd say. As a general kind of rule.'

'I'm sorry,' I said, 'I don't really drink.'

'Listen,' he leaned forward. 'I was sitting having a G and T in someone's front room and the wife took Maria upstairs to look at the bloody grouting in the bathroom or something, when this guy comes over to me and I realise about six minutes too late that he plays for bloody Arsenal! If you see what I mean. A *very* ordinary looking guy.

'You have to be careful,' he said. 'And his wife was a cracker.'

When I was a child I used to stare at things as though they knew something I did not. I used to put them into my mouth and chew them to find out what it was. I kept three things under my bed at night; a piece of wood, a metal door-handle and a cloth. I sucked them instead of my thumb.

We climbed the stairs after Malachy and the wife, who were laughing. Malachy was away, I couldn't touch him. He had the same look in his eye as when he came home from a hurling match when the right team won.

The husband was talking in a low, constant voice that I couldn't refuse. I remember looking at the carpet, which had once meant so much to me. Everyone seemed to know what they were doing.

I thought that we were all supposed to end up together and perform and watch and all that kind of thing. I was interested in the power it would give me over breakfast, but I wasn't looking forward to the confusion. I find it difficult enough to arrange myself around one set of limbs, which are heavy things. I wouldn't know what to do with three. Maybe we would get over the awkwardness with a laugh or two, but in my heart of hearts I didn't find the idea of being with a naked woman funny. What would we joke about? Would we be expected to do things?

What I really wanted to see was Malachy's infidelity. I wanted his paunch made public, the look on his face, his bottom in the air. *That* would be funny.

I did not expect to be led down the hall and into the spare room. I did not expect to find myself sitting on my own with an alcoholic and handsome stranger who had a vicious look in his eye. I did not expect to feel anything.

I wanted him to kiss me. He leant over and tried to take off his shoes. He said, 'God, I hate that woman. Did you see her? The way she was laughing and all that bloody lip-gloss. Did you see her? She looks like she's made out of plastic. I can't get a hold of her without slipping around in some body lotion that smells like petrol and dead animals.' He had taken his shoes off and was swinging his legs onto the bed. 'She never changes, you know.' He was trying to take his trousers off. 'Oh I know she's sexy. I mean, you saw her. She is sexy. She is sexy. She is sexy. I just prefer if somebody else does it. If you don't mind.' I still wanted him to kiss me. There was the sound of laughter from the other room.

I rolled off the wet patch and lay down on the floor with my cheek on the carpet, which was warm and rough and friendly. I should go into floor-coverings. I remember when I wet the bed as a child. First it is warm then it gets cold. I would go into my parents' bedroom, with its smell, and start to cry. My mother gets up. She is half-asleep but she's not cross. She is huge. She strips the bed of the wet sheet and takes off the rubber under-blanket which falls with a thick sound to the floor. She puts a layer of newspaper on the mattress and pulls down the other sheet. She tells me to take off my wet pyjamas. I sleep in the raw between the top sheet and the rough blanket and when I turn over, all the warm newspaper under me makes a noise.

CHOIRMASTER

Elspeth Davie

Elspeth Davie (1918–1995) was a Scottish author. Although she wrote novels, she is best known for her short stories. Davie won the Katherine Mansfield Prize in 1978.

One day, out of the blue, it came to Sam, the choirmaster, that God must be very tired of people constantly flopping to the ground and begging for this and that. Rows of men, women and children on their knees – whispering, imploring, pleading, whether in song or prayer. What way was that to ask for anything? God, it was said, was all-powerful and could do anything on earth or in heaven. Heaven was an unknown quantity, of course. But, looking around the earth, people could see things had gone badly, drastically wrong. Drought and famine had ravished some lands more ferociously than others. The sickening stench of death rose from the hot earth, and from the baked mud of the riverbanks. Birth and death arrived suddenly together. Scarcely was there time to dispose of the afterbirth than the burial cloths were unwound. Gone were the days when any choir could sing cheerfully of the good seed being sown and scattered regularly by men and watered just as punctually by God. The eyes of all those in this land dried up in their sockets while staring at the terrible, brazen sky. At each dawn all the vessels in the place were brought out – the jugs, the pitchers, basins and baths in order to catch every drop of the miraculous, God-given liquid when it fell. No water fell. No water had fallen for weeks and months. Obviously, as the old choirmaster now believed, God must be weary of the bent knee and the humble, bowed head. Perhaps it was bold, abusive songs and outraged shouts He was hoping for, not the quiet, muttered prayer and the thanks which would make the lesser gods shrivel with shame. Was it not possible that God wished to be commanded for a change, not cajoled at all?

Sam had always been a lusty shouter himself. He had formed his choir as he travelled, and as he travelled continually, he gathered together a huge company of men, women and children from the remoter parts of the world. He picked his singers from the desperate and hungry, from the ill and even the dying, from people too weak to work and from some who had been almost beaten to the ground by servitude. He therefore knew that wherever they went in the world, his choir would be singing to companions in suffering; and so, whatever else it sounded like, whatever words or music were used – the song must ring true. His singers understood this, and if they were forced to compete with tornadoes, the pounding of huge waves, claps of thunder, the last rumblings of earthquake – the more they tried to rise to Sam's demands. It was true they had their own demands, but never for anything petty. Depending on what piece of land they were passing through, the men asked for what they imagined were the simple rights of every man. They demanded work, water, bread, decent huts and medicine. Occasionally they might pray to God for death. The women asked for all these as well as care and comfort for their children. Occasionally they might ask for fewer babies and sometimes even for more, as long as they still had milk to give them.

As time went on some desperate people asked if it were possible that God might be a little deaf on account of His great age. Perhaps He was no music-lover, in spite of some talk of angelic choirs. Then the choirmaster saw that he would have his work cut out, teaching, explaining, reprimanding and generally dealing with the strong emotions of his singers.

'Look,' he said one day to his hungry and unhappy crowd. 'Please, if you can possibly help it, don't cry when you're begging for anything. Begging's bad enough, but begging *and* crying must make God feel really mean. Do you want Him to feel mean?'

'Yes, I do,' said a blind old man with fly-encrusted sores around his eyes and down his legs. His feet were bound in grey bandages and he leant on a stick. It was true he was on his last legs, yet might still live for a day or so.

'No, I don't think *I* do,' said a gaunt-faced, middle-aged woman with four small children behind her, two others clutching at her cloak, and a bulge-eyed baby in her arms. 'They are all beautiful,' she said, indicating each child with a nod of her head, 'but will I have the strength to love and feed them all?'

It was true that hundreds of people in the huge choir had hardly enough strength to raise their voices. A few could do nothing but lie on the ground and wait for death for themselves and their children. This would often come quickly. But a decent burial took strength from the living and many died in the doing of it.

Not everyone in the choir agreed with Sam's method of singing loudly all the time with scarcely a break.

'Hadn't we better stop and listen once in a while?' asked one old-fashioned believer. 'Wasn't there something about a still, small voice?'

'Yes, I've heard that, but I've always been against the idea,' said the choirmaster. 'As long as we've got the strength, we're here to sing, not to listen. Sure, people want to join my choir for all kinds of reasons. They tell me they've got great voices, clear voices, that they can reach the highest notes and the lowest. And, naturally, people like that have ambitions to be the star singer. Or maybe they've no voice at all, but just want to get away from a plaguing family back home. Whatever they've come for, what help are they to a company like ours, especially if they're interested in small voices? Isn't it hard enough to get people to stand up straight and open their mouths?'

Yet for a time the old choirmaster did think of adding to his singers. And it was not only here that he looked. There were plenty of good voices back in his own country to which he returned for a short time. Many there had joined in processions and stood on platforms, for one cause or another. Groups with banners gathered outside hospitals, colleges and churches. Some he brought back to his choir, whether they had fine voices or not. He needed to make up for all he had lost through sickness or death. But he himself changed a great deal as he grew older. He had seen so much of horror, pain and misery in the land that the idea of singing songs of love or thanks for anything on earth seemed out of the question. Nowadays, outrage towards heaven was what he looked for in his singers – anything that gave force and fury to the human voice, his only rule being that they sing with chests out and heads flung back. Always they must be defiant, never suppliant.

Sam would have liked the suffering creatures of the earth to be heard in his choir – birds and animals as well as men. For he believed that many creatures might find more protection there than those outside who suffered the cruelty of human beings – the trap-setters, the cage-builders and the money-makers behind the bleeding hell of the slaughterhouses. Yet, on second thoughts, he decided to stick only to humans and allowed them to sing exactly as they pleased, whether in fear, pain, fury or sorrow. As long as they made a loud enough noise they might curse or weep as much as they liked. There was, he told them, no one God to cry to – or, if only one, he had obviously been created by all races of men, in all ages of Time, and out of every belief that had ever been attempted on earth. The choirmaster again reminded his singers that thanksgiving must sometimes be very tough on God. No doubt He might rather be bullied a bit, scolded, and even openly threatened for a change.

The choirmaster was growing old and tired. These days he was often hard put to vary the singing to every catastrophe. They came so thick and fast there was hardly time to draw breath before the next shattered the community; the flood and famine, dust and drought, disease and death, and all followed by endless questions: 'Why, why, why?' Then the hopeless non-answers. Finally silence.

But the old man kept on with his training. Above all, it was essential to teach his choir, the loud and soft notes in the human voice. They had to sing as loud as possible to be heard through the landslides and earthquakes, or simply to alert the desperate inhabitants of lonely places that help was on the way. It also took great skill to teach them to change from the loudest possible crescendo to a sound so quiet that the cry of an infant or even the whisper of a dying child might be located under some mountain of rubble.

By this time the outrage choir was pretty well established, but one day the choirmaster – ever on the look out for likely singers – picked up another possible member. His company was passing a forest one evening when a young man appeared out of the darkness between two trees. The trees were tall, their broad jungle-leaves casting great shadows around the newcomer, giving the impression that he was delicate. This was an illusion. He was thin but sturdy with strong, muscular legs and large, workman's hands. He had the unusual attraction of a darkish brown skin and clear, blue eyes. It was hard to tell whether he came from the north, the south, the east or the west.

'I heard you coming a long way off,' he said. 'What sort of procession is it?'

'No procession at all,' Sam answered. 'This is a choir, and monstrously hard work it is too, dealing with an unruly crowd like this. But I'm not grumbling because that's exactly what I want them to be – unruly and complaining!'

'What are they complaining about?' the young man asked.

'Complaining's a poor word. I was wrong to use it,' replied the choirmaster. 'They're not girning or whingeing about some paltry thing, some petty grudge.

Those who still have strength are shouting to high heaven about the hopelessness of this earth – the thirst, the hunger, the pain, the misery. Some are still singing quite sweetly, of course. Most are cursing.'

'Lord, but it must be a tough job leading a choir like that!' exclaimed the stranger.

'It certainly is. But one day I might get them to sing properly as well as shout. I confess it was I who worked them up. But still, it *is* supposed to be a choir, not only a furious rabble.'

'May I join your choir?' the young man asked.

'It all depends on the voice,' said the choirmaster.

'A tenor,' the other replied.

'Then I doubt if I can take you on,' said Sam. 'Tenors tend to sing about sweetness, peace, love, harmony and the rest of it. All the things this world is almost totally lacking in. Myself, I believed in all that once. Not now, of course.'

'And I can sing solos,' the young man went on, as if not having heard the last remark.

'Sorry, but I never allow solo singing,' said the choirmaster firmly. 'Soloists always become vain, no matter how modest they seem to be at the start. They tend to be temperamental too, and before you know where you are, they're acting like spoilt children. There is this terrific silence whenever a tenor solo gets up to sing – you must have noticed that yourself – as if he were a prince or god or some such being. People can even fall in love with tenors before the last note's out. It all plays havoc with a well-trained choir, and this *is* a well-trained choir! Once they've settled down you'll hear them sing. And I've worked so hard with them. A good choir is my one real aim in life. As in every art it's a case of balance and gravity, if you like. We can't afford too much emotion.'

'Nevertheless, you need a hell of a lot of emotion to sing well,' said the young man. 'To put anything across at all – that's a lifetime's work. Anyway, you're certainly putting it over. There's no doubt it will reach this Almighty Person you're singing to.'

'You mean He has huge, listening ears as well as everything else?'

'Possibly,' said the other. 'I've never thought about His different parts.'

'Wherever He is, I seldom think about Him nowadays,' said the old choirmaster. 'He has allowed such fearful things to happen here. I can hardly bring myself to look up at all, far less utter a respectful word. I think I'd choke if I did. Yet I can still manage to train a good choir. Imagine that!'

'You're probably best to choke and have done with it,' the newcomer replied. 'And I like people who speak their minds. Myself, I'm not so fond of the meek as I was sometimes thought to be when I was young.'

'You certainly still look young enough to me!' exclaimed the choirmaster.

'No, no, I can scarcely remember what that was like. I think I never was really young at all.'

'Well, I'll let you join us for a bit,' said the older man, 'and we can judge what kind of voice you have. Naturally, I can't promise anything right now. A great many people have wanted to join, but the moment they find it's not a church outing with picnic included, they fall away at once.'

'I've no interest in church choirs myself, nor Sunday School picnics, for that matter,' the young man assured him.

So it turned out that this newcomer was allowed to practise with the rest. But the choirmaster knew he was taking a big risk. The choir itself was never too pleased with his rare, haphazard choice of new members. Moreover, it was no longer as straightforward as in the old days when the choirmaster had been full of optimism and simple belief. Nowadays any new recruits he chose for his choir were strangely mixed. Either they would show too little anger in their voices – falling back into the old, placating tone, or else they allowed out-of-hand fury to spoil the rhythm and tempo of the song.

Yet the old choirmaster didn't hurry his new member into song. He allowed him to find his feet before he even opened his mouth. The young man was simply encouraged to walk along with the choir for a while, not singing, but just chatting with them, finding out how much strength they could still summon up for practice, hearing how they could still manage to sing in harmony even while often hating one another's guts. Some would confess how deeply they resented what they'd heard of other choirs in the cities of the world – choirs used to all the perks of wealthy companies – applause that went on for hours with endless flower-throwing, plus banquets and bouquets and beautiful women. Many, in fact, were bitter that they'd ever met up with the old choirmaster who, for reasons of his own, had, early on, gathered them into this company where they now suffered the humiliation of becoming a crowd of travelling beggars under a one-time raving idealist who could offer no food, no water, no medicine and no comfort of any kind, while gradually letting his own hopes and beliefs peter out as the arid, blazing days went on. Sometimes he appeared unsteady on his feet as the starving inhabitants of each village pressed around him, trying to claw pity from his heart. Often, at night, he would wonder what would become of him if pity ever deserted him.

As for the choir, the reasons for their present suffering gradually became clear. Long ago, when Sam took over, he had forced them to sing – no, not merely to sing but to shout – loud and triumphantly about the Love of God. Love! The scorn, the fury, the disappointment and bitterness in their singing gradually grew to a raucous crescendo as they realized what they had walked into, unawares. And now, even the old choirmaster was disintegrating before their eyes.

'So he's seen no more of this enormous love than we have!' they cried. 'This old man's taken us through deadly heat and freezing cold with nowhere to camp – through forests and deserts, all of us hungry and filthy as pariah dogs. He thinks we'll follow for the rest of our lives, like fools. Let's sing something different, so furiously blasphemous it will frighten the life out of him. Then we can run back to our homes, if there's still a home to run to. But where will our children be now? Will our husbands and wives have left long ago? They will curse us for leaving, then curse us for coming back! What a fix the old one has got us into! May he be damned!'

The new singer held up his hand. 'Wait!' he shouted. 'Don't forget your God gave you freedom – the freedom to come or to go, to turn good into bad and bad into good. But have you taken your freedom?'

Again the air was filled with furious muttering. More fierce cries and curses went up into the sky. 'There must be silence!' the young leading singer reminded them, 'or else the God will not hear that He is loved and forgiven!'

'Never! How we have suffered!' came shouts from every side. 'Where is this love? He had no love. Now we have none ourselves!'

The great trees whistled and creaked in accord. Hissing came through the dripping leaves. At least a quarter of the choir left immediately and ran back as fast as they could down the way they had come. The new singer watched them go sympathetically, while the rest hesitated, in two minds whether to follow or to stay. Many were still pondering on this unknown Love of God.

'What kind of love is this?' they demanded, this love that allows terror and torture to innocent men and beasts?' There had been loving parents in some lucky lives, of course: a few loving friends, a loving teacher or two, loving cats and dogs. A few admitted that, not clearly knowing what love meant, they had recklessly given it to all sorts of undeserving persons, and been let down, dropped, deserted, and swiftly passed over or replaced. So did this God-love have infinite meanings then – all different from anything known on earth? If so, what was the use of talking about it?

'Time to talk or sing if we ever get to heaven!' came a shout. 'Right now, let's keep our mouths shut!'

There was complete silence, so much so that the old choirmaster came back to see what had happened. 'Are you working them up about something?' he asked the new member. 'If so I'll have to ask you to leave at once. I've put a life's work into training them, and I can't afford to hear it all go for nothing. What's more, I'm afraid I've changed my mind about the love-singing and even the love-talk. I'm into *Justice* now. *Justice* is the greatest thing on earth!'

'But will you let me stay and sing with your choir a little longer?' the young man asked.

'That's fair enough, of course. And I will stand and listen as hard as I can,' said Sam, stepping from the fringe of the forest into the sunlight.

The sound he heard was like light itself – sometimes flashing up through the trees and descending again into blackness through thick leaves, and once more climbing up a scale of brilliance till it reached a sunburst of sound. Bells, flutes and cymbals like those that herald the appearance of a new king were heard, and then a second descent into the dark evening shadow moving swiftly along the ground.

'Have they fallen on their knees to pray and praise then?' Sam asked incredulously, peering at the men and women on the ground.

'Not yet,' said the new singer. 'How on earth could they sing with tongues parched dry with thirst, with stomachs blown tight as drums with hunger?'

'But have they sung up forgiveness to God yet?' the old man asked.

'No, no,' the other answered again. 'He will not be forgiven for a long, long time. Only when the desert is green as an orchard, when the dying children get their milk and lose the look of wizened age. Only then.'

The old choirmaster stepped forward defiantly. 'Of course the *singing* sounded good,' he said. 'But I'm not sure what you're trying to do. Are you trying to be different from all other singers?'

'Yes, I suppose I am,' the other conceded.

'Then what exactly are you aiming at?' the old choirmaster went on. He had known all along that this particular singer was proud, if not actually arrogant. He had met all types in his profession – the cringing and the confident, loud-voiced braggarts and soft-voiced hypocrites, bullying voices and begging ones. Yet it was difficult to know where this particular voice fitted in. All he could vouch for was that it was a totally new and beautiful one. And so powerful it was that the man was automatically taken as leader.

The young man was silent for a while before answering Sam's question. 'You ask what I'm aiming at. I am helping people to forgive the Almighty One for all the terrible things He has allowed on earth – the unbelievable wretchedness and frightful pain. He has forgiven them for many things. Now they can forgive Him. *He* can never be human. *They* can never be gods, but at least they can show they are human and be proud of it.'

'Don't try to change my singers,' said the old choirmaster. 'It has taken me long enough to prevent the bending knee and that horrible, begging note.'

'There'll be none of that if I have anything to do with it,' the new member assured him. 'They must go on shouting and cursing for as long as they wish. First the God must be shown fearlessly all they have endured. Then He might be forgiven. You will let me stay a short time with your singers, then?'

Again the old choirmaster could only agree. He waited, rather jealously, to hear what other sound this newcomer would bring from his choir. The old man believed that he had heard all sounds produced by animal and human throat. But this was something else. Fearful sounds and words evoking frightful images; young men, women and children of every race sliced to the bone by guns, be-headed by bombs; the frightened breath of children waiting for doors to open in the night; the roar of the wounded lion, the scream of the trapped hare, the terrified bellow of beasts with rolling eyes, slung up for slaughter; the rumbling of earthquakes spurting from unknown depths. These were not sounds only from throat or ground. These were the sounds of Hell on earth.

The young leader lifted up his arms, urging the choir to louder and louder shouts of outrage. Then he raised his hand for silence. 'That was excellent!' he called. 'You have shown a magnificent fury for the things allowed by God. Now you can show forgiveness to match!'

Again the air was filled with furious mutterings and cries of complaint.

'You see, they are not stupid,' the old choirmaster explained. 'Most of the things we heard are the fault of Man. They have nothing to do with God. Anyway, He is above thanks or blame. To think anything else would be blasphemy.'

Old Sam had once hoped to be a popular preacher in a large city church with a decent stipend and a gathering of well-dressed ladies and gentlemen who would listen to him with unquestioning respect. How he longed, after all these years in the wilderness, to arrive at a cool, Christian building where there was no cursing, no obscenity, no endless questions and no striving on his part to offer quickfire explanations for every single horror that had ever happened upon earth!

He sidetracked a good deal of the argument nowadays. Yet he was still left with the humiliating desire to keep on with his own nagging questions, whether directed to an angel or devil in his own mind or even to some interloper who might happen, in passing, to step out of a dark wood. He turned again to the young singer for reassurance. 'It *is* the fault of human beings, isn't it?' he asked anxiously. 'The old barbaric gods would have allowed these horrors, of course, but not the great, good God of Love we have prayed and sung to day after day, year in year out.'

'I can promise great changes will come one day,' the younger man replied.

'One day, one year, one eternity,' added the old choirmaster, shaking his head dolefully.

The young man smiled. He had always foreseen more doubt than hope. One had to wait aeons and aeons of time for hope. Suddenly he left the path. He entered the forest again. Black darkness hid him.

'Is that young man gone for good?' asked one of the singers. 'I liked him. His standards were far too high, of course. He will never be popular.'

'He may well come again,' the choirmaster replied. 'He was simply here to see the damage and the pain for himself.'

'But who brought it on us?' the singer asked again.

'No doubt we brought it on ourselves,' said the old man.

'That is an easy answer,' said the other.

'Yes, I believe you're right,' the choirmaster agreed. 'It would take some superhuman power to bring all the catastrophe that has occurred on earth.'

'So that is the only answer you can find?'

'Well, I am only human,' said the old man. 'And I am tired. What more can I say? For the whole of my life I have been dumbfounded.'

Hearing this, the rest of the choir circled protectively around him. They were no longer angry. Doubt was more lovable than an iron faith, they decided. This looser circle they had formed let in both light and shadow. People felt free to break away from it and to come back again, to stand still, argue or be silent, to sing in tune or discord, to listen or to stop their ears. It was no sacred circle. Those who left were not followed or persuaded by love, the binding ties of friendship or the community spirit – to come back.

Over the centuries came changing groups of singers with their choirmasters. Rules changed. Tunes changed. Hopes rose and fell. Only music itself remained and the great forest of ancient trees. But every choirmaster taught his group not only how to sing, but to listen intently and to count the beat. Sometimes the songs were strident with bitterness, sometimes mellow with hope. Often for end-less time there was no singing at all in the forest. But always an ardent listening for the return of a young leader hacking down branches to let in light – and for the terrible and confident crackle of His approaching footsteps over aeon upon aeon of fallen twigs.

ILSE'S HOUSE

Alison Lurie

Alison Lurie (b. 1926) is an American novelist and academic. She won
the Pulitzer Prize in 1984 for her novel *Foreign Affairs*. She has published
ten novels, one collection of short stories, and a non-fiction work entitled
The Language of Clothes.

Sure, I'm aware that people still theorise about why I never married
Gregor Spiegelman. I can understand that Greg was a madly eligible man:
good-looking, successful, charming, sexy. He reminded me of those European film stars of the thirties you see on TV reruns; he had that same suave low-key
style. And then not only was he chairman of the department, he was important
in his field. Everyone agreed that there were only two people in the world who
knew as much as he did about Balkan economic history – some said only one.

Whereas I was just a fairly attractive young woman with a good job as a mar-
ket-research analyst. It seemed kind of a fluke that I should have caught Greg,
when so many had tried and failed. Women had been after him for years, ever
since his marriage ended and his wife went back to Europe. I was rather pleased
myself. Though I didn't let on to anyone, privately I thought Dinah Kieran was
about the luckiest girl in upstate New York.

Of course some of my friends thought Greg was way too old for me. But he
didn't look anywhere near fifty-four. His springy light-brown hair was scarcely
grey at all, and he was really fit: he played squash and ran two miles every day. I
didn't see why his chronological age should bother me. Back in the past it used to
be regarded as a coup to marry a man who was already established, instead of taking a chance on some untried boy like my poor old Ma did, to her lifelong regret.

A couple of people I knew said Greg was a male chauvinist, but I couldn't see
it. I wasn't exactly a feminist then anyhow. Sure, I was for equal rights and equal
pay; I was making as much as any man in my department, and I'd had to fight
for that. But when one of my girlfriends started complaining about how having
a chair pulled out for her in a restaurant was insulting, I got really bored. Holy
God, why shouldn't a guy treat a woman with courtesy and consideration if he
felt like it?

I rather liked being Greg's little darling, if you want to know the truth. I liked
it when he helped me into my coat and gave me a secret squeeze as he settled it
round me. I liked having him bring me old-fashioned presents: expensive perfume and flowers and sexy lingerie in the anemone colours that go best with my
black-Irish looks: red and lavender and hot pink. I suppose he spoiled me, really,
but after the kind of childhood I had there was a lot to make up for.

When we split some people blamed it on the age difference, and others said I wasn't intellectual enough for Gregor, or mature enough. Or they said our backgrounds were too different; what that meant was that I grew up in a trailer camp and didn't attend the right schools. Well, it ended so suddenly, that always makes talk. The date had been announced, the wedding invitations sent out, the caterer hired, the University chapel reserved – and then, two weeks before the ceremony, kaflooey, the whole thing was off.

In fact I was the one who broke it off. Everybody knew that, we didn't make a secret of it, and the reason we gave was the real one in a way; that I didn't want to live in Greg's house. People thought that was completely nuts, since I'd been more or less living there for months.

Greg didn't usually let on that I claimed his kitchen was haunted, because in his view that was just a crazy excuse. After all, I might not be an academic, as he said once, but I wasn't an ignorant uneducated person. I had a Master's in statistics and ought to be more rational than most women, not less. He never believed I'd really seen anything. Nobody else had had any funny experiences there, not even his hippie cleaning-lady, who believed in astrology and past lives.

You've got to understand, there was nothing intrinsically spooky about Greg's house. It was the kind of place you see in ads for paint and lawn care; a big white modern Colonial, on a broad tree-lined street in Corinth Heights. Ma would have died for it. Greg bought it when he got married, and the kitchen had been totally redone before his wife left. It was a big room with lots of cupboards and all the top-of-the-line equipment anyone could want: two ovens, microwave, disposal, dishwasher, you name it. It had avocado-green striped-and-flowered wallpaper, and the stove and fridge and cupboards and counters were that same pale sick green. Not my favourite colour, and it was kind of dark in the daytime, because of the low ceiling and the pine trees growing so close. Still, it was just about the last place you'd expect to meet a ghost.

But I did see something. At least I thought I saw something. What I thought I saw was Ilse Spiegelman, Greg's ex-wife. Of course that didn't make any sense, because how could Ilse be a ghost if she wasn't dead? And as far as I knew she was alive and well back in Czechoslovakia, or as well as you could be under the government they had then, and teaching at the university where Greg had met her.

She was probably better off there, he said. She'd liked his house, but she never cared much for the rest of America. Even after eight years she hadn't really adjusted.

'I blame myself,' he told me once. 'I didn't think enough about what I was doing, taking a woman away from her country, her family, her career. I only thought of how narrow and restricted Ilse's life was. I thought of the cold cramped two-room apartment she had to share with her sister and her parents, and how she couldn't afford a warm winter coat or the books and journals she needed for her research. I imagined how happy and grateful she would be here, but I was wrong.'

Greg said that naturally he'd expected Ilse would soon learn English. He was born in Europe himself and only came to America when he was ten, though you'd never know it. But Ilse wasn't good at languages, and she never got to the point where she was really comfortable in English, which made a problem when she started looking for work. Eventually she found a couple of temporary research jobs, and she did some part-time cataloguing for the library; but it wasn't what she wanted or was used to.

After a while Ilse didn't even try to find a job, Greg said, and she didn't make many friends. She wasn't as adaptable as he'd thought. In fact she turned out to be a very tense, stubborn, high-strung person, and rather selfish. When things didn't go exactly as she liked she became touchy and withdrawn.

For instance, he said, Ilse got so she didn't want to go places with him. A concert was possible, or a film, especially if it was in some language she knew. But she didn't like parties. She claimed that people talked so fast she couldn't understand them, and that they didn't want to speak to her anyhow: she was only invited because she was Gregor's wife. Everyone would be happier if she didn't go, she insisted.

When Ilse stayed home she wasn't happy either, because she imagined Greg was flirting with other women at the party. I could sort of understand how she got that idea. Greg liked women and was comfortable with them. He had a way of standing close to someone attractive and lowering his voice and speaking to her with this little quiet smile. Sometimes he would raise just his left eyebrow. It wasn't deliberate; he couldn't actually move the right one, because of a bicycle accident he'd had years ago; but it was devastating.

The way he talked to women even bothered me a bit at first, though I told myself it didn't mean anything. But it made Ilse really tense and touchy. Though she must have known what a gregarious person Greg naturally was, she started trying to get him to decline invitations. And when he did persuade her to go to some party, he told me, she followed him around, holding tight to his arm. And she always wanted to leave before he did. Well, of course that wasn't much fun for either of them, so it's no wonder that after a while Greg stopped trying to persuade her to come along.

When he went out alone, he said, Ilse would always wait up for him, even though he'd asked her over and over again not to. Then while she was waiting she'd open a bottle of liqueur, Amaretto or crème de menthe or something like that, and start sipping, and by the time he came home she'd be woozy and argumentative. When Greg told her it worried him to think of her drinking alone, Ilse got hysterical. 'You have drink, at your party, why should I not have drink?' she shouted. And when Greg pointed out to her that she had finished nearly a whole bottle of Kahlúa that had been his Christmas present from his graduate students, she screamed at him and called him a tightwad, or whatever the Czech word for that is.

Finally one evening Greg came home at about one-thirty a.m. It was completely innocent, he told me: he'd been involved in a discussion about politics and forgotten the time. At first he thought Ilse had gone to sleep, but she wasn't in the bedroom and didn't answer when he called. He was worried and went all round the house looking for her. Finally he went into the kitchen and turned on the light and saw her sitting on the floor, wedged into the space between the refrigerator and the wall where the brooms and mops were kept.

Greg said he asked her what she was doing there. I could hear just how his voice would have sounded: part anxious, part irritated, part jokey. But Ilse wouldn't answer.

'So what did you do?' I said.

'Nothing.' Greg shrugged.

'Nothing?' I repeated. I didn't think he would have lost his temper, because he never did; only sometimes when he was disappointed in someone or something he'd give them this kind of cold, tight look. I expected he would have looked at Ilse like that, and then hauled her out of there and helped her upstairs.

'What could I do, darling? I knew she'd been drinking and wanted to make a scene, even though she knew how much I dislike scenes. I went upstairs and got ready for bed, and after I was almost asleep I heard her come in and fall into the other bed. Next morning she didn't apologise or say anything about what had happened, and I thought it would be kinder not to bring it up. But that was when it became clear to me that it wasn't going to work out for Ilse here.'

The next time I was alone in Greg's house I went into the kitchen and looked at the space between the fridge and the wall. It didn't seem wide enough for anyone to sit in. But when I pushed the brooms and mops and vacuum back and tried it myself I discovered that there was just barely enough room. I felt weird in there, like a kid playing hide-and-seek who's been forgotten by the other kids. All I could see was a section of avocado-green cupboard and a strip of vinyl floor in the yellowish-green swirly seasick pattern that I'd never liked too much. The cleaning-rags and the dustpan brushed against my head and neck. I wouldn't have wanted to sit there for any length of time, even if I was a kid. And I thought that anybody who did must have been in a bad way.

I think that was a mistake, trying it out, because now I had a kind of idea of how Ilse Spiegelman must have felt. But then for a while I forgot the whole thing, because Greg asked me to marry him. Up till then he had never even mentioned marriage, and neither had I. I certainly wasn't going to hint around the way he'd said his last live-in girlfriend had, or pressure him like the one before that.

That was the year there was so much excitement in the media about a survey which claimed to prove that college-educated women over thirty had just about no chance of getting married. A couple of times people said to me, Dinah, you're a statistician, aren't you worried? Well, Jesus, of course I was worried, because I was nearly twenty-nine, but I just smiled and said that everybody in my field knew that study was really badly flawed technically.

By Christmas of that year, I'd begun to sense a rising curve of possibility in the relationship; but I waited and kept my cool. Then Greg told me he'd been invited to the Rockefeller Foundation Study Center on Lake Como for a month the next summer. He said he wished I could come with him, but you weren't allowed to bring anyone but a spouse. I didn't make any suggestions. When he told me how luxurious and scenic the study centre was, I just said, 'Oh, really?' and, 'That's great.'

Three days later he brought it up again, and asked me what I'd think of our getting married before he went, because he knew I'd enjoy seeing Italy and he really didn't like the idea of leaving me behind. I didn't shriek with joy and rush into his arms, though that was what I wanted to do; I just smiled and said it sounded like a fairly good idea, as long as he didn't want us to be divorced as soon as we got back, because my poor old Ma couldn't take that.

It was the next day that I saw Ilse for the first time. I still had my apartment downtown, but I was spending a lot of time at Greg's, and sleeping over most nights. I got up early on Sunday to make sausages and waffles with maple syrup, because we'd been talking about American country breakfasts a couple of days before and he said he'd never had a good one.

It was a wet dark late-winter morning and the kitchen windows were streaked with half-frozen rain like transparent glue. When I went into the room the first thing I noticed was what looked like somebody's legs and feet in grey tights and worn black low-heel pumps sticking out between the refrigerator and the wall. I kind of screamed, but nothing came out except a sort of gurgle. Then I took a step nearer and saw a pale woman in a dark dress sitting wedged in there.

I didn't think of Ilse. If I thought anything, I thought we must have left the back door unlocked and some miserable homeless person or schizo graduate student had got in. 'Jesus Christ, what the hell!' I screeched and backed away and turned on the light.

And then I looked again and nobody was there. All I saw was Greg's black rubber galoshes, left to drip when we'd come in from a film the night before, and his long grey wool scarf hanging from a hook by the dusters. I couldn't see how my brain had assembled these variables into the figure of a woman, but the brain does funny things sometimes.

Later, after I got my breath back, I thought of Greg's story and realised that what I'd seen or imagined was Ilse Spiegelman. I didn't like that, because it meant that Greg's ex-wife was on my mind to an extent I hadn't suspected.

I didn't say anything about it. I damn sure wasn't going to tell Greg, who said sometimes that one of the things he loved most about me, besides my naturally pointed breasts, was my well-organised mind. 'You're a wonder, Dinah,' he used to tell me. 'Under those wild black curls, you're as clear-headed as any man I ever met.' Like a lot of guys his age, he believed that no matter how much education they got most women never became rational beings and their heads were essentially full of unconnected light-weight ideas, like those little white Styrofoam bubbles they pack stereo equipment in.

So I didn't say anything to anybody. What I did was, I tried to find out what Ilse had looked like. My idea was that if she was really different from the thing I thought I'd seen, it would prove I'd had a hallucination. That wouldn't be so great, but it would be better than a ghost.

Greg didn't have any photos of Ilse as far as I knew; at least I couldn't find any around the house. When I asked him what she was like he only said she was blonde and shorter than me. Then I asked if she was pretty. He looked at me and laughed out loud and said, 'Not anywhere near as pretty as you are, my lovely little cabbage.'

After that I did a sample among his friends. I didn't take it too far; I didn't want people to think I was going into some type of retrospective jealous fit. So I didn't have a significant data base, and when I averaged their statements out all I got was the profile of a medium-sized woman in her early forties with dirty-blonde hair. Some said it was wavy and others said it was straight. They

all agreed that she didn't have much to say and her accent was hard to understand, but she was attractive, at least to start with. Later on, some of them said,
she seemed to kind of let herself go, and towards the end she looked ill a lot
of the time.

Greg's department secretary told me Ilse was slim but a little broad in the
beam; but that information isn't much use if you're trying to identify somebody
sitting on the floor behind a refrigerator. A couple of people said she looked
'foreign', whatever that meant; and a colleague of Greg's said she had a 'small
sulky hot-looking mouth', but I had to discount that because he was always on
the make.

Finally I decided that it could just possibly have been Ilse, but most likely it
was my imagination. That was bad enough, because I'd never been the imaginative type, and I didn't like the idea that I was starting to see things, like one of
Ma's superstitious old-lady neighbours.

The trouble was, though, I began to feel uncomfortable about Greg's kitchen.
I didn't like going in there much any more; and I always made sure to switch on
the overhead light first, even if it was a bright day. I had the theory that if the
light was on I wouldn't think I saw Ilse Spiegelman, and in fact I didn't.

Weeks went by and my weird feeling about the kitchen should have gone away,
only somehow it hung on. So one day I asked Greg casually what he thought of
our moving after we married. We'd been to a cocktail party at my boss's new
house on the lake. It had a big fieldstone fireplace and sliding glass doors onto a
deck and a really super view. I said I'd love to live in a place like that. I think it
was the first time I ever asked Greg to do anything more for me than stop at the
store for a bottle of Chardonnay on his way home. Up to then he'd more or less
anticipated my every wish.

Well, Greg didn't see the point of it, and from a practical view there was no
point. His house was in good condition and its location was ideal: less than a
mile from the University, so that on most days he could walk to his office. He
said that for one thing it would be a real drag for both of us to drive to town in
the kind of weather they have here from December through March. Then he reminded me how much work he'd done on his garden and grounds over the years.
Next year his asparagus bed would be bearing for the first time, I wouldn't want
to miss that, he said and laughed and kissed me.

So I let it pass. By that time I'd just about convinced myself that I hadn't seen
anything.

Then one day in March I came in after work with two bags of groceries and set
them on the counter and turned, and Holy Mother of God, there she was again,
squeezed in by the refrigerator. It was nearly dark out and darker inside, but I
knew it was the same woman: the hair like frayed rope, the shapeless dress and
shiny grey tights and black clunky pumps, scuffed at the toes, sticking out into
the room.

She didn't seem to see me. She wasn't looking in my direction anyhow, but
down at the seasick-green floor, just sitting there, not moving, as if she were drunk
or stunned. It was much worse than the first time. Then I was just surprised and

uneasy, the way anyone would be if they found a strange woman in their kitchen, but now I was like really terrified.

I almost couldn't breathe, but somehow I stumbled back and put on the light, and when I looked round she'd disappeared again. But I was sure I'd seen someone, and I was practically sure it had been Ilse. And what was worse, I got the idea that she'd been sitting there on the floor for a long while. Or maybe she was always sitting there, only most of the time I couldn't see her.

I can tell you I was in a bad state. I figured either I'd seen a ghost, or I was losing my mind. But I didn't feel crazy, except whenever I had to go into the kitchen I panicked. The main idea I had was that I had to leave that house.

Next day at breakfast I brought up moving again, but I didn't get anywhere. Greg made all the points he'd made before, and also he mentioned the financial aspects for the first time. It turned out he had no savings to speak of and not much equity in the house. But he had an eight per cent mortgage; he couldn't possibly get that kind of rate again, he said. I was a little surprised that Greg didn't have more net worth, but it made sense when I thought about it. He liked to live well: trips to New York and to conferences all over the world, expensive food and liquor, and a new Volvo every five years.

He assumed the issue was settled, but I didn't want to let it drop. I said I was making enough money to help out and I had some savings besides; and I knew I'd be happier in a new place. Greg lowered his newspaper for a moment and glanced up at me, and for the first time I saw, just for a second, that thin cold look he gave people and things he didn't like.

But then Greg smiled slowly and folded the newspaper and put it down and came over and kissed me and said I mustn't ever worry about money. He wouldn't think of touching my little savings, he said; he had plenty for both of us.

I kissed him back, of course, and felt all warm and loved again, but at the same time just for a moment I remembered something a friend of mine at work had said when I first started going out with Greg. 'He's a really sweet guy until you cross him,' she said. 'Then, watch out.'

In a couple of days I'd more or less forgotten about that look Greg had flashed at me; but I realised I'd stuck myself with Ilse's kitchen, and my morale slid way down the chart. I didn't know what the hell to do. If I said anything to anybody they'd think I was nuts, and maybe they'd be right. Maybe I ought to just drive up to the state hospital and turn myself in. I thought of telling Ma; she believed in ghosts, and a couple of her friends had seen them; but those were always ghosts of the dead.

Then I remembered something I read in an anthropology book in college. There were sorcerers in Mexico and Central America, it said, that could project an image of themselves to anywhere they chose. The author hadn't seen it done herself, but all the locals were convinced it could happen. Well, I thought, it could be. There were some weird things in the world. Maybe Ilse Spiegelman was some kind of Czechoslovakian witch, and if she wanted to keep me from marrying Greg and moving into her house and her kitchen she might do it that way. The distance wouldn't faze her – for that kind of project two thousand miles was the same as two yards.

If I told Ma, she'd probably say I should go to a priest and ask for an exorcism. But I knew if I did that he'd give me a lot of grief for not having been to confession for three years, and living in sin with Greg. And besides, how the hell could I ask Greg to have his kitchen exorcised? I considered trying to sneak a priest into the house when Greg was at the University, but I decided it was too risky.

So I told myself okay, let's assume it was Ilse, trying to scare me off. Well, I wouldn't let her. The next time she appeared I'd make the sign of the cross and tell her to get the hell out and leave me alone. Listen, sister, I'd tell her, you had your chance with Greg, now it's my turn.

After that, instead of praying I wouldn't see Ilse, I actually tried to catch her at it. For a couple of weeks, whenever Greg went out, I set my jaw and said a Hail Mary and marched into the room. I never saw a damn thing. Then, late one evening after I'd rinsed our coffee mugs in the sink and turned out the light and was leaving the kitchen, I saw her again, sitting shadowy by the refrigerator. I wasn't expecting her, so I screamed out, 'Jesus Christ!'

Greg had gone up to bed already, and he heard me and called out, 'What's the matter, darling?' I was frightened and confused, and I called back, 'Nothing, I just cut my hand on the bread knife.' Then I switched on the light, and of course nobody was there.

I thought, oh God. That's what she wanted. She's never going to appear when I'm ready for her; she wants to surprise me, and hurt me. And now she had, because of course then I had to get out the bread knife and saw a hole in my hand to show Greg.

After that I was in a bad way. I didn't want to see Ilse when I wasn't expecting her; but I couldn't think of her the whole time. Plus I was developing a full-blown phobia about her kitchen. So I came right out and told Greg that there were things I didn't like about his house.

He was very sweet and sympathetic. He put his arms round me and kissed one of his favourite places – the back of my neck just above the left shoulder, where I have a circle of freckles. Then he asked me to tell him what it was I didn't like and maybe it could be fixed. 'I want you to be perfectly happy here, Dinah my love,' he said.

Well, I told him there were three things. I said I'd like the downstairs bathroom repapered, because I'd never cared for goldfish, they had such stupid expressions; and I'd like a deck by the dining-room so that we could eat outdoors in the summer. 'If that's what you want, why not?' Greg said, holding me and stroking me.

Then I said I'd also like a new cabinet built in the kitchen, between the refrigerator and the wall. That was the only thing I really cared about, because I thought that if there wasn't any space there Ilse couldn't come and sit in it; and that was the only thing Greg objected to. If we put a cabinet there, he said, where would I keep my cleaning equipment? Well, I told him I'd move it out to the back entry. No, I didn't think that would be inconvenient, I said; anyhow I'd always thought a kitchen looked messy if there were old brooms and rags hanging around. I was terrified that he'd suggest building a broom cupboard, which would have been worse than nothing, but luckily it didn't occur to him.

'You want your kitchen just like your graphs, all squared away,' Greg said. 'All right, darling.' And he laughed. He liked to tease me sometimes about my passion for order.

Greg promised to have the improvements made before the wedding and he carried through. The day the new cabinet was installed I went into the kitchen the minute I got home. Just as I'd planned, it completely filled the space where Ilse had sat. There was a drawer under the counter, and a shelf under that; nobody could possibly get in there. I stooped down and looked to make sure, and then I put in a couple of baking tins and some bags of paper cups and plates.

I've done it, I thought, and I was really happy. I thought how generous and brilliant and good-looking Greg was, and how smart I was, and how we were going to Montreal for our honeymoon and then to Europe. I'd bought a beautiful wedding dress: heavy ecru silk with a sexy low square neck and yards of lace.

Well, it got to be two weeks before the wedding. I was so high I was even starting to feel a little sorry for Ilse. I thought about how she was probably back in those two nasty little rooms again with her family. I knew what that was like, from the years I spent with my mother and sisters in the trailer camp, with cold sour air leaking through the window-frames and the kitchen faucet spitting rust and the neighbours playing the radio or screaming at each other all night. No wonder she was jealous.

Then the term was nearly over, and Greg's department was giving a reception. He called me that Friday afternoon from his office to say they were short of paper plates and could I drop some by after work? So when I got home I went into the kitchen and opened the new cabinet by the refrigerator.

It was a good thing I was alone, because I let out a real burglar-alarm screech. There was Ilse Spiegelman, just like before, only now she was shrunken down into some kind of horrible little dwarf about two and a half feet high. I didn't even try the light. I just howled and stumbled out into the hall.

It took me nearly thirty-five minutes to get up my nerve to go back into the kitchen – where of course Ilse wasn't any more, or at least I couldn't see her – and put my hand into that cabinet, maybe right through her, and take out those paper plates that Greg was waiting for.

After that I knew I was beaten. If Ilse could shrink herself like that she could appear any size, and anywhere she goddamn wanted to. Maybe she'd get into the flour bin in the pantry next, or maybe some day when I took the lid off the top of the sugar bowl she'd be in there, all scrunched up.

I was really depressed and sort of desperate. But then I thought that maybe Ilse wouldn't mind my living with Greg as long as we weren't married. After all, she hadn't even appeared until we got engaged.

So that evening I told Greg I didn't think I could go through with it. I said I was terrified of the responsibility of marriage. At first he was wonderful. He held me and kissed me and petted me and said that was perfectly natural: marriage *was* frightening. And of course, he added, I was probably apprehensive about becoming a department chairman's wife.

'Yeah, that's right,' I said, though that thought hadn't occurred to me.

He understood, Greg said. I might not think I was up to the job, but he would help me; and if anybody tried to make me feel incompetent or not worthy of him, he would give them hell.

When I kept on insisting that I didn't want to get married, Greg asked what had changed my mind. I was still afraid to tell him about Ilse; I didn't want him to think I'd gone off the deep end. So I came up with the kind of stuff you read everywhere these days about marriage being an outmoded patriarchal contract, and how the idea of owning another human being was fascist. I probably didn't make a very good presentation, because I didn't believe in what I was saying. Anyhow, Greg didn't buy it.

'You surprise me, Dinah,' he said, raising his left eyebrow. 'I've never heard you talk like this before. Who's been brainwashing you, I wonder?'

Well, I swore nobody had. I burbled on, saying I loved him so much, but I was frightened, and why couldn't we just go on the way we were? After all, I said, he'd been with other women and he hadn't wanted to marry them. That was a mistake. Greg's face changed, and he gave me that bad look again. Then he dropped his arm and sort of pushed me aside.

'What is this?' he said, laughing in an unfriendly way. 'The revenge of the bimbos?'

'Huh?' I was completely at a loss; but finally I got what he meant. There were maybe four or five women in town who had wanted to marry Greg, and some of them were still pretty hurt and angry according to rumour. He meant, was I doing it for them?

'Jesus, no,' I said. 'I don't owe those women anything. They're none of them my friends.' Then he seemed convinced and quieted down.

But I still said I didn't want to get married. Greg tried to reassure me some more, but I could see he was getting impatient. He asked if I realised that if I broke off our engagement it would embarrass him in front of everyone and make him a local joke. He'd already had to take some kidding from friends because he'd sworn so often that he was never going to marry again. And there were quite a few people on campus who weren't Greg's friends: people who envied his success and would have loved for him to mess up somehow.

I felt awful about that, and I said he could blame it all on me: he could tell everybody I was being silly and neurotic. But Greg explained that this would be almost as bad, because people would think less of him for having a relationship with someone like that.

Then he sat back and looked at me in that hard considering way, as if I was a student who'd plagiarised a paper, or some article he didn't approve of, and finally he said slowly, 'There's something else behind this, Dinah. And I can take a guess at what it is.'

What it turned out to be was, Greg thought I must have got involved with somebody else, probably some guy nearer my own age, only I was afraid to admit it. I swore there wasn't anybody. I kept saying I loved him, that he was the only person I loved, but he didn't seem to hear me any more. He pushed his face up close to mine so it filled my whole visual field and looked all distorted, like something you see in the previews of a horror film for a split second: not long enough to be sure what it is, but long enough to know it's something awful.

'All right, who is it, you bitch? Who?' he shouted, and when I kept saying

'Nobody,' he took hold of me and shook me as if I were a bottle of ketchup and he could shake out some man's name, only there wasn't any name.

When Greg let go, and I could stop trembling and crying, I told him the truth, only he didn't believe me. Instead he started going over all the other explanations he'd thought up. Gradually things got really strange and scary. Greg was cursing in this tight hard voice and saying that if I really thought I'd seen Ilse sitting in the kitchen cabinet I must be going crazy; and I was weeping. I said that if I were going crazy it would be wicked of me to marry him and ruin his life, and he said I already had.

It went on like that all weekend. We hardly slept, and finally I got so miserable and mixed-up and exhausted that I started agreeing with everything Greg said. That I had probably been brainwashed by feminists and that I was sometimes attracted to younger men; and that I was basically irrational, deceptive, coward-ly, neurotic and unconsciously envious of Greg because he was a superior person and I was nobody to speak of. The weird thing was that I didn't just agree to all this; in the state I was in by then, I'd started to believe whatever he said.

On Monday morning we were in the kitchen trying to have breakfast. I was in really bad shape; I hadn't had a bath or done anything about my hair for two days, and over my nightgown I had on an old red terry-cloth bathrobe with cof-fee stains. I had got to the point where I didn't care any more if I was crazy or not. I thought that if Ilse Spiegelman meant to haunt me for the rest of my life it couldn't be worse than this.

So when Greg came downstairs I told him I wanted to forget the whole thing and go ahead with the wedding. I put two pieces of Pepperidge Farm raisin toast on his plate and he looked at them. And then he looked at me and I could see that he didn't want to marry me any more, and also he didn't want to live with me.

I was right too. Later that morning Greg called my office and said that he thought it would be best if we didn't see each other or speak to each other again. So he was putting all my 'debris' out in the back entry, and would I please collect it before six p.m.?

Well, after work I went round. I could tell how upset and furious Greg still was by the way he'd pitched my belongings out the kitchen door. My lavender nightgown looked as if it had been strangled and there was raisin granola spilled everywhere; and a bottle of conditioner that he hadn't bothered to close had leaked over everything. It was a total mess. All the time I was cleaning it up I was crying and carrying on, because I still thought I was in love with Greg and that everything that had happened was my fault. And I couldn't help it, I didn't want to, but I looked through the glass of the kitchen door once more to see if Ilse was there. Maybe she would be smiling now, I thought, or even laughing. The cabinet door was hanging open, but it was empty.

I piled everything into the car and drove to my apartment; thank God the lease still had a month to run. But the place looked awful. I'd hardly been there for weeks and there was dust everywhere and the windows were grimed over with soot. I managed to unload the car and carry everything upstairs, and dumped a heap of clothes sticky with conditioner and granola into the bathtub and knelt down to turn on the water.

Then it really hit me. I felt so defeated and crazy and miserable that I slid down onto the dirty yellow vinyl and sat there in a heap between the tub and the toilet. I felt like killing myself, but I didn't have enough energy to move. I thought that maybe in a little while I would crawl across the floor and put my head in the gas oven.

Then all of a sudden I realised that I was sitting on the floor in a cramped space, just like Ilse. She'd finally reduced me to her own miserable condition.

But maybe she wasn't the only one who had done that, I thought. And for the first time I wondered if Greg had ever said the kind of things to Ilse he'd been saying to me all weekend, till she blamed herself for everything and was totally wiped out and beaten down. I remembered how his face had turned into a horror-film preview, and suddenly I felt kind of lucky to have got out of his house. I thought that even if he changed his mind now and took me back, and was as charming and affectionate as before, I would always remember this weekend and wonder if it would happen again, and I would have to sort of tiptoe round him for the rest of my life.

What if I was wrong to believe Ilse had been trying to stop me marrying Greg? I thought. What if she had been trying to warn me?

I still don't know for sure if that's right. Now that everything's changed over there, I'd really like to go to Czechoslovakia and look her up and ask her. But I don't see how I can, what with my husband and the baby.

Gregor's never married again, though he's been with a lot of different women since we separated. I wonder sometimes if any of them have seen Ilse. But maybe she hasn't had to appear, because none of his relationships seem to last very long.

IN THE SHADOW

Alison Lurie

Alison Lurie (b. 1926) is an American novelist and academic. She won
the Pulitzer Prize in 1984 for her novel *Foreign Affairs*. She has published
ten novels, one collection of short stories, and a non-fiction work entitled
The Language of Clothes.

Celia Zimmern was about the last person she, or anyone else, would have
expected to see a ghost. To the other women who worked at the American Embassy in London that year, she seemed almost unnaturally cool
and rational. Nothing ever rattled her, or – as far as they could observe – deeply
excited her.

Celia didn't even seem excited by her undoubted effect on men – which she
should have been, they thought, because there was really no explanation for it.
She wasn't beautiful, only rather pretty: slight, small, with a halo of crinkly dark-
oak hair and oak-brown eyes with lashes so long and dense that some thought
them false. Her manner wasn't flirtatious or seductive, and she always dressed
quietly. Most people didn't realise that Celia's fawn wool suit was a thrift-shop
Chanel, and her navy crêpe a Jean Muir; they only noticed that she wore the
same clothes over and over again.

For Celia, such monotony was preferable to its alternative. If she had a failing,
she knew, it was that she wanted the best or nothing. Unfortunately, the best is
usually expensive, and as a result not only Celia's closet but her tiny elegant flat
in Knightsbridge was almost empty. She would rather shiver all day than wear a
cheap synthetic sweater, rather sit on an Afghan cushion or even her beautifully
waxed parquet floor than in a plastic sling chair. Her acquisitiveness expressed
itself so fastidiously that most of the time it seemed more like asceticism. But
anyone who had watched Celia in a shop, stroking the surface of a beige suede
skirt or lifting a perfect peach from green tissue paper, would have known otherwise.

Celia made no public show of her good taste – or of any other preference. On
the job, especially, she maintained a very low profile; she took in information
rather than giving it out. She'd never understood why most people strove to
voluntarily repeat facts and anecdotes and opinions they already knew. Whereas
by listening carefully one might hear something interesting, even something that
would turn out to be useful.

Because Celia's manner was so low-key, members of the public tended to assume that she was employed at the Embassy in some low-grade clerical capacity.
In fact she was a career diplomat with a responsible position in the Information

Section. Her attitude at work was one of polite attention to the matter at hand; but underneath this was an almost formidable administrative intelligence and decisiveness.

Though a few of Celia's female colleagues considered her somewhat poor in spirit as well as in wardrobe, most liked and even admired her. From their point of view her only fault was that she attracted too many men, and that she continued to go out with ones in whom she had no serious interest, constantly accompanying them to restaurants, concerts, theatres, and films. She was nearly thirty, they said to each other; why couldn't she settle on one guy and give some-body else a chance? It wasn't fair. 'I don't even believe she sleeps with most of them,' one irritable young woman from the Visa Office asserted, calling Celia 'a bitch in the manger'.

Celia herself was modest and a little cynical about her social success. She knew it was mostly her gift as a listener that attracted and held men, just as it soothed irritated officials and calmed impatient journalists. Somehow, she had the ability to focus her entire attention on whomever she was with, letting them speak at length without intruding any personal opinions. 'That's very interest-ing,' she would say if the monologue faltered. 'Tell me more,' or 'Really! I never knew that.'

What still rather surprised her was that none of the men she knew ever caught on. They took her ready responsiveness for granted, as they would that of a superior computer system. Indeed, she sometimes privately compared herself to those computer programs that can imitate psychotherapy and even produce a transference. A similar transference usually appeared in any man Celia went out with more than once or twice: a feeling of love and trust, and the conviction that she was deeply sympathetic with all his views. So strong was this conviction that often, even when Celia declined to put out, they wanted to continue seeing her, to engross her attention for life.

Celia was aware that her acquaintances wished she would settle on one guy, and also that she was twenty-nine. Even from the point of her career, marriage would be advisable. In this connection, her mind turned most often to an economist named Dwayne Mudd. He was a large handsome young man among whose many assets were good manners, sexual energy, professional competence and a declared wish to have children. When she admitted to her friends that Dwayne was talking of marriage, they told her she could hardly do better. He was perfect, they said.

It was true, Celia admitted to herself, that Dwayne Mudd was a Rhodes Schol-ar, a member of a well-known midwestern political family, a former college track star, a *magna cum laude* graduate of Dartmouth, and an alumnus of Yale Law School, with what was probably a brilliant career ahead of him. Why was it, then, that when she imagined being married to him her strongest feeling was one of restless depression? Was it just his ridiculous name?

Or did it have something to do with the fact that Dwayne seemed to assume Celia was fortunate to be courted by him? When he told her that she was really very pretty, or that she would make an ideal diplomat's or politician's wife, she somehow felt he was giving himself a pep talk. He was excusing himself for not having chosen someone richer and more beautiful; above all, someone from an-other prominent midwestern family, because as he had once remarked, in politics it's a big advantage to have a wife with good connections.

When Celia told Dwayne that she didn't think she would ever want to marry him, he didn't seem to hear her. 'You can't mean that seriously, darling,' he said. Even though she repeated it, he insisted on treating her reluctance as feminine coquettishness. 'You'll come round,' he said, smiling. 'I can wait.'

But Celia, though she told herself that she could hardly do better, was more and more determined not to come round. Privately, she had begun to refer to Dwayne as the Wombat; not only because of his admiration for Australia, where he had spent his last posting, but because of his cropped furry hair, broad and somewhat furry hands, solid build, and stubborn tenacity.

Usually Celia kept her growing annoyance with Dwayne to herself, but occasionally it slipped out. Once, for instance, he called her office four times in a single day, mainly to say that he was thinking of her and of what he referred to as 'last night'.

'He must love you very much,' said her boss's secretary, Crystal, who was softly pretty and romantically inclined.

'Dwayne Mudd is a sentimentalist,' replied Celia. 'He probably read somewhere that women like this sort of constant nuisance and interruption.'

A few days later, a cornucopia of sugar-pink rosebuds appeared on her desk at lunchtime.

'Oh, how lovely!' Crystal exclaimed.

'Well. Maybe,' Celia said. 'What I think is, if you're going to buy flowers, you should go to a flower shop. Anything you find on those stalls outside the underground is going to be dead before you get it home.' She held the crumpled paper cone out horizontally, so that the weak stems, studded with knots of crumpled, rusting pink silk, drooped downwards.

'But it's the thought that counts, isn't it?' Crystal asked.

Celia, who disagreed, did not contradict her. 'You know what they always remind me of, flowers like these? Those shoddy cut-price umbrellas they sell in the same place, outside Bond Street station. They never open right either, and quite soon they collapse completely.'

They're kind of sweet now, though, you know.

Crystal looked at the roses in a way that caused Celia to ask, 'Would you like them?'

'Oh, yes! Thank you.' Crystal raised the paper cornucopia to her lace-trimmed blouse and buried her nose in the faint fragrance.

'I guess Dwayne still wants to marry you,' she said finally, exhaling.

'Yes.' Celia gave a little apologetic laugh. 'Of course that's impossible. I couldn't marry a man whose name was Dwayne Mudd. Imagine what it would mean – a lifetime of bad jokes.'

'You could keep your own last name. Lots of girls do that now,' Crystal suggested.

'You'd still be married to him and have to hear the jokes,' said Celia. 'Just for instance, Dwayne told me once that in elementary school he was known as "Muddy Drain".'

Crystal giggled. 'But he must believe he still has a chance,' she said. 'After all, you keep seeing him. And you still have his mother's gold watch.'

'Yes,' Celia admitted. She lifted her slim hand, admiring again an exquisite bracelet watch made in the nineteen-thirties by Cartier, with a woven gold-mesh band and a tiny oblong dial elegantly engraved with Roman numerals. 'But it's only a loan, you know. I've promised to return it the moment Dwayne finds someone else to marry.'

'He'll never find anyone as long as you go on encouraging him,' Crystal predicted.

'I don't encourage him,' Celia protested mildly.

'You must, or he wouldn't still be hanging around. He'd find another girl-friend. I think really maybe you should give back his watch and tell him you don't want to see him any more.' Crystal's voice shook slightly.

'But I do want to see Dwayne,' Celia said, smiling, not offended – indeed, Crystal had never seen her offended. 'He's quite pleasant to be with and he knows a great deal about international economics and the Common Market. I just don't want to marry him. He realises that.'

'I don't think he does,' said Crystal, who already had the difficult last name of Freeplatzer and felt she could reconcile herself to a lifetime of bad jokes quite easily if it should become Mudd. 'But I suppose he'll figure it out in time.'

Either Crystal was wrong, or Dwayne Mudd didn't have enough time. He was still stubbornly pursuing Celia when, two months later, driving home from a party in what was later determined to be a condition of .12 blood-alcohol content, he turned the wrong way up a one-way street in Belgravia and collided fatally with a heavy lorry.

Celia, in the opinion of some, didn't take this news as hard as she might have – as she should have, one of them said at lunch in the canteen.

'I don't see that,' protested Crystal loyally. 'I know Celia was really, really shocked by what happened to Dwayne.'

'Well, we all were. I'm not claiming she doesn't feel as bad as we do. But she ought to feel worse. After all, she was going out with him.'

'Yes, but she's been going out with a lot of other men too, you know. Three at least.'

Crystal's friends nodded. Oh, they knew that, they said crossly.

'I don't see how she can just go on as if nothing had happened,' one complained. 'As if she didn't really care.'

Celia *does* care, Crystal thought. She's still wearing Dwayne Mudd's mother's gold watch; doesn't that prove it?

It was true that Celia was wearing the watch. After Dwayne died she'd asked herself if perhaps she should return it – but to whom? Dwayne had no brothers or sisters; she'd have to ask someone at the Embassy who his legal heirs were, which meant appearing in the embarrassing and false public role of grieving girlfriend. Possibly Dwayne had some cousin who would want the watch, but that wasn't likely. Most people – especially people in Iowa, was the thought that crossed Celia's mind, though she quickly suppressed it as snobbish – wouldn't appreciate Dwayne's mother's watch. They'd think it old-fashioned and inconvenient; they'd much prefer the latest glittery Rolex that never had to be wound

and would tell them the day of the month and the time in Hong Kong. And anyhow, wouldn't Dwayne have wanted her to have it; if he'd known – ?

A month later, as if the Fates had finally harkened to Crystal's friends, Celia
abruptly removed herself from competition: not by accepting another of her current beaus, but by requesting and receiving a job transfer. What amazed everyone
was her destination: a small hot West African country of no political importance.

'Of course it's a fairly responsible position: Cultural Affairs Officer,' a secretary in the department involved reported to her friends later in the canteen. 'And
the salary is good, because it's a hardship post.'

'But gee, really: Goto,' Crystal exclaimed.

'I know. Nobody's ever heard of it. My boss told Celia that if she'd just hang
on a while he could probably find her something much better. But Celia said she
wanted to leave as soon as possible. I don't get it.'

'Maybe it's because of Dwayne Mudd,' suggested another young woman.
'Maybe she can't forget him as long as she's here in London. She might feel
guilty, even.'

'I don't know,' Crystal said. 'Guilty doesn't exactly sound like her.'

All the same, she thought later, there was definitely something on Celia's mind.
She had a new distracted manner, a kind of preoccupation – could she have realised that she'd been in love with Dwayne after all?

'I think I can guess why you asked for a transfer,' Crystal said when Celia took
her for a farewell lunch at Wheeler's. 'It was because of Dwayne Mudd.'

Celia started as if she'd taken hold of a defective electrical appliance. 'How
did you know?' she half-whispered; looking round the restaurant as if it were
full of undercover agents. 'I mean, what makes you say that?' she amended, recovering her cool.

'It's – well, the way you've been sort of tense ever since he died,' Crystal said.
'I figured you might still be thinking about Dwayne and kind of, you know, imagining him everywhere in London.'

'Yes,' Celia said after a considerable pause. She lowered her fork, speared a
slice of cucumber, raised it. 'Not everywhere,' she added, addressing the cucumber, 'I only see him at certain times … Whenever I'm, you know, with somebody
else.'

'You mean, in your mind's eye,' Crystal said, stirring her salad for concealed
bits of shrimp.

'What?' Celia lowered the fork again.

'I mean you don't, like, really see Dwayne? Not like a spirit apparition.' Crystal leaned forward, her mouth half-open.

'Oh, no; of course not,' Celia lied. She was reminded that Crystal, though reasonably discreet, was the daughter of small-town spiritualists and had a residual
fascination with their beliefs.

The truth was, though, that Celia was seeing Dwayne Mudd, or something
that looked a lot like him. Mostly he appeared as a sort of wavery grey semi-
transparent image printed on the scene like a weak carbon copy when someone's

forgotten to change the ribbon. He wasn't there all the time, only very occasionally – only, she realised after the first week, when she was alone with a man.

The first time Celia saw Dwayne she was in a taxi with a handsome, slightly stupid young merchant banker. As he bent and kissed her, she imagined or
perceived something like Dwayne Mudd sitting on the jump seat. She sat up
abruptly and it vanished.

It was dusk and raining, and Celia attributed the illusion to a trick of the wet
half-light. But she couldn't really get into it again with the merchant banker, and
when they reached her flat in Knightsbridge she checked her little gold watch,
exclaimed at the lateness of the hour and didn't ask him in.

The next time Dwayne Mudd appeared was worse, because it was daylight.
Celia was on a Sunday outing with an American legal expert called Mark. They
were sitting in a little wood at the top of Hampstead Heath, looking out through
a stand of ancient beeches at a Constable landscape of towering cumulus clouds
and descending fields of grass and flowers. Celia had just had a first-rate lunch
and learnt several useful things about libel law; she felt pleased, at peace.

But when Mark put his arm round her and stroked her bare shoulder the grey
shadow of the Wombat wavered into view beneath the branches of a nearby
tree. This time what she saw was difficult to explain as a trick of the light: it was
clearly the two-dimensional image of a man; not grey now, but weakly coloured
like a tinted black-and-white photograph.

'What is it?' Mark asked, following her start and fixed stare.

'I heard thunder,' Celia said, improvising. 'We'd better get back, we'll be
drenched.'

When Mark, clearly much disappointed and even cross, had returned Celia to
her flat and not been invited in, she poured herself a vodka and grapefruit juice
and sat down to face the situation.

She refused to consider Crystal's idea that what she had seen was a 'spirit apparition' i.e. a ghost. Not only did ghosts not exist, the very idea of them was in
bad taste; it went with woozy New Age music, the fingering of greasy tarot cards
and the search for people's former incarnations, who somehow always turned
out to be upscale or celebrity personages.

No, there was no ghost, Celia said to herself. Rather, for some reason, she
was psychologically haunted by the death of Dwayne Mudd, about which she
consciously felt only a mild sadness, and also – for Dwayne had become quite a
nuisance in the final month or so – a little relief.

But, Celia thought, there must be more going on subconsciously. I must believe that if I'd agreed to marry Dwayne he wouldn't be dead. Some irrational,
infantile part of me must think that if I'd gone to that stuffy dinner-party with
him he wouldn't have drunk too much and there wouldn't have been an accident.
That's what he would probably want me to think if he were alive.

'Don't be Silly,' she told herself sharply, capitalising the adjective, which had
been her nickname as a small child – perhaps on the principle of opposites, for
if there was anything Celia hadn't been for a long while, it was silly. That's total
nonsense about Dwayne, it's just what something neurotic in you imagines. Maybe you ought to see a shrink.

But almost as rapidly as this idea came to Celia she rejected it. She couldn't afford private therapy, she'd have to go through the Embassy medical plan. And when anyone did that it got into their medical records and stayed there. Of course no one was supposed to know what was in the records; but people often did know, because someone had to file them.

And when you came up for promotion, it usually came out. Then, even if there'd only been a minor problem, insomnia, for instance, or fear of flying, it could hurt your career. And hers wasn't a minor problem: she was having what a shrink would call delusions. Possibly she was actually coming down with a full-blown psychosis.

Celia, who up to now had always taken her mental stability for granted, began to feel depressed and even frightened. But she was a young woman of considerable courage and determination. The only thing to do, she finally decided, was to ignore her hallucinations and assume they would eventually go away.

An opportunity to test this theory appeared the following weekend; Celia was at home, making lunch for a former lover from America, a painter named Nat. She knew, and he knew, that this lunch would probably end in bed, for old times' sake. But as she was adding fresh cream to the vichyssoise, Nat came up close behind and embraced her; and there was the greyish shape of Dwayne Mudd again, sliding about on the sunlit wall among the shadows of the hanging Swedish ivy. As Nat caressed her right breast the shape seemed to grow darker.

'No,' she said aloud.

'Sorry, love,' Nat grinned. 'Okay, I'll leave you alone while you cook.'

The shadow wavered, faded. But it reappeared after lunch as Celia stood to clear the table.

'I've missed you,' Nat said, standing also, looking directly at her.

'Yes.' They moved towards each other and then, entwined, towards the bedroom. Dwayne's image followed them from room to room, sliding over the walls and furniture.

As they sank down on the bed, Celia deliberately shut her eyes. 'You want to watch, Wombat, go ahead,' she told him silently in her mind, where of course he was located.

As if she had spoken, a voice – Dwayne Mudd's voice, though flatter now, dead-pan – in fact, dead – replied. – That's a filthy person you're with, it said. – Literally. He hasn't had a shower since Thursday.

Celia, with considerable effort, did not look round or even open her eyes. It was clear that Nat had heard nothing, for he went on kissing her enthusiastically. She cooperated, holding him close, although now his light-brown hair had an – imagined? – odour of stale turpentine.

– You like dirt and paint, look at his hands, Dwayne Mudd's voice said. – And wait till you smell how long he's been wearing those socks.

You're lying, Celia thought, but in spite of herself she glanced at Nat's hand as it lifted her grey silk Nicole Farhi jersey. There was a sour-green smudge across the knuckles and the square-cut nails were black. And when, in spite of her resolution, she raised her eyes, there was the shadow of Dwayne Mudd in the desk chair. Irrationally, because he was merely a figment of her imagination, she felt deeply embarrassed that he, fully clothed, should see her lying there naked.

The event that followed, though clearly great fun for Nat, was unsatisfactory to Celia. She concentrated on keeping her eyes shut, but she couldn't help hearing the voice.

– Well, look at that. He still doesn't wear underpants. Kind of disgusting, isn't it? Dwayne said, while Nat gasped and cried out, 'Oh, love!'

– And get a whiff of those armpits. That was why you broke up with him, wasn't it?

'Celia, my darling,' Nat murmured, subsiding, then turning to look at her. 'Are you all right?' he asked. 'I mean, is something the matter? You didn't – You usually –'

'I'm fine,' Celia assured him. 'That was lovely. But I think … Well, the thing is,' she continued, 'I'm rather involved with someone else just now.'

'Really? Oh, hell,' Nat said.

That was how it began; and it rapidly became worse. Soon, whenever Celia even shook hands with a man, the wavering image of Dwayne Mudd appeared and spoke. In life the Wombat's language had been decorous; now it was coarse.

– He's got zits on his ass.

– Notice how he stinks of stale smoke, from his lousy nicotine habit. Shit, you can smell it, you're close enough.

– How can you stand that moustache, so red and bristly, like a hog I knew in Iowa. Got a face like a goddamn hog, too, hasn't he?

– I suppose you know he's fucking the wife of the MP from that place in Surrey where he lives.

This last remark was directed at the merchant banker, whom Celia had been spending most of her time with lately – not because she liked him best but because he was the most imperceptive of her suitors and thus least apt to notice her distracted condition. But after she'd made discreet inquiries and discovered that Dwayne was right about the MP's wife, she crossed the banker off her list. Someone must have mentioned the affair and I must have remembered it subconsciously, she told herself. But she wasn't sure; she wasn't sure of anything any more.

I'm falling apart, Celia thought. I've got to get out of London before I completely crack up. No, out of England.

When she first heard of Goto, Celia had seen in her mind a comic-book panorama of jungle and swamp, crocodiles, giant snakes, political violence and malarial heat. But in fact it wasn't bad. Though she arrived in July the temperature was tolerable. The heavy rains had passed and the landscape was densely green, layered like a Henri Rousseau painting with palms and banana trees and tall grasses studded with red and magenta and white flowers. The atmosphere at the Embassy was agreeable and relaxed, and there was an Olympic-size outdoor pool embraced by blossoming shrubs.

Popti, the capital, turned out to be a seaside city of broad boulevards and red sandy alleys; of low blond and ochre and terracotta houses and shops, with here and there a shimmering high-rise hotel or bank. For years it had been a French colony; French was still the official language and there were visible survivals of French cuisine and French fashion.

There might be advantages in a place like this, Celia realised. She could practise her French and develop some regional expertise. Moreover, her professional situation was greatly improved; she had an office of her own, a secretary and the occasional use of an Embassy car and driver. She also had authority; she could cause events to happen. In just a month she'd started two film series; she was reorganising the library and negotiating with USIS in Washington for interesting speakers.

What's more, she had been assigned a four-bedroom air-conditioned villa with cook, cleaner, part-time gardener and twenty-four-hour guard service. It was not far from the Embassy and next door to the home and shop of the city's most fashionable dressmaker, Madame Miri (to some of her European clients, Madame Marie). Celia's own house was usually quiet except for the faint, almost domestic hum of the radio that would communicate instantly with the Marine guard station at the Embassy in case of emergency.

But there was always something going on in Madame's deep, leafy compound, which besides the shop contained five buildings and a large and shifting population of relatives and employees, from infants in cotton hip slings to toothless grandmothers. Celia was becoming quite friendly with Madame, who like herself was a perfectionist where dress was concerned; she had already copied a complex Issey Miyake for Celia in a remarkable black and indigo-grey local batik.

Most restful of all, Celia hadn't seen Dwayne Mudd since she arrived. That proved nothing, though, for as yet she had touched no man except to shake hands. Now that she had her life organised, she knew, it was time to test her safety – her sanity, really. Because what was the alternative? The alternative was a possibly lifelong nervous celibacy.

As a sympathetic listener, Celia had not only rapidly become popular in the European community, she had also acquired two admirers. She decided to go out with the one she liked least, an Oklahoma businessman – probably married, she guessed, though he claimed not – called Gary Mumpson. She therefore allowed Gary to take her to the most expensive French restaurant and, after dinner, to drive to the beach and park. It was pitch dark there, under a sky of intense tropical blackness speckled with stars. As Gary leant over to kiss her, rather sweatily, Celia held her breath. For a moment nothing happened; then, mixed with the sound of the heavy, treacherous surf, she seemed to discern an unmistakable voice.

– Yeah, give the creep a big hug, it said, – so you can feel that rubber tyre.

You're imagining things, Celia told herself; but her arms were already around Gary and she could not help following the Wombat's instructions.

– Anyhow, you're wasting your time, the voice seemed to say. – Not only is he married, his cock is only three inches long.

No, it was no use. 'Come on, let's drive back,' Celia said miserably, struggling upright.

'Nah, what for – oh, sure. Great idea!' Gary panted, imagining (mistakenly) that this was an invitation to Celia's apartment.

The next day was Saturday. Celia, after a sleepless night, left her house in the hope of jogging off some of her depression. The morning was cool and fresh, the street nearly empty, but as she reached the gate of the compound next door she was greeted by Madame Miri.

In the strong sunlight her landlady was an imposing figure. Her skin shone like polished mahogany and she wore a brilliant ballooning orange robe and turban printed with blue birds-of-paradise.

'What is it, *chérie*?' she inquired in her excellent French, putting a broad vermilion-nailed hand on Celia's arm.

'What?' Celia said stupidly. 'What is what?'

'You are troubled this morning.'

'No, not at all.' Celia tried to make her voice light and unconcerned.

Madame shook her head. 'I see it, in the air around you. Please, come into the shop.' She lifted a hanging curtain printed with giant golden flowers.

Blurrily, Celia followed. Madame Miri indicated that she should seat herself beside the big cutting-table heaped with fashion magazines and bolts of multi-coloured cloth, and brought her a cup of scalding French coffee.

'You don't sleep well last night,' Madame Miri stated rather than inquired.

'Not very well, no,' Celia admitted.

'You have the nightmare, perhaps?'

'Well, yes, sometimes,' said Celia, thinking that the appearances of Dwayne Mudd were a kind of nightmare.

'I shall give you something.' Madame Miri rose and swept through another curtain at the dim back of the room, where she seemed to be opening drawers and unscrewing bottles, murmuring to herself in a sing-song.

I'm not going to swallow any strange medicine, Celia promised herself.

'*Voilà*.' Returning, Madame laid before Celia a small bag of reddish home-spun tied with a strip of leather.

'Take this, *chérie*. You don't open it, but tonight you put it under your pillow, yes?'

'All right,' Celia promised, relieved. She knew or could guess what was in the bag: a selection of the magical and medicinal herbs and bits of bone sold at stalls in the village markets and even here in the capital. It was what people called a *gris-gris* – a protective charm.

'It's good,' Madame urged, smiling, holding out the little bag. 'Good against fear.'

Of course Madame Miri believes in spirits, she thought; almost everyone does here. The principal religion of Goto, after all, was animism: the worship of ancestors and of certain trees, rivers, and mountains. Ghosts and demons inhabited the landscape and the fields and groves often displayed, instead of a scarecrow, a bundle of leaves and powders and bones given power by spells and hung from a branch or wedged into the fork of a tree. According to local belief, it protected the crops not only against birds and animals but against thieves and evil spirits.

'Thank you,' Celia said.

When she could Celia kept her promises. She therefore put the *gris-gris* under her pillow that night and, because of it or not, slept more easily the rest of the week. Somewhat revived in spirits, she decided to risk going out with the second of her current admirers, the Marine Master Sergeant in charge of the guard at the Embassy. Jackson was an amusing young Southerner of considerable native wit who looked well in his uniform and magnificent in swim trunks. On the down side, he was four years younger than Celia, badly educated, and had terrible political convictions.

This did not surprise Celia: in her opinion, many people had peculiar views. But however much she might disagree, she made no attempt to protest or correct them. She'd always disliked argument, which in her experience never convinced anyone – only facts did that, and even then not very often. Whenever she seriously disagreed with someone she repeated a phrase her father had taught her when she was fourteen: 'You may be right.' ('It took me fifty-five years to learn to say that,' he had told her. 'Maybe it'll save you a little trouble.')

At the last moment before Jackson arrived in his red Corvette, Celia, with a superstitious impulse of which she was rather ashamed, placed Madame Miri's *gris-gris* in the bottom of her handbag. But when her date handed – or, more accurately, handled – her into the car, she thought for a moment that she saw Dwayne's image, wavering but distinct, on the whitewashed wall of the compound. It was transformed almost at once into the blowing shadows of a banyan tree, and Celia scolded herself for succumbing to nerves.

Unlike Gary, Jackson did not wait to make his move till after supper. As soon as they pulled up in front of the open-air restaurant, from which noisy, thumping local music was soaking, he turned towards Celia. 'Hey, you really look super tonight,' he said, grabbing her expertly.

Dwayne Mudd reappeared at once, sitting on the hood of the Corvette: strangely grey and semi-transparent against the sun-flooded tropical shrubbery, as if the light that shone on him was still the humid grey light of London. You better watch your step with this one, he announced.

Oh, shut up, Celia said silently. I've come all this way; I'm going to enjoy myself if I feel like it.

– He goes with whores, Dwayne continued relentlessly, pressing his grey face up against the windshield. – You should find out when he was last tested for AIDS. And check if he has a cut on his lip.

Involuntarily, Celia ran the tip of her tongue over Jackson's wide mouth. Mistaking her intention, he gasped and pulled her closer, murmuring, 'Oh, baby.'

That night, oppressed by both anxiety and frustrated desire, Celia slept worse than ever – as was immediately apparent to Madame Miri when she appeared next morning.

'But it is not yet well, *ma petite*,' she announced, after lowering herself into a chair and accepting coffee.

'No,' Celia admitted. 'I guess your charm doesn't work on Europeans.' She laughed nervously.

Madame ignored this. 'There is something heavy on your mind, is it not so?' she asked.

'No – well, yes.' Giving in, Celia told Madame Miri, gradually, everything. She'll know I'm insane now, she thought as the grotesque words fell from her mouth like the toads and snakes of the old fairy tale. She'll tell me to see a doctor.

'My poor child,' Madame said instead, when Celia fell nervously silent. 'I see how it is. This individual, he is jealous. Since he cannot have you, he wants to keep all other men away. That I have seen before, *eh oui.*' She sighed. 'And so for nothing you made this long journey.' For the first time, she used the intimate second person singular. 'Though perhaps not for nothing,' she added almost to herself.

'I thought, if I was so far from London –'

'*Chérie*, two, three thousand miles, they are like this' (she snapped her fingers) 'to a spirit. They don't figure space like we do.'

'A spirit?' Celia echoed.

'*Exactement.*' Madame Miri smiled, and Celia remembered a verse from a tribal chant that had been recited to her by the Deputy Chief of Mission.

> Those who are dead have not gone.
> They are in the shadow that brightens,
> They are in the shadow that fades,
> They are in the shadow that trembles.

'And how was he called in life, this *personnage*?' Madame asked.

'Dwayne Mudd,' Celia said.

Madame frowned. 'Mudd. *C'est la boue, n'est-ce pas*?'

'Yes, I suppose so,' Celia admitted.

'A bad name. Ill-omened.'

'Evidently,' Celia said. She tried an uneasy laugh, but Madame ignored the pathetic result.

'It takes a spirit to catch a spirit,' she said in a low voice, leaning across the table towards Celia as if Dwayne Mudd might be listening. 'You know perhaps some very powerful woman gone over to the other side, your mother, your grandmother *peut-être*?'

Celia shook her head. 'No, I'm sorry. They're both still alive. And my other grandmother, my father's mother – I don't know. I never liked her much and I don't think she liked me either.' She looked up at Madame Miri, who was still waiting patiently, and then down into the dark reflections of her coffee cup.

'There is someone,' she said after a pause. 'I never knew her, but I'm named after her. She was my father's stepmother.'

'*Une belle-mère, mais sympathique.*'

'Oh yes, so my father claims. He never uses the word "wonderful" about anyone or anything, but he said once that she was a wonderful woman – I'm supposed to be like her, even though we weren't related.'

'That's well. Perhaps you have her soul.'

'Maybe,' Celia said, recalling that according to local belief ancestral spirits returned after death to inhabit their newborn descendants.

'*En tout cas*, she's without doubt watching over you, or you would not have thought of her now.' Madame Miri smiled.

'I'm not so sure about that,' Celia said. 'I mean, if she is, I guess she hasn't been watching very often, or I wouldn't be in this fix now.'

'*Pas certain, chérie.* This *belle-mère*, she was perhaps a very polite lady?'

'What?' Celia asked, feeling disorientated. Lack of sleep, she thought. 'Oh, yes. My father said she had perfect manners.'

'That explains it. She's watching over you, *oui*, but when you and some type are becoming close,' (Madame made a somewhat obscene gesture) '*elle est bien élevée*, she averts her eyes. And, *tu me l'as raconté*, that's the only time this evil spirit appears.'

'Yes,' Celia agreed. Am I really having this conversation? she thought.

'Very well, I tell you, this is what you do. Next time you see him, you call for *la belle-mère*. Not necessary to shout her name out loud, just whisper in your mind, "*Venez, venez à moi, aidez-moi*."'

'All right,' Celia promised.

For a few minutes after Madame Miri had left, she felt better. Perhaps she wasn't mad after all, only haunted. In Goto the existence of supernatural beings did not seem so impossible. Out in the country, almost every village was guarded by one or more fetish figures, which resembled large grey stone fire hydrants hung with coloured rags and garlands of flowers. They had broad faces, staring eyes and huge sexual organs, and gave off, even to a sceptic like Celia, an ominous and powerful aura.

Even here in the capital, the totemic animal of the dominant local tribe, the pigeon, was honoured by a monumental sculpture of a huge white bird, described in tourist brochures as the 'Pigeon of Peace'. Closer at hand, in a shadowy corner of Madame Miri's courtyard, squatted two household gods, smaller versions of the village fetish figures. They wore bright, constantly renewed garlands of red and orange flowers, and each day Madame's cook fed them: their open stone mouths were always smeared with dried blood and rice and fruit pulp.

But Celia's euphoria lasted only briefly. She realised that if she began to take all this seriously she would be mentally worse off than before: not only having delusions, but starting to believe in ghosts, and thinking that she could exorcise them by invoking the name of an ancestor whom she had never met and who wasn't even an ancestor. Going native, in fact, she thought. She had already heard stories about people, anthropologists mostly, who began by taking the local belief system too seriously and ended up partly or wholly off their rockers.

Some of these tales, and most of the information about Gotolese superstition, had come from a man in whom Celia was becoming seriously interested: the Deputy Chief of Mission himself, a career diplomat and former anthropologist named Charles Fenn. He was a tall, thin, very intelligent, slightly odd-looking man of about forty, with a long face, skewed eyebrows, a beaky nose, and a satirical, melancholy manner. She had liked him from the start, without ever thinking of him as a possible beau. But then, everyone at the Embassy liked Charles, from the Ambassador (a fat, elderly Texan magnate whose contributions to the Republican party had earned him this honorary post) down to the twelve-year-old Gotolese undergardener.

According to Embassy gossip, melancholy was not Charles' normal mood, but the result of events beyond his control. He was recently separated and in the process of being divorced: his ex-wife, everyone said, had been a cute and even lovable airhead, but terminally indiscreet and totally unable to adjust to West Africa. Since she left, Charles had been under the weather emotionally, while remaining unvaryingly hard-working and sympathetic to his staff. 'He really listens to you,' people often said.

'Yes, I know,' Celia always replied, feeling mildly uneasy, because this was what people often said about her.

Her unease escalated to panic at her next one-to-one meeting with Charles, after her skilled attentiveness had drawn him into describing his years as an anthropologist.

'It's a very cluttered field,' he was telling her. 'In more ways than one. You know what they say about the Navaho, that the typical family consists of a grandparent, the parents, 3.2 children, and an anthropologist. It was almost like that where I was. I realised I wasn't only going to be unnecessary and ineffectual, I was going to be superfluous.'

'Tell me more,' Celia murmured encouragingly as he paused and gazed out the window into the glossy green crown of an Embassy avocado tree.

Charles turned and looked at her. 'You always say that, don't you?' he remarked with what struck Celia as a dangerous casualness. '"Tell me more."'

'No – well, not always,' she stammered.

Charles smiled. 'Or else you say, "That's really interesting." Persuading the other person to go on talking, so you'll get to know them, and they won't know you. I recognise the technique, you see, because I do it, too.'

'I don't ...' Celia began, and swallowed the rest of the fib.

'But now I think it's your turn. *You* tell me more.' He did not take his eyes off her. They were a strange colour, she saw, between dark gold and green.

'More about what?'

'I don't care. Your childhood, your opinions, your ambitions, your dreams, whatever you like. As long as it's the truth, of course.' Charles smiled.

'I – uh.' Celia hesitated; her heart seemed to flop in her chest like a fish.

'I know. Tell me about your time in the Peace Corps, what you liked most about that.' He glanced at the wall clock. 'You have ten minutes, all right?'

'All right,' Celia said. She swallowed. 'I think it was the way the villages looked at night,' she was surprised to hear herself say. 'Especially when there was a moon ...' Why did I agree? she asked herself. Why didn't I just laugh it off and say – Not today or – I don't feel like it? I could still say that. But instead she heard her voice going on, beginning to speak of things she'd not told anyone, not because they were private or shocking, but because nobody had ever really listened, they were all just waiting their turn to talk.

It's the way he looks at me, she thought, glancing at Charles. He knows I'm here. Is that how I make people feel?

'That's very interesting,' Charles said as she paused, glancing at the clock and then back at Celia. 'Go on.'

'Well. It's because, you see, the desert isn't quiet at night. There are all the sounds in the trees and scrub outside the village, rustlings and squeaks and sighs, and you're there, you're part of it ... you feel ...' She looked at Charles Fenn. He was still listening; he heard her, every word. This could be important, she thought. It is important.

She thought it again after she left Charles' office, and that evening back home. She told herself that Charles was a most unusual man. That without his flighty wife he would probably go far; with Celia, even farther – if she were ever her normal self again. Otherwise she would simply screw up his career, not to mention her own, she thought wretchedly. Then she reminded herself that there was no reason to worry about this, because nothing Charles had yet done or said suggested he wanted to go anywhere with her. But for some reason that made Celia feel even more miserable.

Things were still in this condition when Charles asked Celia to accompany him and another staff member to a reception at the French Embassy. The Commercial Attaché was in the front seat with the driver; Charles and Celia in the back, and as they drove through streets illuminated by the mauve and vermilion afterglow of a tropical sunset Charles described the rank, history and personal peculiarities of the people she was about to meet.

'There's a lot of rather odd characters in the local diplomatic corps, I'm afraid,' he concluded. 'But I hope you're going to like it here all the same.' The car lurched suddenly round a corner, flinging Celia, in her gossamer-light pale mauve muslin dress, abruptly against him.

'Thanks, I think I will,' she replied distractedly, trying to catch her breath, not moving away.

'I'm very glad to hear that.' Charles also did not move; under the cover of the attaché case on his lap, he put his hand on hers.

– You're making another mistake, said the flat dead voice of Dwayne Mudd. At first Celia could not see him; then she realised he was sitting, grey and squeezed up, between Charles and the door.

– You think he's so fucking great. He's got –'

I don't want to hear it, Celia thought desperately, feeling the steady, disturbing, desirable pressure of Charles' shoulder, arm and hand against hers.

– Athlete's foot, and –

Remembering Madame Miri, she cried out silently in her mind to the other Celia Zimmern. *Venez à moi, aidez-moi!* How stupid it sounded: like calling on herself.

Miraculously, the horrible flat voice ceased. My God, it worked, Celia thought. But the shadow of Dwayne Mudd did not vanish: it remained in the car, silently moving its greyish lips, until they reached the French Embassy.

'So, how does it go?' Madame Miri asked next morning, waylaying Celia as she went out for an early run. Narrowing her eyes in the brilliant sun, she added, 'Perhaps not completely well, yes?'

'He's still there,' Celia admitted. 'I can't hear him any more, but he's there, trying to speak, opening and shutting his mouth. Half the way to the French Embassy yesterday evening in the car, and all the way back – well, whenever I – you know. I can't bear it any more!' she cried suddenly. 'I think I'm going mad.'

'*Ah non, chérie. Come, come chez moi.* We shall consider this further.'

In a dazed condition, weakened by another night without sleep, Celia followed Madame to her shop and then, for the first time, through the curtain into the back room. It was low, dimly lit, hung with thick woven and embroidered fabrics and dominated by a kind of altar covered with an embroidered red cloth and crowded with flowers and images, including what looked like a lion with wings.

'Sit down, please.' Madame Miri indicated a low multicoloured leather pouf.

'There is something,' she said, opening her eyes after some moments of silent concentration. 'I think this spirit of mud has got some hold on you.'

'I don't know –' Celia said. 'Maybe I feel guilty –'

'Guilty, that is nothing. This is not your husband, only a stupid, jealous spirit. But I think perhaps there is some object that he has given to you, and through this he has power to come to you when he desires.'

Involuntarily, Celia glanced at her left wrist; at Dwayne's mother's gold watch. Madame Miri followed her gaze. 'So that is his?' she asked.

'Yes; well, it was his mother's.'

'So, even worse. In it, her power is joined to his. I understand well now.' She nodded several times.

'You think I shouldn't wear this watch when I go out with someone?'

'Never you should wear it,' Madame said solemnly. 'It is dangerous to you always. Give it to me; I will take care of it.'

Somewhat stunned by this development, Celia did not move.

'You must hold to persons; not to things,' said Madame Miri, putting out her hand.

Slowly, Celia unfastened the gold-mesh band and placed her Cartier watch in Madame's broad black-rimmed apricot-tinted palm, where it looked strangely small.

'But if it's so dangerous,' she said, watching what she had come to think of as her property disappear into Madame's fist. 'I mean, if you have the watch, won't he come to you?'

Madame Miri laughed. 'If he comes, let him come. He will have a large surprise, will he not?' She laughed again, more fully. 'Don't derange yourself, *ma petite*,' she said gently. 'I know how to deal with such as him, *je te le jure.*'

Five months later, Celia Zimmern and Charles Fenn were married in the garden of the American Embassy in Goto. There were well over a hundred guests; strings of coloured lanterns – ruby, sapphire, topaz, and jade-green – laced the tropical evening; fireworks were set off beside the pool. Madame Miri, who had created Celia's spectacular white tulle and lace wedding dress from a Givenchy pattern, sat at one end of the long head table, resplendent in vermilion silk brocaded in gold, with a matching fantastically folded headdress.

'A day of joy,' she said when Celia, circulating among the company, stopped beside her. 'I see that all is well with you.'

'Oh, yes.' Celia looked at Madame again. On both broad, glowing mahogany arms she wore a mass of gold bangles; among them was the gold Cartier watch. But that's mine, Celia wanted to say; then she faltered, realising that the statement was false, and that anyhow this was the wrong time and place for it; that perhaps there would never be a right time or place.

Madame Miri, unembarrassed, followed the direction of her gaze. 'That one has not appeared again to you, *n'est-ce pas?*'

'No, not since –' Celia glanced at her own slim wrist, on which there was now only a faint band of untanned skin. Out of practical necessity she had purchased a Timex from the Embassy commissary, but usually kept it in her handbag. 'Has he appeared to you?' she added, registering the emphasis in Madame's phrasing.

'*Ah oui*; I have seen him, with his little moustache,' replied Madame Miri. 'A good appearance, that fellow. But not interesting, no. *Jamais.* Not like that man of yours there, eh?' She gave an intimate laugh, bubbly with champagne, and gestured towards Charles, who was also moving among the guests.

'No,' Celia said, trying to remember if she had ever told Madame Miri that the Wombat had a small moustache. She knew she had told Charles; indeed, a month ago, without really intending to do so, she had found herself telling Charles everything about Dwayne Mudd.

His reaction, as always, was interested and sympathetic. 'I think most people see their former lovers sometimes, though not as clearly as you did. I used to see my wife; almost see her anyhow. And if you live in a place like this for a while you're not surprised by anything.'

Somehow after that Celia had at last succeeded in forgetting Dwayne Mudd. But now, dizzied by happiness and champagne, she imagined him as a fretful ghost eternally bound to Goto, a country he would probably have deplored and detested – he hated what he called 'the sticks'. She even wondered if he were present this evening, invisible and inaudible except to Madame Miri.

'Do you think Dwayne's at the party, then?' she asked, glancing round uneasily, and then back at Madame Miri. In the jewelled light of the paper lanterns Madame looked larger and more formidable than ever. What she really resembled, Celia thought, was the female of the pair of larger-than-life mahogany figures in the local museum. Heavy-limbed, heavy-lidded, they had been roughly carved a century or more ago; they were identified on their label as *Gardes des portes de l'enfer* – guardians of the gates of Hell.

'No.' Madame Miri shook her turbaned head slowly, so that her heavy earrings swayed. 'He is not here.' She was no longer laughing. 'He has gone where he should go.' She pointed down, towards the earth. But then she smiled and raised her glass. 'Do not think more of him, *chérie*,' she told Celia. 'He will not trouble you again.'

THE WATCH TRICK

Jennifer Egan

Jennifer Egan (b. 1962) is an American writer. She has published short fiction in the *New Yorker* and *Harper's*, and her journalism appears frequently in the *New York Times Magazine*. Egan's novel *A Visit from the Goon Squad* won the 2011 Pulitzer Prize and the National Book Critics Circle Award.

S onny drove his boat straight into the middle of the lake and cut the engine. They rocked in silence, the deep, prickling hush of a Midwestern summer. The lake was flat as a rug, pushed against a wall of pale sky.

The four of them were celebrating Sonny's engagement to Billie, a girl with soft hair and a Southern accent. She kept to herself, leaning back in a chair with her legs propped on the rail. She had met Sonny the week before, at a party before her own wedding to someone else. This turn of events would have been more shocking in some lives than it was in Sonny's; he was a man who lived by his own egregiousness, who charmed, offended, and was talked about at other people's dinner parties. Stealing a bride was right up his alley.

Diana watched Sonny measure, shake, and pour martinis with the ease of a cardsharp shuffling. She was forty-two, with a worn, pretty face. Her husband, James, sat beside her, looking amused. He and Sonny had been best friends since the army. James leaned back and looked from Sonny to his bride. 'So tell us how you two happened,' he said.

Sonny just grinned, his eyes fine and vacant as crystal.

Billie swung down her legs and leaned forward, animated for the first time that day. In two sips she had finished half her martini. 'Let me tell,' she said. 'I'm dying to.'

On the night before her wedding, she explained, her father had thrown a party aboard an old steamboat. Sonny had pursued her, flirting openly whenever he found her alone, eyeing her from a distance the rest of the time. Late in the evening they were standing alone on the deck when abruptly he took off his gold Rolex, held it up in the moonlight, and threw it in the water: 'Baby, when I'm with you,' he said, 'time just stops.'

Billie narrowed her eyes as she spoke. She was very young, and strands of roller-curled hair spiraled like ribbons down her back. 'I'm like, please,' she said, 'could you possibly be more corny? But' – and here she seemed to struggle, reaching for Sonny's hand – 'it was like when you're half asleep and you hear voices, you know, from the real world, and you just think, No, I want to stay asleep and have this dream.'

She paused and tried to catch their eyes, but James and Diana were looking as far away as possible. They'd been hearing the story for years in various forms – from the Hawaiian tour guide Sonny fell in love with while gazing at the view from Kaala Peak, threatening to jump unless she agreed to come back to Chicago with him; from the astrologer who had obsessed him from the moment she divined that his mother had been killed in a small plane crash when Sonny was five. This very boat – a 34-foot Chris-Craft flybridge – he had bought twelve years before in the certainty that he would marry a professional water-skier he'd seduced the previous night. That was Sonny: music, a few drinks under his belt, the light falling a certain way, and any pretty waitress might receive a declaration of love, an impassioned lecture on their two converging fates. If she was smart, she would laugh it off and bring him his change. Not that Sonny didn't mean it – he could mean almost anything. But his attention span was short.

'So we escaped in a lifeboat,' Billie concluded. 'Daddy was mad as hell.' She grinned irrepressibly now, a young, mischievous girl whose life had taken a sudden turn for the thrilling.

'That's quite a story,' James said, with a sly look at Diana.

Sonny mixed another round of drinks. It was August, one of those hot, hot days when the sky seems to vibrate. Diana longed to strip down to her bathing suit, but her legs embarrassed her. Veins had risen to the surface in recent years. These seemed more offensive now, in the presence of Billie, who had long, gleaming legs and knees delicate as teeth.

'I hope Daddy will forgive me after Sonny and I get married,' Billie said, suddenly despondent. 'And Bobby, too, my fiancé. I've known him since the fifth grade.'

'Your ex-fiancé,' James reminded her.

'Oh yeah,' she said. 'Ex.'

James and Diana's friendship with Sonny had had its perfect moment twenty years before, in the early seventies, when Diana wore short polyester dresses and thick pale lipstick. Sonny would squire them from one Chicago nightclub to the next, and each time they went inside she felt they were expected, that the party could really begin now that they had arrived. In pictures from those days James and Sonny looked surprisingly big-eared and eager. They were typewriter salesmen for IBM, and had started a side business marketing inventions – a solar bicycle, aerosol tanning lotion – that failed one by one and left them nearly bankrupt. In the end James quit and went to law school; Sonny later cashed in on fast-food investments he'd had the prescience to make early on. But in those first days they'd been convinced success was imminent, and would wedge fat cigars between their teeth and talk about the good life. Diana pictured it coming suddenly and with violence, a shock that would leave them reeling. But like so many things, success took longer than they thought to arrive, and by the time it came, it merely seemed their due.

After a second round of drinks, Diana went down to the cabin. The sun hurt her eyes – it had been like that since she'd started researching her dissertation, 'Crisis and Catharsis in the Films of Alfred Hitchcock'. She had promised James she would cut down the hours she spent viewing, but lately she found that everything in her life – the telephone calls, the endless, hopeful pounding of their son Daniel's basketball against the garage door as he struggled to match his father, the bills and invitations – seemed like nothing but distractions from Hitchcock's tense, dreamlike world, where even the clicking of heels was significant. Diana often felt weirdly nostalgic as she watched, as if her own life had been like that once – dreamy, Technicolor – but had lost these qualities through some misstep of her own.

James came down to the cabin. He glanced up toward the deck, smiling, and shook his head. 'Nothing changes,' he said.

'Am I crazy,' Diana said, 'or is it more romantic this time?'

'You're crazy,' James said.

'I guess it's always romantic when two people fall in love,' Diana mused. 'Even if it turns out not to be real.'

'Turns out!'

'Well, never was.'

'It's been a long time since the last one,' James said, washing his hands in the sink. 'I thought maybe he was outgrowing it.'

'Oh, let's hope not!' Diana said.

James gave her an odd look, then opened the small refrigerator and peered inside it. He'd been a star basketball forward at the University of Michigan, and still had the ropey limbs and urgent, visible veins of an athlete. Lately Diana had wakened sometimes in the middle of the night to find James's eyes wide open. 'What are you thinking about?' she would ask repeatedly, nervously, though he writhed under her scrutiny. She was worried he was having an affair, or wishing he were having one.

'You know,' she said, moving near him, 'today makes me think of the old days.'

'Me, too,' James said. He was tossing things into a bowl: mayonnaise, ketchup, Tabasco, chopped celery.

Diana watched his face. 'We've changed since then,' she said. 'More than Sonny.'

'Let's hope so.' James looked up, meeting her eyes. 'How?'

'I'm not sure.'

She had noticed that she and her husband were more affectionate in public than in private nowadays, as if the presence of other people relieved some pressure between them. 'I mean, back then,' she said, 'how do you think we expected our lives to turn out?'

James picked up an egg and rolled it from one palm to the other a few times, then set it gently on the counter.

'We were kids,' he said.

Years before, while she and James were dating, Diana had once been seduced by Sonny. At the time she was twenty-three and fresh out of Smith. Sonny didn't like her. She'd been trying for weeks to win him over, but he seemed hardly to notice. She and James were staying on Lake Erie at the house Sonny had borrowed that summer, and while James made crayfish stew for dinner in the main house, Diana brought Sonny a Scotch in the cabin he used as a painting studio. He painted copies: Pollock, Motherwell, Kline, de Kooning – anything really, as long as it was abstract (he drew badly). He worked from small reproductions cut from the pages of books, and his results were uncannily good. They filled the walls of his Clark Street apartment, and first-time visitors were astonished by the daunting collection he seemed to have amassed.

Sonny surprised Diana that day by looking pleased to see her. It was raining, and while she shook the drops from her hair, Sonny shut the door behind her and lifted the drink from her hand. He sipped, then handed it back for her to share. 'I'm pretty hard on James's girlfriends,' he observed.

'I've noticed. Is that a policy?' She was nervous, and held the glass in both hands.

'I keep the boundaries clear, nobody gets the wrong idea,' he said.

It took Diana a moment to understand. 'God, it's not like anyone would,' she said. 'I mean, you're James's best friend.'

'That's why it scares me.'

He went to the window and looked outside at the rain. Diana sipped his drink, relieved it was only this he'd had against her, not something worse.

'You think I should relax about it?' he asked.

'Sonny, you have to promise.'

She crossed the room and stood beside him. She had finished the Scotch, and now she felt loopy, bold. Setting the glass at her feet, she took Sonny's hand. 'Friends?' she asked.

He nodded, then shyly put his arms around her. As they hugged, Diana teased herself, imagining what it would be like to make love to Sonny. Then he drew back, took her face in his hands, and kissed her.

Diana was as stunned as if he had slapped her. Gently she tried to pull away, but Sonny was running his palms along her back and kissing her neck as if this were all something they had agreed on. She tried to take it as a joke. 'I've heard of self-contradiction,' she said, 'but this is outrageous.' Sonny didn't pause, and as the moments passed, Diana felt drawn in by his fierce arousal, by the very fact that something so unthinkable was actually happening. The feeling was not quite desire, but something like it. It held her still while Sonny eased her onto the concrete floor, pushing a folded rag behind her head. She was crying by then, and tears ran from her eyes into both ears. She pulled Sonny to her, hooking her fingers over the thick ridges of muscle along his spine. He felt heavy and strange in her arms. His belt buckle struck the concrete – once, then again, over and over again with a thick, blunt sound. She closed her eyes at the end. When Sonny was done he stood up, slapped the dust from his hands, and picked up his paintbrush. Diana touched the floor beneath her, thinking she might have bled, though there was no reason. She ran through the rain back to the house, convinced her life would never be the same.

But nothing happened. No mention of the incident was ever made, and Sonny never again laid a hand on her except in the most benign affection. Only one thing changed: he liked her after that. It was as if she had passed some test or – and she tried not to think about this – as if she were partly his. What troubled her most was that she couldn't forget it; not Sonny himself so much as the paintbrushes soaking in their jars of cloudy water, the rolls of unstretched canvas, each detail bringing with it an ache of longing that still haunted her sometimes.

When Diana returned to the deck, Sonny and Billie were on the flybridge. 'This baby measures depth,' Sonny said, and sipped his drink. 'There's where you pump out the bilge.'

'What's a bilge?' Billie asked.

She was wearing a captain's hat, and Diana wondered if it was the same one her son, Daniel, used to wear as a little boy when they took him out on this boat. He was Danny then, and although he cringed to hear it now, Diana secretly preferred the childish name. He would sit on the tall seat, the hat nearly covering his eyes, and swing his legs while Uncle Sonny let him steer the boat. Sonny always kept one hand on the wheel; for all his recklessness, he'd been careful with Danny. 'Kid, I'm raising you for the fast lane,' he'd say.

Diana went to the stern and gazed at the lake. She was jealous of Sonny and Billie, though clearly this was absurd – they'd be lucky to last out the week. Yet in a sense it was this she envied: the fantasy, its tinge of the illicit. She stared toward shore and tried to block out Sonny's voice. A narrow strip of land was barely visible through the haze, yet it seemed, for a moment, to hold out some whispery promise – tennis courts, gin and tonics, secret, sweaty unions behind flowerbeds … Lord, what was wrong with her?

When James came up on deck, Sonny pulled a bottle of champagne from an ice chest and popped the cork. Billie held the glasses while he poured, champagne spilling over her fingers and along the frosted stems.

'It's suicide drinking in this heat,' Sonny said with relish.

James collapsed in a chair and set the bowl of tuna salad at his feet. 'Make mine a double,' he said.

'That's a bit morbid,' Diana said, but he didn't laugh.

Sonny passed the glasses around. His white shirt was transparent with sweat, and through it Diana noticed the darkness of his chest hair, the belly rearing up under his ribcage. Today would be one more day in a long spree for Sonny, and she found this comforting. Somewhere, at least, the party never ended.

'James, baby, I toast to you,' Sonny, said, slinging an arm around James and thumping his back. He must have noticed James was down, Diana thought – Sonny was quick to notice things like that. 'You ought to be reminded every half hour you're a saint from heaven,' he declared, breathing hard.

'Should've married you, Sonny,' James said.

'Bingo,' Sonny said. 'Would've saved us both a heap of trouble.'

'Now, wait a minute,' Diana said, laughing.

Billie watched with rapt attention, her legs drawn under her chin. 'You all must've had some nice adventures, being friends so long,' she said.

'Adventures. Christ,' Sonny said, flopping onto a chair. He turned to James and Diana and all three of them laughed, helpless at how many there were.

'I wish I could've been there,' Billie said.

Sonny took her hand and swung it gently in the space between their chairs. His own hands were small and over-muscled, crowded with jeweled rings he'd smuggled in from somewhere. Billie ran her fingers over the rings.

A lazy silence fell, and they lolled back in their chairs. Diana reached for James's hand, pleased to feel his fingers relax into her own. She thought of the old days; stories they still told about parties that started calmly – like Hitchcock's movies – and then spun out of control. 'Am I imagining it,' she said, 'or was life completely different twenty years ago?'

Sonny laughed. 'Not mine.'

'Nothing changes but your body,' James said, patting Sonny's gut.

'I could have some fun in yours, that's for sure,' Sonny said.

'It's not like you're doing so badly,' Diana pointed out.

Sonny turned to her. 'I mean, what does he need it for? Parking himself in that stodgy office?'

'I work pretty hard,' James said, 'believe it or not.'

Sonny pulled another bottle from the ice chest and shot the cork into the lake. When James covered his glass, Sonny poured right over his hand until James yanked it away, shaking champagne from his fingers. Sonny filled each glass to the top, so it spilled in their laps when they tried to drink. His unflagging excess lifted Diana's spirits. She could already hear herself, weeks from now at someone's dinner party: 'We were out on Sonny's boat. His stolen bride was there, and Sonny'd been drinking for days ...'

'What will the two of you do after you're married?' she asked, unable to resist. 'What kind of lives will you have?'

James stared at her in disbelief.

'We'll give parties,' Billie said. 'Right?'

'Sure, lots of parties,' Sonny said. 'Parties every night.'

'I hope you'll invite us,' Diana said.

'Of course,' Sonny assured her. 'You'll be the guests of honor.' He waited for James to speak. 'Come on, buddy. Crash course on married life. Should we get a dog? One of those basketball hoops above the garage? Cheez Whiz and Ritz Crackers?'

Billie listened with a frown, her idea of marriage to Sonny having clearly assumed a rather different shape.

'Follow your instincts,' James said mockingly. 'You're made for marriage, Sonny. It's written all over you.'

The sarcasm caught Sonny off guard. He studied James. 'So it's that easy,' he said. 'And here I've been admiring you all these years.'

'You've kept that a secret.'

'What do you mean? I tell everyone.' Sonny refilled the glasses and shoved the bottle back inside the ice chest. 'There was a time,' he explained to Billie, 'when James and I were in business together.'

'Don't, Sonny,' James said. He hadn't touched his last drink.

'We introduced a few inventions before the world was ready for them. Then James abandoned ship.'

'The ship was sinking. I had a wife and a kid.' He, too, spoke to Billie, as if a word from her would determine, finally, who had lived the better life. She looked from one to the other, flushed from their sudden attention.

'Anyway, being a lawyer isn't so bad,' Sonny said, draining his glass and setting it on the deck. 'It's just boring as hell.'

Billie stood up and moved behind Sonny's chair. She reached her arms around his chest and rested her head on his shoulder, closing her eyes. Her long hair gathered in his lap. Sonny wound a strand around his finger. James looked away.

'What's boring as hell,' James said, 'is hearing you tell the same lies year after year.'

Sonny burst out laughing. 'Less boring than the truth,' he cried.

'What're you talking about?' Billie demanded, letting go of Sonny and turning on James.

James shook his head. Sonny continued laughing in a loud, forced way. Now Billie marched over to James and stood before him. 'How dare you insult my husband,' she declared, using a voice she must have heard somewhere and liked the sound of.

'He's not your husband yet, and I wouldn't be in such a hurry.'

Sonny let out a whoop. 'Bastard!'

'James,' Diana said.

But James was looking up at Billie, who loomed over him now, hands on her hips, her pointy elbows shaking. 'I'd marry him before you any day of the week,' she said.

'No one's asking you to marry me,' James said quietly.

They stared at each other, Billie in a stance of pure childish defiance, James with a kind of confusion, as if the anger he felt toward this young, beautiful girl were a mystery to him.

'I'd go back to my fiancé first,' Billie muttered.

'Give that some thought,' James said. 'Because if Sonny still remembers your name next month, you'll have done better than most.'

Billie hesitated, smiling uneasily. She looked unsure of what James meant at first. Then she said, 'I don't believe you. You're just jealous.'

James said nothing. He looked suddenly tired.

'And even if he used to be like that,' Billie said more loudly, 'I couldn't care less, because Sonny loves me.' She turned to Sonny. 'Right?'

But Sonny's eyes were closed, and he appeared lost in some private contemplation. Billie watched him, waiting. Finally he managed to open his eyes and look at her, squinting as if she were a piece of bright foil. 'That's right, baby,' he said. 'It's different this time.'

Billie held very still, as if waiting to experience the comfort of these words. Then she began to cry. Her shoulders curled, and she lifted her hands to her face. Diana left her chair and took the girl in her arms.

Sonny shut his eyes again. Sunlight poured over his face, and sweat glittered in the creases of his skin. He opened his eyes and looked at James. 'I slept with your wife,' he said.

Diana froze, still holding the sobbing Billie. Everything seemed to tilt, and a finger of nausea rose in her throat. 'James, it was a hundred years ago,' she said.

'I don't remember it,' Sonny said, 'but I know it happened.'

James rose slowly from his chair, and went to the edge of the boat. He gazed toward the shore. Billie had quieted down and was looking with smeary, fascinated eyes from Sonny to James.

James turned and veered toward Sonny, who rose halfway out of his chair before James hit him twice in the face, knocking him backward over the chair and into the rail. Billie screamed and clung to Diana. Sonny lay with his mouth open, blood running from his nose.

Billie and Diana went to Sonny, took his arms and tried to haul him to his feet, but he shook them off and stood up slowly. His breath stank of alcohol, not just a few drinks but a thick, rotten sweetness. Drops of red bloomed on his collar. He hovered unsteadily, pushing the hair from his eyes. 'I'm gonna kill you,' he said to James, 'I swear to God.'

'Do it,' James said.

Sonny came at James and attempted a clumsy punch, which James blocked easily. But Sonny followed almost instantly with a second, jabbing James high under his ribs, seeming to force the breath from him. Then again, in the chin, so James staggered backward.

'Stop it!' Diana screamed, and tried with Billie to come between them, but it was impossible; the men shoved them away and lunged for one another in a frenzy, pounding, grunting, as if each believed his own survival hinged purely on the other's annihilation. Blood ran from Sonny's nose over his teeth, gathering in the cracks between them. He choked and started to cough, then went at James again, slugging his ear before finally James caught him in that boxing hold Diana had seen on TV, when the fighters seem to hug each other, heads down, so neither can move.

A perfect stillness opened around them. Everyone seemed to wait. Diana noticed the whiteness of Sonny's cuffs, a scar behind James's ear from his basketball days, the slick, marmalade-colored planks at her feet. The world disappeared; the only sound was the men's breathing.

Finally James let Sonny go and waited, poised for a response. But Sonny was barely able to stand. His eyes were running – it could have been the sun or the blow to his nose. Diana had never seen him cry in all the years she had known him, and found it hard to watch. But Billie couldn't take her eyes away from Sonny. She wore a look Diana recognized, the sick, scared look of a girl whose mischief has gotten her in trouble, who suspects her life will never be the same.

Sonny went to a chair and sat down heavily. He picked up a glass and downed what was left inside it, then fumbled for the bottle. 'I can't kill you, buddy, I just realized,' he said, making an effort to smile. 'I'd be too lonely without you.'

It was not until James started the motor that the world seemed to move again. A wind blew, the boat shook, and Diana inhaled the smell of gasoline. From the deck she watched her husband swing the boat around, his knuckles on the wheel, the hollow of his spine against his shirt. She was afraid to go near him. Sonny hadn't moved from his chair. His head was thrown back, and under his nose he held a towel filled with ice Billie had brought him. One eye was already going black.

Slowly Diana inched toward James, hesitating behind him on the flybridge. He had not glanced at her once since the fight with Sonny, and she felt as if he never would again. Finally she went around in front of him and touched his cheek, which was swollen and bloody. To her surprise, James grinned. Diana studied him, not sure what this meant. 'The good old days,' he said, and shook his head.

He put an arm around Diana, and they stood side by side watching Billie, who was hunched alone at the bow. As the boat thumped over the lake, she leaned forward, watching the thick folds of water peel aside. Her curls had vanished, and now her thin, straight hair whipped madly around her head. Diana had an urge to go to her, to promise Billie she would thank God one day that none of this had worked. But she doubted the girl would believe her.

More than a year passed before James and Diana saw much of Sonny again. By then Diana had earned her PhD and was teaching in the Film Studies Department at the U of I's Circle Campus. Sonny had grown even fatter, and his complexion was the color of raw oysters. The doctor issued continual warnings, but Sonny's only response had been to take up occasional smoking. Diana noticed that he flicked the cigarette constantly, so that it never had time to gather any ash.

'Remember that time I almost killed you?' he would ask James sometimes when they'd had a few drinks. 'I should've let you have it – don't know what stopped me.'

'Willpower,' James said, grinning at Diana. 'Pure self-restraint.'

'Don't kid yourself, buddy. It was pity.'

This was one story James and Diana never told at parties. Except sometimes the beginning, where Sonny made off with a bride on the eve of her own wedding. The rest they kept to themselves, hardly mentioning it, lest it take on that eerie power of old movies and faded snapshots, an allure against which the present day could only pale.

Now and then Diana still thought of Billie, who had gone back to her original fiancé and married him. Somewhere in the Deep South, Diana guessed, the girl must occasionally tell the story of her brief elopement with a madman. 'It was terrible!' she would say. 'It was something out of hell.' Yet Diana guessed that when Billie looked at the familiar trappings of her life and recalled that strange day, she was sometimes wistful.

ATLANTIC CROSSING

Jeanette Winterson

Jeanette Winterson (b. 1959) is a British writer. Her first novel, *Oranges are Not the Only Fruit,* won the 1985 Whitbread Prize for a First Novel and was adapted into a BAFTA-winning television programme. Winterson was awarded an OBE in 2006 for services to literature.

I met Gabriel Angel in 1956. The year Arthur Miller married Marilyn Monroe. I was going home. Gabriel Angel was leaving home. We were both going to the same place. We were going to London. The Millers were there too at the time.

The *Cowdenbeath* was a pre-war liner with a mahogany lining. She looked like a bath-time boat with two fat black funnels and a comfortable way of sitting in the water. She had been money and ease, the Nancy Astor generation, not the frugal fifties.

She had been requisitioned as a troop ship during the war, and now her cruising days were over, she was faded, just a ferry, when I got to her. Once a month she sailed from Southampton to St Lucia and once a month she sailed back again. One end of the bath to the other in eight days. She didn't have glamour but she had plenty of stories to tell and I've always liked that in a woman. It is what I liked about Gabriel Angel.

Journeys make me nervous, so I was up too early on the morning of my leaving, opening and shutting my trunk and bothering the porters about safe storage. The gangway up to the *Cowdenbeath* was busy with bodies run random like ants before ants. There was freight to be loaded, food to get on board, everything to be cleared before eleven o'clock embarkation.

Invisible worlds, or worlds that are supposed to be invisible interest me. I like to see the effort it takes for some people to make things go smoothly for other people. Don't misunderstand me; mostly I'm part of the invisible world myself.

A couple of hours after I had permanently creased my permanent press suit by sitting hunched up in a roll of rope, I saw a good-looking black woman, maybe twenty, maybe twenty-five, standing with her feet together, a little brown suitcase in her hand. She was staring at the boat as if she intended to buy it. If the sea hadn't been on one side; she would have walked right round, her head cocked like a spaniel, her eyes eager and thoughtful.

After a few moments she was joined by a much older woman with a particular dignity. The younger one said something to her, then spread out her arm towards the ship. Whatever it was, they both laughed, which did nothing for my nerves. I wanted to be reassured by the imposing vessel before me, not have it picked at like a cotton bale.

I climbed out of my rope hole, grabbed my hat, and sauntered towards them. They didn't give me a glance, but I heard the older one asking to be sent a tin of biscuits with a picture of the Queen on the lid. It is the same all over the Commonwealth; they all love the latest Queen. She's too young for me.

The steward showed me to my cabin. Mr Duncan Stewart D22. I opened my hand luggage, spread a few things on the lower bunk, and went back up on deck to watch the spectacle. I like to see the people arriving. I like to imagine their lives. It keeps me from thinking too much about my own. A man shouldn't be too introspective. It weakens him. That is the difference between Tennessee Williams and Ernest Hemingway. I'm a Hemingway man myself although I don't believe it is right to hunt lions.

Look at these two coming on deck right now; lesbians I'll bet. Both about sixty-five, shrunk into their cotton suits and wearing ancient Panamas. The stout one has a face the colour and texture of a cricket ball and the thin one looks as if she's been folded once too often.

What brogues the stout one is wearing; polished like conkers and laced too tight. Shoe lacing is a revealing and personal matter. There are criss-cross lacers; the neat brisk people who like a pattern under the surface. There are straight-lacers; who pretend to be tougher than they are but when they come undone, boy, are they undone. There are the tie-tights; the ones who need to feel secure, and there are the slack-jacks, who like to leave themselves a little loose, the ones who would rather not wear shoes at all. I've met people who always use a double knot. They are liars. I'm telling you because I know.

Once the lesbians had gone by, trailing their old woman smell of heavy scent and face powder, I went back downstairs, intending to nap for an hour. I was suddenly very tired. I wanted to get my jacket off, let my feet smell, and wake up an hour later to a Scotch and Soda. In my mind I was through the sleep and tasting the drink.

I opened the door to my cabin. There was the young woman I had noticed earlier on the dock. She turned at the noise of the door and looked surprised.

'Can I help you?' she said.

'There must be some mistake' I said, 'this is my cabin.' She frowned and picked up a cabin list from the top of her little suitcase. Her voice lilted.

'D22. G Angel and D Stewart.'

'That's right. I am Duncan Stewart.'

'And I am Gabriel Angel.'

'You should be a man.'

She looked confused and examined herself in the mirror. I tried to pursue this obvious line. Obvious to me.

'Gabriel is a man's name.'

'Gabriel is an angel's name,' she said.

'Angels are men. Look at Raphael and Michael.'

'Look at Gabriel.'

I did look at her. No wings but great legs. Still I was tired and did not want to argue theology with a young woman I had never met. I thought about the bunk and the Scotch and started feeling sorry for myself. I decided to go and tackle the Purser.

'You stay here until I get back' I commanded, 'I'll straighten it out.'

I didn't straighten it out. The ship was crammed to the lifeboats. The Purser, like me, like any normal person guided by Bible basics, had assumed Gabriel was a man's name. That's why we had been yoked together. Second Class ticket holders can't be choosy. I had to explain all this to her but she didn't flinch. Either she was as innocent as she looked or she was an old hand. Some of these girls have been milking men since breast-swell. I didn't want any trouble.

'Top or bottom?' I asked, getting ready to move my stuff.

'Top' she said. 'I like heights.'

She climbed up and lay down and I eased myself below, keeping my shoes on, in case my feet smelled. I was disappointed. I had expected to share but I had hoped for some tough guy who wanted late night Scotch and a pack of cards. When you dig under the surface, past the necessities, men and women don't mix.

Her head came dipping over the side of the bunk.

'Are you asleep?'

'Yes.'

'So am I.'

There was a pause, then she asked me what I did for a living.

'I'm a business man. I do business.'

She was looking at me upside down, like a big brown bat. She was making me feel sea-sick.

'What about you?' I said, not caring.

'I'm an aviator.'

Eight days at sea. One day longer than God needed to invent the whole world, including its holiday pattern. Two days longer than he took to make her Grandmother Eve and my Grandfather Adam. This time I am not falling for the apple.

We sat up on deck today, Gabriel Angel and myself. She told me she was born in 1937, the day that Amelia Earhart had become the first woman to complete the Atlantic crossing, solo flight. Her granddaddy, as she calls him, told her it was an omen, and that's why they called her Gabriel, 'bringer of Good News', a bright flying thing.

Her granddaddy taught her to fly in the mail planes he ran between the islands. He told her she had to be smarter than life, find a way of beating gravity, and to believe in herself as angels do, their bodies bright as dragonflies, great gold wings cut across the sun.

I'm not against anyone fastening their life to an event of some significance and that way making themselves significant. God knows, we need what footholds we can find on the glass mountain of our existence. Trouble is, you climb and climb, and around middle age, you discover you have spent all the time in the same spot. You thought you were going to be somebody until you slip down into the nobody that you are. I'm telling you because I know.

She said, 'I am poor but even the poorest inherit something, their daddy's eyes, their mother's courage. I inherited the dreams.'

I leaned back. I could see in her a piece of the bright hope I once had in myself and it made me sour and angry. It made me feel sorry for her too. I wanted to take both her hands in mine, look her in the eye, and let her see that the world isn't interested in a little black girl's dreams.

She said, 'Mr Stewart, have you ever been in love?' She was leaning over the side, watching the ocean. I watched the curve of her spine, the slender tracings of her hips, beneath her dress. I wanted to touch her. I don't know why. She's too young for me.

Before I could answer, although I don't know how I would have answered, she started talking about a man with stars in his hair and arms stretched out like wings to hold her.

I moved away as soon as I could.

What is there to say about love? You could sweep up all the words and stack them in the gutter and love wouldn't be any different, wouldn't feel any different, the hurt in the heart, the headachy desire that hardly submits to language. What we can't tame we talk about. I'm talking a lot about Gabriel Angel.

If I were able to speak the truth, I'd say I had a fiancée before the War, and we're going back to 1938 now. She had a thick plait of hair that ran all the way down her back. She could wrap her hair around her as though it were a snake. I was no snake charmer.

She was a farmer's daughter, had a heart like a tractor to pull any man out of himself. Her hair was red the way the sun is red first thing in the morning. She had a look about her that took everything seriously, even the wood pile. There were plenty of men who would have traded their bodies for a split log, just to be under her hands for five minutes. I know I would. We didn't touch much. She didn't seem to want it. When we said goodnight at the bottom of her lane she let me run my index finger from her temple to her throat. Such soft hair she had on her face, invisible, but not to my hand.

If I were young again, I would have bounced up to Gabriel Angel on the dock and asked her to come with me on the later sailing. That would have been the Italian line, the real cruise ship. SS *Garibaldi* softly rocking the Mediterranean. Forget the direct Atlantic crossing, carrying workers and immigrants to a cold place they've never seen. I could have held her hand through Martinique, Las Palmas, Tenerife. I could have put my arm around her waist through the straits of Gibraltar. At Barcelona I would have bought her gem Madonnas and seed pearls. Then we would have continued by sea to Genoa and met the boat-train for England. That railway, through Italy, Switzerland and France was laid in the 1850s and was one of the first to be constructed. I'm told that Robert Browning, poet, and Mrs Elizabeth Barrett Browning, also poet, travelled along its length. I would have enjoyed that connection. I should like to run away with Gabriel Angel.

As it is, we're on this ferry boat to Southampton, the short direct brutal route, and Gabriel Angel has never been in my arms.

It turns out that the two lesbians are missionaries. Miss Bead, the one with a face like a love-note somebody crushed in his fist, tells me they have been in Trinidad for thirty years. Miss Quim, the cricket ball, has taught three generations of hockey teams. They are on their way home to buy a farmhouse together in Wales and get a dog called Rover. I realise they are happy.

I am not sleeping well. Below my cabin is dormitory accommodation, the cheapest way to travel. That's all right, what's wrong is the Barbados Banjo Band, twenty-five of them, on their way to the dancehalls of England. It isn't easy to sleep well piled on top of fifty feet, five hundred fingers and toes and forty-six eyes. Above me are the maddening curves of Gabriel Angel.

In the ship's lounge, proudly displayed, is a large map of the Atlantic threaded through with the red line of our route. Every day one of the stewards moves a gay green flag further along the red line, so that we can see where we are. Today we have reached the middle; the point of no return. Today the future is nearer than the past.

I don't have anyone to go to in England. No one will be waiting for me at Southampton or Victoria. I have a two-bedroomed terraced house in London. I have had it let for the past twelve years and I'll have to live in a boarding house until it becomes vacant again next month. I won't recognise anything familiar. I had the agents furnish it cheaply for me.

Later, my cargo will arrive and I'll start selling Caribbean crafts and trinkets and I suppose I'll go on doing that until something better comes along or until I die. Looking at my future is like looking at a rainy day through a dirty window.

'You must be excited Mr Stewart.'

'What about, Miss Angel?'

She has been reading my copy of *Wuthering Heights* by Emily Brontë and now she wishes she could live in Yorkshire. I must be careful not to lend her *Rob Roy*.

Is compassion possible between a man and a woman? When I say (as I have not said), 'I want to take care of you', do I mean 'I want you to take care of me?'

I am materially comfortable. I can provide. I could protect. I have a lot to offer a young woman in a strange place without friends or money.

'Will you marry me Miss Angel?'

It is early in the morning, not yet six o'clock. I have dressed carefully. My tie is even and my shoes are well polished and double knotted. Anyone can look at me now. Up on deck the sea chops at the boat, the waves are like grey icing, forked over. The wind is whipping my coat sleeves and making my eyes water.

Today we will dock at Southampton and I will catch the train to Victoria station and shake hands with my fellow travellers and we will wish each other well and forget each other at once. I think I'll spend tonight in a good hotel.

Last night I could not sleep, so I climbed the bunk ladder and stared at Gabriel

Angel, lying peacefully under the dim yellow safety lamp. Why doesn't she want me?

The sun is rising now, but it is 93,000,000 miles away and I can't get warm. Soon Gabriel Angel will come on deck in her short sleeved blouse and carrying a pair of borrowed binoculars. She won't be cold. She has the sun inside her.

I wish the wind would drop. A man looks silly with tears in his eyes.

MY SON THE HERO

Clare Boylan

Clare Boylan (1948–2006) was an Irish author, journalist and critic. Born in Dublin, she began her career as a journalist, winning the Journalist of the Year award in 1974 when working for the *Evening Press*. Boylan went on to concentrate on fiction, and published seven novels and three collections of short stories.

On his way home from the pub my son Ken rescued a kitten up a tree. 'Must have been a big kitten,' I said when I saw the state of his shirt. Bits of it had stuck to his chest where something had clawed through fabric and flesh.

'No,' Ken said solemnly. 'It was only small.' He made a shape with his hands about the size of a rat. His nose was cut and there were great big rusty tracks down his face.

There was something about the shirt – all bloody and chewed, like a hen left by a fox. Already I didn't like that kitten. 'If it was up a tree' – gingerly, I peeled it off and pushed it into a bucket – 'you should have left it. Cats know how to get out of trees.'

Ken scoured his head with the insides of his eyes. He had a way of considering the simplest question as if it were complex and profound, of looking back into his head for answers. 'There was a gang of kids standing round the tree. They had a dog – big, fat bastard. Cat was afraid.'

'Weren't you afraid?' I touched him and he trembled. 'They give you a hard time?'

'Yeah.' He put his hand to his bloody nose. With his fingers close to his face he gave a start and then drew back to study the purple semicircle behind the thumb, as if his hand had been caught in a gin trap. He put his two hands away carefully between his knees. 'She bit me,' he said indignantly.

'Who bit you?'

'Bloody dog.'

'Mind your language, Ken!'

To tell the truth I didn't care about the language, or the shirt. I was proud of Ken. He's not bright. People think I've wasted my life on him. Even his own father said that. Then he left us. Well, there's worse things to waste your life on. I know there's not much going on but there's courage and there's tenderness. That's worth something. You need some tenderness in the world today. Every day you read terrible things in the papers – babies murdered, old women robbed, their jaws broken and their false teeth smashed. Only the next day there was a story of some poor young girl missing. It gave me a start because it was in our own neighbourhood. I did a wash to take my mind off things, but when I went to get Ken's shirt, it was gone. 'Ken!' I said. 'Did you take that shirt from the soak?'

'N-no!' he said, and he looked as guilty as a dog.

He was watching telly, so I went upstairs and searched his room. Break your heart to go in there – trainers, size 12, and a bed full of teddies – everything in a heap on the floor. Under the mattress a stack of chocolate wrappers, and the wet shirt, seeping into a pile of magazines. It was when I looked at those magazines that my heart went through me. They were men's magazine's – not the girlie ones with women showing what they'd had for breakfast, but dirty, cruel filth. I sat there shaking as I turned the sodden pages. Then I bawled down the stair. 'Ken!'

He lumbered up and peered round the door. 'You mad at me?'

'Why would I be mad?'

'My good shirt – all torn.'

'What about these?' I held out the magazines.

He gave a sort of sneer. 'Where did you get them, Ken?' He shook his head and looked away.

'Can't say. Reg told me not to say.'

Reg Fuller? 'What have you got to do with that scum, boy?'

'I'm not a boy.' His eyes filled with tears. 'I'm a man. Reg called me a man. He said men were mad for magazines like these. He sold me them.'

I swatted him with the bundle of wet filth. 'Did you like them, son? Is that the kind of thing you like?' I was scared. To me Ken's still a child. He began to cry. I put my arms around him. 'Men don't like those magazines, pet,' I told him. 'Reg Fuller was lying. They're just dirty rubbish. Where do we put dirty rubbish?'

'In the stove,' he snivelled.

'That's right, Ken. Put them in the stove.'

Poor Ken doesn't understand much. He put the shirt in the stove along with the magazines. Wet smoke belched out and I thought I could smell blood rising over the stench of burning fabric.

He didn't go out that night, maybe because his face was scratched and bloody or it might have been that gang. We watched the news, but it was all about that poor woman appealing for information about her missing daughter. A picture of the girl was put on the screen – little blonde, face like a flower. She was last seen talking to a man with a raincoat. 'Please don't hurt Denise,' the mother kept saying, but I could tell from the way her voice squeezed on the name that she knew Denise was already dead. Ken's face mimicked the anguish of the mother. 'He knows too,' I thought. People like him often do. 'Come on, love,' I said. 'Let's go down the pub for a drink.'

Off we went, him hanging on to my arm – the odd couple. Funny to think how much we share. The instinct to protect, for one. I've passed that on to him. Then there's the other thing, never admitted, the need for sex or love, the need to connect. I've taken magazines to bed too, stupid bare-assed hunks – probably gay. We're outcasts, Ken and me. All we've got is each other. No one will have him because of the way he is and no one will have me because I've got him. Something stuck in my brain like a splinter on that walk, but it couldn't work its way out because Reg Fuller turned up with his mates and started teasing my son.

'Got a girl, have you, Ken? We saw you with a little blonde. What have you done with your girlfriend?'

'You leave him alone,' I said. Ken sank his face in his collar, puffy and bright pink. 'Have you got a girlfriend, Ken?' I said gently. He shook his head.

'Wouldn't know what to do with a girl, would you Ken?' they called after him

He shuffled on for a bit, then turned back jerkily. 'I would!'

'How would you know, Ken?'

I hurried him on. I hadn't much covered that side of life with him. Best not to stir up what's never going to crop up. 'Those magazines,' he mumbled.

'Oh, Ken, no!' I held his face. 'That's not what you do with a girl.' He didn't understand. He didn't understand anything.

Denise Carroll's body was found in a wheelie bin. Terrible things had been done to her. She was 21, an economics student, out for a drink with some friends. The thing that struck me was how she had fought to live. Bits of the man's skin and clothing were under her nails. His hair was in her fists. Extraordinary how people cling to life, even when it is most debased. Extraordinary how human evil can make an ordinary thing like a bin sinister. Ken felt it too. When I asked him to put out the bin he gave a shudder. I watched him standing in the rain, just staring at the bin. 'Where's your raincoat, Ken?' I called out. He peered down at his body as if he expected to see it there.

'Gone,' he said in surprise.

'Where?' You get exasperated, but it's no use.

'I left it somewhere.'

'Weren't you wearing it when you went to the pub the other night?' I said and suddenly I remembered what it was that had stuck in my head. He couldn't have rescued a kitten from a tree on his way home from the pub. There are no trees on that walk.

'Ken,' I said. 'Show me where the kitten was.' I grabbed his hand and dragged him back to the pub.

'It was there!' He stabbed his big blunt hand in several different directions.

'There's no tree there, Ken.' I was trying to be patient but my voice was shaking. 'You have to show me the tree.'

He looked around blankly. 'Gone,' he said with interest.

I forced him to look at me, trying to find a way past that blank expression, trying to imagine how she must have felt when she faced him. 'There was a girl, Ken, wasn't there?'

He looked vague for a minute and then he nodded.

'Why didn't you tell me about the girl?' I seized him and shook him. It was like trying to shake a bear.

'I forgot about her,' he said.

'Jesus, Ken. She must have been scared to death.'

He thought about this inside his head. He gave a sentimental smile and nodded. 'Yeah. She was really scared.'

'How could you do such a thing?'

'Because, because … ' I sometimes thought his brain must be like an old rubbish skip, where he had to throw out nearly everything before he could find anything that was useful. 'Because she wanted me to.'

That evening the police came. They said it was a routine enquiry, house to house. I had bathed Ken, scrubbed his nails, brushed his hair until it more or less sat down but I saw the way they looked at those gouge marks down his face. 'Where were you on Friday night?' they asked him. Ken peered back into his head. There was nothing I could do. There were witnesses who'd seen him – Reg Fuller, people in the pub.

'I can't remember,' he said. The thing that kept going round my head was the same phrase Denise Carroll's mother had used: 'Please don't hurt him.'

'We found a raincoat,' they said. 'We'd like you to come and take a look at it.'

Ken's face brightened. 'I lost my raincoat.'

After they'd left I gave Ken an early supper in bed – a hamburger with plenty of ketchup and four sleeping pills. I had told the police I'd bring him round the station in the morning. They were decent about that, said they'd send a car for him. Ken was quite excited about getting a ride in a cop car. When he'd eaten I sat by the side of his bed and held his hand. He's no beauty, but my heart caught on the innocent arch of his eyebrows, the mild curve of his mouth, bits of my features woven into his unfinished face. How had evil got into him? Was it evil, or just a man's desire coming through some twisted circuit, like carbon monoxide forced through a car window? Anyway, he was mine. I couldn't let them get him. I settled his pillows, slipping out the one that raised his head too high. I watched him a moment to remember how he looked asleep and then pressed the pillow over his head. I did it carefully, like pressing a cutter over pastry. It was very peaceful. Suddenly Ken's arms shot out; he reached out, wildly clawing at me. I lifted the pillow and saw the look on his face. Oh God, that face. I pressed down with all my might. Ken's strong, but the sleeping pills were against him. His arms fell. The doorbell rang. Bloody cops, back again! Of course they didn't trust me to bring him to the station. When I removed the pillow Ken looked like a squashed doll. I stood there clutching the pillow to my chest while the doorbell shrilled. As I turned to go downstairs there was a shudder from the bed and Ken regained his breathing with a mighty snore. I touched his forehead and he smiled.

At first there seemed to be no one at the door, but when I looked down there was a little girl, eight or nine. 'Is Ken there?' she said.

'Ken's in bed.' I kept my hand to my face to hide the scratches. 'So should you be.'

'I only found out tonight where he lives,' she said. 'I had to come and thank him. He got my kitten, Susie, down a tree.'

'Oh, my God,' I said.

'It was being chased by these big boys with a dog and it ran into someone's garden. They went in after it; I was terrified. Then Ken came along. He's very brave,' she, said admiringly. 'Those boys gave him a right going over. They set their dog on him.' She was about to go when she remembered the large carrier bag she was holding. 'Here's Ken's coat. He asked me to mind it when he went up the tree.'

She watched me oddly. 'Don't cry,' she said. 'Susie's all right. Oh, and she says she's very sorry. She gave Ken a terrible scraping, but we all do foolish things when we're frightened.'

THE ARTIST

Maggie Gee

Maggie Gee (b. 1948) is a British novelist who has written eleven novels and a collection of short stories. She was the first female Chair of the Royal Society of Literature, and is now one of the Vice-Presidents of the organisation. Her 2003 novel, *The White Family*, was shortlisted for the Orange Prize. She was awarded an OBE in 2012.

When Boris had only been with her a month, he came in from the garden holding a rose, a dark red complicated knot of velvet. Bowing slightly, he placed it in her fingers. 'Broke in accident,' he explained (he was repointing the brick at the back). It was her own rose he was offering her with that graceful, cavalier flourish. 'Put in water, Emma, please.'

'Beautiful, Boris,' she said, inhaling deeply, once, then again. The scent of the rose was so intense it shocked her, made her throat catch and her eyes prickle, as if life was suddenly all around her, as if she was breathing for the first time in years. Emma had hay fever, and avoided flowers. 'So beautiful, I shall write about it.' (She wrote novels, which had never been published, but she had a study, and told people she wrote.)

'I am artist,' said Boris, grinning at her with self-deprecating, dark-eyed charm. His teeth were very white, but one was chipped; he had a handsome, cherubic face. 'I am artist, you see, Emma. I am artist like you.' He jabbed his brown finger towards her, laughing. 'I make beautiful house for you.'

'Wonderful, Boris. Thank you. But really I just need the tiles laying out in squares. One black, one white, and so on.'

'Emma, I like you very much. I make you a beautiful floor, it is my present to you.' He bowed extravagantly, a knight. How old was he? Forty, fifty? 'I am artist, Emma,' he continued, showing her a piece of paper on which he had sketched an elaborate black and white design. 'You don't want one square – two square – one square – two square, black, white, same thing always. Very boring. No good!'

She took the paper from him, folded it narrowly, and slipped it back into the pocket of his jacket. 'That's just what I do want. Black, white, black, white. Like a chessboard. Simple. The tiles are in the garage. Now, I must go and work.'

Boris smiled at her forgivingly. 'Yes, you do your work, Emma, you write your books, beautiful. I like this very much, to work for an artist, like me.'

The rose was lovely, though slightly battered. She kissed it lightly before throwing it away.

*

'He's impossible,' she complained lazily to her husband as they lay in bed with their books, looking at Edward over her glasses, his familiar pinched profile in the cool blue room. She wanted to tell him, she wanted to tell someone, that Boris had given her a rose. 'Impossible. Edward? I'm talking to you.'

'Who is? For heaven's sake, I'm reading my book.'

'Boris,' she said.

He sat up and stared. 'Why do you keep talking about *this person*? Get a proper builder, an English one.'

'I tried, if you remember. You said the price was outrageous.'

'When you heard Boris's quote, you were very happy.'

'You found him, not me.'

'You agreed we should ask him.'

Edward couldn't deny it. He changed tack. 'You can't manage tradesmen, you never could. The cleaners never do what you tell them to.'

'The cleaners always leave. Because you won't let me pay them enough.'

'I'll talk to the fellow. I'll sort him out.'

'– No, Edward. It's fine, really.' She knew how Edward would talk to Boris, He would send him away, as he had threatened to do. Then the house would be empty every day. She liked Boris's voice, and his accent, which spoke to her of strange wide spaces somewhere far away in southeast Europe, hot stony fields, bright market-places, somewhere she would never go, she supposed, since now she so rarely went out at all. She could never tell Edward about the rose. Her memory of it wilted, faded. 'It's okay, Edward. Boris is – different.'

'What the hell does that mean?' How scornfully he spoke. Had he always spoken to her like that?

'Boris feels he's an artist. He isn't, of course. But he wants to be.' She enjoyed this thought. Poor Boris. What Emma did, he only dreamed of.

'Fraud and con man, like all the others. I want him out by the end of the week. Now could I *please* get on with my book?'

But she saw he was reading his Antiques Almanac, which surely could not have much of a plot-line. 'He lost everything, you know. In that bloody awful war. He didn't choose to come here. But now we can help him.' Saying it, Emma was suffused with love.

Edward sighed with irritation. 'He's just an illegal. That's why you're using him. Because he's cheap.' He snapped his book shut, lay down abruptly, and presented her with his navy silk back, taking off his glasses, clicking down the arms. 'A guy in the office said Afghans are cheaper. Good night, Emma.' In minutes he was snoring.

In September, when he should have been clearing out the drains, Boris had brought round his wife and daughter in a rusty, dust-covered grey saloon.

'Van break down. Very sorry.'

'Never mind, come in and get started.'

'No can do. I am in car, with wife, daughter … I can come in for cup of coffee, Emma, only.'

Boris loved her real coffee, which reminded him of home. 'Actually, I'm writing,' she protested, but he had already barrelled past her, sighing.

'What about your wife, your daughter?'

'They are well, thank you, Emma. Except only daughter –'

'I mean, you can't leave them out in the car, Boris.' It was a bore, but good manners demanded it.

'Yes, they love it.'

'Of course they don't love it. Go and ask them in.'

They trooped up the path, very straight-faced, in front of Boris, who drove them before him like sheep, looking off contemptuously to one side with a smile that seemed to say to the neighbours, 'I know, but these were all I could get.' 'Wife,' he jabbed one finger towards a thickset, grey-faced woman with hostile, uncomprehending eyes. 'Daughter,' and he put his hand on the girl's shoulder, but this time his voice was tinged with love and regret. 'Anna,' he added. 'Seventeen.' She was pretty, with her fathers white teeth and cherub nose, but her skin and lips were pale, too pale, her eyes had a slightly sunken look, and she was leaning on her mother.

'Hallo, Anna,' Emma smiled at the daughter. To the wife she tried, 'I'm sorry, I don't know your name,' but the woman's reply meant nothing to her. The words were guttural, unfamiliar.

'Will they have tea or coffee?' she asked Boris.

'No, they don't like,' said Boris, pushing them into the drawing-room, while trying to shepherd Emma back into the dining-room where the serious business of coffee would go on. 'Maybe daughter will have water.'

'Lemonade? Biscuits?'

'They don't want.'

'Water? I can hardly give them just *water*.'

Emma had broken away from Boris, doing her duty, reluctantly, and followed the two women into the drawing-room, where she found them standing together in front of the fireplace. 'Sit down,' Emma said, and they did, too promptly. 'Cake? Fruit juice? Milk? Herbal tea?'

The daughter took pity on her and explained. 'My mother speaks nothing,' she said. 'We like water, thank you, only water.'

'Water, okay then,' Emma said, reluctantly.

She got two glasses, but forgot to fill them, dreaming while Boris's coffee brewed. In the dining-room, Boris was inspecting, with what was surely self-conscious over-emphasis, the prints on the walls, frowning upwards, pursing his lips, nodding judiciously. 'Yes, very beautiful,' he said aloud, looking, not by accident, she thought, at a Lucian Freud of a naked woman. He must want her to see that he liked bare flesh. Such a terrible flirt! Though of course, she was flattered … He made as if to notice her a few seconds later. 'Daughter is ill,' he hissed.

'Oh dear, Boris.'

'Yes, I take to the doctor. But she need clean air. Air here very dirty. She cannot breathe, Emma. London very bad. Is dust, where we live, damp also. No good.'

'Oh, has she got asthma? What a shame –'

'Asthma, yes. In my country, she hasn't got it. Now she pray every day to Virgin, but she get it very bad.'

'I am so sorry, Boris. But don't worry. I myself have atrocious hay fever. They're all allergies. Have you considered acupuncture?' She mimed little needles jabbing into her arm. 'Maybe aromatherapy?'

He shook his heavy, curly head mournfully. 'Injection? No. Too much – never mind. More coffee, please, Emma.'

Invited in, at first, on a strictly limited basis, to repoint the fireplace, then repaint the drawing-room, Boris's role slowly became a roving one, as different parts of the house demanded his attention. He would announce these impending tasks to Emma, with a mixture of sorrow and glee.

Their relationship progressed in fits and starts. Boris nearly always complimented her. She had striking blue eyes, she had always known that, but he noticed the effect of different colours that she wore, and one day told her he would like to paint her. 'First paint my house,' she said, fondly, and he looked at her with a strange regret that made her think he was a little in love. It wasn't so surprising; she was still quite pretty, and his benefactor, and a writer. But her books became a stumbling block. Boris took everything literally; she had told him she wrote books, when he first came to the house. After a few months he asked if he could see one, just to flatter her, she thought, of course, and she deflected it. But he kept on asking, becoming more pressing, and in the end she had been forced to explain: she hadn't actually published any books. He seemed unreasonably disappointed. Was there a slight dimming of his admiration?

Boris was doing the exterior paintwork when Edward put his foot down. 'When will this clown get the job finished?' he raged at his wife.

'It's been very wet.'

'It isn't now. Has he been here today?'

'His daughter's been ill this week, so he's hardly been in,' Emma said, placatingly, but Edward glared at Boris's paint-pots straggling across the patio, and his brushes in tins of cloudy white spirit, sticking up at the sky at an irritating angle.

'He's never going to darken my doors again if he doesn't get the bloody job done and this mess out of the way before Friday!' he exploded. 'I mean it, Emma. Don't think I don't. We'll get in a decent English builder at last.'

Next day Boris arrived around four, looking worried. After giving up for months, he smelled of smoke again, 'Anna is in the hospital,' he explained. 'I just come to tell you how she is, Emma.'

She didn't make him tea. 'Edward says you have to finish the job by Friday or never come back, and he means it,' she said.

'She is very bad, Emma. Tea with sugar, please.'

'No, he is *serious*,' she said. 'You have to get it done.'

But Boris suddenly clutched her fingers, with an odd little moan. 'Last night they make us stay with her in hospital. Daughter's face goes blue ...'

She pulled her hand away. 'Boris what are you going to do?' she yelled at him, feeling her power at last, losing her temper with his handsome tanned face, his white broken teeth, his thick stupid curls, his foreign problems, the swamp of his need, sucking down tea and coffee and kindness, the scruples that stopped him making love to her, his pallid, boneless daughter and grey hopeless wife, the way he'd made her husband cross with her.

He looked shocked. 'Not to shout, Emma. I am sensitive, like you. I am artist. Not to shout.' He looked as though he was going to cry.

'All right, Boris. But you must get the job done.'

He rang on the door at seven thirty next morning, half an hour earlier than ever before. Emma was bleary and vague, in a hastily donned jade silk kimono. Boris's eyes ran automatically over her body, but his mouth was a line, and his eyes were bloodshot. 'Daughter very sick last night,' he said. 'Van is no good again. And I haven't car, because wife must have it to visit hospital. Emma, you will drive me.'

'Drive you where?'

'Drive me to find men.'

'Why haven't you found them already?' she screamed at him.

Boris was frightened of this new savage woman, so different from the mild, flirtatious one he knew. 'Please, Emma. I know where we find men. But quick, drive me now, please.'

'I'm not dressed,' she said. Not that she often did get completely dressed, nowadays, for why go out? Most days Boris came in.

'Emma, put on clothes now,' he insisted. She liked him sounding masterful, and went off upstairs without protesting, returning dressed in the first thing she found in her cupboard, a smart Chanel-copy suit with gold buttons and pink braid.

He looked at her strangely as she came downstairs, but he bowed slightly, and she felt exalted. She was excited: it was an outing. She didn't listen to what he was saying.

'Slow down,' he said, in the northern suburbs. 'Here we find men, Emma.' His mobile rang and he swore and dived for it. As the traffic waited at a bottleneck, he listened intently, then shouted at the phone, finally clicking it off after an explosion of furious consonants. Emma was surprised to see tears in his eyes.

'Are you all right, Boris?' she asked him, tentative.

'Yes, Emma. Now I do work.'

'But you're crying, Boris.'

'Is only dust.'

'Oh. That's good.'

Her attention was distracted. She was driving down a long desolate road, straight, running between Victorian terraces, but there was something in front of the terraces, something that at first she mistook for trees, grey shapeless trees with aimless branches, one or two hundred metres of trees, something that struck her as strange in a city, but then she realised they were not trees. They were thickets of men, standing in clumps, mostly silent, staring at the traffic, men in rough clothes with worn brown skin, men looking furtive, men looking hungry, men with no colour beneath their tans. Dozens of them. Scores. Hundreds? Not a single woman among those thin faces. Washed out tracksuits, ill-fitting trousers. Some of their hair was white with dust. Most of them were smoking lethargically. The slogans on their chests looked tired, dated.

'What is it, Boris? What's going on?'

'Here we find men. Stop car. I do it.'

'I don't want these people!' she found herself shouting. They looked ill and strange, not exotic like Boris. Scenting interest, some had turned towards the car. They were calling out, but she couldn't understand them. Then she caught some broken English: 'Only fifty!' 'Only forty!' She felt naked and stupid in her pink Chanel ribbons and terrible glittering golden buttons.

'Not to shout, Emma.' He looked very weary. 'Is okay. You leave to me.'

'They're not coming in my house. I want proper workmen.'

'Is workmen, Emma.' His phone rang again. He cursed, and threw it down on the back seat, got out of the car and left her alone.

On the pavement, Boris started talking to people. She sat inside trembling, clutching the steering-wheel. What if they suddenly rushed the car, snatched her handbag, raped her, mugged her? The phone rang again, urgent, painful. After thirteen rings she picked it up. A woman's voice shouted in an unknown language. 'I don't understand,' Emma whispered. The woman's cries became more desperate. 'I don't understand. Speak English, please,' Emma said. 'You're in England now. Please speak English.'

She felt better as she said it, briefly, in this unfamiliar place, that had no rules; she stood up for something she thought she believed in, but then the phone went silent, dead, and she laid it on the seat, and felt worse than ever. It must have been his wife. She spoke no English.

Boris came back with three hangdog giants. They got into the back without speaking a word. There was a smell of metal, and old cigarette smoke. They would make her car smell of men – for Edward was not, in that sense, a man.

'I think your wife phoned,' she said to Boris.

He shrugged. He would not look at her. 'Drive home please Emma. We finish the painting.'

The cloud had cleared by the time they got back, and the sun drilled through, fiercely hot. That long dark road with its unhealthy armies had left her with a spreading weight of terror. Boris had come to her on false pretences; he had let her imagine him framed by blue mountains, aromatic meadows, sturdy flocks, but now she saw he just came from this, a sour sad place where no one was happy.

They worked all day, the three strangers and Boris. She heard him shout at them from time to time. She went out twice, nervously, to see what they were doing, and offer tea, but Boris refused, waving one hand in dismissal, going on painting with the other one. She felt unsettled, sitting bowed in her study, trying to invent a love story, safe in her room in the cool pleasant house but uneasily aware of the four male bodies crawling all over it, obsessed, intent, locked to her hot surfaces, sweating, grunting.

The men stayed till seven, and then filed in, burnt red by the sun, hair splashed with white, lips grey-coated, refusing to look her in the eyes. They seemed barely human. She went out and inspected. The job was finished. Boris spoke to the others, who looked only at him, as if Emma herself hardly existed.

She needed Boris to smile at her, 'Would you like a drink, Boris?' she pleaded. 'You must be thirsty after all that work. While I put the money in an envelope.'

'No thank you, Emma. Men wait outside.'

'Oh, they'll be all right. They'll be perfectly happy.'

'No thank you, Emma. I go now, please.'

When Edward arrived, they had just disappeared. He was itching for a fight: the train was hellish, boiling. 'Did he bloody well turn up?' he shouted in the hallway.

'Go out and have a look,' said her voice from the study.

Five minutes later, Edward came back in and appeared at her door, actually smiling. 'At long last,' he said. 'Doesn't look too bad. And he's finally cleared all his paint pots away. The whole bloody lot. Why are you crying?'

In November, some tiles blew off the roof, and Edward instructed her to telephone Boris. She had missed him, sharply, day by day. When she tried his number, it was unobtainable. She rang it repeatedly, swearing and weeping.

Next day she got dressed as soon as Edward was gone and drove to the suburbs, remembering. Boris's sweet dark eyes, the slight roughness of his jaw. He had opened doors for her. Surely he liked her. He gave her a rose. He … admired her.

The forest of men was there, as before. She kept nearly stopping, was afraid, drove on, and finally drew up beside a young, slight man. He had a thin clever face, and black eyes like Boris's. Perhaps he came from the same country. She thought his mouth was quite appealing.

At twelve o'clock she called him in for coffee. 'Thirsty on the roof,' she said, kindly, with elaborate mime to help things along.

'I understand you,' he said. 'It's okay. Nearly everything, I understand. In my own country, I learned good English. I am a student. I *was* a student –' (Yes, she thought, they are all students. The minicab drivers all claimed to be students.) '… sixteenth and seventeenth century history … I am here because of the war.' He started to talk about invasions, displacements. Oh dear, she thought, he may be a bore.

'Where are you from?' she cut in. He told her.

'My last man came from there,' she said. She felt a rush of hope and pleasure. She told him the name. 'Perhaps you know him. Very hard workers, your countrymen.'

His face had changed. It was charged with interest. 'But Boris is a great man,' he said.

'Excellent worker,' she agreed.

'Is a great artist,' he said.

She laughed. It was charming, how they all praised each other. Every single one was a genius.

'No, really,' he said. 'He is an artist. We think he is a genius.'

'Yes, Boris liked to think he was an artist. That's why we got on. I am artistic, too.'

'In my country, Boris is a very great artist. Abroad you don't know him, but in my country … But now I think he says he will do no more painting.'

She wasn't sure she had understood him. For a moment she'd thought he meant actual art. 'Yes, he's stopped working for me, since the summer,' she said. 'That's why we need a new man, really.'

She went to the kitchen to fetch some biscuits. He carried on talking in the rich, empty room. 'Boris says he will do no more painting. Is a great loss for my country. He says life is over, since his daughter died. His beautiful daughter died, in August.'

The packet wouldn't open; she was wrenching it, noisily, crashing bourbon biscuits on to bone china, but she managed to pick out the single word 'daughter', and remembered Boris's wife, her misery, the apples she ate, her grey distance. The wife and daughter had spoiled it all. 'Are you married?' she called back through from the kitchen.

He shook his head. 'Life is too hard to marry,' he said. 'Life is beautiful, but life is short.'

'I see you are sensitive,' she said, 'like me. I am an artist, you know. I write. There will be other jobs for you,' she said, smiling.

KENNY

Colette Paul

Colette Paul is a Scottish author. She has published one book of short stories, *Whoever You Choose to Love*, which was shortlisted for the Glenfiddich Spirit of Scotland Writer's Award. She won the Royal Society of Authors Tom-Gallon Trust Award in 2005.

Kenny told her last week that sometimes he forgot they weren't living together any more. Sometimes, he said, he would turn to say something to her, or switch off the telly and reach for her. It would take him a few moments to realize she wasn't there.

'Our home used to be my sanctuary,' he said. 'Not any more.'

He looked at her face for a response, and June looked away. She concentrated on a patch of wallpaper above the radiator, cream with tiny gold Chinese symbols spread along it. They were probably Chinese for Peace or Love or something. The wallpaper was torn away at one edge, and underneath someone had drawn a willy, resplendent with pubic hair.

'June,' he said, 'd'you hear me?'

'I hear you.'

He sighed and turned away. He wasn't in the habit of being serious or articulating his feelings, and it embarrassed him.

'I don't care what's wrong with you,' he said, 'you'll do for me, June.'

It seemed to June that there'd been a kind of profound silence inside her, for the past few weeks now, and she didn't know if she wanted, or even if she was able, to break it. She supposed she was depressed. She had thought, in a vague, unfocused way, that moving away might help, but nothing had changed. She was still the same.

This morning she wakes early. She lies still, looking out of the window, the sky heaped blue upon blue. A car horn beeps outside and then it's quiet except for the clock ticking. The clock ticking seems to deepen the silence. Mornings are the worst time for her. She tried to describe it to Kenny once, how what she felt, just after waking, was like grief. It was like being overcome with grief, although she didn't know what for.

'I don't understand,' he'd said. 'I don't know what you're talking about.'

'It's like being neither dead nor alive,' she said another time, and Kenny took that as an insult and reminded her of all she had to be happy about.

She gets up and walks to the kitchen, drinks a glass of water, then another one. Things used to be different; she can still remember when things were different.

Remembers Kenny, up at six in the morning getting ready for work while she drifted in and out of sleep. The noise of the bathroom taps running, Kenny spitting out toothpaste and washing his face. He's very thorough when it comes to his oral hygiene, hates people with bad breath and embarrassed by the state of his own teeth. He told her once that he used to try not to smile because of them. June was surprised; she hadn't imagined he felt self-conscious about a single aspect of himself.

'They're the only charmless thing about me,' he'd said, nibbling her shoulder, 'so I can't be doing that badly.'

And then, still naked, coming into the bedroom, by the mirror, combing his hair. Him coming over to her, his face, smelling of soap, on her neck, saying, 'Aren't I a handsome devil?' and her laughing. Telling him he looked alarming, telling him to let her sleep.

'Come on, Boo, refresh me,' he'd say, and he'd make her sit up and talk to him.

He called her Boo because when they first met she was too shy to speak to him. He was staying in the hotel she was working in, doing some building work on the west wing extension. One night there'd been a party in the hotel bar and Kenny had come over and spoken to her. He asked her why she never said hello to him, and June said she did say hello to him. She'd blushed and Kenny had said he'd been watching her and he'd decided that she wouldn't say boo to a goose.

They got to know each other over that one summer. On her nights off Kenny took her to expensive restaurants, the funfair on the other side of Ayr pier, to the ten-pin bowling and the cinema. He was earning a lot from the hotel job and was angry if she tried to pay for anything. It violated his sense of what it was to be a man. Also, he liked to spend money, and liked other people knowing he spent money. One night, walking along the beach in the rain, he asked her how much she thought his socks cost.

'Have a look,' he said and lifted up his trouser leg. 'How much?'

June said she didn't know, two pairs for a fiver? Kenny roared with laughter. He said they were Armani, fifteen pounds a pop. She'd been horrified.

'Aren't you ashamed,' she said, 'of spending that kind of money on socks?'

'Ashamed? Why should I be ashamed? I left school a dunderhead with one standard grade, and now I'm wearing Armani socks. Why should I be ashamed?' He put his arm around her and said, 'I'm still a dunderhead right enough, but we all have our crosses to bear.'

Kenny liked to turn everything into a party. He knew how to tell a story, gleefully, how to make his digressions more interesting than his original story. He dealt efficiently with interruptions, knowing when it was best to hand the floor over to someone else, and when to dismiss them. And though he never laughed at his own jokes, there was always this feeling that he was deliberately reining himself in, that he wouldn't be able to stop laughing if he started. Kenny was funny. Instinctively he understood the comic value of certain words, words that other people knew but never used. He made everyone sound ridiculous, but lovably so. Regularly, at the end of the night, June would be sitting, quiet, surrounded by a bunch of people she barely knew. Kenny would be holding court, getting higher and higher, making everyone laugh. At two or three or four in the morning, in that dismal Royale Hotel bar, Kenny'd leap up and fetch the night watchman, Mr Henry, to their table. June was frightened of Mr Henry. He seemed ancient, his face lean and ferocious, dark brown and creviced from the sun. He'd once accused June of stealing a fibreglass maid that stood at the door of the hotel.

'Right, what is it?' Mr Henry would say. Kenny would point at June and shout that they couldn't shut her up. She hadn't taken her medication, he'd shout, she was a troublemaker, and they wanted her thrown out. Everyone would scream with laughter, and Mr Henry would be furious, telling Kenny he'd no time for his tomfoolery.

'But you're laughing inside,' Kenny would say, slinging his arm over Mr Henry's shoulder.

After breakfast she cleaned the rooms on the top floor where Kenny and his workmates were staying. He would take his break at eleven and meet her up there. They would sit on the edge of the hard bed eating the complimentary shortcake and watching *Colombo*. They didn't talk much when they were alone. One morning he said he thought they should take their clothes off.

'You can keep your hat on,' he said.

'Thank goodness for that,' said June.

'If you think I'm the kind of guy who would put a girl's modesty in jeopardy,' said Kenny, 'then think again.'

Light came through the cheap blue curtains, the bed sheets hadn't been changed yet, and June could feel the grit which Kenny trailed with him from work press into her back. Afterwards he put his arm behind her neck and kissed her face.

'I didn't know you'd never, you know, done the deed,' he said.

'Well, I didn't tell you.'

'Was it okay? I didn't hurt you?'

'It was okay. I wanted to.'

They lay in silence, and after a while June said, 'You look sad.'

Sometimes she thought she could sense a sort of sadness from him. It was his eyes, she'd decided. They were pale, luminous blue, dark-lashed, and sometimes, seeing him by the door, or alone in repose, they had a dignified, sober melancholy about them.

'I am sad,' said Kenny, 'I've just missed the *Colombo* double bill.'

'Seriously,' she said, laughing. 'Aren't you ever sad?'

Kenny scrunched up his face meditatively and said, 'Do you remember when Jamie died in *EastEnders*? On Christmas fucking Eve, when Sonia was waiting for him, when he'd just bought her an engagement ring? He was all happy and excited and then that bastard Martin Fowler had to run him over. There was a definite lump in my throat that night.'

She laughed, and Kenny kissed her cheek and said, 'Why would I ever be sad? Not one bad thing's ever happened to me in my whole life.'

June said, 'It must be terrible to have a happy childhood. It doesn't prepare you for all the crap to come. I'm glad,' she said, 'that I'd such a bad one.'

'How was it so bad?'

'You tell me about yours first.'

Kenny shrugged and said there was nothing to tell. It was just happy.

'Tell me one thing you remember,' she said, 'anything at all.'

Kenny paused and then smiled. 'There was this one time in primary school,' he said. 'We had to draw pictures of Britain during the war. So I drew a wee boy with a banana skin in his hand and a big smile and one of those bubbles coming out his mouth saying YUM. And then the teacher comes round to look at all our drawings, and everyone else's drawn unhappy people and rubbly buildings and stuff. So she comes to mine and looks at it and says, "What's that?" and points to the banana skin. And I say, "A banana skin," and she goes, "But there weren't any bananas during the war," and I say, "That's why the boy's so happy. 'Cause he's found a banana." There,' Kenny said, 'will that do?'

'Yes,' she said, laughing, 'that'll do.'

June goes into the bedroom to wake Billy. He's lying with his eyes open and starts smiling when she bends down to him. He's got blue eyes and dark hair, like Kenny, and also Kenny's sunny disposition. He looks around as if he's willing the world to delight him. When he was first born, June was scared of holding him. What if she tripped, what if she dropped him? He was as breakable, as miraculous, as an eggshell, while around her the world of things had taken on a frightening solidity – the world of uncovered sockets, matches, stairs, and cookers. If you were vigilant you could guard against the danger of things, although not against cot death, measles, whooping cough. She read handbooks, memorized symptoms; Kenny got annoyed and said she was morbid. She read a story in a magazine about a woman who'd mistakenly put her baby in the microwave when she was in a psychotic trance.

'That's enough, June,' Kenny had said when she told him about it. 'If you want to scare yourself, read a horror book.'

Sometimes, watching Kenny sling Billy over his shoulder, she was envious of how easily everything came to him. He didn't think about the precariousness of life, it didn't terrify him the way it terrified her. His love for Billy, and for her too, is unsparing, without anxiety. This is the way, she thinks, that he will love whoever he chooses to love.

She dresses Billy and feeds him porridge in the kitchen. He's getting bigger and more substantial every day – Billy Bunting, Kenny calls him – his skin soft, and fine as icing sugar, tender rolls of fat under his chin, over his knees and wrists. She lifts up his legs and kisses his feet. One day, she realizes, she won't be able to do this any more, and a terrible feeling of loss comes over her. It's not an unwelcome feeling; she's glad to feel anything. There've been days recently when she thinks that someone could drive a nail through her arm and she wouldn't even blink. She lifts Billy from his highchair and carries him round the kitchen. There's a mouldy cauliflower in the fridge, and hardly anything else. She finished the milk this morning, and there's no washing powder left. She takes out the cauliflower and puts it down on the counter, staring at it, wondering what to do next. The more she stares at the cauliflower, the more unrecognizable it becomes, the more incomprehensible. When Billy starts to wriggle, she shakes herself and throws it in the bin.

The dishes need washing, clothes need washing, she needs to buy food. If she'd bothered to get the phone connected, she could ring Kenny and ask him to bring some stuff over tonight when he picks up Billy. She could go to the shops herself, but the thought fills her with dread and she pushes it out of her mind.

She's been living here two months now. It was the first flat the council offered her, and the man who showed her round asked her if she was sure she didn't want to wait for something better to come up. No, she said, it was fine. She didn't care where she lived as long as it was away from where she'd been. She would have gone anywhere. So she found herself here. In a high-rise, nine storeys above the ground. There's a lift, but it's usually broken, and she doesn't like it anyway. It's claustrophobic and airless, full of the breath and germs of everyone who's been inside it. The stairs are just as bad, dark, smelling of urine. If you tripped and fell down the stairs you would die, and when June is on the stairs she thinks about this, and starts forgetting how to walk at all. One day last week she'd stopped on the eighth landing, Billy in her arms, too frightened to go any further.

She turns on *Sesame Street* and sits Billy on her knee. They play a game where June pretends to disappear, dropping her face behind her hand and counting one, two, three. Billy looks at her with his big serious eyes, laughing hysterically when she pops her face up over her hands. She blows raspberries onto his stomach, and then gets out his books to read. He can't talk yet, although she and Kenny used to try to decipher his gurgles, re-forming and shaping them into English. They were confident that he was going to be a genius. The book she's reading him today is about a little girl walking down a street, naming all the objects she passes. June points to the pictures and reads out the words underneath – mummy, tree, cherry, dog – until she can no longer make sense of what she's saying, pure meaningless sounds coming out of her mouth. Billy touches her lips with his fingers; he knows he's losing her. Soon he gets sleepy, and she puts him back in his cot for a nap.

She worries that she's becoming a capricious mother. Some days she'll play with Billy for hours and hours, desperately using her energy to think up new games for him. It's Billy who eventually crawls away to play by himself. Other days she can hardly be bothered to talk to him. This upsets her because, above all, she wants to be a good mum. She doesn't want Billy to go through what she went through. The days when her mother would lie in bed, tears falling silently down her face. Once June wiped her cheeks and her mother had looked up at her blankly, as if she didn't recognize her. Her Aunt Helen used to come over to clean the house and make dinner, wash her school uniform. She told June one night that her mother was ill, but that it didn't mean she didn't love her. The same night, getting out of bed for a glass of water, June overheard them talking in the kitchen.

'You have options, Elizabeth,' she heard Helen say. 'I know you don't think so, but you do.'

Her mother didn't reply.

'June could come and live with me,' said her aunt.

'I couldn't do that,' said her mum.

'You could go into hospital, get some proper medical help. See a psychiatrist.'

'I couldn't do that.'

Her aunt went on and on, until at last June heard her say, 'You don't want to die. No one wants to die.'

When her mother didn't respond, June froze. It felt as if the whole world had suddenly been stilled.

'There,' said Helen, 'that's lots of options. Let's go through them again.'

And June had stood in the hall in her nightdress, her heart thumping, listening to them haggle over her mother's life.

She goes back into the kitchen, at a loss what to do first. She starts running water for the dishes although when the basin's full she turns off the tap and looks out of the window instead. She can see the Fancy Café, where she went once for a cup of tea, the waitresses cooing over Billy; and Corinne's Hair, and Rajou's with an iron grille over the cash desk. On the other side of the road is Pollokmews train station, looking surprisingly quaint and rural amidst all the graffiti and junk and concrete ugliness of the rest of the area. At first she thought it'd be good living somewhere where everything was so close together. It'd be easier, she'd thought, to manage herself here. But it's not turned out that way: she's spent more time looking out of the window than she's spent outside. The things she sees from the window have taken on a nebulous, impalpable quality, as if they exist in a film or a dream. She finds herself concentrating on one thing at a time – a woman's hands moving, her feet, her face – unable to merge the features together to make a whole living person.

Today she looks towards the train station, watches a bald man lurch like a sleepwalker down the platform. He's got a plastic Somerfield bag round his arm; it swings as it blows in the wind. She turns to look at the clock and when she looks back, he's falling backwards over the edge of the platform. It happens in a second, the movement as neat and final as a domino toppling over. She presses her face to the window but can only see the empty platform. It takes her a few seconds to move, running to Billy's cot, pulling him up, Billy crying. Running to the door, her hands sweating, sweat all over her. Billy screaming in her arms. She's not even out of the front door when she hears the train coming. Running back to the window, she sees it gather speed and roar past the station. Then everything's exactly the same again. The sky arches on.

Inside the flat June screams, and the noise mixes with Billy wailing and a Tina Turner song someone's playing at top volume in the flat below.

When Kenny arrives she's sitting with Billy on her lap. He asks what's happened, the door was standing open. He stops and looks at her.

'What's wrong?' he says, coming close and directing her face towards him. 'What's happened?'

'I can't talk just now,' she says.

He asks if it has anything to do with Billy, and she shakes her head. He sits beside her, taking Billy from her arms.

'I think I'll stay,' he says.

When Billy goes back off to sleep, Kenny makes them a coffee. The room gets darker and darker but neither of them switches on the light.

'June,' he says.

She hears it faintly, as if it's coming over great distances to reach her.

'June.'

He kneels down in front of her, and puts his head on her lap, his arms tight around her legs.

'I'm sorry,' he says.

'Please,' she says, putting her hand on his head. 'Shh.'

REACH

Rachel Seiffert

Rachel Seiffert (b. 1971) is a British novelist and short story writer. Her first novel, *The Dark Room*, was shortlisted for the 2001 Man Booker Prize, and won the LA Times Prize for First Fiction. Her collection of short stories, *Field Study*, received an award from International PEN in 2004 and her novel, *Afterwards*, was longlisted for the 2007 Orange Prize.

Wednesday, and Kim's mother goes up to the school for parents' evening.

– She's doing badly, then.

– Well, no, not exactly. She can read and write. Quite well for a seven year old, as it happens.

Her daughter's class teacher pushes Kim's report around on the desk with her fingertips and Alice waits for her to pull the words together.

– She's just not an easy child to reach, Mrs Bell.

———

Home is the end house of the terrace above the seafront. From her bedroom window, Kim can see over the rooftops to the old pier and, beyond it, the last curve of sand before the headland. Seagulls hover on thermals, suspended, and Kim watches them at the window, swaying, waiting. From here she will see her mother when she comes home from the school.

In the door and then chopping, no sitting down between and no hello either. But this is not unusual. Kim's description of her mother in one of her schoolbooks: she always cooks with her coat on.

Kim waits after her mother has passed along the path beneath her windowsill to the back door and the kitchen. Face still pressed to the wall, and so still hidden from the street below, Kim listens a while to the pot and pan noises, then goes downstairs to find Alice. Early evening, getting dark, her mother is working by the blue light of the grill-flame, chops spitting underneath. Kim stands in the doorway a minute or so, but Alice does not turn. An evening like any other: potato peelings on the counter, mother's back at the sink. Kim wonders briefly if she got the day right, if Alice has been to the parents' evening after all, but decides against mentioning it. Joins her brother in the sitting room instead, watches TV with Joseph until dinner.

If she's staying, Alice will take her coat off and eat with her children. Tonight, she has a cup of tea and makes sure the washing-up is underway before she heads off out to work again. A reminder of bedtimes and a brisk kiss each on her way to the door. This too is normal, so Kim breathes a little easier, dries the plates slowly that Joseph washes fast. Watches the familiar sight of her mother's back receding down the garden path. She can close her eyes and see Alice making her way down the hill to the seafront. Keys gripped in her right hand, left holding her collar together against the wind.

Kim's eyes are sore tonight, scratchy, her lids heavy. She keeps them closed, keeps her mind's eye on her mother a little longer. Imagines the sea flat behind Alice as she opens the salon door, surface skimmed into ripples by the wind. She knows her mother chose the shop for its view across the beach, along the seafront. Has heard her telling the customers, watched her polish the wide glass window clean of rain and salt. Alice plays no music in her salon, she does not talk much. There is calm when she cuts and sets hair. In the summer with the door open and the sea air. In the winter with the hum of the dryers and the wide window misted against the dark afternoons.

Kim opens her eyes again at the kitchen window, her mother long gone, brother back in front of the television. She dries her hands on the damp tea towel, flicks the last crumbs of dinner off the kitchen table. Kim tries to rest her forehead on the cool surface, but can't; her neck stiff, resisting, caught somehow by her shoulders. The days before the parents' evening have been edgy, and she can't relax now, not sure what to do with all the worry.

—

When Alice is asked about her business, she says she makes a decent living for her family. Margins are tight with debts like hers, but she has no gaps in her appointment book to speak of, few concerns to raise with her accountant.

When Alice thinks about her daughter, as she does this evening, she sees her pale eyes and paler hair, the solid flesh of her face with its closed, impassive expression. Stubby thumbs sucked white and soft and drawn into tight, damp fists.

Alice has long fingers and strong nails; neat ovals without cuticles. She does them last thing before she leaves the salon, after the work is done. Alone with her thoughts and files. Rubbing the cream in, hand over hand over hand.

She didn't argue with what the teacher said this afternoon. *Not an easy child.* Alice has heard those words before now: from different sources, in different disguises, so many times she has come to expect them. Would never say so, but she agrees.

With Joseph it was simple: love arrived with him. Fury when the midwife carried him away from her across the delivery room to be washed and weighed. Kim was early. Only a few weeks after Frank had gone. Gas and air, and Alice kept telling the midwife she wasn't ready for the baby, but she came anyway. No tears and not much pain either. And then it took Alice years to get used to her: her rare smiles, her uncooperative arms and legs.

Alice hears the pigeons shuffling in the eaves above the doorway as she locks up. The soft, quivering noise they make in their throats. The water behind her is calm, just a slight breeze coming in across the sands. Breaking up the surface a little, touching her cheek as she turns the key in the lock and up the street towards home.

—

Thursday and Kim is ill.

She vomits once at school. A pile of sawdust and a smell in the corridor. Again when she gets home. Joseph heats the dinner Alice has left in the fridge for them, and when Kim throws up a third time, he phones the shop.

– Can you come home now, Mum?
– Run her a bath and put her to bed, love. Please. I'll not be late. Make sure she drinks something.

Joseph does as he is told, and his sister is silent, compliant. When Alice comes home it is dark and Kim is running a fever: dry heat and then sudden sweats which glue her pale hair to her forehead.

Friday morning, Kim can't stand up to walk to the toilet, and so when she needs to throw up again, her mother finds her crawling out into the bright hall.

– No school for you, then.

An unwieldy dead weight with limbs, Alice carries her daughter to the bathroom.

—

Cold black tea. Chalky taste of the aspirin mashed into jam and eaten with a teaspoon. Alice is home for fifteen minutes at lunchtime, keeps her coat on. Stands her daughter naked by the radiator, washes her down with a flannel and hot water in a red plastic bowl. Kneeling next to her clammy body, its awkward joints and dimples, soft belly. Kim's eyes are half-closed and she sways as Alice works. Hot cloth on face and neck, round ears, down spine, between toes and fingers. Skin turning cool where the flannel has been.

Kim lies in new pyjamas when Alice leaves for work again. Under new sheets and tucked blankets, curtains drawn against the day. The slats of the bunk above her shift and birds' eyes peep from the mattress. Beaks and wings. Kim calls for her mum, but she's gone now, back down the road. The hairspray smell of Alice left with her, and Kim is alone with the birds again. They fly out from between the slats, grey wings beating the hot air against her cheeks.

—

Alice always hoped it would come. Read about it in the leaflets she got from the midwives and the library. You will not always bond with your baby immediately, but this is normal and no cause for worry.

Kim arrived and Alice had two to care for. Frank gone and only one of her didn't seem nearly enough. Joseph was four then and she would pick him up from nursery school early. To feel his hand holding her skirt as they walked home along the seafront, to have his arms fold around her neck when she lifted him up.

Alice tried holding Kim after her evening bottle, after Joseph was asleep and they could have some quiet time together, like it said in the leaflets. But it was hard and sometimes it frightened her: sitting with her baby and still feeling so little.

—

Red-brown spots gather in the afternoon. On the soles of Kim's feet, behind her ears, inside her eyelids. Joseph sees them when the doctor shines his torch in his sister's dark bedroom. He pulls the girl's eyelids down with his thumbs.

– I'll need to use your telephone. Call an ambulance and your mother.

Joseph tells Kim later that they drove away with the siren on, but Kim remembers silence inside the ambulance. Looking at her mother and then following Alice's gaze to the trees and lamp-posts passing. The strip of world visible through the slit of clear window above the milk-glass in the doors.

—

Alice Bell's girl had meningitis and nearly died.

The customers in the salon ask concerned questions, and Alice gets a call from the health visitor, too. The woman has a good look at the clean hall, the tidy kitchen Alice leads her to. The grass in the garden is long, falls this way and that, but Alice is sure that everything else is in good order. Thinks she recognises the health visitor, too; that she has maybe cut her hair before.

Alice gets more leaflets from her. Is told about the tumbler test: roll a glass against the rash, she says. Alice thanks the woman, but thinks it's not really any good to her, this information. It's happened now, over, Kim will be home again soon.

The house is quiet after the health visitor leaves. Small. Alice sweeps her leaflets off the kitchen table, dumps them in the bin on the front on her way back to the salon.

—

Kim has scars. A tiny, round wound in the small of her back, where they tapped the fluid from her spine. And one on the back of her hand from the drip: skin and vein still slightly raised, puncture-mark already healing, fading with the black-turning-yellow bruise. She has fine, white scratch-lines on the soles of her feet, too, but these are more memory than reality. Pin-tip traces to check for sensation, pricks in the tops of her toes that drew blood-drops, which later become blood-spots on the hospital sheets.

The real scar is at her throat. Tracheotomy. Kim can't say the word, but this is where her fingers go at night in her hospital bed, and when she wakes. To feel the way the skin is pulled over, small folds overlapping and grown together. Like melted plastic, the beaker which fell in on itself when Joseph left it on the stove. At first the hairy ends of the stitches are there too. Six black bristles for Kim's fingertips to brush against under the dressing, to investigate in the bathroom mirror when no one else is there to be looking. One hand on the wheely drip, the other pushing herself up on the sink, closer to the long, clean mirror and the grey-pink pucker of skin in her reflection.

—

Kim is back at home now, back at school. Weeks have passed already, but Alice still sees the first days in the hospital with her daughter. The pictures come at her from nowhere. When she is doing the books, while she is cutting, shopping, walking, on her way home.

From her bedroom window, Kim watches her mother in the dusk light, coming up the road. She walks with her coat unbuttoned and sometimes she stops, head down, hands deep in her pockets. Stays like that for a minute or two on the pavement before walking on.

The nurses held Kim's body curled and still and Alice watched. Daughter's spine turned towards her, small feet pulled up below her bum. Brown iodine swirled on to her skin, and then her toes splayed as the needle went in: five separate soft pads on each foot, reaching.

They had a bed free for Alice in a room down the hall, but she stayed in the chair by her daughter's bed and didn't sleep much. Awake when Kim's temperature rose again and she swallowed her tongue. The doctors drew the curtain round the bed and the fitting girl while they worked. So Alice couldn't see what they were doing any longer but still she didn't move. Stayed put, listening, while they made the hole for the tube in her daughter's neck, and took her temperature down with wet sheets around her legs. No one asked Alice to leave and she sat in the chair, shoes off, coat on, pulled tight around her chest.

—

Kim has headaches, too.

Joseph watches while his sister ties the belt round her head. One of Granddad's old ones. Big buckle, cracked leather, round her forehead, over her temples. He pulls it tight for her and then she lies down, head under the blankets, nose showing. Brows pulled into a frown by the belt, jaw clenching, neck held taut against the pain.

Kim's drinks have to be warm because her teeth feel everything, and she is clumsy. Legs bruised from falls and corners, clothes stained colourful by spills. Kim has no sense of edges these days; where a glass can be placed safely, where her body can pass without damage. She creates noise and mess and the mumbling speech that the doctor said should improve quickly takes weeks to go away.

—

The school calls Alice in again. No parents' everting this time: a meeting with Kim's class teacher and headmistress, attendance register open on the desk between them.

– When does Kim leave the house, Mrs Bell?
– Quarter to nine. With her brother.
– Every morning

Alice nods, doesn't tell them that she leaves the house at eight twenty to open the salon. Thinks they are doubtless capable of working that one out. She reminds them.

– My daughter has been very ill.
– Yes.

They are writing things down and Alice is remembering again. That Kim couldn't stop herself looking at her tracheotomy wound. That the peeled ends of the dressing curled up off her neck, giving her away, gathering dust like magnets, tacky traces on her skin turning black. Alice visited her at visiting time, whispered: it'll get infected. She smiled when she said it. Didn't want to tell her daughter off, just to tell her. Let her know that she had noticed. That she understood it, her curiosity.

Kim looked at her. Skin under her eyes flushing. Hands moving up to cover the dressing. Alice didn't know what that meant: whether her daughter was surprised or pleased or angry.

– Kim is what we call On Report now, Mrs Bell.
– She could have died.
– Yes.

They blink at her across the desk. Sympathetic, insistent.

– I'm afraid her attendance record has to improve.

—

Kim finds different places to spend her days. Sometimes the coast path over the headland where the wind cuts into her legs. Sometimes the burnt stubble of the fields inland, where she flies her kites made out of plastic bags. Most days it is the beach, though, where she lies down under the old pier. On her back on the cracking shingle, waves at her feet, sea wall behind her. Sodden wood, salt, seaweed and litter.

Above her, she can see the gulls' flapping battles through the gappy planks of the old walkway. Lies still, watching the starlings fly their swooping arcs around the splintered columns and rails. Cloud and wind over the water. Storm of black beak and wing reeling above her head.

—

Alice shuts the salon early and is home before her children. Joseph acts as though it is normal for his mother to open the door for him; Kim steps into the hallway, clutching her school bag as if it were proof of something, tell-tale damp of the day in her clothes and hair. Joseph slips upstairs to his bedroom, Kim stays silent, eyes on the wallpaper white Alice asks her where she has been, and why. She watches Kim's face for a reaction but cannot read anything from her daughter's expression.

– Whatever. You'll be leaving the house with me from now on.
– No.

Later Alice goes over the scene again. In bed, light out, eyes open. Feels something closing down, tight around her ribs. Remembers the screaming battles they had when Kim was three, four, five. Doesn't want to repeat those years again. Her daughter smelled of sea and air this afternoon, it filled the corridor. Alice didn't know what to do, what to say, so she said nothing. An almost eight-year-old stranger standing in front of her. Mouth open, breath passing audibly over her small, wet teeth.

—

Kim doesn't know it, but the school keeps close tabs on her. Her teachers know she comes for registration and then dodges out of the gate behind the playing fields. They don't confront her; instead they call her mother and then Alice hangs up the phone in the back room of the salon, behind the closed curtain, under the noise of the dryers, and cries.

Alice doesn't know it, but some mornings her daughter comes down to the front. The smell leads her there: hot air, warm skin and hair, shampoo. She doesn't go in; instead she watches her mother's face at the salon window. Eyes and cheekbones amongst the reflections. Blank sky, cold sea, ragged palms. Her mother's eyes blinking, face not moving. Lamp-posts with lights strung between, rocking in the breeze.

—

Another Wednesday, another week or two later, and Kim stands in the salon doorway. Alice has had the phone call already. Knows her daughter hasn't been to school, didn't expect her to show up here. The rain slides down the window-pane and, through the open shop door, she can hear it singing in the drains.

Alice takes her daughter's coat from her, sits her down in an empty chair. The salon is quiet and Kim spends the next few minutes watching her mother working in the mirror. She sees that Alice doesn't look at her, only out of the window, or down at her fingers, turning grey hair around the pastel shades of the plastic rollers, pink and yellow and green. Her mother's cheeks are flushed, lips drawn in, and the skin around her eyes pulled taut.

When Alice steps over to her, Kim looks away. Sees the old lady's eyes on them, under the dryer. Alice knows she is watching them, too. Has felt her customers observing her ever since Kim was ill, has grown accustomed to the scrutiny. She stands behind her daughter now. A second or two passes, and she finds herself still there. Not shouting, not angry. Just looking at the slope of her daughter's shoulders, the nape of her neck, her sodden hair.

Alice gets a clean towel from the shelves at the back and then plugs in a dryer, sets to work. At first Kim watches the rain, the gulls fighting on the rail outside, but soon she closes her eyes. Feels the pressure of her mother's fingers, how strong her hands are, how warm the air is, the low noise of the dryer.

FIELD STUDY

Rachel Seiffert

Rachel Seiffert (b. 1971) is a British novelist and short story writer. Her first novel, *The Dark Room*, was shortlisted for the 2001 Man Booker Prize, and won the LA Times Prize for First Fiction. Her collection of short stories, *Field Study*, received an award from International PEN in 2004 and her novel, *Afterwards*, was longlisted for the 2007 Orange Prize.

Summer and the third day of Martin's field study. Morning, and he is parked at the side of the track, looking out over the rye he will walk through shortly to reach the river. For two days he has been alone, gathering his mud and water samples, but not today.

A boy shouts and sings in the field. His young mother carries him piggyback through the rye. Martin hears their voices, thin through the open window of his car. He keeps still. Watching, waiting for them to pass.

The woman's legs are hidden in the tall stalks of the crop and the boy's legs are skinny. He is too big to be carried comfortably, and mother and son giggle as she struggles on through the rye. The boy wears too-large trainers, huge and white, and they hang heavy at his mother's sides. Brushing the ears of rye as she walks, bumping at her thighs as she jogs an unsteady step or two. Then swinging out wide as she spins on the spot: whirling, stumbling around and around. Twice, three times, four times, laughing, lurching as the boy screams delight on her back.

They fall to the ground and Martin can't see them any more. Just the rye and the tops of the trees beyond: where the field slopes down and the river starts its wide arc around the town. Three days Martin has been here. Only another four days to cover the area, pull enough data together for his semester paper, already overdue. The young woman and her child have gone. Martin climbs out of the car, gathers his bags and locks the doors.

This river begins in the high mountains Martin cannot see but knows lie due south of where he stands. Once it passes the coal and industry of the foothills, it runs almost due west into these flat, farming lands, cutting a course through the shallow valley on which his PhD studies are centred. Past the town where he is staying and on through the provincial capital, until it finally mouths in the wide flows which mark the border between Martin's country and the one he is now in.

Not a significant stretch of water historically, commercially, not even especially pretty. But a cause for concern nonetheless: here, and even more so in Martin's country, linking as it does a chemical plant on the eastern side of the border with a major population centre to the west.

Martin has a camera, notebooks and vials. Some for river water, others for river mud. Back in the town, in his room at the guesthouse, he has chemicals and a microscope. More vials and dishes. The first two days' samples, still to be analysed, a laptop on which to record his results.

The dark, uneven arc of the trees is visible for miles, marking the course of the river through the yellow-dry countryside. The harvest this year will be early and poor. Drought, and so the water level of the river is low, but the trees along its banks are still full of new growth, thick with leaves, the air beneath them moist.

Martin drinks the first coffee of the day from his flask by the water's edge. The river has steep banks, and roots grow in twisted detours down its rocky sides. He has moved steadily west along the river since the beginning of the week, covering about a kilometre each day, with a two-kilometre gap in between. Up until now, the water has been clear, but here it is thick with long fronds of weed. Martin spreads a waterproof liner on the flat rock, lays out vials and spoons in rows. He writes up the labels while he drinks his second coffee, then pulls on his long waterproof gloves. Beyond the branches, the field shimmers yellow-white and the sun is strong; under the trees, Martin is cool. Counting, measuring, writing, photographing. Long sample spoon scratching river grit against the glass of the vials.

Late morning and hot now, even under the trees. The water at this point in the river is almost deep enough to swim. Martin lays out his vials, spoons and labels for the third time that morning. Wonders a moment or two what it would be like to lie down in the lazy current, the soft weed. Touches his gloved fingertips to the surface and counts up all the toxic substances he will test his samples for later. He rolls up his trouser legs as high as they will go before he pulls on the waders, enjoys the cool pressure of the water against the rubber against his skin as he moves carefully out to about mid-stream. The weed here is at its thickest, and Martin decides to take a sample of that, too. The protective gauntlets make it difficult to get a grip, but Martin manages to pull one plant from the river bed with its root system still reasonably intact. He stands a while, feeling the current tug its way around his legs, watching the fingers of weed slowly folding over the gap he has made. Ahead is a sudden dip, a small waterfall that Martin had noted yesterday evening on the map. The noise of the cascade is loud, held in close by the dense green avenue of trees. Martin wades forward and when he stops again, he hears voices, a laugh-scream.

The bushes grow dense across the top of the drop, but Martin can just see through the leaves: young mother and son, swimming in the pool hollowed out by the waterfall. They are close. He can see the boy take a mouthful of water and spray it at his mother as she swims around the small pool. Can see the mud between her toes when she climbs out and stands on the rock at the water's edge. The long black-green weed stuck to her thigh. She is not naked, but her underwear is pale, pink-white like her skin, and Martin can also see the darker wet of nipples and pubic hair. He turns quickly and wades back to the bank, weed sample held carefully in gauntleted hands.

He stands for a moment by his bags, then pulls off the waders, pulls on his shoes again. He will walk round them, take a detour across the fields and they will have no cause to see him. He has gathered enough here already, after all. The pool and waterfall need not fall within his every 100 metres remit. No problem.

—

Martin sleeps an hour when he gets back to the guesthouse. Open window providing an occasional breeze from the small back court and a smell of bread from the kitchen. When he wakes the sun has passed over the top of the building and his room is pleasantly cool and dim.

He works for an hour or two on the first day's mud and water vials, and what he finds confirms his hypothesis. Everything within normal boundaries, except one particular metal, present in far higher concentrations than one should expect.

His fingers start to itch as he parcels up a selection of samples to send back to the university lab for confirmation. He knows this is psychosomatic, that he has always been careful to wear protection: doesn't even think that poisoning with this metal is likely to produce such a reaction. He includes the weed sample in his parcel, with instructions that a section be sent on to botany, and a photocopy of the map, with the collection sites clearly marked. In the post office, his lips and the skin around his nostrils burn, and so, despite his reasoning, he allows himself another shower before he goes down to eat an early dinner in the guesthouse café.

—

The boy from the stream is sitting on one of the high stools at the bar doing his homework, and the waitress who brings Martin his soup is his mother. She wishes him a good appetite in one of the few phrases he understands in this country, and when Martin thanks her using a couple of words picked up on his last visit, he thinks she looks pleased.

Martin watches her son while he eats. Remembers the fountain of river-water the boy aimed at his mother, wonders how much he swallowed, if they swim there regularly, how many years they might have done this for. Martin thinks he looks healthy enough, perhaps a little underweight.

His mother brings Martin a glass of wine with his main course, and when he tries to explain that he didn't order it, she just puts her finger to her lips and winks. She is thin, too, but she looks strong; broad shoulders and palms, long fingers, wide nails. She pulls her hands behind her back, and Martin is aware now that he has been staring. He lowers his eyes to his plate, watches her through his lashes as she moves on to the next table. Notes: *good posture, thick hair*. But Martin reasons while he eats that such poisons can take years to make their presence felt; nothing for a decade or two, then suddenly tumours and shortness of breath in middle age.

The woman is sitting at the bar with her son when Martin finishes his meal. She is smoking a cigarette and checking through his maths. The boy watches, kicking his trainers against the high legs of his barstool, as Martin walks towards them.

– I'm sorry. I don't really speak enough of your language. But I wanted to tell you something.

The woman looks up from her son's exercise book and blinks as Martin speaks. He stops a moment, waits to see if she understands, if she will say something, but after a small smile and a small frown, she just nods and turns away from him, back to her son. At first Martin thinks they are talking about him, and that they might still respond, but the seconds pass and the boy and his mother keep talking, and then Martin can't remember how long he has been standing there looking at the back of her head, so he looks away. Sees his tall reflection in the mirror behind the bar. One hand, *left, no right*, moving up to cover his large forehead, *sunburnt*, and red hair.

– What you want to say to my mother?

The boy speaks Martin's language. He shrugs when Martin looks at him. Martin lets his hand drop back down to his side.

– Oh, okay. Okay, good. Can you translate for me then?

The boy shrugs again, which Martin takes to be assent, and so he starts to explain. About the river, how he saw them swimming in the morning and he didn't want to disturb them, but that he has been thinking about it again this evening. And then Martin stops talking because he sees that the boy is frowning.

– Should I start again?
– You were watching my mother swimming.
– No.

The boy whispers to his mother, who flushes and then puts her hand over her mouth and laughs.

– No. No, that's not right.

Martin shakes his head again, holds both hands up, but it is loud, the woman's laughter in the quiet café, and the other two customers look up from their meals.

– I was not watching. Tell her I was not watching. I was taking samples from the river, that' s all. I'm a scientist. And I think you should know that it is polluted. The river is dirty and you really shouldn't swim there. That's all. Now please tell your mother.

The young woman keeps laughing while Martin speaks, and though he avoids looking in the mirror again, he can feel the blush making his sunburn itch, the pulse in his throat. The boy watches him a second or two, lips moving, not speaking. Martin thinks the boy doesn't believe him.

– You could get sick. The river will make you sick. I just thought you should know. Okay?

Martin is angry now. With the suspicious boy, his laughing mother. He counts out enough to pay for his meal, including the wine. Leaves it on the table without a tip and goes to his room.

—

In the morning, a man serves Martin his breakfast, but before he leaves for the river again the young mother comes into the café, pushing her son in front of her. She speaks in a low whisper to the boy, who translates for Martin in a monotone.

– My mother say she is sorry. We are both sorry. She is Ewa, I am Jacek. She say you should tell me about the river so I can tell her.

—

Martin is still annoyed when he gets back from the river in the afternoon. Doesn't expect the woman and her boy to stick to their appointment, half hopes they won't turn up, still hasn't analysed day two and three's samples. But when he comes downstairs after his shower, he finds them waiting for him in the café as arranged.

The boy helps Martin spread out his maps, asks if he can boot up the laptop. His mother murmurs something, and her son sighs.

– She says I should say please. Please.
– It's okay.

Martin shows them the path of the river from the mountains to the border and where the chemical plant lies, almost a hundred kilometres upstream from the town. Amongst his papers, he finds images of what the metal he has found in the river looks like, its chemical structure and symbol, and he tells them its common name. He says that as far as they know, the body cannot break it down, so it stores it, usually in the liver. He speaks a sentence at a time and lets the boy translate. Shows them the graphs he has plotted on his computer. Waits while the boy stumbles over his grammar, watches his mother listening, thinks: *Jacek and Ewa.*

– Where do you come from?

Ewa speaks in Martin's language, points at the map. Martin looks at her, and Jacek clears his throat.

– I am teaching her.

Martin smiles. He shows them where he is studying and then, a little further to the west, the city where he was born. And then Jacek starts to calculate how many kilometres it is from Martin's university to the border and from the border to the town. Martin asks Ewa:

– How old is he?
– Nearly eleven.

He nods. Thinks she must have been very young when she got pregnant.

– He's just about bilingual already.

An exaggeration, a silly thing to say, and Martin can see in Ewa's eyes that she knows it, but she doesn't contradict him.

– School. He is good student. Also good teacher.

She smiles and Martin is glad that they came today, Ewa and her son. Pushes last night's laughter to the back of his mind. Sees that Ewa's smile is wide and warm and that her tongue shows pink behind her teeth.

—

Day five and Martin works his way along the river again. The hot fields are empty, the road quiet. The water here is wider, deeper; flies dance above the surface.

Mid-morning and Jacek crashes through the undergrowth.

– Martin! There you are. I am here.

Martin looks up from the water, startled. He nods, then he doesn't know what to say to the boy, so he carries on working. Jacek watches him a while, and then pulls off his trainers, rolls up his trousers, picks up a vial.

– No! You shouldn't come in.
– I can help you. You work faster when I can pass them to you.
– Shouldn't you be at school?

Jacek frowns.

– Does your mother know you are here?
– She don't mind.

Martin thinks a moment.

– We don't know enough yet about this metal, you see. It's too much of a risk.

Jacek avoids eye contact, rubs his bare ankles.

– You really can't help me without boots and gloves, Jacek. I only have one pair of each. I'm sorry.

An hour later the boy is back with pink washing-up gloves and a pair of outsize rubber boots, soles caked in mud. He holds up a bag of apples.

– For you. From my mother.

—

In the evening the café is crowded and Ewa is busy; another waitress brings Martin his dinner. His table is near the bar, where Jacek is doing his homework again. New vocabulary, and he asks Martin to correct his spelling. Ewa makes a detour past his table on her way to the kitchen.

– Thank you.
– No problem.

He scratches his sunburn, stops. Feels huge at the small table after she has gone.

Jacek brings his mother with him on day six. Ewa stands at the water's edge while her son changes into his boots and washing-up gloves. Midday already, and the sky is clear, the sun high. Martin has sweat patches under his arms, on his back. He watches Ewa hold the front of her T-shirt away from her chest, and then flap it back and forth to get cool air at the hot skin beneath. He sees yellow pollen on her shoes, the hem of her skirt, damp hair at her temples.

They work for a while, and Jacek asks questions which Martin answers. Ewa says very little. She crouches on the bank and looks at the water. Lids down, lips drawn together, arms wrapped around her shins. When Martin says it's time to move downstream 100 metres, Jacek says he wants to come with him and Ewa says she will go home.

Jacek watches Martin watching his mother as she wades through the long grass back to the road.

– She used to swim here with my Tata, I think.
– Your father?

Martin tries to remember a wedding ring. Sees Ewa's strong palms, her long fingers.

– He is in your country.
– Oh?
– He is illegal. Too much problems at the border, so he don't come home.

Martin watches Jacek as they unpack the bags again. Fair with freckles. Narrow lips, pale eyes, broad nose. A good-looking boy, but not at all like his mother.

—

Day seven and Martin doesn't go to the river. After breakfast he sets up his computer, a new graph template, and plots the data from days two and three. Both agree with day one's graph, with Martin's predictions, and he starts sketching out a structure for his argument, writes a first draft conclusion. The sample results should have come back from the university yesterday, including the mud and weed from day four, which would speed up Martin's analysis. He goes downstairs to the small office mid-morning to check for faxes again, but the guesthouse is quiet, café closed, reception deserted. Sunday. So there won't be anybody at the labs, either, but Martin walks out to the phone boxes in the town square anyway.

Jacek hammers on the glass.

– Where were you?
– Wait.

Martin holds up one finger, but the phone just keeps ringing out at the other end. Jacek peels his pink gloves off while Martin leaves a message on the lab answerphone. The boy cups his hands around his eyes, presses them up to the glass, watching him. It is stifling inside the phone box and Jacek's hands leave a sweaty streak on the pane outside.

When Martin opens the door, Jacek has his fists on his hips. Rubber boots on the paving stones beside him.

– Why didn't you come?
– I've finished. I only need to do a couple more tests.
– Oh.

Jacek picks up his boots and falls into step with Martin. The sun is strong and they walk together on the shady side of the narrow street which leads back up to the guesthouse.

– I'm going home tomorrow.
– Tomorrow?

He looks up at Martin for a second or two, then turns heel and runs.

—

Martin sleeps in the afternoon and is woken by the landlady's husband with a message.

– Is it from the university?
– No. From my wife's sister.

Martin stares at the man. Eyes unfocused, face damp with heat and sleep.

– From Ewa. Jacek's mother. She works here. My wife's sister.
– Oh, yes. Yes, sorry.
– She says you should come to her house. She will cook you something to eat this evening. To say thank you.

—

Martin showers and sits down at his computer again but finds he can't work. Looks out at the birds instead, washing in a puddle on the flat roof of the building opposite. The concrete is mossy and Martin wonders where the water came from. He has been here a week and it's been 30 degrees straight through and hasn't rained once. The skin on his back is damp again, and under his arms, and he thinks he hasn't anything clean to wear this evening, so he takes a T-shirt down the hall with him and washes it in the bathroom, lays it out on his windowsill to dry.

It is still slightly damp when he goes out to find Ewa's. Bottle of wine bought from the guesthouse bar under one arm, map and address on a scrap of paper from the landlady's husband. There is a slight breeze and the T-shirt is cool against his skin. He catches sight of himself in the bakery window as he passes, pushes his hair down over his forehead a little as he turns the corner. An involuntary gesture he hopes nobody saw.

—

Jacek opens the door.

– You're early!
– Sorry.

He leads Martin up the stairs, two at a time, cartons of cigarettes and cake mix piled high along one wall. The narrow entrance hall of Ewa's flat is similarly crowded: disposable nappies, tuna fish, toothbrushes in different shades, pink and green and yellow. Jacek sees Martin looking at the boxes.

– The man we rent from. He keep things here, we pay him not so much. Every week is something new coming for him to sell.

A table stands in the middle of the room, a wardrobe in the corner. Mattress leant up against the wall and draped with a sheet. The window is open and the radio on. Martin recognises the song, a current hit, but can't understand what the announcer says afterwards. He goes into the kitchen, where Ewa is chopping and Jacek stirring.

– Can I help?
– No!

Ewa pours him a glass of wine and pushes him out into the bedroom-dining room again.

– Five minutes.

The wind is blowing into town from the river, and Martin can hear church bells ringing out the evening service.

They eat, Martin and Ewa smiling and nodding, Jacek concentrating on his food, not worried by the silence.

– Jacek, can you ask your mother to tell me a little about the town, please?

The boy looks up with his mouth full, Martin swallows.

– I know very little. I would like to know.

It is not true. He knows what she tells him already, what the boy translates for her about the nine churches, the resistance during the war and occupation, the failed collectivisation of the fruit growers during the communist era.

– There was a jam factory here when she was my age. Everybody was working there, or they were farmers. Apricots, pears, apples, and I don't know how you say those small ones. Berries?

Martin asks about the communist years.

– You want to hear about no food and unhappiness, yes?

Martin rubs his sunburn, and Ewa slaps her son's hands.

– Jacek! Sorry. I don't understand him, but I see he was bad. You translate only, yes? Yes?

Ewa points at her son and then pours them all more wine, offers to make Martin some tea.

– The way we drink it here.

Jacek's translation is sulky, sleepy. Black, in a glass so you can see the leaves floating. Boiling water, hot glass with no handles so your fingerprints get smooth and hard from the holding. Martin looks at the tips of his fingers, Ewa smiles.

– I didn't know your sister owns the guesthouse.
– Yes.

Ewa smiles, Jacek yawns.

– She gives my mother work.
– And her husband?
– Tadeusz?
– Uncle Tadeusz does no work.
– Sh! Not true.

Ewa speaks more herself now, interrupts her son's translations. She tells him her brother-in-law is a plumber. That he put his faith in the church. Her explanations are ungrammatical, sometimes nonsensical, but Martin enjoys listening to her. She says that they built new houses a year or two after the elections, a whole row, right in the centre. New times, new buildings. Flats above, shop spaces below. Brick, solid, good windows. And Tadeusz put in all the pipes, toilets, baths, taps, sinks. He got a loan to pay for all the materials. Copper piping and ceramics, imported from the west. He had the houses blessed when they were finished, but not yet painted. The priest came and threw his holy water around the empty rooms and Tadeusz was so proud. She remembers the wet, dark spots on the pink-red plasterwork, that it was a hot day, and that the dark spots left white marks behind when they dried.

– He never got paid, Tadeusz, and he cries often now.

Each time he defaults on his loan, and the houses are still empty. A while ago there was new graffiti on the wall of the last one in the row: send the nuns abroad and the priests to the moon.

Ewa looks at Jacek, who isn't listening any more, eyes half closed, head propped in his hands. She whispers to Martin:

– I think Tadeusz write that.

Martin feels her breath on his neck as she speaks, can smell wine and soap mixed.

– My sister, she wanted that Jacek and me should live with her. After Piotr left.
– Your husband?

Ewa doesn't answer, her eyes are unfocused.

– I couldn't. Not live with Tadeusz. He's not a bad man, but so much bitterness.

Martin is drunk and so is Ewa.

– I don't want my son be bitter, you see. I want that he like his life, this town, his country.

Martin nods.

– There is not so much here now, but I show him places, take him to the river.

Ewa sighs. They sit with the breeze from the open window on their bright cheeks and Jacek has his head on the tablecloth, asleep.

– I don't make him be at school this week. I think he can't swim in the river now, but it is good that he speak with you. Has some nice time, learn someone new. More than in a classroom.

Ewa smiles into the middle distance and Martin looks at her. Only half a metre between them, the corner of the table, knees almost touching underneath.

He leans towards her. But Ewa catches him.

– No.

One hand on each of his shoulders, she holds him at arms' length. Martin blinks.

An empty wine glass rolls on the table. Ewa shakes her head.

– Sorry, no.

She smiles and then Martin sits back in his chair again, sunburn itching, sweat prickling in his scalp.

He doesn't look at her and for a minute or so they sit in silence. Jacek's even breathing in the room and the church bells sounding again outside. When Martin looks up, Ewa is blinking, smiling at him.

– I am sorry.

She rights the glass on the table, then covers her mouth with her hand and laughs.

———

In the morning there is a fax from the department lab. Martin has a hangover, asks for coffee and water to be sent up to his room. His eyes skim the figures, cannot settle. He boots up the laptop, plots the lab's figures onto his graph, though he already sees the disparity between the last set of results and his predictions. Days one and two show serious levels of contamination in mud and water, and correspond with Martin's own data. Day three's samples, however, are almost low enough to be considered clear.

Martin sits on the narrow bed a while, trying to decide if he is relieved or disappointed. The weedy water, the pool under the waterfall: *Clean. As good as*. But the premise of his paper: *Void*. His headache is bad, the day hot already, the shame of yesterday evening still fresh. Martin presses the heels of his palms against his eyes.

He wants to go home, he needs to get dressed. He goes to the bathroom where the window is open, the air much cooler than in his room. He stands under the shower a long time, warm flow on face and shoulders taking the edge off his headache, filling his ears, closing his eyes, replacing Ewa and her laughter with water falling on tile.

The room he returns to is strewn with papers and clothes.

Martin works his way round it methodically, folding and sorting into piles. Before he packs, he checks through the lab technician's tidy columns once more, notes the memo at the end of the fax: the weed sample has been sent on to botany.

On the way downstairs, he reasons with himself: if the weed results are interesting, he can propose to further investigate the river fauna in the conclusion to his paper. Over breakfast, he thinks he could propose a joint venture with botany, perhaps. Something to please the department. Zoology might even be interested: the weed may be thriving, but crowding other species out. At the very least, it is good news for Ewa. She is not working this morning, but Martin thinks he will leave a note for her, tell her it's okay to take Jacek swimming again. He finishes his roll. Thinks he made a mess of the field study, the week in general, but there are still ways to make amends.

Martin stands in the narrow reception hall with his bags, sees Ewa happy by the waterfall while he waits for her sister to calculate his bill. Then he remembers how sad she looked the day she came with Jacek to the river, and he is shocked at the satisfaction the memory gives him.

There is paper on the counter in front of him. He has a pencil in his back pocket, but he doesn't get it out. He pays and picks up his bags. While he loads up the car he tells himself it is too soon to know for certain. He has yet to test all his samples, examine all the possibilities; swimming at the waterfall could still be dangerous.

On the road out of town, he sees Ewa's hand over her mouth, her eyes pressed shut, Jacek woken by her laughter and staring at him.

At the border, the road runs parallel with the river for a kilometre or so, and the traffic moves slowly. To his right, trees grow tall along the riverbanks and in his rear-view mirror Martin can see the rest of the country spread out behind him, dry and flat. His chest is tight with shame, but the border guard is waving him through now, and he is driving on again.

LOVE IN THE MARKETPLACE

Yiyun Li

Yiyun Li (b. 1972) is a Chinese American author. Her debut short story collection, *A Thousand Years of Good Prayers*, won the 2005 Frank O'Connor International Short Story Award, and her second collection, *Gold Boy, Emerald Girl*, was shortlisted for the same award. Her debut novel, *The Vagrants*, was shortlisted for the 2011 IMPAC Dublin Literary Award. She is an editor of the Brooklyn-based literary magazine, *A Public Space*.

Sansan is known to her students as Miss Casablanca. A beautiful nickname if one does not pay attention to the cruel, almost malicious smiles when the name is mentioned, and she chooses not to see. Sansan, at thirty-two, does not have a husband, a lover, or a close friend. Since graduation from college, she has been teaching English at the Educators' School in the small town where she grew up, a temporary job that has turned permanent. For ten years she has played *Casablanca*, five or six times a semester, for each class of students. The pattern of their response has become familiar, and thus bearable for her. At the beginning, they watch in awe, it being the first real American movie they have watched, without Chinese dubbing or subtitles. Sansan sees them struggle to understand the dialogue, but the most they can do is catch a phrase or two now and then. Still, they seem to have no trouble understanding the movie, and always, some girls end the class with red teary eyes. But soon they lose their interest. They laugh when the women in the movie cry; they whistle when a man kisses a woman on the screen. In the end, Sansan watches the movie alone, with the added sound track from the chatting students.

That is what Sansan is doing with her morning class when someone taps on the door. Only when the knocking becomes urgent does she pause the tape.

"Your mother's waiting for you outside. She wants to see you," the janitor says when Sansan opens the door.

"What for?"

"She didn't say."

"Can't you see I'm busy with my students?"

"It's your mother waiting outside," the janitor says, one foot planted firmly inside the door.

Sansan stares at the janitor. After a moment, she sighs. "OK, tell her I'm coming," she says. The students all watch on amused. She tells them to keep watching the movie, and knows they will not.

Outside the school gate, Sansan finds her mother leaning onto the wooden wheelbarrow she pushes to the marketplace every day. Stacked in it are a coal stove, a big aluminum pot, packs of eggs, bottles of spices, and a small wooden stool. For forty years. Sansan's mother has been selling hard-boiled eggs in the marketplace by the train station, mostly to travelers. Sitting on the stool for all her adult life has made her a tiny stooped woman. Sansan hasn't seen her mother for a year, since her father's funeral. Her mother's hair is thinner and grayer, but so will Sansan's own be in a few years, and she feels no sentiment for either of them.

"Mama, I heard you were looking for me," Sansan says.

"How else would I know that you're alive?"

"Why? I thought people talked about me to you all the time."

"They can lie to me."

"Of course." Sansan grins.

"But whose problem is it when you make people talk about you?"

"Theirs."

"You've never known how to spell the word 'shame.'"

"Do you come just to tell me that I should be ashamed of myself? I know it by heart now."

"What god did I offend to deserve you as a daughter?" Her mother raises her voice. A few passersby slow down and look at them with amused smiles.

"Mama, do you have something to say? I'm busy."

"It won't be long before you will become an orphan, Sansan. One day I'll be drowned by all the talk about you."

"People's words don't kill a person."

"What killed your dad, then?"

"I was not the only disappointment for dad," Sansan says. Hard as she tries, she feels her throat squeezed tight by a sudden grief. Her father, before his death, worked as a meter reader, always knocking on people's doors around dinnertime, checking their gas and water meters, feeling responsible for the ever-rising rates and people's anger. One evening he disappeared after work. Later he was discovered by some kids in a pond outside the town, his body planted upside down. The pond was shallow, waist deep at most; he had plunged himself into the mud, with the force of a leap maybe, but nobody could tell for sure how he did it, or why Sansan's mother believed that it was Sansan's failure at marriage that killed him.

"Think of when you first went to college. Your dad and I thought we were the most accomplished parents in the world," her mother says, ready to reminisce and cry.

"Mama, we've been there many times. Let's not talk about it."

"Why? You think I toil all these years just to raise a daughter to shut me up?"

"I'm sorry, but I have to go," Sansan says.

"Don't go yet. Stay with me longer," her mother says, almost pleading.

Sansan tries to soften her voice. "Mama, I'm in the middle of a class."

"Come home tonight, then. I have something important to tell you."

"Why don't you tell me now? I can spare five minutes."

"Five minutes are not enough. It's about Tu." Sansan's mother steps closer and whispers, "Tu is divorced."

Sansan stares at her mother for a long moment. Her mother nods at her. "Yes, he's unoccupied now."

"I don't know what you're talking about," Sansan says.

"His parents want you to go back to him."

"Mama. I don't understand."

"That's why you have to come home and talk to me. Now go teach," Sansan's mother says, and pushes the wheelbarrow forward before Sansan replies.

Sansan discovered *Casablanca* the year Tu wrote a short and apologetic letter from America, explaining his decision not to marry her. Before the letter's arrival, she showed *The Sound of Music* to her students, humming with every song, ready to abandon the students for America at any minute. After the letter, she has never sung again. *Casablanca* says all she wants to teach the students about life.

Sansan goes back to the classroom and resumes her place on the windowsill, letting her legs dangle the way she remembers her American teachers did in college. At the end of the Paris scene, when Rick gets soaked on the platform in the pouring rain, and then boards the train, a boy says, "How funny. His coat is dry as a camel's fur now."

Sansan is surprised that she has missed the detail all along. She thinks of praising the boy for his keen observation, but changes her mind. "One of life's mysteries is its inexplicability," she raises her voice and says.

The students roar with laughter. Certainly the line will be passed on, along with the nickname, to the next class, but Sansan does not care. The students, recent graduates from junior high, will be teaching elementary students after the two years of studying in the Educators' School. Most of them are from villages, and the school is their single chance to escape heavy farm labor. English is taught only to comply with a regulation set by the Education Department; they will never understand what she means, these kids living out their petty desires.

After two classes, Sansan decides to take off, complaining to her colleagues of a headache. Nobody believes her excuse, she knows, but nobody would contradict her, either. They indulge her the way people do a person with a mild and harmless craziness, whose eccentricity adds color to their otherwise dull lives. Among the few people in town who have college degrees, Sansan is the best-educated one. She was one of the two children from the town who have ever made it to the most prestigious college in Beijing, and the only one to have returned. The other one, Tu, the childhood companion and classmate and boyfriend and fiancé at one time or another in her life, is in America, married to a woman more beautiful than Sansan.

And divorced now, ten years too late. Back in her rented room, Sansan sits on her bed and cracks sunflower seeds. The shells rain down onto the sheet and the floor, and she lets them pile up. She craves the popping sounds in her skull, and the special flavor in her mouth. It is the sunflower seeds, sweet and salty and slightly bitter from the nameless spices Gong's Dried Goods Shop uses to process its sunflower seeds, and the English novels she bought in college – a full shelf of them, each one worthy of someone's lifetime to study – that make her life bearable. But the sunflower seeds taste different today, Tu's divorce, like a fish bone stabbed in her throat, distracts her.

Tu would never imagine her sitting among the shells of sunflower seeds and pondering his failed marriage, but she still imagines him on a daily basis. Not a surprise, as she promised Tu at their engagement ceremony. "I'll be thinking of you until the day when all the seas in the world dry up," she said. Tu must have said something similar, and Min, the only witness of the ceremony and then Tu's legal wife on paper, hugged both of them. It was odd, in retrospect, that Min did not take a vow. After all, the engagement between Sansan and Tu, just as the marriage between Min and Tu, was the contract for all three of them.

Min was the most beautiful girl Sansan had met in college, and is, ten years later, the most beautiful person in her memory. In college they lived in the same dorm with four other girls, but for a long time in their first year, they were not close. Min was a city girl, attractive, outgoing, one of the girls who would have anything they set their eyes on, and of course they only set their eyes on the best. Sansan, a girl from a small town, with a heavy accent and a plain face, was far from the best for Min, as a confidante or a friend.

Toward the end of their freshman year, the demonstrations in Tiananmen Square disrupted their study. Min became an active protester in the Square. Miss Tiananmen, the boys voted her; she dressed up as the Statue of Liberty and gestured victory to the Western reporters' cameras. After the crashing down, she had to go through a difficult time, being checked and rechecked; she ended up belonging to the category that did not need imprisonment but did not have a right to any legal job after graduation, either. When Min came back to school, still beautiful but sad and defeated, Sansan was the first and the only person in the dorm who dared to express sympathy and friendliness toward Min. Sansan was among the few who had not attended any protests. She and Tu had been the only students showing up for classes when their classmates had gone on a strike; later, when the teachers had stopped coming to classes, they had become intimate, falling in love as their parents and the whole town back home had expected them to.

Sansan never thought of her friendly gesture to Min as anything noble or brave; it was out of a simple wish to be nice to someone who deserved a better treatment from life. Sansan was overwhelmed with joy and gratitude, then, when Min decided to return the goodwill and become her best friend. Sansan felt a little uneasy, too, as if she had taken advantage of Min's bad fortune; they would have never become friends under normal circumstances, but then, what was wrong with living with the exceptional, if that's what was given by life?

At the end of their sophomore year, the Higher Education Department announced a new policy that allowed only those students who had American relatives to be granted passports for studying abroad, something that made no sense at all, but such was their life at the time, living with all the ridiculous rules that changed their lives like a willy-nilly child. Min's only hope for her future – going to America after graduation – became a burst bubble, and Sansan, when she could not stand the heartbreakingly beautiful face of Min, started to think and act with resolution.

"Are you out of your mind?" Tu said when she announced to him her plan – that he would apply to an American graduate school and help Min out through a false marriage. "I don't have any American relatives."

"Your grandfather's brother – didn't he go to Taiwan after the Liberation War? Why couldn't he have gone to America later? Listen, nobody will go to America to check your family history. As long as we get a certificate saying that he's in America …"

"But who'll give us the certificate?"

"I'll worry about that. You think about the application," Sansan said. She saw the hesitation in Tu's eyes, but there was also a spark of hope, and she caught it before it dimmed. "Don't you want to go to America, too? We don't have to go back home after graduation, and work at some boring jobs because we don't have city residency. Nobody will care about whether you are from a small town when you get to America."

"But to marry Min?"

"Why not?" Sansan said. "We have each other, but she doesn't have anyone. The city boys – they all become turtles in their shells once she's in trouble."

Tu agreed to try. It was one of the reasons Sansan loved him – he trusted her despite his own doubt; he followed her decision. Persuading Min seemed easy, even though she too questioned the plan. Sansan alone nudged Tu and Min toward the collective American dream for all three of them; she went back to her hometown, and through bribing and pleading got a false certificate about the American grand-uncle of Tu. The plan could have gone wrong but it went right at every step. Tu was accepted by a school in Pennsylvania; Min, with the marriage certificate, got her own paperwork done to leave the country as Tu's dependent. The arrangement, a secret known only to the three of them, was too complicated to explain to outsiders, but none of the three had a doubt then. One more year and the plan would be complete, when Min would find a way to sponsor herself and Tu, with a marriage and a divorce under his belt, would come home and marry Sansan.

It did not occur to Sansan that she should have had sex with Tu before he took off. In fact, he asked for it, but she refused. She remembered reading, in her college course, *Women in Love*, and one detail had stuck with her ever since. One of the sisters, before her lover went to war, refused to have sex with him, afraid that it would make him crave women at a time when only death was available. But Tu was not going to a war but a married life with another woman. How could a man resist falling in love with a beautiful woman whose body ate, slept, peed, and menstruated in the same apartment, a thin door away from him?

Sansan started to imagine the lovemaking between Tu and Min when, after the short letter informing her of their intention to stay in the marriage, neither would write to her again. She stripped them, put them in bed, and studied their sex as if it would give her an answer. Min's silky long hair brushed against the celery stalk of Tu's body, teasing him, calling out to him; Tu pushed his large cauliflower head against Min's heavy breasts, a hungry, ugly piglet looking for his nourishment. The more she imagined, the more absurd they became. It was unfair of her, Sansan knew, to make Tu into a comic image, but Min's beauty, like a diamond, was impenetrable. Sansan had never worried about the slightest possibility of their falling in love – Min was too glamorous a girl for Tu, the boy with a big head, a thin body, and a humble smile. She had put her faith in the love between Tu and herself, and she had believed in the sacrifice they had to go through to save a friend. But inexplicable as life was, Min and Tu fell in love, and had mismatched sex in Sansan's mind. Sometimes she replaced Min with herself, and masturbated. Tu and she looked more harmonious – they had been playmates when Sansan had been a toddler sitting by her mother's stove, where Tu had been a small boy from the next stall, the fruit vendor's son; the sex, heart-breakingly beautiful, made her cry afterward.

Sansan took up the habit of eating sunflower seeds when she could no longer stand her imagination. Every night, she sits for hours cracking sunflower seeds; she reaches for the bag the first thing when she wakes up, before she gets out of bed. She calms down when the shells pop in her brain, and is able to imagine Tu and Min in their clothes. The fact that they both broke their promises to her, hurtful as it is and it will always be, no longer matters. What remains meaning-ful is Tu and Min's marriage vows to each other. She was the one to make them husband and wife, and even if they would be too ashamed to admit it to each other, she would always hover above their marriage bed, a guardian angel that blesses and curses them with her forgiveness.

What, then, has led them to end their marriage, ten years too late? Once they broke their promises to her; twice they did. With a divorce, what will become of her, when neither of them will be obliged to think about her nobleness?

When the bag of sunflower seeds runs out, Sansan decides to go find her mother and ask about Tu's divorce. The marketplace, the only one in town, is next to the railway station. The trains running between Beijing and the southern cities stop several times a day at the station for ten-minute breaks, and many vendors rely on these trains for their businesses.

The one-fifteen train has just pulled into the station when Sansan arrives. A few passengers show up stretching their legs and arms, and soon more flood into the marketplace. Sansan stands a few steps away and watches her mother hitting the side of the pot with a steel ladle and chanting, "Come and try – come and buy – the eight-treasure eggs – the best you'll ever taste."

A woman stops and lifts the lid, and her kid points to the biggest egg in the pot. More people slow down at the good smell of tea leaves, spices, and soy sauce. Some take out their wallets to pay; others, seeing more egg sellers, walk on without knowing they've missed the best hard-boiled eggs in the world. When Sansan was young, she was infuriated by the people who did not choose her mother's eggs – the other vendors were all stingy, never adding as many spices and tea leaves to their pots as her mother did. But when Sansan became older, she grew angry, instead, at her mother's stubbornness. All those people who buy her eggs – strangers that come and go and will not remember this place or her mother's face even if they remember the taste of the eggs – they will never know that her mother spends more money on the best spices and tea leaves.

When the train leaves, Sansan finds a brick and puts it next to her mother's stool. She sits down and watches her mother add eggs and more spices to the pot.

"Isn't it a waste of money to put in so much of the expensive spices?" Sansan says.

"Don't tell me how to boil eggs. I have done this for forty years, and have brought you up boiling eggs my way."

"But even if people can taste the difference, they will never come back to look for your eggs."

"Why not give them their one chance to eat the best eggs in the world, then?" her mother says, raising her voice. A few vendors look at them, winking at one another. The marketplace is full of eyes and ears. By dinnertime, the whole town will have known that Sansan has shown up and attacked her poor mother, and children of the town will be warned, at the dinner tables, not to follow Sansan's example, a daughter not fulfilling her filial duty, who spends money on renting when her mother has kept a room ready for her.

"Mama, why don't you think of retirement?" Sansan says in a lower voice.

"Who will feed me then, a poor old widow?"

"I will."

"You don't even know how to take care of yourself," her mother says. "What you need is a man like Tu."

Sansan looks at her own shadow on the ground, and the fragments of egg-shells by her leather sandals. The eggshells were her only toys before she befriended Tu from the next stall, the fruit vendor's son. Tu's parents have retired, living in a two-bedroom flat that Tu bought for them. The next stall now sells cigarettes and lighters and palm-sized pictures of blond women whose clothes, when put close to the flame, disappear. After a moment, Sansan asks, "What happened to Tu?"

"His parents came by yesterday, and asked if you wanted to go back to him."

"Why?"

"A man needs a woman. You need a husband, too."

"Is that what I am, a substitute?"

"Don't act willful. You're not a young girl anymore."

"Why did he get a divorce?"

"People change their minds. Sansan, if you ask me, I would say just go back to Tu without questioning."

"Is that what Tu wants? Or is it his parents' idea?"

"What's the difference? He'll marry you if you want to go back to him, that's what his parents said."

"That would make it an arranged marriage."

"Nonsense. We've seen you two grow up together from the beginning," Sansan's mother says. "Even in arranged marriages, people fall in love."

Sansan feels a sting in her heart. "Sure, people fall in love in arranged marriages, but that's not the love I want."

"What do you want, then, Miss Romantic?"

Sansan does not reply. A romance is more than a love story with a man. A promise is a promise, a vow remains a vow; such is the grandeur of *Casablanca*, such is the true romance that keeps every day of her life meaningful.

Neither of them speaks. Sansan watches her mother pick up the fresh eggs with the ladle, and crack the shells carefully with a spoon so that the spices will soak the eggs well. When her mother finishes, she scoops up an egg and puts it into Sansan's hands without a word. The egg is hot but Sansan does not drop it.

She looks at the cracks on the shell, darkened by the spices and soy sauce like a prophet's fractured turtle shell. When she was younger, she had to beg her mother for a long time before she was given an egg to eat, but when Tu was around, her mother always gave them each an egg without hesitation. Sansan wonders if her mother still remembers such things, the nourishing of their relationship long before she and Tu became lovers.

A few minutes pass, and then, across the street, two jeeps stop with screeching noises. Sansan looks up and sees several cops jump out and surround Gong's Dried Goods Shop. Soon the customers are driven out the door. "What's going on?" the vendors ask one another. Sansan's mother stands up and looks across the street for a minute, and hands the ladle to Sansan.

"Take care of the stove for me," her mother says, and walks across the street with a few other curious vendors.

Sansan watches her mother pushing to the front of the store, where the cops have set up red warning tapes. She wonders why, after forty years in the marketplace, her mother is still interested in other people's business.

Ten minutes later, her mother returns and says to the vendors, "You'll never imagine this – they've found opium in Gong's goods."

"What?"

"No wonder their business is always so good – they add opium when they make their nuts and seeds so people will always want to go back to them," Sansan's mother says. "What black-hearted people they are!"

"How did the police find out?" the vendor across the aisle asks.

"Someone working in the shop must have told on them."

More vendors come back. Sansan listens to them talking about Gong's opium business, her palms wet and sticky. She was planning to go to Gong's to buy more sunflower seeds before the end of the day; even the thought of the sunflower seeds makes her eager to go home and hide herself in a pile of cracked shells, letting the taste on her tongue take her over and carry her away to a safe place, where she watches over Tu and Min serenely. Is that what she is living on, a poisoned food, a drugged dream?

Sansan's mother turns to her. "But let's not talk about other people's trouble. What do you think of the proposal, Sansan?"

"To marry Tu? No, I don't want to marry him."

"You've been waiting for him all these years. Don't be silly."

"I've never waited for him."

"But that's a lie. Everyone knows you're waiting for him."

"Everyone?"

"Why else do you never get married? Everyone knows he did this horrible thing to you, but men make mistakes. Even his parents apologized yesterday. It's time to think about forgiveness."

"What's to forgive?"

"He *had* you, and then left you for another woman. Listen, it would not be that bad a thing if you went back to him. As the old saying goes – *what belongs to someone will belong to him eventually.*"

"Wait a minute, Mama. What do you mean he had me?"

Sansan's mother blushes. "You know what I mean."

"No, I don't know. If you mean sex, no, he's never had me."

"There's nothing to be ashamed of. It was understandable, and it was no-body's fault."

Sansan, for the first time, understands the town's tolerance of her, a pitiful woman used and then abandoned by a lover, a woman unmarriable because she will never be able to demonstrate her virginity on the snow-white sheet spread on the wedding bed. "Mama, I have nothing to do with Tu. We never had sex."

"Are you sure?" Sansan's mother asks, hopeful disbelief in her eyes.

"I'm a spinster losing my mind. If you don't believe me, why don't you ask the town to vote on my virginity?"

Sansan's mother stares at her for a long moment, and claps her hands. "That's even better. I didn't know you loved him so much. I'll go talk to his parents to-night, and tell them you've kept your *cleanness* for him all these years."

"I did nothing for him."

"But why wouldn't you get married, if he never had you?"

Sansan does not reply. She wonders how much of the gossip about her lost virginity burdened her father before his death. She wonders why her mother has never confronted her all these years; but then, how could her mother, a proud yet humble woman of tradition, ask her daughter such a thing when they have never talked about sex in her family?

"If you can't answer the question, it's time to make up your mind," Sansan's mother says.

"My mind has been made up all along. I won't marry Tu."

"Are you going crazy?"

"Mama, why do you want to be the best egg seller in the world?"

Sansan's mother shakes her head. "I don't know what you're talking about."

"Mama, why do you put more spices in?"

"If I'm telling people I sell the best eggs in the world, I have to keep my prom-ise."

"But nobody cares about it. You're keeping a promise that matters only to you."

"Don't talk to me like that. I'm an illiterate. Besides, what has that to do with your marriage?"

"I have my own promise to keep."

"Why are you so stubborn? Do you know we'll both end up as crazy women if you don't get married?" Sansan's mother says, and starts to cry.

Another train pulls into the station with a long whistle. Sansan listens to her mother chanting in a trembling voice, and wipes a drop of tear off. Indeed she is going crazy, hurting her mother so, the only person who loves her despite who she is. But she has no other choice. People in this world can discard their prom-ises like used napkins, but she does not want to be one of them.

A man enters the marketplace, in a dirty shirt and jeans and carrying a shape-less bag. He hugs the bag close to his body as if it were a woman. Sansan watches the man sit down at the open space between the two stalls across the aisle from her mother's stove. He takes a flattened cardboard box and a knife out of the bag, the kind with a long and sharp blade that fruit vendors use to cut watermelons. Then he takes off his shirt, points the knife to his left arm, and with a push, carefully slices open his flesh, from the elbow to the shoulder. He seems so calm and measured in his movements that Sansan and a few other people who have noticed him all watch with quiet amazement. The man dips his index finger in the blood, checks his finger as if he is a calligrapher, and writes down the words on the cardboard box: *Give me ten yuan and I will let you slice me once wherever you like; if you finish my life with one cut, you owe me nothing.*

The man has to shout out the words twice before more people gather.

"What a crazy man," an old woman says.

"An inventive way to beg, though," another woman says.

"Why not just begging?"

"Who'd give him money? He's a strong man. He should be able to find some work."

"Young people don't like to work now. They like easy money," an old man says.

"What's easy about hurting oneself?"

"Hey, what's your story?" a young man asks. "Don't you know you have to make up some really good tragedies to beg?"

People laugh. The man sits quietly in the middle of the circle, the blood dripping from his elbow onto his jeans, but he seems not to notice it. After a while, he shouts the words again.

Sansan's mother sighs. She fumbles in her cash box and then walks to the man. "Here is ten yuan. Take it, young man, and go find a job. Don't waste your life with this nonsense."

"But there's no job to find."

"Take the money then."

The man holds the blade between his two palms, and offers the knife handle to Sansan's mother, "Here you go, Auntie."

"Why? I don't want to cut you."

"But you have to, I can't take your money without you cutting me. It's written here," the man says.

"Just take it."

"I'm not a beggar."

"What are you, then?" someone in the crowd asks.

"An idiot," someone else says, and people break out laughing. The man does not move, still holding out the knife for Sansan's mother. She shakes her head and lets the bill drop onto the cardboard. The man returns the bill to the foot of Sansan's mother, and sits back at his spot.

Sansan picks up the bill and walks to the man. The man looks up at her, and she looks into his eyes. Without a word, he puts the knife in her hand. She studies his body, the naked skin smooth and tanned, and the wound that's quietly bleeding. She touches his upper arm with one finger, testing and calculating, and then moves her fingertip to his shoulder. The man shivers slightly as her finger traces his flesh.

"Sansan, are you crazy?" her mother says.

The man's muscles loosen under her caressing finger; after all these years, she finally meets someone who understands what a promise is. Crazy as they may seem to the world, they are not alone, and they will always find each other. Such is the promise of life; such is the grandeur. "Don't worry, Mama," Sansan says, and turns to smile at her mother before she points the knife at the man's shoulder and slices, slowly opening his flesh with love and tenderness.

MOTHER TONGUE

Nadine Gordimer

Nadine Gordimer (b. 1923) is a South African writer, political activist and recipient of the 1991 Nobel Prize in Literature. She won the Man Booker Prize for her 1974 novel *The Conservationist*, and has since won numerous awards and recognition worldwide. A fierce defender of equality, Gordimer refused to accept her shortlisting for the 1998 Orange Prize because the award recognises only women writers.

But everything's by chance – how else would she ever have met him? Been here.

They fell in love in her country. Met there.

A taxi he had taken skidded into her small car. It was raining the way Europe weeps in winter, and the taxi driver slammed out of his vehicle and accosted her from the other side of her window, streaming water as if dissolving in anger. His passenger intervened, exonerating her and citing the weather as responsible. The damage to taxi and car was minimal; names, addresses and telephone numbers were exchanged for the purpose of insurance claims. – A hoo-hah about nothing. – He said that to her as if this was something he and she, in their class as taxi patron and private car owner, would rate it before the level of indignation of the Pakistani or whatever the taxi man was. The passenger spoke in English, native to him, but saw through the blur of rain the uncertain nod of one who has heard but not quite understood. He didn't know a colloquial turn of phrase to translate the passing derision into that country's language.

How he came to call her had to do with a document he was to sign, as witness; couldn't have been an opportunity to follow up any attraction to a pretty face, because the rain had made hers appear smeary as the image in a tarnished mirror. So they met again, over a piece of paper in a café near the lawyer's office where she worked. It was of course still raining, and he was able to make conversation with his cobbled-together vocabulary in the country's language, remarking that you didn't have days on end like this where he came from; that's how she learnt: from Africa. *South Africa. Mandela.* The synapses and neurons made the identifying connection in the map of every European mind. Yes, he had picked up something of her language, although the course he'd taken in preparation hadn't proved of much use when he arrived and found himself where everybody spoke it all the time and not in phrase-book style and accent. They laughed together at the way *he* spoke it, a mutual recognition closer, with the flesh-and-bone structure, shining fresh skin, deep-set but frank eyes, before him in place of the image in the tarnished mirror. Blond hair – real blond, he could tell from experience of his predilection for Nordic types, genuine or chemically concocted (once naked, anyway, they carelessly showed their natural category). She knew little of his language, the few words she remembered, learnt at school. But the other forms of recognition were making communication between them. They began to see each other every day; she would take his calls on her mobile, carried into the corridor or the women's room out of earshot of others in the lawyer's office. There among the wash-basins and toilet booths the rendezvous was decided.

He worked for one of the vast-tentacled international advertising agencies, and had got himself sent to her country by yet another kind of recognition; the director's, of his intelligence, adaptability, and sanguine acceptance of the need to learn the language of the country to which he would be sent as one of the co-ordinator's of the agency's conglomerate hype (global, they called it). He was not a copywriter or designer, he was a businessman who, as he told her, had many friends and contacts of his generation in different enterprises and might – as they were all on the lookout for – move on to some other participation in the opportunities of their world. By this he also meant his and hers, both of them young. He saw that world of theirs, though they were personally far apart geographically, turning round technology as the earth revolves round the sun.

She shared an apartment with a girl-friend; the first love-making was in his apartment where he lived, alone, since coming to Germany some months past. He had had his share of affairs at home – that surely must be, in view of his composed, confidently attractive face, the lean sexual exuberance of his body, and his quick mind; by lapse of e-mails and calls between them, the affair with someone back there was outworn. The girl met by chance probably had had a few experiments. She spoke of a boy-friend who had emigrated somewhere. Of course she might just be discreet and once they were in their sumptuous throes of love-making, what went before didn't matter. Her flesh was not abundant but alertly responsive – a surprising find. He'd thought of German female types as either rather hefty, athletic, or fat.

But it was her tenderness to him, the loving*ness* in the sexuality that made this foreign affair somewhat different from the others, so that – he supposed it's what's called falling in love – they married. In love. Passed that test. An odd move in his life, far from what would have been expected, among his circle at home. But powerful European countries are accustomed to all sorts of invasions, both belligerent and peaceful, and this foreign one was legal, representing big business, an individual proof of the world's acceptance of Germany's contrition over the past. He was suitably well received when she took him to her family, and as a welcome novelty among her friends. With their easy company he became more fluent in the to-and-fro of their language. And of course it was the language of the love affair and the marriage that had been celebrated in true German style, a traditional festivity which her circle of friends, who had moved on to an unceremonious life-style, nevertheless delightedly animated around the veiled bride and three-piece-suited groom. His was a personality and a growing adeptness in exchanges that, in their remaining months there, made Germany a sort of his-and-hers.

She knew when she began to love this man that the condition would be that she would live in another country. A country she had never seen, touched the earth, felt the wind or sun, rain, heard in its expression by its inhabitants, except through him, touch of his skin, sound of his voice; a country landscaped by his words. Love goes wherever the beloved must. The prospect of going home with him to Africa: her friends saw that she was – first time since they'd all grown up together – exalted. The anticipation actually showed in the burnish of the shine over her fine cheekbones and the eagerness in her readied eyes. She ceased to see the Bauhaus façade of the building where the lawyer's offices were, the familiar tower of the ancient church that had survived the bombs of the parents' war, the beer *stube* where she was among those friends. Her parents: how did that church's marriage ceremony put it? An old biblical injunction along with many of the good precepts she had learnt at the Lutheran Sunday school they had sent her to as a child. 'Leave thy father and thy mother and cleave only ...' Something like that. The emotional parting with the parents, handed from the arms of one to the other, each jealous to have the last embrace of the daughter, was not a parting but an arrival in the embrace of a beloved man.

They were in Africa. His Africa, now defined out of a continent. Further defined: his city there. The property market, he was told by his friends who wanted to bring him up-to-date with what was happening while he was away 'doing the disappearing act into the married man', was 'flat on its arse' and this was the time to do what married men did, quit the bachelor pad and buy a house. So they spent only a month in his apartment that was to her a hotel room vacated by a previous occupant. She didn't know any of the objects in it which must have been personal to the man she had not known while he lived there. She looked through his books, took down one here and there as if she were in a library expecting to find some particular subject, but even when he was absent did not touch letters she saw lying in a drawer she had pulled out to find a ballpoint likely to be at hand in the unit of desk, computer, fax and photocopier. When they bought a house and he decided the only furniture worth taking along was the complex of his communications outfit, he cleared into a garbage bin the bundle of letters along with other papers, outlived.

The house new to them was in fact an old house, as age is measured in a city founded as a gold-mining camp 120 years ago. His white parents' generation were all for steel and glass or fake Californian-Spanish, didn't want to live with wooden verandah rails and coal-burning fire-places. To their offspring generation the Frank Lloyd Wright and Hispano-Californian look-alikes were symbolic of people looking to take on an identity outside the one they weren't sure of. Even if they didn't think in this way of their impulse to be worldly-fashionable, the assumed shell was also another shelter in their chosen isolation from the places, the manner in which the black people who surrounded, outnumbered them, lived: in hovels and shacks. Young whites on an economic level of choice found the old high-ceilinged, corrugated-iron-roofed houses more interestingly built, spacious for adaptation to ways of a life open to the unexpected. Everyone was doing it; fixing up old places. Blacks too, the professionals, media people and civil servants in what was called the new dispensation – civic term for what used to be called freedom. The houses were short of bathrooms, but those were easily installed, just as the kitchen, in the house he bought, was at once renovated with the equipment she knew – as the model of her mother's in Germany – was essential.

Home. A real his-and-hers. Friends came to help him thin overgrown trees, she had the beer chilled and the snacks ready for this male camaraderie. She planted flowers she had never seen before, didn't bloom where she came from. She hadn't found work yet – that wasn't urgent, anyway, her share in the creation of the house was a new and fulfilling occupation, as anything in the service of devotion is, centred by the big bed where they made love. There was the suggestion that she might find part-time employment to interest her at the local Goethe Institute. But she didn't want to be speaking German – English was her language now. She was introduced to, plunged into immersion in his circle. She talked little, although back in her own country, her circle where he'd made a place for himself so easily, she was rather animated. Here, she listened; it seemed to be her place. She was happy to feel she was understanding everything said in his language, even if she couldn't use it confidently enough to speak up.

There were many parties. Even without any special occasion, his friends black and white clustered instinctively in this or that apartment, house or bar, like agents of some cross-pollination of lives.

On a terrace the sunken sun sends pale searchlights to touch a valance of clouds here and there, the darkness seems to rise from damp grass as the drinking ignites animation in his friends. She has asked him to stop the car on the way, where there's a flower-seller on a corner. – What for? No-one's birthday, far as I know. – He forgets it's the rule, in her country, to take flowers or chocolates- – some gift – to a party. – Wine'd have been a better idea, my sweet. – And it happens that the host or one of the hosts – it's a combined get-together – dumps the bunch of lilies on a table where they are soon pushed aside by glasses and ashtrays.

When they arrived she sat beside him. At these gatherings married people don't sit together, it's not what one does, bringing a cosy domesticity into a good-time atmosphere. But she's still a newcomer, innocent of the protocol and he's too fond to tell her she should – well, circulate. She's one of the prettiest women there: looks fresh-picked; while the flowers she brought wilt. She's younger than most of the women. She sits, with the contradiction of knees and feet primly aligned and the lovely foothills of breasts showing above the neckline of her gauzy dress. Perhaps the difference between her and the others is she's prepared herself to look her best to honour him, not to attract other men.

He gets up to go over and greet someone he thinks has forgotten him – he's been away in Europe a whole year – and when the shoulder-grasping embrace, the huge laughter, is over, comes back, but by chance in the meantime someone has been waved to the seat next to his wife. So he pulls up a chair on the woman's other side. He hasn't deserted – it's a three-some. His newly imported wife happens to have already met this woman on some other occasion within the circle. The woman is very attractive, not really young any more but still wild, riling the company with barbed remarks, running hands up through her red-streaked plumage as if in a switch to despair at herself. People are distracted from their own talk by her spectacle. More wine is tilted into glasses as they come up to laugh, interject. The husband is one of her butts. He's challenging a reminiscence of an incident in the friends' circle his neighbour is recounting, flourishing loudly. All around the wife are references back and forth, a personal lingo – every clique has this, out of common experience. It was the same among her friends in that past life in Germany. Jokes you don't understand even if you know the words; understand only if you're aware what, who's being sent up. She doesn't know, either, the affectionate, patronising words, phrases, that are the means of expression of people who adapt and mix languages, exclamations, word-combinations in some sort of English that isn't the usage of educated people like themselves. There are so many languages in this country of theirs that his friends don't speak, but find it amusing to bring the flavours of into their own with the odd word or expression; so much more earthy, claiming an identity with their country as it is, now. Anecdotes are being argued – interruptions flying back and forth as voices amplify over re-filled glasses.

... so *they threw him with a stone*, right? – the director's office, *nogal* ...

... *In your face.* That's her always ... *Hai! Hamba kahle* ...

... *Awesome!* Something to do with a sports event or, once, a dessert someone made? They use the word often in talk of many different kinds; she's looked it up in a dictionary but there it means 'inspiring awe, an emotion of mingled reverence, dread and wonder'. And there are forms of address within the circle borrowed from other groups, other situations and experiences they now share. Someone calls out – *Chief*, I want to ask you something – when neither the speaker nor the pal hailed, white or black (for the party is mixed), is tribal – as she knows the title to be, whether in Indonesia, Central America, Africa, anywhere she could think of. Some address one another as *My China*. How is she to know this is some comradely endearment, cockney rhyming slang – 'my mate, my china plate' – somehow appropriated during the days of apartheid's army camps.

Smiling, silent; to be there with him is enough.

The party becomes a contest between him and the woman who sits between them. Each remembers, insists on a different version of what the incident was.

– You're confounding it with that time everyone was shagging in the bushes! –

– Well, you would be reliable about *that* –

– listen, listen, listen to me! – He slaps his arm round the back of her neck, under the hair she's flung up, laughing emphasis. She puts a hand on his thigh: – *You* never listen –

It's a wrestling match of words that come from the past, with touch that comes from the past. The hand stays on him. Then he snatches it up palm to palm, shaking it to contradict what she's jeering, laughing close to his face and drowning our the calls of others. – O-O-O you were still in *kort broek*, My China! Loverboy – you remember Isabella that time water skiing? Kama Sutra warns against games under water—

– No ways! You're the one to talk – also did some deep-diving in search of marine life, *ek sê*. No-oo, *kahle-kahle* was my line! –

– And what happened to your great fancy from where was it, Finland? That

Easter. Well, why not – whatever you did's politically correct with me, they say the grave's a fine and private place but no *okes* do there embrace – Among the well-read of the friends this adaptation of Marvell was uproariously appreciated.

She was alone and laughed – she did not know what at. She sat beside the woman and her husband who were hugging, celebrating each other in the easy way of those who have old connections of intimacy encoded in exchanges of a mother tongue, released by wine and a good time had by all. She laughed when everyone else did. And then sat quiet and nobody noticed her. She understood she didn't know the language.

The only mother tongue she had was his in her mouth, at night.

THE SHARED PATIO

Miranda July

Miranda July (b. 1974) is an American filmmaker, artist and writer. Her body of work includes film, fiction, monologue and live performance art. She wrote, directed and starred in the films *Me and You and Everyone We Know* (2005) and *The Future* (2011). Her fiction has appeared in the *Paris Review*, *Harper's* and the *New Yorker*. Her collection of stories, *No One Belongs Here More Than You*, won the Frank O'Connor International Short Story Award.

I t still counts, even though it happened when he was unconscious. It counts doubly because the conscious mind often makes mistakes, falls for the wrong person. But down there in the well, where there is no light and only thousand-year-old water, a man has no reason to make mistakes. God says do it and you do it. Love her and it is so. He is my neighbor. He is of Korean descent. His name is Vincent Chang. He doesn't do hapkido. When you say the word "Korean," some people automatically think of Jackie Chan's South Korean hapkido instructor, Grandmaster Kim Jin Pal; I think of Vincent.

What is the most terrifying thing that has ever happened to you? Did it involve a car? Was it on a boat? Did an animal do it? If you answered yes to any of these questions, then I am not surprised. Cars crash, boats sink, and animals are just scary. Why not do yourself a favor and stay away from these things.

Vincent has a wife named Helena. She is Greek with blond hair. It's dyed. I was going to be polite and not mention that it was dyed, but I really don't think she cares if anyone knows. In fact, I think she is going for the dyed look, with the roots showing. What if she and I were close friends. What if I borrowed her clothes and she said, That looks better on you, you should keep. it. What if she called me in tears, and I had to come over and soothe her in the kitchen, and Vincent tried to come into the kitchen and we said, Stay out, this is girl talk! I saw something like that happen on TV; these two women were talking about some stolen underwear and a man came in and they said, Stay out, this is girl talk! One reason Helena and I would never be close friends is that I am about half as tall as she. People tend to stick to their own size group because it's easier on the neck. Unless they are romantically involved, in which case the size difference is sexy. It means: I am willing to go the distance for you.

If you are sad, ask yourself why you are sad. Then pick up the phone and call someone and tell him or her the answer to the question. If you don't know anyone, call the operator and tell him or her. Most people don't know that the operator has to listen, it is a law. Also, the postman is not allowed to go inside your house, but you can talk to him on public property for up to four minutes or until he wants to go, whichever comes first.

Vincent was on the shared patio. I'll tell you about this patio. It is shared. If you look at it, you will think it is only Helena and Vincent's patio, because their back door opens on to it. But when I moved in, the landlord said that it was the patio for both the upstairs and downstairs units. I'm upstairs. He said, Don't be shy about using it, because you pay just as much rent as they do. What I don't know for sure is if he told Vincent and Helena that it is a shared patio. I have tried to demonstrate ownership by occasionally leaving something down there, like my shoes, or one time I left an Easter flag. I also try to spend exactly the same amount of time on the patio as they do. That way I know we are each getting our value. Every time I see them out there, I put a little mark on my calendar. The next time the patio is empty, I go sit on it. Then I cross off the mark. Sometimes I lag behind and have to sit out there a lot toward the end of the month to catch up.

Vincent was on the shared patio. I'll tell you about Vincent. He is an example of a New Man. You might have read the article about the New Men in *True* magazine last month. New Men are more in touch with their feelings than even women, and New Men cry. New Men want to have children, they long to give birth, so sometimes when they cry, it is because they can't do this; there is just nowhere for a baby to come out. New Men just give and give and give. Vincent is like that. Once I saw him give Helena a massage on the shared patio. This is kind of ironic, because it is Vincent who needs the massage. He has a mild form of epilepsy. My landlord told me this when I moved in, as a safety precaution. New Men are often a little frail, and also Vincent's job is art director, and that is very New Man. He told me this one day when we were both leaving the building at the same time. He is the art director of a magazine called *Punt*. This is an unusual coincidence because I am the floor manager of a printer, and we sometimes print magazines. We don't print *Punt*, but we print a magazine with a similar name, *Positive*. It's actually more like a newsletter; it's for people who are HIV-positive.

Are you angry? Punch a pillow. Was it satisfying? Not hardly. These days people are too angry for punching. What you might try is stabbing. Take an old pillow and lay it on the front lawn. Stab it with a big pointy knife. Again and again and again. Stab hard enough for the point of the knife to go into the ground. Stab until the pillow is gone and you are just stabbing the earth again and again, as if you want to kill it for continuing to spin, as if you are getting revenge for having to live on this planet day after day alone.

Vincent was on the shared patio. I was already behind in my patio use, so it made me a little anxious to see him there so late in the month. Then I had an idea;

I could sit there with him. I put on Bermuda shorts and sunglasses and suntan oil. Even though it was October, I still felt summery; I had a summery tableau in mind. In truth, though, it was quite windy, and I had to run back for a sweater. A few minutes later, I ran back for pants. Finally, I sat in a lawn chair beside Vincent on the shared patio and watched the suntan oil soak through the fabric of my khakis. He said he always liked the smell of suntan oil. This was a very graceful way of acknowledging my situation. A man with grace, that's the New Man. I asked him how things were going at *Punt*, and he told me a funny story about a typo. Because we are in the same business, he didn't have to explain that "typo" is short for "typographical error." If Helena had come out, we would have had to stop using our industry lingo so that she could understand us, but she didn't come out because she was still at work. She's a physician's assistant, which may or may not be the same thing as a nurse.

I asked Vincent more questions, and his answers became longer and longer until they hit a kind of cruising altitude and I didn't have to ask, he just orated. It was unexpected, like suddenly finding oneself at work on a weekend. What was I doing here? Where was my Roman Holiday? My American in Paris? This was just more of the same, an American in America. Finally he paused and squinted up at the sky, and I guessed he was constructing the perfect question for me, a fantastic question that I would have to rise up to, drawing from everything I knew about myself and mythology and this black earth. But he was pausing only to emphasize what he was saying about how the cover design was not actually his fault, and then at last he did ask me something; he asked, Did *I* think it was his fault, you know, based on everything he had just told me? I looked at the sky just to see what it felt like. I pretended I was pausing before telling him about the secret feeling of joy I hide in my chest, waiting, waiting, waiting for someone to notice that I rise each morning, seemingly with nothing to live for, but I do rise, and it is only because of this secret joy, God's love, in my chest. I looked down from the sky and into his eyes and I said, It wasn't your fault. I excused him for the cover and for everything else. For not yet being a New Man. We fell into silence then; he did not ask me any more questions. I was still happy to sit there beside him, but that is only because I have very, very low expectations of most people, and he had now become Most People.

Then he lurched forward. With a sudden motion, he leaned forward at an inhuman angle and stayed there. It was not the behavior of Most People, nor of New Men; it was perhaps something that an old man would do, an elderly man. I said, Vincent. Vincent. I yelled, Vincent Chang! But he only leaned forward silently, his chest almost to his knees. I knelt down and looked into his eyes. They were open, but closed like a store that is closed and looking ghostly with all the lights off. With the lights off, I could now see how luminous he had been the moment before, even in his selfishness. And it struck me that maybe *True* magazine had been wrong. Maybe there are no New Men. Maybe there are only the living and the dead, and all those who are living deserve each other and are equal to each other. I pushed his shoulders back so that he was upright in his chair again. I didn't know anything about epilepsy, but I had imagined more shaking. I moved his hair out of his face. I put my hand under his nose and felt gentle, even breaths. I pressed my lips against his ear and whispered again, It's not your fault. Perhaps this was really the only thing I had ever wanted to say to anyone, and be told.

I pulled up my chair and leaned my head against his shoulder. And although I was genuinely scared about this epileptic seizure I was in charge of, I slept. Why did I do this dangerous and inappropriate thing? I'd like to think I didn't do it, that it was in fact done to me. I slept and dreamed that Vincent was slowly sliding his hands up my shirt as we kissed. I could tell my breasts were small from the way his palms were curved. Larger breasts would have required a less acute angle. He held them as if he had wanted to for a long time, and suddenly, I saw things as they really were. He loved me. He was a complex person with layers of percolating emotions, some of them spiritual, some tortured in a more secular way, and he burned for me. This complicated flame of being was mine. I held his hot face and asked him the hard question.

What about Helena?

It's okay, because she's in the medical profession. They have to do whatever is the best for health.

That's right, the Hippocratic oath.

She'll be sad, but she won't interfere with us because of the oath.

Will you move your things up to my apartment?

No. I have to keep living with Helena because of our vows.

Your vows? What about the oath?

It'll be okay. All that is nothing compared to our thing.

Did you ever really love her?

Not really, no.

But me?

Yes.

Even though I have no pizzazz?

What are you talking about, you perfect thing.

You can see that I'm perfect?

It's in each thing that you do. I watch you when you hang your bottom over the side of the bathtub to wash it before bed.

You can see me do this?

Every night.

It's just in case.

I know. But no one will ever enter you in your sleep.

How can you promise that?

Because I'm watching you.

I thought I would have to wait until I died for this.

From now on I am yours.

No matter what? Even when you are with Helena and I am just the short woman upstairs, am I still yours then?

Yes, it is a fact between us, even if we never speak of it again.

I can't believe this is really happening.

And then Helena was there, shaking us both. But Vincent kept sleeping, and I wondered if he was dead and, if so, had he said the things in the dream before or after he passed away, and which was more authentic. Also, was *I* a criminal? Would I be arrested for negligence? I looked up at Helena; she was a swarm of action in her physician's-assistant clothes. All the motion made me dizzy; I shut my eyes again and was about to reenter the dream when Helena yelled, When did the seizure start? And, Why the fuck were you sleeping? But she was checking his vital signs with professional flourish, and the next time she looked at me, I knew I would not have to answer these questions because I had somehow become her assistant, the physician's assistant's assistant. She told me to run into their apartment for a plastic bag that would be on top of the refrigerator. I ran inside gratefully and shut the door.

Their apartment was very quiet. I tiptoed across the kitchen and pressed my face against the freezer, breathing in the complex smells of their life. They had pictures of children on their refrigerator. They had friends, and these friends had given birth to more friends. I had never seen anything as intimate as the pictures of these children. I wanted to reach up and grab the plastic bag from the top of the refrigerator, but I also wanted to look at each child. One was named Trevor, and he was having a birthday party this Saturday. *Please come!* the invitation said. *We'll have a whale of a time!* and there was a picture of a whale. It was a real whale, a photograph of a real whale. I looked into its tiny wise eye and wondered where that eye was now. Was it alive and swimming, or had it died long ago, or was it dying now, right this second? When a whale dies, it falls down through the ocean slowly, over the course of a day. All the other fish see it fall, like a giant statue, like a building, but slowly, slowly. I focused my attention on the eye; I tried to reach down inside of it, toward the real whale, the dying whale, and I whispered, It's not your fault.

Helena slammed through the back door. She briefly pressed her breasts against my back as she reached over me to grab the bag, and then she ran back outside. I turned and watched her through the window. She was giving Vincent a shot. He was waking up. She was kissing Vincent, and he was rubbing his neck. I wondered what he remembered. She was sitting on his lap now, and she had her arms wrapped around his head. They did not look up when I walked past.

The interesting thing about *Positive* is that it never mentions HIV. If it weren't for the advertisements – Retrovir, Sustiva, Viramune – you would think it was a magazine about staying positive, as in upbeat. For this reason it is my favorite magazine. All the other ones build you up just to knock you down, but the editors at *Positive* understand that you have already been knocked down, again and again, and at this point you really don't need to fail a quiz called "Are You So Sexy or Just So-So?" *Positive* prints lists of ways to feel better, kind of like "Hints from Heloise." They seem easy to write, but that's the illusion of all good advice. Common sense and the truth should feel authorless, writ by time itself. It is actually hard to write something that will make a terminally ill person feel better. And *Positive* has rules, you can't just lift your guidance from the Bible or a book about Zen; they want original material. So far none of my submissions has been accepted, but I think I'm getting closer.

> *Do you have doubts about life? Are you unsure if it is worth the trouble? Look at the sky: that is for you. Look at each person's face as you pass on the street: those faces are for you. And the street itself, and the ground under the street, and the ball of fire underneath the ground: all*

these things are for you. They are as much for you as they are for other people. Remember this when you wake up in the morning and think you have nothing. Stand up and face the east. Now praise the sky and praise the light within each person under the sky. It's okay to be unsure. But praise, praise, praise.

THE THING AROUND YOUR NECK

Chimamanda Ngozi Adichie

Chimamanda Ngozi Adichie (b. 1977) is a Nigerian author. She has published three novels, the second of which, *Half of a Yellow Sun*, won the Orange Prize, as well as an acclaimed collection of short stories, *The Thing Around Your Neck*. In 2010 she was listed in the *New Yorker's* '20 Under 40' Fiction Issue.

You thought everybody in America had a car and a gun; your uncles and aunts and cousins thought so too. Right after you won the American visa lottery, they told you: In a month, you will have a big car. Soon, a big house. But don't buy a gun like those Americans.

They trooped into the room in Lagos where you lived with your father and mother and three siblings, leaning against the unpainted walls because there weren't enough chairs to go round, to say goodbye in loud voices and tell you with lowered voices what they wanted you to send them. In comparison to the big car and house (and possibly gun), the things they wanted were minor – handbags and shoes and perfumes and clothes. You said okay, no problem.

Your uncle in America, who had put in the names of all your family members for the American visa lottery, said you could live with him until you got on your feet. He picked you up at the airport and bought you a big hot dog with yellow mustard that nauseated you. Introduction to America, he said with a laugh. He lived in a small white town in Maine, in a thirty-year-old house by a lake. He told you that the company he worked for had offered him a few thousand more than the average salary plus stock options because they were desperately trying to look diverse. They included a photo of him in every brochure, even those that had nothing to do with his unit. He laughed and said the job was good, was worth living in an all-white town even though his wife had to drive an hour to find a hair salon that did black hair. The trick was to understand America, to know that America was give-and-take. You gave up a lot but you gained a lot, too.

He showed you how to apply for a cashier job in the gas station on Main Street and he enrolled you in a community college, where the girls had thick thighs and wore bright-red nail polish, and self-tanner that made them look orange. They asked where you learned to speak English and if you had real houses back in Africa and if you'd seen a car before you came to America. They gawped at your hair. Does it stand up or fall down when you take out the braids? They wanted to know. All of it stands up? How? Why? Do you use a comb? You smiled tightly when they asked those questions. Your uncle told you to expect it; a mixture of ignorance and arrogance, he called it. Then he told you how the neighbors said, a few months after he moved into his house, that the squirrels had started to disappear. They had heard that Africans ate all kinds of wild animals.

You laughed with your uncle and you felt at home in his house; his wife called you *nwanne*, sister, and his two school-age children called you Aunty. They spoke Igbo and ate *garri* for lunch and it was like home. Until your uncle came into the cramped basement where you slept with old boxes and cartons and pulled you forcefully to him, squeezing your buttocks, moaning. He wasn't really your uncle; he was actually a brother of your father's sister's husband, not related by blood. After you pushed him away, he sat on your bed – it was his house, after all – and smiled and said you were no longer a child at twenty-two. If you let him, he would do many things for you. Smart women did it all the time. How did you think those women back home in Lagos with well-paying jobs made it? Even women in New York City?

You locked yourself in the bathroom until he went back upstairs, and the next morning, you left, walking the long windy road, smelling the baby fish in the lake. You saw him drive past – he had always dropped you off at Main Street – and he didn't honk. You wondered what he would tell his wife, why you had left. And you remembered what he said, that America was give-and-take.

You ended up in Connecticut, in another little town, because it was the last stop of the Greyhound bus you got on. You walked into the restaurant with the bright, clean awning and said you would work for two dollars less than the other waitresses. The manager, Juan, had inky-black hair and smiled to show a gold tooth. He said he had never had a Nigerian employee but all immigrants worked hard. He knew, he'd been there. He'd pay you a dollar less, but under the table; he didn't like all the taxes they were making him pay.

You could not afford to go to school, because now you paid rent for the tiny room with the stained carpet. Besides, the small Connecticut town didn't have a community college and credits at the state university cost too much. So you went to the public library, you looked up course syllabi on school Web sites and read some of the books. Sometimes you sat on the lumpy mattress of your twin bed and thought about home – your aunts who hawked dried fish and plantains, cajoling customers to buy and then shouting insults when they didn't; your uncles who drank local gin and crammed their families and lives into single rooms; your friends who had come out to say goodbye before you left, to rejoice because you won the American visa lottery, to confess their envy; your parents who often held hands as they walked to church on Sunday mornings, the neighbors from the next room laughing and teasing them; your father who brought back his boss's old newspapers from work and made your brothers read them; your mother whose salary was barely enough to pay your brothers' school fees at the secondary school where teachers gave an A when someone slipped them a brown envelope.

You had never needed to pay for an A, never slipped a brown envelope to a teacher in secondary school. Still, you chose long brown envelopes to send half your month's earnings to your parents at the address of the parastatal where your mother was a cleaner; you always used the dollar notes that Juan gave you because those were crisp, unlike the tips. Every month. You wrapped the money carefully in white paper but you didn't write a letter. There was nothing to write about.

In later weeks, though, you wanted to write because you had stories to tell. You wanted to write about the surprising openness of people in America, how eagerly they told you about their mother fighting cancer, about their sister-in-laws' preemie, the kinds of things that one should hide or should reveal only to the family members who wished them well. You wanted to write about the way people left so much food on their plates and crumpled a few dollar bills down, as though it was an offering, expiation for the wasted food. You wanted to write about the child who started to cry and pull at her blond hair and push the menus off the table and instead of the parents making her shut up, they pleaded with her, a child of perhaps five years old, and, then, they all got up and left. You wanted to write about the rich people who wore shabby clothes and tattered sneakers, who looked like the night watchmen in front of the large compounds in Lagos. You wanted to write that rich Americans were thin and poor Americans were fat and that many did not have a big house and car; you still were not sure about the guns, though, because they might have them inside their pockets.

It wasn't just to your parents you wanted to write, it was also to your friends, and cousins and aunts and uncles. But you could never afford enough perfumes and clothes and handbags and shoes to go around and still pay your rent on what you earned at the waitressing job, so you wrote nobody.

Nobody knew where you were, because you told no one. Sometimes you felt invisible and tried to walk through your room wall into the hallway, and when you bumped into the wall, it left bruises on your arms. Once, Juan asked if you had a man that hit you because he would take care of him and you laughed a mysterious laugh.

At night, something would wrap itself around your, neck, something that very nearly choked you before you fell asleep.

Many people at the restaurant asked when you had come from Jamaica, because they thought that every black person with a foreign accent was Jamaican. Or some who guessed that you were African told you that they loved elephants and wanted to go on a safari.

So when he asked you, in the dimness of the restaurant after you recited the daily specials, what African country you were from, you said Nigeria and expected him to say that he had donated money to fight AIDS in Botswana. But he asked if you were Yoruba or Igbo, because you didn't have a Fulani face. You were surprised – you thought he must be a professor of anthropology at the state university, a little young in his late twenties or so, but who was to say? Igbo, you said. He asked your name and said Akunna was pretty. He did not ask what it meant, fortunately, because you were sick of how people said, "Father's Wealth? You mean, like, your father will actually sell you to a husband?"

He told you he had been to Ghana and Uganda and Tanzania, loved the poetry of Okot p'Bitek and the novels of Amos Tutuola and had read a lot about sub-Saharan African countries, their histories, their complexities. You wanted to feel disdain, to show it as you brought his order, because white people who liked Africa too much and those who liked Africa too little were the same – condescending. But he didn't shake his head in the superior way that Professor Cobbledick back in the Maine community college did during a class discussion on decolonization in Africa. He didn't have that expression of Professor Cobble-dick's, that expression of a person who thought himself better than the people he knew about. He came in the next day and sat at the same table and when you asked if the chicken was okay, he asked if you had grown up in Lagos. He came in the third day and began talking before he ordered, about how he had visited Bombay and now wanted to visit Lagos, to see how real people lived, like in the shantytowns, because he never did any of the silly tourist stuff when he was abroad. He talked and talked and you had to tell him it was against restaurant policy. He brushed your hand when you set the glass of water down. The fourth day, when you saw him arrive, you told Juan you didn't want that table anymore. After your shift that night, he was waiting outside, earphones stuck in his ears, asking you to go out with him because your name rhymed with *hakuna matata* and *The Lion King* was the only maudlin movie he'd ever liked. You didn't know what *The Lion King* was. You looked at him in the bright light and noticed that his eyes were the color of extra-virgin olive oil, a greenish gold. Extra-virgin olive oil was the only thing, you loved, truly loved, in America.

He was a senior at the state university. He told you how old he was and you asked why he had not graduated yet. This was America, after all, it was not like back home, where universities closed so often that people added three years to their normal course of study and lecturers went on strike after strike and still were not paid. He said he had taken a couple of years off to discover himself and travel, mostly to Africa and Asia. You asked him where he ended up finding himself and he laughed. You did not laugh. You did not know that people could simply choose not to go to school, that people could dictate to life. You were used to accepting what life gave, writing down what life dictated.

You said no the following four days to going out with him, because you were uncomfortable with the way he looked at your face, that intense, consuming way he looked at your face that made you say goodbye to him but also made you reluctant to walk away. And then, the fifth night, you panicked when he was not standing at the door after your shift. You prayed for the first time in a long time and when he came up behind you and said hey, you said yes, you would go out with him, even before he asked. You were scared he would not ask again.

The next day, he took you to dinner at Chang's and your fortune cookie had two strips of paper. Both of them were blank.

You knew you had become comfortable when you told him that you watched *Jeopardy* on the restaurant TV and that you rooted for the following, in this order: women of color, black men, and white women, before, finally, white men – which meant you never rooted for white men. He laughed and told you he was used to not being rooted for, his mother taught women's studies.

And you knew you had become close when you told him that your father was really not a schoolteacher in Lagos, that he was a junior driver for a construction company. And you told him about that day in Lagos traffic in the rickety Peugeot 504 your father drove; it was raining and your seat was wet because of the rust-eaten hole in the roof. The traffic was heavy, the traffic was always heavy in Lagos, and when it rained it was chaos. The roads became muddy ponds and cars got stuck and some of your cousins went out and made some money pushing the cars out. The rain, the swampiness, you thought, made your father step on the brakes too late that day. You heard the bump before you felt it. The car your father rammed into was wide, foreign, and dark green, with golden headlights like the eyes of a leopard. Your father started to cry and beg even before he got out of the car and laid himself flat on the road, causing much blowing of horns. Sorry, sir, sorry, sir, he chanted. If you sell me and my family, you cannot buy even one tire on your car. Sorry, sir.

The Big Man seated at the back did not come out, but his driver did, examining the damage, looking at your father's sprawled form from the corner of his eye as though the pleading was like pornography, a performance he was ashamed to admit he enjoyed. At last he let your father go. Waved him away. The other cars' horns blew and drivers cursed. When your father came back into the car, you refused to look at him because he was just like the pigs that wallowed in the marshes around the market. Your father looked like *nsi*. Shit.

After you told him this, he pursed his lips and held your hand and said he understood how you felt. You shook your hand free, suddenly annoyed, because he thought the world was, or ought to be, full of people like him. You told him there was nothing to understand, it was just the way it was.

He found the African store in the Hartford yellow pages and drove you there. Because of the way he walked around with familiarity, tilting the bottle of palm wine to see how much sediment it had, the Ghanaian store owner asked him if he was African, like the white Kenyans or South Africans, and he said yes, but he'd been in America for a long time. He looked pleased that the store owner had believed him. You cooked that evening with the things you had bought, and after he ate *garri* and *onugbu* soup, he threw up in your sink. You didn't mind, though, because now you would be able to cook *onugbu* soup with meat.

He didn't eat meat because he thought it was wrong the way they killed animals; he said they released fear toxins into the animals and the fear toxins made people paranoid. Back home, the meat pieces you ate, when there was meat, were the size of half your finger. But you did not tell him that. You did not tell him either that the *dawadawa* cubes your mother cooked everything with, because curry and thyme were too expensive, had MSG, *were* MSG. He said MSG caused cancer, it was the reason he liked Chang's; Chang didn't cook with MSG.

Once, at Chang's, he told the waiter he had recently visited Shanghai, that he spoke some Mandarin. The waiter warmed up and told him what soup was best and then asked him, "You have girlfriend in Shanghai now?" And he smiled and said nothing.

You lost your appetite, the region deep in your chest felt clogged. That night, you didn't moan when he was inside you, you bit your lips and pretended that you didn't come because you knew he would worry. Later you told him why you were upset, that even though you went to Chang's so often together, even though you had kissed just before the menus came, the Chinese man had assumed you could not possibly be his girlfriend, and he had smiled and said nothing. Before he apologized, he gazed at you blankly and you knew that he did not understand.

He bought you presents and when you objected about the cost, he said his grandfather in Boston had been wealthy but hastily added that the old man had given a lot away and so the trust fund he had wasn't huge. His presents mystified you. A fist-size glass ball that you shook to watch a tiny shapely doll in pink spin around. A shiny rock whose surface took on the color of whatever touched it. An expensive scarf hand-painted in Mexico. Finally you told him, your voice stretched in irony, that in your life presents were always useful. The rock, for instance, would work if you could grind things with it. He laughed long and hard but you did not laugh. You realized that in his life, he could buy presents that were just presents and nothing else, nothing useful. When he started to buy you shoes and clothes and books, you asked him not to, you didn't want any presents at all. He bought them anyway and you kept them for your cousins and uncles and aunts, for when you would one day be able to visit home, even though you did not know how you could ever afford a ticket *and* your rent. He said he really wanted to see Nigeria and he could pay for you both to go. You did not want him to pay for you to visit home. You did not want him to go to Nigeria, to add it to the list of countries where he went to gawk at the lives of poor people who could never gawk back at *his* life. You told him this on a sunny day, when he took you to see Long Island Sound; and the two of you argued, your voices raised as you walked along the calm water. He said you were wrong to call him self-righteous. You said he was wrong to call only the poor Indians in Bombay the real Indians. Did it mean he wasn't a real American, since he was not like the poor fat people you and he had seen in Hartford? He hurried ahead of you, his upper body bare and pale, his flip-flops raising bits of sand, but then he came back and held out his hand for yours. You made up and made love and ran your hands through each other's, hair, his soft and yellow like the swinging tassels of growing corn, yours dark and bouncy like the filling of a pillow. He had got too much sun and his skin turned the color of a ripe watermelon and you kissed his back before you rubbed lotion on it.

The thing that wrapped itself around your neck, that nearly choked you before you fell asleep, started to loosen, to let go.

You knew by people's reactions that you two were abnormal – the way the nasty ones were too nasty and the nice ones too nice. The old white men and women who muttered and glared at him, the black men who shook their heads at you, the black women whose pitying eyes bemoaned your lack of self-esteem, your self-loathing. Or the black women who smiled swift solidarity smiles; the black men who tried too hard to forgive you, saying a too-obvious hi to him; the white men and women who said, "What a good-looking pair" too brightly, too loudly as though to prove their own open-mindedness to themselves.

But his parents were different; they almost made you think it was all normal. His mother told you that he had never brought a girl to meet them, except for his high school prom date, and he grinned stiffly and held your hand. The tablecloth shielded your clasped hands. He squeezed your hand and you squeezed back and wondered why he was so stiff, why his extra-virgin-olive-oil-colored eyes darkened as he spoke to his parents. His mother was delighted when she asked if you'd read Nawal el Saadawi and you said yes. His father asked how similar Indian food was to Nigerian food and teased you about paying when the check came. You looked at them and felt grateful that they did not examine you like an exotic trophy, an ivory tusk.

Afterwards, he told you about his issues with his parents, how they portioned out love like a birthday cake, how they would give him a bigger slice if only he'd agree to go to law school. You wanted to sympathize. But instead you were angry.

You were angrier when he told you he had refused to go up to Canada with them for a week or two, to their summer cottage in the Quebec countryside. They had even asked him to bring you. He showed you pictures of the cottage and you wondered why it was called a cottage because the buildings that big around your neighborhood back home were banks and churches. You dropped a glass and it shattered on the hardwood of his apartment floor and he asked what was wrong and you said nothing, although you thought a lot was wrong. Later, in the shower you started to cry. You watched the water dilute your tears and you didn't know why you were crying.

You wrote home finally. A short letter to your parents, slipped in between the crisp dollar bills, and you included your address. You got a reply only days later, by courier. Your mother wrote the letter herself; you knew from the spidery penmanship, from the misspelled words.

Your father was dead; he had slumped over the steering wheel of his company car. Five months now, she wrote. They had used some of the money you sent to give him a good funeral. They killed a goat for the guests and buried him in a good coffin. You curled up in bed, pressed your knees to your chest and tried to remember what you had been doing when your father died, what you had been doing for all the months when he was already dead. Perhaps your father died on the day your whole body had been covered in goosebumps, hard as uncooked rice, that you could not explain, Juan teasing you about taking over from the chef so that the heat in the kitchen would warm you up. Perhaps your father died on one of the days you took a drive to Mystic or watched a play in Manchester or had dinner at Chang's.

He held you while you cried, smoothed your hair, and offered to buy your ticket, to go with you to see your family. You said no, you needed to go alone. He asked if you would come back and you reminded him that you had a green card and you would lose it if you did not come back in one year. He said you knew what he meant, would you come back, come back?

You turned away and said nothing, and when he drove you to the airport, you hugged him tight for a long, long moment, and then you let go.

THE REDEMPTION OF GALEN PIKE

Carys Davies

Carys Davies is a British short story writer. She won the Society of Authors 2010 Olive Cook Short Story Award for 'The Quiet', and was then awarded the V. S. Pritchett Memorial Prize in 2011 for 'The Redemption of Galen Pike'. She curates the short fiction programme for Lancaster's literature festival, Litfest, where she hosts readings and discussions with other writers of short fiction.

They'd all seen Sheriff Nye bringing Pike into town: the two shapes snaking down the path off the mountain through the patches of melting snow and over the green showing beneath, each of them growing bigger as they moved across the rocky pasture and came down into North Street to the jailhouse – Nye on his horse, the tall gaunt figure of Galen Pike following behind on the rope.

The current Piper City jailhouse was a low cramped brick building containing a single square cell, Piper City being at this time, in spite of the pretensions of its name, a small and thinly populated town of a hundred and ninety-three souls in the foothills of the Colorado mountains. Aside from the cell, there was a scrubby yard behind, where the hangings took place, a front office with a table, a chair and a broom; a hook on the wall where the cell keys hung from a thick ring; a small stove where Knapp the jailer warmed his coffee and cooked his pancakes in the morning.

For years, Walter's sister Patience had been visiting the felons who found themselves incarcerated for any length of time in the Piper City jail. Mostly they were outsiders – drifters and vagrants drawn to the place by the occasional but persistent rumours of gold – and whenever one came along, Patience visited him.

Galen Pike's crime revolted Patience more than she could say, and on her way to the jailhouse to meet him for the first time, she told herself she wouldn't think of it; walking past the closed bank, the shuttered front of the general store, the locked-up haberdasher's, the drawn blinds of the dentist, she averted her gaze.

She would do what she always did with the felons; she would bring Galen Pike something to eat and drink, she would sit with him and talk to him and keep him company in the days that he had left. She would not recite scripture, or lecture him about the Commandments or the deadly sins, and she would only read to him if he desired it – a psalm or a prayer or a few selected verses she thought might be helpful to someone in his situation but that was all.

She was a thin, plain woman, Patience Haig.

Straight brown hair scraped back from her forehead so severely that there was a small bald patch where the hair was divided in the centre. It was tied behind in a long dry braid. Her face, too, was long and narrow, her features small and unremarkable, except for her nose which was damaged and lopsided, the right nostril squashed and flattened against the bridge. She wore black flat-heeled boots and a grey dress with long sleeves and a capacious square collar. She was thirty-six years old.

If the preparation of the heart is taken seriously the right words will come. As she walked, Patience silently repeated the advice Abigail Warner had given her when she'd passed on to Patience the responsibility of visiting the jail. Patience was always a little nervous before meeting a new prisoner for the first time, and as she came to the end of Franklin Street and turned the corner into North, she reminded herself that the old woman's advice had always stood her in good stead: if she thought about how lonely it would be – how bleak and frightening and uncomfortable – to be shut up in a twelve foot box far from home without company or kindness, then whatever the awfulness of the crime that had been committed, she always found that she was able, with the help of her basket of biscuits and strawberry cordial, to establish a calm and companionable atmosphere in the grim little room. Almost always, she had found the men happy to see her.

"Good morning, Mr Pike," she said, stepping through the barred door and hearing it clang behind her.

Galen Pike loosened the phlegm in his scrawny throat, blew out his hollow cheeks and hawked on the ground.

"I have warm biscuits," continued Patience, setting her basket on the narrow table between them, "and strawberry cordial."

Pike looked her slowly up and down. He looked at her flat-heeled tightly laced boots, her grey long-sleeved dress and scraped-back hair and asked her, in a nasty smoke-cracked drawl, if she was a preacher.

"No," said Patience, "I am your friend."

Pike burst out laughing.

He bared his yellow teeth and threw back his mane of filthy black hair and observed that if she was his friend she'd have brought him something a little stronger than strawberry cordial to drink.

If she was his friend, he said, lowering his voice and pushing his vicious ravenous-looking face close to hers and rocking forward on the straight-backed chair to which he was trussed with rope and a heavy chain, she'd have used her little white hand to slip the key to his cell off its hook on her way in and popped it in her pretty Red Riding Hood basket instead of leaving it out there on the goddamn wall with that fat pancake-scoffing fucker of a jailer.

Patience blinked and took a breath and replied crisply that he should know very well she couldn't do the second thing, and she certainly wouldn't do the first because she didn't believe anyone needed anything stronger than strawberry cordial to refresh themselves on a warm day.

She removed the clean white cloth that covered the biscuits. The cloth was damp from the steam and she used it to wipe the surface of the greasy little table which was spotted and streaked with thick unidentifiable stains, and poured out three inches of cordial into the pewter mug she'd brought from home that belonged to her brother Walter.

She told Galen Pike that she would sit with him; that she would come every morning between now and Wednesday unless he told her not to, and on Wednesday she would come too, to be with him then also, if he desired it. In the meantime, if he wanted to, he could unburden himself about what he had done, she would not judge him. Or they could talk about other things, or if he liked she would read to him, or they might sit in silence if he preferred. She didn't mind in the least, she said, if they sat in silence, she was used to silence, she liked it almost more than speaking.

Pike looked at her, frowning and wrinkling his big hooked nose, as if he was trying to figure out whether he'd been sent a mad person. When he didn't make any reply to what she'd said, Patience settled herself in the chair opposite him and took out her knitting and for half an hour neither she nor Galen Pike spoke a word, until Pike, irritated perhaps by the prolonged quiet or the rapid clickety-clack of her wooden needles, leaned across the table with the top half of his scrawny body and twisted his face up close to hers like before and asked, what was a dried-up old lady like her doing knitting a baby's bootie?

Patience coloured at the insult but ignored it and told Pike that she and the other women from the Franklin Street Friends' Meeting House were preparing a supply of clothing for Piper City's new hostel for unwed mothers. A lot of girls, she said, ended up coming this way, dragging themselves along the Boulder Road, looking for somewhere to lay their heads.

Pike slouched against the back of his chair. He twisted his grimy-fingered hands which were fastened together in a complicated knot and roped tightly, one on top of the other, across his lap.

"Unwed mothers?" he said in a leering unpleasant way. "Where all is that then?"

"Nowhere at present," Patience replied, looking up from her work, "but when it opens it will be here on North Street. The application is with the mayor."

When Patience Haig wasn't visiting the occasional residents of the Piper City jail, she was fighting the town's Republican mayor, Byron Lym.

Over the years, she and her brother Walter and the other Friends from the Franklin Street Meeting House had joined forces with the pastor and congregation of the Episcopalian church and a number of other Piper City residents to press for certain improvements in the town: a new roof for the dilapidated schoolhouse; a road out to Piet Larson's so they could get a cart out there from time to time and bring the old man into town so he could feel a bit of life about him; a library; a small fever hospital; a hostel on North Street for unwed mothers.

So far, Lym had blocked or sabotaged each and every one of the projects. He'd said no to the new roof for the school, no to Piet Larson's road, no to the library, no to the hospital and a few days from now, they would find out if he was going to say no to the hostel too.

"He is a difficult man, the mayor," said Patience, but Pike wasn't listening, he was looking out through the cell's tiny window at the maroon peaks of the mountains and when, at the end of an hour, he had asked no more questions about the hostel or anything else, or shown any desire at all to enter into any kind of conversation, Patience put her needles together and placed the finished bootie in her basket and told him that she would come again in the morning if he'd like her to.

Pike yawned and without turning his eyes from the window told her to suit herself, it was all the same to him whether she came or not. In another week he would be dead and that would be that.

Over the next three days, Patience visited Galen Pike every morning.

She brought fresh biscuits and cordial and asked Pike if he wished to talk, or have her read to him. When he didn't reply she took out her knitting and they sat together in silence.

On the fifth morning, a Sunday, Patience arrived a little later than usual, apologising as she stepped in past Knapp when he unlocked, and then locked, the barred door behind her; she'd been at Meeting for Worship, she said, and there'd been a great quantity of notices afterwards, mostly on the subject of the hostel, as the mayor had indicated he'd be making his decision shortly, possibly as early as tomorrow.

Pike yawned and spat on the floor and said he didn't give a shit where she'd been or what she'd been doing and the only thing he wanted to know was how she'd got that pretty nose.

Knapp, in his office, peeped out from behind his newspaper. He'd never known any of the men to be so unmannerly to Miss Haig. He craned his neck a little farther to see if anything interesting would happen now, if Patience Haig would put Pike in his place, or maybe get up and walk out and leave him to rot in there by hisself for the last three days of his life like he deserved.

"I fell off a gate, Mr Pike," said Patience. "When I was nine."

"Ain't that a shame," said Pike in his nasty drawl, and Knapp kept his eye on Patience, but all she said was that it was quite all right, she'd got used to it a long time ago and didn't notice it unless people remarked on it, which in her experience they never did unless they meant to be rude or unkind, and after that the two of them settled into their customary silence.

Patience took out her knitting.

In his office Knapp folded up the newspaper and began heating his coffee and cooking his pancakes. The fat in his skillet began to pop and smoke and then he poured in the batter and when the first pancake was cooked he slid it onto a plate and then he cooked another and another and when he had a pile of half a dozen he drew his chair up to his table and began to eat. Every so often he looked up and over into the cell where Patience Haig and Galen Pike sat together, as if he was still hoping for some significant event or exchange of words, something he might tell his wife about on Wednesday when he was done keeping an eye on Pike and could go home. It was creepy, he thought, as he munched on his pancakes and gulped his coffee, the way the fellow was so scrawny and thin.

"QUIT SNOOPING!" yelled Pike all of a sudden into the silence, opening his mouth wide in a big yellow-toothed snarl that made Knapp jump like a frightened squirrel and drop his fork.

"Jesus Christ," growled Pike. "Nosy fat curly-tailed fuckin' hog."

He turned to Patience. "What all d'y'all do then? At the worship meeting?"

Patience laid down her knitting and explained that there were nineteen members of the Piper City Friends' Meeting, including herself and her brother Walter, and on Sunday mornings they gathered together at the Franklin Street Meeting House where they sat on two rows of benches arranged around a small central table.

"What about the preacher?"

"No preacher," said Patience. Instead, they abided in silence and sought the light of God within themselves and no one spoke out loud unless the spirit moved them.

"What light of God?" said Galen Pike.

"The light of God that shines in every man," said Patience.

On the following day Byron Lym summoned Patience Haig and the pastor of the Episcopalian church and a handful of the other Piper City residents who supported the creation of the hostel for unwed mothers and told them they couldn't have it.

Afterwards, walking home, Patience passed Mayor Lym's big yellow house with its screened-in porch and its magical square of mown green lawn and its herbaceous borders and its sweeping driveway of twinkling smooth-rolled macadam out in front. She passed the schoolhouse with its perished square of flapping tarpaulin tethered to the beams of the broken roof; she passed the plot of unused ground next to the lumber yard where they'd hoped to build the library; the empty warehouse that could so easily be converted into a fever hospital; and by the time she reached Franklin Street she felt so low, so crushed and despondent and depressed, that she didn't go to the jail at all that day to visit Galen Pike.

She ate lunch with her brother Walter and let loose a tirade against the mayor. "Byron Lym has no interest in the unfortunate people of this world," she said, speaking quickly and breathlessly. Boiling fury and exasperated irritation bordering on despair made her burst out: "He is selfish and corrupt and bad for the town."

Walter served the macaroni cheese and Patience sat without eating, fuming.

Byron Lym had won every election in Piper City for fifteen years. The margin was narrow, but on election day, the Republican vote always seemed to win out: there were enough people in Piper City who didn't seem to mind Byron Lym stealing their taxes and spending them on himself, as long as he kept them low.

"It's wrong, Walter," she declared, "the way that man manages to hold onto those votes. It's like a greedy child with a handful of sticky candies and it shouldn't be allowed when there's not one ounce of goodness in him, not one single solitary drop."

Walter raised his eyebrows and looked at his sister with his mild smile. "No light of God, sister?"

Patience threw her napkin at him across the table. "Don't tease me, Walter. Doubtless it is there in some dark silk-lined pocket of his embroidered waistcoat but if it is he keeps it well hidden."

When they'd finished eating she asked her brother to please excuse her, she was going out for some air and for an hour Walter could hear her out on the porch glider, rocking furiously back and forth, the rusty rings creaking and tugging in the porch roof as if they might pull the whole thing down at any moment.

In his cell, Pike sat with the rope cutting into his wrists, the chain grinding against his hips every time he shifted himself in the chair. He looked around at the bare brick walls and the thick bars, at Knapp reading his newspaper or hunched over his skillet or dragging the twigs of his old broom across the office floor.

He closed his eyes and sat listening to the rustle of the aspen trees outside, and from time to time he turned his head and looked out through the tiny window at the maroon peaks of the mountains.

Eleven o'clock had come and gone, then twelve and the woman in the grey dress with the lopsided nose had not appeared. Three o'clock, four, still no sign, and Galen Pike discovered that he missed her.

He missed the gentle tapping of her knitting needles, the soft reedy tooting of the stale air of his cell as it went in and out of her squashed nostril. He realised that from the moment he woke up in the mornings, he was listening for her quick light step in the street outside. From the moment Knapp pushed his oatmeal through the bars and reached in for his potty, he was looking over at the office door and waiting for it to open. She was the only person in the world who did not recoil from him in disgust. In the courthouse people had held themselves against the wall, gawping at his wild black hair and straggly vagabond's beard, shaking their heads as if they had seen the devil. This one, with her neat hair and her long plain face and her flat polished shoes, sat there straight and stiff and looked him in the eye. He felt bad about calling her an old lady and being rude about her nose. He missed the way she gathered the silence of his cell about her like something warm that did not exclude him from it. He'd even come to enjoy the strawberry cordial.

Slowly, inch by careful inch, and with the greatest difficulty, he began working his hands loose from the tight coils of the rope.

"Forgive me, Mr Pike," said Patience when she came in the morning.

She would have come yesterday, she said, but the mayor had turned down their application for the hostel. He said it would be "a blister in the eye of any visitor to Piper City and an affront to the respectability of its inhabitants." Afterwards her spirits had been so low she'd gone straight home. "My company would have been very poor I'm afraid, Mr Pike, even for someone who makes as few demands on it as you."

Pike wished Knapp wasn't there. He hated the way the fat jailer spied on them.

"Ain't that a shame," he said, his voice low, hoarse.

"Yes."

Suddenly there were tears in Patience Haig's eyes. Her plain narrow face looked even longer than ever, pulled down by the twitching corners of her thin mouth.

Pike studied her. He didn't know what to say.

Knapp had edged closer, attracted no doubt by the soft sound of Patience Haig crying. When Pike saw him he jumped up with his chair on his back and shook his chains and roared and rushed towards the bars like a gorilla, sending the terrified Knapp scurrying back to his stove on the far side of his little office. When Pike returned to the table he found Patience laughing quietly.

"He's like the winged lion in the Book of Revelation," she said, blowing her nose. "Full of eyes before, behind and within."

"Ain't that the truth."

Patience sniffed and dried her cheeks with a half-made bootie. She straightened her long dry braid and squared her bony shoulders.

"Well," she said. "Enough of my disappointments, Mr Pike. How are you today?"

Pike wanted to tell her he'd missed her yesterday when she hadn't come.

"I'm okay," he said.

"That's good," said Patience.

"I have something for you," said Galen Pike, laying his hand upon the table.

He had made it, he said, to brighten her frock.

It was a kind of rosette, or flower, woven from what appeared to be loose threads from the rope that had been twined about his hands, which Patience saw now was no longer there. Four rough stringy petals; at the centre a button from his putrid blood-soaked shirt. Patience held it for a moment in the palm of her hand. The rough petals scraped her skin. She wondered if Pike meant it as a romantic gesture of some sort.

If the preparation of the heart is taken seriously the right words will come.

"Thank you, Mr Pike," she said gently. Thank you but she couldn't accept it, she was against adornment, material decoration.

She placed the flower back in the hollow of his cupped hand. His dirty fingers closed around it.

"You hate me."

"No."

Knapp held his breath. He watched Pike turn the rope flower over in his hand and shake his head, the foul matted tangle of snakes and rat-tails, and heard him tell Patience Haig she was wrong about the light of God being in every man. He didn't have it. It had passed him by. Where he was, was dark and swampy and bad.

"Nonsense," said Patience.

It was true, said Pike, looking out through the tiny window at the maroon-coloured peaks beyond. Since his mother died he'd done all manner of wicked things. Since she passed away, years and years and years ago, there'd been no one to tell him how to behave; no one in the world he'd wanted to please, whose good opinion mattered at all. If he'd wanted to do something, he'd gone ahead and done it. He looked at Patience. What was her name? he asked.

"Patience," she said. "Patience Haig."

"You remind me, a little, Miss Haig, of my mother."

Knapp's beady eyes moved from Galen Pike to the thin Quaker lady in her drab frock. It was hard to tell from her expression if she enjoyed this comparison with Pike's mother. Her face showed no emotion, her long braid lay neatly down her back, her hands folded in her lap.

"I am afraid of the hangman, Miss Haig," said Galen Pike.

He touched his hand to his throat. Would she shave him, in the morning? And cut his hair? Would she bring him a clean shirt so he wouldn't look so dirty and overgrown when they came for him in the morning? That is, he added with an awkward kind of grimace, if she didn't disapprove too much of him being anxious about his appearance.

Patience looked at her hands. Of course she would shave him, she said softly. If he thought it would help.

And then, because she wanted very much to lighten the heaviness of the moment, she smiled, and said she hoped she wouldn't make too much of a mess of it; she'd watched her brother Walter shaving a few times but had no experience herself. Pike said he was sure it would be all right. He trusted her not to hurt him.

When she'd finished shaving him the next morning, and given him Walter's clean shirt to put on instead of his stinking one, Patience asked him if he wanted her to read something. The twenty-third Psalm was beautiful, she said. It would give him strength, she was sure. Pike said all he wanted was for her to go with him. For ten minutes more they sat quietly. There was the sound of Knapp's broom moving across the floor of his little office, outside in the yard the rustle of the aspen trees, and then Knapp came with the key, and Sheriff Nye and two of his men, and Dr Harriman and the hangman from Boulder.

Nye unlocked the chain around Pike's waist and untied the remaining rope that fastened his legs to the chair, and took him by the arm.

In the yard he asked him if he had any last words and in a strong voice Pike said he wanted to thank Miss Patience Haig for the tasty biscuits and the cordial and the clean shirt and the shave but most of all he wanted to thank her for her sweet quiet company. She was the best and kindest person he had ever known. He had not deserved her but he was grateful and he wished he had something to give her, some small remembrance or lasting token of appreciation to show his gratitude, but he had nothing and all he could hope was that if she ever thought of him after he was dead, it would not be badly.

It was hard to tell, Knapp said later to his wife, what effect this short speech of Pike's had on Patience Haig, but when the burlap bag came smartly down over Pike's black eyes and repulsive ravenous features and the floor opened beneath his feet, he was certain Miss Haig struggled with her famous composure; that behind the rough snap of the cloth and the clatter of the scaffold's wooden machinery, he heard a small high cry escape from her plain upright figure.

When it was over Patience asked Knapp if she might sit for while in the empty cell. She looked for the rope flower but it wasn't there. Knapp must have spirited it away, or perhaps Pike had taken it with him.

It seemed an eternity since he'd first wandered into town. There'd still been snow on the ground, though the worst of the winter had been over. For months before there'd been talk of a little gold to the south, and she remembered seeing the four Piper City men heading off on their expedition to look for it, Pike making the fifth as bag-carrier and general dogsbody, loaded up with cooking pots and shovels, dynamite, fuel, picks.

She walked slowly away from the jailhouse, trying to empty her mind of everything that had happened since the four Piper City men had failed to return and their horrible fate had been discovered. She tried to empty her mind of the quiet hours she'd spent with Galen Pike at the jail, of Byron Lym's crushing rejection of her latest project, of the terrible hanging. She had never felt so miserable in her entire life. She turned out of North Street into Franklin and passed in front of the shuttered front of the general store, the closed bank, the locked-up haberdasher's, the drawn blinds of the dentist. She paused before the heavy pine doors of the bank. On the brass knocker someone had tied an evergreen wreath with a thick black ribbon. Poor Mr Shrigley, she thought. Poor Mr Palgrave. Poor Damon Archer and Dawson Mew.

She walked on a little way and then she stopped and turned and looked back at the silent premises of the four dead men.

It had not occurred to her before.

"Oh dear Lord," she whispered, thinking of Byron Lym's stubborn but wafer-thin majority at the polls.

In Piper City everyone knew how everyone else voted and if Patience's memory served her and she was not mistaken, there'd been forty-eight Republican voters at the last election, and since then Galen Pike had eaten four of them. It was doubtful Lym could succeed next time without them.

Patience turned on her heel.

She squared her bony shoulders and tucked her basket into the crook of her arm.

Quickened her step along Franklin Street towards home.

Ran up the steps onto the porch and in through the screen door, to tell Walter the news.

THE HEART OF DENIS NOBLE

Alison MacLeod

Alison MacLeod is a British novelist, short story writer and essayist. She was awarded the Society of Authors Tom-Gallon Trust Award in 2008 and was shortlisted for the BBC National Short Story Award in 2011 for 'The Heart of Denis Noble'.

As Denis Noble, Professor of Cardiovascular Physiology, succumbs to the opioids – a meandering river of fentanyl from the IV drip – he is informed his heart is on its way. In twenty, perhaps thirty minutes' time, the Cessna air ambulance will land in the bright, crystalline light of December, on the small landing strip behind the Radcliffe Hospital.

A bearded jaw appears over him. From this angle, the mouth is oddly labial. Does he understand? Professor Noble nods from the other side of the ventilation mask. He would join in the team chat but the mask prevents it, and in any case, he must lie still so the nurse can shave the few hairs that remain on his chest.

No cool-box then. No heart on ice. This is what they are telling him. Instead, the latest technology. He remembers the prototype he was once shown. His new heart will arrive in its own state-of-the-art reliquary. It will be lifted, beating, from a nutrient-rich bath of blood and oxygen. So he can rest easy, someone adds. It's beating well at 40,000 feet, out of range of all turbulence. 'We need your research, Professor,' another voice jokes from behind the ECG. 'We're taking no chances!'

Which isn't to say that the whole thing isn't a terrible gamble.

The nurse has traded the shaver for a pair of nail-clippers. She sets to work on the nails on his right hand, his plucking hand. Is that necessary? he wants to ask. It will take him some time to grow them back, assuming of course he still has 'time'. As she slips the pulse-oximeter over his index finger, he wonders if Joshua will show any interest at all in the classical guitar he is destined to inherit, possibly any day now. According to his mother, Josh is into electronica and urban soul.

A second nurse bends and whispers in his ear like a lover. 'Now all you have to do is relax, Denis. We've got everything covered.' Her breath is warm. Her breast is near. He can imagine the gloss of her lips. He wishes she would stay by his ear forever. 'We'll have you feeling like yourself again before you know it.'

He feels he might be sick.

Then his choice of pre-op music – the second movement of Schubert's Piano Trio in E-Flat Major – seems to flow, sweet and grave, from her mouth into his ear, and once more he can see past the red and golden treetops of Gordon Square to his attic room of half a century ago. A recording of the Schubert is rising through the floorboards, and the girl beside him in his narrow student bed is warm; her lips brush the lobe of his ear; her voice alone, the whispered current of it, is enough to arouse him. But when her fingers find him beneath the sheet, they surprise him with a catheter, and he has to shut his eyes against the tears, against the absurdity of age.

The heart of Denis Noble beat for the first time on the fifth of March, 1936 in the body of Ethel Noble as she stitched a breast pocket to a drape-cut suit in an upstairs room at Wilson & Jeffries, the tailoring house where she first met her husband George, a trainee cutter, across a flashing length of gold silk lining.

As she pierced the tweed with her basting needle, she remembered George's tender, awkward kiss to her collarbone that morning, and, as if in reply, Denis's heart, a mere tube at this point, beat its first of more than two billion utterances – da dum. Unknown to Ethel, she was twenty-one days pregnant. Her thread dangled briefly in mid-air.

Soon, the tube that was Denis Noble's heart, a delicate scrap of mesoderm, would push towards life. In the dark of Ethel, it would twist and grope, looping blindly back towards itself in the primitive knowledge that circulation, the vital whoosh of life, deplores a straight line. With a tube, true, we can see from end to end, we can blow clear through or whistle a tune – a tube is nothing if not straightforward – but a loop, a *loop*, is a circuit of energy understood only by itself.

In this unfolding, intra-uterine drama, Denis Noble – a dangling button on the thread of life – would begin to take shape, to hold fast. He would inherit George's high forehead and Ethel's bright almond-shaped, almost Oriental, eyes. His hands would be small but unusually dexterous. A birthmark would stamp itself on his left hip. But inasmuch as he was flesh, blood and bone, he was also, deep within Ethel, a living stream of sound and sensation, a delicate flux of stimuli, the influence of which eluded all known measure, then as now.

He was the cloth smoothed beneath Ethel's cool palm, and the pumping of her foot on the pedal of the Singer machine. He was the hiss of her iron over the sleeve press and the clink of brass pattern-weights in her apron pocket. He was the soft spring light through the open window, the warmth of it bathing her face, and the serotonin surging in her synapses at the sight of a magnolia tree in flower. He was the manifold sound waves of passers-by: of motor cars hooting, of old men hawking and spitting, and delivery boys teetering down Savile Row under bolts of cloth bigger than they were. Indeed it is impossible to say where Denis stopped and the world began.

Only on a clear, cloudless night in November 1940 did the world seem to un-stitch itself from the small boy he was and separate into something strange, something other. Denis opened his eyes to the darkness. His mother was scooping him from his bed and running down the stairs so fast, his head bumped up and down against her shoulder.

Downstairs, his father wasn't in his armchair with the newspaper on his lap, but on the sitting room floor cutting cloth by the light of a torch. Why was Father camping indoors? 'Let's sing a song,' his mother whispered, but she forgot to tell him which song to sing.

The kitchen was a dark place and no, it wasn't time for eggs and soldiers, not yet, she shooshed, and even as she spoke, she was depositing him beneath the table next to the fat yellow bundle that was his sister, and stretching out beside him, even though her feet in their court shoes stuck out the end. 'There, there,' she said as she pulled them both to her. Then they turned their ears towards a sky they couldn't see and listened to the planes that droned like wasps in the jar of the South London night.

When the bang came, the floor shuddered beneath them and plaster fell in lumps from the ceiling. His father rushed in from the sitting room, pins still gripped between his lips. Before his mother had finished thanking God, Denis felt his legs propel him, without permission, not even his own, to the window to look. Beneath a corner of the black-out curtain, at the bottom of the garden, flames were leaping. 'Fire!' he shouted, but his father shouted louder, nearly swallowing his pins – 'GET AWAY from the window!' – and plucked him into the air.

They owed their lives, his mother would later tell Mrs West next door, to a cabinet minister's suit. Their Anderson shelter, where they would have been huddled were it not for the demands of bespoke design, had taken a direct hit.

That night, George and a dicky stirrup pump waged a losing battle against the flames until neighbours joined in with rugs, hoses and buckets of sand. Denis stood behind his mother's hip at the open door. His baby sister howled from her Moses basket. Smoke gusted as he watched his new red wagon melt in the heat. Ethel smiled down at him, squeezing his hand, and it seemed very odd because his mother shook as much as she smiled and she smiled as much as she shook. It should have been very difficult, like rubbing your tummy and patting your head at the same time, and as Denis beheld his mother – her eyes wet with tears, her hair unpinned, her arms goose-pimpled – he felt something radiate through his chest. The feeling was delicious. It warmed him through. He felt light on his toes. If his mother hadn't been wearing her heavy navy blue court shoes, the two of them, he thought, might have floated off the doorstep and into the night.

At the same time, the feeling was an ache, a hole, a sore inside him. It made him feel heavy. His heart was like something he'd swallowed that had gone down the wrong way. It made it hard to breathe. Denis Noble, age four, didn't understand. As the tremor in his mother's arm travelled into his hand, up his arm, through his armpit and into his chest, he felt for the first time the mysterious life of the heart.

He had of course been briefed in the weeks prior to surgery. His consultant, Mr Bonham, had sat at his desk – chins doubling with the gravity of the situation – reviewing Denis's notes. The tests had been inconclusive but the 'rather urgent' need for transplantation remained clear.

Naturally he would, Mr Bonham said, be familiar with the procedure. An incision in the ribcage. The removal of the pericardium – 'a slippery business, but routine'. Denis's heart would be emptied, and the aorta clamped prior to excision. 'Textbook.' The chest cavity would be cleared, though the biatrial cuff would be left in place. Then the new heart would be 'unveiled – voilà!', and the aorta engrafted, followed by the pulmonary artery.

Most grafts, Mr Bonham assured him, recovered normal ventricular function without intervention. There were risks, of course: bleeding, RV failure, brady-arrhythmias, conduction abnormalities, sudden death …

Mr Bonham surveyed his patient through his half-moon specs. 'Atheist, I presume?'

'I'm afraid not.' Denis regarded his surgeon with polite patience. Mr Bonham was widely reputed to be one of the last eccentrics still standing in the NHS.

'A believer then. Splendid. More expedient at times like this. And fear not. The Royal Society won't hear it from me!'

'Which is perhaps just as well,' said Denis, 'as I'm afraid I make as poor a "believer" as I do an atheist.'

Mr Bonham removed his glasses. 'Might be time to sort the muddle out.' He huffed on his specs, gave them a wipe with a crumpled handkerchief, and returned them to the end of his nose. 'I have a private hunch, you see, that agnostics don't fare quite as well in major surgery. No data for *The Lancet* as yet but' – he ventured a wink – 'even so. See if you can't muster a little … certainty.'

A smile crept across Denis's face. 'The Buddhists advise against too much metaphysical certainty.'

'You're a Buddhist?' A Buddhist at Oxford? At Balliol?

Denis's smile strained. 'I try to keep my options open.'

'I see.' Mr Bonham didn't. There was an embarrassment of categories. A blush spread up his neck, and as Denis watched his surgeon shuffle his notes, he felt his chances waver.

The *allegro* now. The third movement of the Piano Trio – *faster, faster* – but the Schubert is receding, and as Denis surfaces from sleep, he realises he's being whisked down the wide, blanched corridors of the Heart Unit. His trolley is a precision vehicle. It glides. It shunts around corners. There's no time to waste – the heart must be fresh – and he wonders if he has missed his stop. Kentish Town. Archway. Highgate. East Finchley. The names of the stations flicker past like clues in a dream to a year he cannot quite summon. Tunnel after tunnel. He mustn't nod off again, mustn't miss the stop, but the carriage is swaying and rocking, it's only quarter past five in the morning, and it's hard to resist the ramshackle lullaby of the Northern Line.

West Finchley. Woodside Park.

1960.

That's the one.

It's 1960, but no one, it seems, has told the good people of Totteridge. Each time he steps onto the platform at the quaint, well-swept station, he feels as if he has been catapulted back in time.

The slaughterhouse is a fifteen-minute walk along a B-road, and Denis is typically the first customer of the day. He feels underdressed next to the workers in their whites, their hard hats, their metal aprons and steel-toed Wellies. They stare, collectively, at his loafers.

Slaughter-men aren't talkers by nature, but nevertheless, over the months,

Denis has come to know each by name. Front of house, there's Alf the Shackler, Frank the Knocker, Jimmy the Sticker, Marty the Plucker, and Mike the Splitter. Frank tells him how, years ago, a sledgehammer saw him through the day's routine, but now it's a pneumatic gun and a bolt straight to the brain; a few hundred shots a day, which means he has to wear goggles, 'cos of all the grey matter flying'. He's worried he's developing 'trigger-finger', and he removes his plastic glove so Denis can see for himself 'the finger what won't uncurl.'

Alf is brawny but soft-spoken with kind, almost womanly eyes. Every morning on the quiet, he tosses Denis a pair of Wellies to spare his shoes. No one mentions the stink of the place, a sharp kick to the lungs of old blood, manure and offal. The breeze block walls exhale it and the floor reeks of it, even though the place is mopped down like a temple every night.

Jimmy is too handsome for a slaughterhouse, all dirty blond curls and American teeth, but he doesn't know it because he's a farmboy who's never been further than East Finchley. Marty, on the other hand, was at Dunkirk. He has a neck like a battering ram and a lump of shrapnel in his head. Every day, at the close of business, he brings his knife home with him on the passenger seat of his Morris Mini-Minor. He explains to Denis that he spends a solid hour each night sharpening and sanding the blade to make sure it's smooth with no pits. 'An' 'e wonders,' bellows Mike, 'why 'e can't get a bird!'

Denis pays £4 for two hearts a day, a sum that left him stammering with polite confusion on his first visit. At Wilson and Jeffries, his father earns £20 per week.

Admittedly, they bend the rules for him. Frank 'knocks' the first sheep as usual. Alf shackles and hoists. But Jimmy, who grasps his sticking knife – Jimmy, the youngest, who's always keen, literally, to 'get stuck in' – doesn't get to slit the throat and drain the animal. When Denis visits, there's a different protocol. Jimmy steps aside, and Marty cuts straight into the chest and scoops out 'the pluck'. The blood gushes. The heart and lungs steam in Marty's hands. The others tssktssk like old women at the sight of the spoiled hide, but Marty is butchery in motion. He casts the lungs down a chute, passes the warm heart to Denis, rolls the stabbed sheep down the line to Mike the Splitter, shouts 'Chop, chop, ha ha' at Mike, and waits like a veteran for Alf to roll the second sheep his way.

Often Denis doesn't wait to get back to the lab. He pulls a large pair of scissors from his hold-all, grips the heart at arm's length, cuts open the meaty ventricles, checks to ensure the Purkinje fibres are still intact, then pours a steady stream of Tyrode solution over and into the heart. When the blood is washed clear, he plops the heart into his Thermos and waits for the next heart as the gutter in the floor fills with blood. The Tyrode solution, which mimics the sugar and salts of blood, is a simple but strange elixir. Denis still can't help but take a schoolboy sort of pleasure in its magic. There in his Thermos, at the core of today's open heart, the Purkinje fibres have started to beat again in their Tyrode bath. Very occasionally, a whole ventricle comes to life as he washes it down. On those occasions, he lets Jimmy hold the disembodied heart as if it is a wounded bird fluttering between his palms.

Then the Northern Line flickers past in reverse until Euston Station re-appears, where Denis hops out and jogs – Thermos and scissors clanging in the hold-all – down Gower Street, past the main quad, through the Anatomy entrance, up the grand, century-old staircase to the second floor, and into the empty lab before the clock on the wall strikes seven.

In the hush of the Radcliffe's principal operating theatre, beside the anaesthetised, intubated body of Denis Noble, Mr Bonham assesses the donor heart for a final time.

The epicardial surface is smooth and glistening. The quantity of fat is negligible. The aorta above the valve reveals a smooth intima with no atherosclerosis. The heart is still young, after all; sadly, just seventeen years old, though – in keeping with protocol – he has revealed nothing of the donor identity to the patient, and Professor Noble knows better than to ask. The lumen of the coronary artery is large, without any visible narrowing. The muscular arterial wall is of sound proportion.

Pre-operative monitoring has confirmed strong wall motion, excellent valve function, good conduction and regular heart rhythm.

It's a ticklish business at the best of times, he reminds his team, but yes, he is ready to proceed.

In the lab of the Anatomy Building, Denis pins out the heart like a valentine in a Petri dish. The buried trove, the day's booty, is nestled at the core; next to the red flesh of the ventricle, the Purkinje network is a skein of delicate yellow fibres. They gleam like the bundles of pearl cotton his mother used to keep in her embroidery basket.

Locating them is one thing. Getting them is another. It is tricky work to lift them free; trickier still to cut away sections without destroying them. He needs a good eye, a small pair of surgical scissors, and the steady cutting hand he inherited, he likes to think, from his father. If impatience gets the better of him, if he sneezes, if his scissors slip, it will be a waste of a fresh and costly heart. Beyond the lab door, an undergrad class thunders down the staircase. Outside, through the thin Victorian glass panes, Roy Orbison croons 'Only the Lonely' on a transistor radio.

Denis drops his scissors and reaches for a pair of forceps. He works like a watchmaker, lifting another snipped segment free. A second Petri dish awaits. A fresh bath of Tyrode solution, an oxygenated variety this time, will boost their recovery. If all goes well, he can usually harvest a dozen segments from each heart. But the ends will need to close before the real work can begin. Sometimes they need an hour, sometimes longer.

Coffee. He needs a coffee. He boils water on the Bunsen burner someone pinched from the chemistry lab. The instant coffee is on the shelf with the belljars. He pours, using his sleeve as a mitt, and, in the absence of a spoon, uses the pencil that's always tucked behind his ear.

At the vast chapel-arch of a window, he can just see the treetops of Gordon Square, burnished with autumn, and far below, the gardeners raking leaves and lifting bulbs. Beyond it, from this height, he can see as far as Tavistock Square, though the old copper beech stands between him and a view of his own attic window at the top of Connaught Hall.

He tries not to think about Ella, whom he hopes to find, several hours from now, on the other side of that window, in his room – i.e., his bed – where they have agreed to meet to 'compare the findings' of their respective days. Ella, a literature student, has been coolly bluffing her way into the Press Box at the Old Bailey for the last week or so. For his part, he'd never heard of the infamous novel until the headlines got hold of it, but Ella is gripped and garrulous, and even the sound of her voice in his ear fills him with a desire worthy of the finest dirty book.

He paces, mug in hand. He can't bring himself to leave his fibres unattended while they heal.

He watches the clock.

He checks the fibres. Too soon.

He deposits his mug on the windowsill and busies himself with his prep. He fills the first glass micro-pipette with potassium chloride, inserts the silver thread-wire and connects it to the valve on his home-made amp. The glass pipette in his hand always brings to mind the old wooden dibber, smooth with use, that his father used during spring planting. Denis can see him still, in his weekend pullover and tie, on his knees in the garden, as he dibbed and dug for a victory that was in no hurry to come. Only his root vegetables ever rewarded his efforts.

Soon, Antony and Günter, his undergrad assistants, will shuffle in for duty. He'll post Antony, with the camera and a stockpile of film, at the oscilloscope's screen. Günter will take to the darkroom next to the lab, and emerge pale and blinking at the end of the day.

Outside, the transistor radio and its owner take their leave. He drains his coffee, glances at the clock, and checks his nails for sheep's blood. How much longer? He allows himself to wander as far as the stairwell and back again. He doodles on the blackboard – a sickle moon, a tree, a stick man clinging to a branch – and erases all three.

At last, at last. He prepares a slide, sets up the Zeiss, switches on its light and swivels the lens into place. At this magnification, the fibre cells are pulsing minnows of life. His 'dibbers' are ready; Günter passes him the first and checks its connection to the amp. Denis squints over the Zeiss and inserts the micro-pipette into a cell membrane. The view is good. He can even spot the two boss-eyed nuclei. If the second pipette penetrates the cell successfully, he'll make contact with the innermost life of the cell.

His wrist is steady, which means every impulse, every rapid-fire excitation, should travel up the pipette through the thread-wire and into the valve of the amplifier. The oscilloscope will 'listen' to the amp. Fleeting waves of voltage will rise and fall across its screen, and Antony will snap away on the Nikon, capturing every fluctuation, every trace. Günter, for his part, has already removed himself like a penitent to the darkroom. There, if all goes well, he'll capture the divine spark of life on Kodak paper, over and over again.

Later still, they'll convert the electrical ephemera of the day into scrolling graphs; they'll chart the unfolding peaks and troughs; they'll watch on paper the ineffable currents that compel the heart to life.

Cell after cell. Impulse upon impulse. An ebb and flow of voltage. The unfolding story of a single heartbeat in thousandths of a second.

*

'Tell me,' says Ella, 'about your excitable cells. I like those.' Their heads share the one pillow. Schubert's piano trio is rising through the floorboards of the student hall. A cellist he has yet to meet lives below.

'I'll give you excitable.' He pinches her bottom. She bites the end of his nose. Through the crack of open window, they can smell trampled leaves, wet pavement and frostbitten earth. In the night above the attic window, the stars throb.

She sighs luxuriously and shifts, so that Denis has to grip the mattress of the narrow single bed to steady himself. 'Excuse me, Miss, but I'm about to go over the edge.'

'Of the bed or your mental health? Have you found those canals yet?'

'Channels.'

'Precisely. Plutonium channels. See? I listen. You might not think I do, but I do.'

'Potassium. Potassium channels.'

'That's what I said.'

'I'm afraid you didn't. Which means …'

'Which means …?'

He rumples his brow in a display of forethought. 'Which means – and I say this with regret – I might just have to spank you.' He marvels at his own audacity. He is someone new with her and, at the same time, he has never felt more himself.

'Cheek!' she declares, and covers her own with the eiderdown. 'But I'm listening now. Tell me again. What do you do with these potassium channels?'

'I map their electrical activity. I demonstrate the movement of ions – electrically charged particles – through the cell membranes.' From the mattress edge, he gets a purchase by grabbing hold of her hip.

'Why aren't you more pleased?'

'Tell me about the trial today.'

'I thought you said those channels of yours were *the* challenge. The new discovery. The biologist's New World.'

'I'm pleased. Yes. Thanks. It's going well.' He throws back the eiderdown, springs to his feet and rifles through her shoulder bag for her notebook. 'Is it in here?'

'Is what?'

'Your notebook.'

'A man's testicles are never at their best as he bends,' she observes.

'So did The Wigs put on a good show today?'

She folds her arms across the eiderdown. 'I'm not talking dirty until you tell me about your potassium what-nots.'

'Channels.' From across the room, his back addresses her. 'They're simply passages or pores in the cell membrane that allow a mass of charged ions to be shunted into the cell – or out of it again if there's an excess.'

She sighs. 'If it's all so matter of fact, why are you bothering?'

He returns to her side, kisses the top of her head and negotiates his way back into the bed. 'My supervisor put me on the case, and, like I say, all's well. I'm getting the results, rather more quickly than I expected, so I'm pleased. Relieved even. Because in truth, I would have looked a little silly if I hadn't found them.

They're already known to exist in muscle cells, and the heart is only another muscle after all.'

'Only another muscle?'

'Yes.' He nips through her notebook.

'But this is something that has you running through Bloomsbury in the middle of the night and leaving me for a date with a computer.'

He kisses her shoulder. 'The computer isn't nearly so amiable.'

'Denis Noble, are you doing interesting work or aren't you?'

'I have a dissertation to produce.'

'Please. Never be, you know ... take it or leave it. Never be bored. Men who are bored bore me.'

'Then I shall stifle every yawn.'

'You'll have to do better than that. Tell me what you aim to discover next.' She divests him of his half of the eiderdown, and he grins, in spite of the cold.

'Whatever it is, you'll be the first to know.'

'Perhaps it isn't an "it",' she muses. 'Have you thought of that?'

'How can "it" not be an "it"?'

'I'm not sure,' she says, and she wraps herself up like the Queen of Sheba. The eiderdown crackles with static, and her fine, shiny hair flies away in the light of the desk-lamp. 'But a book, for example, is not an "it".'

'Of course it's an "it". It's an object, a thing. Ask any girl in her deportment class, as she walks about with one on her head.'

'Then I'll re-phrase, shall I? A story is not an "it". If it's any good, it's more alive than an "it". Every part of a great story "contains" every other part. Every small part anticipates the whole. Nothing can be passive or static. Nothing is just a part. Not really. Because the whole, if it's powerful enough that is, cannot be divided. That's what a great creation is. It has its own marvellous unity.' She pauses to examine the birthmark on his hip, a new discovery. 'Of course, I'm fully aware I sound like a) a girl and b) a dreamy arts student, but I suspect the heart *is* a great creation and that the same rule applies.'

'And which *rule* might that be?' He loves listening to her, even if he has no choice but to mock her, gently.

'The same principle then.'

He raises an eyebrow.

She adjusts her generous breasts. 'The principle of Eros. Eros is an attractive force. It binds the world; it makes connections. At best, it gives way to a sense of wholeness, a sense of the sacred even; at worst, it leads to fuzzy vision. Logos, your contender, particularises. It makes the elements of the world distinct. At best, it is illuminating; at worst, it is reductive. It cheapens. Both are vital. The balance is the thing. You need Eros, Denis. You're missing Eros.'

He passes her her notebook and taps it. 'On that point, we agree entirely. I wait with the utmost patience.'

She studies him with suspicion, then opens the spiral-bound stenographer's notebook. In the days before the trial, she taught herself shorthand in record time simply to capture, like any other putative member of the press, the banned passages of prose. She was determined to help carry their erotic charge into the world. 'T. S. Eliot was supposed to give evidence for the defense today, but apparently he sat in his taxi and couldn't bring himself to "do the deed".'

'Old men – impotent. Young men' – he smiles shyly and nods to his exposed self – 'ready.' He opens her notebook to a random page of shorthand. The ink is purple.

'My little joke,' she says. 'A sense of humour is *de rigueur* in the Press Box.' She nestles into the pillow and relinquishes his half of the eiderdown. He pats down her fly-away hair. 'From Chapter Ten,' she begins. '"Then with a quiver of exquisite pleasure he touched the warm soft body, and touched her navel for a moment in a kiss. And he had to come into her at once, to enter the peace on earth of her soft quiescent body. It was the moment of pure peace for him, the entry into the body of a woman." '

'That gamekeeper chap doesn't hang about,' he says, his smile twitching.

'Quiet,' she chides. 'He is actually a very noble sort. Not sordid like you.'

'My birth certificate would assure you that I'm a Noble sort.'

'Ha ha.'

Denis lays his head against her breast and listens to the beat of her heart as she reads. Her voice enters him like a current and radiates through him until he feels himself almost hum with it, as if he is the body of a violin or cello that exists only to amplify her voice. He suspects he is not in love with her – and that is really just as well – but it occurs to him that he has never known such sweetness, such delight. He tries to stay in the moment, to loiter in the beats between the words she reads, between the breaths she takes. He runs his hand over the bell of her hip and tries not to think that in just four hours he will set off into the darkened streets of Bloomsbury, descend a set of basement steps and begin his night shift in the company of the only computer at the University of London powerful enough to crunch his milliseconds of data into readable equations.

As a lowly biologist, an ostensible lightweight among the physicists and computer guys, he has been allocated the least enviable slot on the computer, from two till four a.m. By five, he'll be on the Northern Line again, heading for the slaughterhouse.

Ella half wakes as he leaves.

'Go back to sleep,' he whispers. He grabs his jacket and the hold-all.

She sits up in bed, blinking in the light of the lamp which he has turned to the wall. 'Are you going now?'

'Yes.' He smiles, glancing at her, finds his wallet and checks he has enough for the hearts of the day.

'Goodbye, Denis,' she says softly.

'Sweet dreams,' he says.

But she doesn't stretch and settle back under the eiderdown. She remains upright and naked even though the room is so cold, their breath has turned to frost on the inside of the window. He wonders if there isn't something odd in her expression. He hovers for a moment before deciding it is either a shadow from the lamp or the residue of a dream. Whatever the case, he can't be late for his shift. If he is, the porter in the unit won't be there to let him in – which means he has no more time to think on it.

He switches off the lamp.

*

In his later years, Denis Noble has allowed himself to wonder, privately, about the physiology of love. He has loved – with gratitude and frustration – parents, siblings, a spouse and two children. What, he asks himself, is love if not a force within? And what is a force within if not something *lived through* the body? Nevertheless, as Emeritus Professor of Cardiovascular Physiology, he has to admit he knows little more about love than he did on the night he fell in love with his mother; the night their shelter was bombed; the night he felt with utter certainty the strange and secret life of the heart within his chest.

Before 1960 drew to a close, he would – like hundreds of thousands of other liberated readers – buy the banned book and try to understand it as Ella had understood it. Later still in life, he would dedicate himself to the music and poetry of the Occitan troubadours. (*'I only know the grief that comes to me, to my love-ridden heart, out of over-loving …'*) He would read and re-read the ancient sacred-sexual texts of the Far East. He would learn, almost by heart, St Theresa's account of her vision of the seraph: *'I saw in his hands a long spear of gold, and at the iron's point there seemed to be a little fire. He appeared to me to be thrusting it at times into my heart, and to pierce my very entrails; when he drew it out, he seemed to draw them out also, and to leave me all on fire with a great love of God. The pain was so great that it made me moan; and yet so surpassing was the sweetness of this excessive pain that I could not wish to be rid of it.'*

But *what*, he wanted to ask St Theresa, could the heart, that feat of flesh, blood and voltage, have to do with love? *Where*, he'd like to know, is love? *How* is love?

On the train to Totteridge, he can still smell the citrus of Ella's perfume on his hands, in spite of all the punched paper-tape offerings he's been feeding to the computer through the night. He only left its subterranean den an hour ago. These days, the slots of his schedule are his daily commandments.

He is allowed 'to live' and to sleep from seven each evening to half past one the next morning, when his alarm wakes him for his shift in the computer unit. He closes the door on the darkness of Connaught Hall and sprints across Bloomsbury. After his shift, he travels from the Comp. Science basement to the Northern Line, from the Northern Line to the slaughterhouse, from the slaughterhouse to Euston, and from Euston to the lab for his twelve-hour day. 'Seven to seven,' he declares to his supervisor. He arrives home to Connaught Hall for supper at seven-thirty, Ella at eight, sleep at ten and three hours' oblivion until the alarm rings and the cycle starts all over again.

He revels briefly in the thought of a pretty girl still asleep in his bed, a luxury he'd never dared hope to win as a science student. Through the smeared carriage windows, the darkness is thinning into a murky dawn. The Thermos jiggles in the hold-all at his feet, the carriage door rattles and clangs, and his head falls back.

Up ahead, Ella is standing naked and grand on a bright woodland path in Tavistock Square. She doesn't seem to care that she can be seen by all the morning commuters and the students rushing past on their way to classes. She slips through the gate at the western end of the square and turns, closing it quickly. As he reaches it, he realises it is a kissing-gate. She stands on the other side but refuses him her lips. 'Gates open,' she says tenderly, 'and they close.' He tries to go through but she shakes her head. When he pulls on the gate, he gets an electric shock. 'Why are you surprised?' she says. Then she's disappearing through another gate into Gordon Square, and her hair is flying away in the morning light, as if she herself is electric. He pulls again on the gate, but it's rigid.

The dream returns to him only later as Marty is scooping the pluck from the first sheep on the line.

He feels again the force of that electric shock.

The gate was conductive …

It opened … It closed.

It *closed.*

He receives from Marty the first heart of the day. It's hot between his palms but he doesn't reach for his scissors. He doesn't open the Thermos. He hardly moves. Deep within him, it's as if his own heart has been jump-started to life.

In the operating theatre, Mr Bonham and his team have been at work for three-and-a-half hours, when at last he gives the word. Professor Noble can be disconnected from the bypass machine. His pulse is strong. The new heart, declares Mr Bonham, 'is going great guns'.

His dream of Ella at the gate means he can't finish at the slaughterhouse quickly enough. On the train back into town, he swears under his breath at the eternity of every stop. In the lab, he wonders if the ends of the Purkinje fibres will ever close and heal. He has twelve hours of lab time. Seven to seven. Will it be enough?

Twelve hours pass like two. The fibres are tricky today. He botched more than a few in the dissection, and the insertion of the micro-pipette has been hit and miss. Antony and Günter exchange looks. They discover he has amassed untold quantities of film, and he tells Antony he wants a faster shutter speed. When they request a lunch break, he simply stares into the middle distance. When Günter complains that his hands are starting to burn from the fixatives, Denis looks up from his micro-pipette, as if at a tourist who requires something of him in another language.

Finally, when the great window is a chapel arch of darkness and rain, he closes and locks the lab door behind him. There is nothing in his appearance to suggest anything other than a long day's work. No one he passes on the grand staircase of the Anatomy Building pauses to look. No one glances back, pricked by an intuition or an afterthought. He has remembered his hold-all and the Thermos for tomorrow's hearts. He has forgotten his jacket, but the sight of a poorly dressed student is nothing to make anyone look twice.

Yet as he steps into the downpour of the night, every light is blazing in his head. His brain is Piccadilly Circus, and in the dazzle, he hardly sees where he's going but he's running, across Gordon Square and on towards Tavistock … He wants to shout the news to the winos who shelter from the rain under dripping trees. He wants to holler it to every lit window, to every student in his or her numinous haze of thought. He wants to dash up the stairs of Connaught Hall, knock on the door of the mystery cellist, and blurt out the words. Tomorrow at the slaughterhouse, he tells himself, he might even have to hug Marty and Alf. 'They *close*!'

He saw it with his own eyes: potassium channels that *closed*.

They did just the opposite of what everyone expected.

He assumed some sort of experimental error. He went back through Günter's contact sheets. He checked the amp and the connections. He wondered if he wasn't merely observing his own wishful thinking. He started again. He shook things up. He subjected the cells to change – changes of voltage, of ions, of temperature. Antony asked, morosely, for permission to leave early. He had an exam – Gross Anatomy – the next day. Didn't Antony understand? 'They're not simply open,' he announced over a new ten-pound cylinder of graph paper. 'They *opened*.'

Antony's face was blank as an egg.

Günter suggested they call it a day.

But the channels opened. They were active. They opened *and*, more remarkably still, they *closed*.

Ella was right. He'll tell her she was. He'll be the first to admit it. The channels aren't merely passive conduits. They're not just machinery or component parts. They're alive and responsive.

Too many ions inside the cell – too much stress, exercise, anger, love, lust or despair – and they close. They stop all incoming electrical traffic. They preserve calm in the midst of too much life. They allow the ion gradient to stabilise.

He can hardly believe it himself. The heart 'listens' to itself. Causation isn't just upward; it's unequivocally downward too. It's a beautiful loop of feedback. The parts of the heart listen to each other as surely as musicians in an ensemble listen to each other. That's what he's longing to tell Ella. *That's* what he's discovered. Forget the ensemble. The heart is an *orchestra*. It's the BBC Proms. It's the Boston Pops. Even if he only understands its rhythm section today he knows this now. The heart is infinitely more than the sum of its parts.

And he can prove it mathematically. The super computer will vouch for him, he feels sure of it. He'll design the equations. He'll come up with a computer model that will make even the physicists and computer scientists stand and gawp.

Which is when it occurs to him: what if the heart doesn't stop at the heart? What if the connections don't end?

Even he doesn't quite know what he means by this.

He will ask Ella. He will tell her of their meeting at the kissing-gate. He will ask for the kiss her dream-self refused him this morning. He'll enjoy the sweet confusion on her face.

Ella at eight.

Ella always at eight.

He waits by the window until the lights go out over Tavistock Square and the trees melt into darkness.

He waits for three days. He retreats under the eiderdown. He is absent from the slaughterhouse, the lab and the basement.

A fortnight passes. A month. The new year.

When the second movement of the Piano Trio rises through the floorboards, he feels nothing. It has taken him months, but finally, he feels nothing.

*

As he comes round, the insult of the tube down his throat assures him he hasn't died.

The first thing he sees is his grandson by the foot of his bed tapping away on his new mobile phone. 'Hi, Granddad,' Josh says, as if Denis has only been napping. He bounces to the side of the ICU bed, unfazed by the bleeping monitors and the tubes. 'Put your index finger here, Denis. I'll help you … No, like right *over* the camera lens. That's it. This phone has an Instant Heart Rate App. We'll see if you're working yet.'

'Cool,' Denis starts to say, but the irony is lost to the tube in his throat.

Josh's brow furrows. He studies his phone screen like a doctor on a medical soap. 'Sixty-two beats per minute at rest. Congratulations, Granddad. You're like … alive.' Josh squeezes his hand and grins.

Denis has never been so glad to see him.

On the other side of the bed, his wife touches his shoulder. Her face is tired. The fluorescence of the lights age her. She has lipstick on her front tooth and tears in her eyes as she bends to whisper, hoarsely, in his ear, 'You came back to me.'

The old words.

After a week, he'd given up hope. He realised he didn't even know where she lived, which student residence, which flat, which telephone exchange. He'd never thought to ask. Once he even tried waiting for her outside The Old Bailey, but the trial was over, someone told him. Days before. Didn't he read the papers?

When she opened his door in January of '61, she stood on the threshold, like an apparition who might at any moment disappear again. She simply waited, her shiny hair still flying away from her in the light of the bare bulb on the landing. He was standing at the window through which he'd given up looking. On the other side, the copper beech was bare with winter. In the room below, the Schubert recording was stuck on a scratch.

Her words, when they finally came, were hushed and angry. They rose and fell in a rhythm he'd almost forgotten. 'Why don't you *know* that you're in love with me? What's wrong with you, Denis Noble?'

Cooking smells – boiled vegetables and mince – wafted into his room from the communal kitchen on the floor below. It seemed impossible that she should be here. Ella. Not Ella at eight. *Ella.*

Downstairs, the cellist moved the needle on the record.

'You came back to me,' he said.

His eyes filled.

As his recuperation begins, he will realise, with not a little impatience, that he knows nothing at all about the whereabouts of love. He knows only where it isn't. It is not in the heart, or if it is, it is not only in the heart. The organ that first beat in the depths of Ethel in the upstairs room of Wilson & Jeffries is now consigned to the scrap heap of cardiovascular history. Yet in this moment, with a heart that is not strictly his, he loves Ella as powerfully as he did the night she re-appeared in his room on Tavistock Square.

But if love is not confined to the heart, nor would it seem is memory confined to the brain. The notion tantalises him. Those aspects or qualities which make the human condition human – love, consciousness, memory, affinity – are, Denis feels more sure than ever, *distributed* throughout the body. The single part, as Ella once claimed so long ago, must contain the whole.

He hopes his new heart will let him live long enough to see the proof. He'll have to chivvy the good folk at the Physiome Project along.

He wishes he had a pencil.

In the meantime, as Denis adjusts to his new heart hour by hour, day by day, he will demonstrate, in Josh's steadfast company, an imperfect but unprecedented knowledge of the lyrics of Jay-Z and OutKast. He will announce to Ella that he is keen to buy a BMX bike. He won't be sure himself whether he is joking or not. He will develop an embarrassing appetite for doner kebabs, and he will not be deterred by the argument, put to him by Ella, his daughter and Josh, that he has never eaten a doner kebab in his entire life.

He will surprise even himself when he hears himself tell Mr Bonham, during his evening rounds, that he favours Alton Towers over the Dordogne this year.

THE LOST SEED

Emma Donoghue

Emma Donoghue (b. 1969) is an Irish-born playwright, literary historian and novelist. She has published seven novels, eleven plays and four collections of short stories. Her 2010 novel, *Room*, was a finalist for the Man Booker Prize.

In this world we are as seed scattered from God's hand. Some fall on the fat soil and thrive. Some fall among thorns and are choked as they grow. Some fall on hard ground, and their roots get no purchase, for the bitter rocks lie all around.

I, Richard Berry, make this record in the margins of the Good Book for those who come after, lest our plantation fail and all trace of our endeavors be wiped from the earth. Shielded by the Lord's arm, our ship has traveled safe across the ocean through all travails, to make landfall at the colony of Plymouth. Today we stretched our legs on land again. The snow reaches our knees. We never saw stuff like this before. It is bright as children's teeth and squeaks underfoot.

On the first day of June came the quake. So powerful is the mighty hand of the Lord, it makes both the earth and the sea to shake. Many of our thatched huts fell down.

But we and the settlers who came before us keep faith with our Maker and our mission. We go on hacking ourselves a space in the wilderness of Cape Cod: our settlement is to be called Yarmouth. The mosquitoes bite us till we are striped with blood. May we cast off the old sins of England like dust from our boots.

I have written nothing in this book for a time, being much occupied with laboring for the good of the Lord and this plantation. We have made new laws, and set down on paper the liberties of all freemen. The Indians have shown us how to bury dead fish with our seeds to sweeten the soil. We have sold them guns.

I am still unmarried. I thought on Sarah White but she laughs overmuch.

Of late I have been troubled by a weakness of spirit. I dwell on my mother and father and come near to weeping, for I will never see them again in this life. But I must remember that those who till the soil beside me are my brethren.

There are few enough of our congregation aboveground. Edward Preston lost his wife this past month, and so did Teague Joanes, a godly man whose field lies next to mine. For ye know not the hour. There are others in Yarmouth who seek to stir up division like mud in a creek. At Meeting they grasp at privilege and make much of themselves. But our dissensions must be thrust aside. If we do not help each other, who will help us? We are all sojourners in a strange land: we must lend aid, and stand guard against attack, and carry our faith like a precious stone. We hear of other plantations where there is not a Christian left alive.

Our court sentenced Seb Mitchel to be fined three pounds for his unseemly and blasphemous speeches. He spoke against his Maker for taking all three of Seb's children. He will have to give his hog to pay the fine.

Our numbers in Yarmouth are increased with the coming of ships, yet I dislike these incomers, who are all puffed up and never think of our sweat that built this town. I pray they be not like the seed that springs up quick and eager but is soon parched and blasted by the noonday sun.

Sarah White is married to Hugh Norman these two months past. She is lightsome of countenance and speech. She forgets the saying of the Apostle, that wives should submit. If she does not take care, her behavior will be spoken of at Meeting. I went by her house the other day, and she was singing a song. I could not make out the words, but it was no hymn.

These days some play while others work. Things that are lawful in moderation, whether archery or foot-racing, tobacco or ale, are become traps for the weak. Each man goes his own way, it seems; there is little concord or meekness of spirit. I remind my brethren that we are not separate, one from the other. Another bad winter could extinguish us. In this rough country we stand together or we fall.

God has not yet granted me a helpmeet. I look about me diligently at the sisters in our plantation, but some are shrewish, and others have a barren look about them, or a limp, or a cast in the eye.

In the first days, I remember, we were all one family in the Lord. But now each household shuts its doors at night. Every man looks to his own wife and his own children. I think on the first days, when there was great fellowship, through all trials.

Last night there was a snow so heavy that the whole plantation was made one white. I stood in my door and saw some flakes as wide as my hand, that came down faster than the others. Every flake falls alone, and yet on the ground they are all one.

Twice in these last months a woman has come big-bellied to be married, and she and the man put a shame-face on and paid their fine to the court, but it is clear think little of their sin.

Our court sentenced Joan Younge's master to pay her fine of two pounds, for she was rude to her mistress on the Lord's day and blocked her ears when the Bible was read, and the master should have kept her under firm governance. I would have had the girl whipped down to the bone.

Teague Joanes is the only man now who says more to me than yea or nay.

At sunset most evenings I meet him where our cornfields join. He tells me that though marriage be our duty, it brings much grief, and from the hour a child is born his father is never without fear.

Hugh Norman's daughter was found in the well, five years old. I went by their house and offered a word of succor to the mother, Sarah, but she would not leave off howling like a beast. One of John Vincent's daughters was there.

Good news on the last ship. King Charles has been cast down for his Popish wickedness. Men of conscience govern England. Heathenish festivities no longer defile the name of the Lord, and there is no more Christmas.

Here we work till the light fails. We have indentured men, some blacks among them, to hoe the land, but still too much of the crop is lost in the weeds, and strangled in rankness.

Mary Vincent is fifteen, and comely, but not overmuch.

Our court found Nathaniel Hatch and his sister Lydia Hatch guilty of unclean practices. They have strayed so far from the path, they are sheep who cannot be brought home. He is to be banished to the south and she to the north. We are not to break bread with them, or so much as throw them a crust. If we happen to pass either of them in the road, we are to turn our faces away. If either tries to speak to any of our community, we are to stop up our ears. No other town in Plymouth, or any other Christian plantation, will take in a cast-out.

I gave my view in Meeting that the pair should have been put to death for their incest, as a sign to waverers. (And after all, to be cast out is itself a sort of death, for who would wish to roam this wilderness alone?) It has seemed to me for some time that our laws are too soft. If any man go after strange flesh, or children, or fowl or other beasts, even if the deed be not accomplished, it should be death. If any man act upon himself so as to spill his seed on the ground, it should be exile, at least. For the seed is most precious in these times and must not be lost.

I spoke to Mary Vincent's father, and he was not opposed, but the girl would not have me.

I am a fruitless man. My grievous sins of pride and hard-heartedness have made me to bury my coin in the ground, like the bad servant in the parable. I have begot no children to increase our plantation. All I can do is work.

There is talk of making a law against the single life, so that every unmarried man or woman would have to go and live in some godly family. But what house would take me in?

Nathaniel Hatch is rumored to be living still in the woods to the south of Yarmouth. I wonder if he has repented of his filth. Even if the wolves have spared him, he has no people now. As for his sister, no one has set eyes on her.

Mary Vincent is to marry Benjamin Hammon.

My face is furrowed like a cornfield. The ice leaves its mark, and the burning summer turns all things brown. But I will cast off vanity. The body is but the husk that is tossed aside in the end.

Benjamin Hammon said to Teague Joanes that Sarah Norman told his wife I was an old killjoy.

It matters not.

Sin creeps around like a fog in the night. Too many of us forget to be watchful. Too many have left their doors open for the Tempter to slip in. I puzzle over it as I lie on my bed in the darkness, but I cannot tell why stinking lusts and things fearful to name should arise so commonly among us. It may be that our strict laws stop up the channel of wickedness, but it searches everywhere and at last breaks out worse than before.

I consider it my pressing business to stand sentry. Where vice crawls out of the shadows, I shine a light on it. Death still seizes so many of our flock each winter, we cannot spare a single soul among the survivors. Better I should anger my neighbor than stand by and watch the Tempter pluck up his soul as the eagle fastens on the lamb. Better I should be spurned and despised, and feel myself to be entirely alone on this earth, than that I should relinquish my holy labor. They call me killjoy, but let them tell me this, what business have we with joy? What time have we to spare for joy, and what have we done to deserve it?

The Lord has entered into the Temple and the cleansing has begun. Let the godless tremble, but the clean of heart rejoice.

This day by my information charges were laid against Sarah Norman, together with Mary Hammon, fifteen years old and newly a wife, the more her shame. I testified to what I witnessed. With my own eyes I saw them, as I stood by Hugh Norman's window in the heat of the day. His wife and Benjamin Hammon's were lying on the one bed together. They were naked as demons, and there was not a hand-span between their bodies.

It is time now to put our feet to the spades to dig up evil and all its roots.

But already there is weakening. Our court was prevailed upon to let the girl go, with only an admonition, on account of her youth. The woman's case has been held over until the weight of business allows it to be heard. But I have faith she will be brought to judgment at last after all these years of giddiness. In the meantime, Hugh Norman has sworn he will put her and her children out of his house. I gave my belief that she should be cast out of Yarmouth.

Teague Joanes came to my house last night after dark, a thing he has never done before. He said, was it not likely the woman and the girl were only comforting each other when I saw them through the window, and what soul did not need some consolation in these hard times? I reminded him that consolation was not to be sought nor found in this life, but the next. He would have prevailed upon me to show mercy, as the Father did to his Prodigal. But I gave my belief that by their transgression Sarah Norman and Mary Hammon have strayed far beyond the reach of mercy.

Then he asked me a curious thing, did I never feel lonely? In the depth of winter, say, when the snow fills up all the pathways.

I told him I never did. But this was akin to a lie.

Teague said he could not believe I was such a hard man. I gave him no answer, for my thoughts were all confounded. Then he said at any rate he would not part with me on bad terms, and came up to me and held on to me, and his leg lay against my leg.

All that was last night. And today charges were laid by my information against Teague Joanes for an attempt at sodomy.

These are bitter times. The wind of opposition blows full in my face, but I must not turn aside, for fear of my soul.

At last our court found Sarah Norman guilty of lewd behavior with Mary Hammon, but sentenced her merely to make a public acknowledgment on the Lord's day following. She lives now in a mud hut on the edge of our plantation, and her children with her, as Hugh Norman has taken ship back to England. With my own eyes I have seen some of the brethren stop to speak with her on the road. I ask why she has not been exiled, and there is none will answer me.

The case against Teague Joanes has not yet been heard. He is well liked among those who are deceived by a show of friendliness and the Tempter's own sweet smile. Many whisper that the charges should be struck out as unfounded. No one says a word to me these days. But I know what I know.

Our paths crossed on the Lord's day, and he spat on my back.

I am not a dreaming man, but last night the most dreadful sight was shown to me. I saw Teague Joanes and Sarah Norman consorting uncleanly on a bed, the man behind the woman, turning the natural use to that which is against nature, and laughing all the while.

And when I woke I knew this was no fancy but a true vision, granted me by the Lord, so that with the eyes of sleep I could witness what is hidden in the light of day. So I walked to the court and laid charges against them both for sodomy.

The clerk did not want to write down my dream. So I took him by the collar and I asked, would he wrestle with God's own angel?

In the whole town there is none who will greet me. I hear the slurs they cast upon me as I go down the street.

I work in my own field, though these days my bones creak like dead trees. I keep my head down if ever someone passes by. I wait for the court to hear my evidence. I must stand fast.

Today I was called to the court. I stepped out my door, and over my head were hanging icicles as thick as my fist and sharp like swords of glass.

There in the court were Teague Jones and Sarah Norman and Benjamin Hammon and his wife Mary together with many others, the whole people of Plymouth. And I read on their faces that they were my enemies and God's.

At first I spoke up stoutly and told of the wickedness that is spreading through this plantation, and of the secrets that hide in the folds of men's hearts. And then Teague Joanes stood up and shouted out that I was a madman and that I had no heart.

It was quiet for a moment, a quietness I have never heard before.

Then I was asked over and over again about what I had seen, and what I had imagined, and what I knew for sure. But I could not answer. I felt a terrible spinning. All I could think on was the evening Teague Joanes walked in my door. Not of the words he spoke, but the way he stood there, looking in my eyes as few know how to in these times. The way he laid his arms around me, fearless, and pressed me to him, as one brother to another. And all of a sudden I remembered the treacherous stirring between us, the swelling of evil, and I knew whose body began it.

So I said out very loud in front of the whole court that I had perjured myself and that I withdrew the charges and that I was damned for all time. And when I walked to the door, the people moved out of my way so as not to touch me.

I went across the fields for fear of meeting any human creature on the road. And it seemed to me the snow was like a face, for its crust is an image of perfection, but underneath is all darkness and slime. And I wept, a thing I have not done since I was a child, and the water turned to ice on my cheeks.

THE TURTLE

Roshi Fernando

Roshi Fernando was born in London. She was awarded the Impress Prize for New Writers in 2009 for her composite novel *Homesick*, which portrays a community of Sri Lankan immigrants in London through a series of interlinked short stories. In 2011, her story, 'The Fluorescent Jacket', was shortlisted for The Sunday Times EFG Private Bank Short Story Award.

In the dark they are back to the people they always were, Jenny and Mike with their son Lucas. They are three stumbling human beings, walking in black air, with multitudinous stars above them, and Jenny and Mike, with Lucas in between, can just be people on holiday.

With her pashmina wrapped about her, and Mike holding Lucas's other hand, she feels safer in their family, stronger in her belief in it. The guide with the torch is far ahead, and a group of worthy Germans and Italians walk his invisible footsteps in the sand one step behind. Mike and Jenny and Lucas take their time because Lucas is only four and Lucas does not like the feel of the sand as it enters the holes of his Crocs. 'I like wet sand,' he says to Jenny, 'but not *this* sand.'

'That's funny, because I would have thought it would be the other way round,' Mike says.

'No, no, Daddy. It is *this* way round,' Lucas says. 'I think this sand is yucky,' he says to Jenny, conspiratorially. She nods in the dark. 'I SAID ...' Lucas shouts –

'Yes, sorry, I heard you,' Jenny whispers. 'Remember the deal, Lucas? We whisper, and then the turtles will come out. Do you remember?' she asks urgently. Up ahead, she has seen a few of the Germans' heads turning towards them.

'Would you like a carry, littley?' Mike says.

'No, Daddy,' Lucas says. He has developed a habit of calling Mike 'Daddy' in a formal manner, as if addressing a newly bought dog that needs to learn his name. It is done kindly, but Jenny hears it every time as an admonishment to them both.

'Let me carry you,' Mike continues. 'We could catch up, and see the turtles sooner.' Jenny feels the change in the air as he stoops to pick his son up. She stiffens as she feels the child's hand become rigid in her own.

'No, Mike, don't ...' she says sharply, and it is nearly too late, but he has learnt, from her emails and her sobbing phone calls in the middle of the night, to stop as soon as she says no, to do as she says, at least where Lucas is concerned. They walk on, but she feels she is dragging Lucas, and she realises he has let go of Mike's hand.

There are dips in the sand, great hollows where her foot thinks there will be ground and instead there is air and she unbalances two or three times, giggling embarrassedly, without humour. She pulls Lucas down with her once, and he shouts again. Mike lags behind, then comes up unexpectedly at her shoulder, holding her arm with his hand. She wants to shake him off, but she contains the anger.

They reach the group, and the group acknowledge them, Jenny is sure, with stares and disapprobation, but she can't see; it is so dark she cannot see her own hand. She looks down at Lucas; his face reflects the guide's red light and is an ecstasy of expectation. She only notices now that the guide is still waiting for a group of Japanese who straggle up behind them.

'Where is the turtle?' Lucas asks, quite reasonably, she thinks. It is a rational request in this circumstance. It is fine for him to ask that, at that pitch of voice. The guide does not reply, simply looks ahead towards the older Japanese couple still struggling towards them. Lucas steps forward and tugs at the guide's *dish dasha*. 'I said,' he says louder, 'where is the turtle?' The guide flicks Lucas's hand away. Jenny hushes him, takes Lucas's hand, leads him off into the dark. Mike follows.

'Can I have attention, *please*?' the guide says. 'My assistant is now looking for turtle. There is turtle nearby, but we have to wait, so please to sit. Sit …' He gestures expansively. He has wide eyes, a broad smile, satanic in the red-bulbed torch he uses to search out the laying turtles. Mike and Jenny take Lucas up a dune, behind the rest of the group, and kneel gingerly. Lucas does not want to sit.

'The sand is yucky,' he repeats.

'Look,' Mike says, 'look at the stars,' and slowly he coaxes Lucas into sitting between his knees, with stories about Hercules and Orion. Stars shoot across the wide sky, as Mike's story takes hold. Jenny imagines this as ordinary, imagines they could live here, as Mike wants them to, and she could take for granted stars that transverse the sky.

Twenty minutes later, when they are starting to cramp and Lucas is beginning to shiver, there is sudden movement, an exchange of texts and the guide says, 'Please! Please! Quiet! There is a turtle very near here! She is in process of laying eggs, please!'

'Did you hear that, Lucas? We're going to see a turtle now,' Mike says. Lucas is still with the stars.

'Lukey, did you hear?' Jenny whispers. 'A real turtle!'

He is dreamy, tired perhaps. They get up, Mike lifting Lucas to his feet, and Jenny notices he is careful not to do more. She is grateful. The group all stand and murmur. Suddenly Lucas shouts, 'We're going to see a turtle!' and Mike and Jenny gasp, shush him, tell him no. Some of the group laugh.

The guide says 'Quiet! Quiet …' He tells them facts and figures about the turtle, how she will not lay until she is between thirty-six and forty-two years old. She is two metres long. She swims back to the same beach every year, and the turtles that are born on this beach will return to lay their eggs. He says the turtle lays, then she covers them in a large mound and goes back to the water. Jenny takes the information and speaks it into Lucas's ear. Lucas interrupts her sometimes, to ask her to repeat the words; she knows he is encapsulating the knowledge. She knows these words will stay now, that each kick of a turtle's flipper is a neural pathway opened and connected to another in her son's brain. She is an enabler, that is all, helpless in this assimilation of facts, lacking courage to deny it and make him play as any other child. She fills him up, day after day, and it seems to make him stronger, seems to make him more.

'Come now,' the guide says. 'Let us go. But when we approach, be calm and quiet please. The mother lays eggs *now*! Now!' They follow his torchlight down on to the main beach, falling in and out of holes which Jenny now realises must be old nests. The assistant is squatting next to a hole containing a dark green, hexagonally patterned rock. The rock has a head, which moves from side to side like a toy. Lucas has started to tremble.

'See, it's a turtle, Lukey, can you see it?' Mike and Jenny and Lucas stand back, away from the rest of the group, letting Lucas understand.

'I need to see,' he whispers. He allows Mike to pick him up. Jenny watches him crane forward, his arm carelessly about Mike's neck. She does not look at the turtle, only at that arm, the skin in full contact with Mike's skin. It is simply there, and she is nearly faint with not breathing.

'Come!' the guide whispers to them. 'Come and see the eggs!' As they approach, the guide asks others to stand and move away. He kneels again, shows them where they should sit. He takes Lucas's chin in his hand and points it, just so, like a midwife. 'Look!' he says, and Lucas does not object to his touch, simply looks and there are large pearls dropping from the turtle's tail, precise and round, a pile of luminescent blobs of matter, perfect in their potential.

'Oohhhh!' Lucas says wildly. The guide nods, pats Lucas's head. He does not move them away:

It was the hottest night of the year, the night Lucas was born. He was stuck in her birth canal, his English head too wide for her. 'You are made for round-headed Sri Lankan babies,' the Chinese midwife said. 'We need to unhook him. Episiotomy ... forceps.' Words mentioned, not understood: she was feral with fear and pain and anxiety for the child. Mike stood between her and the doctor, stood with his eyes to hers, cradling her head as cuts were made, holding her hands as tight as she clung to his, while cold metal plunged high into her abdomen to retrieve the tiny man stuck inside.

'It hurts, Mike!' she screamed, and he held her, telling her she was the bravest, telling her the baby was nearly there. 'Ohhhh!' she screamed.

And it was this noise she heard, when Lucas cried out. It was this red-hot anguish she thought of, the white light, the blackness inside her skull.

Jenny looks down at the turtle: there are tears rolling from the creature's eyes. 'She's crying,' she says to the guide.

'Yes, tears. But she is secreting excess salt, nothing more. It is not pain. It is not sadness!' He laughs, as if it were a joke. His phone beeps, and he reads the message. 'Oh! My goodness! You are lucky group! There is baby here! Baby!' He turns to Lucas. 'Come! You see baby?' Mike and Lucas stand and follow the others. But Jenny stays there, in the dark with the turtle, in fellowship.

Much later, in bed finally, Lucas's limbs are still, and he settles into her. She holds him close, as if he were a normal child. 'My egg,' he says. His T-shirt is damp with sweat in the closeness of the night room.

'You're a little egg, all tucked up and safe in our bed,' she coos.

'No. *My* egg.' He struggles awake. 'Be careful with it. It's in my pocket.'

When he's asleep, she looks in his trouser pockets. There is an egg there, dented, worn by the world it seems, still pale but its skin dull, dead. Mike is making tea in the kitchen of their suite. She shows him, and he reverently washes out a yoghurt pot, places tissues inside, and puts the egg in, tucking more tissues around it. Its value to Lucas somehow brings them together. Yet, when they go to bed, they say goodnight, nothing more, and stares at the ceiling, listening to the waves outside their window, knowing the sky above them is still full of stars.

The egg focuses Lucas, Mike thinks. There are fewer scenes than in England. Perhaps Lucas is growing out of it, he thinks, but he knows it is a foolish thought. He has always chosen to ignore the worst of Lucas's foibles: the way he crawled back and forth on top of the patch that was burnt by a falling iron in the carpet in their sitting room, running his hand along its texture, then crawling, then backing up and doing the whole procedure over and over, as they both watched helplessly. His mouth dribbling from a sticking-out tongue. Jenny's anxiety made Mike ashamed – of himself, of his family.

'You were the same,' his mother said, when he broached the subject. Had he been? He asked his eldest sister, who was ten when he was born. Had he been madly obsessive, too bright, easily upset? She was part of the problem – she had the same symptoms, so could not provide the solution. 'But we did OK, didn't we?' she emailed back. Did we, he wonders? Did we? Jenny and he on this cusp – and his brothers and sisters all divorced or near enough. Lucas is going to be happy, he decides. This holiday, this childhood, this life.

They wake up early every morning, and Lucas is awake before them, singing in his bed, as if in answer to the call to prayer at five.

His egg sits by his bed: it is the first thing he sees when he wakes. He has replaced the tissue with sand from the beach at Ras Al Jinz: he brought it back in his jacket pocket. Lucas had taken in everything. The guide said, 'The sand of this beach is the mother of these turtles, and it is to their mother they return when they too become mothers!' Lucas's egg is at the bottom of the yoghurt cup, weighed down by sand. Sometimes he tops the sand up from other beaches, but he is careful not to allow the cup to tip so that the 'Mummy sand', as he calls it, stays integral to the egg.

'How can you tell the difference?' Mike asks.

'Oh, I can,' Lucas says, showing the fineness of the Ras Al Jinz sand compared to the rice-like desiccated shells of the Ras Al Haad sand. He is now an expert on turtles and an expert on sand.

As they have travelled about, Lucas has held the egg in its carton, with its clingfilm (with holes) lid, on his lap in the back of the car. He has refused air conditioning, preferring the temperature of the car to be the temperature of the warm dry air of Oman. As they drive past mountain after mountain of pinky orange rock and plains of sandy earth, Lucas looks steadily and calmly about him, understanding little, 'not engaging' as Jenny puts it, but holding his yoghurt pot. Mike is fine with this. It *is* fine, he thinks. It is perfectly ordinary for a four-year-old child to behave in this way.

The driving makes Jenny talk to him, and Mike is grateful and quick to reply, so that the friendship that began their relationship is rekindled soon enough. They do not laugh yet, as they used to, but the interest shown and given is enough for Mike to be encouraged.

'I used to love stick insects when I was his age, you know.'

'Really?' she smiles. She is the most beautiful of women, pale brown, with her long black hair making her seem paler in this deeply coloured, heavily sunned country. He cannot see her eyes under her over-large sunglasses, but he has noticed that she has steadily lost weight since Lucas was born, and her wrists are tiny, her cheekbones too prominent. He dares not look at her breasts, her waist. He looks at the empty road as he drives and they speak. He does not dare imagine making love to her.

When he was offered the job in Oman, he expected her to be negative. The vehemence, though, her downright refusal to contemplate a move, disquieted them both. But the break away from the family, from the pity, from the routine visits to various caring professions: all would be banished, he argued, and we could do it ourselves. It would be just *us*, he said, bringing up *our* child. She had not considered it. Had not thought it through, he realised. He took the job. He knew it was the right moment, the right opportunity, and she would follow or she would not. And with the extra money Oman offered, he would be able to pay for Lucas and Jenny to have the life they needed, in Oman or England. There were no other choices. He came to Oman.

'I had a snail farm,' she says. 'I collected snails for a whole week or so – you know, those ugly grey-brown things that eat everything, and I let them crawl up my arm, and Mum took pictures and thought I was some sort of science genius, but I wasn't.' He notices a line of sweat-dots glistening on her upper lip. He would like to lick them off. She looks out of the open window.

'Camel!' she cries. 'Did you see, Lucas? Oh, slow down, Mike!' and she puts her hand out and touches his forearm. It tingles; the warmth of her fingers he feels down in the base of his penis. He cannot help his erection, and he slows the car down, stops on the hard shoulder of the highway, so she can hang out of the window with a camera, and he adjusts himself, and shifts in his seat. Lucas is asleep behind him, and the pot is sideways in his lap. Mike leans over and takes the yoghurt pot, puts it into the drinks holder at the front. He starts the car again.

'You don't have to be a tourist, Jen,' he says.

'Let's not talk about it,' she says.

'Why? Why not?'

She does not say anything. He drives up the last hill, in a culvert cut through orange cliffs. He knows at the top there will be the first sight of the ocean, navy and straight, the dash of a child's loaded brush across this white day. They are on their way back to Sur. They will soon be passing the Sur lagoon where young men play football at dusk. Sometimes, he plays football with the office crowd in a park in Muttrah, a rowdy, good-humoured game where often he finds himself floored by a handsome Omani who picks him up and slaps his back. Football is the language here – even in the desert, a Bedouin served them coffee in a Beckham shirt. He could teach Lucas, he thinks, and then smiles at his optimism.

'Shall we stop for a drink?' he asks, pointing to the hotel on the lagoon. Its door stands open invitingly. The tide is receding, and here the water is yellow with silt and glinting around the already stranded dhows lying on their sides.

'Lucas is still asleep,' she says.

'We can leave him in the car. It's safe here. We can sit over there, look,' he says, pulling in through the gates. In England he is never so decisive. In England Jenny tells him where to park.

'OK,' she says.

They sit at the table, and he drinks a mango lassi, and she drinks lime juice through a delicate, opaque straw. Everything about her looks taut, as if about to break. They are Mike and Jenny, Jenny and Mike, who hold hands and drink in pubs by the river.

'Please, Jenny?' he says. And just this question brings it all pouring out, the misgivings, the resentment, the torture of being left by herself in England, the 'I will *never* …' that she has stored up for this occasion, the quiet reflection after the tears, the talk of divorce. And he hears it all, but it is as if it is something that can be dealt with in the morning, on a fresh day, like a bad Excel spreadsheet that has come in at 5.30. Tomorrow it will seem easier, and when she has finished her drink, and takes off her sunglasses to really look at him (a technique he is wise to), he only says, 'Oh, my, you are lovely,' and she smiles, she – smiles. At least, she smiles.

Just down the road, he can see the men pulling up in their cars, in shorts and vests and mirrored shades. They don't wear shoes, but slip swiftly over the rocks on to the lagoon bed. Lucas's scream, 'My egg!' he greets calmly, and Mike walks steadily to the car, takes his son from his seat and the yoghurt pot from the front, and they stay for another drink and watch the sunset game.

Jenny wakes up abruptly on the beach. She watches a bird fly out across the waves. It has come to her, the sudden idea. It does not make her lift her head from the towel. She lies there, still, and thinks – if he is to drown Lucas, he must do it soon. Now. I will give him *this moment*.

Just as suddenly as the idea has come, it becomes anathema, and she sits up, curling her legs beneath her. She feels the breath judder into her, her head twitching to the side. In the distance, Mike and Lucas walk along the sea edge, hand in hand, looking down at the water. They stop to silently watch an Omani family in the sea. A father struggles with a ball against the tide and two boys run in and out of the water. She hears the boys' laughter, and she turns away.

On their last day, they stop in Muttrah. He has taken them to the Grand Mosque, and round the Sultan Qaboos University Campus, should she be tempted to take up the provisional teaching post he has begged for. He drove past the International School. He did not need to point it out. She saw it: he saw her head turn.

They sit at a juice bar, opposite the bay, fanning themselves with menus, the heat swabbing them, getting between them. Will she launch into another tirade? Not yet. She sips. He hears the sigh.

'You see, what I'm afraid of …' she says. Here it comes. 'You see me as some kind of catalogue bride. Bring me out here and I'll facilitate for you. I'll look after your fucked-up son …' His fucked-up son is playing with an ugly black street cat under the next table.

'… and be waiting at home with my sexed-up clothes under my hijab …' And so she goes on. He waits silently for her to finish. She can see his jaw twitch in patient frustration. 'I don't want to talk about it any more,' she finishes.

'Have you thought,' he says suddenly, 'that Lucas may benefit –' But she does not let him carry on. Off again, the het-up, angry words, female and hot. He talks over them: 'Maybe a new country … maybe it is not stepping backwards. Maybe a new culture … Maybe you'll be free to be *you* …' But Jenny does not see the new culture, the new life. She sees a turtle, in a hole, flapping its back flippers to bury its eggs, its head nodding this way and that in exhaustion. She sees the lady on the next table, her hijab-ed head nodding this way and that.

'No, Mike. I *can't*. I can't be *trapped* … ' but as she says it, she thinks of the turtle climbing out of her hole, walking down to the foam, swimming out to sea.

'Oh, Jen. I hate to say it, but you have got to – *shut up*!' He sees she is shocked. He has spoilt her, being so polite, so gentle. 'I'm sorry, but you have to *listen*.'

She will not, and she stumbles up, he knows in tears, and takes Lucas's hand roughly, so that as he stands, he glances his head against the corner of the table. He shouts, and begins to cry, but a painful, ordinary child's cry.

'Be quiet, Lucas,' she says, in anger, and Lucas is quiet. She starts to march away, pulling at his wrist. Lucas drags back, and they tug at each other. Lucas says: 'I want Daddy. I want to stay with Daddy.' Mike takes three Omani Real from his wallet and tucks them under the ashtray. He picks up Lucas's rucksack and takes Lucas's hand. Lucas shakes Jenny away.

They walk back into the soukh, Jenny ahead of them. Around them, men offer pashminas, perfume. The smoke of frankincense carries them through.

'You know you're going on the aeroplane tonight, don't you?' Mike says.

'Yes. Can you check my egg?' It is a ritual now. Where is the egg? It is in the main pocket on the right side. It is in the dark, under your muslin. Mike opens the bag, makes a pantomime one-eyed probe, and Lucas giggles. Jenny has disappeared around a corner into the gold soukh. He saw which way she went, but he is in no hurry to find her.

'Lucas. So you know you're going home, don't you?' He wants to appeal to the logic in the child, make it easier, the way things were made easier when he was a child, by teachers at boarding school.

'Yes,' Lucas says. But unexpectedly, he says, 'And when will you come for us?'

'Come for you?'

'Yes,' Lucas says. 'When?' And he has learnt that use of a deep, direct look into Mike's eyes.

'I don't want you to go,' Mike says, and he looks away, towards Jenny.

At the airport, they are dreadfully alone. Mike has kissed Lucas again and again, and Lucas has kissed Mike tenderly and carefully. Jenny allows him to kiss her cheek. It is night, almost ten. Lucas is tired as Mike picks him up, holds his full length against him as if to memorise it. Lucas walks backwards through the security doors. Jenny looks back once, sees Mike brush a tear away. She and Lucas have to become a team again. She pushes the trolley, and he carries his rucksack.

She tries to check in, but they have not opened the desk yet, so she sits Lucas on the trolley and they wait, watching the men and women in their flowing robes. She is grateful for the air conditioning, the vacuum of the airport. An Omani manager is kind and beckons them to a different desk. The bags are on the conveyor belt when Lucas says, 'My turtle.' It is a low-pitched gurgle of a noise.

'Did you pack these bags yourself?'

'Yes.'

'Mummy,' he whispers. 'My turtle.'

'Lucas,' she says sharply. '*Wait!*' She has learnt that his feelings are not always precious, and that he will not break.

'Did anyone ask you to carry any packages for them?'

'No,' she says, talking to both of them. Lucas looks as if he needs the toilet. 'Do you need to go?'

'Yes,' he says urgently. 'Mummy, my turtle. It's hatching. It is.'

The man at the desk smiles at Lucas.

'It isn't, Lucas,' she says, chattily. She wants to get through this, get back to England, and the cold and dark, which make her safe. The taxi is booked to meet their flight. The old shuffling George who takes them to Lucas's appointments will be there, white bristles on his cheeks; hair unkempt and the black anorak pervading smoke and Fisherman's Friends. Lucas jumps from one foot to the other. He is going red.

'He needs toilet?' the man says.

'I think so.' She is embarrassed, the way she always is, in a matter-of-fact, my-child-is-special-needs way.

'Go – go,' he says with a smile, and points towards the lavatories across the hall. She takes Lucas's hand roughly and they go through the double doors.

'See?' Lucas says, unzipping his rucksack. Inside, clambering over his muslin, his colouring pencils and his shells is a small black creature. It is comical, its head bobbing about, and it tries to climb up the black nylon interior. Its eyes look up at her, and Jenny yelps. Someone is coming in. Jenny pulls Lucas into the toilet and locks it.

'Oh, God, what are we going to do?'

'I want to take him home,' Lucas says stoutly. He slides to the floor with the bag on his lap. Jenny looks at him and sees Mike. She thinks of Mike carrying the yoghurt pot through Oman, and it makes her cry, the suddenness of the turtle's appearance. Oh, Mike, she thinks.

'We have to take him home,' Lucas whines. He is looking at Jenny, the way he looks at her when she is to say no, no, Lucas, we can't.

'Take him home? Where to?' she asks him. She will not say no.

'To the beach, of course,' he says. She was sure he meant his little room, with its dinosaur mural and plastic animals on the floor.

'Lucas! We're just about to get on a plane! We're going home!'

'No! Jenny.' He calls her Jenny in moments of crisis, like an old man, like a friend. 'We need to take him to his beach.'

'Lucas …' As Lucas begins to shout, she realises she had never imagined a time when Mike was not part of her, when she was simply Jenny again.

She calls Mike from the desk, but he is not home. She cannot remember his mobile number in her fluster. She takes the bags off the conveyor belt, tells the man they are not going. They fight their way out of security, and all the while Lucas laughs, and is manic, allowing his rucksack to be held safely by his mother, while running up and down the concourse, skidding on his knees, getting in the way of busy men and tourists. It is nearly midnight. She should take a cab, but instead she goes to a desk and hires a car.

She asks the man for a map, pays by credit card, loads the bags in with no help from anyone, straps the rucksack into the seat next to Lucas. 'You do *not* touch him, understand? You allow him air to breathe, but you do *not* touch him, OK?'

'I won't hurt him … '

'Lucas. I'm warning you … what did the man do when you saw the baby turtle?'

'He guided him down the beach with his torch.'

'Exactly. We will do the same.'

'At Ras Al Jinz?' Lucas's eyes are wide, excited.

'No. I don't know,' she says. 'We'll ask Daddy.'

They stand at Ras Al Haad, watching the sea. Lucas's shoulders still heave from the crying, and the singing of the muezzin is unexpected and disturbs them. The sun will come up soon. Lucas holds Mike's hand, and Jenny stands apart from them. It will take time, she thinks. And later, months and years later, when Lucas and her daughters are willowy and stand tall next to her, she thinks of this moment, on this beach, as the moment of knowledge. The moment she covered what was exposed. The moment she opened what was shut away.

EVEN PRETTY EYES COMMIT CRIMES

M. J. Hyland

M. J. Hyland (b. 1968) is a British-born author who grew up in Australia. Her first short story was published when she was seventeen. She has written three novels, the second of which, *Carry Me Down,* was shortlisted for the 2006 Man Booker Prize.

M y father WAS sitting on my doorstep. He was wearing khaki shorts, his bare head was exposed to the full bore of the sun, and he was holding a pineapple. I hadn't a clue what he was doing there. He hadn't given me any warning.

As I crossed the street, I raised my hand, but his eyes were closed, and he didn't see me until I was standing right in front of him.

'Dad. What are you doing here so early?'

'Relax,' he said. 'There's nothing to worry about.'

I looked at my watch. It wasn't yet eight-thirty and I wasn't in the mood for him. I'd walked home to save on bus fares after working a ten-hour night shift and I needed a shower and sleep.

'Did you knock?'

'No,' he said. 'I didn't knock. I didn't want to wake anybody. I was just going to leave the pineapple on your doorstep, but then I sat down to rest for a minute and you turned up.'

The neighbour's dogs were barking. My father frowned at the pampas grass that grew wild along the length of the broken fence.

'Your neighbours need to train those bloody kelpies to stop barking.'

I held out my hand.

'Here, Dad. Grab hold.'

'I'm alright,' he said. 'No need.'

I'd had twenty-nine years to get used to Australia; its boiling summers, long days with no distinct parts – hot in the morning, noon and night – but I still couldn't stomach the heat or the glare that came off every footpath and every parked car. My father was the opposite. He was made better by the sun; it made him buoyant and though he was sixty-five, on that morning, I was much more beaten and tired than he'd ever been.

'Do you want to come into the flat for a minute,' I said.

'If that's alright.'

'We'd best be quiet, though. Janice won't be out of bed yet.'

But Janice wasn't home. As soon as we were inside the hall I saw she'd left the bedroom door open and it was clear the bed hadn't been slept in. I'd made the bed and it was just as I'd left it. We'd had an argument about money before I left for work and when I was walking out the door she said, 'You're boring now, Paul.'

She said this in the cool and expert way my mother used to say things about couples who sit in cafés reading the newspaper and not talking to each other. 'They're boring each other,' she used to say. 'They're probably only days away from divorce.'

My father looked into the bedroom, just as I had done. He suspected Janice of straying, just as he'd suspected my mother.

'Janice must be out,' I said.

I straightened my shoulders and tried to hide my worry and fatigue. I was at the end of a long run of night shifts, and I wasn't in the mood for the grilling he'd give me if he knew about my marriage troubles.

'Where's your uniform?' he asked.

'In my locker. I don't like walking home wearing it. I get changed first.'

'So, you have a clean one for tomorrow's shift?'

'Yes, Dad. I have a few.'

He looked into the bedroom again. 'Where do you think she is?'

'Keep your hat on, Dad. She's probably just popped out to do some shopping.'

I owed my father some money, and mentioning shops was a mistake. He was well-off and enjoyed his riches, but he didn't like giving money away, not without arrangements for its 'fair return'.

When I was eighteen my father asked me to have a drink with him. It was the first time he'd asked to meet me in a pub and he picked the day and time of the meeting months in advance.

'It's time we had a proper man-to-man chat,' he said.

It was a perfect spring day, a gentle day, and we sat in the corner of the dark pub under a TV screen, in a suburb miles from his surgery, and even further away from my university digs.

'It's time I told you a few home-truths,' he said.

'OK,' I said. 'Go ahead.'

'Well, for starters, I knew your mother was up to no good years before she left us.'

As far as I was concerned, she hadn't left *us* when I was ten years old, she'd left *him*. She'd got sick of him and found somebody else. I was only ten, but I wasn't stupid. I'd heard her say, 'Men shouldn't talk as much as you do, Richard.'

My father sipped his beer slowly and looked at the TV screen above my head.

'She was a very good liar, your mother,' he said.

I was too angry to speak. What he'd said got me in the gut, a weird kind of wetness low in my stomach. I'd have got blind drunk that day if I'd had some spare money of my own but I had to listen to him curse my mother with nothing but a warm glass of beer froth in front of me.

When he came back to the table after ordering another round, he put the drinks down on our corner table and sat close and, after a moment, as though he was a different person, he put his hand on my knee.

'I'll tell you something now,' he said. 'Even pretty eyes commit crimes. You should bear that in mind when you start making lady friends.'

'Right,' I said.

'You prefer ladies, don't you?'

'Of course I do,' I said. 'Jesus Christ!'

My father didn't like sitting close to people, and he didn't like touching, and said he loathed displays of affection of any kind, but he was sitting very close, and his hand stayed on my knee a bit too long, and he softly squeezed, and my knee got hotter and hotter, and he kept looking at me, as though waiting for me to do something, and I had an idea that he was going to ask if we could have sex, father and son. It was a crazy idea, but I was certain of it. I moved my leg.

'Well then,' he said, 'you've been warned. You thought your mother was an angel because she looked like one, but you were completely wrong about that.'

I didn't want to hear any more. I told him I needed to use the toilet and I went to the bar and used the last of my money to pay for our drinks. I wasn't going to say goodbye, I couldn't stand him anymore, but he came round the corner, and saw me.

'What are you doing?' he said.

'I need to go back to Uni. I just remembered I have to meet my tutor.'

My father and I had lived alone together for seven years and, for seven years, when he got home from work, I'd be stuck with him, trapped with his talking in the kitchen or lounge, and if he wanted me when I went into my bedroom, he'd barge in, and I'd have to yawn my head right off its hinges to get rid of him. Nearly every weekend I'd pretend to be going into the city to see a film with friends and instead, catch the bus to an internet café three suburbs away, and drink coffee and play games online.

He followed me to the front door of the pub. 'Did you hear what I said? Were you listening?'

'Yes, but I have to go to a lecture.'

'You're a stinking liar,' he said. 'I'm staying on and I'll finish these beers. I don't like people who waste time and money. Do you follow me?'

'Yes,' I said.

He opened the door for me, and saw me out to the street.

We saw very little of each other after that spring afternoon; once or twice a year, my birthday and Christmas, but that changed when I married Janice. On our wedding day, at a small outdoor ceremony by the lake, he gave me our wedding gift; a Tartan picnic flask, six blue plastic cups, and a matching rug.

'You'll have a family of your own, soon,' he said. 'And I want to help you along. I can help you get on with things. I can help you sort things out.'

After the wedding, he formed a habit of stopping by the flat, donating furniture, giving me loans, calling me late in the night and saying things like, 'I'm just around the corner. Have you got a minute?'

*

And here he was again, only two months since his last visit, standing beside my kitchen table and holding a pineapple in the crook of his arm.

I turned my back to him and checked the whiteboard on the fridge to see if Janice had left me a message. She hadn't. I pretended to check the clock over the sink and looked into the backyard. Her bike was leaning against the shed, but her helmet wasn't in the basket. She might be gone for good and my father would be here to see it happen.

As I turned round to face him, he gave me the pineapple, offered it to me as though it were something of great value.

'It fell off the tree when I was heading home last night,' he said. 'What a glorious country, eh?'

'I don't really like pineapples, Dad. Why don't you give it to somebody at work?'

'Give it back to me, then. It's not going to waste.'

I gave it back to him.

'You should eat more fruit,' he said.

'You're right,' I said. 'I should.'

I thought he was going to leave but he sat at the table and put the pineapple in his lap. He was going to stay, and there was nothing I could do about it.

'What do you want to drink?' I said. 'Will a cup of tea do?'

'That'd be nice.'

I opened the fridge and looked out to the backyard again. The neighbour's ginger cat was curled up, asleep, on the Greek family's trampoline.

'Sorry, Dad. There's no milk.'

There was always milk in the fridge. Janice bought two litres every night when she went to the 7-Eleven on the corner for her cigarettes.

'Then I'll have water,' he said. 'Do you have ice?'

'You don't want a beer?'

'Christ, no,' he said. 'It's too early. I'm working today.'

'What time do you start?'

'I'm supposed to be there by nine. But there's no mad rush. I've arranged for the locum to do the mornings.'

There was no ice in the ice-tray, but I rummaged in the freezer as though there was hope it might be found. The breeze from the frost took some of the heat off my hands.

'There's no ice,' I said.

'Forget the water, then. I'll suck on one of these.'

He took a packet of *Fisherman's Friends* from the back pocket of his khaki shorts.

'Do you want one?'

'No thanks, Dad. They make me cough.'

As soon as I sat at the table, he stood and went to the sink and put the pineapple on the draining board, tried to stand it upright. When it toppled, he held its bottom and moved it round 'til he was sure it wouldn't budge.

'Thanks for the pineapple,' I said. 'Janice will love it.'

'Does she usually go out so early in the morning?'

'Sometimes,' I lied. 'She likes going for walks.'

'Is she still selling buttons?'

'No, she quit. And it wasn't buttons, it was sewing equipment ...'

'I know that.'

He sat down again, but didn't pull his chair under the table. I thought he'd be leaving soon.

'How have you been?' he said. 'How are you keeping?'

'I've been well-enough, thanks, Dad. The nights are hard, but I like the quiet hours when the patients are sleeping. And the walk home is good.'

He looked at the ceiling fan.

'Is that broken?'

'Yes. The landlord's coming to fix it soon.'

He looked at the window.

'Didn't she leave you a note or anything? Didn't she tell you where she was going?'

'No, Dad. I'm not her minder.'

I sat up in the chair and put my shoulders back, tried to make my body look bigger, tried to hide my panic. But it made no difference. I was work-wrecked and nervous and he could see it. Janice was gone somewhere, and it might be for good this time.

'How about you, Dad?'

'I could use a bit more help. The locum's pretty good, but my secretary's always behind. Things are getting to be too much for us. I've been wondering if I should retire.'

We were silent then and the only sound came from the traffic in Ormond Road, the delivery trucks beeping as they reversed out of the Mornflake warehouse. He wasn't troubled by the silence, or the lack of something to do with his hands. He was tidy and ambitious and he liked his own company. Even a stranger could see it; the way he sat with his hands on the knees of his khaki shorts, the creases just as they were when he pulled them, brand new from the box.

'Maybe you need a new secretary,' I said.

'Don't be daft, son. I've spent too long training her. Anyway, the patients like her. She keeps teddy bears behind the desk for the kiddies.'

'That's good then, Dad,' I said. 'Surely the fact that the patients like your secretary's much more important than paperwork.'

'You're right, son,' he said. 'Of course, you're right.'

The baby in the flat upstairs started howling.

'It's too hot in here,' I said.

I stood and opened the back door and, as soon as it was open, the ginger cat jumped off the trampoline and ran into the kitchen and sniffed at the cupboard door under the sink, walked to the door and looked at us for a moment, then sat.

'Is that yours?' he said.

'No. It belongs to the upstairs neighbour.'

'Why does it come in here?'

'That's what cats do,' I said. 'It wants food, I suppose.'

'It stinks,' he said. 'Is it neutered? You should tell those Greeks upstairs that neutering is a relatively cheap and simple operation.'

There was no air coming through the kitchen door and the backs of my knees were sweating.

I stood up from the table.

'Listen, Dad. I might have a bit of a sleep now, if that's alright.'

'Won't you be waking up again soon?' he said. 'When Janice gets home?'

'Not necessarily. I'm a heavy sleeper.'

He stood and looked over at the pineapple on the draining board.

'I'll get out of your hair then, will I?'

We faced each other across the table, and we were breathing in unison.

'OK. Stay for a bit,' I said. 'I can sleep later. Let's go into the lounge room.'

I stopped in the hallway and told him I'd be in soon.

'I just want to open the bedroom window.'

Janice had cleared out most of her clothes. I couldn't check the bedside drawers, without my father wondering what I was doing, but I knew the drawers would be empty, too. She'd threatened leaving, but I didn't believe she would, not like this, not this suddenly, not without a final warning, not without a last chance. People didn't end marriages this way, without warning, without second chances.

I got two glasses of orange juice and brought them into the lounge. My father was standing by the window and he'd unclenched his jaw, let his mouth hang open. I saw how he might look in repose, when there was nobody else around. He'd let me see him, not as strong, and not as calm. He was thinking about my mother, and I sensed it there in his slackened mouth and, for a moment, I thought of her too, the memory that always came to me first, though I didn't want it to.

It was a few months before she left home, a winter's day, and the three of us were eating lunch in a café. She told the waitress she wanted something that wasn't on the menu. She asked for a 'large onion sandwich'. The waitress was still at our table when my father laughed at her. 'Precisely how large is a large onion?' he said.

My mother got out of her seat.

'The waitress knew what I meant,' she said. 'Everybody else knew what I meant.'

He tried to apologise, as he often did, by saying, 'Oh, pet. Don't feel that way.'

She came round to my father's side of the table. She'd hung her coat over the back of his chair and she needed him to sit forward to get at it.

'Move,' she said.

He turned round to her, put his hand on her arm, and tried to console her as best he could, as he often did, by holding onto a part of her.

'I said move,' she said, 'you slow, deaf pig! I need my coat.'

My father didn't move quickly enough. She wrenched the coat from behind his back.

'You're embarrassing me, Richard,' she said. 'Get off my bloody coat!'

*

I stood in the lounge room doorway and held the glasses of orange juice and looked at him, waited for him to see me.

'Oh, hi,' he said. 'I've turned on the fan for you.'

'Thanks, Dad. Here's your OJ.'

I sat down on the end of the settee and he sat in the armchair near the door. As we sat, we crossed our legs, left over right, a genetic tic, something we always did when we sat down.

'So, where do you think that young wife of yours has got to?'

'She's probably meeting a friend for coffee or something.'

He looked at his watch. 'It's very early for that.'

I said nothing, and he sat forward, moved his legs round so that his knees and feet were aimed in my direction.

'I think I'll call Janice,' I said. 'I'll ask her to bring some milk and ice back with her.'

'Alright,' he said. 'I should be heading off soon anyway.'

'OK,' I said and felt the phone warm in my hand.

He waited for me to check for messages, but there were none. She was gone.

'She's on her way home,' I said. 'She says she'll be back soon.'

'Where is she?'

'I don't know yet. But I think I'll try and get some sleep now.'

I thought he'd leave then, but he didn't. He was going to stick it out, wait with me until she came home – or didn't.

'I've been meaning to ask you,' he said. 'Have you given any more thought to taking the exam?'

He was talking about the mature-age medical school exam. He'd reminded me of it the last time we met, and the time before that.

'Not yet,' I said, 'but I will.'

'Do you think you'll work as a nurse for the rest of your life?'

'I might, Dad. I like it.'

'How's your blood-pressure been of late?'

'Normal, Dad. It's normal.'

'Do you still get those dizzy spells? Maybe while I'm here I could check your pulse?'

'I can check my own bloody pulse. There's no need.'

'You look a bit flushed. A bit iffy around the gills.'

'There's nothing wrong with me. I'm just real hot, Dad. It's just stuffy in here. I feel like I'm wearing a bear suit.'

'I see,' he said. 'You never did warm to the heat.'

He laughed at himself, like a school-boy.

'Good one,' I said. 'That's a good one.'

We were silent and he scratched his arm while looking out the window. A Morn-flake truck was reversing out of the factory warehouse.

'There might be fleas in here,' he said, 'from that cat. Have you been bitten?'

'No. I haven't been bitten. It was probably a mozzie.'

'There's a lot of sand,' he said. 'In the carpet.'

We lived fifteen minutes from Bondi Beach and that's part of the reason why we paid so much rent for such a cramped, gloomy flat. I wanted to move out to the suburbs, just for a few years, and save some money for an air-conditioner and a trip back to London, but Janice couldn't stand the stench of the suburban sticks and so we stayed and bought three fans; so that made four fans, including the overhead in the kitchen that was busted.

I looked at him and jiggled my glass, swirled the juice round as though it had ice in it, and said nothing about the sand.

'You can check your mobile phone again if you want,' he said.

'I'm not worried, Dad. She'll be here in a minute.'

He stood. 'I should be going,' he said. 'I'll see myself out.'

'OK, Dad. Thanks for coming over. I'm sorry I wasn't very good company.'

'You're tired, that's all. You've never liked the heat.'

We stood in the hallway, near the front door. His hands were stuffed inside his khaki pockets and he didn't look like he was ready to go. In this in-between state, this waiting, this not coming or going, he'd usually be the one to make the first move to action. But on that morning, he stood stock still, and looked at me. I didn't want to speak, and he didn't either, so I opened the front door and stepped outside and waited for him to follow. I was in a bad state, sweating and nervous, and even though I didn't want to be left alone, I didn't know how to be this way with him watching me.

'Goodbye,' I said.

'Goodbye, son.'

I'd already turned to go back inside when he stepped back onto the porch and took hold of me. He hugged me, long enough for me to feel what went on beneath his chest, and I closed my eyes as he held me, and there was no rush from either of us to get it over with, and I held him with the same strength as he held me.

He let go first, but it wasn't to be rid of me. He wanted to say something. He took hold of my wrist.

'I hope you can find a way out of this situation, son. I wish you luck.'

And so he knew Janice had gone, and he'd probably known for a long time that she'd leave me, and maybe he hadn't come to rub my nose in it. Maybe it wasn't that at all.

'OK,' I said. 'OK, Dad.'

Saying 'OK' said nothing, and meant nothing, but as I held my breath, and watched him walk down the path, I hoped he'd realise that I wanted to say more, and that I just didn't know how to take the chance. He'd know, wouldn't he, that I was too surprised to speak? Maybe he'd have seen that I was too afraid to do anything, or say anything, that might bring my emotions to the boil. I was too busy shuddering to say anything more, and I hoped he knew that, and that he realised, that morning, I loved him.

THE GIFT

Emma Donoghue

Emma Donoghue (b. 1969) is an Irish-born playwright, literary historian and novelist. She has published seven novels, eleven plays and four collections of short stories. Her 2010 novel, *Room*, was a finalist for the Man Booker Prize.

Mrs. Sarah Bell
177 3rd Street
Jersey City

March 5, 1877

I need to put my little one with you. Her name is Lily May Bell, she is of one hundred per cent American parentage. Her father John Bell died unexpected when she was only three months old leaving me alone in the world and I cannot supply her needs tho' not for want of trying. I would work and take care of her but no one will have me and her too, some say they would if she was 2 or 3 years old. She is just from the breast, her bowels have not been right for a long time. I have cried and worried over her so much I think my milk hurt her. I boarded Lily May out for some months so I could work at dressmaking but she did not thrive, and the woman said it might be the best in the end for a fatherless mite. A neighbor told me in confidence that woman is no better than a baby farmer and doses them all stupid with syrup so I have taken Lily May out and can see no way except to throw myself on the mercy of your famous New York Society. Be kind to her for God's sake. You must not think that I neglected her. Do not be afraid of her face, it is nothing but an old ringworm. I will try hard to relieve you of her care as soon as ever can be.

Mrs. Sarah Bell
177 3rd Street
Jersey City

March 10, 1877

Thank you for your reply and for all your goodness. I hope Lily May does not "make strange" with the nurses for long but I suppose it is only to be expected. I do get some consolation from knowing I have done the best for her in my straitened circumstances. You say every child is assigned a place to sleep and a chair in the dining room which I am glad of, except that my baby cannot sit at table on her own yet so I hope there is someone to prop her up. I appreciate how busy the Rev. Brace and you all must be what with taking those unfortunates off the streets (and more swarming off every ship it seems), but if I may I will write from time to time to ask how mine is doing.

I am very sorry that I have nothing to send you but trust will come a day when I shall be able to pay you for all your trouble. I am in hopes of claiming Lily May before too long and God grant she will not recall a bit of it.

Please find herewith the form you sent.

This is to certify that I MRS. SARAH BELL *am the mother and only legal guardian of* LILY MAY BELL. *I hereby freely and of my own will agree for the New York Children's Aid Society to provide a home until* she *is of age or bind* her *out as the Managers may judge best. I hereby promise not to interfere in any way with the views and directions of the Managers.*

Mrs. Sarah Bell
177 3rd Street
Jersey City

April 2, 1877

I am relieved to hear about Lily May's bowels. You say a visit is not thought advisable, well once she is more settled in it might be a different story. I believe I could keep a hold of my feelings and not frighten her by giving way.

No one knows how awful it is to be separate from their child but a mother. You refer twice to "the orphans" but remember she is only a half, she has got one parent living. If I am spared and nothing prevents, the father of us all will permit me to have my little one back. Every night on my bended knees I pray for her.

Mrs. Sarah Bell
177 3rd Street
Jersey City

March 3, 1878

I have thought long and hard about what you say of the special trains going out west every week and the fresh air and placing out in farm homes. Institutions are confining to the young it is true and New York famously unhealthy. Do you pay these country women to take the children in? I fear that some would do it for mercenariness not kindness. Or perhaps they pay your Society, I have heard of such arrangements. But then that sounds like buying a horse at market. I am very much bewildered in my mind at the thought of my Lily May going off who knows where.

I planned by now to have put enough by to bring her back to Jersey with me but living is so dear. A home and friends is what I should wish for my little girl, at least until we can be reunited. I do recall the paper I signed last year but circumstances forced my hand. Do not take this as ingratitude, if I do not see her again I will never be worth anything on this earth. How far off do these trains go? If she is taken in by some family, do pass on my request that they will not change her name. Perhaps you will think me too particular but only consider how any mother would feel and you will excuse me.

In answer to your question there was never anything like that in my family or my husband's to my knowledge. Lily May is not two years old yet after all and my mother always said I was silent as the grave till I was three.

Mr. Bassett, Sheriff
Andes
New York

August 14, 1878

My wife and I have no children living, only one stillborn some twenty years back. Mrs. Bassett would like a girl between the ages of two and four, young enough to forget all that has gone before. No particular eye or hair color, except that if she is a foreigner she would stand out in Delaware County. So long as there is no hereditary taint we do not object to her being a foundling or illegitimate. In fact, we would prefer no relations. We do not particularly require the girl to be the student type, but want a happy-natured, responsive one and refined enough to take into our home. We would want to give her a High School education and if possible have her join the church choir.

I quite understand about no money changing hands, and signing the indenture. If a grievance arises can it be canceled?

We have gone to the hotel twice before, when orphan trains have come in, and enjoyed the songs and recitations, but never found anyone quite to our liking. There seemed a lot of older, rough-looking children. Mrs. Bassett would be afraid to take a boy, as harder to raise, and you never know. (It is not for farm work we want a child, unlike some fellow citizens we have seen squeezing boys' arms at the hotel.) I have talked to our doctor, who is on the town's Selection Committee. He said to write to the New York Society direct, and if you had a little girl who may answer our purposes, you might sew our request number right onto her hem, so she would not be given to anyone else.

Mr. Bassett, Sheriff
Andes
New York

November 3, 1878

My wife and I are so far much pleased with the child. At the hotel we took one good look at her, and then I nodded at Mrs. Bassett who could not speak, so I went up, and shook hands, and said, "You are going to be our little girl." She seemed queemish at first, but is getting used to the animals and no longer makes a face at the milk warm from the cow. She has a funny habit of keeping her arms on the table at meals; I suppose she learned it to prevent any other orphan from snatching her food.

We will keep her on trial for now, just in case. But barring serious misbehavior or disease, we mean to keep her and give her our name, Bassett I mean. Her first will be Mabel which keeps two of her old names – May Bell – in a hidden way as it were. She will have her room to herself, and more bonnets than she can wear. I can assure you we will take her to school and church and treat her as "no different."

Mrs. Sarah Bell
347 Grove Street
Jersey City

December 7, 1878

I could not give a proper answer to your letter last month as my heart was running over and remains the same. I am not ungrateful for this foster couple's Christianity but I could wish the circumstances otherwise. I write now just to inform you that I have changed my residence to the above and to ask to be informed the minute if anything should happen to my Lily as I have awful dreams. In the country between dogs and barb wire and rivers there is no knowing what could befall a little stranger.

Mr. Bassett, Sheriff
Andes
New York

February 6, 1879

Our Mabel is now one of the most content of children, and growing out of all her clothes. She has a rosy face and is most affectionate. She speaks more than before, though not quite clearly, but my wife can always make her out, so fears of feeblemindedness have been put to rest. She has quite forgotten her old name.

People here are civil, although I fear when she starts school, there will be a certain dose of meanness, as always among children. Such epithets as "bad blood" get thrown around with no thought for the hurt caused. Mrs. Bassett and I look on Mabel as quite our own, and could not love her more if she truly were. Your Agent can call on us anytime, we have nothing to hide.

I can appreciate that mothers do not like to part with their children, even to get them into much better situations. Can you assure us though that this Mrs. Bell will not be given our address? I have heard of cases where a woman abandons her child, and then lands up at the new home and makes scenes.

Mr. Bassett
Battle Creek
Iowa

November 3, 1879

Your last has, after some delay, reached us here in our new home. Please mark all future communications "Private," and do not use headed paper as nobody here knows of our connection with the Society. That in fact was one reason for our fresh start, though land and opportunity were others. It is mostly Germans round here, and no one seems to suspect Mabel is anything other than flesh of our flesh, a late gift from above. Keeping the secret we hope will shield her from the "pauper taint." She is a good girl and a talented singer, though her speech is still somewhat less plain than could be wished.

Thank you for sending the "adoption form," but on consideration we see no need for further fuss, and the risk of further publicity attendant on going through the courts. My wife holds to the principle that Mabel is our own already. We have made wills to provide for her future, all signed and sealed.

Mrs. Samuel Adams (Mrs. Sarah Bell as was)
697 2nd Avenue
Jersey City

April 23, 1880

I write to let you know of my change of fortune, as you will see from the above I am married again. We have "a good home" also (just as much as the couple who have got Lily May) and my husband Samuel who is in business is willing to welcome her into that home for which I thank God on bended knee as not every man would do the same.

If you have the slightest reservations you can send one of your Agents to ask the neighbors what you like. I will always acknowledge your kindness and what these folks on the farm did in giving refuge to my Lily in a time of calamity but that time is over. Let me know how soon she can be brought back. I will hardly know my little one now!

Mr. Bassett
Battle Creek
Iowa

May 12, 1880

It shows heart that the mother has inquired, but there is no question of return like some parcel. My wife is upset the matter has been raised so cavalierlike, and says she will defy anyone to even talk of taking our girl away when we have already adopted her "in spirit." To my mind it is the day to day that makes a family, *de facto* if not *de jure*, and since your Society thought fit to give Mabel into our care, there have passed some five hundred days. She is going on four and we are all she knows in the world.

If as you say this woman has a new husband, why can't she make the best of it? Perhaps she will have more children with him, whereas Mrs. Bassett and self are past any chance of that.

I enclose a recent photograph so you can see how pleasant looking Mabel is turning out. I am in two minds about whether you ought to show the mother the picture. It might ease her to see how well the child is getting on, but then again it might increase the longing. On second thoughts, as it has the address of the studio on it, you had best not let her look at it.

Mrs. Samuel Adams
697 2nd Avenue
Jersey City

January 18, 1884

You may recognize my name as Mrs. Sarah Bell as I was before my present marriage. Since I wrote asking for my child Lily May near to four years ago and was refused, which I took very much to heart, circumstances have gone against Mr. Adams's ventures. But things are looking up again and we have moved to the above, which if you send an Agent as I asked you last time they will see is a gracious home fit for any young person. The Lord knows I am not the first mother to have been obliged to let go of a little one in a time of trouble but now I am in a position to keep house and reclaim my own Lily May.

I think of her all the time, at seven years old what kind of life can it be in the wilds of Iowa when she was always nervous of a cat even? You say this couple treat her as "their own" but that is only make do and make believe as they must know in their heart of hearts. What is done can be undone if there is a will and a way. Surely if you pass this letter on to them so they can hear a mother's misery then they would have mercy if they are such good folks as you keep saying.

Mr. Bassett
Battle Creek
Iowa

September 24, 1885

I thank you for your two last. I apologize if mine had a "testy tone," only Mrs. Bassett was ill at the time, and sometimes it seems as if we will never be left at peace with our girl.

No, we do not think it advisable to enter into any kind of correspondence with this Adams woman (Bell as was), or encourage hopes of a visit. Is it not a queer thing for her to resume her talk of retrieving her child after all these years?

I fear she has hopes of being paid off, as it is well known that the blood relations only kick up a fuss if they sniff money in it.

Mabel is so much our daughter, we look back on the time before God gave her to us, and cannot imagine how we got through the lonesome days. She goes to school and Sunday School regularly and learns quickly. She regards tardiness almost as a crime. She is largish and has good health on the whole, though hardly what you would call rugged. She has not the least notion of being an adopted. My wife and I abide by "least said soonest mended."

Mr. Bassett
Battle Creek
Iowa

May 14, 1887

Enclosed please find the form completed as per and the fee of twenty-five dollars for the attorney. We never grudged the sum, it was only that my wife stood out against the intrusion and kept saying it smacked of having to pay for our beloved. But I have prevailed, since I live in terror of the mother turning up on our doorstep some day.

The NEW YORK CHILDREN'S AID SOCIETY hereby adopts to <u>Mr.</u> *and* <u>Mrs. Bassett</u> *an orphan* <u>named Mabel Bassett formerly Lily May Bell</u> *as our child, to keep, protect and treat as our own. We covenant with said Society to provide said orphan with suitable food, clothing, lodging and medical attendance, in health and in sickness, and to instruct* <u>her</u> *adequately in usefuless, as well as to advance and settle* <u>her</u> *in life according as circumstances may permit.*
Witness our hands and seals this <u>12th</u> *day of* <u>May 1887</u>.

Mrs. Sarah Bell
214 Beckman Avenue
Jersey City

February 20, 1889

As you will see I am going by my old name again, Mrs. Sarah Bell. I have suffered a divorce since I wrote last but will likely be married again shortly to a much more worthy man. Just now I can be reached at the house of my father Mr. Joseph Prettyman, address above, if you wish to send me any word.

It seems I have known no luck in this world since the day my first husband Mr. John Bell up and died on me when Lily May my one and only was on my breast. These ties are mysterious and unbreakable, you call her "Mabel" but I will never use that name. Child stealing is what I call it, to send innocents by the trainload into the most backward parts of the country and hand them over to God knows who all, even when they have family living back East. All I asked was to take my

Lily home with me and who better to love her than her own mother whose only crime was poverty?

It occurs to me now that my darling is past twelve. I wonder does she think of me at all or have her "folks" so-called kept her in the blackest ignorance of who she is.

Mrs. Sarah C. Mulkins
Davenport Center
New York

October 26, 1894

You may remember me as Mrs. Sarah Bell. I have been married again for some years to a good man called Mulkins and we have a very comfortable residence, see above. The other day I was thinking about my Lily May as I often and will always do and nothing can prevent a mother's heart from grieving, when I remembered that she comes of age next month. Surely at eighteen she should know the truth, that she has a loving mother who has never ceased from inquiring for her and never "abandoned" her as you cruelly put it, only gave her over for temporary safekeeping to preserve her from starvation. If she contacts your Society I trust you will in Christian charity give her my address, you can do that much for all your cant of "legalities." Won't you please tell me how my Lily May is and whether I will be permitted to lay eyes on her again in this lifetime?

Mr. Bassett
Sioux City
Iowa

November 30, 1897

In response to your last several letters, I will tell you that Mabel was married this October 12th to a fine young man from Cedar County. We are much obliged to the Society for its concern over these long years, but now she is a grown woman and a wife, it seems to us her file should by rights be closed and as if it never were. You ask if she is ever to know who she is, which question Mrs. Bassett and I call impertinent, as she knows she is our beloved Mabel. We must insist that neither Mrs. Bell nor any other former connection shall ever learn anything about Mabel's whereabouts. We keep the papers locked up safe and whoever passes first, the other will burn them. We are not wealthy folk but this one gift we can leave to our girl and will.

MILLIE AND BIRD

Avril Joy

Avril Joy is a British author. In 2003 she won a Northern Promise award from *New Writing North*. Her short story 'Millie and Bird' won the inaugural Costa Short Story Award in 2013.

It was the kind of summer when the grass grew too long to cut and your toes stubbed at the damp end of your trainers, the summer I was sixteen. It rained all through May and June. It rained on my birthday. It never let up and the weeds in the yard grew taller than the gate post. Jonty Angel, our next-door neighbour, gave Millie the bird that summer, a white zebra finch, and she spent all her time coaxing it onto her shoulder, whispering to it and feeding it titbits. He gave her a cage too and she put it in her bedroom out of harm's way. It was the summer of Bird, it was the summer I fell in love.

'Why the hell does she have to go round the house with that stupid bird on her shoulder, for Christ's sake? What girl her age does that?'

'I don't know but she's only thirteen. Where's the harm?' I say.

'When I was thirteen I had better things to think of, like school for one thing. No time for pets. No time to whisper sweet nothings at a stupid bloody bird.'

I watch Millie walk into the yard and up through the garden. Bird on her shoulder, its beak buried in her hair. She disappears behind the shed. Behind the shed it's mostly overgrown with nettles. There's an old crabapple, a sink which coats over every spring with a skin of spawn, a rusty bike and a couple of broken cold frames.

'Why don't I make you a cup of tea Mum? See if there's anything on the radio, a concert or something? There might be a play on.' I say.

As if she doesn't hear me she goes to the sideboard, opens the door and reaches inside to the stash she keeps behind the pile of old records we're not allowed to touch. She lifts it out like she's won a raffle, like it's a surprise, like she didn't know there was a half-full bottle of vodka there. She pours herself a mug, holds it up and smiles like she doesn't ever need to be put to bed, or ever get sick, or rant and rave about it all being our fault.

I go out into the garden and look for Millie. I won't go behind the shed into the nettles as I don't want my legs all messed up with stings. I want them silky smooth and ready for the fake tan. 'Millie, what are you doing?'

'Nothing.'

'Come over here then and sit for a bit.' I'm on the bench in front of the shed. It moves when you sit on it. The grass is shorter here on account of it having to work its way up through crazy paving and gravel. 'Come on.' I want her to come but not for her sake. I'm not worried about her getting nettle rash and besides she's got Bird. That's what she calls the bird: Bird. When I asked her why, she said it seemed for the best, that naming leads to attachment and I said where the hell did she get that idea from, and she said she read it on the internet.

Millie sits next to me. Bird is on her shoulder moving from one red foot to the other like he's stepping up and down in time to music we can't hear, clawing at her t-shirt.

He turns his head and looks at me with a black eye. I think about Otis and his smoky, black skin that smells of walnut and vanilla. 'You going out tonight?' asks Millie.

'Yes, seven o'clock, Elaine's first, we're meeting there then going into town.'

'Can I come?'

'Don't be daft, you're thirteen.'

'Well *you're* only sixteen and one week.'

'Next year maybe, anyway I don't think Bird would appreciate it, in Jelly's, with all that noise and all those people.'

Bird is still now. A cabbage white floats past and a swarm of midges hover above the long grass. I think I should do something about the grass, like ask Jonty if I can borrow his mower, though he said it needed to be cut down first. A crow flies out of the lilac tree above us and Bird jumps up onto Millie's head.

'Is it stupid or what, that bird? It'll get eaten by the crows if it's not careful.'

'He's just nervous,' says Millie and puts her hand up and grasps the bird and brings it down into her lap where she cups it in both hands. 'His heart's beating like crazy,' she says, 'feel it.'

She goes to pass the bird to me but I pull away, 'don't give it to me,' I say, 'I don't like birds.' But it's not that I don't like birds, it's that I don't want to feel its heart beating like that, not when its skin is all feathers and a puff of wind coming by could break its bones.

'What's not to like? He's beautiful, feel him, he's like silk and he smells of grass.' She holds the bird towards me.

'Don't bring it near me,' I say. 'Keep it to yourself. Come on, I'll make us tea before I go out.'

I make egg and chips because it's easy, oven chips cook themselves. It's just for us. Mum's in the front room with the telly and her bottle. Millie feeds the bird a chip. He's not normally allowed at the table. We clear away and then go upstairs to my room. Millie puts Bird in his cage and then comes and sits on the bed and watches me get ready. We share a bottle of coke and I smoke a cigarette out of the window as best I can, but it's hard because it's raining and the cig is getting damp.

Millie does my nails with the purple varnish I bought especially. She's good at doing things like hair and nails although you wouldn't think so to look at her. 'You could be a hairdresser or a beautician,' I say, 'if you weren't so brainy.' She smiles. Millie is clever; the cleverest girl in her class, although how she's going to be anything beats me. I used to think about being a lawyer. I fancied that, but now, well I'm not sure. Jonty Angel says he might be able to get me a job in the auction house where he works. Sometimes you have to be realistic and scale things down, the kind of things you'd been hoping for. I used to pray about that kind of stuff but then your prayers they get rained on like the grass.

I like it when Millie takes my hand and then each of my fingers, one by one, and holds them while she paints the nail. She's just dipping into the thick, pearly varnish when we hear stumbling on the stairs and the bathroom door banging shut. Millie puts the brush back in the bottle and we wait. I listen hard. I'm good at listening, it comes with practice. I've got dolphin ears. Dolphins hear fourteen times better than humans. After a minute or two we start up again and one by one my nails take on a glossy purple sheen. I look at Millie, at her bitten-down nails and I think – tomorrow I'll paint them purple.

The toilet flushes and the bathroom door opens. Her bedroom door closes. 'She's gone to sleep it off,' I say. 'She'll be snoring like an old bag lady soon.' Millie stops, brush mid-way between bottle and the little finger of my left hand. I can tell she doesn't like what I've said. But I laugh and before long she laughs and then we both laugh and we roll about on the bed laughing, only not too loud and me with my hands in the air to stop my nails smudging.

'Can I wait up for you?' Millie says.

'It'll be late.'

'I'll get into your bed.'

'Not with that bird you won't.'

'I'll leave Bird in his cage. Promise.'

'All right then.'

It's gone eight when we wake in the grey light I hear the rain outside and a cheeping noise at my ear. What the hell. I told her no bird. 'Millie,' I turn. The bird hops away from my ear and onto Millie's pillow. 'I thought I said no bird.'

Millie opens her eyes. 'I couldn't leave him. Mum got up after you went out and came downstairs and said I'd got to give Bird back to Jonty or else she'd get rid of him. I was scared she'd hurt him.'

'Well put him back in his cage now or get his box or something, just get it out of the bed.' I turn over and push my head back in the pillow and replay last night's kiss, and then I hear her.

'Breakfast!' She shouts up the stairs, 'Come on, up you get.'

I turn back to Millie and raise my eyebrows in a kind of here-we-go-again way. 'Better get up,' I say. 'It's going to be one of those *happy-family days*.'

No one makes pancakes like she does and she's cut up fruit and there's syrup and sugar and lemon and a clean cloth on the table. When we finish eating, she says, 'The rain's stopped. Think it's about time we saw to the garden. There's a scythe somewhere in the shed. I'll find it. You go next door and borrow Jonty's mower.'

It's true, the rain has stopped and the sun is out and it's warm enough to be outside in a t-shirt, and I don't care that I've had less than five hours sleep, what with getting in so late, because I'm in love and, as it turns out, it is one of those *happy-family-days* and who knows when the next one might come around.

The garden looks different by the time we finish, like it's doubled its size. The sky is cloudless and we've got the old car rugs out on the lawn. Mum reads the paper. I doze on and off and think about Otis walking me home. I think about him kissing me in the lane; kissing Otis is like sucking chicken from a bone, and I think about how when I went round to his house his Mum made us a whole plate of chicken sandwiches for supper. If things carry on like today, then maybe I can invite him back, that's what I'm thinking when I hear the click of a lighter and look up to see Jonty leaning on the fence.

'All right girls? Looks a bit more like it,' he says, lighting his rollie with the Zippo flame. Jonty's got a pierced tongue and a tattoo of an eagle on the back of his neck and he's wearing a t-shirt that says *The World is Disappearing*. It's black and it's got a line of blue-green worlds across the front that get smaller and smaller until they disappear round the back. I used to think Jonty was a messenger. Well for one thing 'angel,' means messenger, Millie told me that, and for another, because of his t-shirts which said things like: *I Just Wanna Be Myself, Love Kills, No More Pain*. I used to think he was speaking to me until I realised he was the drummer in an old punk-rock band and it was his uniform. He doesn't play in the band anymore on account of him nearly losing his foot in a motorbike accident.

I wonder if Jonty is really worried about the world disappearing: the land sinking, the seas rising, polar ice caps melting. I know all about it from school and Mrs Allen in geography but I can't be worrying about it. I've got too many other things and besides it's not exactly news to me; my world's been disappearing from as far back as I can remember, mostly into the bottom of a vodka bottle. Today, just for once, I wish Jonty was wearing something to make us smile, like that t-shirt of his that says, *If You Want Breakfast in Bed, Sleep in the Kitchen*, or best of all, the red one with, *Save the Drama for Your Llama*, in big white letters across the front.

'Fancy a Barbie? I've got a few burgers in the freezer, veggie as well as meat.'

Millie's eyes light up. She likes being around Jonty, we both like being around Jonty because you can rely on him. Jonty is reliable which you have to be if you've got an aviary full of birds to look after. Millie is the only one he lets help him. Mum likes him too, she's known him since she and Dad first moved in, further back than we can remember. Sometimes they play old records together, sometimes he calls her *Blondie* and you can tell she likes that.

'Come on then before it decides to set away raining again. I'll get it lit. If you want ketchup you'll have to bring it with you.'

By the time we've eaten our burgers the sky is the colour of wet tarmac. We sit sipping coke and waiting for the rain. Nobody speaks. I'm praying it won't rain, praying for the end of the summer when rain washed the baby wood pigeons out of their nests in the plane trees and into the gutter. I think of Otis and I pray: let everyday be like today, so I can bring him home; no more sideboards and vodka, no more coming in from school and her sparked out on the sofa. I let that fantasy loose in the air around me and I wonder if we're all, in our own way, dreaming of the same kind of thing. I'm sure Millie is because she's got that faraway look and a half-smile on her face and for once she isn't petting Bird.

'We should go away on holiday,' says Mum, 'get away from this sodding, sand-bag summer, somewhere hot – Greece. I went there once with your Dad.'

I hold my breath.

'Let's drink to it,' she says.

We all hold our breath. Jonty gives me a quick look then says, 'Aye, good idea, why don't I make us a cup of tea?'

Jonty brings a pot of tea and a packet of digestives on a tray with four mugs. We drink tea and listen to the birds shushing and chirruping in the aviary. The rain clouds pass and the sky turns blue again and I'm starting to think that everything seems OK and maybe I'll get out tonight, so I take my phone out of my pocket. I'll text Otis, who knows I might even go round his house for a bit. And I'm thinking how his Mum might make us chicken sandwiches again for supper, when I look up and see Millie's gone.

Don't ask me where it comes from or why but I can feel it, like a wild animal feels the coming storm, something moving on the air; it's my dolphin ears and most likely my nose too. I know something isn't right. I put my phone down. 'Where's Millie?' 'Gone to put Bird away,' says Jonty, 'she's going to give us a hand feeding that lot,' he nods in the direction of the aviary. Mum's drinking tea and smoking, her head buried in Jonty's newspaper. She doesn't look up as I get to my feet.

I call for Millie in the house but there's no reply. I walk through the garden, following my dolphin nose, down to the shed, then round the back to the nettle patch. Millie is there, squatting by the old sink with her hands in the water.

'Millie, what's up?' I say but I don't need an answer because Millie takes her hands out of the water and I can see what's up, right there, under that clear blue sky, shining in the sink, I can see it, see him: Bird, floating lifeless, his feathers slicked onto his tiny body. 'Millie, what, how …?'

'I'm going to take him out now, find something to wrap him in, then bury him.'

'But Millie, what happened?'

'Some things are too hard to bear,' says Millie laying his body on the grass. 'Some things you just couldn't bear.' She looks up at me with a look that says *you know what I mean*, and I don't need to think about it because I do. I know exactly what she means.

I nod. 'We'll bury him,' I say. 'Then you can go and help Jonty with the aviary, and after that I'll paint your nails purple.'

Millie already has a trowel and she's digging a hole at the base of the crab apple. She takes an old crepe bandage from her pocket and wraps it around Bird. She lays him in the hole and covers him with wet leaves and soil. 'Say a prayer,' she says. And I do.

LOSS

THE CANARY

Katherine Mansfield

Katherine Mansfield (1888–1923) was born in Wellington, New Zealand. After moving to England at nineteen, Mansfield secured her reputation as a writer with the story collection *Bliss*, published in 1920. She reached the height of her powers with her 1922 collection *The Garden Party*. Her last five years were shadowed by tuberculosis; she died from the disease at the age of thirty-four.

… You see that big nail to the right of the front door? I can scarcely look at it even now and yet I could not bear to take it out. I should like to think it was there always even after my time. I sometimes hear the next people saying, 'There must have been a cage hanging from there.' And it comforts me. I feel he is not quite forgotten.

… You cannot imagine how wonderfully he sang. It was not like the singing of other canaries. And that isn't just my fancy. Often, from the window I used to see people stop at the gate to listen, or they would lean over the fence by the mock-orange for quite a long time – carried away. I suppose it sounds absurd to you – it wouldn't if you had heard him – but it really seemed to me he sang whole songs, with a beginning and an end to them.

For instance, when I'd finished the house in the afternoon, and changed my blouse and brought my sewing on to the verandah here, he used to hop, hop, hop from one perch to the other, tap against the bars as if to attract my attention, sip a little water, just as a professional singer might, and then break into a song so exquisite that I had to put my needle down to listen to him. I can't describe it; I wish I could. But it was always the same, every afternoon, and I felt that I understood every note of it.

… I loved him. How I loved him! Perhaps it does not matter so very much what it is one loves in this world. But love something one must! Of course there was always my little house and the garden, but for some reason they were never enough. Flowers respond wonderfully, but they don't sympathise. Then I loved the evening star. Does that sound ridiculous? I used to go into the backyard, after sunset, and wait for it until it shone above the dark gum tree. I used to whisper, 'There you are, my darling.' And just in that first moment it seemed to be shining for me alone. It seemed to understand this … something which is like longing, and yet it is not longing. Or regret – it is more like regret. And yet regret for what? I have much to be thankful for!

… But after he came into my life I forgot the evening star; I did not need it any more. But it was strange. When the Chinaman who came to the door with birds to sell held him up in his tiny cage, and instead of fluttering, fluttering, like the poor little goldfinches, he gave a faint, small chirp, I found myself saying, just as I had said to the star over the gum tree, 'There you are, my darling.' From that moment he was mine!

... It surprises even me now to remember how he and I shared each other's lives. The moment I came down in the morning and took the cloth off his cage he greeted me with a drowsy little note. I knew it meant 'Missus! Missus!' Then I hung him on the nail outside while I got my three young men their breakfasts, and I never brought him in, to do his cage, until we had the house to ourselves again. Then, when the washing-up was done, it was quite a little entertainment. I spread a newspaper over a corner of the table and when I put the cage on it he used to beat with his wings, despairingly, as if he didn't know what was coming. 'You're a regular little actor,' I used to scold him. I scraped the tray, dusted it with fresh sand, filled his seed and water tins, tucked a piece of chickweed and half a chili between the bars. And I am perfectly certain he understood and appreciated every item of this little performance. You see by nature he was exquisitely neat. There was never a speck on his perch. And you'd only to see him enjoy his bath to realise he had a real small passion for cleanliness. His bath was put in last. And the moment it was in he positively leapt into it. First he fluttered one wing, then the other, then he ducked his head and dabbled his breast feathers. Drops of water were scattered all over the kitchen, but still he would not get out. I used to say to him, 'Now that's quite enough. You're only showing off.' And at last out he hopped and standing on one leg he began to peck himself dry. Finally he gave a shake, a flick, a twitter and he lifted his throat – Oh, I can hardly bear to recall it. I was always cleaning the knives by then. And it almost seemed to me the knives sang too, as I rubbed them bright on the board.

... Company, you see, that was what he was. Perfect company. If you have lived alone you will realise how precious that is. Of course there were my three young men who came in to supper every evening, and sometimes they stayed in the dining-room afterwards reading the paper. But I could not expect them to be interested in the little things that made my day. Why should they be? I was nothing to them. In fact, I overheard them one evening talking about me on the stairs as 'the Scarecrow'. No matter. It doesn't matter. Not in the least. I quite understand. They are young. Why should I mind? But I remember feeling so especially thankful that I was not quite alone that evening. I told him, after they had gone. I said, 'Do you know what they call Missus?' And he put his head on one side and looked at me with his little bright eye until I could not help laughing. It seemed to amuse him.

... Have you kept birds? If you haven't, all this must sound, perhaps, exaggerated. People have the idea that birds are heartless, cold little creatures, not like dogs or cats. My washerwoman used to say every Monday when she wondered why I didn't keep 'a nice fox terrier', 'There's no comfort, Miss, in a canary.' Untrue! Dreadfully untrue! I remember one night. I had had a very awful dream – dreams can be terribly cruel – even after I had woken up I could not get over it. So I put on my dressing-gown and came down to the kitchen for a glass of water. It was a winter night and raining hard. I suppose I was half asleep still, but through the kitchen window, that hadn't a blind, it seemed to me the dark was staring in, spying. And suddenly I felt it was unbearable that I had no one to whom I could say 'I've had such a dreadful dream,' or – 'Hide me from the dark.' I even covered my face for a minute. And then there came a little 'Sweet! Sweet!' His cage was on the table, and the cloth had slipped so that a chink of light shone through. 'Sweet! Sweet!' said the darling little fellow again, softly, as much as to say, 'I'm here, Missus. I'm here!' That was so beautifully comforting that I nearly cried.

... And now he's gone. I shall never have another bird, another pet of any kind. How could I? When I found him, lying on his back, with his eye dim and his claws wrung, when I realised that never again should I hear my darling sing, something seemed to die in me. My breast felt hollow, as if it was his cage. I shall get over it. Of course. I must. One can get over anything in time. And people always say I have a cheerful disposition. They are quite right. I thank God I have.

... All the same, without being morbid, or giving way to – to memories and so on, I must confess that there does seem to me something sad in life. It is hard to say what it is. I don't mean the sorrow that we all know, like illness and poverty and death. No, it is something different. It is there, deep down, deep down, part of one, like one's breathing. However hard I work and tire myself I have only to stop to know it is there, waiting. I often wonder if everybody feels the same. One can never know. But isn't it extraordinary that under his sweet, joyful little singing it was just this – sadness? – Ah, what is it? – that I heard.

A WALK IN THE WOODS

Elizabeth Bowen

Elizabeth Bowen (1899–1973) was an Irish novelist and short story writer. She published her first book, a collection of short stories entitled *Encounters*, in 1923. During World War II Bowen wrote the novel, *The Heat of the Day* and a collection of stories, *The Demon Lover and Other Stories*, which won her universal praise for their depiction of wartime London. She was awarded a CBE in 1948. Her final novel, *Eva Trout, or Changing Scenes* won the James Tait Black Memorial Prize in 1969 and was shortlisted for the Man Booker Prize.

The mysterious thing was that the woods were full of people – though they showed a front of frondy depth and silence, inviolable and sifted through with sun. They looked like a whole element, like water, possible to behold but not to enter, in which only the native creature can exist. But this was a deception. Once inside them, it was only at a few moments that the solitary walker could feel himself alone, and lovers found it hard to snatch unregarded kisses. For those few moments when nobody was in sight, the glades of bronze bracken, the wet, green rides leading off still seemed to be the edge of another world. The brown distances, the deep hollows welled with magic, forlorn silence, as though they were untrodden. But what was likely to be the last fine Sunday of autumn had brought Londoners, or people from suburbs on this side of the city, in hundreds into these woods, which lay open, the People's property – criss-crossed by tarmac roads on which yellow leaves stuck. The people who came here were mostly well-to-do, for you needed a car to get here without effort. So saloon cars, run off the roads between the wide-apart birch-trees, were packed flank to flank, like shining square-rumped tin pigs, in the nearby glades. Inside a few of these cars people remained sitting with the wireless on – but mostly they had got out, yawned, stretched, and scattered in threes and fours.

Most of the Londoners lacked a sense of direction. Directly they were out of the sight of the road, an atavistic fear of the woods invaded them. Willing or unwilling they walked in circles, coming back again and again to make certain they had not lost their cars – in which had often been left a tea-basket, an overcoat of some value, or an old lady, an aunt or a grandmother. Not to be sure where one is induces panic – and yet the sensation of being lost was what they unconsciously looked for on this holiday – they had come to the woods. The sounds of bolder people whistling to dogs, of mackintoshes rustling against the bracken reassured them made them strike in deeper.

Walking between the pillars of the trees, the men squared their shoulders – as though they inherited savage dignity. The matronly women, heavy in fur coats – which, just taken out after the summer, shed a smell of camphor – protestingly rolled as they walked on their smart heels. They looked about them, dissatisfied, acquisitive, despising the woods because they belonged to everyone. Had they not profoundly dreaded to trespass, they would have preferred the property of some duke. Now and then, recalling a pottery vase at home, they would strip off their gloves and reach for a fanlike spray of gold beech leaves. Or, unwillingly stooping, they tugged at a frond of bracken – but that is hard to pick. Their faces stayed unrelaxed: there is no poetry for the middle-class woman in her middle years. Nature's disturbing music is silent for her; her short phase of instinctive life is over. She is raising, forcing upward the children she has, and driving her man on. Her features become bleak with narrow intention: she is riveted into society. Still, to touch the edge of Nature stands for an outing – you pack baskets and throng to the edge of forest or sea. The still, damp, glittering woods, the ma-jestic death of the year were reflected in the opaque eyes of these women – hardly more human, very much less pathetic, than the glass eyes of the foxes some of them wore. In family parties the women and men parted; they did not speak to each other. The women walked more slowly to act as a brake. Where tracks narrowed between thickets or bracken the families went in files. The children escaped and kept chasing each other, cat-calling, round the trees. They were not allowed to run down the wet green rides.

Sometimes the thud of hooves was heard, and young people on horseback crossed the end of a glade in coloured jerseys, with chins up, flaunting their bold happiness. The walkers, with a sort of animal envy, lowered their eyes and would not look after them. From couples of lovers clashing through the bracken, or standing suspended in love, fingers touching, in patches of sun, eyes were averted in a commenting way.

The riders thudding, across a glade were heard, not seen, by a couple in a thicket. These two, in a secret clearing at the foot of an oak, sat on a mackintosh eating sandwiches. They were very hungry. They had come to the edge of the woods in a Green Line bus, struck in and wandered for a long time now, looking for the place their fancy wanted. The woman, a city woman, refused to believe the woods had no undiscovered heart, if one could only come on it. Each time she had sighted the black of another tarmac road she had let out a persecuted sigh. The young man saw she was flagging, and he was hungry. He had found what she wanted by fighting through this thicket to the foot of the oak, then pulling her after him. In here they at least *saw* no one. They had spread the mack-intosh, kissed, and opened the sandwiches.

'Listen,' she said. 'There go people riding.'

'Did you ever ride?'

'I did once.'

'On that farm?'

'Yes, that time,' she said, smiling quickly, touched that he should remember. She spoke often about her childhood, never about her girlhood – which was past, for she was ten years older than he. And her girlhood had been brief: she had married young. She watched him reach out for another sandwich, then gently and wilfully detained him by making her thumb and finger into a bracelet round his thin wrist. He pulled his wrist up to his lips and kissed the joint of her thumb. They enjoyed this play as seriously as lions. She shut her eyes, dropped her head back to let the sun through the branches fall on her forehead – then let his wrist go. He took the sandwich he wanted; she opened her eyes and saw him. 'You greedy boy.'

'Yes, I *am* greedy,' he said. '*You* know I'm greedy.'

She thrust both hands up to her cheeks and said: 'That's no good – *here*.'

'No, we've struck unlucky. I thought woods in winter—'

'It's still autumn. It's the fine Sunday.' Her face went narrow, as though she heard the crack of a whip: she opened a gap in their thicket by bending a branch back. With cautious, angry eyes they both looked through. A party of five people were filing through the bracken, about ten yards away. 'There they go,' she said. 'There go the neighbours. That's my life. Oh, God! Henry—'

'They can't hurt us.'

'You know they can. Look, eat that last sandwich, do.'

'What about you?'

'I don't want it: I cut them for you. Turkey and ham, that should be.'

'*I'm* a spoilt boy,' said Henry, taking the sandwich without any more fuss. She crumbled up the paper, drove it with the point of his stick into the soft earth at the foot of the oak and earthed it up alive. Then she brushed crumbs from the mackintosh with a downcast face, making a bed in which they dare not be. But Henry drew his long legs up, scrambled round like a dog and lay across the mackintosh with his head in Carlotta's lap. She stroked his stubborn dark hair back, leaned her bosom over his face and stroked his forehead with a terrible held-in tenderness. The whole weight of his body seemed to have gone into his head, which lay as heavy as a world on her thighs. His clerk's face was exposed to her touch and to the sky – generally so intent, over-expressive, nervous, the face was wiped into blank repose by her touch. He flung one hand across his chest and held a fold of her skirt. His spectacles, by reflecting the sky's light, hid his eyes from her, so she leaned over further and lifted them off gently. She looked into the blotted darkness of his pupils which, from being exposed like this, looked naked. Then he shut his eyes and put on the withdrawn smile of someone expecting sleep. 'You are so good,' he said.

'Sleep then … go on, sleep … '

'Will you?'

'Maybe. Sleep … '

But she watched, with the bend of her spine against the tree, while he lay with his eyes shut. She saw that his will to sleep was a gentle way of leaving her for a little. She felt a tide of peace coming in – but then the tide turned: his forehead twitched. A bird trilled its unhopeful autumn song. He opened his eyes and said: 'It's awful, having no place.'

'But we make a place of our own.'

'But I get so tired – all this doesn't seem natural.'

'Oh, Henry – what's the good?'

'Well, *you've* often said that.'

'Then *you've* said, what's the good?'

'It was all very well at first,' he said, 'just knowing you. Just coming round to your place. Seeing you before Joe got back, or even: with Joe. I used to like you to have a place of your own – that was why I'd rather go with you than a girl.'

'That's what you want,' she said, 'just mothering. That's what Joe thinks; he doesn't think any harm. "Here comes your boy," he says; I think he's right, too: that's all you're really after.' She gently outlined his mouth with one of her fingertips.

But his mouth tightened. 'No, it's more than that now,' he said. '*You* know it's more than that.' He stared at the sky with his unfocused eyes – like a hare's eyes. 'I wanted what I've got; I wanted that all the time; I wanted that from the first – though it may once have been mixed up in the other dung. But ever *since* that, ever since we—'

'Do you wish we hadn't?'

'You don't know what you're saying. But I used to like your home; it was such a snug little place. I was happy there in a way: that's all gone now. I used to like Joe, too, one time. And now – it's awful … *This* isn't what I imagined the first time I saw you. Hiding in woods like this – it isn't fit for you … really.'

'It's my only life. You're my only life. My only way out. Before you came, I was walled in alive. I didn't know where to turn, I was burning myself out … I don't mind where we go; so long as we get *away* from them … And we do have these days when Joe's gone to his mother's.'

'But we've got no place … When I was young I used to believe there was really some tremendous world and that one would get to it. A sort of a Shakespeare world. And I heard it in music, too. And I lived there for three days after I first met you. I once used to believe—'

'But you're young still.'

'Well, perhaps I do still.'

'I always have. That's our place.'

'But we ought to have some real place – I mean, I want you.'

'Oh, shut up,' she said. 'I—'

'Look, come on,' he said, getting up. 'Better walk on. This does no good. Let's walk on into the woods.'

'They're so full.'

'But they look empty.'

'Kiss once—'

They kissed. It was he who pulled apart. He gathered up her mackintosh on his arm and began to fight a way out for her through the thickets. As she stepped between the branches he held back, her lips shook and she looked quite blind. Her look attracted the notice of Muffet and Isabella, two schoolgirls who, walking arm-in-arm through the woods, had already started to stare and nudge each other on seeing the thicket of purple leaves shake. Any man and woman together made them giggle. They saw a haggard woman with dark red hair and a white face: something in her expression set them off giggling all the more. Henry disentangled the mackintosh from the last of the thicket; his consciousness of the girls staring and giggling made him look very young. His pride in Carlotta was wounded; his pity for her abased him. She was a married woman out with her neighbour's lodger. They both came from a newly developed suburb, and had met at the local debating society.

As he saw the girls' pink faces stuck open with laughter he saw why Carlotta hated her life. He saw why she towered like a statue out of place. She was like something wrecked and cast up on the wrong shore. When they met she had been one of these women going through life dutifully, and at the same time burning themselves up. Across the hall where they met, her forehead like no other woman's forehead, her impatient carriage, her deep eyes and held-in mouth, had been like a signal to him. He could not turn away. When they had talked, she excited, released, soothed him. Pride and a bitter feeling of misdirection had, up to that meeting, isolated them both. Passion broke down a wall in each of their lives. But her spirit was stronger than his, and so he was frightened of her ... Carlotta stumbled stepping out of the thicket, and put a hand on his elbow for support. Henry twitched his elbow away and strode ahead of her, lashing round at the bracken with his stick.

'Henry—'

'Look out, they're looking. Those girls behind. *Don't* look round—'

'All right,' she said. 'We can't be too careful, can we.' Henry did not know if she spoke in irony or sheer pain.

Muffet was spending the Sunday with Isabella, whose family lived not far from the Green Line bus stop. The girls were friends at the High School. They both wore dark-blue overcoats and walked bare-headed; their lively faces showed no particular character. They were allowed by their mothers to walk in the woods so long as they did not get talking to men: they had been told what happens to girls who do that – their minds were bulging with cautionary horrors. They had neither of them got boys yet: when they had got boys they would stop walking together. At present their walks were gay and enjoyable – on fine Sundays the woods were a great show for them: too soon this would be over, winter silence would fall.

This afternoon, in a fairly retired glade, they had come on a lonely car in which a couple embraced. They also inspected cars parked nearer the roadside, squinting in at grandmothers and the picnic baskets, running away in alarm from pairs of well-got-up women, upright in backs of cars like idols under glass cases, discontentedly waiting for their men to return. Or, intercepting a bar of wireless music, Isabella and Muffet would take a few dancing steps. They envied the thundering riders, the young lovers, the imperious owners of well-bred dogs ... Isabella and Muffet, anything but reluctant, hopped with impatience where brook and river meet. They were fifteen. They stared at everyone. At the same time they had a sense of propriety which was very easily offended.

They peered at the broken thicket, then turned to stare after the couple.

'My goodness,' said Isabella, '*she* looked silly!'

'Breaking trees, too,' said Muffet. 'That's against the law.'

'Besides being old enough to be his mother. She *was* old. Did you see her?'

'Perhaps she was his mother.'

'Mother my eye! But he gave her the push all right – did you see that? Did you see?'

'Going on at him like that.'

'Well, I call it a shame. It's a shame on him. He's a nice boy.'

'No, I call him sappy. I mean, at her age. Fancy him letting her.'

'Well, I tell you, I call it a shame.'

'Well, I tell you, it makes me laugh … Look, let's go down there: I see people down there.' Isabella dug a bag of sweets out of her pocket and they sauntered on, both sucking, talking with cheeks blocked. 'Supposing you got offered a fur coat, what kind would you go for, nutria or kolinsky? … If a boy that always went racing but that you were sweet on asked you to marry him, would you? … Supposing you were going with a boy, then found out he was a trunk murderer …'

'Oh, there's such a sweet dog, such a sweet fellow. Come, then!'

'My goodness,' said Isabella, 'it isn't half getting dark.'

'Well, what *do* you expect?'

'No, but the sun's gone in. And that's not mist, now; that's fog, that is.'

'They're starting two of those cars up.'

'Mother'll be starting to worry. Better be getting home.'

Yes, mist that had been the natural breath of the woods was thickening to fog, as though the not-distant city had sent out an infection. At dusk coming so suddenly and so early, the people felt a touch of animal fear – quickening their steps, they closed on each other in a disordered way, as though their instinct were to bolt underground. Wind or thunder, though more terrible in woods, do not hold this same threat of dissolution. The people packed back into their cars; the cars lurched on to the roads and started back to London in a solid stream. Down the rides, beginning to be deserted, the trees with their leaves still clinging looked despoiled and tattered. All day the woods had worn an heroic dying smile; now they were left alone to face death.

But this was still somebody's moment. There was still some daylight. The small lake, or big pool, clearly reflected in its black mirror the birches and reeds. A tall girl, with a not quite young porcelain face, folding her black fur collar round her throat with both hands, stood posing against a birch, having her photograph taken across the water by two young men at the other side of the lake. Bob, busy over the camera on a portable tripod, was an 'art' photographer: he could photograph Nature in the most difficult light. Therefore he could go far in search of her strange moods. He felt, thought, loved, even in terms of the Lens. He sold his work to papers, where it appeared with lines of poetry underneath. This girl over the water in the fog-smudged woods was to be called 'Autumn Evening'. Cecil, an old friend, behind Bob's shoulder, looked across at the girl.

Without breaking her pose, a born model's, she coughed, and shook under her fur coat. Cecil said cautiously: 'She's getting a bit cold, Bob.'

'*Tsssss*!' said Bob sharply. He had become his camera. His whole temperament crouched over his subject, like a lion over a bit of meat.

'Won't be long,' Cecil called across the lake.

'I'm all right,' said the girl, coughing again.

'Tell her not to grab her collar up,' Bob muttered. 'She's not supposed to look cold. She's got her coat all dragged up; it spoils the figure.'

'He says, not to grab your collar,' Cecil shouted.

'Right-o.' She let her collar fall open: Turning her head inside the fur corolla, she looked more obliquely across the lake. 'Is that better?'

'O.K … *Ready*!' The slow exposure began.

People taking photographs in this half-light, this dream-light, made Carlotta and Henry stop to wonder. They stood back among the birches to be out of the way. Then the artistic tensity broke up; signals were exchanged across the water; the girl came round the lake to join the two young men. 'What's that floating?' she said. But they were busy packing up the camera. 'Should that be all right?' she said, but no one answered. Bob handed Cecil the tripod, shouldered his camera and they walked away from the lake with Bob's hand on his girl's shoulder.

'Do you think that photo will ever come out?' said Carlotta.

'I suppose he knows what he's doing … I'd like to try with a camera … '

'I'd sooner paint,' said Carlotta. They walked round the edge of the lake, looking across to where the girl had stood. 'She was pretty,' Carlotta said. She thought; 'She'll get her death. But I'd like to stand like that. I wish Henry *had* a camera. I wish I could give him one … Against the photographer's shoulder-blade eternalized minutes were being carried away. Carlotta and Henry were both tired, what they saw seemed to belong in the past already. The light seemed to fade because of their own nerves. And still water in woods, in any part of the world, continues an everlasting terrible fairy tale, in which you are always lost, in which giants oppress. Now the people had gone, the lovers saw that this place was what they had been looking for all today. But they were so tired, each stood in an isolated dream.

'What *is* that floating?' she said.

Henry screwed up his eyes. 'A thermos.' He picked up a broken branch and, with an infinity of trouble, started to claw in, with the tip of the branch, the floating flask towards himself. Its cap was gone.

'But we don't want it, Henry.'

She might never have spoken – Henry's face was intent; he recklessly stood with one toe in the water. The ribbed aluminium cylinder, twirling under the touches of the branch, rode reluctantly in. Henry reached it eagerly out of the water, shook it. Its shattered inner glass coating rattled about inside – this, the light hollowness, the feel of the ribs in his grasp made Henry smile with almost crazy pleasure. 'Treasure!' he said, with a checked, excited laugh.

Carlotta smiled, but she felt her throat tighten. She saw Henry's life curve off from hers, like one railway line from another, curve off to an utterly different, and far-off destination. When she trusted herself to speak, she said as gently as possible: 'We'll have to be starting back soon. You know it's some way. The bus—'

'No, we won't miss that,' said Henry, rattling the flask and smiling.

SENTIMENT

Dorothy Parker

Dorothy Parker (1893–1967) was an American critic, satirical poet, and short story writer. Best known for her wit and eye for 20th-century foibles, Parker wrote book reviews, poetry and short fiction for the fledgling magazine the *New Yorker*. She wrote the screenplay for the Hitchcock film *Saboteur*, but her involvement with Communism led to her being blacklisted in Hollywood.

O h, anywhere, *driver, anywhere – it doesn't matter. Just keep driving.* It's better here in this taxi than it was walking. It's no good my trying to walk. There is always a glimpse through the crowd of someone who looks like him – someone with his swing of the shoulders, his slant of the hat. And I think it's he. I think he's come back. And my heart goes to scalding water and the buildings away and bend above me. No, it's better to be here. But I wish the driver would go fast, so fast that people walking by would be a long gray blur, and I could see no swinging shoulders, no slanted hat. It's bad stopping still in the traffic like this. People pass too slowly, too clearly, and always the next one might be – No, of course it couldn't be. I know that. Of course I know it. But it might be, it might.

And people can look in and see me, here. They can see if I cry. Oh, let them – it doesn't matter. Let them look and be damned to them.

Yes, you look at me. Look and look and look, you poor, queer tired woman. It's a pretty hat, isn't it? It's meant to be looked at. That's why it's so big and red and new, that's why it has these great soft poppies on it. Your poor hat is all weary and done with. It looks like a dead cat, a cat that was run over and pushed out of the way against the curbstone. Don't you wish you were I and could have a new hat whenever you pleased? You could walk fast, couldn't you, and hold your head high and raise your feet from the pavement if you were on your way to a new hat, a beautiful hat, a hat that cost more than ever you had? Only I hope you wouldn't choose one like mine. For red is mourning, you know. Scarlet red for a love that's dead. Didn't you know that?

She's gone now. The taxi is moving and she's left behind forever. I wonder what she thought when our eyes and our lives met. I wonder did she envy me, so sleek and safe and young. Or did she realize how quick I'd be to fling away all I have if I could bear in my breast the still, dead heart that she carries in hers. She doesn't feel. She doesn't even wish. She is done with hoping and burning, if ever she burned and she hoped. Oh, that's quite nice, it has a real lilt. She is done with hoping and burning, if ever she – Yes, it's pretty. Well – I wonder if she's gone her slow way a little happier, or, perhaps, a little sadder for knowing that there is one worse off than herself.

This is the sort of thing he hated so in me. I know what he would say. "Oh, for heaven's sake!" he would say. "Can't you stop that fool sentimentalizing? Why do you have to do it? Why do you *want* to do it? Just because you see an old charwoman on the street, there's no need to get sobbing about her. She's all right. She's fine. 'When your eyes and your lives met' – oh, come on now. Why, she never even saw you. And her 'still, dead heart,' nothing! She's probably on her way to get a bottle of bad gin and have a roaring time. You don't have to dramatize *everything*. You don't have to insist that *everybody's* sad. Why are you always so sentimental? Don't *do* it Rosalie." That's what he would say. I know.

But he won't say that or anything else to me, any more. Never anything else, sweet or bitter. He's gone away and he isn't coming back. "Oh, of course I'm coming back!" he said. "No, I don't know just when – I told you that. Ah, Rosalie, don't go making a national tragedy of it. It'll be a few months, maybe – and if ever two people needed a holiday from each other! It's nothing to cry about. I'll be back. I'm not going to stay away from New York forever."

But I knew. I knew. I knew because he had been far away from me long before he went. He's gone away and he won't come back. He's gone away and he won't come back, he's gone away and he'll never come back. Listen to the wheels saying it on and on and on. That's sentimental, I suppose. Wheels don't say anything Wheels can't speak. But I *hear* them.

I wonder why it's wrong to be sentimental. People are so contemptuous of feeling. "You wouldn't catch *me* sitting alone and mooning," they say. "Moon" is what they say when they mean remember, and they are so proud of not remembering. It's strange, how they pride themselves upon their lacks. "I never take anything seriously," they say. "I simply couldn't imagine," they say, "letting myself care so much that I could be hurt." They say. "No one person could be that important to *me*." And why, why do they think they're right?

Oh, who's right and who's wrong and who decides? Perhaps it was I who was right about that charwoman. Perhaps she *was* weary and still-hearted, and perhaps, for just that moment, she knew all about me. She needn't have been all right and fine and on her way for gin, just because he said so. Oh. Oh, I forgot. He didn't say so. He wasn't here; he isn't here. It was I, imagining what he would say. And I thought I heard him. He's always with me, he and all his beauty and his cruelty. But he mustn't be any more. I mustn't think of him. That's it, don't think of him. Yes. Don't breathe, either. Don't hear. Don't see. Stop the blood in your veins.

I can't go on like this. I can't, I can't. I cannot stand this frantic misery. If I knew it would be over in a day or a year or two months, I could endure it. Even if it grew duller sometimes and wilder sometimes, it could be borne. But it is always the same and there is no end.

"Sorrow like a ceaseless rain

Beats upon my heart.
People twist and scream in pain –
Dawn will find them still again;
This has neither wax nor wane.
Neither stop nor start."

Oh, let's see – how does the next verse go? Something, something, something, something, something to rhyme with "wear." Anyway, it ends:

"All my thoughts are slow and brown:
Standing up or sitting down
Little matters, or what gown
Or what shoes I wear."

Yes, that's the way it goes. And it's right, it's so right. What is it to me what I wear? Go and buy yourself a big red hat with poppies on it – that ought to cheer you up. Yes – go buy it and loathe it. How am I to go on, sitting and staring and buying big red hats and hating them, and then sitting and staring again – day upon day upon day upon day? Tomorrow and tomorrow and tomorrow. How am I to drag through them like this?

But what else is there for me? "Go out and see your friends and have a good time," they say. "Don't sit alone and dramatize yourself." Dramatize yourself! If it be drama to feel a steady – no, a *ceaseless* rain beating upon my heart, then I do dramatize myself. The shallow people, the little people, how can they know what suffering is, how could their thick hearts be torn? Don't they know, the empty fools, that I could not see again the friends we saw together, could not go back to the places where he and I have been? For he's gone, and it's ended. It's ended, it's ended. And when it ends, only those places where you have known sorrow are kindly to you. If you revisit the scenes of your happiness, your heart must burst of its agony.

And that's sentimental, I suppose. It's sentimental to know that you cannot bear to see the places where once all was well with you, that you cannot bear reminders of a dead loveliness. Sorrow is tranquillity, remembered in emotion. It – oh, I think that's quite good. "Remembered in emotion" – that's a really nice reversal. I wish I could say it to him. But I won't say anything to him, ever again, ever, ever again. He's gone, and it's over, and I dare not think of the dead days. All my thoughts must be slow and brown, and I must—

Oh, no, no, no! Oh, the driver shouldn't go through this street! This was our street, this is the place of our love and our laughter. I can't do this, I can't, I can't. I will crouch down here, and hold my hands tight, tight over my eyes, so that I cannot look. I must keep my poor heart still, and I must be like the little, mean, dry-souled people who are proud not to remember.

But oh, I see it, I see it, even though my eyes are blinded. Though I had no eyes, my heart would tell me this street, out of all streets. I know it as I know my hands, as I know his face. Oh, why can't I be let to die as we pass through?

We must be at the florist's shop on the corner now. That's where he used to stop to buy me primroses, little yellow primroses massed tight together with a circle of their silver-backed leaves about them, clean and cool and gentle. He always said that orchids and camellias were none of my affair. So when there were no spring and no primroses, he would give me lilies-of-the-valley and little, gay rosebuds and mignonette and bright blue cornflowers. He said he couldn't stand the thought of me without flowers – it would be all wrong; I cannot bear flowers near me, now. And the little gray florist was so interested and so glad – and there was the day he called me "madam"! Ah, I can't, I can't.

And now we must be at the big apartment house with the big gold doorman. And the evening the doorman was holding the darling puppy on a big, long leash, and we stopped to talk to it, and he took it up in his arms and cuddled it, and that was the only time we ever saw the doorman smile! And next is the house with the baby, and he always would take off his hat and bow very solemnly to her, and sometimes she would give him her little starfish of a hand. And then is the tree with the rusty iron bars around it, where he would stop to turn and wave to me, as I leaned out the window to watch him. And people would look at him, because people always had to look at him, but he never noticed. It was our tree, he said; it wouldn't dream of belonging to anybody else. And very few city people had their own personal tree, he said. Did I realize that, he said.

And then there's the doctor's house, and the three thin gray houses and then – oh, God, we must be at our house now! Our house, though we had only the top floor. And I loved the long, dark stairs, because he climbed them every evening. And our little prim pink curtains at the windows, and the boxes of pink geraniums that always grew for me. And the little stiff entry and the funny mail-box, and his ring at the bell. And I waiting for him in the dusk, thinking he would never come; and yet the waiting was lovely, too. And then when I opened the door to him – Oh, no, no, no! Oh, no one could bear this. No one, no one.

Ah, why, why, why must I be driven through here? What torture could there be so terrible as this? It will be better if I uncover my eyes and look. I will see our tree and our house again, and then my heart will burst and I will be dead. I will look, I will look.

But where's the tree? Can they have cut down our tree – *our* tree? And where's the apartment house? And where's the florist's shop? And where – oh, where's our house, where's—

Driver, what street is this? Sixty-Fifth? Oh. No. Nothing, thank you. I – I thought it was Sixty-Third …

THE LOTTERY

Shirley Jackson

Shirley Jackson (1916–1965) was an American author best known for her story, 'The Lottery'. A prolific short story writer, Jackson also wrote six novels, one of which, *The Haunting of Hill House*, was nominated for the National Book Award in 1960. The Shirley Jackson Awards were established in 2007 to recognise outstanding achievement in the literature of psychological suspense, horror and the dark fantastic.

The morning of June 27th was clear and sunny, with the fresh warmth of a fun-summer day; the flowers were blossoming profusely and the grass was richly green. The people of the village began to gather in the square, between the post office and the bank, around ten o'clock; in some towns there were so many people that the lottery took two days and had to be started on June 26th, but in this village, where there were only about three hundred people, the whole lottery took less than two hours, so it could begin at ten o'clock in the morning and still be through in time to allow the villagers to get home for noon dinner.

The children assembled first, of course. School was recently over for the summer, and the feeling of liberty sat uneasily on most of them; they tended to gather together quietly for a while before they broke into boisterous play, and their talk was still of the classroom and the teacher; of books and reprimands. Bobby Martin had already stuffed his pockets full of stones, and the other boys soon followed his example, selecting the smoothest and roundest stones; Bobby and Harry Jones and Dickie Delacroix – the villagers pronounced this name "Deflacroy" – eventually made a great pile of stones in one corner of the square and guarded it against the raids of the other boys. The girls stood aside, talking among themselves, looking over their shoulders at the boys, and the very small children rolled in the dust or clung to the hands of their older brothers or sisters.

Soon the men began to gather, surveying their own children, speaking of planting and rain, tractors and taxes. They stood together, away from the pile of stones in the corner, and their jokes were quiet and they smiled rather than laughed. The women, wearing faded house dresses and sweaters, came shortly after their menfolk. They greeted one another and exchanged bits of gossip as they went to join their husbands. Soon the women, standing by their husbands, began to call to their children, and the children came reluctantly, having to be called four or five times. Bobby Martin ducked under his mother's grasping hand and ran, laughing, back to the pile of stones. His father spoke up sharply, and Bobby came quickly and took his place between his father and his oldest brother.

The lottery was conducted – as were the square dances, the teenage club, the Halloween program – by Mr. Summers, who had time and energy to devote to civic activities. He was a round-faced, jovial man and he ran the coal business, and people were sorry for him, because he had no children and his wife was a scold. When he arrived in the square, carrying the black wooden box, there was a murmur of conversation among the villagers, and he waved and called, "Little late today, folks." The postmaster, Mr. Graves, followed him, carrying a three-legged stool, and the stool was put in the center of the square and Mr. Summers set the black box down on it. The villagers kept their distance, leaving a space between themselves and the stool, and when Mr. Summers said, "Some of you fellows want to give me a hand?" there was a hesitation before two men, Mr. Martin and his oldest son, Baxter, came forward to hold the box steady on the stool while Mr. Summers stirred up the papers inside it.

The original paraphernalia for the lottery had been lost long ago, and the black box now resting on the stool had been put into use even before Old Man Warner, the oldest man in town, was born. Mr. Summers spoke frequently to the villagers about making a new box, but no one liked to upset even as much tradition as was represented by the black box. There was a story that the present box had been made with some pieces of the box that had preceded it, the one that had been constructed when the first people settled down to make a village here. Every year, after the lottery, Mr. Summers began talking again about a new box, but every year the subject was allowed to fade off without anything's being done. The black box grew shabbier each year, by now it was no longer completely black but splintered badly along one side to show the original wood color, and in some places faded or stained.

Mr. Martin and his oldest son, Baxter, held the black box securely on the stool until Mr. Summers had stirred the papers thoroughly with his hand. Because so much of the ritual had been forgotten or discarded, Mr. Summers had been successful in having slips of paper substituted for the chips of wood that had been used for generations. Chips of wood, Mr. Summers had argued, had been all very well when the village was tiny, but now that the population was more than three hundred and likely to keep on growing, it was necessary to use something that would fit more easily into the black box. The night before the lottery, Mr. Summers and Mr. Graves made up the slips of paper and put them in the box, and it was then taken to the safe of Mr. Summers' coal company and locked up until Mr. Summers was ready to take it to the square next morning. The rest of the year, the box was put away, sometimes one place, sometimes another; it had spent one year in Mr. Graves's barn and another year underfoot in the post office, and sometimes it was set on a shelf in the Martin grocery and left there.

There was a great deal of fussing to be done before Mr. Summers declared the lottery open. There were the lists to make up – of heads of families, heads of households in each family, members of each household in each family. There was the proper swearing-in of Mr. Summers by the postmaster, as the official of the lottery; at one time, some people remembered, there had been a recital of some sort, performed by the official of the lottery, a perfunctory, tuneless chant that had been rattled off duly each year; some people believed that the official of the lottery used to stand just so when he said or sang it, others believed that he was supposed to walk among the people, but years and years ago this part of the ritual had been allowed to lapse. There had been, also, a ritual salute, which the official of the lottery had had to use in addressing each person who came up to draw from the box, but this also had changed with time, until now it was felt necessary only for the official to speak to each person approaching. Mr. Summers was very good at all this; in his clean white shirt and blue jeans, with one hand resting carelessly on the black box, he seemed very proper and important as he talked interminably to Mr. Graves and the Martins.

Just as Mr. Summers finally left off talking and turned to the assembled villagers, Mrs. Hutchinson came hurriedly along the path to the square, her sweater thrown over her shoulders, and slid into place in the back of the crowd. "Clean forgot what day it was," she said to Mrs. Delacroix, who stood next to her, and they both laughed softly. "Thought my old man was out back slacking wood," Mrs. Hutchinson went on, "and then I looked out the window and the kids was gone, and then I remembered it was the twenty-seventh and came a-running." She dried her hands on her apron, and Mrs. Delacroix said, "You're in time, though. They're still talking away up there."

Mrs. Hutchinson craned her neck to see through the crowd and found her husband and children standing near the front. She tapped Mrs. Delacroix on the arm as a farewell and began to make her way through the crowd. The people separated good-humoredly to let her through; two or three people said, in voices just loud enough to be heard across the crowd, "Here comes your Missus Hutchinson," and "Bill, she made it after all." Mrs. Hutchinson reached her husband, and Mr. Summers, who had been waiting, said cheerfully, "Thought we were going to have to get on without you, Tessie." Mrs. Hutchinson said, grinning, "Wouldn't have me leave m'dishes in the sink, now, would you, Joe?" and soft laughter ran through the crowd as the people stirred back into position after Mrs. Hutchinson's arrival.

"Well, now," Mr. Summers said soberly, "guess we better get started, get this over with, so's we can go back to work. Anybody ain't here?"

"Dunbar," several people said. "Dunbar, Dunbar."

Mr. Summers consulted his list. "Clyde Dunbar," he said. "That's right. He's broke his leg, hasn't he? Who's drawing for him?"

"Me, I guess," a woman said, and Mr. Summers turned to look at her. "Wife draws for her husband," Mr. Summers said. "Don't you have a grown boy to do it for you, Janey?" Although Mr. Summers and everyone else in the village knew the answer perfectly well, it was the business of the official of the lottery to ask such questions formally. Mr. Summers waited with an expression of polite interest while Mrs. Dunbar answered.

"Horace's not but sixteen yet," Mrs. Dunbar said regretfully. "Guess I gotta fill in for the old man this year."

"Right," Mr. Summers said. He made a note on the list he was holding. Then he asked, "Watson boy drawing this year?"

A tall boy in the crowd raised his hand. "Here," he said. "I'm drawing for m'mother and me." He blinked his eyes nervously and ducked his head as several voices in the crowd said things like "Good fellow, Jack," and "Glad to see your mother's got a man to do it."

"Well," Mr. Summers said, "guess that's everyone. Old Man Warner make it?"

"Here," a voice said, and Mr. Summers nodded.

A sudden hush fell on the crowd as Mr. Summers cleared his throat and looked at the list. "All ready?" he called. "Now, I'll read the names – heads of families first – and the men come up and take a paper out of the box. Keep the paper folded in your hand without looking at it until everyone has had a turn. Everything clear?"

The people had done it so many times that they only half listened to the directions; most of them were quiet, wetting their lips, not looking around. Then Mr. Summers raised one hand high and said, "Adams." A man disengaged himself from the crowd and came forward. "Hi, Steve," Mr. Summers said, and Mr. Adams said, "Hi, Joe." They grinned at one another humorlessly and nervously. Then Mr. Adams reached into the black box and took out a folded paper. He held it firmly by one corner as he turned and went hastily back to his place in the crowd, where he stood a little apart from his family, not looking down at his hand.

"Allen," Mr. Summers said. "Anderson … Bentham."

"Seems like there's no time at all between lotteries any more," Mrs. Delacroix said to Mrs. Graves in the back row. "Seems like we got through with the last one only last week."

"Time sure goes fast," Mrs. Graves said.

"Clark … Delacroix."

"There goes my old man," Mrs. Delacroix said. She held her breath while her husband went forward.

"Dunbar," Mr. Summers said, and Mrs. Dunbar went steadily to the box while one of the women said, "Go on, Janey," and another said, "There she goes."

"We're next," Mrs. Graves said. She watched while Mr. Graves came around from the side of the box, greeted Mr. Summers gravely, and selected a slip of paper from the box. By now, all through the crowd there were men holding the small folded papers in their large hands, turning them over and over nervously. Mrs. Dunbar and her two sons stood together, Mrs. Dunbar holding the slip of paper.

"Harburt … Hutchinson."

"Get up there, Bill," Mrs. Hutchinson said, and the people near her laughed.

"Jones."

"They do say," Mr. Adams said to Old Man Warner, who stood next to him, "that over in the north village they're talking of giving up the lottery."

Old Man Warner snorted. "Pack of crazy fools," he said. "Listening to the young folks, nothing's good enough for *them*. Next thing you know, they'll be wanting to go back to living in caves, nobody work any more, live *that* way for a while. Used to be a saying; about 'Lottery in June, corn be heavy soon.' First thing you know, we'd all be eating stewed chickweed and acorns. There's *always* been a lottery," he added petulantly. "Bad enough to see young Joe Summers up there joking with everybody."

"Some places have already quit lotteries," Mrs. Adams said.

"Nothing but trouble in *that*," Old Man Warner said stoutly. "Pack of young fools."

"Martin." And Bobby Martin watched his father go forward. "Overdyke ... Percy."

"I wish they'd hurry," Mrs. Dunbar said to her older son. "I wish they'd hurry."

"They're almost through," her son said.

"You get ready to run tell Dad," Mrs. Dunbar said.

Mr. Summers called his own name and then stepped forward precisely and selected a slip from the box. Then he called, "Warner."

"Seventy-seventh year I been in the lottery," Old Man Warner said as he went through the crowd. "Seventy-seventh time."

"Watson." The tall boy came awkwardly through the crowd. Someone said, "Don't be nervous, Jack," and Mr. Summers said, "Take your time, son."

"Zanini."

After that, there was a long pause, a breathless pause, until Mr. Summers, holding his slip of paper in the air, said, "All right, fellows." For a minute, no one moved, and then all the slips of paper were opened. Suddenly, all the women began to speak at once, saying, "Who is it?" "Who's got it?" "Is it the Dunbars?" "Is it the Watsons?" Then the voices began to say, "It's Hutchinson. It's Bill," "Bill Hutchinson's got it."

"Go tell your father," Mrs. Dunbar said to her older son.

People began to look around to see the Hutchinsons. Bill Hutchinson was standing quiet, staring down at the paper in his hand. Suddenly, Tessie Hutchinson shouted to Mr. Summers, "You didn't give him time enough to take any paper he wanted. I saw you. It wasn't fair!"

"Be a good sport, Tessie," Mrs. Delacroix called, and Mrs. Graves said, "All of us took the same chance."

"Shut up, Tessie," Bill Hutchinson said.

"Well, everyone," Mr. Summers said, "that was done pretty fast, and now we've got to be hurrying a little more to get done in time." He consulted his next list. "Bill," he said, "you draw for the Hutchinson family. You got any other households in the Hutchinsons?"

"There's Don and Eva," Mrs. Hutchinson yelled. "Make *them* take their chance!"

"Daughters draw with their husbands' families, Tessie," Mr. Summers said gently. "You know that as well as anyone else."

"It wasn't *fair*," Tessie said.

"I guess not, Joe," Bill Hutchinson said regretfully. "My daughter draws with her husband's family, that's only fair. And I've got no other family except the kids."

"Then, as far as drawing for families is concerned, it's you," Mr. Summers said in explanation, "and as far as drawing for households is concerned, that's you, too. Right?"

"Right," Bill Hutchinson said.

"How many lads, Bill?" Mr. Summers asked formally.

"Three," Bill Hutchinson said. "There's Bill, Jr., and Nancy, and little Dave. And Tessie and me."

"All right, then," Mr. Summers said. "Harry, you got their tickets back?"

Mr. Graves nodded and held up the slips of paper. "Put them in the box, then," Mr. Summers directed. "Take Bill's and put it in."

"I think we ought to start over," Mrs. Hutchinson said, as quietly as she could. "I tell you it wasn't *fair*. You didn't give him time enough to choose, everybody saw that."

Mr. Graves had selected the five slips and put them in the box, and he dropped all the papers but those onto the ground, where the breeze caught them and lifted them off.

"Listen, everybody," Mrs. Hutchinson was saying to the people around her.

"Ready, Bill?" Mr. Summers asked, and Bill Hutchinson, with one quick glance around at his wife and children, nodded.

"Remember," Mr. Summers said, "take the slips and keep them folded until each person has taken one. Harry, you help little Dave." Mr. Graves took the hand of the little boy, who came willingly with him up to the box. "Take a paper out of the box, Davy," Mr. Summers said. Davy put his hand into the box and laughed. "Take just one paper," Mr. Summers said. "Harry, you hold it for him." Mr. Graves took the child's hand and removed the folded paper from the tight fist and held it while little Dave stood next to him and looked up at him wonderingly.

"Nancy next," Mr. Summers said. Nancy was twelve, and her school friends breathed heavily as she went forward, switching her skirt, and took a slip daintily from the box. "Bill, Jr.," Mr. Summers said, and Billy, his face red and his feet over-large, nearly knocked the box over as he got a paper out. "Tessie," Mr. Summers said. She hesitated for a minute, looking around defiantly, and then set her lips and went up to the box. She snatched a paper out and held it behind her.

"Bill," Mr. Summers said, and Bill Hutchinson reached into the box and felt around, bringing his hand out at last with the slip of paper in it.

The crowd was quiet. A girl whispered, "I hope it's not Nancy," and the sound of the whisper reached the edges of the crowd.

"It's not the way it used to be," Old Man Warner said clearly. "People ain't the way they used to be."

"All right," Mr. Summers said. "Open the papers. Harry, you open little Dave's."

Mr. Graves opened the slip of paper and there was a general sigh through the crowd as he held it up and everyone could see that it was blank. Nancy and Bill, Jr., opened theirs at the same time, and both beamed and laughed, turning around to the crowd and holding their slips of paper above their heads.

"Tessie," Mr. Summers said. There was a pause, and then Mr. Summers looked at Bill Hutchinson, and Bill unfolded his paper and showed it. It was blank.

"It's Tessie," Mr. Summers said, and his voice was hushed. "Show us her paper, Bill."

Bill Hutchinson went over to his wife and forced the slip of paper out of her hand. It had a black spot on it, the black spot Mr. Summers had made the night before with the heavy pencil in the coal-company office. Bill Hutchinson held it up, and there was a stir in the crowd.

"All right, folks," Mr. Summers said. "Let's finish quickly."

Although the villagers had forgotten the ritual and lost the original black box, they still remembered to use stones. The pile of stones the boys had made earlier was ready; there were stones on the ground with the blowing scraps of paper that had come out of the box. Mrs. Delacroix selected a stone so large she had to pick it up with both hands and turned to Mrs. Dunbar. "Come on," she said. "Hurry up.'

Mrs. Dunbar had small stones in both hands, and she said, gasping for breath, "I can't run at all. You'll have to go ahead and I'll catch up with you."

The children had stones already, and someone gave little Davy Hutchinson a few pebbles.

Tessie Hutchinson was in the center of a cleared space by now, and she held her hands out desperately as the villagers moved in on her. "It isn't fair," she said. A stone hit her on the side of the head.

Old Man Warner was saying, "Come on, come on, everyone." Steve Adams was in the front of the crowd of villagers, with Mrs. Graves beside him.

"It isn't fair, it isn't right," Mrs. Hutchinson screamed, and then they were upon her.

THE LIFE YOU SAVE MAY BE YOUR OWN

Flannery O'Connor

Flannery O'Connor (1925–1964) was an American writer. An important voice in American literature, O'Connor published two novels and thirty-two short stories, as well as reviews and commentaries. Her *Complete Stories* won the US National Book Award for Fiction in 1972, and was voted Best of the National Book Awards in 2009.

The old woman and her daughter were sitting on their porch when Mr. Shiftlet came up their road for the first time. The old woman slid to the edge of her chair and leaned forward, shading her eyes from the piercing sunset with her hand. The daughter could not see far in front of her and continued to play with her fingers. Although the old woman lived in this desolate spot with only her daughter and she had never seen Mr. Shiftlet before, she could tell, even from a distance, that he was a tramp and no one to be afraid of. His left coat sleeve was folded up to show there was only half an arm in it and his gaunt figure listed slightly to the side as if the breeze were pushing him. He had on a black town suit and a brown felt hat that was turned up in the front and down in the back and he carried a tin tool box by a handle. He came on, at an amble, up her road, his face turned toward the sun which appeared to be balancing itself on the peak of a small mountain.

The old woman didn't change her position until he was almost into her yard; then she rose with one hand fisted on her hip. The daughter, a large girl in a short blue organdy dress, saw him all at once and jumped up and began to stamp and point and make excited speechless sounds.

Mr. Shiftlet stopped just inside the yard and set his box on the ground and tipped his hat at her as if she were not in the least afflicted; then he turned toward the old woman and swung the hat all the way off. He had long black slick hair that hung flat from a part in the middle to beyond the tips of his ears on either side. His face descended in forehead for more than half its length and ended suddenly with his features just balanced over a jutting steel-trap jaw. He seemed to be a young man but he had a look of composed dissatisfaction as if he understood life thoroughly.

"Good evening," the old woman said. She was about the size of a cedar fence post and she had a man's gray hat pulled down low over her head.

The tramp stood looking at her and didn't answer. He turned his back and faced the sunset. He swung both his whole and his short arm up slowly so that they indicated an expanse of sky and his figure formed a crooked cross. The old woman watched him with her arms folded across her chest as if she were the owner of the sun, and the daughter watched, her head thrust forward and her fat helpless hands hanging at the wrists. She had long pink-gold hair and eyes as blue as a peacock's neck.

He held the pose for almost fifty seconds and then he picked up his box and came on to the porch and dropped down on the bottom step. "Lady," he said in a firm nasal voice, "I'd give a fortune to live where I could see me a sun do that every evening."

"Does it every evening," the old woman said and sat back down. The daughter sat down too and watched him with a cautious sly look as if he were a bird that had come up very close. He leaned to one side, rooting in his pants pocket, and in a second he brought out a package of chewing gum and offered her a piece. She took it and unpeeled it and began to chew without taking her eyes off him. He offered the old woman a piece but she only raised her upper lip to indicate she had no teeth.

Mr. Shiftlet's pale sharp glance had already passed over everything in the yard – the pump near the corner of the house and the big fig tree that three or four chickens were preparing to roost in – and had moved to a shed where he saw the square rusted back of an automobile. "You ladies drive?" he asked.

"That car ain't run in fifteen year," the old woman said. "The day my husband died, it quit running."

"Nothing is like it used to be, lady," he said. "The world is almost rotten."

"That's right," the old woman said. "You from around here?"

"Name Tom T. Shiftlet," he murmured, looking at the tires.

"I'm pleased to meet you," the old woman said. "Name Lucynell Crater and daughter Lucynell Crater. What you doing around here, Mr. Shiftlet?"

He judged the car to be about a 1928 or '29 Ford. "Lady," he said, and turned and gave her his full attention, "lemme tell you something. There's one of these doctors in Atlanta that's taken a knife and cut the human heart – the human heart," he repeated, leaning forward; "out of a man's chest and held it in his hand," and he held his hand out, palm up, as if it were slightly weighted with the human heart, "and studied it like it was a day-old chicken, and lady," he said, allowing a long significant pause in which his head slid forward and his clay-colored eyes brightened, "he don't know no more about it than you or me."

"That's right," the old woman said.

"Why, if he was to take that knife and cut into every corner of it, he still wouldn't know no more than you or me. What you want to bet?"

"Nothing," the old woman said wisely. "Where you come from, Mr. Shiftlet?"

He didn't answer. He reached into his pocket and brought out a sack of tobacco and a package of cigarette papers and rolled himself a cigarette, expertly with one hand, and attached it in a hanging position to his upper lip. Then he took a box of wooden matches from his pocket and struck one on his shoe. He held the burning match as if he were studying the mystery of flame while it traveled dangerously toward his skin. The daughter began to make loud noises and to point to his hand and shake her finger at him, but when the flame was just before touching him, he leaned down with his hand cupped over it as if he were going to set fire to his nose and lit the cigarette.

He flipped away the dead match and blew a stream of gray into the evening. A sly look came over his face. "Lady," he said, "nowadays, people'll do anything anyways. I can tell you my name is Tom T. Shiftlet and I come from Tarwater, Tennessee, but you never have seen me before: how you know I ain't lying? How you know my name ain't Aaron Sparks, lady, and I come from Singleberry, Georgia, or how you know it's not George Speeds and I come from Lucy, Alabama, or how you know I ain't Thompson Bright from Toolafalls, Mississippi?"

"I don't know nothing about you," the old woman muttered, irked.

"Lady," he said, "people don't care how they lie. Maybe the best I can tell you is, I'm a man; but listen lady," he said and paused and made his tone more ominous still, "what is a man?"

The old woman began to gum a seed. "What you carry in that tin box, Mr. Shiftlet?" she asked.

"Tools," he said, put back. "I'm a carpenter."

"Well, if you come out here to work, I'll be able to feed you and give you a place to sleep but I can't pay. I'll tell you that before you begin," she said.

There was no answer at once and no particular expression on his face. He leaned back against the two-by-four that helped support the porch roof. "Lady," he said slowly, "there's some men that some things mean more to them than money." The old woman rocked without comment and the daughter watched the trigger that moved up and down in his neck. He told the old woman then that all most people were interested in was money, but he asked what a man was made for. He asked her if a man was made for money, or what. He asked her what she thought she was made for but she didn't answer, she only sat rocking and wondered if a one-armed man could put a new roof on her garden house. He asked a lot of questions that she didn't answer. He told her that he was twenty-eight years old and had lived a varied life. He had been a gospel singer, a foreman on the railroad, an assistant in an undertaking parlor, and he had come over the radio for three months with Uncle Roy and his Red Creek Wranglers. He said he had fought and bled in the Arm Service of his country and visited every foreign land and that everywhere he had seen people that didn't care if they did a thing one way or another. He said he hadn't been raised thataway.

A fat yellow moon appeared in the branches of the fig tree as if it were going to roost there with the chickens. He said that a man had to escape to the country to see the world whole and that he wished he lived in a desolate place like this where he could see the sun go down every evening like God made it to do.

"Are you married or are you single?" the old woman asked.

There was a long silence. "Lady," he asked finally, "where would you find you an innocent woman today? I wouldn't have any of this trash I could just pick up."

The daughter was leaning very far down, hanging her head almost between her knees, watching him through a triangular door she had made in her overturned hair; and she suddenly fell in a heap on the floor and began to whimper. Mr. Shiftlet straightened her out and helped her get back in the chair.

"Is she your baby girl?" he asked.

"My only," the old woman said, "and she's the sweetest girl in the world. I wouldn't give her up for nothing on earth. She's smart too. She can sweep the floor, cook, wash, feed the chickens, and hoe. I wouldn't give her up for a casket of jewels."

"No," he said kindly, "don't ever let any man take her away from you."

"Any man come after her," the old woman said, "I'll have to stay around the place."

Mr. Shiftlet's eye in the darkness was focused on a part of the automobile bumper that glittered in the distance. "Lady," he said, jerking his short arm up as if he could point with it to her house and yard and pump, "there ain't a broken thing on this plantation that I couldn't fix for you, one-arm jackleg or not. I'm a man," he said with a sullen dignity, "even if I ain't a whole one. I got," he said, tapping his knuckles on the floor to emphasize the immensity of what he was going to say, "a moral intelligence!" and his face pierced out of the darkness into a shaft of doorlight and he stared at her as if he were astonished himself at this impossible truth.

The old woman was not impressed with the phrase. "I told you you could hang around and work for food," she said, "if you don't mind sleeping in that car yonder."

"Why listen, Lady," he said with a grin of delight, "the monks of old slept in their coffins!"

"They wasn't as advanced as we are," the old woman said.

The next morning he began on the roof of the garden house while Lucynell, the daughter, sat on a rock and watched him work. He had not been around a week before the change he had made in the place was apparent. He had patched the front and back steps, built a new hog pen, restored a fence, and taught Lucynell, who was completely deaf and had never said a word in her life, to say the word "bird." The big rosy-faced girl followed him everywhere, saying "Burrttddt ddbirrrttdt," and clapping her hands. The old woman watched from a distance, secretly pleased. She was ravenous for a son-in-law.

Mr. Shiftlet slept on the hard narrow back seat of the car with his feet out the side window. He had his razor and a can of water on a crate that served him as a bedside table and he put up a piece of mirror against the back glass and kept his coat neatly on a hanger that he hung over one of the windows.

In the evenings he sat on the steps and talked while the old woman and Lucynell rocked violently in their chairs on either side of him. The old woman's three mountains were black against the dark blue sky and were visited off and on by various planets and by the moon after it had left the chickens, Mr. Shiftlet pointed out that the reason he had improved this plantation was because he had taken a personal interest in it. He said he was even going to make the automobile run.

He had raised the hood and studied the mechanism and he said he could tell that the car had been built in the days when cars were really built. You take now, he said, one man puts in one bolt and another man puts in another bolt and another man puts in another bolt so that it's a man for a bolt. That's why you have to pay so much for a car: you're paying all those men. Now if you didn't have to pay but one man, you could get you a cheaper car and one that had had a personal interest taken in it, and it would be a better car. The old woman agreed with him that this was so.

Mr. Shiftlet said that the trouble with the world was that nobody cared, or stopped and took any trouble. He said he never would have been able to teach Lucynell to say a word if he hadn't cared and stopped long enough.

"Teach her to say something else," the old woman said.

"What you want her to say next?" Mr. Shiftlet asked.

The old woman's smile was broad and toothless and suggestive. "Teach her to say 'sugarpie,' " she said.

Mr. Shiftlet already knew what was on her mind.

The next day he began to tinker with the automobile and that evening he told her that if she would buy a fan belt, he would be able to make the car run.

The old woman said she would give him the money. "You see that girl yonder?" she asked, pointing to Lucynell who was sitting on the floor a foot away, watching him, her eyes blue even in the dark. "If it was ever a man wanted to take her away, I would say, 'No man on earth is going to take that sweet girl of mine away from me!' but if he was to say, 'Lady, I don't want to take her away, I want her right here,' I would say, 'Mister, I don't blame you none. I wouldn't pass up a chance to live in a permanent place and get the sweetest girl in the world myself. You ain't no fool,' I would say."

"How old is she?" Mr. Shiftlet asked casually.

"Fifteen, sixteen," the old woman said. The girl was nearly thirty but because of her innocence it was impossible to guess.

"It would be a good idea to paint it too," Mr. Shiftlet remarked. "You don't want it to rust out."

"We'll see about that later," the old woman said.

The next day he walked into town and returned with the parts he needed and a can of gasoline. Late in the afternoon, terrible noises issued from the shed and the old woman rushed out of the house, thinking Lucynell was somewhere having a fit. Lucynell was sitting on a chicken crate, stamping her feet and screaming, "Burrddttt! Bddurrddtttt!" but her fuss was drowned out by the car. With a volley of blasts it emerged from the shed, moving in a fierce and stately way. Mr. Shiftlet was in the driver's seat, sitting very erect. He had an expression of serious modesty on his face as if he had just raised the dead.

That night, rocking on the porch, the old woman began her business at once, "You want you an innocent woman, don't you?" she asked sympathetically. "You don't want none of this trash."

"No'm, I don't," Mr. Shiftlet said.

"One that can't talk," she continued, "can't sass you back or use foul language. That's the kind for you to have. Right there," and she pointed to Lucynell sitting cross-legged in her chair, holding both feet in her hands.

"That's right," he admitted. "She wouldn't give me any trouble."

"Saturday," the old woman said, "you and her and me can drive into town and get married."

Mr. Shiftlet eased his position on the steps.

"I can't get married right now," he said. "Everything you want to do takes money and I ain't got any."

"What you need with money?" she asked.

"It takes money," he said. "Some people'll do anything anyhow these days, but the way I think, I wouldn't marry no woman that I couldn't take on a trip like she was somebody. I mean take her to a hotel and treat her. I wouldn't marry the Duchesser Windsor," he said firmly, "unless I could take her to a hotel and give her something good to eat.

"I was raised thataway and there ain't a thing I can do about it. My old mother taught me how to do."

"Lucynell don't even know what a hotel is," the old woman muttered. "Listen here, Mr. Shiftlet," she said, sliding forward in her chair, "you'd be getting a permanent house and a deep well and the most innocent girl in the world. You don't need no money. Lemme tell you something: there ain't any place in the world for a poor disabled friendless drifting man."

The ugly words settled in Mr. Shiftlet's head like a group of buzzards in the top of a tree. He didn't answer at once. He rolled himself a cigarette and lit it and then he said in an even voice, "Lady, a man is divided into two parts, body and spirit."

The old woman clamped her gums together.

"A body and a spirit," he repeated. "The body, lady, is like a house: it don't go anywhere; but the spirit, lady, is like a automobile: always on the move, always ..."

"Listen, Mr. Shiftlet," she said, "my well never goes dry and my house is always warm in the winter and there's no mortgage on a thing about this place. You can go to the courthouse and see for yourself. And yonder under that shed is a fine automobile." She laid the bait carefully. "You can have it painted by Saturday. I'll pay for the paint."

In the darkness, Mr. Shiftlet's smile stretched like a weary snake waking up by a fire. After a second he recalled himself and said, "I'm only saying a man's spirit means more to him than anything else. I would have to take my wife off for the weekend without no regards at all for cost. I got to follow where my spirit says to go."

"I'll give you fifteen dollars for a weekend trip," the old woman said in a crabbed voice. "That's the best I can do."

"That wouldn't hardly pay for more than the gas and the hotel," he said. "It wouldn't feed her."

"Seventeen-fifty," the old woman said. "That's all I got so it isn't any use you trying to milk me. You can take a lunch."

Mr. Shiftlet was deeply hurt by the word "milk." He didn't doubt that she had more money sewed up in her mattress but he had already told her he was not interested in her money. "I'll make that do," he said and rose and walked off without treating with her further.

On Saturday the three of them drove into town in the car that the paint had barely dried on and Mr. Shiftlet and Lucynell were married in the Ordinary's office while the old woman witnessed. As they came out of the courthouse, Mr. Shiftlet began twisting his neck in his collar. He looked morose and bitter as if he had been insulted while someone held him. "That didn't satisfy me none," he said. "That was just something a woman in an office did, nothing but paper work and blood tests. What do they know about my blood? If they was to take my heart and cut it out," he said, "they wouldn't know a thing about me. It didn't satisfy me at all."

"It satisfied the law," the old woman said sharply.

"The law," Mr. Shiftlet said and spit. "It's the law that don't satisfy me."

He had painted the car dark green with a yellow band around it just under the windows. The three of them climbed in the front seat and the old woman said, "Don't Lucynell look pretty? Looks like a baby doll." Lucynell was dressed up in a white dress that her mother had uprooted from a trunk and there was a Panama hat on her head with a bunch of red wooden cherries on the brim. Every now and then her placid expression was changed by a sly isolated little thought like a shoot of green in the desert. "You got a prize!" the old woman said.

Mr. Shiftlet didn't even look at her.

They drove back to the house to let the old woman off and pick up the lunch. When they were ready to leave, she stood staring in the window of the car, with her fingers clenched around the glass. Tears began to seep sideways out of her eyes and run along the dirty creases in her face. "I ain't ever been parted with her for two days before," she said.

Mr. Shiftlet started the motor.

"And I wouldn't let no man have her but you because I seen you would do right. Good-by, Sugarbaby," she said, clutching at the sleeve of the white dress. Lucynell looked straight at her and didn't seem to see her there at all. Mr. Shiftlet eased the car forward so that she had to move her hands.

The early afternoon was clear and open and surrounded by pale blue sky. Although the car would go only thirty miles an hour, Mr. Shiftlet imagined a terrific climb and dip and swerve that went entirely to his head so that he forgot his morning bitterness. He had always wanted an automobile but he had never been able to afford one before. He drove very fast because he wanted to make Mobile by nightfall.

Occasionally he stopped his thoughts long enough to look at Lucynell in the seat beside him. She had eaten the lunch as soon as they were out of the yard and now she was pulling the cherries off the hat one by one and throwing them out the window. He became depressed in spite of the car. He had driven about a hundred miles when he decided that she must be hungry again and at the next small town they came to, he stopped in front of an aluminum-painted eating place called The Hot Spot and took her in and ordered her a plate of ham and grits. The ride had made her sleepy and as soon as she got up on the stool, she rested her head on the counter and shut her eyes. There was no one in The Hot Spot but Mr. Shiftlet and the boy behind the counter, a pale youth with a greasy rag hung over his shoulder. Before he could dish up the food, she was snoring gently.

"Give it to her when she wakes up," Mr. Shiftlet said. "I'll pay for it now."

The boy bent over her and stared at the long pink-gold hair and the half-shut sleeping eyes. Then he looked up and stared at Mr. Shiftlet. "She looks like an angel of Gawd," he murmured.

"Hitch-hiker," Mr. Shiftlet explained. "I can't wait. I got to make Tuscaloosa."

The boy bent over again and very carefully touched his finger to a strand of the golden hair and Mr. Shiftlet left.

He was more depressed than ever as he drove on by himself. The late afternoon had grown hot and sultry and the country had flattened out. Deep in the sky a storm was preparing very slowly and without thunder as if it meant to drain every drop of air from the earth before it broke. There were times when Mr. Shiftlet preferred not to be alone. He felt too that a man with a car had a responsibility to others and he kept his eye out for a hitchhiker. Occasionally he saw a sign that warned: "Drive carefully. The life you save may be your own."

The narrow road dropped off on either side into dry fields and here and there a shack or a filling station stood in a clearing. The sun began to set directly in front of the automobile. It was a reddening ball that through his windshield was slightly flat on the bottom and top. He saw a boy in overalls and a gray hat standing on the edge of the road and he slowed the car down and stopped in front of him. The boy didn't have his hand raised to thumb the ride, he was only standing there, but he had a small cardboard suitcase and his hat was set on his head in a way to indicate that he had left somewhere for good. "Son," Mr. Shiftlet said, "I see you want a ride."

The boy didn't say he did or he didn't but he opened the door of the car and got in, and Mr. Shiftlet started driving again. The child held the suitcase on his lap and folded his arms on top of it. He turned his head and looked out the window away from Mr. Shiftlet. Mr. Shiftlet felt oppressed. "Son," he said after a minute, "I got the best old mother in the world so I reckon you only got the second best."

The boy gave him a quick dark glance and then turned his face back out the window.

"It's nothing so sweet," Mr. Shiftlet continued, "as a boy's mother. She taught him his first prayers at her knee, she give him love when no other would, she told him what was right and what wasn't, and she seen that he done the right thing. Son," he said, "I never rued a day in my life like the one I rued when I left that old mother of mine."

The boy shifted in his seat but he didn't look at Mr. Shiftlet. He unfolded his arms and put one hand on the door handle.

"My mother was a angel of Gawd," Mr. Shiftlet said in a very strained voice. "He took her from heaven and giver to me and I left her." His eyes were instantly clouded over with a mist of tears. The car was barely moving.

The boy turned angrily in the seat. "You go to the devil!" he cried. "My old woman is a flea bag and yours is a stinking pole cat!" and with that he flung the door open and jumped out with his suitcase into the ditch.

Mr. Shiftlet was so shocked that for about a hundred feet he drove along slowly with the door still open. A cloud, the exact color of the boy's hat and shaped like a turnip, had descended over the sun, and another, worse looking, crouched behind the car. Mr. Shiftlet felt that the rottenness of the world was about to engulf him. He raised his arm and let it fall again to his breast, "Oh Lord!" he prayed. "Break forth and wash the slime from this earth!"

The turnip continued slowly to descend. After a few minutes there was a guffawing peal of thunder from behind and fantastic raindrops, like tin-can tops, crashed over the rear of Mr. Shiftlet's car. Very quickly he stepped on the gas and with his stump sticking out the window he raced the galloping shower into Mobile.

THE BLUSH

Elizabeth Taylor

Elizabeth Taylor (1912–1975) was a popular British novelist and short story writer. Her first novel, *At Mrs Lippincote's*, was published in 1945 and was followed by eleven more. Her short stories were published in various magazines and collected in four volumes. She also wrote a children's book.

They were the same age – Mrs Allen and the woman who came every day to do the housework. 'I shall never have children now,' Mrs Allen had begun to tell herself. Something had not come true; the essential part of her life. She had always imagined her children in fleeting scenes and intimations; that was how they had come to her, like snatches of a film. She had seen them plainly, their chins tilted up as she tied on their bibs at meal-times; their naked bodies had darted in and out of the water sprinkler on the lawn; and she had listened to their voices in the garden and in the mornings from their beds. She had even cried a little dreaming of the day when the eldest boy would go off to boarding-school; she pictured the train going out of the station; she raised her hand and her throat contracted and her lips trembled as she smiled. The years passing by had slowly filched from her the reality of these scenes – the gay sounds; the grave peace she had longed for; even the pride of grief.

She listened – as they worked together in the kitchen – to Mrs Lacey's troubles with her family, her grumblings about her grown-up son who would not get up till dinner-time on Sundays and then expected his mother to have cleaned his shoes for him; about the girl of eighteen who was a hairdresser and too full of dainty ways which she picked up from the women's magazines, and the adolescent girl who moped and glowered and answered back.

'My children wouldn't have turned out like that,' Mrs Allen thought, as she made her murmured replies. 'The more you do for some, the more you may,' said Mrs Lacey. But from gossip in the village which Mrs Allen heard she had done all too little. The children, one night after another, for years and years, had had to run out for parcels of fish and chips while their mother sat in the Horse and Jockey drinking brown ale. On summer evenings, when they were younger, they had hung about outside the pub: when they were bored they pressed their foreheads to the window and looked in at the dark little bar, hearing the jolly laughter, their mother's the loudest of all. Seeing their faces, she would swing at once from the violence of hilarity to that of extreme annoyance and, although ginger-beer and packets of potato crisps would be handed out through the window, her anger went out with them and threatened the children as they ate and drank.

'And she doesn't always care who she goes there *with*,' Mrs Allen's gardener told her.

'She works hard and deserves a little pleasure – she has her anxieties,' said Mrs Allen, who, alas, had none.

She had never been inside the Horse and Jockey, although it was nearer to her house than the Chequers at the other end of the village where she and her husband went sometimes for a glass of sherry on Sunday mornings. The Horse and Jockey attracted a different set of customers – for instance, people who sat down and drank, at tables all round the wall. At the Chequers no one ever sat down, but stood and sipped and chatted as at a cocktail party, and luncheons and dinners were served, which made it so much more respectable: no children hung about outside, because they were all at home with their nannies.

Sometimes in the evenings – so many of them – when her husband was kept late in London, Mrs Allen wished that she could go down to the Chequers and drink a glass of sherry and exchange a little conversation with someone; but she was too shy to open the door and go in alone: she imagined heads turning, a surprised welcome from her friends, who would all be safely in married pairs; and then, when she left, eyes meeting with unspoken messages and conjecture in the air.

Mrs Lacey left her at midday and then there was gardening to do and the dog to be taken for a walk. After six o'clock, she began to pace restlessly about the house, glancing at the clocks in one room after another, listening for her husband's car – the sound she knew so well because she had awaited it for such a large part of her married life. She would hear, at last, the tyres turning on the soft gravel, the door being slammed, then his footsteps hurrying towards the porch. She knew that it was a wasteful way of spending her years – and, looking back, she was unable to tell one of them from another – but she could not think what else she might do. Humphrey went on earning more and more money and there was no stopping him now. Her acquaintances, in wretched quandaries about where the next term's school-fees were to come from, would turn to her and say cruelly: 'Oh, *you're* all right, Ruth. You've no idea what you are spared.'

And Mrs Lacey would be glad when Maureen could leave school and 'get out earning'. ' "I've got my geometry to do," she says, when it's time to wash up the tea-things. "I'll geometry you, my girl," I said. "When I was your age, I was out earning." '

Mrs Allen was fascinated by the life going on in that house and the children seemed real to her, although she had never seen them. Only Mr Lacey remained blurred and unimaginable. No one knew him. He worked in the town in the valley, six miles away, and he kept himself to himself; had never been known to show his face in the Horse and Jockey. 'I've got my own set,' Mrs Lacey said airily. 'After all, he's nearly twenty years older than me. I'll make sure neither of my girls follow my mistake. "I'd rather see you dead at my feet," I said to Vera.' Ron's young lady was lucky; having Ron, she added. Mrs Allen found this strange, for Ron had always been painted so black; was, she had been led to believe, oafish, ungrateful, greedy and slow to put his hands in his pockets if there was any paying out to do. There was also the matter of his shoe-cleaning, for no young woman would do what his mother did for him – or said she did.

Always, Mrs Lacey would sigh and say: 'Goodness me, if only I was their age and knew what I know now.'

She was an envious woman: she envied Mrs Allen her pretty house and her clothes and she envied her own daughters their youth. 'If I had your figure,' she would say to Mrs Allen. Her own had gone: what else could be expected, she asked, when she had had three children? Mrs Allen thought, too, of all the brown ale she drank at the Horse and Jockey and of the reminiscences of meals past which came so much into her conversations. Whatever the cause was, her flesh, slackly corseted, shook as she trod heavily about the kitchen. In summer, with bare arms and legs she looked larger than ever. Although her skin was very white, the impression she gave was at once colourful – from her orange hair and bright lips and the floral patterns that she always wore. Her red-painted toe-nails poked through the straps of her fancy sandals; turquoise-blue beads were wound round her throat.

Humphrey Allen had never seen her; he had always left for the station before she arrived, and that was a good thing, his wife thought. When she spoke of Mrs Lacey, she wondered if he visualised a neat, homely woman in a clean white overall. She did not deliberately mislead him, but she took advantage of his indifference. Her relationship with Mrs Lacey and the intimacy of their conversations in the kitchen he would not have approved, and the sight of those calloused feet with their chipped nail-varnish and yellowing heels would have sickened him.

One Monday morning, Mrs Lacey was later than usual. She was never very punctual and had many excuses about flat bicycle-tyres or Maureen being poorly. Mrs Allen, waiting for her, sorted out all the washing. When she took another look at the clock, she decided that it was far too late for her to be expected at all. For some time lately Mrs Lacey had seemed ill and depressed; her eyelids, which were chronically rather inflamed, had been more angrily red than ever and, at the sink or ironing-board, she would fall into unusual silences, was absent-minded and full of sighs. She had always liked to talk about the 'change' and did so more than ever as if with a desperate hopefulness.

'I'm sorry, but I was ever so sick,' she told Mrs Allen, when she arrived the next morning. 'I still feel queerish. Such heartburn. I don't like the signs, I can tell you. All I crave is pickled walnuts, just the same as I did with Maureen. I don't like the signs one bit. I feel I'll throw myself into the river if I'm taken that way again.'

Mrs Allen felt stunned and antagonistic. 'Surely not at your age,' she said crossly.

'You can't be more astonished than me,' Mrs Lacey said, belching loudly. 'Oh, pardon. I'm afraid I can't help myself.'

Not being able to help herself, she continued to belch and hiccough as she turned on taps and shook soap-powder into the washing-up bowl. It was because of this that Mrs Allen decided to take the dog for a walk. Feeling consciously fastidious and aloof she made her way across the fields, trying to disengage her thoughts from Mrs Lacey and her troubles; but unable to. 'Poor woman,' she thought again and again with bitter animosity.

She turned back when she noticed how the sky had darkened with racing, sharp-edged clouds. Before she could reach home, the rain began. Her hair, soaking wet, shrank into tight curls against her head; her woollen suit smelt like a damp animal. 'Oh, I am drenched,' she called out, as she threw open the kitchen door.

She knew at once that Mrs Lacey had gone, that she must have put on her coat and left almost as soon as Mrs. Allen had started out on her walk, for nothing was done; the washing-up was hardly started and the floor was unswept. Among the stacked-up crockery a note was propped; she had come over funny, felt dizzy and, leaving her apologies and respects, had gone.

Angrily, but methodically, Mrs Allen set about making good the wasted morning. By afternoon, the grim look was fixed upon her face. 'How dare she?' she found herself whispering, without allowing herself to wonder what it was the woman had dared.

She had her own little ways of cosseting herself through the lonely hours, comforts which were growing more important to her as she grew older, so that the time would come when not to have her cup of tea at four-thirty would seem a prelude to disaster. This afternoon, disorganised as it already was, she fell out of her usual habit and instead of carrying the tray to the low table by the fire, she poured out her tea in the kitchen and drank it there, leaning tiredly against the dresser. Then she went upstairs to make herself tidy. She was trying to brush her frizzed hair smooth again when she heard the door bell ringing.

When she opened the door, she saw quite plainly a look of astonishment take the place of anxiety on the man's face. Something about herself surprised him, was not what he had expected. 'Mrs Allen?' he asked uncertainly and the astonishment remained when she had answered him.

'Well, I'm calling about the wife,' he said. 'Mrs Lacey that works here.'

'I was worried about her,' said Mrs Allen.

She knew that she must face the embarrassment of hearing about Mrs Lacey's condition and invited the man into her husband's study, where she thought he might look less out-of-place than in her brocade-smothered drawing-room. He looked about him resentfully and glared down at the floor which his wife had polished. With this thought in his mind, he said abruptly: 'It's all taken its toll.'

He sat down on a leather couch with his cap and his bicycle-clips beside him.

'I came home to my tea and found her in bed, crying,' he said. This was true. Mrs Lacey had succumbed to despair and gone to lie down. Feeling better at four o'clock, she went downstairs to find some food to comfort herself with; but the slice of dough-cake was ill-chosen and brought on more heartburn and floods of bitter tears.

'If she carries on here for a while, it's all got to be very different,' Mr Lacey said threateningly. He was nervous at saying what he must and could only bring out the words with the impetus of anger. 'You may or may not know that she's expecting.'

'Yes,' said Mrs Allen humbly. 'This morning she told me that she thought ...'

'There's no "thought" about it. It's as plain as a pikestaff.' Yet in his eyes she could see disbelief and bafflement and he frowned and looked down again at the polished floor.

Twenty years older than his wife – or so his wife had said – he really, to Mrs Allen, looked quite ageless, a crooked, bow-legged little man who might have been a jockey once. The expression about his blue eyes was like a child's: he was both stubborn and pathetic.

Mrs Allen's fat spaniel came into the room and went straight to the stranger's chair and began to sniff at his corduroy trousers.

'It's too much for her,' Mr Lacey said. 'It's too much to expect.'

To Mrs Allen's horror she saw the blue eyes filling with tears. Hoping to hide his emotion, he bent down and fondled the dog, making playful thrusts at it with his fist closed.

He was a man utterly, bewilderedly at sea. His married life had been too much for him, with so much in it that he could not understand.

'Now I know, I will do what I can,' Mrs Allen told him. 'I will try to get some-one else in to do the rough.'

'It's the late nights that are the trouble,' he said. 'She comes in dog-tired. Night after night. It's not good enough. "Let them stay at home and mind their own children once in a while," I told her. "We don't need the money." '

'I can't understand,' Mrs Allen began. She was at sea herself now, but felt peri-lously near a barbarous, unknown shore and was afraid to make any movement towards it.

'I earn good money. For her to come out at all was only for extras. She likes new clothes. In the daytimes I never had any objection. Then all these cocktail parties begin. It beats me how people can drink like it night after night and pay out for someone else to mind their kids. Perhaps you're thinking that it's not my business, but I'm the one who has to sit at home alone till all hours and get my own supper and see next to nothing of my wife. I'm boiling over some nights. Once I nearly rushed out when I heard the car stop down the road. I wanted to tell your husband what I thought of you both.'

'My husband?' murmured Mrs Allen.

'What am I supposed to have, I would have asked him? Is she my wife or your sitter-in? Bringing her back at this time of night. And it's no use saying she could have refused. She never would.'

Mrs Allen's quietness at last defeated him and dispelled the anger he had tried to rouse in himself. The look of her, too, filled him with doubts, her grave, uncer-tain demeanour and the shock her age had been to him. He had imagined some-one so much younger and – because of the cocktail parties – flighty. Instead, he recognised something of himself in her, a yearning disappointment. He picked up his cap and his bicycle-clips and sat looking down at them, turning them round in his hands. 'I had to come,' he said.

'Yes,' said Mrs Allen.

'So you won't ask her again?' he pleaded. 'It isn't right for her. Not now.'

'No, I won't,' Mrs Allen promised and she stood up as he did and walked over to the door. He stooped and gave the spaniel a final pat. 'You'll excuse my coming, I hope.'

'Of course.'

'It was no use saying any more to her. Whatever she's asked, she won't refuse. It's her way.'

Mrs Allen shut the front door after him and stood in the hall, listening to him wheeling his bicycle across the gravel. Then she felt herself beginning to blush. She was glad that she was alone, for she could feel her face, her throat, even the tops of her arms burning, and she went over to a looking-glass and studied with great interest this strange phenomenon.

THE SOUND
OF THE RIVER

Jean Rhys

Jean Rhys (1890–1979) was a novelist from Dominica, educated in
the UK from the age of sixteen. Introduced in 1924 to the writer Ford
Madox Ford, Rhys began to write short stories under his patronage. She
is best known for her novel *Wide Sargasso Sea*, written as a 'prequel' to
Charlotte Brontë's *Jane Eyre*.

The electric bulb hung on a short flex from the middle of the ceiling, and
there was not enough light to read so they lay in bed and talked. The
night air pushed out the curtains and came through the open window
soft and moist.

'But what are you afraid of? How do you mean afraid?'

She said, 'I mean afraid like when you want to swallow and you can't.'

'All the time?'

'Nearly all the time.'

'My dear, really. You are an idiot.'

'Yes, I know.'

Not about this, she thought, not about this.

'It's only a mood,' she said. 'It'll go.'

'You're so inconsistent. You chose this place and wanted to come here, I
thought you approved of it.'

'I do. I approve of the moor and the loneliness and the whole set-up, especially
the loneliness. I just wish it would stop raining occasionally.'

'Loneliness is all very well,' he said, 'but it needs fine weather.'

'Perhaps it will be fine tomorrow.'

If I could put it into words it might go, she was thinking. Sometimes you can
put it into words – almost – and so get rid of it – almost. Sometimes you can tell
yourself I'll admit I was afraid today. I was afraid of the sleek smooth faces, the
rat faces, the way they laughed in the cinema. I'm afraid of escalators and doll's
eyes. But there aren't any words for this fear. The words haven't been invented.

She said, 'I'll like it again when the rain stops.'

'You weren't liking it just now, were you? Down by the river?'

'Well,' she said, 'no. Not much.'

'It was a bit ghostly down there tonight. What can you expect? Never pick a
place in fine weather.' (Or anything else either he thought.) 'There are too many
pines about,' he said. 'They shut you in.'

'Yes.'

But it wasn't the black pines, she thought, or the sky without stars, or the thin hunted moon, or the lowering, flat-topped hills, or the tor and the big stones. It was the river.

'The river is very silent,' she'd said. 'Is that because it's so full?'

'One gets used to the noise, I suppose. Let's go in and light the bedroom fire. I wish we had a drink. I'd give a lot for a drink, wouldn't you?'

'We can have some coffee.'

As they walked back he'd kept his head turned towards the water.

'Curiously metallic it looks by this light. Not like water at all.'

'It looks smooth as if it were frozen. And much wider.'

'Frozen – no. Very much alive in an uncanny way. Streaming hair,' he'd said as if he were talking to himself. So he'd felt it too. She lay remembering how the brown broken-surfaced, fast-running river had changed by moonlight. Things are more powerful than people. I've always believed that. (You're not my daughter if you're afraid of a horse. You're not my daughter if you're afraid of being seasick. You're not my daughter if you're afraid of the shape of a hill, or the moon when it is growing old. In fact you're not my daughter.)

'It isn't silent now is it?' she said. 'The river I mean.'

'No, it makes a row from up here.' He yawned. 'I'll put another log on the fire. It was very kind of Ransom to let us have that coal and wood. He didn't promise any luxuries of that sort when we took the cottage. He's not a bad chap, is he?'

'He's got a heart. And he must be wise to the climate after all.'

'Well I like it,' he said as he got back into bed, 'in spite of the rain. Let's be happy here.'

'Yes, let's.'

That's the second time. He said that before. He'd said it the first day they came. Then too she hadn't answered 'yes let's' at once because fear which had been waiting for her had come up to her and touched her, and it had been several seconds before she could speak.

'That must have been an otter we saw this evening,' he said, 'much too big for a water rat. I'll tell Ransom. He'll be very excited.'

'Why?'

'Oh, they're rather rare in these parts.'

'Poor devils, I bet they have an awful time if they're rare. What'll he do? Organize a hunt? Perhaps he won't, we've agreed that he's soft-hearted. This is a bird sanctuary, did you know? It's all sorts of things. I'll tell him about that yellow-breasted one. Maybe he'll know what it was.'

That morning she had watched it fluttering up and down the window pane – a flash of yellow in the rain. 'Oh what a pretty bird.' Fear is yellow. You're yellow. She's got a broad streak of yellow. They're quite right, fear is yellow. 'Isn't it pretty? And isn't it persistent? It's determined to get in …'

'I'm going to put this light out,' he said. 'It's no use. The fire's better.'

He struck a match to light another cigarette and when it flared she saw the deep hollows under his eyes, the skin stretched taut over his cheekbones, and the thin bridge of his nose. He was smiling as if he knew what she'd been thinking.

'Is there anything you're not afraid of in these moods of yours?'

'You,' she said. The match went out. Whatever happened, she thought. Whatever you did. Whatever I did. Never you. D'you hear me?

'Good.' He laughed. 'That's a relief.'

'Tomorrow will be fine, you'll see. We'll be lucky.'

'Don't depend on our luck. You ought to know better by this time,' he muttered. 'But you're the sort who never knows better. Unfortunately we're both the sort who never knows better.'

'Are you tired? You sound tired.'

'Yes,' He sighed and turned away, 'I am rather.' When she said, 'I must put the light on, I want some aspirin,' he didn't answer, and she stretched her arm over him and touched the switch of the dim electric bulb. He was sleeping. The lighted cigarette had fallen on to the sheet.

'Good thing I saw that,' she said aloud. She put the cigarette out and threw it through the window, found the aspirin, emptied the ashtray, postponing the moment when she must lie down stretched out straight, listening, when she'd shut her eyes only to feel them click open again.

'Don't go to sleep,' she thought lying there. 'Stay awake and comfort me. I'm frightened. There's something here to be frightened of, I tell you. Why can't you feel it? When you said, let's be happy, that first day, there was a tap dripping somewhere into a full basin, playing a gay and horrible tune. Didn't you hear it? I heard it. Don't turn away and sigh and sleep. Stay awake and comfort me.'

Nobody's going to comfort you, she told herself, you ought to know better. Pull yourself together. There was a time when you weren't afraid. Was there? When? When was that time? Of course there was. Go on. Pull yourself together, pull yourself to pieces. There was a time. There was a time. Besides I'll sleep soon. There's always sleeping, and it'll be fine tomorrow.

'I knew it would be fine today,' she thought when she saw the sunlight through the flimsy curtains. 'The first fine day we've had.'

'Are you awake,' she said. 'It's a fine day. I had such a funny dream,' she said, still staring at the sunlight. 'I dreamt I was walking in a wood and the trees were groaning and then I dreamt of the wind in telegraph wires, well a bit like that, only very loud. I can still hear it – really I swear I'm not making this up. It's still in my head and it isn't anything else except a bit like the wind in telegraph wires.'

'It's a lovely day,' she said and touched his hand.

'My dear, you are cold. I'll get a hot water bottle and some tea. I'll get it because I'm feeling very energetic this morning, you stay still for once!'

'Why don't you answer,' she said sitting up and peering at him. 'You're frightening me,' she said, her voice rising. 'You're frightening me. Wake up,' she said and shook him. As soon as she touched him her heart swelled till it reached her throat. It swelled and grew jagged claws and the claws clutched her driving in deep. 'Oh God,' she said and got up and drew the curtains and saw his face in the sun. 'Oh God,' she said staring at his face in the sun and knelt by the bed with his hand in her two hands not speaking not thinking any longer.

The doctor said, 'You didn't hear anything during the night?'

'I thought it was a dream.'

'Oh! You thought it was a dream. I see. What time did you wake up?'

'I don't know. We kept the clock in the other room because it had a loud tick. About half past eight or nine, I suppose.'

'You knew what had happened of course.'

'I wasn't sure. At first I wasn't sure.'

'But what did you do? It was past ten when you telephoned. What did you do?'

Not a word of comfort. Suspicion. He has small eyes and bushy eyebrows and he looks suspicious.

She said, 'I put on a coat and went to Mr Ransom's, where there's a telephone, I ran all the way but it seemed a long way.'

'But that oughtn't to have taken you more than ten minutes at the most.'

'No, but it seemed very long. I ran but I didn't seem to be moving. When I got there everybody was out and the room where the telephone is was locked. The front door is always open but he locks that room when he goes out. I went back into the road but there was no one there. Nobody in the house and nobody in the road and nobody on the slope of the hill. There were a lot of sheets and men's shirts hanging on a line waving. And the sun of course. It was our first day. The first fine day we've had.'

She looked at the doctor's face, stopped, and went on in a different voice.

'I walked up and down for a bit. I didn't know what to do. Then I thought I might be able to break the door in. So I tried and I did. A board broke and I got in. But it seemed a long time before anybody answered.'

She thought, Yes, of course I knew. I was late because I had to stay here listening. I heard it then. It got louder and closer and it was in the room with me. I heard the sound of the river.

I heard the sound of the river.

A VISIT

Anna Kavan

Anna Kavan (1901–1968) was a British writer and painter. Having begun her career under her married name, Helen Ferguson, she suffered a nervous breakdown and became Anna Kavan, the protagonist of her 1930 novel *Let Me Alone*. Suffering from long-term drug addiction and bouts of mental illness, Kavan's life featured prominently in her work. She died of heart failure in 1968, soon after the publication of her most celebrated work, the novel *Ice*.

One hot night a leopard came into my room and lay down on the bed beside me. I was half asleep, and did not realize at first that it was a leopard. I seemed to be dreaming the sound of some large, soft-footed creature padding quietly through the house, the doors of which were wide open because of the intense heat. It was almost too dark to see the lithe, muscular shape coming into my room, treading softly on velvet paws, coming straight to the bed without hesitation, as if perfectly familiar with its position. A light spring, then warm breath on my arm, on my neck and shoulder, as the visitor sniffed me before lying down. It was not until later, when moonlight entering through the window revealed an abstract spotted design, that I recognized the form of an unusually large, handsome leopard stretched out beside me.

His breathing was deep though almost inaudible, he seemed to be sound asleep. I watched the regular contractions and expansions of the deep chest, admired the elegant relaxed body and supple limbs, and was confirmed in my conviction that the leopard is the most beautiful of all wild animals. In this particular specimen I noticed something singularly human about the formation of the skull, which was domed rather than flattened, as is generally the case with the big cats, suggesting the possibility of superior brain development inside. While I observed him, I was all the time breathing his natural odour, a wild primeval smell of sunshine, freedom, moon and crushed leaves, combined with the cool freshness of the spotted hide, still damp with the midnight moisture of jungle plants. I found this non-human scent, surrounding him like an aura of strangeness, peculiarly attractive and stimulating.

My bed, like the walls of the house, was made of palm-leaf matting stretched over stout bamboos, smooth and cool to the touch, even in the great heat. It was not so much a bed as a room within a room, an open staging about twelve feet square, so there was ample space for the leopard as well as myself. I slept better that night than I had since the hot weather started, and he too seemed to sleep peacefully at my side. The close proximity of this powerful body of another species gave me a pleasant sensation I am at a loss to name.

When I awoke in the faint light of dawn, with the parrots screeching outside, he had already got up and left the room. Looking out, I saw him standing, statuesque, in front of the house on the small strip of ground I keep cleared between it and the jungle. I thought he was contemplating departure, but I dressed and went out, and he was still there, inspecting the fringe of the dense vegetation, in which huge heavy hornbills were noisily flopping about.

I called him and fed him with some meat I had in the house. I hoped he would speak, tell me why he had come and what he wanted of me. But though he looked at me thoughtfully with his large, lustrous eyes, seeming to understand what I said, he did not answer, but remained silent all day. I must emphasize that there was no hint of obstinacy or hostility in his silence, and I did not resent it. On the contrary, I respected him for his reserve; and, as the silence continued unbroken, I gave up expecting to hear his voice. I was glad of the pretext for using mine and went on talking to him. He always appeared to listen and understand me.

The leopard was absent during much of the day. I assumed that he went hunting for his natural food; but he usually came back at intervals, and seldom seemed to be far away. It was difficult to see him among the trees, even when he was quite close, the pattern of his protective spots blended so perfectly with the pattern of sun-spots through savage branches. Only by staring with concentrated attention could I distinguish him from his background; he would be crouching there in a deep-shaded glade, or lying extended with extraordinary grace along a limb of one of the giant kowikawas, whose branch-structure supports less robust trees, as well as countless creepers and smaller growths. The odd thing was that, as soon as I'd seen him, he invariably turned his head as if conscious that I was watching. Once I saw him much further off, on the beach, which is only just visible from my house. He was standing darkly outlined against the water, gazing out to sea; but even at this distance, his head turned in my direction, though I couldn't possibly have been in his range of vision. Sometimes he would suddenly come indoors and silently go all through the house at a quick trot, unexpectedly entering one room after another, before he left again with the same mysterious abruptness. At other times he would lie just inside or outside, with his head resting on the threshold, motionless except for his watchful moving eyes, and the twitching of his sensitive nostrils in response to stimuli which my less acute senses could not perceive.

His movements were always silent, graceful, dignified, sure; and his large, dark eyes never failed to acknowledge me whenever we met in our daily comings and goings.

I was delighted with my visitor, whose silence did not conceal his awareness of me. If I walked through the jungle to visit someone, or to buy food from the neighbouring village, he would appear from nowhere and walk beside me, but always stopped before a house was in sight, never allowing himself to be seen. Every night, of course, he slept on the bed at my side. As the weeks passed he seemed to be spending more time with me during the day, sitting or lying near me while I was working, now and then coming close to gaze attentively at what I was doing.

Then, without warning, he suddenly left me. This was how it happened. The rainy season had come, bringing cooler weather; there was a chill in the early morning air, when he returned to my room as I finished dressing, and leaned against me for a moment. He had hardly ever touched me in daylight, certainly never in that deliberate fashion. I took it to mean that he wished me to do something for him, and asked what it was. Silently he led the way out of the house, pausing to look back every few steps to see whether I was coming, and into the jungle. The stormy sky was heavily clouded, it was almost dark under the trees, from which great drops of last night's rain splashed coldly on my neck and bare arms. As he evidently wanted me to accompany him further, I said I would go back for a coat.

However, he seemed to be too impatient to wait, lunging forward with long, loping strides, his shoulders thrusting like steel pistons under the velvet coat, while I reluctantly followed. Torrential rain began streaming down, in five minutes the ground was a bog, into which my feet sank at each step. By now I was shivering, soaked to the skin, so I stopped and told him I couldn't go on any further. He turned his head and for a long moment his limpid eyes looked at me fixedly, with an expression I could not read. Then the beautiful head turned away, the muscles slid and bunched beneath patterned fur, as he launched himself in a tremendous leap through the shining curtain of raindrops, and was instantly hidden from sight. I walked home as fast as I could, and changed into dry clothes. I did not expect to see him again before evening, but he did not come back at all.

Nothing of any interest took place after the leopard's visit. My life resumed its former routine of work and trivial happenings. The rains came to an end, winter merged imperceptibly into spring. I took pleasure in the sun and the natural world. I felt sure the leopard meant to return, and often looked out for him, but throughout this period he never appeared. When the sky hung pure and cloudless over the jungle, many-coloured orchids began to flower on the trees. I went to see one or two people I knew; a few people visited me in my house. The leopard was never mentioned in our conversations.

The heat increased day by day, each day dawned glassily clear. The atmosphere was pervaded by the aphrodisiac perfume of wild white jasmine, which the girls wove into wreaths for their necks and hair. I painted some large new murals on the walls of my house, and started to make a terrace from a mosaic of coloured shells. For months I'd been expecting to see the leopard, but as time kept passing without a sign of him, I was gradually losing hope.

The season of oppressive heat came round in due course, and the house was left open all night. More than at any other time, it was at night, just before falling asleep, that I thought of the leopard, and, though I no longer believed it would happen, pretended that I'd wake to find him beside me again. The heat deprived me of energy, the progress of the mosaic was slow. I had never tried my hand at such work before, and being unable to calculate the total quantity of shells that would be required, I constantly ran out of supplies, and had to make tiring trips to the beach for more.

One day while I was on the shore, I saw, out to sea, a young man coming towards the land, standing upright on the crest of a huge breaker, his red cloak blowing out in the wind, and a string of pelicans solemnly flapping in line behind him. It was so odd to see this stranger, with his weird escort, approaching alone from the ocean on which no ships ever sailed, that my thoughts immediately connected him with the leopard: there must be some contact between them; perhaps he was bringing me news. As he got nearer, I shouted to him, called out greetings and questions, to which he replied. But because of the noise of the waves and the distance between us, I could not understand him. Instead of coming on to the beach to speak to me, he suddenly turned and was swept out to sea again, disappearing in clouds of spray. I was puzzled and disappointed. But I took the shells home, went on working as usual, and presently forgot the encounter.

Some time later, coming home at sunset, I was reminded of the young man of the sea by the sight of a pelican perched on the highest point of my roof. Its presence surprised me: pelicans did not leave the shore as a rule, I had never known one come as far inland as this. It suddenly struck me that the bird must be something to do with the leopard, perhaps bringing a message from him. To entice it closer, I found a small fish in the kitchen, which I put on the grass. The pelican swooped down at once, and with remarkable speed and neatness, considering its bulk, skewered the fish on its beak, and flew off with it. I called out, strained my eyes to follow its flight; but only caught a glimpse of the great wings flapping away from me over the jungle trees, before the sudden black curtain of tropical darkness came down with a rush.

Despite this inconclusive end to the episode, it revived my hope of seeing the leopard again. But there were no further developments of any description; nothing else in the least unusual occurred.

It was still the season when the earth sweltered under a simmering sky. In the afternoons the welcome trade wind blew through the rooms and cooled them, but as soon as it died down the house felt hotter than ever. Hitherto I had always derived a nostalgic pleasure from recalling my visitor; but now the memory aroused more sadness than joy, as I had finally lost all hope of his coming back.

At last the mosaic was finished and looked quite impressive, a noble animal with a fine spotted coat and a human head gazing proudly from the centre of the design. I decided it needed to be enclosed in a border of yellow shells, and made another expedition to the beach, where the sun's power was intensified by the glare off the bright green waves, sparkling as if they'd been sprinkled all over with diamonds. A hot wind whistled through my hair, blew the sand about, and lashed the sea into crashing breakers, above which flocks of sea birds flew screaming, in glistening clouds of spray. After searching for shells for a while I straightened up, feeling almost dizzy with the heat and the effort. It was at this moment, when I was dazzled by the violent colours and the terrific glare, that the young man I'd already seen reappeared like a mirage, the red of his flying cloak vibrating against the vivid emerald-green waves. This time, through a haze of shimmering brilliance, I saw that the leopard was with him, majestic and larger than life, moving as gracefully as if the waves were solid glass.

I called to him, and though he couldn't have heard me above the thundering of the surf, he turned his splendid head and gave me a long, strange, portentous look, just as he had that last time in the jungle, sparkling rainbows of spray now taking the place of rain. I hurried towards the edge of the water, then suddenly stopped, intimidated by the colossal size of the giant rollers towering over me.

I'm not a strong swimmer, it seemed insane to challenge those enormous on-coming walls of water, which would certainly hurl me back contemptuously on to the shore with all my bones broken. Their exploding roar deafened me, I was half-blinded by the salt spray, the whole beach was a swirling, glittering dazzle, in which I lost sight of the two sea-borne shapes. And when my eyes brought them back into focus, they had changed direction, turned from the land, and were already a long way off, receding fast, diminishing every second, reduced to vanishing point by the hard, blinding brilliance of sun and waves.

Long after they'd disappeared, I stood there, staring out at that turbulent sea, on which I had never once seen any kind of boat, and which now looked emptier, lonelier, and more desolate than ever before. I was paralysed by depression and disappointment, and could hardly force myself to pick up the shells I'd collected and carry them home.

That was the last time I saw the leopard. I've heard nothing of him since that day, or of the young man. For a little while I used to question the villagers who lived by the sea, some of them said they vaguely remembered a man in a red cloak riding the water. But they always ended by becoming evasive, uncertain, and making contradictory statements, so that I knew I was wasting my time.

I've never said a word about the leopard to anyone. It would be difficult to describe him to these simple people, who can never have seen a creature even remotely like him, living here in the wilds as they do, far from zoos, circuses, cinemas and television. No carnivora, no large or ferocious beasts of any sort have ever inhabited this part of the world, which is why we can leave our houses open all night without fear.

The uneventful course of my life continues, nothing happens to break the monotony of the days. Sometime, I suppose, I may forget the leopard's visit. As it is I seldom think of him, except at night when I'm waiting for sleep to come. But, very occasionally he still enters my dreams, which disturbs me and makes me feel restless and sad. Although I never remember the dreams when I wake, for days afterwards they seem to weigh me down with the obscure bitterness of a loss which should have been prevented, and for which I am myself to blame.

OBSESSIONAL

Anna Kavan

Anna Kavan (1901–1968) was a British writer and painter. Having begun her career under her married name, Helen Ferguson, she suffered a nervous breakdown and became Anna Kavan, the protagonist of her 1930 novel *Let Me Alone*. Suffering from long-term drug addiction and bouts of mental illness, Kavan's life featured prominently in her work. She died of heart failure in 1968, soon after the publication of her most celebrated work, the novel *Ice*.

It happened between nine and ten in the evening, his usual time. The inner door of the lobby suddenly opened, just as if he'd let himself in with his key, and she turned her head.

The sheer, mad impossibility of his reappearing, now, all these months afterwards, did not check the instantaneous charge of purest joy that went through her like an electric shock. Many miracles had occurred in connection with him, and this could be one more, since cosmic rays and the mystery of mutation had committed them to each other – might they not come together without the body, and not only in dreams?

Already, before her reasoning brain killed the illusion, the words of welcome took shape, her muscles tensed for the suddenly youthful springing up that would take her to meet him, hands outstretched to bring him quickly into the room. 'Oh, I'm so glad you've come ...' Already, while in the act of turning, she'd seen his face crumpled in the hunted expression which always struck her as unbearably touching, though she could never decide if it was genuine or assumed, as he said with heart-tending humility – real or false, what did it matter? ... 'You must not be angry with me because I did not come to see you these last days. I wanted to come – but it has not been possible ...'

'Of course I'm not angry,' she would answer. 'All that matters is that you're here now.' And everything would be perfect and understood, any need for explanation, any hint of criticism or sadness past would fade out with his troubled expression, his mouth widening in the warm, amused smile of his usual greeting, in confident anticipation of happiness.

Only of course he was not there this time. The door had opened, but nobody had come in. She got up to shut it, the flying fantasy leaving a black hiatus; in the midst of which she remembered that for once she was not alone, and, feeling the visitor's eyes following her with a question, turned back to him, her own eyes painful from straining to see what had never been visible.

'The wind must somehow have blown it open. Unless a ghost opened it.' She closed the door firmly, with unnecessary force, and returned to the friend; one of the very few who still – out of pity? Curiosity? Force of habit? – spent an occasional evening with her.

He nodded, smiling, with the amiable easy pretence of the unbeliever, tolerant enough to admit to ghosts of his own, before, rather obviously, changing the subject. Conversation continued, sounding unnaturally loud in her quiet room, which seemed to take on an air of pained surprise at the unaccustomed clatter of voices. But it was an effort for her to go on talking, and she soon fell silent, remaining absent, dispirited, more aware of the apparition that had failed to materialize than she was of the living guest, who left early, discouraged by her lack of interest in him, or in anything he could say, and was forgotten almost before he was out of the room.

It was always the same now, the ghost always coming between her and her life in the world, so much more important, since that lost being was still her only companion, and their now-obsolete relationship the one true human contact she would ever have.

The last time she had seen him in the flesh, all the vital force of his life stripped away, his sharpened face had confronted her with such a fearful fixed finality of sightless indifference that she had been frozen in mortal terror, engulfed by abysmal despair. After all the years of unfailing support, his huge, inhuman, deaf, blind inaccessibility was horrifying. He had not kept his promise. He had abandoned her, left her to suffer alone.

Since he'd gone, the world had become unnervingly strange. There was nothing she could do and nowhere she could go. She felt lost, lonely, dazed, deprived of everything, even of her identity, which was not strong enough to survive without his constant encouragement and reassurance. Isolation clamped down on her. For days she saw no one, spoke to no one. The telephone seldom rang. The strangers in the streets seemed frightening, as if they belonged to a different species, pushing, hard-faced, hurrying past her without a glance. Waiting to cross, standing in the middle of the road, traffic tearing in both directions, she had a sense of utter estrangement from the noisy, inconsequential chaos around her, as if she stood in a no-world, peering doubtfully at shadows, wondering if any of them were real.

Despite the frightful blow he'd inflicted on her by the act of ceasing to be, the man who had formerly filled her life was still her only reality. He had gone from the world. She would never see him again. And yet he was always with her, speaking to her, sharing her perceptions; he occupied her completely, leaving no room for life, excluding her from the world. Incapable of living without him, she had made him her ghostly reality. His ghost was better than nothing; it gave her no sense of the supernatural, in which she'd never believed, but at times seemed almost identical with the real man. Even more than while he had been alive, she was obsessed by him in a way that was not altogether pleasant, although, like an addiction, it was essential to her.

He waylaid her everywhere: in avenues with prancing equestrian statues, in tree-lined squares, tube stations, libraries, shops. She knew he was waiting for her in other countries: beside lakes and mountains, in hotels and clinics, at a certain café where all one evening he'd written verses and made drawings for her, under the doomed goggling eyes of the crowded trout in their tank. He naturally frequented the streets and parks where they'd walked so often. Forgotten conversations sprang up and struck her among the tables of restaurants where they'd been together. In the quiet streets of her own district, any half-glimpsed face of a passer-by was likely to startle her with the possibility of being his. She would wake in the morning with the conviction that he was coming to see her, and sit all day watching the door, afraid of missing him if she moved. Or she would suddenly feel him waiting impatiently for her somewhere, and in nightmare anxiety race from one of their old meeting places to another, hours later finding herself at home, exhausted, desolated, almost in tears, not sure whether she'd really been to all those places or only imagined she had.

A flimsy crumpled advertisement she took from the letterbox would, for a split second, become one of his scribbled notes, with an obscene cat drawn in the corner, the message scrawled in soft purple crayon illegible but for the words, 'The poor M was here …' She would rush to the telephone when it rang, expecting, for the first moment before the voice at the other end spoke in her ear, to hear his distraught voice utter her name. Almost daily, in her comings and goings about the town, a distant figure in a dark blue suit sliced her heart with an imagined resemblance. Hurrying out one day for a loaf of bread, suddenly she had a premonition. And, yes, there he was, walking in the same direction, among the people in front of her, bending forward slightly as if to thrust his way through them, hands and arms held a little away from him – there was no mistaking that characteristic prowling walk. But when she darted forward, eager and smiling, he became an elderly stranger with a heavy, morose face, and the ghostly illusion dissolved in the roar and diesel fumes of a passing bus. She did not wish to escape the consciousness of him, which nevertheless was a burden, like a dead body she carried about everywhere and couldn't bear to relinquish. Going into her workroom, she was half-surprised not to find him scrutinizing her latest paintings with a wry, enigmatic smile. Her disappointment darkened these paintings, already discoloured and splashed by the boredom and futility of her present existence. All her activities had become distasteful, dreary, a weariness to her. Everything she had ever done had been done for him. Why should she try to do anything now?

She wandered out restlessly into the darkening garden, feeling the cool dusk rising round her like water, filling the small space, already full of his inescapable aura. He had been in the habit of dropping in for a few minutes at about this time, roaming round the garden or sitting there till it got dark. Sometimes, if she'd been specially preoccupied with her work, she had wished he would not interrupt her, and this memory caused her a fresh pang. She never did any work these days, so he could come whenever he pleased – why wasn't he here now? As if the thought had invoked it, his hatless, hairless, dignified skull glimmered transparently for a second against the leaves at a spot where in other years he had planted beans. But directly afterwards there was only the deserted garden where nobody came any more, enclosed like a dark pool of twilight by trees and high walls, and containing nothing except her sadness and solitude and the silent watery chill of the rapidly deepening dusk. In the house, certain parts of the rooms, certain objects, always vividly evoked his image, and for these she could be prepared. It was the chance reminders, come upon unawares, that stabbed her most cruelly: a coat left on the settee, simulating his collapsed form sprawled on the green cushions, taking his pulse with two fingers, motionless with the fated calm of a man long familiar with the idea that any moment may be his last.

The haunted vacancy of these darkening ghostly rooms drove her out into the streets to calm herself by the effort of walking. But still the relentless seconds assailed her like arrows one after the other with piercing loneliness, loss. The lights came on, outlining the shapes of strangers, whose faces, limbs, voices, gestures, tormented her with momentary fragments of similarity, which flew away at a second glance. She even caught sight once, in a dark entry, of his spectral monocled countenance smiling inscrutably as it did from so many snapshots, leaving her with a famished longing so acute that it seemed physical, and hardly to be endured. If only, just once more, he would come in the reassuring solidity she had valued so lightly while it was accessible to her. She knew exactly how they would meet, his eyes finding hers with absolute certainty, but at once moving on, while his mouth undermined this pretence by breaking into the glad, intimate smile of greeting that always made her forget the other look of pretended indifference – distance – what? What was that element of elusiveness which had been there from the start, confirming itself in the end by his broken promise, like some ancient curse nobody believed in, which had finally come true after all?

The question remained unanswered. Deciding that she was tired enough to go home, she walked, dragging her feet wearily, through the emptying streets, not noticing anything, until arrested by the strong sense of his proximity, a few yards from the house where he'd lived all the time she had known him. Immediately she recalled the last painful occasion she'd been inside it, when his absence had been like a scream in the little rooms, where it was distressingly evident that no one now ever looked at the pictures, or took the books from the shelves. Certain small objects, special favourites he'd often stroked and held in his hands while he talked – a white jade fish, a painted Bengal tiger with a stiff string tail – had been incarcerated behind the glass doors of a cabinet, and glared out mournfully from their prison. She could not bear to see his beloved possessions uncared for, and, as soon as she was left alone for a minute, went out on to the stairs; where something impelled her to put her head round the door of his room, and she had instantly been struck down by most violent grief, as, in the act of reaching out to draw her towards the bed, his soft, strong hands disintegrated in thin air.

It seemed to her now that the door of the garage – the only place where there was room for his piano – was open and that he was playing inside; an illusion so powerful that she moved involuntarily to join him; then, collecting herself with an effort, walked on in the direction of her own street. Familiar music he'd often played followed her as she went, floating after her in the dark; muted, melancholy, incomplete passages that seemed to come from the middle of some long piece which never ended, the beginning of which she had never heard. The wistful, wandering notes affected her with an intolerable sadness. Nevertheless, at the corner she stopped to listen again; but now the faint sounds had faded out and she was alone in the silent and empty darkness.

Walking on, she wondered if it was safe to go to bed, if she would sleep now. Her legs ached with tiredness as she climbed the stairs and opened her door.

The house looked dark and desolate inside. She went into the lobby, putting out one hand to switch off the outside light, and as she turned her head – never sure which switch controlled which bulb – to look down the staircase, a ghostly face glinted into her vision with an expression so heart-breakingly apologetic that she almost said aloud, 'Don't look like that. Nothing matters now that you're here.'

THE FIRST YEAR
OF MY LIFE

Muriel Spark

Muriel Spark (1918–2006) was a Scottish novelist best known for her novel, *The Prime of Miss Jean Brodie*. In 2008 *The Times* named her in its list of the '50 Greatest British Writers Since 1945'. Spark was twice shortlisted for the Man Booker Prize and was awarded the Golden PEN Award in 1998 by English PEN for her services to literature. She became Dame Commander of the Order of the British Empire in 1993.

I was born on the first day of the second month of the last year of the First World War, a Friday. Testimony abounds that during the first year of my life I never smiled. I was known as the baby whom nothing and no one could make smile. Everyone who knew me then has told me so. They tried very hard, singing and bouncing me up and down, jumping around, pulling faces. Many times I was told this later by my family and their friends; but, anyway, I knew it at the time.

You will shortly be hearing of that new school of psychology, or maybe you have heard of it already, which after long and far-adventuring research and experiment has established that all of the young of the human species are born omniscient. Babies, in their waking hours, know everything that is going on everywhere in the world, they can tune in to any conversation they choose, switch on to any scene. We have all experienced this power. It is only after the first year that it was brainwashed out of us, for it is demanded of us by our immediate environment that we grow to be of use to it in a practical way. Gradually, our know-all brain-cells are blacked out although traces remain in some individuals in the form of ESP, and in the adults of some primitive tribes.

It is not a new theory. Poets and philosophers, as usual, have been there first. But scientific proof is now ready and to hand. Perhaps the final touches are being put to the new manifesto in some cell at Harvard University. Any day now it will be given to the world, and the world will be convinced.

Let me therefore get my word in first, because I feel pretty sure, now, about the authenticity of my remembrance of things past. My autobiography, as I very well perceived at the time, started in the very worst year that the world had ever seen so far. Apart from being born bedridden and toothless, unable to raise myself on the pillow or utter anything but farmyard squawks or police-siren wails, my bladder and my bowels totally out of control, I was further depressed by the curious behaviour of the two-legged mammals around me. There were those black-dressed people, females of the species to which I appeared to belong, saying they had lost their sons. I slept a great deal. Let them go and find their sons. It was like the special pin for my nappies which my mother or some other hoverer dedicated to my care was always losing. These careless women in black lost their husbands and their brothers. Then they came to visit my mother and clucked and crowed over my cradle. I was not amused.

'Babies never really smile till they're three months old,' said my mother. 'They're not *supposed* to smile till they're three months old.'

My brother, aged six, marched up and down with a toy rifle over his shoulder.

> The grand old Duke of York
> He had ten thousand men;
> He marched them up to the top of the hill
> And he marched them down again.

> And when they were up, they were up
> And when they were down, they were down.
> And when they were neither down nor up
> They were neither up nor down.

'Just listen to him!'

'Look at him with his rifle!'

I was about ten days old when Russia stopped fighting. I tuned in to the Czar, a prisoner, with the rest of his family, since evidently the country had put him off his throne and there had been a revolution not long before I was born. Everyone was talking about it. I tuned in to the Czar. 'Nothing would ever induce me to sign the treaty of Brest-Litovsk,' he said to his wife. Anyway, nobody had asked him to.

At this point I was sleeping twenty hours a day to get my strength up. And from what I discerned in the other four hours of the day I knew I was going to need it. The Western Front on my frequency was sheer blood, mud, dismembered bodies, blistered crashes, hectic flashes of light in the night skies, explosions, total terror. Since it was plain I had been born into a bad moment in the history of the world, the future bothered me, unable as I was to raise my head from the pillow and as yet only twenty inches long. 'I truly wish I were a fox or a bird,' D. H. Lawrence was writing to somebody. Dreary old creeping Jesus. I fell asleep.

Red sheets of flame shot across the sky. It was 21st March, the fiftieth day of my life, and the German Spring Offensive had started before my morning feed. Infinite slaughter. I scowled at the scene, and made an effort to kick out. But the attempt was feeble. Furious and impatient for some strength, I wailed for my feed. After which I stopped wailing but continued to scowl.

> The grand old Duke of York
> He had ten thousand men …

They rocked the cradle. I never heard a sillier song. Over in Berlin and Vienna the people were starving, freezing, striking, rioting and yelling in the streets. In London everyone was bustling to work and muttering that it was time the whole damn business was over.

The big people around me bared their teeth; that meant a smile, it meant they were pleased or amused. They spoke of ration cards for meat and sugar and butter.

Where will it all end?

I went to sleep. I woke and tuned in to Bernard Shaw who was telling someone to shut up. I switched over to Joseph Conrad who strangely enough, was saying precisely the same thing. I still didn't think it worth a smile, although it was expected of me any day now. I got on to Turkey. Women draped in black huddled and chattered in their harems; yak-yak-yak. This was boring, so I came back to home base.

In and out came and went the women in British black. My mother's brother, dressed in his uniform, came coughing. He had been poison-gassed in the trenches. '*Tout le monde à la bataille!*' declaimed Marshal Foch the old swine. He was now Commander-in-Chief of the Allied Forces. My uncle coughed from deep within his lungs, never to recover but destined to return to the Front. His brass buttons gleamed in the firelight. I weighed twelve pounds by now, I stretched and kicked for exercise seeing that I had a lifetime before me, coping with this crowd. I took six feeds a day and kept most of them down by the time the *Vindictive* was sunk in Ostend harbour, on which day I kicked with special vigour in my bath.

In France the conscripted soldiers leapfrogged over the dead on the advance and littered the fields with limbs and hands, or drowned in the mud. The strongest men on all fronts were dead before I was born. Now the sentries used bodies for barricades and the fighting men were unhealthy from the start. I checked my toes and fingers, knowing I was going to need them. *The Playboy of the Western World* was playing at the Court Theatre in London, but occasionally I beamed over to the House of Commons which made me drop off gently to sleep. Generally, I preferred the Western Front where one got the true state of affairs. It was essential to know the worst, blood and explosions and all, for one had to be prepared, as the boy scouts said. Virginia Woolf yawned and reached for her diary. Really, I preferred the Western Front.

In the fifth month of my life I could raise my head from my pillow and hold it up. I could grasp the objects that were held out to me. Some of these things rattled and squawked. I gnawed on them to get my teeth started. 'She hasn't smiled yet?' said the dreary old aunties. My mother, on the defensive, said I was probably one of those late smilers. On my wavelength Pablo Picasso was getting married and early in that month of July the Silver Wedding of King George V and Queen Mary was celebrated in joyous pomp at St Paul's Cathedral. They drove through the streets of London with their children. Twenty-five years of domestic happiness. A lot of fuss and ceremonial handing over of swords went on at the Guildhall where the King and Queen received a cheque for £53,000 to dispose of for charity as they thought fit. *Tout le monde à la bataille!* Income tax in England had reached six shillings in the pound. Everyone was talking about the Silver Wedding yak-yak-yak, and ten days later the Czar and his family, now in Siberia, were invited to descend to a little room in the basement. Crack, crack, went the guns; screams and blood all over the place, and that was the end of the Romanoffs. I flexed my muscles, 'A fine healthy baby,' said the doctor; which gave me much satisfaction.

Tout le monde à la bataille! That included my gassed uncle. My health had improved to the point where I was able to crawl in my playpen. Bertrand Russell was still cheerily in prison for writing something seditious about pacifism. Tuning in as usual to the Front Lines it looked as if the Germans were winning all the battles yet losing the war. And so it was. The upper-income people were upset about the income tax at six shillings to the pound. But all women over thirty got the vote. 'It seems a long time to wait,' said one of my drab old aunts, aged twenty-two. The speeches in the House of Commons always sent me to sleep which was why I missed, at the actual time, a certain oration by Mr Asquith following the armistice on 11th November. Mr Asquith was a greatly esteemed former prime minister later to be an Earl, and had been ousted by Mr Lloyd George. I clearly heard Asquith, in private, refer to Lloyd George as 'that damned Welsh goat'.

The armistice was signed and I was awake for that. I pulled myself on to my feet with the aid of the bars of my cot. My teeth were coming through very nicely in my opinion, and well worth all the trouble I was put to in bringing them forth. I weighed twenty pounds. On all the world's fighting fronts the men killed in action or dead of wounds numbered 8,538,315 and the warriors wounded and maimed were 21,219,452. With these figures in mind I sat up in my high chair and banged my spoon on the table. One of my mother's black-draped friends recited:

> I have a rendezvous with Death
> At some disputed barricade,
> When spring comes back with rustling shade
> And apple blossoms fill the air –
> I have a rendezvous with Death.

Most of the poets, they said, had been killed. The poetry made them dab their eyes with clean white handkerchiefs.

Next February on my first birthday, there was a birthday cake with one candle. Lots of children and their elders. The war had been over two months and twenty-one days. 'Why doesn't she smile?' My brother was to blow out the candle. The elders were talking about the war and the political situation. Lloyd George and Asquith, Asquith and Lloyd George. I remembered recently having switched on to Mr Asquith at a private party where he had been drinking a lot. He was playing cards and when he came to cut the cards he tried to cut a large box of matches by mistake. On another occasion I had seen him putting his arm around a lady's shoulder in a Daimler motor car, and generally behaving towards her in a very friendly fashion. Strangely enough she said, 'If you don't stop this nonsense immediately I'll order the chauffeur to stop and I'll get out.' Mr Asquith replied, 'And pray, what reason will you give?' Well anyway it was my feeding time.

The guests arrived for my birthday. It was so sad, said one of the black widows, so sad about Wilfred Owen who was killed so late in the war, and she quoted from a poem of his:

> What passing-bells for these who die as cattle?
> Only the monstrous anger of the guns.

The children were squealing and toddling around. One was sick and another wet the floor and stood with his legs apart gaping at the puddle. All was mopped up. I banged my spoon on the table of my high chair.

> But I've a rendezvous with Death
> At midnight in some flaming town;
> When spring trips north again this year,
> And I to my pledged word am true,
> I shall not fell that rendezvous.

More parents and children arrived. One stout man who was warming his behind at the fire, said, 'I always think those words of Asquith's after the armistice were so apt ... '

They brought the cake close to my high chair for me to see, with the candle shining and flickering above the pink icing. 'A pity she never smiles.'

'She'll smile in time,' my mother said, obviously upset.

'What Asquith told the House of Commons just after the war,' said that stout gentleman with his backside to the fire, '– so apt, what Asquith said. He said that the war has cleansed and purged the world, by God! recall his actual words: "All things have become new. In this great cleansing and purging it has been the privilege of our country to play her part ... "'

That did it, I broke into a decided smile and everyone noticed it, convinced that it was provoked by the fact that my brother had blown out the candle on the cake. 'She smiled!' my mother exclaimed. And everyone was clucking away about how I was smiling. For good measure I crowed like a demented raven. 'My baby's smiling!' said my mother.

'It was the candle on her cake,' they said.

The cake be damned. Since that time I have grown to smile quite naturally, like any other healthy and housetrained person, but when I really mean a smile, deeply felt from the core, then to all intents and purposes it comes in response to the words uttered in the House of Commons after the First World War by the distinguished, the immaculately dressed and the late Mr Asquith.

INDIGNITIES

Ellen Gilchrist

Ellen Gilchrist (b. 1935) is an American author and poet who studied
creative writing under Eudora Welty. Her 1981 collection of stories, *In
the Land of Dreamy Dreams*, received immense critical acclaim and, in
1984, she won the National Book Award for her collection of stories,
Victory Over Japan.

Last night my mother took off her clothes in front of twenty-six invited
guests in the King's Room at Antoine's. She took off her Calvin Klein
evening jacket and her beige silk wrap-around blouse and her custom-made
brassiere and walked around the table letting everyone look at the place where
her breasts used to be.

She had had them removed without saying a word to anyone. I'm surprised
she told my father. I'm surprised she invited him to the party. He never would
have noticed. He hasn't touched her in years except to hand her a check or a
paper to sign.

After mother took off her blouse the party really warmed up. Everyone stayed
until the restaurant closed. Teddy Lanier put the make on a waiter. Alice Lemle
sang "A Foggy Day in London Town." A poet called Cherokee stood up on an
antique chair, tore open her dress, and drew the sign for infinity on her chest with
a borrowed Flair pen. Amalie DuBois sat down by the baked Alaska and began
eating the meringue with her fingers.

Everyone followed us home. Someone opened the bar and Clarence Josephy
sat down at the baby grand and began improvising. He always makes himself at
home. There was a terrible period in my childhood when I thought he was going
to be my father. I started going to mass with a little girl from Sacred Heart to
pray he wouldn't move in and have breakfast with us every day. I even bought
a crucifix. I had worked up to forty-six Hail Marys a day by the time my father
came home from Australia and the crisis passed.

As soon as everyone was settled with a drink Mother went upstairs to change
and I followed her. "Well, Mother," I said, "this takes the cake. You could have
given me some warning. I thought I was coming home for a birthday party."

"I'm leaving it all to you, Melissa," she said. "Take my advice. Sell everything
and fly to Paris."

I threw myself down on the bed with my hands over my ears, but she went
tirelessly and relentlessly on. "This is your chance to rise above the categories,"
she said. "God knows I've done my best to teach you the relativity of it all."
She sighed and shook her head, stepping into a long white dressing gown. I had

always been a disappointment to her, that's for certain. No illicit drugs, no un-wanted pregnancies, no lesbian affairs, no irate phone calls from teachers, never a moment's doubt that I was living up to my potential.

Melissa was born old, my mother always tells everyone, born with her fingers crossed.

"Why do you think you're dying, Mother?" I said. "Just tell me that, will you? Lots of women get breast cancer. It doesn't mean you're going to die."

"It means I'm going to die," she said. "And I'll tell you one thing. I am never setting foot inside that hospital again. I've never run across such a humorless unimaginative group in my life. And the food! Really, it's unforgivable."

"Mother," I said, trying to put my arms around her.

"Now, Melissa," she said, "let's save the melodrama for the bourgeoisie. I have a book for you to read." She always has a book for me to read. She has a book about everything. She reads the first chapter and the table of contents and the last three paragraphs and if she likes the theory she says APPROVED and goes on to the next book.

If she really likes the theory she writes the author and the publisher and buys twenty copies and gives them away to friends. She has ruined a lot of books for me that way. What real book could live up to one of mother's glowing and inac-curate descriptions?

It must be interesting to be her daughter, people say to me.

I don't know, I tell them. I've never tried it. I use her for a librarian.

The book she pressed upon me now was *Life after Life* by Raymond A. Moody, Jr., M.D. It was full of first-person accounts by men and women who were snatched from the jaws of death and came back to tell of their ecstatic ex-periences on the brink of nonbeing. The stories are remarkably similar. It seems the soul lifts off from the body like a sort of transparent angel and floats around the corpse. Then the person sees someone he is dying to talk to standing at the end of a tunnel swinging a lantern and waiting for him.

"But who are you in such a hurry to see, Mother," I said, "all of your friends are downstairs and you never liked your own parents."

"Perhaps Leonardo will be there. Perhaps Blake is waiting for me. Or Margaret Mead or Virginia Woolf."

"How old will you be in heaven, Mother?" I ask, being drawn into the fantasy.

"Oh, thirty-four I think. Attractive, yet intelligent enough to be interesting. What color was my hair at that age? The only thing I regret about all this is that I never had time to grow out my gray hair. I kept putting it off. Vanity, vanity."

"Mother, let's stop this."

"Right. Not another word." She sprayed herself with Shalimar and giving me a pat on the cheek went downstairs to her guests, leaving me alone in her room.

Her room is half of the second floor of a Queen Anne house designed by Thomas Sully in 1890.

There is a round bed on a dais with dozens of small soft pillows piled against a marble headboard. There is a quilt made by her great-grandmother's slaves and linen sheets the colors of the sky at evening.

Everything else in the room is white, white velvet, white satin, white silk, white marble, white painted wood.

There is a dressing table six feet long covered with every product ever manufactured by Charles of the Ritz.

There is a huge desk littered with papers and books, her unpublished poems, her short stories, her journals, her unfinished novels.

"Mother," I called, following her into the hall, "what about the novels. Who will finish the novels?"

"We'll give them to somebody who needs them," she called back. "Some poor person who doesn't have any."

I went downstairs to find her reclining on a love seat with her admirers sitting at her feet drinking brandy and helping plan the funeral.

I was surprised at how traditional her plans have become. Gone was the flag-shaped tombstone saying IT SEEMED LIKE A GOOD IDEA AT THE TIME. Gone the videotape machine in the mausoleum.

"Some readings from García Márquez," she was saying. "Lionel can do them in Spanish. Spanish always sounds so *religious*, don't you agree?"

"How long do you think it will be," Bartlett said.

"Not more than six months surely," Mother said. "February."

"I like a winter funeral myself," Eric said. "Especially in this climate."

The weather was perfect for the funeral. "Don't you know she *arranged* this," everyone kept saying. As we were entering the chapel a storm blew up quite suddenly. Rain beat on the walls and lightning flashed through the stained-glass windows.

Then, just as we were carrying the coffin outside, the sun broke from the clouds. "That was going too far," everyone agreed.

Later, a wind blew up from the east and continued to blow while we shoveled dirt on the coffin. "Really!" everyone muttered.

"Melissa," she had said to me, "swear you will never let strangers lower my box." So, while the gravediggers sat politely nearby wondering if we belonged to some new kind of cult, we cranked the coffin down and picked up the shovels.

Clarence turned on the tape player and we shoveled to Mahler for a while, then to Clementi, then Bach.

"I remember the night she chartered a plane and flew to California for the earthquake," Lionel said, pulling a feather out of his hat and dropping it in the hole. He was wearing a velvet suit and an enormous green hat with feathers. He looked like a prehistoric bird.

"Remember the year she learned to scuba dive," Selma said, weeping all over her white tuxedo and dropping an onyx ring on top of the feather. "She didn't even know how to *swim*."

"I remember the week she played with me," I said. "I was four years old. She called and had a piano crate delivered and we turned it into a house and painted murals all over the walls. The title of our mural was Welsh Fertility Rites with Sheepdogs Rampant."

The wind kept on blowing and I kept on shoveling, staring down at all that was left of my childhood, now busily growing out yards and yards of two-toned hair.

THE PILL-BOX

Penelope Lively

Penelope Lively (b. 1933) is a critically acclaimed British author of fiction for both children and adults. She won the Carnegie Medal for children's fiction in 1973, for *The Ghost of Thomas Kempe*, and also the Man Booker Prize for her 1987 novel, *Moon Tiger*. Lively was made Dame Commander of the Order of the British Empire in the 2012 New Year Honours list.

The writer of a story has an infinity of choices. An infinity of narratives; an infinity of endings. The process of choosing, of picking this set of events rather than that, of ending up here rather than there – well, call it what you like: craft, art, accident, intuition.

Call it what you like, it's a curious process.

I teach Eng. Lit. Consequently I try to point this sort of thing out to the young. Life and literature – all that. Parallels; illuminations. I'm no mystic, but there's one thing that never ceases to astonish me: the fixity of things. That we live with it, accept it as we do. That we do not question that the course of events is thus, and never could be other. When you think of how nearly, at every moment, it is not.

Think of it. Stare it in the face and think of it.

I come out of my front gate, I bump into old Sanders next door, we have a chat … Shift the point at which I emerge by ever so little, and I do not meet Sanders, we do not have a word about the cricket club dinner, he does not offer to drop over later with his Black & Decker and fix that shelf for me.

I cross the street, looking first to right and left, a lorry passes, I alight upon the pavement opposite.

I cross the street, not looking, first to right and left; the lorry driver's concentration lapses for a second, I am so much meat under his wheels.

Some bloke is gunned down in Sarajevo. In another country, evil is bred. And then and then and then … A tired voice comes from a crackling wireless: there is war. "May God bless you all," he says.

A trigger jams. Elsewhere, a mad house-painter dies young of polio. And then, and then, and then … 3rd September 1939 is a fine day, sunshine with a hint of showers.

Oh well *of course* you say, any fool can play those games. Intriguing but unproductive. We inhabit, after all, a definite world; facts are facts. The sequence of my life, of your life, of the public life.

Listen, then. I went up to the pill-box this evening – the wartime pill-box on the top.

The pill-box is on the brow of the hill and faces square down the lane. I take my time getting up there; it's a steep pull up and the outlook's half the point of the walk. I have a rest at the first gate, and then at the end by the oak, and again at the gate to Clapper's field. You get the view from there: the village down below you and the fields reaching away to the coast and the sea hanging at the edge of the green, a long grey smear with maybe a ship or two and on clear days the white glimmer of the steelworks over on the Welsh coast.

It was sited to cover anything coming up and heading on over the hill. Heading for the main road – that would have been the idea, I suppose. It would have had the village covered, too, and a good part of the valley. Very small it looks now, stuck there at the edge of the field: barely room for a couple of blokes inside. I never know why it's not been taken away – much longer and it'll be a historical monument I daresay and they'll slap a protection order on it. The field is rough grazing and always has been so I suppose no one's felt any great call to get rid of it. Dalton's field, it is; from time to time you find he's stashed some cattle feed away in the pill-box, or a few bags of lime. It comes in handy for the village lads, too, always has done: get your girl up there, nice bit of shelter ... I've made use of it that way myself in my time. Back in – oh, forty-seven or thereabouts. Yes, forty-seven, that spring it rained cats and dogs and there was flooding right left and centre. Rosie Parks, black curly hair and an answer to everything. Lying in there with the rain coming down in spears outside; "You lay off, Keith Harrison, I'm telling you ...", "Ah, come on, Rosie ..." Giggle giggle.

The rain started this evening when I was at the oak, just a sprinkle, and by the time I got to the top it was coming down hard and looked set in for a while so I ducked down into the pill-box to sit it out.

I was thinking about the past, in a vague kind of way – the war, being young. Looking out from inside the pill-box you see the countryside as a bright green rectangle, very clear, lots of detail, like a photo. And I've got good eyesight anyway, even at fifty-seven, just about a hundred per cent vision. I could see the new houses they've put up on the edge of the village and I was thinking that the place has changed a lot since I was a boy, and yet in other ways it hasn't. The new estate, the shop, cars at every door, telly aerials, main drainage; but the same names, by and large, same families, same taste to the beer, same stink from Clapper's silage in hot weather.

I can see the house where I was born, from the pill-box. And the one I live in now. The churchyard, where my parents are, God bless 'em. The recreation ground beside the church hall where we used to drill in 1941; those of us left behind, too old like Jim Blockley at sixty-odd, too young like me at seventeen-and-a-half, too wonky like the postmaster with his bronchitis, too valuable like the farmers and the doctor.

I can see the road, too – the road that takes me daily to work. Ten miles to Scarhead to try to drum a bit of sense and a bit of knowledge into forty fifteen-year-old heads. Full cycle. Back then, mine was the empty head, the bloke at the blackboard was ... was old Jenkins, Jenks. It's not been a mistake, coming back. I'd always thought I'd like to. The day I saw the advert, in the *Times Ed. Supp.*, I knew at once I'd apply. Yes, I thought, that's it, that's for me, end up back at home, why not? I've always thought of it as home, down here, wherever I've been – Nottingham, up in the north-east, London. Not that it's local boy made good, exactly. Teaching's a tidy enough occupation, they reckon down here, but not high-flying. Farmers do a sight better. I don't drive a Jag, like Tim Matlock who was in my class at the grammar and farms up on the county border now. Not that I care tuppence.

I lit a pipe to keep the midges off; the rain was coming down harder than ever. It looked as though I might have to pack in the rest of my walk. I opened the newspaper: usual stuff, miners reject pay offer, Middle East talks, rail fares up.

When I heard the first voice I thought there was someone outside in the field – some trick of the acoustics, making it sound as though it were in the pill-box.

"They're bloody coming!" he said.

And then another bloke, a young one, a boy, gave a sort of grunt. You knew, somehow, he was on edge. His voice had that crack to it, that pitch of someone who's keyed up, holding himself in. Shit-scared.

"Can I have a look, Mr Barnes? Oh God – I see them. Heading straight up."

How can I put it? Describe how it was. The words that come to mind are banal, clichés: eery, unearthly, uncanny.

They were there, but they were not. They were in the head, but yet were outside it. There were two men, an old and a younger, who spoke from some other dimension; who were there with me in the pill-box and yet also were not, could not be, had never been.

Listen again.

"Give me them field-glasses … They've set Clapper's barn on fire. There's more tanks on the Scarhead road – six, seven … They'll be at the corner in a few minutes now, son."

And the young chap speaks again. "O.K.," he says. "O.K., I'm ready."

The voices, you understand, are overlaid by other noises, ordinary noises: the rain on the roof of the pill-box, sheep, a tractor in the lane. The tractor goes past but the voices don't take a blind bit of notice. The old bloke tells the other one to pass him another clip of ammo. "You all right, son?" he says, the boy answers that he is all right. There is that high sharp note in his voice, in both their voices.

There is a silence.

And then they come back.

"I can see him now. Armoured car. Two."

"O.K. Yes. I've got them."

"Hold it. Hold it, son …"

"Yes. Right …"

"Hold it. Steady. When they get to the oak."

"O.K., Mr Barnes."

And everything is quiet again. A quiet you could cut with a knife. The inside of the pill-box is tight-strung, waiting; it is both a moment in time and a time that is going on for ever, will go on for ever. I drop my tobacco tin and it clatters on the concrete floor but the sound does not break that other quiet, which, I now realise, is somewhere else, is something else.

The old bloke says, "Fire!"

And then they are both talking together. There is no other sound, nothing, just their voices. And the rain.

The boy says, "I got him, my God. I got him!" and the other one says, "Steady. Re-load now. Steady. Wait till the second one's moving again. Right. Fire!"

"We hit him!"

"He's coming on …"

"Christ there's another behind!"

"Bastards! Jerry bastards!"

And the boy cries, "That's for my dad! And that's for my mum! Come on then, bloody come on then …"

"Steady, son. Hold it a minute, there's a …"

"What's he doing, Christ he's …"

"He's got a grenade. Keep on firing, for God's sake. Keep him covered."

And suddenly they go quiet. Quite quiet. Except that just once the old bloke says something. He says, "Don't move, Keith, keep still, I'm coming over, I …"

He says, "Keith?"

And there is nothing more.

I went on sitting there. The quietness left the inside of the pill-box, that other quietness. The tractor came back down the lane again. The rain stopped. A blackbird started up on the roof of the pill-box. Down in the valley there was a patch of sunlight slap on the village; the church very bright, a car windscreen flashing, pale green of the chestnuts in the pub car park.

I knew, now, that from the first moment there'd been something about that young chap's voice. The boy.

Mr Barnes. Joe Barnes worked the manor farm in the war. He left here some time ago, retired to Ilfracombe; he died a year or two back.

I was in his platoon, in 1941. I've not thought of him in years. Couldn't put a face to him, now. He died of cancer in a nursing-home in Ilfracombe. Didn't he?

Or.

Or he died in a pill-box up on the hill above the village, long ago. Him and a boy called Keith. In which case the pill-box is no longer there nor I take it the village nor the whole bloody place at least not in any way you or I could know it.

No young fellow called Keith ever put his hand up the skirt of Rosie Parks in that pill-box, nor did another bloke, a fifty-seven year old teacher of English, walk up that way of an evening for a smoke and a look at the view.

I came out, filled my pipe, looked down at the village. All right, yes, I thought to myself – interesting, the imaginative process. The mind churning away, putting pictures to a line of thought. I dozed off in there.

Later I knew I did not imagine it. I heard it. Heard them. So what do you make of that? Eh? What can anyone make of it? How, having glimpsed the possibility of the impossible, can the world remain as steady as you had supposed?

Suppose that the writer of a story were haunted, in the mind, for ever, by all those discarded alternatives, by the voices of all those assorted characters. Forced to preserve them always as the price of creative choice.

Then suppose, by the same token, that just once in a while it is given to any one of us to experience the inconceivable. To push through the barrier of what we know into the heady breathtaking unbearable ozone of what we cannot contemplate. Did that happen to me? In the pill-box on the hill on a summer Monday evening, with the world steady under my feet and the newspaper in my hand, telling me what's what, how the world is, where we are?

MILES CITY, MONTANA

Alice Munro

Alice Munro (b. 1931) is a Canadian short story writer and winner of the 2009 Man Booker International Prize, which honours her complete body of work. She has been awarded Canada's Governor General's Award for Fiction three times, the Giller Prize twice and is a perennial contender for the Nobel Prize for Fiction. She was awarded the National Book Critics Circle Award in 1998 for her collection *The Love of a Good Woman*.

My father came across the field carrying the body of the boy who had been drowned. There were several men together, returning from the search, but he was the one carrying the body. The men were muddy and exhausted, and walked with their heads down, as if they were ashamed. Even the dogs were dispirited, dripping from the cold river. When they all set out, hours before, the dogs were nervy and yelping, the men tense and determined, and there was a constrained, unspeakable excitement about the whole scene. It was understood that they might find something horrible.

The boy's name was Steve Gauley. He was eight years old. His hair and clothes were mud-colored now and carried some bits of dead leaves, twigs, and grass. He was like a heap of refuse that had been left out all winter. His face was turned in to my father's chest, but I could see a nostril, an ear, plugged up with greenish mud.

I don't think so. I don't think I really saw all this. Perhaps I saw my father carrying him, and the other men following along, and the dogs, but I would not have been allowed to get close enough to see something like mud in his nostril. I must have heard someone talking about that and imagined that I saw it. I see his face unaltered except for the mud – Steve Gauley's familiar, sharp-honed, sneaky-looking face – and it wouldn't have been like that; it would have been bloated and changed and perhaps muddied all over after so many hours in the water.

To have to bring back such news, such evidence, to a waiting family, particularly a mother, would have made searchers move heavily, but what was happening here was worse. It seemed a worse shame (to hear people talk) that there was no mother, no woman at all – no grandmother or aunt, or even a sister – to receive Steve Gauley and give him his due of grief. His father was a hired man, a drinker but not a drunk, an erratic man without being entertaining, not friendly but not exactly a troublemaker. His fatherhood seemed accidental, and the fact that the child had been left with him when the mother went away, and that they continued living together, seemed accidental. They lived in a steep-roofed, gray-shingled hillbilly sort of house that was just a bit better than a shack – the father fixed the roof and put supports under the porch, just enough and just in time – and their life was held together in a similar manner; that is, just well enough to keep the Children's Aid at bay. They didn't eat meals together or cook for each other, but there was food. Sometimes the father would give Steve money to buy food at the store, and Steve was seen to buy quite sensible things, such as pancake mix and macaroni dinner.

I had known Steve Gauley fairly well. I had not liked him more often than I had liked him. He was two years older than I was. He would hang around our place on Saturdays, scornful of whatever I was doing but unable to leave me alone. I couldn't be on the swing without him wanting to try it, and if I wouldn't give it up he came and pushed me so that I went crooked. He teased the dog. He got me into trouble – deliberately and maliciously, it seemed to me afterward – by daring me to do things I wouldn't have thought of on my own: digging up the potatoes to see how big they were when they were still only the size of marbles, and pushing over the stacked firewood to make a pile we could jump off. At school, we never spoke to each other. He was solitary, though not tormented. But on Saturday mornings, when I saw his thin, self-possessed figure sliding through the cedar hedge, I knew I was in for something and he would decide what. Sometimes it was all right. We pretended we were cowboys who had to tame wild horses. We played in the pasture by the river, not far from the place where Steve drowned. We were horses and riders both, screaming and neighing and bucking and waving whips of tree branches beside a little nameless river that flows into the Saugeen in southern Ontario.

The funeral was held in our house. There was not enough room at Steve's father's place for the large crowd that was expected because of the circumstances. I have a memory of the crowded room but no picture of Steve in his coffin, or of the minister, or of wreaths of flowers. I remember that I was holding one flower, a white narcissus, which must have come from a pot somebody forced indoors, because it was too early for even the forsythia bush or the trilliums and marsh marigolds in the woods. I stood in a row of children, each of us holding a narcissus. We sang a children's hymn, which somebody played on our piano: "When He Cometh, When He Cometh, to Make Up His Jewels." I was wearing white ribbed stockings, which were disgustingly itchy, and wrinkled at the knees and ankles. The feeling of these stockings on my legs is mixed up with another feeling in my memory. It is hard to describe. It had to do with my parents. Adults in general but my parents in particular. My father, who had carried Steve's body from the river, and my mother, who must have done most of the arranging of this funeral. My father in his dark-blue suit and my mother in her brown velvet dress with the creamy satin collar. They stood side by side opening and closing their mouths for the hymn, and I stood removed from them, in the row of children, watching. I felt a furious and sickening disgust. Children sometimes have an access of disgust concerning adults. The size, the lumpy shapes, the bloated power. The breath, the coarseness, the hairiness, the horrid secretions. But this was more. And the accompanying anger had nothing sharp and self-respecting about it. There was no release, as when I would finally bend and pick up a stone and throw it at Steve Gauley. It could not be understood or expressed, though it died down after a while into a heaviness, then just a taste, an occasional taste – a thin, familiar misgiving.

Twenty years or so later, in 1961, my husband, Andrew, and I got a brand-new car, our first – that is, our first brand-new. It was a Morris Oxford, oyster-colored (the dealer had some fancier name for the color) – a big small car, with plenty of room for us and our two children. Cynthia was six and Meg three and a half.

Andrew took a picture of me standing beside the car. I was wearing white pants, a black turtleneck, and sunglasses. I lounged against the car door, canting my hips to make myself look slim.

"Wonderful," Andrew said. "Great. You look like Jackie Kennedy." All over this continent probably, dark-haired, reasonably slender young women were told, when they were stylishly dressed or getting their pictures taken, that they looked like Jackie Kennedy.

Andrew took a lot of pictures of me, and of the children, our house, our garden, our excursions and possessions. He got copies made, labelled them carefully, and sent them back to his mother and his aunt and uncle in Ontario. He got copies for me to send to my father, who also lived in Ontario, and I did so, but less regularly than he sent his. When he saw pictures he thought I had already sent lying around the house, Andrew was perplexed and annoyed. He liked to have this record go forth.

That summer, we were presenting ourselves, not pictures. We were driving back from Vancouver, where we lived, to Ontario, which we still called "home," in our new car. Five days to get there, ten days there, five days back. For the first time, Andrew had three weeks' holiday. He worked in the legal department at B. C. Hydro.

On a Saturday morning, we loaded suitcases, two thermos bottles – one filled with coffee and one with lemonade – some fruit and sandwiches, picture books and coloring books, crayons, drawing pads, insect repellent, sweaters (in case it got cold in the mountains), and our two children into the car. Andrew locked the house, and Cynthia said ceremoniously, "Goodbye, house."

Meg said, "Goodbye, house." Then she said, "Where will we live now?"

"It's not goodbye forever," said Cynthia. "We're coming back. Mother! Meg thought we weren't ever coming back!"

"I did not," said Meg, kicking the back of my seat.

Andrew and I put on our sunglasses, and we drove away, over the Lions Gate Bridge and through the main part of Vancouver. We shed our house, the neighborhod, the city, and – at the crossing point between Washington and British Columbia – our country. We were driving east across the United States, taking the most northerly route, and would cross into Canada again at Sarnia, Ontario. I don't know if we chose this route because the Trans-Canada Highway was not completely finished at the time or if we just wanted the feeling of driving through a foreign, a very slightly foreign, country – that extra bit of interest and adventure.

We were both in high spirits. Andrew congratulated the car several times. He said he felt so much better driving it than our old car, a 1951 Austin that slowed down dismally on the hills and had a fussy-old-lady image. So Andrew said now.

"What kind of image does this one have?" said Cynthia. She listened to us carefully and liked to try out new words such as "image." Usually she got them right.

"Lively," I said. "Slightly sporty. It's not show-off."

"It's sensible, but it has class," Andrew said. "Like my image."

Cynthia thought that over and said with a cautious pride, "That means like you think you want to be, Daddy?"

As for me, I was happy because of the shedding. I loved taking off. In my own house, I seemed to be often looking for a place to hide – sometimes from the children but more often from the jobs to be done and the phone ringing and the sociability of the neighborhood. I wanted to hide so that I could get busy at my real work, which was a sort of wooing of distant parts of myself. I lived in a state of siege, always losing just what I wanted to hold on to. But on trips there was no difficulty. I could be talking to Andrew, talking to the children and looking at whatever they wanted me to look at – a pig on a sign, a pony in a field, a Volkswagen on a revolving stand – and pouring lemonade into plastic cups, and all the time those bits and pieces would be flying together inside me. The essential composition would be achieved. This made me hopeful and lighthearted. It was being a watcher that did it. A watcher, not a keeper.

We turned east at Everett and climbed into the Cascades. I showed Cynthia our route on the map. First I showed her the map of the whole United States, which showed also the bottom part of Canada. Then I turned to the separate maps of each of the states we were going to pass through. Washington, Idaho, Montana, North Dakota, Minnesota, Wisconsin. I showed her the dotted line across Lake Michigan, which was the route of the ferry we would take. Then we would drive across Michigan to the bridge that linked the United States and Canada at Sarnia, Ontario. Home.

Meg wanted to see, too.

"You won't understand," said Cynthia. But she took the road atlas into the back seat.

"Sit back," she said to Meg. "Sit still. I'll show you."

I could hear her tracing the route for Meg, very accurately, just as I had done it for her. She looked up all the states' maps, knowing how to find them in alphabetical order.

"You know what that line is?" she said. "It's the road. That line is the road we're driving on. We're going right along this line."

Meg did not say anything.

"Mother, show me where we are right this minute," said Cynthia.

I took the atlas and pointed out the road through the mountains, and she took it back and showed it to Meg. "See where the road is all wiggly?" she said. "It's wiggly because there are so many turns in it. The wiggles are the turns." She flipped some pages and waited a moment. "Now," she said, "show me where we are." Then she called to me, "Mother, she understands! She pointed to it! Meg understands maps!"

It seems to me now that we invented characters for our children. We had them firmly set to play their parts. Cynthia was bright and diligent, sensitive, courteous, watchful. Sometimes we teased her for being too conscientious, too eager to be what we in fact depended on her to be. Any reproach or failure, any rebuff, went terribly deep with her. She was fair-haired, fair-skinned, easily showing the effects of the sun, raw winds, pride, or humiliation. Meg was more solidly built, more reticent – not rebellious but stubborn sometimes, mysterious. Her silences seemed to us to show her strength of character, and her negatives were taken as signs of an imperturbable independence. Her hair was brown, and we cut it in straight bangs. Her eyes were a light hazel, clear and dazzling.

We were entirely pleased with these characters, enjoying the contradictions as well as the confirmations of them. We disliked the heavy, the uninventive, approach to being parents. I had a dread of turning into a certain kind of mother – the kind whose body sagged, who moved in a woolly-smelling, milky-smelling fog, solemn with trivial burdens. I believed that all the attention these mothers paid, their need to be burdened, was the cause of colic, bed-wetting, asthma. I favored another approach – the mock desperation, the inflated irony of the professional mothers who wrote for magazines. In those magazine pieces, the children were splendidly self-willed, hard-edged, perverse, indomitable. So were the mothers, through their wit, indomitable. The real-life mothers I warmed to were the sort who would phone up and say, "Is my embryo Hitler by any chance over at your house?" They cackled clear above the milky fog.

We saw a dead deer strapped across the front of a pickup truck.

"Somebody shot it," Cynthia said. "Hunters shoot the deer."

"It's not hunting season yet," Andrew said. "They may have hit it on the road. See the sign for deer crossing?"

"I would cry if we hit one," Cynthia said sternly.

I had made peanut-butter-and-marmalade sandwiches for the children and salmon-and-mayonnaise for us. But I had not put any lettuce in, and Andrew was disappointed.

"I didn't have any," I said.

"Couldn't you have got some?"

"I'd have had to buy a whole head of lettuce just to get enough for sandwiches, and I decided it wasn't worth it."

This was a lie. I had forgotten.

"They're a lot better with lettuce."

"I didn't think it made that much difference." After a silence, I said, "Don't be mad."

"I'm not mad. I like lettuce on sandwiches."

"I just didn't think it mattered that much."

"How would it be if I didn't bother to fill up the gas tank?"

"That's not the same thing."

"Sing a song," said Cynthia. She started to sing:

> "*Five little ducks went out one day,*
> *Over the hills and far away.*
> *One little duck went*
> *'Quack-quack-quack.'*
> *Four little ducks came swimming*
> *back.*"

Andrew squeezed my hand and said, "Let's not fight."

"You're right. I should have got lettuce."

"It doesn't matter that much."

I wished that I could get my feelings about Andrew to come together into a serviceable and dependable feeling. I had even tried writing two lists, one of things I liked about him, one of things I disliked – in the cauldron of intimate life, things I loved and things I hated – as if I hoped by this to prove something, to come to a conclusion one way or the other. But I gave it up when I saw that all it proved was what I already knew – that I had violent contradictions. Sometimes the very sound of his footsteps seemed to me tyrannical, the set of his mouth smug and mean, his hard, straight body a barrier interposed – quite consciously, even dutifully, and with a nasty pleasure in its masculine authority – between me and whatever joy or lightness I could get in life. Then, with not much warning, he became my good friend and most essential companion. I felt the sweetness of his light bones and serious ideas, the vulnerability of his love, which I imagined to be much purer and more straightforward than my own. I could be greatly moved by an inflexibility, a harsh propriety, that at other times I scorned. I would think how humble he was, really, taking on such a ready-made role of husband, father, breadwinner, and how I myself in comparison was really a secret monster of egotism. Not so secret, either – not from him.

At the bottom of our fights, we served up what we thought were the ugliest truths. "I know there is something basically selfish and basically untrustworthy about you," Andrew once said. "I've always known it. I also know that that is why I fell in love with you."

"Yes," I said, feeling sorrowful but complacent.

"I know that I'd be better off without you."

"Yes. You would."

"You'd be happier without me."

"Yes."

And finally – finally – racked and purged, we clasped hands and laughed, laughed at those two benighted people, ourselves. Their grudges, their grievances, their self-justification. We leapfrogged over them. We declared them liars. We would have wine with dinner, or decide to give a party.

I haven't seen Andrew for years, don't know if he is still thin, has gone completely gray, insists on lettuce, tells the truth, or is hearty and disappointed.

We stayed the night in Wenatchee, Washington, where it hadn't rained for weeks. We ate dinner in a restaurant built about a tree – not a sapling in a tub but a tall, sturdy cottonwood. In the early-morning light, we climbed out of the irrigated valley, up dry, rocky, very steep hillsides that would seem to lead to more hills, and there on the top was a wide plateau, cut by the great Spokane and Columbia rivers. Grainland and grassland, mile after mile. There were straight roads here, and little farming towns with grain elevators. In fact, there was a sign announcing that this county we were going through, Douglas County, had the second-highest wheat yield of any county in the United States. The towns had planted shade trees. At least, I thought they had been planted, because there were no such big trees in the countryside.

All this was marvellously welcome to me. "Why do I love it so much?" I said to Andrew. "Is it because it isn't scenery?"

"It reminds you of home," said Andrew. "A bout of severe nostalgia." But he said this kindly.

When we said "home" and meant Ontario, we had very different places in mind. My home was a turkey farm, where my father lived as a widower, and though it was the same house my mother had lived in, had papered, painted, cleaned, furnished, it showed the effects now of neglect and of some wild sociability. A life went on in it that my mother could not have predicted or condoned. There were parties for the turkey crew, the gutters and pluckers, and sometimes one or two of the young men would be living there temporarily, inviting their own friends and having their own impromptu parties. This life, I thought, was better for my father than being lonely, and I did not disapprove, had certainly no right to disapprove. Andrew did not like to go there, naturally enough, because he was not the sort who could sit around the kitchen table with the turkey crew, telling jokes. They were intimidated by him and contemptuous of him, and it seemed to me that my father, when they were around, had to be on their side. And it wasn't only Andrew who had trouble. I could manage those jokes, but it was an effort.

I wished for the days when I was little, before we had the turkeys. We had cows, and sold the milk to the cheese factory. A turkey farm is nothing like as pretty as a dairy farm or a sheep farm. You can see that the turkeys are on a straight path to becoming frozen carcasses and table meat. They don't have the pretense of a life of their own, a browsing idyll, that cattle have, or pigs in the dappled orchard. Turkey barns are long, efficient buildings – tin sheds. No beams or hay or warm stables. Even the smell of guano seems thinner and more offensive than the usual smell of stable manure. No hints there of hay coils and rail fences and songbirds and the flowering hawthorn. The turkeys were all let out into one long field, which they picked clean. They didn't look like great birds there but like fluttering laundry.

Once, shortly after my mother died, and after I was married – in fact, I was packing to join Andrew in Vancouver – I was at home alone for a couple of days with my father. There was a freakishly heavy rain all night. In the early light, we saw that the turkey field was flooded. At least, the low-lying parts of it were flooded – it was like a lake with many islands. The turkeys were huddled on these islands. Turkeys are very stupid. (My father would say, "You know a chicken? You know how stupid a chicken is? Well, a chicken is an Einstein compared with a turkey.") But they had managed to crowd to higher ground and avoid drowning. Now they might push each other off, suffocate each other, get cold and die. We couldn't wait for the water to go down. We went out in an old rowboat we had. I rowed and my father pulled the heavy, wet turkeys into the boat and we took them to the barn. It was still raining a little. The job was difficult and absurd and very uncomfortable. We were laughing. I was happy to be working with my father. I felt close to all hard, repetitive, appalling work, in which the body is finally worn out, the mind sunk (though sometimes the spirit can stay marvellously light), and I was homesick in advance for this life and this place. I thought that if Andrew could see me there in the rain, red-handed, muddy, trying to hold on to turkey legs and row the boat at the same time, he would only want to get me out of there and make me forget about it. This raw life angered him. My attachment to it angered him. I thought that I shouldn't have married him. But who else? One of the turkey crew?

And I didn't want to stay there. I might feel bad about leaving, but I would feel worse if somebody made me stay.

Andrew's mother lived in Toronto, in an apartment building looking out on Muir Park. When Andrew and his sister were both at home, his mother slept in the living room. Her husband, a doctor, had died when the children were still too young to go to school. She took a secretarial course and sold her house at Depression prices, moved to this apartment, managed to raise her children, with some help from relatives – her sister Caroline, her brother-in-law Roger. Andrew and his sister went to private schools and to camp in the summer.

"I suppose that was courtesy of the Fresh Air fund?" I said once, scornful of his claim that he had been poor. To my mind, Andrew's urban life had been sheltered and fussy. His mother came home with a headache from working all day in the noise, the harsh light of a department-store office, but it did not occur to me that hers was a hard or admirable life. I don't think she herself believed that she was admirable – only unlucky. She worried about her work in the office, her clothes, her cooking, her children. She worried most of all about what Roger and Caroline would think.

Caroline and Roger lived on the east side of the park, in a handsome stone house. Roger was a tall man with a bald, freckled head, a fat, firm stomach. Some operation on his throat had deprived him of his voice – he spoke in a rough whisper. But everybody paid attention. At dinner once in the stone house – where all the dining-room furniture was enormous, darkly glowing, palatial – I asked him a question. I think it had to do with Whittaker Chambers, whose story was then appearing in the *Saturday Evening Post*. The question was mild in tone, but he guessed its subversive intent and took to calling me Mrs. Gromyko, referring to what he alleged to be my "sympathies." Perhaps he really craved an adversary, and could not find one. At that dinner, I saw Andrew's hand tremble as he lit his mother's cigarette. His Uncle Roger had paid for Andrew's education, and was on the board of directors of several companies.

"He is just an opinionated old man," Andrew said to me later. "What is the point of arguing with him?"

Before we left Vancouver, Andrew's mother had written, "Roger seems quite intrigued by the idea of your buying a small car!" Her exclamation mark showed apprehension. At that time, particularly in Ontario, the choice of a small European car over a large American car could be seen as some sort of declaration – a declaration of tendencies Roger had been sniffing after all along.

"It isn't that small a car," said Andrew huffily.

"That's not the point," I said. "The point is, it isn't any of his business!"

We spent the second night in Missoula. We had been told in Spokane, at a gas station, that there was a lot of repair work going on along Highway 2, and that we were in for a very hot, dusty drive, with long waits, so we turned onto the interstate and drove through Coeur d'Alene and Kellogg into Montana. After

Missoula, we turned south toward Butte, but detoured to see Helena, the state capital. In the car, we played Who Am I?

Cynthia was somebody dead, and an American, and a girl. Possibly a lady. She was not in a story. She had not been seen on television. Cynthia had not read about her in a book. She was not anybody who had come to the kindergarten, or a relative of any of Cynthia's friends.

"Is she human?" said Andrew, with a sudden shrewdness.

"No! That's what you forgot to ask!"

"An animal," I said reflectively.

"Is that a question? Sixteen questions!"

"No, it is not a question. I'm thinking. A dead animal."

"It's the deer," said Meg, who hadn't been playing.

"That's not fair!" said Cynthia. "She's not playing!"

"What deer?" said Andrew.

I said, "Yesterday."

"The day before," said Cynthia. "Meg wasn't playing. Nobody got it."

"The deer on the truck," said Andrew.

"It was a lady deer, because it didn't have antlers, and it was an American and it was dead," Cynthia said.

Andrew said, "I think it's kind of morbid, being a dead deer."

"I got it," said Meg.

Cynthia said, "I think I know what morbid is. It's depressing."

Helena, an old silver-mining town, looked forlorn to us even in the morning sunlight. Then Bozeman and Billings, not forlorn in the slightest – energetic, strung-out towns, with miles of blinding tinsel fluttering over used-car lots. We got too tired and hot even to play Who Am I? These busy, prosaic cities reminded me of similar places in Ontario, and I thought about what was really waiting there – the great tombstone furniture of Roger and Caroline's dining room, the dinners for which I must iron the children's dresses and warn them about forks, and then the other table a hundred miles away, the jokes of my father's crew. The pleasures I had been thinking of – looking at the countryside or drinking a Coke in an old-fashioned drugstore with fans and a high, pressed-tin ceiling – would have to be snatched in between.

"Meg's asleep," Cynthia said. "She's so hot. She makes me hot in the same seat with her."

"I hope she isn't feverish," I said, not turning around.

What are we doing this for, I thought, and the answer came – to show off. To give Andrew's mother and my father the pleasure of seeing their grandchildren. That was our duty. But beyond that we wanted to show them something. What strenuous children we were, Andrew and I, what relentless seekers of approbation. It was as if at some point we had received an unforgettable, indigestible message – that we were far from satisfactory, and that the most commonplace success in life was probably beyond us. Roger dealt out such messages, of course – that was his style – but Andrew's mother, my own mother and father couldn't have meant to do so. All they meant to tell us was "Watch out. Get along." My father, when I was in high school, teased me that I was getting to think I was so smart I would never find a boyfriend. He would have forgotten that in a week. I never forgot it. Andrew and I didn't forget things. We took umbrage.

"I wish there was a beach," said Cynthia.

"There probably is one," Andrew said. "Right around the next curve."

"There isn't any curve," she said, sounding insulted.

"That's what I mean."

"I wish there was some more lemonade."

"I will just wave my magic wand and produce some," I said. "Okay, Cynthia? Would you rather have grape juice? Will I do a beach while I'm at it?"

She was silent, and soon I felt repentant. "Maybe in the next town there might be a pool," I said. I looked at the map. "In Miles City. Anyway, there'll be something cool to drink."

"How far is it?" Andrew said.

"Not so far," I said. "Thirty miles, about."

"In Miles City," said Cynthia, in the tones of an incantation, "there is a beautiful blue swimming pool for children, and a park with lovely trees."

Andrew said to me, "You could have started something."

But there was a pool. There was a park, too, though not quite the oasis of Cynthia's fantasy. Prairie trees with thin leaves – cotton-woods and poplars – worn grass, and a high wire fence around the pool. Within this fence, a wall, not yet completed, of cement blocks. There were no shouts or splashes; over the entrance I saw a sign that said the pool was closed every day from noon until two o'clock. It was then twenty-five after twelve.

Nevertheless I called out, "Is anybody there?" I thought somebody must be around, because there was a small truck parked near the entrance. On the side of the truck were these words: "We have Brains, to fix your Drains. (We have Roto-Rooter too.)"

A girl came out, wearing a red lifeguard's shirt over her bathing suit. "Sorry, we're closed."

"We were just driving through," I said.

"We close every day from twelve until two. It's on the sign." She was eating a sandwich.

"I saw the sign," I said. "But this is the first water we've seen for so long, and the children are awfully hot, and I wondered if they could just dip in and out – just five minutes. We'd watch them."

A boy came into sight, behind her. He was wearing jeans and a T-shirt with the words "Roto-Rooter" on it.

I was going to say that we were driving from British Columbia to Ontario, but I remembered that Canadian place names usually meant nothing to Americans. "We're driving right across the country," I said. "We haven't time to wait for the pool to open. We were just hoping the children could get cooled off."

Cynthia came running up barefoot behind me. "Mother. Mother, where is my bathing suit?" Then she stopped, sensing the serious adult negotiations. Meg was climbing out of the car – just wakened, with her top pulled up and her shorts pulled down, showing her pink stomach.

"Is it just those two?" the girl said.

"Just the two. We'll watch them."

"I can't let any adults in. If it's just the two, I guess I could watch them. I'm having my lunch." She said to Cynthia, "Do you want to come in the pool?"

"Yes, please," said Cynthia firmly.

Meg looked at the ground.

"Just a short time, because the pool is really closed," I said. "We appreciate this very much," I said to the girl.

"Well, I can eat my lunch out there, if it's just the two of them." She looked toward the car as if she thought I might try to spring some more children on her.

When I found Cynthia's bathing suit, she took it into the changing room. She would not permit anybody, even Meg, to see her naked. I changed Meg, who stood on the front seat of the car. She had a pink cotton bathing suit with straps that crossed and buttoned. There were ruffles across the bottom.

"She *is* hot," I said. "But I don't think she's feverish."

I loved helping Meg to dress or undress, because her body still had the solid unself-consciousness, the sweet indifference, something of the milky smell, of a baby's body. Cynthia's body had long ago been pared down, shaped and altered, into Cynthia. We all liked to hug Meg, press and nuzzle her. Sometimes she would scowl and beat us off, and this forthright independence, this ferocious bashfulness, simply made her more appealing, more apt to be tormented and tickled in the way of family love.

Andrew and I sat in the car with the windows open. I could hear a radio playing, and thought it must belong to the girl or her boyfriend. I was thirsty, and got out of the car to look for a concession stand, or perhaps a soft-drink machine, somewhere in the park. I was wearing shorts, and the backs of my legs were slick with sweat. I saw a drinking fountain at the other side of the park and was walking toward it in a roundabout way, keeping to the shade of the trees. No place became real till you got out of the car. Dazed with the heat, with the sun on the blistered houses, the pavement, the burned grass, I walked slowly. I paid attention to a squashed leaf, ground a Popsicle stick under the heel of my sandal, squinted at a trash can strapped to a tree. This is the way you look at the poorest details of the world resurfaced, after you've been driving for a long time – you feel their singleness and precise location and the forlorn coincidence of your being there to see them.

Where are the children?

I turned around and moved quickly, not quite running, to a part of the fence beyond which the cement wall was not completed. I could see some of the pool. I saw Cynthia, standing about waist-deep in the water, fluttering her hands on the surface and discreetly watching something at the end of the pool, which I could not see. I thought by her pose, her discretion, the look on her face, that she must be watching some byplay between the lifeguard and her boyfriend. I couldn't see Meg. But I thought she must be playing in the shallow water – both the shallow and deep ends of the pool were out of my sight.

"Cynthia!" I had to call twice before she knew where my voice was coming from. "Cynthia! Where's Meg?"

It always seems to me, when I recall this scene, that Cynthia turns very gracefully toward me, then turns all around in the water – making me think of a ballerina on point – and spreads her arms in a gesture of the stage. "Dis-ap-peared!"

Cynthia was naturally graceful, and she did take dancing lessons, so these movements may have been as I have described. She did say "Disappeared" after looking all around the pool, but the strangely artificial style of speech and gesture, the lack of urgency, is more likely my invention. The fear I felt instantly when I couldn't see Meg – even while I was telling myself she must be in the shallower water – must have made Cynthia's movements seem unbearably slow and inappropriate to me, and the tone in which she could say "Disappeared" before the implications struck her (or was she covering, at once, some ever-ready guilt?) was heard by me as quite exquisitely, monstrously self-possessed.

I cried out for Andrew, and the lifeguard came into view. She was pointing toward the deep end of the pool, saying, "What's that?"

There, just within my view, a cluster of pink ruffles appeared, a bouquet, beneath the surface of the water. Why would a lifeguard stop and point, why would she ask what that was, why didn't she just dive into the water and swim to it? She didn't swim; she ran all the way around the edge of the pool. But by that time Andrew was over the fence. So many things seemed not quite plausible – Cynthia's behavior, then the lifeguard's – and now I had the impression that Andrew jumped with one bound over this fence, which seemed about seven feet high. He must have climbed it very quickly, getting a grip on the wire.

I could not jump or climb it, so I ran to the entrance, where there was a sort of lattice gate, locked. It was not very high, and I did pull myself over it. I ran through the cement corridors, through the disinfectant pool for your feet, and came out on the edge of the pool.

The drama was over.

Andrew had got to Meg first, and had pulled her out of the water. He just had to reach over and grab her, because she was swimming somehow, with her head underwater – she was moving toward the edge of the pool. He was carrying her now, and the lifeguard was trotting along behind. Cynthia had climbed out of the water and was running to meet them. The only person aloof from the situation was the boyfriend, who had stayed on the bench at the shallow end, drinking a milkshake. He smiled at me, and I thought that unfeeling of him, even though the danger was past. He may have meant it kindly. I noticed that he had not turned the radio off, just down.

Meg had not swallowed any water. She hadn't even scared herself. Her hair was plastered to her head and her eyes were wide open, golden with amazement.

"I was getting the comb," she said. "I didn't know it was deep."

Andrew said, "She was swimming! She was swimming by herself. I saw her bathing suit in the water and then I saw her swimming."

"She nearly drowned," Cynthia said. "Didn't she? Meg nearly drowned."

"I don't know how it could have happened," said the lifeguard. "One moment she was there, and the next she wasn't."

What had happened was that Meg had climbed out of the water at the shallow end and run along the edge of the pool toward the deep end. She saw a comb that somebody had dropped lying on the bottom. She crouched down and reached in to pick it up, quite deceived about the depth of the water. She went over the edge and slipped into the pool, making such a light splash that nobody heard – not the lifeguard, who was kissing her boyfriend, or Cynthia, who was watching them. That must have been the moment under the trees when I thought, Where are the children? It must have been the same moment. At that moment, Meg was slipping, surprised, into the treacherously clear blue water.

"It's okay," I said to the lifeguard, who was nearly crying. "She can move pretty fast." (Though that wasn't what we usually said about Meg at all. We said she thought everything over and took her time.)

"You swam, Meg," said Cynthia, in a congratulatory way. (She told us about the kissing later.)

"I didn't know it was deep," Meg said. "I didn't drown."

We had lunch at a take-out place, eating hamburgers and fries at a picnic table not far from the highway. In my excitement, I forgot to get Meg a plain hamburger, and had to scrape off the relish and mustard with plastic spoons, then wipe the meat with a paper napkin, before she would eat it. I took advantage of the trash can there to clean out the car. Then we resumed driving east, with the car windows open in front. Cynthia and Meg fell asleep in the back seat.

Andrew and I talked quietly about what had happened. Suppose I hadn't had the impulse just at that moment to check on the children? Suppose we had gone uptown to get drinks, as we had thought of doing? How had Andrew got over the fence? Did he jump or climb? (He couldn't remember.) How had he reached Meg so quickly? And think of the lifeguard not watching. And Cynthia, taken up with the kissing. Not seeing anything else. Not seeing Meg drop over the edge.

Disappeared.

But she swam. She held her breath and came up swimming.

What a chain of lucky links.

That was all we spoke about – luck. But I was compelled to picture the opposite. At this moment, we could have been filling out forms. Meg removed from us, Meg's body being prepared for shipment. To Vancouver – where we had never noticed such a thing as a graveyard – or to Ontario? The scribbled drawings she had made this morning would still be in the back seat of the car. How could this be borne all at once, how did people bear it? The plump, sweet shoulders and hands and feet, the fine brown hair, the rather satisfied, secretive expression – all exactly the same as when she had been alive. The most ordinary tragedy. A child drowned in a swimming pool at noon on a sunny day. Things tidied up quickly. The pool opens as usual at two o'clock. The lifeguard is a bit shaken up and gets the afternoon off. She drives away with her boyfriend in the Roto-Rooter truck. The body sealed away in some kind of shipping coffin. Sedatives, phone calls, arrangements. Such a sudden vacancy, a blind sinking and shifting. Waking up groggy from the pills, thinking for a moment it wasn't true. Thinking if only we hadn't stopped, if only we hadn't taken this route, if only they hadn't let us use the pool. Probably no one would ever have known about the comb.

There's something trashy about this kind of imagining, isn't there? Something shameful. Laying your finger on the wire to get the safe shock, feeling a bit of what it's like, then pulling back. I believed that Andrew was more scrupulous than I about such things, and that at this moment he was really trying to think about something else.

When I stood apart from my parents at Steve Gauley's funeral and watched them, and had this new, unpleasant feeling about them, I thought that I was understanding something about them for the first time. It was a deadly serious thing. I was understanding that they were implicated. Their big, stiff, dressed-up bodies did not stand between me and sudden death, or any kind of death. They gave consent. So it seemed. They gave consent to the death of children and to my death not by anything they said or thought but by the very fact that they had made children – they had made me. They had made me, and for that reason my death – however grieved they were, however they carried on – would seem to them anything but impossible or unnatural. This was a fact, and even then I knew they were not to blame.

But I did blame them. I charged them with effrontery, hypocrisy. On Steve Gauley's behalf, and on behalf of all children, who knew that by rights they should have sprung up free, to live a new, superior kind of life, not to be caught in the snares of vanquished grown-ups, with their sex and funerals.

Steve Gauley drowned, people said, because he was next thing to an orphan and was let run free. If he had been warned enough and given chores to do and kept in check, he wouldn't have fallen from an untrustworthy tree branch into a spring pond, a full gravel pit near the river – he wouldn't have drowned. He was neglected, he was free, so he drowned. And his father took it as an accident, such as might happen to a dog. He didn't have a good suit for the funeral, and he didn't bow his head for the prayers. But he was the only grownup that I let off the hook. He was the only one I didn't see giving consent. He couldn't prevent anything, but he wasn't implicated in anything, either – not like the others, saying the Lord's Prayer in their unnaturally weighted voices, oozing religion and dishonor.

At Glendive, not far from the North Dakota border, we had a choice – either to continue on the interstate or head northeast, toward Williston, taking Route 16, then some secondary roads that would get us back to Highway 2.

We agreed that the interstate would be faster, and that it was important for us not to spend too much time – that is, money – on the road. Nevertheless we decided to cut back to Highway 2.

"I just like the idea of it better," I said.

Andrew said, "That's because it's what we planned to do in the beginning."

"We missed seeing Kalispell and Havre. And Wolf Point. I like the name."

"We'll see them on the way back."

Andrew's saying "on the way back" was a surprising pleasure to me. Of course, I had believed that we would be coming back, with our car and our lives and our family intact, having covered all that distance, having dealt somehow with those loyalties and problems, held ourselves up for inspection in such a foolhardy way. But it was a relief to hear him say it.

"What I can't get over," said Andrew, "is how you got the signal. It's got to be some kind of extra sense that mothers have."

Partly I wanted to believe that, to bask in my extra sense. Partly I wanted to warn him – to warn everybody – never to count on it.

"What I can't understand," I said, "is how you got over the fence."

"Neither can I."

So we went on, with the two in the back seat trusting us, because of no choice, and we ourselves trusting to be forgiven, in time, for everything that had first to be seen and condemned by those children: whatever was flippant, arbitrary, careless, callous – all our natural, and particular, mistakes.

FRAGILITY

Carol Shields

Carol Shields (1935–2003) was an American-born Canadian writer. She is best known for her 1993 novel *The Stone Diaries,* which won the Pulitzer Prize as well as the Governor General's Award in Canada. Shields published ten novels, three collections of poetry and five collections of short stories.

We are flying over the Rockies on our way to Vancouver, and there sits Ivy with her paperback. I ask myself Should I interrupt and draw her attention to the grandeur beneath us?

In a purely selfish sense, watching Ivy read is as interesting as peering down at those snowy mountains. She turns the pages of a book in the same way she handles every object, with a peculiar respectful gentleness, as though the air around it were more tender than ordinary air. I've watched her lift a cup of tea with this same abstracted grace, cradling a thick mug in a way that transforms it into something precious and fragile. It's a gift some people have.

I decide not to disturb her; utterly absorbed in what she's reading, she's seen the Rockies before.

In the seat ahead of us is a young man wearing a bright blue jacket – I remember that once I had a similar jacket in a similar hue. Unlike us, he's clearly flying over the Rockies for the first time. He's in a half-standing position at the window, snapping away with his camera, pausing only to change the film. From where I'm sitting I can see his intense, eager trigger hand, his steadying elbow, his dropped lower lip. In a week he'll be passing his slides around the office, holding them delicately at their edges up to the light. He might set up a projector and screen them one evening in his living room; he might invite a few friends over, and his wife – who will resemble the Ivy of fifteen years ago – will serve coffee and wedges of cheese cake; these are the Rockies, he'll say – magnificent, stirring, one of the wonders of the continent.

I tell myself that I would give a great deal to be in that young man's shoes, but this is only a half-truth, the kind of lie Ivy and I sometimes spin for our own amusement. We really don't want to go back in time. What we envy in the young is that fine nervous edge of perception, the ability to take in reality afresh. I suppose, as we grow older, that's what we forfeit, acquiring in its place a measure of healthy resignation.

Ivy puts down her book suddenly and reaches for my hand. A cool, light, lazy touch. She's smiling.

"Good book?"

"Hmmm," she says, and stretches.

Now, as a kind of duty, I point out the Rockies.

"Beautiful," she exclaims, leaning toward the window.

And it is beautiful. But unfortunately the plane is flying at a height that extracts all sense of dimension from the view. Instead of snow-capped splendor, we see a kind of Jackson Pollock dribbling of white on green. It's a vast abstract design, a linking of incised patterns, quite interesting in its way, but without any real suggestion of height, or majesty.

"It looks a little like a Jackson Pollock," Ivy says in that rhythmic voice of hers.

"Did you really say that?"

"I think so." Her eyebrows go up, her mouth crimps at the edges. "At least, if I didn't, someone did."

I lift her hand – I can't help myself – and kiss her fingertips.

"And what's that for?" she asks, still smiling.

"An attack of poignancy."

"A serious new dietary disease, I suppose," Ivy says, and at that moment the steward arrives with our lunch trays.

Ivy and I have been to Vancouver fairly often on business trips or for holidays. This time it's different; in three months we'll be moving permanently to Vancouver, and now the two of us are engaged in that common-enough errand, a house-hunting expedition.

Common, I say, but not for us.

We know the statistics: that about half of all North Americans move every five years, that we're a rootless, restless, portable society. But for some reason, some failing on our part or perhaps simple good fortune, Ivy and I seem to have evaded the statistical pattern. The small stone-fronted, bow-windowed house we bought when Christopher was born is the house in which we continue to live after twenty years.

If there had been another baby, we would have considered a move, but we stayed in the same house in the middle of Toronto. It was close to both our offices and close too to the clinic Christopher needed. Curiously enough, most of our neighbors also stayed there year after year. In our neighborhood we know everyone. When the news of my transfer came, the first thing Ivy said was, "What about the Mattisons and the Levensons? What about Robin and Sara?"

"We can't very well take everyone on the street along with us."

"Oh Lordy," Ivy said, and bit her lip. "Of course not. It's only—"

"I know," I said.

"Maybe we can talk Robin and Sara into taking their holidays on the coast next year. Sara always said—"

"And we'll be back fairly often. At least twice a year."

"If only—"

"If only what?"

"Those stupid bulbs." (I love the way Ivy pronounces the word *stupid: stewpid*, giving it a patrician lift.)

"Bulbs?"

"Remember last fall, all those bulbs I put in?"

"Oh," I said, remembering.

She looked at me squarely: "You don't mind as much as I do, do you?"

"Of course I do. You know I do."

"Tell me the truth."

What could I say? I've always been impressed by the accuracy of Ivy's observations. "The truth is—"

"The truth is—?" she helped me along.

"I guess I'm ready."

"Ready for what?" Her eyes filled with tears. This was a difficult time for us. Christopher had died in January. He was a tough kid and lived a good five years longer than any of us ever thought he would. His death was not unexpected, but still, Ivy and I were feeling exceptionally fragile.

"Ready for what?" she asked again.

"For something," I admitted. "For anything, I guess."

The first house we look at seems perfect. The settled neighborhood is dense with trees and shrubbery, and reminds us both of our part of Toronto. There are small repairs that need doing but nothing major. Best of all, from the dining room there can be seen a startling lop of blue water meeting blue sky.

I point this out to Ivy; a view was one of the things we had put on our list. There is also a fireplace, another must, and a capacious kitchen with greenhouse windows overlooking a garden.

"And look at the bulbs," I point out. "Tulips halfway up. Daffodils."

"Lilies," Ivy says.

"I think we've struck it lucky," I tell the real-estate woman who's showing us around, a Mrs. Marjorie Little. ("Call me Marge," she'd said to us with west-coast breeziness.)

Afterward, in the car, Ivy is so quiet I have to prompt her. "Well?"

Marge Little, sitting at the wheel, peers at me, then at Ivy.

"It's just," Ivy begins, "it's just so depressing."

Depressing? I can't believe she's saying this. A view, central location, a fireplace. Plus bulbs.

"Well," Ivy says slowly, "it's a divorce house. You must have noticed?"

I hadn't. "A divorce house? How do you know?"

"I looked in the closets. Her clothes were there but *his* weren't."

"Oh."

"And half the pictures had been taken off the wall. Surely you noticed that."

I shake my head.

"I know it sounds silly, but wouldn't you rather move into a house with some good" – she pauses – "some good vibrations?"

"Vibrations?"

"Did you notice the broken light in the bathroom? I'll bet someone threw something at it. In a rage."

"We could always fix the light. And the other things. And with our own furniture—"

Ivy is an accountant. Once I heard a young man in her firm describe her as a *crack* accountant. For a number of years now she's been a senior partner. When this same young man heard she was leaving because of my transfer, he couldn't help ragging her a little, saying he thought women didn't move around at the whim of their husbands anymore, and that, out of principle, she ought to refuse to go to Vancouver or else arrange some kind of compromise life – separate apartments, for instance, with weekend rendezvous in Winnipeg.

Ivy had howled at this. She's a positive, good-natured woman and, as it turned out, she had no trouble finding an opening in a good Vancouver firm, at senior level. As I say, she's positive. Which is why her apprehension over good or bad vibrations is puzzling. Can it be she sees bad times ahead for the two of us? Or is it only that she wants solid footing after these long years with Christopher? Neither of us is quite glued back together again. Not that we ever will be.

"I can't help it," Ivy is saying. "It just doesn't feel like a lucky house. There's something about—"

Marge Little interrupts with a broad smile. "I've got all kinds of interesting houses to show you. Maybe you'll like the next one better."

"Does it have good vibes?" Ivy asks, laughing a little to show she's only half-serious.

"I don't know," Marge Little says. "They don't put that kind of info on the fact sheet."

The next house is perched on the side of the canyon. No, that's not quite true. It is, in fact, falling into the canyon. I notice, but don't mention, the fact that the outside foundation walls are cracked and patched. Inside, the house is alarmingly empty; the cool settled air seems proof that it's been vacant for some time.

Marge consults her fact sheet. Yes, the house has been on the market about six months. The price has been reduced twice. But – she glances at us – perhaps we noticed the foundation ...

"Yes," I say. "Hopeless."

"Damn," Ivy says.

We look at two more houses; both have spectacular views and architectural distinction. But one is a bankruptcy sale and the other is a divorce house. By now I'm starting to pick up the scent: it's a compound of petty carelessness and strenuous neglect, as though the owners had decamped in a hurry, angry at the rooms themselves.

To cheer ourselves up, the three of us have lunch in a sunny Broadway restaurant. It seems extraordinary that we can sit here and see mountains that are miles away; the thought that we will soon be able to live within sight of these mountains fills us with optimism. We order a little wine and linger in the sunlight. Vancouver is going to be an adventure. We're going to be happy here. Marge Little, feeling expansive, tells us about her three children and about the problem she has keeping her weight down. "Marge Large they'll be calling me soon," she says. It's an old joke, we sense, and the telling of it makes us feel we're old friends. She got into the business, she says, because she loves houses. And she has an instinct for matching houses with people. "So don't be discouraged," she tells us. "We'll find the perfect place this afternoon."

We drive through narrow city streets to a house where a famous movie idol grew up. His mother still lives in the house, a spry, slightly senile lady in her eighties. The tiny house – we quickly see it is far too small for us – is crowded with photographs of the famous son. He beams at us from the hallway, from the dining room, from the bedroom bureau.

"Oh, he's a good boy. Comes home every two or three years," his mother tells us, her large teeth shining in a diminished face. "And once I went down there, all the way down to Hollywood, on an airplane. He paid my way, sent me a ticket, I saw his swimming pool. They all have swimming pools. He has a cook, a man who does all the meals, so I didn't have to lift a finger for a whole week. What an experience, like a queen. I have some pictures someplace I could show you—"

"That would be wonderful," Marge Little says, "but" – she glances at her watch – "I'm afraid we have another appointment."

"—I saw those pictures just the other day. Now where—? I think they're in this drawer somewhere. Here, I knew it. Take a look at this. Isn't that something? That's his swimming pool. Kidney-shaped. He's got another one now, even bigger."

"Beautiful," Ivy says.

"And here he is when he was little. See this? He'd be about nine there. We took a trip east. That's him and his dad standing by Niagara Falls. Here's another—"

"We really have to—"

"A good boy. I'll say that for him. Didn't give any trouble. Sometimes I see his movies on the TV and I can't believe the things he does; with women and so on. I have to pinch myself and say it's only pretend—"

"I think—"

"I'm going into this senior-citizen place. They've got a nice TV lounge, big screen, bigger than this little, bitty one, color too. I always—"

"Sad," Ivy says, when we escape at last and get into the car.

"The house or the mother?" I ask her.

"Both."

"At least it's not a D.H." (This has become our shorthand expression for divorce house.)

"Wait'll you see the next place," Marge Little says, swinging into traffic. "The next place is fabulous."

Fabulous, yes. But far too big. After that, in a fit of desperation, we look at a condo. "I'm not quite ready for this," I have to admit.

"No garden," Ivy says in a numb voice. She looks weary, and we decide to call it a day.

The ad in the newspaper reads: WELL-LOVED FAMILY HOME. And Ivy and Marge Little and I are there, knocking on the door, at nine-thirty in the morning.

"Come in, come in," calls a young woman in faded jeans. She has a young child on one hip and another – they must be twins – by the hand. Sunlight pours in the front window and there is freshly baked bread cooling on the kitchen counter.

But the house is a disaster, a rabbit warren of narrow hallways and dark corners. The kitchen window is only feet away from a low brick building where bodywork is being done on imported sports cars. The stairs are uneven. The bedroom floors slope, and the paint is peeling off the bathroom ceiling.

"It just kills us to leave this place," the young woman says. She's following us through the rooms, pointing with unmistakable sorrow at the wall where they were planning to put up shelving, at the hardwood floors they were thinking of sanding. Out of the blue, they got news of a transfer.

Ironically, they're going to Toronto, and in a week's time they'll be there doing what we're doing, looking for a house they can love. "But we just know we'll never find a place like this," she tells us with a sad shake of her head. "Not in a million zillion years."

After that we lose track of the number of houses. The day bends and blurs, square footage, zoning regulations, mortgage schedules, double-car garages, cedar siding only two years old – was that the place near that little park? No, that was the one on that little crescent off Arbutus. Remember? The one without the basement.

Darkness is falling as Marge Little drives us back to our hotel. We are passing hundreds – it seems like thousands – of houses, and we see lamps being turned on, curtains being closed. Friendly smoke rises from substantial chimneys. Here and there, where the curtains are left open, we can see people sitting down to dinner. Passing one house, I see a woman in a window, leaning over with a match in her hand, lighting a pair of candles. Ivy sees it too, and I'm sure she's feeling as I am, a little resentful that everyone but us seems to have a roof overhead.

"Tomorrow for sure," Marge calls cheerily. (Tomorrow is our last day. Both of us have to be home on Monday.)

"I suppose we could always rent for a year." Ivy says this with low enthusiasm.

"Or," I say, "we could make another trip in a month or so. Maybe there'll be more on the market."

"Isn't it funny? The first house we saw, remember? In a way, it was the most promising place we've seen."

"The one with the view from the dining room? With the broken light in the bathroom?"

"It might not look bad with a new fixture. Or even a skylight."

"Wasn't that a divorce house?" I ask Ivy.

"Yes," she shrugs, "but maybe that's just what we'll have to settle for."

"It *was* listed at a good price."

"I live in a divorce house," Marge Little says, pulling in front of our hotel. "It's been a divorce house for a whole year now."

"Oh, Marge," Ivy says. "I didn't mean—" she stops. "Forgive me."

"And it's not so bad. Sometimes it's darned cheerful."

"I just—" Ivy takes a breath. "I just wanted a lucky house. Maybe there's no such thing—"

"Are you interested in taking another look at the first house? I might be able to get you an appointment this evening. That is, if you think you can stand one more appointment today."

"Absolutely," we say together.

This time we inspect the house inch by inch. Ivy makes a list of the necessary repairs, and I measure the window for curtains. We hadn't realized that there was a cedar closet off one of the bedrooms. The lights of the city are glowing through the dining-room window. A spotlight at the back of the house picks out the flowers just coming into bloom. There'll be room for our hi-fi across from the fireplace. The basement is dry and very clean. The wallpaper in the downstairs den is fairly attractive and in good condition. The stairway is well proportioned and the banister is a beauty. (I'm a sucker for banisters.) There's an alcove where the pine buffet will fit nicely. Trees on both sides of the house should give us greenery and privacy. The lawn, as far as we can tell, seems to be in good shape. There's a lazy Susan in the kitchen, also a built-in dishwasher, a later model than ours. Plenty of room for a small table and a couple of chairs. The woodwork in the living room has been left natural, a wonder since so many people, a few years back, were painting over their oak trim.

Ivy says something that makes us laugh. "Over here," she says, "over here is where we'll put the Christmas tree." She touches the edge of one of the casement windows, brushes it with the side of her hand and says, "It's hard to believe that people could live in such a beautiful house and be unhappy."

For a moment there's silence, and then Marge says, "We could put in an offer tonight. I don't think it's too late. What do you think?"

And now, suddenly it's the next evening, and Ivy and I are flying back to Toronto. Here we are over the Rockies again, crossing them this time in darkness. Ivy sits with her head back, eyes closed, her shoulders so sharply her own; she's not quite asleep, but not quite awake either.

Our plane seems a fragile vessel, a piece of jewelry up here between the stars and the mountains. Flying through dark air like this makes me think that life itself is fragile. The miniature accidents of chromosomes can spread unstoppable circles of grief. A dozen words carelessly uttered can dismantle a marriage. A few gulps of oxygen are all that stand between us and death.

I wonder if Ivy is thinking, as I am, of the three months ahead, of how tumultuous they'll be. There are many things to think of when you move. For one, we'll have to put our own house up for sale. The thought startles me, though I've no idea why.

I try to imagine prospective buyers arriving for appointments, stepping through our front door with polite murmurs and a sharp eye for imperfections.

They'll work their way through the downstairs, the kitchen (renewed only four years ago), the living room (yes, a real fireplace, a good draft), the dining room (small, but you can seat ten in a pinch). Then they'll make their way upstairs (carpet a little worn, but with lots of wear left). The main bedroom is fair size (with good reading lamps built in, also bookshelves).

And then there's Christopher's bedroom.

Will the vibrations announce that here lived a child with little muscular control, almost no sight or hearing and no real consciousness as that word is normally perceived? He had, though – and perhaps the vibrations will acknowledge the fact – his own kind of valor and perhaps his own way of seeing the world. At least Ivy and I always rewallpapered his room every three years or so out of a conviction that he took some pleasure in the sight of ducks swimming on a yellow sea. Later, it was sail boats; then tigers and monkeys dodging jungle growth, then a wild op-art checkerboard; and then, the final incarnation, a marvelous green cave of leafiness with amazing flowers and impossible birds sitting in branches.

I can't help wondering if these prospective buyers, these people looking for God only knows what, if they'll enter this room and feel something of his fragile presence alive in a fragile world.

Well, we shall see. We shall soon see.

THE MERRY WIDOW

Margaret Drabble

Margaret Drabble (b. 1939) is a British novelist, biographer and critic. Awarded a CBE in 1980, Drabble was promoted to Dame Commander of the Order of the British Empire in the 2008 Birthday Honours. In 2011, she was awarded the Golden PEN Award by English PEN for a lifetime's distinguished service to literature.

When Philip died, his friends and colleagues assumed that Elsa would cancel the holiday. Elsa knew that this would be their assumption. But she had no intention of cancelling. She was determined upon the holiday. During Philip's unexpectedly sudden last hours, and in the succeeding weeks of funeral and condolence and letters from banks and solicitors, it began to take an increasingly powerful hold upon her imagination. If she were honest with herself, which she tried to be, she had not been looking forward to the holiday while Philip was alive: it would have been yet another dutifully endured, frustrating, saddening attempt at reviving past pleasures, overshadowed by Philip's increasing ill health and ill temper. But without Philip, the prospect brightened. Elsa knew that she would have to conceal her growing anticipation, for it was surely not seemly for so recent a widow to look forward so eagerly to something as mundane as a summer holiday – although it was not, she reasoned with herself, as though she were contemplating an extravagant escapade. Their plans had been modest enough – no Swans tour of the Greek isles, no luxury hotel, not even a little family pension with check tablecloths and local wine in the Dordogne, but a fortnight in a rented cottage in Dorset. A quiet fortnight in late June. An unambitious arrangement, appropriate for such a couple as Philip and Elsa, Elsa and Philip.

Perhaps, she thought, as she threw away old socks and parcelled suits for Oxfam and the Salvation Army, as she cancelled subscriptions to scholarly periodicals, perhaps she should try to imply to these well-meaning acquaintances that she felt a spiritual *need* to go to Dorset, a need for solitude, for privacy, a need to recover in tranquillity and new surroundings from the shock (however expected a shock) of Philip's death? And indeed, such an implication would not be so far from the truth, except for the fact that the emotion she expected to experience in Dorset was not grief, but joy. She needed to be alone, to conceal from prying eyes her relief, her delight in her new freedom and, yes, her joy.

This was unseemly, but it was so. She had been absolutely fed up to the back teeth with Philip, she said to herself, gritting those teeth tightly as she wrote to increase the standing order for oil delivery, as she rang the plumber to arrange to have a shower attachment fitted to the bathroom tap. Why on earth shouldn't she have a shower attachment, at her age, with her pension and savings? Her jaw ached with retrospective anger. How mean he had become, how querulous, how determined to thwart every pleasure, to interfere with every friendship. Thanks to Philip, she had no friends left, and that was why she was looking forward with a voluptuous, sensuous, almost feverish longing to the delights of solitude. To get away, away from all these ruined relationships, these false smiles, these old tweed suits and pigeonholes full of papers – to be alone, not to have to pretend, to sleep and wake alone, unobserved.

It had not been Philip's fault, she told others, that he had become 'difficult'. It had been the fault of the illness. It had been bad luck, to be struck down like that when not yet sixty, bad luck to have such constant nagging pain, bad luck to be denied one's usual physical exercise and pleasures, one's usual diet. But of course in her heart she thought it *was* Philip's fault. Illness had merely accentuated his selfishness, his discreet malice, his fondness for putting other people in their place. Illness gave him excuses for behaving badly – but he had *always* behaved badly. He had seized upon illness as a gift, had embraced it as his natural state. When younger, he had made efforts to control his tongue, his witticisms at the expense of others, his desire to prove the rest of the world ignorant, foolish, ill-mannered. Illness had removed the controls, had given him licence. He had seemed to enjoy humiliating her in public, complaining about her behind her back, undermining her when they sat alone together watching television. It had reached the stage where she could not express the slightest interest in any television programme without his launching an attack on her taste, her interests, her habits of mind. If she watched the news, she was news-obsessed, media-obsessed, brain-washed into submission by the news-madness of the programme planners; if she watched tennis or athletics or show-jumping, he would lecture her on the evils of competitive sport; if she watched wildlife documentaries, he would mock her for taking an interest in badgers and butterflies when she ought to be attending to the problems of the inner cities; if she watched a comedy series, he would call her escapist, and the comedy would be attacked as cosy middle-class fantasy or as a glorification of working-class subculture. Whatever she watched was wrong, and if she watched nothing – why, she was a television snob, unable to share the simple pleasures of Everyman. Night after night, at an oblique angle, through the small screen, he had abused her. It was not television he hated, it was her.

There was no television in Dorset. Apologetically, the owners of the little Mill House had explained that the valley was too deep for good reception, the picture quality too poor to make it worth providing a set. Good, Philip had said, but he had not meant it. If he had lived, if he had been alive to go on this Dorset holiday, he would undoubtedly have found some devious way to complain about its absence. Her lack of conversation, perhaps, would have been trundled out: better a mindless television programme, he would have declared, than your small talk, your silences.

Dead he was, now, and there would be no complaints. No television, and no complaints. There would be silence.

The evening before her departure, Elsa Palmer sat alone in the drawing-room with a tray of bread and cheese and pickle, and tomato salad, and milk chocolate digestive biscuits, and a pile of road maps, and her bird book, and her butterfly book, and her flower book, and her Pevsner. The television was on, but she was not watching it. She ate a bit of cheese, and wrote down road numbers in an orderly way. A10, A30, A354. There didn't seem to be any very obvious way of getting to Dorset from Cambridge, but that made the exercise of plotting a route all the more entertaining. She would pass through towns she did not know, get stuck in high streets she had never seen, drive past hedgerows banked with unfamiliar flowers. Alone, with her car radio. If she took a wrong turning, nobody would reprimand her. If she chose to listen to Radio 2, nobody would know. She could stop for a cup of coffee, she could eat a sandwich from her knee and drop crumbs on her skirt. And, at the end of the journey, there would be the Mill House, where nothing would remind her of Philip. She would lose herself in the deep Dorset countryside, so different from these appalling, over-farmed, open East Anglian wastes. There would be a whole fortnight of walkings and wanderings, of scrambling up coastal paths and rambling through woods, of collecting specimens and identifying them from her books in the long, light, solitary evenings. Unobserved, uncriticized.

Philip, of late, had taken increasingly strongly against her passion for identifications. 'What's in a name?' he would say, when she tried to remember a variety of sweet pea, or to spot a distant little brown bird at the end of the garden. As he always beat her down in argument by sheer persistence (and anyway, was it fair to argue with an ill man?) she had never been able to defend her own pleasure in looking things up in reference books. It had seemed a harmless pleasure, until Philip attacked it. Harmless, innocent, and proper for the wife of a university lecturer. An interest in flowers and butterflies. What could be wrong with that? By some sleight of reasoning he had made it seem sinister, joyless, life-denying. He had made her feel it to be a weakness, a symptom of a character defect. She would never work out quite how he had managed it.

The Lulworth Skipper. A local little butterfly that haunts Lulworth Cove. She looked at its portrait and smiled approvingly. Yes, she would walk along the Dorset Coast Path, with the Ordnance Survey map in her pocket, and go to Lulworth, and search for the Lulworth Skipper. And if she did not find it, nobody would know she had been defeated. Her pleasure would be her own, her disappointment her own.

Marriage has warped me, thought Elsa Palmer the next day, as she dawdled through Biggleswade. Marriage is unnatural, thought Elsa Palmer, as she stopped at the red light of some roadworks ini Aylesbury.

Marriage and maternity. She thought of her children, her grandchildren. They had all attended the funeral, dutifully. She had found herself bored by them, irritated with them. After years and years of cravenly soliciting their favours, of begging them to telephone more often, of blackmailing them into coming for Christmas (or, lately, into inviting herself and Philip for Christmas), she now, suddenly, had found herself bored, had admitted herself to be bored. Stuart was a slob, Harriet was a pedantic chip off the old block (and always ill, my God, what stories of migraines and backaches, and she was only twenty-nine) and even young Ben had been incredibly tedious about his new car. And the grandchildren – whining, sniffing, poking their noses, kicking the furniture, squabbling, with their awful London accents and their incessant demands for sweets. Spoiled brats, the lot of them. Elsa smiled, comfortably, to herself, as she sailed through the landscape, divinely, enchantingly, rapturously alone. The weather responded to her mood; the sun shone, huge white clouds drifted high, vast shadows fell on the broad trees and the green-gold trees. An Indian summer, in June.

She had cautioned herself against disappointment at her journey's end; could the mill really be as charming as it appeared in its photographs? Was there some undisclosed flaw, some blot in the immediate landscape, some pylon or pig farm on its doorstep? Maybe, maybe: but some charm it must surely have, and the description of the little river flowing through the house and the garden, dividing the front garden from the little paddock at the back, could not be wholly fictitious. There were trout in the stream, she was assured. She pictured herself reclining in a deckchair, lying on a rug on the grass, reading a book, sipping a drink, looking up every now and then to gaze at the trout in the shallows, the waving weed. Inexpressibly soothing, she found this image of herself.

And the mill, when finally she arrived in the late afternoon, was no disappointment. It was smaller than it looked in the photographs, but houses always are, and it was right on the road, but the road was a small road, a country road, a delightful road, and she liked the way the garden gate opened onto a flinty courtyard where she parked her car. Rustic, unpretentious. A little lawn, with a wooden table; creepers growing up the house; a nesting blackbird watching anxiously, boldly, curiously; and beyond the lawn, the little river, the River Cerne itself, which flowed right through what was to be, for a whole fortnight, her own little property. The border was paved, and next to the idle mill wheel was a low stone wall, warm from the day's sun. She sat on it, and saw the promised trout flicker. It was all that she had hoped. There was a little bridge over the river, leading to the tree-shaded, thickly hedged paddock, part also of her property. You can sit there, the owners had assured her, quite out of sight of the road. If you don't like to sit down on the lawn at the front, they had said, it's quite private, through the back.

Quite private. She savoured the concept of privacy. She would save her exploration of it until she had collected the key and been shown round, until she had unpacked and made herself at home.

The interior of the house, as displayed to her by Mrs Miller from the village, was perhaps a little too rustic-smart: she was introduced to a shining wooden kitchen table and benches with diamond-shaped holes carved in them, a lot of glossy bright brown woodwork, an open light wooden staircase up to an upper floor and a semi-galleried sitting-room, a brass horseshoe and a brass kettle, and a disconcerting fox's mask grinning down from a wall. It was all newly decorated, spick and span. But the millstone was still there, and the ancient machinery of the mill could still be seen in the back rooms of the house, and through the heart of the house flowed the noisy, companionable sound of water. Elsa liked it all very much. She even liked the varnished wood and the fox's mask. Philip would have hated them, would have been full of witticisms about them, but she liked them very much. They were not to her taste, but she felt instantly at home with them. 'It's lovely,' she said, brightly, to Mrs Miller, hoping Mrs Miller would take herself off as soon as she had explained the intricacies of the electricity meter and revealed the contents of the kitchen cupboards. 'Oh, I'm sure I'll find everything I need,' she said, noting that milk, bread and butter had been provided. She was touched by the thoughtfulness of her absent landlords.

Mrs Miller vanished, promptly, tactfully. Elsa Palmer was alone. She wandered from room to room, examining the objects that make themselves at home in holiday cottages – an earthenware jug of dried flowers, a songbook open on the piano, a Visitors' Book, an umbrella-stand, a children's tricycle under the stairs, a stone hot-water bottle, a clock in a glass case, a print of a hunting scene. They made her feel amazingly irresponsible. She felt that for the first time for years she had no housekeeping cares in the world. She could live on Kit Kat or KiteKat and no one would comment. She could starve, and no one would care. Contemplating this freedom, she unpacked her clothes and laid them neatly in empty, paper-lined, mothballed, impersonal drawers, and made up the double bed in the low-ceilinged bedroom, and went downstairs. It was early evening. She could hear the sound of the mill stream. She unpacked her groceries: eggs, cheese, long-life milk, tins of tuna fish, onions, potatoes, a little fruit. A bottle of gin, a bottle of white wine, a few bottles of tonic.

With a sense of bravado, she poured herself a gin and tonic. Philip had always poured the drinks; in his lifetime she would no more have thought of pouring one for herself than she would have expected Philip to make an Irish stew. The thought of Philip struggling with an Irish stew struck her as irresistibly comic; she smliled to herself. Now Philip was dead, she could laugh at him at last. She adorned her gin and tonic with ice cubes and a slice of lemon. A merry widow.

The evening sun was mellow. It was one of the longest days of the year. She wandered out into the flinty courtyard and over to the little lawn. She sat on the low stone wall and sipped her drink. She watched a flock of long-tailed finches fluttering in a small tree. Tomorrow, if they returned, she would sit here and identify them. She thought they would return.

The weeds swayed and poured in the stream. Water crowfoot blossomed above the surface, its roots trailing. Trout rippled, stationary yet supple and subtle, motionless yet full of movement.

She sat and gazed as water and time flowed by. Then she rose and wandered over the little hidden wooden bridge to inspect the unseen paddock on the far side. As she crossed the bridge, a startled moorhen dislodged itself with great noise and splashing and she saw some chicks scrambling clumsily upstream. And there was the paddock – a long, triangular plot of land, planted with fruit trees, bordered on one side by a fence, on another by the stream and on the third by a high, irregular, ancient row of mixed tree and hedge, at the bottom of which ran another little tributary. The paddock, she discovered, was a sort of island. The music of the water was soft and reassuring. The grass was deep, knee-high. The stream was fringed with all sorts of wild flowers, growing in rich profusion and disorder – forget-me-not, valerian, comfrey, buttercup and many other species that she could not at once distinguish. A wild garden, overgrown, secret, mysterious. Nobody could overlook her here.

She sipped her gin and tonic and wandered through the long grasses in the cool of the evening. A deep, healing peace possessed her. She stood on the little triangular point of her island, where the two streams met, and stood on a tree root at the end of her promontory, gazing at a view that could not have altered much in a thousand years. A field of wheat glowed golden to her left, rising steeply to a dark purple wood. Long shadows fell. A small, steep view. The small scale of her little kingdom was peculiarly comforting. A few hundred yards of modest wilderness. She would sit here, perhaps, in the afternoons. Perhaps she would sleep a little, on a rug, under a fruit tree, in the sun, listening to the sound of water. Pleasant plans formed themselves in her imagination as she wandered slowly back and over the little bridge, plucking as she went a spray of blue forget-me-not. She would look it up, after her supper, in the flower book. How impatient Philip would have been with such a plan! It's *obviously* a forget-me-not, *anyone* can see it's a forget-me-not, Philip would have said, and anyway, who cares what it is? But he would have put it more wittily than that, more hurtfully than that, in words that, thank God, she did not have to invent for him. For he was not here, would never be there again.

Later, reading her flower book, examining the plant more closely, she discovered that it wasn't a forget-me-not at all. Its leaves were all wrong, and it was too tall. It was probably a borage, hairy borage – and after a while, she settled for green alkanet. *Anchusa sempervirens.* 'Small clusters of flat white-eyed bright blue flowers, rather like a forget-me-not or speedwell ...' Yes, that was it. *Rather like*. Rather like, but not identical. Similar, but not the same. This distinction delighted her. She would forget it, she knew, but for the moment it delighted her. She was not very good at flowers, and forgot most of the names she so painstakingly established. At her age she found it difficult to retain new information, almost impossible to enlarge her store of certainties from the hundred names she had learned, half a century ago, as a brownie in the Yorkshire Dales. But the inability did not diminish her pleasure, it increased it. Philip had never been able to understand this. The safety, the comfort of the familiar well-thumbed pages; the safety, the comfort of the familiar process of doubt, comparison, temporary certainty. Yes, there it was. Green alkanet.

Her dreams that night were violent and free. Horses raced through dark fields, waterfalls plunged over crags, clouds heaped ominously in a black sky. But when she woke, the morning was serene and blue and filled with birdsong. She made herself a mug of coffee and sat outside, watching the odd car pass, the village bus, an old woman walking a dog. She planned her day. She would walk the mile and a half into the village, do a little shopping, visit the church, buy a newspaper, wander back, read her novel, eat a little lunch, then go and lie on a rug on the long grass in the paddock. The next day, she would be more ambitious perhaps, she would go for a real walk, a mapped walk. But today, she would be quiet. The luxury of knowing that nothing and no one could interfere with her prospect made her feel momentarily a little tearful. Had she really been so unhappy for so long? She saw the little long-tailed finches fluttering in the tree. They had returned to charm her.

Philip, she reflected, as she sat on the wall reading, would not have approved her choice of novel. She was reading a Margery Allingham omnibus, nostalgically, pointlessly. Philip had despised detective stories. He had mocked her pleasure in them. And indeed they *were* a bit silly, but that was the point of them. Yes, that was the point. After lunch, she took Margery Allingham into the paddock, with a rug and her sunhat, and lay under an apple tree. Impossible to explain, to the young, the satisfaction of sleeping in the afternoon. How can you *enjoy* being asleep, her children used to ask her. Now they too, parents themselves, were glad of a siesta, of an afternoon nap. Elsa lay very still. She could hear the moorhen with its chicks. She lifted her eyes from the page and saw a little brown water rat swimming upstream. A fringe of tall plants and weeds shimmered and blurred before her eyes. Sedges, reeds, cresses … yes, later she would look them all up. She nodded, drooped. She fell asleep.

After an hour she woke, from dreams of grass and gardens, to find her dream continuing. She was possessed by a great peace. She lay there, gazing at the sky. She could feel her afflictions, her irritations, her impatiences leaving her. They loosened their little hooks and drifted off. She would be redeemed, restored, forgiven.

The day passed smoothly into the evening, and gin and tonic, and the identification of long-tailed finches, and a reading of Pevsner. She marked churches she might or might not visit, and smiled at Pevsner's use of the phrase 'life-size angels'. Who was to know the life size of an angel? Had it not once been thought that millions of them might dance on the point of a pin? Might not an angel be as tall as an oak tree, as vast and powerful as a leviathan?

She slept like an angel, and woke to another blue uninterrupted day of laziness. She decided not to make a long excursion. She would spend another whole day in the delights of her new terrain. She repeated her walk to the village of the previous morning, she returned to a little lunch, she took herself off again to the paddock with her rug and her Margery Allingham. Already she had established the charm of routine, of familiarity. She felt as though she had been here forever. She read, nodded, dozed, and fell asleep.

When she woke, half an hour later, she knew at once that she was no longer alone. She sat up hastily, guiltily, rearranging her hat, straightening her cotton skirt over her bare knees, reaching for her glasses, trying to look as though she had never dozed off in an afternoon in her life. Where was the intruder? Who had aroused her? Discreetly, but with mounting panic, she surveyed her triangle of paddock – and yes, there, at the far end, she could see another human being. An old man, with a scythe. She relaxed, slightly; a rustic old character, a gardener of some sort, annoying and embarrassing to have been caught asleep by him, but harmless enough, surely? Yes, quite harmless. What was he up to? She shaded her eyes against the afternoon sun.

He appeared to be cutting the long grass. The long grass of her own paddock.

Oh dear, thought Elsa Palmer to herself. What a shame. She wanted him to stop, to go away at once. But what right had she to stop him? He must belong to the Mill House, he was clearly fulfilling his horticultural obligations to his absentee employers.

Slowly, as she sat and watched him, the full extent of the disaster began to sink in. Not only was her solitude invaded, not only had she been observed asleep by a total stranger, but this total stranger was even now in the act of cutting back the very foliage, the very grasses that had so pleased her. She watched him at work.

He scythed and sawed. He raked and bundled. Could he see her watching him? It made her feel uncomfortable, to watch this old man at work, in the afternoon, on a hot day, as she sat idling with Margery Allingham on a rug. She would have to get up and go. Her paddock was ruined, at least for this afternoon. Furtively she assembled her possessions and began to creep away back to the house. But he spotted her. From the corner of the triangle, a hundred yards and more away, he spotted her. He saluted her with an axe and called to her. 'Nice day,' he called. 'Not disturbing you, am I?'

'No, no, of course not,' she called back, faintly, edging away, edging back towards the little wooden bridge. Stealthily she retreated. He had managed to hack only a few square yards; it was heavy going, it would take him days, weeks to finish off the whole plot ...

Days, weeks. That evening, trapped in her front garden, on her forecourt, she saw him cross her bridge, within yards of her, several times, with his implements, with his wheelbarrows full of rubbish. She had not dared to pour herself a gin and tonic; it did not seem right. Appalled, she watched him, resisting her impulse to hide inside her own house. On his final journey, he paused with his barrow. 'Hot work,' he said, mopping his brow. He was a terrible old man, gnarled, brown, toothless, with wild white hair. 'Yes, hot work,' she faintly agreed. What was she meant to do? Offer him a drink? Ask him in? Make him a pot of tea? He stood, resting on his barrow, staring at her.

'Not in your way, am I?' he asked.

She shook her head.

'On your own, are you?' he asked. She nodded, then shook her head. 'A peaceful spot,' he said.

'Yes,' she said.

'I'll be back in the morning,' he said. But, for the moment, did not move. Elsa stood, transfixed. They stared at one another. Then he sighed, bent down to tweak out a weed from the gravel, and moved slowly, menacingly on.

Elsa was shattered. She retired into her house and poured herself a drink, more for medicine than pleasure. Could she trust him to have gone? What if he had forgotten something? She lurked indoors for twenty minutes, miserably. Then, timidly, ventured out. She crept back across the bridge to inspect the damage he had done at the far end of the paddock. Well, he was a good workman. He had made an impression on nature; he had hacked and tidied to much effect. Cut wood glared white, severed roots in the river bank bled, great swathes of grass and flowers and sedge lay piled in a heap. He had made a devastation. And at this rate, it would take him a week, a fortnight, to work his way round. To level the lot. If that was his intention, which it must be. I'll be back in the morning, he had said. Distractedly plucking at sedges, she tried to comfort herself. She could go for walks, she could amuse herself, further afield, she could lie firmly in her deckchair on the little front lawn. She had a right. She had paid. It was her holiday.

Pond sedge. *Carex acutiformis*. Or great pond sedge, *Carex riparia*? She gazed at the flower book, as night fell. It did not seem to matter much what kind of sedge it was. Carnation sedge, pale sedge, drooping sedge. As Philip would have said, who cared? Elsa drooped. She drooped with disappointment.

Over the next week the disappointment intensified. Her worst fears were fulfilled. Day by day, the terrible old man returned with his implements, to hack and spoil and chop. She had to take herself out, in order not to see the ruination of her little kingdom. She went for long walks, along white chalky ridges, through orchid-spotted shadows, through scrubby little woods, past fields of pigs, up Roman camps, along the banks of other rivers, as her own river was steadily and relentlessly stripped and denuded. Every evening she crept out to inspect the damage. The growing green diminished, retreated, shrank. She dreaded the sight of the old man with the scythe. She dreaded the intensity of her own dread. Her peace of mind was utterly destroyed. She cried, in the evenings, and wished she had a television set to keep her company. At night she dreamed of Philip. In her dreams he was always angry, he shouted at her and mocked her, he was annoyed beyond the grave.

I am going mad, she told herself, as the second week began, as she watched the old man once more cross the little bridge, after the respite of Sunday. I must have been mad already, to let so small a thing unbalance me. And I thought I was recovering. I thought I could soon be free. But I shall never be free, when so small a thing can destroy me.

She felt cut to the root. The sap bled out. She would be left a dry low stalk.

I might as well die, she said to herself, as she tried to make herself look again at her flower book, at her Pevsner, at her old companions. No others would she ever have, and these had now failed her.

Worst of all were the old man's attempts at conversation. He liked to engage her, despite her obvious reluctance, and she, as though mesmerized, could not bring herself to avoid him. It was the banality of these conversational gambits that delayed her recognition of his identity, his identification. They misled her. For he was an old bore, ready to comment on the weather, the lateness of the bus, the cricket. Elsa Palmer had no interest in cricket, did not wish to waste time conversing with an old man about cricket, but found herself doing so nevertheless. For ten minutes at a time she would listen to him as he rambled on about names that meant nothing to her, about matches of yesteryear. Why was she so servile, so subdued? What was this extremity of fear that gripped her as she listened?

He was hacking away her own life, this man with a scythe. Bundling it up, drying it out for the everlasting bonfire. But she did not let herself think this. Not yet.

It was on the last evening of his hacking and mowing that Elsa Palmer defeated the old man. She had been anticipating his departure with mixed feelings, for when he had finished the paddock would be flat and he would be victorious. He would have triumphed over Nature, he would depart triumphant, this old man of the river bank.

She saw him collect his implements for the last time, saw him pause with his wheelbarrow for the last time. Finished, now, for the year, he said. A good job done. Feebly, she complimented him, thinking of the poor shaven discoloured pale grass, the amputated stumps of the hedgerow. For the last time they discussed the weather and the cricket. He bade her goodbye, wished her a pleasant holiday.

She watched him trundle his barrow through the gate, and across the road, and on, up the hillside, to the farm. He receded. He had gone.

And I, thought Elsa, am still alive.

She leaned on the gate and breathed deeply. She gathered her courage. She summoned all her strength.

I am still alive, thought Elsa Palmer. Philip is dead, but I, I have survived the Grim Reaper.

And it came to her as she stood there in the early evening fight that the old man was not Death, as she had feared, but Time. Old Father Time. *He* is the one with the scythe. She had feared that the old man was Death calling for her, as he had called for Philip, but no, he was only Time, Time friendly, Time continuing, Time healing. What had he said, of the paddock? 'Finished for the year,' he had said. But already, even now at this instant, it was beginning to grow again, and next June it would be as dense, as tangled, as profuse as ever, awaiting his timely, friendly scythe. Not Death, but Time. Similar, but not identical. She had named him, she had identified him, she had recognized him, and he had gone harmlessly away, leaving her in possession of herself, of her place, of her life. She breathed deeply. The sap began to flow. She felt it flow in her veins. The frozen water began to flow again under the bridge. The trout darted upstream. Yes, Old Father Time, *he* is the one with the scythe. Death is that other one. Death is the skeleton. Already, the grass was beginning to grow, the forget-me-nots and green alkanets were recovering.

Rejoicing, she went indoors, to her flower book. It glowed in the lamplight, it lived again. She settled down, began to turn the pages. Yes, there they were, forget-me-not, green alkanet – and what about brooklime? Was it a borage or a speedwell? She gazed at the colour plates, reprieved, entranced. Widespread and common in wet places. She turned the pages of her book, naming names. Time had spared her, Time had trundled his scythe away. Philip had been quite wrong, wrong all along. Elsa smiled to herself in satisfaction. Philip was dead because he had failed to recognize his adversary. Death had taken him by surprise, death un-named, unrecognized, unlabelled. Lack of recognition had killed Philip. Whereas I, said Elsa, I have conversed with and been spared by the Grim Reaper.

She turned the pages, lovingly. *Carex acutiformis, Carex riparia*. Tomorrow she would get to grips with the sedges. There were still plenty left, at the far end of the paddock, in the difficult corner by the overhanging alder. Tomorrow she would go and pick some specimens. And maybe, when she went back to Cambridge, she would enrol for that autumn course on Italian Renaissance Art and Architecture. She didn't really know much about iconography, but she could see that it had its interest. Well, so did everything, of course. Everything was interesting.

She began to wish she had not been so mean, so unfriendly. She really ought to have offered that old man a cup of tea.

THE I OF IT

A. M. Homes

A. M. Homes (b. 1961) is an American writer known for her controversial novels and unusual stories. She released her first collection of short stories, *The Safety of Objects*, in 1990. In 2013 she won the Women's Prize for Fiction with her novel *May We Be Forgiven*.

I am sitting naked on a kitchen chair, staring at it. My jeans and underwear are bunched up at my ankles. I walked from the bathroom to here, shuffling one foot in front of the other as though in shackles.

This has been a terrible week. I have been to the doctor. It is evening and I am sitting at my table staring down. I half wish that it had done what was threatened most in cases of severe abuse and fallen off. If I had found it lying loose under the sheets or pushed down to the bottom of the bed, rubbing up against my ankle, I could have picked it up lovingly, longingly. I could have brought it to eye level and given it the kind of inspection it truly deserved; I would have admired it from every angle, and then kept it in my dresser drawer.

I have an early memory of discovering this part of myself, discovering it as something neither my mother or sisters had. I played with it, knowing mine was the only one in the house, admiring its strength, enjoying how its presence seemed to mean so much to everyone. They were always in one way or another commenting on its existence from the manner in which they avoided it when they dried me from the tub to the way they looked out the car window when we stopped on long road trips and I stood by the highway releasing a thin yellow stream that danced in the wind.

This stab of maleness was what set me apart in a house of women; it was what comforted me most in that same house, knowing that I would never be like them.

From the time I first noticed that it filled me with warmth as I twirled my fingers over its top, I felt I had a friend. I walked to and from school and noisily up and down the stairs in our house, carrying it with me, slightly ahead of me, sharing its confidence.

I was a beautiful boy, or so they said. If I stood in my school clothes in front of the mirror I did not see anything special. My haircut was awful, my ears stuck out like telephone receivers, my eyes, while blue, seemed to disappear entirely when I smiled. And yet when I stood in front of the same mirror naked, I danced at the sight of myself, incredibly and inexcusably male.

I had no desire to be beautiful or good. Somehow, I suspect because it did not come naturally, I longed to be bad. I wanted to misbehave, to prove to myself that I could stand the sudden loss of my family's affection. I wanted to do terrible, horrible things and then be excused simply because I was a boy and that's what boys do, especially boys without fathers. I had the secret desire to frighten others. But I was forever a pink-skinned child, with straight blond hair, new khaki pants, white socks, and brown shoes.

My only true fear was of men. Having grown up without fathers, brothers, or uncles, men were completely unfamiliar to me, their naked selves only accidentally seen in bathhouses or public restrooms. They lived behind extra long zippers, hidden, like something in a freak show you'd pay to see once and only once. Their ungraceful parts hung deeply down, buried in a weave of hair that wound itself denser as it got closer as if to protect the world from the sight of such a monster. As I grew older, I taught myself to enjoy what was frightening.

I never wore underwear. Inside my jeans, it lay naked, rubbing the blue denim white. I went out in the evenings to roam among men, to display myself, to parade, to hunt. I was what everyone wanted, white, clean, forever a boy. They wanted to ruin me as a kind of revenge. It was part of my image to look unavailable but the truth was anyone could have me. I liked ugly men. Grab your partner and do-si-do. Change partners. I kissed a million of them. I opened myself to them and them to me. I walked down the street nearly naked with it in the lead. It was pure love in the sense of loving oneself and loving the sensation.

I was alive, incredibly, joyously. Even in the grocery store or the laundromat, every time someone's eyes passed over me, holding me for a second, I felt a boost that sent me forward and made me capable of doing anything. Every hour held a sensuous moment, a romantic possibility. Each person who looked at me and smiled, cared for me. To be treasured by those who weren't related, to whom I meant nothing, was the highest form of a compliment.

Men, whose faces I didn't recognize, bent down to kiss me as I sat eating lunch in sidewalk cafes. I kissed them back and whispered, It was good seeing you. And when my lunch dates asked who that was, I simply smiled.

I felt celebrated. Every dream was a possibility. It was as though I would never be afraid again. I remember being happy.

I look down on it and begin to weep. I do not understand what has happened or why. I am sickened by myself, and yet cannot stand the sensation of being so revolted. It is me, I tell myself. It is me, as though familiarity should be a comfort.

I remember when the men I met were truly strangers; our private parts went off in search of each other like dogs on a leash sniffing each other while the owners look away. I remember still, after that, meeting a man, and looking at him, looking at him days and months in a row and each time loving him.

I feel like I should wear rubber gloves for fear of touching myself or someone else. I have never felt so dangerous. I am weeping and it frightens me.

A friend told me about a group of men who make each other feel better, more hopeful, good about their bodies.

I picture a room full of men, sitting on folding chairs. They begin as any sort of meeting that welcomes strangers; they go around the room, first names only. They talk a little bit, and then finally, as though the talking is the obligatory introductory prayer, the warning of what is to follow, the cue to begin the incantation, they slowly take off their clothing, sweaters and shoes first. They silently stand up, and drop their pants to the floor. The sight of a circle of naked men and folding chairs is exciting. Those who can, rise to the occasion and fire their poison jets into the air. It is wonderful. A great relief. They are saying something. They are angry. Men shuffle around in a circle doing it until they collapse. I imagine that one time someone died at a meeting. He came and he died. When he fell, the group used it as inspiration. They did it again, over him, and it was all so much better then.

I can no longer love. I cannot possess myself as I did before. I can never again possess it, as it possessed me.

I am in my apartment screaming at nothing. This is the most horrible thing that ever happened, I am furious. I deserve better than this. I am a good boy. Truly I am. I am sorry. I am so sorry.

I look down on it and it seems to look up at me. I want it to apologize for wanting the world, literally. I have the strongest desire to punish it, to whack it until it screams, beat it until it is bloody and runs off to hide, shaking in a corner, but I can't. I cannot turn my back so quickly, and besides it is already lying there pale and weak, as if it is dead.

I see sick men, friends that have shriveled into strangers, unwelcome in hospitals and at home. They can't think or breathe, and still as they go rattling towards death, it never loses an ounce, it lies fattened, untouched in the darkness between their legs. It is strikingly an ornament, a reminder of the past.

Should I ask for a divorce? A separation from myself on the grounds that this part of me that is more male than I alone could ever be has betrayed me. We no longer have anything in common except profound depression and disbelief. I have lost my best friend, my playmate from childhood, myself. I have lost what I loved most deeply. I wish to be compensated.

I let a napkin from the table fall across it, and then quickly whisk it away, *Voilà*, like I am doing a magic trick. I look down upon my lap as if expecting to see a bunch of flowers or a white rabbit in its place.

I remember the first man who unzipped my pants while I stood motionless, eyes turned down. I allowed myself to peek, to see it in his hand.

"It is a beautiful thing," he said, lifting it like a treasure and touching it gently.

I kick off my jeans and run from room to room. I look out onto the city that once seemed so big and has now shrunken so that it is no more than a garden surrounding my apartment. I stand naked in the window, my hands flat against the glass. My reflection is clear. There is no escaping myself. My lips press against the window. I am a beautiful boy. I feel the familiar warmth that rises when I am being taken in. In the apartment directly across from mine I see a man watching me, his hand upon himself. He seems wonderful through the glass, someone I could be with forever. He smiles. I slide the window open and lean towards the air. I am no longer safe, I step up onto the sill and spring forward into the night.

THE FIRST TIME

Marina Warner

Marina Warner (b. 1946) is a British writer of fiction, criticism and history. Her works include novels and short stories as well as studies of art, myths, symbols and fairytales. Her 1988 novel, *The Lost Father*, was shortlisted for the Man Booker Prize and she won the 2012 National Book Critics Circle Award for her non-fiction work, *Stranger Magic*. Warner was elected a Fellow of the Royal Society of Literature in 1984 and she was awarded a CBE in 2008.

The serpent had decided to diversify; the market economy demanded it. Jeans, soft drinks, bicycles and sunglasses had learned to present themselves in subtly different guises; so could he.

He took a training course in nutrition. In his first job (for he showed talent), he was issued with an instantly printed label identifying him as 'Lola – Trainee Customer Service Assistant', and he wangled himself a pitch on the Tropical Fruit stand in the Tropical Fruit promotion that was taking place in order to add a little cheer to the London winter.

To attract the customers' attention, the serpent now known as Lola was togged up in tropical splendour and he put on his deepest and brownest syrupy voice to match. There were OAPs with plastic shopping bags on wheels and hair in their noses; they tasted the little cubes of fragrant juicy this and that which Lola had cut up and flagged with their proper name and country of origin, but one said he would think about it, dear, and another made a face and said the stringy bits were too stringy. Lola wasn't sure the game was worth the candle in their case. She was after brighter prizes. The serpent in her liked fresh material; he hoped for a challenge. (Though pity, it would turn out after all, wasn't unknown to him.)

Then Lola spotted a candidate: a likely lass, a young one made just as she fancied, quite ready for pleasure, pleasure of every sort, a hard green bright slip of a girl, barely planted but taking root, and so she held out in her direction a nifty transparent plastic cup like a nurse's for measuring out dosages in hospital, with one of the tasty morsels toothpicked and labelled inside it, and urged her to eat. (She was speaking aloud in the new soft brown demerara voice, but under her breath she was cooing and hissing in another voice altogether which she hoped her young shopper would listen to, secretly. This was a trick the serpent had perfected over centuries of practice.)

'Come here, my little girly, I have just the thing for a cold day, bring some sunshine back into your life.

(I know what it's like, it's written all over you. He fucked you to death three days ago – oh, is it a whole week? – and you haven't heard from him since. Your face is pale, your brow is wan and you can't understand what you did wrong. Well, you can tell me all about it)

'There's nothing Lola your Trainee Customer Service Assistant can't provide. It's Tropical Fruit week – just move over this way – we have passion fruit and pawpaw (that's papaya by another name) and prickly pear and pitahaya and guava and tamarillo and phylaris and grenadilla. Not to mention passion fruit. Each one has been flown here from the lands of milk and honey where they grow naturally, as in the original garden of paradise, and they're full of just that milk and honey, I'm telling you, you can hear the palm trees bending in the breeze on the beach and the surf breaking in creamy froth on the sand and they reach the parts other things don't reach

(the tingly bits, the melting bits and rushes-to-the head and the rushes to places elsewhere than the head – well I shan't go on, but your troubles are at an end if you just come a little bit closer, so I can pick up the signals in your dear little fluttering heart, my sweet, and whisper in your ear)

'As I say, it's Tropical Fruit week and this is the Tropical Fruit stand! With a dozen different varieties of fruit from all over the world, many new, exciting and delicious flavours for you to sample, and

(let me add this under my breath so only you can hear – they all have different powers they can work wonders in all kinds of different ways – they're guaranteed to fix up your little problems before you can snap your fingers and say What the hell, and what the hell, I know all about that, I know the hell you're in, believe me.

And I also know – I do – how to stop it hurting, my dear little one)

'I should know, because I'm fresh from the Healthy Eating consultancy course in our company headquarters in Stanton St James, Gloucestershire. We were given an intensive fortnight of nutritional experience, and so there's nothing I can't tell you now about fruit–'

And the serpent, to his great joy, saw that the young girl was getting interested and coming closer, with her shopping list crumpled under one hand on the bar of the supermarket trolley and the other twiddling a strand of her hair near her chin, as she drew near to look at Lola's spread of little plastic cups with pieces of fruit in each one, so close that Lola could hear her thinking,

i was all clenched up cos i was scared it's not everyday i do it you know in fact i don't do it very often though looking at me you might think so and i like to make out i'm a one cos otherwise you look a bit of a wimp don't you i mean everyone else is doing it, aren't they? and my mother said keep smiling the men don't like scenes they don't like glooms if you want to drive a man away just keep that down at the mouth look on your face and the wind'll change men don't like a woman all down in the dumps who'd want to spend a minute with you it'd be like passing the time of day with a ghoul

And Lola took charge of the situation, it was her job to bring a little sunshine back into winter; pleasure was her speciality. So she began,

'Take mango for instance, now the instructions say, "Make sure the rind is rosy-yellow and slightly yielding to the touch – green mangoes are inedible." Just like it says there, on the label, a mango, when it's properly ripe and ready, is full and juicy and its sweetness runs all over your hands and gives off this deep rich scent –'

(I don't have to go on, do I? A good man is going to know that and if he don't know it, he's no good and you can drop him, my sweet, and find another one who understands these things. The first point you must get into your little head, sweetheart, is that if you were clenched up like you said it wasn't anybody's fault but his –)

i tried to be lighthearted and cheerful while it was going on but it kept getting to me all the same and making me sad, sex does that to you it lifts you up but it doesn't last it drops you down again from a great height and now i can't concentrate on anything cos i keep seeing him doing things to me and me doing them back i was trying to keep a brave face on it but i know i was disappointing not passionate like he knows it from other girls it wasn't new to him like it was to me he knows that i could sense it but i don't like the neighbours to hear anything cos when they're at it and i hear and mum is out and i'm alone it makes me feel funny

Lola carries on, talking over the girl's thoughts, which are coming across to her loud and clear. 'Take this guava for instance,' she tells her. 'It's in perfect condition. Sometimes when you pierce one of these fruits, they're not quite ripe yet. You have to wait for the ones that aren't ready, you can't rush them. But the ones that are overripe, gone soft and spongy, you have to throw those away ...'

(don't you worry any more, my little girly, you'll be fine. You're just lacking confidence, that's all it is, and you wanted to please him, when really you should just think how much pleasure there's in it for you. Never forget that, it's the first rule. My sweet little girly, you're a perfect little girly and he's a fool if I know men – and I do – forget him and find another one who'll appreciate you)

it's a bit shocking, really, i didn't expect such a mess, both of us leaking this and that, i did melt at first, stickiness afterwards he seemed to like it, he held on to me tight, he asked me if i cared for him and i said i did; and his heart was thumping and it seemed like a promise it was a promise, it must have been some kind of a promise ... but then nothing not another sight of him not a word what did I do wrong what can i do now

(when he comes back and he will you know he'll be round with his tongue hanging out you must be ready so come closer still – you are a sweet and tender pretty little girl, aren't you, yum yum, no wonder he liked you he's probably just frightened of coming back because your hold on him's too strong believe me, I know. You're at just that dangerous age, and your hair smells good, vanilla and grass and peach and a trace of sweat, that's good, very good –)

The young girl's head was very near Lola now, as she bent over the little measuring cups with their pink and yellow and crimson offerings, sniffing at this one and that one, daring, daring to taste one.

'Peaches don't count as Tropical but they have restorative powers too, I'm telling you, and now we can grow them all the year round, that's the wonder of modern agronomy – agronomy – the science of growing foods

(anyhow, darling, just any one of these Tropical Fruits will give him what he wants from you and then you'll have him in the palm of your hand. Try slipping him a fat cactus fruit, with the spines cut off, mind – or if you're ambitious, try pawpaw – papaya by another name as I was saying and it's no accident that this is papa-fare, ha ha. It's a fruit for daddy's girls, firm and slippery, yes!)

'and its juice makes an excellent meat tenderiser if you want to add it to a marinade or you can just open it and eat it all, yes, seeds and all – Or there's tamarillo here, it's full of rich pulp under the tight shiny skin and the flavour's sweet and sour when it's ripe, and has many culinary uses, in desserts as well as savoury dishes ... Eat it when the skin's turned a deep red, and the fruit's firm but yielding to gentle pressure ...'

(that's right, you start giggling, you'll be fine even if it's all over with him there'll soon be another one – I'm telling you, live for passion there's nothing better and that's the second rule and all men and women are fools who don't grasp it)

it began like that he said, Trust me, and then you open up first your mouth and his mouth and then, well ... sometimes i envy men, they know what other women are like, i wonder if i'm like the other ones, he must have had lots he felt like he knew what he was doing, i was a bit scared, he's older than me just two years but it makes a difference and he's got a reputation at school that's what made me interested in the first place so i bit down on my fears, other girls do it all the time i must get on with mum's shopping it might give that assistant ideas, my hanging around here maybe i should try one of her fruits she looks silly standing there in that tropical outfit with the headcloth and the fruit earrings dangling and the bangles over her surgical gloves she's using a little sharp knife with these funny knobbly and lumpy fruits she's egging on to Customers, the OAPs with their shopping bags on wheels and their nose hair sprouting, so now it's my turn and i point to one of the little plastic cups with the fruit inside on a toothpick and she's saying to me,

'Go on try, you're under no obligation to purchase – I don't even have the fruits here on my stand, you have to go to the fruit and veg. section and choose your own. We're here to educate the public, to raise the standards of nutrition and health in the households of this country, especially where there are children and young people, growing up

(like you, my dear, so silky and soft and lovely with just that whiff of unwashed ...)

'There's pitahaya for you too – firm as a pear and slightly perfumed, like rose petals – it's refreshing! Here, you can eat it like a dessert fruit, you peel it like this, lengthways, the rind comes off smoothly, it's related to the prickly pear but this one hasn't got any prickles. Or you can slice it into salads – add a dash of colour to your salad bowl, keep the winter at bay with Tropical Fruit from the parts of the world where frost can't reach and the sun always shines, scoop out the pink flesh and taste the sunshine!'

we didn't use anything it seemed mean to ask him to as if i thought he was diseased or something so now i don't know i could be pregnant – are you happy to be pregnant? the ads ask – i could be i suppose – i can feel something inside me it's like a letter y it's either a sperm wriggling or it's one of those cells they go on about on the telly reproducing itself all wrong and giving me aids

(now that was silly very silly you can't have the pleasure that's due to you, my girl, if you're careless, that's the third rule. But if you bend your ear I'll let you in on the way to have fun – never do that again, this time you'll be all right, I can tell, I can see and hear things other people can't and)

'There's nothing like fresh fruit to build up your immune system, clean out your insides, keep you healthy and lean and full of energy ...

(as I say, you're in luck this time but don't try anything like that again)

'... in these days of pollution and other problems – I mean we've all wised up to the devastation of the rain forests and their connection to ... well, I shan't talk about meat-eating because we still have a butcher's counter here – all free range, of course – but anyway what with acid rain and the hole in the ozone layer and the thinning of the oxygen supply and the little creepy-crawly things out of the tap in your water – you need Fruit! Fresh fruit, goes straight to the immune system and kick-starts it into a new life ...'

Eventually, the serpent was successful: his fresh, young, sad target dropped her mother's shopping list somewhere on the floor of the supermarket and forgot everything that was on it and came home instead with

1 mango
1 pitahaya
2 pawpaws
4 guavas
2 tamarillos
6 passion fruit
and 13p change

Her mother said, 'Where's the shopping I asked you to get?' And so her daughter told her about Lola, about the Tropical Fruit stand and Tropical Fruit week. She kept quiet, however, about some of the other matters that had passed between her and the sales assistant.

Her mother scolded, her mother railed: 'In my day, an apple a day kept the doctor away – now you have to have –' she picked up the guavas and the soft but firm mango and the tubular and prickle-free pitahaya and smooth and slippery pawpaw – 'What do you do with this stuff anyway?'

'I've brought the leaflet – look!'

'Apples were good enough for us, and they should be good enough for you. And when I write down a pound of apples on the shopping list I mean a pound of apples, I don't mean any of this fancy rubbish. Your generation doesn't understand the meaning of no – you just believe in self, self, self, you want mote, more, more. You think only of your own pleasure. You'll be the ruin of me. I don't know, I try to bring you up right ...'

'Plump and rounded or long and thin, it has a distinctive firmness of texture and delicacy of aroma ...' her daughter began, reading from the recipe leaflet provided, and she thought she heard her mother stifle a snort as she kept on with the Tropical Fruit week promotion package.

if he doesn't come back that lady was right i'll just find another one what she said made sense he thought he was something but was he anything to write home about anyhow i feel better about it already I'll go back to school and i'll just make out it meant nothing to me nothing and i don't care about him she was wicked she was strong i liked her

Lola was still at the stand, back in the shop, doing her patter, to other customers passing by:

'Guava, passion fruit, tamarillo! Let me just tell you exactly how you can put each one to good use –'

And meanwhile she was thinking,

(my little girly, you're young, you're inexperienced, but you'll soon know so much. You'll look back on this and you'll laugh or you won't even remember that you ever felt so pale and wan. In fact you might even look back and wish that you could feel something as sweet and real and true as this first-time pain you were feeling till I taught you the three principles of pleasure and set you on my famous primrose path)

The mother took the leaflet out of her daughter's hand and scanned it impatiently; and read:

> For a happy and healthy life!
> Take fresh fruit in season.
> Squeeze.

INSIDE INFORMATION

Nicola Barker

Nicola Barker (b. 1966) is a British novelist and short story writer. Her novel, *Wide Open*, won the IMPAC Dublin Literary Award in 2000, and another, *Darkmans,* was shortlisted for the Man Booker Prize in 2007.

Martha's social worker was under the impression that by getting herself pregnant, Martha was looking for an out from a life of crime. She couldn't have been more wrong.

'First thing I ever nicked,' Martha bragged, when her social worker was initially assigned to her, 'very first thing I ever stole was a packet of Lil-lets. I told the store detective I took them as a kind of protest. You pay 17½ per cent VAT on every single box. Men don't pay it on razors, you know, which is absolutely bloody typical.'

'But you stole other things, too, on that occasion, Martha.'

'Fags and a bottle of Scotch. So what?' she grinned. 'Pay VAT on those too, don't you?'

Martha's embryo was unhappy about its assignment to Martha. Early on, just after conception, it appealed to the higher body responsible for its selection and placement. This caused something of a scandal in the After-Life. The World-Soul was consulted – a democratic body of pinpricks of light, an enormous institution – which came, unusually enough, to a rapid decision.

'Tell the embryo,' they said, 'hard cheese.'

The embryo's social worker relayed this information through a system of vibrations – a language which embryos alone in the Living World can produce and receive. Martha felt these conversations only as tiny spasms and contractions.

Being pregnant was good, Martha decided, because store detectives were much more sympathetic when she got caught. Increasingly, they let her off with a caution after she blamed her bad behaviour on dodgy hormones.

The embryo's social worker reasoned with the embryo that all memories of the After-Life and feelings of uncertainty about placement were customarily eradicated during the trauma of birth. This was a useful expedient. 'Naturally,' he added, 'the nine-month wait is always difficult, especially if you've drawn the short straw in allocation terms, but at least by the time you've battled your way through the cervix, you won't remember a thing.'

The embryo replied, snappily, that it had never believed in the maxim that Ignorance is Bliss. But the social worker (a corgi in its previous incarnation) restated that the World-Soul's decision was final.

As a consequence, the embryo decided to take things into its own hands. It would communicate with Martha while it still had the chance and offer her, if not an incentive, at the very least a moral imperative.

Martha grew larger during a short stint in Wormwood Scrubs. She was seven months gone on her day of release. The embryo was now a well-formed foetus, and, if its penis was any indication, it was a boy. He calculated that he had, all things being well, eight weeks to change the course of Martha's life.

You see, the foetus was special. He had an advantage over other, similarly situated, disadvantaged foetuses. This foetus had Inside Information.

In the After-Life, after his sixth or seventh incarnation, the foetus had worked for a short spate as a troubleshooter for a large pharmaceutical company. During the course of his work and research, he had stumbled across something so enormous, something so terrible about the World-Soul, that he'd been compelled to keep this information to himself, for fear of retribution.

The rapidity of his assignment as Martha's future baby was, in part, he was convinced, an indication that the World-Soul was aware of his discoveries. His soul had been snatched and implanted in Martha's belly before he'd even had a chance to discuss the matter rationally. In the womb, however, the foetus had plenty of time to analyse his predicament. *It was a cover-up!* He was being gagged, brainwashed and railroaded into another life sentence on earth.

In prison, Martha had been put on a sensible diet and was unable to partake of the fags and the sherry and the Jaffa cakes which were her normal dietary staples. The foetus took this opportunity to consume as many vital calories and nutrients as possible. He grew at a considerable rate, exercised his knees, his feet, his elbows, ballooned out Martha's belly with nudges and pokes.

In his seventh month, on their return home, the foetus put his plan into action. He angled himself in Martha's womb, at just the right angle, and with his foot, gave the area behind Martha's belly button a hefty kick. On the outside, Martha's belly was already a considerable size. Her stomach was about as round as it could be, and her navel, which usually stuck inwards, had popped outwards, like a nipple.

By kicking the inside of her navel at just the correct angle, the foetus – using his Inside Information – had successfully popped open the lid of Martha's belly button like it was an old-fashioned pill-box.

Martha noticed that her belly button was ajar while she was taking a shower. She opened its lid and peered inside. She couldn't have been more surprised. Under her belly button was a small, neat zipper, constructed out of delicate bones. She turned off the shower, grabbed hold of the zipper and pulled it. It unzipped vertically, from the middle of her belly to the top. Inside she saw her foetus, floating in brine. 'Hello,' the foetus said. 'Could I have a quick word with you, please?'

'This is incredible!' Martha exclaimed, closing the zipper and opening it again. The foetus put out a restraining hand. 'If you'd just hang on a minute I could tell you how this was possible …'

'It's so weird!' Martha said, closing the zipper and getting dressed.

Martha went to Tesco's. She picked up the first three items that came to hand, unzipped her stomach and popped them inside. On her way out, she set off the alarms – the bar-codes activated them, even from deep inside her – but when she was searched and scrutinized and interrogated, no evidence could be found of her hidden booty. Martha told the security staff that she'd consider legal action if they continued to harass her in this way.

When she got home, Martha unpacked her womb. The foetus, squashed into a corner, squeezed up against a tin of Spam and a packet of sponge fingers, was intensely irritated by what he took to be Martha's unreasonable behaviour.

'You're not the only one who has a zip, you know,' he said. 'All pregnant women have them; it's only a question of finding out how to use them, from the outside, gaining the knowledge. But the World-Soul has kept this information hidden since the days of Genesis, when it took Adam's rib and reworked it into a zip with a pen-knife.'

'Shut it,' Martha said. 'I don't want to hear another peep from you until you're born.'

'But I'm trusting you,' the foetus yelled, 'with this information. It's my salvation!'

She zipped up.

Martha went shopping again. She shopped sloppily at first, indiscriminately, in newsagents, clothes shops, hardware stores, chemists. She picked up what she could and concealed it in her belly.

The foetus grew disillusioned. He re-opened negotiations with his social worker. 'Look,' he said, 'I know something about the World-Soul which I'm willing to divulge to my earth-parent Martha if you don't abort me straight away.'

'You're too big now,' the social worker said, fingering his letter of acceptance to the Rotary Club which preambled World-Soul membership. 'And anyway, it strikes me that Martha isn't much interested in what you have to say.'

'Do you honestly believe,' the foetus asked, 'that any woman on earth in her right mind would consider a natural birth if she knew that she could simply unzip?'

The social worker replied coldly: 'Women are not kangaroos, you cheeky little foetus. If the World-Soul has chosen to keep the zipper quiet then it will have had the best of reasons for doing so.'

'But if babies were unzipped and taken out when they're ready,' the foetus continued, 'then there would be no trauma, no memory loss. Fear of death would be a thing of the past. We could eradicate the misconception of a Vengeful God.'

'And all the world would go to hell,' the social worker said.

'How can you say that?'

The foetus waited for a reply, but none came.

Martha eventually sorted out her priorities. She shopped in Harrods and Selfridges and Liberty's. She became adept at slotting things of all conceivable shapes and sizes into her belly. Unfortunately, the foetus himself was growing quite large. After being unable to fit in a spice rack, Martha unzipped and addressed him directly. 'Is there any possibility,' she asked, 'that I might be able to take you out prematurely so that there'd be more room in there?'

The foetus stared back smugly. 'I'll come out,' he said firmly, 'when I'm good and ready.'

Before she could zip up, he added, 'And when I do come out, I'm going to give you the longest and most painful labour in Real-Life history. I'm going to come out sideways, doing the can-can.'

Martha's hand paused, momentarily, above the zipper. 'Promise to come out very quickly,' she said, 'and I'll nick you some baby clothes.'

The foetus snorted in a derisory fashion. 'Revolutionaries,' he said, 'don't wear baby clothes. Steal me a gun, though, and I'll fire it through your spleen.'

Martha zipped up quickly, shocked at this vindictive little bundle of vituperation she was unfortunate enough to be carrying. She smoked an entire packet of Marlboro in one sitting, and smirked, when she unzipped, just slightly, at the coughing which emerged.

The foetus decided that he had no option but to rely on his own natural wit and guile to foil both his mother and the forces of the After-Life. He began to secrete various items that Martha stole in private little nooks and crannies about her anatomy.

On the last night of his thirty-sixth week, he put his plan into action. In his arsenal: an indelible pen, a potato, a large piece of cotton from the hem of a dress, a thin piece of wire from the supports of a bra, all craftily reassembled. In the dead of night, while Martha was snoring, he gradually worked the zip open from the inside, and did what he had to do.

The following morning, blissfully unaware of the previous night's activities, Martha went out shopping to Marks and Spencer's. She picked up some Belgian chocolates and a bottle of port, took hold of her zipper and tried to open her belly. It wouldn't open. The zipper seemed smaller and more difficult to hold.

'That bastard,' she muttered, 'must be jamming it up from the inside.' She put down her booty and headed for the exit. On her way out of the shop, she set off the alarms.

'For Chrissakes!' she told the detective, 'I've got nothing on me!' And for once, she meant it.

Back home, Martha attacked her belly with a pair of nail scissors. But the zip wasn't merely jammed, it was meshing and merging and disappearing, fading like the tail end of a bruise. She was frazzled. She looked around for her cigarettes. She found her packet and opened it. The last couple had gone, and instead, inside, was a note.

> Martha, [the note said] *I have made good my escape, fully intact. I sewed a pillow into your belly. On the wall of your womb I've etched and inked an indelible bar-code. Thanks for the fags.*
> *Love, Baby.*

'But you can't do that!' Martha yelled. 'You don't have the technology!' She thought she heard a chuckle, behind her. She span around. On the floor, under the table, she saw a small lump of afterbirth, tied up into a neat parcel by an umbilical cord. She could smell a whiff of cigarette smoke. She thought she heard laughter, outside the door, down the hall. She listened intently, but heard nothing more.

DESIDERATUS

Penelope Fitzgerald

Penelope Fitzgerald (1916–2000) was a Man Booker Prize-winning British novelist, poet, essayist and biographer. In 2008, *The Times* included her in a list of the '50 Greatest British Writers Since 1945' and, in 2012, the *Observer* named her final novel, *The Blue Flower*, as one of 'The 10 Best Historical Novels'. A collection of Fitzgerald's short stories, *The Means of Escape*, and a volume of her non-fiction writings, *A House of Air*, were published posthumously.

Jack Digby's mother never gave him anything. Perhaps, as a poor woman, she had nothing to give, or perhaps she was not sure how to divide anything between the nine children. His godmother, Mrs Piercy, the poulterer's wife, did give him something, a keepsake, in the form of a gilt medal. The date on it was September the 12th, 1663, which happened to be Jack's birthday, although by the time she gave it him he was eleven years old. On the back there was the figure of an angel and a motto, *Desideratus*, which, perhaps didn't fit the case too well, since Mrs Digby could have done with fewer, rather than more, children. However, it had taken the godmother's fancy.

Jack thanked her, and she advised him to stow it away safely, out of reach of the other children. Jack was amazed that she should think anywhere was out of the reach of his little sisters. 'You should have had it earlier, when you were born,' said Mrs Piercy, 'but those were hard times.' Jack told her that he was very glad to have something of which he could say, This is my own, and she answered, though not with much conviction, that he mustn't set too much importance on earthly possessions.

He kept the medal with him always, only transferring it, as the year went by, from his summer to his winter breeches. But anything you carry about with you in your pocket you are bound to lose sooner or later. Jack had an errand to do in Hending, but there was nothing on the road that day, neither horse nor cart, no hope of cadging a lift, so after waiting for an hour or so he began to walk over by the hill path.

After about a mile the hill slopes away sharply towards Watching, which is not a village and never was, only a single great house standing among its outbuildings almost at the bottom of the valley. Jack stopped there for a while to look down at the smoke from the chimneys and to calculate, as anyone might have done, the number of dinners that were being cooked there that day.

If he dropped or lost his keepsake he did not know it at the time, for as is commonly the case he didn't miss it until he got home again. Then he went through his pockets, but the shining medal was gone and he could only repeat, 'I had it when I started out.' His brothers and sisters were of no help at all. They had seen nothing. What brother or sister likes being asked such questions?

The winter frosts began and at Michaelmas Jack had the day off school and thought, I had better try going that way again. He halted, as before, at the highest point, to look down at the great house and its chimneys, and then at the ice under his feet, for all the brooks, ponds, and runnels were frozen on every side of him, all hard as bone. In a little hole or depression just to the left hand of the path, something no bigger than a small puddle, but deep, and by now set thick with greenish ice as clear as glass, he saw, through the transparency of the ice, at the depth of perhaps twelve inches, the keepsake that Mrs Piercy had given him.

He had nothing in his hand to break the ice. Well then, Jack Digby, jump on it, but that got him nowhere, seeing that his wretched pair of boots was soaked right through. 'I'll wait until the ice has gone,' he thought. 'The season is turning, we'll get a thaw in a day or two.'

On the next Sunday, by which time the thaw had set in, he was up there again, and made straight for the little hole or declivity, and found nothing. It was empty, after that short time, of ice and even of water. And because the idea of recovering the keepsake had occupied his whole mind that day, the disappointment made him feel lost, like a stranger to the country. Then he noticed that there was an earthenware pipe laid straight down the side of the hill, by way of a drain, and that this must very likely have carried off the water from his hole, and everything in it. No mystery as to where it led, it joined another pipe with a wider bore, and so down, I suppose, to the stable-yards, thought Jack. His Desideratus had been washed down there, he was as sure of that now as if he'd seen it go.

Jack had never been anywhere near the house before, and did not care to knock at the great kitchen doors for fear of being taken for a beggar. The yards were empty. Either the horses had been taken out to work now that the ground was softer or else – which was hard to believe – there were no horses at Watching. He went back to the kitchen wing and tried knocking at a smallish side entrance. A man came out dressed in a black gown, and stood there peering and trembling.

'Why don't you take off your cap to me?' he asked.

Jack took it off, and held it behind his back, as though it belonged to someone else.

'That is better. Who do you think I am?'

'No offence, sir,' Jack replied, 'but you look like an old schoolmaster.'

'I am a schoolmaster, that is, I am tutor to this great house. If you have a question to ask, you may ask it of me.'

With one foot still on the step, Jack related the story of his godmother's keepsake.

'Very good,' said the tutor, 'you have told me enough. Now I am going to test your memory. You will agree that this is not only necessary, but just.'

'I can't see that it has anything to do with my matter,' said Jack.

'Oh, but you tell me that you dropped this-or-that in such-and-such a place, and in that way lost what had been given to you. How can I tell that you have truthfully remembered all this? You know that when I came to the door you did not remember to take your cap off.'

'But that—'

'You mean that was only lack of decent manners, and shows that you come from a family without self-respect. Now, let us test your memory. Do you know the Scriptures?'

Jack said that he did, and the tutor asked him what happened, in the fourth chapter of the Book of Job, to Eliphaz the Temanite, when a vision came to him in the depth of the night.

'A spirit passed before his face, sir, and the hair of his flesh stood up.'

'The hair of his flesh stood up,' the tutor repeated. 'And now, have they taught you any Latin?' Jack said that he knew the word that had been on his medal, and that it was *Desideratus*, meaning long wished-for.

'That is not an exact translation,' said the tutor. Jack thought, he talks for talking's sake.

'Have you many to teach, sir, in this house?' he asked, but the tutor half closed his eyes and said, 'None, none at all. God has not blessed Mr Jonas or either of his late wives with children. Mr Jonas has not multiplied.'

If that is so, Jack thought, this schoolmaster can't have much work to do. But now at last here was somebody with more sense, a house-keeperish-looking woman, come to see why the side-door was open and letting cold air into the passages. 'What does the boy want?' she asked.

'He says he is in search of something that belongs to him.'

'You might have told him to come in, then, and given him a glass of wine in the kitchen,' she said, less out of kindness than to put the tutor in his place. 'He would have been glad of that, I daresay.'

Jack told her at once that at home they never touched wine. 'That's a pity,' said the housekeeper. 'Children who are too strictly prohibited generally turn out drunkards.' There's no pleasing these people, Jack thought.

His whole story had to be gone through again, and then again when they got among the servants in one of the pantries. Yet really there was almost nothing to tell, the only remarkable point being that he should have seen the keepsake clearly through almost a foot of ice. Still nothing was said as to its being found in any of the yards or ponds.

Among all the to-ing and fro-ing another servant came in, the man who attended on the master, Mr Jonas, himself. His arrival caused a kind of disquiet, as though he were a foreigner. The master, he said, had got word that there was a farm-boy, or a schoolboy, in the kitchens, come for something that he thought was his property.

'But all this is not for Mr Jonas's notice,' cried the tutor. 'It's a story of child's stuff, a child's mischance, not at all fitting for him to look into.'

The man repeated that the master wanted to see the boy.

The other part of the house, the greater part, where Mr Jonas lived, was much quieter, the abode of gentry. In the main hall Mr Jonas himself stood with his back to the fire. Jack had never before been alone or dreamed of being alone with such a person. What a pickle, he thought, my godmother, Mrs Piercy, has brought me into.

'I daresay you would rather have a sum of money,' said Mr Jonas, not loudly, 'than whatever it is that you have lost.'

Jack was seized by a painful doubt. To be honest, if it was to be a large sum of money, he would rather have that than anything. But Mr Jonas went on, 'However, you had better understand me more precisely. Come with me.' And he led the way, without even looking round to see that he was followed.

At the foot of the wide staircase Jack called out from behind, 'I think, sir, I won't go any further. What I lost can't be here.'

'It's poor-spirited to say "I won't go any further",' said Mr Jonas.

Was it possible that on these dark upper floors no one else was living, no one was sleeping? They were like a sepulchre, or a barn at the end of winter. Through the tall passages, over uneven floors, Mr Jonas, walking ahead, carried a candle in its candlestick in each hand, the flames pointing straight upwards. I am very far from home, thought Jack. Then, padding along behind the master of the house, and still twisting his cap in one hand, he saw in dismay that the candle flames were blown over to the left, and a door was open to the right.

'Am I to go in there with you, sir?'

'Are you afraid to go into a room?'

Inside it was dark and in fact the room probably never got much light, the window was so high up. There was a glazed jug and basin, which reflected the candles, and a large bed which had no curtains, or perhaps, in spite of the cold, they had been drawn back. There seemed to be neither quilts nor bedding, but a boy was lying there in a linen gown, with his back towards Jack, who saw that he had red or reddish hair, much the same colour as his own.

'You may go near him, and see him more clearly,' Mr Jonas said. 'His arm is hanging down, what do you make of that?'

'I think it hangs oddly, sir.'

He remembered what the tutor had told him, that Mr Jonas had not multiplied his kind, and asked, 'What is his name, sir?' To this he got no answer.

Mr Jonas gestured to him to move nearer, and said, 'You may take his hand.'

'No, sir, I can't do that.'

'Why not? You must touch other children very often. Wherever you live, you must sleep the Lord knows how many in a bed.'

'Only three in a bed at ours,' Jack muttered.

'Then touch, touch.'

'No, sir, no, I can't touch the skin of him!'

Mr Jonas set down his candles, went to the bed, took the boy's wrist and turned it, so that the fingers opened. From the open fingers he took Jack's medal, and gave it back to him.

'Was it warm or cold?' they asked him later. Jack told them that it was cold. Cold as ice? Perhaps not quite as cold as that.

'You have what you came for,' said Mr Jonas. 'You have taken back what was yours. Note that I don't deny it was yours.'

He did not move again, but stood looking down at the whiteish heap on the bed. Jack was more afraid of staying than going, although he had no idea how to find his way through the house, and was lucky to come upon a back staircase which ended not where he had come in but among the sculleries, where he managed to draw back the double bolts and get out into the fresh air.

'Did the boy move,' they asked him, 'when the medal was taken away from him?' But by this time Jack was making up the answers as he went along. He preferred, on the whole, not to think much about Watching. It struck him, though, that he had been through a good deal to get back his godmother's present, and he quite often wondered how much money Mr Jonas would in fact have offered him, if he had had the sense to accept it. Anyone who has ever been poor – even if not as poor as Jack Digby – will sympathize with him in this matter.

AGNES OF IOWA

Lorrie Moore

Lorrie Moore (b. 1957) is an American writer, known for her humorous and poignant short stories. Moore has published three collections: *Self-Help*, *Like Life*, and *Birds of America*, which was a *New York Times* bestseller. She has contributed to the *Paris Review* and the *New Yorker* and published three novels, one of which, *A Gate at the Stairs*, was shortlisted for the 2010 Orange Prize.

Her mother had given her the name Agnes, believing that a good-looking woman was even more striking when her name was a homely one. Her mother was named Cyrena, and was beautiful to match, but had always imagined her life would have been more interesting, that she herself would have had a more dramatic, arresting effect on the world and not ended up in Cassell, Iowa, if she had been named Enid or Hagar or Maude. And so she named her first daughter Agnes, and when Agnes turned out not to be attractive at all, but puffy and prone to a rash between her eyebrows, her hair a flat and bilious hue, her mother backpedaled and named her second daughter Linnea Elise (who turned out to be a lovely, sleepy child with excellent bones, a sweet, full mouth, and a rubbery mole above her lip that later in life could be removed without difficulty, everyone was sure).

Agnes herself had always been a bit at odds with her name. There was a brief period in her life, in her mid-twenties, when she had tried to pass it off as French – she had put in the accent grave and encouraged people to call her "On-yez." This was when she was living in New York City, and often getting together with her cousin, a painter who took her to parties in TriBeCa lofts or at beach houses or at mansions on lakes upstate. She would meet a lot of not very bright rich people who found the pronunciation of her name intriguing. It was the rest of her they were unclear on. "On-yez, where are you from, dear?" asked a black-slacked, frosted-haired woman whose skin was papery and melanomic with suntan. "Originally." She eyed Agnes's outfit as if it might be what in fact it was: a couple of blue things purchased in a department store in Cedar Rapids.

"Where am I from?" Agnes said it softly. "Iowa." She had a tendency not to speak up.

"*Where?*" The woman scowled, bewildered.

"Iowa," Agnes repeated loudly.

The woman in black touched Agnes's wrist and leaned in confidentially. She moved her mouth in a concerned and exaggerated way, like a facial exercise. "No, dear," she said. "*Here* we say O-*hi*-o."

That had been in Agnes's mishmash decade, after college. She had lived improvisationally then, getting this job or that, in restaurants or offices, taking a class or two, not thinking too far ahead, negotiating the precariousness and subway flus and scrimping for an occasional manicure or a play. Such a life required much exaggerated self-esteem. It engaged gross quantities of hope and despair and set them wildly side by side, like a Third World country of the heart. Her days grew messy with contradictions. When she went for walks, for her health, cinders would spot her cheeks and soot would settle in the furled leaf of each ear. Her shoes became unspeakable. Her blouses darkened in a breeze, and a blast of bus exhaust might linger in her hair for hours. Finally, her old asthma returned and, with a hacking, incessant cough, she gave up. "I feel like I've got five years to live," she told people, "so I'm moving back to Iowa so that it'll feel like fifty."

When she packed up to leave, she knew she was saying good-bye to something important, which was not that bad, in a way, because it meant that at least you had said hello to it to begin with, which most people in Cassell, Iowa, she felt, could not claim to have done.

A year and a half later, she married a boyish man twelve years her senior, a Cassell realtor named Joe, and together they bought a house on a little street called Birch Court. She taught a night class at the Arts Hall and did volunteer work on the Transportation Commission in town. It was life like a glass of water: half-empty, half-full. Half-full. Half-full. Oops: half-empty. Over the years, she and Joe tried to have a baby, but one night at dinner, looking at each other in a lonely way over the meat loaf, they realized with shock that they probably never would. Nonetheless, after six years, they still tried, vandalizing what romance was left in their marriage.

"Honey," she would whisper at night when he was reading under the reading lamp and she had already put her book away and curled toward him, wanting to place the red scarf over the lamp shade but knowing it would annoy him and so not doing it. "Do you want to make love? It would be a good time of month."

And Joe would groan. Or he would yawn. Or he would already be asleep. Once, after a long, hard day, he said, "I'm sorry, Agnes. I guess I'm just not in the mood."

She grew exasperated. "You think *I'm* in the mood?" she said. "I don't want to do this any more than you do," and he looked at her in a disgusted way, and it was two weeks after that that they had the sad dawning over the meat loaf.

At the Arts Hall, formerly the Grange Hall, Agnes taught the Great Books class, but taught it loosely, with cookies. She let her students turn in poems and plays and stories that they themselves had written; she let them use the class as their own little time to be creative. Someone once even brought in a sculpture: an electric one with blinking lights.

After class, she sometimes met with students individually. She recommended things for them to write about or read or consider in their next project. She smiled and asked if things were going well in their lives. She took an interest.

"You should be stricter," said Willard Stauffbacher, the head of the Instruction Department; he was a short, balding musician who liked to tape on his door pictures of famous people he thought he looked like. Every third Monday, he conducted the monthly departmental meeting – aptly named, Agnes liked to joke, since she did indeed depart mental. "Just because it's a night course doesn't mean you shouldn't impart standards," Stauffbacher said in a scolding way. "If it's piffle, use the word *piffle*. If it's meaningless, write *meaningless* across the top of every page." He had once taught at an elementary school and once at a prison. "I feel like I do all the real work around here," he added. He had posted near his office a sign that read RULES FOR THE MUSIC ROOM:

I will stay in my seat unless [sic] permission to move.
I will sit up straight.
I will listen to directions.
I will not bother my neighbor.
I will not talk when Mr. Stauffbacher is talking.
I will be polite to others.
I will sing as well as I can.

Agnes stayed after one night with Christa, the only black student in her class. She liked Christa a lot – Christa was smart and funny, and Agnes sometimes liked to stay after with her to chat. Tonight, Agnes had decided to talk Christa out of writing about vampires all the time.

"Why don't you write about that thing you told me about that time?" Agnes suggested.

Christa looked at her skeptically. "What thing?"

"The time in your childhood, during the Chicago riots, walking with your mother through the police barricades."

"Man, I lived that. Why should I want to write about it?"

Agnes sighed. Maybe Christa had a point. "It's just that I'm no help to you with this vampire stuff," Agnes said. "It's formulaic, genre fiction."

"You would be of more help to me with *my childhood*?"

"Well, with more serious stories, yes."

Christa stood up, perturbed. She grabbed her vampire story back. "You with all your Alice Walker and Zora Hurston. I'm just not interested in that anymore. I've done that already. I read those books years ago."

"Christa, please don't be annoyed." *Please do not talk when Mr. Stauffbacher is talking.*

"You've got this agenda for me."

"Really, I don't at all," said Agnes. "It's just that – you know what it is? It's that I'm just sick of these vampires. They're so roaming and repeating."

"If you were black, what you're saying might have a different spin. But the fact is, you're not," Christa said, and picked up her coat and strode out – though ten seconds later, she gamely stuck her head back in and said, "See you next week."

"We need a visiting writer who's black," Agnes said in the next depart mental meeting. "We've never had one." They were looking at their budget, and the readings this year were pitted against Dance Instruction, a program headed up by a redhead named Evergreen.

"The Joffrey is just so much central casting," said Evergreen, apropos of nothing. As a vacuum cleaner can start to pull up the actual thread of a carpet, her brains had been sucked dry by too much yoga. No one paid much attention to her.

"Perhaps we can get Harold Raferson in Chicago," Agnes suggested.

"We've already got somebody for the visiting writer slot," said Stauffbacher coyly. "An Afrikaner from Johannesburg."

"What?" said Agnes. Was he serious? Even Evergreen barked out a laugh.

"W. S. Beyerbach. The university's bringing him in. We pay our five hundred dollars and we get him out here for a day and a half."

"Who?" asked Evergreen.

"This has already been decided?" asked Agnes.

"Yup." Stauffbacher looked accusingly at Agnes. "I've done a lot of work to arrange for this. *I've* done all the work!"

"Do less," said Evergreen.

When Agnes first met Joe, they'd fallen madly upon each other. They'd kissed in restaurants; they'd groped, under coats, at the movies. At his little house, they'd made love on the porch, or the landing of the staircase, against the wall in the hall by the door to the attic, filled with too much desire to make their way to a real room.

Now they struggled self-consciously for atmosphere, something they'd never needed before. She prepared the bedroom carefully. She played quiet music and concentrated. She lit candles – as if she were in church, praying for the deceased. She donned a filmy gown. She took hot baths and entered the bedroom in nothing but a towel, a wild fishlike creature of moist, perfumed heat. In the nightstand drawer she still kept the charts a doctor once told her to keep, still placed an X on any date she and Joe actually had sex. But she could never show these to her doctor; not now. It pained Agnes to see them. She and Joe looked like worse than bad shots. She and Joe looked like idiots. She and Joe looked dead.

Frantic candlelight flickered on the ceiling like a puppet show. While she waited for Joe to come out of the bathroom, Agnes lay back on the bed and thought about her week, the bloody politics of it, how she was not very good at politics. Once, before he was elected, she had gone to a rally for Bill Clinton, but when he was late and had kept the crowd waiting for over an hour, and when the sun got hot and bees began landing on people's heads, when everyone's feet hurt and tiny children began to cry and a state assemblyman stepped forward to announce that Clinton had stopped at a Dairy Queen in Des Moines and that was why he was late – Dairy Queen! – she had grown angry and resentful and apolitical in her own sweet-starved thirst and she'd joined in with some other people who had started to chant, "Do us a favor, tell us the flavor."

Through college she had been a feminist – basically: she shaved her legs, *but just not often enough*, she liked to say. She signed day-care petitions, and petitions for Planned Parenthood. And although she had never been very aggressive with men, she felt strongly that she knew the difference between feminism and Sadie Hawkins Day – which some people, she believed, did not.

"Agnes, are we out of toothpaste or is this it – oh, okay, I see."

And once, in New York, she had quixotically organized the ladies' room line at the Brooks Atkinson Theatre. Because the play was going to start any minute and the line was still twenty women long, she had gotten six women to walk across the lobby with her to the men's room. "Everybody out of there?" she'd called in timidly, allowing the men to finish up first, which took a while, especially with other men coming up impatiently and cutting ahead in line. Later, at intermission, she saw how it should have been done. Two elderly black women, with greater expertise in civil rights, stepped very confidently into the men's room and called out, "Don't mind us, boys. We're coming on in. Don't mind us."

"Are you okay?" asked Joe, smiling. He was already beside her. He smelled sweet, of soap and minty teeth, like a child.

"I think so," she said, and turned toward him in the bordello light of their room. He had never acquired the look of maturity anchored in sorrow that burnished so many men's faces. His own sadness in life – a childhood of beatings, a dying mother – was like quicksand, and he had to stay away from it entirely. He permitted no unhappy memories spoken aloud. He stuck with the same mild cheerfulness he'd honed successfully as a boy, and it made him seem fatuous – even, she knew, to himself. Probably it hurt his business a little.

"Your mind's wandering," he said, letting his own eyes close.

"I know." She yawned, moved her legs onto his for warmth, and in this way, with the candles burning into their tins, she and Joe fell asleep.

The spring arrived cool and humid. Bulbs cracked and sprouted, shot up their green periscopes, and on April first, the Arts Hall offered a joke lecture by T. S. Eliot, visiting scholar. "The Cruelest Month," it was called. "You don't find that funny?" asked Stauffbacher.

April fourth was the reception for W. S. Beyerbach. There was to be a dinner afterward, and then Beyerbach was to visit Agnes's Great Books class. She had assigned his second collection of sonnets, spare and elegant things with sighing and diaphanous politics. The next afternoon there was to be a reading.

Agnes had not been invited to the dinner, and when she asked about this, in a mildly forlorn way, Stauffbacher shrugged, as if it were totally out of his hands. I'm a *published poet*, Agnes wanted to say. She *had* published a poem once – in *The Gizzard Review*, but still!

"It was Edie Canterton's list," Stauffbacher said. "I had nothing to do with it."

She went to the reception anyway, annoyed, and when she planted herself like a splayed and storm-torn tree near the cheese, she could actually feel the crackers she was eating forming a bad paste in her mouth and she became afraid to smile. When she finally introduced herself to W. S. Beyerbach, she stumbled on her own name and actually pronounced it "On-yez."

"On-yez," repeated Beyerbach in a quiet Englishy voice. Condescending, she thought. His hair was blond and white, like a palomino, and his eyes were blue and scornful as mints. She could see he was a withheld man; although some might say *shy*, she decided it was *withheld*: a lack of generosity. Passive-aggressive. It was causing the people around him to squirm and blurt things nervously. He would simply nod, the smile on his face faint and vaguely pharmaceutical. Everything about him was tight and coiled as a door spring. From living in *that country*, thought Agnes. How could he live in that country?

Stauffbacher was trying to talk heartily about the mayor. Something about his old progressive ideas, and the forthcoming convention center. Agnes thought of her own meetings on the Transportation Commission, of the mayor's leash law for cats, of his new squadron of meter maids and bicycle police, of a councilman the mayor once slugged in a bar. "Now, of course, the mayor's become a fascist," said Agnes in a voice that sounded strangely loud, bright with anger.

Silence fell all around. Edie Canterton stopped stirring the punch. Agnes looked about her. "Oh," she said. "Are we not supposed to use *that word* in this room?" Beyerbach's expression went blank. Agnes's face burned in confusion.

Stauffbacher appeared pained, then stricken. "More cheese, anyone?" he asked, holding up the silver tray.

After everyone left for dinner, she went by herself to the Dunk 'N Dine across the street. She ordered the California BLT and a cup of coffee, and looked over Beyerbach's work again: dozens of images of broken, rotten bodies, of the body's mutinies and betrayals, of the body's strange housekeeping and illicit pets. At the front of the book was a dedication – *To DFB (1970–1989)*. Who could that be? A political activist, maybe. Perhaps it was the young woman referred to often in his poems, "a woman who had thrown aside the unseasonal dress of hope," only to look for it again "in the blood-blooming shrubs." Perhaps if Agnes got a chance, she would ask him. Why not? A book was a public thing, and its dedication was part of it. If it was too personal a question for him, *tough*. She would find the right time, she decided. She paid the check, put on her jacket, and crossed the street to the Arts Hall, to meet Beyerbach by the front door. She would wait for the moment, then seize it.

He was already at the front door when she arrived. He greeted her with a stiff smile and a soft "Hello, Onyez," an accent that made her own voice ring coarse and country-western.

She smiled and then blurted, "I have a question to ask you." To her own ears, she sounded like Johnny Cash.

Beyerbach said nothing, only held the door open for her and then followed her into the building.

She continued as they stepped slowly up the stairs. "May I ask to whom your book is dedicated?"

At the top of the stairs, they turned left down the long corridor. She could feel his steely reserve, his lip-biting, his shyness no doubt garbed and rationalized with snobbery, but so much snobbery to handle all that shyness, he could not possibly be a meaningful critic of his country. She was angry with him. *How can you live in that country?* she again wanted to say, although she remembered when someone had once said that to her – a Danish man on Agnes's senior trip abroad to Copenhagen. It had been during the Vietnam War and the man had stared meanly, righteously. "The United States – how can you live in that country?" the man had asked. Agnes had shrugged. "A lot of my stuff is there," she'd said, and it was then that she first felt all the dark love and shame that came from the pure accident of home, the deep and arbitrary place that happened to be yours.

"It's dedicated to my son," Beyerbach said finally.

He would not look at her, but stared straight ahead along the corridor floor. Now Agnes's shoes sounded very loud.

"You lost a son," she said.

"Yes," he said. He looked away, at the passing wall, past Stauffbacher's bulletin board, past the men's room, the women's room, some sternness in him broken, and when he turned back, she could see his eyes filling with water, his face a plethora, reddened with unbearable pressure.

"I'm so sorry," Agnes said.

Side by side now, their footsteps echoed down the corridor toward her classroom; all the anxieties she felt with this mournfully quiet man now mimicked the anxieties of love. What should she say? It must be the most unendurable thing to lose a child. Shouldn't he say something of this? It was his turn to say something.

But he would not. And when they finally reached her classroom, she turned to him in the doorway and, taking a package from her purse, said simply, in a reassuring way, "We always have cookies in class."

Now he beamed at her with such relief that she knew she had for once said the right thing. It filled her with affection for him. Perhaps, she thought, that was where affection began: in an unlikely phrase, in a moment of someone's having unexpectedly but at last said the right thing. *We always have cookies in class.*

She introdnced him with a bit of flourish and biography. Positions held, universities attended. The students raised their hands and asked him about apartheid, about shantytowns and homelands, and he answered succinctly, after long sniffs and pauses, only once referring to a question as "unanswerably fey," causing the student to squirm and fish around in her purse for something, nothing, Kleenex perhaps. Beyerbach did not seem to notice. He went on, spoke of censorship, how a person must work hard not to internalize a government's program of censorship, since that is what a government would like best, for *you* to do it *yourself*, and how he was not sure he had not succumbed. Afterward, a few students stayed and shook his hand, formally, awkwardly, then left. Christa was the last. She, too, shook his hand and then started chatting amiably. They knew someone in common – Harold Raferson in Chicago! – and as Agnes quickly wiped the seminar table to clear it of cookie crumbs, she tried to listen, but couldn't really hear. She made a small pile of crumbs and swept them into one hand.

"Good night," sang out Christa when she left.

"Good night, Christa," said Agnes, brushing the crumbs into the wastebasket.

Now she stood with Beyerbach in the empty classroom. "Thank you so much," she said in a hushed way. "I'm sure they all got quite a lot out of that. I'm very sure they did."

He said nothing, but smiled at her gently.

She shifted her weight from one leg to the other. "Would you like to go somewhere and get a drink?" she asked. She was standing close to him, looking up into his face. He was tall, she saw now. His shoulders weren't broad, but he had a youthful straightness to his carriage. She briefly touched his sleeve. His suitcoat was corduroy and bore the faint odor of clove. This was the first time in her life that she had ever asked a man out for a drink.

He made no move to step away from her, but actually seemed to lean toward her a bit. She could feel his dry breath, see up close the variously hued spokes of his irises, the grays and yellows in the blue. There was a sprinkling of small freckles near his hairline. He smiled, then looked at the clock on the wall. "I would love to, really, but I have to get back to the hotel to make a phone call at ten-fifteen." He looked a little disappointed – not a lot, thought Agnes, but certainly a little.

"Oh, well," she said. She flicked off the lights and in the dark he carefully helped her on with her jacket. They stepped out of the room and walked together in silence, back down the corridor to the front entrance of the hall. Outside on the steps, the night was balmy and scented with rain. "Will you be all right walking back to your hotel?" she asked. "Or—"

"Oh, yes, thank you. It's just around the corner."

"Right. That's right. Well, my car's parked way over there. So I guess I'll see you tomorrow afternoon at your reading."

"Yes," he said, "I shall look forward to that."

"Yes," she said. "So shall I."

The reading was in the large meeting room at the Arts Hall and was from the sonnet book she had already read, but it was nice to hear the poems again, in his hushed, pained tenor. She sat in the back row, her green raincoat sprawled beneath her on the seat like a leaf. She leaned forward, onto the seat ahead of her, her back an angled stem, her chin on double fists, and she listened like that for some time. At one point, she closed her eyes, but the image of him before her, standing straight as a compass needle, remained caught there beneath her lids, like a burn or a speck or a message from the mind.

Afterward, moving away from the lectern, Beyerbach spotted her and waved, but Stauffbacher, like a tugboat with a task, took his arm and steered him elsewhere, over toward the side table with the little plastic cups of warm Pepsi. We are both men, the gesture seemed to say. We both have *back* in our names. Agnes put on her green coat. She went over toward the Pepsi table and stood. She drank a warm Pepsi, then placed the empty cup back on the table. Beyerbach finally turned toward her and smiled familiarly. She thrust out her hand. "It was a wonderful reading," she said. "I'm very glad I got the chance to meet you." She gripped his long, slender palm and locked thumbs. She could feel the bones in him.

"Thank you," he said. He looked at her coat in a worried way. "You're leaving?"

She looked down at her coat. "I'm afraid I have to get going home." She wasn't sure whether she really had to or not. But she'd put on the coat, and it now seemed an awkward thing to take off.

"Oh," he murmured, gazing at her intently. "Well, all best wishes to you, Onyez."

"Excuse me?" There was some clattering near the lectern.

"All best to you," he said, something retreating in his expression.

Stauffbacher suddenly appeared at her side, scowling at her green coat, as if it were incomprehensible.

"Yes," said Agnes, stepping backward, then forward again to shake Beyerbach's hand once more; it was a beautiful hand, like an old and expensive piece of wood. "Same to you," she said. Then she turned and fled.

For several nights, she did not sleep well. She placed her face directly into her pillow, then turned it some for air, then flipped over to her back and opened her eyes, staring at the far end of the room through the stark angle of the door frame toward the tiny light from the bathroom which illumined the hallway, faintly, as if someone had just been there.

For several days, she thought perhaps he might have left her a note with the secretary, or that he might send her one from an airport somewhere. She thought that the inadequacy of their good-bye would haunt him, too, and that he might send her a postcard as elaboration.

But he did not. Briefly, she thought about writing him a letter, on Arts Hall stationery, which for money reasons was no longer the stationery, but photocopies of the stationery. She knew he had flown to the West Coast, then off to Tokyo, then Sydney, then back to Johannesburg, and if she posted it now, perhaps he would receive it when he arrived. She could tell him once more how interesting it had been to meet him. She could enclose her poem from *The Gizzard Review*. She had read in the newspaper an article about bereavement – and if she were her own mother, she could send him that, too.

Thank God, thank God, she was not her mother.

Spring settled firmly in Cassell with a spate of thundershowers. The perennials – the myrtle and grape hyacinths – blossomed around town in a kind of civic blue, and the warming air brought forth an occasional mosquito or fly. The Transportation Commission meetings were dreary and long, too often held over the dinner hour, and when Agnes got home, she would replay them for Joe, sometimes bursting into tears over the parts about the photoradar or the widening interstate.

When her mother called, Agnes got off the phone fast. When her sister called about her mother, Agnes got off the phone even faster. Joe rubbed her shoulders and spoke to her of carports, of curb appeal, of asbestos-wrapped pipes.

At the Arts Hall, she taught and fretted and continued to receive the usual memos from the secretary, written on the usual scrap paper – except that the scrap paper this time, for a while, consisted of the extra posters for the Beyerbach reading. She would get a long disquisition on policies and procedures concerning summer registration, and she would turn it over and there would be his face – sad and pompous in the photograph. She would get a simple phone message – "Your husband called. Please phone him at the office" – and on the back would be the ripped center of Beyerbach's nose, one minty eye, an elbowish chin. Eventually, there were no more, and the scrap paper moved on to old contest announcements, grant deadlines, Easter concert notices.

*

At night, she and Joe did yoga to a yoga show on TV. It was part of their effort not to become their parents, though marriage, they knew, held that hazard. The functional disenchantment, the sweet habit of each other had begun to put lines around her mouth, lines that looked like quotation marks – as if everything she said had already been said before. Sometimes their old cat, Madeline, a fat and pampered calico reaping the benefits of life with a childless couple during their childbearing years, came and plopped herself down with them, between them. She was accustomed to much nestling and appreciation and drips from the faucet, though sometimes she would vanish outside, and they would not see her for days, only to spy her later, in the yard, dirty and matted, chomping a vole or eating old snow.

For Memorial Day weekend, Agnes flew with Joe to New York, to show him the city for the first time. "A place," she said, "where if you're not white and not born there, you're not automatically a story." She had grown annoyed with Iowa, the pathetic thirdhand manner in which the large issues and conversations of the world were encountered, the oblique and tired way history situated itself there – if ever. She longed to be a citizen of the globe!

They roller-skated in Central Park. They looked in the Lord & Taylor windows. They went to the Jofffey. They went to a hair salon on Fifty-seventh Street and there she had her hair dyed red. They sat in the window booths of coffee shops and got coffee refills and ate pie.

"So much seems the same," she said to Joe. "When I lived here, everyone was hustling for money. The rich were. The poor were. But everyone tried hard to be funny. Everywhere you went – a store, a manicure place – someone was telling a joke. A *good* one." She remembered it had made any given day seem bearable, that impulse toward a joke. It had been a determined sort of humor, an intensity mirroring the intensity of the city, and it seemed to embrace and alleviate the hard sadness of people having used one another and marred the earth the way they had. "It was like brains having sex. It was like every brain was a sex maniac." She looked down at her pie. "People really worked at it, the laughing," she said. "People need to laugh."

"They do," said Joe. He took a swig of coffee, his lips out over the cup in a fleshy flower. He was afraid she might cry – she was getting that look again – and if she did, he would feel guilty and lost and sorry for her that her life was not here anymore, but in a far and boring place now with him. He set the cup down and tried to smile. "They sure do," he said. And he looked out the window at the rickety taxis, the oystery garbage and tubercular air, seven pounds of chicken giblets dumped on the curb in front of the restaurant where they were. He turned back to her and made the face of a clown.

"What are you doing?" she asked.

"It's a clown face."

"What do you mean, 'a clown face?'" Someone behind her was singing "I Love New York," and for the first time she noticed the strange irresolution of the tune.

"A regular clown face is what I mean."

"It didn't look like that."

"No? What did it look like?"

"You want me to do the face?"

"Yeah, do the face."

She looked at Joe. Every arrangement in life carried with it the sadness, the sentimental shadow, of its not being something else, but only itself: she attempted the face – a look of such monstrous emptiness and stupidity that Joe burst out in a howling sort of laughter, like a dog, and then so did she, air exploding through her nose in a snort, her head thrown forward, then back, then forward again, setting loose a fit of coughing.

"Are you okay?" asked Joe, and she nodded. Out of politeness, he looked away, outside, where it had suddenly started to rain. Across the street, two people had planted themselves under the window ledge of a Gap store, trying to stay dry, waiting out the downpour, their figures dark and scarecrowish against the lit window display. When he turned back to his wife – his sad young wife – to point this out to her, to show her what was funny to a man firmly in the grip of middle age, she was still bent sideways in her seat, so that her face fell below the line of the table, and he could only see the curve of her heaving back, the fuzzy penumbra of her thin spring sweater, and the garish top of her bright, new, and terrible hair.

CURVED IS THE LINE OF BEAUTY

Hilary Mantel

Hilary Mantel (b. 1952) is a British writer who has twice been awarded the Man Booker Prize. She won her first Booker for the 2009 novel, *Wolf Hall*, and her second, in 2012, for *Bring Up the Bodies*, making her the first woman to receive the award twice. She has published twelve novels and one collection of short stories, *Learning to Talk*.

When I was in my middle childhood my contemporaries started to disappear. They vanished from the mill-town conurbations and the Manchester back-streets, and their bodies – some of them, anyway – were found buried on the moors. I was born on the edge of this burial ground, and had been instructed in its ways. Moorland punished those who were in the wrong place at the wrong time. It killed those who were stupid and those who were unprepared. Ramblers from the city, feckless boys with bobble hats, would walk for days in circles, till they died of exposure. The rescue parties would be baffled by dank fogs, which crept over the landscape like sheets drawn over corpses. Moorland was featureless except for its own swell and eddy, its slow waves of landscape rising and falling, its knolls, streams and bridle paths which ran between nowhere and nowhere; its wetness underfoot, its scaly patches of late snow, and the tossing inland squall that was its typical climate. Even in mild weather its air was wandering, miasmic, like memories that no one owns. When raw drizzle and fog invaded the streets of the peripheral settlements, it was easy to feel that if you stepped out of your family house, your street, your village, you were making a risky move; one mistake, and you would be lost.

The other way of being lost, when I was a child, was by being damned. Damned to hell that is, for all eternity. This could happen very easily if you were a Catholic child in the 1950s. If the speeding driver caught you at the wrong moment – let us say, at the midpoint between monthly confessions – then your dried-up soul could snap from your body like a dead twig. Our school was situated handily, so as to increase the risk, between two bends in the road. Last-moment repentance is possible, and stress was placed on it. You might be saved, if, in your final welter of mashed bones and gore, you remembered the correct formula. So it was really all a matter of timing. I didn't think it might be a matter of mercy. Mercy was a theory that I had not seen in operation. I had only seen how those who wielded power extracted maximum advantage from every situation. The politics of the playground and classroom are as instructive as those of the parade ground and the Senate. I understood that, as Thucydides would later tell me, 'the strong exact what they can, and the weak yield what they must'.

Accordingly, if the strong said, 'We are going to Birmingham,' to Birmingham you must go. We were going to make a visit, my mother said. To whom, I asked; because we had never done this before. To a family we had not met, she said, a family we did not yet know. In the days after the announcement I said the word 'family' many times to myself, its crumbly soft sound like a rusk in milk, and I carried its scent with me, the human warmth of chequered blankets and the yeast smell of babies' heads.

In the week before the visit, I went over in my mind the circumstances that surrounded it. I challenged myself with a few contradictions and puzzles which these circumstances threw up. I analysed who *we* might be, we who were going to make the visit: because that was not a constant or a simple matter.

The night before the visit I was sent to bed at eight – even though it was the holidays and Saturday next day. I opened the sash window and leaned out into the dusk, waiting till a lonely string of street lights blossomed, far over the fields, under the upland shadow. There was a sweet grassy fragrance, a haze in the twilight; *Dr Kildare's* Friday-night theme tune floated out from a hundred TV sets, from a hundred open windows, up the hill, across the reservoir, over the moors; and as I fell asleep I saw the medics in their frozen poses, fixed, solemn and glazed, like heroes on the curve of an antique jar.

I once read of a jar on which this verse was engraved:

> Straight is the line of duty;
> Curved is the line of beauty.
> Follow the straight line; thou shalt see
> The curved line ever follow thee.

At five o'clock, a shout roused me from my dreams. I went downstairs in my blue spotted pyjamas to wash in hot water from the kettle, and I saw the outline of my face, puffy, in the light like grey linen tacked to the summer window. I had never been so far from home; even my mother had never, she said, been so far. I was excited and excitement made me sneeze. My mother stood in the kitchen in the first uncertain shaft of sun, making sandwiches with cold bacon and wrapping them silently, sacramentally, in greaseproof paper.

We were going in Jack's car, which stood the whole night, these last few months, at the kerb outside our house. It was a small grey car, like a jelly mould, out of which a giant might turn a foul jelly of profanity and grease. The car's character was idle, vicious and sneaky. If it had been a pony you would have shot it. Its engine spat and steamed, its underparts rattled; it wanted brake shoes and new exhausts. It jibbed at hills and sputtered to a halt on bends. It ate oil, and when it wanted a new tyre there were rows about having no money, and there was slamming the door so hard that the glass of the kitchen cupboard rattled in its grooves.

The car brought out the worst in everybody who saw it. It was one of the first cars on the street, and the neighbours, in their mistaken way, envied it. Already sneerers and ill-wishers of ours, they were driven to further spite when they saw us trooping out to the kerb carrying all the rugs and kettles and camping stoves and raincoats and wellington boots that we took with us for a day at the seaside or the zoo.

There were five of *us*, now. Me and my mother; two biting, snarling, pinching little boys; Jack. My father did not go on our trips. Though he still slept in the house – the room down the corridor, the one with the ghost – he kept to his own timetables and routines, his Friday jazz club, and his solitary sessions of syncopation, picking at the piano, late weekend afternoons, with a remote gaze. This had not always been his way of life. He had once taken me to the library. He had taken me out with my fishing net. He had taught me card games and how to read a racecard; it might not have been a suitable accomplishment for an eight-year-old, but any skill at all was a grace in our dumb old world.

But those days were now lost to me. Jack had come to stay with us. At first he was just a visitor and then without transition he seemed to be always there. He never carried in a bag, or unpacked clothes; he just came complete as he was. After his day's work he would drive up in the evil car, and when he came up the steps and through the front door, my father would melt away to his shadowy evening pursuits. Jack had a brown skin and muscles beneath his shirt. He was your definition of a man, if a man was what caused alarm and shattered the peace.

To amuse me, while my mother combed the tangles out of my hair, he told me the story of David and Goliath. It was not a success. He tried his hardest – as I tried also – to batten down my shrieks. As he spoke his voice slid in and out of the London intonations with which he had been born; his brown eyes flickered, caramel and small, the whites jaundiced. He made the voice of Goliath, but – to my mind – he was lacking in the David department.

After a long half-hour, the combing was over. My vast weight of hair studded to my skull with steel clips, I pitched exhausted from the kitchen chair. Jack stood up, equally exhausted, I suppose; he would not have known how often this needed to happen. He liked children, or imagined he did. But (owing to recent events and my cast of mind) I was not exactly a child, and he himself was a very young man, too inexperienced to navigate through the situation in which he had placed himself, and he was always on the edge, under pressure, chippy and excitable and quick to take offence. I was afraid of his flaring temper and his irrationality: he argued with brute objects, kicked out at iron and wood, cursed the fire when it wouldn't light. I flinched at the sound of his voice, but I tried to keep the flinch inwards.

When I look back now I find in myself – in so far as I can name what I find – a faint stir of fellow feeling that is on the way to pity.

It was Jack's quickness of temper, and his passion for the underdog, that was the cause of our trip to Birmingham. We were going to see a friend of his, who was from Africa. You will remember that we have barely reached the year 1962, and I had never seen anyone from Africa, except in photographs, but the prospect in itself was less amazing to me than the knowledge that Jack had a friend. I thought friends were for children. My mother seemed to think that you grew out of them. Adults did not have friends. They had relatives. Only relatives came to your house. Neighbours might come, of course. But not to our house. My mother was now the subject of scandal and did not go out. We were all the subject of scandal, but some of us had to. I had to go to school, for instance. It was the law.

It was six in the morning when we bundled into the car, the two little boys dropped sleep-stunned beside me on to the red leather of the back seat. In those days it took a very long time to get anywhere. There were no motorways to speak of. Fingerposts were still employed, and we did not seem to have the use of a map. Because my mother did not know left from right, she would cry 'That way, that way!' whenever she saw a sign and happened to read it. The car would swerve off in any old direction and Jack would start cursing and she would shout back. Our journeys usually found us bogged in the sand at Southport, or broken down by the drystone wall of some Derbyshire beauty spot, the lid of the vile spitting engine propped open, my mother giving advice from the wound-down window: fearful advice, which went on till Jack danced with rage on the roadway or on the uncertain sand, his voice piping in imitation of a female shriek; and she, heaving up the last rags of self-control, heaving them into her arms like some dying diva's bouquet, would drop her voice an octave and claim, 'I don't talk like that.'

But on this particular day, when we were going to Birmingham, we didn't get lost at all. It seemed a miracle. At the blossoming hour of ten o'clock, the weather still fine, we ate our sandwiches, and I remember that first sustaining bite of salted fat, sealing itself in a plug to the hard palate: the sip of Nescafé to wash it down, poured steaming from the flask. In some town we stopped for petrol. That too passed without incident.

I rehearsed, in my mind, the reason behind the visit. The man from Africa, the friend, was not now but had once been a workmate of Jack. And they had spoken. And his name was Jacob. My mother had told me, don't say 'Jacob is black', say 'Jacob is coloured'.

What, coloured? I said. What, striped? Like the towel which, at that very moment, was hanging to dry before the fire? I stared at it; the stripes had run together to a patchy violet-grey. I felt it; the fibres were stiff as dried grass. Black, my mother said, is not the term polite people use. And stop mauling that towel!

So now, the friend, Jacob. He had been, at one time, living in Manchester, working with Jack. He had married a white girl. They had gone to get lodgings. At every door they had been turned away. No room at the inn. Though Eva was expecting. Especially because she was expecting. Even the stable door was bolted, it was barred against them, NO COLOUREDS, the signs said.

Oh, merrie England! At least people could spell in those days. They didn't write NO COLOURED'S or 'NO' COLOUREDS. That's about all you can say for it.

So: Jacob unfolded to Jack this predicament of his: no house, the insulting notices, the pregnant Eva. Jack, quickly taking fire, wrote a letter to a tabloid newspaper. The newspaper, quick to spot a cause, took fire also. There was naming and shaming; there was a campaign. Letters were written and questions were asked. The next thing you knew, Jacob had moved to Birmingham, to a new job. There was a house now, and a baby, indeed two. Better days were here. But Jacob would never forget how Jack had taken up the cudgels. That, my mother said, was the phrase he had used.

David and Goliath, I thought. My scalp prickled, and I felt steel pins cold against it. Last night had been too busy for the combing. My hair fell smoothly down my back, but hidden above the nape of my neck there was a secret pad of fuzziness which, if slept on for a second night, would require a howling hour to unknot.

The house of Jacob was built of brick in a quiet colour of brown, with a white-painted gate and a tree in a tub outside. One huge window stared out at a grass verge, with a sapling; and the road curved away, lined with similar houses, each in their own square of garden. We stepped out of the heat of the car and stood jelly-legged on the verge. Behind the plate glass was a stir of movement, and Jacob opened the front door to us, his face breaking into a smile. He was a tall slender man, and I liked the contrast of his white shirt with the soft sheen of his skin. I tried hard not to say, even to think, the term that is not the one polite people use. Jacob, I said to myself, is quite a dark lavender, verging on purple on an overcast day.

Eva came out from behind him. She had a compensatory pallor, and when she reached out, vaguely patting at my little brothers, she did it with fingers like rolled dough. Well, well, the adults said. And, this is all very nice. Lovely, Eva. And fitted carpets. Yes, said Eva. And would you like to go and spend a penny? I didn't know this phrase. Wash your hands, my mother said. Eva said, run upstairs, poppet.

At the top of the stairs there was a bathroom, not an arrangement I had reason to take for granted. Eva ushered me into it, smiling, and clicked the door behind her. Standing at the basin and watching myself in the mirror, I washed my hands carefully with Camay soap. Maybe I was dehydrated from the journey, for I didn't seem to need to do anything else. I hummed to myself, 'You'll look a little lovelier ... each day ... with fabulous *Camay*.' I didn't look around much. Already I could hear them on the stairs, shouting that it was their turn. I dried carefully between my fingers with the towel behind the door. There was a bolt on this door and I thought for a moment of bolting myself in. But a familiar pounding began, a head-butting, a thudding and a giggling, and I opened the door so that my brothers fell in at it and I went downstairs to do the rest of the day.

Everything had been fine, till the last hour of the journey. 'Not long to go,' my mother had said, and suddenly swivelled in her seat. She watched us, silent, her neck craning. Then she said, 'When we are visiting Jacob, don't say "Jack". It's not suitable. I want you to say,' and here she began to struggle with words, '"Daddy ... Daddy Jack".'

Her head, once more, faced front. Studying the line of her cheek, I thought she looked sick. It had been a most unconvincing performance. I was almost embarrassed for her. 'Is this just for today?' I asked. My voice came out cold. She didn't answer.

When I got back into the downstairs room they were parading Eva's children, a toddler and a baby, and remarking that it was funny how it came out, so you had one butter-coloured and one bluish, and Jacob was saying, too, that it was funny how it came out and you couldn't ever tell, really, it was probably beyond the scope of science as we know it today. The sound of a pan rocking on the gas jet came from the kitchen, and there was a burst of wet steam, and some clanking; Eva said, carrots, can't take your eye off them. Wiping her hands on her apron, she made for the door and melted into the steam. My eyes followed her. Jacob smiled and said, so how is the man who took up the cudgels?

We children ate in the kitchen – my family, that is, because the two babies sat in their own high chairs by Eva and sucked gloop from a spoon. There was a little red table with a hinged flap, and Eva propped the back door open so that the sunlight from the garden came in. We had vast pale slices of roast pork, and gravy that was beige and so thick it kept the shape of the knife. Probably if I am honest about what I remember, I think it is the fudge texture of this gravy that stays in my mind, better even than the afternoon's choking panic, the tears and prayers that were now only an hour or so away.

After our dinner Tabby came. She was not a cat but a girl, and the niece of Jacob. Enquiries were made of me: did I like to draw? Tabby had brought a large bag with her, and from it she withdrew sheets of rough coloured paper and a whole set of coloured pencils, double-ended. She gave me a quick, modest smile, and a flicker of her eyes. We settled down in a corner, and began to make each other's portrait.

Out in the garden the little boys grubbed up worms, shrieked, rolled the lawn with each other and laid about with their fists. I thought that the two coloured babies, now snorting in milky sleep, would be doing the same thing before long. When one of the boys fetched the other a harder clout than usual, the victim would howl, 'Jack! Jack!'

My mother stood looking over the garden. 'That's a lovely shrub, Eva,' she said. I could see her through the angle made by the open door of the kitchen; her high-heeled sandals planted squarely on the lino. She was smaller than I had thought, when I saw her beside the floury bulk of Eva, and her eyes were resting on something further than the shrub: on the day when she would leave the moorland village behind her, and have a shrub of her own. I bent my head over the paper and attempted the blurred line of Tabby's cheek, the angle of neck to chin. The curve of flesh, its soft bloom, eluded me; I lolled my pencil point softly against the paper, feeling I wanted to roll it in cream, or in something vegetable-soft but tensile, like the fallen petal of a rose. I had already noticed, with interest, that Tabby's crayons were sharpened down in a similar pattern to the ones I had at home. She had little use for gravy colour and still less for bl***k. Almost as unpopular was the double-ended crayon in morbid mauve/dark pink. Most popular with her was gold/green: as with me. On those days when I was tired of crayoning, and started to play that the crayons were soldiers, I had to imagine that gold/green was a drummer boy, so short was he.

On the rough paper, my pencil snagged; at once, my reverie was interrupted. I took in a breath. I bit my lip. I felt my heart begin to beat: an obscure insult, trailing like the smell of old vegetable water, seemed to hang in the air. This paper is for kids, I thought; it's for babies who don't know how to draw. My fingers gripped the crayon. I held it like a dagger. My hand clenched around it. At my toppest speed, I began to execute cartoon men, with straight jointless limbs, and brown 'O's for heads, with wide grinning mouths, jug ears; petty Goliaths with slatted mouths, with five fingerbones splaying from their wrists.

Tabby looked up. Shh, shh … she said; as if soothing me.

I drew children rolling in the grass, children made of two circles with a third 'O' for their bawling mouths.

Jacob came in, laughing, talking to Jack over his shoulder, '… so I tell him, if you want a trained draughtsman for £6 a week, man, you can whistle for him!'

I thought, I won't call Jack anything, I won't give him a name. I'll nod my head in his direction so they'll know who I mean. I'll even point to him, though polite people don't point. Daddy Jack! *Daddy Jack!* They can whistle for him!

Jacob stood over us, smiling softly. The crisp turn of his collar, the top button released, disclosed his velvet, quite dark-coloured throat. 'Two nice girls,' he said. 'What have we here?' He picked up my paper. 'Talent!' he said. 'Did you do this, honey, by yourself?' He was looking at the cartoon men, not my portrait of Tabby, those tentative strokes in the corner of the page; not at the tilt of her jaw, like a note in music. 'Hey, Jack,' he said, 'now this is good, I can't believe it at her young age.' I whispered, 'I am nine,' as if I wanted to alert him to the true state of affairs. Jacob waved the paper around, delighted. 'I could well say this is a prodigy,' he said. I turned my face away. It seemed indecent to look at him. In that one moment it seemed to me that the world was blighted, and that every adult throat bubbled, like a garbage pail in August, with the syrup of rotting lies.

I see them, now, from the car window, children any day, on any road; children going somewhere, disconnected from the routes of adult intent. You see them in twos or threes, in unlikely combinations, sometimes a pair with a little one tagging along, sometimes a boy with two girls. They carry, it might be, a plastic bag with something secret inside, or a stick or box, but no obvious plaything; sometimes a ratty dog processes behind them. Their faces are intent and their missions hidden from adult eyes; they have a geography of their own, urban or rural, that has nothing to do with the milestones and markers that adults use. The country through which they move is older, more intimate than ours. They have their private knowledge of it. You do not expect this knowledge to fail.

There was no need to ask if we were best friends, me and Tabby, as we walked the narrow muddy path by the water. Perhaps it was a canal, but a canal was not a thing I'd seen, and it seemed to me more like a placid inland stream, silver-grey in colour, tideless though not motionless, fringed by sedge and tall grasses. My fingers were safely held in the pad of Tabby's palm, and there was a curve of light on the narrow, coffee-coloured back of her hand. She was a head taller than me, willowy, cool to the touch, even at the hot end of this hot afternoon. She was ten and a quarter years old, she said; lightly, almost as if it were something to shrug away. In her free hand she held a paper bag, and in this bag – which she had taken from her satchel, her eyes modestly downcast – were ripe plums.

They were – in their perfect dumpling under my fingertips, in their cold purple blush – so fleshy that to notch your teeth against their skin seemed like becoming a teatime cannibal, a vampire for a day. I carried my plum in my palm, caressing it, rolling it like a dispossessed eye, and feeling it grow warm from the heat of my skin. We strolled, so, abstinent; till Tabby pulled at my hand, stopped me, and turned me towards her, as if she wanted a witness. She clenched her hand. She rolled the dark fruit in her fist, her eyes on mine. She raised her fist to her sepia mouth. Her small teeth plunged into ripe flesh. Juice ran down her chin. Casually, she wiped it. She turned her face full to mine, and for the first time I saw her frank smile, her lips parted, the gap between her front teeth. She flipped my wrist lightly, with the back of her fingers; I felt the sting of her nails. 'Let's go on the wrecks,' she said.

It meant we must scramble through a fence. Through a gap there. I knew it was illicit. I knew no would be said: but then what, this afternoon, did I care for no? Under the wire, through the snag of it, the gap already widened by the hands of forerunners, some of whom must have worn double-thickness woollen double-knit mittens to muffle the scratch against their flesh. Once through the wire, Tabby went, 'Whoop!'

Then soon she was bouncing, dancing in the realm of the dead cars. They were above our head to the height of three. Her hands reached out to slap at their rusting door-sills and wings. If there had been glass in their windows, it was strewn now at our feet. Scrapes of car paint showed, fawn, banana, a degraded scarlet. I was giddy, and punched my fingers at metals: it crumbled, I was through it. For that moment only I may have laughed; but I do not think so.

She led me on the paths to the heart of the wrecks. We play here, she said, and towed me on. We stopped for a plum each. We laughed. 'Are you too young to write a letter?' she asked. I did not answer. 'Have you heard of penfriends? I have one already.'

All around us, the scrapyard showed its bones. The wrecks stood clear now, stack on stack, against a declining yellow light. When I looked up they seemed to foreshorten, these carcasses, and bear down on me; gaping windows where faces once looked out, engine cavities where the air was blue, treadless tyres, wheel arches gaping, boots unsprung and empty of bags, unravelling springs where seats had been; and some wrecks were warped, reduced as if by fire, bl∗∗kened. We walked, sombre, cheeks bulging, down the paths between. When we had penetrated many rows in, by blind corners, by the swerves enforced on us by the squishy corrosion of the sliding piles, I wanted to ask, why do you play here and who do you mean by *we*, can I be one of your friends or will you forget me, and also can we go now please?

Tabby ducked out of sight, around some rotting heap. I heard her giggle. 'Got you!' I said. 'Yes!' She ducked, shying away, but my plum stone hit her square on the temple, and as it touched her flesh I tasted the seducing poison which, if you crack a plum stone, your tongue can feel. Then Tabby broke into a trot, and I chased her: when she skidded to a halt, her flat brown sandals making brakes for her, I stopped too, and glanced up, and saw we had come to a place where I could hardly see the sky. Have a plum, she said She held the bag out. I am lost, she said. We are, we are, lost. I'm afraid to say.

What came next I cannot, you understand, describe in clock-time. I have never been lost since, not utterly lost, without the sanctuary of sense; without the reasonable hope that I will and can and deserve to be saved. But for that next buried hour, which seemed like a day, and a day with fading light, we ran like rabbits: pile to pile, scrap to scrap, the wrecks towering, as we went deeper, for twenty feet above our heads. I could not blame her. I did not. But I did not see how I could help us either.

If it had been the moors, some ancestral virtue would have propelled me, I felt, towards the metalled road, towards a stream bed or cloud that would have conveyed me, soaked and beaten, towards the A57, towards the sanctuary of some stranger's car; and the wet inner breath of that vehicle would have felt to me, whoever owned it, like the wet protective breathing of the belly of the whale. But here, there was nothing alive. There was nothing I could do, for there was nothing natural. The metal stretched, friable, bl***k, against evening light. We shall have to live on plums for ever, I thought. For I had the sense to realise that the only incursion here would be from the wreckers' ball. No flesh would be salvaged here; there would be no rescue team. When Tabby reached for my hand, her fingertips were cold as ball-bearings. Once, she heard people calling. Men's voices. She said she did. I heard only distant, formless shouts. They are calling our names, she said. Uncle Jacob, Daddy Jack. They are calling for us.

She began to move, for the first time, in a purposive direction. 'Uncle Jacob!' she called. In her eyes was that shifty light of unconviction that I had seen on my mother's face – could it be only this morning? 'Uncle Jacob!' She paused in her calling, respectful, so I could call in my turn. But I did not call. I would not, or I could not? A scalding pair of tears popped into my eyes. To know that I lived, I touched the knotted mass of hair, the secret above my nape: my fingers rubbed and rubbed it, round and round. If I survived, it would have to be combed out, with torture. This seemed to militate against life; and then I felt, for the first time and not the last, that death at least is straightforward. Tabby called, 'Uncle Jacob!' She stopped, her breath tight and short, and held out to me the last plum stone, the kernel, sucked clear of flesh.

I took it without disgust from her hand. Tabby's troubled eyes looked at it. It sat in my palm, a shrivelled brain from some small animal. Tabby leaned forward. She was still breathing hard. The edge of her littlest nail picked at the convolutions. She put her hand against her ribs. She said, 'It is like the map of the world.'

There was an interval of praying. I will not disguise it. It was she who raised the prospect. 'I know a prayer,' she said. I waited. 'Little Jesus, meek and mild ...'

I said, 'What's the good of praying to a baby?'

She threw her head back. Her nostrils flared. Prayers began to run out of her. 'Now I lay me down, to sleep,

– I pray the Lord my soul to keep'

Stop, I said.

'If I should die before I wake—'

My fist, before I even knew it, clipped her across the mouth.

After a time, she raised her hand there. A fingertip trembled against the corner of her lip, the crushed flesh like velvet. She crept her lip downwards, so that for a moment the inner membrane showed, dark and bruised. There was no blood.

I said, 'Aren't you going to cry?'

She said, 'Are you?'

I couldn't say, I never cry. It was not true. She knew it. She said softly, it is all right if you want to cry. You're a Catholic, aren't you? Don't you know a Catholic prayer?

Hail Mary, I said. She said, teach it me. And I could see why: because night was falling: because the sun lay in angry streaks across farther peaks of the junkyard. 'Don't you have a watch?' she whispered. 'I have one it is Timex, but it is at home, in my bedroom.' I said, I have a watch it is Westclox, but I am not allowed to wind it, it is only to be wound by Jack. I wanted to say, and often he is tired, it is late, my watch is winding down, it is stopping but I dare not ask, and when next day it's stopped there's bellowing, only I can do a bleeding thing in this bleeding house. (Door slam.)

There is a certain prayer which never fails. It is to St Bernard; or by him, I was never quite clear. Remember oh most loving Virgin Mary, that it is a thing *unheard of* that anyone *ever* beseeched thy aid, craved thy intercession or implored thy help and was left forsaken. I thought that I had it, close enough – they might not be the exact words but could a few errors matter, when you were kicking at the very gate of the Immaculate herself? I was ready to implore, ready to crave: and this prayer, I knew, was the best and most powerful prayer ever invented. It was a clear declaration that heaven must help you, or go to hell! It was a taunt, a challenge, to Holy Mary, Mother of God. Get it fixed! Do it now! It is a thing *unheard* of! But just as I was about to begin, I realised I must not say it after all. Because if it didn't work …

The strength seemed to drain away then, from my arms and legs. I sat down, in the deep shadows of the wrecks, when all the indications were that we should keep climbing. I wasn't about to take a bet on St Bernard's prayer, and live my whole life knowing it was useless. My life might be long, it might be very long. I must have thought there were worse circumstances, in which I'd need to deal this final card from my sleeve.

'Climb!' said Tabby. I climbed. I knew – did she? – that the rust might crumble beneath us and drop us into the heart of the wrecks. Climb, she said, and I did: each step tested, so that I learned the resistance of rotting metal, the play and the give beneath my feet, the pathetic cough and wheeze of it, its abandonment and mineral despair. Tabby climbed. Her feet scurried, light, skipping, the soles of her sandals skittering and scratching like rats. And then, like stout Cortez, she stopped, pointed, and stared. 'The woodpiles!' I gazed upwards into her face. She swayed and teetered, six feet above me. Evening breeze whipped her skirt around her stick legs. 'The woodpiles!' Her face opened like a flower.

What she said meant nothing to me, but I understood the message. We are out! she cried. Her arm beckoned me. Come on, come on! She was shouting down to me, but I was crying too hard to hear. I worked myself up beside her: crab arms, crab legs, two steps sideways for every step forward. She reached down and scooped at my arm, catching at my clothes, pulling, hauling me up beside her. I shook myself free. I pulled out the stretched sleeve of my cardigan, eased the shape into the wool, and slid it back past my wrist. I saw the light on the still body of water, and the small muddy path that had brought us there.

*

'Well, you girls,' Jacob said, 'don't you know we came calling? Didn't you hear us?'

Well, suppose I did, I thought, Suppose she was right. I can just hear myself, can't you, bawling, here, Daddy Jack, here I am! Come and save me, Daddy Jack!

It was seven o'clock. They had been composing sandwiches and Jacob had been for ice cream and wafers. Though missed, we had never been a crisis. The main point was that we should be there for the right food at the right time.

The little boys slept on the way home, and I suppose so did I. The next day, next week, next months are lost to me. It startles me now that I can't imagine how I said goodbye to Tabby, and that I can't even remember at what point in the evening she melted away, her crayons in her satchel and her memories in her head. Somehow, with good fortune on our side for once, my family must have rolled home; and it would be another few years before we ventured so far again.

The fear of being lost comes low these days on the scale of fears I have to live with. I try not to think about my soul, lost or not (though it must be thirty years since my last confession), and I don't generally have to resort to that covert shuffle whereby some women turn the map upside down to count off the road junctions. They say that females can't read maps and never know where they are, but in the year 2000 the Ordnance Survey appointed its first woman director, so I suppose that particular slander loses its force. I married a man who casts a professional eye on the lie of the land, and would prefer me to direct with reference to tumuli, stream beds and ancient monuments. But a finger tracing the major routes is enough for me, and I just say nervously, 'We are about two miles from our turn-off or maybe, of course, we are not.' Because they are always tearing up the contour lines, ploughing under the map, playing hell with the cartography that last year you were sold as *le dernier cri*.

As for the moorland landscape, I know now that I have left it far behind. Even those pinching little boys in the back seat share my appreciation of wild-flower verges and lush arable acres. It is possible, I imagine, to build a home on firm ground, a home with long views. I don't know what became of Jacob and his family: did I hear they went home to Africa? Of Tabby, I never heard again. But in recent years, since Jack has been wandering in the country of the dead, I see again his brown skin, his roving caramel eyes, his fretting rage against power and its abuses: and I think perhaps that he was lost all his life, and looking for a house of justice, a place of safety to take him in.

In the short term, though, we continued to live in one of those houses where there was never any money, and doors were slammed hard. One day the glass did spring out of the kitchen cupboard, at the mere touch of my fingertips. At once I threw up my hands, to protect my eyes. Between my fingers, for some years, you could see the delicate scars, like the ghosts of lace gloves, that the cuts left behind.

FATHER, FATHER

Susan Hill

Susan Hill (b. 1942) is a British author, best known for her novel *The Woman in Black,* which was adapted into a long-running stage show in London's West End. She won the Somerset Maugham Award in 1971 for *I'm the King of the Castle*, and was awarded a CBE in 2012.

'I never realised,' Nita said, standing beside the washbasin rinsing out a tooth glass. Kay was turning a face flannel over and over between her hands, quite pointlessly.

'Dying. Do you mean about dying?'

'That. Yes.'

They were silent, contemplating it, the truth sinking in at last with the speaking of the word. In the room across the landing their mother was dying.

'I really meant Father.'

Naturally they had always seemed happy. Theirs had been the closest of families for thirty-seven years, Raymond and Elinor, Nita and Kay the two little girls. People used to point them out: 'The happy family.'

So they had taken it for granted that he loved her, as they loved her, fiercely and full of pride in her charm and her warmth and her skill, loved her more than they loved him, if they had ever had to choose. Not that they did not love their father. But he was a man, and that itself set him outside their magic ring. They simply did not know him. Not as they knew one another, and knew her.

'But not this.'

Not this desperate, choking, terrified devotion, this anguish by her bed, this distraught clinging. This was a love they could not recognise and did not know how to deal with – and even, in a way, resented. And so they fussed over him, his refusal to eat, his red eyes, the flesh withering on his frame; they took him endless cups of tea, coffee, hot water with lemon, but otherwise could not face his anguished, embarrassing love, and the fear on his face, his openness to grief.

The end was agony, though perhaps it was more so for them, for their mother seemed unaware of it all now. She had slipped down out of reach.

It lasted for hours. There was a false alarm. The doctor came. Next she rallied, and even seemed about to wake briefly, before drowning again.

They had both gone to sleep, Nita on the sewing-room sofa under a quilt, Kay in the kitchen rocking chair, slumped awkwardly across her arm. But some change woke them and they both went into the hall, looking at one another in terror, scarcely believing, icy calm. They went up the stairs without speaking.

Afterwards, and for the rest of their lives, the picture was branded on their minds and the branding marks became deeper and darker and more ineradicable with everything that happened. So that what might have been a tender, fading memory became a bitter scar. Their father was kneeling beside the bed. He had her hand between both of his and clutched to his breast, and his tears were splashing down onto it and running over it. Every few minutes a groan came from him, a harsh, raw sound which appalled them.

The lamp was on, tipped away from her face and the golden-yellow curtains she had chosen for their cheerful brightness during the day were now dull topaz. The bedside table was a litter of bottles and pots of medicines.

Her breathing was hoarse, as if her chest was a gravel bed through which water was trying to strain. Now and then it heaved up and collapsed down again. But the rest of her body was almost flat to the bed, almost a part of it. She was so thin, the bedclothes were scarcely lifted.

Nita felt for Kay's hand and pressed until it hurt, though neither of them was aware of it. Their father was still bent over the figure on the bed, still holding, holding on.

And then, shocking them, everything stopped. There was a rasping breath, and after it, nothing, simply nothing at all, and the world stopped turning and waited, though what was being waited for they could not have told.

That split second fell like a drop of balm in the tumult of her dying and their distress, so that long afterwards each of them would try to recall it for comfort. But almost at once it was driven out by the cataract of grief and rage that poured from their father. The bellow of pain that horrified them so that in the end they fled down to the sitting room, and held each other and wept, but quietly, and with a restraint and dignity that was shared and unspoken.

There was to be a funeral tea, though not many would come. She had outlived most of her relatives and had needed few friends, their family unit had been so tight, yielding her all she had wanted.

But those who did come must be properly entertained.

Nita and Kay arrived back before the rest to prepare, though the work had been done by Mrs Willis and her daughter.

The hall was cool. Nita, standing in front of the mirror to take off her hat and tidy her hair, caught her sister's eye. They were exhausted. The whole day, like the whole week, seemed unreal, something they had floated through. Their father had wept uncontrollably in the church, and at the graveside bent forward so far, as the coffin was lowered, that they had half-feared he was about to pitch himself in after it.

Behind Nita, Kay's face was pinched, the eye sockets bruise-coloured. There was everything to say. There was nothing to say. The clock ticked.

She will never hear it tick again, Nita thought.

For a second, then, the truth found an entrance and a response, but there was no time, the cars had returned, there were footsteps on the path, voices. The truth retreated again.

They turned, faces composed. Nita opened the door.

*

Every day for the next six months they thought that he would die too. If he did not, it was not any will to live that prevented it. He scarcely ate. He saw no one. He scarcely spoke. He had always been interested in money, money was his work, his hobby, his passion. Now, the newspapers lay unopened, bank letters and packets of company reports gathered dust. For much of the time he sat in the drawing room opposite his wife's chair. Often he wept. Whenever he could persuade Nita or Kay to sit with him he talked about their mother. Within the half-year she had achieved sainthood and become perfect in the memory, every detail about her sacred, every aspect of their marriage without flaw.

'I miss her,' Kay said, one evening in October. They were in the kitchen, tidying round, putting away, laying the table for breakfast.

Nita sat down abruptly. The kitchen went silent. It had been said. Somehow, until now, they had not dared.

'Yes.'

'I miss laughing with her over the old photographs, I miss watching her embroider. Her hands.'

'People don't now, do they? There used to be all those little shops for silks and threads and transfers.'

They thought of her sewing box, in the drawing room by the French windows, and the last, intricate piece, unfinished on the round wood frame.

'Things will never be the same, Kay.'

'But they will get better. Surely they'll get better.'

'I suppose so.'

'Perhaps – we ought at least to start looking at some of the things.'

The sewing box, her desk, the drawers and wardrobe in her bedroom. Clothes, earrings, hair-brushes, letters, embroidery silks were spread out for inspection in their minds.

'You read about people quarrelling with their mothers.'

'We never quarrelled.'

'You couldn't.'

'You read about it being the natural way of things.'

'Quarrelling is not obligatory.'

They caught one another's eye and Nita laughed. The laughter grew, and took them gradually over; they laughed until they cried, and sat back exhausted, muscles aching, and the laughter broke something, some seal that had been put on life to keep it down.

Outside Nita's room, they held one another, knowing that the laughter had marked a change. In the study, hearing their laughter coming faintly from the distant kitchen, their father let misery and loneliness and self-pity wash over him, and sank back, submerging himself under the wave.

What would life be like? They did not know. Each morning they went out of the house together, at the same time, and parted at the end of the next street. Nita walked on, to her hospital reception desk. Kay caught her bus to the department store where she was Ladies' Fitter.

At six they met again, and walked home. And so, life was the same, it went on in the old way – yet it did not. Even the shape of the trees in the avenue seemed changed. When they neared the house something came over them, some miasma of sorrow and fear and uncertainty, and a sort of dread.

Each knew that the other felt it, but neither spoke of it; they spoke, as before, of the ordinary details of the day, the weather, the news of the town.

And in each of their minds was always the question – will today be different? Will this be the day when he wakes from the terrible paralysis of misery?

But when the door opened into the cool, silent hall and the light caught the bevel of the mirror, they knew at once that after all, this was not the day, and went in to hang their coats and empty this or that bag, to wash and tidy before going in to him.

The medicines had been thrown away and a few bills and receipts and shopping lists, otherwise he would allow nothing to be sorted or moved or cleared.

Everything must remain as she had left it.

Once, a few days after the funeral, Kay had crept into her mother's bedroom and sat on the bed, which the nurse had stripped and re-made with fresh linen, as if, somehow, her mother might come back and it must be ready for her. And she had been everywhere in the room. Kay had touched the dressing gown behind the door, and the touch had disturbed the faint fine smell of the violet talcum powder and soap her mother had used, and brought her back even more vividly.

Six months later, nothing had been moved, but going into the room again, in search of her mother's old address book, she had sensed the difference at once. There was a hollow, she was no longer there. The bedroom was quite empty of her.

Kay had found, as she stood for a few moments at the window looking out over the garden, that she could not conjure her mother up in any way, could not picture her, could not remember the sound of her voice. When she touched the dressing gown, the smell had gone.

'Father ought to go in there now,' she said, going in to Nita. 'Surely it might …'

Her sister shook her head.

'Perhaps Dr Boyle—'

'But he isn't ill.'

'I suppose not.'

'Perhaps you are right though, about the room.'

'What should we say?'

They imagined what words might conceivably serve, where they might possibly begin.

'It would be best to be straightforward,' Nita said at last.

'Could you?'

'I – I think I must.'

But two days later, it was Kay who spoke, coming into the drawing room and finding it in darkness, so that she startled him by clicking on the light.

There had been some petty irritations during the day and she was suffering from a cold; if it had not been for those things she might never have confronted him, would never have had the courage.

'Whatever are you doing sitting here in the dark again, Father? Whatever good is this going to do any of us?'

She saw that she had shocked him and his shock gave her nerve.

'It is six months since Mother died, half a year. What good are you doing? We have to go out, carry on a life. That's how it should be, how it has to be. Do you think we haven't felt it and missed her as much as you? Do you suppose she would think well of you, hiding away, wringing your hands? You've interest in nothing, concern for nothing. You're in the half-dark. Have you wondered how it is for us, coming back to it at the end of every day?'

She heard herself as she might hear someone in a play. She was not startled or made afraid by her own voice, or the passion with which she had spoken. She simply heard herself, with interest but without emotion and when she stopped speaking she heard the silence.

Her father was staring at her, his face brick-red, his mouth working.

She began to shake.

It was Nita who saved them, coming without any warning into the room.

'Kay?'

She looked at her sister, at her father, at the two shocked faces and though she had heard nothing of what had been said, the force of it seemed to press down upon the silence that filled the room and Nita understood the enormity of what had happened.

'Kay?'

But Kay was frozen, she could neither speak nor move, could scarcely even breathe.

And then he got up and without looking at either of them, blundered out of the room, and through the hall towards the stairs.

When they returned home the following evening he was not in the house. He had left before ten, Mrs Willis said, in a taxi which was taking him in to the city.

By the time he returned they had gone to bed, though both were lying awake, turning the events over in their minds. Both heard his key in the lock, his foot-steps, the closing of his bedroom door. Both thought of creeping along the corridor to the other. Neither did.

The next day, the pattern was the same, and so, until the end of that week, on the Saturday, he ate lunch and supper with them. But something in his look forbade them to refer to any of it. Kay was terrified of catching his eye.

'He is my father, why should I be afraid of him?'

The news was on the television, the one programme they always watched, as they had watched it every night with their mother. Somehow, speaking over the voices on it seemed to Kay like not quite speaking at all.

The news ended. Nita got up.

'He should be grateful to us,' she said and her voice rose. 'Grateful!'

Her sister's face had flushed and Kay saw that there were tears in her eyes.

'It had to stop and I didn't have the courage to say it.'

She went quickly out of the room. Kay stared at the blank screen, and quite suddenly, her mother's face came to mind; she saw her as she had been, long before the illness, saw her grey, neatly parted hair and the soft cheeks, saw her smiling, pleased, patient expression. She had gone and now she had come back.

The television screen remained opaque and grey.

'Yes,' Kay said to herself. 'Yes.'

As she left the sewing room where they kept the television set her father came out of his study and instinctively Kay stepped back, acutely conscious of what had been said earlier.

'Kay.'

She found herself reaching out, and then held by him, her face against his sleeve, pressed into the cloth, smelling his soap and the faint smell of his city day which brought her childhood back to envelop her and hold her as he held her himself.

Nothing else was said after the one word 'Kay' and in a second or two he disengaged himself gently and went down the passage towards the side door that led to the garden. Every night, until the last weeks of her mother's life, he had gone there at the end of the evening to smoke a single small cigar. Kay went up to her bedroom and opened the window and after a moment the smell of the smoke came to her from the garden below.

She felt a rush of the most exhilarating happiness, as the anxiety and gloom of the past weeks fell away. The house had been sunk into the dreary aftermath of their mother's death for so long that she had forgotten even the small, pleasant details of everyday life until now, when one of them had been given back. They were all weary, their flesh felt dead, their skins grey, their movements were slow; there had been no lightness in anything, the subdued atmosphere had become usual, their father's isolated uncommunicated grief suffocating everything that might have been enjoyed or anticipated.

She leaned further out of the window, intent on catching as much as possible of the smell of his cigar smoke.

We have come through it, she thought. We have come through.

She was not rash enough to expect life to be everything that it had been. Their mother was dead. Nothing could alter that, nothing lessened the pain though the death had been 'a blessing'.

But something had changed at last. They had all moved on and surely for good.

She waited at the open window until the last trace of smoke had faded from the air and the only smell was of night, and grass and the earth. Then she got into bed, and slept like something new born.

And indeed, slowly, gradually the mood in the house lightened. Their father spoke to them, went out, returned with the evening paper, opened letters, worked at his desk. There was no laughter yet, and no social life. Friends and neighbours were not invited. But they had all of them lost the habit of that and did not feel any particular need yet to re-acquire it.

'In the summer,' Nita said.

'Perhaps we could have one of the old summer garden parties.'

'I wonder – do you think Father has given any thought to a holiday?'

Such small exchanges lightened their days. There was no sense of urgency or anxiety, no need to push forward too fast. But when they spoke of their mother now it was with smiling reminiscence, only tinged at the edges with sorrow.

On a Wednesday evening, almost eight months after the death, they walked down the avenue together as usual, and into the house.

'Hello?'

Sometimes they returned first, sometimes he did, and so one or other always called out.

'Hello?'

It was late spring but exceptionally warm. The drawing-room door was open. Nita went through.

The French windows were also open. From the garden came voices speaking quietly together.

'Kay.'

'What's wrong?'

'There is – there's someone in the garden with Father.'

They looked at one another, recognising the next step taken, the next stage reached.

'Good,' Kay said. 'Isn't that good?'

Though they had to wait and absorb it, take in the feeling of strangeness. No one else had been in the house since the day of the funeral. Now someone was here, some old friend of his, some neighbour, and although if asked they would each have said that they welcomed it, nevertheless it felt like a violation of something that had grown to become sacred.

The clock ticked in the hall behind them.

'Oh goodness,' Kay said, half-laughing with impatience at their own hesitation, and walked boldly out through the open windows onto the terrace.

The scene, and the next moments that passed, took their place in the series of ineradicable pictures etched into their minds, joining their mother's deathbed, the funeral, the sight of their father leaning over the grave.

Two garden chairs were drawn up on either side of the small table. Two cups and saucers, the teapot, milk jug and sugar bowl stood on the table. That fact alone they had difficulty in absorbing, and wondered wildly how the tea had come to be made and found its way out there.

Hearing them, their father turned, but did not get up.

Kay and Nita hesitated like children uncertain of what to say or do next, needing permission to come forward. They were on the outside of a charmed circle.

'Here you are!' he said.

After another moment, and as one, they began to cross the grass.

'This is a friend of mine – Leila. Leila Crocker.' He gestured expansively. 'My daughters. Nita. Kay.'

They knew, Nita said afterwards. They knew absolutely and at once and their stomachs plunged like lifts down a deep shaft, leaving only nausea.

The garden froze, the colours were blanched out of everything, the leaves stiffened, the trees went dead. Unbelievably, instinctively, impossibly, they knew.

She stood. Said, 'How very nice.'

Under their feet, deep below the grass and turf, the earth seemed to shift and heave treacherously, shaking their confidence, throwing them off balance. The sky tipped and ended up on its side, like a house after a bomb had fallen.

At the moment of death, it is said, a person's past rushes towards them, but it was the whole of the future that they saw, in the instant between taking in the presence of the woman with their father, and her words; and in composing themselves to greet her, they saw what was to come in every aspect and detail, it seemed.

'But that cannot have been so,' Nita said, years later. Yet it had. They knew that absolutely.

But all they saw was a woman, of perhaps forty-five, perhaps a few years less or a few years more, who wore a cherry-red suit and had hair formed in an extraordinary bolster above her brow, and who was called Leila Crocker.

'Leila,' she said quickly; 'please call me that.'

They would not. At once they retreated into themselves like snails touched on the tenderest tips of their horns. They could not possibly call her Leila, and so they called her nothing at all.

'I'm afraid the tea will have gone cold.' And she touched the china pot with the blue ribbon pattern. Nita and Kay flinched, though giving no outward sign. The last woman to have touched the blue ribbon teapot had been their mother.

'Not that we've left much of it I'm afraid.'

Their father's voice sounded quite different to them. Lighter, younger, the tone oddly jovial. Everything about him was lighter and younger. He sat back smiling, leaning back in the garden chair, looking at the blue ribbon teapot, and at the woman.

'No please.' Nita made a strange little gesture, like a half-bow. 'Don't worry. We always make tea freshly.'

No one moved then. No one else spoke.

We make a tableau, Kay thought, or one of those old pictures. 'Tea in the Garden' – no, 'A Visitor to Tea'.

Their father might have spoken then, might have told them to take their freshly made tea into the garden to join them. The woman might have said, observing their evening routine, that she must go. But he did not, she did not; they sat, as if waiting to resume an interrupted conversation, so that in the end it was Nita who broke the tableau, by turning and going quickly back across the lawn and through the open French window into the house. Kay gave a half-smile, as if in some kind of hopeless explanation or apology – though meaning neither – before following her sister. Just at the window, she glanced quickly back, expecting them to be watching, feeling their eyes on her. But her father and the woman were turned towards one another, both leaning forwards slightly, their eager conversation eagerly resumed.

We might not have been here, Kay thought.

In the kitchen, Nita dropped the lid of the kettle and the sound went on reverberating on the tiled floor, even after she had bent impatiently to pick it up.

Rain poured off the roofs of the houses they walked past and the early blossom lay in sad, sodden little heaps in the gutter. Spring had retreated behind banked, swollen clouds and a cold wind.

'Perhaps it is time for us to leave home,' Kay said into the umbrella with which she was trying to shield her head and face. Nita stopped dead and lifted her own umbrella to stare at her sister and the rain flowed off it down her neck.

'Even without ... well, there will surely be changes. Perhaps we should institute our own.'

'Why must there be changes?'

'Aren't we rather too old to be living at home still?'

Kay was thirty-five, Nita about thirty-seven. They looked older. Felt older.

'But wherever would we go to? Where would you want to go?'

'A flat?'

'Do you like flats?'

'Not particularly.'

'We are perfectly happy and comfortable as we are.'

'Yes.'

They turned the corner. Each had had a private inner glimpse into the rooms of a small flat, and looked quickly away.

'Besides.'

The rest was unspoken, and perfectly understood. Besides, Nita would have continued, now that she has come to the house there is all the more reason than ever for us to stay.

Every afternoon since that first day when they had stepped into the garden and seen their father sitting with Leila Crocker over the blue ribbon teapot, they had dreaded coming home and finding her there again. Twice already they had done so. Once, the two of them had been seated in exactly the same place in the garden, the table and the tea things between them so that they might never have moved at all.

The next time, Leila Crocker had been coming along the passage from the downstairs cloakroom as they opened the front door. None of them had known what to say.

Now, Kay turned her key in the lock, pushed the door slowly and waited. They both waited, listening. But the house was empty, they could feel at once. It felt and sounded and smelled empty. The clock ticked. Nita took both umbrellas out to the scullery.

At the end of the television news, when Kay had switched off the set, their father had not come home.

'He has never said anything.'

'Perhaps he has nothing to say.'

'He has told us nothing about her. Wouldn't it be usual – to tell something?'

'What is "usual"? I don't think I know.'

'No.'

It was not that he had behaved secretively, or evasively, or avoided them. Things had gone on exactly as before. Except that in some vital, deep-rooted way, they had not. Because always, no matter how he behaved, the woman was between the three of them.

The taxi came for him each morning. He went out, returned, sometimes very late, opened his letters, read the newspaper, worked at his desk, smoked his single late cigar. When they were all together, he ate with them. When he was not at home, they had no idea of where he was and could not ask.

The house seemed suddenly imbued with meaning, redolent of their past and precious to them. Every door handle and window-pane and cupboard. Every book and curtain and step on the stairs. The mirror in the hall and the clock and the blue ribbon teapot, all seemed to hold the life of their family within every atom, to be infinitely more than household objects made of wood and glass and metal and china and paint. Every touch and footstep, the echo of every word spoken, was part of the fabric and substance of the house. At night they lay and wrapped it round themselves and held it to them.

They were possessive, passionate and jealous of it and everything it contained. The feeling they had for it was as strong and vital as their love for their father and the memory of their mother. They were shocked by the power of it.

They could not say that they liked Leila Crocker. They could not say that they disliked her.

'Her hair is very tightly permed,' Kay said.

'But her shoes are good.'

At the department store during one lunch hour Kay had suddenly told the other fitter about it. Anne McKay's hirsute face had lit up.

'Oh, Kay, that is so very nice! Isn't that nice for him? I think that's lovely.'

What is 'lovely'? Kay thought, panicking. I have told her that he brought a woman to tea. Her face betrayed her terror. Anne McKay reached out and touched her arm. They were seated in the old broken-down basket chairs in the dusty little staffroom.

'I meant how lovely for him to have some companionship. I know you miss your mother, of course you do, but life has to move on.'

Does it? Why does it? Why can it not stay as it is? Kay took a bite from her sandwich but could not swallow it.

'You won't be at home for ever, will you? Either of you.'

Won't we? Why not? Why should we ever leave? Who could make us?

Kay jumped up, and went to the cloakroom and there spat the piece of sandwich violently into the lavatory basin.

'I suppose,' Nita said, hearing about it later, 'that companionship is important.'

'He has us. He isn't alone.'

'We should try to be fair.'

'What is "unfair"?'

'We are – well, isn't it quite different?'

'From what?'

'I mean, it is just a different kind of companionship – friendship. Of course it is, Kay.'

But what the nature of the friendship or companionship was they could not have said.

It had been raining for almost a week, but now, as they walked the last hundred yards down the avenue, the sun came out and shone in their faces and reflected watery gold on the wet pavement and the house roof.

'We must try to be fair,' Nita said again.

They quickened their steps.

But the house was empty, as it was empty every evening for the next week, and after that, it seemed, was never empty again. It was the speed of it all that horrified them, the speed which was, Kay said, unnecessary and unseemly.

'And rather hurtful.'

But their father was now oblivious to everything except the woman he was to marry. For he would marry Leila Crocker, he said, telling them, with neither warning nor ceremony, the next time he spent an evening at home with them.

'I should like you to know,' he had said, laying down his soup spoon, 'that I have asked Leila to be my wife.'

The room went deathly silent and, it seemed to Kay and Nita, deathly cold. A chill mist seemed to creep in under the door and the window frame, curling itself round them so that they actually shivered. They could not look at him or at one another. They could do nothing.

'I have found a very dear companion, a very fine person with whom to share the rest of my life. Your mother – her illness and her death – were – very diffi-cult. I had not imagined – of course you hardly know Leila, but you will come to know her, and to love and admire her, I am quite certain of it. Quite certain.'

He beamed innocently from one to the other.

'This is going to be a very happy home once more.'

It was like their bereavement all over again but in a way worse, because death was the final certainty, and this was uncertain, this would go on and on. Their whole lives would change but they did not know how. Their future would be entirely different but they could not picture it.

That first night, after he had told them, the silence had been so terrible, his ea-ger, beaming face so open and expectant, that Nita had prayed to die, then, there, rather than have to face any of it and Kay had wished her tongue cut out, for any words she might feel able to utter would be wrong and false and surely choke her.

In the end, after what might have been a minute or a lifetime, their father said, 'I hope very much that you are pleased.'

Kay swallowed.

'Of course, your mother—'

Nita leaped up, pushing her chair back with such force that it toppled and crashed over behind her. 'She – Mother has nothing to do with this – please do not talk about Mother.'

'Perhaps—' Kay heard her own voice, strangled and peculiar. 'Perhaps you may be able to understand what a shock this is.'

'But you *are* happy for me? You do share this happiness with me?'

His face was that of a child anxious for approval, and their feelings as they looked at him were impossible, confused, painful.

'She has given me a new life.'

They fled.

The next morning Nita woke Kay up before seven o'clock.

'I am going to the service. Will you come?'

Kay turned onto her back. They had not been to church since the Sunday after the funeral.

'What will you pray for?'

'Guidance.'

'For him?'

'For ourselves.'

'For it to end – for this – this thing to be over.'

Nita sat down on her sister's bed. 'I think,' she said carefully, 'that it will not.'

'No.'

'And I find I cannot cope with – I have never felt like this in my life.'

'What do you feel?'

'I think it is hatred. And anger. Great anger.'

'Betrayal.'

'Is it?'

'But not us – it is not us he is betraying.'

'No.'

'It is indecent. He is an old man.'

'Perhaps if it had been in a few years' time.'

'That is the worst, isn't it? Think of all those tears. All that – and how to think it was all lies and falseness.'

'Oh I don't think it was. He did—'

'Love Mother?'

'Yes.'

'Then how could he?'

'If I don't deal with this terrible hatred it will become destructive of everything. I hardly slept.'

'Burrowing.'

'Yes. It's like that. A canker. Will you come?'

'No.'

'We have to try. We must try.'

'For her sake?'

'No, for him. Of course for him.'

'Do you like her?'

'We barely know her. I only say we should try.'

'You are too good.'

Kay turned over and pressed her face hard into her pillow. Her mother seemed to be somewhere in the depths of it, as she was everywhere now, smiling, patient. Betrayed. 'You will have to go by yourself,' Kay said, tears pouring down her face.

The city restaurant had been full at ten minutes past one and so they had been obliged to share a table. That was how they had met.

'I suppose she had been on the lookout for just such a man, eating alone.'

'Kay—'

'Unfair?'

'Yes.'

'It is all unfair.'

'She is very nice to us.'

'Why should she not be?'

'We have not been altogether nice to her – we have perhaps been rather un-welcoming.'

'Of course we have. She is unwelcome.'

Though so far Leila Crocker had behaved impeccably. She had been reserved, friendly hut never effusive. Pleasant and careful.

'It really is difficult to dislike her,' Nita said.

'I don't care for her clothes.'

'Well they are perfectly good clothes.'

'Oh yes. *Good* clothes.'

Leila Crocker wore smart suits in plain colours, alternating them week by week, cherry-red, ice-blue, camel, mauve. She was, she said, personal assistant to a managing director. The second rime she came to the house, she told them that she was forty-four.

'Why did she suppose her age was of any interest to us? It is no business of ours.'

Their father was almost thirty years older. They could not talk to him.

'I hope that things will go on as they always have,' he said.

'How can they? How can anything ever be as it was?'

Kay ran her finger over and over the closed lid of the piano.

'He is destroying all of it.'

'Do stop doing that.'

'Do you suppose he ever thinks – thinks of Mother?'

'Surely he must.'

'What? What can he think?'

'You will take off the veneer.'

'There is no one else left to defend her memory.'

'Is that what we are for?'

'What else?'

'It is almost as though thirty-seven years had somehow—'

'Well they have not.' Kay spoke in a raw, furious whisper.

'Do stop doing that. I think I shall go mad,' Nita shouted, then went quite silent. They stared at one another fearfully.

'Look,' Kay said after a moment. 'Look what is happening, what it is making us do. Everything is cracking and splintering and being destroyed. Even us.'

A month after Leila Crocker had first come to the house, Nita found her in the kitchen one evening.

'I am cooking for us all.'

'Oh, there is no need. I was going to make omelettes with a salad.'

'I'm sure you would prefer roast chicken.'

'And then,' Nita said, going in, trembling, to her sister's room, 'I noticed it.'

'Noticed what?'

'How can he think of doing such a thing? How can he?'

The light had caught the ring on Leila Crocker's hand as she had reached out to one of the kitchen taps.

Kay laid down her pen. Her diary was open on the desk in front of her.

'The diamond hoop with the small sapphires?'

'Yes.'

Though their mother had rarely worn it, saying it was too special, too dressy, it was to be kept for very special occasions, and those had rarely come, in such quiet, self-contained lives.

'Are you sure?'

The words came out of Kay's mouth as heavy and cold and separate as marbles.

'Go down and see for yourself. If he has to give her a ring – well, people naturally do—'

'Not the ring that belonged to their wife of thirty-seven years who has been dead for under a year. I think not.'

At two o'clock in the morning, Kay went into her sister's room and, after hesitating a moment, her bed.

'Ninny?' She had not used the name for twenty years.

'I'm not asleep.'

'1 don't think I can bear it.'

'I know.'

'I feel as if I were a child.'

'What would other people do? Different kinds of people?'

Kay thought of Anne McKay, and Mrs Willis. 'Do you – do you believe she can know?'

They lay, picturing their mother, floating somewhere nearby, smiling, patient.

Is it for her? Nita thought, feeling her sister's warmth to the side of her. As children they had often crept into one another's beds. Is it really for Mother's sake that I mind what is happening more than I have ever minded anything apart from her dying?

But in the end she turned on her side and took her sister's hand and, after a few moments, slept, exhausted by the impossible, unanswerable questions.

'We cannot possibly go to the wedding,' Kay had said. But of course they did, and somehow got through the service, at which there were three hymns and two readings and Leila Crocker wore cream lace. The church and the hotel room afterwards were full of strangers. Their father's face was flushed with excitement and open devotion.

Somehow, they got through all of it. Somehow, they stayed until the car had left the hotel courtyard, waved at by the strangers.

In the avenue, Kay stopped, took off her jacket and shook it out until the few paper rose petals drifted into the gutter.

The two weeks that followed were extraordinarily happy. They felt an unreal sense of freedom and contentment, in the house by themselves, answerable to no one. The sun shone; they set the table up on the terrace and ate supper there, and, at the weekend, breakfast and lunch as well.

They put a shield around themselves. Neither referred to their father or to the marriage. When postcards arrived, first from Rome, and then from Florence, they read and then discarded them without a word.

But on the morning they were due to return Nita cut fresh branches of phila-delphus and put them in jugs about the house.

'We have to try. We have a duty to try. Things may go perfectly well.'

From the very beginning they did not, though whose fault it was none of them could have told.

It was difficult to share their home with another, difficult to accept her as having precedence over them, difficult that she and their father slept in the same room, the old room in which their mother had slept in the years before her last illness, difficult to get used to changes of daily routine and the presence of their stepmother's possessions hanging in wardrobes, filling drawers, displacing the old order of things. Difficult to find someone else in the house every evening when they returned home, at supper, at breakfast and for the whole of every weekend.

'Difficult, difficult, difficult,' Kay said, walking faster than usual up the avenue.

But difficult might have become less so. They might perhaps have adapted themselves to the new arrangement, in the end. Difficult was not painful or hurt-ful and it was pain and hurt which came very quickly.

'What is happening?' Nita said as they rounded the corner, and saw the removal van outside the house. 'What is happening?'

They almost ran.

It was nearly over. The work had been going on for most of the day. All the old furniture from their mother's sewing room and the small sitting room, as well as from the bedroom in which she had died, had gone. In the sitting room were a new, bright-blue sofa and chair, and a glass-fronted cabinet. The sewing room and bedroom were empty.

Their father met them in the hall, saw their faces, but could not manage to meet their eyes.

After that everything disintegrated, everything was swept away, or so it felt. Their mother's clothes were cleared, and her papers. The photographs of her about the drawing room and their father's study disappeared, though her pearls and her two pairs of good earrings did not go, their stepmother wore them.

'How dare she?' Kay said, banging into her father's study. 'How dare she take Mother's things, her personal things, how could you let her?'

'Please lower your voice. I remember that when your mother passed away –'

'Died. She died.'

'—you – and Nita – you said you would prefer not to have those things. As I understood.'

'That did not give – your wife – the right to appropriate them.'

He stood up. 'I gave them to her. I wanted her to have them. Leila took nothing.'

'How could you give them – you?'

'I think, I believe, that it is what—'

'If you say it is what Mother would have wanted, I think I shall kill you.'

'Kay—'

'You let her throw out our mother's furniture – clear her things.'

'We did it together. It was time.'

'For who?'

'For me.'

'You are a blind, cruel, besotted, foolish old man.'

At the top of the stairs, she almost collided heavily with Nita.

'Whatever is happening? Why were you screaming?'

In her own room, Kay sobbed tears of bitter pain and rage.

Nita had closed the door. 'It is very hard,' she said. 'I hate this. I mind it as much as you do. I mind it for Mother's sake and for us, but screaming at Father is not right – he loves her, he is besotted with her. He cannot see that she is doing anything wrong.'

'He is being treacherous, utterly treacherous. He was married to Mother for almost forty years. He loved her, he saw her die and almost went mad with grief. We had to watch all that, bear all that. He has utterly, utterly betrayed her, bringing that woman here, marrying her in such haste, such a few months after – and making that – that vulgar display, that wedding – giving her Mother's jewellery, helping her throw Mother's things away – taking down the photographs.

'She has no idea, none. She is completely insensitive and I do not care for her, I wish she had never come here – but I don't blame her and I do not hate her. I blame him. I hate him. I can't forgive him – I cannot –'

The tears this time were not of anger, but of misery and grief at everything lost, and after a moment Nita cried with her for the same loss, of their mother and of everything that had been hers, and for the loss of him, the loss of all love, for it seemed that their father had taken everything from them, and given it to his wife, taken his love for them and for their mother and theirs for him, taken his loyalty and sense of what was right. Taken their home and their place in it.

They sat holding one another on Kay's bed as the light faded, and the empty room below and the empty room next door were like hollow caves carved out of their own hearts.

They lived in the house for another five months, and in that time everything changed, piece by piece. Everything that was old and familiar and belonged to their past went and was replaced by the new, the strange, until only their father's study and their own rooms remained unaltered. They scarcely spoke to him, avoided him altogether if they could. To their stepmother they were polite, with all the careful, wary courtesy of strangers, but they saw, in her face, in her eyes, that she was indifferent to them.

'They neither need nor want us,' Nita said, 'that much is clear without anything being said.'

They felt invisible, quite supplanted, quite irrelevant. One evening they drew a circle on the street map, and began to look within it. They could not have borne to change their routine, the walk to the same bus stop, the return together. It was all that was left to them, apart from their jobs, and their own shared life.

When they found a flat which would do, Kay told their father, who said nothing. 'You have your own lives to lead,' their stepmother said brightly; 'naturally you do.'

The flat was really quite pleasant. The sitting room had wide windows over-looking the chestnut trees that lined the quiet street. The rooms were freshly painted. They grew used to not having a garden, particularly as it was winter when they moved in.

They wondered from time to time whether they had judged Leila Crocker, as they still thought of her, correctly, whether she had cornered their father into a meeting, marriage, the clearing away of his past, or whether she had in fact been blameless and the fault was his, but it came to matter less and less just as, to their surprise, they were able to remember their mother more clearly in the flat than they had in the old house. She had come with them, she was there every evening on their return, in her photograph, which was everywhere, and with her invisible yet smiling, patient presence.

They thought as little as possible about their father and their old home, though it was the memories of home which gave them the greatest pain, striking without warning, because of the way the sun shone suddenly through a window, or the banging of a gate. At these moments, the past would wash over them and drown them in itself. Their years of childhood and young womanhood were fresher and more vivid than the previous day so that it seemed they might simply have opened the door and walked back into them.

Their habits firmed, hardened, their natures set. Routine became all-important. They came to dread any disturbance, any hint of the unfamiliar.

Their father's new marriage had nothing to do with them.

'It is far better,' Kay said; 'it is the only way.' And all the while believed it.

But very occasionally, Nita got up before her and went to the early service. Kay could never be persuaded. It was the only rift between them, and slight enough, apart from the day Nita let the blue ribbon teapot slip out of her hands onto the floor of the kitchenette, where it smashed into far too many pieces for there to be the slightest hope of repair. Walking into the room a moment later, Kay found her sister standing, staring down at the shards of china and, recog-nising them, she began to scream, furiously, uncontrollably, her voice rising and rising, until Nita's face took on a look of pain, and panic, and, as Kay's scream intensified, of fear.

RENAISSANCE

Colette Paul

Colette Paul is a Scottish author. She has published one book of short stories, *Whoever You Choose to Love*, which was shortlisted for the Glenfiddich Spirit of Scotland Writer's Award. She won the Royal Society of Authors Tom-Gallon Trust Award in 2005.

My mum was generally a cheerful person. It was her misfortune that she had borne a child who was neither cheerful, nor endowed with finer feelings, as she was. She was always telling me that when I was a baby I used to lie completely quiet and still for hours and people would say to her, 'Are you sure that baby's alive?' and sometimes she herself wondered. She couldn't understand it because she came from a family of lookers-on-the-bright-side. It was in the genes.

'Our family motto,' she said, 'was if you break a leg, just be thankful you didn't break two legs.'

We only went up to Granny Philips's twice a year, and I never found her and Grandpa very cheery. There was plastic covering the sofa and tables, and the only time they smiled was when their dog, Gertrude, came into the room. The conversation revolved around Gertrude – they loved her more than they loved each other – and Sam, Mum's brother, who had depression, and still lived at home.

'You *think* you've got depression,' Mum would say to him, 'but answer me this. Do people in Africa have depression? Do they have time to get depressed when they've got to walk to the well and work in the fields? Can they just stay in bed all day, watching cartoons and thinking how miserable they are?'

'I suppose not,' Sam would say, slumped in his seat, looking more and more depressed.

Mum's one beef was that she never went to university. This was the only subject that was immune to her abrasive brand of looking on the bright side. If she had gone, she said, she would have studied English. She had won a prize at school for an essay entitled 'Why We Read'. She could remember whole poems, and could recite them off by heart to prove it. One of them was 'The Donkey' by Chesterton. For this one she adopted a low, sad voice, and stood rooted to the spot as if she were possessed by the spirit of the donkey. When it came to *Fools! For I also had my hour* she would fairly belt the line out. I disliked these performances. I found them sentimental, and never knew what to say when she had finished and was looking at me with such sad triumph. Once I asked her what happened to the donkey afterwards, and she got annoyed and said he just went back to being an ugly donkey, but that that wasn't the point.

Mum cited my dad as the reason she didn't go to university. She said she would have thrived in such an atmosphere, but that he didn't want her thriving. He wanted a good little doctor's wife. Dad said the real reason was that Mum didn't have the qualifications to get into university, and that having a good head for poetry didn't mean she was brainy anyway. It just meant she had a good memory. This was the one thing he could say that truly enraged Mum. Usually she ignored his drunken rants, the rants where he would call everyone he knew rotten bastards and elaborate endlessly on the ways they had wronged him. But she couldn't let a slur on her intelligence pass by without comment.

'I'm not the one who had to re-sit their exams three times,' she'd say.

Other times she'd mention her IQ, or the fact that Dad had been scared to try a tomato until he was twenty-one, or that he'd only ever read one book in his life. She never mentioned the most obvious thing, that he was killing off what was left of his brain with alcohol. She ignored what she didn't want to face, and made it seem somehow bad-mannered to mention the obvious. So I never mentioned it either.

I spent most of my time with Mum, and didn't see Dad very much. He worked late, and often wouldn't be home until I'd gone to bed. My response to him was complicated by the fact that he was so changeable. When he was sober he was gentle and easy to be with. We would play draughts or chess together, or take a walk to the beach and skim pebbles. He didn't talk very much and was more comfortable showing me how to do things. By the time I was nine I could put someone in the recovery position, wire a plug, and tie knots to shame the Boy Scouts. Dad never talked about his life, but I felt he was sad, and when he was sober I felt sorry for him. He had a doleful, refugee look about him, as if he didn't belong with the people around him and was ready to apologize at any moment for his presence. I never thought about him being a doctor, and I was always surprised at Christmas time when he would bring home presents his patients had given him. (Unfortunately it was mostly bottles of whisky, which meant a lot of Xmas cheer for Dad, and not much for Mum and me.) For a little while his black bag with his medical equipment inside – his props, Dad called them – fascinated me. The props looked so alien and authoritative, yet Dad could wield them and interpret their signals. When I asked him about them he explained what they were used for, and said they were easy to handle once you knew how.

'Anyone can do it,' he said, and I believed him and stopped being impressed.

By the time I was twelve he was drunk or hung over more often than he was sober. One afternoon, just before the summer holidays, Mum came into my room and told me we were moving.

'Your father's lost his job,' she said. 'He's in disgrace.'

'What'd he do?' I said.

Mum walked over to the window and stared outside. Then she came over and put her hands on my shoulders.

'Don't hunch,' she said, 'it makes you look like an old woman.'

'I'm not hunching,' I said.

She said it would be good for us to live somewhere new, but she didn't sound as if she believed it.

'You'll miss your friends,' she said, 'but you'll make new ones. And so will I. It'll be exciting.'

'I don't have any friends,' I said, which was true.

'Well, that's even better then,' she said, 'you won't miss anyone. I'll tell you what I'll miss. I'll miss Lucy, and I'll miss the book group –'

I interrupted to remind her that she didn't even like the book group, and when she denied it I cited the week before when she told me they weren't a very bright bunch, and all they wanted to do was gossip and read Joanna Trollope novels.

'I did not say that,' said Mum, 'and even if I did, it doesn't mean I won't miss them. When I think of them discussing *Pride and Prejudice* without me ... I have a lot to say about that book,' she added ominously.

I said I was sure they'd miss her too, and Mum surprised me by smiling hesitantly and saying, 'Do you think they will?'

It was on the tip of my tongue to say, *No, they'll crack open the party poppers*, but I looked at her face and said, 'Of course they'll miss you. You're the life and soul of that book group.'

'I'm sure that's not true,' she said, in a way that made me believe she thought it was very true indeed, 'but it's very nice of you to say so.'

She went on for another ten minutes about what she'd miss – the beach, the house, the weather – until she stopped and said there must be *something* I'd miss.

'I don't know yet,' I said. 'I won't know until we're gone.'

I saw her looking at me, willing me to mention something we could share together.

'I might miss the tree,' I said, 'in the front garden.'

'Oh, the tree!' she said in sudden delight. 'I love that tree. When you were little, you and I used to sit under that tree for hours in the summertime. You used to stare up at the leaves and there wouldn't be a peep out of you. I used to wonder what you were thinking, you looked so serious for a baby.'

'I was probably thinking I wish Mum wouldn't stick me under this stupid tree for hours,' I said, and Mum laughed.

'And there was me,' she said, 'thinking you were deep.'

It was an eternal disappointment to her that I wasn't deep, as she had hoped, but just quiet. Mum's criteria for deepness were pretty arbitrary anyway – they involved liking poetry and crying at sad films, as she did. I scuppered my chances of ever being deep by laughing during the graveyard scene in *Who Will Love My Children*.

'Anyway,' she said, 'we'll be together, you and me. That's what matters.'

'And Dad,' I said, but Mum kissed the back of my head and didn't say anything to that.

We arrived in Glasgow one rainy Friday night, two days into my summer holidays. Mum said Glasgow meant dear green place, but it didn't look very green. We passed groups of dark high-rise flats, shabby rows of shops, huge billboard stands. A fat girl behind the counter of a fish-and-chip shop stuck her two fingers up at me as we waited at the traffic lights.

'Would you look at that,' said Mum, 'she must be very unhappy.'

But the girl didn't look unhappy at all. She looked like she wanted to bash someone, preferably me. When I said this to Mum, she replied that my outlook on life was superficial.

'Any psychologist worth his salt will tell you,' she said, 'that behind every bully is a very scared, very sad person.'

I rolled my eyes and looked out of the window. It had begun to strike me, in the past year, that Mum could be a bit dim. It wouldn't matter, I thought, if she wasn't so pleased with herself.

'I agree with Cara,' Dad said suddenly. It startled me to hear his voice because I'd forgotten he was there. What can you say to someone who agrees with you? I said nothing and we rolled into Waver Street in silence.

The delivery van arrived the next morning, and we spent the next few days unpacking. The house was too small for all our things, and we had to start piling stuff into cupboards. The first things to go were Mum's pictures, which looked wrong on the murky, floral walls. Then old photo albums, vases, toiletry sets, my old christening gown, her old christening gown. Hoarding was the one indulgence Mum allowed herself. She never threw anything away without a wrench of her heart. She got nostalgic about an old clay bear she'd made at school, and angry and disappointed reading my old school reports, which, apart from maths which Mum didn't rate anyway, were roundly bad. One entry particularly incensed her for its inelegance and atrocious spelling:

Cara' may be a good student if she paid atention in class. As it is, she pays no attention, and is not a good student.

'She certainly didn't beat around the bush,' Mum said. We were sitting on the living-room floor, the papers scattered around us.

'They all say the same,' she said. 'Why do you think that is?' She gave me a concentrated look, as if my answer was the most important thing in the whole world. I hated that look.

'I don't know,' I said and shrugged. 'Because I don't pay attention?'

From upstairs came the sound of Dad laughing. I'd taken his lunch up to their room earlier and he'd been watching a Jerry Springer show about people who wanted to marry their pets. He'd pointed to the telly with his vodka bottle and said it just wasn't right to get engaged to your horse.

'Well,' said Mum sharply, 'you'll need to start paying attention. You're going into second year after the summer, that's when the wheat's separated from the chaff. I want to see you in the wheat pile.'

I said what if I liked it in the chaff pile, and Mum said to stop being facetious. 'Stupidness doesn't suit anyone,' she said.

This brought on a reverie about her own thwarted ambition, what she could have excelled in (anything she wanted!) if she'd been given the chances and opportunities I had.

'I just soaked up knowledge,' she said. 'I was thankful for it. How many other people,' she said, 'can recite the whole of "Hail to thee blithe spirit! Bird that never wert" off by heart?'

*

That same day, Mum decided we should introduce ourselves to the neighbours. Only one woman answered our knock, and we had to call out our business before she would open the door.

'I thought you were those Jehovah Witnesses,' she said.

'Oh no,' said Mum. 'Though hopefully we bring good news,' she added in an excruciatingly jolly voice.

Shelia was round and solid as a Christmas pudding. Her t-shirt said FCUK OFF although her expression alone conveyed this message. I was intimidated by her, but also impressed by the short thrift she gave Mum.

'Well then, I'm busy,' she said after a few minutes, practically shutting the door in our faces. I'd never seen Mum dismissed before: she was used to regimenting people's emotional responses to match her own.

'Not a congenial person at all,' Mum said when we got home.

'Behind every bully is a very scared, very sad person,' I said, pleased with myself.

We saw Shelia again a few nights later. She came to the door late on Saturday night to tell Mum that Dad was passed out at the bottom of the street. At first Mum tried to pretend she didn't know what Shelia was talking about. This was pretty futile, as Dad had been sitting in the garden for the past two days saluting everyone who went past.

'Well, he must have a twin,' said Shelia, 'and it's conked out down the road.'

'Okay, well thank you for letting us know,' said Mum brightly.

We went down the road to get him. He had a cut down one side of his face, and was muttering something about shitheads. Mum gave him a hanky for his face, but he groggily swiped it away.

'You! What do you care?' he said, slurring his words.

'We both care,' I said, desperate to get him off the street.

'She doesn't. She wouldn't spit on me if I was on fire.'

'Don't be ridiculous,' said Mum. 'Grab his other arm, Cara.'

'You'd probably laugh your head off,' he said, a note of girlish hysteria creeping into his voice. 'You'd have a ball!'

I tried to lift his arm to pull him up, but it was no use. He was too heavy and making no attempt to help us. He stumbled up himself, calling us a couple of fuckers before he lurched away.

Things got back to normal pretty quickly. Dad got a job, I don't know how he managed it, working in a doctor's surgery in Bearsden. His drinking eased up, and became confined to frantic, demented bouts of one or two days. We hardly noticed him except when he was drunk. It was like realizing you had a ghost only when you heard its manacles rattle. Sometimes he would come into my room. He always used a pretext: he wanted to seal my window, bleed the radiator. He would hang around afterwards and maybe say something like: 'That was five flus today. There's something going around.'

'Mmm,' I'd say.

'Have you been feeling okay? No temperature, no aches and pains?'

'Nope.'

'Good.' He would muse on this quietly for a few minutes. Then he would get up and say, 'Well, tell me if you feel anything coming on.'

A month after we moved in he came in to show me a big card everyone had signed for his birthday. He pointed out all the names and told me what job each of them did at the surgery. Everyone had written a message, which he read out in embarrassed pleasure.

'They all call you Teddy,' I said. 'Not William?'

'I know,' said Dad. 'That's their nickname for me.'

He told me that the last time he'd had a nickname was at school. The boys in his class called him walnut face, because of his acne. But, as Dad pointed out, that wasn't really a nickname.

'That was just people being cruel,' he said.

Later that night I asked Mum if she'd seen the card. We were side by side at the sink, Mum washing, me drying. She was humming a tune and broke off, smiling at me as if she'd just realized I was there.

'The card,' I said, 'did you see it?'

'Of course I saw it,' she said. 'It was very nice.'

'He seems quite popular,' I said, handing her back a plate with a tomato sauce stain. It was one of her principles to be sloppy about housework.

'Yes, people always take to your father. He has a very modest way about him, people like that.'

'Is that why you liked him?' I asked, and Mum said she supposed it must have been.

'It's so long ago now,' she said. 'I was just turned eighteen when we got married. You don't know your own mind at that age. All I wanted was to be grown-up, have a house, a husband, a big wedding. Idiotic,' she said, 'that was just the word for me at that age.'

She smiled fondly at the thought of her younger, idiotic self, and went back to humming her tune.

If anything, Mum was happier after we moved to Glasgow. She joined a hill-walking club and went on jaunts with them every Saturday. She came back late in the evening, full of the joys. Scotland had the most beautiful scenery – she described it rapturously – and the people in the group were the most interesting and well-informed people you could hope to meet.

'It's so invigorating,' she said after the first meeting, 'to meet people who understand you. People you can talk to.'

'Are they all loonies too, then?' I said, but Mum was in a good mood and just laughed.

I got to know everyone in the hill-walking group on a first-name basis. Velma, a retired schoolteacher, wonderful for her age, but you didn't want to get stuck as her partner because her arthritis slowed her down considerably. Gina and Tom, the couple who got on well, and Clair and Philip, who didn't. Betty the librarian, who didn't seem interested when Mum tried to engage her on the subject of literature. The person she talked most about, though, was a divorcee called Brian. He taught a communication course in a college in Hamilton, and his life had been a life compounded of misfortune. His parents died in a car crash, his sister was a recovering drug-addict, his ex-wife a jealous psychotic.

'But he doesn't let life get him down,' said Mum, admiration shining through her voice. 'He just refuses.'

He revealed his life to her on these walks, supposedly because she was a good listener, and empathetic to boot. He said these were rare qualities.

We finished the dishes, and Mum dried her hands and said she'd better get ready. She was meeting the hill-walking group in the pub at seven.

'That's the second time this week you're going out,' I said. 'Not including Saturday.'

Mum said she was in the house all day with me, wasn't she allowed to see her friends at night? 'Humans are social animals,' she said, 'they need other people to spark off.'

'For hearty outdoor types, you spend a lot of time in the pub,' I said.

'I don't know why you're being like this. You've got Barbara now. I don't stop you seeing her.'

In fact, I wished Mum would stop me seeing Barbara. She was someone I was scared *not* to be friends with. She was thirteen, a year older than me, and none of the other girls in the street would hang around with her. Barbara said it was because they were snobs, but the real reason was that she hit them. I didn't know if she hit them because they didn't like her, or if they didn't like her because she hit them. The thing was that Barbara insisted on being involved in everything they were doing. There were four girls, all about our ages, that lived in Waver Street. When it was hot as it had been for weeks, they spread blankets on the street and lounged around on them. They read magazines, painted each other's nails, plaited their hair with beads. Barbara was bony, with a greyish, old-china tinge to her skin. She had heavy, greasy black hair, thick eyebrows, and a huge nose that she often stroked self-consciously. She didn't look like the kind of girl who could get away with thinking she was pretty, or worth decorating.

The first time I met her was one of those hot days. I was sitting with the girls, whose names I'd instantly forgotten, trying to decide how I could escape home without seeming rude. I was going through what Mum called a beefy stage, and I towered above them in height and girth. They were asking each other questions from a 'How Good A Friend Are You?' quiz in a magazine. Barbara came along and stood beside the blanket.

'Ask me,' she said fiercely, halfway between a threat and a plea. One of the girls, a bossy, vicious blonde, said, 'Why, Barbara? You don't have any friends.'

'I do so,' said Barbara. 'and they're better than any of you.'

'Unless you count her nits,' another girl said, and they all tittered.

'I don't have nits,' Barbara said flatly. 'You have nits.'

'Very clever,' said the blonde one. 'How long did it take you to think that one up, Barbara?'

They all ignored her after that, but Barbara kept standing there. And then suddenly she swooped down and walloped one of them on the face. The girls jumped apart, shouting, but not before Barbara had managed to rain a few more blows on them. It all lasted only a few minutes. Barbara stopped abruptly and walked away, giving me a half-hearted push on her way past.

A few days later I was down at the disused railway line at the back of Waver Street. I was walking up and down the tracks, bored, when Barbara appeared.

'Hey, you,' she said, 'what's your name?'

'Cara,' I said.

'What kind of name's that?' she said, and I shrugged. She sat at the edge of the platform and swung her legs over the edge.

'Everyone says your dad's an alkie,' she said.

'He's not. He's a doctor.'

'Doesn't matter anyway. They say things about me, too, that aren't true. They make me so mad.'

'I'd better go,' I said after a few minutes of silence.

She was picking a scab on her knee and didn't look up. 'See you around,' she said as I walked away.

Barbara was very definite about what she wanted to do, and more and more she wanted me to accompany her while she did it. Even though I didn't like her, it never occurred to me to say no to her. At first we just walked around the streets. Then Barbara started to invite me to her house. The curtains were never open, but the sun shone through them and showed up dust everywhere. There were ashtrays, and old newspapers, and dirty plates and cups lying around; a smell of old cat-food permeated the house. Barbara's room was the worst. There were clothes all over the floor, mixed up with plates and bowls crusted with dried-on food. A box of cereal with cornflakes spilling out of it lay in the corner of her room for weeks. The only things that Barbara took care of were her old, beat-up trumpet, and her cassette player. She had two tapes – Simply Red and Louis Armstrong – and she made us listen to them right through, in total silence. The other thing she liked to do was rifle through her mum's bedroom. She would pull all her clothes out of the wardrobe, onto the bed, and run her hands tenderly through them, as if she were touching skin.

'Has your mum got this many clothes?' she asked me once.

I didn't know what to say: her mum's clothes were cheap and pretty ordinary looking. I couldn't understand their appeal.

'I don't know,' I said. 'I suppose so.'

'One day I'm going to have even more than this.'

She held up a red, silky blouse, smelt it, and then passed it to me.

'That's the perfume she wears,' she said. 'It costs thirty-two pounds, and that's just for a tiny bottle.'

It was in her mum's bedroom that she showed me the photographs. She got them out of a drawer where they'd been hidden under piles of underwear. They were of normal size, bad quality. A woman bending over and spreading her bum cheeks; lying on her back with her legs splayed; on all fours like a dog. On and on. Barbara looked at each of them carefully, seriously, before passing them to me. Someone was playing a radio outside, and apart from that it was deadly quiet.

'Why's your mum got these?' I said at last.

'They're of her, stupid.'

'They're disgusting,' I said, and Barbara said, 'I know,' and gathered them up and hid them away again.

A few days later I met her mum for the first time. I was sitting in Barbara's room, listening to her practise her trumpet. She couldn't play a note on it; she just blew into it as hard as she could and wiggled her fingers about. She told me that the best musicians in the world were self-taught. We heard the front door open, and then someone's feet coming up the stairs. Barbara stopped and shouted, 'Mum?'

'You don't need to holler like that, Barbara,' said her mum. She stood in the doorway, a dumpy, baggy woman wearing jeans and a denim jacket. Her brown hair was tied in a ponytail, and she had a weary, fleshy face that looked like it couldn't be bothered to decide on an expression. She looked round the room blankly; she didn't say hello, or ask me my name, as all the mums I'd ever met did.

'Do you want to hear my trumpet Mum?' said Barbara in a plaintive voice I'd never heard her use before.

'Not just now,' she sighed. 'I've got to go out again.'

I felt myself staring at her, and turned away. Trying to connect her with the woman in the photographs was like trying to imagine what ice-cream sprinkled with salt would taste like. Except more disturbing.

'Where're you going?' said Barbara.

'Phil's taking me out.'

She left and we heard her bedroom door close.

'You need to go now,' said Barbara, pushing me towards the door. 'I want to see my mum.'

I got home, relieved at how normal and orderly everything looked. The gate, the curtains pulled efficiently at either side of the window. They made Barbara's house seem a Gothic extravagance of my imagination, and my involvement in her life slipped away: I forgot her.

The kitchen door was open. I could hear Mum's voice. And then a man's voice. They were at the kitchen table drinking tea.

'I ask you,' Mum was saying, 'whoever heard of Lady Macbeth urinating in the middle of the stage? And then the three witches wearing sunglasses! I nearly fell off my seat.'

'It's just shock value these days,' the man said. 'They want to grind your face in the shit, as Pinter said.'

'Oh,' said Mum, and paused. I could tell she didn't know who Pinter was. 'Just lamentable,' she said after a few seconds, 'that's what it was.'

'What was?' I said suddenly, walking into the kitchen. They hadn't noticed me and Mum was surprised.

'Well hello to you too,' she said. 'Cara, this is Brian from the group, Brian this is Cara.'

'Hello there,' he said.

'Hi.'

I walked over to the cupboard and got out a packet of crisps. 'Put those back,' Mum shouted over. 'It'll be lunch soon, I don't want you stuffing your face with rubbish.'

'I'm *starving*.'

'You don't look starving. Quite the opposite.'

I sat down at the table and Mum told me they were talking about the play they'd seen last night. I'd been asleep when she came in.

'To be fair,' said Brian, talking precisely as if he were picking insects from his food, 'the ending was good. It meant we got to go home.'

Mum flashed him a brilliant smile. 'That's right,' she said. 'And the seats,' she said, 'those little hard seats!'

'We should go to the pantomime next time,' Brian said, 'I bet you get a comfy seat there.'

Mum started talking about how she'd never been to the theatre until she was seventeen – 'It was *Death of a Salesman*,' she said. 'I just sat there, gripped' – and how she'd hardly been since because she had no one to go with.

'You've never invited me,' I said.

'That's because you wouldn't like it.'

She looked at me absent-mindedly and then directed her attention back to Brian. 'She'd fidget, like her dad. I took him to see *The Silver Darlings* once and he fidgeted the whole time. He only perked up when I bought him a Cornetto at the interval.'

Brian started talking about his ex-wife, the one Mum told me about who had tried to poison him and phoned him up late at night to screech at him. He didn't look the kind of man anyone would screech down the phone at. There was something well tended and carefully refined about him – his fine black sweater, gold-rimmed glasses, the considered smile on his face. A certain amount of woody aftershave floated around him and got up my nose.

Mum made us bacon and eggs for lunch. It took her ten minutes to notice I hadn't touched my bacon.

'What's wrong with it?' she said. 'Why aren't you eating?'

'You've given me all the fatty bits,' I said, looking down at my plate and pushing the bacon around with my fork.

'Don't be ridiculous,' she said.

I was angry and more upset than the situation warranted. I sat staring at the table until Mum cleared the plates away and said that it was up to me if I didn't want to eat it.

'Missing a meal won't kill you,' she said.

I never saw Brian after that, although Mum went out with him at night. He waited for her in his car, the engine purring. They still went hill-walking on Saturdays, and during the week there were poetry readings, plays, the foreign cinema, folk-singing evenings at the Scotia bar.

'Why don't you go along?' I said to Dad one night. He was sitting in the living room, reading the paper. Mum was getting changed in the bedroom.

'It's not really my cup of tea,' he said. 'I just get bored at that kind of thing.'

'You might like it,' I said. 'You won't know if you never go.'

'Who'd look after you?' he said, and I said I could look after myself. I wanted to say something about Brian, although I didn't know what. I didn't know how to say it.

'Do you want to try and beat me at chess?' Dad said.

'No thanks.'

'Scared I'll thrash you,' he said, tugging me gently on the arm. I was angry at him suddenly, angry because he seemed so piteous, so clumsy and needy in his affection.

'I just don't feel like it,' I said, and left the room.

During this period – I remember it as a few weeks, although it was probably longer – Mum was positively incandescent. She laughed all the time, she acted silly, thrilled at her own silliness, and spoke constantly about what she'd seen and done, and who said what to whom. She didn't speak about the old house any more, she said moving to Glasgow was the best decision she'd ever made. 'This is my renaissance,' she was fond of saying. She enrolled for an Open University course in English literature after the summer, and read through the brochures during dinner.

'Don't get your hopes up,' Dad said. 'You might find it too difficult. It's been years since you've had to write an essay.'

'I'll manage,' said Mum serenely. She was as untouched by him recently as a Buddha is untouched by worldly possessions. She ate her dinner, enchanted with whatever she was thinking about. When Dad told her about his day, she didn't even feign interest.

One night she never returned home. We'd bought my school uniform that afternoon. It was a week till the end of the school holidays. I'd woken up because Dad had fallen against the Welsh dresser, which banged off the wall.

'Is Mum not home yet?' I said, rubbing my eyes.

Dad shrugged and let his hands fall into his lap. 'She's old enough to look after herself,' he said. 'She'll be back.'

I stood at the window and looked out at the street. It was two in the morning. The street was empty and all the lights in the houses were off.

'Phone her friends,' I said, turning round to Dad. 'Ask them if they've seen her.'

'At least she has friends,' said Dad. He was holding his head in his hands as if it were a piece of precious, over-ripe fruit. 'You don't know what it's like,' he said. 'Loneliness. Having no one care about you. They say, they say you can't name things you can't see, but try loneliness. You can't see it but it's there. It's in me.'

He patted his chest and shut his eyes very slowly and then opened them again.

'Try the soul,' he said.

I went through to the kitchen to look for her address book, but I couldn't find it. When I went back into the living room Dad was snoring. I emptied his vodka into the sink, and then stood at the window again. Still nothing. At some point I must have fallen asleep. I woke up on the couch the next morning. It took me a few minutes to remember something was wrong, and then I ran through the house, checking all the rooms. All her clothes were still there, everything she owned still there. I woke up Dad. He phoned the hospitals, police stations, all the people they knew in Dorset, Gran and Grandpa. No one knew anything. We couldn't find any numbers for the hill-walking group.

'We'll just have to wait,' said Dad.

*

A letter came for me the next day. I knew right away it was Mum's writing. Dad read it after me. He didn't say a word. Then he put his arms around me and said, 'I'm sorry, I'm so sorry.' I pushed him away and shouted that it was all his fault. I ripped the letter up, but later Dad Sellotaped it together and brought it up to my room.

'You might want to keep it,' he said, and put it down on my desk. And in the end, I did.

A few days later I was with Barbara. We were straddling the roof of a tenement flat, having climbed up the scaffolding on Barbara's insistence. It was windy and I grabbed onto the edge, terrified.

'I've not seen you for a while,' she said. She was hardly holding on at all. I shrugged and looked over the rooftops.

'I'm going to jump,' she said. She slid down the roof on her bum and disappeared. I shouted her name, but there was no reply. My voice echoed into the silence. I kept shouting, expecting her to reappear, but she didn't. I was scared to move and had to force myself to slide down. There was a narrow row of steel stairs scaling the building, and I went down them gingerly, my hands sweating. She was lying on the pavement, one arm flung out behind her head. I was crouched over her, screaming, when her eyes flew open and she began to laugh.

'Got you,' she said.

'That's not funny,' I said, walking away. I was still shaking.

'As if you'd care,' she said, 'if I was dead.' She looked at me out of the corners of her eyes as if she had asked me a question and was waiting for a reply.

'I would care,' I said, 'and so would your mum.'

'Shows how much you know,' said Barbara. She started walking alongside me.

'Would your mum care?' she asked me. She spoke in her usual flat voice, but she was looking at me slyly.

'Yeah, of course,' I said.

'Hmm,' said Barbara. 'I thought friends were meant to tell each other everything,' she said.

I stopped and stared at her. 'Well, you're not my friend,' I said. 'And I don't want to know your stupid secrets anyway. I don't want to go to your smelly house, and look at your smelly mum's photographs.'

'At least my mum doesn't abandon me,' Barbara shouted. 'Shows how much she loves you.'

'She does. I mean, she's not. Abandoned me, she's not.'

'Everyone knows. *Everyone*,' said Barbara in a quieter voice.

And the next thing I knew, I was hitting her as hard as I could. I gave her a black eye, but the next day she came to my door and acted as if nothing had happened.

'You okay?' she said.

'Yeah,' I said. 'You?'

'Yeah. Want to go to Superdrug?' she said, and I said okay.

For years I looked for her. In the street, on buses, in shops. I felt she would look exactly the same as she did when I was twelve. Even when I was almost definite it wasn't her, I had to check. Always a strange tugging of my heart when it wasn't her.

She moved to Nice with Brian, and wrote me letters that I didn't reply to. She remained, remains, colossal.

I graduated with a good maths degree. Dad and Peter, my boyfriend, came to the graduation. Dad stood in the middle of the aisle and took my picture. And then again, outside in the quadrangles, drinking complimentary Bucks Fizz, laughing, toasting the end of my university days. Even then, throughout the whole time, I could hear Mum say, in her tone of tender and complicated disappointment, 'Anyone can be a counter, Cara.'

AFTER A LIFE

Yiyun Li

Yiyun Li (b. 1972) is a Chinese American author. Her debut short story collection, *A Thousand Years of Good Prayers*, won the 2005 Frank O'Connor International Short Story Award, and her second collection, *Gold Boy, Emerald Girl*, was shortlisted for the same award. Her debut novel, *The Vagrants*, was shortlisted for the 2011 IMPAC Dublin Literary Award. She is an editor of the Brooklyn-based literary magazine, *A Public Space*.

Mr. and Mrs. Su are finishing breakfast when the telephone rings. Neither moves to pick it up at first. Not many people know their number; fewer use it. Their son, Jian, a sophomore in college now, calls them once a month to report his well-being. He spends most of his holidays and school breaks with his friends' families, not offering even the most superficial excuses. Mr. and Mrs. Su do not have the heart to complain and remind Jian of their wish to see him more often. Their two-bedroom flat, small and cramped as it is, is filled with Beibei's screaming when she is not napping, and a foul smell when she dirties the cloth sheets beneath her. Jian grew up sleeping in a cot in the foyer and hiding from his friends the existence of an elder sister born with severe mental retardation and cerebral palsy. Mr. and Mrs. Su sensed their son's elation when he finally moved into his college dorm. They have held on to the secret wish that after Beibei dies – she is not destined for longevity, after all – they will reclaim their lost son, though neither says anything to the other, both ashamed by the mere thought of the wish.

The ringing stops for a short moment and starts again. Mr. Su walks to the telephone and puts a hand on the receiver. "Do you want to take it?" he asks his wife.

"So early it must be Mr. Fong," Mrs. Su says.

"Mr. Fong is a man of courtesy. He won't disturb other people's breakfast," Mr. Su says. Still, he picks up the receiver, and his expression relaxes. "Ah, yes, Mrs. Fong. My wife, she is right here," he says, and signals to Mrs. Su.

Mrs. Su does not take the call immediately. She goes into Beibei's bedroom and checks on her, even though it is not time for her to wake up yet. Mrs. Su strokes the hair, light brown and baby-soft, on Beibei's forehead. Beibei is twenty-eight going on twenty-nine; she is so large it takes both her parents to turn her over and clean her; she screams for hours when she is awake, but for Mrs. Su, it takes a wisp of hair to forget all the imperfections.

When she returns to the living room, her husband is still holding the receiver for her, one hand covering the mouthpiece. "She's in a bad mood," he whispers.

Mrs. Su sighs and takes the receiver. "Yes, Mrs. Fong, how are you today?"

"As bad as it can be. My legs are killing me. Listen, my husband just left. He said he was meeting your husband for breakfast and they were going to the stockbrokerage afterward. Tell me it was a lie."

Mrs. Su watches her husband go into Beibei's bedroom. He sits with Beibei often; she does, too, though never at the same time as he does. "My husband is putting on his jacket so he must be going out to meet Mr. Fong now," Mrs. Su says. "Do you want me to check with him?"

"Ask him," Mrs. Fong says.

Mrs. Su walks to Beibei's room and stops at the door. Her husband is sitting on the chair by the bed, his eyes closed for a quick rest. It's eight o'clock, early still, but for an aging man, morning, like everything else, means less than it used to. Mrs. Su goes back to the telephone and says, "Mrs. Fong? Yes, my husband is meeting your husband for breakfast."

"Are you sure? Do me a favor. Follow him and see if he's lying to you. You can never trust men."

Mrs. Su hesitates, and says, "But I'm busy."

"What are you busy with? Listen, my legs are hurting me. I would've gone after him myself otherwise."

"I don't think it looks good for husbands to be followed," Mrs. Su says.

"If your husband goes out every morning and comes home with another woman's scent, why should you care about what looks good or bad?"

It is not her husband who is having an affair, Mrs. Su retorts in her mind, but she doesn't want to point out the illogic. Her husband is indeed often used as a cover for Mr. Fong's affair, and Mrs. Su feels guilty toward Mrs. Fong. "Mrs. Fong, I would help on another day, but today is bad."

"Whatever you say."

"I'm sorry," Mrs. Su says.

Mrs. Fong complains for another minute, of the untrustworthiness of husbands and friends in general, and hangs up. Mrs. Su knocks on the door of Beibei's room and her husband jerks awake, quickly wiping the corner of his mouth. "Mrs. Fong wanted to know if you were meeting Mr. Fong," she says.

"Tell her yes."

"I did."

Mr. Su nods and tucks the blanket tight beneath Beibei's soft, shapeless chin. It bothers Mrs. Su when her husband touches Beibei for any reason, but it must be ridiculous for her to think so. Being jealous of a daughter who understands nothing and a husband who loves the daughter despite that! She will become a crazier woman than Mrs. Fong if she doesn't watch out for her sanity, Mrs. Su thinks, but still, seeing her husband smooth Beibei's hair or rub her cheeks upsets Mrs. Su. She goes back to the kitchen and washes the dishes, while her husband gets ready to leave. When he says farewell, she answers politely without turning to look at him.

At eight-thirty Mr. Su leaves the apartment, right on time for the half-hour walk to the stockbrokerage. Most of the time he is there only to study the market; sometimes he buys and sells, executing the transactions with extraordinary prudence, as the money in his account does not belong to him. Mr. Fong has offered the ten-thousand yuan as a loan, and has made it clear many times that he is not in any urgent need of the money. It is not a big sum at all for Mr. Fong, a retired senior officer from a military factory, but Mr. Su believes that *for each drop of water one received, one has to repay with a well.* The market and the economy haven't helped him much in returning Mr. Fong's generosity. Mr. Su, however, is not discouraged. A retired mathematics teacher at sixty-five, Mr. Su believes in exercising one's body and mind – both provided by his daily trip to the stockbrokerage – and being patient.

Mr. Su met Mr. Fong a year ago at the stockbrokerage. Mr. Fong, a year senior to Mr. Su, took a seat by him, and conversation started between the two men. He was there out of curiosity, Mr. Fong said; he asked Mr. Su if indeed the stock system would work for the country, and if that was the case, how Marxist political economics could be adapted for this new, clearly capitalistic, situation. Mr. Fong's question, obsolete and naive as it was, moved Mr. Su. With almost everyone in the country going crazy about money, and money alone, it was rare to meet someone who was nostalgic about the old but also earnest in his effort to understand the new. "You are on the wrong floor to ask the question," Mr. Su replied. "Those who would make a difference are in the VIP lounges upstairs."

The stockbrokerage, like most of the brokerage firms in Beijing, rented space from bankrupted state-run factories. The one Mr. Su visited used to manufacture color TVs, a profitable factory until it lost a price war to a monopolizing corporation. The laid-off workers were among the ones who frequented the ground floor of the brokerage, opening accounts with their limited means and hoping for good luck. Others on the floor were retirees, men and women of Mr. Su's age who dreamed of making their money grow instead of letting the money die in banks, which offered very low interest rates.

"What are these people doing here if they don't matter to the economy?" Mr. Fong asked.

"*Thousands of sand grains make a tower,*" Mr. Su said. "Together their investments help a lot of factories run."

"But will they make money from the stock market?"

Mr. Su shook his head. He lowered his voice and said, "Most of them don't. Look at that woman there in the first row, the one with the hairnet. She buys and sells according to what the newspapers and television say. She'll never earn money that way. And there, the old man – eighty-two he is, a very fun and healthy oldster but not a wise investor."

Mr. Fong looked at the people Mr. Su pointed out, every one an example of bad investing. "And you, are you making money?" Mr. Fong asked.

"I'm the worst of all," Mr. Su said with a smile. "I don't even have money to get started." Mr. Su had been observing the market for some time. With an imaginary fund, he had practiced trading, dutifully writing down all the transactions in a notebook; he had bought secondhand books on trading and developed his own theories. His prospects of earning money from the market were not bleak at all, he concluded after a year of practice. His pension, however, was small. With a son going to college, a wife and a daughter totally dependent on him, he had not the courage to risk a penny on his personal hobby.

Very quickly, Mr. Fong and Mr. Su became close friends. They sat at teahouses or restaurants, exchanging opinions about the world, from prehistorical times to present day. They were eager to back up each other's views, and at the first sign of disagreement, they changed topics. It surprised Mr. Su that he would make a friend at his age. He was a quiet and lonely man all his life, and most people he knew in his adult life were mere acquaintances. But perhaps this was what made old age a second childhood – friendship came out of companionship easily, with less self-interest, fewer social judgments.

After a month or so, at dinner, Mr. Fong confessed to Mr. Su that he was in a painful situation. Mr. Su poured a cup of rice wine for Mr. Fong, waiting for him to continue.

"I fell in love with this woman I met at a street dance party," Mr. Fong said.

Mr. Su nodded. Mr. Fong had once told him about attending a class to learn ballroom dancing, and had discussed the advantages: good exercise, a great chance to meet people when they were in a pleasant mood, and an aesthetic experience. Mr. Su had thought of teasing Mr. Fong about his surrendering to Western influences, but seeing Mr. Fong's sincerity, Mr. Su had given up the idea.

"The problem is, she is a younger woman," Mr. Fong said.

"How much younger?" Mr. Su asked.

"In her early forties."

"Age should not be a barrier to happiness," Mr. Su said.

"But it's not quite possible."

"Why, is she married?"

"Divorced," Mr. Fong said. "But think about it. She's my daughter's age."

Mr. Su looked Mr. Fong up and down. A soldier all his life, Mr. Fong was in good shape; except for his balding head, he looked younger than his age. "Put on a wig and people will think you are fifty," Mr. Su said. "Quite a decent bridegroom, no?"

"Old Su, don't make fun of me," Mr. Fong said, not concealing a smile. It vanished right away. "It's a futile love, I know."

"Chairman Mao said, *One can achieve anything as long as he dares to imagine it.*"

Mr. Fong shook his head and sullenly sipped his wine. Mr. Su looked at his friend, distressed by love. He downed a cup of wine and felt he was back in his teenage years, consulting his best friend about girls, being consulted. "You know something?" he said. "My wife and I are first cousins. Everybody opposed the marriage, but we got married anyway. You just do it."

"That's quite a courageous thing," Mr. Fong said. "No wonder I've always had the feeling that you're not an ordinary person. You have to introduce me to your wife. Why don't I come to visit you tomorrow at your home? I need to pay respect to her."

Mr. Su felt a pang of panic. He had not invited a guest to his flat for decades. "Please don't trouble yourself," he said finally. "A wife is just the same old woman after a lifelong marriage, no?" It was a bad joke, and he regretted it right away.

Mr. Fong sighed. "You've got it right, Old Su. But the thing is, a wife is a wife and you can't ditch her like a worn shirt after a life."

It was the first time Mr. Fong mentioned a wife. Mr. Su had thought Mr. Fong a widower, the way he talked only about his children and their families. "You mean, your wife's well and" – Mr. Su thought carefully and said – "she still lives with you?"

"She's in prison," Mr. Fong said and sighed again. He went on to tell the story of his wife. She had been the Party secretary of an import-export branch for the Agriculture Department, and naturally, there had been money coming from subdivisions and companies that needed her approval on paperwork. The usual cash-for-signature transactions, Mr. Fong explained, but someone told on her. She received a *within-the-Party* disciplinary reprimand and was retired. "Fair enough, no? She's never harmed a soul in her life," Mr. Fong said. But unfortunately, right at the time of her retirement, the president issued an order that for corrupt officials who had taken more than a hundred and seventy thousand yuan, the government would seek heavy punishments. "A hundred and seventy thousand is nothing compared to what he's taken!" Mr. Fong hit the table with a fist. In a lower voice, he said, "Believe me, Old Su, only the smaller fish pay for the government's face-lift. The big ones – they just become bigger and fatter."

Mr. Su nodded. A hundred and seventy thousand yuan was more than he could imagine, but Mr. Fong must be right that it was not a horrific crime. "So she had a case with that number?"

"Right over the limit, and she got a sentence of seven years."

"Seven years!" Mr. Su said. "How awful, and unfair."

Mr. Fong shook his head. "In a word, Old Su, how can I abandon her now?"

"No," Mr. Su said. "That's not right."

They were silent for a moment, and both drank wine as they pondered the dilemma. After a while, Mr. Fong said, "I've been thinking: before my wife comes home, we – the woman I love and I – maybe we can have a temporary family. No contract, no obligation. Better than those, you know what they call, one night of something?"

"One-night stands?" Mr. Su blurted out, and then was embarrassed to have shown familiarity with such improper, modern vocabularies. He had learned the term from tabloids the women brought to the brokerage; he had even paid attention to those tales, though he would never admit it.

"Yes. I thought ours could be better than that. A *dew marriage before the sunrise.*"

"What will happen when your wife comes back?" Mr. Su asked.

"Seven years is a long time," Mr. Fong said. "Who knows what will become of me in seven years? I may be resting with Marx and Engels in heaven then."

"Don't say that, Mr. Fong," Mr. Su said, saddened by the eventual parting that they could not avoid.

"You're a good friend, Old Su. Thank you for listening to me. All the other people we were friends with – they left us right after my wife's sentence, as if our bad luck would contaminate them. Some of them used to come to our door and beg to entertain us!" Mr. Fong said, and then, out of the blue, he brought out the suggestion of loaning Mr. Su some money for investing.

"Definitely not!" Mr. Su said. "I'm your friend not because of your money."

"Ah, how can you think of it that way?" Mr. Fong said. "Let's look at it this way: it's a good experiment for an old Marxist like me. If you make a profit, great; if not, good for my belief, no?"

Mr. Su thought Mr. Fong was drunk, but a few days later, Mr. Fong mentioned the loan again, and Mr. Su found it hard to reject the offer.

Mrs. Fong calls again two hours later. "I have a great idea," she says when Mrs. Su picks up the phone. "I'll hire a private detective to find out whom my husband is seeing."

"Private detective?"

"Why? You think I can't find the woman? Let me be honest with you – I don't trust that husband of yours at all. I think he lies to you about my husband's whereabouts."

Mrs. Su panics. She didn't know there were private detectives available. It sounds foreign and dangerous. She wonders if they could do some harm to her husband, his being Mr. Fong's accomplice in the affair. "Are you sure you'll find a reliable person?" she says.

"People will do anything if you have the money. Wait till I get the solid evidence," Mrs. Fong says. "The reason I'm calling you is this: if your husband, like you said, is spending every day away from home, wouldn't you be suspicious? Don't you think it possible that they are both having affairs, and are covering up for each other?"

"No, it's impossible."

"How can you be so sure? I'll hire a private detective for both of us if you like."

"Ah, please no," Mrs. Su says.

"You don't have to pay."

"I trust my husband," Mrs. Su says, her legs weakened by sudden fear. Of all the people in the world, a private detective will certainly be the one to find out about Beibei.

"Fine," Mrs. Fong says. "If you say so, I'll spare you the truth."

Mrs. Su has never met Mrs. Fong, who was recently released from prison because of health problems after serving a year of her sentence. A few days into her parole, she called Su's number – it being the only unfamiliar number in Mr. Fong's list of contacts – and grilled Mrs. Su about her relationship with Mr. Fong. Mrs. Su tried her best to convince Mrs. Fong that she had nothing to do with Mr. Fong, nor was there a younger suspect in her household – their only child was a son, Mrs. Su lied. Since then, Mrs. Fong has made Mrs. Su a confidante, calling her several times a day. Life must be hard for Mrs. Fong now, with a criminal record, all her old friends turning their backs on her, and a husband in love with a younger woman. Mrs. Su was not particularly sympathetic with Mrs. Fong when she first learned of the sentence – one hundred and seventy thousand yuan was an astronomical number to her – but now she does not have the heart to refuse Mrs. Fong's friendship. Her husband is surely having a secret affair, Mrs. Fong confesses to Mrs. Su over the phone. He has developed some alarming and annoying habits – flossing his teeth after every meal, doing sit-ups at night, tucking his shirts in more carefully, rubbing hair-growing ointment on his head. "As if he has another forty years to live," Mrs. Fong says. He goes out and meets Mr. Su every day, but what good reason is there for two men to see each other so often?

The stock market, Mrs. Su explains unconvincingly. Mrs. Fong's calls exhaust Mrs. Su, but sometimes, after a quiet morning, she feels anxious for the phone to ring.

Mrs. Su has lived most of her married life within the apartment walls, caring for her children and waiting for them to leave in one way or another. Beyond everyday greetings, she does not talk much with the neighbors when she goes out for groceries. When Mr. and Mrs. Su first moved in, the neighbors tried to pry information from her with questions about the source of all the noises from the apartment. Mrs. Su refused to satisfy their curiosity, and in turn, they were enraged by the denial of their right to know Su's secret. Once when Jian was four or five, a few women trapped him in the building entrance and grilled him for answers; later Mrs. Su found him on the stairs in tears, his lips tightly shut.

Mrs. Su walks to Beibei's bedroom door, which she shut tightly so that Mrs. Fong would not hear Beibei. She listens for a moment to Beibei's screaming before she enters the room. Beibei is behaving quite agitatedly today, the noises she makes shriller and more impatient. Mrs. Su sits by the bed and strokes Beibei's eyebrows; it fails to soothe her into her usual whimpering self. Mrs. Su tries to feed Beibei a few spoonfuls of gruel, but she sputters it all out onto Mrs. Su's face.

Mrs. Su gets up for a towel to clean them both. The thought of a private detective frightens her. She imagines a ghostlike man tagging along after Mr. Fong and recording his daily activities. Would the detective also investigate her own husband if Mrs. Fong, out of curiosity or boredom, spends a little more money to find out other people's secrets? Mrs. Su shudders. She looks around the bedroom and wonders if a private detective, despite the curtains and the window that are kept closed day and night, will be able to see Beibei through a crack in the wall. Mrs. Su studies Beibei and imagines how she looks to a stranger: a mountain of flesh that has never seen the sunshine, white like porcelain. Age has left no mark on Beibei's body and face; she is still a newborn, soft and tender, wrapped up in an oversized pink robe.

Beibei screeches and the flesh on her cheeks trembles. Mrs. Su cups Beibei's plump hand in her own and sings in a whisper, "The little mouse climbs onto the counter. The little mouse drinks the cooking oil. The little mouse gets too full to move. Meow, meow, the cat is coming and the little mouse gets caught."

It was Beibei's favorite song, and Mrs. Su believes there is a reason for that. Beibei was born against the warning of all the relatives, who had not agreed with the marriage between the cousins in the first place. At Beibei's birth, the doctors said that she would probably die before age ten; it would be a miracle if she lived to twenty. They suggested the couple give up the newborn as a specimen for the medical college. She was useless, after all, for any other reason. Mr. and Mrs. Su shuddered, at the image of their baby soaked in a jar of formaldehyde, and never brought Beibei back to the hospital after mother and baby were released. Being in love, the couple were undaunted by the calamity. They moved to a different district, away from their families and old neighbors, he changing his job, she giving up working altogether to care for Beibei. They did not invite guests to their home; after a while, they stopped having friends. They applauded when Beibei started making sounds to express her need for comfort and company; they watched her grow up into a bigger version of herself. It was a hard life, but their love for each other, and for the daughter, made it the perfect life Mrs. Su had dreamed of since she had fallen in love at twelve, when her cousin, a year older and already a lanky young man, had handed her a book of poems as a present.

The young cousin has become the stooping husband. The perfect life has turned out less so. The year Beibei reached ten – a miracle worth celebrating, by all means – her husband brought up the idea of a second baby. Why? she asked, and he talked about a healthier marriage, a more complete family. She did not understand his reasoning, and she knew, even when Jian was growing in her belly, that they would get a good baby and that it would do nothing to save them from what had been destroyed. They had built a world around Beibei, but her husband decided to turn away from it in search of a family more like other people's. Mrs. Su found it hard to understand, but then, wasn't there an old saying about men always being interested in change, and women in preservation? A woman accepted anything from life and made it the best; a man bargained for the better but also the less perfect.

Mrs. Su sighs, and looks at Beibei's shapeless features. So offensive she must be to other people's eyes that Mrs. Su wishes she could shrink Beibei back to the size that she once carried in her arms into this room; she wishes she could sneak Beibei into the next world without attracting anybody's attention. Beibei screams louder, white foam dripping by the corner of her mouth. Mrs. Su cleans her with a towel, and for a moment, when her hand stops over Beibei's mouth and muffles the cry, Mrs. Su feels a desire to keep the hand there. Three minutes longer and Beibei could be spared all the struggles and humiliations death has in store for every living creature, Mrs. Su thinks, but at the first sign of blushing in Beibe's pale face, she removes the towel. Beibei breathes heavily. It amazes and saddens Mrs. Su that Beibei's life is so tenacious that it has outlived the love that once made it.

With one finger, Mr. Su types in his password – a combination of Beibei's and Jian's birthdays – at a terminal booth. He is still clumsy in his operation of the computer, but people on the floor, aging and slow as most of them are, are patient with one another. The software dutifully produces graphs and numbers, but Mr. Su finds it hard to concentrate today. After a while, he quits to make room for a woman waiting for a booth. He goes back to the seating area and looks for a good chair to take a rest. The brokerage, in the recent years of a downward economy, has slackened in maintenance, and a lot of chairs are missing orange plastic seats. Mr. Su finally finds a good one among homemade cotton cushions, and sits down by a group of old housewives. The women, in their late fifties or early sixties, are the happiest and chattiest people on the floor. Most of them have money locked into stocks that they have no other choice but to keep for now, and perhaps forever; the only reason for them to come every day is companionship. They talk about their children and grandchildren, unbearable in-laws, soap operas from the night before, stories from tabloids that must be discussed and analyzed at length.

Mr. Su watches the rolling numbers on the big screen. The PA is tuned in to a financial radio station, but the host's analysis is drowned by the women's stories. Most of the time, Mr. Su finds them annoyingly noisy, but today he feels tenderness, almost endearment, toward the women. His wife, quiet and pensive, will never become one of these chatty old hens, but he wishes, for a moment, that one of them were his wife, cheered up by the most mundane matters, mindlessly happy.

After taking note of the numbers concerning him, Mr. Su sighs. Despite all the research he had done, his investment does not show any sign more positive than the old women's. Life goes wrong for the same reason that people miscalculate. Husband and wife promise each other a lifelong love that turns out shorter than a life; people buy stocks with good calculations, but they do not take into consideration life's own preference for, despite the laws of probability, the unlikely. Mr. Su fell in love with his wife at thirteen, and she loved him back. What were the odds for first lovers to end up in a family? Against both families' wills, they married each other, and against everybody's warning, they decided to have a baby. Mr. Su, younger and more arrogant then, calculated and concluded that the odds for a problematic baby were very low, so low that fate was almost on their side. Almost, but not quite, and as a blunt and mean joke, Beibei was born with major problems in her brain and spinal cord. It would not be much of a misfortune except when his wife started to hide herself and the baby from the world; Beibei must have reminded his wife every day that their marriage was less legitimate. There's nothing to be ashamed of, Mr. Su thought of telling her, but he did not have the heart. It was he who suggested another baby. To give them a second chance, to save his wife from the unnecessary shame and pain that she had insisted on living with. Secretly he also wished to challenge fate again. The odds of having another calamity were low, very low, he tried to convince his wife; if only they could have a normal baby, and a normal family! The new baby's birth proved his calculation right – Jian was born healthy, and he grew up into a very handsome and bright boy, as if his parents were awarded doubly for what had been taken away the first time – but who would've thought that such a success, instead of making their marriage a happier one, would turn his wife away from him? How arrogant he was to make the same mistake a second time, thinking he could outsmart life. What had survived the birth of Beibei did not survive Jian's birth, as if his wife, against all common wisdom, could share misfortune with him but not happiness. For twenty years, they have avoided arguments carefully; they have been loving parents, dutiful spouses, but something that had made them crazy for each other as young cousins has abandoned them, leaving them in unshareable pain.

A finger taps Mr. Su's shoulder. He opens his eyes and realizes that he has fallen asleep. "I'm sorry," he says to the woman.

"You were snoring," she says with a reproachful smile.

Mr. Su apologizes again. The woman nods and returns to the conversation with her companions. Mr. Su looks at the clock on the screen, too early for lunch still, but he brings out a bag of instant noodles and a mug from his bag anyway, soaking the noodles with boiling water from the drinking stand. The noodles soften and swell. Mr. Su takes a sip of soup and shakes his head. He thinks of going home and talking to his wife, asking her a few questions he has never gathered enough courage to ask, but then decides that things unsaid had better remain so. Life is not much different from the stock market – you invest in a stock and you stick, and are stuck, to the choice, despite all the possibilities of other mistakes.

At noon, the restaurant commissioned by the stockbrokerage delivers the lunch boxes to the VIP lounges, and the traders on the floor heat lunches in the microwave or make instant noodles. Mr. Su, who is always cheered up by the mixed smells of leftovers from other dinner tables, goes into a terminal booth in a hopeful mood. Someday, he thinks, when his wife is freed from taking care of Beibei, he'll ask her to accompany him to the stockbrokerage. He wants her to see other people's lives, full of meaningless but happy trivialities.

Mr. Su leaves the brokerage promptly at five o'clock. Outside the building, he sees Mr. Fong, sitting on the curb and looking up at him like a sad, deserted child.

"Mr. Fong," Mr. Su says. "Are you all right? Why didn't you come in and find me?"

Mr. Fong suggests they go for a drink, and then holds out a hand and lets Mr. Su pull him to his feet. They find a small roadside diner, and Mr. Fong orders a few cold plates and a bottle of strong yam wine. "Don't you sometimes wish a marriage doesn't go as long as our lives last?" Mr. Fong says over the drink.

"Is there anything wrong?" Mr. Su asks.

"Nothing's right with the wife after she's released," Mr. Fong says.

"Are you going to divorce her?"

Mr. Fong downs a cup of wine. "I wish I could," he says and starts to sob. "I wish I didn't love her at all so I could just pack up and leave."

By late afternoon Mrs. Su is convinced that Beibei is having problems. Her eyes, usually clear and empty, glisten with a strange light, as if she is conscious of her pain. Mrs. Su tries in vain to calm her down, and when all the other ways have failed, she takes out a bottle of sleeping pills. She puts two pills into a small porcelain mortar, and then, after a moment of hesitation, adds two more. Over the years she has fed the syrup with the pill powder to Beibei so that the family can have nights for undisturbed sleep.

Calmed by the syrup, Beibei stops screaming for a short moment, and then starts again. Mrs. Su strokes Beibei's forehead and waits for the medicine to take over her limited consciousness. When the telephone rings, Mrs. Su does not move. Later, when it rings for the fifth time, she checks Beibei's eyes, half closed in drowsiness, and then closes the bedroom door before picking up the receiver.

"Why didn't you answer the phone? Are you tired of me, too?" Mrs. Fong says.

Mrs. Su tries to find excuses, but Mrs. Fong, uninterested in any of them, cuts her off. "I know who the woman is now."

"How much did it cost you to find out?"

"Zero. Listen, the husband – shameless old man – he confessed himself."

Mrs. Su feels relieved. "So the worst is over, Mrs. Fong."

"Over? Not at all. Guess what he said to me this afternoon? He asked me if we could all three of us live together in peace. He said it as if he was thinking on my behalf. 'We have plenty of rooms. It doesn't hurt to give her a room and a bed. She is a good woman, she'll take good care of us both.' Taking care of his *thing*, for sure."

Mrs. Su blushes. "Does she want to live with you?"

"Guess what? She's been laid off. Ha ha, not a surprise, right? I'm sure she wants to move in. Free meals. Free bed. Free man. What comes better? Maybe she's even set her eyes on our inheritance. Imagine what the husband suggested? He said I should think of her as a daughter. He said she lost her father at five and did not have a man good to her until she met him. So I said, Is she looking for a husband, or a stepfather? She's *honey-mouthing him*, you see? But the blind-man! He even begged me to feel for her pain. Why didn't he ask her to feel for me?"

Something hits the door with a heavy thump, and then the door swings open. Mrs. Su turns and sees an old man leaning on the door, supported by her husband. "Mr. Fong's drunk," her husband whispers to her.

"Are you there?" Mrs. Fong says.

"Ah, yes, Mrs. Fong, something's come up and I have to go."

"Not yet. I haven't finished the story."

Mrs. Su watches the two men stumble into the bathroom. After a moment, she hears the sounds of vomiting and the running of tap water, her husband's low comforting words, Mr. Fong's weeping.

"So I said, Over my dead body, and he cried and begged and said all these ridiculous things about opening one's mind. Many households have two women and one man living in peace now, he said. It's the marriage revolution, he said. Revolution? I said. It's retrogression. You think yourself a good Marxist, I said, but Marx didn't teach you bigamy. Chairman Mao didn't tell you to have a concubine."

Mr. Su helps Mr. Fong lie down on the couch and he closes his eyes. Mrs. Su watches the old man's tear-smeared face twitch in pain. Soon Mrs. Fong's angry words blend with Mr. Fong's snoring.

With Mr. Fong fast asleep, Mr. Su stands up and walks into Beibei's room. One moment later, he comes out and looks at Mrs. Su with a sad and calm expression that makes her heart tremble. She lets go of the receiver with Mrs. Fong's blabbering and walks to Beibei's bedroom. There she finds Beibei resting undisturbed, the signs of pain gone from her face, porcelain white, with a bluish hue. Mrs. Su kneels by the bed and holds Beibei's hand, still plump and soft, in her own. Her husband comes close and strokes her hair, gray and thin now, but his touch, gentle and timid, is the same one from a lifetime ago, when they were children playing in their grandparents' garden, where the pomegranate blossoms, fire-hued and in the shape of bells, kept the bees busy and happy.

SORRY?

Helen Simpson

Helen Simpson (b. 1959) is a British novelist and short story writer. She worked at *Vogue* for five years before becoming a writer full-time. Her first collection, *Four Bare Legs in a Bed and Other Stories*, won the Sunday Times Young Writer of the Year award, and her second, *Hey Yeah Right Get A Life*, won the Hawthornden Prize. In 1993 she was selected as one of *Granta*'s top twenty novelists under the age of forty.

'Sorry?' said Patrick. 'I didn't quite catch that.'

'Soup of the day is wild mushroom,' bellowed the waiter.

'No need to shout,' said Patrick, putting his hand to his troublesome ear.

The new gadget shrieked in protest.

'They take a bit of getting used to,' grimaced Matthew Herring, the deaf chap he'd been fixed up with for a morale-boosting lunch.

'You don't say,' he replied.

Some weeks ago Patrick had woken up to find he had gone deaf in his right ear – not just a bit deaf but profoundly deaf. There was nothing to be done, it seemed. It had probably been caused by a tiny flake of matter dislodged by wear-and-tear change in the vertebrae, the doctor had said, shrugging. He had turned his head on his pillow, in all likelihood, sometimes that was all it took. This neck movement would have shifted a minuscule scrap of detritus into the river of blood running towards the brain, a fragment that must have finished by blocking the very narrowest bit of the entire arterial system, the ultra-fine pipe leading to the inner ear. Bad luck.

'I don't hear perfectly,' said Matthew Herring now. 'It's not magic, a digital hearing aid, it doesn't turn your hearing into perfect hearing.'

'Mine's not working properly yet,' said Patrick. 'I've got an appointment after lunch to get it seen to.'

'Mind you, it's better than the old one,' continued Matthew comfortably. 'You used to be able to hear me wherever I went with the analogue one, it used to go before me, screeching like a steam train.'

He chuckled at the memory.

Patrick did not smile at this cosy reference to engine whistles. He had been astonished at the storm of head noise that had arrived with deafness, the whistles and screeches over a powerful cloud of hissing just like the noise from Elizabeth's old pressure cooker. His brain was generating sound to compensate for the loss of hearing, he had been told. Apparently that was part and parcel of the deafness, as well as dizzy episodes. Ha! Thanks to the vertigo which had sent him arse over tip several times since the start of all this, he was having to stay with his daughter Rachel for a while.

'Two girls,' he said tersely in answer to a question from his tedious lunch companion. He and Elizabeth had wished for boys, but there you were. Rachel was the only one so far to have provided him with grandchildren. The other daughter, Ruth, had decamped to Australia some time ago. Who knew what she was up to, but she was still out there so presumably she had managed to make a go of it, something that she had signally failed to do in England.

'I used to love music,' Matthew Herring was saying, nothing daunted. 'But it's not the same now I'm so deaf. Now it tires me out; in fact, I don't listen any more. I deliberately avoid it. The loss of it is a grief, I must admit.'

'Oh well, music means nothing to me,' said Patrick. 'Never has. So I shan't miss *that*.'

He wasn't about to confide in Matthew Herring, but of all his symptoms it had been the auditory hallucinations produced by the hearing aid which had been the most disturbing for him. The low violent stream of nonsense issuing from the general direction of his firstborn had become insupportable in the last week, and he had had to turn the damned thing off.

At his after-lunch appointment with the audiologist, he found himself curiously unable to describe the hallucinatory problem.

'I seem to be picking up extra noise,' he said eventually. 'It's difficult to describe.'

'Sounds go into your hearing aid where they are processed electronically,' she intoned, 'then played back to you over a tiny loudspeaker.'

'Yes, I know that,' he snapped. 'I am aware of that, thank you. What I'm asking is, might one of the various settings you programmed be capable of, er, amplifying sounds that would normally remain unheard?'

'Let's see, shall we,' she said, still talking to him as though he were a child or a halfwit. 'I wonder whether you've been picking up extra stuff on the Loop.'

'The Loop?'

'It works a bit like Wi-Fi,' she said. 'Electromagnetic fields. If you're in an area that's on the Loop, you can pick up on it with your hearing aid when you turn on the T-setting.'

'The T-setting?'

'That little extra bit of kit there,' she said, pointing at it. 'I didn't mention it before, I didn't want to confuse you while you were getting used to the basics. You must have turned it on by mistake from what you're saying.'

'But what *sort* of extra sounds does it pick up?' he persisted.

Rachel's lips had not been moving during that initial weird diatribe a week ago, he was sure of it, nor during the battery of bitter little remarks he'd had to endure since then.

'Well, it can be quite embarrassing,' she said, laughing merrily. 'Walls don't block the magnetic waves from a Loop signal, so you might well be able to listen in to confidential conversations if neighbouring rooms are also on it.'

'Hmm,' he said, 'I'm not sure that quite explains this particular problem. But I suppose it might have something to do with it.'

'Look, I've turned off the T-setting,' she said. 'If you want to test what it does, simply turn it on again and see what happens.'

'Or hear,' he said. 'Hear what happens.'

'You're right!' she declared, with more merry laughter.

He really couldn't see what was so amusing, and said so.

Back at Rachel's, he made his way to the armchair in the little bay window and whiled away the minutes until six o'clock by rereading the *Telegraph*. The trouble with this house was that it had been knocked through, so you were all in it hugger-mugger together. He could not himself see the advantage of being forced to witness every domestic detail. Frankly, it was bedlam, with the spin cycle going and Rachel's twins squawking and Rachel washing her hands at the kitchen sink yet again like Lady Macbeth. Now she was doing that thing she did with the brown paper bag, blowing into it and goggling her eyes, which seemed to amuse the twins at least.

Small children were undoubtedly tiresome, but the way she indulged hers made them ten times worse. Like so many of her generation she seemed to be making a huge song and dance about the whole business. She was ridiculous with them, ludicrously over-indulgent and lacking in any sort of authority. It was when he had commented on this in passing that the auditory hallucinations had begun.

'I don't want to do to them what you did to me, you old beast,' the voice had growled, guttural and shocking, although her lips had not been moving. 'I don't want to hand on the misery. I don't want that horrible Larkin poem to be true.' He had glared at her, amazed, and yet it had been quite obvious she was blissfully unaware of what he had heard. Or thought he had heard.

He must have been hearing things.

Now he held up his wrist and tapped his watch at her. She waved back at him, giving one last puff into the paper bag before scurrying to the fridge for the ice and lemon. As he watched her prepare his first drink of the evening, he decided to test out the audiologist's theory.

'Sit with me,' he ordered, taking the clinking glass.

'I'd love to, Dad, but the twins ...' she said.

'Nonsense,' he said. 'Look at them, you can see them from here, they're all right for now.'

She perched on the arm of the chair opposite his and started twisting a strand of her lank brown hair.

'Tell me about your day,' he commanded.

'My day?' she said. 'Are you sure? Nothing very much happened. I took the twins to Tumbletots, then we went round Asda ...'

'Keep talking,' he said, fiddling with his hearing aid. 'I want to test this gadget out.'

'... then I had to queue at the post office, and I wasn't very popular with the double buggy,' she droned on.

He flicked the switch to the T-setting.

'... never good enough for you, you old beast, you never had any time for me, you never listened to anything I said,' came the low growling voice he remembered from before. 'You cold old beast, Ruth says you're emotionally autistic, definitely somewhere on the autistic spectrum anyway, that's why she went to the other side of the world, but she says she still can't get away from it there, your lack of interest, you blanked us, you blotted us out, you don't even know the names of your grandchildren let alone their birthdays ...'

He flicked the switch back.

'... after their nap, then I put the washing on and peeled some potatoes for tonight's dinner while they watched CBeebies ...' she continued in her toneless everyday voice.

'That's enough for now, thanks,' he said crisply. He took a big gulp of his drink, and then another. 'Scarlett and, er, Mia. You'd better see what they're up to.'

'Are you OK, Dad?'

'Fine,' he snapped. 'You go off and do whatever it is you want to do.' He closed his eyes. He needed Elizabeth now. She'd taken no nonsense from the girls. He had left them to her, which was the way she'd wanted it. All this hysteria! Elizabeth had known how to deal with them.

He sensed he was in for another bad night, and he was right. He lay rigid as a stone knight on a tomb, claustrophobic in his partially closed-down head and its frantic brain noise. The deafer he got the louder it became; that was how it was, that was the deal. He grimaced at the future, his other ear gone, reduced to the company of Matthew Herring and his like, a shoal of old boys mouthing at each other.

The thing was, he had been the breadwinner. Children needed their mothers. It was true he hadn't been very interested in them, but then, frankly, they hadn't been very interesting. Was he supposed to pretend? Neither of them had amounted to much. And he had had his own life to get on with.

He'd seen the way they were with their children these days – 'Oh, that's wonderful, darling! You *are* clever' and 'Love you!' at the end of every exchange, with the young fathers behaving like old women, cooing and planting big sloppy kisses on their babies as if they were in a Disney film. The whole culture had gone soft, it gave him the creeps; opening up to your feminine side! He shuddered in his pyjamas.

Elizabeth was dead. That was what he really couldn't bear.

The noise inside his head was going wild, colossal hooting and zooming and pressure-cooker hiss; he needed to distract his brain with – what had the doctor called it? – 'sound enrichment'. Give it some competition, fight fire with fire: that was the idea. Fiddling with the radio's tuning wheel in the dark, he swore viciously and wondered why it was you could never find the World Service when you needed it. He wanted talk but there was only music, which would have to do. Nothing but a meaningless racket to him, though at least it was a different *sort* of racket; that was the theory.

No, that was no better. If anything, it was worse.

Wasn't the hearing aid supposed to help cancel tinnitus? So the doctor had suggested. Maybe the T-setting would come into its own in this sort of situation.

He turned on the tiny gadget, made the necessary adjustments, and poked it into his ear.

It was like blood returning to a dead leg, but in his head and chest. What an extraordinary sensation! It was completely new to him. Music was stealing hotly, pleasurably through his veins for the first time in his life, unspeakably delicious. He heard himself moan aloud. The waves of sound were announcing bliss and at the same time they brought cruel pain. He'd done his best, hadn't he? He didn't know what the girls expected from him. He'd given them full financial support until they were eighteen, which was more than many fathers could say. What was it exactly that he was supposed not to have done?

Lifting him on a dark upsurge into the night, the music also felled him with inklings of what he did not know and had not known, intimations of things lovely beyond imagination which would never now be his as death was next. A tear crept down his face.

He hadn't cried since he was a baby. Appalling! At this rate he'd be wetting himself. When his mother had died, he and his sisters had been called into the front room and given a handkerchief each and told to go to their bedrooms until teatime. Under the carpet. Into thin air.

The music was so astonishingly beautiful, that was the trouble. Waves of entrancing sound were threatening to breach the sea wall. Now he was coughing dry sobs.

This was not on. Frankly he preferred any combination of troublesome symptoms to getting in this state. He fumbled with the hearing aid and at last managed to turn the damned thing *off*. Half-unhinged, he tottered to the bathroom and ran a basin of water over it, submerged the beastly little gadget, drowned it. Then he fished it out and flushed it down the lavatory. Best place for it.

No more funny business, he vowed. That was that. From now on he would put up and shut up, he swore it on Elizabeth's grave. Back in bed, he once again lowered his head onto the pillow.

Straight away the infernal noise factory started up; he was staggering along beat by beat in a heavy shower of noise and howling.

'It's not real,' he whispered to himself in the dark. 'Compensatory brain activity, that's what this is.'

Inside his skull all hell had broken loose. He had never heard anything like it.

UP AT A VILLA

Helen Simpson

Helen Simpson (b. 1959) is a British novelist and short story writer. She worked at *Vogue* for five years before becoming a writer full-time. Her first collection, *Four Bare Legs in a Bed and Other Stories*, won The Sunday Times Young Writer of the Year award, and her second, *Hey Yeah Right Get A Life*, won the Hawthornden Prize. In 1993 she was selected as one of *Granta*'s top twenty novelists under the age of forty.

They were woken by the deep-chested bawling of an angry baby. Wrenched from wine-dark slumber, the four of them sat up, flustered, hair stuck with pine needles, gulping awake with little light breaths of concentration. They weren't supposed to be here, they remembered that.

They could see the baby by the side of the pool, not twenty yards away, a furious geranium in its parasol-shaded buggy, and the large pale woman sagging above it in her bikini. Half an hour ago they had been masters of that pool, racing topless and tipsy round its borders, lithe Nick chasing sinewy Tina and wrestling her, an equal match, grunting, snaky, toppling, crashing down into the turquoise depths together. Neither of them would let go underwater. They came up fighting in a chlorinated spume of diamonds. Joe, envious, had tried a timid imitation grapple, but Charlotte was having none of it.

'Get off!' she snorted, kind, mocking, and slipped neatly into the pool via a dive that barely broke the water's skin. Joe, seeing he was last as usual, gave a foolish bellow and launched his heavy self into the air, his aimless belly slapping down disastrously like an explosion.

After that, the sun had dried them off in about a minute, they had devoured their picnic of *pissaladière* and peaches, downed the bottles of pink wine and gone to doze in the shade behind the ornamental changing screen.

Now they were stuck. Their clothes and money were heaped under a bush of lavender at the other end of the pool.

'Look,' whispered Tina as a man came walking towards the baby and its mother. 'Look, they're English. He's wearing socks.'

'What's the matter with her now,' said the man, glaring at the baby.

'How should I know,' said the woman. 'I mean, she's been fed. She's got a new nappy.'

'Oh, plug her on again,' said the man crossly, and wandered off towards a cushioned sun-lounger. 'That noise goes straight through my skull.'

The woman muttered something they couldn't hear, and shrugged herself out of her bikini top. They gasped and gaped in fascination as she uncovered huge brown nipples on breasts like wheels of Camembert.

'Oh gross!' whispered Tina, drawing her lips back from her teeth in a horrified smirk.

'Be quiet,' hissed Nick as they all of them heaved with giggles and snorts and their light eyes popped, over-emphatic in faces baked to the colour of flowerpots.

They had crept into the grounds of this holiday villa, one of a dozen or more on this hillside, at slippery Nick's suggestion, since everything was *fermé le lundi* down in the town and they had no money left for entrance to hotel pools or even to beaches. Anyway they had fallen out of love over the last week with the warm soup of the Mediterranean, its filmy surface bobbing with polystyrene shards and other unsavoury orts.

'Harvey,' called the woman, sagging on the stone bench with the baby at her breast. 'Harvey, I wish you'd ...'

'Now what is it,' said Harvey testily, making a great noise with his two-day-old copy of *The Times*.

'Some company,' she said with wounded pathos. 'That's all.'

'Company,' he sighed. 'I thought the idea was to get away from it all.'

'I thought we'd have a chance to talk on holiday,' said the woman.

'All right, all right,' said Harvey, scrumpling up *The Times* and exchanging his sun-lounger for a place on the stone bench beside her. 'All right. So what do you want to talk about?'

'Us,' said the woman.

'Right,' said Harvey. 'Can I have a swim first?' And he was off, diving clumsily into the pool, losing his poise at the last moment so that he met the water like a flung cat.

'She's hideous,' whispered Tina. 'Look at that gross stomach, it's all in folds.' She glanced down superstitiously at her own body, the high breasts like halved apples, the handspan waist.

'He's quite fat too,' said Charlotte. 'Love handles, anyroad.'

'I'm never going to have children,' breathed Tina. 'Not in a million years.'

'Shush,' said Joe, straining forward for the next instalment. The husband was back from his swim, shaking himself like a Labrador in front of the nursing mother.

'"Us"', he said humorously, wiggling a finger inside each ear, then drubbing his hair with the flats of his hands. 'Fire away then.'

She started immediately, as if she knew she only had two or three minutes of his attention, and soon the air was thick with phrases like Once she's on solids, and You'd rather be reading the paper, and Is it because you wanted a boy? He looked dull but resigned, silent except for once protesting, What's so special about bathtime. She talked on, but like a loser, for she was failing to find the appropriate register, flailing around, pulling clichés from the branches. At some subliminal level each of the eavesdropping quartet recognised their own mother's voice in hers, and glazed over.

'You've never moaned on like this before,' marvelled Harvey at last. 'You were always so independent. Organised.'

'You think I'm a mess,' she said. 'A failure as a mother.'

'Well, you're obviously not coping,' he said. 'At home all day and you can't even keep the waste bins down.'

Nick and Tina were laughing with silent violence behind the screen, staggering against each other, tears running down their faces. Joe was mesmerised by the spectacle of lactation. As for Charlotte, she was remembering another unwitting act of voyeurism, a framed picture from a childhood camping holiday.

It had been early morning, she'd gone off on her own to the village for their breakfast baguettes, and the village had been on a hill like in a fairy-tale, full of steep little flights of steps which she was climbing for fun. The light was sweet and glittering and as she looked down over the rooftops she saw very clearly one particular open window, so near that she could have lobbed in a ten-franc piece, and through the window she could see a woman dropping kisses onto a man's face and neck and chest. He was lying naked in bed and she was kissing him lovingly and gracefully, her breasts dipping down over him like silvery peonies. Charlotte had never mentioned this to anyone, keeping the picture to herself, a secret snapshot protected from outside sniggerings.

'The loss of romance,' bleated the woman, starting afresh.

'We haven't changed,' said Harvey stoutly.

'Yes, we have! Of course we have!'

'Rubbish.'

'But we're supposed to change, it's all different now, the baby's got to come first.'

'I don't see why,' said Harvey. 'Mustn't let them rule your life.'

The baby had finished at last, and was asleep; the woman gingerly detached her from her body and placed her in the buggy.

'Cheer up,' said Harvey, preparing for another dip. 'Once you've lost a bit of weight, it'll all be back to normal. Romance et cetera. Get yourself in shape.'

'You don't fancy me any more,' she wailed in a last-ditch attempt to hold him.

'No, no, of course I do,' he said, eyeing the water. 'It's just a bit … different from before. Now that you've gone all, you know, sort of floppy.'

That did it. At the same moment as the woman unloosed a howl of grief, Nick and Tina released a semi-hysterical screech of laughter. Then – 'Run!' said Joe – and they all shot off round the opposite side of the pool, snatching up their clothes and shoes and purses at the other end. Harvey was meanwhile shouting, 'Hoi! Hoi! What the hell d'you think you're playing at!' while his wife stopped crying and his daughter started.

The four of them ran like wild deer, leaping low bushes of lavender and thyme, whooping with panicky delight, lean and light and half-naked – or, more accurately, nine-tenths naked – through the pine trees and *après-midi* dappling. They ran on winged feet, and their laughter looped the air behind them like chains of bubbles in translucent water.

High up on the swimming-pool terrace the little family, frozen together for a photographic instant, watched their flight open-mouthed, like the ghosts of summers past; or, indeed, of summers yet to come.

PLUNDER

Edna O'Brien

Edna O'Brien (b. 1930) is an Irish novelist, playwright, poet and short story writer. Her first novel, *The Country Girls*, is often credited with breaking silence on sexual matters and social issues in Ireland following World War II. Due to the controversy caused by the book, O'Brien left Ireland for London where she has remained. She has written over twenty works of fiction and received the Irish PEN Lifetime Achievement Award in 2001.

One morning we wakened to find that there was no border – we had been annexed to the fatherland. Of course we did not hear of it straightaway as we live in the wilds, but a workman who comes to gather wood and fallen boughs told us that soldiers had swarmed the town and occupied the one hotel. He said they drank there, got paralytic, demanded lavish suppers, and terrorised the maids. The townspeople hid, not knowing which to fear most, the rampaging soldiers or their huge dogs that ran loose without muzzles. He said they had a device for examining the underneath of cars – a mirror on wheels to save themselves the inconvenience of stooping. They were lazy bastards.

The morning we sighted one of them by the broken wall in the back avenue we had reason to shudder. His camouflage was perfect, green and khaki and brown, the very colours of this mucky landscape. Why they should come to these parts baffled us and we were sure that very soon they would scoot it. Our mother herded us all into one bedroom, believing we would be safer that way – there would be no danger of one of us straying and we could keep turns at the watch. As luck had it, only the week before we had gathered nuts and apples and stored them on wooden trays for the winter. Our mother worried about our cow, said that by not being milked her poor udder would be pierced with pain, said the milk would drip all over the grass. We could have used that cow's milk. Our father was not here, our father had disappeared long before.

On the third morning they came and shouted our mother's name – Rosanna. It sounded different, pronounced in their tongue, and we wondered how they knew it. They were utter hooligans. Two of them roughed her out, and the elder tugged on the long plait of her hair.

Our mother embraced each of us and said she would be back presently. She was not. We waited, and after a fearful interval we tiptoed downstairs but could not gain entry to the kitchen because the door between it and the hall was barricaded with stacked chairs. Eventually we forced our way through, and the sight was grisly. Her apron, her clothes, and her underclothes were strewn all over the floor, and so were hairpins and her two side combs. An old motorcar seat was raised onto a wooden trough in which long ago she used to put the feed for hens and chickens. We looked in vain through the window, thinking we might see her in the back avenue or better still coming up the path, shattered, but restored to us. There was one soldier down there, his rifle cocked. Where was she? What had they done to her? When would she be back? The strange thing is that none of us cried and none of us broke down. With a bit of effort we carried the stinking car seat out and threw it down the three steps that led from the back door. It was all we could do to defy our enemies. Then we went up to the room and waited. Our cow had stopped moaning, and we realised that she too had been taken and most likely slaughtered. The empty field was ghost-like, despite the crows and jackdaws making their usual commotion at evening time. We could guess the hours roughly by the changing light and changing sky. Later the placid moon looked in on us. We thought, if only the workman would come back and give us news. The sound of his chainsaw used to jar on us, but now we would have welcomed it as it meant a return to the old times, the safe times, before our mother and our cow were taken. Our brother's wooden flute lay in the fire grate, as he had not the heart to play a tune, even though we begged for it.

On the fifth morning we found some reason to jubilate. The sentry was gone from his post, and no one came to stand behind that bit of broken wall. We read this as deliverance. Our mother would come back. We spoke of things that we would do for her. We got her clean clothes out of the wardrobe and lay them neatly on the bed. Her lisle stockings hanging down, shimmered pink in a shaft of sunlight, and we could imagine her legs inside them. We told each other that the worst was over. We bit on apples and pelted each other with the butts for fun. Our teeth cracked with a vengeance on the hazelnuts and the walnuts, and picking out the tasty, fleshy particles, we shared them with one another like true friends, like true family. Our brother played a tune. It was about the sun setting on a place called 'Boulevouge'.

Our buoyancy was shortlived. By evening we heard gunshot again, and a soldier had returned to the broken bit of wall, a shadowy presence. Sleep was impossible and so we watched and we prayed. We did that for two whole days and nights, and what with not eating and not sleeping, our nerves got the better of us and, becoming hysterical, we had to slap each other's faces, slap them smartly, to bring common sense into that room.

The hooligans in their camouflage have returned. They have come by a back route, through the dense woods and not up the front avenue as we expected.

They are in the kitchen, laughing and shouting in their barbarous tongues. Fear starts to seep out of us, like blood seeping. If we are taken all together, we might muster some courage, but from the previous evidence it is likely that we will be taken separately. We stand, each in our corner, mute, petrified, like little effigies, our eyes fastened to the knob of the door, our ears straining beyond it, to gauge which step of stairs they are already stomping on.

How beautiful it would be if one of us could step forward and volunteer to become the warrior for the others. What a firmament of love ours would be.

A deathly emptiness to the whole world, to the fields and the sacked farmyards and the tumbledown shacks. Not a soul in sight. Not an animal. Not a bird. Here and there mauled carcasses and bits of torn skins where animals must have fought each other in their last frenzied hungers. I almost got away. I was walking towards somewhere that I didn't know, somewhere safe. There had been no soldiers for weeks. They'd killed each other off. It was hard to know which side was which, because they swapped sides the way they swapped uniforms. My mother and later my brother and my two sisters had been taken. I was out foraging and when I came back our house was a hulk of smoke. Black ugly smoke. I only had the clothes I stood up in, a streelish green dress and a fur coat that was given to my mother once. It used to keep us warm in bed, and sometimes when it slipped onto the floor I would get out to pick it up. It felt luxurious, the hairs soft and tickling on bare feet. That was the old world, the other world, before the barbarians came. Why they came here at all is a mystery, as there was no booty, no gold mines, no silver mines – only the woods, the tangly woods, and in some parts tillage, small patches of oats or barley. Even to think of corn, first green and then a ripening yellow, or the rows of cabbage, or any growing thing, was pure heartbreak. Maybe my brother and sisters are across the border or maybe they are dead. I moved at dusk and early night, bunched inside the fur coat. I wanted to look old, to look a hag. They did not fancy the older women; they wanted young women and the younger the better, like wild strawberries. It was crossing a field that I heard the sound of a vehicle, and I ran, not knowing there was such swiftness in me. They were coming, nearer and nearer, the wheels slurping over the ridged earth that bordered the wood that I was heading into. The one who jumped out picked me up and tossed me to the Head Man. They spluttered with glee. He sat me on his lap, wedged my mouth open, wanting me to say swear words back to him. His eyes were hard as steel and the whites a yellowy gristle. Their faces were daubed with paint and they all had puce tattoos. The one that drove was called Gypsy. That drive was frantic. Me screaming, screaming, and the Head Man slapping me like mad and opening me up as though I was a mess of potage. They stopped at a disused lime kiln. He was first. When he splayed me apart I thought I was dead, except that I wasn't. You don't die when you think you do. The subordinates used their hands as stirrups. When I was turned over I bit on the cold lime floor to clean my mouth of them. Their shouts, their weight, their tongues, their slobber, the way they bore through me, wanting to get up into my head, to the God particle. That's what an old woman in the village used to call it, that last cranny where you say prayers and confide in yourself the truth of what you feel about everything and everyone. They couldn't get to it. I had stopped screaming. The screams were stifled. Through the open roof I saw a buzzard glide in a universe of blue. It was waiting for another to be with it, and after a time that other came that was its comrade and they glided off into those crystalline nether-reaches. Putting on their trousers, they kept telling each other to hurry the fuck up. The Head Man stood above me, straddled, the fur coat over his shoulders, and he looked spiteful, angry. The blood was pouring out of me and the ground beneath was warm. I saw him through the slit in my nearly shut eyes. For a minute I thought he might kill me and then he turned away as if it wasn't worth the bother, the mess. The engine had already started when Gypsy ran back and placed a cigarette across my upper lip. I expect he was trying to tell me something. As children we were told that why we have a dent in our upper lip is because when we are born an angel comes and places a forefinger there for silence, for secrecy. By degrees I came back. Little things, the air sidling through that small clammy enclosure and the blood drying on me, like resin. Long ago, we had an aluminium alarm clock with the back fallen off, that worked on a single battery, but batteries were scarce. Our mother would take out the battery and we'd guess the time by the failing light, by the dusk, by the cockcrow and the one cow, the one faithful cow that stood, lowing, at the paling, waiting to be milked. One of us would go out with a bucket and the milking stool. When she put the battery back the silver needle would start up and then the two hands, like two soft black insects, crept over each other in their faithful circuit. The lime-green dress that I clung to, that I clutched, that I dug my fingernails into, is splotched with flowers, blood-red and prodigal, like poppies. Soon as I can walk I will set out. To find another, like me. We will recognise each other by the rosary of poppies and the speech of our eyes. We, the defiled ones, in our thousands, scattered, trudging over the land, the petrified land, in search of a safe haven, if such a place exists.

Many and terrible are the roads to home.

AUNT TELEPHONE

Edith Pearlman

Edith Pearlman (b. 1936) is an American short story writer. She has published more than 250 works of short fiction and non-fiction in national magazines, literary journals, anthologies and online publications. She was awarded the PEN/Malamud Award in 2011, and her latest collection, *Binocular Vision*, won the 2012 National Book Critics Circle Award.

I got my first taste of raw flesh when I was nine years old. I had been taken to an adult party. My father was out of town at an investors' conference and my brother was spending the night at a friend's; and my babysitter got sick at the last minute, or said she did. What was my mother to do – stay home? So she brought me along. The affair was cocktails and a buffet featuring beef tartare on pumpernickel rounds and a bowl of icy seviche – this was thirty years ago, before such delicacies had been declared lethal. The party was given by the Plunkets, family therapists: two fatties who dressed in similar sloppy clothing as if to demonstrate that glamour was not a prerequisite for rambunctious sex.

My mother and I and Milo walked over to the party in the glowing September afternoon. Our house and Milo's and the Plunkets' all lay within a mile of each other in Godolphin, a leafy wedge of Boston, as did the homes of most of the other guests – the psychiatrists and clinical psychologists and social workers who made up this crowd. They were all friends, they referred patients to one another, they distributed themselves into peer-supervision subsets – a collegial, talkative crew, their envy vigorously tamped down. Their kids were friends, too – some as close as cousins. I already hated groups, but I was willy-nilly part of the bunch.

Among the adults, Milo was first among peers. He produced paper after acclaimed paper: case histories of children with symptoms like elective mutism and terror of automobiles and willful constipation lasting ten days. I longed to become one of his fascinating patients, but I knew to my sadness that therapists rarely treated their friends' children no matter how sick and I knew, also, that I wasn't sick anyway, just ornery and self-centered. In his published work Milo gave the young sufferers false first names and surname initials. "What would you call *me*?" I asked him once, still hoping for immortality.

"Well, Susan, what would you like to be called?"

"Catamarina M."

He warmed me with his brown gaze. ("The eyes," Dr. Lenore once remarked to my mother, "thoroughly compensate for the absence of chin.")

Milo said: "Catamarina is your name forever."

So I had an appellation if not symptoms. All I had to do was stop talking or moving my bowels. Alas, nature proved too strong for me.

Milo's colleagues respected his peaceable bachelordom: they recognized asexuality as an unpathological human preference, also as a boon to society. He had been born in cosmopolitan Budapest, which gave him further cachet. His liberal parents, who were in the bibelot business, had gotten out just before World War II. So Milo was brought up in New York by a pair of Hungarians, penniless at first, soon rich again. He inherited a notable collection of ancient Chinese figurines.

On the day of that party Milo was wearing his standard costume: flannel slacks, turtleneck sweater, tweed jacket. He was then almost fifty, a bit older than my parents and their friends. His hair, prematurely gray, rose high and thick from a narrow forehead. It swung at his nape like a soft broom. He was very tall and very thin.

Dr. Will Plunket gave me beef tartare in a hamburger bun. But the Plunket boys wouldn't let me join their game of Dungeons and Dragons. So, munching my feral sandwich, I wandered in the fall garden still brightened by a glossy sun. On a chaise on the flagstone terrace sat a woman I didn't know. She looked sulky and bored. Dr. Judah joined me for a while and wondered aloud if fairies nested under the chrysanthemums. I frowned at him, but when he went inside I knelt and peered under the mums. Nothing. After a while Milo found me. In his soft voice he talked about the greenery near the stone wall – basil was rumored to cure melancholy, marjoram headaches, ground ivy conjunctivitis. He bent, picked up a handful of the ivy, stood, and crushed a few leaves into my palm. "Not to be taken internally." Then he, too, went in.

I drifted toward the terrace. "How lucky you are," drawled the woman on the chaise, and she drank some of her cocktail.

"Yes. Why?"

"To have such an attentive aunt," she said, and drank some more.

"My aunt lives in Michigan."

"She's here on a visit?"

"She's in Europe this month."

"I mean the aunt you were just talking to."

"Milo?"

"Her name is Milo?"

I raced into the house. I found my mother standing with Dr. Margaret and Dr. Judah. "You'll never believe it, that patient on the terrace, she thought Milo was my aunt!" My mother gave me a ferocious stare. "My *aunt*," I heedlessly repeated to Dr. Margaret, and then turned to Dr. Judah. "My—" but I couldn't finish because my mother was yanking me out of the room.

"Stop talking, Susan, stop right now, do not say that again. It would hurt Milo's feelings dreadfully." She let go of me and folded her arms. "There's dirt on your knees," she said, though dirt was not usually denigrated in this circle. "Filth."

"Garden soil," I corrected.

My mother sighed. "The woman on the terrace is Dr. Will's sister."

"I wish Milo *was* my aunt."

"Were."

"Were? Why?"

"Condition contrary to fact." As our conversation slid into the safe area of grammar, we returned to the party. Milo was now listening to Dr. Will. It didn't seem to me that Milo's longish hair was more feminine than Dr. Will's black smock. But this once I would obey my mother. I would not again relate the error of the woman on the terrace. I hoped that Milo hadn't heard my earlier exclamation. Not for the world would I hurt his feelings; or so I thought.

Milo celebrated thanksgiving here, Passover there, Christmas twice in one day, first at the Collinses and then at the Shapiros. He smoked his after-dinner cigar in everybody's backyard. He came to our annual New Year's Day open house, which I was required to attend for fifteen minutes. I spent that quarter hour behind a lamp. My parents, shoulder to shoulder, greeted their guests. Sometimes my mother slipped her hand into my father's pocket, like a horse nuzzling for sugar.

Milo went to piano recitals and bar mitzvahs and graduations. In August he visited four different families, one each week. He *was* an aunt, my aunt, aunt to many children born into our therapeutic set, if an aunt is someone always ready to talk on the telephone to worried parents – especially to mothers, who do most of the worrying. Those mothers of ours, full of understanding for their patients, were helpless when their own offspring gave them trouble. Then they became frantic kid sisters, reaching for the phone. Bad report cards, primitive behavior on the playground, sass, lying, staying out all night, playing hooky – for all such troubles Milo was ready with advice and consolation. He knew, also, when a child needed outside help – strangling the cat was a sure indication. Usually, though, it was the parent who required an interpretation and also a recommendation to back off. "No, a joint today is not a crack pipe tomorrow," he memorably assured Dr. Lenore. Dr. Lenore's daughter was, of course, listening on the extension. We were all masters of domestic wiretapping – slipping a forefinger between receiver and the button on which it rested, lifting the receiver to our ear, releasing the button with the caution of a surgeon until a connection was soundlessly established.

The July I was twelve I ran away from overnight camp. The day after I arrived home, surly and triumphant, I eavesdropped on Milo and my mother. Milo was suggesting that my mother praise me for taking the bus rather than hitchhiking on the highway.

"She stole the bus money from her counselor," my mother said.

"Borrowed, I think. Encourage her to return the money by mail."

"Shouldn't she be encouraged to return herself to camp?"

Milo said: "To the hated place?" There was a talcum pause as he drew on his cigar. "To the place she had the resourcefulness to escape from?"

"It's difficult to have her home," my mother said, with a little sob.

"Yes, Ann, I can imagine," said Milo. And then: "It is her home, too."

There was a silence – Milo's the silence of someone who has delivered a truth and my mother's the silence of someone who has received it. And a third silence, a silence within a silence: mine. "It is her home, too," I heard. The gentle living room. The kitchen whose window looked out on birds and squirrels and sometimes a pheasant that had strayed from the more suburban part of Godolphin. The attached office where my mother saw patients during the day. The bedroom where in the evenings she received those patients' panicky calls and where she herself called Milo. My brother's room with his construction projects in various stages of completion – though a year younger than I, he was already an adept mechanic. My own room: posters, books, toys outgrown but not discarded, clothing pooled on the floor and draped on lamps. A long window led from my room onto a little balcony. My mother had once planted impatiens in boxes on the balcony but I let the flowers die. Without recrimination she had watched me neglect – desecrate, even – a generous space in the house. The house that was hers, too.

For the remainder of July I babysat for the kids next door, treating them with a pretend affection I ended up feeling. ("Hypocrisy is the first step toward sincerity," Milo had written.) I made a small effort to straighten my room. ("A token is a cheap coin, but it is not counterfeit" – same source.) In August we went to Cape Cod.

Our determinedly modest bungalow faced the sea; there was no sandy beach, but we had become used to lying on our strip of shingle. The house had four small bedrooms. The walls were thin, providing perfect acoustics. There was a grille and an outdoor shower. Sometimes my father grilled fish; sometimes he and my mother prepared meals together in the inconvenient kitchen, where they bumped into each other and laughed.

As always Milo came for the third week. I could hear him, too, turning over in bed or splashing in the bathroom, just as I could hear my parents' soft conversations, my brother's indiscriminate farting. The small family – still too large a group for me. "I want to work in a private office," I said one morning.

"You could be a psychiatrist," said my unimaginative brother.

"Private! By myself! Nobody comes in."

"Ah. You could be a bank president," Milo said. "They are rarely interrupted."

"Or a hotel housekeeper," my mother said. "Just you and piles of linen."

"Or an astronomer, alone with her telescope," my father said. That was the best offer. "The work requires a bit of math," he added, mildly.

Later that day Milo took my brother and me to Bosky's Wild Animal Preserve. We visited Bosky's once or twice each summer. The wildest animals there were a pair of foxes. Foxes are devoted parents while their offspring require care. Then they separate, and next season they find new partners. But Bosky's two downcast specimens were stuck with each other year after year. The male peacock didn't seem to have much fun, either. His occasional halfhearted display revealed gaps in his feathers. A pichi, a female rock snake, a few monkeys chattering nonsense – these were our wild animals. But beyond the pathetic cages was a large working farm, with chickens and turkeys and an apple orchard and a field of corn. A pony in a straw hat dragged a cart around the cornfield. Two other chapeaued ponies could be ridden around a ring, though not independently: you had to endure, walking beside you, one of the local teenagers who worked at Bosky's. These louts did not hide their contempt for nag and rider.

The rock snake was fed a live white mouse every two weeks. This public meal was unadvertised but word got around. When we got to Bosky's that day with Milo, there were a dozen small children already gathered in front of the snake's cage. Their parents, wearing doubtful expressions, milled at a distance. My brother went off to the ponies. Milo and I were tall enough to see over the children's heads, so we two and the kids viewed the entire performance – the lowering of the mouse into the cage by Mr. Bosky, the terrified paralysis of the rodent, the expert constriction by the snake, and then the mouse's slow incorporation into the snake's hinged mouth. She fed herself the mouse, whose bones were all broken but who still presumably breathed. In it went, farther in, still farther, until all we could see was its tiny rump and then only its thin white tail.

The little kids, bored once the tail had disappeared, drifted toward their pained parents. One skinny mother vomited into a beach bag. Milo looked at her with sympathy. Not I, though.

"A recovering bulimic," I told him as we moved away.

"Giving herself a thrill?" he wondered. "Could be," he said, generously admitting me into the company of interpreters.

I love you, Milo, I might have said if we said that sort of thing.

In the fall I began to attend school regularly, forcing myself to tolerate groups at least for a classroom hour. I had to choose a sport so I went out for track, the least interpersonal of activities. I did my homework in most subjects. I made up the math I had flunked the year before.

My mother needed to call Milo less often.

I even achieved a kind of intimacy. My best friend – almost my only one, really, unless you counted Dr. Judah's daughter and Dr. Lenore's daughter and the younger Plunket boy, who were all in my grade – was an extra-tall girl with an extra-long neck. Her parents had been born in India. They both practiced radiology. Their daughter planned a career in medicine, too, as casually as a child of other parents might look forward to taking over the family store. Anjali – such a beautiful name – was plain and dark, with drooping lids and wide nostrils. Her last name was Nezhukumatathil – "Where my father comes from, the equivalent of Smith."

She lived a few blocks from us. She and I walked home along the same streets every day, rarely bothering to talk. Our route took us past the stretch of row houses that included Milo's, past his small, low-maintenance garden: a dogwood tree, a cast iron white love seat below it, pachysandra around it. Milo's front door had two bells, one for the living quarters, one for the office and playroom. He was always working in the late afternoon, and so I didn't tell Anjali that I knew the owner of that particular narrow house.

But one May at five o'clock there he was on the lacy bench, he and his cigar. A patient had canceled, I immediately understood. There was an exchange of hellos and an introduction; and then – after Milo had poked the cigar into a tin of sand beside the love seat – we were inside; and Milo was telling Anjali the provenance of some of his figurines and showing her his needlepoint utensils. How had he guessed that this mute camel liked small things and delicate handiwork? If I'd been walking with Sarah – another girl I sometimes made myself pal around with, a very good runner – he'd have known to put "Hair" on the stereo and discuss stretching exercises. Ah, it was his business. I sipped a can of Coke. You might guess that it tasted like wormwood, that I was full of jealousy – but no: I was full of admiration for Milo, performing his familial role for this schoolgirl, comfortably limited by the imminent arrival of the next patient; within ten minutes he'd give us the gate. And he did, first looking with a rueful expression at his watch. "Good-bye, Anjali," he said at the door. "See you soon, Susan. Thank you for bringing your friend," as if I had done it on purpose to display my hard-won sociability.

A block or so later Anjali made a rare disclosure – she'd like to live like Milo.

"In what way?" I asked, expecting mention of the figurines, the needlepoint, even the dogwood.

"Alone."

Me, too! I wanted to confide. But the confidence would have been false. I already guessed that someday I would marry and produce annoying children. I was not as bold as Milo, as Anjali. Nature would again prove too strong for me.

August: just before senior year. I ran every morning; it was no longer an obligation but a pleasure. The third week Anjali came to the Cape to visit me, and one of my brother's friends came to visit him, and Milo came to visit the family. He swam and baked blueberry pies and treated us to impromptu lectures on this and that – the nature of hurricanes; stars, though I had already dismissed astronomy as a career; the town of Scheveningen, where, at the age of four, he had spent the summer. He liked to recall an ancient Dutch waiter who had brought him lemonade every afternoon and talked about his years as a circus acrobat. "Lies, beautiful lies, essential to amour propre."

"To the waiter's amour propre?" I asked.

"And to mine. Taking lies seriously, it's a necessary skill."

In bathing briefs, muscular and tanned, Milo could not be mistaken for a woman. But my brother's friend, whose schoolteacher parents were not part of our exalted circle, told my brother that Milo was so fucking helpful he was probably some cast-off queen. My brother didn't hesitate to repeat the evaluation to me. "A queen!"

"There's filth on your knees," I snapped, but of course he didn't get the reference. I was furious with all three of them: the unappreciative guest, my unfeeling brother, and Milo, who had brought the accusation on himself with his pies and his reminiscences. He'd encouraged the taciturn Anjali to talk about ancient artifacts, too. Apparently they were her prime interest nowadays. Apparently Anjali and Milo had run into each other at the museum during the spring – some dumb exhibition, pre-Columbian telephones, maybe. Afterward he had treated her to tea.

On Thursday of that week Milo and I drove Anjali through a light rain to the bus station – she had to get back to town for a family party. She jumped out of the backseat and threw her traveling sack, studded with tiny mirrors, over her bony shoulder. "Thanks," she said in her toneless voice. (She had properly thanked my mother back in the bungalow.) She slammed the door and strode toward the bus.

Milo opened his window and stuck his head into the drizzle. "There's a netsuke exhibition in October," he called.

She stopped and turned, and smiled at him, a smile that lasted several seconds too long. Then she boarded the bus.

We watched the vehicle pull out.

"Shall we take a run to Bosky's?" Milo said.

"The place is swarming with ants," I said. "Bosky's fornicates," I showed off. Milo was silent. "Sure," I relented. It was his vacation, too.

On that damp day Milo paid his usual serious attention to the wild animals: the foxes forced into monogamy, the impotent peacock, the dislocated monkeys. He glanced at the languid snake, still digesting last week's meal. He stopped for an irritatingly long while at the cage of an animal new to the preserve, an agouti from Belize that was (an ill-painted sign mentioned) a species of rodent. "Among Belizeans he's considered a tasty meal," Milo told me; he knew more than the sign painter. "The agouti himself is herbivorous. A sociable little fellow. He shares a common burrow system with others of his kind."

"Does he. Like you."

He gave me his interested stare. "I eat meat— "

"I shouldn't have said that," I muttered.

" – though it's true that I have lost my taste for beef tartare. It wasn't a terrible thing to say, Catamarina M. We all do live, your parents and I and our friends, in a kind of mutual burrow, and the telephone makes it even more intimate, especially when one of you children sneaks onto the line – it's like a hiccup, I listen for it. In what way did you insult me?"

"I suggested you were a rat," I said, confessing to the lesser sin. What I had suggested, as I feared he knew, was that he was an inquisitive dependent animal, exchanging advice for friendship; that for all his intuition and clinical wisdom he did not know firsthand the rage that flared between individuals, the urge to eat each other up. Strong emotions were not part of his repertoire. But they had become part of mine during Anjali's visit as I watched her unfold under his radiant friendship – envy, hatred, fury ... *Once I saved you from ridicule, you ridiculous man.*

"A rat," he echoed. "Nevertheless, you are my favorite ... niece."

"I'm supposed to take that lie seriously? Up your goulash, Milo."

"Susan—"

"Go home." I took several steps away from him and his friend the agouti. Then I whirled and began to run. I ran past the pichi and the monkeys and into the farm area, scattering hens and chickens and little kids. "Hey!" yelled Mr. Bosky. I vaulted the railing of the ponies' riding ring and ran around it and vaulted back. "She's crazy," remarked one of the local boys, in surprised admiration. Perhaps I could sneak out one night and meet him in a haystack. I ran straight into the corn, between stag lines of stalks.

Past the corn was another field where lettuce grew close to the ground. I skirted it – I had no wish to do damage to Bosky's. I ran, faster still, enjoying one of those spurts our track coach taught us to take advantage of – a coach who, without concern for feelings or individuality, made us into athletes. I slowed down when I reached the woods, and padded through it like a fox free of her partner; I slithered, like a snake who has to catch her own mouse. On the other side of the woods was the highway. I crossed it carefully – I had no wish to grieve my parents, either. Another narrow road led to the rocky beach, a couple of miles from our house. I walked the rest of the way. My brother and his friend were sitting on the porch, amiably talking with Milo – Aunt Milo, Queen Milo, Dr. Milo, who so evenly distributed his favors. He and I waved to each other, and I went around to the outside shower and turned it on and stood under it, with all my clothes on.

As I had noticed, my mother was calling Milo less frequently. By that last year in high school, it seemed, she didn't call him at all except to remind him of the New Year's party.

And later, talking with children of the other therapists when we were home from college, or, still later, when we ran into each other in New York or San Francisco, I learned that all of our mothers eventually stopped consulting Milo. Partly, I think, they had less need for his advice. We kids were at last growing up. And our parents had incorporated and so no longer needed to hear Milo's primary rule about offspring – "They owe you and society a minimal courtesy. Everything else is their business" – just as they had incorporated his earlier observation about physical punishment: "It's addictive. Rather than strike your child, light up a cigar."

And perhaps, too, they had to flee their older sibling, the one who had seen their wounds.

A few of them may have even believed the rumor about Milo: that he was paying so much attention to Anjali N., a high school girl, that her parents had to warn him off. That fable had been astonishingly easy to launch. I merely related it to Dr. Margaret's daughter – two years younger than I, grateful for my attention. Then I swore her to secrecy.

At any rate, we grown offspring discovered from each other that Milo himself began to initiate the telephone calls, eager to know the progress of the patients, the anecdotes from the latest trips, the news of the children – especially the news of the children.

"Nosy," said Dr. Lenore's daughter.

"Avaricious," said Benjy Plunket, who had practically lived at Milo's house during his parents' divorce. "When I was in college he wanted to study everything I was studying – he even bought himself a copy of my molecular biology textbook, stuff new since his time."

"He managed to tag along on the Apfels' Las Vegas trip," said Dr. Lenore's daughter.

"People outlive their usefulness," Dr. Judah's daughter summed up.

"It's sad," we all agreed, with offhand malice.

My mother still answered when Milo called (machines allowed other old friends to screen him out) and she tolerated his increasingly discursive monologues. And she kept inviting him to our Cape Cod house, and when he joined our family on a cruise to Scandinavia it was because she and my father enthusiastically insisted. Others were less generous. The Apfels, who had lost heavily in Las Vegas, broke with him entirely.

We are adults now. We prefer e-mail to the telephone. Many of us still live in Godolphin. None of us has entered the mental-health professions. Even Anjali failed to follow her parents into medicine. She teaches art history in Chicago, and has three daughters. Nature proved too strong for her, too.

Some of our children have problems. But though the aged Milo is still working – is esteemed adviser to an inner-city child-guidance center, has done pioneering work with juvenile offenders – we don't consult him. He reminds us too much of our collective childhood in that all-knowing burrow; and of our anxious mothers; and of the unnerving power of empathy. We're a different generation: the tough love crowd. And there's always Ritalin.

I do keep in touch with Milo. It's not a burden: my husband and I are both linguists, and Milo is interested in language. "There is a striving for design in the utterances even of the schizophrenic," he has written.

I inherited the Cape Cod house, and Milo comes to visit every summer. He and I and my two sons always pay a visit to Bosky's. The wild-animal preserve has dwindled to one desperate moose, one raccoon, and those poor foxes, or some other pair. The snake has retired and the agouti is gone, too. But the farm in back continues to flourish, and the ponies get new straw hats every season. My kids have outgrown the place but they understand that old Milo is to be indulged.

A white mustache coats Milo's upper lip. His hair, also white, is still long. His hairline has receded considerably, and he's subject to squamous carcinomas on the exposed brow. Advised by his dermatologist, he covers his head. In the winter he sports a beret, in the summer a cloth hat with a soft brim.

Today, wearing the summer hat and a pair of oversize cargo pants that look like a split skirt, he is riding one of the ponies. That saddle must be punishing his elderly bones. Maybe he's trying to amuse my sons. Certainly they are entertained. When he reaches the far side of the ring they release unseemly snickers. "Granny Wild West," snorts one. "Madame Cowpoke," returns the other. Meanwhile Milo is bending toward the kid who's leading his pony – eliciting a wretched story, no doubt; offering a suggestion that may change the boy's life or at least make his afternoon a little better.

I'd like to smack both my sons and *also* smoke a cigar. Instead I inform them that Milo represents an evolved form of human life that they might someday emulate or even adopt. That sobers them. So I don't mention that he was once valued and then exploited and then betrayed and finally discarded; that, like his displaced parents, he adjusted gracefully to new circumstances.

We stand there, elbows on the railing, as Milo on his pony plods toward us. We smile at him. Within the rim of his bonnet, his face creases; below the soapy mustache his lips part to reveal brown teeth. He is grinning back at us as if he shared our mild mockery of his performance: as if it were his joke, too.

VANITAS

Emma Donoghue

Emma Donoghue (b. 1969) is an Irish-born playwright, literary historian and novelist. She has published seven novels, eleven plays and four collections of short stories. Her 2010 novel, *Room*, was a finalist for the Man Booker Prize.

This afternoon I was so stone bored, I wrote something on a scrap of paper and put it in a medicine bottle, sealed it up with the stub of a candle. I was sitting on the levee; I tossed the bottle as far as I could (since I throw better than girls should) and the Mississippi took it, lazily. If you got in a boat here by the Duparc-Locoul Plantation, and didn't even row or raise a sail, the current would take you down fifty miles of slow curves to New Orleans in the end. That's if you didn't get tangled up in weed.

What I wrote on the scrap was *Au secours!* Then I put the date, *3 juillet 1839*. The Americans if drowning or in other trouble call out, *Help!* which doesn't capture the attention near as much, it's more like a little sound a puppy would make. The bottle was green glass with *Poison* down one side. I wonder who'll fish it out of the brown water, and what will that man or woman or child make of my message? Or will the medicine bottle float right through the city, out into the Gulf of Mexico, and my scribble go unread till the end of time?

It was a foolish message, and a childish thing to do. I know that; I'm fifteen, which is old enough that I know when I'm being a child. But I ask you, how's a girl to pass an afternoon as long and scalding as this one? I stare at the river in hopes of seeing a boat go by, or a black gum tree with muddy roots. A week ago I saw a blue heron swallow down a wriggling snake. Once in a while a boat will have a letter for us, a boy attaches it to the line of a very long fishing rod and flicks it over to our pier. I'm supposed to call a nègre to untie the letter and bring it in; Maman hates when I do it myself. She says I'm a gateur de nègres, like Papa, we spoil them with soft handling. She always beats them when they steal things, which they call only *taking*.

I go up the pecan alley toward the Maison, and through the gate in the high fence that's meant to keep the animals out. Passers-by always know a Creole house by the yellow and red, not like the glaring white American ones. Everything on our Plantation is yellow and red – not just the houses but the stables, the hospital, and the seventy slave cabins that stretch back like a village for three miles, with their vegetable gardens and chicken pens.

I go in the Maison now, not because I want to, just to get away from the bam-bam-bam of the sun on the back of my neck. I step quietly past Tante Fanny's room, because if she hears me she might call me in for some more lessons. My parents are away in New Orleans doing business; they never take me. I've never been anywhere, truth to tell. My brother, Emile, has been in the Lycee Militaire in Bordeaux for five years already, and when he graduates, Maman says perhaps we will all go on a voyage to France. By all, I don't mean Tante Fanny, because she never leaves her room, nor her husband, Oncle Louis, who lives in New Orleans and does business for us, nor Oncle Flagy and Tante Marcelite, quiet sorts who prefer to stay here always and see to the nègres, the field ones and the house ones. It will be just Maman and Papa and I who go to meet Emile in France. Maman is the head of the famille ever since Grandmère Nannette Prud'Homme retired; we Creoles hand the reins to the smartest child, male or female (unlike the Americans, whose women are too feeble to run things). But Maman never really wanted to oversee the family enterprise, she says if her brothers Louis and Flagy were more useful she and Papa could have gone back to la belle France and stayed there. And then I would have been born a French mademoiselle. "Creole" means born of French stock, here in Louisiana, but Maman prefers to call us French. She says France is like nowhere else in the world, it's all things gracious and fine and civilized, and no sacrés nègres about the place.

I pass Millie on the stairs, she's my maid and sleeps on the floor of my room but she has to help with everything else as well. She's one of Pa Philippe's children, he's very old (for a nègre), and has VPD branded on both cheeks from when he used to run away, that stands for Veuve Prud'Homme Duparc. It makes me shudder a little to look at the marks. Pa Philippe can whittle anything out of cypress with his little knife: spoons, needles, pipes. Since Maman started our breeding program, we have more small nègres than we know what to do with, but Millie's the only one as old as me. "Allo, Millie," I say, and she says, "Mam'zelle Aimée," and grins back but forgets to curtsy.

"Aimée" means beloved. I've never liked it as a name. It seems it should belong to a different kind of girl.

Where I am bound today is the attic. Though it's hotter than the cellars, it's the one place nobody else goes. I can lie on the floor and chew my nails and fall into a sort of dream. But today the dust keeps making me sneeze. I'm restless, I can't settle. I try a trick my brother, Emile, once taught me, to make yourself faint. You breathe in and out very fast while you count to a hundred, then stand against the wall and press as hard as you can between your ribs. Today I do it twice, and I feel odd, but that's all; I've never managed to faint as girls do in novels.

I poke through some wooden boxes but they hold nothing except old letters, tedious details of imports and taxes and engagements and deaths of people I never heard of. At the back there's an old-fashioned sheepskin trunk, I've tried to open it before. Today I give it a real wrench and the top comes up. Ah, now here's something worth looking at. Real silk, I'd say, as yellow as butter, with layers of tulle underneath, and an embroidered girdle. The sleeves are huge and puffy, like sacks of rice. I slip off my dull blue frock and try it on over my shift. The skirt hovers, the sleeves bear me up so I seem to float over the splinters and dust of the floorboards. If only I had a looking glass up here. I know I'm short and homely, with a fat throat, and my hands and feet are too big, but in this sun-colored dress I feel halfway to beautiful. Grandmere Nannette, who lives in her Maison de

Reprise across the yard and is descended from Louis XV's own physician, once said that like her I was pas jolie but at least we had our skin, un teint de roses. Maman turns furious if I go out without my sunhat or a parasol, she says if I get freckled like some Cajun farm girl, how is she supposed to find me a good match? My stomach gets tight at the thought of a husband, but it won't happen before I'm sixteen, at least. I haven't even become a woman yet, Maman says, though I'm not sure what she means.

I dig in the trunk. A handful of books; the collected poetry of Lord Byron, and a novel by Victor Hugo called *Notre-Dame de Paris*. More dresses – a light violet, a pale peach – and light shawls like spiders' webs, and, in a heavy traveling case, some strings of pearls, with rings rolled up in a piece of black velvet. The bottom of the case lifts up, and there I find the strangest thing. It must be from France. It's a sort of bracelet – a thin gold chain – with trinkets dangling from it. I've never seen such perfect little oddities. There's a tiny silver locket that refuses to open, a gold cross, a monkey (grimacing), a minute kneeling angel, a pair of ballet slippers. A tiny tower of some sort, a snake, a crouching tiger (I recognize his toothy roar from the encyclopedia), and a machine with miniature wheels that go round and round; I think this must be a locomotive, like we use to haul cane to our sugar mill. But the one I like best, I don't know why, is a gold key. It's so tiny, I can't imagine what door or drawer or box in the world it might open.

Through the window, I see the shadows are getting longer; I must go down and show myself, or there'll be a fuss. I pack the dresses back into the trunk, but I can't bear to give up the bracelet. I manage to open its narrow catch, and fasten the chain around my left arm above the elbow, where no one will see it under my sleeve. I mustn't show it off, but I'll know it's there; I can feel the little charms moving against my skin, pricking me.

"*Vanitas*," says Tante Fanny. "The Latin word for— ?"

"Vanity," I guess.

"A word with two meanings. Can you supply them?"

"A, a desire to be pretty, or finely dressed," I begin.

She nods, but corrects me: "Self-conceit. The holding of too high an opinion of one's beauty, charms or talents. But it also means futility," she says, very crisp. "Worthlessness. What is done *in vain*. Vanitas paintings illustrate the vanity of all human wishes. Are you familiar with Ecclesiastes, chapter one, verse two?"

I hesitate. I scratch my arm through my sleeve, to feel the little gold charms.

My aunt purses her wide mouth. Though she is past fifty now, with the sallow look of someone who never sees the sun, and always wears black, you can tell that she was once a beauty. "*Vanity of vanities, saith the Preacher, vanity of vanities*," she quotes; "*all is vanity.*"

That's Cousine Eliza on the wall behind her mother's chair, in dark oils. In the picture she looks much older than sixteen to me. She is sitting in a chair with something in her left hand, I think perhaps a handkerchief; has she been crying? Her white dress has enormous sleeves, like clouds; above them, her shoulders slope prettily. Her face is creamy and perfectly oval, her eyes are dark, her hair is coiled on top of her head like a strange plum cake. Her lips are together, it's a perfect mouth, but it looks so sad. Why does she look so sad?

"In this print here," says Tante Fanny, tapping the portfolio in her lap with one long nail (I don't believe she ever cuts them), "what does the hourglass represent?"

I bend to look at it again. A grim man in seventeenth-century robes, his desk piled with objects. "Time?" I hazard.

"And the skull?"

"Death."

"Très bien, Aimée."

I was only eight when my uncle and aunt came back from France, with – among their copious baggage – Cousine Eliza in a lead coffin. She'd died of a fever. Papa came back from Paris right away, with the bad news, but the girl's parents stayed on till the end of the year, which I thought strange. I was not allowed to go to the funeral, though the cemetery of St. James is only ten miles upriver. After the funeral was the last time I saw my Oncle Louis. He's never come back to the Plantation since, and for seven years Tante Fanny hasn't left her room. She's shut up like a saint; she spends hours kneeling at her little prie-dieu, clutching her beads, thumping her chest. Millie brings all her meals on trays, covered to keep off the rain or the flies. Tante Fanny also sews and writes to her old friends and relations in France and Germany. And, of course, she teaches me. Art and music, French literature and handwriting, religion and etiquette (or, as she calls it, les convenances and comme il faut). She can't supervise my piano practice, as the instrument is in the salon at the other end of the house, but she leaves her door open, when I'm playing, and strains her ears to catch my mistakes.

This morning instead of practicing I was up in the attic again, and I saw a ghost, or at least I thought I did. I'd taken all the dresses out of the old sheepskin trunk, to admire and hold against myself; I'd remembered to bring my hand mirror up from my bedroom, and if I held it at arm's length, I could see myself from the waist up, at least. I danced like a gypsy, like the girl in *Notre-Dame de Paris*, whose beauty wins the heart of the hideous hunchback.

When I pulled out the last dress – a vast white one that crinkled like paper – what was revealed was a face. I think I cried out; I know I jumped away from the trunk. When I made myself go nearer, the face turned out to be made of something hard and white, like chalk. It was not a bust, like the one downstairs of poor Marie Antoinette. This had no neck, no head; it was only the smooth, pitiless mask of a girl, lying among a jumble of silks.

I didn't recognize her at first; I can be slow. My heart was beating loudly in a sort of horror. Only when I'd sat for some time, staring at those pristine, lidded eyes, did I realize that the face was the same as the one in the portrait of Cousine Eliza, and the white dress I was holding was the dress she wore in the painting. These were all her clothes that I was playing with, it came to me, and the little gold bracelet around my arm had to be hers too. I tried to take it off and return it to the trunk, but my fingers were so slippery I couldn't undo the catch. I wrenched at it, and there was a red line around my arm; the little charms spun.

Tante Fanny's room is stuffy; I can smell the breakfast tray that waits for Millie to take it away. "Tante Fanny," I say now, without preparation, "why does Cousine Eliza look so sad?"

My aunt's eyes widen violently. Her head snaps.

I hear my own words too late. What an idiot, to make it sound as if her daughter's ghost was in the room with us! "In the picture," I stammer, "I mean in the picture, she looks sad."

Tante Fanny doesn't look round at the portrait. "She was dead," she says, rather hoarse.

This can't be right. I look past her. "But her eyes are open."

My aunt lets out a sharp sigh and snaps her book shut. "Do you know the meaning of the word 'posthumous'?"

"Eh …"

"After death. The portrait was commissioned and painted in Paris in the months following my daughter's demise."

I stare at it again. But how? Did the painter prop her up somehow? She doesn't look dead, only sorrowful, in her enormous, ice-white silk gown.

"Eliza did not model for it," my aunt goes on, as if explaining something to a cretin. "For the face, the artist worked from a death mask." She must see the confusion in my eyes. "A sculptor pastes wet plaster over the features of a corpse. When it hardens he uses it as a mold, to make a perfect simulacrum of the face."

That's it. That's what scared me, up in the attic this morning: Eliza's death mask. When I look back at my aunt, there's been a metamorphosis. Tears are chasing down her papery cheeks. "Tante Fanny—"

"Enough," she says, her voice like mud. "Leave me."

I don't believe my cousin – my only cousin, the beautiful Eliza, just sixteen years old – died of a fever. Louisiana is a hellhole for fevers of all kinds, that's why my parents sent Emile away to Bordeaux. It's good for making money, but not for living, that's why Napoleon sold it so cheap to the Americans thirty-six years ago. So how could it have happened that Eliza grew up here on the Duparc-Locoul Plantation, safe and well, and on her trip to Paris – that pearly city, that apex of civilization – she succumbed to a fever? I won't believe it, it smells like a lie.

I'm up in the attic again, but this time I've brought the Bible. My brother, Emile, before he went away to France, taught me how to tell fortunes with the Book and Key. In those days we used an ugly old key we'd found in the cellars, but now I have a better one; the little gold one that hangs on my bracelet. (Eliza's bracelet, I should say.) What you do is, you open the Bible to the Song of Solomon, pick any verse you like, and read it aloud. If the key goes clockwise, it's saying yes to the verse, and vice versa. Fortune-telling is a sin when gypsies or conjurers do it, like the nègres making their nasty gris-gris to put curses on each other, but it can't be wrong if you use the Good Book. The Song of Solomon is the most puzzling bit of the Bible but it's my favorite. Sometimes it seems to be a man speaking, and sometimes a woman; she says *I am black but comely*, but she can't be a nègre, surely. They adore each other, but at some points it sounds as if they are brother and sister.

My first question for the Book today is, did Cousine Eliza die a natural death? I pull the bracelet down to my wrist, and I hold all the other little charms still, letting only the key dangle. I shake my hand as I recite the verse I've chosen, one that reminds me of Eliza: *Thy cheeks are comely with rows of jewels, thy neck with chains of gold.* When my hand stops moving, the key swings, most definitely anticlockwise. I feel a thrill all the way down in my belly. So! Not a natural death; as I suspected.

What shall I ask next? I cross my legs, to get more comfortable on the bare boards, and study the Book. A verse gives me an idea. Was she – is it possible – she was murdered? Not a night goes by in a great city without a cry in the dark, I know that much. *The watchmen that went about the city found me*, I whisper, *they smote me, they wounded me*. I shake my wrist, and the key dances, but every which way; I can't tell what the answer is. I search for another verse. Here's one: *Every man hath his sword upon his thigh because of fear in the night*. What if … I rack my imagination. What if two young Parisian gallants fought a duel over her, after glimpsing her at the opera, and Eliza died of the shock? I chant the verse, my voice rising now, because no one will hear me up here. I wave my hand in the air, and when I stop moving, the key continues to swing, counterclockwise. No duel, then; that's clear.

But what if she had a lover, a favorite among all the gentlemen of France who were vying for the hand of the exquisite Creole maiden? What if he was mad with jealousy and strangled her, locking his hands around her long pale neck rather than let Tante Fanny and Oncle Louis take her back to Louisiana? *For love is strong as death; jealousy is cruel as the grave*, I croon, and my heart is thumping, I can feel the wet break out under my arms, in the secret curls there. I've forgotten to wave my hand. When I do it, the key swings straight back and forward, like the clapper of a bell. Like the thunderous bells in the high cathedral of Notre-Dame de Paris. Is that an answer? Not jealousy, then, or not exactly; some other strange passion? Somebody killed Eliza, whether they meant to or not, I remind myself; somebody is to blame for the sad eyes in that portrait. For Tante Fanny walled up in her stifling room, and Oncle Louis who never comes home.

I can't think of any more questions about Eliza; my brain is fuzzy. Did she suffer terribly? I can't find a verse to ask that. How can I investigate a death that happened eight years ago, all the way across the ocean, when I'm only a freckled girl who's never left the Plantation? Who'll listen to my questions, who'll tell me anything?

I finish by asking the Book something for myself. Will I ever be pretty, like Eliza? Will these dull and round features ever bloom into perfect conjunction? Will I grow a face that will take me to France, that will win me the love of a French gentleman? Or will I be stuck here for the rest of my life, my mother's harried assistant and perhaps her successor, running the Plantation and the wine business and the many complex enterprises that make up the wealth of the Famille Duparc-Locoul? That's too many questions. Concentrate, Aimée. Will I be pretty when I grow up? *Behold, thou art fair, my love*, I murmur, as if to make it so; *behold, thou art fair*. But then something stops me from shaking my hand, making the key swing. Because what if the answer is no?

I stoop over the trunk and take out the death mask, as I now know it's called. I hold it very carefully in my arms, and I lie down beside the trunk. I look into the perfect white oval of my cousin's face, and lay it beside mine. *Eliza, Eliza.* I whisper my apologies for disturbing her things, for borrowing her bracelet, with all its little gold and silver trinkets. I tell her I only want to know the truth of how she died so her spirit can be at rest. My cheek is against her cool cheek, my nose aligns itself with hers. The plaster smells of nothing. I set my dry lips to her smooth ones.

"Millie," I ask, when she's buttoning up my dress this morning, "you remember my Cousine Eliza?"

The girl makes a little humming sound that could mean yes, no, or maybe. That's one of her irritating habits. "You must," I say. "My beautiful cousin who went away to Paris. They say she died of a fever."

This time the sound she makes is more like *hmph*.

I catch her eye, its milky roll. Excitement rises in my throat. "Millie," I say, too loud, "have you ever heard anything about that?"

"What would I hear, Mam'zelle Aimée?"

"Oh, go on! I know you house nègres are always gossiping. Did you ever hear tell of anything strange about my cousin's death?"

Millie's glance slides to the door. I step over there and shut it. "Go on. You can speak freely."

She shakes her head, very slowly.

"I know you know something," I say, and it comes out too fierce. Governing the nègres is an art, and I don't have it; I'm too familiar, and then too cross. Today, watching Millie's purple mouth purse, I resort to a bribe. "I tell you what, I might give you a present. What about one of these little charms?" Through my sleeve, I tug the gold bracelet down to my wrist. I make the little jewels shake and spin in front of Millie's eyes. "What about the tiger, would you like that one?" I point him out, because how would she know what a tiger looks like? "Or maybe these dance slippers. Or the golden cross, which Jesus died on?" I don't mention the key, because that's my own favorite.

Millie looks hungry with delight. She's come closer; her fingers are inches away from the dancing trinkets.

I tuck the bracelet back under my wrist ruffle. "Tell me!"

She crosses her arms and leans in close to my ear. She smells a little ripe, but not too bad. "Your cousine?"

"Yes."

"Your oncle and tante killed her."

I shove the girl away, the flat of my hand against her collarbone. "How dare you!"

She gives a luxurious shrug. "All I say is what I hear."

"Hear from whom?" I demand. "Your Pa Philippe, or your Ma?" Millie's mother works the hoe-gang, she's strong as a man. "What would they know of my family's affairs?"

Millie is grinning as she shakes her head. "From your tante."

"Tante Marcelite? She'd never say such a thing."

"No, no. From your Tante Fanny."

I'm so staggered I have to sit down. "Millie, you know it's the blackest of sins to lie," I remind her. "I think you must have made up this story. You're saying that my Tante Fanny told you – you – that she and Oncle Louis murdered Eliza?"

Millie's looking sullen now. "I don't make up nothing. I go in and out of that dusty old room five times a day with trays, and sometimes your tante is praying or talking to herself, and I hear her."

"But this is ridiculous." My voice is shaking. "Why would – what reason could they possibly have had for killing their own daughter?" I run through the plots I invented up in the attic. Did Eliza have a French lover? Did she *give herself* to him and fall into ruin? Could my uncle and aunt have murdered her, to save the Famille from shame? "I won't hear any more of such stuff."

The nègre has the gall to put her hand out, cupped for her reward.

"You may go now," I tell her, stepping into my shoes.

Next morning, I wake up in a foul temper. My head starts hammering as soon as I lift it off the pillow. Maman is expected back from New Orleans today. I reach for my bracelet on the little table beside my bed and it's gone.

"Millie?" But she's not there, on the pallet at the foot of my bed; she's up already. She's taken my bracelet. I never mentioned giving her more than one little trinket; she couldn't have misunderstood me. Damn her for a thieving little nègre.

I could track her down in the kitchen behind the house, or in the sewing room with Tante Marcelite, working on the slave clothes, or wherever she may be, but no. For once, I'll see to it that the girl gets punished for her outrageous impudence.

I bide my time; I do my lessons with Tante Fanny all morning. My skin feels greasy, I've a bouton coming out on my chin; I'm a martyr to pimples. This little drum keeps banging away in the back of my head. And a queasiness, too; a faraway aching. What could I have eaten to put me in such a state?

When the boat arrives I don't rush down to the pier; my mother hates such displays. I sit in the shady gallery and wait. When Maman comes to find me, I kiss her on both cheeks. "Perfectly well," I reply. (She doesn't like to hear of symptoms, unless one is seriously ill.) "But that dreadful brat Millie has stolen a bracelet from my room." As I say it, I feel a pang, but only a little one. Such a story for her to make up, calling my aunt and uncle murderers of their own flesh! The least the girl deserves is a whipping.

"Which bracelet?"

Of course, my mother knows every bit of jewelry I own; it's her memory for detail that's allowed her to improve the family fortunes so much. "A, a gold chain, with trinkets on it," I say, with only a small hesitation. If Eliza got it in Paris, as she must have done, my mother won't ever have seen it on her. "I found it."

"Found it?" she repeats, her eyebrows soaring.

I'm sweating. "It was stoppered up in a bottle," I improvise; "it washed up on the levee."

"How peculiar."

"But it's mine," I repeat. "And Millie took it off my table while I was sleeping!"

Maman nods judiciously and turns away. "Do tidy yourself up before dinner, Aimée, won't you?"

We often have a guest to dinner; Creoles never refuse our hospitality to anyone who needs a meal or a bed for the night, unless he's a beggar. Today it's a slave trader who comes up and down the River Road several times a year; he has a long beard that gets things caught in it. Millie and two other house nègres carry in the dishes, lukewarm as always, since the kitchen is so far behind the house. Millie's face shows nothing; she can't have been punished yet. I avoid her eyes. I pick at the edges of my food; I've no appetite today, though I usually like poule d'eau – a duck that eats nothing but fish, so the Church allows it on Fridays. I listen to the trader and Maman discuss the cost of living, and sip my glass of claret. (Papa brings in ten thousand bottles a year from his estates at Chateau Bon-Air; our Famille is the greatest wine distributor in Louisiana.) The trader offers us our pick of the three males he has with him, fresh from the auction block at New Orleans, but Maman says with considerable pride that we breed all we need, and more.

After dinner I'm practicing piano in the salon – stumbling repeatedly over a tricky phrase of Beethoven's – when my mother comes in. "If you can't manage this piece, Aimée, perhaps you could try one of your Schubert's?" Very dry.

"Certainly, Maman."

"Here's your bracelet. A charming thing, if eccentric. Don't make a habit of fishing things out of the river, will you?"

"No, Maman." Gleeful, I fiddle with the catch, fitting it around my wrist.

"The girl claimed you'd given it to her as a present."

Guilt, like a lump of gristle in my throat.

"They always claim that, strangely enough," remarks my mother, walking away. "One would think they might come up with something more plausible."

The next day I'm in Tante Fanny's room, at my lessons. There was no sign of Millie this morning, and I had to dress myself; the girl must be sulking. I'm supposed to be improving my spelling of verbs in the subjunctive mode, but my stomach is a rat's nest, my dress is too tight, my head's fit to split. I gaze out the window to the yard, where the trader's saddling his mules. He has four nègres with him, their hands lashed to their saddles.

"Do sit down, child."

"Just a minute, Tante—"

"Aimée, come back here!"

But I'm thudding along the gallery, down the stairs. I trip over my hem, and catch the railing. I'm in the yard, and the sun is piercing my eyes. "Maman!"

She turns, frowning. "Where is your sunhat, Aimée?"

I ignore that. "But Millie – what's happening?"

"I suggest you use your powers of deduction."

I throw a desperate look at the girl, bundled up on the last mule, her mute face striped with tears. "Have you sold her? She didn't do anything so very bad. I have the bracelet back safe. Maybe she only meant to borrow it."

My mother sighs. "I won't stand for thieving, or back-answers, and Millie has been guilty of both."

"But Pa Philippe, and her mother – you can't part her from them—"

Maman draws me aside, her arm like a cage around my back. "Aimée, I won't stoop to dispute my methods with an impudent and sentimental girl, especially in front of strangers. Go back to your lesson."

I open my mouth, to tell her that Millie didn't steal the bracelet, exactly; that she thought I had promised it to her. But that would call for too much explanation, and what if Maman found out that I've been interrogating the nègres about private family business? I shut my mouth again. I don't look at Millie; I can't bear it. The trader whistles to his mules to start walking. I go back into the house. My head's bursting from the sun; I have to keep my eyes squeezed shut.

"What is it, child?" asks Tante Fanny when I open the door. Her anger has turned to concern; it must be my face.

"I feel ... weak."

"Sit down on this sofa, then. Shall I ring for a glass of wine?"

Next thing I know, I'm flat on my back, choking. I feel so sick. I push Tante Fanny's hand away. She stoppers her smelling salts. "My dear."

"What—"

"You fainted."

I feel oddly disappointed. I always thought it would be a luxuriant feeling – a surrendering of the spirit – but it turns out that fainting is just a sick sensation, and then you wake up.

"It's very natural," she says, with the ghost of a smile. "I believe you have become a woman today."

I stare down at myself, but my shape hasn't changed.

"Your petticoat's a little stained," she whispers, showing me the spots – some brown, some fresh scarlet – and suddenly I understand. "You should go to your room and ask Millie to show you what to do."

At the mention of Millie, I put my hands over my face.

"Where did you get that?" asks Tante Fanny, in a changed voice. She reaches out to touch the bracelet that's slipped out from beneath my sleeve. I flinch. "Aimée, where did you get that?"

"It was in a trunk, in the attic," I confess. "I know it was Eliza's. Can I ask you, how did she die?" My words astonish me as they spill out.

My aunt's face contorts. I think perhaps she's going to strike me. After a long minute, she says, "We killed her. Your uncle and I."

My God. So Millie told the truth, and in return I've had her sold, banished from the sight of every face she knows in the world.

"Your cousin died for our pride, for our greed." Tante Fanny puts her fingers around her throat. "She was perfect, but we couldn't see it, because of the mote in our eyes."

What is she talking about?

"You see, Aimée, when my darling daughter was about your age she developed some boutons."

Pimples? What can pimples have to do with anything?

My aunt's face is a mask of creases. "They weren't so very bad, but they were the only defect in such a lovely face, they stood out terribly. I was going to take her to the local root doctor for an ointment, but your papa happened to know a famous skin specialist in Paris. I think he was glad of the excuse for a trip to his native country. And we knew that nothing in Louisiana could compare to France. So your papa accompanied us – Eliza and myself and your Oncle Louis – on the long voyage, and he introduced us to this doctor. For eight days" – Tante Fanny's tone has taken on a biblical timbre – "the doctor gave the girl injections, and she bore it bravely. We waited for her face to become perfectly clear again – but instead she took a fever. We knew the doctor must have made some terrible mistake with his medicines. When Eliza died—" Here the voice cracks, and Tante Fanny lets out a sort of barking sob. "Your oncle wanted to kill the doctor; he drew his sword to run him through. But your papa, the peacemaker, persuaded us that it must have been the cholera or some other contagion. We tried to believe that; we each assured each other that we believed it. But when I looked at my lovely daughter in her coffin, at sixteen years old, I knew the truth as if God had spoken in my heart."

She's weeping so much now, her words are muffled. I wish I had a handkerchief for her.

"I knew that Eliza had died for a handful of pimples. Because in our vanity, our dreadful pride, we couldn't accept the least defect in our daughter. We were ungrateful, and she was taken from us, and all the years since, and all the years ahead allotted to me, will be expiation."

The bracelet seems to burn me. I've managed to undo the catch. I pull it off, the little gold charms tinkling.

Tante Fanny wipes her eyes with the back of her hand. "Throw that away. My curse on it, and on all glittering vanities," she says hoarsely. "Get rid of it, Aimée, and thank God you'll never be beautiful."

Her words are like a blow to the ribs. But a moment later, I'm glad she said it. It's better to know these things. Who'd want to spend a whole life hankering?

I go out of the room without a word. I can feel the blood welling, sticky on my thighs. But first I must do this. I fetch an old bottle from the kitchen, and a candle stub. I seal up the bracelet in its green translucent tomb, and go to the top of the levee, and throw it as far as I can into the Mississippi.

GRAVEL

Alice Munro

Alice Munro (b. 1931) is a Canadian short story writer and winner of the 2009 Man Booker International Prize, which honours her complete body of work. She has been awarded Canada's Governor General's Award for fiction three times, the Giller Prize twice and is a perennial contender for the Nobel Prize for Fiction. She was awarded the National Book Critics Circle Award in 1998 for her collection, *The Love of a Good Woman*.

At that time we were living beside a gravel pit. Not a large one, hollowed out by monster machinery, just a minor pit that a farmer must have made some money from years before. In fact, the pit was shallow enough to lead you to think that there might have been some other intention for it – foundations for a house, maybe, that never made it any further.

My mother was the one who insisted on calling attention to it. "We live by the old gravel pit out the service-station road," she'd tell people, and laugh, because she was so happy to have shed everything connected with the house, the street – the husband – with the life she'd had before.

I barely remember that life. That is, I remember some parts of it clearly, but without the links you need to form a proper picture. All that I retain in my head of the house in town is the wallpaper with teddy bears in my old room. In this new house, which was really a trailer, my sister, Caro, and I had narrow cots, stacked one above the other. When we first moved there, Caro talked to me a lot about our old house, trying to get me to remember this or that. It was when we were in bed that she talked like this, and generally the conversation ended with me failing to remember and her getting cross. Sometimes I thought I did remember, but out of contrariness or fear of getting things wrong I pretended not to.

It was summer when we moved to the trailer. We had our dog with us. Blitzee. "Blitzee loves it here," my mother said, and it was true. What dog wouldn't love to exchange a town street, even one with spacious lawns and big houses, for the wide-open countryside? She took to barking at every car that went past, as if she owned the road, and now and then she brought home a squirrel or a groundhog she'd killed. At first Caro was quite upset by this, and Neal would have a talk with her, explaining about a dog's nature and the chain of life in which some things had to eat other things.

"She gets her dog food," Caro argued, but Neal said, "Suppose she didn't? Suppose someday we all disappeared and she had to fend for herself?"

"I'm not going to," Caro said. "I'm not going to disappear, and I'm always going to look after her."

"You think so?" Neal said, and our mother stepped in to deflect him. Neal was always ready to get on the subject of the Americans and the atomic bomb, and our mother didn't think we were ready for that yet. She didn't know that when he brought it up I thought he was talking about an atomic bun. I knew that there was something wrong with this interpretation, but I wasn't about to ask questions and get laughed at.

Neal was an actor. In town there was a professional summer theater, a new thing at the time, which some people were enthusiastic about and others worried about, fearing that it would bring in riffraff. My mother and father had been among those in favor, my mother more actively so, because she had more time. My father was an insurance agent and travelled a lot. My mother had got busy with various fund-raising schemes for the theater and donated her services as an usher. She was good-looking and young enough to be mistaken for an actress. She'd begun to dress like an actress too, in shawls and long skirts and dangling necklaces. She'd let her hair go wild and stopped wearing makeup. Of course, I had not understood or even particularly noticed these changes at the time. My mother was my mother. But no doubt Caro had noticed. And my father must have. Though, from all that I know of his nature and his feelings for my mother, I think he may have been proud to see how good she looked in these liberating styles and how well she fit in with the theater people. When he spoke about this time, later on, he said that he had always approved of the arts. I can imagine now how embarrassed my mother would have been, cringing and laughing to cover up her cringing, if he'd made this declaration in front of her theater friends.

Well, then came a development that could have been foreseen and probably was, but not by my father. I don't know if it happened to any of the other volunteers. I do know, though I don't remember it, that my father wept and for a whole day followed my mother around the house, not letting her out of his sight and refusing to believe her. And, instead of telling him anything to make him feel better, she told him something that made him feel worse.

She told him that the baby was Neal's.

Was she sure?

Absolutely. She had been keeping track.

What happened then?

My father gave up weeping. He had to get back to work. My mother packed up our things and took us to live with Neal in the trailer he had found, out in the country. She said afterwards that she had wept too. But she said also that she had felt alive. Maybe for the first time in her life, truly alive. She felt as if she had been given a chance; she had started her life all over again. She'd walked out on her silver and her china and her decorating scheme and her flower garden and even on the books in her bookcase. She would live now, not read. She'd left her clothes hanging in the closet and her high-heeled shoes in their shoe trees. Her diamond ring and her wedding ring on the dresser. Her silk nightdresses in their drawer. She meant to go around naked at least some of the time in the country, as long as the weather stayed warm.

That didn't work out, because when she tried it Caro went and hid in her cot and even Neal said he wasn't crazy about the idea.

What did he think of all this? Neal. His philosophy, as he put it later, was to welcome whatever happened. Everything is a gift. We give and we take.

I am suspicious of people who talk like this, but I can't say that I have a right to be.

He was not really an actor. He had got into acting, he said, as an experiment. To see what he could find out about himself. In college, before he dropped out, he had performed as part of the Chorus in *Oedipus Rex*. He had liked that – the giving yourself over, blending with others. Then one day, on the street in Toronto, he ran into a friend who was on his way to try out for a summer job with a new small-town theater company. He went along, having nothing better to do, and ended up getting the job, while the other fellow didn't. He would play Banquo. Sometimes they make Banquo's Ghost visible, sometimes not. This time they wanted a visible version and Neal was the right size. An excellent size. A solid ghost.

He had been thinking of wintering in our town anyway, before my mother sprang her surprise. He had already spotted the trailer. He had enough carpentry experience to pick up work renovating the theater, which would see him through till spring. That was as far ahead as he liked to think.

Caro didn't even have to change schools. She was picked up by the school bus at the end of the short lane that ran alongside the gravel pit. She had to make friends with the country children, and perhaps explain some things to the town children who had been her friends the year before, but if she had any difficulty with that I never heard about it.

Blitzee was always waiting by the road for her to come home.

I didn't go to kindergarten, because my mother didn't have a car. But I didn't mind doing without other children. Caro, when she got home, was enough for me. And my mother was often in a playful mood. As soon as it snowed that winter she and I built a snowman and she asked, "Shall we call it Neal?" I said okay, and we stuck various things on it to make it funny. Then we decided that I would run out of the house when his car came and say, Here's Neal, here's Neal, but be pointing up at the snowman. Which I did, but Neal got out of the car mad and yelled that he could have run me over.

That was one of the few times that I saw him act like a father.

Those short winter days must have seemed strange to me – in town, the lights came on at dusk. But children get used to changes. Sometimes I wondered about our other house. I didn't exactly miss it or want to live there again – I just wondered where it had gone.

My mother's good times with Neal went on into the night. If I woke up and had to go to the bathroom, I'd call for her. She would come happily but not in any hurry, with some piece of cloth or a scarf wrapped around her – also a smell that I associated with candlelight and music. And love.

Something did happen that was not so reassuring, but I didn't try to make much sense of it at the time. Blitzee, our dog, was not very big, but she didn't seem small enough to fit under Caro's coat. I don't know how Caro managed to do it. Not once but twice. She hid the dog under her coat on the school bus, and then, instead of going straight to school, she took Blitzee back to our old house in town, which was less than a block away. That was where my father found the dog, on the winter porch, which was not locked, when he came home for his solitary lunch. There was great surprise that she had got there, found her way home like a dog in a story. Caro made the biggest fuss, and claimed not to have seen the dog at all that morning. But then she made the mistake of trying it again, maybe a week later, and this time, though nobody on the bus or at school suspected her, our mother did.

I can't remember if our father brought Blitzee back to us. I can't imagine him in the trailer or at the door of the trailer or even on the road to it. Maybe Neal went to the house in town and picked her up. Not that that's any easier to imagine.

If I've made it sound as though Caro was unhappy or scheming all the time, that isn't the truth. As I've said, she did try to make me talk about things, at night in bed, but she wasn't constantly airing grievances. It wasn't her nature to be sulky. She was far too keen on making a good impression. She liked people to like her; she liked to stir up the air in a room with the promise of something you could even call merriment. She thought more about that than I did.

She was the one who most took after our mother, I think now.

There must have been some probing about what she'd done with the dog. I think I can remember some of it. "I did it for a trick."

"Do you want to go and live with your father?"

I believe that was asked, and I believe she said no.

I didn't ask her anything. What she had done didn't seem strange to me. That's probably how it is with younger children – nothing that the strangely powerful older child does seems out of the ordinary.

Our mail was deposited in a tin box on a post, down by the road. My mother and I would walk there every day, unless it was particularly stormy, to see what had been left for us. We did this after I got up from my nap. Sometimes it was the only time we went outside all day. In the morning, we watched children's television shows – or she read while I watched. (She had not given up reading for very long.) We heated up some canned soup for lunch, then I went down for my nap while she read some more. She was quite big with the baby now and it stirred around in her stomach, so that I could feel it. Its name was going to be Brandy – already was Brandy – whether it was a boy or a girl.

One day when we were going down the lane for the mail, and were in fact not far from the box, my mother stopped and stood quite still.

"Quiet," she said to me, though I hadn't said a word and wasn't even playing the shuffling game with my boots in the snow.

"I was being quiet," I said.

"Shush. Turn around."

"But we didn't get the mail."

"Never mind. Just walk."

Then I noticed that Blitzee, who was always with us, just behind or ahead of us, wasn't there anymore. Another dog was, on the opposite side of the road, a few feet from the mailbox.

My mother phoned the theater as soon as we got home and let in Blitzee, who was waiting for us. Nobody answered. She phoned the school and asked someone to tell the bus driver to drive Caro up to the door. It turned out that the driver couldn't do that, because it had snowed since Neal last plowed the lane, but he – the driver – did watch until she got to the house. There was no wolf to be seen by that time.

Neal was of the opinion that there never had been one. And if there had been, he said, it would have been no danger to us, weak as it was probably from hibernation.

Caro said that wolves did not hibernate. "We learned about them in school."

Our mother wanted Neal to get a gun.

"You think I'm going to get a gun and go and shoot a goddam poor mother wolf who has probably got a bunch of babies back in the bush and is just trying to protect them, the way you're trying to protect yours?" he said quietly.

Caro said, "Only two. They only have two at a time."

"Okay, okay. I'm talking to your mother."

"You don't know that," my mother said. "You don't know if it's got hungry cubs or anything."

I had never thought she'd talk to him like that.

He said, "Easy. Easy. Let's just think a bit. Guns are a terrible thing. If I went and got a gun, then what would I be saying? That Vietnam was okay? That I might as well have gone to Vietnam?"

"You're not an American."

"You're not going to rile me."

This is more or less what they said, and it ended up with Neal not having to get a gun. We never saw the wolf again, if it was a wolf. I think my mother stopped going to get the mail, but she may have become too big to be comfortable doing that anyway.

The snow dwindled magically. The trees were still bare of leaves and my mother made Caro wear her coat in the mornings, but she came home after school dragging it behind her.

My mother said that the baby had got to be twins, but the doctor said it wasn't.

"Great. Great," Neal said, all in favor of the twins idea. "What do doctors know."

The gravel pit had filled to its brim with melted snow and rain, so that Caro had to edge around it on her way to catch the school bus. It was a little lake, still and dazzling under the clear sky. Caro asked with not much hope if we could play in it.

Our mother said not to be crazy. "It must be twenty feet deep," she said.

Neal said, "Maybe ten."

Caro said, "Right around the edge it wouldn't be."

Our mother said yes it was. "It just drops off," she said. "It's not like going in at the beach, for fuck's sake. Just stay away from it."

She had started saying "fuck" quite a lot, perhaps more than Neal did, and in a more exasperated tone of voice.

"Should we keep the dog away from it, too?" she asked him.

Neal said that that wasn't a problem. "Dogs can swim."

*

A Saturday. Caro watched *The Friendly Giant* with me and made comments that spoiled it. Neal was lying on the couch, which unfolded into his and my mother's bed. He was smoking his kind of cigarettes, which could not be smoked at work so had to be made the most of on weekends. Caro sometimes bothered him, asking to try one. Once he had let her, but told her not to tell our mother.

I was there, though, so I told.

There was alarm, though not quite a row.

"You know he'd have those kids out of here like a shot," our mother said. "Never again."

"Never again," Neal said agreeably. "So what if he feeds them poison Rice Krispies crap?"

In the beginning, we hadn't seen our father at all. Then, after Christmas, a plan had been worked out for Saturdays. Our mother always asked afterwards if we had had a good time. I always said yes, and meant it, because I thought that if you went to a movie or to look at Lake Huron, or ate in a restaurant, that meant that you had had a good time. Caro said yes, too, but in a tone of voice that suggested that it was none of our mother's business. Then my father went on a winter holiday to Cuba (my mother remarked on this with some surprise and maybe approval) and came back with a lingering sort of flu that caused the visits to lapse. They were supposed to resume in the spring, but so far they hadn't.

After the television was turned off, Caro and I were sent outside to run around, as our mother said, and get some fresh air. We took the dog with us.

When we got outside, the first thing we did was loosen and let trail the scarves our mother had wrapped around our necks. (The fact was, though we may not have put the two things together, the deeper she got into her pregnancy the more she slipped back into behaving like an ordinary mother, at least when it was a matter of scarves we didn't need or regular meals. There was not so much championing of wild ways as there had been in the fall.) Caro asked me what I wanted to do, and I said I didn't know. This was a formality on her part but the honest truth on mine. We let the dog lead us, anyway, and Blitzee's idea was to go and look at the gravel pit. The wind was whipping the water up into little waves, and very soon we got cold, so we wound our scarves back around our necks.

I don't know how much time we spent just wandering around the water's edge, knowing that we couldn't be seen from the trailer. After a while, I realized that I was being given instructions.

I was to go back to the trailer and tell Neal and our mother something.

That the dog had fallen into the water.

The dog had fallen into the water and Caro was afraid she'd be drowned.

Blitzee. Drownded.

Drowned.

But Blitzee wasn't in the water.

She could be. And Caro could jump in to save her.

I believe I still put up some argument, along the lines of she hasn't, you haven't, it could happen but it hasn't. I also remembered that Neal had said dogs didn't drown.

Caro instructed me to do as I was told.

Why?

I may have said that, or I may have just stood there not obeying and trying to work up another argument.

In my mind I can see her picking up Blitzee and tossing her, though Blitzee was trying to hang on to her coat. Then backing up, Caro backing up to take a run at the water. Running, jumping, all of a sudden hurling herself at the water. But I can't recall the sound of the splashes as they, one after the other, hit the water. Not a little splash or a big one. Perhaps I had turned towards the trailer by then – I must have done so.

When I dream of this, I am always running. And in my dreams I am running not towards the trailer but back towards the gravel pit. I can see Blitzee floundering around and Caro swimming towards her, swimming strongly, on the way to rescue her. I see her light-brown checked coat and her plaid scarf and her proud successful face and reddish hair darkened at the end of its curls by the water. All I have to do is watch and be happy – nothing required of me, after all.

What I really did was make my way up the little incline towards the trailer. And when I got there I sat down. Just as if there had been a porch or a bench, though in fact the trailer had neither of these things. I sat down and waited for the next thing to happen.

I know this because it's a fact. I don't know, however, what my plan was or what I was thinking. I was waiting, maybe, for the next act in Caro's drama. Or in the dog's.

I don't know if I sat there for five minutes. More? Less? It wasn't too cold.

I went to see a professional person about this once and she convinced me – for a time, she convinced me – that I must have tried the door of the trailer and found it locked. Locked because my mother and Neal were having sex and had locked it against interruptions. If I'd banged on the door they would have been angry. The counsellor was satisfied to bring me to this conclusion, and I was satisfied, too. For a while. But I no longer think that was true. I don't think they would have locked the door, because I know that once they didn't and Caro walked in and they laughed at the look on her face.

Maybe I remembered that Neal had said that dogs did not drown, which meant that Caro's rescue of Blitzee would not be necessary. Therefore she herself wouldn't be able to carry out her game. So many games, with Caro.

Did I think she could swim? At nine, many children can. And in fact it turned out that she'd had one lesson the summer before, but then we had moved to the trailer and she hadn't taken any more. She may have thought she could manage well enough. And I may indeed have thought that she could do anything she wanted to.

The counsellor did not suggest that I might have been sick of carrying out Caro's orders, but the thought did occur to me. It doesn't quite seem right, though. If I'd been older, maybe. At the time, I still expected her to fill my world.

How long did I sit there? Likely not long. And it's possible that I did knock. After a while. After a minute or two. In any case, my mother did, at some point, open the door, for no reason. A presentiment.

Next thing, I am inside. My mother is yelling at Neal and trying to make him understand something. He is getting to his feet and standing there speaking to her, touching her, with such mildness and gentleness and consolation. But that is not what my mother wants at all and she tears herself away from him and runs out the door. He shakes his head and looks down at his bare feet. His big helpless-looking toes.

I think he says something to me with a singsong sadness in his voice. Strange.

Beyond that I have no details.

My mother didn't throw herself into the water. She didn't go into labor from the shock. My brother, Brent, was not born until a week or ten days after the funeral, and he was a full-term infant. Where she was while she waited for the birth to happen I do not know. Perhaps she was kept in the hospital and sedated as much as possible under the circumstances.

I remember the day of the funeral quite well. A very pleasant and comfortable woman I didn't know – her name was Josie – took me on an expedition. We visited some swings and a sort of dollhouse that was large enough for me to go inside, and we ate a lunch of my favorite treats, but not enough to make me sick. Josie was somebody I got to know very well later on. She was a friend my father had made in Cuba, and after the divorce she became my stepmother, his second wife.

My mother recovered. She had to. There was Brent to look after and, most of the time, me. I believe I stayed with my father and Josie while she got settled in the house that she planned to live in for the rest of her life. I don't remember being there with Brent until he was big enough to sit up in his high chair.

My mother went back to her old duties at the theater. At first she may have worked as she had before, as a volunteer usher, but by the time I was in school she had a real job, with pay, and year-round responsibilities. She was the business manager. The theater survived, through various ups and downs, and is still going now.

Neal didn't believe in funerals, so he didn't attend Caro's. He never saw Brent. He wrote a letter – I found this out much later – saying that since he did not intend to act as a father it would be better for him to bow out at the start. I never mentioned him to Brent, because I thought it would upset my mother. Also because Brent showed so little sign of being like him – like Neal – and seemed, in fact, so much more like my father that I really wondered about what was going on around the time he was conceived. My father has never said anything about this and never would. He treats Brent just as he treats me, but he is the kind of man who would do that anyway.

He and Josie have not had any children of their own, but I don't think that bothers them. Josie is the only person who ever talks about Caro, and even she doesn't do it often. She does say that my father doesn't hold my mother responsible. He has also said that he must have been sort of a stick-in-the-mud when my mother wanted more excitement in her life. He needed a shaking-up, and he got one. There's no use being sorry about it. Without the shaking-up, he would never have found Josie and the two of them would not have been so happy now.

"Which two?" I might say, just to derail him, and he would staunchly say, "Josie. Josie, of course."

My mother cannot be made to recall any of those times, and I don't bother her with them. I know that she has driven down the lane we lived on, and found it quite changed, with the sort of trendy houses you see now, put up on unproduc-tive land. She mentioned this with the slight scorn that such houses evoke in her. I went down the lane myself but did not tell anyone. All the eviscerating that is done in families these days strikes me as a mistake.

Even where the gravel pit was a house now stands, the ground beneath it levelled.

I have a partner, Ruthann, who is younger than I am but, I think, somewhat wiser. Or at least more optimistic about what she calls routing out my demons. I would never have got in touch with Neal if it had not been for her urging. Of course, for a long time I had no way, just as I had no thought, of getting in touch. It was he who finally wrote to me. A brief note of congratulations, he said, after seeing my picture in the *Alumni Gazette*. What he was doing looking through the *Alumni Gazette* I have no idea. I had received one of those academic honors that mean something in a restricted circle and little anywhere else.

He was living hardly fifty miles away from where I teach, which also happens to be where I went to college. I wondered if he had been there at that time. So close. Had he become a scholar?

At first I had no intention of replying to the note, but I told Ruthann and she said that I should think about writing back. So the upshot was that I sent him an e-mail, and arrangements were made. I was to meet him in his town, in the un-threatening surroundings of a university cafeteria. I told myself that if he looked unbearable – I did not quite know what I meant by this – I could just walk on through.

He was shorter than he used to be, as adults we remember from childhood usually are. His hair was thin, and trimmed close to his head. He got me a cup of tea. He was drinking tea himself.

What did he do for a living?

He said that he tutored students in preparation for exams. Also, he helped them write their essays. Sometimes, you might say, he wrote those essays. Of course, he charged.

"It's no way to get to be a millionaire, I can tell you."

He lived in a dump. Or a semi-respectable dump. He liked it. He looked for clothes at the Sally Ann. That was okay too.

"Suits my principles."

I did not congratulate him on any of this, but, to tell the truth, I doubt that he expected me to.

"Anyway, I don't think my lifestyle is so interesting. I think you might want to know how it happened."

I could not figure out how to speak.

"I was stoned," he said. "And, furthermore, I'm not a swimmer. Not many swimming pools around where I grew up. I'd have drowned, too. Is that what you wanted to know?"

I said that he was not really the one that I was wondering about.

Then he became the third person I'd asked, "What do you think Caro had in mind?"

The counsellor had said that we couldn't know. "Likely she herself didn't know what she wanted. Attention? I don't think she meant to drown herself. Attention to how bad she was feeling?"

Ruthann had said, "To make your mother do what she wanted? Make her smarten up and see that she had to go back to your father?"

Neal said, "It doesn't matter. Maybe she thought she could paddle better than she could. Maybe she didn't know how heavy winter clothes can get. Or that there wasn't anybody in a position to help her."

He said to me, "Don't waste your time. You're not thinking what if you had hurried up and told, are you? Not trying to get in on the guilt?"

I said that I had considered what he was saying, but no.

"The thing is to be happy," he said. "No matter what. Just try that. You can. It gets to be easier and easier. It's nothing to do with circumstances. You wouldn't believe how good it is. Accept everything and then tragedy disappears. Or tragedy lightens, anyway, and you're just there, going along easy in the world."

Now, good-bye.

I see what he meant. It really is the right thing to do. But, in my mind, Caro keeps running at the water and throwing herself in, as if in triumph, and I'm still caught, waiting for her to explain to me, waiting for the splash.

THE EYE

Alice Munro

Alice Munro (b. 1931) is a Canadian short story writer and winner of the 2009 Man Booker International Prize, which honours her complete body of work. She has been awarded Canada's Governor General's Award for fiction three times, the Giller Prize twice and is a perennial contender for the Nobel Prize for Fiction. She was awarded the National Book Critics Circle Award in 1998 for her collection, *The Love of a Good Woman*.

When I was five years old my parents all of a sudden produced a baby boy, which my mother said was what I had always wanted. Where she got this idea I did not know. She did quite a bit of elaborating on it, all fictitious but hard to counter.

Then a year later a baby girl appeared, and there was another fuss but more subdued than with the first one.

Up until the time of the first baby I had not been aware of ever feeling different from the way my mother said I felt. And up until that time the whole house was full of my mother, of her footsteps her voice her powdery yet ominous smell that inhabited all the rooms; even when she wasn't in them.

Why do I say ominous? I didn't feel frightened. It wasn't that my mother actually told me what I was to feel about things. She was an authority on that without having to question a thing. Not just in the case of a baby brother but in the matter of Red River cereal which was good for me and so I must be fond of it. And in my interpretation of the picture that hung at the foot of my bed, showing Jesus suffering the little children to come unto him. Suffering meant something different in those days, but that was not what we concentrated on. My mother pointed out the little girl half hiding round a corner because she wanted to come to Jesus but was too shy. That was me, my mother said, and I supposed it was though I wouldn't have figured it out without her telling me and I rather wished it wasn't so.

The thing I really felt miserable about was Alice in Wonderland huge and trapped in the rabbit hole, but I laughed because my mother seemed delighted.

It was with my brother's coming, though, and the endless carryings-on about how he was some sort of present for me, that I began to accept how largely my mother's notions about me might differ from my own.

I suppose all this was making me ready for Sadie when she came to work for us. My mother had shrunk to whatever territory she had with the babies. With her not around so much, I could think about what was true and what wasn't. I knew enough not to speak about this to anybody.

The most unusual thing about Sadie – though it was not a thing stressed in our house – was that she was a celebrity. Our town had a radio station where she played her guitar and sang the opening welcome song which was her own composition.

"Hello, hello, hello, everybody—"

And half an hour later it was, "Good-bye, good-bye, good-bye, everybody." In between she sang songs that were requested, as well as some she picked out herself. The more sophisticated people in town tended to joke about her songs and about the whole station which was said to be the smallest one in Canada. Those people listened to a Toronto station that broadcast popular songs of the day – three little fishes and a momma fishy too – and Jim Hunter hollering out the desperate war news. But people on the farms liked the local station and the kind of songs Sadie sang. Her voice was strong and sad and she sang about loneliness and grief.

Leanin' on the old top rail,
In a big corral.
Lookin' down the twilight trail
For my long lost pal –

Most of the farms in our part of the country had been cleared and settled around a hundred and fifty years ago, and you could look out from almost any farmhouse and see another farmhouse only a few fields away. Yet the songs the farmers wanted were all about lone cowhands, the lure and disappointment of far-off places, the bitter crimes that led to criminals dying with their mothers' names on their lips, or God's.

This was what Sadie sang with such sorrow in a full-throated alto, but in her job with us she was full of energy and confidence, happy to talk and mostly to talk about herself. There was usually nobody to talk to but me. Her jobs and my mother's kept them divided most of the time and somehow I don't think they would have enjoyed talking together anyway. My mother was a serious person as I have indicated, one who used to teach school before she taught me. She maybe would have liked Sadie to be somebody she could help, teaching her not to say "youse." But Sadie did not give much indication that she wanted the help anybody could offer, or to speak in any way that was different from how she had always spoken.

After dinner, which was the noon meal, Sadie and I were alone in the kitchen. My mother took time off for a nap and if she was lucky the babies napped too. When she got up she put on a different sort of dress as if she expected a leisurely afternoon, even though there would certainly be more diapers to change and also some of that unseemly business that I tried never to catch sight of, when the littlest one guzzled at a breast.

My father took a nap too – maybe fifteen minutes on the porch with the *Saturday Evening Post* over his face, before he went back to the barn.

Sadie heated water on the stove and washed the dishes with me helping and the blinds down to keep out the heat. When we were finished she mopped the floor and I dried it, by a method I had invented – skating around and around it on rags. Then we took down the coils of sticky yellow flypaper that had been put up after breakfast and were already heavy with dead or buzzing nearly dead black flies, and hung up the fresh coils which would be full of newly dead ones by suppertime. All this while Sadie was telling me about her life.

I didn't make easy judgments about ages then. People were either children or grown-ups and I thought her a grown-up. Maybe she was sixteen, maybe eighteen or twenty. Whatever her age, she announced more than once that she was not in any hurry to get married.

She went to dances every weekend but she went by herself. By herself and for herself, she said.

She told me about the dance halls. There was one in town, off the main street, where the curling rink was in the winter. You paid a dime for a dance, then went up and danced on a platform with people gawking all around, not that she cared. She always liked to pay her own dime, not to be beholden. But sometimes a fellow got to her first. He asked if she wanted to dance and the first thing she said was, Can you? Can you dance? she asked him bluntly. Then he would look at her funny and say yes, meaning why else would he be here? And it would turn out usually that what he meant by dance was shuffling around on two feet with his sweaty big meats of hands grabbing at her. Sometimes she just broke off and left him stranded, danced by herself – which was what she liked to do anyway. She finished up the dance that had been paid for, and if the moneymaker objected and tried to make her pay for two when it was only one, she told him that was enough out of him. They could all laugh at her dancing by herself if they liked.

The other dance hall was just out of town on the highway. You paid at the door there and it wasn't for one dance but the whole night. The place was called the Royal-T. She paid her own way there too. There was generally a better class of dancer, but she did try to get an idea of how they managed before she let them take her out on the floor. They were usually town fellows while the ones at the other place were country. Better on their feet – the town ones – but it was not always the feet you had to look out for. It was where they wanted to get hold of you. Sometimes she had to read them the riot act and tell them what she would do to them if they didn't quit it. She let them know she'd come there to dance and paid her own way to do it. Furthermore she knew where to jab them. That would straighten them out. Sometimes they were good dancers and she got to enjoy herself. Then when they played the last dance she bolted for home.

She wasn't like some, she said. She didn't mean to get caught.

Caught. When she said that, I saw a big wire net coming down, some evil little creatures wrapping it around and around you and choking you so you could never get out. Sadie must have seen something like this on my face because she said not to be scared.

"There's nothing in this world to be scared of, just look out for yourself."

"You and Sadie talk together a lot," my mother said.

I knew something was coming that I should watch for but I didn't know what.

"You like her, don't you?"

I said yes.

"Well of course you do. I do too."

I hoped that was going to be all and for a moment I thought it was.

Then, "You and I don't get so much time now we have the babies. They don't give us much time, do they?

"But we do love them, don't we?"

Quickly I said yes.

She said, "Truly?"

She wasn't going to stop till I said truly, so I said it.

My mother wanted something very badly. Was it nice friends? Women who played bridge and had husbands who went to work in suits with vests? Not quite, and no hope of that anyway. Was it me as I used to be, with my sausage curls that I didn't mind standing still for, and my expert Sunday School recitations? No time for her to manage that anymore. And something in me was turning traitorous, though she didn't know why, and I didn't know why either. I hadn't made any town friends at Sunday School. Instead, I worshipped Sadie. I heard my mother say that to my father. "She worships Sadie."

My father said Sadie was a godsend. What did that mean? He sounded cheerful. Maybe it meant he wasn't going to take anybody's side.

"I wish we had proper sidewalks for her," my mother said. "Maybe if we had proper sidewalks she could learn to roller-skate and make friends."

I did wish for roller skates. But now without any idea why, I knew that I was never going to admit it.

Then my mother said something about it being better when school started. Something about me being better or something concerning Sadie that would be better. I didn't want to hear.

Sadie was teaching me some of her songs and I knew I wasn't very good at singing. I hoped that wasn't what had to get better or else stop. I truly did not want it to stop.

My father didn't have much to say. I was my mother's business, except for later on when I got really mouthy and had to be punished. He was waiting for my brother to get older and be his. A boy would not be so complicated.

And sure enough my brother wasn't. He would grow up to be just fine.

Now school has started. It started some weeks ago, before the leaves turned red and yellow. Now they were mostly gone. I am not wearing my school coat but my good coat, the one with the dark velvet cuffs and collar. My mother is wearing the coat she wears to church, and a turban covers most of her hair.

My mother is driving to whatever place it is that we are going to. She doesn't drive often, and her driving is always more stately and yet uncertain than my father's. She peeps her horn at any curve.

"Now," she says, but it takes a little while for her to get the car into place.

"Here we are then." Her voice seems meant to be encouraging. She touches my hand to give me a chance to hold hers, but I pretend not to notice and she takes her hand away.

The house has no driveway or even a sidewalk. It's decent but quite plain. My mother has raised her gloved hand to knock but it turns out we don't have to. The door is opened for us. My mother has just started to say something encouraging to me – something like, It will go more quickly than you think – but she doesn't get finished. The tone in which she spoke to me had been somewhat stern but slightly comforting. It changes when the door is opened into something more subdued, softened as if she was bowing her head.

The door has been opened to let some people go out, not just to let us go in. One of the women going out calls back over her shoulder in a voice that does not try to be soft at all.

"It's her that she worked for, and that little girl."

Then a woman who is rather dressed up comes and speaks to my mother and helps her off with her coat. That done, my mother takes my coat off and says to the woman that I was especially fond of Sadie. She hopes it was all right to bring me.

"Oh the dear little thing," the woman says and my mother touches me lightly to get me to say hello.

"Sadie loved children," the woman said. "She did indeed."

I notice that there are two other children there. Boys. I know them from school, one being in the first grade with me, and the other one older. They are peering out from what is likely the kitchen. The younger one is stuffing a whole cookie into his mouth in a comical way and the other, older, one is making a disgusted face. Not at the cookie stuffer, but at me. They hate me of course. Boys either ignored you if they met you somewhere that wasn't school (they ignored you there too) or they made these faces and called you horrid names. If I had to go near one I would stiffen and wonder what to do. Of course it was different if there were adults around. These boys stayed quiet but I was slightly miserable until somebody yanked the two of them into the kitchen. Then I became aware of my mother's especially gentle and sympathetic voice, more ladylike even than the yoke of the spokeswoman she was talking to, and I thought maybe the face was meant for her. Sometimes people imitated her voice when she called for me at school.

The woman she was talking to and who seemed to be in charge was leading us to a part of the room where a man and a woman sat on a sofa, looking as if they did not quite understand why they were here. My mother bent over and spoke to them very respectfully and pointed me out to them.

"She did so love Sadie," she said. I knew that I was supposed to say something then but before I could the woman sitting there let out a howl. She did not look at any of us and the sound she made seemed like a sound you might make if some animal was biting or gnawing at you. She slapped away at her arms as if to get rid of whatever it was, but it did not go away. She looked at my mother as if my mother was the person who should do something about this.

The old man told her to hush.

"She's taking it very hard," said the woman who was guiding us. "She doesn't know what she's doing." She bent down lower and said, "Now, now. You scare the little girl."

"Scare the little girl," the old man said obediently.

By the time he finished saying that, the woman was not making the noise anymore and was patting her scratched arms as if she didn't know what had happened to them.

My mother said, "Poor woman."

"An only child too," said the conducting woman. To me she said, "Don't you worry."

I was worried but not about the yelling.

I knew Sadie was somewhere and I did not want to see her. My mother had not actually said that I would have to see her but she had not said that I wouldn't have to, either.

Sadie had been killed when walking home from the Royal-T dance hall. A car had hit her just on that little bit of gravel road between the parking space belonging to the dance hall and the beginning of the proper town sidewalk. She would have been hurrying along just the way she always did, and was no doubt thinking cars could see her, or that she had as much right as they did, and perhaps the car behind her swerved or perhaps she was not quite where she thought she was. She was hit from behind. The car that hit her was getting out of the way of the car that was behind it, and that second car was looking to make the first turn onto a town street. There had been some drinking at the dance hall, though you could not buy liquor there. And there was always some honking and yelling and whipping around too fast when the dancing was over. Sadie scurrying along without even a flashlight would behave as if it was everybody's business to get out of her way.

"A girl without a boyfriend going to dances on foot," said the woman who was still being friends with my mother. She spoke quite softly and my mother murmured something regretful.

It was asking for trouble, the friendly woman said still more softly.

I had heard talk at home that I did not understand. My mother wanted something done that might have had to do with Sadie and the car that hit her, but my father said to leave it alone. We've got no business in town, he said. I did not even try to figure this out because I was trying not to think about Sadie at all, let alone about her being dead. When I had realized that we were going into Sadie's house I longed not to go, but didn't see any way to get out of it except by behaving with enormous indignity.

Now after the old woman's outburst it seemed to me we might turn around and go home. I would never have to admit the truth, which was that I was in fact desperately scared of any dead body.

Just as I thought this might be possible, I heard my mother and the woman she seemed now to be conniving with speak of what was worse than anything.

Seeing Sadie.

Yes, my mother was saying. Of course, we must see Sadie. Dead Sadie.

I had kept my eyes pretty well cast down, seeing mostly just those boys who were hardly taller than I was, and the old people who were sitting down. But now my mother was taking me by the hand in another direction.

There had been a coffin in the room all the time but I had thought it was something else. Because of my lack of experience I didn't know exactly what such a thing looked like. A shelf to put flowers on, this object we were approaching might have been, or a closed piano.

Perhaps the people being around it had somehow disguised its real size and shape and purpose. But now these people were making way respectfully and my mother spoke in a new very quiet voice.

"Come now," she said to me. Her gentleness sounded hateful to me, triumphant.

She bent to look into my face, and this, I was sure, was to prevent me from doing what had just occurred to me – keeping my eyes squeezed shut. Then she took her gaze away from me but kept my hand tightly held in hers. I did manage to lower my lids as soon as she took her eyes off me, but I did not shut them quite lest I stumble or somebody push me right where I didn't want to be. I was able to see just a blur of the stiff flowers and the sheen of polished wood.

Then I heard my mother sniffling and felt her pulling away. There was a click of her purse being opened. She had to get her hand in there, so her hold on me weakened and I was able to get myself free of her. She was weeping. It was attention to her tears and sniffles that had set me loose.

I looked straight into the coffin and saw Sadie.

The accident had spared her neck and face but I didn't see all of that at once. I just got the general impression that there was nothing about her as bad as I had been afraid of. I shut my eyes quickly but found myself unable to keep from looking again. First at the little yellow cushion that was under her neck and that also managed to cover her throat and chin and the one cheek I could easily see. The trick was in seeing a bit of her quickly, then going back to the cushion, and the next time managing a little bit more that you were not afraid of. And then it was Sadie, all of her or at least all I could reasonably see on the side that was available.

Something moved. I saw it, her eyelid on my side moved. It was not opening or halfway opening or anything like that, but lifting just such a tiny bit as would make it possible, if you were her, if you were inside her, to be able to see out through the lashes. Just to distinguish maybe what was light outside and what was dark.

I was not surprised then and not in the least scared. Instantly, this sight fell into everything I knew about Sadie and somehow, as well, into whatever special experience was owing to myself. And I did not dream of calling anybody else's attention to what was there, because it was not meant for them, it was completely for me.

My mother had taken my hand again and said that we were ready to go. There were some more exchanges, but before any time had passed, as it seemed to me, we found ourselves outside.

My mother said, "Good for you." She squeezed my hand and said, "Now then. It's over." She had to stop and speak to somebody else who was on the way to the house, and then we got into the car and began to drive home. I had an idea that she would like me to say something, or maybe even tell her something, but I didn't do it.

There was never any other appearance of that sort and in fact Sadie faded rather quickly from my mind, what with the shock of school, where I learned somehow to manage with an odd mixture of being dead scared and showing off. As a matter of fact some of her importance had faded in that first week in September when she said she had to stay home now to look after her father and mother, so she wouldn't be working for us anymore.

And then my mother had found out she was working in the creamery.

Yet for a long time when I did think of her, I never questioned what I believed had been shown to me. Long, long afterwards, when I was not at all interested in any unnatural display, I still had it in my mind that such a thing had happened. I just believed it easily, the way you might believe and in fact remember that you once had another set of teeth, now vanished but real in spite of that. Until one day, one day when I may even have been in my teens, I knew with a dim sort of hole in my insides that now I didn't believe it anymore.

BEFORE HE LEFT THE FAMILY

Carrie Tiffany

Carrie Tiffany (b. 1965) is a British-born Australian author. Her first novel, *Everyman's Rules for Scientific Living*, was published in 2005 and made the shortlist of both the Guardian First Book Award and the Orange Prize. Her second novel, *Mateship with Birds*, won the 2013 inaugural Stella Prize and was shortlisted for the Women's Prize for Fiction.

Before he left the family, my father worked as a sales representative for a pharmaceutical company. He travelled from chemist to chemist with samples of pills and lotions and pastes in the back of his Valiant station wagon. The best sales representatives visited modern chemists in the city and suburbs. My father had to drive long distances to country chemists who had stocked the same product lines for years and weren't interested in anything new. As he drank more and more, my father called on fewer and fewer chemists, but the cardboard boxes of samples kept arriving. They no longer fitted in the back of the car, so my father stored them in the corrugated iron shed next to the house. Summer in Perth is very hot. For months and months the bitumen boiled on the roads and we had to use the ends of our t-shirts to open the iron lid of the mailbox, or risk getting burnt. The pharmaceutical samples expanded in the heat of the shed. The lotions and pastes burst their tubes and tubs and seeped through the cardboard boxes. It smelt good in the shed – sweet and clean and surgical. My brother and I went in there often and sat among the sodden boxes as we read our father's *Playboy* magazines.

In the last weeks of their marriage, our parents battled out the terms of their separation at the dinner table in between the ice-cream bowls. My mother, small and freckled, wrote lists of their possessions on a Nordette® Low Dose Oral Contraceptive notepad. She looked like a teenage girl playing a board game. Nathan and I listened in as we watched television on the other side of the vinyl concertina doors that marked the division between the lounge room and the dining room. We watched *MASH*. Nathan sang along to the theme song, and for the first time I noticed how high and piping his voice was. And there was something creepy about his pink skin and the cowlick at the front of his fine white hair. I wondered if we hadn't created a masculine enough environment for our father. I tipped my brother out of his chair and started boxing his arms and chest. He wailed. The doors were dragged open.

'Kevin, what are you doing?' my mother said, leaning against the buckled vinyl as if she was too young to stand unsupported. I let Nathan squirm out from underneath me.

'He's a sissy,' I said. 'He sings like a girl. Tell him he's not allowed to sing.'

She looked from me to Nathan and back to me again; then she forced her eyes open wide so they boggled with exasperation.

The playmates in the *Playboy* magazines are always smiling. Or, if they aren't smiling they have a gasping, pained expression as if they've just stood on a drawing pin. None of them have someone special in their lives at this time, but with the right man they can be hot to handle. They like the feeling of silk against their bare skin, and they appreciate the outdoors and candle-lit dinners. Miss July says she likes the heat (she's from Queensland), but on the next page she says she would like to make love in the snow. This contradiction seems to have slipped past the *Playboy* editor. I wonder if this is a concern to other readers? The skin of the playmates can be matched to the samples of different timber stains that we have in woodwork class. The brunettes are teak or mahogany, the blondes are stained pine if they have a tan, or unstained pine if they are from Sweden, Finland, Denmark, or the Netherlands. The playmates don't have veins showing through their skin – it is just the one colour – like a pelt. And none of them have freckles or bits of hardened sleep in the corner of their eyes like tiny potatoes.

My father agreed to take only his personal items; his clothes, shoes, records, golf clubs, and alcohol. On the morning that he left I stood in the driveway and waved him off. My mother and brother watched from the kitchen window. My father's work shirts hung in rows down each side of the rear of the station wagon. It looked neat – like it had been designed for that purpose – like a gentleman's wardrobe on wheels. My father waved his forearm out of the window as he drove off. Just as he rounded the bend in the road and the car moved out of sight, he tooted his horn. I stood and watched for a few minutes. When I finally turned to walk away, I noticed my mother and brother were still looking out of the kitchen window; but now they were looking at me.

My father married my mother when she was eighteen, because he had made her pregnant. It was just the one time; the one date. My mother had a job interview at the shoe shop where my father was working. She didn't get the job, but my father, the junior sales clerk, asked her out. When my brother and I were little we often asked our father to tell us the story of how he met our mother. He always said the same thing. He said that our mother had the best pair of knockers he'd ever seen. For many years my brother and I believed that knockers were a brand of shoe. It was through reading the *Playboy* magazines hidden among the boxes of pharmaceutical samples in the shed that I realised my mistake. And although we never spoke of it, I believe that Nathan, who is three years younger than me, was also enlightened this way.

I heard my father's car in the driveway a few days after he left. My mother was at her bootscooting class and Nathan had gone along to watch. The Valiant was empty and I wanted to ask my father where he was living, where all his shirts were hanging now, but it felt too intrusive. My father called me over to help him load the stereo, the fan, a china dinner service that had never been out of its box, an Esky, and a bodybuilding machine into the back of his car. I knew that my mother would be angry, but I felt flattered my father had asked me for help with the lifting. No man ever refused to help another man lift.

A week later, my father came back again and tried to remove some of the boxes of pharmaceutical samples from the shed. My mother rushed out of the house as soon as she saw his car. She shrieked at him and tried to block the doorway to the shed. My father pushed past her. Nathan started to whimper. I stood near the tailgate of the Valiant – I hoped that my father would think I was trying to help him, and that my mother would think I was trying to stop him. My mother saw one of our neighbours working in his garden over the fence and she called out to him. She insisted that he help her, saying that my father was trying to steal her property. Ron looked uncomfortable, but he came and leant against the fence, holding his small soil-stained trowel in his hand.

'G'day, Ron,' my father said, cheerfully, as he carried a stack of cardboard boxes towards the car. My mother rushed at him then, and they grappled with the boxes. Some of the boxes disintegrated as my mother and father snatched at them. Ron banged his trowel against the fence palings to signal his disapproval. I was embarrassed for all of us. It was unseemly. The pieces of soft cardboard on the ground looked dirty and cheap. The value of us – the whole family enterprise – seemed to be symbolised by them.

My father never came to the house again. He took a job interstate. The telephone calls became less and less frequent, then they stopped. The first year, with the anticipation that he might write or ring on our birthdays or at Christmas, was confusing, but things settled down after that.

Because my father left Western Australia and my mother didn't know where he was working, she was unable to have any maintenance payments taken out of his wages. Money was tight. When the windscreen of the Torana shattered, my mother covered it in gladwrap and kept driving. She took a job with the local real estate agent. She didn't have her licence, so she answered the telephone and wrote down messages. On the weekends the owner of the agency let her put up directional signs in the streets surrounding houses they had listed for sale. He told her it was good experience and would help her when she sat the exam for her estate agent's licence.

One Saturday morning Nathan and I went along to help our mother with the signs. The signs were metal; they attached to a steel stake with wire. There was a rubber mallet to bang the steel stakes into the ground. The house for sale was on a recent estate behind the tip. A new road had been built to get into the estate so that the residents didn't have to go past the tip, but everyone knew it was there. In summer the tip stank as the rubbish decayed in the heat. It was better in winter when people lit fires there and the smoke was rich and fruity. We parked on the side of the road and tried to hammer the first stake into the ground. It only went in a few inches before it hit rock. We took turns. Each of us thought the other wasn't doing it right, until we had tried for ourselves. As I hit the stake with the mallet and the force reverberated, not into the ground, but back up my arm and shoulder, I knew we were no longer a family. A woman and two boys is not a family. We had no muscle. We had no way of breaking through.

It rained overnight. My mother insisted that we go back and try to erect the signs the next day, as the ground would be softer. With my father gone I had to sit next to my mother in the front seat of the car as she drove. She was wearing Nathan's old raincoat from scouts and a red gingham headscarf over her hair. I told her that it would suit her better if she tied it under her throat like the Queen.

'This way,' I said, as I turned in the seat and knotted it under her chin, 'is more dignified.' I was already a foot taller than her and I was worried someone from school might see us and think she was my girlfriend, instead of my mother. My brother sat in the back of the car while my mother swung at the stake with the mallet. The rain had muddied the surface of the ground, but barely soaked in at all. It was still hard going. It started to drizzle. I held the Lorazepam® High-Potency Benzodiazepine golf umbrella over my mother's head with my arm out-stretched so I didn't have to stand too close to her. If anyone drove past and saw us I hoped they would think I was more in the role of caddy than lover.

Increasingly, when I thought about my father, my memories of him were not so much of actual events or incidents, but of the things he left behind. My father had a moustache and one of his eyes was sleepy. The sleepy eye was more noticeable in photographs than in real life. Not many adults have a sleepy eye – or perhaps it's difficult to tell because so many of them wear glasses. There was a framed photograph of my parents on their wedding day next to the telephone in the hall. My mother is wearing a too-big navy suit in the photograph. Her cheeks are uneven and she looks seasick. My father seems happier – his moustache, if not his mouth, is smiling. His eyes are downcast though. He is looking at the most striking thing in the photograph – his massive white wrists. My father told me the story of the photograph one night when he'd been drinking and my mother wouldn't let him in the house. He climbed through my window and spent the night on the floor next to my bed. The story was this: a few months after the date with my mother, my father had another date. This date was with a girl he really liked, a girl he wanted to marry. He paid a friend who worked in a garage to give him the keys to a sports car for the evening so he could take the first rate girl out. Showing off, he took a corner too fast and crashed into a brick wall. The girl was unhurt, but my father broke both of his wrists. Because of this he was wearing plaster casts on his wrists when he married my mother a couple of months later. The casts give my father a serious and masculine appearance in the wedding photograph. The weight of them on his wrists make his arms look heavy, almost burdened, with muscle. And the thickness and hardness of the casts straining at his shirt cuffs is menacing. He doesn't look like a sales clerk, he looks like a boxer.

Underneath the photograph, in the drawer of the hall table, there are three boxes of white biros with blue writing on them – Aldactone® Spironolactone Easy To Swallow Tablets. One afternoon after school I try all of the biros on the back cover of the phone book. Out of fifty-four biros, only seven work.

Because my mother goes on a few dates with one of the real estate agents and it doesn't work out, she has to leave her job. She goes on benefits and is made to do courses. Her course at the local neighbourhood house is called 'Starting Again for the Divorced and Separated'. My mother does her homework in her

My New Life Workbook in front of the television. When she gets up to go to the toilet during a commercial break I take a look at what she's written. Under '*What motivates me?*' she has answered, '*flowers*'.

My mother asks me and Nathan to go with her to a Parents without Partners picnic. It's at an animal nursery. I can tell that Nathan doesn't mind the sound of it, that he would like to pet the lambs and the rabbits. But I say we are too old, that it's dumb, and by holding Nathan's eye for long enough I get him to agree. My mother goes without us. She meets a man who works on prawn trawlers in the Gulf of Carpentaria. The man has a daughter whom he sees sometimes when he's in town. My mother has a lot of late-night telephone conversations with the man on the prawn trawler. She has to say 'over' when she finishes what she is saying, because he is using a radio telephone. When the prawn season finishes, my mother's new boyfriend moves in with us.

I have become so familiar with the playmates in my father's *Playboy* magazines that they don't work anymore, so I read the articles. In *Playboy* forum, men write in and describe how they meet women in ordinary places; the petrol station, the laundromat or the video library, and they have sex with them against the bowser, the dryers, or on the counter. When this happens a friend of the woman with different-coloured hair often arrives unexpectedly and has no hesitation joining in. And if the first woman at the petrol station, the laundromat, or the video library has small breasts, her friend will always have large breasts – or the other way around. After I've read all of the articles I look at the ads and the fashion pages and choose things. I choose Rigs Pants, Lord Jim Bionic Hair Tonic, Manskins jocks, Laredo heeled cowboy boots with a fancy shaft, and Aramis Devin aftershave – the world's first great sporting fragrance for men. I think I hear someone outside, but it's just a pair of dusty boxing gloves that hang from a nail on the back door of the shed. When it's windy the gloves bang into each other. I can no longer remember if the boxing gloves belonged to my father, or if they were in the shed before we came to live here.

Nathan joins the gymnastics team at school and I get a checkout job on Thursday nights and Saturday mornings. Nathan's legs are bowed and he doesn't have any strength in his upper arms. When he does his exercises his shorts ride up and his orange jocks show. The gymnastics teacher says his vaulting technique is poor. He tells me that Nathan doesn't look like he's trying to jump over the horse, more like he's trying to fuck it. He tells me this because I am standing next to my mother in the school quadrangle at open day where we are watching a display of gymnastics. I am wearing my Coles New World tie and the gymnastics teacher must think I am my mother's boyfriend. Nathan is best at the type of gymnastics where he has to throw a stick or play with a ball – a type of gymnastics that might have been invented by puppies. Because Nathan's wrists are weak he wears special white tape around them. He brings some of the tape home – he says the gymnastics teacher gave it to him, but I doubt it. Nathan wears the tape on his wrists every day during the school holidays. When the tape gets grubby he puts more over the top until his wrists are so thick he can't hold his fork properly. When he's talking he throws his hands around in the air and watches them. This is something I've seen my mother do when she has just changed her nail polish.

By over-ringing the total on a number of small sales, it is safe to take around five dollars out of the till at work each week. It's better not to take an even amount. Four dollars thirty-nine is good. *Playboy* magazine costs two dollars. I don't buy it every month. I buy it when the cover looks like it will go with the covers of my father's magazine already in the shed.

My mother takes her wedding photograph out of the frame on the hall table and replaces it with a picture of herself and her new boyfriend on a fishing trip. The photograph shows my mother and Wayne standing on a jetty together, each holding a fishing line with a white fish dangling from it. My mother's face is puffy with the strain of holding the fish aloft. Her lips are open and stretched tight, just like the fishes' lips. If it were a group portrait you would have said my mother and the fish were related. My parents' wedding photograph is relegated to a drawer in the hall table where the envelopes and takeaway menus are kept. The photograph rises to the surface every time I search for a piece of paper to take down a message. It is crumpled now and smells of soy sauce.

There is a letter in the latest *Playboy* that I think might be from my father. In the letter a man describes an encounter he has with a woman at a bodybuilding centre. The man describes himself as well built, with a full head of hair and a moustache. He is lifting weights on his own late one night when a beautiful girl comes in to clean the equipment.

The girl is wearing a short pink cleaner's dress which fits poorly across the chest. Because her washing machine has broken down and she is poor and has no change for the laundromat, she is not wearing any underpants. The girl says hello to the man shyly and starts cleaning. The man is sweating heavily – sweat is running off his biceps like he's standing under a waterfall. The man notices that the girl is watching him. He decides to do a few rounds with the punching bag. He calls the girl (she has been bent over rubbing the weight-lifting bars with a cloth), and asks her to help him lace up his boxing gloves. As soon as the girl gets close to the man, she is intoxicated by his sweat. She ties the laces of the boxing gloves together so he is her prisoner. She tells the man to sit down on the bench press, then she takes her dress off and rides him like he's a bucking bronco.

The letter is signed, *Hot and Sweaty, Tweed Heads*. I hope that it is my father's letter. I hope the girl in the story is the same girl my father took out on a date when he broke his wrists, and when she finally takes off his boxing gloves and they hold hands, I hope they are not joined by one of her friends with different-coloured hair. I place the magazine on the top of the pile so Nathan will read it too. I hope Nathan will think that our father is happy. I want Nathan to understand that our mother was never going to make things work with our father. She was the wrong girl. And because she was the wrong girl, Nathan and I were the wrong sons. It could never have been any other way.

DIVING BELLES

Lucy Wood

Lucy Wood is a British author. She grew up in Cornwall and completed a Master's degree in Creative Writing at Exeter University. The short story collection, *Diving Belles*, is her first published work.

I ris crossed her brittle ankles and folded her hands in her lap as the diving bell creaked and juddered towards the sea. At first, she could hear Demelza shouting and cursing as she cranked the winch, but as the bell was can-ulevered away from the deck her voice was lost in the wind. Cold air rushed through the open bottom of the bell, bringing with it the rusty smell of *The Matriarch*'s liver-spotted flanks and the brackish damp of seaweed. The bench Iris was sitting on was narrow and every time the diving bell rocked she pressed against the footrest to steady herself. She kept imagining that she was inside a church bell and that she was the clapper about to ring out loudly into the water, announcing something. She fixed her eyes on the small window and didn't look down. There was no floor beneath her feet, just a wide open gap, and the sea peaked and spat. She lurched downwards slowly, metres away from the side of the trawler, where a layer of barnacles and mussels clung on like the survivors of a shipwreck.

She fretted with her new dress and her borrowed shoes. She tried to smooth her white hair, which turned wiry when it was close to water. The wooden bench was digging into her and the wind was rushing up her legs, snagging at the dress and exposing the map of her veins. She'd forgotten tights; she always wore trousers and knew it was a mistake to wear a dress. She'd let herself get talked into it, but had chosen brown, a small victory. She gathered the skirt up and sat on it. If this was going to be the first time she saw her husband in forty-eight years she didn't want to draw attention to the state of her legs. 'You've got to be heartbreaking as hell,' Demelza advised her customers, pointing at them with her cigarette. 'Because you've got a lot of competition down there.'

Salt and spray leapt up to meet the bell as it slapped into the sea. Cold, dark water surged upwards. Iris lifted her feet, waiting for the air pressure in the bell to level off the water underneath the footrest. She didn't want anything oily or foamy to stain Annie's shoes. She went through a checklist – Vanish, cream clean-er, a bit of bicarb – something would get it out but it would be a fuss. She pulled her cardigan sleeves down and straightened the life-jacket. Thousands of bubbles forced themselves up the sides of the diving bell, rolling over the window like marbles. She peered out but couldn't see anything beyond the disturbed water.

As she was lowered further the sea calmed and stilled. Everything was silent. She put her feet back down and looked into the disc of water below them, which was flat and thick and barely rippled. She could be looking at a lino or slate floor rather than a gap that opened into all those airless fathoms. A smudged grey shape floated past. The diving bell jolted and tipped, then righted itself and sank lower through the water.

Iris held her handbag against her chest and tried not to breathe too quickly. She had about two hours' worth of oxygen but if she panicked or became over-excited she would use it up more quickly. Her fingers laced and unlaced. 'I don't want to have to haul you back up here like a limp fish,' Demelza had told her each time she'd gone down in the bell. 'Don't go thinking you're an expert or anything. One pull on the cord to stop, another to start again. Two tugs for the net and three to come back up. Got it?' Iris had written the instructions down the first time in her thin, messy writing and put them in her bag along with tissues and mints, just in case. The pull-cord was threaded through a tube that ran alongside the chain attaching the bell to the trawler. Demelza tied her end of it to a cymbal that she'd rigged on to a tripod, so that it crashed loudly whenever someone pulled on it. The other end of the cord drooped down and brushed roughly against the top of Iris's head.

She couldn't see much out of the window; it all looked grey and endless, as if she were moving through fog rather than water. The diving bell dropped down slowly, slower, and then stopped moving altogether. The chain slackened and for a second it seemed as though the bell had been cut off and was about to float away. Then the chain straightened out and Iris rocked sideways, caught between the tension above and the bell's heavy lead rim below. She hung suspended in the mid-depths of the sea. This had happened on her second dive as well. Demelza had suddenly stopped winching, locked the handle and gone to check over her co-ordinates one last time. She wouldn't allow the diving bell to land even a foot off the target she'd set herself.

The bell swayed. Iris sat very still and tried not to imagine the weight of the water pressing in. She took a couple of rattling breaths. It was like those moments when she woke up in the middle of the night, breathless and alone, reaching across the bed and finding nothing but a heap of night-chilled pillows. She just needed to relax and wait, relax and wait. She took out a mint and crunched down hard, the grainy sugar digging into her back teeth.

After a few moments Demelza started winching again and Iris loosened her shoulders, glad to be on the move. Closer to the seabed, the water seemed to clear. Then, suddenly, there was the shipwreck, looming upwards like an unlit bonfire, all splints and beams and slumped funnels. The rusting mainframe arched and jutted. Collapsed sheets of iron were strewn across the sand. The diving bell moved between girders and cables before stopping just above the engine. The *Queen Mary*'s sign, corroded and nibbled, gazed up at Iris. Empty cupboards were scattered to her left. The cargo ship had been transporting train carriages and they were lying all over the seabed, marooned and broken, like bodies that had been weighed down with stones and buried at sea. Orange rust bloomed all over them. Green and purple seaweed drifted out through the windows. Red man's fingers and dead man's fingers pushed up from the wheel arches.

Demelza thought that this would be a good place to trawl. She'd sent Iris down to the same spot already. 'Sooner or later,' she said, 'they all come back.

They stay local, you see. They might go gallivanting off for a while, but they always come back to the same spot. They're nostalgic bastards, sentimental as hell. That makes them stupid. Not like us though, eh?' she added, yanking Iris's life-jacket straps tighter.

A cuckoo wrasse weaved in and out of the ship's bones. Cuttlefish mooned about like lost old men. Iris spat on her glasses, wiped them on her cardigan, hooked them over her ears, and waited.

Over the years, she had tried to banish as many lonely moments as possible. She kept busy. She took as many shifts as she could at the hotel, and then when that stopped she became addicted to car boot sales – travelling round to different ones at the weekends, sifting through chipped plates and dolls and candelabra, never buying anything, just sifting through. She joined a pen pal company and started writing to a man in Orkney; she liked hearing about the sudden weather and the seals hauled out on the beach, his bus and his paintings. 'I am fine as always,' she would write, but stopped when he began to send dark, tormented paintings, faces almost hidden under black and red.

She knew how to keep busy most of the day and, over time, her body learned to shut down and nap during the blank gap straight after lunch. It worked almost every time, although once, unable to sleep and sick of the quiet humming of the freezer – worse than silence she often thought – she turned it off and let the food melt and drip on the floor. Later, regretting the waste, she'd spent hours cooking, turning it into pies and casseroles and refreezing it for another day.

She ate in front of films she borrowed from the library. She watched anything she could get her hands on. It was when the final credits rolled, though, when the music had stopped and the tape rewound, that her mind became treacherous and leapt towards the things she tried not to think about during the day. That was when she lay back in the chair – kicking and jolting between wakefulness and sleep as if she were thrashing about in shallow water – and let her husband swim back into the house.

Then, she relived the morning when she had woken to the smell of salt and damp and found a tiny fish in its death throes on the pillow next to her. There was only a lukewarm indent in the mattress where her husband should have been. She swung her legs out of bed and followed a trail of sand down the stairs, through the kitchen and towards the door. Her heart thumped in the soles of her bare feet. The door was open. Two green crabs high-stepped across the slates. Bladderwrack festooned the kitchen, and here and there, on the fridge, on the kettle, anemones bloomed, fat and dark as hearts. It took her all day to scrub and bleach and mop the house back into shape. By the time she'd finished he could have been anywhere. She didn't phone the police; no one ever phoned the police. No one was reported missing.

Despite the bleach, the smell lingered in cupboards and corners. Every so often, an anemone would appear overnight; she would find a translucent shrimp darting around inside an empty milk bottle. Sometimes, all the water in the house turned into brine and she lugged huge bottles of water home from the supermarket. The silence waxed and waned. Life bedded itself down again like a hermit crab in a bigger, emptier shell.

*

Once in a while, Annie and her husband Westy came round to see Iris. They lived on the same street and came over when Annie had something she wanted to say or if she was bored. She could smell out bad news and liked to talk about it, her own included. Westy went wherever she went. He was a vague man. He'd got his whole Scout group lost when he was twelve because he'd read the compass wrong, so he was nicknamed Westy and it stuck – everyone used it, even his wife; sometimes Iris wondered if he could even remember his real name. When Annie dies, she sometimes thought, his mind will go, just like that, and mentally she would snap her fingers, instantly regretting thinking it.

When she heard them coming up the path she would rush round the house, checking water filters, tearing thrift off the shelves. If she ever missed something, a limpet shell, a watery cluster of sea moss, Annie and Westy would look away, pretending not to notice.

Last month, they came over on a Sunday afternoon. 'I don't like Sundays,' Annie said, drinking her tea at scalding point. 'They make me feel like I'm in limbo.' She was short and spread herself out over the chair. She made Iris want to stoop over.

It was damp outside and the kitchen windows had steamed up. Annie had brought over saffron cake and Iris bit at the edges, feeling she had to but hating the chlorine taste of it. She'd told Annie that before but she kept bringing it over anyway.

'Don't forget the envelope,' Westy said.

Annie shot him a quick look. 'I'll come to that.' She glanced down at her bag. 'Have you heard about the burglaries around King's Road?'

'I read something about it,' Iris said. She crossed her arms, knowing that Annie was trying to ease into something.

'Five over two weeks. All in the middle of the day. The owners came back to stripped houses – everything gone, even library books.'

'Library books?' Iris said. She saw that Annie and Westy were wearing the same fleece in different colours – one purple, one checked red and green.

'Exactly. One of the owners said they saw a van driving away. They saw the men in there looking at them.' Annie paused, looked at Westy. 'Imagine going in there, seeing the bare walls, knowing that someone had gone through everything, valuing it.'

'Their shoes,' Westy said.

'Everything,' said Annie. 'And no chance of ever getting it back.' She stopped, waiting for Iris to speak, but Iris didn't say anything. Annie reached down into her bag and got out a blue and gold envelope and put it on the table, cleared her throat. 'Ever heard of Diving Belles?' she asked bluntly.

Iris didn't look at the envelope. 'I suppose so,' she said. She saw Annie take a deep breath – she was bad at this, had never liked giving out gifts. Iris's mind raced through ways she could steer the conversation away; she snatched at topics but couldn't fasten on to any.

'When Kayleigh Andrews did it,' Annie told her, 'it only took one go. They found her husband as quick as anything.'

Iris didn't reply. She tightened her lips and poured out more tea.

'It seems like a very lucrative business,' Annie said, pressing on. 'A good opportunity.'

'Down on the harbour,' said Westy. 'By the old lifeboat hut.'

Iris knocked crumbs into her cupped palm from the table edge and tipped them into her saucer. The clock on the fridge ticked loudly into the silence. The old anger swept back. She could break all these plates.

'A good opportunity,' Annie said again.

'For some people,' Iris replied. A fly buzzed over and she banged a plate down hard on to it.

'What you need is one of those electric swatters,' Westy told her.

'You shouldn't have gone to the trouble,' Iris said. She gripped the sides of her chair.

Annie pushed the envelope so it was right in front of her. 'The voucher's redeemable for three goes,' she said.

'It's kind of you.'

They looked around the room as if they had never seen it before, the cream walls and brown speckled tiles. A sea snail crawled over the window-sill.

'I can't swim. I won't be able to do it if I can't swim,' Iris said suddenly.

'You don't need to swim. You just sit in this bell thing and get lowered down,' Annie said. 'The voucher gives you three goes, Iris. You don't have to swim anywhere.'

Iris stood up, stacked the cups and plates, and took them to the sink. Soon Annie would say something like, 'Nothing ventured, nothing gained.' Her hands trembled slightly, the crockery clattering together like pebbles flipping over.

After they'd left, she watched the envelope out of the corner of her eye. She did small jobs that took her closer towards it: she swept the floor, straightened the chairs, the tablecloth. Later, lying in bed, she pictured it sitting there. It was very exposed in the middle of the table like that – what if somebody broke in? It would be a waste of Annie's money if the voucher was stolen. She went downstairs, picked up the envelope, brought it back upstairs and tucked it under her pillow.

The reception at Diving Belles was in an old corrugated-iron Portakabin on the edge of the harbour. Iris knocked tentatively on the door. The wind hauled itself around the town, crashing into bins and slumping into washing, jangling the rigging on the fishing boats. There were piles of nets and lobster pots and orange buoys that smelled of fish and stagnant water. No one answered the door. She stepped back to check she had the right place, then knocked again. There was a clanging above her head as a woman walked across the roof. She was wearing khaki trousers, a tight black vest and jelly shoes. Her hair was short and dyed red. She climbed down a ladder and stood in front of Iris, staring. Her hands were criss-crossed with scars and her broad shoulders and arms were covered in tattoos. Iris couldn't take her eyes off them. She watched an eel swim through a hollow black heart on the woman's bicep.

'Is it, I mean, are you Demelza?' Iris asked.

'Demelza, Demelza ... Yes, I suppose I am.' Demelza looked up at the roof and stepped back as if to admire something. There was a strange contraption up there – it looked like a metal cage with lots of thick springs. 'That ought to do it,' Demelza muttered to herself.

Iris looked up. Was that a seagull sprawled inside or a plastic bag?

Demelza strode off towards the office without saying anything else. Iris hesitated, then followed her.

The office smelled like old maps and burnt coffee. Demelza sat behind a desk which had a hunting knife skewered into one corner. Iris perched on the edge of a musty deckchair. Paperwork and files mixed with rusty boat parts. There was a board on the wall with hundreds of glinting turquoise and silver scales pinned to it.

Demelza leaned back in her chair and lit a cigarette. 'These are herbal,' she said. 'Every drag is like death.' She inhaled deeply then rubbed at her knuckles, rocking back and forth on the chair's back legs.

Iris tensed her back, trying to keep straight so that her deckchair wouldn't collapse. The slats creaked. She felt too warm even though the room was cold.

'So,' Demelza barked suddenly. 'What are we dealing with here? Husband taken?'

Iris nodded.

Demelza rummaged around in the desk drawer and pulled out a form. 'How many nights ago?'

'I'm not exactly sure.'

'Spit it out. Three? Seven? If you haven't counted the nights I don't know why you're pestering me about it.'

'Seventeen thousand, six hundred and thirty-two,' Iris said.

'What the hell? There's not room for that on this form.' Demelza looked at her. Her eyes were slightly bloodshot and she didn't seem to blink.

'If it doesn't fit on the form then don't trouble yourself,' Iris said. She started to get up, relief and disappointment merging.

'Hang on, hang on.' Demelza gestured for her to sit back down. 'I didn't say I wouldn't do it. It makes more sense anyway now I come to think about it. I've never known them to be bothered by an old codger before.' She sniggered to herself.

'He was twenty-four.'

'Exactly, exactly.' Demelza scribbled something down on the form. 'But this is going to be damn tricky, you know. There's a chance he will have migrated; he could have been abandoned; he could be anywhere. You understand that?' Iris nodded again. 'Good. I need you to sign here – just a simple legal clause about safety and the like, and to confirm you know that I'm not legally obliged to produce the husband. If I can't find him it's tough titties, OK?'

Iris signed it.

'And how I track them is business secrets,' Demelza said. 'Don't bother asking me about it. I don't want competition.'

A plastic singing fish leered down at Iris from the wall. She could feel tendrils of her hair slipping from behind their pins. She always wore her hair up, but once she'd left it down and nobody in her local shop had recognised her. When she'd ventured back she'd had to pretend that she'd been away for a while. She dug a pin in deeper. Was Demelza smirking at her? She hunched down in the chair, almost wishing it would fold up around her. She shouldn't have come. She waited for Demelza to say something but she was just rocking back and forth, one leg draped over the desk.

'The weather's warming up.' Iris said eventually, although it was colder than ever.

Demelza said something through her teeth about seagulls and tourists then sighed and stood up. 'Come on,' she said. They walked to the end of the harbour. Small waves lifted up handfuls of seaweed at the bottom of the harbour wall. Demelza pointed to an old beam trawler. 'There she is.'

'There she is,' Iris said. *The Matriarch* was yellow and haggard as an old fingernail. Rust curled off the bottom. It looked like it was struggling to stay afloat. Its figurehead was a decapitated mermaid and the deck smelled of tar and sewage. None of the other boats had anchored near it.

Demelza took a deep sniff. 'Beautiful, isn't she?' Without waiting for an answer she walked up the ramp and on to the boat. The diving bell was sitting on a platform next to the wheel. It looked ancient and heavy, like a piece of armour. For the first time, Iris realised she'd be going right under the sea. Picturing herself inside, she remembered a pale bird she had once seen hanging in a cage in a shop window.

Demelza ran her hand across the metal. She explained how the diving bell worked. 'See, when it's submerged the air and the water pressure balance so the water won't come in past the bench. The oxygen gets trapped in the top. Of course, modern ones do it differently; there are pipes and things that pump oxygen down from the boat. Apparently that's "safer". They have all this crap like phones in there but they're not as beautiful as this one. This one is a real beauty. Why would you need a goddamn phone under the sea?' She looked at Iris as if she expected an answer.

Iris thought about comfort and calling for help. 'Well,' she said. 'No one likes change, do they?'

Demelza clapped her hard on the back. 'My sentiment exactly.' They walked back along the harbour. 'Give me a few days to track any signs then I'll give you a buzz,' she said.

Fifteen minutes passed inside the diving bell. It could have been seconds or hours. The hulk of the *Queen Mary* was dark and still. Iris noticed every small movement. A spider crab poked its head out of a hole. A sea slug pulsed across the keel. The seaweed swayed and rocked in small currents and, following them with her eyes, Iris rocked into a thin sleep, then jolted awake with a gasp, thinking she had fallen into the water, feeling herself hit the cold and start to sink. She hadn't slept well the night before but it was ridiculous and dangerous to fall asleep here, to come all this way and sleep. She pinched her wrist and shifted on the bench, wishing Demelza had put some sort of cushion on it.

Time passed. A ray swam up and pasted itself to the glass like a wet leaf. It had a small, angry face. Its mouth gaped. The diving bell became even darker inside and Iris couldn't see anything out of the window. 'Get away,' she said. Nothing happened. She leaned forwards and banged hard on the glass until the ray unpeeled itself and disappeared. Her heart beat fast and heavy. Every time she glimpsed a fish darting, or saw a small shadow, she thought that it was him swimming towards her. She worked herself up and then nothing happened. Her heart slowed down again.

Demelza was sure there would be a sighting. She said that she'd recorded a lot more movement around the wreck in the past few days, but to Iris it seemed as empty and lonely as ever.

Something caught her eye and she half stood on the footrest to look out. Nothing – probably seaweed. Her knees shook, not up to the task of hefting her about in such a narrow gap. She sat back down. Even if he did appear, even if she made him follow the diving bell until Demelza could reach him with the net, what would she say to him on deck? What was that phrase Annie had picked up? 'Long time no see'? She practised saying it. 'Long time no see.' It sounded odd and caught in her throat. She cleared it and tried again. 'Actually, long time lots of sea,' she joked into the hollow metal. It fell flat. She thought of all the things she wanted to tell him. There were so many things but none of them were right. They stacked up in front of her like bricks, dense and dry. She had a sudden thought and colour seeped up her neck and into her cheeks. Of course, he was going to be naked. She had forgotten about that. She'd be standing there, thinking of something to say, and Demelza would be there, and he'd be naked. It had been so long since … She didn't know whether she would … Was she a wife or a stranger? She picked at the fragile skin around her nails, tearing it to pieces.

On the first dive, Iris had got a sense of how big it all was, how vast; emptier and more echoing than she had thought possible. It made her feel giddy and sick. She had presumed that there would be something here – she didn't know what – but she hadn't imagined this nothingness stretching on and on. She shuddered, hating the cold and the murk, regretting ever picking up the envelope from the table. The silence bothered her. She didn't like to think of him somewhere so silent.

As she went deeper, small memories rose up to meet her. A fine net of flour over his dark hair; a song on his lips that went, 'My old man was a sailor, I saw him once a year'; a bee, but she didn't know what the bee was connected to.

She saw something up ahead: a small, dark shape swimming towards her. Her stomach lurched. It had to be him – he had sensed her and was coming to meet her! She pulled on the cord, once, hard, to stop. The bell drifted down for a few moments then lurched to a halt. Iris craned her neck forwards, trying to make him out properly. She should have done this years ago.

He came closer, swimming with his arms behind him. What colour was that? His skin looked very dark; a kind of red-brown. He swam closer and her heart dropped down into her feet. It was an octopus. Its curled legs drifted out behind as it swam around the bell, its body like a bag snagged on a tree. She had thought this octopus was her husband! Shame and a sudden tiredness coursed through her. She tried to laugh but only the smallest corner of her mouth twitched, then wouldn't stop. 'You silly fool,' she told herself. 'You silly fool.' She watched its greedy eyes inspecting the bell, then pulled three times on the cord. A spasm of weariness gripped her. She told Demelza she hadn't seen anything.

'I thought you had, when you wanted to stop suddenly,' Demelza said. She took a swig from a hip flask and offered it to Iris, who sipped until her dry lips burned. 'Wouldn't have thought they'd have been mid-water like that, but still, they can be wily bastards at times.' She turned round and squinted at Iris, who was sitting very quietly with her eyes closed. 'No sea legs,' Demelza said to herself. 'You know what the best advice I heard was?' she asked loudly. 'You can't chuck them back in once they're out.' She shook her head and bit her knuckles. 'I had a woman yesterday, a regular. She comes every couple of weeks. Her husband is susceptible to them, she says. So she goes down, we net him up and lug him back on to the deck, all pale and fat, dripping salt and seaweed like a goddamn seal. And all the time I'm thinking, what the hell's the point? Leave him down there. But she's got it in her head that she can't live without him so that's that.'

'Maybe she loves him,' Iris said.

'Bah. There are plenty more fish in the sea,' Demelza said. She laughed and laughed, barking and cawing like a seagull. 'There are plenty more fish in the sea,' she said again, baring her teeth to the wind. 'Plenty, fish, sea,' she muttered over and over as she steered back to the harbour.

On her second dive Iris heard the beginning of a song threading through the water towards her. It was slow and deep, more of an ache in her bones than something she heard in her ears. There was a storm building up but Demelza thought it would hold off long enough to do the dive. At firsr Iris thought the sound was the wind, stoked right up and reaching down into the water – it was the same noise as the wind whistling through gaps in boats, or over the mouth of a milk bottle, but she knew that the wind wouldn't come down this far. It thrummed through the metal and into her bones, maybe just her old body complaining again, playing tricks, but she felt so light and warm. The song grew louder, slowing Iris's heart, pressing her eyes closed like kind thumbs. It felt good to have her eyes closed. The weight of the water pressed in but it was calm, inviting; it beckoned to her. She wanted to get out of the bell, just get up and slip through the gap at the bottom. She almost did it. She was lifting herself stiffly from the bench when the song stopped and slipped away like a cloud diffusing into the sky, leaving her cold and lonely inside the bell. Then the storm began, quietly thumping far away like someone moving boxes around in a dusty attic.

Iris waited, shuffling and sighing. She felt tired and uncomfortable. Her last dive. She wanted tea and a hot-water bottle. It was chilly and there were too many shapes, too many movements – she couldn't keep hold of it all at once, things moved then vanished, things shifted out of sight. She was sick and tired of half glimpsing things. It had all been a waste of time. She cursed Annie for making her think there was a chance, that it wasn't all over and done with. She would give the dress away and after a while she would see somebody else walking round in it. Her glasses dug into her nose.

She felt for the cord, ready to pull it and get Demelza to haul her back up. She had never felt so old. She stretched the skin on the backs of her hands and watched it go white, and then wrinkle up into soft pouches. Her eyes were dry and itchy. She saw a flicker of something bright over to one side of the wreck. It was red, or maybe gold; she had just seen a flash. Then a large shape moved into the collapsed hollow of the ship, followed by two more shapes. There were a group of them, all hair and muscled tails and movement. They were covered in shells and kelp and their long hair was tangled and matted into dark, wet ropes. They eddied and swirled like pieces of bright, solidified water.

Then he was there. He broke away from the group and drifted through the wreck like a pale shaft of light. Iris blinked and adjusted her glasses. The twists and turns of his body – she knew it was him straight away, although there was something different, something more muscular, more streamlined and at home in the water about his body than she had ever seen. She leaned forwards and grabbed for the cord bur then her throat tightened.

No one had told her he would be young. At no point had she thought he would be like this, unchanged since they'd gone to sleep that night all those years before. His skin! It was so thin, almost translucent, fragile and lovely with veins branching through him like blown ink. She had expected to see herself mirrored in him. She touched her own skin. His body moved effortlessly through the water. He was lithe, just as skinny, but more moulded, polished like a piece of sea glass.

He swam closer and she leaned back on the bench and held her breath, suddenly not wanting him to see her. She kept as still as possible, willing his eyes to slide past; they were huge and bright and more heavily lidded than she remembered. She leaned back further. He didn't look at the bell. Bubbles streamed out of his colourless mouth. He was so beautiful, so strange. She couldn't take her eyes off him.

There were spots on her glasses and she couldn't see him as well as she wanted to. She breathed on the lenses and wiped them quickly. Her hands shook and she fumbled with them, dropping them into the open water under the bench. They floated on the surface and she bent down to scoop them out but couldn't reach. Her hips creaked and locked; she couldn't reach down that far. One lens dipped into the water and then they sank completely. Iris blinked. Everything mixed together into a soft, light blur. She peered out, desperately trying to see him. He was still there. He was keeping close to the seabed, winging his way around the wreck, but everything about him had seeped into a smudgy paleness, like a running watercolour or an old photograph exposed to light. He was weaving in and out of the train carriages, in through a door and out through a window, threading his body through the silence and the rust. Iris tried to keep him in focus, tried to concentrate on him so that she wouldn't lose him. But she couldn't tell if he had reappeared from one of the carriages. Where was he, exactly? It was as if he were melting slowly into the sea, the water infusing his skin; his skin becoming that bit of light, that bit of movement. Iris watched and waited until she didn't know if he was there or not there, near or far away, staying or leaving.

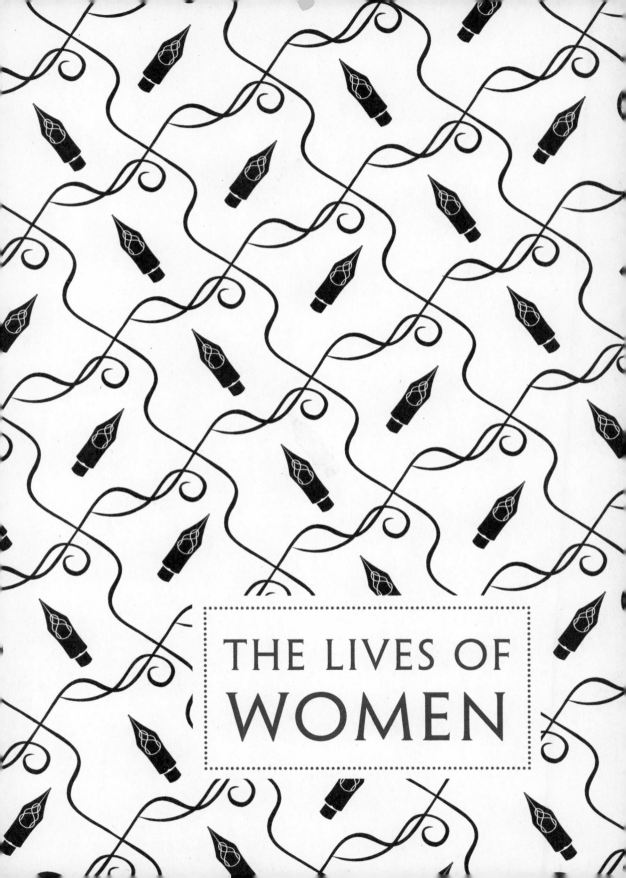

THE LIVES OF
WOMEN

CONSEQUENCES

Willa Cather

Willa Cather (1873–1947) was an American author who wrote highly praised novels depicting frontier life on the Great Plains. She was awarded the Pulitzer Prize in 1923 for her novel *One of Ours*. Cather received the Gold Medal for Fiction from the National Institute of Arts and Letters in 1944, an award given once a decade for an author's complete body of work.

Henry Eastman, a lawyer, aged forty, was standing beside the Flatiron Building in a driving November rainstorm, signaling frantically for a taxi. It was six-thirty, and everything on wheels was engaged. The streets were in confusion about him, the sky was in turmoil above him, and the Flatiron Building, which seemed about to blow down, threw water like a mill-shoot. Suddenly, out of the brutal struggle of men and cars and machines and people tilting at each other with umbrellas, a quiet, well-mannered limousine paused before him, at the curb, and an agreeable, ruddy countenance confronted him through the open window of the car.

"Don't you want me to pick you up, Mr. Eastman? I'm running directly home now."

Eastman recognized Kier Cavenaugh, a young man of pleasure, who lived in the house on Central Park South, where he himself had an apartment.

"Don't I?" he exclaimed, bolting into the car. "I'll risk getting your cushions wet without compunction. I came up in a taxi, but I didn't hold it. Bad economy. I thought I saw your car down on Fourteenth Street about half an hour ago."

The owner of the car smiled. He had a pleasant, round face and round eyes, and a fringe of smooth, yellow hair showed under the brim of his soft felt hat. "With a lot of little broilers fluttering into it? You did. I know some girls who work in the cheap shops down there. I happened to be downtown and I stopped and took a load of them home. I do sometimes. Saves their poor little clothes, you know. Their shoes are never any good."

Eastman looked at his rescuer. "Aren't they notoriously afraid of cars and smooth young men?" he inquired.

Cavenaugh shook his head. "They know which cars are safe and which are chancy. They put each other wise. You have to take a bunch at a time, of course. The Italian girls can never come along; their men shoot. The girls understand, all right; but their fathers don't. One gets to see queer places, sometimes, taking them home."

Eastman laughed drily. "Every time I touch the circle of your acquaintance, Cavenaugh, it's a little wider. You must know New York pretty well by this time."

"Yes, but I'm on my good behavior below Twenty-third Street," the young man replied with simplicity. "My little friends down there would give me a good character. They're wise little girls. They have grand ways with each other, a romantic code of loyalty. You can find a good many of the lost virtues among them."

The car was standing still in a traffic block at Fortieth Street, when Cavenaugh suddenly drew his face away from the window and touched Eastman's arm. "Look, please. You see that hansom with the bony gray horse – driver has a broken hat and red flannel around his throat. Can you see who is inside?"

Eastman peered out. The hansom was just cutting across the line, and the driver was making a great fuss about it, bobbing his head and waving his whip. He jerked his dripping old horse into Fortieth Street and clattered off past the Public Library grounds toward Sixth Avenue. "No, I couldn't see the passenger. Someone you know?"

"Could you see whether there was a passenger?" Cavenaugh asked.

"Why, yes. A man, I think. I saw his elbow on the apron. No driver ever behaves like that unless he has a passenger."

"Yes, I may have been mistaken," Cavenaugh murmured absent-mindedly.

Ten minutes or so later, after Cavenaugh's car had turned off Fifth Avenue into Fifty-eighth Street, Eastman exclaimed, "There's your same cabby, and his cart's empty. He's headed for a drink now, I suppose." The driver in the broken hat and the red flannel neck cloth was still brandishing the whip over his old gray. He was coming from the west now, and turned down Sixth Avenue, under the elevated.

Cavenaugh's car stopped at the bachelor apartment house between Sixth and Seventh Avenues where he and Eastman lived, and they went up in the elevator together. They were still talking when the lift stopped at Cavenaugh's floor, and Eastman stepped out with him and walked down the hall, finishing his sentence while Cavenaugh found his latch-key. When he opened the door, a wave of fresh cigarette smoke greeted them. Cavenaugh stopped short and stared into his hallway. "Now how in the devil – !" he exclaimed angrily.

"Someone waiting for you? Oh, no, thanks. I wasn't coming in. I have to work tonight. Thank you, but I couldn't." Eastman nodded and went up the two flights to his own rooms.

Though Eastman did not customarily keep a servant he had this winter a man who had been lent to him by a friend who was abroad. Rollins met him at the door and took his coat and hat.

"Put out my dinner clothes, Rollins, and then get out of here until ten o'clock. I've promised to go to a supper tonight. I shan't be dining. I've had a late tea and I'm going to work until ten. You may put out some kumiss and biscuit for me."

Rollins took himself off, and Eastman settled down at the big table in his sitting-room. He had to read a lot of letters submitted as evidence in a breach of contract case, and before he got very far he found that long paragraphs in some of the letters were written in German. He had a German dictionary at his office, but none here. Rollins had gone, and anyhow, the bookstores would be closed. He remembered having seen a row of dictionaries on the lower shelf of one of Cavenaugh's bookcases. Cavenaugh had a lot of books, though he never read anything but new stuff. Eastman prudently turned down his student's lamp very low – the thing had an evil habit of smoking – and went down two flights to Cavenaugh's door.

The young man himself answered Eastman's ring. He was freshly dressed for the evening, except for a brown smoking jacket, and his yellow hair had been brushed until it shone. He hesitated as he confronted his caller, still holding the door knob, and his round eyes and smooth forehead made their best imitation of a frown. When Eastman began to apologize, Cavenaugh's manner suddenly changed. He caught his arm and jerked him into the narrow hall. "Come in, come in. Right along!" he said excitedly. "Right along," he repeated as he pushed Eastman before him into his sitting-room. "Well I'll—" He stopped short at the door and looked about his own room with an air of complete mystification. The back window was wide open and a strong wind was blowing in. Cavenaugh walked over to the window and stuck out his head, looking up and down the fire escape. When he pulled his head in, he drew down the sash.

"I had a visitor I wanted you to see," he explained with a nervous smile. "At least I thought I had. He must have gone out that way," nodding toward the window.

"Call him back. I only came to borrow a German dictionary, if you have one. Can't stay. Call him back."

Cavenaugh shook his head despondently. "No use. He's beat it. Nowhere in sight."

"He must be active. Has he left something?" Eastman pointed to a very dirty white glove that lay on the floor under the window.

"Yes, that's his."

Cavenaugh reached for his tongs, picked up the glove, and tossed it into the grate, where it quickly shriveled on the coals. Eastman felt that he had happened in upon something disagreeable, possibly something shady, and he wanted to get away at once. Cavenaugh stood staring at the fire and seemed stupid and dazed; so he repeated his request rather sternly, "I think I've seen a German dictionary down there among your books. May I have it?"

Cavenaugh blinked at him. "A German dictionary? Oh, possibly! Those were my father's. I scarcely know what there is." He put down the tongs and began to wipe his hands nervously with his handkerchief.

Eastman went over to the bookcase behind the Chesterfield, opened the door, swooped upon the book he wanted and stuck it under his arm. He felt perfectly certain now that something shady had been going on in Cavenaugh's rooms, and he saw no reason why he should come in for any hang-over. "Thanks. I'll send it back tomorrow," he said curtly as he made for the door.

Cavenaugh followed him. "Wait a moment. I wanted you to see him. You did see his glove," glancing at the grate.

Eastman laughed disagreeably. "I saw a glove. That's not evidence. Do your friends often use that means of exit? Somewhat inconvenient."

Cavenaugh gave him a startled glance. "Wouldn't you think so? For an old man, a very rickety old party? The ladders are steep, you know, and rusty." He approached the window again and put it up softly. In a moment he drew his head back with a jerk. He caught Eastman's arm and shoved him toward the window. "Hurry, please. Look! Down there." He pointed to the little patch of paved court four flights down.

The square of pavement was so small and the walls about it were so high, that it was a good deal like looking down a well. Four tall buildings backed upon the same court and made a kind of shaft, with flagstones at the bottom, and at the top a square of dark blue with some stars in it. At the bottom of the shaft Eastman saw a black figure, a man in a caped coat and a tall hat stealing cautiously around, not across the square of pavement, keeping close to the dark wall and avoiding the streak of light that fell on the flagstones from a window in the opposite house. Seen from that height he was of course fore-shortened and probably looked more shambling and decrepit than he was. He picked his way along with exaggerated care and looked like a silly old cat crossing a wet street. When he reached the gate that led into an alley way between two buildings, he felt about for the latch, opened the door a mere crack, and then shot out under the feeble lamp that burned in the brick arch over the gateway. The door closed after him.

"He'll get run in," Eastman remarked curtly, turning away from the window. "That door shouldn't be left unlocked. Any crook could come in. I'll speak to the janitor about it, if you don't mind," he added sarcastically.

"Wish you would." Cavenaugh stood brushing down the front of his jacket, first with his right hand and then with his left. "You saw him, didn't you?"

"Enough of him. Seems eccentric. I have to see a lot of buggy people. They don't take me in any more. But I'm keeping you and I'm in a hurry myself. Good night."

Cavenaugh put out his hand detainingly and started to say something; but Eastman rudely turned his back and went down the hall and out of the door. He had never felt anything shady about Cavenaugh before, and he was sorry he had gone down for the dictionary. In five minutes he was deep in his papers; but in the half hour when he was loafing before he dressed to go out, the young man's curious behavior came into his mind again.

Eastman had merely a neighborly acquaintance with Cavenaugh. He had been to a supper at the young man's rooms once, but he didn't particularly like Cavenaugh's friends; so the next time he was asked, he had another engagement. He liked Cavenaugh himself, if for nothing else than because he was so cheerful and trim and ruddy. A good complexion is always at a premium in New York, especially when it shines reassuringly on a man who does everything in the world to lose it. It encourages fellow mortals as to the inherent vigor of the human organism and the amount of bad treatment it will stand for. "Footprints that perhaps another," etc.

Cavenaugh, he knew, had plenty of money. He was the son of a Pennsylvania preacher, who died soon after he discovered that his ancestral acres were full of petroleum, and Kier had come to New York to burn some of the oil. He was thirty-two and was still at it; spent his life, literally, among the breakers. His motor hit the Park every morning as if it were the first time ever. He took people out to supper every night. He went from restaurant to restaurant, sometimes to half-a-dozen in an evening. The head waiters were his hosts and their cordiality made him happy. They made a life-line for him up Broadway and down Fifth Avenue. Cavenaugh was still fresh and smooth, round and plump, with a lustre to his hair and white teeth and a clear look in his round eyes. He seemed absolutely unwearied and unimpaired; never bored and never carried away.

Eastman always smiled when he met Cavenaugh in the entrance hall, serenely going forth to or returning from gladiatorial combats with joy, or when he saw him rolling smoothly up to the door in his car in the morning after a restful night in one of the remarkable new roadhouses he was always finding. Eastman had seen a good many young men disappear on Cavenaugh's route, and he admired this young man's endurance.

Tonight, for the first time, he had got a whiff of something unwholesome about the fellow – bad nerves, bad company, something on hand that he was ashamed of, a visitor old and vicious, who must have had a key to Cavenaugh's apartment, for he was evidently there when Cavenaugh returned at seven o'clock. Probably it was the same man Cavenaugh had seen in the hansom. He must have been able to let himself in, for Cavenaugh kept no man but his chauffeur; or perhaps the janitor had been instructed to let him in. In either case, and whoever he was, it was clear enough that Cavenaugh was ashamed of him and was mixing up in questionable business of some kind.

Eastman sent Cavenaugh's book back by Rollins, and for the next few weeks he had no word with him beyond a casual greeting when they happened to meet in the hall or the elevator. One Sunday morning Cavenaugh telephoned up to him to ask if he could motor out to a road-house in Connecticut that afternoon and have supper; but when Eastman found there were to be other guests he declined.

On New Year's eve Eastman dined at the University Club at six o'clock and hurried home before the usual manifestations of insanity had begun in the streets. When Rollins brought his smoking coat, he asked him whether he wouldn't like to get off early.

"Yes, sir. But won't you be dressing, Mr. Eastman?" he inquired.

"Not tonight." Eastman handed him a bill. "Bring some change in the morning. There'll be fees."

Rollins lost no time in putting everything to rights for the night, and Eastman couldn't help wishing that he were in such a hurry to be off somewhere himself. When he heard the hall door close softly, he wondered if there were any place, after all, that he wanted to go. From his window he looked down at the long lines of motors and taxis waiting for a signal to cross Broadway. He thought of some of their probable destinations and decided that none of those places pulled him very hard. The night was warm and wet, the air was drizzly. Vapor hung in clouds about the *Times* Building, half hid the top of it, and made a luminous haze along Broadway. While he was looking down at the army of wet, black carriage-tops and their reflected headlights and tail-lights, Eastman heard a ring at his door. He deliberated. If it were a caller, the hall porter would have telephoned up. It must be the janitor. When he opened the door, there stood a rosy young man in a tuxedo, without a coat or hat.

"Pardon. Should I have telephoned? I half thought you wouldn't be in."

Eastman laughed. "Come in, Cavenaugh. You weren't sure whether you wanted company or not, eh, and you were trying to let chance decide it? That was exactly my state of mind. Let's accept the verdict." When they emerged from the narrow hall into his sitting-room, he pointed out a seat by the fire to his guest. He brought a tray of decanters and soda bottles and placed it on his writing table.

Cavenaugh hesitated, standing by the fire. "Sure you weren't starting for somewhere?"

"Do I look it? No, I was just making up my mind to stick it out alone when you rang. Have one?" He picked up a tall tumbler.

"Yes, thank you. I always do."

Eastman chuckled. "Lucky boy! So will I. I had a very early dinner. New York is the most arid place on holidays," he continued as he rattled the ice in the glasses. "When one gets too old to hit the rapids down there, and tired of gobbling food to heathenish dance music, there is absolutely no place where you can get a chop and some milk toast in peace, unless you have strong ties of blood brotherhood on upper Fifth Avenue. But you, why aren't you starting for somewhere?"

The young man sipped his soda and shook his head as he replied:

"Oh, I couldn't get a chop, either. I know only flashy people, of course." He looked up at his host with such a grave and candid expression that Eastman decided there couldn't be anything very crooked about the fellow. His smooth cheecks were positively cherubic.

"Well, what's the matter with them? Aren't they flashing tonight?"

"Only the very new ones seem to flash on New Year's eve. The older ones fade away. Maybe they are hunting a chop, too."

"Well" – Eastman sat down – "holidays do dash one. I was just about to write a letter to a pair of maiden aunts in my old home town, up-state; old coasting hill, snow-covered pines, lights in the church windows. That's what you've saved me from."

Cavenaugh shook himself. "Oh, I'm sure that wouldn't have been good for you. Pardon me," he rose and took a photograph from the bookcase, a handsome man in shooting clothes. "Dudley, isn't it? Did you know him well?"

"Yes. An old friend. Terrible thing, wasn't it? I haven't got over the jolt yet."

"His suicide? Yes, terrible! Did you know his wife?"

"Slightly. Well enough to admire her very much. She must be terribly broken up. I wonder Dudley didn't think of that."

Cavenaugh replaced the photograph carefully, lit a cigarette, and standing before the fire began to smoke. "Would you mind telling me about him? I never met him, but of course I'd read a lot about him, and I can't help feeling interested. It was a queer thing."

Eastman took out his cigar case and leaned back in his deep chair. "In the days when I knew him best he hadn't any story, like the happy nations. Everything was properly arranged for him before he was born. He came into the world happy, healthy, clever, straight, with the right sort of connections and the right kind of fortune, neither too large nor too small. He helped to make the world an agreeable place to live in until he was twenty-six. Then he married as he should have married. His wife was a Californian, educated abroad. Beautiful. You have seen her picture?"

Cavenaugh nodded. "Oh, many of them."

"She was interesting, too. Though she was distinctly a person of the w⟨orld, she⟩ had retained something, just enough of the large Western manner. She ⟨had the⟩ habit of authority, of calling out a special train if she needed it, of usin⟨g all our⟩ ingenious mechanical contrivances lightly and easily, without over-ratir⟨...⟩ She and Dudley knew how to live better than most people. Their house⟨...⟩ most charming one I have ever known in New York. You felt freedom ⟨...⟩ a zest of life, and safety – absolute sanctuary – from everything sordi⟨...⟩ A whole society like that would justify the creation of man and woul⟨...⟩ planet shine with a soft, peculiar radiance among the constellation⟨s...⟩ I'm putting it on thick?"

The young man sighed gently. "Oh, no! One has always felt t⟨...⟩ people like that. I've never known any."

"They had two children, beautiful ones. After they had been marrie⟨d...⟩ years, Rosina met this Spaniard. He must have amounted to somethin⟨g...⟩ wasn't a flighty woman. She came home and told Dudley how matters stoo⟨d...⟩ persuaded her to stay at home for six months and try to pull up. They were bo⟨th⟩ fair-minded people, and I'm as sure as if I were the Almighty, that she did try. But at the end of the time, Rosina went quietly off to Spain, and Dudley went to hunt in the Canadian Rockies. I met his party out there. I didn't know his wife had left him and talked about her a good deal. I noticed that he never drank anything, and his light used to shine through the log chinks of his room until all hours, even after a hard day's hunting. When I got back to New York, rumors were creeping about. Dudley did not come back. He bought a ranch in Wyoming, built a big log house and kept splendid dogs and horses. One of his sisters went out to keep house for him, and the children were there when they were not in school. He had a great many visitors, and everyone who came back talked about how well Dudley kept things going.

"He put in two years out there. Then, last month, he had to come back on business. A trust fund had to be settled up, and he was administrator. I saw him at the club; same light, quick step, same gracious handshake. He was getting gray, and there was something softer in his manner; but he had a fine red tan on his face and said he found it delightful to be here in the season when everything is going hard. The Madison Avenue house had been closed since Rosina left it. He went there to get some things his sister wanted. That, of course, was the mistake. He went alone, in the afternoon, and didn't go out for dinner – found some sherry and tins of biscuit in the sideboard. He shot himself sometime that night. There were pistols in his smoking-room. They found burnt-out candles beside him in the morning. The gas and electricity were shut off. I suppose there, in his own house, among his own things, it was too much for him. He left no letters."

Cavenaugh blinked and brushed the lapel of his coat. "I suppose," he said slowly, "that every suicide is logical and reasonable, if one knew all the facts."

Eastman roused himself. "No, I don't think so. I've known too many fellows who went off like that – more than I deserve, I think – and some of them were absolutely inexplicable. I can understand Dudley; but I can't see why healthy bachelors, with money enough, like ourselves, need such a device. It reminds me of what Dr. Johnson said, that the most discouraging thing about life is the

ohnson? The specialist? Oh, the old fellow!" said Cavenaugh imperturb-
es, that's interesting. Still I fancy if one knew the facts – Did you know
Wyatt?"

don't think so."

You wouldn't, probably. He was just a fellow about town who spent money.
wasn't one of the *forestieri*, though. Had connections here and owned a fine
d place over on Staten Island. He went in for botany, and had been all over,
unting things; rusts, I believe. He had a yacht and used to take a gay crowd
down about the South Seas, botanizing. He really did botanize, I believe. I never
knew such a spender – only not flashy. He helped a lot of fellows and he was
awfully good to girls, the kind who come down here to get a little fun, who don't
like to work and still aren't really tough, the kind you see talking hard for their
dinner. Nobody knows what becomes of them, or what they get out of it, and
there are hundreds of new ones every year. He helped dozens of 'em; it was he
who got me curious about the little shop girls.

"Well, one afternoon when his tea was brought, he took prussic acid instead.
He didn't leave any letters, either; people of any taste don't. They wouldn't leave
any material reminder if they could help it. His lawyers found that he had just
$314.72 above his debts when he died. He had planned to spend all his money,
and then take his tea; he had worked it out carefully."

Eastman reached for his pipe and pushed his chair away from the fire. "That
looks like a considered case, but I don't think philosophical suicides like that
are common. I think they usually come from stress of feeling and are really, as
the newspapers call them, desperate acts; done without a motive. You remember
when Anna Karenina was under the wheels, she kept saying, 'Why am I here?'"

Cavenaugh rubbed his upper lip with his pink finger and made an effort to
wrinkle his brows. "May I, please?" reaching for the whiskey. "But have you," he
asked, blinking as the soda flew at him, "have you ever known, yourself, cases
that were really inexplicable?"

"A few too many. I was in Washington just before Captain Jack Purden was
married and I saw a good deal of him. Popular army man, fine record in the
Philippines, married a charming girl with lots of money; mutual devotion. It
was the gayest wedding of the winter, and they started for Japan. They stopped
in San Francisco for a week and missed their boat because, as the bride wrote
back to Washington, they were too happy to move. They took the next boat,
were both good sailors, had exceptional weather. After they had been out for
two weeks, Jack got up from his deck chair one afternoon, yawned, put down
his book, and stood before his wife. 'Stop reading for a moment and look at
me.' She laughed and asked him why. 'Because you happen to be good to look
at.' He nodded to her, went back to the stern and was never seen again. Must
have gone down to the lower deck and slipped overboard, behind the machinery. It was the luncheon hour, not many people about; steamer cutting through
a soft green sea. That's one of the most baffling cases I know. His friends raked
up his past, and it was as trim as a cottage garden. If he'd so much as dropped
an ink spot on his fatigue uniform, they'd have found it. He wasn't emotional

or moody; wasn't, indeed, very interesting; simply a good soldier, fond of all the pompous little formalities that make up a military man's life. What do you make of that, my boy?"

Cavenaugh stroked his chin. "It's very puzzling, I admit. Still, if one knew everything –"

"But we do know everything. His friends wanted to find something to help them out, to help the girl out, to help the case of the human creature."

"Oh, I don't mean things that people could unearth," said Cavenaugh uneasily. "But possibly there were things that couldn't be found out."

Eastman shrugged his shoulders. "It's my experience that when there are 'things' as you call them, they're very apt to be found. There is no such thing as a secret. To make any move at all one has to employ human agencies, employ at least one human agent. Even when the pirates killed the men who buried their gold for them, the bones told the story."

Cavenaugh rubbed his hands together and smiled his sunny smile.

"I like that idea. It's reassuring. If we can have no secrets, it means that we can't, after all, go so far afield as we might," he hesitated, "yes, as we might."

Eastman looked at him sourly. "Cavenaugh, when you've practised law in New York for twelve years, you find that people can't go far in any direction, except –" He thrust his forefinger sharply at the floor. "Even in that direction, few people can do anything out of the ordinary. Our range is limited. Skip a few baths, and we become personally objectionable. The slightest carelessness can rot a man's integrity or give him ptomaine poisoning. We keep up only by incessant cleansing operations, of mind and body. What we call character is held together by all sorts of tacks and strings and glue."

Cavenaugh looked startled. "Come now, it's not so bad as that, is it? I've always thought that a serious man, like you, must know a lot of Launcelots." When Eastman only laughed, the younger man squirmed about in his chair. He spoke again hastily, as if he were embarrassed. "Your military friend may have had personal experiences, however, that his friends couldn't possibly get a line on. He may accidentally have come to a place where he saw himself in too unpleasant a light. I believe people can be chilled by a draft from outside, somewhere."

"Outside?" Eastman echoed. "Ah, you mean the far outside! Ghosts, delusions, eh?"

Cavenaugh winced. "That's putting it strong. Why not say tips from the outside? Delusions belong to a diseased mind, don't they? There are some of us who have no minds to speak of, who yet have had experiences. I've had a little something in that line myself and I don't look it, do I?"

Eastman looked at the bland countenance turned toward him. "Not exactly. What's your delusion?"

"It's not a delusion. It's a haunt."

The lawyer chuckled. "Soul of a lost Casino girl?"

"No; an old gentleman. A most unattractive old gentleman, who follows me about."

"Does he want money?"

Cavenaugh sat up straight. "No. I wish to God he wanted anything – but the pleasure of my society! I'd let him clean me out to be rid of him. He's a real article. You saw him yourself that night when you came to my rooms to borrow a dictionary, and he went down the fire escape. You saw him down in the court."

"Well, I saw somebody down in the court, but I'm too cautious to take it for granted that I saw what you saw. Why, anyhow, should I see your haunt? If it was your friend I saw, he impressed me disagreeably. How did you pick him up?"

Cavenaugh looked gloomy. "That was queer, too. Charley Burke and I had motored out to Long Beach, about a year ago, sometime in October, I think. We had supper and stayed until late. When we were coming home, my car broke down. We had a lot of girls along who had to get back for morning rehearsals and things; so I sent them all into town in Charley's car, and he was to send a man back to tow me home. I was driving myself, and didn't want to leave my machine. We had not taken a direct road back; so I was stuck in a lonesome, woody place, no houses about. I got chilly and made a fire, and was putting in the time comfortably enough, when this old party steps up. He was in shabby evening clothes and a top hat, and had on his usual white gloves. How he got there, at three o'clock in the morning, miles from any town or railway, I'll leave it to you to figure out. *He* surely had no car. When I saw him coming up to the fire, I disliked him. He had a silly, apologetic walk. His teeth were chattering and I asked him to sit down. He got down like a clothes-horse folding up. I offered him a cigarette, and when he took off his gloves I couldn't help noticing how knotted and spotty his hands were. He was asthmatic, and took his breath with a wheeze. 'Haven't you got anything – refreshing in there?' he asked, nodding at the car. When I told him I hadn't, he sighed. 'Ah, you young fellows arc greedy. You drink it all up. You drink it all up, all up – up!' he kept chewing it over."

Cavenaugh paused and looked embarrassed again. "The thing that was most unpleasant is difficult to explain. The old man sat there by the fire and leered at me with a silly sort of admiration that was – well, more than humiliating. 'Gay boy, gay dog!' he would mutter, and when he grinned he showed his teeth, worn and yellow – shells. I remembered that it was better to talk casually to insane people; so I remarked carelessly that I had been out with a party and got stuck.

"'Oh yes, I remember,' he said, 'Flora and Lottie and Maybelle and Marcelline, and poor Kate.'

"He had named them correctly; so I began to think I had been hitting the bright waters too hard.

"Things I drank never had seemed to make me woody; but you can never tell when trouble is going to hit you. I pulled my hat down and tried to look as uncommunicative as possible; but he kept croaking on from time to time, like this: 'Poor Katie! Splendid arms, but dope got her. She took up with Eastern religions after she had her hair dyed. Got to going to a Swami's joint, and smoking opium. Temple of the Lotus, it was called, and the police raided it.'

"This was nonsense, of course; the young woman was in the pink of condition. I let him rave, but I decided that if something didn't come out for me pretty soon, I'd foot it across Long Island. There wasn't room enough for the two of us. I got up and took another try at my car. He hopped right after me.

"'Good car,' he wheezed, 'better than the little Ford.'

"I'd had a Ford before, but so has everybody; that was a safe guess.

"'Still,' he went on, 'that run in from Huntington Bay in the rain wasn't bad. Arrested for speeding, he-he.'

"It was true I had made such a run, under rather unusual circumstances, and had been arrested. When at last I heard my life-boat snorting up the road, my visitor got up, sighed, and stepped back into the shadow of the trees. I didn't wait to see what became of him, you may believe. That was visitation number one. What do you think of it?"

Cavenaugh looked at his host defiantly. Eastman smiled.

"I think you'd better change your mode of life, Cavenaugh. Had many returns?" he inquired.

"Too many, by far." The young man took a turn about the room and came back to the fire. Standing by the mantel he lit another cigarette before going on with his story.

"The second visitation happened in the street, early in the evening, about eight o'clock. I was held up in a traffic block before the Plaza. My chauffeur was driving. Old Nibbs steps up out of the crowd, opens the door of my car, gets in and sits down beside me. He had on wilted evening clothes, same as before, and there was some sort of heavy scent about him. Such an unpleasant old party! A thorough-going rotter; you knew it at once. This time he wasn't talkative, as he had been when I first saw him. He leaned back in the car as if he owned it, crossed his hands on his stick and looked out at the crowd – sort of hungrily.

"I own I really felt a loathing compassion for him.

"We got down the avenue slowly. I kept looking out at the mounted police. But what could I do? Have him pulled? I was afraid to. I was awfully afraid of getting him into the papers.

"'I'm going to the New Astor,' I said at last. 'Can I take you anywhere?'

"'No, thank you,' says he. 'I get out when you do. I'm due on West Forty-fourth. I'm dining tonight with Marcelline – all that is left of her!'

"He put his hand to his hat brim with a gruesome salute. Such a scandalous, foolish old face as he had! When we pulled up at the Astor, I stuck my hand in my pocket and asked him if he'd like a little loan.

"'No, thank you, but' – he leaned over and whispered, ugh! – 'but save a little, save a little. Forty years from now – a little – comes in handy. Save a little.'

"His eyes fairly glittered as he made his remark. I jumped out. I'd have jumped into the North River. When he tripped off, I asked my chauffeur if he'd noticed the man who got into the car with me. He said he knew someone was with me, but he hadn't noticed just when he got in. Want to hear any more?"

Cavenaugh dropped into his chair again. His plump cheeks were a trifle more flushed than usual, but he was perfectly calm. Eastman felt that the young man believed what he was telling him.

"Of course I do. It's very interesting. I don't see quite where you are coming out though."

Cavenaugh sniffed. "No more do I. I really feel that I've been put upon. I haven't deserved it any more than any other fellow of my kind. Doesn't it impress you disagreeably?"

"Well, rather so. Has anyone else seen your friend?"

"You saw him."

"We won't count that. As I said, there's no certainty that you and I saw the same person in the court that night. Has anyone else had a look in?"

"People sense him rather than see him. He usually crops up when I'm alone or in a crowd on the street. He never approaches me when I'm with people I know, though I've seen him hanging about the doors of theatres when I come out with a party; loafing around the stage exit, under a wall; or across on the street, in a doorway. To be frank, I'm not anxious to introduce him. The third time, it was I who came upon him. In November my driver, Harry, had a sudden attack of appendicitis. I took him to the Presbyterian Hospital in the car, early in the evening. When I came home, I found the old villain in my rooms. I offered him a drink, and he sat down. It was the first time I had seen him in a steady light, with his hat off.

"His face is lined like a railway map, and as to color – Lord, what a liver! His scalp grows tight to his skull, and his hair is dyed until it's perfectly dead, like a piece of black cloth."

Cavenaugh ran his fingers through his own neatly trimmed thatch, and seemed to forget where he was for a moment.

"I had a twin brother, Brian, who died when we were sixteen. I have a photograph of him on my wall, an enlargement from a kodak of him, doing a high jump, rather good thing, full of action. It seemed to annoy the old gentleman. He kept looking at it and lifting his eyebrows, and finally he got up, tip-toed across the room, and turned the picture to the wall.

"'Poor Brian! Fine fellow, but died young,' says he.

"Next morning, there was the picture, still reversed."

"Did he stay long?" Eastman asked interestedly.

"Half an hour, by the clock."

"Did he talk?"

"Well, he rambled."

"What about?"

Cavenaugh rubbed his pale eyebrows before answering.

"About things that an old man ought to want to forget. His conversation is highly objectionable. Of course he knows me like a book; everything I've ever done or thought. But when he recalls them, he throws a bad light on them, somehow. Things that weren't much off color, look rotten. He doesn't leave one a shred of self-respect, he really doesn't. That's the amount of it." The young man whipped out his handkerchief and wiped his face.

"You mean he really talks about things that none of your friends know?"

"Oh, dear, yes! Recalls things that happened in school. Anything disagreeable. Funny thing, he always turns Brian's picture to the wall."

"Does he come often?"

"Yes, oftener, now. Of course I don't know how he gets in downstairs. The hall boys never see him. But he has a key to my door. I don't know how he got it, but I can hear him turn it in the lock."

"Why don't you keep your driver with you, or telephone for me to come down?"

"He'd only grin and go down the fire escape as he did before. He's often done it when Harry's come in suddenly. Everybody has to be alone sometimes, you know. Besides, I don't want anybody to see him. He has me there."

"But why not? Why do you feel responsible for him?"

Cavenaugh smiled wearily. "That's rather the point, isn't it? Why do I? But I absolutely do. That identifies him, more than his knowing all about my life and my affairs."

Eastman looked at Cavenaugh thoughtfully. "Well, I should advise you to go in for something altogether different and new, and go in for it hard; business, engineering, metallurgy, something this old fellow wouldn't be interested in. See if you can make him remember logarithms."

Cavenaugh sighed. "No, he has me there, too. People never really change; they go on being themselves. But I would never make much trouble. Why can't they let me alone, damn it! I'd never hurt anybody, except, perhaps –"

"Except your old gentleman, eh?" Eastman laughed. "Seriously, Cavenaugh, if you want to shake him, I think a year on a ranch would do it. He would never be coaxed far from his favorite haunts. He would dread Montana."

Cavenaugh pursed up his lips. "So do I!"

"Oh, you think you do. Try it, and you'll find out. A gun and a horse beats all this sort of thing. Besides losing your haunt, you'd be putting ten years in the bank for yourself. I know a good ranch where they take people, if you want to try it."

"Thank you. I'll consider. Do you think I'm batty?"

"No, but I think you've been doing one sort of thing too long. You need big horizons. Get out of this."

Cavenaugh smiled meekly. He rose lazily and yawned behind his hand. "It's late, and I've taken your whole evening." He strolled over to the window and looked out. "Queer place, New York; rough on the little fellows. Don't you feel sorry for them, the girls especially? I do. What a fight they put up for a little fun! Why, even that old goat is sorry for them, the only decent thing he kept."

Eastman followed him to the door and stood in the hall, while Cavenaugh waited for the elevator. When the car came up Cavenaugh extended his pink, warm hand. "Good night."

The cage sank and his rosy countenance disappeared, his round-eyed smile being the last thing to go.

Weeks passed before Eastman saw Cavenaugh again. One morning, just as he was starting for Washington to argue a case before the Supreme Court, Cavenaugh telephoned him at his office to ask him about the Montana ranch he had recommended; said he meant to take his advice and go out there for the spring and summer.

When Eastman got back from Washington, he saw dusty trunks, just up from the trunk room, before Cavenaugh's door. Next morning, when he stopped to see what the young man was about, he found Cavenaugh in his shirt sleeves, packing.

"I'm really going; off tomorrow night. You didn't think it of me, did you?" he asked gaily.

"Oh, I've always had hopes of you!" Eastman declared. "But you are in a hurry, it seems to me."

"Yes, I am in a hurry." Cavenaugh shot a pair of leggings into one of the open trunks. "I telegraphed your ranch people, used your name, and they said it would be all right. By the way, some of my crowd are giving a little dinner for me at Rector's tonight. Couldn't you be persuaded, as it's a farewell occasion?" Cavenaugh looked at him. hopefully.

Eastman laughed and shook his head. "Sorry, Cavenaugh, but that's too gay a world for me. I've got too much work lined up before me. I wish I had time to stop and look at your guns, though. You seem to know something about guns. You've more than you'll need, but nobody can have too many good ones." He put down one of the revolvers regretfully. "I'll drop in to see you in the morning, if you're up."

"I shall be up, all right. I've warned my crowd that I'll cut away before midnight."

"You won't, though," Eastman called back over his shoulder as he hurried downstairs.

The next morning, while Eastman was dressing, Rollins came in greatly excited.

"I'm a little late, sir. I was stopped by Harry, Mr. Cavenaugh's driver. Mr. Cavenaugh shot himself last night, sir."

Eastman dropped his vest and sat down on his shoe-box. "You're drunk, Rollins," he shouted. "He's going away today!"

"Yes, sir. Harry found him this morning. Ah, he's quite dead, sir. Harry's telephoned for the coroner. Harry don't know what to do with the ticket."

Eastman pulled on his coat and ran down the stairway. Cavenaugh's trunks were stripped and piled before the door. Harry was walking up and down the hall with a long green railroad ticket in his hand and a look of complete stupidity on his face.

"What shall I do about this ticket, Mr. Eastman?" he whispered. "And what about his trunks? He had me tell the transfer people to come early. They may be here any minute. Yes, sir. I brought him home in the car last night, before twelve, as cheerful as could be."

"Be quiet, Harry. Where is he?"

"In his bed, sir."

Eastman went into Cavenaugh's sleeping-room. When he came back to the sitting-room, he looked over the writing table; railway folders, time-tables, receipted bills, nothing else. He looked up for the photograph of Cavenaugh's twin brother. There it was, turned to the wall. Eastman took it down and looked at it; a boy in track clothes, half lying in the air, going over the string shoulders first, above the heads of a crowd of lads who were running and cheering. The face was somewhat blurred by the motion and the bright sunlight. Eastman put the picture back, as he found it. Had Cavenaugh entertained his visitor last night, and had the old man been more convincing than usual?

"Well, at any rate, he's seen to it that the old man can't establish identity. What a soft lot they are, fellows like poor Cavenaugh!" Eastman thought of his office as a delightful place.

A SOCIETY

Virginia Woolf

Virginia Woolf (1882–1941) was a British writer and one of the foremost modernists of the 20th-century. She was a significant figure in London literary society and a central figure in the influential Bloomsbury Group. Her most famous works include the novels *Mrs Dalloway*, *To the Lighthouse* and *Orlando* and the long essay *A Room of One's Own*.

This is how it all came about. Six or seven of us were sitting one day after tea. Some were gazing across the street into the windows of a milliner's shop where the light still shone brightly upon scarlet feathers and golden slippers. Others were idly occupied in building little towers of sugar upon the edge of the tea tray. After a time, so far as I can remember, we drew round the fire and began as usual to praise men – how strong, how noble, how brilliant, how courageous, how beautiful they were – how we envied those who by hook or by crook managed to get attached to one for life – when Poll, who had said nothing, burst into tears. Poll, I must tell you, has always been queer. For one thing her father was a strange man. He left her a fortune in his will, but on condition that she read all the books in the London Library. We comforted her as best we could; but we knew in our hearts how vain it was. For though we like her, Poll is no beauty; leaves her shoe laces untied; and must have been thinking, while we praised men, that not one of them would ever wish to marry her. At last she dried her tears. For some time we could make nothing of what she said. Strange enough it was in all conscience. She told us that, as we knew, she spent most of her time in the London Library, reading. She had begun, she said, with English literature on the top floor; and was steadily working her way down to *The Times* on the bottom. And now half, or perhaps only a quarter, way through a terrible thing had happened. She could read no more. Books were not what we thought them. 'Books,' she cried, rising to her feet and speaking with an intensity of desolation which I shall never forget, 'are for the most part unutterably bad!'

Of course we cried out that Shakespeare wrote books, and Milton and Shelley.

'Oh, yes,' she interrupted us. 'You've been well taught, I can see. But you are not members of the London Library.' Here her sobs broke forth anew. At length, recovering a little, she opened one of the pile of books which she always carried about with her – 'From a Window' or 'In a Garden' or some such name as that it was called, and it was written by a man called Benton or Henson or something of that kind. She read the first few pages. We listened in silence. 'But that's not a book,' someone said. So she chose another. This time it was a history, but I have forgotten the writer's name. Our trepidation increased as she went on. Not a word of it seemed to be true, and the style in which it was written was execrable.

'Poetry! Poetry!' we cried, impatiently. 'Read us poetry!' I cannot describe the desolation which fell upon us as she opened a little volume and mouthed out the verbose, sentimental foolery which it contained.

'It must have been written by a woman,' one of us urged. But no. She told us that it was written by a young man, one of the most famous poets of the day. I leave you to imagine what the shock of the discovery was. Though we all cried and begged her to read no more she persisted and read us extracts from the Lives of the Lord Chancellors. When she had finished, Jane, the eldest and wisest of us, rose to her feet and said that she for one was not convinced.

'Why,' she asked, 'if men write such rubbish as this, should our mothers have wasted their youth in bringing them into the world?'

We were all silent; and, in the silence, poor Poll could be heard sobbing out, 'Why, why did my father teach me to read?'

Clorinda was the first to come to her senses. 'It's all our fault,' she said. 'Every one of us knows how to read. But no one, save Poll, has ever taken the trouble to do it. I, for one, have taken it for granted that it was a woman's duty to spend her youth in bearing children. I venerated my mother for bearing ten; still more my grandmother for bearing fifteen; it was, I confess, my own ambition to bear twenty. We have gone on all these ages supposing that men were equally industrious, and that their works were of equal merit. While we have borne the children, they, we supposed, have borne the books and the pictures. We have populated the world. They have civilised it. But now that we can read, what prevents us from judging the results? Before we bring another child into the world we must swear that we will find out what the world is like.'

So we made ourselves into a society for asking questions. One of us was to visit a man-of-war; another was to hide herself in a scholar's study; another was to attend a meeting of business men; while all were to read books, look at pictures, go to concerts, keep our eyes open in the streets, and ask questions perpetually. We were very young. You can judge of our simplicity when I tell you that before parting that night we agreed that the objects of life were to produce good people and good books. Our questions were to be directed to find out how far these objects were now attained by men. We vowed solemnly that we would not bear a single child until we were satisfied.

Off we went then, some to the British Museum; others to the King's Navy; some to Oxford; others to Cambridge; we visited the Royal Academy and the Tate; heard modern music in concert rooms, went to the Law Courts, and saw new plays. No one dined out without asking her parents certain questions and carefully noting his replies. At intervals we met together and compared our observations. Oh, those were merry meetings! Never have I laughed so much as I did when Rose read her notes upon 'Honour' and described how she had dressed herself as an Aethiopian Prince and gone aboard one of His Majesty's ships. Discovering the hoax, the Captain visited her (now disguised as a private gentleman) and demanded that honour should be satisfied. 'But how?' she asked. 'How?' he bellowed. 'With the cane of course!' Seeing that he was beside himself with rage and expecting that her last moment had come, she bent over and received, to her amazement, six light taps upon the behind. 'The honour of the

British Navy is avenged!' he cried, and, raising herself, she saw him with the sweat pouring down his face holding out a trembling right hand. 'Away!' she exclaimed, striking an attitude and imitating the ferocity of his own expression. 'My honour has still to be satisfied!' 'Spoken like a gentleman!' he returned, and fell into profound thought. 'If six strokes avenge the honour of the King's Navy,' he mused, 'how many avenge the honour of a private gentleman?' He said he would prefer to lay the case before his brother officers. She replied haughtily that she could not wait. He praised her sensibility. 'Let me see,' he cried suddenly, 'did your father keep a carriage?' 'No,' she said. 'Or a riding horse?' 'We had a donkey,' she bethought her, 'which drew the mowing machine.' At this his face lightened. 'My mother's name—' she added. 'For God's sake, man, don't mention your mother's name!' he shrieked, trembling like an aspen and flushing to the roots of his hair, and it was ten minutes at least before she could induce him to proceed. At length he decreed that if she gave him four strokes and a half in the small of the back at a spot indicated by himself (the half conceded, he said, in recognition of the fact that her great-grandmother's uncle was killed at Trafalgar) it was his opinion that her honour would be as good as new. This was done; they retired to a restaurant; drank two bottles of wine for which he insisted upon paying; and parted with protestations of eternal friendship.

Then we had Fanny's account of her visit to the Law Courts. At her first visit she had come to the conclusion that the Judges were either made of wood or were impersonated by large animals resembling man who had been trained to move with extreme dignity, mumble and nod their heads. To test her theory she had liberated a handkerchief of bluebottles at the critical moment of a trial, but was unable to judge whether the creatures gave signs of humanity for the buzzing of the flies induced so sound a sleep that she only woke in time to see the prisoners led into the cells below. But from the evidence she brought we voted that it is unfair to suppose that the Judges are men.

Helen went to the Royal Academy, but when asked to deliver her report upon the pictures she began to recite from a pale blue volume, 'O! for the touch of a vanished hand and the sound of a voice that is still. Home is the hunter, home from the hill. He gave his bridle reins a shake. Love is sweet, love is brief. Spring, the fair spring, is the year's pleasant King. O! to be in England now that April's there. Men must work and women must weep. The path of duty is the way to glory —' We could listen to no more of this gibberish.

'We want no more poetry!' we cried.

'Daughters of England!' she began, but here we pulled her down, a vase of water getting spilt over her in the scuffle.

'Thank God!' she exclaimed, shaking herself like a dog. 'Now I'll roll on the carpet and see if I can't brush off what remains of the Union Jack. Then perhaps —' here she rolled energetically. Getting up she began to explain to us what modern pictures are like when Castalia stopped her.

'What is the average size of a picture?' she asked. 'Perhaps two feet by two and a half,' she said. Castalia made notes while Helen spoke, and when she had done, and we were trying not to meet each other's eyes, rose and said, 'At your wish I spent last week at Oxbridge, disguised as a charwoman. I thus had access to the rooms of several Professors and will now attempt to give you some idea – only,' she broke off,

'I can't think how to do it. It's all so queer. These Professors,' she went on, 'live in large houses built round grass plots each in a kind of cell by himself. Yet they have every convenience and comfort. You have only to press a button or light a little lamp. Their papers are beautifully filed. Books abound. There are no children or animals, save half a dozen stray cats and one aged bullfinch – a cock. I remember,' she broke off, 'an Aunt of mine who lived at Dulwich and kept cactuses. You reached the conservatory through the double drawing-room, and there, on the hot pipes, were dozens of them, ugly, squat, bristly little plants each in a separate pot. Once in a hundred years the Aloe flowered, so my Aunt said. But she died before that happened –' We told her to keep to the point. 'Well,' she resumed, 'when Professor Hobkin was out I examined his life work, an edition of Sappho. It's a queer looking book, six or seven inches thick, not all by Sappho. Oh, no. Most of it is a defence of Sappho's chastity, which some German had denied, and I can assure you the passion with which these two gentlemen argued, the learning they displayed, the prodigious ingenuity with which they disputed the use of some implement which looked to me for all the world like a hairpin astounded me; especially when the door opened and Professor Hobkin himself appeared. A very nice, mild, old gentleman, but what could *he* know about chastity?' We misunderstood her.

'No, no,' she protested, 'he's the soul of honour I'm sure – not that he resembles Rose's sea captain in the least. I was thinking rather of my Aunt's cactuses. What could they know about chastity?'

Again we told her not to wander from the point, – did the Oxbridge professors help to produce good people and good books? – the objects of life.

'There!' she exclaimed. 'It never struck me to ask. It never occurred to me that they could possibly produce anything.'

'I believe,' said Sue, 'that you made some mistake. Probably Professor Hobkin was a gynaecologist. A scholar is a very different sort of man. A scholar is overflowing with humour and invention – perhaps addicted to wine, but what of that? – a delightful companion, generous, subtle, imaginative – as stands to reason. For he spends his life in company with the finest human beings that have ever existed.'

'Hum,' said Castalia. 'Perhaps I'd better go back and try again.'

Some three months later it happened that I was sitting alone when Castalia entered. I don't know what it was in the look of her that so moved me; but I could not restrain myself, and dashing across the room, I clasped her in my arms. Not only was she very beautiful; she seemed also in the highest spirits. 'How happy you look!' I exclaimed, as she sat down.

'I've been at Oxbridge,' she said.

'Asking questions?'

'Answering them,' she replied.

'You have not broken our vow?' I said anxiously, noticing something about her figure.

'Oh, the vow,' she said casually. 'I'm going to have a baby if that's what you mean. You can't imagine,' she burst out, 'how exciting, how beautiful, how satisfying –'

'What is?' I asked.

'To – to – answer questions,' she replied in some confusion. Whereupon she told me the whole of her story. But in the middle of an account which interested and excited me more than anything I had ever heard, she gave the strangest cry, half whoop, half holloa –

'Chastity! Chastity! Where's my chastity!' she cried. 'Help ho! The scent bottle!'

There was nothing in the room but a cruet containing mustard, which I was about to administer when she recovered her composure.

'You should have thought of that three months ago,' I said severely.

'True,' she replied. 'There's not much good in thinking of it now. It was unfortunate, by the way, that my mother had me called Castalia.'

'Oh, Castalia, your mother –' I was beginning when she reached for the mustard pot.

'No, no, no,' she said shaking her head. 'If you'd been a chaste woman yourself you would have screamed at the sight of me – instead of which you rushed across the room and took me in your arms. No, Cassandra. We are neither of us chaste.' So we went on talking.

Meanwhile the room was filling up, for it was the day appointed to discuss the results of our observations. Everyone, I thought, felt as I did about Castalia. They kissed her and said how glad they were to see her again. At length, when we were all assembled, Jane rose and said that it was time to begin. She began by saying that we had now asked questions for over five years, and that though the results were bound to be inconclusive – here Castalia nudged me and whispered that she was not so sure about that. Then she got up, and, interrupting Jane in the middle of a sentence, said:

'Before you say any more, I want to know – am I to stay in the room? Because,' she added, 'I have to confess that I am an impure woman.'

Everyone looked at her in astonishment.

'You are going to have a baby?' asked Jane.

She nodded her head.

It was extraordinary to see the different expressions on their faces. A sort of hum went through the room, in which I could catch the words 'impure', 'baby', 'Castalia', and so on. Jane, who was herself considerably moved, put it to us:

'Shall she go? Is she impure?'

Such a roar filled the room as might have been heard in the street outside.

'No! No! No! Let her stay! Impure? Fiddlesticks!' Yet I fancied that some of the youngest, girls of nineteen or twenty, held back as if overcome with shyness. Then we all came about her and began asking questions, and at last I saw one of the youngest, who had kept in the background, approach shyly and say to her:

'What is chastity then? I mean is it good, or is it bad, or is it nothing at all?' She replied so low that I could not catch what she said.

'You know I was shocked,' said another, 'for at least ten minutes.'

'In my opinion,' said Poll, who was growing crusty from always reading in the London Library, 'chastity is nothing but ignorance – a most discreditable state of mind. We should admit only the unchaste to our society. I vote that Castalia shall be our President.'

This was violently disputed.

'It is as unfair to brand women with chastity as with unchastity,' said Poll.

'Some of us haven't the opportunity either. Moreover, I don't believe Cassy herself maintains that she acted as she did from a pure love of knowledge.'

'He is only twenty-one and divinely beautiful,' said Cassy, with a ravishing gesture.

'I move,' said Helen, 'that no one be allowed to talk of chastity or unchastity save those who are in love.'

'Oh, bother,' said Judith, who had been enquiring into scientific matters, 'I'm not in love and I'm longing to explain my measures for dispensing with prostitutes and fertilising virgins by Act of Parliament.'

She went on to tell us of an invention of hers to be erected at Tube stations and other public resorts, which, upon payment of a small fee, would safeguard the nation's health, accommodate its sons, and relieve its daughters. Then she had contrived a method of preserving in sealed tubes the germs of future Lord Chancellors 'or poets or painters or musicians,' she went on, 'supposing, that is to say, that these breeds are not extinct, and that women still wish to bear children –'

'Of course we wish to bear children!' cried Castalia impatiently. Jane rapped the table.

'That is the very point we are met to consider,' she said. 'For five years we have been trying to find out whether we are justified in continuing the human race. Castalia has anticipated our decision. But it remains for the rest of us to make up our minds.'

Here one after another of our messengers rose and delivered their reports. The marvels of civilisation far exceeded our expectations, and as we learnt for the first time how man flies in the air, talks across space, penetrates to the heart of an atom, and embraces the universe in his speculations a murmur of admiration burst from our lips.

'We are proud,' we cried, 'that our mothers sacrificed their youth in such a cause as this!' Castalia, who had been listening intently, looked prouder than all the rest. Then Jane reminded us that we had still much to learn, and Castalia begged us to make haste. On we went through a vast tangle of statistics. We learnt that England has a population of so many millions, and that such and such a proportion of them is constantly hungry and in prison; that the average size of a working man's family is such, and that so great a percentage of women die from maladies incident to childbirth. Reports were read of visits to factories, shops, slums, and dockyards. Descriptions were given of the Stock Exchange, of a gigantic house of business in the City, and of a Government Office. The British Colonies were now discussed, and some account was given of our rule in India, Africa and Ireland. I was sitting by Castalia and I noticed her uneasiness.

'We shall never come to any conclusion at all at this rate,' she said. 'As it appears that civilisation is so much more complex than we had any notion, would it not be better to confine ourselves to our original enquiry? We agreed that it was the object of life to produce good people and good books. All this time we have been talking of aeroplanes, factories, and money. Let us talk about men themselves and their arts, for that is the heart of the matter.'

So the diners out stepped forward with long slips of paper containing answers to their questions. These had been framed after much consideration. A good man, we had agreed, must at any rate be honest, passionate, and unworldly. But whether or not a particular man possessed those qualities could only be discovered by asking questions, often beginning at a remote distance from the centre. Is Kensington a nice place to live in? Where is your son being educated – and your daughter? Now please tell me, what do you pay for your cigars? By the way, is Sir Joseph a baronet or only a knight? Often it seemed that we learnt more from trivial questions of this kind than from more direct ones. 'I accepted my peerage,' said Lord Bunkum, 'because my wife wished it.' I forget how many titles were accepted for the same reason. 'Working fifteen hours out of the twenty-four, as I do –' ten thousand professional men began.

'No, no, of course you can neither read nor write. But why do you work so hard?' 'My dear lady, with a growing family –' 'But *why* does your family grow?' Their wives wished that too, or perhaps it was the British Empire. But more significant than the answers were the refusals to answer. Very few would reply at all to questions about morality and religion, and such answers as were given were not serious. Questions as to the value of money and power were almost invariably brushed aside, or pressed at extreme risk to the asker. 'I'm sure,' said Jill, 'that if Sir Harley Tightboots hadn't been carving the mutton when I asked him about the capitalist system he would have cut my throat. The only reason why we escaped with our lives over and over again is that men are at once so hungry and so chivalrous. They despise us too much to mind what we say.'

'Of course they despise us,' said Eleanor. 'At the same time how do you account for this – I made enquiries among the artists. Now no woman has ever been an artist, has she, Poll?'

'Jane–Austen–Charlotte–Bronte–George–Eliot,' cried Poll, like a man crying muffins in a back street.

'Damn the woman!' someone exclaimed. 'What a bore she is!'

'Since Sappho there has been no female of first rate –' Eleanor began, quoting from a weekly newspaper.

'It's now well known that Sappho was the somewhat lewd invention of Professor Hobkin,' Ruth interrupted.

'Anyhow, there is no reason to suppose that any woman ever has been able to write or ever will be able to write,' Eleanor continued. 'And yet, whenever I go among authors they never cease to talk to me about their books. Masterly! I say, or Shakespeare himself! (for one must say something) and I assure you, they believe me.'

'That proves nothing,' said Jane. They all do it. 'Only,' she sighed, 'it doesn't seem to help *us* much. Perhaps we had better examine modern literature next. Liz, it's your turn.'

Elizabeth rose and said that in order to prosecute her enquiry she had dressed as a man and been taken for a reviewer.

'I have read new books pretty steadily for the past five years,' said she. 'Mr Wells is the most popular living writer; then comes Mr Arnold Bennett; then Mr Compton Mackenzie; Mr McKenna and Mr Walpole may be bracketed together.' She sat down.

'But you've told us nothing!' we expostulated. 'Or do you mean that these gentlemen have greatly surpassed Jane–Eliot and that English fiction is – where's that review of yours? Oh, yes, "safe in their hands."'

'Safe, quite safe,' she said, shifting uneasily from foot to foot. 'And I'm sure that they give away even more than they receive.'

We were all sure of that. 'But,' we pressed her, 'do they write good books?'

'Good books?' she said, looking at the ceiling. 'You must remember,' she began, speaking with extreme rapidity, 'that fiction is the mirror of life. And you can't deny that education is of the highest importance, and that it would be extremely annoying, if you found yourself alone at Brighton late at night, not to know which was the best boarding house to stay at, and suppose it was a dripping Sunday evening – wouldn't it be nice to go to the Movies?'

'But what has that got to do with it?' we asked.

'Nothing – nothing – nothing whatever,' she replied.

'Well, tell us the truth,' we bade her.

'The truth? But isn't it wonderful,' she broke off – 'Mr Chitter has written a weekly article for the past thirty years, upon love or hot buttered toast and has sent all his sons to Eton –'

'The truth!' we demanded.

'Oh, the truth,' she stammered, 'the truth has nothing to do with literature,' and sitting down she refused to say another word.

It all seemed to us very inconclusive.

'Ladies, we must try to sum up the results,' Jane was beginning when a hum, which had been heard for some time through the open window, drowned her voice.

'War! War! War! Declaration of War!' men were shouting in the stteet below.

We looked at each other in horror.

'What war?' we cried. 'What war?' We remembered, too late, that we had never thought of sending anyone to the House of Commons. We had forgotten all about it. We turned to Poll, who had reached the history shelves in the London Library, and asked her to enlighten us.

'Why,' we cried, 'do men go to war?'

'Sometimes for one reason, sometimes for another,' she replied calmly. 'In 1760, for example –' The shouts outside drowned her words. 'Again in 1797 – in 1804 – It was the Austrians in 1866 – 1870 was the Franco-Prussian – In 1900 on the other hand –'

'But it's now 1914!' we cut her short.

'Ah, I don't know what they're going to war for now,' she admitted.

The war was over and peace was in process of being signed, when I once more found myself with Castalia in the room where our meetings used to be held. We began idly turning over the pages of our old minute books. 'Queer,' I mused, 'to see what we were thinking five years ago.' 'We are agreed,' Castalia quoted, reading over my shoulder, 'that it is the object of life to produce good people and good books.' We made no comment upon *that*. 'A good man is at any rate honest, passionate and unworldly.' 'What a woman's language!' I observed. 'Oh, dear,' cried Castalia, pushing the book away from her, 'what fools we were! It was all Poll's father's fault,' she went on. 'I believe he did it on purpose – that ridiculous will, I mean, forcing Poll to read all the books in the London Library.

If we hadn't learnt to read,' she said bitterly, 'we might still have been bearing children in ignorance and that, I believe, was the happiest life after all. I know what you're going to say about war,' she checked me, 'and the horror of bearing children to see them killed, but our mothers did it, and their mothers, and their mothers before them. And *they* didn't complain. They couldn't read. I've done my best,' she sighed, 'to prevent my little girl from learning to read, but what's the use? I caught Ann only yesterday with a newspaper in her hand and she was beginning to ask me if it was "true". Next she'll ask me whether Mr Lloyd George is a good man, then whether Mr Arnold Bennett is a good novelist, and finally whether I believe in God. How can I bring my daughter up to believe in nothing?' she demanded.

'Surely you could teach her to believe that a man's intellect is, and always will be, fundamentally superior to a woman's?' I suggested. She brightened at this and began to turn over our old minutes again. 'Yes,' she said, 'think of their discoveries, their mathematics, their science, their philosophy, their scholarship –' and then she began to laugh, 'I shall never forget old Hobkin and the hairpin,' she said, and went on reading and laughing and I thought she was quite happy, when suddenly she threw the book from her and burst out, 'Oh, Cassandra, why do you torment me? Don't you know that our belief in man's intellect is the greatest fallacy of them all?' 'What?' I exclaimed. 'Ask any journalist, school-master, politician or public house keeper in the land and they will all tell you that men are much cleverer than women.' 'As if I doubted it,' she said scornfully. 'How could they help it? Haven't we bred them and fed and kept them in comfort since the beginning of time so that they may be clever even if they're nothing else? It's all our doing!' she cried. 'We insisted upon having intellect and now we've got it. And it's intellect,' she continued, 'that's at the bottom of it. What could be more charming than a boy before he has begun to cultivate his intellect? He is beautiful to look at; he gives himself no airs; he understands the meaning of art and literature instinctively; he goes about enjoying his life and making other people enjoy theirs. Then they teach him to cultivate his intellect. He becomes a barrister, a civil servant, a general, an author, a professor. Every day he goes to an office. Every year he produces a book. He maintains a whole family by the products of his brain – poor devil! Soon he cannot come into a room without making us all feel uncomfortable; he condescends to every woman he meets, and dares not tell the truth even to his own wife; instead of rejoicing our eyes we have to shut them if we are to take him in our arms. True, they console themselves with stars of all shapes, ribbons of all shades, and incomes of all sizes – but what is to console us? That we shall be able in ten years' time to spend a weekend at Lahore? Or that the least insect in Japan has a name twice the length of its body? Oh, Cassandra, for Heaven's sake let us devise a method by which men may bear children! It is our only chance. For unless we provide them with some innocent occupation we shall get neither good people nor good books; we shall perish beneath the fruits of their unbridled activity; and not a human being will survive to know that there once was Shakespeare!'

'It is too late,' I replied. 'We cannot provide even for the children that we have.'

'And then you ask me to believe in intellect,' she said.

While we spoke, men were crying hoarsely and wearily in the street, and, listening, we heard that the Treaty of Peace had just been signed. The voices died away. The rain was falling and interfered no doubt with the proper explosion of the fireworks.

'My cook will have bought the *Evening News*,' said Castalia, 'and Ann will be spelling it out over her tea. I must go home.'

'It's no good – not a bit of good,' I said. 'Once she knows how to read there's only one thing you can teach her to believe in – and that is herself.'

'Well, that would be a change,' said Castalia.

So we swept up the papers of our Society, and though Ann was playing with her doll very happily, we solemnly made her a present of the lot and told her we had chosen her to be President of the Society of the future – upon which she burst into tears, poor little girl.

GENEROUS PIECES

Ellen Gilchrist

Ellen Gilchrist (b. 1935) is an American author and poet who studied creative writing under Eudora Welty. Her 1981 collection of stories, *In the Land of Dreamy Dreams*, received immense critical acclaim and, in 1984, she won the National Book Award for her collection of stories, *Victory Over Japan*.

I am poking around the house looking for change to spend at the Sweet Shoppe. It is afternoon, November. The light coming through the windows of my parents' room is flat and gray and casts thick shadows on the rug my father brought home from China after the war.

I am going through the pockets of his gabardine topcoat. The pockets are deep and cool. The rubbers are in the right-hand pocket. I pull them out, look at them for a moment, then stick my hand back in the pocket and leave it there. I stand like that for a long time, halfway into the closet with my hand deep in the pocket, listening to the blood run through my body, to the sound of my own breathing.

I smell the cold safety of his suits and shirts. I stare down at the comforting order of his shoes and boots. I hold one of the little packets between my fingers, feeling the hard rim, the soft yielding center. It gives way, like the hide of a mouse.

Behind me is the walnut bed in which he was born far away in Georgia. Beside it, the old-fashioned dresser with a silver tray onto which he empties his pockets in the evenings. While he dreams the tray holds his daytime life, his plumb bob, his pocketknife, his pens and pencils, his onyx Kappa Sigma ring, his loose change, his money clip.

How do I know what the rubbers are? How do I know with such absolute certainty that they are connected with Christina Carver's mother and the pall that has fallen over our house on Calvin Boulevard?

I stand in the closet door for a long time. I want to take out the little package and inspect it more closely, but I cannot bring myself to withdraw it from the pocket, as if to pull it out into the light would make it real. After a while I become afraid my mother will come home and find me in her room so I take my hand from the pocket and leave.

I wander into the kitchen and make a sugar sandwich and talk for a while to the elderly German housekeeper. She is a kindly woman with a thick accent who smiles all the time. She has a small grandson who is deaf, and occasionally she brings him to work and talks with him in the language deaf people make with their hands. I feel sorry for her because of the deaf child and try to remember to pick up my clothes so she won't have to bend over to reach them. When I am good about this she bakes me gingerbread men with buttons and smiles made out of raisins.

I leave the house and begin walking aimlessly across the small Indiana town. Usually I go by Christina's after school. We are best friends. We spend the night together on weekends. We stand by each other in lines. I work hard to make Christina my friend. I need her for an ally as we have only lived in this town six months and she is the most popular girl in the class.

We have lived in five towns in three years. Every time we move my father makes more money. Every place we live we have a nicer house. This time we are not going to move anymore he promises. This time we are going to stay put.

I want to stay put. When the junior-high cheerleader elections are held in the spring the girls will try out in pairs. If I try out with Christina I know I will win.

My mother was a cheerleader at the University of Georgia. Her senior year in college she was voted Most Popular Girl. There is a full-page photograph of her in the 1929 University of Georgia yearbook. She is wearing a handmade lace dress the color of snow, the color of marble. Her face is small and sweet and full of sadness. Underneath her feet in black letters it says, *Most Popular Girl.*

I will never be popular. But at least I can get elected cheerleader. I do Christina's homework. I write her book reports. I carry messages to her secret boyfriend. He is a college boy named Dawson who plays the saxophone and is dying of cancer in an apartment behind his Jewish grandmothers mansion. I carry their messages. I stand guard when she goes to visit him. I listen to her love stories. They lie down together on a bed with their clothes on and strange things happen. One thing they do is called dryfucking. I don't really understand what it is but I feel funny and excited when she talks about it.

Once I went with her to Dawson's apartment, some rooms above a brick garage of the only mansion in Seymour, Indiana. There were phonograph albums and cartoons nailed to the walls. Dawson was very nice to me. He kept making me listen to something called *Jazz at the Philharmonic.* I pretended to like it. I pretended to like the worst part of all when someone named Jojo plays the drums for about fifteen minutes.

I pass the grade school and turn onto Duncan Street where Christina has lived every day of her life. Next door to her house is a vacant lot. A bicycle I used to own is rusting in a corner of the lot. It has a flat tire but I have never bothered walking it to the service station to get it fixed. I have a new bicycle with shiny fenders. Christina's mother always teases me about the old bike. "It must be nice to be rich," she says, laughing.

She thinks it is funny that no one makes me do anything about it. Christina has to do all kinds of things my mother would never dream of making me do. She has to help with the dishes and iron her own clothes and practice the piano for an hour every day and go horseback riding on Saturday.

When I get to Christina's house she is in the dining room with her mother looking at the fabrics they have spread out all over the dining room table. They have been to a sale and the dining room table is covered with bright plaid wools and gold and blue corduroy and a heavy quilted cotton with little flowers on a green background.

"Here's Margaret now," her mother says, smiling at me, moving closer, her small, brisk body making me feel heavy and awkward and surprised. "Margaret, look at these bargains we got at Hazard's. We're going to make skirts and weskits. Look, we bought something for you. So you and Christina can have twin outfits." She holds up the quilted fabric. "Isn't it darling? Isn't it the darlingest thing you've ever seen?"

She is always so gay, so full of plans. I think of her getting into the Packard with my father the night they went off to Benton to the ballgame, the night my mother wouldn't go. Christina's father was out of town and I stood on the porch watching my father put her into his big car. My mother stood in the dark doorway not saying a word and later she went into the bedroom and locked the door. My mother has not been well lately. She is worn out. She has hot flashes. She takes hormones and writes long letters to Mississippi and is always mad at me.

"Do you like it?" Christina's mother says, holding the fabric against her body as if she were a model.

"Oh, my," I say, taking the material. "I love it. It's darling. Is it really for me?"

"Look," Christina says, "the one with the green background is for you, to go with your red hair. We got the same print with a blue background for me. Won't we look great together? You aren't supposed to mix blue and green together but who cares. We can wear them to the Christmas Follies if we get them made in time."

"You're going to *make* it tor me?" I say.

"Of course we are," her mother says. "I'll get started on it tomorrow morning. I can't wait to see how cute you'll look together. Besides I need to do something to pay your father back for all the help he's been to us with our taxes. I'll have to measure you first, though. Can I do it now?"

"I can't stay that long today," I say quickly, not wanting her to know how big my waist is. It is twenty-six. I will never be a belle. "I'll come back tomorrow and let you do it, if that's O.K."

"Whenever you have time," she says. "I can go on and start on Christina's."

Christina walks me out into the yard. "She's going to a horse show on Saturday," she says. "Do you want to go with me to see Dawson?"

"Sure," I say.

"I don't know what I'd do without you," Christina says. "I don't know what I did before you moved here. Dawson says you're darling. He thinks you're smart as a whip. He wants you to come back over. He wants you to meet a friend of his from college."

"I'll see you tomorrow then," I say. "I'll come by in the morning. And thanks a lot about the skirt. That's really nice of your mother."

I walk off down Duncan Street for a few blocks, then change my mind about going home. I decide to walk out toward the railroad tracks and get some exercise to make myself smaller before I get measured.

It will be light for another hour. I think about going by Janet Ingram's house to see what she is doing. Janet lives on the edge of town in a house that is very different from the ones Christina and I live in. There are stained red carpets on the floors and over the mantel is a collection of china bulls her father wins at carnivals. I know I am not supposed to go there although my mother has never actually told me so.

Janet's father sleeps in the daytime and works at night in a factory. Once I was there in the afternoon and he was just getting up, walking around the house in a sleeveless T-shirt. I walk along, thinking about the way Janet's house smells, warm and close and foreign, as though the air were full of germs.

I try not to think about Christina's mother. If I think of her I remember how she leans over my father's chair handing him things when they have dinner at our house. I think of him putting her into his car. Then I think of the beautiful quilted material. I think of Christina and me walking into the junior high together, wearing our matching outfits.

I am walking along a new street where houses are under construction. Two men are still hammering on the high beams of one. They are standing on the slanting half-finished roof. I am afraid they will fall while I am watching them and I turn my face away. It is terrible for people to have dangerous jobs like that. I'm glad my father doesn't have a dangerous job. People who are poor have to have jobs like that. Perhaps it doesn't matter as much what happens to them.

Janet comes to the door. Her father is in the living room putting on his shoes. "I can't ask you to stay," she says. "My dad's getting ready to leave for work and I have to help with dinner."

"That's all right," I say. "I was just walking around. I just came by to see what you were doing."

I am staring at Janet's breasts, which are even larger than mine. I wonder if it is true that Janet lets boys touch her breasts.

I begin walking home. Dark is falling faster than I expected. The days grow shorter. It is almost Thanksgiving.

A group of children playing in a yard begins following me. One of them recognizes me from school. He picks up a dirt clod and throws it at me. It hits my coat. I don't know what to do. No one has ever thrown anything at me before. I look up. Another dirt clod hits me on the shoulder. I begin to run, trying to figure out what is going on. I run through the darkening streets as fast as I can. Streetlights flicker and come on. Here and there a yellow porch light shines brightly. I run and run, afraid of falling down, afraid of every shadow, afraid to look up, afraid of the trees, afraid of the moon.

Now it is full dark. How did it get dark so quickly? I fear the dark. I never sleep without a light in my room. If I wake in the night in the dark I am terrified and jump out of bed and run down to my parents' room and tremble between them until morning.

The night is so still I can hear the branches of the trees reaching out their arms for me. A huge moon has appeared in the eastern sky. I run past the construction site. The exposed beams stand out against the dark blue sky. I think if I looked inside I would find the bodies of the carpenters broken and bleeding on the floor.

I run past an alley where I found an automatic card shuffler in a trashcan once when my grandmother was visiting us. When I brought it home she flew into hysterics and bathed me with lye soap, lecturing me about diseases I could catch from strangers.

Now I am on my own street. I run past the Dustins' house. I run into my house and down the hall and turn around and around and run into the kitchen and find my father sitting at the table with my brother. They are laughing and cutting fat green olives into generous pieces.

I throw myself upon him screaming, "Look what they did to me! Look what they did to me! Look what they did!"

He takes me into the bedroom and sits on the bed with me. He holds me in his arms. My face is against his shirt. I burrow into the strength of his body. Once I look up and there are tears running down his cheeks.

My mother is touching my hair. "It's from living like this," she says. "This insane life in this hick Yankee town. I don't know who she's with half the time. God knows who she plays with. God knows what she's doing."

"What do you want me to do?" he says. "Go home and starve in Waycross? Run a hardware store the rest of my life?"

"I don't know," she says. "I don't know what I want you to do."

After a while my mother undresses me and puts me in bed in her soft flowered nightgown. She brings me a hot toddy and feeds it to me with a spoon. The hot liquor runs down my throat and soothes me. My mother promises to stay with me till I sleep. She turns off the lamp. She sits touching my arm with her soft hands. And the terror draws in its white arms and is still, watching me with cold eyes from the mirror on my father's dresser.

THE WALTZ

Dorothy Parker

Dorothy Parker (1893–1967) was an American critic, satirical poet, and short story writer. Best known for her wit and eye for 20th-century foibles, Parker wrote book reviews, poetry and short fiction for the fledgling magazine the *New Yorker*. She wrote the screenplay for the Hitchcock film *Saboteur*, but her involvement with Communism led to her being blacklisted in Hollywood.

Why, *thank you so much. I'd adore to.*

I don't want to dance with him. I don't want to dance with anybody. And even if I did, it wouldn't be him. He'd be well down among the last ten. I've seen the way he dances; it looks like something you do on Saint Walpurgis Night. Just think, not a quarter of an hour ago, here I was sitting, feeling so sorry for the poor girl he was dancing with. And now *I'm* going to be the poor girl. Well, well. Isn't it a small world?

And a peach of a world, too. A true little corker. Its events are so fascinatingly unpredictable, are not they? Here I was, minding my own business, not doing a stitch of harm to any living soul. And then he comes into my life, all smiles and city manners, to sue me for the favor of one memorable mazurka. Why, he scarcely knows my name, let alone what it stands for. It stands for Despair, Bewilderment, Futility, Degradation, and Premeditated Murder, but little does he wot. I don't wot his name, either; I haven't any idea what it is. Jukes, would be my guess from the look in his eyes. How do you do, Mr. Jukes? And how is that dear little brother of yours, with the two heads?

Ah, now why did he have to come around me, with his low requests? Why can't he let me lead my own life? I ask so little – just to be left alone in my quiet corner of the table, to do my evening brooding over all my sorrows. And he must come, with his bows and his scrapes and his may-I-have-this-ones. And I had to go and tell him that I'd adore to dance with him. I cannot understand why I wasn't struck right down dead. Yes, and being struck dead would look like a day in the country, compared to struggling out a dance with this boy. But what could I do? Everyone else at the table had got up to dance, except him and me. There was I, trapped. Trapped like a trap in a trap.

What can you say, when a man asks you to dance with him? I most certainly will *not* dance with you, I'll see you in hell first. Why, thank you, I'd like to awfully, but I'm having labor pains. Oh, yes, *do* let's dance together – it's so nice to meet a man who isn't a scaredy-cat about catching my beri-beri. No. There was nothing for me to do, but say I'd adore to. Well, we might as well get it over with. All right, Cannonball, let's run out on the field. You won the toss; you can lead.

Why, I think it's more of a waltz, really. Isn't it? We might just listen to the music a second. Shall we? Oh, yes, it's a waltz. Mind? Why, I'm simply thrilled. I'd love to waltz with you.

I'd love to waltz with you. I'd love to waltz with you, I'd love to have my tonsils out, I'd love to be in a midnight fire at sea. Well, it's too late now. We're getting under way. *Oh.* Oh, dear. Oh, dear, dear, dear. Oh, this is even worse than I thought it would be. I suppose that's the one dependable law of life – everything is always worse than you thought it was going to be. Oh, if I had any real grasp of what this dance would be like, I'd have held out for sitting it out. Well, it will probably amount to the same thing in the end. We'll be sitting it out on the floor in a minute, if he keeps this up.

I'm so glad I brought it to his attention that this is a waltz they're playing. Heaven knows what might have happened, if he had thought it was something fast; we'd have blown the sides right out of the building. Why does he always want to be somewhere that he isn't? Why can't we stay in one place just long enough to get acclimated? It's this constant rush, rush, rush, that's the curse of American life. That's the reason that we're all of us so – *Ow!* For God's sake, don't *kick*, you idiot; this is only second down. Oh, my shin. My poor, poor shin, that I've had ever since I was a little girl!

Oh, no, no, no. Goodness, no. It didn't hurt the least little bit. And anyway it was my fault. Really it was. Truly. Well, you're just being sweet, to say that. It really was all my fault.

I wonder what I'd better do – kill him this instant with my naked hands, or wait and let him drop in his traces. Maybe it's best not to make a scene. I guess I'll just lie low, and watch the pace get him. He can't keep this up indefinitely – he's only flesh and blood. Die he must, and die he shall, for what he did to me. I don't want to be of the over-sensitive type, but you can't tell me that kick was unpremeditated. Freud says there are no accidents. I've led no cloistered life, I've known dancing partners who have spoiled my slippers and torn my dress; but when it comes to kicking, I am Outraged Womanhood. When you kick me in the shin, *smile.*

Maybe he didn't do it maliciously. Maybe it's just his way of showing his high spirits. I suppose I ought to be glad that one of us is having such a good time. I suppose I ought to think myself lucky if he brings me back alive. Maybe it's captious to demand of a practically strange man that he leave your shins as he found them. After all, the poor boy's doing the best he can. Probably he grew up in the hill country, and never had no larnin'. I bet they had to throw him on his back to get shoes on him.

Yes it's lovely, isn't it? It's simply lovely. It's the loveliest waltz. Isn't it? Oh, I think it's lovely too.

Why, I'm getting positively drawn to the Triple Threat here. He's my hero. He has the heart of a lion, and the sinews of a buffalo. Look at him – never a thought of the consequences, never afraid of his face, hurling himself into every scrimmage, eyes shining, cheeks ablaze. And shall it be said that I hung back? No, a thousand times no. What's it to me if I have to spend the next couple of years in a plaster cast? Come on, Butch, right through them! Who wants to live forever?

Oh. Oh, dear. Oh, he's all right, thank goodness. For a while I thought they'd have to carry him off the field. Ah, I couldn't bear to have anything happen to him. I love him. I love him better than anybody in the world. Look at the spirit he gets into a dreary, commonplace waltz; how effete the other dancers seem, beside him. He is youth and vigor and courage, he is strength and gaiety and – *Ow!* Get off my instep, you hulking peasant! What do you think I am, anyway – a gangplank? *Ow!*

No, of course it didn't hurt. Why, it didn't a bit. Honestly. And it was all my fault. You see, that little step of yours – well, it's perfectly lovely, but it's just a tiny bit tricky to follow at first. Oh, did you work it up yourself? You really did? Well, aren't you amazing! Oh, now I think I've got it. Oh, I think it's lovely. I was watching you do it when you were dancing before. It's awfully effective when you look at it.

It's awfully effective when you look at it. I bet I'm awfully effective when you look at me. My hair is hanging along my cheeks, my skirt is swaddling about me. I can feel the cold damp of my brow. I must look like something out of "The Fall of the House of Usher." This sort of thing takes a fearful toll of a woman my age. And he worked up his little step himself, he with his degenerate cunning. And it was just a tiny bit tricky at first, but now I think I've got it. Two stumbles, slip, and a twenty-yard dash; yes. I've got it. I've got several other things, too, including a split shin and a bitter heart. I hate this creature I'm chained to. I hated him the moment I saw his leering, bestial face. And here I've been locked in his noxious embrace for the thirty-five years this waltz has lasted. Is that orchestra never going to stop playing? Or must this obscene travesty of a dance go on until hell burns out?

Oh, they're going to play another encore. Oh, goody. Oh, that's lovely. Tired? I should say I'm not tired. I'd like to go on like this forever.

I should say I'm not tired. I'm dead, that's all I am. Dead, and in what a cause! And the music is never going to stop playing, and we're going on like this, Double Time Charlie and I, throughout eternity. I suppose I won't care any more, after the first hundred thousand years. I suppose nothing will matter then, not heat nor pain nor broken heart nor cruel, aching weariness. Well. It can't come too soon for me.

I wonder why I didn't tell him I was tired. I wonder why I didn't suggest going back to the table. I could have said let's just listen to the music. Yes, and if he would, that would be the first bit of attention he has given it all evening. George Jean Nathan said that the lovely rhythms of the waltz should be listened to in stillness and not be accompanied by strange gyrations of the human body. I think that's what he said. I think it was George Jean Nathan. Anyhow, whatever he said and whoever he was and whatever he's doing now, he's better off than I am. That's safe. Anybody who isn't waltzing with this Mrs. O'Leary's cow I've got here is having a good time.

Still if we were back at the table, I'd probably have to talk to him. Look at him – what could you say to a thing like that! Did you go to the circus this year, what's your favorite kind of ice cream, how do you spell cat? I guess I'm as well off here. As well off as if I were in a cement mixer in full action.

I'm past all feeling now. The only way I can tell when he steps on me is that I can hear the splintering of bones. And all the events of my life are passing before my eyes. There was the time I was in a hurricane in the West Indies, there was the day I got my head cut open in the taxi smash, there was the night the drunken lady threw a bronze ash-tray at her own true love and got me instead, there was that summer that the sailboat kept capsizing. Ah, what an easy, peaceful time was mine, until I fell in with Swifty, here. I didn't know what trouble was, before I got drawn into this *danse macabre*. I think my mind is beginning to wander. It almost seems to me as if the orchestra were stopping. It couldn't be, of course; it could never, never be. And yet in my ears there is a silence like the sound of angel voices …

Oh they've stopped, the mean things. They're not going to play any more. Oh, darn. Oh, do you think they would? Do you really think so, if you gave them twenty dollars? Oh, that would be lovely. And look, do tell them to play this same thing. I'd simply adore to go on waltzing.

THROUGH THE TUNNEL

Doris Lessing

Doris Lessing (b. 1919) is a British novelist, poet, playwright, biographer and short story writer. In 2001, Lessing was awarded the David Cohen Prize for a lifetime's achievement in British Literature and she was ranked fifth on *The Times* list of the '50 Greatest British Writers Since 1945'. Lessing was awarded the 2007 Nobel Prize in Literature.

Going to the shore on the first morning of the vacation, the young English boy stopped at a turning of the path and looked down at a wild and rocky bay, and then over to the crowded beach he knew so well from other years. His mother walked on in front of him, carrying a bright striped bag in one hand. Her other arm, swinging loose, was very white in the sun. The boy watched that white naked arm, and turned his eyes, which had a frown behind them, towards the bay and back again to his mother. When she felt he was not with her, she swung around. "Oh, there you are, Jerry!" she said. She looked impatient, then smiled. "Why, darling, would you rather not come with me? Would you rather—" She frowned, conscientiously worrying over what amusements he might secretly be longing for, which she had been too busy or too careless to imagine. He was very familiar with that anxious, apologetic smile. Contrition sent him running after her. And yet, as he ran, he looked back over his shoulder at the wild bay; and all morning, as he played on the safe beach, he was thinking of it.

Next morning, when it was time for the routine of swimming and sunbathing, his mother said, "Are you tired of the usual beach, Jerry? Would you like to go somewhere else?"

"Oh, no!" he said quickly, smiling at her out of that unfailing impulse of contrition – a sort of chivalry. Yet, walking down the path with her, he blurted out, "I'd like to go and have a look at those rocks down there."

She gave the idea her attention. It was a wild-looking place, and there was no one there; but she said, "Of course, Jerry, When you've had enough, come to the big beach. Or just go straight back to the villa, if you like." She walked away, that bare arm, now slightly reddened from yesterday's sun, swinging. And he almost ran after her again, feeling it unbearable that she should go by herself, but he did not.

She was thinking, Of course he's old enough to be safe without me. Have I been keeping him too close? He mustn't feel he ought to be with me. I must be careful.

He was an only child, eleven years old. She was a widow. She was determined to be neither possessive nor lacking in devotion. She went worrying off to her beach.

As for Jerry, once he saw that his mother had gained her beach, he began the steep descent to the bay. From where he was, high up among red-brown rocks, it was a scoop of moving blueish green fringed with white. As he went lower, he saw that it spread among small promontories and inlets of rough, sharp rock, and the crisping, lapping surface showed stains of purple and darker blue. Finally, as he ran sliding and scraping down the last few yards, he saw an edge of white surf and the shallow, luminous movement of water over white sand, and, beyond that, a solid, heavy blue.

He ran straight into the water and began swimming. He was a good swimmer. He went out fast over the gleaming sand, over a middle region where rocks lay like discoloured monsters under the surface, and then he was in the real sea – a warm sea where irregular cold currents from the deep water shocked his limbs.

When he was so far out that he could look back not only on the little bay but past the promontory that was between it and the big beach, he floated on the buoyant surface and looked for his mother. There she was, a speck of yellow under an umbrella that looked like a slice of orange peel. He swam back to shore, relieved at being sure she was there, but all at once very lonely.

On the edge of a small cape that marked the side of the bay away from the promontory was a loose scatter of rocks. Above them, some boys were stripping off their clothes. They came running, naked, down to the rocks. The English boy swam towards them, but kept his distance at a stone's throw. They were of that coast; all of them were burned smooth dark brown and speaking a language he did not understand. To be with them, of them, was a craving that filled his whole body. He swam a little closer; they turned and watched him with narrowed, alert dark eyes. Then one smiled and waved. It was enough. In a minute, he had swum in and was on the rocks beside them, smiling with a desperate, nervous supplication. They shouted cheerful greetings at him; and then, as he preserved his nervous, uncomprehending smile, they understood that he was a foreigner strayed from his own beach, and they proceeded to forget him. But he was happy. He was with them.

They began diving again and again from a high point into a well of blue sea between rough, pointed rocks. After they had dived and come up, they swam around, hauled themselves up, and waited their turn to dive again. They were big boys – men, to Jerry. He dived, and they watched him; and when he swam around to take his place, they made way for him. He felt he was accepted and he dived again, carefully, proud of himself.

Soon the biggest of the boys poised himself, shot down into the water, and did not come up. The others stood about, watching. Jerry, after waiting for the sleek brown head to appear, let out a yell of warning; they looked at him idly and turned their eyes back towards the water. After a long time, the boy came up on the other side of a big dark rock, letting the air out of his lungs in a sputtering gasp and a shout of triumph. Immediately the rest of them dived in. One moment, the morning seemed full of chattering boys; the next, the air and the surface of the water were empty. But through the heavy blue, dark shapes could be seen moving and groping.

Jerry dived, shot past the school of underwater swimmers, saw a black wall of rock looming at him, touched it, and bobbed up at once to the surface, where the wall was a low barrier he could see across. There was no one visible; under him, in the water, the dim shapes of the swimmers had disappeared. Then one, and then another of the boys came up on the far side of the barrier of rock, and he understood that they had swum through some gap or hole in it. He plunged down again. He could see nothing through the stinging salt water but the blank rock. When he came up the boys were all on the diving rock, preparing to attempt the feat again. And now, in a panic of failure, he yelled up, in English, "Look at me! Look!" and he began splashing and kicking in the water like a foolish dog.

They looked down gravely, frowning. He knew the frown. At moments of failure, when he clowned to claim his mother's attention, it was with just this grave, embarrassed inspection that she rewarded him. Through his hot shame, feeling the pleading grin on his face like a scar that he could never remove, he looked up at the group of big brown boys on the rock and shouted, *"Bonjour! Merci! Au revoir! Monsieur, monsieur!"* while he hooked his fingers round his ears and waggled them.

Water surged into his mouth; he choked, sank, came up. The rock, lately weighted with boys, seemed to rear up out of the water as their weight was removed. They were flying down past him now, into the water; the air was full of falling bodies. Then the rock was empty in the hot sunlight. He counted one, two, three …

At fifty, he was terrified. They must all be drowning beneath him, in the watery caves of the rock! At a hundred, he stared around him at the empty hillside, wondering if he should yell for help. He counted faster, faster, to hurry them up, to bring them to the surface quickly, to drown them quickly – anything rather than the terror of counting on and on into the blue emptiness of the morning. And then, at a hundred and sixty, the water beyond the rock was full of boys blowing like brown whales. They swam back to the shore without a look at him.

He climbed back to the diving rock and sat down, feeling the hot roughness of it under his thighs. The boys were gathering up their bits of clothing and running off along the shore to another promontory. They were leaving to get away from him. He cried openly, fists in his eyes. There was no one to see him, and he cried himself out.

It seemed to him that a long time had passed, and he swam out to where he could see his mother. Yes, she was still there, a yellow spot under an orange umbrella. He swam back to the big rock, climbed up, and dived into the blue pool among the fanged and angry boulders. Down he went, until he touched the wall of rock again. But the salt was so painful in his eyes that he could not see.

He came to the surface, swam to shore and went back to the villa to wait for his mother. Soon she walked slowly up the path, swinging her striped bag, the flushed, naked arm dangling beside her. "I want some swimming goggles," he panted, defiant and beseeching.

She gave him a patient, inquisitive look as she said casually, "Well, of course, darling."

But now, now, now! He must have them this minute, and no other time. He nagged and pestered until she went with him to a shop. As soon as she had bought the goggles, he grabbed them from her hand as if she were going to claim them for herself, and was off, running down the steep path to the bay.

Jerry swam out to the big barrier rock, adjusted the goggles, and dived. The impact of the water broke the rubber-enclosed vacuum, and the goggles came loose. He understood that he must swim down to the base of the rock from the surface of the water. He fixed the goggles tight and firm, filled his lungs, and floated, face down, on the water. Now he could see. It was as if he had eyes of a different kind – fish eyes that showed everything clear and delicate and wavering in the bright water.

Under him, six or seven feet down, was a floor of perfectly clean, shining white sand, rippled firm and hard by the tides. Two greyish shapes steered there, like long, rounded pieces of wood or slate. They were fish. He saw them nose towards each other, poise motionless, make a dart forward, swerve off, and come around again. It was like a water dance. A few inches above them the water sparkled as if sequins were dropping through it. Fish again – myriads of minute fish, the length of his fingernail – were drifting through the water, and in a moment he could feel the innumerable tiny touches of them against his limbs. It was like swimming in flaked silver. The great rock the big boys had swum through rose sheer out of the white sand – black, tufted lightly with greenish weed. He could see no gap in it. He swam down to its base.

Again and again he rose, took a big chestful of air, and went down. Again and again he groped over the surface of the rock, feeling it, almost hugging it in the desperate need to find the entrance. And then, once, while he was clinging to the black wall, his knees came up and he shot his feet out forward and they met no obstacle. He had found the hole.

He gained the surface, clambered about the stones that littered the barrier rock until he found a big one, and, with this in his arms, let himself down over the side of the rock. He dropped, with the weight, straight to the sandy floor. Clinging tight to the anchor of stone, he lay on his side and looked in under the dark shelf at the place where his feet had gone. He could see the hole. It was an irregular, dark gap; but he could not see deep into it. He let go of his anchor, clung with his hands to the edges of the hole, and tried to push himself in.

He got his head in, found his shoulders jammed, moved them in sidewise, and was inside as far as his waist. He could see nothing ahead. Something soft and clammy touched his mouth; he saw a dark frond moving against the greyish rock, and panic filled him. He thought of octopuses, of clinging weed. He pushed himself out backward and caught a glimpse, as he retreated, of a harmless tentacle of seaweed drifting in the mouth of the tunnel. But it was enough. He reached the sunlight, swam to shore, and lay on the diving rock. He looked down into the blue well of water. He knew he must find his way through that cave, or hole, or tunnel, and out the other side.

First, he thought, he must learn to control his breathing. He let himself down into the water with another big stone in his arms, so that he could lie effortlessly on the bottom of the sea. He counted. One, two, three. He counted steadily. He could hear the movement of blood in his chest. Fifty-one, fifty-two … His chest was hurting. He let go of the rock and went up into the air. He saw that the sun was low. He rushed to the villa and found his mother at her supper. She said only "Did you enjoy yourself?" and he said "Yes."

All night the boy dreamed of the water-filled cave in the rock, and as soon as breakfast was over he went to the bay.

That night, his nose bled badly. For hours he had been underwater, learning to hold his breath, and now he felt weak and dizzy. His mother said, "I shouldn't overdo things, darling, if I were you."

That day and the next, Jerry exercised his lungs as if everything, the whole of his life, all that he would become, depended upon it. Again his nose bled at night, and his mother insisted on his coming with her the next day. It was a torment to him to waste a day of his careful self-training, but he stayed with her on that other beach, which now seemed a place for small children, a place where his mother might lie safe in the sun. It was not his beach.

He did not ask for permission, on the following day, to go to his beach. He went, before his mother could consider the complicated rights and wrongs of the matter. A day's rest, he discovered, had improved his count by ten. The big boys had made the passage while he counted a hundred and sixty. He had been counting fast, in his fright. Probably now, if he tried, he could get through that long tunnel, but he was not going to try yet. A curious, most unchildlike persistence, a controlled impatience, made him wait. In the meantime, he lay underwater on the white sand, littered now by stones he had brought down from the upper air, and studied the entrance to the tunnel. He knew every jut and corner of it, as far as it was possible to see. It was as if he already felt its sharpness about his shoulders.

He sat by the clock in the villa, when his mother was not near, and checked his time. He was incredulous and then proud to find he could hold his breath without strain for two minutes. The words "two minutes," authorised by the clock, brought close the adventure that was so necessary to him.

In another four days, his mother said casually one morning, they must go home. On the day before they left, he would do it. He would do it if it killed him, he said defiantly to himself. But two days before they were to leave – a day of triumph when he increased his count by fifteen – his nose bled so badly that he turned dizzy and had to lie limply over the big rock like a bit of seaweed, watching the thick red blood flow on to the rock and trickle slowly down to the sea. He was frightened. Supposing he turned dizzy in the tunnel? Supposing he died there, trapped? Supposing – his head went around, in the hot sun, and he almost gave up. He thought he would return to the house and lie down, and next summer, perhaps, when he had another year's growth in him – *then* he would go through the hole.

But even after he had made the decision, or thought he had, he found himself sitting up on the rock and looking down into the water; and he knew that now, this moment, when his nose had only just stopped bleeding, when his head was still sore and throbbing – this was the moment when he would try. If he did not do it now, he never would. He was trembling with fear that he would not go; and he was trembling with horror at the long, long tunnel under the rock, under the sea. Even in the open sunlight, the barrier rock seemed very wide and very heavy; tons of rock pressed down on where he would go. If he died there, he would lie until one day – perhaps not before next year – those big boys would swim into it and find it blocked.

He put on his goggles, fitted them tight, tested the vacuum. His hands were shaking. Then he chose the biggest stone he could carry and slipped over the edge of the rock until half of him was in the cool enclosing water and half in the hot sun. He looked up once at the empty sky, filled his lungs once, twice, and then sank fast to the bottom with the stone. He let it go and began to count. He took the edges of the hole in his hands and drew himself into it; wriggling his shoulders in sidewise as he remembered he must, kicking himself along with his feet.

Soon he was clear inside. He was in a small rock-bound hole filled with yellowish-grey water. The water was pushing him up against the roof. The roof was sharp and pained his back. He pulled himself along with his hands – fast, fast – and used his legs as levers. His head knocked against something; a sharp pain dizzied him. Fifty, fifty-one, fifty-two ... He was without light, and the water seemed to press upon him with the weight of rock. Seventy-one, seventy-two ... There was no strain on his lungs. He felt like an inflated balloon, his lungs were so light and easy, but his head was pulsing.

He was being continually pressed against the sharp roof, which felt slimy as well as sharp. Again he thought of octopuses, and wondered if the tunnel might be filled with weed that could tangle him. He gave himself a panicky, convulsive kick forward, ducked his head, and swam. His feet and hands moved freely, as if in open water. The hole must have widened out. He thought he must be swimming fast, and he was frightened of banging his head if the tunnel narrowed.

A hundred, a hundred and one ... The water paled. Victory filled him. His lungs were beginning to hurt. A few more strokes and he would be out. He was counting wildly; he said a hundred and fifteen, and then, a long time later, a hundred and fifteen again. The water was a clear jewel-green all around him. Then he saw, above his head, a crack running up through the rock. Sunlight was falling through it, showing the clean, dark rock of the tunnel, a single mussel shell, and darkness ahead.

He was at the end of what he could do. He looked up at the crack as if it were filled with air and not water, as if he could put his mouth to it to draw in air. A hundred and fifteen, he heard himself say inside his head – but he had said that long ago. He must go on into the blackness ahead, or he would drown. His head was swelling, his lungs cracking. A hundred and fifteen, a hundred and fifteen pounded through his head, and he feebly clutched at rocks in the dark, pulling himself forward, leaving the brief space of sunlit water behind. He felt he was dying. He was no longer quite conscious. He struggled on in the darkness between lapses into unconsciousness. An immense, swelling pain filled his head, and then the darkness cracked with an explosion of green light. His hands, groping forward, met nothing; and his feet, kicking back, propelled him out into the open sea.

He drifted to the surface, his face turned up to the air. He was gasping like a fish. He felt he would sink now and drown; he could not swim the few feet back to the rock. Then he was clutching it and pulling himself up onto it. He lay face down, gasping. He could see nothing but a red-veined, clotted dark. His eyes must have burst, he thought; they were full of blood. He tore off his goggles and a gout of blood went into the sea. His nose was bleeding, and the blood had filled the goggles.

He scooped up handfuls of water from the cool, salty sea, to splash on his face, and did not know whether it was blood or salt water he tasted. After a time, his heart quieted, his eyes cleared, and he sat up. He could see the local boys diving and playing half a mile away. He did not want them. He wanted nothing but to get back home and lie down.

In a short while, Jerry swam to shore and climbed slowly up the path to the villa. He flung himself on his bed and slept, waking at the sound of feet on the path outside. His mother was coming back. He rushed to the bathroom, thinking she must not see his face with bloodstains, or tearstains, on it. He came out of the bathroom and met her as she walked into the villa, smiling, her eyes lighting up.

"Have a nice morning?" she asked, laying her hand on his warm brown shoulder a moment.

"Oh, yes, thank you," he said.

"You look a bit pale." And then, sharp and anxious, "How did you bang your head?"

"Oh, just banged it," he told her.

She looked at him closely. He was strained; his eyes were glazed-looking. She was worried. And then she said to herself, Oh, don't fuss! Nothing can happen. He can swim like a fish.

They sat down to lunch together.

"Mummy," he said, "I can stay underwater for two minutes – three minutes, at least." It came bursting out of him.

"Can you, darling?" she said. "Well, I shouldn't overdo it. I don't think you ought to swim any more today."

She was ready for a battle of wills, but he gave in at once. It was no longer of the least importance to go to the bay.

THE AXE

Penelope Fitzgerald

Penelope Fitzgerald (1916–2000) was a Man Booker Prize-winning British novelist, poet, essayist and biographer. In 2008, *The Times* included her in a list of the '50 Greatest British Writers Since 1945' and, in 2012, the *Observer* named her final novel, *The Blue Flower*, as one of 'The 10 Best Historical Novels'. A collection of Fitzgerald's short stories, *The Means of Escape*, and a volume of her non-fiction writings, *A House of Air*, were published posthumously.

Y ou will recall that when the planned redundancies became necessary as the result of the discouraging trading figures shown by this small firm – in contrast, so I gather from the Company reports, with several of your other enterprises – you personally deputed to me the task of 'speaking' to those who were to be asked to leave. It was suggested to me that if they were asked to resign in order to avoid the unpleasantness of being given their cards, it might be unnecessary for the firm to offer any compensation. Having glanced personally through my staff sheets, you underlined the names of four people, the first being that of my clerical assistant, W. S. Singlebury. Your actual words to me were that he seemed fairly old and could probably be frightened into taking a powder. You were speaking to me in your 'democratic' style.

From this point on I feel able to write more freely, it being well understood, at office-managerial level, that you do not read more than the first two sentences of any given report. You believe that anything which cannot be put into two sentences is not worth attending to, a piece of wisdom which you usually attribute to the late Lord Beaverbrook.

As I question whether you have ever seen Singlebury, with whom this report is mainly concerned, it may be helpful to describe him. He worked for the Company for many more years than myself, and his attendance record was excellent. On Mondays, Wednesdays and Fridays, he wore a blue suit and a green knitted garment with a front zip. On Tuesdays and Thursdays he wore a pair of grey trousers of man-made material which he called 'my flannels', and a fawn cardigan. The cardigan was omitted in summer. He had, however, one distinguishing feature, very light blue eyes, with a defensive expression, as though apologizing for something which he felt guilty about, but could not put right. The fact is that he was getting old. Getting old is, of course, a crime of which we grow more guilty every day.

Singlebury had no wife or dependants, and was by no means a communicative man. His room is, or was, a kind of cubby-hole adjoining mine – you have to go through it to get into my room – and it was always kept very neat. About his 'things' he did show some mild emotion. They had to be ranged in a certain pattern in respect to his in and out trays, and Singlebury stayed behind for two or three minutes every evening to do this. He also managed to retain every year the complimentary desk calendar sent to us by Dino's, the Italian cafe on the corner. Singlebury was in fact the only one of my personnel who was always quite certain of the date. To this too his attitude was apologetic. His phrase was, 'I'm afraid it's Tuesday.'

His work, as was freely admitted, was his life, but the nature of his duties – though they included the post-book and the addressograph – was rather hard to define, having grown round him with the years. I can only say that after he left, I was surprised myself to discover how much he had had to do.

Oddly connected in my mind with the matter of the redundancies is the irritation of the damp in the office this summer and the peculiar smell (not the ordinary smell of damp), emphasized by the sudden appearance of representatives of a firm of damp eliminators who had not been sent for by me, nor is there any record of my having done so. These people simply vanished at the end of the day and have not returned. Another firm, to whom I applied as a result of frequent complaints by the female staff, have answered my letters but have so far failed to call.

Singlebury remained unaffected by the smell. Joining, very much against his usual habit, in one of the too frequent discussions of the subject, he said that he knew what it was; it was the smell of disappointment. For an awkward moment I thought he must have found out by some means that he was going to be asked to go, but he went on to explain that in 1942 the whole building had been requisitioned by the Admiralty and that relatives had been allowed to wait or queue there in the hope of getting news of those missing at sea. The repeated disappointment of these women, Singlebury said, must have permeated the building like a corrosive gas. All this was very unlike him. I made it a point not to encourage anything morbid. Singlebury was quite insistent, and added, as though by way of proof, that the lino in the corridors was Admiralty issue and had not been renewed since 1942 either. I was astonished to realize that he had been working in the building for so many years before the present tenancy. I realized that he must be considerably older than he had given us to understand. This, of course, will mean that there are wrong entries on his cards.

The actual notification to the redundant staff passed off rather better, in a way, than I had anticipated. By that time everyone in the office seemed inexplicably conversant with the details, and several of them in fact had gone far beyond their terms of reference, young Patel, for instance, who openly admits that he will be leaving us as soon as he can get a better job, taking me aside and telling me that to such a man as Singlebury dismissal would be like death. Dismissal is not the right word, I said. But death is, Patel replied. Singlebury himself, however, took it very quietly. Even when I raised the question of the Company's Early Retirement pension scheme, which I could not pretend was over-generous, he said very little. He was generally felt to be in a state of shock. The two girls whom you asked me to speak to were quite unaffected, having already found themselves employments as hostesses at the Dolphinarium near here. Mrs Horrocks, of Filing, on the other hand, *did* protest, and was so offensive on the question of severance pay that I was obliged to agree to refer it to a higher level. I consider this as one of the hardest day's work that I have ever done for the Company.

Just before his month's notice (if we are to call it that) was up, Singlebury, to my great surprise, asked me to come home with him one evening for a meal. In all the past years the idea of his having a home, still less asking anyone back to it, had never arisen, and I did not at all want to go there now. I felt sure, too, that he would want to reopen the matter of compensation, and only a quite unjustified feeling of guilt made me accept. We took an Underground together after work, travelling in the late rush-hour to Clapham North, and walked some distance in the rain. His place, when we eventually got to it, seemed particularly inconvenient, the entrance being through a small cleaner's shop. It consisted of one room and a shared toilet on the half-landing. The room itself was tidy, arranged, so it struck me, much on the lines of his cubby-hole, but the window was shut and it was oppressively stuffy. This is where I bury myself, said Singlebury.

There were no cooking arrangements and he left me there while he went down to fetch us something ready to eat from the Steakorama next to the cleaner's. In his absence I took the opportunity to examine his room, though of course not in an inquisitive or prying manner. I was struck by the fact that none of his small store of stationery had been brought home from the office. He returned with two steaks wrapped in aluminium foil, evidently a special treat in my honour, and afterwards he went out on to the landing and made cocoa, a drink which I had not tasted for more than thirty years. The evening dragged rather. In the course of conversation it turned out that Singlebury was fond of reading. There were in fact several issues of a colour-printed encyclopaedia which he had been collecting as it came out, but unfortunately it had ceased publication after the seventh part. Reading is my hobby, he said. I pointed out that a hobby was rather something that one did with one's hands or in the open air – a relief from the work of the brain. Oh, I don't accept that distinction, Singlebury said. The mind and the body are the same. Well, one cannot deny the connection, I replied. Fear, for example, releases adrenalin, which directly affects the nerves. I don't mean connection, I mean identity, Singlebury said, the mind is the blood. Nonsense, I said, you might just as well tell me that the blood is the mind. It stands to reason that the blood can't think.

I was right, after all, in thinking that he would refer to the matter of the redundancy. This was not till he was seeing me off at the bus-stop, when for a moment he turned his grey, exposed-looking face away from me and said that he did not see how he could manage if he really had to go. He stood there like someone who has 'tried to give satisfaction' – he even used this phrase, saying that if the expression were not redolent of a bygone age, he would like to feel he had given satisfaction. Fortunately we had not long to wait for the 45 bus.

At the expiry of the month the staff gave a small tea-party for those who were leaving. I cannot describe this occasion as a success.

The following Monday I missed Singlebury as a familiar presence and also, as mentioned above, because I had never quite realized how much work he had been taking upon himself. As a direct consequence of losing him I found myself having to stay late – not altogether unwillingly, since although following general instructions I have discouraged overtime, the extra pay in my own case would be instrumental in making ends meet. Meanwhile Singlebury's desk had not been cleared – that is, of the trays, pencil-sharpener and complimentary calendar which were, of course, office property. The feeling that he would come back – not like Mrs Horrocks, who has rung up and called round incessantly – but simply come back to work out of habit and through not knowing what else to do, was very strong, without being openly mentioned. I myself half expected and dreaded it, and I had mentally prepared two or three lines of argument in order to persuade him, if he *did* come, not to try it again. Nothing happened, however, and on the Thursday I personally removed the 'things' from the cubby-hole into my own room.

Meanwhile in order to dispel certain quite unfounded rumours I thought it best to issue a notice for general circulation, pointing out that if Mr Singlebury should turn out to have taken any unwise step, and if in consequence any inquiry should be necessary, we should be the first to hear about it from the police. I dictated this to our only permanent typist, who immediately said, oh, he would never do that. He would never cause any unpleasantness like bringing police into the place, he'd do all he could to avoid that. I did not encourage any further discussion, but I asked my wife, who is very used to social work, to call round at Singlebury's place in Clapham North and find out how he was. She did not have very much luck. The people in the cleaner's shop knew, or thought they knew, that he was away, but they had not been sufficiently interested to ask where he was going.

On Friday young Patel said he would be leaving, as the damp and the smell were affecting his health. The damp is certainly not drying out in this seasonably warm weather.

I also, as you know, received another invitation on the Friday, at very short notice, in fact no notice at all; I was told to come to your house in Suffolk Park Gardens that evening for drinks. I was not unduly elated, having been asked once before after I had done rather an awkward small job for you. In our Company, justice has not only not to be done, but it must be seen not to be done. The food was quite nice; it came from your Caterers Grade 3. I spent most of the evening talking to Ted Hollow, one of the area sales-managers. I did not expect to be introduced to your wife, nor was I. Towards the end of the evening you spoke to me for three minutes in the small room with a green marble floor and matching wallpaper leading to the ground-floor toilets. You asked me if everything was all right, to which I replied, all right for whom? You said that nobody's fault was nobody's funeral. I said that I had tried to give satisfaction. Passing on towards the washbasins, you told me with seeming cordiality to be careful and watch it when I had had mixed drinks.

I would describe my feeling at this point as resentment, and I cannot identify exactly the moment when it passed into unease. I do know that I was acutely uneasy as I crossed the hall and saw two of your domestic staff, a man and a woman, holding my coat, which I had left in the lobby, and apparently trying to brush it. Your domestic staff all appear to be of foreign extraction and I personally feel sorry for them and do not grudge them a smile at the oddly assorted guests. Then I saw they were not smiling at my coat but that they seemed to be examining their fingers and looking at me earnestly and silently, and the collar or shoulders of my coat was covered with blood. As I came up to them, although they were still both absolutely silent, the illusion or impression passed, and I put on my coat and left the house in what I hope was a normal manner.

I now come to the present time. The feeling of uneasiness which I have described as making itself felt in your house has not diminished during this past weekend, and partly to take my mind off it and partly for the reasons I have given, I decided to work over-time again tonight, Monday the twenty-third. This was in spite of the fact that the damp smell had become almost a stench, as of something putrid, which must have affected my nerves to some extent, because when I went out to get something to eat at Dino's I left the lights on, both in my own office and in the entrance hall. I mean that for the first time since I began to work for the Company I left them on deliberately. As I walked to the corner I looked back and saw the two solitary lights looking somewhat forlorn in contrast to the glitter of the Arab-American Mutual Loan Corporation opposite. After my meal I felt absolutely reluctant to go back to the building, and wished then that I had not given way to the impulse to leave the lights on, but since I had done so and they must be turned off, I had no choice.

As I stood in the empty hallway I could hear the numerous creakings, settlings and faint tickings of an old building, possibly associated with the plumbing system. The lifts for reasons of economy do not operate after 6.30 p.m., so I began to walk up the stairs. After one flight I felt a strong creeping tension in the nerves of the back such as any of us feel when there is danger from behind; one might say that the body was thinking for itself on these occasions. I did not look round, but simply continued upwards as rapidly as I could. At the third floor I paused, and could hear footsteps coming patiently up behind me. This was not a surprise; I had been expecting them all evening.

Just at the door of my own office, or rather of the cubby-hole, for I have to pass through that, I turned, and saw at the end of the dim corridor what I had also expected, Singlebury, advancing towards me with his unmistakable shuffling step. My first reaction was a kind of bewilderment as to why he, who had been such an excellent timekeeper, so regular day by day, should become a creature of the night. He was wearing the blue suit. This I could make out by its familiar outline, but it was not till he came halfway down the corridor towards me, and reached the patch of light falling through the window from the street, that I saw that he was not himself – I mean that his head was nodding or rather swivelling irregularly from side to side. It crossed my mind that Singlebury was drunk. I had never known him drunk or indeed seen him take anything to drink, even at the office Christmas party, but one cannot estimate the effect that trouble will have upon a man. I began to think what steps I should take in this situation. I turned on the light in his cubby-hole as I went through and waited at the entrance of my own office. As he appeared in the outer doorway I saw that I had not been correct about the reason for the odd movement of the head. The throat was cut from ear to ear so that the head was nearly severed from the shoulders. It was this which had given the impression of nodding, or rather, lolling. As he walked into his cubby-hole Singlebury raised both hands and tried to steady the head as though conscious that something was wrong. The eyes were thickly filmed over, as one sees in the carcasses in a butcher's shop.

I shut and locked my door, and not wishing to give way to nausea, or to lose all control of myself, I sat down at my desk. My work was waiting for me as I had left it – it was the file on the matter of the damp elimination – and, there not being anything else to do, I tried to look through it. On the other side of the door I could hear Singlebury sit down also, and then try the drawers of the table, evidently looking for the 'things' without which he could not start work. After the drawers had been tried, one after another, several times, there was almost total silence.

The present position is that I am locked in my own office and would not, no matter what you offered me, indeed I could not, go out through the cubby-hole and pass what is sitting at the desk. The early cleaners will not be here for seven hours and forty-five minutes. I have passed the time so far as best I could in writing this report. One consideration strikes me. If what I have next door is a visitant which should not be walking but buried in the earth, then its wound cannot bleed, and there will be no stream of blood moving slowly under the whole width of the communicating door. However, I am sitting at the moment with my back to the door, so that, without turning round, I have no means of telling whether it has done so or not.

BETTY

Margaret Atwood

Margaret Atwood (b. 1939) is a Canadian writer and environmental activist. She is amongst the most honoured authors of fiction in recent history. She is a winner of the Arthur C. Clarke Award and has been shortlisted for the Man Booker Prize five times, winning in 2000 for her novel *The Blind Assassin*. She is the author of more than fifty volumes of poetry, children's literature, fiction and non-fiction.

When I was seven we moved again, to a tiny wooden cottage on the Saint Marys River, upstream from Sault Sainte Marie. We were only renting the cottage for the summer, but for the time being it was our house, since we had no other. It was dim and mousy-smelling and very cramped, stuffed with all the things from the place before that were not in storage. My sister and I preferred to spend most of our time outside it.

There was a short beach, behind which the cottages, with their contrasting trim – green against white, maroon against robin's-egg blue, brown against yellow – were lined up like little shoeboxes, each with its matching outhouse at an unsanitary distance behind. But we were forbidden to swim in the water, because of the strong current. There were stories of children who had been swept away, down toward the rapids and the locks and the Algoma Steel fires of the Soo which we could sometimes see from our bedroom window on overcast nights, glowing dull red against the clouds. We were allowed to wade though, no further than the knee, and we would stand in the water, strands of loose weed tangling against our ankles, and wave at the lake freighters as they slid past, so close we could see not only the flags and sea gulls at their stems but the hands of the sailors and the ovals of their faces as they waved back to us. Then the waves would come, washing over our thighs up to the waists of our bloomered and skirted seersucker bathing suits, and we would scream with delight.

Our mother, who was usually on the shore, reading or talking to someone but not quite watching us, would sometimes mistake the screams for drowning. Or she would say later, "You've been in over your knees," but my sister would explain that it was only the boat waves. My mother would look at me to see if this was the truth. Unlike my sister, I was a clumsy liar.

The freighters were huge, cumbersome, with rust staining the holes for their anchor chains and enormous chimneys from which the smoke spurted in grey burps. When they blew their horns, as they always did when approaching the locks, the windows in our cottage rattled. For us, they were magical. Sometimes things would drop or be thrown from them, and we would watch these floating objects eagerly, running along the beach to be there when they landed, wading out to fish them in. Usually these treasures turned out to be only empty cardboard boxes or punctured oil cans, oozing dark brown grease and good for nothing. Several times we got orange crates, which we used as cupboards or stools in our hideouts.

We liked the cottage partly because we had places to make these hideouts. There had never been room before, since we had always lived in cities. Just before this it was Ottawa, the ground floor of an old three-tiered red-brick apartment building. On the floor above us lived a newly married couple, the wife English and Protestant, the husband French and Catholic. He was in the Air Force, and was away a lot, but when he came back on leave he used to beat up his wife. It was always about eleven o'clock at night. She would flee downstairs to my mother for protection, and they would sit in the kitchen with cups of tea. The wife would cry, though quietly, so as not to wake us – my mother insisted on that, being a believer in twelve hours of sleep for children – display her bruised eye or cheek, and whisper about his drinking. After an hour or so there would be a discreet knock on the door, and the airman, in full uniform, would ask my mother politely if he could have his wife back upstairs where she belonged. It was a religious dispute, he would say. Besides, he'd given her fifteen dollars to spend on food and she had served him fried Kam. After being away a month, a man expected a good roast, pork or beef, didn't my mother agree? "I kept my mouth shut and my eyes open," my mother would say. He never seemed that drunk to her, but with the polite kind you couldn't tell what they would do.

I wasn't supposed to know about any of this. I was considered either too young or too good; but my sister, who was four years older, was given hints, which she passed along to me with whatever she thought fit to add. I saw the wife a number of times, going up or down the stairs outside our door, and once she did have a black eye. I never saw the man, but by the time we left Ottawa I was convinced he was a murderer.

This might have explained my father's warning when my mother told him she had met the young couple who lived in the right-hand cottage. "Don't get too involved," he said. "I don't want her running over here at all hours of the night." He had little patience with my mother's talents as a sympathetic listener, even when she teased him by saying, "But I listen to you, dear." She attracted people he called sponges.

He didn't seem to have anything to worry about. This couple was very different from the other one. Fred and Betty insisted on being called Fred and Betty, right away. My sister and I, who had been drilled to call people Mr. and Mrs., had to call them Fred and Betty also, and we could go over to their house whenever we wanted to. "I don't want you to take that at face value," our mother said. Times were hard but our mother had been properly brought up, and we were going to be, too. Nevertheless, at first we went to Fred and Betty's as often as we could.

Their cottage was exactly the same size as ours, but since there was less furniture in it it seemed bigger. Ours had Ten-Test walls between the rooms, painted lime green, with lighter squares on the paint where other people had once hung pictures. Betty had replaced her walls with real plywood and painted the inside bright yellow, and she'd made yellow and white curtains for the kitchen, a print of chickens coming out of eggshells. She'd sewed herself a matching apron from the leftover material. They owned their cottage rather than renting it; as my mother said, you didn't mind doing the work then. Betty called the tiny kitchen a kitchenette. There was a round ironwork table tucked into one corner, with two scrolled ironwork chairs, painted white, one for Betty and one for Fred. Betty called this corner the breakfast nook.

There was more to do at Fred and Betty's than at our house. They had a bird made of hollow coloured glass that perched on the edge of a tumbler of water, teetering back and forth until it would finally dip its head into the water and take a drink. They had a front door knocker in the shape of a woodpecker, you pulled a string, and the woodpecker pecked at the door. They also had a whistle in the shape of a bird that you could fill with water and blow into and it would warble, "like a canary," Betty said. And they took the Saturday coloured funnies. Our parents didn't, and they didn't like us reading trash, as they called it. But Fred and Betty were so friendly and kind to us, what, as my mother said, could they do?

Beyond all these attractions there was Fred. We both fell in love with Fred. My sister would climb into his lap and announce that he was her boyfriend and she was going to marry him when she grew up. She would then make him read the funnies to her and tease him by trying to take the pipe out of his mouth or by tying his shoelaces together. I felt the same way, but I knew it was no good saying so. My sister had staked her claim, when she said she was going to do a thing she usually did it. And she hated my being what she called a copycat. So I would sit in the breakfast nook on one of the scrolled ironwork chairs while Betty made coffee, watching my sister and Fred on the living-room couch.

There was something about Fred that attracted people. My mother, who was not a flirtatious woman – she went in for wisdom, instead – was livelier when he was around. Even my father liked him, and would sometimes have a beer with him when he got back from the city. They would sit on the porch of Fred's cottage in Betty's yellow wicker chairs, swatting at the sand flies and discussing baseball scores. They seldom mentioned their jobs. I'm not sure what Fred did, but it was in an office. My father was "in wallpaper," my mother said, but I was never very clear about what that meant. It was more exciting when they talked about the war. My father's bad back had kept him out of it, much to his disgust, but Fred had been in the Navy. He never said too much about it, though my father was always prompting him; but we knew from Betty that they were engaged just before Fred left and married right after he came back. Betty had written letters to him every single night and mailed them once a week. She did not say how often Fred had written to her. My father didn't like many people, but he said that Fred wasn't a fool.

Fred didn't seem to make any efforts to be nice to people. I don't think he was even especially handsome. The difficulty is that though I can remember Betty down to the last hair and freckle, I can't remember what Fred looked like. He had dark hair and a pipe, and he used to sing to us if we pestered him enough. "Sioux City Sue," he would sing, "Your hair is red, your eyes are blue, I'd swap my horse and dog for you … " Or he would sing "Beautiful Brown Eyes" to my sister, whose eyes were brown as compared with my own watery blue. This hurt my feelings, as the song contained the line, "I'll never love blue eyes again." It seemed so final, a whole lifetime of being unloved by Fred. Once I cried, which was made worse by the fact that I couldn't explain to anyone what was wrong; and I had to undergo the humiliation of Fred's jocular concern and my sister's scorn, and the worse humiliation of being comforted by Betty in the kitchenette. It was a humiliation because it was obvious even to me that Betty didn't grasp things very well. "Don't pay any attention to *him*," she said, having guessed that my tears had something to do with Fred. But that was the one piece of advice I couldn't take.

Fred, like a cat, wouldn't go two steps out of his way for you really, as my mother said later. So it was unfair that everyone was in love with Fred, but no one, despite her kindness, was in love with Betty. It was Betty who always greeted us at the door, asked us in, and talked to us while Fred slouched on the couch reading the paper. She fed us cookies and milk shakes and let us lick out the bowls when she was baking. Betty was such a nice person; everyone said so, but no one would have called Fred exactly that. Fred, for instance, did not laugh much, and he only smiled when he was making rude remarks, mostly to my sister. "Stuffing your face again?" he would say. "Hey, baggy pants." Whereas Betty never said things like that, and she was always either smiling or laughing.

She laughed a lot when Fred called her Betty Grable, which he did at least once a day. I couldn't see why she laughed. It was supposed to be a compliment, I thought. Betty Grable was a famous movie star; there was a picture of her thumb-tacked to the wall in Fred and Betty's outhouse. Both my sister and I preferred Fred and Betty's outhouse to our own. Theirs had curtains on the window, unlike ours, and it had a little wooden box and a matching wooden scoop for the lye. We only had a cardboard box and an old trowel.

Betty didn't really look like Betty Grable, who was blonde and not as plump as our Betty. Still, they were both beautiful, I thought. I didn't realize until much later that the remark was cruel; for Betty Grable was renowned for her legs, whereas our Betty had legs that started at her waist and continued downwards without a curve or a pause until they reached her feet. At the time they seemed like ordinary legs. Sitting in the kitchenette, I saw a lot of Betty's legs, for she wore halter tops and shorts, with her yellow apron over them. Somehow Betty could never get her legs to tan, despite the hours she spent crocheting in her wicker chair, the top part of her in the shade of the porch but her legs sticking out into the sun.

My father said that Betty had no sense of humour. I couldn't understand this at all. If you told her a joke she would always laugh, even if you got it mixed up, and she told jokes of her own, too. She would print the word "BED," making the E smaller and thicker than the B and the D. "What's this?" she would say. "It's the little dark E in BED." I didn't get this joke the first time she told it and she had to explain it to me. "Little darkie," she said, her slightly protruding teeth shining with good humour. We had never been to the United States, even though we could see it across the river, a strip of green trees that faded west into the blue of Lake Superior, and the only black people I had seen were the characters in the comics. There was L'il 8-Ball, and the Africans in Tarzan, and Lothar in

Mandrake the Magician, who wore a lion skin. I couldn't see what any of them had to do with the word "bed."

My father also said that Betty had no sex appeal. This didn't seem to bother my mother in the least. "She's a very nice girl," she would answer complacently, or, "She has very nice colouring." My mother and Betty were soon collaborating on a scheme for making the preserving easier. Most people still had Victory gardens, though the war was over, and the months of July and August were supposed to be spent putting up as many jars of fruit and vegetables as you could. My mother's garden was half-hearted, like most of her housekeeping efforts. It was a small patch beside the outhouse where squash vines rambled over a thicket of overgrown tomato plants and a few uneven lines of dwarfed carrots and beets. My mother's talent, we had heard her say, was for people. Betty and Fred didn't have a garden at all. Fred wouldn't have worked in it, and when I think of Betty now I realize that a garden would have been too uncontained for her. But she had Fred buy dozens of six-quart baskets of strawberries, peaches, beans, tomatoes and Concord grapes, on his trips into the city; and she persuaded my mother to give up on her own garden and join her in her mammoth canning sessions.

My mother's wood stove was unbearably hot for such an operation, and Betty's little electric range was too small; so Betty got "the boys," as she called Fred and my father, to set up the derelict wood stove that until then had been rusting behind Betty's outhouse. They put it in our backyard, and my mother and Betty would sit at our kitchen table, which had been carried outside, peeling, slicing and talking, Betty with her round pincushion cheeks flushed redder than usual by the heat and my mother with an old bandanna wrapped around her head, making her look like a gypsy. Behind them the canning kettles bubbled and steamed, and on one side of the table the growing ranks of Crown jars, inverted on layers of newspapers, cooled and sometimes leaked or cracked. My sister and I hung around the edges, not wanting to be obvious enough to be put to work, but coveting the empty six-quart baskets. We could use them in our hideout, we felt; we were never sure what for, but they fitted neatly into the orange crates.

I learned a lot about Fred during Betty's canning sessions: how he liked his eggs, what size socks he took (Betty was a knitter), how well he was doing at the office, what he refused to eat for dinner. Fred was a picky eater, Betty said joyfully. Betty had almost nothing else to talk about, and even my mother, veteran of many confidences, began to talk less and smoke more than usual when Betty was around. It was easier to listen to disasters than to Betty's inexhaustible and trivial cheer. I began to think that I might not want to be married to Fred after all. He unrolled from Betty's mouth like a long ribbon of soggy newspaper printed from end to end with nothing but the weather. Neither my sister nor I was interested in sock sizes, and Betty's random, unexciting details diminished Fred in our eyes. We began to spend less of our playtime at Fred and Betty's and more in our hideout; which was in a patch of scrubby oak on a vacant lot along the shore. There we played complicated games of Mandrake the Magician and his faithful servant Lothar, with our dolls as easily hypnotized villains. My sister was always Mandrake. When we tired of this we would put on our bathing suits and go wading along the shore, watching for freighters and throwing acorns into the river to see how quickly they would be carried away by the current.

It was on one of these wading expeditions that we met Nan. She lived ten lots down, in a white cottage with red trim. Unlike many of the other cottages, Nan's had a real dock, built out into the river and anchored around the posts with piles of rocks. She was sitting on this dock when we first saw her, chewing gum and flipping through a stack of airplane cards from Wings cigarettes. Everyone knew that only boys collected these. Her hair and her face were light brown, and she had a sleek plump sheen, like caramel pudding.

"What're you doing with *those*?" were my sister's first words. Nan only smiled.

That same afternoon Nan was allowed into our hideout, and after a cursory game of Mandrake, during which I was demoted to the lowly position of Narda, the two of them sat on our orange crates and exchanged what seemed to me to be languid and pointless comments.

"You ever go to the store?" Nan asked. We never did. Nan smiled some more. She was twelve, my sister was only eleven and three-quarters.

"There's cute boys at the store," Nan said. She was wearing a peasant blouse with a frill and an elastic top that she could slide down over her shoulders if she wanted to. She stuck her airplane cards into her shorts pocket and we went to ask my mother if we could walk to the store. After that, my sister and Nan went there almost every afternoon.

The store was a mile and a half from our cottage, a hot walk along the shore past the fronts of other cottages where fat mothers basked in the sun and other, possibly hostile children paddled in the water; past rowboats hauled up on the sand, along cement breakwaters, through patches of beach grass that cut your ankles if you ran through it and beach peas that were hard and bitter-tasting. In some places we could smell the outhouses. Just before the store, there was an open space with poison ivy, which we had to wade around.

The store had no name. It was just "the store," the only store for the cottagers since it was the only one they could walk to. I was allowed to go with my sister and Nan, or rather, my mother insisted that I go. Although I hadn't said anything to her about it, she could sense my misery. It wasn't so much my sister's desertion that hurt, but her blithe unconsciousness of it. She was quite willing to play with me when Nan wasn't around.

Sometimes, when the sight of my sister and Nan conspiring twenty paces ahead of me made me too unhappy, I would double back and go to Fred and Betty's. There I would sit facing backwards on one of Betty's kitchen chairs, my two hands rigid in the air, holding a skein of sky blue wool while Betty wound it into balls. Or, under Betty's direction, I crocheted sweaty, uneven little pink and yellow dolls' dresses for the dolls my sister was, suddenly, too old to play with.

On better days I would make it as far as the store. It was not beautiful or even clean, but we were so used to wartime drabness and grime that we didn't notice. It was a two-storey building of unpainted wood which had weathered grey. Parts of it were patched with tar paper, and it had coloured metal signs nailed around the front screen door and windows: Coca-Cola, 7-Up, Salada Tea. Inside, it had the sugary, mournful smell of old general stores, a mixture of the cones for the icecream cones, the packages of Oreo cookies, the open boxes of jawbreakers and licorice whips that lined the counter, and that other smell, musky and sharp, part dry-rot and part sweat. The bottles of pop were kept in a metal cooler with a heavy lid, filled with cold water and chunks of ice melted to the smoothness of the sand-scoured pieces of glass we sometimes found on the beach.

The owner of the store and his wife lived on the second floor, but we almost never saw them. The store was run by their two daughters, who took turns behind the counter. They were both dark and they both wore shorts and polka-dot halter tops, but one was friendly and the other one, the thinner, younger one, was not. She would take our pennies and ring them into the cash register without saying a word, staring over our heads out the front window with its dangling raisin-covered fly-papers as if she was completely detached from the activity her hands were performing. She didn't dislike us; she just didn't see us. She wore her hair long and done in a sort of roll at the front, and her lipstick was purplish.

The first time we went to the store we found out why Nan collected airplane cards. There were two boys there, sitting on the grey, splintery front steps, their arms crossed over their knees. I had been told by my sister that the right thing to do with boys was to ignore them, otherwise they would pester you. But these boys knew Nan, and they spoke to her, not with the usual taunts, but with respect.

"You got anything new?" one of them said.

Nan smiled, brushed back her hair and wiggled her shoulders a little inside her peasant blouse. Then she slid her airplane cards slowly out of her shorts pocket and began riffling through them.

"You got any?" the other boy said to my sister. For once she was humbled. After that, she got my mother to switch brands and built up her own pack. I saw her in front of the mirror about a week later, practising that tantalizing slide, the cards coming out of her pocket like a magician's snake.

When I went to the store I always had to bring back a loaf of wax-papered bread for my mother, and sometimes a package of "Jiffy" Pie Crust, if they had any. My sister never had to: she had already discovered the advantages of being unreliable. As payment, and, I'm sure, as compensation for my unhappiness, my mother gave me a penny a trip, and when I had saved five of these pennies I bought my first Popsicle. Our mother had always refused to buy them for us, although she permitted ice-cream cones. She said there was something in Popsicles that was bad for you, and as I sat on the front steps of the store, licking down to the wooden stick, I kept looking for this thing. I visualized it as a sort of core, like the white fingernail-shaped part in a kernel of corn, but I couldn't find anything.

My sister and Nan were sitting beside me on the front steps. There were no boys at the store that day, so they had nothing else to do. It was even hotter than usual, and airless; there was a shimmer over the river, and the freighters wavered as they passed through it. My Popsicle was melting almost before I could eat it. I had given my sister half of it; which she had taken without the gratitude I had hoped for. She was sharing it with Nan.

Fred came around the corner of the building and headed towards the front door. This was no surprise, as we had seen him at the store several times before.

"Hi, beautiful," he said to my sister. We moved our rumps along the step to let him in the door.

After quite a long time he came out, carrying a loaf of bread. He asked us if we wanted a lift with him in his car: he was just coming back from the city, he said. Of course we said yes. There was nothing unusual about any of this, except that the daughter, the thinner, purple one, stepped outside the door and stood on the steps as we were driving off. She folded her arms across her chest in that slump-shouldered pose of women idling in doorways. She wasn't smiling. I thought she had come out to watch the Canada Steamship lines freighter that was going past, but then I saw that she was staring at Fred. She looked as if she wanted to kill him.

Fred didn't seem to notice. He sang all the way home. "Katy, oh beautiful Katy," he sang, winking at my sister, whom he sometimes called Katy since her name was Catherine. He had the windows open, and dust from the rutted gravel road poured over us, whitening our eyebrows and turning Fred's hair grey. At every jolt my sister and Nan screamed gleefully, and after a while I forgot my feelings of exclusion and screamed too.

It seemed as if we had lived in the cottage for a long time, though it was only one summer. By August I could hardly remember the apartment in Ottawa and the man who used to beat up his wife. That had happened in a remote life; and, despite the sunshine, the water, the open space, a happier one. Before, our frequent moves and the insecurities of new schools had forced my sister to value me: I was four years younger, but I was loyal and always there. Now those years were a canyon between us, an empty stretch like a beach along which I could see her disappearing ahead of me. I longed to be just like her, but I could no longer tell what she was like.

In the third week of August the leaves started to turn, not all at once, just a single red one here and there, like a warning. That meant it would soon be time for school and another move. We didn't even know where we would be moving to this time, and when Nan asked us what school we went to, we were evasive.

"I've been to eight different schools," my sister said proudly. Because I was so much younger, I had only been to two. Nan, who had been to the same one all her life, slipped the edge of her peasant blouse over her shoulders and down to her elbows to show us that her breasts were growing. The rings around her nipples had softened and started to puff out; otherwise she was as flat as my sister.

"So what," said my sister, rolling up her jersey. This was a competition I couldn't be part of. It was about change, and, increasingly, change frightened me. I walked back along the beach to Betty's house, where my latest piece of grubby crocheting was waiting for me and where everything was always the same.

I knocked on the screen door and opened it. I meant to say, "Can I come in?" the way we always did, but I didn't say it. Betty was sitting by herself at the iron table of the breakfast nook. She had on her shorts and a striped sailor top, navy blue and white with a little anchor pin, and the apron with the yellow chickens coming out of their eggs. For once she wasn't doing anything, and there was no cup of coffee in front of her. Her face was white and uncomprehending, as if someone had just hit her for no reason.

She saw me, but she didn't smile or ask me in. "What am I going to do?" she said.

I looked around the kitchen. Everything was in its place: the percolator gleamed from the stove, the glass bird was teetering slowly down, there were no broken dishes, no water on the floor. What had happened?

"Are you sick?" I said.

"There's nothing I can do," Betty said.

She looked so strange that I was frightened. I ran out of the kitchen and across the hillocky grass to get to my mother, who always knew what should be done.

"There's something wrong with Betty," I said.

My mother was mixing something in a bowl. She rubbed her hands together to get the dough off, then wiped them on her apron. She didn't look surprised or ask me what it was. "You stay here," she said. She picked up her package of cigarettes and went out the door.

That evening we had to go to bed early because my mother wanted to talk to my father. We listened, of course; it was easy through the Ten-Test walls.

"I saw it coming," my mother said. "A mile away."

"Who is it?" my father said.

"She doesn't know," said my mother. "Some girl from town."

"Betty's a fool," my father said. "She always was." Later, when husbands and wives leaving each other became more common, he often said this, but no matter which one had left it was always the woman he called the fool. His highest compliment to my mother was that she was no fool.

"That may be," said my mother. "But you'd never want to meet a nicer girl. He was her whole life,"

My sister and I whispered together. My sister's theory was that Fred had run away from Betty with another woman. I couldn't believe this: I had never heard of such a thing happening. I was so upset I couldn't sleep, and for a long time after that I was anxious whenever my father was away overnight, as he frequently was. What if he never came back?

We didn't see Betty after that. We knew she was in her cottage, because every day my mother carried over samples of her tough and lumpy baking, almost as if someone had died. But we were given strict orders to stay away, and not to go peering in the windows as our mother must have known we longed to do. "She's having a nervous breakdown," our mother said, which for me called up an image of Betty lying disjointed on the floor like a car at the garage.

We didn't even see her on the day we got into my father's second-hand Studebaker, the back seat packed to the window-tops with only a little oblong space for me to crouch in, and drove out to the main highway to begin the six hundred-mile journey south to Toronto. My father had changed jobs again; he was now in building materials, and he was sure, since the country was having a boom, that this was finally the right change. We spent September and part of October in a motel while my father looked for a house. I had my eighth birthday and my sister turned twelve. Then there was another new school, and I almost forgot about Betty.

But a month after I had turned twelve myself Betty was suddenly there one night for dinner. We had people for dinner a lot more than we used to, and sometimes the dinners were so important that my sister and I ate first. My sister didn't care, as she had boyfriends by that time. I was still in public school and had to wear lisle stockings instead of the seamed nylons my sister was permitted. Also, I had braces. My sister had had braces at that age too, but she had somehow managed to make them seem rakish and daring, so that I had longed for a mouthful of flashing silver teeth like hers. But she no longer had them, and my own mouth in its shackles felt clumsy and muffled.

"You remember Betty," my mother said.

"Elizabeth," Betty said.

"Oh yes, of course," said my mother.

Betty had changed a lot. Before, she had been a little plump; now she was buxom. Her cheeks were as round and florid as two tomatoes, and I thought she was using too much rouge until I saw that the red was caused by masses of tiny veins under her skin. She was wearing a long black pleated skirt, a white short-sleeved angora sweater with a string of black beads, and open-toed black velvet pumps with high heels. She smelled strong of Lily of the Valley. She had a job, my mother told my father later; a very good job. She was an executive secretary, and now called herself Miss instead of Mrs.

"She's doing very well," my mother said, "considering what happened. She's pulled herself together."

"I hope you don't start inviting her to dinner all the time," said my father, who still found Betty irritating in spite of her new look. She laughed more than ever now, and crossed her legs frequently.

"I feel I'm the only real friend she has," said my mother. She didn't say Betty was the only real friend she had, though when my father said "your friend" everyone knew who he meant My mother had a lot of friends, and her talent for wise listening was now a business asset for my father.

"She says she'll never marry again," said my mother.

"She's a fool," my father said.

"If I ever saw anyone cut out for marriage, it was her," said my mother. This remark increased my anxiety about any own future. If all Betty's accomplishments had not been enough for Fred, what hope was there for me? I did not have my sister's natural flair, but I had thought there would be some tricks I could learn, dutifully, painstakingly. We were taking Home Economics at school and the teacher kept saying that the way to a man's heart was through his stomach. I knew this wasn't true – my mother was still a slapdash cook, and when she gave the best dinners she had a woman in to help – but I laboured over my blanc-mange and Harvard beets as if I believed it.

My mother started inviting Betty to dinner with men who were not married. Betty smiled and laughed and several of the men seemed interested, but nothing came of it.

"After the way she was hurt, I'm not surprised," my mother said. I was now old enough to be told things, and besides, my sister was never around. "I heard it was a secretary at his company he ran off with. They even got married, after the divorce." There was something else about Betty, she told me, although I must never mention it as Betty found it very distressing. Fred's brother, who was a dentist, had killed his wife because he got involved – my mother said "involved" richly, as if it was a kind of dessert – with his dental technician. He had put his wife into the car and run a tube in from the exhaust pipe, and then tried to pretend it was suicide. The police had found out though, and he was in jail.

This made Betty much more interesting in my eyes. It was in Fred's blood, then, the tendency towards involvement. In fact it could just as easily have been

Betty herself who had been murdered. I now came to see Betty's laugh as the mask of a stricken and martyred woman. She was not just a wife who had been deserted. Even I could see that this was not a tragic position, it was a ridiculous and humiliating one. She was much more than that: she was a woman who had narrowly escaped death. That Betty herself saw it this way I soon had no doubt. There was something smug and even pious about the way she kept Mother's single men at a polite distance, something faintly nunlike. A lurid aura of sacrificial blood surrounded her. Betty had been there, she had passed through it, she had come out alive, and now she was dedicating herself to, well, to something else.

But it was hard for me to sustain this version of Betty for long. My mother soon ran out of single men and Betty, when she came to dinner, came alone. She talked as incessantly about the details surrounding the other women at her office as she had about Fred. We soon knew how they all took their coffee, which ones lived with their mothers, where they had their hair done, and what their apartments looked like. Betty herself had a darling apartment on Avenue Road, and she had redone it all herself and even made the slipcovers. Betty was as devoted to her boss as she had once been to Fred. She did all his Christmas shopping, and each year we heard what he had given to his employees, what to his wife and children, and what each item had cost. Betty seemed, in a way, quite happy.

We saw a lot of Betty around Christmas; my mother said she felt sorry for her because she had no family. Betty was in the habit of giving us Christmas presents that made it obvious she thought we were younger than we were. She favoured Parcheesi sets and angora mittens a size too small. I lost interest in her. Even her unending cheerfulness came to seem like a perversion, or a defect almost like idiocy. I was fifteen now and in the throes of adolescent depression. My sister was away at Queen's; sometimes she gave me clothes she no longer wanted. She was not exactly beautiful – both her eyes and her mouth were too large – but everyone called her vivacious. They called me nice. My braces had come off, but it didn't seem to make any difference. What right had Betty to be cheerful? When she came to dinner, I excused myself early and went to my room.

One afternoon, in the spring of Grade Eleven, I came home from school to find my mother sitting at the dining-room table. She was crying, which was so rare that my immediate fear was that something had happened to my father. I didn't think he had left her, that particular anxiety was past. But perhaps he had been killed in a car crash.

"Mum, what is it?" I said.

"Bring me a glass of water," she said. She drank some of it and pushed back her hair. "I'm all right now," she said. "I just had a call from Betty. It was very upsetting; she said horrible things to me."

"Why?" I said. "What did you do?"

"She accused me of … horrible things." My mother swabbed at her eyes. "She was screaming. I've never heard Betty scream in my life before. After all that time I spent with her. She said she never wanted to speak to me again. Where would she get such an idea?"

"What idea?" I said. I was just as mystified as my mother was. My mother was a bad cook, but she was a good woman. I could not imagine her doing anything that would make anyone want to scream at her.

My mother held back slightly. "Things about Fred," she said. "She must be crazy. I hadn't seen her for a couple of months, and then suddenly, just like that."

"There must be something wrong with her," my father said at dinner that night. Of course he was right. Betty had an undetected brain tumour, which was discovered when her strange behaviour was noticed at the office. She died in the hospital two months later, but my mother didn't hear about it till afterwards. She was contrite; she felt she should have visited her friend in the hospital, despite the abusive phone call.

"I ought to have known it was something like that," she said. "Personality change, that's one of the clues." In the course of her listening, my mother had picked up a great deal of information about terminal illnesses.

But for me, this explanation wasn't good enough. For years after that, Betty followed me around, waiting for me to finish her off in some way more satisfactory to both of us. When I first heard about her death I felt doomed. This, then, was the punishment for being devoted and obliging, this was what happened to girls such as (I felt) myself. When I opened the high-school yearbook and my own face, in pageboy haircut and tentative, appeasing smile, stared back at me, it was Betty's eyes I superimposed on mine. She had been kind to me when I was a child, and with the callousness of children towards those who are kind but not enchanting, I had preferred Fred. In my future I saw myself being abandoned by a succession of Freds who were running down the beach after a crowd of vivacious girls, all of whom looked remarkably like my sister. As for Betty's final screams of hatred and rage, they were screams of protest against the unfairness of life. That anger, I knew, was my own, the dark side of that terrible and deforming niceness that had marked Betty like the aftermath of some crippling disease.

People change, though, especially after they are dead. As I passed beyond the age of melodrama I came to see that if I did not want to be Betty, I would have to be someone else. Furthermore, I was already quite different from Betty. In a way, she had absolved me from making the demanded choices by having made them so thoroughly herself. People stopped calling me a nice girl and started calling me a clever one, and after a while I enjoyed this. Betty herself, baking oatmeal cookies in the ephemeral sunlight of fifteen years before, slid back into three dimensions. She was an ordinary woman who had died too young of an incurable disease. Was that it, was that all?

From time to time I would like to have Betty back, if only for an hour's conversation. I would like her to forgive me for my rejection of her angora mittens, for my secret betrayals of her, for my adolescent contempt. I would like to show her this story I have told about her and ask her if any of it is true. But I can think of nothing I want to ask her that I could phrase in a way that she would care to understand. She would only laugh in her accepting, uncomprehending way and offer me something, a chocolate brownie, a ball of wool.

Fred, on the other hand, no longer intrigues me. The Freds of this world make themselves explicit by what they do and choose. It is the Bettys who are mysterious.

A WORLD OF HER OWN

Penelope Lively

Penelope Lively (b. 1933) is a critically acclaimed British author of fiction for both children and adults. She won the Carnegie Medal for children's fiction in 1973, for *The Ghost of Thomas Kempe*, and also the Man Booker Prize for her 1987 novel, *Moon Tiger*. Lively was made Dame Commander of the Order of the British Empire in the 2012 New Year Honours list.

My sister Lisa is an artist: she is not like other people.

Lisa is two years younger than I am, and we knew quite early on that she was artistic, partly because she could always draw so nicely, but also because of the way she behaved. She lives in a world of her own, our mother used to say. She was always the difficult one, always having tempers and tantrums and getting upset about one thing and another, but once mother realised about her being artistic she made allowances. We all did. She's got real talent, the art master at school said, you'll have to take care of that, Mrs Harris, she's going to need all the help she can get. And mother was thrilled to bits, she's always admired creative people, she'd have loved to be able to write or paint herself but having Lisa turn out that way was the next best thing, or better, even, perhaps. When Lisa was fifteen mother went to work at Luigi's, behind the counter, to save up so there'd be a bit extra in hand for Lisa, when she went to art school. Father had died three years before. It worried me rather, mother going out to work like that; she's had asthma on and off for years now, and besides she felt awkward, serving in a shop. But the trouble is, she's not qualified at anything, and in any case, as she said, a delicatessen isn't quite like an ordinary grocer or a supermarket.

I was at college, by then, doing my teaching diploma. Lisa went to one of the London art schools, and came back at the end of her first term looking as weird as anything, you'd hardly have known her, her hair dyed red and wearing black clothes with pop art cut-outs stuck on and I don't know what. It was just as well mother *had* saved up, because it all turned out much more expensive than we'd thought, even with Lisa's grant. There was so much she had to do, like going to plays and things, and of course she needed smarter clothes, down there, and more of them, and then the next year she had to travel on the continent all the summer, to see great paintings and architecture. She was away for months, we hardly saw anything of her, and when she came back she'd changed completely all over again – her hair was blonde and frizzed out, and she was wearing a lot of leather things, very expensive, boots up to her thighs and long suede coats. She came home for Christmas and sometimes she was gay and chatty and made everybody laugh and other times she was bad-tempered and moody, but as mother said, she'd always been like that, from a little girl, and of course you had to expect it, with her temperament.

Mother had left Luigi's by then, some time before, because of her leg (she got this trouble with her veins, which meant she mustn't stand much) but she started doing a bit of work at home, for pin-money, making cushions and curtains for people: she's always been good at needlework, she sometimes says she wonders if possibly that's where Lisa's creativity came from, if maybe there's something in the family …

It missed me out, if there is. Still, I got my diploma (I did rather well, as it happens, one of the best in my year) and started teaching and not long after that I married Jim, whom I'd known at college, and we had the children quite soon, because I thought I'd go back to work later, when they were at school.

Lisa finished at her art college, and got whatever it is they get, and then she couldn't find a job. At least she didn't want any of the jobs she could have got, like window-dressing or jobs on magazines or for publishers or that kind of thing. And can you blame her, said mother, I mean, what a waste of her talents, it's ridiculous, all that time she's spent developing herself, and then they expect her to be tied down to some nine-to-five job like anyone else!

Lisa was fed up. She had to come and live at home. Mother turned out of her bedroom and had the builders put a skylight in and made it into a studio for Lisa, really very nice, with a bare polished floor and a big new easel mother got by selling that silver tea-set that was a wedding present (she says she never really liked it anyway). But then it turned out Lisa didn't do that kind of painting, but funny things to do with bits of material all sort of glued together, and coloured paper cut out and stuck on to other sheets of paper. And when she did paint or draw it would be squatting on the floor, or lying on her stomach on the sofa.

I can't make head nor tail of the kind of art Lisa does. I mean, I just don't *know* if it's any good or not. But then, I wouldn't, would I? Nor Jim, nor mother, nor any of us. We're not experienced in things like that; it's not up to us to say.

Lisa mooched about at home for months. She said she wouldn't have minded a job designing materials for some good firm – Liberty's or something like that – provided there was just her doing it because she's got this very individual style and it wouldn't mix with other people's, or may be she might arrange the exhibitions at the Victoria and Albert or the Tate or somewhere. She never seemed to get jobs like that, though, and anyway mother felt it would be unwise for her to commit herself because what she really ought to be doing was her own work, that's all any artist should do, it's as simple as that.

Actually Lisa did less and less painting, which mother said was tragic, her getting so disillusioned and discouraged, such a waste of talent. Mother would explain to people who asked what Lisa was doing nowadays about how disgraceful it was that the government didn't see that people like her were given the opportunities and encouragement they need. Goodness knows, she'd say with a sigh, it's rare enough – creative ability – and Mrs Watkins next door, or the vicar, or whoever it was, would nod doubtfully and say yes, they supposed so.

And then Bella Sims arrived and opened up this new gallery in the town. The Art Centre. Before, there'd only been the Craft Shop, which does have some quite odd-looking pictures but goes in for glass animals and corn dollies and all that too; Lisa was vicious about the Craft Shop. But Bella Sims's place was real art, you could see that at once – lots of bare floor and pictures hung very far apart and pottery vases and bowls so expensive they didn't even have a price on them. And Lisa took along some of her things one day and believe it or not Bella Sims said she liked them, and she'd put three of them in her next exhibition which was specially for local artists. Mother was so thrilled she cried when Lisa first told her.

Lisa was a bit off-hand about it all; she seemed to take the attitude that it was only to be expected. She got very thick with Bella Sims.

Bella Sims was fiftyish, one of those people with a loud, posh voice and hair that's just been done at the hairdresser and lots of clunky expensive-looking jewellery. She scared the wits out of me, and mother too, actually, though mother kept saying what a marvellous person she was, and what an asset for the town. I didn't enjoy the preview party for the exhibition, and nor did Jim; I was expecting Judy then, and Clive was eighteen months, so I was a bit done in and nobody talked to us much. But Lisa was having a good time, you could see; she was wearing all peasanty things then, and had her hair very long and shiny, she did look really very attractive. She met Melvyn at that party.

Melvyn was Bella's son. He taught design at the Poly. That meant he was sort of creative too, though of course not a real artist like Lisa. He fell for her, heavily, and who could blame him I suppose, and they started going round together, and then quite soon they said they were getting married. We were all pleased, because Melvyn's nice – you'd never know he was Bella's son – and we didn't realise till later that it was because of Francesca being on the way. Mother was rather upset about that, and felt she might have been a bit to blame, maybe she should have talked to Lisa about things more, but frankly I don't think that would have made any difference. Actually she worried more about Lisa not being able to paint once the baby was born. She was pleased, of course, about Francesca, but she did feel it might be a pity for Lisa to tie herself down so soon.

Actually it didn't work out that way. Lisa got into a habit almost at once of leaving Francesca with mother or with me whenever she wanted some time to herself – she was having to go up and down to London quite a lot by then to keep in touch with her old friends from college, and to try to find openings for her work. I had my two, of course, so, as she said, an extra one didn't make much difference. It did get a bit more of a strain, though, the next year, after she'd had Jason and there was him too. Four children is quite a lot to keep an eye on, but of course mother helped out a lot, whenever her leg wasn't too bad. Bella Sims, I need hardly say, didn't go much for the granny bit.

Lisa had Alex the year after that. I've never understood, I must say, why Lisa has babies so much; I mean, she must *know*. Of course, she is vague and casual, but all the same ... I've had my two, and that's that, barring accidents, and I'm planning to go back to work when I can, eventually. I daresay Lisa would think that all very cold and calculating, but that's the way I am. Lisa says she doesn't believe in planning life, you just let things happen to you, you see what comes next.

Alex had this funny Chinese look from a tiny baby and it took us ages to cotton on, in fact I suppose he was eleven months or so before the penny finally dropped and we realised that, to put it frankly, Melvyn wasn't the father.

It came as a bit of a blow, especially to poor mother. She went all quiet for days, and I must admit she's never really liked Alex ever since, not like she dotes on the others.

The father was someone Lisa knew in London. He was from Thailand, not Chinese, actually. But in fact it was all over apparently sometime before Alex was born and she didn't see him again.

Melvyn took it very well. I suppose he must have known before we did. In fact, Melvyn has been very good to Lisa from the start, nothing of what's happened has been his fault in any way. Not many men would have coped with the children like he has, right from the beginning, which he had to because of Lisa being away quite a bit, or involved in her own things. Truth to tell, he was better with them, too. It's not that Lisa's a bad mother – I mean she doesn't get cross or impatient, specially, she just doesn't bother about them much. She says the worst thing you can do is to be over-protective; she says mother was a bit over-protective with her.

Bella Sims had some fairly nasty things to say; but then soon after that she sold the gallery and moved back to London and we never saw any more of her. This was the wrong kind of provincial town, apparently; art was never going to be a viable proposition.

Things got worse after Alex was born. Lisa went off more and more. Sometimes I'd find we had the children for days on end, or Melvyn would come round, pretty well at the end of his tether, saying could we lend a hand, Lisa was down in London seeing about some gallery which might show her stuff, or she'd gone off to Wales to see a woman who was doing the most fantastic ceramics.

It was after the time Francesca wandered off and got lost for a whole day, and the police found her in the end and then it turned out Lisa had been somewhere with Ravi, this Indian friend of hers, that things rather came to a head. Lisa and Melvyn had a row and Lisa brought all the children round to me, late one night, in their pyjamas, and said she was so upset about everything she'd have to go off on her own for a few days to try to think things over. Jim had flu and I'd just got over it myself so I was a bit sharp with her: I said couldn't Melvyn have them, and she said no, Melvyn had to teach all next day, which was probably true enough. And anyway, she said, they're my children, I'm responsible for them, I've got to work out what to do. She was wearing a long red and blue thing of some hand-blocked stuff, and lots of silver bracelets, and she looked exhausted and very dashing both at the same time, somehow; the children were all crying.

So I took them, of course, and she was gone for a week or so. We talked things over while she was gone. Jim and I talked, and Jim said (which he never had before) that he thought Lisa ought to pull herself together a bit, and I had to agree. It was easier with her not being there; somehow when Lisa's with you, you always end up feeling that she really can't be expected to do what other people do, I actually feel bad if I see Lisa washing a floor or doing nappies or any of the things I do myself every day. It does seem different for her, somehow.

And mother talked to Melvyn, who'd been round to find out where the children were. Mother was very sympathetic; she knows what living with Lisa is like;

we all do. She said to Melvyn that of course Lisa had been silly and irresponsible, nobody could deny that. She told Melvyn, with a little laugh to try to cheer things up a bit, that there'd been occasions when Lisa was a small girl and was being particularly wilful and tiresome that she'd been on the verge of giving her a good smack. And then, she said, one used to remember just in time that there is a point beyond which she – people like her – simply cannot help themselves. One just can't expect the same things you can from other people.

I don't know what Melvyn thought about that; he didn't say. After the divorce came through he married Sylvie Fletcher who works in the library; I was at school with her and she's very nice but quite ordinary. Mother always says it must seem such a come down after Lisa. They've got a little boy now, and Melvyn takes a lot of trouble to see Francesca and Jason (and Alex too, in fact) as much as he can – and it *is* trouble because he has to trail down to London and try to find where Lisa's moved to now, unless it's one of the times Jim and I are having the children, or mother.

Mother and I had to talk, too. I'd gone round there and found her up in Lisa's old studio, just standing looking at a great thing Lisa had done that was partly oil paint slapped on very thick and partly bits of material stuck on and then painted over; in the top corner there was a picture of the Duke of Edinburgh from a magazine, sideways on and varnished over. I think it must have been meant to be funny, or sarcastic or something. We both stood in front of it for a bit and mother said, 'Of course, it is very good, isn't it?'

I said I honestly didn't know.

We both felt a bit awkward in there; Lisa has always been very fussy about her privacy. She says the one thing people absolutely have no right to do is push themselves into other people's lives; she is very strong for people being independent and having individual rights. So mother and I just had a quick tidy because the dust was bothering mother, and then we went downstairs and drank a cup of tea and chatted. Mother talked about this book she'd been reading about Augustus John; she's very interested in biographies of famous poets and artists and people like that. She was saying what a fascinating person he must have been but of course he did behave very badly to people, his wife and all those other women, but all the same it must have been terribly exhilarating, life with someone like that. You could see she was half thinking of Lisa. I was feeling snappish, the children were getting me down rather, and I said Lisa wasn't Augustus John, was she? We don't really know, do we – if she's any good or not.

There was a silence. We looked at each other. And then mother looked away and said, 'No. I know we don't. But she just might be, mightn't she? And it would be so awful if she was and nobody had been understanding and helpful.'

Lisa came back for the children once she'd found a flat. She'd had her hair cut off and what was left was like a little boy's, all smoothed into the back of her neck; it made her look about sixteen. Lisa is very small and thin, I should say; people always offer to carry suitcases for her, if you see her doing anything involving effort you automatically find yourself offering to do it for her because you feel she won't be able to manage and anyway it makes you feel guilty watching her.

She said the hair was symbolic; she was making a fresh start and getting rid of the atmosphere that had been holding her back (I suppose she meant poor Melvyn) and actually everything was going to be good because Ravi's father who was an Indian businessman and quite rich was going to buy a little gallery in Islington that Ravi was going to run and she was frantically busy getting enough stuff together for an exhibition.

The gallery didn't last long because it kept losing money and after a bit Ravi's father, who turned out to be quite an ordinary businessman after all and not as sensitive and interested in art as Lisa had thought, said he was cutting his losses and selling up. In fact Ravi and Lisa weren't living together by then anyway because Lisa had realised that the reason her work wasn't really right was that she'd always been in cities and in fact what she needed to fulfil herself properly was to get away somewhere remote and live a very simple, hard-working life. Actually, she thought, pottery was the right medium for her, once she could scrape up enough for a wheel and everything.

Mother helped out with that, financially, and Lisa took the children down to this place in Somerset where a man she knew, someone quite rich, had this big old house that was a sort of commune for artists, and for parties of young people to come and study nature and the environment. We went down there, once when Lisa wanted us to take Alex for a bit, because he'd not been well and she was finding it a bit of a strain coping with him. There was certainly a lot of environment there, it was miles from anywhere, except the village, and there wasn't much of that, so that there seemed to be more artists than ordinary village people. It was a hot summer and Lisa and the rest were going round with just about no clothes on, more like the south of France than west Somerset and I rather got the impression that some of the older village people didn't like it all that much, and there was an outdoor pop festival one weekend that went on to all hours, and this man who owned the place had made the church into an exhibition room for the artists. It was one of those little grey stone churches with old carvings and so on and it looked queer, all done out inside with huge violent-coloured paintings and peculiar sculptures. Lisa said actually it was frightfully good for these people, to be exposed to a today kind of life, they were so cut off down there, and to be given the sort of visual shock that might get them really looking and thinking.

Eventually Lisa began to feel a bit cut off herself, and there'd been some trouble with the county child care people which Lisa said was a lot of ridiculous fuss, it was just that Francesca had got this funny habit of wandering off sometimes and actually it was good that she felt so free and uninhibited, most people *stifle* their children so. Francesca was six by then, and Jason five. Jason had this bad stammer; he still has, sometimes he can't seem to get a word out for hours.

Lisa came home to mother's for a bit then, because rents in London were sky-high and it would have meant her getting a job, which of course was out of the question, if she was going to keep up her potting, and the weaving she had got very keen on now. And at mother's she had the studio, so it might work out quite well, she thought, provided she kept in touch with people and didn't feel too much out on a limb.

Jim and I had Alex more or less permanently by then; we are very fond of him, he seems almost like ours now which is just as well, I suppose. It is just as well too that Jim is the kind of person he is; Lisa thinks he is dull, I know, but that is just her opinion, and as I have got older I have got less and less certain that she gets things right. In fact, around this time I did have a kind of outburst, with mother, which I suppose was about Lisa, indirectly. She had gone down to London to keep in touch with people, and there had been a business with Francesca at school (sometimes she steals things, it is very awkward, they are going to have the educational psychologist people look at her) and I had had to see to it all. I was feeling a bit fed up too because what with Alex, and having so much to do, I'd realised it wasn't going to be any good trying to go back to work at the end of the year as I'd planned. Maybe you should be like Lisa, and not plan. Anyway, mother was telling me about this biography of Dylan Thomas she'd been reading, and what an extraordinary eccentric person he was and how fascinating to know. Actually I'd read the book too and personally I don't see why you shouldn't write just as good poetry without borrowing money off people all the time and telling lies.

Once, when I was at college, one of the tutors got this well-known poet to come and give a talk to the second-year English. He had glasses with thick rims and a rather old-fashioned-looking suit and frankly he might have been some-body's father, or your bank manager. He was very friendly and he talked to us in the common-room afterwards and he wasn't rude to anyone. I told mother about it, later, and she said she wondered if he was all that good – as a poet, that is.

And I suddenly blew up when she was going on like this about Dylan Thomas. I said – shouted – 'T. S. Eliot worked in an office. Gustav Holst was a bloody schoolteacher.'

Mother looked startled. She said, 'Who?' She's less interested in musicians.

I said crossly, 'Oh, never mind. Just there's more than one way of going about things.' And then the children started squabbling and we were distracted and the subject never came up again, not quite like that.

Lisa got a part-share of a flat in London with a friend; she had to be down there because there was this person who was talking of setting up a craft work-shop for potters and weavers and that, a fantastic new scheme, and she needed to be on the spot for when it came off. It was difficult for her to have the children there, so Francesca stayed with mother and the two little ones with us. Fran-cesca settled down well at school and began to behave a lot better, and Jason's stammer was improving, and then all of a sudden Lisa turned up, as brown as a conker, with her hair long again, and henna-dyed now, and said she'd met these incredible Americans in Morocco, who had this atelier, and she was going to work there and learn this amazing new enamelling technique. That was what she ought to have been doing all along, she said, if only she'd realised, not messing about with pots and fabrics. She was taking the children with her, she said, be-cause growing up in an English provincial town was so stultifying for them, and it was nice and cheap out there.

She took Alex too, but after six months she suddenly sent him back again with a peculiar German friend of hers; we had to collect him at Heathrow. He kept wetting the bed apparently and although Lisa isn't particularly fussy about that kind of thing she said she had the feeling he wasn't very adaptable.

And so it goes on. She came back from Morocco after a couple of years, and there was a spell in London when a rather well-off Dutch person that we thought

she was going to marry bought her a house in Fulham. For six months Francesca
went to a very expensive school where all the teaching was done in French, and
then the Dutch person went off and Lisa found the house was rented, not paid
for like she'd thought, so she came home again for a bit to sort things out, and
Francesca went to the comprehensive.

And then there was Wales with the Polish sculptor, and then the Dordogne
with the tapestry people, and London again, and back here for a bit, and the
cottage in Sussex that someone lent her ...

The last time she was here she had a curious creased look about her, like a
dress that had been put away in a drawer and not properly hung out, and I suddenly realised that she is nearly forty now, Lisa. It doesn't seem right; she is a
person that things have always been in front of, somehow, not behind.

Mother and I cleaned out her old studio, the other day. Mother has this feeling
that Francesca may be talented, in which case she will need to use it. We dusted
and polished and sorted out the cupboard with Lisa's old paintings and collages
and whatnot. They all looked rather shabby, and somehow withered – not quite
as large or bright as one had remembered. Mother said doubtfully, 'I wonder if
she would like any of these sent down to London?' And then, 'Of course it is a
pity she has had such an unsettled sort of life.'

That 'had' did not strike either of us for a moment or two. After a bit mother
began to put the things away in the cupboard again, very carefully; mother is
past seventy now and the stooping was awkward for her. I persuaded her to sit
down and I finished off. There was one portfolio of things Lisa did at school,
really nice drawings of flowers and leaves and a pencil portrait of another girl
whose name neither mother nor I could remember. Mother put these aside; she
thought she might have them framed and hang them in the hall. Holding them,
she said, 'Though with her temperament I suppose you could not expect that she
would settle and at least she has always been free to express herself, which is the
important thing.' When I did not answer she said, 'Isn't it, dear?' and I said, 'Yes.
Yes, I think so, mother.'

SALE

Anita Desai

Anita Desai (b. 1937) is an Indian writer whose published works include novels, children's books and short stories. She is a member of the Advisory Board for English of the National Academy of Letters in Delhi and a Fellow of the Royal Society of Literature in London. She has been shortlisted for the Man Booker Prize three times.

There they are, at the door now, banging. They had met him, written a note and made an appointment – and here they are, as a direct result of it all, rattling. He stands on the other side of the door, in the dusk-mottled room, fingering an unshaven chin and dropping cigarette butts on the floor which is already littered with them. There is a pause in the knocking. He hears their voices – querulous, impatient. He turns and silently goes towards the inner door that opens onto a passage. He pushes it ajar, quietly, holding his breath. At the end of the passage another door stands open: it is like a window or an alcove illuminated by the deep glow of the fire. There his wife sits, kneading dough in a brass bowl, with her head bowed so that her long hair broods down to her shoulders on either side of her heavy, troubled face. The red border of her sari cuts a bright gash through the still tableau. The child sits on the mat beside her, silent, absorbed in the mysteries of a long-handled spoon which he turns over with soft, wavering fingers that are unaccustomed to the unsympathetic steel. His head, too, is bowed so that his father, behind him, can see the small wisps of hair on the back of his neck. He looks at them, holding his breath till it begins to hurt his chest. Then the knocking is resumed and his wife, hearing it, raises her head. She sees him then, at the door, like a dog hanging about, wanting something, and immediately her nostrils flare. 'Can't you answer the door?' she cries. 'What's the matter with you? It must be them – this is your chance.' Startled, the child drops the spoon with a clatter. Quickly he shuts the door. Then he goes and opens the front door and lets them in.

'We were about to give up,' one man cries, laughing, and brings in his friend and also a woman, seeing, whom the artist, who is not expecting her, finds himself dismayed and confused. A woman – therefore someone in league with his wife, he thinks, and stares at her lush, unreluctant face and the bright enamelled earrings that frame it. He is silent. The two men stare at him.

'You *were* expecting us, weren't you?' enquires the jovial man whom he had liked, once. 'We wrote—'

'Yes,' he murmurs. 'Oh yes, yes,' and stands there, on the threshold, with an empty match box in his hand, his face looking like a house from which ghosts had driven away all inhabitants.

Then the man introduces his wife. 'She also paints,' he says, 'and was so interested in seeing your pictures, I brought her along. You don't mind, do you?'

'No,' he says, gathering himself together with a laboured effort, and steps aside to let them in. Then it is they who are silent, staring in dismay at the shambles about them. There are pictures to look at, yes, but one lies on the floor with a bundle of rags and some cigarette stubs on it, another is propped up on a shelf with bottles of hair oil, clay toys and calendars before it, and others have drifted off the wooden divan into corners of the room, peering out from under old newspapers and dirty clothes. The artist watches them, wondering at the imbecility of their appearance as they huddle together and gape. 'Oh,' he says, recovering, 'the light,' and switches it on. It is unshaded and hangs low over the flat table at which he paints so that they are illuminated weirdly from the waist downwards, leaving their faces more confused with shadows than before. The woman is quickest to relax, to make herself known, to become acquainted. 'Ah,' she cries, hurrying to the shelf to pull out a picture. 'What are they?' she asks him, gazing first at the flowers that blaze across the dirty paper, then at him, coaxing him for their secret with an avidly enquiring look. 'Not cannas, not lotuses – what can they be?'

He smiles at her curiosity. 'Nothing,' he says. 'Not real flowers – just anything at all.'

'Really!' she exclaims, shaking her enamelled ear-rings. 'How wonderful to be able to imagine such forms, such colours. Look, Ram, aren't they pretty?' The two men become infected by her exaggerated attitude of relaxation. They begin to prowl about the room, now showing amusement at the litter which is, after all, only to be expected in an artist's studio, then crinkling their noses for, one has to admit, it *does* smell, and then showing surprised interest in the pictures of which they have come to select one for their home which is newly built and now to be furnished. What with the enthusiasm and thoroughness they bring to their task, the rags and grime of the studio are soon almost obliterated by the fanfare of colour that spills forth, a crazy whorl of them, unknown colours that cannot be named, spilling out of forms that cannot be identified. One cannot pinpoint any school, any technique, any style – one can only admit oneself in the presence of a continuous and inspired act of creation: so they tell themselves. The woman gives cry upon cry of excitement and turns again and again to the artist who stands watching them thoughtfully. 'But how did you get this colour? You must tell me because I paint – and I could never get anything like this. What is it?'

'Ahh, Naples Yellow,' he says, as if making a guess.

'No, but there is some orange in it too.'

'Ah yes, a little orange also.'

'And green?'

'Yes, a little perhaps.'

'No, but that special tinge – how did you get it? A little bit of white – or flesh pink? What is it? Ram, Ram, just look, isn't it pretty – this weird bird? I don't suppose it has a name?'

'No, no, it is not real. I am a city man, I know nothing about birds.'

'But you know everything about birds! And flowers. I suppose they *are* birds and flowers, all these marvellous things. And your paintings are full of them. How can it possibly be that you have never seen them?'

He has to laugh then – she is so artless, so completely without any vestige of imagination, and so completely unlike his wife. 'Look,' he says, suddenly buoyant, and points to the window. She has to stand on her toes to look out of the small aperture, through the bars, and then she gazes out with all the intentness she feels he expects of her, at the deep, smoke-ridden twilight wound around the ill-lit slum, the smoking heaps of dung-fires and the dark figures that sit and stand in it hopelessly. Like fog-horns, conch shells begin to blow as tired housewives summon up their flagging spirits for the always lovely, always comforting ritual of evening prayers. She tries to pierce the scene with her sharp eyes, trying to see what he sees in it, till she hears him laughing behind her with a cracked kind of hilarity. 'There you see – my birds and my flowers,' he tells her, clapping his hands as though enjoying a practical joke he has played on her. 'I see a tram – and that is my mountain. I see a letter-box – and that is my tree. Listen! Do you hear my birds?' He raises his hand and, with its gesture, ushers in the evening voices of children uttering those cries and calls peculiar to the time of parting, the time of relinquishing their games, before they enter their homes and disappear into sleep – voices filled with an ecstasy of knowledge, of sensation drawn to an apex, brought on by the realization of imminent departure and farewell: voices panicky with love, with lament, with fear and sacrifice.

The artist watches the three visitors and finds them attentive, puzzled. 'There,' he says, dropping his hand. 'There are my birds. I don't see them – but I hear them and imagine how they look. It is easy, no, when you can hear them so clearly?'

'You are a magician,' says the quiet man, shaking his head and turning to a crayon drawing of pale birds delicately stalking the shallows of a brooding sea. 'Look at these – I can't believe you haven't actually painted them on the spot.'

'No, I have not, but I do know the sea. You know, I am a fisherman! I should have been – my people are. How do you like this one of fishing boats? I used to see them coming in like this, in the evening, with the catch. And then my mother would cook one large one for dinner – oh, it was good, good!'

They all stand around him, smiling at this unexpected burst of childish exuberance. 'You paint from memory then?' enquires one, but the woman cries, 'You like fish? You must come and eat it at our house one day – I cook fish very well.'

'I will, I will,' he cries, scurrying about as though he were looking for something he had suddenly remembered he needed, hunting out seascapes for them to see, and more of the successful flowers. 'Oh, I will love that – to see this new house of yours and eat a meal cooked by you. Yes, I will come. Here, look, another one – a canal scene. Do you like it? That is paddy growing there – it is so green ...' Now he wants to turn out the entire studio for them, bring out his best. He chatters, they laugh. Pictures fall to the floor. Crayons are smeared, oils are smudged – but he does not mind. He does not even sign his pictures. When the woman pauses over a pastel that is blurred by some stroke of carelessness, he says, 'Oh that is nothing, I can touch it up. Do you see the blue? Do you like it? Yes, I will see your paintings and I will tell you plainly what I like and what I don't like, and you will appreciate anyway. Oh, I love fish ...' Only now and then he grows aware of his wife, breathing heavily because of the weight of the child asleep on her arm, straining to hear at the door, frowning because she cannot understand, is not certain, is worried, worried to death … and then he draws down the corners of his mouth and is silent. But when a picture of curled flowers is brought to him, he stares at it till it comes into proper focus and explains it to them. 'Ah,' he says, 'I painted that long ago – for my son, when he was born. I wanted him to have flowers, flowers all about his bed, under his head, at his feet, everywhere. And I did not have any. I did not know of a garden from where I could get some. So I painted them. That is one of them. Ah yes, yes,' he smiles, and the three who watch him grow tender, sympathetic. The woman says, '*This* one? It is your son's? How lovely – how lucky.'

'No,' he cries loudly. 'I mean, you can have it. Do you like it? It is what you want for your new house?'

'Oh no,' she says softly and puts it away. 'You painted it for your child. I can't take it from him.'

The artist finds himself sweating and exhausted – he had not realized how he was straining himself. He has had nothing but tea and cigarettes since early that morning and there is no breath of air coming through the barred window. He wipes his face with his hand and blotches another crayon with his wet fingers as he picks it up and flings it away. 'Then what do you want?' he asks in a flat voice. 'What do you like? What do you want to have – a flower picture or a landscape?'

'Perhaps figures – people always make a room seem bright.'

'I don't paint figures,' he says shortly. 'You told me you wanted a landscape. Here they are – all sizes, big, small, medium; hills, seas, rivers; green, blue, yellow. Is there nothing you like?'

'Yes, yes,' they all assure him together, upset by his change of tone, and one holds up a picture at arm's length to admire it lavishly, another bends to shuffle through the pile on the table. But there are so many, they say, it is hard to choose. That is nothing, he says, *he* will choose for them. Oh no, they laugh, glancing to see if he is serious, for they have something very special in mind – something that will light up their whole house, become its focal point, radiate and give their home a tone, an atmosphere. No, not this one, not *quite* – it is lovely, but … Before he knows it, they are at the door, descending the stairs with one backward look at all the heroic mass of colour inside, saying goodbye. He rushes down the stairs after them, spreading out his arms. Their car stands under the lamp-post. He flings himself at the door, hangs on to it.

'There is not one you liked? I thought you had come to buy – you said – '

'Yes, we wanted to,' says the man whom he had liked, once. 'But not one of these. You see, we have something very special in mind, something quite extraordinary – '

'But – not one of those I showed you? I thought you liked them – you said – '

'I did, I did,' chirps the woman from the soft recesses of the back seat. 'Oh and those lovely flowers you painted for your son – *lucky* child!'

'You liked them? I will paint you another like it, just like it – '

'But we wanted a landscape really,' says the man. 'Something in those cool greys and whites. Perhaps a snow scene – now *that* would be something different.'

'Snow?' shouts the artist. 'I will paint snow. I will paint the Himalayas for you. How big do you want it? So big? So?'

'No, no,' they laugh. 'Not so big. That would be too expensive.'

'All right, smaller. I will paint it. By the end of the week you will have it.'

They laugh at his haste, his trembling, shrill excitement. 'But, my friend, have you ever seen snow?' enquires the jovial one, patting his arm.

'Ah!' he gives such a cry that it halts them in their movements of departure, to turn and see him spread out his arms till his fingers reach out of the smoke of the dung fires and the dust of the unlit lanes, to reach out to the balm of ice and snow and isolation. 'I will paint such snow for you as you have never seen, as no one has ever painted. I can see it all, here,' and he taps his forehead with such emphasis that they smile – he is quite a comic. Or even a bit crazy. Drunk?

'Now, now, my friend,' says the man, patting his arm again. 'Don't be in a hurry about it. You paint it when you are in the mood. Then it will be good.'

'I am in the mood now,' he cries. 'I am always in the mood, don't you see? Tomorrow, tomorrow I will have it ready. I will bring it to your house. Give me the address!'

They laugh. The engine stutters to life and there is a metallic finality in the sound of the doors being shut. But he clings to the handle, thrusts his head in, his eyes blazing. 'And will you give me an advance?' he asks tensely. 'I need money, my friend. Can you give me an advance?'

The woman creeps away into a corner, wrapping herself closely in a white shawl. One man, in embarrassment, falls silent. The other laughs and puts his hands in his pockets, then draws them out to show they are empty. 'Brother, if I had some with me, I would give it to you – all of it – but since we only came to see, I didn't bring any. I'm sorry.'

'I need it.'

'Listen, when you bring the picture, I will give you something, even if I don't want it, I will give you something – in advance, for the one we will buy. But to-day, just now, I have nothing.'

The artist steps back to let them go. As they drive out of the lane and the smoke smudges and obscures the tail-lights, he hears his wife come out on the stairs behind him.

MISCHIEF

Alice Munro

Alice Munro (b. 1931) is a Canadian short story writer and winner of the
2009 Man Booker International Prize, which honours her complete body
of work. She has been awarded Canada's Governor General's Award for
fiction three times, the Giller Prize twice and is a perennial contender for
the Nobel Prize for Fiction. She was awarded the National Book Critics
Circle Award in 1998 for her collection, *The Love of a Good Woman*.

Rose fell in love with Clifford at a party which Clifford and Jocelyn gave
and Patrick and Rose attended. They had been married about three years
at this time, Clifford and Jocelyn a year or so longer.

Clifford and Jocelyn lived out past West Vancouver, in one of those summer
cottages, haphazardly winterized, that used to line the short curving streets between the lower highway and the sea. The party was in March, on a rainy night.
Rose was nervous about going to it. She felt almost sick as they drove through
West Vancouver, watched the neon lights weeping in the puddles on the road,
listened to the condemning tick of the windshield wipers. She would often afterwards look back and see herself sitting beside Patrick, in her low-cut black blouse
and black velvet skirt which she hoped would turn out to be the right thing to
wear; she was wishing they were just going to the movies. She had no idea that
her life was going to be altered.

Patrick was nervous too, although he would not have admitted it. Social life
was a puzzling, often disagreeable business for them both. They had arrived in
Vancouver knowing nobody. They followed leads. Rose was not sure whether
they really longed for friends, or simply believed they ought to have them. They
dressed up and went out to visit people, or tidied up the living room and waited
for the people who had been invited to visit them. In some cases they established steady visiting patterns. They had some drinks, during those evenings, and
around eleven or eleven-thirty – which hardly ever came soon enough – Rose
went out to the kitchen and made coffee and something to eat. The things she
made to eat were usually squares of toast, with a slice of tomato on top, then a
square of cheese, then a bit of bacon, the whole thing broiled and held together
with a toothpick. She could not manage to think of anything else.

It was easier for them to become friends with people Patrick liked than with
people Rose liked because Rose was very adaptable, in fact deceitful, and Patrick
was hardly adaptable at all. But in this case, the case of Jocelyn and Clifford,
the friends were Rose's. Or Jocelyn was. Jocelyn and Rose had known enough
not to try to establish couple-visiting. Patrick disliked Clifford without knowing

him because Clifford was a violinist; no doubt Clifford disliked Patrick because Patrick worked in a branch of his family's department store. In those days the barriers between people were still strong and reliable; between arty people and business people; between men and women.

Rose did not know any of Jocelyn's friends, but understood they were musicians and journalists and lecturers at the University and even a woman writer who had had a play performed on the radio. She expected them to be intelligent, witty, and easily contemptuous. It seemed to her that all the time she and Patrick were sitting in the living rooms, visiting or being visited, really clever and funny people, who had a right to despise them, were conducting irregular lives and parties elsewhere. Now came the chance to be with those people, but her stomach rejected it, her hands were sweating.

Jocelyn and Rose had met in the maternity ward of the North Vancouver General Hospital. The first thing Rose saw, on being taken back to the ward after having Anna, was Jocelyn sitting up in bed reading the Journals of André Gide. Rose knew the book by its colors, having noticed it on the drugstore stands. Gide was on the list of writers she meant to work through. At that time she read only great writers.

The immediately startling and comforting thing to Rose, about Jocelyn, was how much Jocelyn looked like a student, how little she had let herself be affected by the maternity ward. Jocelyn had long black braids, a heavy pale face, thick glasses, no trace of prettiness, and an air of comfortable concentration.

A woman in the bed beside Jocelyn was describing the arrangement of her kitchen cupboards. She would forget to tell where she kept something – rice, say, or brown sugar – and then she would have to start all over again, making sure her audience was with her by saying "Remember on the right hand highest shelf next the stove, that's where I keep the packages of soup but not the canned soup, I keep the canned soup underneath the counter in with the canned goods, well, right next to that—"

Other women tried to interrupt, to tell how they kept things, but they were not successful, or not for long. Jocelyn sat reading, and twiddling the end of a braid between her fingers, as if she was in a library, at college, as if she was researching for a paper, and this world of other women had never closed down on her at all. Rose wished she could manage as well.

She was still dazed from the birth. Whenever she closed her eyes she saw an eclipse, a big black ball with a ring of fire. That was the baby's head, ringed with pain, the instant before she pushed it out. Across this image, in disturbing waves, went the talking woman's kitchen shelves, dipping under their glaring weight of cans and packages. But she could open her eyes and see Jocelyn, black and white, braids falling over her hospital nightgown. Jocelyn was the only person she saw who looked calm and serious enough to match the occasion.

Soon Jocelyn got out of bed, showing long white unshaved legs and a stomach still stretched by pregnancy. She put on a striped bathrobe. Instead of a cord, she tied a man's necktie around her waist. She slapped across the hospital linoleum in her bare feet. A nurse came running, warned her to put on slippers.

"I don't own any slippers."

"Do you own shoes?" said the nurse rather nastily.

"Oh, yes. I own shoes."

Jocelyn went back to the little metal cabinet beside her bed and took out a pair of large, dirty, run-over moccasins. She went off making as sloppy and insolent a noise as before.

Rose was longing to know her.

The next day Rose had her own book out to read. It was *The Last Puritan*, by George Santayana, but unfortunately it was a library copy; the title on the cover was rubbed and dim, so it was impossible that Jocelyn should admire Rose's reading material as Rose had admired hers. Rose didn't know how she could get to talk to her.

The woman who had explained about her cupboards was talking about how she used her vacuum cleaner. She said it was very important to use all the attachments because they each had a purpose and after all you had paid for them. Many people didn't use them. She described how she vacuumed her living-room drapes. Another woman said she had tried to do that but the material kept getting bunched up. The authoritative woman said that was because she hadn't been doing it properly.

Rose caught Jocelyn's eye around the corner of her book.

"I hope you polish your stove knobs," she said quietly.

"I certainly do," said Jocelyn.

"Do you polish them every day?"

"I used to polish them twice a day but now that I have the new baby I just don't know if I'll get around to it."

"Do you use that special stove-knob polish?"

"I certainly do. And I use the special stove-knob cloths that come in that special package."

"That's good. Some people don't."

"Some people will use anything."

"Old dishrags."

"Old snotrags."

"Old snot."

After this their friendship bloomed in a hurry. It was one of those luxuriant intimacies that spring up in institutions; in schools, at camp, in prison. They walked in the halls, disobeying the nurses. They annoyed and mystified the other women. They became hysterical as schoolgirls, from the things they read aloud to each other. They did not read Gide or Santayana but the copies of *True Love* and *Personal Romances* which they had found in the waiting room.

"It says here you can buy false calves," Rose read. "I don't see how you'd hide them, though. I guess you strap them on your legs. Or maybe they just sit here inside your stockings but wouldn't you think they'd show?"

"On your legs?" said Jocelyn. "You strap them on your legs? Oh, false calves! False calves! I thought you were talking about false *calves*! False baby cows!"

Anything like that could set them off.

"False baby cows!"

"False tits, false bums, false baby cows!"

"What will they think of next!"

The vacuum-cleaning woman said they were always butting in and spoiling other people's conversations and she didn't see what was so funny about dirty language. She said if they didn't stop the way they carried on they would sour their milk.

"I've been wondering if maybe mine is sour," Jocelyn said. "It's an awfully disgusting color."

"What color?" Rose asked.

"Well. Sort of blue."

"Good God, maybe it's ink!"

The vacuum-cleaning woman said she was going to tell the nurse they were swearing. She said she was no prude, but. She asked if they were fit to be mothers. How was Jocelyn going to manage to wash diapers, when anybody could see she never washed her dressing gown?

Jocelyn said she planned to use moss, she was an Indian.

"I can believe it," the woman said.

After this Jocelyn and Rose prefaced many remarks with: *I'm no prude, but.*

"I'm no prude but would you look at this pudding!"

"I'm no prude but it feels like this kid has a full set of teeth."

The nurse said, wasn't it time for them to grow up?

Walking in the halls, Jocelyn told Rose that she was twenty-five, that her baby was to be called Adam, that she had a two-year-old boy at home, named Jerome, that her husband's name was Clifford and that he played the violin for a living. He played in the Vancouver Symphony. They were poor. Jocelyn came from Massachusetts and had gone to Wellesley College. Her father was a psychiatrist and her mother was a pediatrician. Rose told Jocelyn that she came from a small town in Ontario and that Patrick came from Vancouver Island and that his parents did not approve of the marriage.

"In the town I come from," Rose said, exaggerating, "everybody says yez. What'll yez have? How're yez doin."

"Yez?"

"Youse. It's the plural of you."

"Oh. Like Brooklyn. And James Joyce. Who does Patrick work for?"

"His family's store. His family has a department store."

"So aren't you rich now? Aren't you too rich to be in the ward?"

"We just spent all our money on a house Patrick wanted."

"Didn't you want it?"

"Not so much as he did."

That was something Rose had never said before.

They plunged into more random revelations.

Jocelyn hated her mother. Her mother had made her sleep in a room with white organdy curtains and had encouraged her to collect ducks. By the time she was thirteen Jocelyn had probably the largest collection in the world of rubber ducks, ceramic ducks, wooden ducks, pictures of ducks, embroidered ducks. She had also written what she described as a hideously precocious story called "The Marvelous Great Adventures of Oliver the Grand Duck," which her mother actually got printed, and distributed to friends and relatives at Christmas time.

"She is the sort of person who just covers everything with a kind of rotten smarminess. She sort of oozes over everything. She never talks in a normal voice, never. She's coy. She's just so filthy coy. Naturally she's a great success as a pediatrician. She has these rotten coy little names for all the parts of your body."

Rose, who would have been delighted with organdy curtains, perceived the fine lines, the ways of giving offence, that existed in Jocelyn's world. It seemed a much less crude and provisional world than her own. She doubted if she could tell Jocelyn about Hanratty but she began to try. She delivered Flo and the store in broad strokes. She played up the poverty. She didn't really have to. The true facts of her childhood were exotic enough to Jocelyn, and of all things, enviable.

"It seems more real," Jocelyn said. "I know that's a romantic notion."

They talked of their youthful ambitions. (They really believed their youth to be past.) Rose said she had wanted to be an actress though she was too much of a coward ever to walk on a stage. Jocelyn had wanted to be a writer but was shamed out of it by memories of the Grand Duck.

"Then I met Clifford," she said. "When I saw what real talent was, I knew that I would probably just be fooling around, trying to write, and I'd be better off nurturing him, or whatever the hell it is I do for him. He is really gifted. Sometimes he's a squalid sort of person. He gets away with it because he is really gifted."

"I think *that* is a romantic notion," Rose said firmly and jealously. "That gifted people ought to get away with things."

"Do you? But great artists always have."

"Not women."

"But women usually aren't great artists, not in the same way."

These were the ideas of most well-educated, thoughtful, even unconventional or politically radical young women of the time. One of the reasons Rose did not share them was that she had not been well educated. Jocelyn said to her, much later in their friendship, that one of the reasons she found it so interesting to talk to Rose, from the start, was that Rose had ideas but was uneducated. Rose was surprised at this, and mentioned the college she had attended in Western Ontario. Then she saw by an embarrassed withdrawal or regret, a sudden lack of frankness in Jocelyn's face – very unusual with her – that that was exactly what Jocelyn had meant.

After the difference of opinion about artists, and about men and women artists, Rose took a good look at Clifford when he came visiting in the evening. She thought him wan, self-indulgent, and neurotic-looking. Further discoveries concerning the tact, the effort, the sheer physical energy Jocelyn expended on this marriage (it was she who fixed the leaky taps and dug up the clogged drains) made Rose certain that Jocelyn was wasting herself, she was mistaken. She had a feeling that Jocelyn did not see much point in marriage with Patrick, either.

At first the party was easier than Rose had expected. She had been afraid that she would be too dressed-up; she would have liked to wear her toreador pants but Patrick would never have stood for it. But only a few of the girls were in slacks. The rest wore stockings, earrings, outfits much like her own. As at any gathering of young women at that time, three or four were noticeably pregnant. And most of the men were in suits and shirts and ties, like Patrick. Rose was relieved. Not only did she want Patrick to fit into the party; she wanted him to accept the people there, to be convinced they were not all freaks. When Patrick was a student he had taken her to concerts and plays and did not seem overly suspicious of the people who participated in them; indeed he rather favored these things, because they were detested by his family, and at that time – the time he chose Rose – he was having a brief rebellion against his family. Once he and Rose had gone to Toronto and sat in the Chinese temple room at the Museum, looking at the frescoes. Patrick told her how they were brought in small pieces from Shansi province; he seemed quite proud of his knowledge, and at the same time disarmingly, uncharacteristically humble, admitting he had got it all on a tour. It was since he had gone to work that he had developed harsh opinions and delivered wholesale condemnations. Modern Art was a Hoax. Avant-garde plays were filthy. Patrick had a special, mincing, spitting way of saying avant-garde, making the words seem disgustingly pretentious. And so they were, Rose thought. In a way, she could see what he meant. She could see too many sides of things; Patrick had not that problem.

Except for some great periodic fights she was very docile with Patrick, she tried to keep in favor. It was not easy to do so. Even before they were married he had a habit of delivering reproving lectures, in response to a simple question or observation. Sometimes in those days she would ask him a question in the hope that he would show off some superior knowledge that she could admire him for, but she was usually sorry she had asked, the answer was so long and had such a scolding tone, and the knowledge wouldn't be so superior, either. She did want to admire him, and respect him; it seemed that was a leap she was always on the edge of taking.

Later she thought that she did respect Patrick, but not in the way he wanted to be respected, and she did love him, not in the way he wanted to be loved. She didn't know it then. She thought she knew something about him, she thought she knew that he didn't really want to be whatever he was zealously making himself into. That arrogance might be called respect; that highhandedness, love. It didn't do anything to make him happy.

A few men wore jeans and turtlenecks or sweatshirts. Clifford was one of them, all in black. It was the time of the beatniks in San Francisco. Jocelyn had called Rose up on the phone and read her *Howl*. Clifford's skin looked very tanned, against the black, his hair was long for the time and almost as light a color as unbleached cotton; his eyes too were very light in color, a bright gray-blue. He looked small and cat-like to Rose, rather effeminate; she hoped Patrick wouldn't be too put off by him.

There was beer to drink, and a wine punch. Jocelyn, who was a splendid cook, was stirring a pot of jambalaya. Rose made a trip to the bathroom to remove herself from Patrick, who seemed to want to stick close to her (she thought he was being a watchdog; she forgot that he might be shy). When she came out he had moved on. She drank three cups of punch in quick succession and was introduced to the woman who had written the play. To Rose's surprise this woman was one of the drabbest, least confident-looking people in the room.

"I liked your play," Rose told her. As a matter of fact she had found if mystifying, and Patrick had thought it was revolting. It seemed to be about a woman who ate her own children. Rose knew that was symbolic, but couldn't quite figure out what it was symbolic of.

"Oh, but the production was terrible!" the woman said. In her embarrassment, her excitement and eagerness to talk about her play, she sprayed Rose with punch. "They made it so literal. I was afraid it would just come across as gruesome and I meant it to be quite delicate, I meant it to be so different from the way they made it." She started telling Rose everything that had gone wrong, the miscasting, the chopping of the most important – the *crucial* – lines. Rose felt flattered, listening to these details, and tried inconspicuously to wipe away the spray.

"But you did see what I meant?" the woman said.

"Oh, yes!"

Clifford poured Rose another cup of punch and smiled at her.

"Rose, you look delicious."

Delicious seemed an odd word for Clifford to use. Perhaps he was drunk. Or perhaps, hating parties altogether as Jocelyn said he did, he had taken on a role; he was the sort of man who told a girl she looked delicious. He might be adept at disguises, as Rose thought she herself was getting to be. She went on talking to the writer and a man who taught English Literature of the Seventeenth Century. She too might have been poor and clever, radical and irreverent for all anybody could tell.

A man and a girl were embracing passionately in the narrow hall. Whenever anybody wanted to get through, this couple had to separate but they continued looking at each other, and did not even close their mouths. The sight of those wet open mouths made Rose shiver. She had never been embraced like that in her life, never had her mouth opened like that. Patrick thought French-kissing was disgusting.

A little bald man named Cyril had stationed himself outside the bathroom door, and was kissing any girl who came out, saying, "Welcome, sweetheart, so glad you could come, so glad you went."

"Cyril is awful," the woman writer said. "Cyril thinks he has to try to act like a poet. He can't think of anything to do but hang around the john and upset people. He thinks he's outrageous."

"Is he a poet?" Rose said.

The lecturer in English Literature said, "He told me he had burned all his poems."

"How flamboyant of him," Rose said. She was delighted with herself for saying this, and with them for laughing.

The lecturer began to think of Tom Swifties.

"I can never think of any of those things," said the writer mournfully, "I care too much about language."

Loud voices were coming from the living room. Rose recognized Patrick's voice, soaring over and subduing everyone else's. She opened her mouth to say something, anything, to cover him up – she knew some disaster was on the way – but just then a tall, curly-haired, elated-looking man came through the hall, pushing the passionate couple unceremoniously apart, holding up his hands for attention.

"Listen to this," he said to the whole kitchen. "There's this guy in the living room you wouldn't believe him. Listen."

There must have been a conversation about Indians going on in the living room. Now Patrick had taken it over.

"Take them away," said Patrick. "Take them away from their parents as soon as they're born and put them in a civilized environment and educate them and they will turn out just as good as whites any day." No doubt he thought he was expressing liberal views. If they thought this was amazing, they should have got him on the execution of the Rosenbergs or the trial of Alger Hiss or the necessity for nuclear testing.

Some girl said mildly, "Well, you know, there is their own culture."

"Their culture is done for," said Patrick. "Kaput." This was a word he was using a good deal right now. He could use some words, clichés, editorial phrases – *massive reappraisal* was one of them – with such relish and numbing authority that you would think he was their originator, or at least that the very fact of his using them gave them weight and luster.

"They want to be civilized," he said. "The smarter ones do."

"Well, perhaps they don't consider they're exactly uncivilized," said the girl with an icy demureness that was lost on Patrick.

"Some people need a push."

The self-congratulatory tones, the ripe admonishment, caused the man in the kitchen to throw up his hands, and wag his head in delight and disbelief. "This has got to be a Socred politician."

As a matter of fact Patrick did vote Social Credit.

"Yes, well, like it or not," he was saying, "they have to be dragged kicking and screaming into the twentieth century."

"Kicking and steaming?" someone repeated.

"Kicking and screaming into the twentieth century," said Patrick, who never minded saying anything again.

"What an interesting expression. So humane as well."

Wouldn't he understand now, that he was being cornered, being baited and laughed at? But Patrick, being cornered, could only grow more thunderous. Rose could not listen any longer. She headed for the back passage, which was full of all the boots, coats, bottles, tubs, toys, that Jocelyn and Clifford had pitched out of the way for the party. Thank God it was empty of people. She went out of the back door and stood burning and shivering in the cool wet night. Her feelings were as confused as anybody's can get. She was humiliated, she was ashamed of Patrick. But she knew that it was his style that most humiliated her, and that made her suspect something corrupt and frivolous in herself. She was angry at those other people who were cleverer, or at least far quicker, than he was. She wanted to think badly of them. What did they care about Indians, really? Given a chance to behave decently to an Indian, Patrick might just come out ahead of them. This was a long shot, but she had to believe it. Patrick was a good person. His opinions were not good, but he was. The core of Patrick, Rose believed, was simple, pure and trustworthy. But how was she to get at it, to reassure herself, much less reveal it to others?

She heard the back door close and was afraid that Jocelyn had come out looking for her. Jocelyn was not someone who could believe in Patrick's core. She thought him stiff-necked, thick-skulled, and essentially silly.

It was not Jocelyn. It was Clifford. Rose didn't want to have to say anything to him. Slightly drunk as she was, woebegone, wet-faced from the rain, she looked at him without welcome. But he put his arms around her and rocked her.

"Oh Rose. Rose baby. Never mind. Rose."

So this was Clifford.

For five minutes or so they were kissing, murmuring, shivering, pressing, touching. They returned to the party by the front door. Cyril was there. He said, "Hey, wow, where have you two been?"

"Walking in the rain," said Clifford coolly. The same light possibly hostile voice in which he had told Rose she looked delicious. The Patrick-baiting had stopped. Conversation had become looser, drunker, more irresponsible. Jocelyn was serving jambalaya. She went to the bathroom to dry her hair and put lipstick on her rubbed-bare mouth. She was transformed, invulnerable. The first person she met coming out was Patrick. She had a wish to make him happy. She didn't care now what he had said, or would say.

"I don't think we've met, sir," she said, in a tiny flirtatious voice she used with him sometimes, when they were feeling easy together. "But you may kiss my hand."

"For crying out loud," said Patrick heartily, and he did squeeze her and kiss her, with a loud smacking noise, on the cheek. He always smacked when he kissed. And his elbows always managed to dig in somewhere and hurt her.

"Enjoying yourself?" Rose said.

"Not bad, not bad."

During the rest of the evening, of course, she was playing the game of watching Clifford while pretending not to watch him, and it seemed to her he was doing the same, and their eyes met, a few times, without expression, sending a perfectly clear message that rocked her on her feet. She saw him quite differently now. His body that had seemed small and tame now appeared to her light and slippery and full of energy; he was like a lynx or a bobcat. He had his tan from skiing. He went up Seymour Mountain and skied. An expensive hobby, but one which Jocelyn felt could not be denied him, because of the problems he had with his image. His masculine image, as a violinist, in this society. So Jocelyn said. Jocelyn had told Rose all about Clifford's background: the arthritic father, the small grocery store in a town in upstate New York, the poor tough neighborhood. She had talked about his problems as a child; the inappropriate talent, the grudging parents, the jeering schoolmates. His childhood left him bitter, Jocelyn said. But Rose no longer believed that Jocelyn had the last word on Clifford.

The party was on a Friday night. The phone rang the next morning, when Patrick and Anna were at the table eating eggs.

"How are you?" said Clifford.

"Fine."

"I wanted to phone you. I thought you might think I was just drunk or something. I wasn't."

"Oh, no."

"I've thought about you all night. I thought about you before, too."

"Yes." The kitchen was dazzling. The whole scene in front of her, of Patrick and Anna at the table, the coffee pot with dribbles down the side, the jar of marmalade, was exploding with joy and possibility and danger. Rose's mouth was so dry she could hardly talk.

"It's a lovely day," she said. "Patrick and Anna and I might go up the mountain."

"Patrick's home?"

"Yes."

"Oh God. That was dumb of me. I forgot nobody else works Saturdays. I'm over here at a rehearsal."

"Yes."

"Can you pretend it's somebody else? Pretend it's Jocelyn."

"Sure."

"I love you, Rose," said Clifford, and hung up.

"Who was that?" said Patrick.

"Jocelyn."

"Does she have to call when I'm home?"

"She forgot. Clifford's at a rehearsal so she forgot other people aren't working." Rose delighted in saying Clifford's name. Deceitfulness, concealment, seemed to come marvelously easy to her; that might almost be a pleasure in itself.

"I didn't realize they'd have to work Saturdays," she said, to keep on the subject. "They must work terribly long hours."

"They don't work any longer hours than normal people, it's just strung out differently. He doesn't look capable of much work."

"He's supposed to be quite good. As a violinist."

"He looks like a jerk."

"Do you think so?"

"Don't you?"

"I guess I never considered him, really."

Jocelyn phoned on Monday and said she didn't know why she gave parties, she was still wading through the mess.

"Didn't Clifford help clean it up?"

"You are joking. I hardly saw him all weekend. He rehearsed Saturday and played yesterday. He says parties are my idea, I can deal with the aftermath. It's true. I get these fits of gregariousness, a party is the only cure. Patrick was interesting."

"Very."

"He's quite a stunning type, really, isn't he?"

"There are lots and lots like him. You just don't get to meet them."

"Woe is me."

This was just like any other conversation with Jocelyn. Their conversations, their friendship, could go on in the same way. Rose did not feel bound by any loyalty to Jocelyn because she had divided Clifford. There was the Clifford Jocelyn knew, the same one she had always presented to Rose; there was also the Clifford Rose knew, now. She thought Jocelyn could be mistaken about him. For instance, when she said his childhood had left him bitter. What Jocelyn called bitterness seemed to Rose something more complex and more ordinary; just the weariness, suppleness, deviousness, meanness, common to a class. Common to Clifford's class, and Rose's. Jocelyn had been insulated in some ways, left stern and innocent. In some ways she was like Patrick.

From now on Rose did see Clifford and herself as being one sort of people, and Jocelyn and Patrick, though they seemed so different, and so disliked each other, as being another sort. They were whole and predictable. They took the lives they were leading absolutely seriously. Compared to them, both Clifford and Rose were shifty pieces of business.

If Jocelyn fell in love with a married man, what would she do? Before she even touched his hand, she would probably call a conference. Clifford would be invited, and the man himself, and the man's wife, and very likely Jocelyn's psychiatrist. (In spite of her rejection of her family Jocelyn believed that going to a psychiatrist was something everybody should do at developing or adjusting stages of life and she went herself, once a week.) Jocelyn would consider the implications; she would look things in the face. Never try to sneak her pleasure. She had never learned to sneak things. That was why it was unlikely that she would ever fall in love with another man. She was not greedy. And Patrick was not greedy either now, at least not for love.

If loving Patrick was recognizing something good, and guileless, at the bottom of him, being in love with Clifford was something else altogether. Rose did not have to believe that Clifford was good, and certainly she knew he was not guileless. No revelation of his duplicity or heartlessness, towards people other than herself, could have mattered to her. What was she in love with, then, what did she want of him? She wanted tricks, a glittering secret, tender celebrations of lust, a regular conflagration of adultery. All this after five minutes in the rain.

Six months or so after that party Rose lay awake all night. Patrick slept beside her in their stone and cedar house in a suburb called Capilano Heights, on the side of Grouse Mountain. The next night it was arranged that Clifford would sleep beside her, in Powell River, where he was playing with the touring orchestra. She could not believe that this would really happen. That is, she placed all her faith in the event, but could not fit it into the order of things that she knew.

During all these months Clifford and Rose had never gone to bed together. They had not made love anywhere else, either. This was the situation: Jocelyn and Clifford did not own a car. Patrick and Rose owned a car, but Rose did not drive it. Clifford's work did have the advantage of irregular hours, but how was he to get to see Rose? Could he ride the bus across the Lions Gate Bridge, then walk up her suburban street in broad daylight, past the neighbors' picture windows? Could Rose hire a baby sitter, pretend she was going to see the dentist, take the bus over to town, meet Clifford in a restaurant, go with him to a hotel room? But they didn't know which hotel to go to; they were afraid that without luggage they would be turned out on the street, or reported to the Vice Squad, made to sit in the Police Station while Jocelyn and Patrick were summoned to come and get them. Also, they didn't have enough money.

Rose had gone over to Vancouver, though, using the dentist excuse, and they had sat in a café, side by side in a black booth, kissing and fondling, right out in public in a place frequented by Clifford's students and fellow musicians; what a risk to take. On the bus going home Rose looked down her dress at the sweat blooming between her breasts and could have fainted at the splendor of herself, as well as at the thought of the risk undertaken. Another time, a very hot August afternoon, she waited in an alley behind the theater where Clifford was rehearsing, lurked in the shadows then grappled with him deliriously, unsatisfactorily. They saw a door open, and slipped inside. There were boxes stacked all around. They were looking for some nesting spot when a man spoke to them.

"Can I do anything for you?"

They had entered the back storeroom of a shoe store. The man's voice was icy, terrifying. The Vice Squad. The Police Station. Rose's dress was undone to the waist.

Once they met in a park, where Rose often took Anna, and pushed her on the swings. They held hands on a bench, under cover of Rose's wide cotton skirt. They laced their fingers together and squeezed painfully. Then Anna surprised them, coming up behind the bench and shouting, "Boo! I caught you!" Clifford turned disastrously pale. On the way home Rose said to Anna, "That was funny when you jumped out behind the bench. I thought you were still on the swing."

"I know," said Anna.

"What did you mean, you'd caught us?"

"I *caught* you," said Anna, and giggled, in what seemed to Rose a disturbingly pert and knowledgeable way.

"Would you like a fudgsicle? I would!" Rose said gaily, with thoughts of blackmail and bargains, Anna dredging this up for *her* psychiatrist in twenty years' time. The episode made her feel shaky and sick and she wondered if it had given Clifford a distaste for her. It had, but only temporarily.

As soon as it was light she got out of bed and went to look at the day, to see if it would be good for flying. The sky was clear; no sign of the fog that often grounded planes at this time of year. Nobody but Clifford knew she was going to Powell River. They had been planning this for six weeks, ever since they knew he was going on tour. Patrick thought she was going to Victoria, where she had a friend whom she had known at college. She had pretended, during the past few weeks, to have been in touch with this friend again. She had said she would be back tomorrow night. Today was Saturday. Patrick was at home to look after Anna.

She went into the dining room to check the money she had saved from Family Allowance checks. It was in the bottom of the silver muffin dish. Thirteen dollars. She meant to add that to what Patrick gave her to get to Victoria. Patrick always gave her money when she asked, but he wanted to know how much and what for. Once when they were out walking she wanted to go into a drugstore; she asked him for money and he said, with no more than customary sternness, "What for?" and Rose began to cry, because she had been going to buy vaginal jelly. She might just as well have laughed, and would have, now. Since she had fallen in love with Clifford, she never quarreled with Patrick.

She figured out again the money she would need. The plane ticket, the money for the airport bus, from Vancouver, and for the bus or maybe it would have to be a taxi into Powell River, something left over for food and coffee. Clifford would pay for the hotel. The thought filled her with sexual comfort, submissiveness, though she knew Jerome needed new glasses, Adam needed rubber boots. She thought of that neutral, smooth, generous bed, which already existed, was waiting for them. Long ago when she was a young girl (she was now twenty-three) she had often thought of bland rented beds and locked doors, with such luxuriant hopes, and now she did again, though for a time in between, before and after she was married, the thought of anything connected with sex irritated her, rather in the way Modern Art irritated Patrick.

She walked around the house softly, planning her day as a series of actions. Take a bath, oil and powder herself, put her diaphragm and jelly in her purse. Remember the money. Mascara, face cream, lipstick. She stood at the top of the two steps leading down into the living room. The walls of the living room were moss green, the fireplace was white, the curtains and slipcovers had a silky pattern of gray and green and yellow leaves on a white background. On the mantel were two Wedgwood vases, white with a circlet of green leaves. Patrick was very fond of these vases. Sometimes when he came home from work he went straight into the living room and shifted them around a bit on the mantel, thinking their symmetrical position had been disturbed.

"Has anybody been fooling around with these vases?"

"Well of course. As soon as you leave for work I rush in and juggle them around."

"I meant Anna. You don't let her touch them, do you?"

Patrick didn't like to hear her refer to the vases in any joking way. He thought she didn't appreciate the house. He didn't know, but maybe could guess what she had said to Jocelyn, the first time Jocelyn came here, and they were standing where Rose stood now, looking down at the living room.

"The department store heir's dream of elegance."

At this treachery even Jocelyn looked abashed. It was not exactly true. Patrick dreamed of getting much more elegant. And it was not true in the implication that it had all been Patrick's choice, and that Rose had always held aloof from it. It had been Patrick's choice, but there were a lot of things she had liked at one time. She used to climb up and polish the glass drops of the dining-room chandelier, using a cloth dipped in water and baking soda. She liked the chandelier; its drops had a blue or lilac cast. But people she admired would not have chandeliers in their dining rooms. It was unlikely that they would have dining rooms. If they did, they would have thin white candles stuck into the branches of a black metal candle-holder, made in Scandinavia. Or else they would have heavy candles in wine bottles, loaded with drippings of colored wax. The people she admired were inevitably poorer than she was. It seemed a bad joke on her, after being poor all her life in a place where poverty was never anything to be proud of, that now she had to feel apologetic and embarrassed about the opposite condition – with someone like Jocelyn, for instance, who could say *middle-class prosperity* so viciously and despisingly.

But if she hadn't been exposed to other people, if she hadn't learned from Jocelyn, would she still have liked the house? No. She must have been souring on it, anyway. When people came to visit for the first time Patrick always took them on a tour, pointing out the chandelier, the powder room with concealed lighting, by the front door, the walk-in closets and the louvered doors opening on to the patio. He was as proud of this house, as eager to call attention to its small distinctions, as if he, not Rose, had grown up poor. Rose had been uneasy about these tours from the start, and tagged along in silence, or made deprecating remarks which Patrick did not like. After a while she stayed in the kitchen, but she could still hear Patrick's voice and she knew beforehand everything he would say. She knew that he would pull the dining-room curtains and point to the small illuminated fountain – Neptune with a fig-leaf – he had put in the garden, and then he would say, "Now there is our answer to the suburban swimming-pool mania!"

After she bathed she reached for a bottle of what she thought was baby oil, to pour over her body. The clear liquid ran down over her breasts and belly, stinging and burning. She looked at the label and saw that this was not baby oil at all, it was nail polish remover. She scrubbed it off, splashed herself with cold water, towelled desperately, thinking of ruined skin, the hospital; grafts, scars, punishment.

Anna was scratching sleepily but urgently at the bathroom door. Rose had locked it, for this preparation, though she didn't usually lock it when she took a bath. She let Anna in.

"Your front is all red," Anna said, as she hoisted herself on to the toilet. Rose found the baby oil and tried to cool herself with it. She used too much, and got oily spots on her new brassiere.

She had thought Clifford might write to her while he was touring, but he did not. He called her from Prince George, and was business-like.

"When do you get into Powell River?"

"Four o'clock."

"Okay, take the bus or whatever they have into town. Have you ever been there?"

"No."

"Neither have I. I only know the name of our hotel. You can't wait there."

"How about the bus depot? Every town has a bus depot."

"Okay, the bus depot. I'll pick you up there probably about five o'clock, and we can get you into some other hotel. I hope to God there's more than one. Okay then."

He was pretending to the other members of the orchestra that he was spending the night with friends in Powell River.

"I could go and hear you play," Rose said. "Couldn't I?"

"Well. Sure."

"I'd be very inconspicuous. I'd sit at the back. I'll disguise myself as an old lady. I love to hear you play."

"Okay."

"You don't mind?"

"No."

"Clifford?"

"Yes?"

"You still want me to come?"

"Oh, Rose."

"I know. It's just the way you sound."

"I'm in the hotel lobby. They're waiting for me. I'm supposed to be talking to Jocelyn."

"Okay I know. I'll come."

"Powell River. The bus depot. Five o'clock."

This was different from their usual telephone conversations. Usually they were plaintive and silly; or else they worked each other up so that they could not talk at all.

"Heavy breathing there."

"I know."

"We'll have to talk about something else."

"What else is there?"

"Is it foggy where you are?"

"Yes. Is it foggy where you are too?"

"Yes. Can you hear the foghorn?"

"Yes."

"Isn't it a horrible sound?"

"I don't mind it, really I sort of like it."

"Jocelyn doesn't. You know how she describes it? She says it's the sound of a cosmic boredom."

They had at first avoided speaking of Jocelyn and Patrick at all. Then they spoke of them in a crisp practical way, as if they were adults, parents, to be outwitted. Now they could mention them almost tenderly, admiringly, as if they were their children.

There was no bus depot in Powell River. Rose got into the airport limousine with four other passengers, all men, and told the driver she wanted to go to the bus depot.

"You know where that is?"

"No," she said. Already she felt them all watching her.

"Did you want to catch a bus?"

"No."

"Just wanted to go to the bus depot?"

"I planned to meet somebody there."

"I didn't even know there was a bus depot here," said one of the passengers.

"There isn't, that I know of," said the driver. "Now there is a bus, it goes down to Vancouver in the morning and it comes back at night, and it stops at the old men's home. The old loggers' home. That's where it stops. All I can do is take you there. Is that all right?"

Rose said it would be fine. Then she felt she had to go on explaining.

"My friend and I just arranged to meet there because we couldn't think where else. We don't know Powell River at all and we just thought, every town has a bus depot!"

She was thinking that she shouldn't have said *my friend*, she should have said *my husband.* They were going to ask her what she and her friend were doing here if neither of them knew the town.

"My friend is playing in the orchestra that's giving a concert here tonight. She plays the violin."

All looked away from her, as if that was what a lie deserved. She was trying to remember if there was a female violinist. What if they should ask her name?

The driver let her off in front of a long two-story wooden building with peeling paint.

"I guess you could go in the sunporch, there at the end. That's where the bus picks them up, anyway."

In the sunporch there was a pool table. Nobody was playing. Some old men were playing checkers; others watched. Rose thought of explaining herself to them but decided not to; they seemed mercifully uninterested. She was worn out by her explanations in the limousine.

It was ten past four by the sunporch clock. She thought she could put in the time till five by walking around the town.

As soon as she went outside she noticed a bad smell, and became worried, thinking it might come from herself. She got out the stick cologne she had bought in the Vancouver airport – spending money she could not afford – and rubbed it on her wrists and neck. The smell persisted, and at last she realized it came from the pulp mills. The town was difficult to walk around in because the streets were so steep, and in many places there was no sidewalk. There was no place to loiter. She thought people stared at her, recognizing a stranger. Some men in a car yelled at her. She saw her own reflection in store windows and understood that she looked as if she wanted to be stared at and yelled at. She was wearing black velvet toreador pants, a tight-fitting highnecked black sweater and a beige jacket which she slung over her shoulder, though there was a chilly wind. She who had once chosen full skirts and soft colors, babyish angora sweaters, scalloped necklines, had now taken to wearing dramatic sexually advertising clothes. The new underwear she had on at this moment was black lace and pink nylon. In the waiting room at the Vancouver airport she had done her eyes with heavy mascara, black eyeliner, and silver eyeshadow; her lipstick was almost white. All this was a fashion of those years and so looked less ghastly than it would seem later, but it was alarming enough. The assurance with which she carried such a disguise fluctuated considerably. She would not have dared parade it in front of Patrick or Jocelyn. When she went to see Jocelyn she always wore her baggiest slacks and sweaters. Nevertheless when she opened the door Jocelyn would say, "Hello, Sexy," in a tone of friendly scorn. Jocelyn herself had become spectacularly unkempt. She dressed exclusively in old clothes of Clifford's. Old pants that didn't quite zip up on her because her stomach had never flattened out after Adam, and frayed white shirts Clifford had once worn for performances. Apparently Jocelyn thought the whole business of keeping your figure and wearing makeup and trying to look in any way seductive was sourly amusing, beneath contempt; it was like vacuuming the curtains. She said that Clifford felt the same way. Clifford, reported Jocelyn, was attracted by the very absence of female artifice and trappings; he liked unshaved legs and hairy armpits and natural smells. Rose wondered if Clifford had really said this, and why. Out of pity, or comradeliness; or as a joke?

Rose found a public library and went in and looked at the titles of the books, but she could not pay attention. There was a fairly incapacitating though not unpleasant buzzing throughout her head and body. At twenty to five she was back in the sunporch, waiting.

She was still waiting at ten past six. She had counted the money in her purse. A dollar and sixty-three cents. She could not go to a hotel. She did not think they would let her stay in the sunporch all night. There was nothing at all that she could do except pray that Clifford might still arrive. She did not believe he would. The schedule had been changed; he had been summoned home because one of the children was sick; he had broken his wrist and couldn't play the violin; Powell River was not a real place at all but a bad-smelling mirage where guilty travelers were trapped for punishment. She wasn't really surprised. She had made the jump that wasn't to be made, and this was how she had landed.

Before the old men went in to supper she asked them if they knew of a concert being given that night in the high school auditorium. They answered grudgingly, no.

"Never heard of them giving no concerts here."

She said that her husband was playing in the orchestra, it was on tour from Vancouver, she had flown up to meet him; she was supposed to meet him here.

Here?

"Maybe got lost," said one of the old men in what seemed to her a spiteful, knowing way. "Maybe your husband got lost, heh? Husbands always getting lost!"

It was nearly dark out. This was October, and further north than Vancouver. She tried to think what to do. The only thing that occurred to her was to pretend to pass out, then claim loss of memory. Would Patrick ever believe that? She would have to say she had no idea what she was doing in Powell River. She would have to say she didn't remember anything she had said in the limousine, didn't know anything about the orchestra. She would have to convince policemen and doctors, be written about in the newspapers. Oh, where was Clifford, why had he abandoned her, could there have been an accident on the road? She thought she should destroy the piece of paper in her purse, on which she had written his instructions. She thought that she had better get rid of her diaphragm as well.

She was going through her purse when a van parked outside. She thought it must be a police van; she thought the old men must have phoned up and reported her as a suspicious character.

Clifford got out and came running up the sunporch steps. It took her a moment to recognize him.

They had beer and hamburgers in one of the hotels, a different hotel from the one where the orchestra was staying. Rose's hands were shaking so that she slopped the beer. There had been a rehearsal he hadn't counted on, Clifford said. Then he had been about half an hour looking for the bus depot.

"I guess it wasn't such a bright idea, the bus depot."

Her hand was lying on the table. He wiped the beer off with a napkin, then put his own hand over hers. She thought of this often, afterwards.

"We better get you checked in here."

"Don't we check in together?"

"Better if it's just you."

"Ever since I got here," Rose said, "it has been so peculiar. It has been so sinister. I felt everybody knew." She started telling him, in what she hoped was an entertaining way, about the limousine driver, the other passengers, the old men in the Loggers' Home. "It was such a relief when you showed up, such a terrible relief. That's why I'm shaking." She told him about her plan to fake amnesia and the realization that she had better throw her diaphragm away. He laughed, but without delight, she thought. It seemed to her that when she spoke of the diaphragm his lips tightened, in reproof or distaste.

"But it's lovely now," she said hastily. This was the longest conversation they had ever had, face to face.

"It was just your guilt-feelings," he said. "Which are natural."

He stroked her hand. She tried to rub her finger on his pulse, as they used to do. He let go. Half an hour later, she was saying, "Is it all right if I still go to the concert?"

"Do you still want to?"

"What else is there to do?"

She shrugged as she said this. Her eyelids were lowered, her lips full and brooding. She was doing some sort of imitation, of Barbara Stanwyck perhaps, in similar circumstances. She didn't intend to do an imitation, of course. She was trying to find some way to be so enticing, so aloof and enticing, that she would make him change his mind.

"The thing is, I have to get the van back. I have to pick up the other guys."

"I can walk. Tell me where it is."

"Uphill from here, I'm afraid."

"That won't hurt me."

"Rose. It's much better this way, Rose. It really is."

"If you say so." She couldn't manage another shrug. She still thought there must be some way to turn things around and start again. Start again; set right whatever she had said or done wrong; make none of this true. She had already made the mistake of asking what she had said or done wrong and he had said, nothing. Nothing. She had nothing to do with it, he said. It was being away from home for a month that had made him see everything differently. Jocelyn. The children. The damage.

"It's only mischief," he said.

He had got his hair cut shorter than she had ever seen it. His tan had faded. Indeed, indeed, he looked as if he had shed a skin, and it was the skin that had hankered after hers. He was again the pale, and rather irritable, but dutiful, young husband she had observed paying visits to Jocelyn in the maternity ward.

"What is?"

"What we're doing. It's not some big necessary thing. It's ordinary mischief."

"You called me from Prince George." Barbara Stanwyck had vanished, Rose heard herself begin to whine.

"I know I did." He spoke like a nagged husband.

"Did you feel like this then?"

"Yes and no. We'd made all the plans. Wouldn't it have been worse if I'd told you on the phone?"

"What do you mean, mischief?"

"Oh, Rose."

"What do you mean?"

"You know what I mean. If we went ahead with this, what good do you think it would do anybody? Rose? Really?"

"Us," Rose said. "It would do us good."

"No it wouldn't. It would end up in one big mess."

"Just once."

"No."

"You said just once. You said we would have a memory instead of a dream."

"Jesus. I said a lot of puke."

He had said her tongue was like a little warmblooded snake, a pretty snake, and her nipples like berries. He would not care to be reminded.

> *Overture to Ruslan and Ludmilla: Glinka*
> *Serenade for Strings: Tchaikovsky*
> *Beethoven's Sixth Symphony, the Pastoral:*
> *First Movement*
> *The Moldau: Smetana*
> *William Tell Overture: Rossini*

She could not hear any of this music for a long time without a specific attack of shame, that was like a whole wall crumbling in on her, rubble choking her.

Just before Clifford left on tour, Jocelyn had phoned Rose and said that her baby sitter could not come. It was the day she went to see her psychiatrist. Rose offered to come and look after Adam and Jerome. She had done this before. She made the long trip on three buses, taking Anna with her.

Jocelyn's house was heated by an oil stove in the kitchen, and an enormous stone fireplace in the small living room. The oil stove was covered with spill-marks; orange peel and coffee grounds and charred wood and ashes tumbled out of the fireplace. There was no basement and no clothes dryer. The weather was rainy, and the ceiling-racks and stand-up racks were draped with damp gray-ing sheets and diapers, hardening towels. There was no washing machine either. Jocelyn had washed those sheets in the bathtub.

"No washer or dryer but she's going to a psychiatrist," said Patrick, to whom Rose sometimes disloyally reported what she knew he would like to hear.

"She must be crazy," Rose said. She made him laugh.

But Patrick didn't like her going to baby-sit.

"You're certainly at her beck and call," he said. "It's a wonder you don't go and scrub her floors for her."

As a matter of fact, Rose did.

When Jocelyn was there, the disorder of the house had a certain willed and impressive quality. When she was gone, it became unbearable. Rose would go to work with a knife, scraping at ancient crusts of Pablum on the kitchen chairs, scouring the coffee pot, wiping the floor. She did spare some time for investigation. She went into the bedroom – she had to watch out for Jerome, a precocious and irritating child – and looked at Clifford's socks and underwear, all crumpled in with Jocelyn's old nursing brassieres and torn garter belts. She looked to see if he had a record on the turntable, wondering if it would be something that would make him think of her.

Telemann. Not likely. But she played it, to hear what he had been hearing. She drank coffee from what she believed to be his dirty breakfast cup. She covered the casserole of Spanish rice from which he had taken his supper the night before. She sought out traces of his presence (he didn't use an electric razor, he used old-fashioned shaving soap in a wooden bowl), but she believed that his life in that house, Jocelyn's house, was all pretense, and waiting, like her own life in Patrick's house.

When Jocelyn came home Rose felt she ought to apologize for the cleaning she had done, and Jocelyn, really wanting to talk about her fight with the psychiatrist who reminded her of her mother, agreed that it certainly was a cowardly mania, this thing Rose had about housecleaning, and she had better go to a psych herself, if she ever wanted to get rid of it. She was joking; but going home on the bus, with Anna cranky and no preparations made for Patrick's supper, Rose did wonder why she always seemed to be on the wrong end of things, disapproved of by her own neighbors because she didn't pay enough attention to housework, and reproved by Jocelyn for being insufficiently tolerant of the natural chaos and refuse of life. She thought of love, to reconcile herself. She was loved, not in a dutiful, husbandly way but crazily, adulterously, as Jocelyn and her neighbors were not. She used that to reconcile herself to all sorts of things: to Patrick, for instance, turning over in bed with an indulgent little clucking noise that meant she was absolved of all her failings for the moment, they were to make love.

The sane and decent things Clifford had said cut no ice with Rose at all. She saw that he had betrayed her. Sanity and decency were never what she had asked of him. She watched him, in the auditorium of the Powell River High School. She watched him playing his violin, with a somber and attentive expression she had once seen directed towards herself. She did not see how she could do without.

In the middle of the night she phoned him, from her hotel to his.

"Please talk to me."

"That's okay," said Clifford, after a moment's silence. "That's okay, Joss."

He must have a roommate, whom the phone might have wakened. He was pretending to talk to Jocelyn. Or else he was so sleepy he really thought she was Jocelyn.

"Clifford, it's me'."

"That's okay," Clifford said. "Take it easy. Go to sleep."

He hung up the phone.

Jocelyn and Clifford are living in Toronto. They are not poor anymore. Clifford is successful. His name is seen on record jackets, heard on the radio. His face and more frequently his hands have appeared on television as he labors at his violin. Jocelyn has dieted and become slender, has had her hair cut and styled; it is parted in the middle and curves away from her face, with a wing of pure white rising from each temple.

They live in a large brick house on the edge of a ravine. There are bird-feeders in the back yard. They have installed a sauna. Clifford spends a good deal of time sitting there. He thinks that will keep him from becoming arthritic, like his father. Arthritis is his greatest fear.

Rose used to go to see them sometimes. She was living in the country, by herself. She taught at a community college and liked to have a place to stay overnight when she came in to Toronto. They seemed glad to have her. They said she was their oldest friend.

One time when Rose was visiting them Jocelyn told a story about Adam. Adam had an apartment in the basement of the house. Jerome lived downtown, with his girlfriend. Adam brought his girls here.

"I was reading in the den," said Jocelyn, "when Clifford was out. I heard this girl, down in Adam's apartment, saying *no, no!* The noise from his apartment comes straight up into the den. We warned him about that, we thought he'd be embarrassed—"

"I didn't think he'd be embarrassed," said Clifford.

"But he just said, we should put on the record player. So, I kept hearing the poor unknown girl bleating and protesting, and I didn't know what to do. I thought these situations are really new, there are no precedents, are you supposed to stop your son from raping some girl if that's what he's doing, right under your nose or at least under your feet? I went downstairs eventually and I started getting all the family skis out of the closet that backs on his bedroom, I stayed there slamming those skis around, thinking I'd say I was going to polish them. It was July. Adam never said anything to me. I wish he'd move out."

Rose told about how much money Patrick had and how he had married a sensible woman even richer than he was, who had made a dazzling living room with mirrors and pale velvet and a wire sculpture like blasted bird cages. Patrick did not mind Modern Art any more.

"Of course it isn't the same," said Rose to Jocelyn, "it isn't the same house. I wonder what she has done with the Wedgwood vases."

"Maybe she has a campy laundry room. She keeps the bleach in one and the detergent in the other."

"They sit perfectly symmetrically on the shelf."

But Rose had her old, old, twinge of guilt.

"Just the same, I like Patrick."

Jocelyn said, "Why?"

"He's nicer than most people."

"Silly rot," said Jocelyn. "And I bet he doesn't like you."

"That's right," Rose said. She started to tell them about her trip down on the bus. It was one of the times when she was not driving her car, because too many things were wrong with it and she could not afford to get it fixed.

"The man in the seat across from me was telling me about how he used to drive big trucks. He said we never seen trucks in this country like they got in the States." She put on her country accent. "In the Yewnited States they got these special roads what they call turnpikes, and only trucks is allowed to go on them. They get serviced on these roads from one end of the country to the other and so most people never sees them at all. They're so big the cab is half the size of a bus and they got a driver in there and an assistant driver and another driver and another assistant driver havin a sleep. Toilet and kitchen and beds and all. They go eighty, ninety miles an hour, because there is never no speed limit on them turnpikes."

"You are getting very weird," said Clifford. "Living up there."

"Never mind the trucks," Jocelyn said. "Never mind the old mythology. Clifford wants to leave me again."

They settled down to drinking and talking about what Clifford and Jocelyn should do. This was not an unfamiliar conversation. What does Clifford really want? Does he really want not to be married to Jocelyn or does he want something unattainable? Is he going through a middle-age crisis?

"Don't be so banal," Clifford said to Rose. She was the one who said middle-age crisis. "I've been going through this ever since I was twenty-five. I've wanted out ever since I got in."

"That is new, for Clifford to say that," said Jocelyn. She went out to the kitchen to get some cheese and grapes. "For him to actually come out and say that," she yelled from the kitchen. Rose avoided looking at Clifford, not because they had any secrets but because it seemed a courtesy to Jocelyn not to look at each other while she was out of the room.

"What is happening now," said Jocelyn, coming back with a platter of cheese and grapes in one hand and a bottle of gin in the other, "is that Clifford is wide open. He used to bitch and stew and some other bilge would come out that had nothing to do with the real problem. Now he just comes out with it. The great blazing truth. It's a total illumination."

Rose had a bit of difficulty catching the tone. She felt as if living in the country had made her slow. Was Jocelyn's talk a parody, was she being sarcastic? No. She was not.

"But then I go and deflate the truth for you," said Clifford, grinning. He was drinking beer from the bottle. He thought beer was better for him than gin. "It's absolutely true I've wanted out ever since I got in. And it's also true that I wanted in, and I wanted to stay in. I wanted to be married to you and I want to be married to you and I couldn't stand being married to you and I can't stand being married to you. It's a static contradiction."

"It sounds like hell," Rose said.

"I didn't say that. I am just making the point that it is no middle-age crisis."

"Well, maybe that was oversimplifying," said Rose. Nevertheless, she said firmly, in the sensible, down-to-earth, countrified style she was adopting for the moment, all they were hearing about was Clifford. What did Clifford really want, what did Clifford need? Did he need a studio, did he need a holiday, did he need to go to Europe by himself? What made him think, she said, that Jocelyn could be endlessly concerned about his welfare? Jocelyn was not his mother.

"And it's your fault," she said to Jocelyn, "for not telling him to put up or shut up. Never mind what he really wants. Get out or shut up. That's all you need to say to him. Shut up or get out," she said to Clifford with mock gruffness. "Excuse me for being so unsubtle. Or frankly hostile."

She didn't run any risk at all by sounding hostile, and she knew it. She would run a risk by being genteel and indifferent. The way she was talking now was a proof that she was their true friend and took them seriously. And so she did, up to a point.

"She's right, you fucking son-of-a-bitch," said Jocelyn experimentally. "Shut up or get out."

When Jocelyn called Rose on the phone, years ago, to read her the poem *Howl*, she was not able, in spite of her usual boldness of speech, to say the word *fuck*. She tried to force herself, then she said, "Oh, it's stupid, but I can't say it. I'm going to have to say eff. You'll know what I mean when I say eff?"

"But she said it's your fault," said Clifford. "You want to be the mother. You want to be the grownup. You want to be long-suffering."

"Balls," said Jocelyn. "Oh, maybe. Maybe, yes. Maybe I do."

"I bet at school you were always latching on to those kids with the problems," said Clifford with his tender grin. "Those poor kids, the ones with acne or awful clothes or speech impediments. I bet you just persecuted those poor kids with friendliness."

Jocelyn picked up the cheese knife and waved it at him.

"You be careful. You haven't got acne or a speech impediment. You are sickeningly good-looking. And talented. And lucky."

"I have nearly insuperable problems coming to terms with the adult male role," said Clifford priggishly. "The psych says so."

"I don't believe you. Psychs never say anything like nearly insuperable. And they don't use that jargon. And they don't make those judgments. I don't believe you, Clifford."

"Well, I don't really go to the psych at all. I go to the dirty movies down on Yonge."

Clifford went off to sit in the sauna.

Rose watched him leave the room. He was wearing jeans, and a T-shirt that said *Just passin thru*. His waist and hips were narrow as a twelve-year-old's. His gray hair was cut in a very short brush cut, showing his skull. Was this the way musicians wore their hair nowadays, when politicians and accountants were bushy and bearded, or was it Clifford's own perversity? His tan looked like pancake makeup, though it was probably all real. There was something theatrical about him altogether, tight and glittery and taunting. Something obscene about his skinniness and sweet, hard smile.

"Is he well?" she said to Jocelyn. "He's terribly thin."

"He wants to look like that. He eats yogurt and black bread."

"You can never split up," Rose said, "because your house is too beautiful." She stretched out on the hooked rug. The living room had white walls, thick white curtains, old pine furniture, large bright paintings, hooked rugs. On a low round table at her elbow was a bowl of polished stones for people to pick up and hold and run through their fingers. The stones came from Vancouver beaches, from Sandy Cove and English Bay and Kitsilano and Ambleside and Dundarave. Jerome and Adam had collected them a long time ago.

Jocelyn and Clifford left British Columbia soon after Clifford returned from his provincial tour. They went to Montreal, then to Halifax, then to Toronto. They seemed hardly to remember Vancouver. Once they tried to think of the name of the street where they had lived and it was Rose who had to supply it for them. When Rose lived in Capilano Heights she used to spend a lot of time remembering the parts of Ontario where she had lived, being faithful, in a way, to that earlier landscape. Now that she was living in Ontario she put the same sort of effort into remembering things about Vancouver, puzzling to get details straight, that were in themselves quite ordinary. For instance, she tried to remember just where you waited for the Pacific Stage bus, when you were going from North Vancouver to West Vancouver. She pictured herself getting on that old green bus around one o'clock, say, on a spring day. Going to baby-sit for Jocelyn. Anna with her, in her yellow slicker and rainhat. Cold rain. The long, swampy stretch of land as you went into West Vancouver. Where the shopping-centers and high-rises are now. She could see the streets, the houses, the old Safeway, St. Mawes Hotel, the thick closing-in of the woods, the place where you got off the bus at the little store. Black Cat cigarettes sign. Cedar dampness as you walked in through the woods to Jocelyn's house. Deadness of early afternoon. Nap time. Young women drinking coffee looking out of rainy windows. Retired couples walking dogs. Pad of feet on the thick mold. Crocuses, early daffodils, the cold bulbs blooming. That profound difference of the air close to the sea, the inescapable dripping vegetation, the stillness. Anna pulling on her hand, Jocelyn's brown wooden cottage ahead. Such a rich weight of apprehension, complications descending as she neared that house.

Other things she was not so keen on remembering.

She had wept on the plane, behind her sunglasses, all the way from Powell River. She wept, sitting in the waiting room at the Vancouver airport. She was not able to stop weeping and go home to Patrick. A plainclothes policeman sat down beside her, opened his jacket to show her his badge, asked if there was anything he could do for her. Someone must have summoned him. Terrified at being so conspicuous, she fled to the Ladies'. She didn't think to comfort herself with a drink, didn't think of looking for the bar. She never went to bars then. She didn't take a tranquilizer, didn't have any, didn't know about them. Maybe there weren't such things.

The suffering. What was it? It was all a waste, it reflected no credit. An entirely dishonorable grief. All mashed pride and ridiculed fantasy. It was as if she had taken a hammer and deliberately smashed her big toe. That's what she thinks sometimes. At other times she thinks it was necessary, it was the start of wrecks and changes, the start of being where she is now instead of in Patrick's house. Life making a gigantic fuss, as usual, for a small effect.

Patrick could not speak when she told him. He had no lecture prepared. He didn't speak for a long time but followed her around the house while she kept justifying herself, complaining. It was as if he wanted her to go on talking, though he couldn't credit what she was saying, because it would be much worse if she stopped.

She didn't tell him the whole truth. She said that she had "had an affair" with Clifford, and by the telling gave herself a dim secondhand sort of comfort, which was pierced, presently, but not really destroyed, by Patrick's look and silence. It seemed ill-timed, unfair of him, to show such a bare face, such an inappropriate undigestible chunk of grief.

Then the phone rang, and she thought it would be Clifford, experiencing a change of heart. It was not Clifford, it was a man she had met at Jocelyn's party. He said he was directing a radio play, and he needed a country girl. He remembered her accent.

Not Clifford.

She would rather not think of any of this. She prefers to see through metal window-frames of dripping cedars and salmonberry bushes and the proliferating mortal greenery of the rain forest some small views of lost daily life. Anna's yellow slicker. The smoke from Jocelyn's foul fire.

"Do you want to see the junk I've been buying?" said Jocelyn, and took Rose upstairs. She showed her an embroidered skirt and a deep-red satin blouse. A daffodil-colored silk pajama suit. A long shapeless rough-woven dress from Ireland.

"I'm spending a fortune. What I would once have thought was a fortune. It took me so long. It took us both so long, just to be able to spend money. We could not bring ourselves to do it. We despised people who had color television. And you know something – color television is great! We sit around now and say, what would we like? Maybe one of those little toaster-ovens for the cottage? Maybe I'd like a hair blower? All those things everybody else has known about for years but we thought we were too good for. You know what we are, we say to each other? We're Consumers! And it's Okay!"

"And not just paintings and records and books. We always knew they were okay. Color T.V.! Hair dryers! Waffle irons!"

"Remote-control birdcages!" Rose cried cheerfully.

"That's the idea."

"Heated towels."

"Heated towel racks, dummy! They're lovely."

"Electric carving knives, electric toothbrushes, electric toothpicks."

"Some of those things are not as bad as they sound. Really they're not."

Another time when Rose came down Jocelyn and Clifford had a party. When everyone had gone home the three of them, Jocelyn and Clifford and Rose, sat around on the living-room floor, all fairly drunk, and very comfortable. The party had gone well. Rose was feeling a remote and wistful lust; a memory of lust, maybe. Jocelyn said she didn't want to go to bed.

"What can we do?" said Rose. "We shouldn't drink any more."

"We could make love," Clifford said.

Jocelyn and Rose said, "Really?" at exactly the same time. Then they linked their little fingers and said, "Smoke goes up the chimney."

Following which, Clifford removed their clothes. They didn't shiver, it was warm in front of the fire. Clifford kept switching his attention nicely from one to the other. He got out of his own clothes as well. Rose felt curious, disbelieving, hardly willing, slightly aroused and, at some level she was too sluggish to reach for, appalled and sad. Though Clifford paid preliminary homage to them both, she was the one he finally made love to, rather quickly on the nubbly hooked rug. Jocelyn seemed to hover above them making comforting noises of assent.

The next morning Rose had to go out before Jocelyn and Clifford were awake. She had to go downtown on the subway. She found she was looking at men with that speculative hunger, that cold and hurtful need, which for a while she had been free of. She began to get very angry. She was angry at Clifford and Jocelyn. She felt that they had made a fool of her, cheated her, shown her a glaring lack, that otherwise she would not have been aware of. She resolved never to see them again and to write them a letter in which she would comment on their selfishness, obtuseness, and moral degeneracy. By the time she had the letter written to her own satisfaction, in her head, she was back in the country again and had calmed down. She decided not to write it. Sometime later she decided to go on being friends with Clifford and Jocelyn, because she needed such friends occasionally, at that stage of her life.

CHANGE OF FACE

Elspeth Davie

Elspeth Davie (1918–1995) was a Scottish author. Although she wrote novels, she is best known for her short stories. Davie won the Katherine Mansfield Prize in 1978.

It was a mistake to imagine that only the vain or the good-looking offered themselves to the man on the street corner. On Fridays he drew passers-by at a pound a face, and more often than not, those who were particularly pleased with their looks walked on with only a passing glance at his work, for it was not work of high quality. He used crayon – not a lasting medium at the best of times – and he was a poor hand at it. The colours tended to be crude and the results smudgy. Yet even if he could have managed it, he was not after the subtleties of the human face. Always, his aim was to make his pound quickly and sometimes, if it was possible, to please. At any rate, he got all kinds of persons willing to pay for things other than likenesses, even if it was only a chair to rest on. Here, too, the natural clowns of the community enjoyed themselves, for by mixing panto-mime with the solemn sitting they could hope to attract a crowd. They were less interested in seeing their own heads on paper.

A few outstanding faces came his way. He almost dreaded their coming and would occasionally ask: 'Do you really want me to draw your face?' If they were already sitting in the chair he'd set out, they would look up, surprised. 'Well, of course. Can't you see – I'm all ready.'

'It takes a long time. You are going to find that chair very hard.' But there was a cushion on it, and he was perfectly capable of throwing off his mediocre sketches in a matter of minutes – fifteen at the very most.

'The thing is,' he would say, 'I'm an amateur at the job, and as a matter of fact, you have an interesting but rather a difficult face.' He would have been incapable of uttering anything more complimentary even if he and his sitter had been in the most private place. Certain encounters during his life had been chilled and checked by this inhibition, but there were some things he could not do or say. That was how he was made. And such sitters did not take the word 'difficult' too badly, though they were puzzled when he suggested they try a more skilled person for the job. 'Someone,' he'd say, 'who could give you a really excellent likeness. Naturally it might take longer. It would certainly be dearer – but at the end of the day worth every bit of time and money!' Usually, however, they sat on calmly, and calmly carried away his botched effort with a good grace.

His difficulties were not all with the handling of crayons. He was susceptible to certain kinds of beauty in human beings. This made him uneasy, for to fall in love in the space of a few minutes at the corner of a city street with no possibility of continuing the relationship was a serious business. Yet at the same time, he felt that so private a human state could scarcely be taken seriously, surrounded as he was by hordes of fast cars, and with the grind of heavy lorries always in his ears. Busy offices clattering with typewriters leaned above him and lines of smiling placards advertising joy. He was simply aware of the occasional wildness, the piercing sorrow within his chest as some person carrying a scrawl, an unpleasing smear of crayon lines, disappeared forever from his eyes.

Other unexpected difficulties turned up in regard to his sitters. Amongst them were a few persons, men and women who had a desire, not only to discover what they looked like in the flesh, but also to know who or what they were deep in the very core of their being. They had turned to him – he with his cheap crayons, his crumbling pinks and blues and greens, had placed themselves trustfully in a pair of clumsy, inept hands. As well hold out their delicate skulls for dissection to a blunt butcher's knife!

The young man had rigged up a kind of shelter for wet and windy days, hardly more than a covering of canvas supported by sticks and with a scrap of curtaining in front. This also provided some privacy for those persons who wanted it, and amongst them were those who so passionately wished to know what might be seen under the skull or behind the black centre of the eye. This was an awkward problem, for these were people who talked while they sat, and however quietly they talked, they managed somehow to make themselves heard above the strident traffic in the street or the constant sound of voices and footsteps on the pavement outside. They made themselves heard even on the wildest days, as though their private storms were more important than those outside and must be listened to at all costs.

He did listen. He listened to many strange things as he rubbed in the smooth pink cheeks, the red lips and brilliant eyes that were so much a part of his trade. It was evident that long ago they had decided that what they had to say could best be said to a stranger. And where was this stranger who had time to stop and talk in the street? This rigged-up shelter, then, came as an unexpected blessing. Yet they had to be quick about it. For the crayoner himself attempted to point out that his temporary shelter was neither a confessional, nor a fortune-teller's booth – tried to make clear the fact that he himself was not a medium, had no psychic power or talent for divination, that his knowledge of the world was limited, that his experiences in love could never be considered either wise or comforting, that he had no advice to give, for he himself had never taken any, that patience was not his strong suit, and, finally, that pounds were important to him and therefore time was of the essence.

Most of all he made it plain that whatever else he was, he was not a talker. On Fridays at this corner, his words had been limited to certain phrases that cropped up over and over again: 'Please raise your eyes a little, would you lower your head, turn a fraction to the right, to the left. Would you mind putting your hair back from your face? Smiling a little, not smiling so much. You have moved, you have changed! Thank you, that is very good, that is much better. Thank you, I am glad you like it, I am sorry you don't like it, I can't help it if you hate it. That will be a pound. No, I cannot discuss its worth, you have seen my charge. No, it does not include a frame. I am sorry that your husband does not like it, that your wife could do better. It is the best portrait you have ever seen? Thank you very much indeed. You do not like the face? No, it is perfectly legal. You cannot call a policeman. There is a litter-bin across the street. You like the face? You think it better than your own? Oh, how could it be better? It is kind of you to say that, very agreeable and kind. You have given me the greatest pleasure. Please stop abusing me, stop threatening me! There are two policemen across the street. Thank you, I am glad you like the eyes. The mouth is too wide? I am sorry I cannot change the mouth. There is someone waiting. Thank you, it is kind of you. *My* face? Oh, how kind of you to say that. I did not know you were looking at it ... '

But those who had discovered his makeshift shelter were not greatly concerned with how much or how little he could talk. Their problem was time, and sometimes it was more than a problem. It could be a torment. For a whole life-story might well have to be crushed into the space of a few minutes. And though it was true they managed to make themselves heard above wheels and horns, it was not always easy to get the gist of it. Sometimes the young man had to piece it together from words and odd phrases, and while doing it would try to persuade himself that it mattered very little to him how short or scrappy their account of themselves had to be. The exchange seemed fair enough – a scrappy, half-told episode for a careless half-done sketch.

There were days when few people were around to have their faces drawn, and at these times he tried his hand at anything that came along. The pigeons came, for it was a windy corner, scattered with seed from a derelict patch of ground behind. For a time he had a line in pigeons. He did them as quickly as possible while they were on the ground, then painstakingly from memory when they had flown. His birds did not sell. Even the most unobservant could see that he knew next to nothing about wings or flight, not even the heavy flight of pigeons, and those who looked closely at birds could see that anything approaching the iridescence of the neck was far beyond the scope of cheap crayons. He fared no better with one or two stray cats that came to sit in his corner when the sun was on it. He adjured everything about these cats from their independence to the sheen on the muscles of their thin loins. He caught nothing of this, however, and he sold nothing. For everyone knew cats or had them, and they could see that the crayon cats were miserable creatures, neither sunlit jungle beasts nor fireside pets, but unnaturally stretched on the comfortless limbo of dead white paper. People wondered, seeing he had failed so badly with fur and feathers, what he could possibly make of the vulnerable human face. He was aware of this and after a while stopped this particular line, for he saw it was no good for his trade.

One Friday in early spring, when he was outside, pinning a new sheet of paper to his board, it started to snow. It came very gently and sparsely at first – a few white crystals dissolving on the white paper and lying here and there amongst his crayons – but then more and more swiftly, until pavement and street were almost levelled under a thin coating. The city quickly became silent. Even the heavy lorry wheels rolled secretly and the sharpest heels sank into softness. The young man quickly closed his crayon box, put his drawing-board under his arm and was all set to go, when an elderly man came round the corner and stopped determinedly beside him. There was no doubt what he'd come for. Briskly he tapped on the closed crayon box and in a word or two indicated his intention of taking a seat in the shelter. He didn't wait for yes or no, but quickly parted the curtain and sat himself down under the canvas covering. Nevertheless, the young man had no intention of starting up again, so there was nothing for it but to stay outside, showing – as he busied himself around the place – that if the other had come for shelter, well and good. But faces were over for the day. As soon as possible he must be off. He waited a long time. Once or twice he looked behind him through the curtain then finally, reluctantly, he stepped inside.

The man was no longer on the edge of his chair, but sitting well back, his feet firmly planted, one hand on each knee. With head up and eyes straight before him, he was holding a pose to the manner born. The crayoner sat down with a deep sigh and studied the face in front of him. Then he opened up his box and looked at the blunt ends of pink, blue and white crayon – and he saw that this time, the task was beyond him. This face was made up as entirely of lines as a piece of old bark. The bones of the jaw were angled. There was no softness or roundness about this head. Even the hairs stood up from the crown in sharp bristling stalks, the red and grey mixed. The young man tapped his crayon box sharply as the old man had done. He confessed that he could deal only in soft-ness and bluntness. 'And I have no way of sharpening these,' he said quickly, 'so your face is not possible. If I had a pen or even a pencil perhaps … but as it is … ' It was no use. He might as well have talked to a statue. The old man's eyes never flickered in his direction. Stubbornly he continued to hold his pose till the other grabbed up a crayon and started to the job.

He had not been long at it when he realised that his sitter, though he kept his head still as a rock, was going to be moving his lips and his eyes without ceasing. Even more than most, he was determined to talk and there was a lot to tell. Before long it became clear that something more than years had been the cause of lines in his face and the strange springing hair of his head – spring-ing as though endlessly astounded. It was his son. Not that this son of his had given him any trouble in the ordinary sense of the word. No better son had lived from his account. Now *there* was a face, he said, any artist in the land might be proud to draw! And it was not only the face. There had been the character of the young man. There was a good deal of sweetness about his nature, he was kind-hearted. Not that he was a paragon – oh, nothing like that! He could be impatient, intolerant to a degree – hard on others and very hard on himself. He had been a graceful person, said his father, hurrying on, he had danced and he had sung. He had been clever, not in the book-learner's way but in the seaman's way – marvellously clever with his hands. Out of almost nothing he could make anything – model boats, miniature harbours and gardens. He could make chairs, furniture of all kinds. Given the time he could have made a house. The young man, said his father, would have gone far.

Would have gone? The crayoner lifted his head from the paper. For that was the crux of the matter. This boy, who had given his father no trouble at all, had given him the very worst possible trouble in the world. He had got himself drowned with two other sailors like himself far out at sea. Their ages put togeth-er, his father said, wouldn't even add up to his own, which was sixty-nine. There were times he could hardly believe he could live so long – to survive three lives so short. His son had been twenty. And where *was* he? Where was he? The crayoner started as he heard such a question addressed to himself.

Yes, where was he, if anywhere? the father asked. He had thought about it for a long time – it was not too much to say he'd thought of it day and night. Not that he was beside himself; for most of the time nowadays he was quite calm. He was calmly trying to work it out, or simply look at it. He had no idea if that was the way to do it. Probably not. But it was his way, though as yet no answers had come up. Perhaps there were none to come, but that never stopped him from asking: Where is he? He'd imagined him in some odd places.

'Tell me,' said the young man, who was slowly putting the blunt crayons back in their box. He did not want to hear.

To begin with, the father explained, he had simply seen him, naturally enough, in the sea – long separated from his companions – going down with his arms above his head and his legs wide, relaxed after his ordeal, and sometimes softly swinging in the current or twirling, head down, as though peering at something in a crack of rock, or floating on his back, one arm above his head as though reaching out to the other element, or trailing a leg, disentangling a foot amongst weeds – all gentle movements, unhurried, as he saw it. And finally leaving the last glimmer of light and the shoals of fish and going down and down into the darkness. Always, when it got very dark he had lost him, the father said, and he was glad to lose him. He needed to see him whole and bright as he had been. The artist would understand.

'What other places?' said the artist. He understood, but again he did not wish to hear.

The man was silent for a moment. 'No doubt it will sound ridiculous, there is no rhyme or reason in it, but I have sometimes thought of him in the air, or out in the very depths of space. Sometimes he is coasting along like an astronaut, but one with a rather tender skin. He had no time to grow himself a metal surface like the rest of us. His outlines are even less distinct than his sea-farm. He is mixed with all the stuff of the sky, spinning in bright dust and dark. I have never imagined his face, can never guess his expression. That is the hardest thing – to have no idea if or what he is feeling. Has he a voice? In the sea he was silent enough. It is to be hoped he has companions of some kind or another. Oh, I hope to God he is not lonely!'

The crayoner would have much preferred not to hear this particular cry, but that was out of the question. The snow had silenced the street and he was forced to listen. He believed he knew something of loneliness himself, but even so he found nothing whatever to say. It seemed to him that his own experience would sound paltry, hardly worth mentioning beside the thing the father had in mind.

'If you think he is nothing and that he is nowhere – say it, by all means,' said the man. 'Many people have said it with the greatest respect, believe me, and by no means the unkindest people either. Far from being angry I'm thankful for every opinion – all have gone through my head at one time or another. And hearing other views can clear the air. It gives a new line on the thing. You look again. You start again from scratch.' The word seemed to remind him of something. 'Have you finished that drawing?' he said.

'I've had to scrap it,' said the young man. 'I told you I hadn't materials for a proper face.'

'Do what you can,' said the other. 'I don't expect a masterpiece.'

Through the slit in the curtain they could see the snow had stopped falling. Muffled footsteps went past and once or twice a face peered in. Reluctantly the young man pinned a new sheet of paper to his board. The other, who had been sitting absolutely still and silent for a long time, at last said: 'I will never find him, of course. And has he found himself? Maybe he will go through every sort of change, but if he is anywhere at all he will find himself sooner or later. I am happy enough with that idea. It is as good as any other.'

The young man had given up all thought of doing a face. But he was a practised hand at the instant sketch on demand, or if there was no demand he would do anything that came into his head. Occasionally, when the faces became too much for him, he had produced fruit and plants, goldfish in bowls, stormy landscapes, lurid landscapes of purple heather, landscapes of snowy mountains. Flowers were the quickest. He had a peculiar creation of his own – a crossbreed between chrysanthemum, cactus and sunflower, and this he now started on. It had the merit that it could not be criticised by any botanist. Today's version had a spiky head of rough red and brown petals and a staring yellow eye rimmed with hard black spots. The head was supported by a tough, green stalk, ribbed and hairy. If the old man was surprised at the sound of the crayon swishing and jagging over the paper, he showed no sign of it, except that once he smoothed his spiky, startled hair as though this might account for the dramatic change in the artist's rhythm.

The sketch took only a matter of minutes, but the young man had the problem of where to place his flower. He was an expert at bowls and pots and jugs, and if hard-pressed, could even produce some hideous vase from its owner's description. Today he decided on something more ambitious. Behind his flower he sketched in a primitive landscape with a few rocks and a hard blue sky beyond. A primitive landscape was all he was capable of. The thing was quickly done, but it was some time before he could bring himself to hand it over, for he felt the moment was an awkward one. His sitter was not after a striking likeness, but he had come for a face – his own face and no other. Cautiously the young man handed over his drawing. 'I am sorry,' he said. 'It was absolutely not on today. I wouldn't insult you with a worthless face … another time perhaps when I'm equipped for it. Naturally I want nothing for that. If you want it, keep it. There is no need to take it.'

The other man, dropping his pose for the first time, looked down at the drawing. If he was taken aback, it took him less than a moment to adjust to what he saw. Quickly he scanned the dry-faced flower for some familiar feature, at the same time feeling along the skin of his cheek with one hand. His fingers rasped round his chin and down his throat as he followed the hard-ribbed stalk with his eyes. With an impassive face he studied the crude desert, only glancing aside once to compare its yellow ridges with the folded white snow-space through the curtain. No, he was not angry, the young man saw with relief – neither pleased nor angry. On the other hand, he had no intention of taking away a plant. His face was what he wanted and he would get it. Without fuss then he had to make the change, to feel his blood as sap, his hair as spiked petals, his neck a tough stalk, desert for snow. He seemed to manage this to his satisfaction. What other feeling he might have was harder to guess.

The old man laid the paper down and began to button up his coat. Then again he picked up the drawing and studied it at arm's length, stubbornly taking his time. He was not flattered. Flower or face – it was no masterpiece. He said nothing, but with a rather caustic smile pointed to a bit of stalk which had been smeared under the young man's thumb and to the desert rock behind, pulverised to crumbs by a broken crayon end. Yet in his expression, as he now carefully rolled up the paper, could be seen some confirmation of his belief that every weird change could be expected in the human form and spirit. Indeed, as he tied the string around, he seemed determined on it. He had by no means come to the end himself. It was now well on in the afternoon. The old man nodded good-bye, and as he went out laid a pound note deep inside the jug which the young man kept for ends of crayon, and the assortment of rags which were used when necessary to scrub down crayoned lips and cheeks to a paler pink.

The young man was alone again. First he carefully extracted the pound note from the jug, and for the second time that day packed up his stuff ready to go. He parted the curtain, and saw that the snow had already almost gone from this end of the street. The boots of pedestrians and the warm breath from office basements had melted it. But in the untrampled distance where the old man was walking, it lay thick. He could see him, still bravely, still incredulously lifting his feet from the early wastes and deserts of spring snow.

A WEIGHT PROBLEM

Elspeth Davie

Elspeth Davie (1918–1995) was a Scottish author. Although she wrote novels, she is best known for her short stories. Davie won the Katherine Mansfield Prize in 1978.

Very occasionally it happens – when all the baggage has been safely stowed and the passengers, their eyes already on the sky, are sitting braced for the revving up – that a plane is pronounced overweight. Everyone is startled to hear a volunteer being asked to leave. It happened like this, coming like a bolt from the blue, late one autumn afternoon. A suave voice came over the intercom asking for such a person, promising that his fare would be cut by half if he would come on by the next plane. In the minute following this request there was no movement to be seen along the lines of seats. Not a head turned. Hands which had been fixing seatbelts or fiddling with the overhead knobs were stilled, but there was no volunteer. The request was repeated more firmly, though still politely, still promising rewards. And now at last there came a movement from the rear. All heads swivelled round as a small, middle-aged man of slight proportions made his way slowly up the long aisle towards the front of the plane.

It was the first thing his fellow-passengers noticed about him, or rather it was the only thing, the first and the last – his thinness. More than a few eyes fixed him, as he went past, with a disbelieving stare. Could the removal of this lightweight make any difference to the huge machine? Could their lives depend perhaps on one thin man? They scanned him hopefully for fat. He had no fat at all. The thin man may have sensed something of this feeling as he edged past without meeting the eyes, scarcely touching the seats, as though he had been searched relentlessly for the very substance of his being and found wanting. Nor did this passenger have any illusions about the value of his action. It was not a heroic one. He did not live in an age of heroes. He had not been asked to jump out of a moving plane nor to take over the controls from a crew of mad pilots. Indeed, far from gaining respect, he thought it more likely he would be judged as mean-minded, a man willing to give himself endless trouble simply to save a pound or two. It was true his fellow-passengers were glad enough to forget him, for in an aircraft the cause of even one instant's unease is not to be tolerated. When he stepped from the plane he disappeared from their eyes and minds as quickly and surely as though he had stepped over the edge of a cliff.

But the spare passenger had simply stepped down on to the ground of his own home town, and once through the genial formalities at the desk, he could go where he liked for the next two hours. The trouble was he had no desire to go anywhere. He was to be away for seven weeks on a long business trip which would take him first to London and from there to the Continent. He had said his farewells to the family. Now his wife would be peacefully filling up the gap with a visit to a neighbour across the way, his two sons would be round the corner regaling themselves and their friends with extra rounds of beer. His daughter would be preparing to meet her boyfriend and re-doing the cheek where one tear had made serious inroads on the make-up. This was no time to return. The passenger therefore decided to walk about for a while, but unobtrusively, as befitting one who had only half-returned – a kind of ghost coming back to his town to have a last look round before returning to the sky. 'If you break my heart I'll go, but I'll be back again!' a transistor sang for him from some far corner, as he walked out through the waiting-room towards the bus for town.

Even as he approached the city he was still thinking about the plane, following its load of people as they circled farther and farther out into the blue evening. And it seemed to him that he grew lighter as he imagined it, that he grew hollow as if he had unguardedly breathed their thinner air. The bus let him off at a familiar corner where there were a café, a boutique and a flower-shop. He entered the café, went directly to a secluded alcove and almost immediately ran into someone he recognized – a man with whom he had a nodding acquaintance inside the long complex of corridors in his own firm. Over a coffee he told his tale, and the other's eyes bulged.

'I've flown enough myself but I'll admit I've never heard that one!'

'Once in a while it does happen.'

'Why not throw out some baggage instead? Anyway – you're lucky!'

'Lucky? You mean I save half my fare?'

'Not only that. Lucky to be asked to make any gesture at all. Who gets the chance these days? Very few.'

'But it wasn't like that,' said the passenger. 'This was a non-event – the same as stepping off the wrong train.'

'Look,' said the other, 'if someone hadn't got off they wouldn't have gone up. Right now they wouldn't have been up there in that sky at all. I wish I'd been given a chance like that. I'm always waiting but it never comes. The most I've ever done is give up my seat in a bus, and even then you can't be absolutely sure of a smile. Just as likely to be insulted. But you! Now there's a stroke of luck!'

The passenger was silent for a while, looking at the other meditatively over the rim of his cup. 'Don't get me wrong,' he said at last. 'I suppose I think just as well of myself as the next man. On the other hand, I'm unable to see myself nowadays as a person of great weight. I have other things of course. No doubt about it. Not weight. That's simply how I feel.'

The other looked him over quickly as though measuring him in feet, weighing him in stones. He even glanced back at the counter as if to see what could be got there to fatten up the man. But he was no fool. He knew it was not only the physical substance they were discussing. He played for time, however. From the counter he brought back two buttered rolls and two more cups of coffee. And at the same time he added the weight of words. 'But for you,' he repeated softly, 'they wouldn't be in the sky at all!'

The passenger sat and thought about this, once more balancing himself in space against the huge machine – against its tons of steel, against elephantine wheels and whirling blades, against its heavy human load. True enough there was something to be said in his favour. His reluctant presence on solid earth at this very instant was the price of their flight. But it did not answer everything.

The other watched him carefully as he ate his roll – and somewhat anxiously – for he had begun to take an interest in this exceedingly thin man with the weight problem. He waited till the last bite of roll had gone, before asking: 'You feel better now? You look better.'

'As far as the stomach goes – yes.'

'You are still worried about weight?'

The passenger smiled. 'Naturally the middle-aged are expected to worry about *overweight*. What isn't always admitted is their worry about the lack of it. At our stage we're expected, aren't we, to make pronouncements of weight, to have opinions that carry weight, to bring our weight to bear, to throw our weight around and all the other phrases related to what should be? Worst of all, and most ridiculous, we're expected to have gathered up some great load of wisdom ...'

'And you?'

'That's the trouble. Less weight. Less with the family, less with the job. My opinions on this and that carry less weight nowadays. My credentials, my references and what have you are exactly the same, of course, but now they weigh less. I very seldom have to weigh my words because they are not listened to anyway.'

'You're weighing them now.'

'Yes, only because you are a sympathetic listener.'

The sympathetic listener looked pleased, but to him it was not enough to listen. He preferred action. Moreover he was afraid that when the thin man began to be really sorry for himself, even listening would be no cure. He suggested a move.

'Where are we going?' said the other as they emerged from the door. 'I've not got much time left.'

'Simply to walk around. Everything's within reach hereabouts. Let's look in here.'

The passenger hesitated on the threshold of a record shop. On window posters and on the sleeves of discs young men were shown singing – gilded youths polished by pink and yellow spotlights, or black-robed, close-cropped with sequined eyelids like frenzied monks, or others again, hairy and sombre as hermits. Song burst from the four walls with ear-splitting fury. 'It is not my scene,' said the thin man. Yet the themes were ancient and universal. Through the raucous, brutal bellow and the rhythmic moan, Love and Freedom were still to the fore.

'Maybe it is not,' said the other in answer, 'but we can go through from here into the boutique.' They stepped through, past beaded curtains and down some steps into a shop at the back. It was quieter here, though the place still throbbed with drumming. Coats and trousers, scarves and dresses swung gently on their hangers. From ceiling hooks the clustered beads and chains vibrated and a subdued rattling came from the boxes of rings and brooches on the table. There was a smell of spice and incense.

'Have you ever looked ...?' said the sympathiser, putting up his hand towards the ropes of neckchains.

'No, never,' said the passenger, stepping back as a cluster of heavy metal crosses swung before his eyes. 'Besides I am not really what you would call ...'

'No need to be any kind of Christian nowadays to wear these,' said the other. 'You can wear anything you fancy – crosses, amulets, wreaths, witch doctors' charms, ankle bells. These strings of worry beads might be worth looking at. There are some beauties here.'

'Worry beads?' a charming, smiling girl stepped from the counter and began unlooping beads of polished wood, strings of chalk-white shells, beads of yellow glass. Over the traveller's head she slipped a string of small green stones. He held them – pleasant to the touch – smooth, warm and slightly waxy as though some stronger sun in another country had melted their surface. The other two stepped back to admire him. 'Definitely yes,' said the man. 'Those are your stones all right.'

'But what am I supposed ...?'

'Anywhere,' said the girl. 'In your pocket, or just leave them on. Keep them hidden if you like.' Cool, firm hands tucked the beads out of sight inside his waistcoat.

'Would you believe it? – the man has a weight problem,' said his companion.

'Oh, nonsense,' said the girl, glancing at his waistline.

'Yes, he feels that he has not, at his age, made sufficient weighty pronouncements to the world. And now of course he thinks it's too late.'

The passenger could not deny this charge, but he gave his own version and for a few minutes, until the girl was called to another customer, they discussed lightness and weight and the formidable heaviness of the great globe itself. The passenger could not help noticing as he glanced around how light everything here appeared to be – airy fabrics stirring, bird and fish mobiles twirling in a breath of air, swinging bells, ruffled feathers, wings and flowers. The whole pile put together could hardly weigh much. Nothing was meant to last. Was that perhaps its value? The records in the adjoining shop still yelled and moaned of Love and Freedom, but it was of its changing and ephemeral nature that they sang.

'I suppose that was not your kind of place either,' said the younger man, as they moved away towards the windows of the expensive flower-shop next door. There were few ordinary bunches or bouquets on display today. Huge funeral wreaths of dark leaves and waxy yellow flowers were propped up against chrysanthemums bound into hard crosses. Tightly packed balls of dried white flowers were strewn about like plushy graveyard cushions.

'Well then – what now?' said the man again with some irritation. 'Is this your scene?'

'Not yet,' said the passenger, briskly for the first time, and in case there was any suggestion that he was already half-dead, he went decisively in past the wreaths and crosses into the back of the shop where all was earthy, damp and aromatic, with pots of leafy plants on shelves and fresh bunches of roses, iris and carnation standing in tubs of water.

'We are looking for a buttonhole – something bright and perfumed,' said the younger man. 'It's for my friend here and it will have to last him through a journey.'

'I am not going to a wedding!' exclaimed the passenger. But the shop assistants, who had been gravely waiting to assist mourners, clustered round as though it was their last chance at the end of the day to forget the showy displays of death in the front of the shop.

'What's more, he has just stepped out of a plane – well, not a moving one, that's asking a bit much of a human being – but he has removed his own weight so that all the others could go on.' Exclamations of admiration and surprise greeted this announcement, and a few light murmurs of disbelief.

'Naturally he got a cut-price fare out of it. Again it would be asking a bit much if he'd had to do it for nothing,' added the man, as he watched a free red carnation being pinned into the passenger's buttonhole. For a while they fussed about him, wondering how long the flower would last, whether it would survive the heat, the pressure, the wind on the tarmac. And again the passenger wondered why he should ever concern himself with weight or lasting things when the whole shop of flowers would fade and pass into memory. But again – did this give it its value? Tonight he believed he would remember every petal of the place.

Time was almost up and the passenger was ready to board the bus back to the airfield. 'Have you everything you need?' asked the other.

'More than enough.'

'But what about something to eat on the journey – a small bar of chocolate?' Disregarding the traveller's protests, he stopped at a small newspaper stall where a few boxes of chocolates were laid out. 'Not even a small bar? Is that all you have?' the thin man heard him ask. He came back with a small twist of golden chocolate sovereigns in a net bag.

'But that's ridiculous. I am not a child!'

'They are simply thin chocolates. There is nothing to them.'

'I have never wanted to gain weight of that kind,' said the thin man.

'Of course not. As to the other kind, you will no doubt think of many wise and weighty things when you are up in the air. People often do when they're removed from the earth or even when they're fast asleep. Goodbye now – and good luck!'

The passenger returned to the airfield with not very much time for the next plane. He was greeted by the familiar officials and hustled through the formalities of the next flight. Indeed it seemed they were genuinely pleased to see him – welcoming him back to this scene like some one-line actor who had accidentally added a hint of farce to the show. 'So you managed to put in a couple of hours,' said one. 'The time didn't hang too heavy, I hope?'

'No, no – not in the least.' The passenger went out onto the tarmac which this evening was living up to its tradition of great wings and high wind. As he walked towards the plane he was almost blown off his feet by a gust from the east. Was he always to be reminded of human lightness?

And yet time had hung something upon him after all. It was not only that he was now decorated with beads, with a flower, with counterfeit gold coin, that he carried a little doubtful praise and some misplaced envy. His responsibilities were enlarged. In his own eyes, for better or worse, he had gained weight of a kind. Ahead the great blank eyes of the machine glared impatiently. But the single, late passenger moved steadily, unhurriedly towards the gangway.

THE PRESCRIPTION

Penelope Fitzgerald

Penelope Fitzgerald (1916–2000) was a Man Booker Prize-winning English novelist, poet, essayist and biographer. In 2008, *The Times* included her in a list of the '50 Greatest British writers since 1945' and, in 2012, the *Observer* named her final novel, *The Blue Flower*, as one of 'The 10 best historical novels'. A collection of Fitzgerald's short stories, *The Means of Escape*, and a volume of her non-fiction writings, *A House of Air*, were published posthumously.

After Petros Zarifi's wife died his shop began to make less and less money. His wife had acted as cashier. That was all over now. The shelves emptied gradually as the unpaid wholesalers refused to supply him with goods. In his tiny room at the back of the shop he had, like many Greek storekeepers, an oleograph in vivid colours of his patron saint, with the motto *Embros* – Forward! But he had now lost all ambition except in the matter of his son Alecco.

The shop was not too badly placed, on the very edge of the Phanar, where Zarifi should have been able to sell to both Greeks and Turks. One of his remaining customers, in fact, was an elderly Stamboullu who worked as dispenser to a prosperous doctor in the Beyazit district. Both old Yousuf and Dr Mehmet drank raki, which they regarded as permissible because it had not been invented in the days of the Prophet. One evening when he was refilling the bottles Zarifi asked Yousuf to speak for him to Mehmet Bey.

'Ask him if he will take my son Alecco, who has just turned fourteen, into his employment.'

'Can't his own relatives provide for him?' asked the old man.

'Don't give a father advice on this matter,' said Zarifi. 'What else does he think about when he lies awake at nights?'

Mehmet Bey took the virtue of compassion seriously. Once he had been told that Zarifi was a *good Greek*, who had won a reputation for honesty, and, possibly as a result, had been unfortunate, he sent word that he would see him.

'Your son can clean my boots and run errands. That is all I have to offer. Don't let him have ambitions. There are too many doctors in Stamboul, and, above all, far too many Greeks.'

'Good, well, I understand you, *bey effendi*, you may trust both my son and me.'

It was arranged that Alecco should work and sleep at the doctor's house in Hayreddin Pasha Street. His room was not much larger than a cupboard, but then, neither had it been at home. Loneliness was his trouble, not discomfort. The doctor's wife, Azizié Hanoum, kept to her quarters, and old Yousuf, who was a poor relation of hers, jealously guarded the dispensary, where the drugs must have been arranged on some kind of system since he was able, given time, to make up a prescription when called upon. As to Mehmet Bey himself, his hours were regular. After a sluggish evening visit to the coffee-house to read the newspaper he would return and spend a few hours more than half asleep in the bosom of his family. But Alecco understood very well, or thought he understood, what it was that his father expected him to do.

Polishing the boots of the *hakim bashi* did not take up much of the day. Always obedient, he went about with the doctor as a servant, keeping several paces behind, carrying his bag and his stethoscope. Once a week Mehmet Bey, as a good Moslem, gave his services to the hospital for the poor on the waterfront, and Alecco learned in the wards to recognize the face of leprosy and of death itself. Then, because he was so quick, he began to help a little with the accounts, and from the ledgers he gathered in a few weeks how the practice was run and which were the commonest complaints and how much could be charged for them in each case – always excepting the bills of the very rich, which were presented by Mehmet Bey in person. The doctor, for his part, recognized that this boy was sharp, and did not much like it. A subject race, he reflected, is a penance to the ruler. But he reminded himself that the father was trustworthy and honourable, and in time the son's sharpness might turn into nothing worse than industry, which is harmless.

Every day Alecco asked himself: have I gone one step forward, or one backward? What have I learned that I didn't know yesterday? Books are teachers to those who have none, but the doctor's library reposed behind the wooden shutters of the cupboards fitted into the walls of his consulting-room. His student *Materia Medica* were there, along with herbals in Arabic and the *Gulistan*, or Rose Garden of Medicines. Lately he had acquired a brand-new book, Gray's *Anatomy* in a French translation. Alecco had seen him turning it over heavily, during the late afternoon. But it was put away with the others, and there was no chance to look at it, still less to copy the illustrations.

The dispensary, also, was kept locked and bolted. But that year the month of Ramazan fell in the hot weather, and both the doctor and old Yousuf, being obliged to fast all day until sunset, went out through the hours of darkness to take refreshment, Mehmet Bey at the homes of his friends, Yousuf at the teahouse. Security was less strict, and the house itself, windowless against the street, seemed to relax at the end of its tedious day. During the second week of the fast, Alecco found the door of the dispensary unfastened.

Just before dawn began to lift, Mehmet Bey returned and saw that a single candle lamp was burning in his dispensary. The Greek boy was standing at the bench, copying out prescriptions. He had also taken down a measuring-glass, a pestle and a number of bottles and jars.

Bath-boy, *tellak*, son of a whore, the doctor thought. The hurt pierced deep. His friends had warned him, his wife had told him he was a fool. But in the end he had made a burden for his own back.

Alecco was so deeply absorbed that his keen sense of danger failed him. He did not move until Mehmet Bey towered close behind him. Then he turned, not dropping the pen and ink which he had stolen but gripping them closely to him, and stared up with the leaden eyes of a woken sleepwalker at his master.

'I see that you are studying my prescriptions,' said Mehmet Bey. 'I know from experience that you learn quickly.'

He picked up the empty glass. 'Now: make up a medicine for yourself.'

Sweating and trembling, Alecco shook in a measure of this and a measure of that, always keeping his eyes on his master. He could not have said what he was doing. Mehmet Bey, however, saw a dose of aphrodisiac go into the glass, and then the dried flowers of *agnus castas*, which inhibits sex, opium, lavender, *ecballium elaterium*, the most violent of all purgatives, *datura*, either 14 grams, inducing insanity, or 22½ grams (death) and finally mustard and cinnamon. Silently he pointed to the fuller's earth, which prevents the patient from vomiting. Alecco added a handful.

'Drink!'

The doctor's voice, raised to a pitch of sacred rage, woke up Azizié Hanoum, and standing terrified in her old wrapper at the door of the women's quarters she saw her husband seize the Greek boy by the nose, from which water poured out, and force his head backwards to dislocation point while something black as pitch ran from the measuring-glass down his throat.

In the morning Alecco, who had been crammed into his room unconscious, appeared smiling with the doctor's cleaned boots in his hands. Mehmet Bey made a sign to avert evil.

'You're well? You're alive?'

'My prescription did me a world of good.'

The doctor called his servants and had him turned out of the house. Picking himself up, Alecco walked away with fourteen-year-old jauntiness along the new horse tramway until he was out of sight. Not until he reached the foot of the Galata Bridge did his will-power give way and he collapsed groaning like vermin on a dung-hill.

Preparing slowly for his rounds, Mehmet Bey at first congratulated himself, since if the boy had died he was not quite certain how he would have stood with the law. But the household's peace was destroyed. Old Yousuf was so perturbed by the mess in the dispensary that he collapsed with a slight stroke. He had never been able to read, and now that the drugs were out of order he could find nothing. Azizié Hanoum poured reproaches on her husband and declared that if the little Greek had been better treated he could have been trained to help Yousuf. Zarifi mourned his son, who did not return either to the Phanar or to Hayreddin Pasha Street. In a few months the grocer's shop was bankrupt.

Alecco had been picked up on the waterfront by a Greek ship's cook, coming back on board after a night's absence. He had some confused idea of conciliating the captain, who, he knew, was short of a boy. The *Andromeda* was an irregular trading vessel carrying mail via Malta and Gibraltar, and by the time she reached London Alecco had been seasick to such an extent that he was clear of the poison's last traces. This seemed a kind of providence; he could never have cheated Death without some help. The captain had fancied him from the start, and when the crew were paid off at Albert Docks he gave him five pounds in English money to make a good start in life.

Ten years later Dr Mehmet's career had reached its highest point and was also (he was sixty-five) approaching its end. Having been called, not for the first time, for consultation at the Old Serail, he settled down for a long waiting period before an attendant arrived to escort him to the ante-rooms. He took a seat overlooking the Sea of Marmara, and resigned himself. In contemplation of the lazing water, he allowed his energies to sleep. The ladies here were the old and the pensioned-off, but the appointment was an honour.

Quite without warning, and faintly disagreeable, was the appearance of a secretary: Lelia Hanoum had wished for a second opinion, and he had the honour to present a distinguished young colleague who had hurried here from another appointment. But when a young man walked in wearing a black *stambouline*, the professional's frock-coat, and followed by a servant carrying his bag and stethoscope, Mehmet Bey knew not only who he was, but that he had been expecting him.

'I decline to accept you as a colleague, Alexander Zarifi.'

'I am qualified,' Dr Zarifi replied.

'Your word is not good enough.'

Alecco took out from the upper pocket of his *stamboulim* a card printed in gilt, which showed that he had recently been appointed to attend the Serail. This could not be contradicted, and after putting it away he said:

'I am honoured, then, to join you as a consultant.' He waited for the usual, in fact necessary, reply: 'The honour is mine,' but instead Mehmet Bey said loudly: 'There is no need for us to waste time in each other's company. I know the case history of Lelia Hanoum, you may consult my notes. I have already made the diagnosis. Last year the patient complained of acute pain in the left side and a distention as though a ball or globe was rising from the abdomen to the throat. Palpitations, fits of crying, quantities of wind passed per rectum. A typical case of hysteria, all too common in the Serail, and entirely the result of an ill-balanced regimen. I advised firm treatment, iron pills and a gentian tonic. Recently, however, she has described the initial pain as on the right side. Accordingly I have changed my diagnosis to acute appendicitis, and I propose to operate as soon as permission can be got from the Palace. She is rather old for the operation to be successful, but that is in God's hands.'

'I cannot agree,' Dr Zarifi replied. 'The very fact that the patient is uncertain whether she feels pain on the left or the right side means that we must look beneath her symptoms for an unconscious or subconscious factor. During my training in Vienna I was fortunate enough to work with Dr Josef Breuer, the great specialist in hysteria. It is for the woman herself to lead us to the hidden factor, perhaps under hypnosis. It is my belief that there is no need for medication, still less surgical interference. We must aim at setting her free.'

'Well, now I have your opinion,' said Mehmet Bey. 'If I reject it, it is because I have studied the art of healing, not so much from personal ambition as to answer the simplest of all appeals – *hastayim*, I am ill. I accept that since we last met you have had the advantage of a good training, but your nature will not have changed. You are still Alexander Zarifi. What is more, there are universal laws, which govern all human beings, not excepting men of science. Cast your memory back, and answer me this question: Knowledge is good, but what is the use of knowledge without honesty?'

Dr Alecco looked down at the ground, and withdrew his diagnosis.

HOW DID I GET AWAY WITH KILLING ONE OF THE BIGGEST LAWYERS IN THE STATE? IT WAS EASY.

Alice Walker

Alice Walker (b. 1944) is an American author, poet, feminist and activist. She is best known for the critically acclaimed novel *The Color Purple*, published in 1982, for which she won the National Book Award and the Pulitzer Prize. Walker's published works include seven novels, four collections of short stories, four children's books and volumes of essays and poetry.

"My mother and father were not married. I never knew him. My mother must have loved him, though; she never talked against him when I was little. It was like he never existed. We lived on Poultry Street. Why it was called Poultry Street I never knew. I guess at one time there must have been a chicken factory somewhere along there. It was right near the center of town. I could walk to the state capitol in less than ten minutes. I could see the top – it was gold – of the capitol building from the front yard. When I was a little girl I used to think it was real gold, shining up there, and then they bought an eagle and put him on top, and when I used to walk up there I couldn't see the top of the building from the ground, it was so high, and I used to reach down and run my hand over the grass. It was like a rug, that grass was, so springy and silky and deep. They had these big old trees, too. Oaks and magnolias; and I thought the magnolia trees were beautiful and one night I climbed up in one of them and got a bloom and took it home. But the air in our house blighted it; it turned brown the minute I took it inside and the petals dropped off.

"Mama worked in private homes. That's how she described her job, to make it sound nicer. 'I work in private homes,' she would say, and that sounded nicer, she thought, than saying 'I'm a maid.'

"Sometimes she made six dollars a day, working in two private homes. Most of the time she didn't make that much. By the time she paid the rent and bought milk and bananas there wasn't anything left.

"She used to leave me alone sometimes because there was no one to keep me – and then there was an old woman up the street who looked after me for a while – and by the time she died she was more like a mother to me than Mama was. Mama was so tired every night when she came home I never hardly got the chance to talk to her. And then sometimes she would go out at night, or bring men home – but they never thought of marrying her. And they sure didn't want to be bothered with me. I guess most of them were like my own father; had children somewhere of their own that they'd left. And then they came to my Mama, who fell for them every time. And I think she may have had a couple of abortions, like some of the women did, who couldn't feed any more mouths. But she tried.

"Anyway, she was a nervous kind of woman. I think she had spells or something because she was so tired. But I didn't understand anything then about exhaustion, worry, lack of a proper diet; I just thought she wanted to work, to be away from the house. I didn't blame her. Where we lived people sometimes just threw pieces of furniture they didn't want over the railing. And there was broken glass and rags everywhere. The place stunk, especially in the summer. And children were always screaming and men were always cussing and women were always yelling about something ... It was nothing for a girl or woman to be raped. I was raped myself, when I was twelve, and my Mama never knew and I never told anybody. For, what could they do? It was just a boy, passing through. Somebody's cousin from the North.

"One time my Mama was doing day's work at a private home and took me with her. It was like being in fairyland. Everything was spotless and new, even before Mama started cleaning. I met the woman in the house and played with her children. I didn't even see the man, but he was in there somewhere, while I was out in the yard with the children. I was fourteen, but I guess I looked like a grown woman. Or maybe I looked fourteen. Anyway, the next day he picked me up when I was coming from school and he said my Mama had asked him to do it. I got in the car with him ... he took me to his law office, a big office in the middle of town, and he started asking me questions about 'how do you all live?' and 'what grade are you in?' and stuff like that. And then he began to touch me, and I pulled away. But he kept touching me and I was scared ... he raped me. But afterward he told me he hadn't forced me, that I felt something for him, and he gave me some money. I was crying, going down the stairs. I wanted to kill him.

"I never told Mama. I thought that would be the end of it. But about two days later, on my way from school, he stopped his car again, and I got in. This time we went to his house; nobody was there. And he made me get into his wife's bed. After we'd been doing this for about three weeks, he told me he loved me. I didn't love him, but he had begun to look a little better to me. Really, I think, because he was so clean. He bathed a lot and never smelled even alive, to tell the truth. Or maybe it was the money he gave me, or the presents he bought. I told Mama I had a job after school baby-sitting. And she was glad that I could buy things I needed for school. But it was all from him.

"This went on for two years. He wouldn't let me get pregnant, he said, and I didn't. I would just lay up there in his wife's bed and work out algebra problems or think about what new thing I was going to buy. But one day, when I got home, Mama was there ahead of me, and she saw me get out of his car. I knew when he was driving off that I was going to get it.

"Mama asked me didn't I know he was a white man? Didn't I know he was a married man with two children? Didn't I have good sense? And do you know what I told her? *I told her he loved me.* Mama was crying and praying at the same time by then. The neighbors heard both of us screaming and crying, because Mama beat me almost to death with the cord from the electric iron. She just hacked it off the iron, still on the ironing board. She beat me till she couldn't raise her arm. And then she had one of her fits, just twitching and sweating and trying to claw herself into the floor. This scared me more than the beating. That night she told me something I hadn't paid much attention to before. She said; 'On top of everything else, that man's daddy goes on the TV every night and says folks like us ain't even human.' It was his daddy who had stood in the school-house door saying it would be over his dead body before any black children would come into a white school.

"But do you think that stopped me? No. I would look at his daddy on TV ranting and raving about how integration was a communist plot, and I would just think of how different his son Bubba was from his daddy! Do you understand what I'm saying. I thought he *loved* me. That *meant* something to me. What did I know about 'equal rights'? What did I care about 'integration'? I was sixteen! I wanted somebody to tell me I was pretty, and he was telling me that all the time. I even thought it was *brave* of him to go with me. History? What did I know about History?

"I began to hate Mama. We argued about Bubba all the time, for months. And I still slipped out to meet him, because Mama had to work. I told him how she beat me, and about how much she despised him – he was really pissed off that any black person could despise him – and about how she had these spells ... Well, the day I became seventeen, the *day* of my seventeenth birthday, I signed papers in his law office, and I had my mother committed to an insane asylum.

"After Mama had been in Carthage Insane Asylum for three months, she managed somehow to get a lawyer. An old slick-headed man who smoked great big black cigars. People laughed at him because he didn't even have a law office, but he was the only lawyer that would touch the case, because Bubba's daddy was such a big deal. And we all gathered in the judge's chambers – because he wasn't about to let this case get out. Can you imagine, if it had? And Mama's old lawyer told the judge how Bubba's daddy had tried to buy him off. And Bubba got up and swore he'd never touched me. And then I got up and said Mama was insane. And do you know what? By that time it was true. Mama *was* insane. She had no mind left at all. They had given her shock treatments or something ... God knows what else they gave her. But she was as vacant as an empty eye socket. She just sat sort of hunched over, and her hair was white.

"And after all this, Bubba wanted us to keep going together. Mama was just an obstacle that he felt he had removed. But I just suddenly – in a way I don't even pretend to understand – woke up. It was like everything up to then had been some kind of dream. And I told him I wanted to get Mama out. But he wouldn't do it; he just kept trying to make me go with him. And sometimes – out of habit, I guess – I did. My body did what it was being paid to do. And Mama died. And I killed Bubba.

"How did I get away with killing one of the biggest lawyers in the state? It was easy. He kept a gun in his desk drawer at the office and one night I took it out and shot him. I shot him while he was wearing his thick winter overcoat, so I wouldn't have to see him bleed. But I don't think I took the time to wipe off my fingerprints, because, to tell the truth, I couldn't stand it another minute in that place. No one came after me, and I read in the paper the next day that he'd been killed by burglars. I guess they thought 'burglars' had stolen all that money Bubba kept in his safe – but I had it. One of the carrots Bubba always dangled before me was that he was going to send me to college: I didn't see why he shouldn't do it.

"The strangest thing was, Bubba's wife came over to the house and asked me if I'd mind looking after the children while she went to Bubba's funeral. I did it, of course, because I was afraid she'd suspect something if I didn't. So on the day he was buried I was in his house, sitting on his wife's bed with his children, and eating fried chicken his wife, Julie, had cooked."

CORRUPTION

Penelope Lively

Penelope Lively (b. 1933) is a critically acclaimed British author of fiction for both children and adults. She won the Carnegie Medal for children's fiction in 1973, for *The Ghost of Thomas Kempe*, and also the Man Booker Prize for her 1987 novel, *Moon Tiger*. Lively was made Dame Commander of the Order of the British Empire in the 2012 New Year Honours list.

The judge and his wife, driving to Aldeburgh for the weekend, carried with them in the back of the car a Wine Society carton filled with pornographic magazines. The judge, closing the hatchback, stared for a moment through the window; he reopened the door and put a copy of *The Times* on top of the pile, extinguishing the garish covers. He then got into the driving seat and picked up the road atlas.

"The usual route, dear?"

"The usual route, I think. Unless we spot anything enticing on the way."

"We have plenty of time to be enticed, if we feel so inclined."

The judge, Richard Braine, was sixty-two; his wife Marjorie, a magistrate, was two years younger. The weekend ahead was their annual and cherished early summer break at the Music Festival; the pornographic magazines were the impounded consignment of an importer currently under trial and formed the contents of the judge's weekend briefcase, so to speak. "Chores?" his wife had said, and he had replied, "Chores, I'm afraid."

At lunch-time, they pulled off the main road into a carefully selected lane and found a gate-way in which to park the car. They carried the rug and picnic basket into a nearby field and ate their lunch under the spacious East Anglian sky in a state of almost flamboyant contentment. Both had noted how the satisfactions of life have a tendency to gain intensity with advancing years. "The world gets more beautiful," Marjorie had once said, "not less so. Fun is even more fun. Music is more musical, if you see what I mean. One hadn't reckoned with that." Now, consuming the thoughtfully constructed sandwiches and the coffee from the thermos, they glowed at one another amid the long thick grass that teemed with buttercup and clover; before them, the landscape retreated into blue distances satisfactorily broken here and there by a line of trees, the tower of a church or a rising contour. From time to time they exchanged remarks of pleasure or anticipation: about the surroundings, the weather, the meal they would eat tonight at the little restaurant along the coast road, tomorrow evening's concert. Richard Braine, who was a man responsive to the moment, took his wife's hand; they sat in the sun, shirt-sleeved, and agreed conspiratorially and without too much guilt that they were quite glad that the eldest married daughter who sometimes accompanied them on this trip had not this year been able to. The daughter was loved, but would just now have been superfluous.

When they arrived at the small hotel it was early evening. The judge carried their suitcase and the Wine Society carton in and set them down by the reception desk. The proprietor, bearing the carton, showed them to their usual room. As she was unpacking, Marjorie said, "I think you should have left that stuff in the car. Chambermaids, you know …" The judge frowned. "That's a point." He tipped the contents of the box into the emptied suitcase and locked it. "I think I'll have a bath before we go out."

He lay in the steamy cubicle, a sponge resting upon his stomach. Marjorie, stripped to a pair of pants, came in to wash. "The dear old avocado suite again. One day we must have an avocado bathroom suite at home." The judge, contemplating the rise of his belly, nodded; he was making a resolution about reduction of the flesh, a resolution which he sadly knew would be broken. He was a man who enjoyed food. His wife's flesh, in the process now of being briskly soaped and scrubbed, was firmer and less copious, as he was fully prepared to concede. He turned his head to watch her and thought for a while in a vague and melancholy way about bodies, about how we inhabit them and are dragged to the grave by them and are conditioned by them. In the course of his professional life he had frequently had occasion to reflect upon the last point: it had seemed to him, observing the faces that passed before him in courtrooms, that confronted him from docks and witness boxes, that not many of us are able to rise above physical appearance. The life of an ugly woman is different from that of a beautiful one; you cannot infer character from appearance, but you can suspect a good deal about the circumstances to which it will have given rise. Abandoning this intetesting but sombre theme, he observed his wife's breasts and muscular but not unshapely thighs and the folds of skin upon her neck and remembered the first time he had seen her with no clothes on. She turned to look at him. "If you're jeering at my knickers, they're a pair of Alison's I grabbed out of the laundry basket by mistake." Alison was their youngest, unmarried daughter. "I hadn't really noticed them," said the judge politely. "I was thinking about something quite different." He smiled. "And don't leer," said his wife, flicking him with her flannel. "It's unbecoming in a man of your age." "It's a tribute to your charms, my dear," said the judge. He sat up and began to wash his neck, thinking still about that first time they had both been embarrassed. Embarrassment had been a part of the pleasure, he reflected. How odd, and interesting.

It was still daylight when they drove to the restaurant, a violet summer twilight in which birds sang with jungle stridency. Marjorie, getting out of the car, said, "That veal and mushroom in cream sauce thing for me, I think. A small salad for you, without dressing."

"No way," said the judge.

"I admire your command of contemporary speech." She went ahead into the restaurant, inspecting the room with bright, observant eyes. When they were sitting at the table she whispered, "There's that same woman we met last year. Remember? The classy type who kept putting you right about Britten."

The judge, cautiously, turned his head. "So it is. Keep a low profile."

"Will do, squire," said Marjorie, applying herself to the menu. "Fifteen all?" she added. "Right?"

"Right," said her husband.

Their acquaintance, leaving before them, stopped to exchange greetings. The judge, mildly resenting the interruption to his meal, left the work to Marjorie. The woman, turning to go, said, "So nice to see you again. And have a lovely break from juries and things." She gleamed upon the judge.

He watched her retreating silk-clad back. "Rather a gushing creature. How the hell does she know what I do?"

"Chatting up the hotel people, I don't doubt. It gives you cachet, you note, your job. Me, on the other hand, she considers a drab little woman. I could see her wondering how I came by you."

"Shall we enlighten her? Sheer unbridled lust ..."

"Talking of which," said Marjorie, "Just how unprincipled would it be to finish off with some of that cheese-cake?"

Back at the hotel, they climbed into bed in a state of enjoyable repletion. The judge put on his spectacles and reached out for the suitcase. "You're not going to start going through that stuff *now* ..." said Marjorie. "At least have one whole day off work."

"You're right," he said. "Tomorrow will do. I'll have that Barbara Pym novel instead."

The judge, waking early the next morning, lay thinking about the current trial. He thought, in fact, not about obscenity or pornography but about the profit motive. He did not, he realised, understand the profit motive; he did not understand it in the same way in which he did not understand what induced people to be cruel. He had never coveted the possessions of others or wished himself richer than he was. He held no stocks or shares; Marjorie, once, had been left a small capital sum by an aunt; neither he nor she had ever been able to take the slightest interest in the financial health of her investments. Indeed, both had now forgotten what exactly the money was in. All this, he realised, was the position of a man with a substantial earned income; were he not paid what he was he might well feel otherwise. But he had not, in fact, felt very much otherwise as an impecunious young barrister. And importers of pornography tend, he understood, to be in an upper income bracket. No – the obstacle, the barrier requiring that leap of the imagination, was this extra dimension of need in some men that sought to turn money into yet more money, that required wealth for wealth's sake, the spawning of figures. The judge himself enjoyed growing vegetables; he considered, now, the satisfaction he got from harvesting a good crop of french beans and tried to translate this into a manifestation of the profit motive. The analogy did not quite seem to work.

The profit motive in itself, of course, is innocuous enough. Indeed, without it societies would founder. This was not the point that was bothering the judge; he was interested in those gulfs of inclination that divide person from person. As a young man he had wondered if this restriction makes us incapable of passing judgement on our fellows, but had come to realise at last that it does not. He remembered being involved in an impassioned argument about apartheid with another law student, an Afrikaner; "You cannot make pronouncements on our policies," the man had said, "when you have never been to our country. You cannot understand the situation." Richard Braine had known, with the accuracy of a physical response, that the man was wrong. Not misguided; simply wrong. A murderer is doing wrong, whatever the circumstances that drive him to his crime.

The profit motive is not wrong; the circumstances of its application may well be. The judge – with a certain irritation – found himself recalling the features of the importer of pornography: a nondescript, bespectacled man memorable only for a pair of rather bushy eyebrows and a habit of pulling an ear-lobe when under cross-examination. He pushed the fellow from his mind, determinedly, and got out of bed. Outside the window, strands of neatly corrugated cloud coasted in a milky-blue sky; it looked as though it would be a nice day.

The Braines spent the morning at Minsmere bird sanctuary; in the afternoon they went for a walk. The evening found them, scoured by fresh air and slightly somnolent, listening to Mozart, Bartok and Mendelssohn. The judge, who had never played an instrument and regarded himself as relatively unmusical, nevertheless responded to music with considerable intensity. It aroused him in various ways; in such different ways, indeed, that, being a thorough and methodical man, he often felt bemused, caught up by the onward rush of events before he had time to sort them out. Stop, he wanted to say to the surging orchestra, just let me have a think about that bit ... But already he would have been swept onwards, into other moods, other themes, other passions. Marjorie, who played the piano in an unspectacular but competent way, had often suggested that the problem might be solved at least in part if he learned to read music.

She was no doubt right, he thought, wrestling now with a tortuous passage. When I retire; just the thing for a man reduced to inactivity. The judge did not look forward to retirement. But a few moments of inattention had been fatal – now the music had got away from him entirely, as though he had turned over two pages of a book. Frowning, he concentrated on the conductor.

Standing at the bar in the interval, he found himself beside their acquaintance from the restaurant, also waiting to order a drink. Gallantry or even basic good manners required that he intervene. "Oh," she said. "How terribly sweet of you. A gin and tonic would be gorgeous." With resignation, he led her back to where Marjorie awaited him.

"Your husband was so sweet and insistent – I'm all on my own this evening, my sister had a splitting headache and decided not to come." She was a tall woman in her early fifties, too youthfully packaged in a flounced skirt and high-heeled boots, her manner towards the judge both sycophantic and faintly roguish. "I was reading about you in *The Times* last month, some case about people had up for embezzling, of course I didn't understand most of it, all terribly technical, but I said to Laura, I *know* him, we had such a lovely talk about Britten at the Festival."

"Ah," said the judge, studying his programme: the Tippett next.

"I'm Moira Lukes, by the way – if you're anything like me names just *evaporate*, but of course I remembered yours from seeing it in the paper!" She turned to Marjorie, "Aren't you loving the concert?"; patronage discreetly flowed, the patronage of a woman with a sexual history towards one who probably had none, of a lavishly clad woman towards a dowdy one. The judge's antennae slightly quivered, though he was not himself sure why. Marjorie blandly agreed that the concert was superb. "Excuse me," she said. "I'm going to make a dash to the loo while there's time."

The judge and Moira Lukes, left alone, made private adjustments so each other's company: the judge cleared his throat and commented on the architecture of the concert hall: Moira moved a fraction closer to him and altered the pitch of her voice, probably without being aware that she did either. "You must lead such a fascinating life," she said. "I mean, you must come across such extraordinary people. Dickensian types. I don't think I've ever set eyes on a criminal."

The judge thought again of the importer of pornography. "Most of them are rather mundane, when it comes to the point."

"But you must get to know so much about people." She was looking very directly at him, with large eyes; a handsome woman, the judge conceded, rather a knock-out as a girl, no doubt. He agreed that yes, one did get a few insights into the ways in which people carry on.

"Fascinating," said Moira Lukes again. "I expect you have the most marvellous stories to tell. I envy your wife no end." The large eyes creased humorously at the corners; a practised device, though the judge did not recognise this. "In fact I think she's a lucky woman – I still remember that interesting chat you and I had last year." And she laid on his arm a hand, which was almost instantly removed – come and gone as briefly as though a bird had alighted for a fleeting second. The judge, startled in several ways, tried to recall this chat: something about when *Peter Grimes* was first performed, or was it *The Turn of the Screw*? The interest of it, now, escaped him. He cast a quick glance across the foyer in search of Marjorie, who seemed to be taking an awfully long time. Moira Lukes was talking now about the area of Sussex in which she lived. Do, she was saying, look in and have lunch, both of you, if you're ever in that part of the world. The judge murmured that yes, of course if ever they were … He noticed the rings on her hand and wondered vaguely what had become of Mr Lukes; somehow one knew that he was no longer around, one way or the other.

"The only time," she said, "I've ever personally had anything to do with the law was over my rather wretched divorce." The judge took a swig of his drink. "And then actually the lawyer was most awfully sweet, in fact he kept my head above water through it all." She sighed, a whiff of a sigh, almost imperceptible; thereby, she implied most delicately, hung a tale. "So I've got rather a soft spot for legal people."

"Good," said the judge heartily. "I'm glad to hear you've been well treated by the profession."

"Oh, *very* well treated."

No sign of Marjorie, still. Actually, the judge was thinking, this Moira Whatshername wasn't perhaps quite so bad after all, behind that rather tiresome manner; appearances, inevitably, deceive. One got the impression, too, of someone who'd maybe had a bit of a rough time. "Well, it's a world that includes all sorts, like most. And it brings you up against life, I suppose, with all that that implies."

The respect with which these banalities were received made him feel a little cheap. In compensation, he told her an anecdote about a case in which he had once been involved; a *crime passionel* involving an apparently wronged husband who had turned out in fact to be the villain of the piece. "A mealy-mouthed fellow, and as plausible as you like, but apparently he'd been systematically persecuting her for years." Moira Lukes nodded sagely. "People absolutely are not what they seem to be."

"Well," said the judge. "Yes and no. On the other hand, plenty of people give themselves away as soon as they open their mouths."

"Oh, goodness," said Moira Lukes. "Now I'll feel I daren't utter a word ever again."

"I had in mind those I come across professionally rather than in private life."

"Ah, then you think I'm safe?"

"Now, whatever could you have to conceal?" said the judge amiably. A bell went. "I wonder where Marjorie's got to. I suppose we'd better start going back in."

Moira Lukes sighed. She turned those large eyes upon him and creased them once again at the corners. "Well, this has been so nice. I'm sure we'll run into each other again over the weekend. But do bear in mind that I'm in the East Sussex phone book. I remember that case I read about was in Brighton – if you're ever judging there again and want a few hours' retreat on your own, do pop over and have a drink." She smiled once more, and walked quickly away into the crowd.

The judge stood for a moment, looking after her. He realised with surprise that he had been on the receiving end of what is generally known as a pass. He realised also that he was finding it difficult to sort out exactly what he felt about this; a rational response and his natural judgement of people (he didn't in fact all that much care for the woman) fought with more reprehensible feelings and a certain complacency (so one wasn't a total old buffer just yet). In this state of internal conflict he made his way back into the concert hall, where he found Marjorie already in her seat.

"What on earth happened to you?"

"Sorry," she said cheerfully. "There was an awful queue in the Ladies and by the time I got out it wasn't worth coming to find you. How did you make out with our friend?"

The judge grunted, and applied himself to the programme. The lights went down, the conductor reappeared, the audience sank into silence ... But the music, somehow, had lost its compulsion; he was aware now of too much that was external – that he could achieve no satisfactory position for his legs, that he had slight indigestion, that the chap in front of him kept moving his head. Beside him, he could see Marjorie's face, rapt. The evening, somehow, had been corrupted.

The next morning was even more seraphic than the one before. "Today," said Marjorie, "we are going to sit on the beach and bask. We may even venture into the sea."

"That sounds a nice idea." The judge had thought during the night of the little episode with that woman and, in the process, a normal balance of mind had returned; he felt irritated – though more with himself than with her – that it had interfered with his enjoyment of the concert. It was with some annoyance, therefore, that he spotted her now across the hotel dining-room, with the sister, lifting her hand in a little finger-waggling wave of greeting.

"What's the matter?" said Marjorie, with marital insight. "Oh ... Her. Well, I'll leave you to hide behind the paper. I'm going upstairs to get sorted out for the beach."

He was half-way through the Home News page when he felt her standing over him. Alone. The sister, evidently, had been disposed of.

"Another heavenly day. Aren't we lucky! All on your own? I saw your wife bustling off ..." She continued to stand, her glance drifting now towards the coffee pot at the judge's elbow.

I am supposed, he thought, to say sit down and join me – have a cup of coffee. And he felt again that quiver of the antennae and knew now the reason. Marjorie does indeed bustle, her walk is rather inelegant, but it is not for you to say so, or to subtly denigrate a person I happen to love. He rattled, slightly, his newspaper. "We're off to the beach shortly."

"Oh, lovely. I daresay we'll go down there later. I wonder ... Goodness, I don't know if I ought to ask you this or not ..." She hesitated, prettily, seized, it seemed, with sudden difference. "Oh, I'll be brave. The thing is, I have this tiresome problem about a flat in London I'm buying, something to do with the leasehold that I simply do not follow, and I just do not have absolute faith in the man who's dealing with it for me – the solicitor, you know – *could* I pick your brains about it at some point?"

The judge, impassive, gazed up at her.

"I don't mean *now* – not in the middle of your holiday weekend. My sister was noticing your address in the hotel register and believe it or not my present flat is only a few minutes away. What would be lovely would be if you could spare an hour or so to look in for a drink on your way home one evening – and your wife too of course, only it might be awfully boring for her if you're going to brief me. Is that the right word? Would it be an imposition? When you're on your own like I am you are so very much at the mercy of ..." – she sighed – "people, the system, I don't know what ... Sometimes I get quite panic-stricken."

I doubt that, thought the judge. He put the newspaper down. "Mrs Lukes ..."

"Oh, Moira ... please."

He cleared his throat. "Conveyancing, as it happens, is not my field. Anything I said might quite possibly be misleading. The only sensible advice I can give is to change your solicitor if you feel lack of confidence in him."

Her eyes flickered; that look of honest appeal dimmed, suddenly. "Oh ... I see. Well, I daresay you're right. I must do that, then. I shouldn't have asked. But of course the invitation stands, whenever you're free."

"How kind," said the judge coolly. He picked up his paper again and looked at her over the top of it; their eyes met in understanding. And he flinched a little at her expression; it was the look of hatred he had seen from time to time, over the years, across a courtroom, on the face in the dock.

"Have a *lovely* day," said Moira Lukes. Composure had returned; she gleamed, and wrinkled her eyes, and was gone. Well, thought the judge, there's no love lost there, now. But it had to be done, once and for all. He folded the paper and went in search of Marjorie.

She was packing a beach-bag with costumes and towels. The judge, unlocking the suitcase, took out a stack of the pornographic magazines and pushed them into the bottom of the bag. "Oh, lor," said Marjorie, "I'd forgotten about them. Must you?"

"'Fraid so. The case resumes tomorrow. It's the usual business of going through them for degrees of obscenity. There are some books too."

"I'll help you," said Marjorie. "There – greater love hath no woman …"

The beach was agreeably uncrowded. Family parties were dotted in clumps about the sand; children and dogs skittered in and out of the surf; gulls floated above the water and a party of small wading birds scurried back and forth before the advancing waves like blown leaves. The judge, who enjoyed a bit of unstrenuous bird-watching, sat observing them with affection. The weather, this particularly delectable manifestation of the physical world and the uncomplicated relish of the people and animals around him had induced a state of general benignity. Marjorie, organising the rug and wind-screen, said, "All right?" "All right?" he replied. They smiled at each other, appreciating the understatement.

Marjorie, after a while, resolutely swam. The judge, more craven, followed her to the water's edge and observed. As they walked back up the beach together he saw suddenly that Moira Lukes and her sister were encamped not for off. She glanced at him and then immediately away. Now, at midday, the beach was becoming more occupied, though not disturbingly so. A family had established itself close to the Braines' pitch: young parents with a baby in a pram and a couple of older children now deeply engaged in the initial stages of sandcastle construction. The judge, who had also made a sandcastle or two in his time, felt an absurd urge to lend a hand; the basic design, he could see, was awry and would give trouble before long. The mother, a fresh-faced young woman, came padding across the sand to ask Marjorie for the loan of a tin-opener. They chatted for a moment; the young woman carried the baby on her hip. "That sort of thing," said Marjorie, sitting down again, "can still make me broody, even at my time of life." She too watched the sandcastle-building; presently she rummaged in the picnic basket and withdrew a plastic beaker. "Turrets," she explained to the judge, a little guiltily. "You can never do a good job with a bucket …" The children received her offering with rewarding glee; the parents gratefully smiled; the sandcastle rose, more stylish.

The judge sighed, and delved in the beach bag. "To work, I suppose," he said. Around them, the life of the beach had settled into a frieze, as though the day were eternal: little sprawled groups of people, the great arc of the horizon against which stood the grey shapes of two far-away ships, like cut-outs, the surface animation of running dogs and children and someone's straw hat, tossed hither and thither by the breeze that had sprung up.

The judge and his wife sat with a pile of magazines each. Marjorie said, "This is a pretty gruesome collection. Can I borrow your hankie, my glasses keep getting salted over."

The judge turned over pages, and occasionally made some notes. Nothing he saw surprised him; from time to time he found himself examining the faces that belonged to the bodies displayed, as though in search of explanations. But they seemed much like any other faces; so presumably were the bodies.

Marjorie said, "Cup of tea? Tell me, why are words capable of so much greater obscenity than pictures?" She was glancing through a book, or something that passed as such.

"That, I imagine, is why people have always gone in for burning them, though usually for quite other reasons."

It was as the judge was reaching out to take the mug of tea from her that the wind came. It came in a great wholesome gust, flinging itself along the beach with a cloud of blown sand and flying plastic bags. It sent newspapers into the air like great flapping birds and spun a spotted football along the water's edge as though it were a top. It lifted rugs and pushed over deck chairs. It snatched the magazines from the judge's lap and from Marjorie's and bore them away across the sand in a helter-skelter whirl of colourful pages, dropping them down only to grab them again and fling them here and there: at the feet of a stout lady snoozing in a deckchair, into the pram of the neighbouring family's baby, onto people's towels and Sunday newspapers.

Marjorie said, "Oh, *lor* ..."

They got up. They began, separately, to tour the beach in pursuit of what the wind had taken. The judge found himself, absurdly, feeling foolish because he had left his jacket on his chair and was plodding along the sand in shirt-sleeves (no tie, either) and tweed trousers. The lady in the deck chair woke and put out a hand to quell the magazine that was wrapping itself around her leg. "Yours?" she said amiably, looking up at the judge, and as she handed him the thing it fell open and for a moment her eyes rested on the central spread, the *pièce de resistance*; her expression changed, rubbed out as it were by amazement, and she looked again at the judge for an instant, and became busy with the knitting on her lap.

Marjorie, stumping methodically along, picked up one magazine and then another, tucking them under her arm. She turned and saw that the children had observed the crisis, abandoned their sandcastle and were scurrying here and there, collecting as though involved in a treasure hunt. The mother, too, had risen and was shaking the sand from a magazine that had come to rest against the wheels of the pram. As Marjorie reached her the little girl ran up with an armful. "Good girl, Sharon," said the mother, and the child – six, perhaps, or seven – virtuously beamed and held out to Marjorie the opened pages of the magazine she held. She looked at it and the mother looked at it and Marjorie looked and the child said, "Are those flowers?". "No, my dear," said Marjorie sadly. "They aren't flowers," and she turned away before she could meet the eyes of the young mother.

The judge collected a couple from a man who handed them over with a wink, and another from a boy who stared at him expressionless, and then he could not find any more. He walked back to their pitch. Marjorie was shoving things into the beach bag. "Shall we go?" she said, and the judge nodded.

It was as they were folding the rug that Moira Lukes came up. She wore neatly creased cotton trousers and walked with a spring. "Yours, apparently," she said; she held the magazine out between a finger and thumb, as though with tongs, and dropped it onto the sand. She looked straight at the judge. "How awfully true," she said, "that people are not what they seem to be." Satisfaction flowed from her; she glanced for an instant, at Marjorie, as though checking that she had heard, and walked away.

The Braines, in silence, completed the assembly of their possessions. Marjorie carried the rug and the picnic basket and the judge bore the beach bag and the wind-screen. They trudged the long expanse of the beach, watched, now, with furtive interest by various eyes.

A REAL DOLL

A. M. Homes

A. M. Homes (b. 1961) is an American writer known for her controversial novels and unusual stories. She released her first collection of short stories, *The Safety of Objects*, in 1990. In 2013 she won the Women's Prize for Fiction with her novel *May We Be Forgiven*.

I'm dating Barbie. Three afternoons a week, while my sister is at dance class, I take Barbie away from Ken. I'm practising for the future.

At first I sat in my sister's room watching Barbie, who lived with Ken, on a doily, on top of the dresser.

I was looking at her but not really looking. I was looking, and all of the sudden realized she was staring at me.

She was sitting next to Ken, his khaki-covered thigh absently rubbing her bare leg. He was rubbing her, but she was staring at me.

"Hi," she said.

"Hello," I said.

"I'm Barbie," she said, and Ken stopped rubbing her leg.

"I know."

"You're Jenny's brother."

I nodded. My head was bobbing up and down like a puppet on a weight.

"I really like your sister. She's sweet," Barbie said. "Such a good little girl. Especially lately, she makes herself so pretty, and she's started doing her nails."

I wondered if Barbie noticed that Miss Wonderful bit her nails and that when she smiled her front teeth were covered with little flecks of purple nail polish. I wondered if she knew Jennifer colored in the chipped chewed spots with purple magic marker, and then sometimes sucked on her fingers so that not only did she have purple flecks of polish on her teeth, but her tongue was the strangest shade of violet.

"So listen," I said. "Would you like to go out for a while? Grab some fresh air, maybe take a spin around the backyard?"

"Sure," she said.

I picked her up by her feet. It sounds unusual but I was too petrified to take her by the waist. I grabbed her by the ankles and carried her off like a Popsicle stick.

As soon as we were out back, sitting on the porch of what I used to call my fort, but which my sister and parents referred to as the playhouse, I started freaking. I was suddenly and incredibly aware that I was out with Barbie. I didn't know what to say.

"So, what kind of a Barbie are you?" I asked.

"Excuse me?"

"Well, from listening to Jennifer I know there's Day to Night Barbie, Magic Moves Barbie, Gift-Giving Barbie, Tropical Barbie, My First Barbie, and more."

"I'm Tropical," she said. I'm Tropical, she said, the same way a person might say I'm Catholic or I'm Jewish. "I came with a one-piece bathing suit, a brush, and a ruffle you can wear so many ways," Barbie squeaked.

She actually squeaked. It turned out that squeaking was Barbie's birth defect. I pretended I didn't hear it.

We were quiet for a minute. A leaf larger than Barbie fell from the maple tree above us and I caught it just before it would have hit her. I half expected her to squeak, "You saved my life. I'm yours, forever." Instead she said, in a perfectly normal voice, "Wow, big leaf."

I looked at her. Barbie's eyes were sparkling blue like the ocean on a good day. I looked and in a moment noticed she had the whole world, the cosmos, drawn in makeup above and below her eyes. An entire galaxy, clouds, stars, a sun, the sea, painted onto her face. Yellow, blue, pink, and a million silver sparkles.

We sat looking at each other, looking and talking and then not talking and looking again. It was a stop-and-start thing with both of us constantly saying the wrong thing, saying anything, and then immediately regretting having said it.

It was obvious Barbie didn't trust me. I asked her if she wanted something to drink.

"Diet Coke," she said. And I wondered why I'd asked.

I went into the house, upstairs into my parents' bathroom, opened the medicine cabinet, and got a couple of Valiums. I immediately swallowed one. I figured if I could be calm and collected, she'd realize I wasn't going to hurt her. I broke another Valium into a million small pieces, dropped some slivers into Barbie's Diet Coke, and swished it around so it'd blend. I figured if we could be calm and collected together, she'd be able to trust me even sooner. I was falling in love in a way that had nothing to do with love.

"So, what's the deal with you and Ken?" I asked later after we'd loosened up, after she'd drunk two Diet Cokes, and I'd made another trip to the medicine cabinet.

She giggled. "Oh, we're just really good friends."

"What's the deal with him really, you can tell me, I mean, is he or isn't he?"

"Ish she or ishn' she," Barbie said, in a slow slurred way, like she was so intoxicated that if they made a Breathalizer for Valium, she'd melt it.

I regretted having fixed her a third Coke. I mean if she o.d.'ed and died Jennifer would tell my mom and dad for sure.

"Is he a faggot or what?"

Barbie laughed and I almost slapped her. She looked me straight in the eye.

"He lusts after me," she said. "I come home at night and he's standing there, waiting. He doesn't wear underwear, you know. I mean, isn't that strange, Ken doesn't own any underwear. I heard Jennifer tell her friend that they don't even make any for him. Anyway, he's always, there waiting, and I'm like, Ken we're friends, okay, that's it. I mean, have you ever noticed, he has molded plastic hair. His head and his hair are all one piece. I can't go out with a guy like that. Besides, I don't think he'd be up for it if you know what I mean. Ken is not what you'd call well endowed ... All he's got is a little plastic bump, more of a hump, really, and what the hell are you supposed to do with that?"

She was telling me things I didn't think I should hear and all the same, I was leaning into her, like if I moved closer she'd tell me more. I was taking every word and holding it for a minute, holding groups of words in my head like I didn't understand English. She went on and on, but I wasn't listening.

The sun sank behind the playhouse, Barbie shivered, excused herself, and ran around back to throw up. I asked her if she felt okay. She said she was fine, just a little tired, that maybe she was coming down with the flu or something. I gave her a piece of a piece of gum to chew and took her inside.

On the way back to Jennifer's room I did something Barbie almost didn't forgive me for, I did something which not only shattered the moment, but nearly wrecked the possibility of our having a future together.

In the hallway between the stairs and Jennifer's room, I popped Barbie's head into my mouth, like lion and tamer, God and Godzilla.

I popped her whole head into my mouth, and Barbie's hair separated into single strands like Christmas tinsel and caught in my throat nearly choking me. I could taste layer on layer of makeup, Revlon, Max Factor, and Maybelline. I closed my mouth around Barbie and could feel her breath in mine. I could hear her screams in my throat. Her teeth, white, Pearl Drops, Pepsodent, and the whole Osmond family, bit my tongue and the inside of my cheek like I might accidently bite myself. I closed my mouth around her neck and held her suspended, her feet uselessly kicking the air in front of my face.

Before pulling her out, I pressed my teeth lightly into her neck, leaving marks Barbie described as scars of her assault, but which I imagined as a New Age necklace of love.

"I have never, ever in my life been treated with such utter disregard," she said as soon as I let her out.

She was lying. I knew Jennifer sometimes did things with Barbie. I didn't mention that once I'd seen Barbie hanging from Jennifer's ceiling fan, spinning around in great wide circles, like some imitation Superman.

"I'm sorry if I scared you."

"Scared me!" she squeaked.

She went on squeaking, a cross between the squeal when you let the air out of a balloon and a smoke alarm with weak batteries. While she was squeaking, the phrase *a head in the mouth is worth two in the bush* started running through my head. I knew it had come from somewhere, started as something else, but I couldn't get it right. *A head in the mouth is worth two in the bush*, again and again, like the punch line to some dirty joke.

"Scared me. Scared me. Scared me!" Barbie squeaked louder and louder until finally she had my attention again. "Have you ever been held captive in the dark cavern of someone's body?"

I shook my head. It sounded wonderful.

"Typical," she said. "So incredibly, typically male."

For a moment I was proud.

"Why do you have to do things you know you shouldn't, and worse, you do them with a light in your eye, like you're getting some weird pleasure that only another boy would understand. You're all the same," she said. "You're all Jack Nicholson."

I refused to put her back in Jennifer's room until she forgave me, until she understood that I'd done what I did with only the truest of feeling, no harm intended.

I heard Jennifer's feet clomping up the stairs. I was running out of time.

"You know I'm really interested in you," I said to Barbie.

"Me too," she said, and for a minute I wasn't sure if she meant she was interested in herself or me.

"We should do this again," I said. She nodded.

I leaned down to kiss Barbie. I could have brought her up to my lips, but somehow it felt wrong. I leaned down to kiss her and the first thing I got was her nose in my mouth. I felt like a St. Bernard saying hello.

No matter how graceful I tried to be, I was forever licking her face. It wasn't a question of putting my tongue in her ear or down her throat, it was simply literally trying not to suffocate her. I kissed Barbie with my back to Ken and then turned around and put her on the doily right next to him. I was tempted to drop her down on Ken, to, mash her into him, but I managed to restrain myself.

"That was fun," Barbie said. I heard Jennifer in the hall.

"Later," I said.

Jennifer came into the room and looked at me.

"What?" I said.

"It's my room," she said.

"There was a bee in it. I was killing it for you."

"A bee. I'm allergic to bees. Mom, Mom," she screamed. "There's a bee."

"Mom's not home. I killed it."

"But there might be another one."

"So call me and I'll kill it."

"But if it stings me I might die." I shrugged and walked out. I could feel Barbie watching me leave.

I took a Valium about twenty minutes before I picked her up the next Friday. By the time I went into Jennifer's room, everything was getting easier.

"Hey," I said when I got up to the dresser.

She was there on the doily with Ken, they were back to back, resting against each other, legs stretched out in front of them.

Ken didn't look at me. I didn't care.

"You ready to go?" I asked. Barbie nodded. "I thought you might be thirsty." I handed her the Diet Coke I'd made for her.

I'd figured Barbie could take a little less than an eighth of a Valium without getting totally senile. Basically, I had to give her Valium crumbs since there was no way to cut one that small.

She took the Coke and drank it right in front of Ken. I kept waiting for him to give me one of those I-know-what-you're-up-to-and-I-don't-like-it looks, the kind my father gives me when he walks into my room without knocking and I automatically jump twenty feet in the air.

Ken acted like he didn't even know I was there. I hated him.

"I can't do a lot of walking this afternoon," Barbie said.

I nodded. I figured no big deal since mostly I seemed to be carrying her around anyway.

"My feet are killing me," she said.

I was thinking about Ken.

"Don't you have other shoes?"

My family was very into shoes. No matter what seemed to be wrong my father always suggested it could be cured by wearing a different pair of shoes. He believed that shoes, like tires, should be rotated.

"It's not the shoes," she said. "It's my toes."

"Did you drop something on them?" My Valium wasn't working. I was having trouble making small talk. I needed another one.

"Jennifer's been chewing on them,"

"What?"

"She chews on my toes."

"You let her chew your footies?"

I couldn't make sense out of what she was saying. I was thinking about not being able to talk, needing another or maybe two more Valiums, yellow adult-strength Pez.

"Do you enjoy it?" I asked.

"She literally bites down on them, like I'm flank steak or something," Barbie said. "I wish she'd just bite them off and have it over with. This is taking forever. She's chewing and chewing, more like gnawing at me."

"I'll make her stop. I'll buy her some gum, some tobacco or something, a pencil to chew on."

"Please don't say anything. I wouldn't have told you except …," Barbie said.

"But she's hurting you."

"It's between Jennifer and me."

"Where's it going to stop?" I asked.

"At the arch, I hope. There's a bone there, and once she realizes she's bitten the soft part off, she'll stop."

"How will you walk?"

"I have very long feet."

I sat on the edge of my sister's bed, my head in my hands. My sister was biting Barbie's feet off and Barbie didn't seem to care. She didn't hold it against her and in a way I liked her for that. I liked the fact she understood how we all have little secret habits that seem normal enough to us, but which we know better than to mention out loud. I started imagining things I might be able to get away with.

"Get me out of here," Barbie said. I slipped Barbie's shoes off. Sure enough, someone had been gnawing at her. On her left foot the toes were dangling and on the right, half had been completely taken off. There were tooth marks up to her ankles. "Let's not dwell on this," Barbie said.

I picked Barbie up. Ken fell over backwards and Barbie made me straighten him up before we left. "Just because you know he only has a bump doesn't give you permission to treat him badly," Barbie whispered.

I fixed Ken and carried Barbie down the hall to my room. I held Barbie above me, tilted my head back, and lowered her feet into my mouth. I felt like a young sword swallower practising for my debut. I lowered Barbie's feet and legs into my mouth and then began sucking on them. They smelled like Jennifer and dirt and plastic. I sucked on her stubs and she told me it felt nice.

"You're better than a hot soak," Barbie said. I left her resting on my pillow and went downstairs to get us each a drink.

We were lying on my bed, curled into and out of each other. Barbie was on a pillow next to me and I was on my side facing her. She was talking about men, and as she talked I tried to be everything she said. She was saying she didn't like men who were afraid of themselves. I tried to be brave, to look courageous and secure. I held my head a certain way and it seemed to work. She said she didn't like men who were afraid of femininity, and I got confused.

"Guys always have to prove how boy they really are," Barbie said.

I thought of Jennifer trying to be a girl, wearing dresses, doing her nails, putting makeup on, wearing a bra even though she wouldn't need one for about fifty years.

"You make fun of Ken because he lets himself be everything he is. He doesn't hide anything."

"He doesn't have anything to hide," I said. "He has tan molded plastic hair, and a bump for a dick."

"I never should have told you about the bump."

I lay back on the bed. Barbie rolled over, off the pillow, and rested on my chest. Her body stretched from my nipple to my belly button. Her hands pressed against me, tickling me.

"Barbie," I said.

"Umm Humm."

"How do you feel about me?"

She didn't say anything for a minute. "Don't worry about it," she said, and slipped her hand into my shirt through the space between the buttons.

Her fingers were like the ends of toothpicks performing some subtle ancient torture, a dance of boy death across my chest. Barbie crawled all over me like an insect who'd run into one too many cans of Raid.

Underneath my clothes, under my skin, I was going crazy. First off, I'd been kidnapped by my underwear with no way to manually adjust without attracting unnecessary attention.

With Barbie caught in my shirt I slowly rolled over, like in some space shuttle docking maneuver. I rolled onto my stomach, trapping her under me. As slowly and unobtrusively as possible, I ground myself against the bed, at first hoping it would fix things and then again and again, caught by a pleasure pain principle.

"Is this a water bed?" Barbie asked.

My hand was on her breasts, only it wasn't really my hand, but more like my index finger. I touched Barbie and she made a little gasp, a squeak in reverse. She squeaked backwards, then stopped, and I was stuck there with my hand on her, thinking about how I was forever crossing a line between the haves and the have nots, between good guys and bad, between men and animals, and there was absolutely nothing I could do to stop myself.

Barbie was sitting on my crotch, her legs flipped back behind her in a position that wasn't human.

At a certain point I had to free myself. If my dick was blue, it was only because it had suffocated. I did the honors and Richard popped out like an escape from maximum security.

"I've never seen anything so big," Barbie said. It was the sentence I dreamed of, but given the people Barbie normally hung out with, namely the bump boy himself, it didn't come as a big surprise.

She stood at the base of my dick, her bare feet buried in my pubic hair. I was almost as tall as she was. Okay, not almost as tall, but clearly we could be related. She and Richard even had the same vaguely surprised look on their faces.

She was on me and I couldn't help wanting to get inside her. I turned Barbie over and was on top of her, not caring if I killed her. Her hands pressed so hard into my stomach that it felt like she was performing an appendectomy.

I was on top, trying to get between her legs, almost breaking her in half. But there was nothing there, nothing to fuck except a small thin line that was supposed to be her ass crack.

I rubbed the thin line, the back of her legs and the space between her legs. I turned Barbie's back to me so I could do it without having to look at her face.

Very quickly, I came. I came all over Barbie, all over her and a little bit in her hair. I came on Barbie and it was the most horrifying experience I ever had. It didn't stay on her. It doesn't stick to plastic. I was finished. I was holding a come-covered Barbie in my hand like I didn't know where she came from.

Barbie said, "Don't stop," or maybe I just think she said that because I read it somewhere. I don't know anymore. I couldn't listen to her. I couldn't even look at her. I wiped myself off with a sock, pulled my clothes on, and then took Barbie into the bathroom.

At dinner I noticed Jennifer chewing her cuticles between bites of tuna-noodle casserole. I asked her if she was teething. She coughed and then started choking to death on either a little piece of fingernail, a crushed potato chip from the casserole, or maybe even a little bit of Barbie footie that'd stuck in her teeth. My mother asked her if she was okay.

"I swallowed something sharp," she said between coughs that were clearly influenced by the acting class she'd taken over the summer.

"Do you have a problem?" I asked her.

"Leave your sister alone," my mother said.

"If there are any questions to ask we'll do the asking," my father said.

"Is everything all right?" my mother asked Jennifer. She nodded. "I think you could use some new jeans," my mother said. "You don't seem to have many play clothes anymore."

"Not to change the subject," I said, trying to think of a way to stop Jennifer from eating Barbie alive.

"I don't wear pants," Jennifer said. "Boys wear pants."

"Your grandma wears pants," my father said.

"She's not a girl."

My father chuckled. He actually fucking chuckled. He's the only person I ever met who could actually fucking chuckle.

"Don't tell her that," he said, chuckling.

"It's not funny," I said.

"Grandma's are pull-ons anyway," Jennifer said, "They don't have a fly. You have to have a penis to have a fly."

"Jennifer," my mother said. "That's enough of that."

I decided to buy Barbie a present. I was at that strange point where I would have done anything for her. I took two buses and walked more than a mile to get to Toys R Us.

Barbie row was aisle 14C. I was a wreck. I imagined a million Barbies and having to have them all. I pictured fucking one, discarding it, immediately grabbing a fresh one, doing it, and then throwing it onto a growing pile in the corner of my room. An unending chore. I saw myself becoming a slave to Barbie. I wondered how many Tropical Barbies were made each year. I felt faint.

There were rows and rows of Kens, Barbies, and Skippers. Funtime Barbie, Jewel Secrets Ken, Barbie Rocker with "Hot Rockin' Fun and Real Dancin' Action." I noticed Magic Moves Barbie, and found myself looking at her carefully, flirtatiously, wondering if her legs were spreadable. "Push the switch and she moves," her box said. She winked at me while I was reading.

The only Tropical I saw was a black Tropical Ken. From just looking at him you wouldn't have known he was black. I mean, he wasn't black like anyone would be black. Black Tropical Ken was the color of a raisin, a raisin all spread out and unwrinkled. He had a short afro that looked like a wig had been dropped down and fixed on his head, a protective helmet. I wondered if black Ken was really white Ken sprayed over with a thick coating of ironed raisin plastic.

I spread eight black Kens out in a line across the front of a row. Through the plastic window of his box he told me he was hoping to go to dental school. All eight black Kens talked at once. Luckily, they all said the same thing at the same time. They said he really liked teeth. Black Ken smiled. He had the same white Pearl Drops, Pepsodent, Osmond family teeth that Barbie and white Ken had. I thought the entire Mattel family must take really good care of themselves. I figured they might be the only people left in America who actually brushed after every meal and then again before going to sleep.

I didn't know what to get Barbie. Black Ken said I should go for clothing, maybe a fur coat. I wanted something really special. I imagined a wonderful present that would draw us somehow closer.

There was a tropical pool and patio set, but I decided it might make her homesick. There was a complete winter holiday, with an A-frame house, fireplace, snowmobile, and sled. I imagined her inviting Ken away for a weekend without me. The six o'clock news set was nice, but because of her squeak, Barbie's future as an anchorwoman seemed limited. A workout center, a sofa bed and coffee table, a bubbling spa, a bedroom play set. I settled on the grand piano. It was $13.00. I'd always made it a point to never spend more than ten dollars on anyone. This time I figured, what the hell, you don't buy a grand piano every day.

"Wrap it up, would ya," I said at the checkout desk.

*

From my bedroom window I could see Jennifer in the backyard, wearing her tutu and leaping all over the place. It was dangerous as hell to sneak in and get Barbie, but I couldn't keep a grand piano in my closet without telling someone.

"You must really like me," Barbie said when she finally had the piano un-wrapped.

I nodded. She was wearing a ski suit and skis. It was the end of August and eighty degrees out. Immediately, she sat down and played "Chopsticks."

I looked out at Jennifer. She was running down the length of the deck, jumping onto the railing and then leaping off, posing like one of those red flying horses you see on old Mobil gas signs. I watched her do it once and then the second time, her foot caught on the railing, and she went over the edge the hard way. A minute later she came around the edge of the house, limping, her tutu dented and dirty, pink tights ripped at both knees. I grabbed Barbie from the piano bench and raced her into Jennifer's room.

"I was just getting warmed up," she said. "I can play better than that, really."

I could hear Jennifer crying as she walked up the stairs.

"Jennifer's coming." I said. I put her down on the dresser and realized Ken was missing.

"Where's Ken?" I asked quickly.

"Out with Jennifer," Barbie said.

I met Jennifer at her door. "Are you okay?" I asked. She cried harder. "I saw you fall."

"Why didn't you stop me?" she said.

"From falling?"

She nodded and showed me her knees.

"Once you start to fall no one can stop you." I noticed Ken was tucked into the waistband of her tutu.

"They catch you," Jennifer said.

I started to tell her it was dangerous to go leaping around with a Ken stuck in your waistband, but you don't tell someone who's already crying that they did something bad.

I walked her into the bathroom, and took out the hydrogen peroxide. I was a first aid expert. I was the kind of guy who walked around, waiting for someone to have a heart attack just so I could practice my CPR technique.

"Sit down," I said.

Jennifer sat down on the toilet without putting the lid down. Ken was stab-bing her all over the place and instead of pulling him out, she squirmed around trying to get comfortable like she didn't know what else to do. I took him out for her. She watched as though I was performing surgery or something.

"He's mine," she said.

"Take off your tights," I said.

"No," she said.

"They're ruined," I said. "Take them off."

Jennifer took off her ballet slippers and peeled off her tights. She was wear-ing my old Underoos with superheroes on them, Spiderman and Superman and Batman all poking out from under a dirty dented tutu. I decided not to say any-thing, but it looked funny as hell to see a flat crotch in boys' underwear. I had the feeling they didn't bother making underwear for Ken because they knew it looked too weird on him.

I poured peroxide onto her bloody knees. Jennifer screamed into my ear. She bent down and examined herself, poking her purple fingers into the torn skin; her tutu bunched up and rubbed against her face, scraping it. I worked on her knees, removing little pebbles and pieces of grass from the area.

She started crying again.

"You're okay," I said. "You're not dying." She didn't care. "Do you want anything?" I asked, trying to be nice.

"Barbie," she said.

It was the first time I'd handled Barbie in public. I picked her up like she was a complete stranger and handed her to Jennifer, who grabbed her by the hair. I started to tell her to ease up, but couldn't. Barbie looked at me and I shrugged. I went downstairs and made Jennifer one of my special Diet Cokes.

"Drink this," I said, handing it to her. She took four giant gulps and immediately I felt guilty about having used a whole Valium.

"Why don't you give a little to your Barbie," I said. "I'm sure she's thirsty too."

Barbie winked at me and I could have killed her, first off for doing it in front of Jennifer, and second because she didn't know what the hell she was winking about.

I went into my room and put the piano away. I figured as long as I kept it in the original box I'd be safe. If anyone found it, I'd say it was a present for Jennifer.

Wednesday Ken and Barbie had their heads switched. I went to get Barbie, and there on top of the dresser were Barbie and Ken, sort of Barbie's head was on Ken's body and Ken's head was on Barbie. At first I thought it was just me.

"Hi," Barbie's head said.

I couldn't respond. She was on Ken's body and I was looking at Ken in a whole new way.

I picked up the Barbie head Ken and immediately Barbie's head rolled off. It rolled across the dresser, across the white doily past Jennifer's collection of miniature ceramic cats, and *boom* it fell to the floor. I saw Barbie's head rolling and about to fall, and then falling, but there was nothing I could do to stop it. I was frozen, paralyzed with Ken's headless body in my left hand.

Barbie's head was on the floor, her hair spread out underneath it like angel wings in the snow, and I expected to see blood, a wide rich pool of blood, or at least a little bit coming out of her ear, her nose, or her mouth. I looked at her head on the floor and saw nothing but Barbie with eyes like the cosmos looking up at me. I thought she was dead.

"Christ, that hurt," she said. "And I already had a headache from these earrings."

There were little red dot/ball earrings jutting out of Barbie's ears.

"They go right through my head, you know. I guess it takes getting used to," Barbie said.

I noticed my mother's pin cushion on the dresser next to the other Barbie/Ken, the Barbie body, Ken head. The pin cushion was filled with hundreds of pins, pins with flat silver ends and pins with red, yellow, and blue dot/ball ends.

"You have pins in your head," I said to the Barbie head on the floor.

"Is that supposed to be a compliment?"

I was starting to hate her. I was being perfectly clear and she didn't understand me.

I looked at Ken. He was in my left hand, my fist wrapped around his waist. I looked at him and realized my thumb was on his bump. My thumb was pressed against Ken's crotch and as soon as I noticed I got an automatic hard-on, the kind you don't know you're getting, it's just there. I started rubbing Ken's bump and watching my thumb like it was a large-screen projection of a porno movie.

"What are you doing?" Barbie's head said. "Get me up. Help me." I was rubbing Ken's bump/hump with my finger inside his bathing suit. I was standing in the middle of my sister's room, with my pants pulled down.

"Aren't you going to help me?" Barbie kept asking. "Aren't you going to help me?"

In the second before I came, I held Ken's head hole in front of me. I held Ken upside down above my dick and came inside of Ken like I never could in Barbie.

I came into Ken's body and as soon as I was done I wanted to do it again. I wanted to fill Ken and put his head back on, like a perfume bottle. I wanted Ken to be the vessel for my secret supply. I came in Ken and then I remembered he wasn't mine. He didn't belong to me. I took him into the bathroom and soaked him in warm water and Ivory liquid. I brushed his insides with Jennifer's toothbrush and left him alone in a cold-water rinse.

"Aren't you going to help me, aren't you?" Barbie kept asking.

I started thinking she'd been brain damaged by the accident. I picked her head up from the floor.

"What took you so long?" she asked.

"I had to take care of Ken."

"Is he okay?"

"He'll be fine. He's soaking in the bathroom." I held Barbie's head in my hand.

"What are you going to do?"

"What do you mean?" I said.

Did my little incident, my moment with Ken, mean that right then and there some decision about my future life as queerbait had to be made?"

"This afternoon. Where are we going? What are we doing? I miss you when I don't see you," Barbie said.

"You see me every day," I said.

"I don't really see you. I sit on top of the dresser and if you pass by, I see you. Take me to your room."

"I have to bring Ken's body back."

I went into the bathroom, rinsed out Ken, blew him dry with my mother's blow dryer, then played with him again. It was a boy thing, we were boys together. I thought sometime I might play ball with him, I might take him out instead of Barbie.

"Everything takes you so long," Barbie said when I got back into the room.

I put Ken back up on the dresser, picked up Barbie's body, knocked Ken's head off, and smashed Barbie's head back down on her own damn neck.

"I don't want to fight with you," Barbie said as I carried her into my room. "We don't have enough time together to fight. Fuck me," she said.

I didn't feel like it. I was thinking about fucking Ken and Ken being a boy. I was thinking about Barbie and Barbie being a girl. I was thinking about Jennifer, switching Barbie and Ken's heads, chewing Barbie's feet off, hanging Barbie from the ceiling fan, and who knows what else.

"Fuck me," Barbie said again.

I ripped Barbie's clothing off. Between Barbie's legs Jennifer had drawn pubic hair in reverse. She'd drawn it upside down so it looked like a fountain spewing up and out in great wide arcs. I spit directly onto Barbie and with my thumb and first finger rubbed the ink lines, erasing them. Barbie moaned.

"Why do you let her do this to you?"

"Jennifer owns me," Barbie moaned.

Jennifer owns me, she said, so easily and with pleasure. I was totally jealous. Jennifer owned Barbie and it made me crazy. Obviously it was one of those relationships that could only exist between women. Jennifer could own her because it didn't matter that Jennifer owned her. Jennifer didn't want Barbie, she had her.

"You're perfect," I said.

"I'm getting fat," Barbie said.

Barbie was crawling all over me, and I wondered if Jennifer knew she was a nymphomaniac. I wondered if Jennifer knew what a nymphomaniac was.

"You don't belong with little girls," I said.

Barbie ignored me.

There were scratches on Barbie's chest and stomach. She didn't say anything about them and so at first I pretended not to notice. As I was touching her, I could feel they were deep, like slices. The edges were rough; my finger caught on them and I couldn't help but wonder.

"Jennifer?" I said, massaging the cuts with my tongue, as though my tongue, like sandpaper, would erase them. Barbie nodded.

In fact, I thought of using sandpaper, but didn't know how I would explain it to Barbie: *you have to lie still and let me rub it really hard with this stuff that's like terrycloth dipped in cement*. I thought she might even like it if I made it into an S&M kind of thing and handcuffed her first.

I ran my tongue back and forth over the slivers, back and forth over the words "copyright 1966 Mattel Inc., Malaysia" tattooed on her back. Tonguing the tattoo drove Barbie crazy. She said it had something to do with scar tissue being extremely sensitive.

Barbie pushed herself hard against me, I could feel her slices rubbing my skin. I was thinking that Jennifer might kill Barbie. Without meaning to she might just go over the line and I wondered if Barbie would know what was happening or if she'd try to stop her.

We fucked, that's what I called it, fucking. In the beginning Barbie said she hated the word, which made me like it even more. She hated it because it was so strong and hard, and she said we weren't fucking, we were making love. I told her she had to be kidding.

"Fuck me," she said that afternoon and I knew the end was coming soon. "Fuck me," she said. I didn't like the sound of the word.

Friday when I went into Jennifer's room, there was something in the air. The place smelled like a science lab, a fire, a failed experiment.

Barbie was wearing, a strapless yellow evening dress. Her hair was wrapped into a high bun, more like a wedding cake than something Betty Crocker would whip up. There seemed to be layers and layers of angel's hair spinning in a circle above her head. She had yellow pins through her ears and gold fuck-me shoes that matched the belt around her waist. For a second I thought of the belt and imagined tying her up, but more than restraining her arms or legs, I thought of wrapping the belt around her face, tying it across her mouth.

I looked at Barbie and saw something dark and thick like a scar rising up and over the edge of her dress. I grabbed her and pulled the front of the dress down.

"Hey, big boy," Barbie said. "Don't I even get a hello?"

Barbie's breasts had been sawed at with a knife. There were a hundred marks from a blade that might have had five rows of teeth like shark jaws. And as if that wasn't enough, she'd been dissolved by fire, blue and yellow flames had been pressed against her and held there until she melted and eventually became the fire that burned herself. All of it had been somehow stirred with the lead of a pencil, the point of a pen, and left to cool. Molten Barbie flesh had been left to harden, black and pink plastic swirled together, in the crater Jennifer had dug out of her breasts.

I examined her in detail like a scientist, a pathologist, a fucking medical examiner. I studied the burns, the gouged-out area, as if by looking closely I'd find something, an explanation, a way out.

A disgusting taste came up into my mouth, like I'd been sucking on batteries. It came up, then sank back down into my stomach, leaving my mouth puckered with the bitter metallic flavor of sour saliva. I coughed and spit onto my shirt sleeve, then rolled the sleeve over to cover the wet spot.

With my index finger I touched the edge of the burn as lightly as I could. The round rim of her scar broke off under my finger. I almost dropped her.

"It's just a reduction," Barbie said. "Jennifer and I are even now."

Barbie was smiling. She had the same expression on her face as when I first saw her and fell in love. She had the same expression she always had and I couldn't stand it. She was smiling, and she was burned. She was smiling, and she was ruined. I pulled her dress back up, above the scarline. I put her down carefully on the doily on top of the dresser and started to walk away.

"Hey," Barbie said, "aren't we going to play?"

YOURS TRULY

A. M. Homes

A. M. Homes (b. 1961) is an American writer known for her controversial novels and unusual stories. She released her first collection of short stories, *The Safety of Objects*, in 1990. In 2013 she won the Women's Prize for Fiction with her novel *May We Be Forgiven*.

I'm hiding in the linen closet writing letters to myself. This is the place where no one knows I am, where I can think without thinking about what anyone else would think or at least it's quiet. I don't want to scare anyone, but things can't go on like this.

Until today I could still go into the living room and talk to my mother's Saturday morning Fat Club. I could say, "Hi, how are you. That's a very nice dress. Magenta's such a good color, it hides the hips. Nice shoes too. I would never have thought of bringing pink and green together like that." I could pretend to be okay, but that's part of the problem.

In here, pressed up against the towels, the sheets, the heating pad, it's clear that everything is not hunky-dory. I've got one of those Itty Bitty Book Lights and I'm making notes.

Today is Odessa's day. At any minute she might turn the knob and let the world, disguised as daylight, come flooding in. She might do that and never know what she's done. She'll open the door and her eyes will get wide. She'll look at me and say, "Lord." She'll say, "You could have given me a heart attack." And I'll think, Yes, I could have, but I'm having one myself and there isn't room for two in the same place at the same time. She'll look at my face and I'll have to look at the floor. She won't know that having someone look directly at me, having someone expect me to look at her, causes a sharp pain that begins in my eyes, ricochets off my skull, and in the end makes my entire skeleton shake. She won't know that I can't look at anything except the towels without being overcome with emotion. She won't know that at the sight of another person I weep, I wish to embrace and be embraced, and then to kill. She won't get that I'm dangerous.

Odessa will open the door and see me standing with this tiny light, clipped to the middle shelf, with the pad of paper on top of some extra blankets, with two extra pencils sticking out of the space between the bath sheets and the Turkish towels. She'll see all this and ask, "Are you all right?" I won't be able to answer. I can't tell her why I'm standing in a closet filled with enough towels to take a small town to the beach. I won't say, I'm not all right. God help me, I'm not. I will simply stand here, resting my arm over my notepad like a child taking a test, trying to make it difficult for cheaters to get their work done.

Odessa will do the talking. She'll say, "Well, if you could excuse me, I need clean sheets for the beds." I'll move over a little bit. I'll twist to the left so she can get to the twin and queen sizes. I'm willing to move for Odessa. I can put one foot on top of the other. I'll do anything for her as long as I don't have to put my feet onto the gray carpet in the hall. I can't. I'm not ready. If I put a foot out there too early, everything will be lost.

Odessa sometimes asks me, "Which sheets do you want on your bed?" She knows I'm particular about these things. She knows her color combinations, dots and stripes together, attack me in my sleep. Sometimes I get up in the middle of the night, pull the sheets off the bed, throw them into the hall, and return to sleep. She will ask me what I want and I'll point to the plain white ones, the ones that seem lighter, cleaner than all the others. Odessa reaches for the sheets and in the instant when they're in her hand but still in the closet, I press my face into them. I press my face into the pile of sheets, into Odessa's hands underneath. I won't feel her skin, her fingers, only cool, clean fabric against my cheek. I inhale deeply as if there were a way to draw the sheets into my lungs, to hold the linen inside me. I breathe and take my head away. Odessa will pull her hands out of the closet and ask, "Do you want the door closed?" I nod. I turn away; draw in my breath, and make myself flat. She closes the door.

I'm hiding in the linen closet sending memos to myself. It's getting complicated. Odessa knows I'm here. She knows but she won't tell anybody. She won't go running into the living room and announce, "Jody's locked herself into the linen closet and she won't come out."

Odessa won't go outside and look for my father. She won't find him pulling weeds on the hill behind the house. Odessa won't tell him, "She's in there with paper, pencils, and that little light you gave her for Christmas." She won't say anything. Odessa understands that this is the way things sometimes are. She'll change the sheets on all the beds, serve the Fat Club ladies their cottage cheese and cantaloupe, and then she'll go downstairs into the bathroom and take a few sips from the bottle of Johnnie Walker she keeps there.

I'm hiding in the closet with my life suspended. I'm hiding and I'm scared to death. I want to come clean, to see myself clearly, in detail, like a hallucination, a death-bed vision, a Kodacolor photograph. I need to know if I'm alive or dead.

I'm hiding in the linen closet and I want to introduce myself to myself. I need to like what I see. If I am really as horrible as I feel, I will spontaneously combust, leaving a small heap of ashes that can be picked up with the Dust-buster. I will explode myself in a flash of fire, leaving a letter of most profuse apology.

Through the wall I hear my mother's Fat Club ladies laugh. I hear the rattle of the group and the gentle tinkling of the individual. It's as though I have more than one pair of ears. Each voice enters in a different place, with a different effect.

I hear them and realize they're laughing for me. They're celebrating the fact that I can no longer pretend. There are tears in my eyes. I'm saying thank you and good-bye. I'm writing it down because I can't simply go out there and stand at the edge of the dining room table until my mother looks up from her copy of the *Eat Yourself Slim Diet* and says, "Yes?"

I can't say that I'm leaving because she'll ask, "When will you be back?"

She'll be looking through the book, flipping through the menus, seeing how many ounces she can eat. If I tell the truth, if I say never, she'll look up at me, peering up higher than usual, above the frameless edges of her reading glasses. She'll say, "A comedian. Maybe Johnny Carson will hire you to guest-host. When will you be back?"

If I go without answering, the other ladies will watch me leave. When I get to where they think I can't hear them, when I get to the kitchen door, they'll put a pause in their meeting and talk about their children.

They'll say they were always the best parents they knew how to be. They'll say they gave their children everything and it was never enough. They'll say they hope their children will grow up and have children exactly like themselves. They'll be thinking about how their children hate them and how they hate their children back because they don't understand what it was they did wrong.

"It has nothing to do with you," I'll have to say. "It's me, it's me, all mine. There is no blame."

"Selfish," the mothers will say.

I'm here in the linen closet, doing my spring cleaning. I'm confessing right and left and Odessa knocks on the door. She knocks and then opens the door. She's carrying a plate with a sandwich and a glass of milk. Only Odessa would serve milk and a sandwich. My mother would give me a Tab with a twist of lemon. My father would make something like club soda with a little bit of syrup in it. He would use maple syrup and spend all afternoon telling me he'd invented something new, something better than other sodas because it had no chemicals, less sugar, and no caffeine. Odessa brings me a sandwich and a glass of milk and it looks like a television commercial. The bread is white, the sandwich cut perfectly in half. There are no finger marks on it, no indentations on the white bread where Odessa put her fingers while she was cutting. The glass is full except for an inch at the top. There are no spots in that inch. The milk looks white and thick, with small bubbles near the top. It looks cool and refreshing.

Odessa hands me the plate. I look at her for a moment. She is perfect. I drink the milk and know that I will have a mustache. I look at Odessa and want to say, "I love you." I want to tell her how no one else would bring me a glass of milk. I want to tell her everything, but she starts talking. Odessa says, "Make sure you don't leave that plate in the closet. I don't want your mother finding it and thinking I've lost my mind. I don't want bugs in here. Bring it out and put it in the dishwasher. Don't stay in there all day or you'll lose your color." I nod and she closes the door.

I'm hiding and I'm eating a cream-cheese-and-cucumber sandwich and having my head examined. I'm in the neighborhood of my soul and getting worried. I'm trying not to hate myself so much, trying not to hate my body, my mind, the thoughts I think. I'm hiding in the linen closet having a sex change. I'm in here with a pad of paper writing things I've thought and then unthought. Thoughts that seemed like incest, like they shouldn't be allowed.

I'm trying to find some piece of myself that is truly me, a part that I would be willing to wear like a jewel around my neck. My foot. I love my foot. If I had to send a part of myself to represent myself in some other country, or in some other way, I would amputate my foot and send it wrapped in white tissue on a silk-embroidered cushion. I would send my foot because it is me, more me than I'm willing to let on. There are other parts that are also good – hands, eyes, mouth – but after a few months I might look at them and not see the truth. After a few years I might look at them and think of someone else. But my foot is mine, all mine, the real thing. There is no mistaking it. I look at it; I take off my sock and it screams my name.

I could go on for hours demonstrating how well I know myself, through my foot, but I won't. It's embarrassing. The foot, my foot, that I wish to wear on a ribbon around my neck is an example of grace twisted and trapped. Chunks of bone and flesh conforming to the dictum: form follows function. It's a wonder I'm not a cripple.

I'm hiding in the linen closet, writing a declaration of independence. I'm in the closet, but the worst is over. There is hope, trapped inside my foot; inside my soul there is possibility. I'm looking at myself and slowly I'm falling in love. I've figured out what it takes to live forever. I'm in love and I'm free.

I want to throw the door open and hear an orchestra swell. I want to run out to the Fat Club ladies and tell them, "Life can go on, I'm in love."

I'll stand in the living room, facing the sofa. I'll stand with my arms spread wide, the violins reaching their pitch. I'll be sweating and shaking, unsteady on my feet, my wonderful, loving, lovable feet. At the end of my proclamation my mother will let her glasses fall from her face and dangle from the cord around her neck.

"Miss Dramatic," she'll say. "Why weren't you an actress?"

The fat ladies will look at each other. They'll look at me and think of other declarations of love. They'll look and one will ask, "Who's the lucky man?"

There will be a silence while they wait for a name, preferably the right kind of a name. If I tell them it isn't a man, their silence will grow and they'll expect what they think is the worst. No one except my mother will have nerve enough to say, "A girl then?"

I'll be forced to tell them, It's not like that. One of the ladies, the one the others think isn't so smart, will ask, "What's it like?"

I'll smile, the orchestra will swell, and I'll look at the four ladies sitting on the sofa, the sofa covered with something modern and green, something that vaguely resembles the turf on a putting green.

"It's like falling in love with life itself," I'll say.

My mother will look around the room. She'll look anywhere except at me.

"Are you all right?" she'll ask when I stop to catch my breath. "You look a little flushed." I'll be singing and dancing.

"I'm fine, I'm wonderful, I'm better than before. I'm in love."

I'll sing and on the end note cymbals will crash and the sound will hold in the air for a minute. And then swinging a top hat and cane, I'll dance away. I'll dance down the hall towards the den.

I want to find my father in the den, the family room, watching tennis on television. I want to catch him in the middle of a set and say that I can't wait for a break. I want to tell him, "Life must go on."

He'll say that it's match point. He'll say that he's been trying to tell me that all along.

"But why didn't you tell me what it really means?"

"It seemed pretty obvious."

And then I'll tell him, "I'm in love." There will be a pause. Someone will have the advantage. My feet will go *clickety-clack* over the parquet floor and he'll say, "Yes, you sound very happy. You sound like you're not quite yourself."

"I'm more myself than I've ever been."

I want to find Odessa. "Life will go on," I'll tell her. "I'm in love." I'll take her by the hand and we'll dance in circles around the recreation room. We'll dance until we're dizzy and Odessa will ask me, "Are you all right?"

I'll only be able to mumble "Ummmm hummm," because my grin will have set like cement. I'm hiding in the linen closet writing love letters to myself.

(SHE OWNS) EVERY THING

Anne Enright

Anne Enright (b. 1962) is an Irish author, born in Dublin. She has published essays, short stories, a work of non-fiction and four novels. Her novel, *The Gathering,* won the 2007 Man Booker Prize.

Cathy was often wrong, she found it more interesting. She was wrong about the taste of bananas. She was wrong about the future of the bob. She was wrong about where her life ended up. She loved corners, surprises, changes of light.

Of all the fates that could have been hers (spinster, murderer, savant, saint), she chose to work behind a handbag counter in Dublin and take her holidays in the sun.

For ten years she lived with the gloves and beside the umbrellas, their colours shy and neatly furled. The handbag counter travelled through navy and brown to a classic black. Yellows, reds, and white were to one side and all varieties of plastic were left out on stands, for the customer to steal.

Cathy couldn't tell you what the handbag counter was like. It was hers. It smelt like a leather dream. It was never quite right. Despite the close and intimate spaces of the gloves and the empty generosity of the bags themselves, the discreet mess that was the handbag counter was just beyond her control.

She sold clutch bags for people to hang on to; folded slivers of animal skin that wouldn't hold a box of cigarettes, or money unless it was paper, or a bunch of keys, 'just a credit card and a condom,' said one young woman to another and Cathy felt the ache of times changing.

She sold the handbag proper, sleek and stiff and surprisingly roomy – the favourite bag, the thoroughbred, with a hard clasp, or a fold-over flap and the smell of her best perfume. She sold sacks to young women, in canvas or in suede, baggy enough to hold a life, a change of underwear, a novel, a deodorant spray.

The women's faces as they made their choice were full of lines going nowhere, tense with the problems of leather, price, vulgarity, colour. Cathy matched blue eyes with a blue trim, a modest mouth with smooth, plum suede. She sold patent to the click of high heels, urged women who had forgotten into neat, swish reticules. Quietly, one customer after another was guided to the inevitable and surprising choice of a bag that was not 'them' but one step beyond who they thought they might be.

Cathy knew what handbags were for. She herself carried everything (which wasn't much) in one pocket, or the other.

*

She divided her women into two categories: those who could and those who could not.

She had little affection for those who could, they had no need of her, and they were often mistaken. Their secret was not one of class, although that seemed to help, but one of belief, and like all questions of belief, it involved certain mysteries. How, for example, does one *believe* in navy?

There were also the women who could not. A woman for example, who could NOT wear blue. A woman who could wear a print, but NOT beside her face. A woman who could wear beads but NOT earrings. A woman who had a secret life of shoes too exotic for her, or one who could neither pass a perfume counter nor buy a perfume, unless it was for someone else. A woman who comes home with royal jelly every time she tries to buy a blouse.

A woman who cries in the lingerie department.

A woman who laughs while trying on hats.

A woman who buys two coats of a different colour.

The problem became vicious when they brought their daughters shopping. Cathy could smell these couples from Kitchenware.

Cathy married late and it was hard work. She had to find a man. Once she had found one, she discovered that the city was full of them. She had to talk and laugh and be fond. She had to choose. Did she like big burly men with soft brown eyes? Did she like that blond man with the eyes of pathological blue? What did she think of her own face, its notches and dents?

She went the easy road with a kind teacher from Fairview and a registry office do. She stole him from a coltish young woman with awkward eyes. Cathy would have sold her a tapestry Gladstone bag, one that was 'wrong' but 'worked' all the same.

Sex was a pleasant surprise. It was such a singular activity, it seemed to scatter and gather her at the same time.

Cathy fell in love one day with a loose, rangy woman, who came to her counter and to her smile and seemed to pick her up with the same ease as she did an Argentinian calf-skin shoulder bag in tobacco brown, with woven leather inset panels, pig-skin lining and snap clasp. It was quite a surprise.

The woman, whose eyes were a tired shade of blue, asked Cathy's opinion, and Cathy heard herself say 'DIVE RIGHT IN, HONEY, THE WATER'S JUST FINE!' – a phrase she must have picked up from the television set. The woman did not flinch. She said 'Have you got it in black?'

Brown was the colour of the bag. Cathy was disappointed by this betrayal. The weave would just disappear in black, the staining was everything. Cathy said, 'It's worth it in brown, even if it means new shoes. It really is a beautiful bag.' The woman, however, neither bought the brown nor argued for black. She rubbed the leather with the base of her thumb as she laid the bag down. She looked at Cathy. She despaired. She turned her wide, sporting shoulders, her dry, bleached hair, and her nose with the bump in it, gave a small sigh, and walked out of the shop.

Cathy spent the rest of the day thinking, not of her hands, with their large knuckles, but of her breasts, that were widely spaced and looked two ways, one towards the umbrellas, the other at the scarves. She also wondered whether the woman had a necklace of lines hanging from her hips, whether she had ever been touched by a woman, what she might say, what Cathy might say back. Whether her foldings and infoldings were the same as her own or as different as daffodil from narcissus. It was a very lyrical afternoon.

Cathy began to slip. She made mistakes. She sold the wrong bags to the wrong women and her patter died. She waited for another woman to pick up the tobacco-brown bag to see what might happen. She sold indiscriminately. She looked at every woman who came her way and she just didn't know anymore.

She could, of course, change her job. She might, for example, work as a hospital maid, in the cardiac ward, which was full of certainties.

Women did not get heart attacks. They would come at visiting time and talk too much or not at all. She could work out who loved simply or in silence. She could spot those who might as well hate. She would look at their bags without judgement, as they placed them on the coverlets, or opened them for tissues. They might even let a tear drip inside.

Cathy emptied out her building-society account and walked up to the hat department with a plastic bag filled with cash. She said, 'Ramona, I want to buy every hat you have.' She did the same at Shoes, although she stipulated size five-and-a-half. She didn't make a fuss when refused. She stuffed the till of her own counter full of notes, called a taxi and hung herself with bags, around her neck and down her arms. All kinds of people looked at her. Then she went to bed for a week, feeling slightly ashamed.

She kept the one fatal bag, the brown calf-skin with a snap clasp. She abused it. She even used it to carry things. She started to sleep around.

WAITING ROOM (THE FIRST)

Elizabeth Jolley

Elizabeth Jolley (1923–2007) was an British-born writer who settled in Western Australia in the late 1950s. She was fifty-three when her first book was published, and went on to write fifteen novels, four short story collections and three works of non-fiction.

These days I live with the need to have something lined up to do next. The way in which I live reminds me of a joke; there are two goldfish swimming round and round in a goldfish bowl and one fish is telling the other fish that there's no time to chat as it's one of those 'get things done' days.

I make little lists because I might forget what I am doing, or more importantly, what I am going to do. Like going to the doctor's to see if my moles are cancer, like throwing away left-over food, old clothes, letters and other papers, especially receipts and bank statements saved over a great many years in case of a possible taxation audit (random).

It's when I am sitting in waiting rooms that I take stock of the way things are, of the way I'm living and of the way I used to live. I compare my life with other people's lives in a rather superficial way. Not comparisons about money but rather on the quality of roof beams, joists, floor boards and the sizes and shapes of windows.

I go back in my thoughts quite often. One time I actually try to remember all the names of the hospitals in the city where I lived for years in the English Midlands. There was, at that time, the Hospital for the Diseases of Women, the Sick Children's, the Ear, Nose and Throat, the Skin Hospital, the Fever, the Cancer, the General, the Accident (Queens) and the Queen Elizabeth. The QE was Maternity as well. I manage to stop the litany before going on to the names of streets, churches, schools and shops, though the names of houses come to mind – Sans Souci, Barclay, The Hollies, Padua, St Cloud and Prenton. Naturally, the hedges follow, the closely watched hedges, the laurel and the privet, the rhododendrons and the holly, evergreens in a series of repetitive quartets.

Those hedges from another country have given way to the honeysuckle, the hibiscus, the oleander, the plumbago, the white and pink climbing roses, the wistaria and the geraniums. There are too the street lawns, the box trees, the plane trees, the peppermints and the cape lilacs. But perhaps it is the blue metal, the smooth and the rough, which I notice the most when we are walking. The habit of closely watching the hedges is not lost, if anything it is more intense, and intensely, too, the roads. The roads are closely watched; Harold Hammond Goldsworthy Bernard the park Thompson Koeppe Princess Caxton Warwick and Queen and back Queen Warwick Caxton ...

I need a shrink, I say to myself, and go on to say that shrink is not a word I use. The use of it, even if not said aloud, is an indication that I need someone with specialist training.

Really this place! All I seem able to do here is to stare at the other people. We all seem stupid sitting here with a conventional obedience which is expected of us.

The chairs here are all joined together, fixed, making a square space in the middle where children can play. There are some little chairs and a low table for the children. I forget about myself for a bit, when I see a small child staggering about with a big plastic bucket. He has thick dark curls and a pale face and I pity him throwing up so much that he has to take a bucket around.

What's the matter with me, I think then, because 'throwing up' is a phrase I never use; neither do I say 'around' instead of round. I dismiss all this immediately when I see that the child is loading up the bucket with all the toys, the building blocks and farm animals, provided for *all* the children to play with, and is hauling them off to the safe harbour between his squatting mother's possessive spread-out legs.

A man sitting diagonally opposite gives his urine specimen to his wife to hold and she takes it and goes on reading her magazine holding the thing as if she was a specimen-glass holder, as if it is meant that she should just sit there, holding this specimen glass while he sits back stroking his chin and raising his eyebrows in every direction in turn round the waiting room; *see here everybody, meet the wife, my specimen-glass holder.*

The receptionist behind the curved desk has a commanding view of the whole room. When I look at her it is clear to me that she would prefer a dress shop in a not too classy department store. A place in which she could peek round the fitting-room curtains saying with emphasis, 'it's *you* dear' either for a dress, a blouse or a hat. It is probable that the pay is better in the Outpatients' Clinic and the hours less barbaric, especially since the decision not to have the clinic open at all on Fridays. I notice every time, without really meaning to, that she wears mostly red dresses or blouses with low V-neck lines exposing the healthy unworried skin of a woman approaching middle age and a suggestion of a similarly healthy and unworried bosom, more or less out of sight.

Certain days are set aside for walking sticks, crutches and wheelchairs. On these days I remind myself often to count my blessings and to remember that there are people worse off etc. For one thing I am only accompanying a patient and am not a patient myself. Without meaning to, against my will, I notice that some of the patients have a perpetually grieved look and some seem actually to be parading their disability. They exaggerate a grieved way of walking with one shoulder higher than the other, the body turned inwards on itself and the head tilted to one side. They seem to have the special skill of taking up the whole width of any place and then there's no way of getting round them like when you're waiting to go down in the small elevator to the Lab for blood tests. Sometimes people, like these people and unfortunates, will take up all the room in the aisles in the supermarket. Walking on two sticks, lurching first to one side and then the other, they make it impossible for anyone else to pass or even reach round for a tin of dog food, a cereal or some soap powder.

I suppose all this sounds cruel and without sympathy. It is not meant to. I might be on two sticks myself one day. Such thoughts, like everything else at present, are very out of character. Like this morning when there are no oranges to squeeze I am shaken to discover how much the disappearance of a small ritual can disturb me and cause an inability to go on to the next thing – just because one insignificant part of the morning routine is missing.

When I ask Mr George what he had for lunch he does not remember and when I ask was it nice, what he had for lunch, he says that it was very nice and, because it was nice, it is a pity that he does not remember what it was.

It is a pity, he says, to forget something nice.

An occupational therapist, with knitting needles pushed into her hair which is dressed in a firm grey bun, approaches. She has cut, she tells me, some pieces, squares and circles, of foam cushion material. She gives them to me saying that she knows relatives and friends enjoy being involved. She says that making little chintzy covers for these is a nice way of spending the long afternoons. She calls her pieces soft splints for pressure areas. She smiles with real pleasure.

I want to tell her that I don't have long afternoons except in my consulting rooms and I am not able to sew there. I nearly explain that I can't sew, it's a bit like not being able to dance, I mean ballroom dancing, it is always an embarrassment to say, 'I can't dance.' It is the same with sewing.

I can imagine all too easily the sense of futility which would all too quickly obliterate the hopefulness accompanying the giving of these chintz covers to some of my afternoon appointments who do, indeed, need occupation and direction but who have, at the same time, the ability in the face of offered activity to make the activity seem useless and unnecessary. This attribute is of course a symptom of the cause which might not be cured by the covering of soft splints with fragments of a cheerful material.

TELEGONY I: GOING INTO A DARK HOUSE

Jane Gardam

Jane Gardam (b. 1928) is a British author, who writes for both children
and adults. Her first novel for adults, *God on the Rocks*, was published
in 1978 and shortlisted for the Man Booker Prize. She has won the
Whitbread Award twice, for *The Queen of the Tambourines* and *The
Hollow Land,* and was awarded an OBE in 2009 in recognition of her
distinguished literary career.

Molly Fielding's mother had been a terrible woman born about the same
time as Tennyson's Maud and as unapproachable.

Nobody knew anything much about her, Molly herself being now
very ancient. Molly had been my grandmother's friend and my mother's, before
she was mine, but with the demise of each generation she seemed to grow younger and freer – to take strength. Her hair, her clothes, her house, all were up to the
minute. So were her investments; and her foreign holidays became farther and
farther flung.

I had found the photograph of her mother before my own mother died. It
was a coffee-coloured thing mounted on thick, fluffy, cream paper, unframed
in a drawer, with the photographer's name in beautiful copperplate across the
corner: 'Settimo'.

I could not believe it. Signor Settimo! He had taken my own photograph when
I was a child. I remembered a delicious little man like a chocolate, with black
hair and eyes and Hitler's square moustache. My Settimo must have been the
son – or even grandson – of course. Molly Fielding's mother must have known
the first. Probably the first Settimo had come over from Italy with the icecream
makers and organ grinders of the *fin de siècle*. It was a long-established firm
when I knew it and a photographer in the English Midlands with a glamorous,
lucky name such as *Settimo* would be almost home and dry. All he'd need would
be flair and a camera and a book of instructions – a match for anyone.

But not for Molly Fielding's mother. Oh, dear me no. There she sits, her strong
jaw raised, its tip pointing straight at the lens. Very watchful. She is examining
the long hump of Mr Settimo beneath the black cloth behind the tripod. Her eyes
– small eyes – are saying, 'Try – but you'll not take me. *I* take.'

Her great face, like his small one, is covered in black cloth. Hers is covered by
a fine veil of silk netting, tied tight round the back of her neck by a broad black
velvet ribbon. It is stitched at the top round the hat brim – a tight hat, expensive

and showy, glittering with jet beads like the head of a snake. Her own head is proudly up, her eyes are very cunning. Oho, how she despises Mr Settimo, the tradesman. She is smiling a most self-satisfied smile. She is armed with a cuirass of necklaces across her beaded front, a palisade of brooches, great gauntlets of rings. She is fair-skinned beneath the veil. She must have been a pretty young girl, and her mouth, above the chin grown fierce, is still small and curly and sexy. No lady. Like somebody's cook but in the way that duchesses can look like somebody's cook. Not born rich, you can see – but now she *is* rich. At this moment, seated before foreign little Mr Settimo, she is rich. I never saw a nastier piece of work than Molly Fielding's mother. I swear it. I don't know how I knew – but I swear it.

'What an awful woman. Who is it?'

My mother said, 'Oh, dear, that's old Molly Fielding's mother. I knew her. She was a character.'

'You *knew* her! She looks before the Punic Wars.'

'She was, just about. God knows. An authentic mid-Victorian. She had Molly very late. She was famous for some sort of reputation but I can't remember what it was. She died about the time Molly married, and that would be all of sixty years ago.'

'What was the husband like?'

'Oh, long gone. Nobody knew him. Molly can't remember him. Maybe there wasn't a husband, but I think I'd have remembered if it was that. I think he was just dispensed with somehow. He was very weak – or silly. But rich.'

'She doesn't look as if she would have needed anyone, ever.'

'Well, she certainly didn't need poor old Molly. Her only child, you know, and she hated her. Molly – such a silent little thing at school. After that she was "at home with mother".'

'Didn't she ever work?'

'Are you mad, child? She had to gather up her mother's shawls and go visiting with her and return the library books.'

'Until she married?'

'Yes. And she'd never have married if her mother could have stopped it. She was always very attractive, Molly. Not beautiful but attractive. She was never let out of her mother's sight – and not let into anyone else's. They lived in hotels, I think, up and down the country. Sometimes in boarding-house places abroad. There had been a big house somewhere but they left it!'

'Were they poor?'

'Rich, dear, rich, just look some time at Molly's rings.'

This conversation was years ago and since then I have often looked at Molly's rings. I looked at them the other day when she came to lunch with me and they still shone wickedly, catching the light of the winter dining room, weighting down her little claws. Molly was a trim, spare, little woman and the claws were smaller now and even sharper-looking than when I'd seen her last, two years ago. Her nails were tiny and beautifully manicured and the prickly old clusters below them looked loose enough at any moment to go sliding off into the chicken supreme.

'Looking at the rings?' she asked. 'You're not getting them, dear. They're for impeccable Alice. My albatrosses. She could have them now if she wanted. I hardly wear them. High days and holidays, like this. I keep them in – no, I'm not going to tell you. You never know. Careless talk … You think they're vulgar, do you?'

'No. I was just – well, remembering them. From way back. They looked smaller then. Your rings were you. Most things look bigger when you're young.'

'I'm smaller,' she said, 'that's all it is. I keep getting them re-made but they can't keep pace with me. I get them done over every year before the insurance runs out. I tell the insurance people the stones rattle. They don't, but you can get them cleaned free if you say that. A jeweller cleans them better than you can yourself. A good jeweller always cleans when he secures. Gin – that's all you can do for yourself, soak them in gin. But it's a waste. You feel you can't drink it afterwards with all the gunge in it.'

The rings shone clear and sharp and there was not a trace of gunge and never had been, for Molly had a code of practice for the maintenance of goods that would have impressed a shipping company; and she had an eye for the free acquisition of necessities and schemes for the painless saving of money that many a government might envy. She also had a talent for the command of luxury. Stories of Molly sharing hotel rooms for which her friends and acquaintances had paid were in my childhood canon. She had slept on the floor of the Hyde Park, for instance, with her daughter's old nanny who had struck it rich with a (now absent) South American lover.

'Nanny had the bed of course – I insisted. Yes, she did fuss about me being on the floor, and we did change over about eleven o'clock, but I'd have been perfectly happy. Who minds sleeping on a floor if it saves two hundred pounds a night? They never notice, you know. I'd been Nanny's dinner guest and we went up to her room after dinner as if to get my coat. No one notices if you don't go home. And it was Harvey Nichols' sale in the morning, just across the road. I felt since I'd saved two hundred pounds I could spend it.'

'But, Molly, you didn't *have* to spend two hundred pounds. You didn't *have* to go into London the night before at all. You only live in Rickmansworth.'

'Oh, but there's nothing in Rickmansworth like the Hyde Park Hotel. Another thing, dear, did you know you can get a jolly good free bath on Paddington Station? There's a very decent bathroom in the Great Western. You just go in there for a coffee and then trot upstairs to the ladies' room and along the corridor and you're in a very nice big bathroom with marble fittings and nice old brass chains to the plugs. Thundering hot water, dear. I take soap and a towel always when I'm in London. In a Harrods bag.'

'You could be arrested.'

'Rubbish. There's not a hint of a sign saying "Private". It says *Bathroom*. Nobody uses it but me because all the rooms are this ghastly thing *En Suite* now. Have you noticed on the motorway – the motels? "*24 En Suites*". I'd never stay in a place like the Great Western now, of course. It's only for commercial travellers. But the bathroom's useful if you have to change for the evening. It saves that nonsense of belonging to a so-called Club. Deadly places – all full of old women. Victoria Station was very good, too, before the War, and at St Pancras,

The Great Northern, you could always stay a night no questions asked if you knew the ropes and wore the right clothes. They used to leave the keys standing in the doors. So unwise.

'And did you know you can spend *such* a pleasant hour or so in the London Library simply by ignoring the Members Only notice? You just walk in looking thoughtful and go upstairs to the Reading Room. It's a pity they've moved the old leather armchairs. They were so comfortable and you could sleep in them before a matinée. I always picked up one of the learned journals from the racks – something like *The John Evelyn Society Quarterly* – so that they'd think I was an old don.'

'They can see you're no don, Molly, with those diamonds.'

'I turn them round, dear. I'm not silly. They used to give you a tray of tea in the London Library once, you know, but all those nice things have stopped since the Conservatives got in. Look – an elastic band. It's the Post Office. I keep these. The postmen drop them all over England – all up the drive of the Final Resting Place. I told the postman they're worth money so now he drops them all through my letter box instead, great showers of them, like tagliatelle.'

We were walking on the common now. Lunch was over. It was a cold day and people were muffled up and pinched of face but Molly looked brisk and scarcely seventy. From the back – her behind neat, her legs and ankles skinny – she might have been forty-five. She wore a beautiful, old, lavender-mixture tweed suit and no glasses and she carried no stick. Trotting around her was a new puppy, a border collie she was training. She walked at a good speed through the spruces, as fast as I did and nearly as fast as the puppy, which she'd let off the lead. Her cheeks were pink, her eyes were bright and several people smiled at her as she went by. One old boy of about sixty gave her the eye and said he agreed about the wastage of elastic bands.

I said we should turn back as it was going to rain and she didn't want to be landed with a cold.

'I never catch cold,' she said. 'It's because I don't use public transport. I like my car. It was quite unnecessary for you to fetch and carry me today, you know. Very nice of you – but I'd have enjoyed crossing London again.'

'Do they let you drive still, Molly?' She had one of the little houses on an estate for the elderly she called the Final Resting Place.

'They can't stop me. Not yet. It's coming up of course – next driving test. Well, yes, they do fuss a bit. I can't remember where I'm going sometimes after I've set off, and the other day I couldn't remember where I'd been.'

'That might be a warning sign, you know, Molly. That it's time to stop.'

'Oh, fish! Wait till I get properly lost, then I'll stop. I've a card in my bag with my telephone number. I haven't forgotten who I am yet.'

'That does happen – '

'Oh, that Alzheimer business. That must be a terrible thing. But it only happens to the old, doesn't it?' She roared with laughter and clipped the dog on the lead.

Molly's dogs have always been wonderfully well behaved and obedient – never smelled or chewed things or wet things or snapped or barked. Rather dispirited animals really. She never appeared to pay much attention to them.

Years ago I remembered that she had said it was her mother who had taught her how to handle dogs.

'Come on,' she cried from the traffic island in the middle of the High Street. 'You'll get run over if you hang about. Make a dash.'

At tea – she'd done well at lunch with a couple of sherries and a glass of chablis with the chicken – she settled down to a crumpet and a long and interesting analysis of her investments. As usual I forgot altogether that Molly had been my grandmother's friend. I forgot the great string of years she had known, the winters and winters and winters, the spring after spring, flowing back and back and back to the first mornings of the century. I forgot the huge number of times she had woken to another day.

When I was a girl, Molly would come breezing by to see us in a fast car, usually with a woman friend, never with a man or her husband who had been, like her father, a shadow. (She had married in ten minutes, my grandmother used to say, when her mother was upstairs in bed having measles of all things: absolutely furious, her mother was, too. In fact she died.) When I was a girl, I had always felt that Molly was empowered with an eternal youth, more formidable, much more effective, than my transient youth that seemed longer ago.

'Well, I'm not clever,' she often said. 'I'm a fool, dear. I know my limitations. No education and not a brain in my head. That's the secret. You're all so clever now – and all so good. It does age people. And also of course I'm frightfully mean. I don't eat or drink much unless I'm out.'

But she wasn't mean. When she gave a present, having said she could afford nothing, it tended to be stupendous. Once she gave me a car. And she did leave me one of the rings. But, 'I'm mean,' she said. 'And I'm not intellectual. I always wanted to be a racing driver after motor cars came in. Not allowed to, of course. D'you think I'm embittered?' (She shrieked with laughter.) 'I've struggled through. I've struggled through.'

And struggle it had sometimes looked to be – her freezing house, her empty hearth and fridge, her beautiful but ancient clothes all mended and pressed and hung in linen bags in the wardrobe. She had often sat wrapped in rugs to save coal. She had never had central heating. An ascetic pauper – until you looked at her investments, and they were wonderful. Whenever you saw her reading the financial columns she was smiling.

'And,' she said, 'hand it to me. I'm rational. That's what gets you through in the end, you know – being rational. I've no imagination, thank God. I give to charity but I've the sense not to watch the news. "Thank God" by the way is jargon. I don't believe in God and I don't believe that half the people I know who go to church and carry on at Christmas and go to the *Messiah* and that sort of thing – that they do either. All my Bridge lot, of course they don't believe in God. Religion's always seemed to me to be fairy stories. I go to church now and then, but it's for keeping up friendships and the look of it. And I quite enjoy weddings and funerals, of course.'

She was awesome, Molly. Awful really. But she was so nice.

She was in the midst of one of these 'I'm rational' conversations, the refrain that had threaded all my association with her, and she was eating her crumpet, and I was wondering why she was still insisting on her – well, on her boringness, and why she didn't bore me, why she never annoyed me; and I had decided it was because she never dissembled, that in my life her total truthfulness was unique. The truth Molly told showed her to be good. A good, straight being. Molly the unimaginative was unable to lie.

At which point she suddenly said, 'By the way, my mother's been seen around again.'

I looked at her.

'Around the village. And the FRP. She's looking for me, you know. But she won't find me.'

I said, 'Your *mother*?'

She said, 'Yes. You didn't know her. You were lucky. I hated her. Of course you know I did. You must have heard. She was very cruel to me. Well, she's back. Darling, are you going to take me home to the house of the near-dead? It's getting dark.'

'Yes, of course. Are you ready?'

'I'll just run upstairs.'

This she did and I waited with her coat and gloves and walking shoes and the basket with the dog's belongings and the dog.

'Yes,' she said coming down the stairs, twisting about at her knickers. 'Yes, she's been around for quite a time, a year or so. I don't know where she was before. I've managed to keep out of her way up to now. I hope that she didn't spot me leaving today, she'd have wanted to come, too.'

So, half an hour later I said, 'Molly, do you mean your *mother*?'

'Yes, dear. I'm afraid she was very unkind. I don't often talk about it. I was very frightened of her. D'you know, dear, I don't know when I've *had* such a wonderful day. Oh, how I've enjoyed it. Now if you turn left here and left again we can take the short cut and get straight to the bypass. You see I know exactly where I am. Now don't come in with me – you must get back before the traffic.'

I said, 'Molly – '

She kissed me, hesitated, and then got out. I saw her standing motionless before her mock-Georgian front door looking first at the lock, then at her key.

'Shall I open it?' I called to her.

'No, no. Of course not. Don't treat me as senile. Ninety-four is nothing. It won't be thought anything of soon. When you're ninety-four there'll be hundreds of you, with all this marvellous new medicine that's going on.'

'Goodbye, dear Molly. I'll wait till you're safe inside.'

'It's just that the lights aren't on.' She said, 'If you could just watch me in from the car. Just watch till I light everything up. It's so silly but I don't greatly like going into a dark house.'

I drove to the estate office and spoke to the lady superintendent who said that Molly was indeed still driving, though they were getting worried about it. She said that Molly was utterly sensible, utterly rational and her eyes and mind were very good. In fact she upset the younger ones by doing her stocks and shares and phoning her broker in the public common room.

'No aberrations? Does her mind wander?'

'*Never*,' she said. 'She is our star turn.'

Yet on the way home I decided to ring up her daughter, Alice, and was walking towards the phone the next morning when it began to ring, and it was Alice calling me. There were the statutory empty screams about how long since we'd spoken and then she asked if it were true that Molly had been to lunch with me. I said yes, and that I'd fetched her and taken her back, of course.

'Not "of course" at all, ducky. Do you know she's still driving?'

I went on like the superintendent for a bit: about the beady eye that saw me look at the rings, the high-speed walk, the psychic hold over the dog, the fearlessness on the High Street, the splendid appetite. 'There was just – '

'Ha!'

'Well, she says her *mother* is about. Alice, her mother'd be about a hundred and thirty years old.'

'I know. Oh, heaven, don't I know. Did she say her mother's looking for her around the village?'

'Yes.'

'And making her clean her nails and polish her shoes and – She rings me up and asks me to bring a cake over because her mother's coming to tea. About twice a week.'

'But I've never heard her mention her mother before.'

'The doctors say it's the supply of oxygen to the brain. It's running uneven, like a car with dirty plugs. There are vacuums or something, and it's in the vacuums she really lives. Maybe it's where we all really live.'

'But all the bossy, sensible, happy years?'

'*All* the years. It was all there underneath, always. The fear.'

FAT PEOPLE

Alison Lurie

Alison Lurie (b. 1926) is an American novelist and academic. She won
the Pulitzer Prize in 1984 for her novel *Foreign Affairs*. She has published
ten novels, one collection of short stories, and a non-fiction work entitled
The Language of Clothes.

I never ran into any spooks in sheets; no headless horsemen, haunted mansions, nothing like that. But there was something weird once –

It was a while ago, when Scott went to India on that research grant. The
first thing that happened was, I began noticing fat people. I saw them snatching
the shrimps and stuffed eggs at parties; I saw them strolling along Cayuga Street
with the swaying sailor's gait of the obese, and pawing through the queen-size
housecoats in J. C. Penney. They were buying tubs of popcorn at the flicks, ahead
of me in line at the post office and the bank, and pumping self-serve gas into their
pickup trucks when I went to the garage.

I didn't pay much attention at first; I figured that since I was dieting I was
more aware of people who should be doing the same. My idea was to lose fifteen
pounds while Scott was away – twenty if possible, because of what he'd said just
before he left.

We were at the county airport on a cold weepy day in March, waiting for
Scott's plane and trying to keep up a conversation, repeating things we'd already
said. I'd seen Scott off on trips before; but this time he'd be gone over three
months. He was saying he wished I were coming, and promising to wire from
Delhi and write twice a week, and telling me he loved me and reminding me
again to check the oil on the Honda. I said I would, and was there anything else
I should do while he was away?

Then the flight was announced and we grabbed each other. But we were both
wearing heavy down jackets, and it didn't feel real. It was like two bundles of
clothes embracing, I said, all choked up. And Scott said, 'Well, there is one thing
we could both do while I'm gone, Ellie; we could lose a few pounds.' He was
kissing my face and I was trying not to break down and howl.

Then Scott was through the X-ray scanner into the boarding lounge, and then
he was crossing the wet tarmac with his carry-on bag, getting smaller and smaller, and climbing the steps. It wasn't till I'd gone back to the main waiting-room
and was standing inside the teary steamed-up window watching his plane shrink
and blur into fog that I really registered his last remark.

I drove back to Pine Grove Apartments and dragged off my fat coat and
looked at myself in the mirror on the back of the closet door. I knew I was a big

girl, at the top of the range for my height, but it had never bothered me before. And as far as I knew it hadn't bothered Scott, who was hefty himself. Maybe when he suggested we lose a few pounds he was just kidding. But it was the last thing I'd hear him say for three months. Or possibly forever, I thought, because India was so far away and full of riots and diseases; and maybe in one of the villages he was going to they wouldn't want to change their thousand-year-old agricultural methods, and they would murder Scott with long wavy decorated knives or serve him curry with thousand-year-old undetectable poisons in it.

I knew it was bad luck to think that way, Scott had said so himself. I looked back at the mirror again, turning sideways. Usually I was pleased by what I saw there, but now I noticed that when I didn't breathe in, my tummy stuck out as far as my breasts.

Maybe I had put on some extra pounds that winter, I thought. Well, it should be pretty easy to take them off. It could be a project, something to do while Scott was gone. I wouldn't write him about it, I'd save it for a surprise when he got back. 'Wow, Ellie,' he would say, 'you look great.'

Only it turned out not to be as easy as all that. After two weeks, I weighed exactly the same. One problem was that all our friends kept asking me over and serving meals it would have been a shame to refuse, not to mention rude. And when I didn't have anywhere to go in the evening I started wandering around the apartment and usually ended up wandering into the kitchen and opening the fridge, just for something to do.

It was about then that I began to notice how many fat people there were in town. All sorts and all ages: overweight country-club types easing themselves out of overweight cars; street people shoving rusted grocery carts jammed with bottles and bundles. Fat old men like off-duty Santa Clauses waddling through the shopping mall, fat teenagers with acne, and babies so plump they could hardly get their thumbs into their mouths.

Of course I'd seen types like this before occasionally, but now they seemed to be everywhere. At first I put it down to coincidence, plus having the subject on my mind. It didn't bother me; in a way it was reassuring. When some bulgy high-school senior came for an interview at the college, and tried to fit their rear end onto the chair by my desk, I would think as I smiled nicely and asked the standard questions, Well, at least I don't look like that.

My folks knew I was trying to lose weight, and wanted to help, but they only made it worse. Every time I went over to the house for Sunday dinner Dad would ask first thing if I'd heard from Scott. It got to be over three weeks, and I still had to say 'No, nothing since the telegram,' and remind them that we'd been warned about how bad the mails were.

Then we'd sit down to the table and Mom would pass my plate, and there'd be this measly thin slice of chicken on it, and a bushel of cooked greens, as if I was in some kind of concentration camp for fatties. The salads all started to have sour low-cal dressing, and there was never anything but fruit for dessert: watery melon, or oranges cut up with a few shreds of dry coconut on top, like little undernourished white worms.

All through the meal Mom and Dad wouldn't mention Scott again, so as not to upset me. There was nothing in the dining-room to remind anybody of Scott either, and of course there wasn't any place set for him at the table. It was as if he'd disappeared or maybe had never even existed. By the time dinner was over I'd be so low in my mind I'd have to stop on the way home for a pint of chocolate marshmallow.

I'd hang up my coat and turn on the television and measure out exactly half a cup of ice cream, 105 calories, less than a bagel. I'd put the rest in the freezer and feel virtuous. But when the next commercial came on I'd open the freezer and have a few more spoonfuls. And then the whole process would repeat, like a commercial, until the carton was scraped clean down to the wax.

It got to be four weeks since Scott had left, and I still didn't weigh any less, even when I shifted my feet on the scale to make the needle wobble downwards. I'd never tried to lose weight before; I'd always thought it was ridiculous the way some people went into agonies over diets. I'd even been kind of shocked when one of my married friends made more fuss about taking a second slice of peach pie than she did about taking a lover. Displaced guilt, I used to think.

Now I was as hysterical about food as any of them. I brooded all afternoon over a fudge brownie I hadn't had for lunch; and if I broke down and ordered one I made up excuses for hours afterwards. 'I didn't promise Scott I'd lose weight,' I would tell myself, or 'It's not fair asking someone to give up both food and love at the same time.'

I started to read all the articles on losing weight that I used to skip before, and I took books out of the library. Over the next couple of weeks I tried one crazy diet after another: no-carbohydrate, no-fat, grapefruit and cornflakes, chipped beef and bananas and skimmed milk. Only I couldn't stick with any of them. Things went wrong at night when I started thinking about how I'd written nine letters to Scott and hadn't got one back. I'd lie in bed asking myself where the hell was he, what was he doing now? And pretty soon I'd feel hungry, starving.

Another thing I kept asking myself, especially when I chewed through some dried-out salad or shook Sweet-N-Low into my coffee, was what Scott, assuming he was still alive, was eating over there on the other side of the world. If he wasn't on a diet, what was the point? I would think, watching my hand reach out for the blue-cheese dressing or the half-and-half. He hadn't meant it seriously, I'd tell myself.

But suppose he had meant it? Suppose Scott was becoming slimmer and trimmer every day; what would he think if he knew I hadn't lost a pound in nearly five weeks?

Trying to do it on my own wasn't working. I needed support, and I thought I knew where to find it. There was a young woman in the Admissions Office called Dale. She was only a couple of years older than me, maybe twenty-six, but in two months she'd just about reorganised our files, and she obviously had her life under control. She was a brunette, with a narrow neat little figure and a narrow neat little poodle face; you got the feeling her hair wouldn't dare get itself mussed up, and she'd never weigh one ounce more than she chose to.

I figured that Dale would have ideas about my problem, because she was always talking about interesting new diets. And whenever some really heavy person came in she'd make a yapping noise under her breath and remark later how awful it was for people to let themselves go physically. 'Heaven knows how that hippopotamus is going to fulfil his athletic requirement,' she would say, or 'That girl's mother ought to be in a circus, she hardly looked human.' And I'd think, do I look human to Dale?

So one day when we were alone in the washroom I let on that I was trying to lose some weight. Dale lit up like a fluorescent tube. 'Yes, I think that's a good idea, Ellie,' she said, looking from herself to me, poodle to hippo, in the mirror over the basins. 'And I'd like to help you, okay?'

'Okay, thanks,' I said. I didn't have any idea what I was getting into.

On our way back to the office, Dale explained to me that being overweight was a career handicap. It was a known fact that heavy people didn't get ahead as fast in business. Besides, fat was low-class: the Duchess of Windsor had said you could never be too rich or too thin. When I told her there wasn't much danger of my ever being either one, Dale didn't laugh. She printed her Duchess of Windsor line out in computer-graphic caps, and fastened it on the side of my filing cabinet with two pineapple magnets.

The next thing Dale did was persuade me to see a doctor to make sure I was healthy, the way they tell you to do in the diet books. Then she started organising my life. She got me enrolled in an aerobics class, and set up a schedule for me to jog every day after work, regardless of the weather. Then she invited herself over to my apartment and cleaned out the cupboards and icebox. Bags of pretzels and fritos, butter and cream cheese and cold cuts, a loaf of cinnamon-raisin bread, most of a pound of Jones bacon – Dale packed everything up, and we hauled it down to the local soup-kitchen. I kind of panicked when I saw all that lovely food disappearing, but I was hopeful too.

The next day Dale brought in a calorie-counter and planned my meals for a week in advance. She kept a chart, and every day she'd ask how much I'd weighed that morning and write it down.

Only the scale still stuck at the same number. If there was nothing in the apartment, there was always plenty in the grocery. I'd go in for celery and cottage cheese and Ry-Krisp, but when I was pushing the cart down the last aisle it was as if the packages of cookies on the shelves were crying out to me, especially the chocolate-covered grahams and the Mallomars. I could almost hear them squeaking inside their cellophane wrappers, in these little high sugary voices: 'Ellie, Ellie! Here we are, Ellie!'

When I confessed to falling off my diet, Dale didn't lose her cool. 'Never mind, Ellie, that's all right,' she said. 'I know what we'll do. From now on, don't you go near a supermarket alone. I'll shop with you twice a week on the way home.'

So the next day she did. But as soon as she got a little ahead of me in the bakery section, I began drifting towards a tray of apricot croissants. Dale looked round and shook her poodle curls and said, 'Naughty, naughty,' – which kind of made me feel crazy, because I hadn't done anything naughty yet – and then she grabbed my arm and pulled me along fast.

There'd been several fat people in the A & P that day, the way there always were lately. When we were in line at the checkout with a load of groceries only a rabbit could love, I noticed one of them, a really heavy blonde girl about my own age, leaving the next register. Her cart was full and a couple of plump bakery boxes, a carton of potato chips and a giant bottle of Coke were bulging out of the brown-paper bags. As she came past the fat girl picked up a package of Hershey bars and tore it open, and half-smiled in my direction as if she were saying, 'Come on, Ellie, have one.'

I looked round at Dale, figuring she would make some negative comment, but she didn't. Maybe she hadn't seen the fat girl yet. The funny thing was, when I looked back I didn't see her either; she must have been in a big rush to get home. And she was going to have a really good time when she got there, too, I thought.

Another week dragged by full of carrots and diet soda and frozen Weight Watchers dinners, and no news from Scott. My diet wasn't making much progress either. I'd take a couple of pounds off, but then I'd go out to dinner or a party and put some back on. Instead of losing I was gaining.

I was still seeing fat people too, more and more of them. I tried to convince myself it was just because they weren't disguised inside winter clothes any longer. The only problem was, the people I was seeing weren't just heavy, they were gross.

The first time I knew for sure that something strange was going on was one day when I was in the shopping plaza downtown, sitting on the edge of a planter full of sticky purple petunias and listening to a band concert instead of eating lunch, which had been Dale's idea, naturally. I was feeling kind of dizzy and sick, and when I touched my head it seemed to vibrate, as if it wasn't attached to my body too well.

Then I happened to glance across the plaza, and through the window of the Home Bakery I saw two middle-aged women, both of them bulging out of flowered blouses and slacks as if they'd been blown up too full. I couldn't make out their faces well because of the way the light shimmered and slid on the shop window; but I could see that one of them was looking straight at me and pointing to a tray of strawberry tarts: big ones with thick ruby glaze and scallops of whipped cream. It was as if she was saying, 'Come and get it, Ellie.'

Without even intending to I stood up and started to push through the crowd. But when I reached the bakery there weren't any fat women, and I hadn't seen them leave either. There'd been a moment when I was blocked by a twin stroller; but it still didn't make sense, unless maybe the fat women hadn't really been there. Suddenly I started feeling sick to my stomach. I didn't want a strawberry tart any more; I just wanted to go somewhere and lie down, only I was due back in the Admissions Office.

When I got there I said to Dale, making my voice casual, 'You know something funny, I keep seeing all these really fat people around lately.'

'There are a lot of them around, Ellie,' Dale said. 'Americans are terribly overweight.'

'But I'm seeing more. I mean, lots more than I ever did before. I mean, do you think that's weird?'

'You're just noticing them more,' Dale said stapling forms together, bang-bang. 'Most people block out unpleasant sights of that sort. They don't see the disgusting rubbish in the streets, or the way the walls are peeling right in this office.' She pointed with her head to a corner above the swing doors, where the cream-coloured paint was swollen into bubbles and flaking away; I hadn't noticed it before. Somehow that made me feel better.

'I guess you could be right,' I said. I knew that Dale was getting impatient with me. She'd stopped keeping my weight chart, and when we went shopping now she read the labels on things aloud in a cross way, as if she suspected I was cheating on my diet and had a package of shortbread or a box of raisins hidden away at home, which was sometimes true.

It was around that time that eating and sex started to get mixed up in my mind. Sometimes at night I still woke up hot and tense and longing for Scott; but more often I got excited about food. I read articles on cooking and restaurants in a greedy lingering way, and had fantasies about veal paprika with sour cream and baby onions, or lemon meringue pie. Once after I'd suddenly gone up to a pushcart and bought a giant hotdog with ketchup and relish I heard myself saying half aloud, 'I just had to have it.' And that reminded me of the way men talked in tough-guy thrillers. 'I had to have her,' they always said, and they would speak of some woman as if she was a rich dessert and call her a dish or a cupcake and describe parts of her as melons or buns. Scott isn't really a macho type, but he's always liked thrillers; he says they relax him on trips. And when he got on the plane that awful day he'd had one with him.

He'd been gone over six weeks by then, and no news since the telegram from Delhi. Either something really terrible had happened to him or he deliberately wasn't writing. Maybe while I was cheating on my diet, Scott was cheating on me, I thought. Maybe he'd found some Indian cupcake to relax him. As soon as I had that idea I tried to shove it out of my head, but it kept oozing back.

Then one sunny afternoon early in June I came home from work and opened the mailbox, and there among the bills and circulars was a postcard from Scott. There wasn't any apology for not writing, just a couple of lines about a beautiful temple he'd visited, and a scrawled 'love and kisses'. On the other side was a picture of a sexy over-decorated Indian woman and a person or god with the head of an elephant, both of them wearing smug smiles.

As I looked at that postcard something kind of exploded inside me. For weeks I'd been telling myself and everyone, 'If only I knew Scott was all right, I'd feel fine.' Now I knew he was all right, but what I felt was a big rush of suspicion and fury.

Pictures from the coffee-table books on India Scott had borrowed from the library crowded into my mind. I saw sleek prune-eyed exotic beauties draped in shiny silk and jewels, looking at me with hard sly expressions; and plump nearly naked blue gods with bedroom eyes; and closeups of temple sculptures in pock-marked stone showing one thousand and one positions for sexual intercourse. The ideas came to me that at that exact moment Scott was making out in one thousand different positions with some woman who had an elephant's head or was completely blue. I knew that was crazy, but still he had to be doing something he didn't want to tell me about and was ashamed of, or he would have written.

I didn't go on upstairs to the apartment. Instead I got back into the car, not knowing where I was going till the Honda parked of its own volition in front of a gourmet shop and cafe that I hadn't been near for weeks. There were five other customers there, which wasn't unusual at that time of day. The unusual thing was, all of them were fat; and not just overweight: humongously huge. All of them looked at me in a friendly way when I came in, as if maybe they knew me and had something to tell me.

For a moment I couldn't move. I just stood there stuck to the indoor-outdoor carpeting and wondered if I was going out of my mind. Five out of five; it wasn't reasonable, but there they were, or anyhow I was seeing them.

The fat people knew about Scott, I thought. They'd known all along. That was what they'd been trying to say to me when they smiled and held up cones or candy bars: 'Come on, honey, why should you deny yourself? You can bet your life Scott isn't.'

A huge guy with a grizzly-bear beard left the counter, giving me a big smile, and I placed my order. A pound of assorted butter cookies, a loaf of cinnamon bread, and a date-walnut coffee ring with white sugar icing. As soon as I got into the car I tore open the box and broke off a piece of the coffee ring, and it was fantastic: the sweet flaky yellow pastry and the sugar-glazed walnuts; a lot better than sex with Scott, I told myself.

For the next four days I pigged out. I finished the cookies and coffee ring that same evening, and on Friday afternoon I sneaked over to the grocery without telling Dale and bought everything I'd dreamt about for weeks: bacon and sausages and sliced Virginia ham, butter and sour cream and baking potatoes, pretzels and barbecue potato chips and frozen french fries. And that was just the beginning.

When I went in to work Monday morning with a box of assorted jam doughnuts I let Dale know I was off my diet for good. Dale tried to shove me back on. It didn't really matter about the weekend binge, she yipped. If I skipped lunch all week and cut way down on dinner and jogged two miles a day I'd be back on track.

'I don't want to be on track,' I told her. 'Eight weeks Scott has been gone, and all I've had from him is one disgusting postcard.'

Dale looked pained and started talking about self-respect and self-image, but I wasn't having any. 'Leave me alone, please,' I said. 'I know what I'm doing.'

Two days and a lot of pork chops and baked potatoes and chicken salad and chocolate almond bark and cherry pie later, I walked into my building, steadied a bag of high-calorie groceries against my hip, and opened the mailbox.

Jesus, I practically dropped the bag. The galvanised-metal slot was crammed with fat white and flimsy blue airmail letters from India. Most of them looked as if they'd been opened and read and crumpled up and walked on, and they were covered with stamps and cancellations.

An hour later, sitting on my sofa surrounded by two months' worth of Scott's letters, I faced facts. He was dieting: his second letter said so, mentioning that he didn't want to look overfed when he walked through a village full of hungry people. All right. I had three weeks, which meant – I went into the bathroom and dragged out the scale from the bottom of the cupboard where I'd shoved it on Friday – which meant, oh God, I'd have to lose over two pounds a week just to get back to where I was when Scott left.

It was an awful three weeks. I had cereal and skimmed milk and fruit for breakfast and lunch, to get through work, but otherwise I didn't eat anything much. Pretty soon I was blurred and headachy most of the time, in spite of all the vitamins and minerals I was scarfing down, and too tired to exercise. And I was still behind schedule on losing weight.

What made it worse was the fat people. I was seeing them again everywhere, only now they didn't look happy or friendly. 'You're making a big mistake, Ellie,' they seemed to be telling me at first. Then they began to get angry and disgusted. 'Sure, he wrote you, stupid,' their expressions said. 'That doesn't prove he's not helping himself to some Indian dish right this minute.'

I quit going out after work; I didn't have the energy. Mostly I just stayed home drinking diet soda and re-reading Scott's letters, kind of to prove to myself that he existed, I guess, because there hadn't been any more. Then I'd watch a little television and go to bed early, hoping to forget about food for a while. But for the first time in my life I was having insomnia, jolting awake in the small hours and lying there starving.

The day Scott was due back, I woke up about four a.m. and couldn't doze off again, even with Valium. For what seemed like hours I thrashed around in bed. Finally I got up and opened a can of diet soda and switched on the TV. Only now, on all the channels that were still broadcasting, everybody was overweight: the third-string newscasters, the punk MTV singers, the comics in an old black-and-white film. On the weather channel I could tell that the girl was hiding thighs like hams under the pleated skirt she kept swishing around as she pointed out the tornado areas. Then the picture changed and a soft plump guy smiled from between chipmunk cheeks and told me that airports were fogged in all over Europe and Scott would never get home.

I turned off the television, dragged on some jeans and a T-shirt, and went out. It was a warm June night full of noises: other tenants' air-conditioners and fans, traffic out on the highway; and planes overhead. There was a hard wind blowing, which made me feel kind of dizzy and slapped about, and it was that uneasy time just before dawn when you start to see shapes but can't make out colours. The sky was a pale sick lemon, but everything else was lumps of blurred grey.

Pine Grove Apartments is surrounded on three sides by an access road, and I'd just turned the corner and was starting towards the dead end. That was when I saw them, way down by the trees. There was a huge sexless person with long stringy hair waving its arms and walking slowly towards me out of the woods, and behind it came more angry fat grey people, and then more and more.

I wanted to run, but I knew somehow that if I turned round the fat people would rush after me the way kids do when you play Giant Steps, and they would catch me and, God, I didn't know what. So I just backed up slowly step by step towards the corner of the building, breathing in shallow gasps.

They kept coming out of the woods in the half-light, more and more, maybe ten or twenty or fifty, I didn't know. I thought I recognised the women from the bakery, and the big guy with the beard – and then I realised I could hear them too, kind of mumbling and wailing. I couldn't take it any more, I turned and raced for home, stumbling over the potholes in the drive.

Well, somehow I made it to the apartment, and slammed the door and double-locked it and put on the chain, and leaned up against the wall panting and gulping. For what seemed like hours I stood there, listening to the sounds of the fat people coming after me, crowding up the stairs, all grey and blubbery, and roaring and sobbing and sliding and thumping against the walls and door.

Then the noises started to change. Gradually they turned into the wind in the concrete stairwell and the air-conditioner downstairs and the six-thirty plane to New York flying over the complex and a dog barking somewhere. It was light out now, nearly seven o'clock. I unbolted my door, keeping the chain on, and eased it open a slow inch. The hall was empty.

I still felt completely exhausted and crazy, but I got myself dressed somehow and choked down some coffee and left for work. On the way I took a detour in the Honda round the corner of the building. At first I was afraid to look, even though I was safe inside the locked car. At the edge of the woods where the mob of fat people had been there was nothing but some big old spirea bushes blowing and tossing about.

That evening Scott came home, ten pounds overweight. A couple of days later, when he was talking about his trip, he said that Indian food was great, especially the sweets, but the women were hard to talk to and not all that good-looking.

'A lot of Indians are heavy too, you know,' he told me.

'Really?' I asked. I wondered if Scott had had some spooky experience like mine, which I still hadn't mentioned: I didn't want him to think I was going to crack up whenever he left town.

'It's a sign of prosperity, actually. You notice them especially in the cities, much more than in this country. I mean, you don't see many fat people around here for instance, do you?'

'No,' I agreed, cutting us both another slice of pineapple upside-down cake. 'Not lately, anyhow.'

G-STRING

Nicola Barker

Nicola Barker (b. 1966) is a British novelist and short story writer. Her novel, *Wide Open*, won the IMPAC Dublin Literary Award in 2000, and another, *Darkmans,* was shortlisted for the Man Booker Prize in 2007.

Ever fallen out with somebody simply because they agreed with you? Well, this is exactly what happened to Gillian and her pudgy but reliable long-term date, Mr Kip.

They lived separately in Canvey Island. Mr Kip ran a small but flourishing insurance business there. Gillian worked for a car-hire firm in Grays Thurrock. She commuted daily.

Mr Kip – he liked to be called that, an affectation, if you will – was an ardent admirer of the great actress Katharine Hepburn. She was skinny and she was elegant and she was sparky and she was intelligent. Everything a girl should be. She was *old* now, too, Gillian couldn't help thinking, but naturally she didn't want to appear a spoilsport so she kept her lips sealed.

Gillian was thirty-four, a nervous size sixteen, had no cheekbones to speak of and hair which she tried to perm. God knows she tried. She was the goddess of frizz. She frizzed but she did not fizz. She was not fizzy like Katharine. At least, that's what Mr Kip told her.

Bloody typical, isn't it? When a man chooses to date a woman, long term, who resembles his purported heroine in no way whatsoever? Is it safe? Is it cruel? Is it downright simple-minded?

Gillian did her weekly shopping in Southend. They had everything you needed there. Of course there was the odd exception: fishing tackle, seaside mementos, insurance, underwear. These items she never failed to purchase in Canvey Island itself, just to support local industry.

A big night out was on the cards. Mr Kip kept telling her how big it would be. A local Rotary Club do, and Gillian was to be Mr Kip's special partner, he was to escort her, in style. He was even taking the cloth off his beloved old Aston Martin for the night to drive them there and back. And he'd never deigned to do that before. Previously he'd only ever taken her places in his H-reg Citroën BX.

Mr Kip told Gillian that she was to buy a new frock for this special occasion. Something, he imagined, like that glorious dress Katharine Hepburn wore during the bar scene in her triumph, *Bringing Up Baby*.

Dutifully, Gillian bought an expensive dress in white chiffon which didn't at all suit her. Jeanie – twenty-one with doe eyes, sunbed-brown and weighing in at ninety pounds – told Gillian that the dress made her look like an egg-box.

All lumpy-humpy. It was her underwear, Jeanie informed her – If only! Gillian thought – apparently it was much too visible under the dress's thin fabric. Jeanie and Gillian were conferring in The Lace Bouquet, the lingerie shop on Canvey High Street where Jeanie worked.

'I tell you what,' Jeanie offered, 'all in one lace bodysuit, right? Stretchy stuff. No bra. No knickers. It'll hold you in an' everything.' Jeanie held up the prospective item. Bodysuits, Gillian just *knew*, would not be Mr Kip's idea of sophisticated. She shook her head. She looked down at her breasts. 'I think I'll need proper support,' she said, grimacing.

Jeanie screwed up her eyes and chewed at the tip of her thumb. 'Bra and pants, huh?'

'I think so.'

Although keen not to incur Jeanie's wrath, Gillian picked out the kind of bra she always wore, in bright, new white, and a pair of matching briefs.

Jeanie ignored the bra. It was functional. Fair enough. But the briefs she held aloft and proclaimed, 'Passion killers.'

'They're tangas,' Gillian said, defensively, proud of knowing the modern technical term for the cut-away pant. 'They're brief briefs.'

Jeanie snorted. 'No one wears these things any more, Gillian. There's enough material here to launch a sailboat.'

Jeanie picked up something that resembled an obscenely elongated garter and proffered it to Gillian. Gillian took hold of the scrap.

'What's this?'

'G-string.'

'My God, girls wear these in Dave Lee Roth videos.'

'Who's that?' Jeanie asked, sucking in her cheeks, insouciant.

'They aren't practical,' Gillian said.

Jeanie's eyes narrowed. 'These are truly modern knickers,' she said. 'These are what *everyone* wears now. And I'll tell you for why. No visible pantie line!'

Gillian didn't dare inform her that material was the whole point of a pantie. Wasn't it?

Oh hell, Gillian thought shifting on Mr Kip's Aston Martin's leather seats, 'maybe I should've worn it in for a few days first.' It felt like her G-string was making headway from between her buttocks up into her throat. She felt like a leg of lamb, trussed up with cheese wire. Now she knew how a horse felt when offered a new bit and bridle for the first time.

'Wearing hairspray?' Mr Kip asked, out of the blue.

'What?'

'If you are,' he said, ever careful, 'then don't lean your head back on to the seat. It's real leather and you may leave a stain.'

Gillian bit her lip and stopped wriggling.

'Hope it doesn't rain,' Mr Kip added, keeping his hand on the gearstick in a very male way, 'the wipers aren't quite one hundred per cent.'

Oh, the G-string was a modern thing, but it looked so horrid! Gillian wanted to be a modern girl but when she espied her rear-end engulfing the sliver of string like a piece of dental floss entering the gap between two great white molars, her heart sank down into her strappy sandals. It tormented her. Like the pain of an old bunion, it quite took off her social edge.

When Mr Kip didn't remark favourably on her new dress; when, in fact he drew a comparison between Gillian and the cone-shaped upstanding white napkins on the fancily made-up Rotary tables, she almost didn't try to smile. He drank claret. He smoked a cigar and tipped ash on her. He didn't introduce her to any of his Rotary friends. Normally, Gillian might have grimaced on through. But tonight she was a modern girl in torment and this kind of behaviour quite simply would not do.

Of course she didn't actually *say* anything. Mr Kip finally noticed Gillian's distress during liqueurs.

'What's got into you?'

'Headache,' Gillian grumbled, fighting to keep her hands on her lap.

Two hours later, Mr Kip deigned to drive them home. It was raining. Gillian fastened her seatbelt. Mr Kip switched on the windscreen wipers. They drove in silence. Then all of a sudden, *wheeeu-woing*! One of the wipers flew off the windscreen and into a ditch. Mr Kip stopped the car. He reversed. He clambered out to look for the wiper, but because he wore glasses, drops of rain impaired his vision.

It was a quiet road. What the hell. Mr Kip told Gillian to get out and look for it.

'In my white dress?' Gillian asked, quite taken aback.

Fifteen minutes later, damp, mussed, muddy, Gillian finally located the wiper. Mr Kip fixed it back on, but when he turned the relevant switch on the dash, neither of the wipers moved. He cursed like crazy.

'Well, that's that,' he said, and glared at Gillian like it was her fault completely. They sat and sat. It kept right on raining.

Finally Gillian couldn't stand it a minute longer. 'Give me your tie,' she ordered. Mr Kip grumbled but did as she'd asked. Gillian clambered out of the car and attached the tie to one of the wipers.

'OK,' she said, trailing the rest of the tie in through Mr Kip's window. 'Now we need something else. Are you wearing a belt?'

Mr Kip shook his head.

'Something long and thin,' Gillian said, 'like a rope.'

Mr Kip couldn't think of anything.

'Shut your eyes,' Gillian said. Mr Kip shut his eyes, but after a moment, naturally, he peeped.

And what a sight! Gillian laboriously freeing herself from some panties which looked as bare and sparse and confoundedly stringy as a pirate's eye patch.

'Good gracious!' Mr Kip exclaimed. 'You could at least have worn some French knickers or cami-knickers or something proper. Those are preposterous!'

Gillian turned on him. 'I've really had it with you, Colin,' she snarled, 'with your silly affected, old-fashioned car and clothes and *everything*.'

From her bag Gillian drew out her Swiss Army Knife and applied it with gusto to the plentiful elastic on her G-string. Then she tied one end to the second wiper and pulled the rest around and through her window. 'Right,' she said, 'start up the engine.'

Colin Kip did as he was told. Gillian manipulated the wipers manually; left, right, left, right. All superior and rhythmical and practical and dour-faced.

Mr Kip was very impressed. He couldn't help himself. After several minutes of driving in silence he took his hand off the gearstick and slid it on to Gillian's lap.

'Watch it,' Gillian said harshly. 'Don't you dare provoke me, Colin. I haven't put my Swiss Army Knife away yet.'

She felt the pressure of his hand leave her thigh. She was knickerless. She was victorious. She was a truly modern female.

WESLEY: BLISTERS

Nicola Barker

Nicola Barker (b. 1966) is a British novelist and short story writer. Her novel, *Wide Open*, won the IMPAC Dublin Literary Award in 2000, and another, *Darkmans,* was shortlisted for the Man Booker Prize in 2007.

L ook,' Trevor said, 'you've got to serve from the back, see?'
Wesley dropped the orange he'd just picked up.
'Put it where it was before,' Trevor said sniffily. 'Exactly.'
Wesley adjusted the placement of the orange. There. Just so. It was neat now. The display looked hunky-dory.

'Let me quickly say something,' Wesley said, as Trevor turned to go and unload some more boxes from the van.

'What?'

'It's just that if you serve people from the back of the stall they immediately start thinking that what you're giving them isn't as good as what's on display.'

Trevor said nothing.

'See what I mean?'

'So what?'

'Well, I'm just saying that if you want to build up customer confidence then it's a better idea to give them the fruit they can see.'

'It's more work that way,' Trevor said, shoving his hands into his pockets.

'Well, I don't care about that,' Wesley responded. 'I'm the one who'll end up having to do most of the serving while you're running the deliveries and I don't mind.'

Trevor gave Wesley a deep look and then shrugged and walked off to the van.

Another new job. Selling fruit off a stall on the Roman Road. Wesley was handsome and intelligent and twenty-three years old and he'd had a run of bad luck so now he was working the markets. No references needed. Actually, on the markets a bad temper was considered something of a bonus. Nobody messed you around. If they did, though, then you had to look out for yourself.

Trevor had red hair and a pierced nose. Wesley looked very strait-laced to him in his clean corduroy trousers and polo-neck jumper, and his hands were soft and he spoke too posh. What Trevor didn't realize however, was that Wesley had been spoilt rotten as a child so was used to getting his own way and could manipulate and wheedle like a champion if the urge took him. Wesley had yet to display to Trevor the full and somewhat questionable force of his personality.

Wesley pulled his weight. That, at least, was something, Trevor decided. After they'd packed up on their first night he invited Wesley to the pub for a drink as a sign of his good faith. Wesley said he wanted something to eat instead. So they went for pie and mash together.

Trevor had some eels and a mug of tea. Wesley ate a couple of meat pies. Wesley liked the old-fashioned tiles and the tables in the pie and mash shop. He remarked on this to Trevor. Trevor grunted.

'My dad was in the navy,' Wesley said, out of the blue.

'Yeah?'

'He taught me how to box.'

'Yeah?'

'Last job I had, I punched my boss in the face. He was up a ladder. I was on a roof. Broke his collar bone.'

'You're kidding!' Trevor was impressed.

'Nope.'

'Fuck.'

'Yeah.'

'What did he do?'

'Tried to prosecute.'

'What!?'

'I buggered off. I live my life,' Wesley said plainly, 'by certain rules. I'll do my whack, but when push comes to shove, I want to be treated decent and to keep my mind free. See?'

Trevor was mystified. He ate his eels, silently.

'I had a brother,' Wesley said, 'and I killed him when I was a kid. An accident and everything. But that's made me think about things in a different way.'

'Yeah?' Trevor was hostile now. 'How did you kill him?'

'Playing.'

'Playing what?'

'None of your fucking business.'

Trevor's eyebrows rose and he returned to his meal.

'I want to do the decent thing,' Wesley said. 'You know? And sometimes that'll get you into all kinds of grief.'

Trevor didn't say anything.

'Watch this.'

Trevor looked up. Wesley had hold of one of the meat pies. He opened his mouth as wide as he could and then pushed the pie in whole. Every last crumb. Trevor snorted. He couldn't help it. Once Wesley had swallowed the pie he asked Jean – the woman who served part-time behind the counter – for a straw. When she gave him one, he drank a whole mug of tea through it up his left nostril.

Trevor roared with laughter. He was definitely impressed.

After a week on the job Wesley started nagging Trevor about the quality of the fruit he was buying from the wholesalers. 'The way I see it, right,' Wesley said, 'if you sell people shit they won't come back. If you sell them quality, they will.'

'Bollocks,' Trevor said, 'this ain't Marks and fucking Spencer's.'

Wesley moaned and wheedled. He told Trevor he'd take a cut in his money if Trevor spent the difference on buying better quality stuff. Eventually Trevor gave in. And he took a cut in his wages too.

After a month, Wesley used his own money to repaint the stall a bright green and bought some lights to hang on it to make it, as he said, 'more of a proposition.'

'Thing is,' Wesley observed, fingering the little string of lights, 'we have to get one of the shops to let us tap into their electricity supply, otherwise we can't use them.'

Trevor didn't really care about the lights but he was grudgingly impressed by the pride Wesley seemed to take in things. He went to the newsagents and the bakery and then finally into the pie and mash shop. Fred, who ran the shop, agreed to let them use his power if they paid him a tenner a week. Wesley said this seemed a reasonable arrangement.

Things were going well. Wesley would spend hours juggling apples for old ladies and did a trick which involved sticking the sharpened end of five or six matches between the gaps in his teeth and then lighting the matches up all at once. He'd burned his lips twice that way and had a permanent blister under the tip of his nose. He'd pick at the blister for something to do until the clear plasma covered his fingers and then he'd say, 'Useful, this, if ever I got lost in a desert. Water on tap.'

After six weeks things had reached a point where Trevor would have done anything Wesley suggested. The stall was flourishing. Business was good. Wesley worked his whack and more so. He kept everyone amused with his tricks and his silly ideas. The customers loved him. He was always clean.

What it was that made Wesley so perfect in Trevor's eyes was the fact that he was a curious combination of immense irresponsibility – he was a mad bastard – and enormous conscientiousness. He wanted to *do* good but this didn't mean he had to *be* good.

One morning, two months after Wesley had started on the stall, Trevor got a flat tyre on his way back from the wholesalers and Wesley was obliged to set up on his own and do a couple of the early deliveries himself into the bargain.

He took Fred at the pie and mash shop his regular bundle of fresh parsley and then asked him for the extension cord so that he could put up his lights on the stall. Fred was busy serving. He indicated with his thumb towards the back of the shop. 'Help yourself, mate. The lead and everything's just behind the door. That's where Trevor stashes them each night.'

Fred liked Wesley and he trusted him. Same as Trevor did and all the others. Wesley, if he'd had any sense, should have realized that he was well set up here.

Wesley wandered out to the rear of the shop. He pulled back the door and picked up the extension lead. Then he paused. It was cold. He looked around him.

A big room. Red, polished, concrete floors. Large, silver fridges. And quiet. He could hear the noise from the shop and, further off, the noise from the market. But in here it was still and the stillness and the silence had a special *sound*. Like water.

Wesley closed his eyes. He shuddered. He opened his eyes again, tucked the lead under his arm and beat a hasty retreat.

He was in a world of his own when Trevor finally arrived that morning. On two occasions Trevor said, 'Penny for them,' and then snapped his fingers in front of Wesley's unfocused eyes when he didn't respond.

'I'm thinking of my dad,' Wesley said. 'Don't ask me why.'

'Why?' said Trevor, who was in a fine good-humour considering his tyre hold-up.

'I was just in the pie and mash shop getting the extension lead for the lights.

Out the back. And then I was suddenly thinking about my dad. You know, the navy and the sea and all the stuff we used to talk about when I was a kid.'

'Your dad still in the navy?' Trevor asked.

Wesley shook his head. 'Desk job,' he said.

'Probably those bloody eels,' Trevor said, bending down and picking up a crate of Coxes.

'What?'

'Those eels out the back. Making you think of the sea.'

'What?'

'In the fridges. He keeps the eels in there.'

'How's that?' Wesley's voice dipped by half an octave. Trevor didn't notice. He was wondering whether he could interest Wesley in selling flowers every Sunday as a side-interest. A stall was up for grabs on the Mile End Road close to the tube station. Sundays only.

'You're telling me he keeps live eels in those fridges?'

'What?'

'Live eels?' Wesley asked, with emphasis.

'In the fridges, yeah.' Trevor stopped what he was doing, straightened up, warned by the tone of Wesley's voice.

'What, like ...' Wesley said, breathing deeply, 'swimming around in a big tank?'

'Nope.' Trevor scratched his head. 'Uh ... like five or six long metal drawers, horizontal, yeah? And when you pull the drawers open they're all in there. Noses at one end and tails at the other. Big fuckers, though. I mean, five foot each or something.'

A woman came up to the stall and wanted to buy a lemon and two bananas. She asked Wesley for what she needed but Wesley paid her no heed.

'Hang on a second,' he said gruffly, holding up his flat hand, 'just shut up for a minute.'

He turned to Trevor. 'You know anything about eels?' he asked. Trevor knew enough about wild creatures to know that if Wesley had been a dog or a coyote his ears would be prickling, his ruff swelling.

'Not to speak of ...' he said.

'Excuse me,' Wesley said to the customer, 'I'll be back in a minute,' and off he went.

Wesley strolled into the pie and mash shop. Fred was serving. Wesley waited patiently in line until it was his turn to be served.

'What can I get you, Wesley?' Fred asked, all jovial.

Wesley smiled back at him. 'Having a few problems with the lights on the stall,' he said. 'Could I just pop out the back and see if the plug's come loose or something?'

'Surely,' Fred said, thumbing over his shoulder. 'You know the lie of the land out there.'

Wesley went into the back room and up to one of the fridges. He took hold of the top drawer and pulled it open. The drawer contained water, and, just as Trevor had described, was crammed full of large, grey eels, all wriggling, eyes open, noses touching steel, tails touching steel. Skin rubbing skin rubbing skin.

Held in limbo, Wesley thought, in this black, dark space. Wanting to move. Wanting to move. Wanting to move. Nowhere to go. Like prison. Like purgatory.

Wesley closed the drawer. He shuddered. He covered his face with his soft hands. He breathed deeply. He hadn't been all that honest. What he'd said about his dad and everything. True enough, his dad had been in the navy, he'd travelled on ships the world over, to India and Egypt and Hong Kong. Only he never came back from the sea. Never came back home. Sort of lost interest in them all. Only sent a card once, a while after ... a while after ... to say he wouldn't ever be back again.

Wesley knew all about the sea, though. Knew all about fishes and currents and stingrays and everything. His mum had bought him a book about it. For his birthday when he was six. And so he knew about eels and how they all travelled from that one special place in the Sargasso Sea. Near the West Indies. That's where they were spawned and that's where they returned to die.

But first, such a journey! Feeding on plankton, the tiny, little transparent eels, newborn, floated to the surface of that great sea from their deep, warm home in its depths, drifted on the Gulf Stream, travelled over the Atlantic, for three summers, then into European waters, in huge numbers, swam upriver, from salt to freshwater. What a journey. And man couldn't tame them or breed them in captivity or stop them. Couldn't do it.

How did they know? Huh? Where to go? How did they know? But they knew! They knew where to go. Moving on, living, knowing, remembering. Something *in* them. Something inside. Passed down through the generations. An instinct.

Wesley uncovered his face and looked around him. He wanted to find another exit. He walked to the rear of the fridges and discovered a door, bolted. He went over and unbolted it, turned the key that had been left in its lock, came back around the fridges and strolled out into the shop.

'Thanks, mate,' Wesley said as he pushed his way past Fred and sauntered back outside again.

Trevor shook his head. 'No way,' he said. And he meant it.

'You've got to fucking do this for me, Trev,' Wesley said.

'Why?'

'You know how old some of those eels are?'

'No.'

'Some could be twenty years old. They've lived almost as long as you have.'

'They get them from a farm,' Trevor said. 'They aren't as old as all that.'

'They can't breed them in captivity,' Wesley said. 'They come from the Sargasso Sea. That's where they go to breed and to die.'

'The what?'

'Near the West Indies. That's where they go. That's what eels do. They travel thousands of miles to get here and then they grow and then they travel thousands of miles to get back again.'

'Sounds a bit bloody stupid,' Trevor said, 'if you ask me.'

'I'm a travelling man,' Wesley said, 'like my dad was. Don't try and keep me in one place. Don't try and lock me away.'

'They're eels, Wesley,' Trevor said, almost losing patience.

'Imagine how they're feeling,' Wesley said, 'caught in those fridges. Needing to travel. Needing it, needing it. Like an illness, almost. Like a fever. Dreaming of those hot waters, the deep ocean. Feeling cold steel on their noses, barely breathing, crammed together. Nowhere to go. No-fucking-where to go.'

'Forget it,' Trevor said, 'I've got no argument with Fred. Forget it, mate.'

'Take the van, Trevor,' Wesley said calmly. 'Drive it round the back, where they make the deliveries. I already unlocked the door.'

Off Wesley strode again. Trevor jangled the keys in his pocket, swore out loud and then ran after him.

Wesley crept in through the back entrance. He stood still a while. He could hear the chattering of customers in the shop and he could hear the sound of a van pulling into the delivery passage. He went outside, smiling wildly, happy to be fucking up, same as he always was.

'OK, Trev,' he said. 'Open the back doors but keep the tail up so's when I dump them in there they don't escape.'

Trevor looked immensely truculent but he did as Wesley asked.

Wesley went back inside, opened up one of the big, silver drawers, pushed his arms in, down and under all that silky, scaleless eel-flesh. He curled his arms right under, five eels, all wriggling, closed his arms around them and lifted. Water splashed and splattered. He looked over to the doorway leading into the shop, bit his lip, couldn't pause. The eels were whipping and lashing and swerving and writhing. He headed for the exit at top speed.

Trevor stood by the tailgate. When he saw the eels he swore. 'Fuck this man! Fuck this!'

Wesley threw the eels into the back of the van. 'Ten minutes,' he said, 'to get them back to water, otherwise they'll suffocate.'

Trevor watched the eels speeding and curling in the back of his van, swimming, almost, on air. He turned to say something but Wesley was gone. A minute later Wesley re-emerged. More eels. Like snakes. Faces like ... faces like cats or otters or something. Little gills. Seal eyes.

As Wesley turned to go back in Trevor caught him by his shirt sleeve. 'I'm not doing this,' he said. 'Things are going well for us here. He's kept eels in this place for years, gets a delivery every week.'

Wesley turned on him. 'Give me the keys.'

'What?'

'Give me the shitting keys and I'll drive them to the canal myself.'

'This is stupid!'

'Don't call me fucking stupid. No one calls me that. Give me the fucking keys.'

Trevor took the keys out of his pocket and dropped them on the floor. He walked off. His eyes were prickling. 'Fuck it!' he shouted, and his voice echoed down the passageway.

Back inside, Wesley pulled open the third drawer, shoved his arms in, took hold of the eels. Water was everywhere now. Thank God it was lunchtime and Fred was busy. He held the fish tight and straightened up. He headed for the back door.

Outside, he met Fred. He was holding the five eels. He looked at Fred.

'What the hell are you doing?' Fred said.

'Why aren't you in the shop?' Wesley asked, stupidly.

'Jean's in,' Fred said, eyeing the eels. 'She's covering.'

'Oh. I didn't know that.'

'What are you doing with my eels?' Fred put out his arms. 'Give them to me.'

'No,' Wesley said. 'You can't own a wild thing.'

As he spoke he took a step back. Fred moved forwards and put himself between Wesley and the tailgate. The eels were itching to get free. Wesley's arms were aching. Fred took a step closer. He was short and square and tough as a boxing hare.

Wesley opened his arms. The eels flew into the air, landed, skidded, flipped, whipped, scissored, dashed. At top speed, they sea-snaked down the passageway, into the market, on to the main road.

'Down the Roman Road,' Wesley yelled. 'Back to the water, back to the frigging sea!'

Fred punched Wesley in the mouth. Jesus, Wesley thought, feels like all my teeth have shifted. He staggered, righted himself, clenched his hands into fists, by way of a diversion, then kicked Fred in the bollocks. Fred buckled.

Wesley skipped past him and sprang into the van. Got the keys in the ignition, started the engine, roared off in a cloud of black exhaust fume.

Beale's Place, Wright's Road, St Stephen's Road. Bollocks to the One Way! Sharp right at the tip of the market. Back on to the Roman Road, screw the traffic, on to the pavement, over the zebra crossing, past the video shop, the church, the intersection, Mile End Park. Sharp left. Over the grass. Tyre tracks. Mud-cut. Foot flat. Brakes.

How long had he taken? He didn't know. He could see the canal, just below. Dirty, dark waters. Dank and littery.

Down with the tailgate! The eels were like flying fish. The air made them pump and shudder. Like spaghetti in a heated pan, boiling and bubbling.

'Get in there!' Wesley yelled at them. 'The Grand Union Canal, the Thames, the Channel, the Ant-bloody-arctic.'

A cluster of eels shuddered down into the grass, rippled on to the concrete path, and then One! Two! Three! Four! Five! Six! Seven! Eight! Into the canal.

One eel split from the others, turned right and darted towards some undergrowth. One stayed in the back of the van, smaller than the others and less agile. Wesley grabbed it by its tail. He swung it in his arms. He ran to the edge of the canal. He threw it. The eel made a whip-cracking motion in the air, shaped itself like a fancy ribbon, just untied from a box of something wrapped and precious. Then splosh! It was under.

Wesley stood by the canal for several minutes. He inspected his hands, he sniffed, he stopped shaking. He started walking. He walked. He walked. He passed by a fisherman. He stopped walking. He looked over his shoulder. 'Which way is it to the sea?' he asked casually. 'From here, I mean?'

The fisherman gave this question some consideration while sucking his tongue and rolling his rod between his two hands.

'I should think,' he said, eventually, 'I should think it's in the exact opposite direction from the one you're travelling.' Then he turned, stared down along the path Wesley had just trodden, and pointed.

EMERALD CITY

Jennifer Egan

Jennifer Egan (b. 1962) is an American writer. She has published short fiction in the *New Yorker* and *Harper's*, and her journalism appears frequently in the *New York Times Magazine*. Egan's novel *A Visit from the Goon Squad* won the 2011 Pulitzer Prize and the National Book Critics Circle Award.

Rory knew before he came to New York what sort of life he would have. He'd read about it in novels by hip young authors who lived there. He saw the apartment, small but high-ceilinged, a tall, sooty window with a fire escape twisting past a chemical-pink sky. Nights in frantic clubs, mornings hunched over coffee in the East Village, warming his hands on the cup, black pants, black turtleneck, pointed black boots. He'd intended to snort cocaine, but by the time he arrived, that was out. He drank instead.

He was a photographer's assistant, loading cameras all day, holding up light meters, waving Polaroids until they were dry enough to tear open. As he watched the models move, he sometimes worried he was still too California. What could you do with sandy blond hair -- cut it off? Short hair was on the wane, at least for men. So there it hung, golden, straight as paper, reminiscent of beaches he'd never seen, being as he was from Chicago (in Chicago there was the lake, but that didn't count). His other option was to gain or lose some weight, but the starved look had lost its appeal – any suggestion of illness was to be avoided. Beefy was the way to go; not fat, just a classic paunch above the belt. But no matter how much Rory ate, he stayed exactly the same. He took up smoking instead, although it burned his throat.

Rory stubbed out his cigarette and checked to make sure the lights were off in the darkroom. He was always the last to leave; his boss, Vesuvi, would hand him the camera as soon as the last shot was done and then swan out through the sea of film containers, plastic cups, and discarded sheets of backdrop paper. Vesuvi was one of those people who always had somewhere to go. He was blessed with a marvelous paunch, which Rory tried not to admire too openly. He didn't want Vesuvi to get the wrong idea.

Rory swept the debris into bags, then he turned out the lights, locked up the studio, and headed down to the street. Twilight was his favorite hour – metal gates sliding down over storefronts, newspapers whirling from the sidewalk into the sky, an air of promise and abandonment. This was the way he'd expected New York to look, and he was thrilled when the city complied.

He took the subway uptown to visit Stacey, a failing model whom he adored against all reason. Stacey – when girls with names like Zane and Anouschka and Brid regularly slipped him their phone numbers during shoots. Stacey refused to change her name. 'If I make it,' she said, 'they'll be happy to call me whatever.' She never acknowledged that she was failing, though it was obvious. Rory longed to bring it up, to talk it over with her, but he was afraid to.

Stacey lay on her bed, shoes still on. A Diet Coke was on the table beside her. She weighed herself each morning, and when she was under 120, she allowed herself a real Coke that day.

'What happened at *Bazaar*?' Rory asked, perching on the edge of the bed. Stacey sat up and smoothed her hair.

'The usual,' she said. 'I'm too commercial.' She shrugged, but Rory could see she was troubled.

'And that was nothing,' Stacey continued. 'On my next go-see the guy kept looking at me and flipping back and forth through my book, and of course I'm thinking, Fantastic, he's going to hire me. So you know what he finally says? I'm not ugly enough. He says, "Beauty today is ugly beauty. Look at those girls, they're monsters – gorgeous, mythical monsters. If a girl isn't ugly, I won't use her." '

She turned to Rory. He saw tears in her eyes and felt helpless. 'What a bastard,' he said.

To his surprise, she began to laugh. She lay back on the bed and let the laughter shake her. 'I mean, here I am,' she said, 'killing myself to stay thin, hot-oiling my hair, getting my nails done, and what does he tell me? I'm not ugly enough!'

'It's crazy,' Rory said, watching Stacey uneasily. 'He's out of his mind.'

She sat up and rubbed her eyes. She looked slaphappy, the way she looked sometimes after a second gin and tonic. Eight months before, after a year's meticulous planning, she had bought her own ticket to New York from Cincinnati. And this was just the beginning; Stacey hoped to ride the wave of her success around the world: Paris, Tokyo, London, Bangkok. The shelves of her tiny apartment were cluttered with maps and travel books, and whenever she met a foreigner – it made no difference from where – she would carefully copy his address into a small leatherbound book, convinced it would not be long before she was everywhere. She was the sort of girl for whom nothing happened by accident, and it pained Rory to watch her struggle when all day in Vesuvi's studio he saw girls whose lives were accident upon accident, from their discovery in whatever shopping mall or hot dog stand to the startling, gaudy error of their faces.

'Rory,' Stacey said. 'Look at me a minute.'

He turned obediently. She was so close he could smell the warm, milky lotion she used on her face. 'Do you ever wish I was uglier?' she asked.

'God no,' Rory said, pulling away to see if she was joking. 'What a question, Stace.'

'Come on. You do this all day long.' She moved close to him again, and Rory found himself looking at the tiny pores on either side of her nose. He tried to think of the studio and the girls there, but when he concentrated on Stacey, they disappeared; and when he thought of the studio, he couldn't see Stacey anymore. It was a world she didn't belong to. As he watched Stacey's tense, expectant face, Rory felt a dreadful power; it would take so little, he thought, to crush her.

'Never mind,' she said when Rory didn't answer. 'I don't want to know.'

She stood and crossed the room, then leaned over and pressed her palms to the floor. She had been a gymnast in high school and was still remarkably limber. This limberness delighted Rory in a way that almost shamed him – in bed she would sit up, legs straight in front of her, then lean over and rest her cheek against her shins. Casually, as if it were nothing! Rory didn't dare tell her how this excited him; if she were aware of it, then it wouldn't be the same.

Stacey stood up, flushed and peaceful again. 'Let's get out of here,' she said.

Her apartment was right off Columbus, a street Rory scorned but one that nevertheless mesmerized him. He and Stacey walked arm in arm, peering into the windows of restaurants as eagerly as diners peered out of them. It was as if they had all been told some friend might pass this way tonight and were keeping their eyes peeled.

'Where should we go?' Stacey asked.

Rory cracked his knuckles one by one. The question made him edgy, as if there were some right answer he should know. Where were the people who mattered? Occasionally Rory would be stricken with a sense that they had been exactly where he was only moments before, but had just left. The worst part was, he didn't know who they were, exactly. The closest he came was in knowing people who seemed to know; his roommate, Charles, a food stylist who specialized in dollops, and of course Vesuvi. Vesuvi was his main source.

They headed downtown, enjoying the last warm days of fall, the pleasant seediness of Seventh Avenue. They passed intersections where patches of old cobblestones were exposed beneath layers of tar, relics of another New York Rory dimly remembered from novels: carriages and top hats, reputations and insults.

'Rory,' Stacey said, 'do you feel more something, now that you've gotten successful?'

Rory turned to her in surprise. 'Who says I'm successful?'

'But you are!'

'I'm no one. I'm Vesuvi's assistant.'

Stacey seemed shocked. 'That's not no one,' she said.

Rory grinned. It was a funny conversation. 'Yeah?' he said. 'Then who is it?'

Stacey pondered this a moment. Suddenly she laughed – the same helpless way she had laughed on the bed, as if the world were funny by accident. Still laughing, she said, 'Vesuvi's assistant.'

At Stacey's suggestion they took a cab to a TriBeCa bistro where Vesuvi often went. It was probably expensive, but Rory had just been paid – what the hell, he'd buy Stacey dinner. Maybe he would even call Charles to see if he was back from LA, where he'd been styling all week for Sara Lee. Rory didn't envy Charles his job, although he made good money; sometimes he was up half the night, using tweezers to paste sesame seeds onto hamburger buns or mixing and coloring the salty dough that looked more like ice cream in pictures than real ice cream did. Rory had been amazed to learn that in breakfast cereal shots it was standard to use Elmer's glue instead of milk. 'It's whiter,' Charles had explained. 'Also it pours more slowly and doesn't soak the flakes.' Rory had found this disturbing in a way he still didn't quite understand.

Inside the restaurant, Rory spotted Vesuvi himself at a large round table in back. Or rather, Vesuvi spotted him, and called out with a heartiness that could only mean he was bored with his present company. With a grand sweep of his arm he beckoned them over.

The waiters pulled up chairs, and Rory and Stacey sat down. Stacey ordered a gin and tonic. Rory could see she was nervous – the girls at the table were faces you saw around a lot: redheaded Daphne, Inge with her guppy-face, others whose names he'd forgotten. What distressed him was seeing Anouschka, a moody girl whose journey from some dour Siberian town to the height of New York fashion seemed to have happened in an afternoon. Once, she had lingered at the studio while Rory cleaned up after work, humming a Fine Young Cannibals song and flipping aimlessly through his copy of *The Great Gatsby*. 'My father is a professor,' she told him. 'He teaches this book.' 'In Russian?' Rory asked incredulously. Anouschka laughed. 'Sure,' she said, curling the word in her accent. 'Why not?'

Outside the studio, Rory and Anouschka had hovered uncertainly in the dusk. Rory was supposed to meet Stacey, but felt awkward saying so to Anouschka. Instead, he blundered forward and hailed a cab, leaving Anouschka standing on the curb, then paid the driver three blocks later and took the subway to Stacey's. He arrived shaking, mystified by his own idiotic behavior.

Anouschka had frightened him ever since; last week, while he was loading Vesuvi's camera, she had casually reported the numerical value of her IQ, then subjected him to a humiliating quiz on the Great Books. 'Have you read much Dostoeysky?' she called up the rickety ladder, where Rory was grappling with a light. '*The Brothers Karamazov*? No? What about *War and Peace*?' When Rory called back down that *War and Peace* was by Tolstoy, Anouschka colored deeply, stalked back onto the set, and did not speak to him again, Rory felt terrible; he'd never read a word of *War and Peace*. He even considered confessing this to Anouschka after the shoot as she grumpily gathered her things. But what the hell, he decided, let her think he was brilliant.

Now Rory looked at Vesuvi sprawled amid the models: sphinxlike, olive-skinned, his close-cropped beard peppered with gray, though his wild curly hair showed no sign of it. He was short, and wore high-heeled boots that Rory found spectacular. Vesuvi was a man of few words, yet he often gave the impression of being on the verge of speech. Conversation would proceed around him tentatively, ready to be swept aside at any moment by whatever Vesuvi might say. Rory watched him adoringly over his glass of bourbon, unable to believe he was sitting with Vesuvi after all the times he had watched him glide away in cabs, feeling as if most of what mattered in the world were disappearing with him. Yet Rory wasn't entirely happy: everyone at the table was watching him, especially Anouschka, and he felt that in return for being included, he was expected to do something stunning.

He glanced at the next table, where conversation seemed more lively. It was a group of downtown types, the men like deposed medieval kings in their bobbed haircuts and gigantic silver medallions. During his first month in New York, Rory had gone out with a girl like the ones at that table – Dave, she'd called herself. She wore nothing but black: bulky sweaters, short loose skirts, woolen tights, and round-toed combat boots. The thrill of the relationship for Rory lay mostly in watching Dave undress – there was something tremendous in the sight of her slender white form emerging from all of that darkness. Once she finished undressing, Rory often wished she would put part of the outfit back on, or better yet, dress completely again and start over.

Vesuvi was eyeing Stacey. 'You look familiar,' he said. 'Did I use you for something?'

'Once,' she said. 'Four and a half months ago.'

'Right, I remember now. It was that … ' He waved a languid hand, which meant he had no idea.

'For *Elle*,' Stacey said. 'Bow ties.' It had been her best job, and she was crushed when the pictures the magazine printed had failed to include her head. To use them in her book would look desperate, her agent said, so she kept them pasted to her bathroom mirror. Rory looked at them while he was shaving.

Vesuvi sat back, satisfied. The question of whether or not he had worked with a girl always troubled him, Rory had noticed, as if the world were divided between girls he had shot and girls he hadn't, and not knowing which side a girl was on caused a cosmic instability.

'You worked for *Elle*?' Anouschka asked Stacey.

'Once,' Stacey said.

'So far,' Rory quickly added.

Anouschka glanced at him, and then at Stacey, with the same startled look she'd worn when Rory left her on the curb. He felt guilty all over again.

'You must've worked for them, too,' Stacey said to Anouschka, who nodded absently.

'I heard you got a cover,' someone said.

'Yes,' Anouschka said dully. Then she seemed to take heart, as if hearing this news for the first time. 'Yes!' she said, grinning suddenly. 'I am the cover for December.'

Rory felt Stacey move in her chair. Anouschka lit a cigarette and smoked; exotic, dragonlike, her black hair tumbling past her shoulders. For a moment all of them watched her, and against his will even Rory was moved by a face so familiar from pictures. Never mind what you thought of Anouschka; she was *that woman* – you recognized her. There was an odd pleasure in this, like finding something you'd been looking for.

'When do you leave for Tokyo?' Anouschka asked Inge.

'Next week,' Inge said. 'Have you been?'

'Two years ago,' Anouschka said in her heavy accent. 'It's okay, but when you take the morning airplanes, you see the Japanese men are coughing their lungs into the trash cans. They smoke like crazy,' she concluded, wagging her cigarette between two fingers. Rory listened miserably; poor Stacey was barely surviving in New York and here was Anouschka, who not only had been to Japan but had the luxury of complaining about it. He rattled the ice in his glass and impatiently cleared his throat.

Anouschka glanced at him and turned serious. 'Still,' she said, 'the culture of Japan is quite important.'

'The culture?' Inge said.

'You know, the museums and this sort of thing.'

Vesuvi, who had seemed on the verge of sleep, roused himself and turned to Anouschka. 'You, inside a museum?' he said. 'That I don't see.'

The girl looked startled.

'You must have gone there on location,' he said.

'Not location! I went for fun. How do you know what I do?'

Vesuvi shrugged and sat back in his chair, his lazy eyes filled with amusement. Anouschka blushed to the neck; the pink tinge seemed at odds with her extravagant face. Helplessly she turned to Stacey. 'You have been to Japan?' she asked.

'I wish.'

'But Milano, yes?'

'No,' Stacey said, and Rory noticed with surprise that her drink was almost gone. Normally one cocktail would last Stacey an entire night, her sips were so tiny.

'Paris?'

Stacey shook her head, and Rory noticed a change in Anouschka's face as she sensed her advantage. The others were quiet. Vesuvi sat forward, looking from Anouschka to Stacey with great interest, as if they were posing for him.

'You never worked in Paris? I think everyone has worked in Paris.'

'I've never been to Paris,' Stacey said.

'London? Munich?' Anouschka turned to the other girls, confirming her surprise. Though she didn't glance at Rory, he sensed that all this was meant for him, and felt a strange, guilty collusion with her. He saw Stacey's hand shake as she lifted her glass, and was overcome with sudden and absolute hatred for Anouschka – he had never hated anyone this way. He stared at her, the gush of hair, the braised-looking mouth; she was ugly, as the man had said today. Ugly and beautiful. Confused, Rory looked away.

'So,' Anouschka said, 'what places you have been?'

Stacey didn't answer at first. She looked double-jointed in her chair, heaped like a marionette.

'I've been to New York,' she said.

There was a beat of silence. 'New York,' Anouschka said.

Vesuvi started to laugh. He had a loud, explosive laugh that startled Rory at first. He had never heard it before. 'New York!' Vesuvi cried. 'That's priceless.'

Stacey smiled. She seemed as surprised as everyone else.

Vesuvi rocked forward in his chair, so that his heavy boots pounded the floor. 'I love it,' he said. 'New York. What a perfect comeback.' Anouschka just stared at him.

It began to seem very funny, all of a sudden.

A chuckle passed through the group like a current. Rory found himself laughing without knowing why; it was enough for him that Vesuvi had a reason. His boss gazed at Stacey in the soft-eyed way he looked at models when a shoot was going well. 'It's a hell of a place, New York,' he said. 'No?'

'The best,' Stacey said.

'But she has gone only here!' Anouschka protested. 'How does she know?'

'Oh, she knows,' Rory said. He felt reckless, dizzy with the urge to make Anouschka angry. 'You don't get it, do you?' he said.

'What can I get when there is nothing?' she retorted. But she looked uncertain.

Vesuvi dabbed with a napkin at his heavy-lidded eyes. 'Next time you go to New York,' he told Stacey, 'take me with you.'

This was too much for Anouschka. 'Fuck you!' she cried, jumping to her feet. 'I am in New York. You are in New York. *Here is New York*!'

But laughter had seized the table, and Anouschka's protests only made it worse. She stood helplessly while everyone laughed, Rory hooting all the louder to keep her in her place.

'That's it,' she said. 'Goodbye.'

'Go back to Japan,' Rory cried. He had trouble catching his breath.

Anouschka fixed her eyes on him. Her makeup made them look burned at the rims, and the irises were a bright, clear green. He thought she might do something crazy – he'd heard she once punctured an ex-boyfriend's upper lip by hurling a fork at him. He stopped laughing and gripped the table's edge, poised for sudden movement. To his astonishment, the charred-looking eyes filled with tears. 'I hate you, Rory,' she said.

She yanked her bag from under the table and hoisted it onto her shoulder. Her long hair stuck to her wet cheeks as she struggled to free her jacket from the chair. Rory thought of his high school lunchroom: girls stalking out, mad, clattering trays, their long, skinny legs skittering on high-heeled shoes. He felt a pang of nostalgia. She was just a kid, Anouschka – so much younger than he was.

'Hey,' Vesuvi said, standing and putting his arms around Anouschka. 'Hey, we're just having a joke.'

'Go to hell with your joke.' She turned her face away so that no one could see her crying.

Vesuvi stroked her back. 'Hey now,' he said.

Chastened, the group sat in guilty silence. Stacey and Rory traded a look and stood up. No one protested as they slid their jackets on, but when Rory opened his wallet to pay for their drinks, Vesuvi winced and waved it away. Anouschka still clung to him, her face buried in his neck.

Vesuvi spoke to Stacey in a lowered voice. 'I've got something coming up you'd be perfect for,' he said. 'Who are you with again?'

Stacey told him the name of her agency, barely able to contain her joy. Rory listened unhappily; Vesuvi said this all the time to girls, and forgot the next minute. It was just a pleasant salutation.

They left the restaurant and headed toward the East Village. Rory longed to reach for Stacey's hand, but she seemed far away from him now, lost in her thoughts. Outside a market, a boy was perched on a stool cutting the heads off beans. A barber swept thick tufts of dark hair into one corner of his shop. From an overhead window came music, and Rory craned his neck to catch a glimpse of someone's arm, a lighted cigarette. The famliarity of it all was sweet and painful to him. He searched the dark shopfronts for something, some final thing at the core of everything else, but he found just his own reflection and Stacey's. Their eyes met in the glass, then flicked away. And it struck him that this was New York: a place that glittered from a distance even when you reached it.

They climbed the four flights of steps to Rory's apartment. A slit of light shone under the door, which meant Charles was back. They found him standing at the kitchen table, wiping a slab of red meat with a paper towel. He had a blowtorch plugged into the wall, and a dismantled smoke alarm lay at his feet.

'You poor thing,' Stacey said, kissing him on the cheek. 'You never stop working.'

Charles's mouth was like a cat's, small and upturned at the corners. It made him seem happy even when he wasn't. 'Meat is my weak point,' he said. 'I've got a job tomorrow doing steak.'

He was prematurely balding, and Rory admired the look of hardship and triumph this gave him. Lately he'd searched his own hairline for signs of recession, but the blond surfer's mane seemed even more prolific Most cruel of all, it was Charles who'd been born and raised in Santa Cruz.

'Here goes,' Charles said, firing up the blowtorch. They watched as he moved the flame slowly over the meat, back and forth as if he were mowing a lawn. Its surface turned a pale gray. When the entire side was done, he flipped the steak over and lightly cooked its other side.

'Ugh,' said Stacey. 'It's still completely raw.'

'Wait,' Charles said.

He held a long metal spit to the flame until it glowed red. Then he pressed the spit to the meat. There was a hiss, a smell of cooking, and when he lifted the spit, a long black stripe branded the steak. He heated the spit several more times and pressed it to the meat at parallel intervals. Soon it was indistinguishable from a medium-rare steak straight off the grill. Rory felt an irrational surge of appetite, a longing to eat the meat in spite of knowing it was raw and cold.

Stacey opened the refrigerator. Rory always kept a supply of Cokes for her in there; Diet, of course, but also some regulars in case she had earned one that day and not yet rewarded herself. To his surprise, she pulled out a can of regular now.

'What the hell,' she said. 'I mean, really, what difference does it make?'

Rory stared at her. She had never said anything like this before. 'What about Vesuvi?' he asked, regretting it even as he spoke.

'Vesuvi won't hire me. You know it perfectly well.'

She was smiling at him, and Rory felt as if she had peered into the lying depths of his soul. 'Vesuvi doesn't know shit,' he said, but it sounded lame even to himself.

Stacey slid open the window and climbed out onto the fire escape. The sky was a strange, sulfurous yellow – beautiful, yet seemingly disconnected from nature. The shabby tree behind Rory's building was empty of leaves, and made a pattern of cracked glass against the sky. Stacey drank her Coke in tiny, careful sips. Rory stood helplessly inside the window, watching her. He needed to say something to her, he knew that, but he wasn't sure how.

He shook a cigarette from his pack and placed it in his mouth. Charles was working on a second steak. 'By the way,' Charles said, pointing with his chin at a spot near Rory's head, 'I baked us a cake – a real one.'

Rory turned in surprise and lifted a plate from above the refrigerator. It was a tall, elegant cake with giant dollops of whipped cream along its edges. 'Charles,' Rory said, confused, 'haven't you been doing this all week?'

'Yeah,' Charles said, 'but always for strangers. And never to eat.'

He bent over the steak, his blowtorch hissing on the damp meat. He looked embarrassed, as if his preference for real cake were a weakness he rarely confided. Charles's honesty shamed Rory – he said what he felt, not caring how it sounded.

Rory climbed out the window and sat beside Stacey. The bars of the fire escape felt cold through his jeans. Stacey held her Coke in one hand and took Rory's hand in the other. They looked at the yellow sky and held hands tightly, as if something were about to happen.

Rory's heart beat quickly. 'So maybe it doesn't work,' he said. 'The modeling. Maybe that just won't happen.'

He searched her face for some sign of surprise, but there was none. She watched him calmly, and for the first time Rory felt that Stacey was older than he, that her mind contained things he knew nothing of. She stood up and handed her Coke to Rory. Then she grasped the railing of the fire escape and lifted her body into a handstand. Rory held his breath, watching in alarmed amazement as the slender wand of her body swayed against the yellow sky. She had no trouble balancing, and hovered there for what seemed a long time before finally bending at the waist, lowering her feet, and standing straight again.

'If it doesn't work,' she said, 'then I'll see the world some other way.'

She took Rory's face in her hands and kissed him on the mouth – hard, with the fierce, tender urgency of someone about to board a train. Then she turned and looked at the sky. Rory stared at her, oddly frightened to think that she would do it, she would find some way. He pictured Stacey in a distant place, looking back on him, on this world of theirs as if it were a bright, glittering dream she had once believed in.

'Take me with you,' he said.

THE SNOBS

Muriel Spark

Muriel Spark (1918–2006) was a Scottish novelist best known for her novel, *The Prime of Miss Jean Brodie*. In 2008 *The Times* named her in its list of the '50 Greatest British Writers Since 1945'. Spark was twice shortlisted for the Man Booker Prize and was awarded the Golden PEN Award in 1998 by English PEN for her services to literature. She became Dame Commander of the Order of the British Empire in 1993.

Snob: A person who sets too much value on social standing, wishing to be associated with the upper class and their mores, and treating those viewed as inferior with condescension and contempt – *Chambers Dictionary*.

I feel bound to quote the above definition, it so well fits the Ringer-Smith couple whom I knew in the nineteen-fifties and of whom I have since met variations and versions enough to fill me with wonder. Snobs are really amazing. They mainly err in failing to fool the very set of people they are hoping to be accepted by, and above all, to seem to belong to, to be taken for. They may live in a democratic society – it does nothing to help. Nothing.

Of the Ringer-Smith couple, he, Jake, was the more snobbish. She, at least, had a certain natural serenity of behaviour which she herself never questioned. She was in fact rather smug. Her background was of small land-owning farmers and minor civil servants. She, Marion, was stingy, stingy as hell. Jake also had a civil service background and, on the mother's side, a family of fruit export-import affairs which had not left her very well off, the inheritance having been absorbed by the male members of the family. Jake and Marion were a fairly suitable match. He was slightly the shorter of the two. Both were skinny. They had no children. Skeletons in the family cupboard do nothing to daunt the true snob, in fact they provoke a certain arrogance, and this was the case with Jake. A family scandal on a national scale had grown to an international one. A spectacular bank robbery with murder on the part of a brother had resulted in the family name being reduced to a byword in every household. The delinquent Ringer-Smith and his associates had escaped to a safe exile in South America leaving Jake and his ageing mother to face the music of the press and TV reporters. Nobody would have taken it out on them in the normal way if it had not been for the contempt with which they treated police, journalists, interrogators, functionaries of the law and the public in general. They put on airs suggesting that they were untouchably 'good family', and they generally carried on as if they were earls and marquises instead of ordinary middle-class people. No earl, no marquis at present alive would in fact be so haughty unless he were completely out of his mind or perhaps an unfortunate drug addict or losing gambler.

I was staying with some friends at a château near Dijon when the Ringer-Smiths turned up. This was in the nineties. I hardly recognized them. The Ringer-Smiths had not just turned up at the château, they were found by Anne, bewildered, outside the village shop, puzzling over a map, uncertain of their way to anywhere. Warming towards their plight as she always would towards those in trouble, Anne invited these lost English people for a cup of tea at the château where they could work out their route.

Anne and Monty, English themselves, had lived in the château for the last eight years. It was a totally unexpected inheritance from the last member of a distant branch of Monty's family. The house and small fortune that went with it came to him in his early fifties as an enormous surprise. He had been a shoe salesman and a bus driver, among other things. Anne had been a stockbroker's secretary. Their two children, both girls, were married and away. The 'fairy tale' story of their inheritance was in the newspapers for a day, but it wasn't everybody who read the passing news.

Monty was out when Anne brought home the Ringer-Smiths. I was watching the television – some programme which now escapes me for ever due to the shock of seeing those people. Anne, tall, merry, blonded-up and carrying her sixties well, took herself off to the kitchen to put on the kettle. She had made the sitting-room as much like England as possible.

'Who does this place belong to?' Jake inquired of me as soon as Anne was out of the room. Obviously, he had not recognized me in the present context, although I felt Marion's eyes upon me in a penetrating stare of puzzlement, of quasi-remembrance.

'It belongs,' I said, 'to the lady who invited you to tea.'

'Oh!' he said.

'Haven't we met?' Marion was speaking to me.

'Yes, you have.' I made myself known.

'What brings you here?' said Jake outright.

'The same as brings you here. I was invited.'

Anne returned with the tea, served with a silver tea service and pretty china cups. She carried the tray while a young girl who was helping in the house followed with hot water and a plate of biscuits.

'You speak English very well,' Jake said.

'Oh, we are English,' said Anne. 'But we live in France now. My husband inherited the château from his family on his mother's side, the Martineaus.'

'Oh, of course,' said Jake.

The factor came in from the farm and took a cup of tea standing up. He addressed Anne as 'Madame'.

Anne was already regretting her impulse in asking the couple to tea. They said very little but just sat on. She was afraid they would miss the last bus to the station. Looking at me, she said, 'The last bus goes at six, doesn't it?'

I said to Marion, 'You don't want to miss the last bus.'

'Could we see round the château?' said Marion. 'The guidebook says it's fourteenth century.'

'Well, not all of it is.' said Anne. 'But today is a bit difficult. We don't, you know, open the house to the public. We live in it.'

'I'm sure we've met,' said Marion to Anne, as if this took care of their catching the last bus – a point which was not lost on Anne. Kindly though she was I knew she hated to have to ferry people by car to the station and take on other chores she was not prepared for. I could see, already in Anne's mind, the thought: 'I have to get rid of these people or they'll stay for dinner and then all night. They are château-grabbers.'

Anne had often lamented to me about the château-grabbers of her later life. People who didn't want to know her when she was obscure and a bus driver's wife now wanted to know her intimately. Monty didn't care much about this, one way or another. But then the work of organizing meals and entertaining in style fell more on Anne than on Monty, who mostly spent his time helping the factor in the grounds, game-keeping and forest-clearing.

Anne could see that the English couple she had invited in 'for a cup of tea' were clingers, climbers, general nuisances, and she especially cast a look of desperation at me when Marion Ringer-Smith said, 'I'm sure we've met.'

'You think so?' Anne said. She had got up and was leading the way to the back door. 'This is the *Cour des Adieux*,' she said; 'it leads quicker to your bus stop.' Marion stooped and took a cake as if it was her last chance of ever eating a cake again.

I was at this moment coming to the end of a novel I was writing. Anne had offered me the peace and quiet of French château life and the informality of her own life-style which made it an ideal arrangement. She had also undertaken to type out the novel from any handwritten manuscripts on to a word-processor. But now at a quarter to six, I could see the rest of our afternoon's plans slipping away.

I doubted that Marion had indeed seen Anne before. It was by some mental process of transference that she had picked on Anne. The one she had actually met was myself, but she wasn't very much aware of it. After a gap of forty years, she remembered very little of me.

Jake Ringer-Smith asked if he could use the bathroom. Oh, you bore, I thought. Why don't you *go*? There are trees and thick bushes all the way down the drive for you to pee on. But no, he had to be shown the bathroom. It was nearly ten minutes to their bus time. Jake kicked his backpack over to his wife and said, 'Take this, will you?'

'I would really like to see round the château,' Marion said, 'while we're here and since we've come all this way.'

I had come across this situation before. There are people who will hold up a party of tired and worn fellow travellers just because *they* have to see a pulpit. There are people who will arrive an hour late for dinner with the excuse that they *had* to see over some art gallery on the way. Marion was very much one of those. If challenged she would have thought nothing of pointing out that, after all, she had paid a plane fare to arrive at where she was. I remember Marion's shapeless cheesecloth dress and her worn sandals and Jake's baggy, ostentatiously patched, grubby trousers, their avidity to get on intimate terms with the lady of the house, to be invited to supper and, no doubt, to spend the night. I was really sorry for

Anne who, I was aware, was sorry for herself and most of all regretting her own impulsive invitation to a cup of tea in her house.

Anne kept a soup kitchen in a building some way from the house, beyond a vegetable garden. She was pledged, I knew, to be there and help whenever possible, at six-thirty every evening. Laboriously, she explained this to the Ringer-Smiths. '… otherwise I'd have been glad to show you the house, not that there's much to see.'

'Soup kitchen!' said Jake. 'May we join it for a bowl of soup? Then perhaps we can stretch out our sleeping-bag for the night under one of your charming archways and see the house tomorrow.'

Does this sound like a nightmare? It was a nightmare. Nothing could throw off these people.

Down at the soup kitchen that evening, dispensing slabs of bread and cheese with bowls of tomato soup, I was not surprised to see the Ringer-Smiths appear.

'We belong to the lower orders,' he said to me with an exaggeratedly self-effacing grin that meant. 'We do not belong to any lower orders and just see how grand we really are – *we* don't care what we look like or what company we keep. We are Us.'

In fact they looked positively shifty among the genuine skin-and-bone tramps and hairy drop-outs and bulging bag-ladies. I dished out their portions to them without a smile. They had missed the last bus. Somehow, Anne and Monty had to arrange for them to have a bedroom for the night. 'We stayed at the château Leclaire de Martineau at Dijon' I could hear them telling their friends.

Before breakfast I advised Anne and Monty to make themselves scarce. 'Otherwise,' I said, 'you'll never get rid of them. Leave them to me.'

'I'm sure,' said Marion, 'I've met Anne before. But I can't tell where.'

'She has been a cook in many houses,' I said. 'And Monty has been a butler.'

'A cook and a butler?' said Jake.

'Yes, the master and mistress are away from home at present.'

'But she *told me she was the owner*,' Marion said, indicating the dining-room door with her head.

'Oh no, you must be mistaken.'

'But I'm sure she said—'

'Not at all,' I said. 'What a pity you can't see over the château. Such lovely pictures. But the Comtesse will be here at any moment. I don't know how you will explain yourselves. So far as I know you haven't been invited.'

'Oh we have,' said Jake. 'The servants begged us to stay. So typical, posing as the lord and lady of the manor! But it's getting late, we'll miss the bus.'

They were off within four minutes, tramping down the drive with their bulging packs.

Anne and Monty were delighted when I told them how it was done. Anne was sure, judging from a previous experience, that the intruders had planned to stay for a week.

'What else can you do with people like that?' said Anne.

'Put them in a story if you are me,' I said. 'And sell the story.'

'Can they sue?'

'Let them sue,' I said. 'Let them go ahead, stand up, and say Yes, that was Us.'

'An eccentric couple. They took the soap with them,' said Anne.

Monty went off about his business with a smile. So did Anne. And I, too. Or so I thought.

It was eleven-thirty, two hours later that morning, when, looking out of the window of my room as I often do when I am working on a novel, I saw them again under one of the trees bordering a lawn. They were looking up towards the house.

I had no idea where Monty and Anne were at that moment, nor could I think how to locate the factor, Raoul, or his wife, Marie-Louise. This was a disturbance in the rhythm of my morning's work, but I decided to go down and see what was the matter. As soon as they saw me Marion said, 'Oh hallo. We decided it was uncivil of us to leave without seeing the lady of the house and paying our respects.'

'We'll wait till the Comtesse arrives,' Jake stated.

'Well, you're unlucky,' I said. 'I believe there's word come through that she'll be away for a week.'

'That's all right,' said Marion. 'We can spare a week.'

'Only civil ...' said Jake.

I managed to alert Anne before she saw them. They were very cool to her when she did at last appear before them. 'The Comtesse would, I'm sure, be offended if we left without a word of thanks,' said Jake.

'Not at all,' said Anne. 'In fact, you *have* to go.'

'Not so,' said Marion.

Raoul tackled them, joined by Monty. Marion had already reclaimed their bedroom. 'As the beds had to be changed anyway,' she said, 'we may as well stay on. We don't mind eating down at the shed.' By this she meant the soup kitchen. 'We are not above eating with the proletariat,' said Jake.

Raoul and I searched the house, every drawer, for a key to the door of their bedroom. Eventually we found one that fitted and succeeded in locking them out. Monty took their packs and dumped them outside the gates of the château. These operations took place while they were feeding in the soup kitchen. We all five (Marie-Louise had joined us) confronted them and told them what we had done.

What happened to them after that none of us quite knows. We do know that they went to retrieve their bags and found themselves locked out by the factor. Anne received a letter, correctly addressed to her as the Comtesse, from Jake, indignantly complaining about the treatment they had received at the hands of the 'staff'.

'Something,' wrote Jake, 'told me not to accept their invitation. I knew instinctively that they were not one of us. I should have listened to my instincts. People like them are such frightful snobs.'

THIRD FLOOR RISING

Hilary Mantel

Hilary Mantel (b. 1952) is a British writer who has twice been awarded the Man Booker Prize. She won her first Booker for the 2009 novel, *Wolf Hall*, and her second, in 2012, for *Bring Up the Bodies*, making her the first woman to receive the award twice. She has published twelve novels and one collection of short stories, *Learning to Talk*.

The summer of my eighteenth birthday I had my first job. It was to fill the time between leaving school and going away to university in London. The previous summer I'd been old enough to work, but I had to stay at home and mind the children, while my mother pursued her glittering career.

For most of the years until I was sixteen, my mother had devoted herself to the care of a sick child. First it was me, until I went to senior school. Then I got abruptly better, by an act of will on my mother's part. My high fevers ceased, or ceased to be noticed, or if they were noticed they stopped being interesting. My youngest brother, his struggles for breath and his night-time cough, were elected to my old place in the household's economy. In my case I had been to school sporadically, but my brother didn't go at all. He played by himself in the garden under a pewter sky, with the fugitive glitter of snow behind it. He lay on his daybed in the room with the television blaring, and turned the pages of a book. One evening we were watching the news when our whole room lit up with a sick white light, and a bolt of ball lightning ripped the lower limbs from the poplar tree and blew the glass from the window frame, whump, fist of God. The shards were strewed over his crocheted blanket, the dog howled, the rain blew into the wreckage of the room and the neighbours squeaked and gibbered in the streets.

A short time after this my mother answered an advertisement for a saleswoman on the fashion floor at Affleck & Brown, which was a small, cramped, old-fashioned department store in Manchester. She had to walk to the station and then travel by train, then walk again to Oldham Street. This was a wonder to me, because I thought she'd given up going out. To do the job she had to have white blouses and black skirts. She bought some at C & A, and this amazed me too, because in our house we got our clothes by less straightforward methods than purchase: by a process of transmogrification, whereby cardigans were unravelled and reappeared as woollen berets and collars were wrenched off to extend hems and what were armholes for the stout became leg holes for the lean. When I was seven I'd had my winter coats made out of two that had belonged to my godmother. Pockets, lapels, everything was miniaturised: except the buttons, which were the originals, and stood out like banqueting plates, or targets for an arrow on my pigeon chest.

My mother had been to school in an age when most people didn't take exams, and she hadn't much to put on her application form. But she got the job, and soon personal disasters began to overtake the people who had appointed her; with them out of the way, she was promoted first to deputy and then to manageress of her department. She developed an airy meringue of white-blonde hair, very tall shoes – not just high heels but little boosts under the soles – and an airy way of talking and gesturing; and she began to encourage her staff to lie about their ages, which seemed to suggest she was lying about her own. She came home late and quarrelsome, with something unlikely in her crocodile bag. It might be a bag of crinkle-cut chips, which tasted of grease and air, a pack of frozen beefburgers which, under the grill, bubbled up with oily spots the grey-yellow colour of a Manchester smog. In time the chip pan got banned, to save the paintwork and to make a class statement, but by then I was living up the road with my friend Anne Terese, and what the others got for rations was something I preferred not to think about.

When I was seventeen I was as unprepared for life as if I had spent my child-hood on a mountainside minding goats. I was given to contemplation of nature, strolling about in the woods and fields. I was given to going to Stockport library and getting seven big books at a time about Latin American revolutions; waiting for an hour in the rain for the bus home, shifting the books at my feet and some-times picking them up in expectation of a bus and cradling them in my arms, rel-ishing their public dirt-edged pages, and the anticipation of finding inside them urgent notes from small-town obsessives: 'NOT Guatemala!!!!' pencilled in the margin, or rather incised into the page with a stub of graphite and the cedar's ragged edge. In our house, too, we never had a pencil sharpener. If you wanted a point you went to my mother and she held the pencil in her fist and swiped chunks off it with the bread knife.

It wasn't the fault of my education that I was so unworldly, because most of my contemporaries were normal, for their time and place and class. But they seemed to be made of a denser, plusher substance than myself. You could imagine them being women, and having upholstery and airing cupboards. There was air in the spaces between my bones, smoke between my ribs. Pavements hurt my feet. Salt sought out ulcers in my tongue. I was given to prodigious vomiting for no reason. I was cold when I woke up and I thought I would go on being it, always. So later, when I was twenty-four and I was offered a chance to migrate to the tropics, I seized on it because I thought now, now at least I will never be cold again.

My holiday job was secured before the interview; who, at Affleck & Brown, would have turned down the daughter of my ever-popular mother? But it was a formality: the mild personnel officer in his dun-coloured suit, in a back office so brown that I thought I had never seen the colour before, in every variety of tobacco spit and jaundice, every texture of Bakelite and Formica. Here I entered, fresh as 1970 in my little cotton shift, and here I was drawn backwards to the fifties, to the brown world of the National Insurance Card, and the yellowed notice from the Wages Council peeling from the distempered wall. Here I was wished luck and walked out on to the carpet, into the public world. 'Draws your feet, this carpet,' said a voice from between the rails.

It came from a shuddering white face, from wagging jowls, from a slow rolling mass of flesh, fiercely corseted inside a dress of stretched black polyester: corseted into the shape of a bulbous flower vase, and the skin with the murky sheen of carnation water two days old. Reek of armpits, rattling cough; these were my colleagues. life in the stores had destroyed them. They had chronic sniffles from the dust and bladder infections from the dirty lavatories. Their veins bulged through elastic stockings. They lived on £15 per week. They didn't work on commission, so they never sold anything if they could help it. Their rheumy malice drove customers back to the escalators and down into the street.

The personnel officer set me to work in the department next to my mother. I was able to study her in action, wafting across the floor in whatever creation she was wearing that day; she was no longer in subfusc, but picked her garments from her own stock. She had developed a manner that was gracious, not to say condescending, combined with a tip-tilted flirtatiousness that she tried out on the wilting gays who were almost the only men in the store; she was liked by her staff – her girls, as she called them – for her prettiness and high spirits.

They didn't seem, the girls, quite so decrepit as the ones who worked for my department, although I soon found out that they had a variety of intractable personal problems, which were meat and drink to my mother, which were in fact what she had instead of meat and drink, because now it was her role in life to stay a size 10, pretend she was a size 8, and so set an example to womankind. The girls had divorces, bad debts, vitamin deficiencies, premenstrual tension, and children with fits and deformities. Their houses were given to subsidence and collapse, floods and moulds, and it seemed to me that they specialised in obsolescent diseases such as smallpox or conditions such as scrapie that only a few morbid-minded people like me had heard of in those days. The worse off they were, the more disorderly and hopeless their lives, the more my mother doted on them. Even today, thirty years on, many of them keep in touch with her. 'Mrs D rang,' she will say. 'The IRA have bombed her house again and her daughter's been engulfed in a tidal wave, but she asked to be remembered to you.' At Christmas, and on the occasions of her falsified birthdays, these girls would buy my mother coloured glass ornaments, and adjuncts to the good life, like soda siphons. They were inner-city women with flat Manchester voices, but my mother and the other department heads talked in peculiar purse-lipped ways designed not to let their vowels show.

I was not employed by the store itself, but by a 'shop-in-shop' called English Lady. There were women, tending to the elderly, who wanted what it offered: dress-and-coat ensembles that I called wedding uniforms, summer frocks and 'separates' in artificial fabrics and pastel shades, washable and easy-iron. In those days people still went out in April to buy a summer coat of pink showerproof poplin, or a light wool with a shadow check, and they bought blazers, boleros and blouses, and trouser ensembles with long tunic tops under which they wore stockings and suspenders, the bumps of the suspenders showing through the polyester. In winter English Lady specialised in camel coats, which their wearers dutifully renewed every few years, expecting exactly the same style and getting it. There were also – for the winter stock was coming in, long before I left for London – coats called llamas, which were an unhealthy silver-grey, and shaggy, like hair shirts turned out, but hair shirts with pockets. For the autumn also there were bristling tweeds, and lumpen stinking sheepskins which we chained to the rails, because English Lady feared for their safety. Herding them was heavy work; they exhaled with a grunt when they were touched, and jostled for *Lebensraum*, puffing out their bulk and testing their bonds inch by squeaky inch.

Customers were scarce that summer. Once the morning dusting was over and we had done the day's updates on varicose veins, there was a desert of time to be got through: days of stupefying heat, thirst and boredom, with no air, no natural light, only a dim fluorescence above which gave a corpse-tint to the freshest skins. Sometimes as I stood I thought furiously about the French Revolution, which had come to preoccupy me. Sometimes my mother tripped across the carpet, fluttering her fingers at me, smiling upon her workforce.

My own boss was called Daphne. She wore goggle-sized fashion specs with coloured rims, behind which swam void pale eyes. In theory she and my mother were friends, but I soon realised, with a sense of shock, that among her peers my mother was a target for envy, and would have been secretly sabotaged if the other bosses had been bright enough to think how to do it. Daphne worked me relentlessly during those summer weeks, finding for me tasks that no one had done in years: cleaning in the stockrooms that were mice-ridden and thick with dust, boxing up great consignments of wire hangers which leapt from their bundles to claw at my arms like rats breaking out of a pet shop. The north-west was filthy in those days, and the rooms behind the scenes at Affleck & Brown were a dark and secret aspect of the filth. The feet-drawing carpets, the thick polythene in which the clothes came swathed, the neglected warp and weft of those garments that failed to sell and were bastilled in distant stockrooms: all these attracted a nap of sticky fluff which magnetised the particles of the Manchester atmosphere, which coated the hands and streaked the face, so that I must often have looked less like a 'junior sales' than a scab in a pit strike, my eyes travelling suspiciously when I surfaced, my hands contaminated, held away from my body in a gesture designed both to placate and ward off.

Sometimes, behind some packed rail draped in yellowing calico, behind some pile of boxes whose labels were faded to illegibility, I could sense a movement, a kind of shifting of feet, a murmur: 'Mrs Solomons?' I would call. 'Mrs Segal?' No answer: just the whispered exhalation of worsted and mohair: the deep intestinal creak of suede and leather: the faint squeal of unoiled metal wheels. Perhaps it was Daphne, spying on me? But sometimes at five thirty when the fitting rooms had to be cleared, I would come across a closed curtain at the end of a row, and I would turn and walk away without pulling it back, afflicted by sudden shyness or by fear of seeing something that I shouldn't see. It is easy to imagine that hanging fabric is bulked out by flesh, or that stitch and seam rehearse, after hours, a human shape without bones.

My colleagues, breathing over me the faint minted aroma of their indigestion remedies, received me with unbounded kindness. My pallor attracted their tut-tutting sanction, and caused them to recommend the red meat that never passed their own lips. Perhaps my remoteness alarmed them, as I stood entranced among the edge-to-edge jackets; and then I would snap back and sell something, which alarmed them too. I liked the challenge of suiting the garments to the women who wanted them, of making a fit, of gratifying harmless desire. I liked tearing off the tickets from the frocks as they were sold, and looping a carrier bag considerately around an arthritic wrist. Sometimes the elderly customers would try to give me tips, which upset me. 'I don't come often now,' said one twisted, gracious old person. 'But when I do come, I always give.'

At the end of each working day my mother and I winced arm in arm to Piccadilly station, up the hill from Market Street, past the hot cafés stewing with grease and the NHS clinic that was always advertising for people to step in and donate blood. (I stepped in as soon as I was eighteen, but they turned me around and stepped me straight back out again.) It seemed to me that my job amounted to standing up for a living, and that no one should have to do it: standing hour after hour, standing when there was no customer in sight, standing in the fuggy heat from nine in the morning till five thirty at night with an hour for lunch in which you sprang out of the building and walked, gulping in the air. You stood long after your feet throbbed and your calves ached, and the ache wasn't gone by next morning when the standing started again. Maybe my mother was better off than me, because she had a tiny shelf of an office to sit in, a chair to perch on. But then she had her shoes, much more pernicious than my small suede sandals; her whole existence was much more high.

Some nights, maybe twice in the week, there were problems with the trains. Once there was an hour's delay. Hunger made us buoyant: talking gaily of the many catastrophes that had beset my mother's girls that day, we nibbled at a green apple she had produced from her bag, turn and turn about. We were not angry or guilty about being late because there was nothing we could do, and our mood was innocent, blithe, until we found ourselves penned up in the hall of our little house with my stepfather snarling. Our giggling stopped: what I have often remarked as brutal is the side of the human hand, tensed, wedge-like, ready to strike like an axe. Something then occurred. I'm not clear what it was. It isn't true that if you're very angry it gives you strength. If you're very angry it gives you a swimming head and limbs weak at the joints, but you do it anyway, a thing you've never done before, you speak the curse, you move, you pin against the wall, you say a certain death formula and what you say you mean; the effect is in proportion to the shock, as if the Meek had got out from the Sermon on the Mount and raked the crossroads with machine-gun fire.

After this, for a while, I left home. My mother and I parted every evening at the end of our road. She was more in sorrow than in anger, but sometimes she was in anger; I realise now that my intervention had interrupted some marital game of hers. When we drew near the end of our day's journey she'd stop chattering about the girls, and she'd move – reluctantly, I often felt – into some remote sniffy territory, putting deliberate distance between us. I would labour on up the hill to where I'd moved in with Anne Terese. She was now alone in the family house. Her parents had parted that summer, and perhaps they hadn't got the hang of it; instead of one going and one staying, both of them had walked out. We didn't compare our families much; we tried on the clothes in the wardrobes, and rearranged the furniture. The house was a peculiar one, prefabricated, contingent but homely, with a stove in the sitting room, and a deep enamel sink, and none of the appliances, like fridges, that people took for granted in the year 1970.

Anne Terese was working for the summer at a factory that made rubber-soled slippers. The work was hard, but every part of her body was hard and efficient too. In the evening, while I sagged feebly on a kitchen chair, she breaded cutlets, and sliced tomato and cucumber on to a glass dish. She made a Polish cake that was heavy with eggs and ripe cherries. At dusk we sat on the porch, in the faint blown scent of old rose. Hope, fine as cobwebs, draped our bare arms and floated across our shoulders, each strand shivering with twilit blue. When the moon rose we moved indoors to our beds, still sleepily murmuring. Anne Terese thought six children would suit her. I thought it would be good if I could stop vomiting.

Sometimes, as I wandered the floor at English Lady, I'd pretend that I was a supervisor at a refugee camp and that the frocks were the inhabitants. When I packed one and threw its ticket into a box I said to myself that I'd resettled it.

Each day began and ended with the count. You took a piece of paper and ruled it into columns for the different types of stock, so that you didn't get the two-pieces mixed up with the dress and jackets, even though they were two pieces also. You had to make categories for the garments that had no name, like the bifurcated items that head office had sent several seasons ago; made of hairy grey-blue tweed, they were some kind of flying suit perhaps, of a kind to be worn by Biggles's nanny. When the sales came around, Daphne would always reduce them, but they remained on the rails, their stiff arms thrust out and their legs wrapped around their necks to keep them from trailing on the carpet.

When you had made your categories you went between the rails and counted, and it was always wrong. You would then patrol the floor looking for English Ladies that had tucked themselves in among the Eastex or Windsmoor. You would haul them back by their necks and thrust them on the rails. But, while it was easy to see why the count should be wrong after the working day, it was less easy to understand why the stock should move around at night. 'Spooks,' I said robustly. I thought they must come down from the third-floor bedding (the sheeted dead) and try on our garments, hissing with spooky excitement, and sliding their phantom limbs into legs and sleeves.

I passed the summer so, in talking to tramps in Piccadilly Gardens; in buying ripe strawberries from the barrows for my lunch; in cooling my forehead against the gunmetal grille of the door of the goods lift. When Daphne castigated me for this failing and that, I would sigh will-do-better, but later I would aim secret kicks at the flying suits, and torture them by wrapping their legs more tightly around their necks and knotting them behind the hanger. To Daphne's face, I was compliance itself. I didn't want my mother to incur even more rancid female hatred, that would snarl invisible about her trim ankles, snag her kitten heels when I was long gone, and marching through London streets.

But then, as September approached, I found that the whole subject of the count was making me restless. Each evening we could only square it with the stock sheets by writing '15 in back' at the end of the dresses and jackets column, and it occurred to me that in all my grovelling and delving I'd never run across these oddments. 'You know,' I said to Daphne, 'where we always write "15 in back"? Where are they?'

'In back,' said Daphne. We were in her office, a scant wedge-shape partitioned off from the sales floor.

'But where?' I said. 'I've never seen them.'

Daphne slotted a cigarette into her mouth. With one hand she flipped a page of a stocklist, in the other hovered a dribbling ballpoint pen. A thin plume of smoke leaked from her lips. 'Don't you smoke yet?' she said 'Aren't you tempted?'

I had wondered, a time or two, why people try to trap you into new vices. Ours was a home that was militantly anti-tobacco. 'I haven't thought about it really … I don't suppose … Well, if your parents don't smoke … I couldn't at home anyway, it would be very bad for my brother.'

Daphne stared at me. A little hoot issued from her, like a hiccup, and then a derisive shout of laughter. 'What! Your mother smokes like a chimney! Every break! Every lunchtime! Haven't you seen her? You must have seen her!'

'No,' I said. 'I have never.' I was the more deceived.

A gobbet of ink dropped from Daphne's pen. 'Have I spoken out of turn?'

'That's all right,' I said.

I told myself I welcomed information, information from any source.

Daphne looked at me glassily. 'Anyway,' she said, 'why should it be bad for your brother?'

I looked at my watch. 'Mrs Segal's lunch,' I smiled. I headed back to the sales floor. I said to myself, it can't matter. Tiny household lies. Pragmatic lies. Amusing, probably: given time. Trivial: like a needle-point snapped under the skin.

But later that afternoon, I sought the 15 in back. I tunnelled my way into lightless holes, where my toes were stubbed by bulging rotten boxes of unknown provenance. The cartons I had made myself, and bound with twine, had never been dispatched by Daphne, but left to squat in collapsing stacks. Now the wire hangers nipped at my calves as they worked their way out. Levering aside the bulky winter stock, thwacking the llamas away from me, I burrowed my way to the farthest corner. Give me that mattock and the wrenching iron.

Nothing. I named every garment I saw, scrabbling inside their shrouds: lifting them by their collars to peep at their labels, or, if I could not lift them, shredding their plastic frills into ruffs around their throats. I saw labels and I saw things that might have been Dress & Jackets but I did not see Dress & Jackets with the label I wanted. The 15 were nowhere to be found. I fought my way back to the air. I never looked back. I scratched it on my pad: zero, nix, nought. Diddly-squat, as the men said. Dress & Jackets, nil. If they had ever been known to exist, they didn't now. I saw how it was; they were to be conjured into being, the 15, to cover a mighty embarrassment, some awesome negligence or theft that had knocked the count to its knees gibbering. They were a fiction, perhaps an antique one; perhaps even older than Daphne. They were an adjustment to reality. They were a tale told by an idiot: to which I had added a phrase or two.

I re-emerged on to the floor. It was three o'clock. One of those dead afternoons, adumbrated, slumberous: not a customer in view. Limp from lack of regard, the stock hung like rags. A long mirror showed a dark smudge across my cheek. My sandals were coated with poisoned grime. I limped to the battered bureau where we kept our duplicate books and spare buttons, and took a duster out of the drawer. I rolled it up and brushed myself down, then moved out on to the floor, between the rails, and dusted between the garments: parting the hangers and polishing the steel spaces between. Somehow the afternoon passed. That night I declined to write '15 in back' at the end of the count; until my colleagues became too upset to bear, and one showed signs of hyperventilating. So in the end I did consent to write the phrase, but I wrote it quite faintly in pencil, with a question mark after it that was fainter still.

When the new school term began, it emerged that there was nothing wrong with my brother any more. He was eleven now, quite fit enough to go to high school. We digested this surprising fact, but no one was quite as glad about it as they should have been. Within months my mother was headhunted, her services sought by mackintosh purveyors and knitwear concessions; she had her pick of jobs, and moved to bigger stores, becoming blonder year by year, rising like a champagne bubble, to command larger numbers of girls and bigger counts and attract even more animosity and spite. At home she pursued her impromptu housekeeping, scouring the bath with powder meant for the washing machine and, when the washing machine broke down, throwing a tablecloth over it and using it as a sort of sideboard while she trained my siblings to go to the launderette.

A few year later Affleck's closed, and the whole district around it went to seed. It was taken over by pornographers, and those kinds of traders who sell plastic laundry baskets, dodgy electric fires and moulded Christmas novelties such as bouncing mince pies and whistling seraphim. The building itself was leased by a high-street clothing store, who traded briefly from its crumbling shell. I was long gone, of course, but I kept friends in the north, and had in my chain of acquaintances a Saturday girl who worked for the new occupiers. They only used the lower floors; from the second floor upwards, the building had been sealed. The fire doors had been closed and locked shut, the escalators had been removed, and the back staircases now ended in blind walls. But the staff were disturbed, said the Saturday girl, by noises from the bricked-in cavity above their heads: by footsteps, and by the sound of a woman screaming.

When I heard this I felt cold and felt sickness in the pit of my stomach, because I knew it was a true ghost story, as true as these things go. It had been no dizzy imp that came down from above and pulled buttons off the frocks, or walked them across the floor and mixed them in with the Jaeger. It was something staler, heavier, grossly sinister and perverse. But I only knew this in retrospect. When I looked back from, say, the age of twenty-three to the age of eighteen, I realised that, in those years, everything had been far worse than it seemed at the time.

THE THING IN THE FOREST

A. S. Byatt

A. S. Byatt (b. 1936) is a British novelist and poet. In 2008, *The Times* named her on its list of the '50 Greatest British Writers Since 1945'. She won the Man Booker Prize in 1990 for her novel *Possession: A Romance*, and was shortlisted again in 2009 for *The Children's Book*, which won the James Tait Black Memorial Prize. She has published five collections of short stories.

There were once two little girls who saw, or believed they saw, a thing in a forest. The two little girls were evacuees, who had been sent away from the city by train, with a large number of other children. They all had their names attached to their coats with safety-pins, and they carried little bags or satchels, and the regulation gas-mask. They wore knitted scarves and bonnets or caps, and many had knitted gloves attached to long tapes which ran along their sleeves, inside their coats, and over their shoulders and out, so that they could leave their ten woollen fingers dangling like a spare pair of hands, like a scarecrow. They all had bare legs and scuffed shoes and wrinkled socks. Most had wounds on their knees in varying stages of freshness and scabbiness. They were at the age when children fall often and their knees were unprotected. With their suitcases, some of which were almost too big to carry, and their other impedimenta, a doll, a toy car, a comic, they were like a disorderly dwarf regiment, stomping along the platform.

The two little girls had not met before, and made friends on the train. They shared a square of chocolate, and took alternate bites at an apple. One gave the other the inside page of her *Beano*. Their names were Penny and Primrose. Penny was thin and dark and taller, possibly older, than Primrose, who was plump and blonde and curly. Primrose had bitten nails, and a velvet collar to her dressy green coat. Penny had a bloodless transparent paleness, a touch of blue in her fine lips. Neither of them knew where they were going, nor how long the journey might take. They did not even know why they were going since neither of their mothers had quite known how to explain the danger to them. How do you say to your child, I am sending you away, because enemy bombs may fall out of the sky, because the streets of the city may burn like forest fires of brick and timber, but I myself am staying here, in what I believe may be daily danger of burning, burying alive, gas, and ultimately perhaps a grey army rolling in on tanks over the suburbs, or sailing its submarines up our river, all guns blazing?

So the mothers (who did not resemble each other at all) behaved alike, and explained nothing, it was easier. Their daughters they knew were little girls, who would not be able to understand or imagine.

The girls discussed on the train whether it was a sort of holiday or a sort of punishment, or a bit of both. Penny had read a book about Boy Scouts, but the children on the train did not appear to be Brownies or Wolf Cubs, only a mongrel battalion of the lost. Both little girls had the idea that these were all perhaps *not very good children*, possibly being sent away for that reason. They were pleased to be able to define each other as 'nice'. They would stick together, they agreed. Try to sit together, and things.

The train crawled sluggishly further and further away from the city and their homes. It was not a clean train – the upholstery of their carriage had the dank smell of unwashed trousers, and the gusts of hot steam rolling backwards past their windows were full of specks of flimsy ash, and sharp grit, and occasional fiery sparks that pricked face and fingers like hot needles if you opened the window. It was very noisy too, whenever it picked up a little speed. The engine gave great bellowing sighs, and the invisible wheels underneath clicked rhythmically and monotonously, tap-tap-tap-CRASH, tap-tap-tap-CRASH. The window-panes were both grimy and misted up. The train stopped frequently, and when it stopped, they used their gloves to wipe rounds, through which they peered out at flooded fields, furrowed hillsides and tiny stations, whose names were carefully blacked out, whose platforms were empty of life.

The children did not know that the namelessness was meant to baffle or delude an invading army. They felt – they did not think it out, but somewhere inside them the idea sprouted – that the erasure was because of them, because they were not meant to know where they were going or, like Hansel and Gretel, to find the way back. They did not speak to each other of this anxiety, but began the kind of conversation children have about things they really disliked, things that upset, or disgusted, or frightened them. Semolina pudding with its grainy texture, mushy peas, fat on roast meat. Listening to the stairs and the window-sashes creaking in the dark or the wind. Having your head held roughly back over the basin to have your hair washed, with cold water running down inside your liberty bodice. Gangs in playgrounds. They felt the pressure of all the other alien children in all the other carriages as a potential gang. They shared another square of chocolate, and licked their fingers, and looked out at a great white goose flapping its wings beside an inky pond.

The sky grew dark grey and in the end the train halted. The children got out, and lined up in a crocodile, and were led to a mud-coloured bus. Penny and Primrose managed to get a seat together, although it was over the wheel, and both of them began to feel sick as the bus bumped along snaking country lanes, under whipping branches, dark leaves on dark wooden arms on a dark sky, with torn strips of thin cloud streaming across a full moon, visible occasionally between them.

They were billeted temporarily in a mansion commandeered from its owner, which was to be arranged to hold a hospital for the long-term disabled, and a secret store of artworks and other valuables. The children were told they were there temporarily, until families were found to take them all into their homes. Penny and Primrose held hands, and said to each other that it would be wizard if they could go to the same family, because at least they would have each other. They didn't say anything to the rather tired-looking ladies who were ordering them about, because with the cunning of little children, they knew that requests were most often counter-productive, adults liked saying no. They imagined possible families into which they might be thrust. They did not discuss what they imagined, as these pictures, like the black station signs, were too frightening, and words might make some horror solid, in some magical way. Penny, who was a reading child, imagined Victorian dark pillars of severity, like Jane Eyre's Mr Brocklehurst, or David Copperfield's Mr Murdstone. Primrose imagined – she didn't know why – a fat woman with a white cap and round red arms who smiled nicely but made the children wear sacking aprons and scrub the steps and the stove. 'It's like we were orphans,' she said to Penny. 'But we're not,' Penny said. 'If we manage to stick together … '

The great house had a double flight of imposing stairs to its front door, and carved griffins and unicorns on its balustrade. There was no lighting, because of the black-out. All the windows were shuttered. No welcoming brightness leaked across door or windowsill. The children trudged up the staircase in their crocodile, hung their coats on numbered makeshift hooks, and were given supper (Irish stew and rice pudding with a dollop of blood-red jam) before going to bed in long makeshift dormitories, where once servants had slept. They had camp-beds (military issue) and grey shoddy blankets. Penny and Primrose got beds together but couldn't get a corner. They queued to brush their teeth in a tiny washroom, and both suffered (again without speaking) suffocating anxiety about what would happen if they wanted to pee in the middle of the night, because the lavatory was one floor down, the lights were all extinguished, and they were a long way from the door. They also suffered from a fear that in the dark the other children would start laughing and rushing and teasing, and turn themselves into a gang. But that did not happen. Everyone was tired and anxious and orphaned. An uneasy silence, a drift of perturbed sleep, came over them all. The only sounds – from all parts of the great dormitory it seemed – were suppressed snuffles and sobs, from faces pressed into thin pillows.

When daylight came, things seemed, as they mostly do, brighter and better. The children were given breakfast in a large vaulted room. They sat at trestle tables, eating porridge made with water and a dab of the red jam, heavy cups of strong tea. Then they were told they could go out and play until lunch-time. Children in those days – wherever they came from – were not closely watched, were allowed to come and go freely, and those evacuated children were not herded into any kind of holding-pen, or transit camp. They were told they should be back for lunch at 12.30, by which time those in charge hoped to have sorted out their provisional future lives. It was not known how they would know when it was 12.30, but it was expected that – despite the fact that few of them had wrist-watches – they would know how to keep an eye on the time. It was what they were used to.

Penny and Primrose went out together, in their respectable coats and laced shoes, on to the terrace. The terrace appeared to them to be vast, and was indeed extensive. It was covered with a fine layer of damp gravel, stained here and there bright green, or invaded by mosses. Beyond it was a stone balustrade, with a staircase leading down to a lawn, which that morning had a quicksilver sheen on the lengthening grass. It was flanked by long flowerbeds, full of overblown annuals and damp clumps of stalks. A gardener would have noticed the beginnings of neglect, but these were urban little girls, and they noticed the jungly mass of wet stems, and the wet, vegetable smell. Across the lawn, which seemed considerably vaster than the vast terrace, was a sculpted yew hedge, with many twigs and shoots out of place and ruffled. In the middle of the hedge was a wicket-gate, and beyond the gate were trees, woodland, a forest, the little girls said, to themselves.

'Let's go into the forest,' said Penny, as though the sentence was required of her.

Primrose hesitated. Most of the other children were running up and down the terrace, scuffing their shoes in the gravel. Some boys were kicking a ball on the grass. The sun came right out, full from behind a hazy cloud, and the trees suddenly looked both gleaming and secret.

'OK,' said Primrose. 'We needn't go far.'

'No. I've never been in a forest.'

'Nor me.'

'We ought to look at it, while we've got the opportunity,' said Penny.

There was a very small child – one of the smallest – whose name, she told everyone, was Alys. With ay she told those who could spell, and those who couldn't, which surely included herself. She was barely out of nappies. She was quite extraordinarily pretty, pink and white, with large pale blue eyes, and sparse little golden curls all over her head and neck, through which her pink skin could be seen. Nobody seemed to be in charge of her, no elder brother or sister. She had not quite managed to wash the tearstains from her dimpled cheeks.

She had made several attempts to attach herself to Penny and Primrose. They did not want her. They were excited about meeting and liking each other. She said now:

'I'm coming too, into the forest.'

'No, you aren't,' said Primrose.

'You're too little, you must stay here,' said Penny.

'You'll get lost,' said Primrose.

'You won't get lost. I'll come with you,' said the little creature, with an engaging smile, made for loving parents and grandparents.

'We don't want you, you see,' said Primrose.

'It's for your own good,' said Penny.

Alys went on smiling hopefully, the smile becoming more of a mask.

'It will be all right,' said Alys.

'Run,' said Primrose.

They ran; they ran down the steps and across the lawn, and through the gate, into the forest. They didn't look back. They were long-legged little girls, not toddlers. The trees were silent round them, holding out their branches to the sun, breathing noiselessly.

*

Primrose touched the warm skin of the nearest saplings, taking off her gloves to feel their cracks and knots. She exclaimed over the flaking whiteness and dusty brown of the silver birches, the white leaves of the aspens. Penny looked into the thick of the forest. There was undergrowth – a mat of brambles and bracken. There were no obvious paths. Dark and light came and went, inviting and mysterious, as the wind pushed clouds across the face of the sun.

'We have to be careful not to get lost,' she said. 'In stories, people make marks on tree-trunks, or unroll a thread, or leave a trail of white pebbles – to find their way back.'

'We needn't go out of sight of the gate,' said Primrose. 'We could just explore a little bit.'

They set off, very slowly. They went on tiptoe, making their own narrow passages through the undergrowth, which sometimes came as high as their thin shoulders. They were urban, and unaccustomed to silence. At first the absence of human noise filled them with a kind of awe, as though, while they would not have put it to themselves in this way, they had got to some original place, from which they, or those before them, had come, and which they therefore recognised. Then they began to hear the small sounds that were there. The chatter and repeated lilt and alarm of invisible birds, high up, further in. The hum and buzz of insects. Rustling in dry leaves, rushes of movement in thickets. Slitherings, dry coughs, sharp cracks. They went on, pointing out to each other creepers draped with glistening berries, crimson, black and emerald, little crops of toadstools, some scarlet, some ghostly-pale, some a dead-flesh purple, some like tiny parasols – and some like pieces of meat protruding from tree-trunks. They met blackberries, but didn't pick them, in case in this place they were dangerous or deceptive. They admired from a safe distance the stiff upright fruiting rods of the Lords and Ladies, packed with fat red berries. They stopped to watch spiders spin, swinging from twig to twig, hauling in their silky cables, reinforcing knots and joinings. They sniffed the air, which was full of a warm mushroom smell, and a damp moss smell, and a sap smell, and a distant hint of dead ashes.

Did they hear it first or smell it first? Both sound and scent were at first infinitesimal and dispersed. Both gave the strange impression of moving in – in waves – from the whole perimeter of the forest. Both increased very slowly in volume, and both were mixed, a sound and a smell fabricated of many disparate sounds and smells. A crunching, a crackling, a crushing, a heavy thumping, combined with threshing and thrashing, and added to that a gulping, heaving, boiling, bursting steaming sound, full of bubbles and farts, piffs and explosions, swallowings and wallowings. The smell was worse, and more aggressive, than the sound. It was a liquid smell of putrefaction, the smell of maggoty things at the bottom of untended dustbins, the smell of blocked drains, and unwashed trousers, mixed with the smell of bad eggs, and of rotten carpets and ancient polluted bedding. The new, ordinary forest smells and sounds, of leaves and humus, fur and feathers, so to speak, went out like lights as the atmosphere of the thing preceded it. The two little girls looked at each other, and took each other's hand. Speechlessly and instinctively they crouched, down behind a fallen tree-trunk, and trembled, as the thing came into view.

Its head appeared to form, or become first visible in the distance, between the trees. Its face – which was triangular – appeared like a rubbery or fleshy mask over a shapeless sprouting bulb of a head, like a monstrous turnip. Its colour was the colour of flayed flesh, pitted with wormholes, and its expression was neither wrath nor greed, but pure misery. Its most defined feature was a vast mouth, pulled down and down at the corners, tight with a kind of pain. Its lips were thin, and raised, like welts from whipstrokes. It had blind, opaque white eyes, fringed with fleshy lashes and brows like the feelers of sea-anemones. Its face was close to the ground, and moved towards the children between its forearms which were squat, thick, powerful and akimbo, like a cross between a monstrous washer-woman and a primeval dragon. The flesh on these forearms was glistening and mottled, every colour, from the green of mould to the red-brown of raw liver, to the dirty white of dry rot.

The rest of its very large body appeared to be glued together, like still-wet papier-mâché, or the carapace of stones and straws and twigs worn by caddis-flies underwater. It had a tubular shape, as a turd has a tubular shape, a provisional amalgam. It was made of rank meat, and decaying vegetation, but it also trailed veils and prostheses of manmade materials, bits of wire-netting, foul dishcloths, wire-wool full of pan-scrubbings, rusty nuts and bolts. It had feeble stubs and stumps of very slender legs, growing out of it at all angles, wavering and rippling like the suckered feet of a caterpillar or the squirming fringe of a centipede. On and on it came, bending and crushing whatever lay in its path, including bushes, though not substantial trees, which it wound between, awk-wardly. The little girls observed, with horrified fascination, that when it met a sharp stone, or a narrow tree-trunk, it allowed itself to be sliced through, flowed sluggishly round in two or three smaller worms, convulsed and reunited. Its progress was achingly slow, very smelly, and apparently very painful, for it moaned and whined amongst its other burblings and belchings. They thought it could not see, or certainly could not see clearly. It and its stench passed within a few feet of their tree-trunk, humping along, leaving behind it a trail of bloody slime and dead foliage, sucked to dry skeletons.

Its end was flat and blunt, almost transparent, like some earthworms.

When it had gone, Penny and Primrose, kneeling on the moss and dead leaves, put their arms about each other, and hugged each other, shaking with dry sobs. Then they stood up, still silent, and stared together, hand in hand, at the trail of obliteration and destruction, which wound out of the forest and into it again. They went back, hand in hand, without looking behind them, afraid that the wicket-gate, the lawn, the stone steps, the balustrade, the terrace and the great house would be transmogrified, or simply not there. But the boys were still play-ing football on the lawn, a group of girls were skipping and singing shrilly on the gravel. They let go each other's hand, and went back in.

They did not speak to each other again.

The next day they were separated and placed with strange families. Their time in these families – Primrose was in a dairy farm, Penny was in a parsonage – did not in fact last very long, though then the time seemed slow-motion and endless.

These alien families seemed like dream worlds into which they had strayed, not knowing the physical or social rules which constructed those worlds. Afterwards, if they remembered the evacuation it was as dreams are remembered, with mnemonics designed to claw back what fleets on waking. So Primrose remembered the sound of milk spurting in the pail, and Penny remembered the empty corsets of the vicar's wife, hanging bony on the line. They remembered dandelion clocks, but you can remember those from anywhere, any time. They remembered the thing they had seen in the forest, on the contrary, in the way you remember those very few dreams – almost all nightmares – which have the quality of life itself, not of fantasm, or shifting provisional scene-set. (Though what are dreams if not life itself?) They remembered too solid flesh, too precise a stink, a rattle and a soughing which thrilled the nerves and the cartilage of their growing ears. In the memory, as in such a dream, they felt, I cannot get out, this is a real thing in a real place.

They returned from evacuation, like many evacuees, so early that they then lived through wartime in the city, bombardment, blitz, unearthly light and roaring, changed landscapes, holes in their world where the newly dead had been. Both lost their fathers. Primrose's father was in the Army, and was killed, very late in the war, on a crowded troop-carrier sunk in the Far East. Penny's father, a much older man, was in the Auxiliary Fire Service, and died in a sheet of flame in the East India Docks on the Thames, pumping evaporating water from a puny coil of hose. They found it hard, after the war, to remember these different men. The claspers of memory could not grip the drowned and the burned. Primrose saw an inane grin under a khaki cap, because her mother had a snapshot. Penny thought she remembered her father, already grey-headed, brushing ash off his boots and trouser-cuffs as he put on his tin hat to go out. She thought she remembered a quaver of fear in his tired face, and the muscles composing themselves into resolution. It was not much, what either of them remembered.

After the war, their fates were still similar and dissimilar. Penny's widowed mother embraced grief, closed her face and her curtains, moved stiffly, like an automat, and read poetry. Primrose's mother married one of the many admirers, visitors, dancing partners she had had before the ship went down, gave birth to another five children, and developed varicose veins and a smoker's cough. She dyed her blonde hair with peroxide when it faded. Both Primrose and Penny were only children who now, because of the war, lived in amputated or unreal families. Penny developed crushes on poetical teachers and in due course – she was clever – went to university, where she chose to study developmental psychology. Primrose had little education. She was always being kept off school to look after the others. She too dyed her blonde curls with peroxide when they turned mousy and faded. She got fat as Penny got thin. Neither of them married. Penny became a child psychologist, working with the abused, the displaced, the disturbed. Primrose did this and that. She was a barmaid. She worked in a shop. She went to help at various church crèches and Salvation Army reunions, and discovered she had a talent for story-telling. She became Aunty Primrose, with her own repertoire. She was employed to tell tales to kindergartens and entertain at children's parties. She was much in demand at Hallowe'en, and had her own circle of bright yellow plastic chairs in a local shopping mall, where she kept an eye on the children of burdened women, keeping them safe, offering them just a *frisson* of fear and terror that made them wriggle with pleasure.

The house aged differently. During this period of time – whilst the little girls became women – it was handed over to the Nation, which turned it into a living museum, still inhabited by the flesh and blood descendants of those who had built it, demolished it, flung out a wing, closed off a corridor. Guided tours took place in it, at regulated times. During these tours, the ballroom and intimate drawing-rooms were fenced off with crimson twisted ropes on little brass one-eyed pedestals. The bored and the curious peered in at four-poster beds and pink silk *fauteuils*, at silver-framed photographs of wartime Royalty, and crackling crazing Renaissance and Enlightenment portraits of long-dead queens and solemn or sweetly musing ancestors. In the room where the evacuees had eaten their rationed meals, the history of the house was displayed, on posters, in glass cases, with helpful notices, and opened copies of old diaries and records. There were reproductions of the famous paintings which had lain here in hiding during the war. There was a plaque to the dead of the house: a gardener, an undergardener, a chauffeur and a second son. There were photographs of military hospital beds, and of nurses pushing wheelchairs in the grounds. There was no mention of the evacuees whose presence appeared to have been too brief to have left any trace.

The two women met in this room on an autumn day in 1984. They had come with a group, walking in a chattering crocodile behind a guide, and had lingered amongst the imagery and records, rather than going on to eavesdrop on the absent ladies and gentlemen whose tidy clutter lay on coffee tables and escritoires. They prowled around the room, each alone with herself in opposite directions, without acknowledging each other's presence. Both their mothers had died that spring, within a week of each other, though this coincidence was unknown to them. It had made both of them think of taking a holiday, and both had chosen that part of the world. Penny was wearing a charcoal trouser suit and a black velvet hat. Primrose wore a floral knit long jacket over a shell-pink cashmere sweater, over a rustling long skirt with an elastic waist, in a mustard-coloured tapestry print. Her hips and bosom were bulky. They coincided because both of them, at the same moment, half saw an image in a medieval-looking illustrated book. Primrose thought it was a very old book. Penny assumed it was nineteenth-century mock-medieval. It showed a knight, on foot, in a forest, lifting has sword to slay something. The knight shone on the rounded slope of the page, in the light, which caught the gilding on his helmet and sword-belt. It was not possible to see what was being slain. This was because, both in the tangled vegetation of the image, and in the way the book was displayed in the case, the enemy, or victim, was in shadows.

Neither of them could read the ancient (or pseudo-ancient) black letter of the text beside the illustration. There was a typed explanation, or description, under the book, done with a faded ribbon and uneven pressure of the keys. They had to lean forward to read it, and to see what was worming its way into, or out of, the deep spine of the book, and that was how they came to see each other's face, close up, in the glass which was both transparent and reflective. Their transparent reflected faces lost detail – cracked lipstick, pouches, fine lines of wrinkles – and looked both younger and greyer, less substantial. And that is how they came to recognise each other, as they might not have done, plump face to bony face. They breathed each other's names, Penny, Primrose, and their breath misted the glass, obscuring the knight and his opponent. I could have died, I could have wet my knickers, said Penny and Primrose afterwards to each other, and both experienced this still moment as pure, dangerous shock. But they stayed there, bent heads together, legs trembling, knees knocking, and read the caption, which was about the Loathly Worm, which, tradition held, had infested the countryside and had been killed more than once by scions of that house, Sir Lionel, Sir Boris, Sir Guillem. The Worm, the typewriter had tapped out, was an English Worm, not a European dragon, and like most such worms, was wingless. In some sightings it was reported as having vestigial legs, hands or feet. In others it was limbless. It had, in monstrous form, the capacity of common or garden worms to sprout new heads or trunks if it was divided, so that two worms, or more, replaced one. This was why it had been killed so often, yet reappeared. It had been reported travelling with a slithering pack of young ones, but these may have been only revitalised segments. The typed paper was held down with drawing-pins and appeared to continue somewhere else, on some not visible page, not presented for viewing.

Being English, the recourse they thought of was tea. There was a tea-room near the great house, in a converted stable at the back. There they stood silently side by side, clutching floral plastic trays spread with briar roses, and purchased scones, superior raspberry jam in tiny jam jars, little plastic tubs of clotted cream. 'You couldn't get cream or real jam in the war,' said Primrose in an undertone as they found a corner table. She said wartime rationing had made her permanently greedy, and thin Penny agreed, it had, clotted cream was still a treat.

They watched each other warily, offering bland snippets of autobiography in politely hushed voices. Primrose thought Penny looked gaunt, and Penny thought Primrose looked raddled. They established the skein of coincidences – dead fathers, unmarried status, child-caring professions, recently dead mothers. Circling like beaters, they approached the covert thing in the forest. They discussed the great house, politely. Primrose admired the quality of the carpets. Penny said it was nice to see the old pictures back on the wall. Primrose said, funny really, that there was all that history, but no sign that they, the children, that was, had ever been there. Penny said no, the story of the family was there, and the wounded soldiers, but not them, they were perhaps too insignificant. Too little, said Primrose, nodding agreement, not quite sure what she meant by too little. Funny, said Penny, that they should meet each other next to that book, with that picture. Creepy, said Primrose in a light, light cobweb voice, not looking at Penny. We saw that thing. When we went in the forest.

Yes we did, said Penny. We saw it.

Did you ever wonder, asked Primrose, if we *really* saw it?

Never for a moment, said Penny. That is, I don't know what it was, but I've always been quite sure we saw it.

Does it change – do you remember all of it?

It was a horrible thing, and yes, I remember all of it, there isn't a bit of it I can manage to forget. Though I forget all sorts of things, said Penny, in a thin voice, a vanishing voice.

And have you ever told anyone of it, spoken of it, asked Primrose more urgently, leaning forward, holding on to the table edge.

No, said Penny. She had not. She said, who would believe it, believe them?

That's what I thought, said Primrose. I didn't speak. But it stuck in my mind like a tapeworm in your gut. I think it did me no good.

It did me no good either, said Penny. No good at all. I've thought about it, she said to the ageing woman opposite, whose face quivered under her dyed goldilocks. I think, I think there are things that are real – more real than we are – but mostly we don't cross their paths, or they don't cross ours. Maybe at very bad times we get into their world, or notice what they are doing in ours.

Primrose nodded energetically. She looked as though sharing was solace, and Penny, to whom it was not solace, grimaced with pain.

'Sometimes I think that thing finished me off,' said Penny to Primrose, a child's voice rising in a woman's gullet, arousing a little girl's scared smile which wasn't a smile on Primrose's face. Primrose said:

'It did finish *her* off, that little one, didn't it? She got into its path, didn't she? And when it had gone by – she wasn't anywhere,' said Primrose. 'That was how it was?'

'Nobody ever asked where she was, or looked for her,' said Penny.

'I wondered if we'd made her up,' said Primrose. 'But I didn't, we didn't.'

'Her name was Alys.'

'With a y.'

There had been a mess, a disgusting mess, they remembered, but no particular sign of anything that might have been, or been part of, or belonged to, a persistent little girl called Alys.

Primrose shrugged voluptuously, let out a gale of a sigh, and rearranged her flesh in her clothes.

'Well, we know we're not mad, anyway,' she said. 'We've got into a mystery, but we didn't make it up. It wasn't a delusion. So it was good we met, because now we needn't be afraid we're mad, need we, we can get on with things, so to speak?'

They arranged to have dinner together the following evening. They were staying in different bed and breakfasts and neither of them thought of exchanging addresses. They agreed on a restaurant in the market square of the local town – *Seraphina's Hot Pot* – and a time, seven-thirty. They did not even discuss spending the next day together. Primrose went on a local bus tour. Penny asked for sandwiches, and took a long solitary walk. The weather was grey, spitting fine rain. Both arrived at their lodgings with headaches, and both made tea with the teabags and kettle provided in their rooms. They sat on their beds. Penny's bed had a quilt with blowsy cabbage roses. Primrose's had a black-and-white checked gingham duvet. They turned on their televisions, watched the same game show, listened to the inordinate jolly laughter. Penny washed herself rather fiercely in her tiny bathroom: Primrose slowly changed her underwear, and put on fresh tights. Between bathroom and wardrobe Penny saw the air in the room fill with a kind of grey smoke. Rummaging in a suitcase for a clean blouse, Primrose felt giddy, as though the carpet was swirling. What would they say to each other, they asked themselves, and sat down, heavy and winded, on the edges of their single beds. Why? Primrose's mind said, scurrying, and Why? Penny asked herself starkly. Primrose put down her blouse and turned up the television. Penny managed to walk as far as the window. She had a view with a romantic bit of moorland, rising to a height that cut off the sky. Evening had caught her: the earth was black: the house-lights trickled feebly into gloom.

Seven-thirty came and went, and neither woman moved. Both, indistinctly, imagined the other waiting at a table, watching a door open and shut. Neither moved. What could they have said, they asked themselves, but only perfunctorily. They were used to not asking too much, they had had practice.

The next day they both thought very hard, but indirectly, about the wood. It was a spring day, a good day for woods, and yesterday's rain-clouds had been succeeded by clear sunlight, with a light movement of air and a very faint warmth. Penny thought about the wood, put on her walking-shoes, and set off obliquely in the opposite direction. Primrose was not given to ratiocination. She sat over her breakfast, which was English and ample, bacon and mushrooms, toast and honey, and let her feelings about the wood run over her skin, pricking and twitching. The wood, the real, and imagined wood – both before and after she had entered it with Penny – had always been simultaneously a source of attraction and a source of discomfort, shading into terror. The light in woods was more golden and more darkly shadowed than any light on city terraces, including the glare of bombardment. The gold and the shadows were intertwined, a promise of liveliness. What they had seen had been shapeless and stinking, but the wood persisted.

So without speaking to herself a sentence in her head – 'I shall go there' – Primrose decided by settling her stomach, setting her knees, and slightly clenching her fists, that she would go there. And she went straight there, full of warm food, arriving as the morning brightened with the first bus-load of tourists, and giving them the slip, to take the path they had once taken, across the lawn and through the wicket-gate.

The wood was much the same, but denser and more inviting in its new greenness. Primrose's body decided to set off in a rather different direction from the one the little girls had taken. New bracken was uncoiling with snaky force. Yesterday's rain still glittered on limp new hazel leaves and threads of gossamer. Small feathered throats above her, and in the depths beyond, whistled and trilled with enchanting territorial aggression and male self-assertion, which were to Primrose simply the chorus. She heard a cackle and saw a flash of the loveliest flesh-pink, in feathers, and a blue gleam. She was not good at identifying birds. She could do 'a robin' – one hopped from branch to branch – 'a black bird' which shone like jet, and 'a tit' which did acrobatics, soft, blue and yellow, a tiny scrap of fierce life. She went steadily on, always distracted by shines and gleams in her eye-corner. She found a mossy bank, on which she found posies of primroses, which she recognised and took vaguely, in the warmth of her heart labouring in her chest, as a good sign, a personal sign. She picked a few, stroked their pale petals, buried her nose in them, smelled the thin, clear honey-smell of them, spring honey without the buzz of summer. She was better at flowers than birds, because there had been *Flower Fairies* in the school bookshelves when she was little, with the flowers painted accurately, wood-sorrel and stitchwort, pimpernel and honeysuckle, flowers she had never seen, accompanied by truly pretty human creatures, all children, from babies to girls and boys, clothed in the blues and golds, russets and purples of the flowers and fruits, walking, dancing, delicate material imaginings of the essential lives of plants. And now as she wandered on, she saw and recognised them, windflower and bryony, self-heal and dead-nettle, and had – despite where she was – a lovely lapping sense of invisible – *just* invisible life swarming in the leaves and along the twigs, despite where she was, despite what she had not forgotten having seen there. She closed her eyes a fraction. The sunlight flickered and flickered. She saw glitter and spangling everywhere. She saw drifts of intense blue, further in, and between the tree-trunks, with the light running over them.

She stopped. She did not like the sound of her own toiling breath. She was not very fit. She saw, then, a whisking in the bracken, a twirl of fur, thin and flaming, quivering on a tree-trunk. She saw a squirrel, a red squirrel, watching her from a bough. She had to sit down, as she remembered her mother. She sat on a hummock of grass, rather heavily. She remembered them all, Nutkin and Moldywarp, Brock and Sleepy Dormouse, Natty Newt and Ferdy Frog. Her mother didn't tell stories and didn't open gates into imaginary worlds. But she had been good with her fingers. Every Christmas during the war, when toys, and indeed materials, were not to be had, Primrose had woken to find in her stocking a new stuffed creature, made from fur fabric with button eyes and horny claws, Or, in the case of the amphibians, made from scraps of satin and taffeta. There had been an artistry to them. The stuffed squirrel was the essence of squirrel, the fox was watchful, the newt was slithery. They did not wear anthropomorphic jackets or caps, which made it easier to invest them with imaginary natures. She believed in Father Christmas, and the discovery that her mother had made the toys, the vanishing of magic, had been a breath-taking blow. She could not be grateful for the skill and the imagination, so uncharacteristic of her flirtatious mother. The creatures continued to accumulate. A spider, a Bambi. She told herself stories at night about a girl-woman, an enchantress in a fairy wood, loved and protected by an army of wise and gentle animals. She slept banked in by stuffed creatures, as the house in the blitz was banked in by inadequate sandbags.

Primrose registered the red squirrel as disappointing – stringier and more rat-like than its plump grey city cousins. But she knew it was rare and special, and when it took off from branch to branch, flicking its extended tail like a sail, gripping with its tiny hands, she set out to follow it as though it was a messenger. It would take her to the centre, she thought, she ought to get to the centre. It could easily have leaped out of sight, she thought, but it didn't. It lingered and sniffed and stared nervily, waiting for her. She pushed through brambles into denser greener shadows. Juices stained her skirts and skin. She began to tell herself a story about staunch Primrose, not giving up, making her way to 'the centre'. She had to have a reason for coming there, it was to do with getting to the centre. Her childhood stories had all been in the third person. 'She was not afraid.' 'She faced up to the wild beasts. They cowered.' She laddered her tights and muddied her shoes and breathed heavier. The squirrel stopped to clean its face. She crushed bluebells and saw the sinister hoods of arum lilies.

She had no idea where she was, or how far she had come, but she decided that the clearing where she found herself was the centre. The squirrel had stopped, and was running up and down a single tree. There was a sort of mossy mound which could almost have had a throne-like aspect, if you were being imaginative. So she sat on it. 'She came to the centre and sat on the mossy chair.'

Now what?

She had not forgotten what they had seen, the blank miserable face, the powerful claws, the raggle-taggle train of accumulated decay. She had come neither to look for it nor to confront it, but she had come because it was there. She had known all her life that she, Primrose, had *really* been in a magic forest. She knew that the forest was the source of terror. She had never frightened the litl'uns she entertained at parties, in schools, in crèches, with tales of lost children in forests. She frightened them with slimy things that came up the plughole, or swarmed out of the U-bend in the lavatory, or tapped on windows at night, and were despatched by bravery and magic. There were waiting hobgoblins in urban dumps beyond the street-lights. But the woods in her tales were sources of glamour, of rich colours and unseen hidden life, flower fairies and more magical beings. They were places where you used words like spangles and sequins for real dewdrops on real dock leaves. Primrose knew that glamour and the thing they had seen came from the same place, that brilliance and the ashen stink had the same source. She made them safe for the litl'uns by restricting them to pantomime flats and sweet illustrations. She didn't look at what she knew, better not, but *she did know she knew*, she recognised confusedly.

Now what?

She sat on the moss, and a voice in her head said, 'I want to go home.' And she heard herself give a bitter, entirely grown-up little laugh, for what was home? What did she know about home?

Where she lived was above a Chinese takeaway. She had a dangerous cupboard-corner she cooked in, a bed, a clothes-rail, an armchair deformed by generations of bottoms. She thought of this place in faded browns and beiges, seen through drifting coils of Chinese cooking-steam, scented with stewing pork and a bubbling chicken broth. Home was not real, as all the sturdy twigs and roots in the wood were real, it had neither primrose-honey nor spangles and sequins. The stuffed animals, or some of them, were piled on the bed and the carpet, their fur rubbed, their pristine stare gone from their scratched eyes. She thought about what one thought was *real*, sitting there on the moss-throne at the centre. When Mum had come in, snivelling, to say Dad was dead, she herself had been preoccupied with whether pudding would be tapioca or semolina, whether there would be jam, and subsequently, how ugly Mum's dripping nose looked, how she looked as though she was *putting it on*. She remembered the semolina and the rather nasty blackberry jam, the taste and the texture, to this day, so was that real, was that home? She had later invented a picture of a cloudy aquamarine sea under a gold sun in which a huge fountain of white curling water rose from a foundering ship. It was very beautiful but not real. She could not remember Dad. She could remember the Thing in the Forest, and she could remember Alys. The fact that the mossy hump had lovely colours – crimson and emerald, she said, maiden-hairs, she named something at random – didn't mean she didn't remember the Thing. She remembered what Penny had said about 'things that are more real than we are'. She had met one. Here at the centre, the spout of water was more real than the semolina, because she was where such things reign. The word she found was 'reign'. She had understood something, and did not know what she had understood. She wanted badly to go home, and she wanted never to move. The light was lovely in the leaves. The squirrel flirted its tail and suddenly set off again, springing into the branches. The woman lumbered to her feet and licked the bramble-scratches on the back of her hands.

Penny had set off in what she supposed to be the opposite direction. She walked very steadily, keeping to hedgerows and field-edge paths, climbing the occasional stile. For the first part of the walk she kept her eyes on the ground, and her ears on her own trudging, as it disturbed stubble and pebbles. She slurred her feet over vetch and stitchwort, looking back over the crushed trail. She remembered the Thing. She remembered it clearly and daily. Why was she in this part of the world at all, if not to settle with it? But she walked away, noticing and not noticing that her path was deflected by fieldforms and the lie of the land into a snaking sickle-shape. As the day wore on, she settled into her stride and lifted her eyes, admiring the new corn in the furrows, a distant skylark. When she saw the wood on the horizon she knew it was the wood, although she was seeing it from an unfamiliar aspect, from where it appeared to be perched on a conical hillock, ridged as though it had been grasped and squeezed by coils of strength. The trees were tufted and tempting. It was almost dusk when she came there. The shadows were thickening, the dark places in the tumbled undergrowth were darkening. She mounted the slope, and went in over a suddenly discovered stile.

Once inside, she moved cautiously, as though she was hunted or hunting. She stood stock-still, and snuffed the air for the remembered rottenness: she listened to the sounds of the trees and the creatures, trying to sift out a distant threshing and sliding. She smelled rottenness, but it was normal rottenness, leaves and stems mulching back into earth. She heard sounds. Not birdsong, for it was too late in the day, but the odd raucous warning croak, a crackle of something, a tremulous shiver of something else. She heard her own heartbeat in the thickening brown air.

She had wagered on freedom and walked away, and walking away had brought her here, as she had known it would. It was no use looking for familiar tree-trunks or tussocks. They had had a lifetime, her lifetime, to alter out of recognition.

She began to think she discerned dark tunnels in the undergrowth, where something might have rolled and slid. Mashed seedlings, broken twigs and fronds, none of it very recent. There were things caught in the thorns, flimsy colourless shreds of damp wool or fur. She peered down the tunnels and noted where the scrapings hung, thickest. She forced herself to go into the dark, stooping, occasionally crawling on hands and knees. The silence was heavy. She found things she remembered, threadworms of knitting wool, unravelled dish-cloth cotton, clinging newsprint. She found odd sausage-shaped tubes of mem-brane, containing fragments of hair and bone and other inanimate stuffs. They were like monstrous owl-pellets, or the gut-shaped hair-balls vomited by cats. Penny went forwards, putting aside lashing briars and tough stems with careful fingers. It had been here, but how long ago? When she stopped, and sniffed the air, and listened, there was nothing but the drowsy wood.

Quite suddenly she came out at a place she remembered. The clearing was larger, the tree-trunks were thicker, but the fallen one behind which they had hidden still lay there. The place was almost the ghost of a camp. The trees round about were hung with threadbare pennants and streamers, like the scorched, hacked, threadbare banners in the chapel of the great house, with their brown stains of earth or blood. It had been here, it had never gone away.

Penny moved slowly and dreamily round, watching herself as you watch your-self in a dream, looking for things. She found a mock tortoiseshell hairslide, and a shoe-button with a metal shank. She found a bird-skeleton, quite fresh, bashed flat, with a few feathers glued to it. She found ambivalent shards and several teeth, of varying sizes and shapes. She found – spread around, half-hidden by roots, stained green but glinting white – a collection of small bones, finger-bones, tiny toes, a rib, and finally what might be a brain-pan and brow. She thought of putting them in her knapsack, and then thought she could not, and heaped them at the foot of a holly. She was not an anatomist. Some at least of the tiny bones might have been badger or fox.

She sat down on the earth, with her back against the fallen trunk. She thought that she should perhaps find something to dig a hole, to bury the little bones, but she didn't move. She thought, now I am watching myself as you do in a safe dream, but then, when I saw it, it was one of those appalling dreams, where you are inside, where you cannot get out. Except that it wasn't a dream.

It was the encounter with the Thing that had led her to deal professionally in dreams. Something which resembled unreality had walked – had rolled, had wound itself, had *lumbered* into reality, and she had seen it. She had been the reading child, but after the sight of the thing, she had not been able to inhabit the customary and charming unreality of books. She had become good at stud-ying what could not be seen. She took an interest in the dead, who inhabited real history. She was drawn to the invisible forces which moved in molecules and caused them to coagulate or dissipate. She had become a psychotherapist 'to be useful'. That was not quite accurate or sufficient as an explanation. The corner of the blanket that covered the unthinkable had been turned back enough for her to catch sight of it. She was in its world. It was not by accident that she had come to specialise in severely autistic children, children who twittered, or banged, or stared, who sat damp and absent on Penny's official lap and told her no dreams, discussed no projects. The world they knew was a real world. Often Penny thought it was *the* real world, from which even their desperate parents were at least partly shielded. Somebody had to occupy themselves with the hope-less. Penny felt she could. Most people couldn't. She could.

All the leaves of the forest began slowly to quaver and then to clatter. Far away there was the sound of something heavy, and sluggish, stirring. Penny sat very still and expectant. She heard the old blind rumble, she sniffed the old stink. It came from no direction; it was on both sides; it was all around; as though the Thing encompassed the wood, or as though it travelled in multiple fragments, as it was described in the old text. It was dark now. What was visible had no distinct colour, only shades of ink and elephant.

Now, thought Penny, and just as suddenly as it had begun, the turmoil ceased. It was as though the Thing had turned away; she could feel the tremble of the wood recede and become still. Quite suddenly, over the tree-tops, a huge disc of white-gold mounted and hung, deepening shadows, silvering edges. Penny remembered her father, standing in the cold light of the full moon, and saying wryly that the bombers would likely come tonight, there was a brilliant, cloudless full moon. He had vanished in an oven of red-yellow roaring, Penny had guessed, or been told, or imagined. Her mother had sent her away before allowing the fireman to speak, who had come with the news. She had been a creep-mouse on stairs and in cubby-holes, trying to overhear what was being imparted, to be given a fragment of reality with which to attach herself to the truth of her mother's pain. Her mother didn't, or couldn't, want her company. She caught odd phrases of talk – 'nothing really to identify', 'absolutely no doubt'. He had been a tired gentle man with ash in his trouser turn-ups. There had been a funeral. Penny remembered thinking there was nothing, or next to nothing, in the coffin his fellow-firemen shouldered, it went up so lightly, it was so easy to set down on the crematorium slab.

They had been living behind the black-out anyway, but her mother went on living behind drawn curtains long after the war was over.

She remembered someone inviting her to tea, to cheer her up. There had been indoor fireworks, saved from before the war. Chinese, set off in saucers. There had been a small conical Vesuvius, with a blue touch-paper and a pink and grey dragon painted on. It had done nothing but sputter until they had almost stopped looking, and then it spewed a coil of fantastically light ash, that rose and rose, becoming five or six times as large as the original, and then abruptly was still. Like a grey bun, or a very old turd. She began to cry. It was ungrateful of her. An effort had been made, to which she had not responded.

The moon had released the wood, it seemed. Penny stood up and brushed leaf mould off her clothes. She had been ready for it and it had not come. She did not know if she had wanted to defy it, or to see that it was as she had darkly remembered it; she felt obscurely disappointed to be released from the wood. But she accepted her release and found her way back to the fields and her village along liquid trails of moonlight.

The two women took the same train back to the city, but did not encounter each other until they got out. The passengers scurried and shuffled towards the exit, mostly heads down. Both women remembered how they had set out in the wartime dark, with their twig-legs and gas-masks. Both raised their heads as they neared the barrier, not in hope of being met, for they would not be, but automatically, to calculate where to go, and what to do. They saw each other's face in the cavernous gloom, two pale, recognisable rounds, far enough apart for speech, and even greetings, to be awkward. In the dimness they were reduced to similarity – dark eyeholes, set mouth. For a moment or two, they stood and simply stared. On that first occasion the station vault had been full of curling steam, and the air gritty with ash. Now, the blunt-nosed sleek diesel they had left was blue and gold under a layer of grime. They saw each other through that black imagined veil which grief, or pain, or despair hang over the visible world. They saw each other's face and thought of the unforgettable misery of the face they had seen in the forest. Each thought that the other was the witness, who made the Thing certainly real, who prevented her from slipping into the comfort of believing she had imagined it, or made it up. So they stared at each other, blankly and desperately, without acknowledgement, then picked up their baggage, and turned away into the crowd.

Penny found that the black veil had somehow become part of her vision. She thought constantly about faces, her father's, her mother's – neither of which would hold their form in her mind's eye. Primrose's face, the hopeful little girl, the woman staring up at her from the glass case, staring at her conspiratorially over the clotted cream. The blonde infant Alys, an ingratiating sweet smile. The half-human face of the Thing. She tried, as though everything depended on it, to remember that face completely, and suffered over the detail of the dreadful droop of its mouth, the exact inanity of its blind squinneying. Present faces were blank discs, shadowed moons. Her patients came and went, children lost, or busy, or trapped behind their masks of vagueness or anxiety or over-excitement. She was increasingly unable to distinguish one from another. The face of the Thing hung in her brain, jealously soliciting her attention, distracting her from dailiness. She had gone back to its place, and had not seen it. She needed to see it. Why she needed it, was because it was more real than she was. It would have been better not even to have glimpsed it, but their paths had crossed. It had trampled on her life, had sucked out her marrow, without noticing who or what she was. She would go and face it. What else was there, she asked herself, and answered herself, nothing.

So she made her way back, sitting alone in the train as the fields streaked past, drowsing through a century-long night under the cabbage-rose quilt in the B&B. This time she went in the old way, from the house, through the garden-gate; she found the old trail quickly, her sharp eye picked up the trace of its detritus, and soon enough she was back in the clearing, where her cairn of tiny bones by the tree-trunk was undisturbed. She gave a little sigh, dropped to her knees, and then sat with her back to the rotting wood and silently called the Thing. Almost immediately she sensed its perturbation, saw the trouble in the branches, heard the lumbering, smelt its ancient smell. It was a greyish, unremarkable day. She closed her eyes briefly as the noise and movement grew stronger. When it came, she would look it in the face, she would see what it was. She clasped her hands loosely in her lap. Her nerves relaxed. Her blood slowed. She was ready.

Primrose was in the shopping mall, putting out her circle of rainbow-coloured plastic chairs. She creaked as she bent over them. It was pouring with rain outside, but the mall was enclosed like a crystal palace in a casing of glass. The floor under the rainbow chairs was gleaming dappled marble. They were in front of a dimpling fountain, with lights shining up through the greenish water, making golden rings round the polished pebbles and wishing-coins that lay there. The little children collected round her: their mothers kissed them goodbye, told them to be good and quiet and listen to the nice lady. They had little transparent plastic cups of shining orange juice, and each had a biscuit in silver foil. They were all colours – black skin, brown skin, pink skin, freckled skin, pink jacket, yellow jacket, purple hood, scarlet hood. Some grinned and some whimpered, some wriggled, some were still. Primrose sat on the edge of the fountain. She had decided what to do. She smiled her best, most comfortable smile, and adjusted her golden locks. Listen to me, she told them, and I'll tell you something amazing, a story that's never been told before.

There were once two little girls who saw, believed they saw, a thing in a forest ...

GOOD PEOPLE

Maggie Gee

Maggie Gee (b. 1948) is a British novelist who has written eleven novels and a collection of short stories. She was the first female Chair of the Royal Society of Literature, and is now one of the Vice-Presidents of the organisation. Her 2003 novel, *The White Family*, was shortlisted for the Orange Prize. She was awarded an OBE in 2012.

Justine wondered, what is the good of these people?

Ten minutes to take-off. They were running late. To Justine, the plane smelled slightly of burning. (She had asked the stewards several times for an aspirin, but they were busy fussing with the old and the young, pillows for two ancient tortoises with sticks, colouring books for two fractious children, one of whom didn't seem quite normal. It wasn't pleasant; she looked away.)

The man came down the gangway at the edge of her vision, hauling his flight-bag, short jacket, lean hips. She sent a silent text message, *sit by me*. It was a nine-hour flight home. She had missed her husband badly while writing her piece on 'Unseen Kampala'.

As the stranger grew nearer, scanning the seat numbers, his image snapped into sharp focus. Hair very black for the colour of his skin. Dark as his sun-glasses. Skin taut. Jaw clenched.

He took the window seat beside her. The smile he gave her was formal, wary. 'Excuse me, ma'am.' He took off his glasses. Sharp against the African sun in the window, the line of his cheek was a clear white cliff. His forehead was remark-ably clear and unlined. Older than she thought, perhaps.

'We are waiting for a final check on a successfully replaced component in one of the turbines,' the captain crackled on the PA system. 'I hope we can still make our scheduled arrival time in London. Some high winds today but they should be behind us.'

The smell of burning seemed stronger, but she ignored it.

'How long have you been in Uganda?' she asked.

'Long enough,' the man answered. 'What a country.'

'I liked it,' she said. 'I loved the people.' Now he had come, her headache was going, though the snot-covered child was still wailing in the arms of one of the blandly smiling stewards.

'Oh there are good people,' he agreed. 'I was lucky enough to work with some very good people.'

'This year was my first time in Africa,' she offered. His teeth were very white and even.

*

Half an hour later they were still on the tarmac. The captain had announced the engineer's arrival. The two stewards were bent over a Ugandan mother with big twin babies who were crying lustily. No one had remembered to bring her aspirin. Reassuring music on a faintly snagged tape puffed cloudlets of travel, escape, romance, into the warm air above their heads.

The economy seats seemed very close together. She was inches away from the stranger's lean thighs. She wondered, craning round for a second at the tens of human beings, belted in, pacified, but buzzing very faintly with desire and frustration, what would happen if suddenly they all released themselves, curled into pairs and made love to each other? She found herself remembering the fault in the turbine. No one could leave now. The great doors were fastened.

The man had been talking; Justine only half listened. There was something slightly odd about the skin under his ears. Money had been stolen from his hotel room, one of the hundred-dollar bills in his jacket.

'Of course, they're poor,' she interrupted. 'It must be hard to see so many rich foreigners.' She saw his mouth twitch with impatience.

'Way I see it, there's right and wrong. If we blur that line, we all get confused. And the Bible can help us with –'

'What do you do?' she interrupted again. The plane was quivering, gathering itself. The strange child pealed with eerie laughter. She heard a steward say 'Good boy' as he hurried past to his position for take-off.

'Pardon me? I'm a freelance evangelist.'

Suddenly the engine note screamed to a climax and they were roaring full-tilt down the runway. The nose rose steeply into blue heaven.

'A freelance evangelist? Oh, I see.'

Perhaps stung by her tone of voice, he began telling her what he had been doing. 'I was working with Mrs Museveni's people. You know, the president's wife? They're good people, around Janet.' The project had been AIDS education.

Justine rushed to show she could relate to this. 'It's so impressive, how Uganda is handling it. AIDS posters all over the place. Were you encouraging them to use protection?'

'Well, first of all, let's get the basics straight. See, I believe the Bible is the Word of God. And the Bible tells us to be pure until marriage –'

'I respect what you're saying,' she said, untruthfully, and raised her voice slightly, putting him right. 'But the reality is, young people have bodies, and their bodies push them in a certain direction.'

'And their souls, ma'am? Shouldn't we be saving their souls?'

The molten lake. The dark flames of hell. She drew a deep breath and prepared to refute him, but the captain came on, sounding cheerful and English. A little light turbulence: fasten your seat-belts.

They sat in silence, turned away from each other. The seat-belt sign went off again. Then the lunch trolley pulled them in the same direction. She wanted the wine, but she didn't want him judging her. 'Just water, please,' the evangelist said. The stewardess had a kind, tired face. The plane juddered and she lurched sideways. 'Are you okay ma'am?' the evangelist asked. A steward came and helped his colleague straighten her trolley, where a dozen little bottles had toppled over, and patted her uniformed arm, consoling. The seat-belt indicator flicked back to life.

Angrily, Justine snatched the red wine, giving the small bottle a rather silly flourish. *I don't have to be a good girl any more.* Once she'd taken a deep drink, she was ready to confront him. 'Did you say Janet Museveni? The president's wife? They say the government is deeply corrupt. Wasn't it a problem working with them?'

His expression of annoyance came slowly, with effort, as if it was pulling against bands of tight tissue, as if his whole head was muscle-bound. 'What I can tell you is that these are good people. All the people round Janet are saved.'

Justine sat there watching him drink his water and read his book: *The Fire this Time.* The sun had moved, and fell directly on him. With a little shiver of triumph and horror, she began to understand his face again, the lean, craggy jaw, the smoothed pale skin. His hair and eyebrows were carefully dyed. His features had all been shifted slightly, spring-cleaned, tightened, purified. She remembered, with a jolt, watching Ugandan TV. A snowy-haired, arthritic, spruce evangelist, a tiny moon-man who must have been near eighty, had solicited gifts of $70, more than the average Ugandan annual income. He had no lines; his eyes were badly skewed.

They're all the same, she thought. Liars. Inhuman. They will not grow old, like the rest of us.

At that moment, the plane fell out of the air.

People were screaming, and a trolley crashed past them, and something hard hit her on the shoulder. Everything was changed, in violent motion. The world left them, they began again –

their arms came together, and they clutched each other's hands, clutched and held, and the plane fell further –

flesh and bone, they gripped each other she was praying to everything and nothing to save her, to some God of love who cared if she fell, to anyone who loved her, to the universe, the great blue unsteadiness outside their thin shell, but it was her neighbour's hand that held her, and she held him –

then the plane stopped falling.

In the relative silence, someone was moaning. A child, or a woman, began to cry. A stewardess lay half under a trolley. The lockers had spewed forth some of their bags. But the engines were still working. There was no fire. Remarkably few people seemed to be hurt. Her neck felt bad, but she could look around. The plane moved confidently through bumpy air.

Now the captain came on to reassure them, sounding out of breath, but more English than ever. Sorry he had not seen that coming. Fortunately able to pull her up again. 'I gather there's some cleaning up to be done, but I hope you will enjoy the rest of the flight.' There was scattered clapping; one man shouted 'Well done.' Then the volume of talk became deafening. Two stewards, glistening with perspiration, something wild about their pupils, came down the aisle, checking who was hurt, calming people down, handing out bandages and consolation.

Justine and her neighbour remembered they were touching, and smiled at each other, washed clean by terror, and gingerly let each other go.

'Thank the Lord,' he said, but his voice was different, his pressed blue shirt black with sweat.

Garrulous with relief she began to tell a story. All round the plane, people turned to each other, talked about what was important to them, the things they had felt in the dying moments which had suddenly, sweetly lifted back into living.

'What you said about the thief who took your hundred-dollar bill. Nothing like that ever happened to me. But one day I got on the wrong *matatu*, and it dropped me off in a rough part of Kampala ... I was being jostled in a crowd of people, and suddenly an old woman pressed up close to me and shouted, in English, "She's with me! She's with me!" and put her arm around me, and said "That youth want to take your bag" and pointed to a thin boy running away. Then she walked with me to some better streets. She did all that to help a stranger. I said "God bless you" from the bottom of my heart. When she left me she asked "Are you saved?" And you know, I'm not religious the way you are,' (she smiled, tried to catch his eye) 'but I told her "Yes," because she *had* saved me.'

The evangelist shifted, his face a reproof. 'But ma'am, excuse me, you are not saved.'

'It was a white lie,' Justine cried, indignant.

'It was false witness,' he insisted.

Her voice rose shrilly in self-defence. 'But when the plane was falling, weren't we both praying? What about love? That woman showed me love.'

Then, angered by the haloes of ice in his eyes, neat in their tight new wallets of skin, she reached out and took his hand again, reached out and locked his fingers in hers, palping him to warmth as he resisted, and he pulled away restrainedly, because she was a woman, but she held him, mercilessly, making him love her, and after a bit she saw he was weeping, but Justine held on, sure she was right, converting him, forcing him to see she was a good person.

(And hidden by their uniforms, unquestioning, the faithful stewards worked on in the background, quietly doing whatever was needed.)

THE CHILD

Ali Smith

Ali Smith (b. 1962) is a Scottish writer whose work has appeared in the *Guardian*, the *Scotsman* and the *Times Literary Supplement*. In 2007 she was elected a Fellow of the Royal Society of Literature. She has published five novels and four collections of short stories.

I went to Waitrose as usual in my lunchbreak to get the weekly stuff. I left my trolley by the vegetables and went to find bouquet garni for the soup. But when I came back to the vegetables again I couldn't find my trolley. It seemed to have been moved. In its place was someone else's shopping trolley, with a child sitting in the little child seat, its fat little legs through the leg-places.

Then I glanced into the trolley in which the child was sitting and saw in there the few things I'd already picked up: the three bags of oranges, the apricots, the organic apples, the folded copy of the Guardian and the tub of Kalamata olives. They were definitely my things. It was definitely my trolley.

The child in it was blond and curly-haired, very fair-skinned and flushed, big-cheeked like a cupid or a chub-fingered angel on a Christmas card or a child out of an old-fashioned English children's book, the kind of book where they wear sunhats to stop themselves getting sunstroke all the postwar summer. This child was wearing a little blue tracksuit with a hood and blue shoes and was quite clean, though a little crusty round the nose. Its lips were very pink and perfectly bow-shaped; its eyes were blue and clear and blank. It was an almost embarrassingly beautiful child.

Hello, I said. Where's your mother?

The child looked at me blankly.

I stood next to the potatoes and waited for a while. There were people shopping all round. One of them had clearly placed this child in my trolley and when he or she came to push the trolley away I could explain these were my things and we could swap trolleys or whatever and laugh about it and I could get on with my shopping as usual.

I stood for five minutes or so. After five minutes I wheeled the child in the trolley to the Customer Services desk.

I think someone somewhere may be looking for this, I said to the woman behind the desk, who was busy on a computer.

Looking for what, Madam? she said.

I presume you've had someone losing their mind over losing him, I said. I think it's a him. Blue for a boy, etc.

The Customer Services woman was called Marilyn Monroe. It said so on her name-badge.

Quite a name, I said pointing to the badge.

I'm sorry? she said.

Your name, I said. You know. Monroe, Marilyn.

Yes, she said. That's my name.

She looked at me like I was saying something dangerously foreign-sounding to her.

How exactly can I help you? she said in a singsong voice.

Well, as I say, this child, I said.

What a lovely boy! she said. He's very like his mum.

Well, I wouldn't know, I said. He's not mine.

Oh, she said. She looked offended. But he's so like you. Aren't you? Aren't you, darling? Aren't you, sweetheart?

She waved the curly red wire attached to her keyring at the child, who watched it swing inches away from its face, nonplussed. I couldn't imagine what she meant. The child looked nothing like me at all.

No, I said. I went round the corner to get something and when I got back to my trolley he was there, in it.

Oh, she said. She looked very surprised. We've had no reports of a missing child, she said.

She pressed some buttons on an intercom thing.

Hello? she said. It's Marilyn on Customers. Good, thanks, how are you? Anything up there on a missing child? No? Nothing on a child? Missing, or lost? Lady here claims she found one.

She put the intercom down. No, Madam, I'm afraid nobody's reported any child that's lost or missing, she said.

A small crowd had gathered behind us. He's adorable, one woman said. Is he your first?

He's not mine, I said.

How old is he? another said.

I don't know, I said.

You don't? she said. She looked shocked.

Aw, he's lovely, an old man, who seemed rather too poor a person to be shopping in Waitrose, said. He got a fifty-pence piece out of his pocket, held it up to me and said: Here you are. A piece of silver for good luck.

He tucked it into the child's shoe.

I wouldn't do that, Marilyn Monroe said. He'll get it out of there and swallow it and choke on it.

He'll never get it out of there, the old man said. Will you? You're a lovely boy. He's a lovely boy, he is. What's your name? What's his name? I bet you're like your dad. Is he like his dad, is he?

I've no idea, I said.

No idea! the old man said. Such a lovely boy! What a thing for his mum to say!

No, I said. Really. He's nothing to do with me, he's not mine. I just found him in my trolley when I came back with the—

At this point the child sitting in the trolley looked at me, raised its little fat arms in the air and said, straight at me: Mammuttm.

Everybody round me in the little circle of baby admirers looked at me. Some of them looked knowing and sly. One or two nodded at each other.

The child did it again. It reached its arms up, almost as if to pull itself up out of the trolley seat and lunge straight at me through the air.

Mummaam, it said.

The woman called Marilyn Monroe picked up her intercom again and spoke into it. Meanwhile the child had started to cry. It screamed and bawled. It shouted its word for mother at me over and over again and shook the trolley with its shouting.

Give him your car keys, a lady said. They love to play with car keys.

Bewildered, I gave the child my keys. It threw them to the ground and screamed all the more.

Lift him out, a woman in a Chanel suit said. He just wants a little cuddle.

It's not my child, I explained again. I've never seen it before in my life.

Here, she said.

She pulled the child out of the wire basket of the trolley seat, holding it at arm's length so her little suit wouldn't get smeared. It screamed even more as its legs came out of the wire seat; its face got redder and redder and the whole shop resounded with the screaming. (I was embarrassed. I felt peculiarly responsible. I'm so sorry, I said to the people round me.) The Chanel woman shoved the child hard into my arms. Immediately it put its arms around me and quietened to fretful cooing.

Jesus Christ, I said because I had never felt so powerful in all my life.

The crowd round us made knowing noises. See? a woman said. I nodded. There, the old man said. That'll always do it. You don't need to be scared, love. Such a pretty child, a passing woman said. The first three years are a nightmare, another said, wheeling her trolley past me towards the fine wines. Yes, Marilyn Monroe was saying into the intercom. Claiming it wasn't. Hers. But I think it's all right now. Isn't it Madam? All right now? Madam?

Yes, I said through a mouthful of the child's blond hair.

Go on home, love, the old man said. Give him his supper and he'll be right as rain.

Teething, a woman ten years younger than me said. She shook her head; she was a veteran. It can drive you crazy, she said, but it's not forever. Don't worry. Go home now and have a nice cup of herb tea and it'll all settle down, he'll be asleep as soon as you know it.

Yes, I said. Thanks very much. What a day.

A couple of women gave me encouraging smiles; one patted me on the arm. The old man patted me on the back, squeezed the child's foot inside its shoe. Fifty pence, he said. That used to be ten shillings. Long before your time, little soldier. Used to buy a week's worth of food, ten shillings did. In the old days, eh? Ah well, some things change and some others never do. Eh? Eh, Mum?

Yes. Ha ha. Don't I know it, I said shaking my head.

I carried the child out into the car park. It weighed a ton.

I thought about leaving it right there in the car park behind the recycling bins, where it couldn't do too much damage to itself and someone would easily find it before it starved or anything. But I knew that if I did this the people in the store would remember me and track me down after all the fuss we'd just had. So I laid it on the back seat of the car, buckled it in with one of the seatbelts and the blanket off the back window, and got in the front. I started the engine.

I would drive it out of town to one of the villages, I decided, and leave it there, on a doorstep or outside a shop or something, when no one was looking, where someone else would report it found and its real parents or whoever had lost it would be able to claim it back. I would have to leave it somewhere without being seen, though, so no one would think I was abandoning it.

Or I could simply take it straight to the police. But then I would be further implicated. Maybe the police would think I had stolen the child, especially now that I had left the supermarket openly carrying it as if it were mine after all.

I looked at my watch. I was already late for work.

I cruised out past the garden centre and towards the motorway and decided I'd turn left at the first signpost and deposit it in the first quiet, safe, vaguely-peopled place I found then race back into town. I stayed in the inside lane and watched for village signs.

You're a really rubbish driver, a voice said from the back of the car. I could do better than that, and I can't even drive. Are you for instance representative of all women drivers or is it just you among all women who's so rubbish at driving?

It was the child speaking. But it spoke with so surprisingly charming a little voice that it made me want to laugh, a voice as young and clear as a series of ringing bells arranged into a pretty melody. It said the complicated words, representative and for instance, with an innocence that sounded ancient, centuries old, and at the same time as if it had only just discovered their meaning and was trying out their usage and I was privileged to be present when it did.

I slewed the car over to the side of the motorway, switched the engine off and leaned over the front seat into the back. The child still lay there helpless, rolled up in the tartan blanket, held in place by the seatbelt. It didn't look old enough to be able to speak. It looked barely a year old.

It's terrible. Asylum-seekers and foreigners come here and take all our jobs and all our benefits, it said preternaturally, sweetly. They should all be sent back to where they come from.

There was a slight endearing lisp on the *s* sounds in the words asylum and seekers and foreigners and jobs and benefits and sent.

What? I said.

Can't you hear? Cloth in your ears? it said. The real terrorists are people who aren't properly English. They will sneak into football stadiums and blow up innocent Christian people supporting innocent English teams.

The little words slipped out of its ruby-red mouth. I could just see the glint of its little coming teeth.

It said: The pound is our rightful heritage. We deserve our heritage. Women shouldn't work if they're going to have babies. Women shouldn't work at all. It's not the natural order of things. And as for gay weddings. Don't make me laugh.

Then it laughed, blondly, beautifully, as if only for me. Its big blue eyes were open and looking straight up at me as if I were the most delightful thing it had ever seen.

I was enchanted. I laughed back.

From nowhere a black cloud crossed the sun over its face, it screwed up its eyes and kicked its legs, waved its one free arm around outside the blanket, its hand clenched in a tiny fist, and began to bawl and wail.

It's hungry, I thought and my hand went down to my shirt and before I knew what I was doing I was unbuttoning it, getting myself out, and planning how to ensure the child's later enrolment in one of the area's better secondary schools.

I turned the car around and headed for home. I had decided to keep the beautiful child. I would feed it. I would love it. The neighbours would be amazed that I had hidden a pregnancy from them so well, and everyone would agree that the child was the most beautiful child ever to grace our street. My father would dandle the child on his knee. About time too, he'd say. I thought you were never going to make me a grandfather. Now I can die happy.

The beautiful child's melodious voice, in its pure RP pronunciation, the pronunciation of a child who's already been to an excellent public school and learned how exactly to speak, broke in on my dream.

Why do women wear white on their wedding day? it asked from the back of the car.

What do you mean? I said.

Why do women wear white on their wedding day? it said again.

Because white signifies purity, I said. Because it signifies—

To match the stove and the fridge when they get home, the child interrupted. An Englishman, an Irishman, a Chineseman and a Jew are all in an aeroplane flying over the Atlantic.

What? I said.

What's the difference between a pussy and a cunt? the child said in its innocent pealing voice.

Language! please! I said.

I bought my mother-in-law a chair, but she refused to plug it in, the child said. I wouldn't say my mother-in-law is fat, but we had to stop buying her Malcolm X t-shirts because helicopters kept trying to land on her.

I hadn't heard a fat mother-in-law joke for more than twenty years. I laughed. I couldn't not.

Why did they send premenstrual women into the desert to fight the Iraqis? Because they can retain water for four days. What do you call an Iraqi with a paper bag over his head?

Right, I said. That's it. That's as far as I go.

I braked the car and stopped dead on the inside lane. Cars squealed and roared past us with their drivers leaning on their horns. I switched on the hazard lights. The child sighed.

You're so politically correct, it said behind me charmingly. And you're a terrible driver. How do you make a woman blind? Put a windscreen in front of her.

Ha ha, I said. That's an old one.

I took the B roads and drove to the middle of a dense wood. I opened the back door of the car and bundled the beautiful blond child out. I locked the car.

I carried the child for half a mile or so until I found a sheltered spot, where I left it in the tartan blanket under the trees.

I've been here before, you know, the child told me. S'not my first time.

Goodbye, I said. I hope wild animals find you and raise you well.

I drove home.

But all that night I couldn't stop thinking about the helpless child in the woods, in the cold, with nothing to eat and nobody knowing it was there. I got up at four a.m. and wandered round in my bedroom. Sick with worry, I drove back out to the wood road, stopped the car in exactly the same place and walked the half-mile back into the trees.

There was the child, still there, still wrapped in the tartan travel rug.

You took your time, it said. I'm fine, thanks for asking. I knew you'd be back. You can't resist me.

I put it in the back seat of the car again.

Here we go again. Where to now? the child said.

Guess, I said.

Can we go somewhere with broadband or wifi so I can look at some porn? the beautiful child said beautifully.

I drove to the next city and pulled into the first supermarket car park I passed. It was 6.45 a.m. and it was open.

Ooh, the child said. My first 24-hour Tesco's. I've had an Asda and a Sainsbury's and a Waitrose but I've not been to a Tesco's before.

I pulled the brim of my hat down over my eyes to evade being identifiable on the CCTV and carried the tartan bundle in through the out doors when two other people were leaving. The supermarket was very quiet but there was a reasonable number of people shopping. I found a trolley, half-full of good things, French butter, Italian olive oil, a folded new copy of the Guardian, left standing in the biscuits aisle, and emptied the child into it out of the blanket, slipped its pretty little legs in through the gaps in the child-seat.

There you go, I said. Good luck. All the best. I hope you get what you need.

I know what you need all right, the child whispered after me, but quietly, in case anybody should hear. Psst, it hissed. What do you call a woman with two brain cells? Pregnant! Why were shopping trolleys invented? To teach women to walk on their hind legs!

Then it laughed its charming peal of a pure childish laugh and I slipped away out of the aisle and out of the doors past the shopgirls cutting open the plastic binding on the morning's new tabloids and arranging them on the newspaper shelves, and out of the supermarket, back to my car, and out of the car park, while all over England the bells rang out in the morning churches and the British birdsong welcomed the new day, God in his heaven, and all being right with the world.

STORY OF MY LIFE

A. L. Kennedy

A. L. Kennedy (b. 1965) is a Scottish writer, known for her characteristically dark tone, which blends realism and fantasy. She has written six novels and six short story collections as well as non-fiction and screenplays. She won the Costa Book of the Year award in 2007 for her novel *Day*.

In this story, I'm like you.

Roughly and on average, I am the same: the same as you.

The same is good. The same is that for which we're meant. It's comforting and gently ties us, makes us unified and neat and it tells us the most pleasant kinds of story, the ones that say how beautifully we fit, the ones that summon up their own attention, make us look.

I understand this.

I understand a lot – very often – almost, all the time – most especially the stories. They are an exercise of will: within them whatever I think, I can wish it to be. They are the worlds that obey me, kinder and finer worlds: in many of them, for example, I'd have no teeth.

Because I believe I'd do better with a beak. So why not have one? That shouldn't be impossible. I feel a beak could make me happy, quite extraordinarily content: sporting something dapper and useful in that line – handy for cracking walnuts, nipping fingers, tweezing seeds. Not that I've ever fancied eating seeds, but one can't predict the path of appetite.

And beaks come in different sizes: that's a plus, along with the range of designs. The toucan would be good for parties, shouting, grievous bodily harm. Ibis: mainly funerals and plumbing. Sparrow: best for online dating and eating crisps. The options, while not infinite, are extensive. In a reasonable world my personality would give rise to my true beak, would nurture it, my proper fit – parrot, hummingbird, bullfinch, albatross – and through it I'd express myself, be jauntily apparent fulfilled, really start going somewhere with my whole appearance – somewhere free from teeth – somewhere other than the dentist.

Story of my life – maybe – going to the dentist.

Because my teeth, they've always been ambitious, problematic, expansive. I never have had enough room for all of them and so out they've come: milk teeth, adult teeth, wisdom teeth: handfuls of them over the years, practically a whole piano's worth. Of course, when I was a kid they still gave you gas for extractions – general, potentially fatal, anaesthetic gas administered, in my case, by an elderly man with unhygienically hairy ears who would bend in at me, eerily grinning, and exclaim – every single time – 'Good Lord, dearie, they're some size, those teeth,' while he flourished that black rubber mask and then cupped me under it, trapped my mouth in one hard, chilly pounce: 'Breathe deeply, dearie. Count backwards from ten.'

I'd shut my eyes and picture his tufted, werewolf earlobes and count until I'd reached as far as seven or so before I'd see these angles of tilting grey that folded in towards a centre point, bolted and sleeked at the backs of my eyes and then rolled me down and away to the dark.

Now, as it happens, I'm not good with chemicals. No choice here – I am made the way I'm made. Sensitive.

In the chair they'd give me nitrous oxide and it put me out nicely enough. I'd swim deep through a cartoony, bendy blank while the dentist did his work – the tugging, the twists – then I'd float straight back up and just bob at the surface like a tiny shore-leave sailor: changeable and land-sick and absolutely smashed.

My first experience of the freedom within incapacity.

That swoop and rock and thunder of delight. It's always best to meet your pleasures before you can tell what they mean.

As I came round some nurse would be attending with her kidney dish and towels: a bit broody perhaps, protective – the motherly type but not a mother and therefore idealistic, if not ridiculous, about kids. She would, shall we say, not entirely expect the violence of my post-operative dismay: my tiny swinging fists and my confusion, my not unjustifiable sense of loss.

I have no idea what I shouted on these occasions – a small person turning expansive, losing it, throwing it, swarming clear out into beautiful rage. I'll pretend, while I tell you the story, that I know.

I'll say I produced – at great speed and with feeling – 'You get away from me! I'll have you! I'll set the Clangers on you. And Bagpuss! Taking my teeth out ... no one ever takes *me* out – except to the dentist – to take out more teeth. I need my teeth for the Tooth Fairy – I'm only five, for Chrissake – that's my one source of income, right there. How else can I save up to run away from here? I could go on the stage – be a sideshow – my manager would want me absolutely as I am – *the Shark Tooth Girl: the more you pull, the more she grows: ivory from head to toes*. I'd be laughing. With all of my teeth, I'd be laughing.'

This is untrue, but diagnostic – it helps to make me plain.

Because I wouldn't ever want to hide from you.

The surprise of my own blood, that's true – thick and live and oddly tasty – I never did get used to that, my inside being outside – on my face, my hands. Even today, if I take a tumble, suffer a lapse, my blood can halt and then amaze me. It's almost hypnotic – seeing myself run. And persons of my type, we run so easily: birds' hearts thumping in us and broad veins full of shocks.

Back from the surgery, next came the hangover – naturally, naturally, naturally – but as I was a child it would be kind, more a mild type of fog than a headache. Beyond it I'd be given soldiers with boiled eggs, gentle food for an affronted mouth and a sudden hunger – oh, such a lively hunger – and a quiet mother comfort to meet it with a little spoon. Then a bath and an early night pelting with lurid dreams of thieves and tunnels and running for my life, right through my life and out the other side and into nowhere: the coppery taste of absence, liquid heat.

Once I was older, I decided I had no more time to waste – people to do and things to be – and avoiding the dental issue became attractive. I brushed regularly, kept my head down, ate everything wholemeal for added wear, but it did no good: my teeth are forceful. They insist.

So when I'm twenty-four, twenty-five, I'm back in the surgery – new dentist – and the first of my wisdom teeth is leaving. Local anaesthetic this time, much more practical and safe, and I haven't enjoyed the injections, but I'm hoping they'll do the trick – mostly my eye's gone a little blurry, but that's nothing to fret about – and here comes the dentist – big man, meaty forearms, substantial grip – and it's plain that he'll check now, tap about to see if I'm numb and therefore happy – except he doesn't. He does not.

And I should pause here briefly, because it lets the story breathe and even possibly give a wink. I step back to let you step forward and see what's next. This way you'll stay with us. With me.

Which is the point.

You staying with me is the point.

And, no, the dentist doesn't check, he is incurious and generally impatient, goes at it fiercely with the pliers and no preamble and here comes a clatter, a turning yank, and then tooth – I am looking at my tooth without me, grinning redly in the light – and I am puzzled because of this feeling, this building feeling which I cannot quite identify – it is large, huge, and therefore moving rather slowly, takes a full *count backwards from tennineeight* to arrive and then I know, then I am wholly, supernaturally aware, I am certain in my soul that I'm in pain. This is hitherto unguessed-at pain – pain of the sort I have tried to anticipate and forestall with insulating activities and assistance. Numb is best – I always aim for numb, for numb of any type – but pain has found me anyway. Worse than imagination, here it is.

To be fair, the dentist was upset – looking down at me and saying, 'Oh, dear,' a number of times before offering a seat in his office and an explanation involving wrongly positioned nerves – it was technically my fault for having provided them. His secretary gave me a comforting and yet excruciating cup of tea.

I walked home – it wasn't far – dizzy and racing with adrenalin. They put it in the anaesthetic, presumably to give it extra zip. Which is to say that you go to the dentist – somebody worrying – and he then injects you with terror – pure fear – you feel it rush your arms, cup its lips hard over that bird inside your chest.

And it is possibly, conceivably, odd that this is so familiar, so really exactly the simple jolt of many mornings and you draw near to your house and wonder, as usual, if so much anxiety should not have a basis in fact. Perhaps a leak under your floorboards has caused rot, perhaps you're ill – genuinely threatened by what, as soon as they knew you weren't suing, your dentist and his secretary called *a head injury* – this making you feel very noble for not complaining, but nevertheless, in many ways it sounds dire. And if you really want to fret, then perhaps you shouldn't lend that guy your money – your guy, your money, but shouldn't they still be apart? You like them both but they should surely be apart? And what if he isn't exclusively your guy, you've had that unease, felt that whisper, about him before – and it's screaming today. And what if your life is, in some degree, wrong or maladjusted when hauling a live tooth raw from the bone leaves you and your state no worse than an average night, a convivial night, a pace or two along your path of joy.

Sensitivity you see? It causes thoughts.

When I reached the flat, I let myself in and sat on the sofa, hands holding each other to dampen their shake and keep out the sense of having gone astray: twenty-five and no real profession, no prudent strategy not much of a relationship.

And too many teeth.

But you try to keep cheery, don't you? And you have time. At twenty-five you've bags of it.

Thirty-five, that's a touch more unnerving – wake up with thirty-five and you'll find that it nags, expects things you don't have: kitchen extensions and dinner parties, DIY, the ability to send out Christmas cards signed *With love from both of us. With love from all of us.*

Instead I'm house-sitting for friends.

And this section of the story is here, for you to like and to let your liking spread to me. Frailty and failure, they're charismatic, they have a kind of nakedness that charms.

So.

Minding the house is company for me.

Well, it *isn't* company – the owners are obviously away, hence my minding – and they've left their cats. And this is domesticity without effort: Brazilian cleaning lady, leather cushions, large numbers of superfluous and troubling ornaments.

This isn't like me owning cats, me living alone with cats, me growing six-inch fingernails and giggling through the letter box when the pizza-delivery man comes, peering out at him and smelling of cats – that's not how it is.

There are these other people who are not me and they are the ones who have the cats and I am treating their animals politely but with an emotional distance, no dependency and no indications of despair. There should be no suggestion that these friends are sorry for me, that the husband is more sorry than the wife and that they have argued about my trustworthiness in their absence and their possessions and have doubted the supervisory skills of a Portuguese-speaking obsessive-compulsive who polishes their every surface twice a week: tables, glasses, apples, doorknobs, the skin between the end of the air and the beginning of my wine. I will not tell you they left behind them a plethora of mildly hysterical notes, or that their act of charity has been overshadowed by a sense of filth, oncoming sadness.

It is only important to mention that I was, on this particular house-sitting evening, chipper and at ease. I had fed both of the creatures and I was going out – out on a date – a variation on a theme of what could be a date. We had reached a transitional stage, the gentleman and I – which is to say, I had reached it and wondered if he had too – and I have to make the best of what I may get, so I was dressed presentably and poised to be charming and, had it not been for the stitches in my mouth, I would have been perfectly on form.

More dentistry – surgical dentistry but with mouthwash and antibiotics and painkillers – big ones.

I like them big.

So I'm all right.

I'm stylish.

And I slip into the restaurant – once I've found it – with what I consider to be grace and it's an agreeable establishment. Italian. So I can have pasta – which is soft.

And here's my date – my approaching a date – and he's looking terrific.

He's looking great. Like a new man.

Truly amazing.

He's looking practically as if he's someone else.

Yes.

Yes, he is.

He is someone else.

I am waving at someone else. The man I am meeting is sitting behind him and to the left and not waving. No one, to be accurate, *is* waving apart from me and I would love to stop waving, but have been distracted by the expression on my almost-date's face.

He is experiencing emotions which will not help me.

But I can still save the evening. I'm a fighter. I calmly and quietly explain the particular story which is presently myself: the drugs I am currently taking – prescribed drugs – the residual levels of discomfort, the trouble I have enunciating – and perhaps he might like to tell me about *his* week and I can listen.

People like it when you listen.

They have stories, too.

But he doesn't give me anything to hear.

And so I talk about my roots – *that* story – a little bit angry, because he should have been better than he is, should have been a comfort. My roots are 23 millimetres long, which is not unimpressive, is almost an inch. I tell him about my root canals. I summarise the activities involved in an apesectomy – the gum slicing, tissue peeling, the jaw drilling, the noise.

This is not romantic, because I no longer wish to be, not any more. I am watching a space just above his head and to the right where another part of my future is closing, folding into nowhere, tasting coppery and hot.

Could be worse, though: could be forty-five, when everything tilts and greys and comes to point behind your eyes and you have not run away, you have waited for the world to come towards you, given it chance after chance. And, besides this, you find it difficult to name what else you have done, or who is yours. After so many years you are aware of certain alterations, additions, the ones that would make you like everyone else, that would join you, tie you gently, allow you to fit.

But they don't make a story – they're only a list.

More dental adventure, that'll keep us right – another practice, another extraction, another tale to tell and that remaining wisdom tooth: it's shy, it lacks direction, the time has come to cut it out.

Cheery dentist, in this instance, talkative, 'This is an extremely straightforward operation. It is, of course, *oral surgery* but you'll be fully anaesthetised.' Which is frankly the least I would hope – and dialogue, that's always a boon – a voice beyond my own, someone in whom I can believe.

He puts his needle in, 'There we are …' and the numbness goes up to my eye. Again. Faulty wiring. So my mouth is now more painful than it was and I'm also half blind. 'Well, I'll just deal with that, then – there you go.'

Oh, that's better, that is good. Thass gread.

And this is my speaking voice, my out-loud voice, the one for everyone but you. *So it's in italics* – that way you'll know.

Thass bedder. Thass suffithiently aneasssetithed. You may protheed.

When we're in private – like now – and I say this, to no one but you, then italics are unnecessary.

We can be normal and alone.

'No, I think you need more than that.'

And this is where the dentist gives me more anaesthetic and I notice his hands smell a little like cornflakes – his gloves, they have this cornflaky scent – which is a detail that makes him seem credible and not simply a nightmare.

'Perhaps a touch more there.'

Whad? No, no thass a bid mush.

'And some more.'

Shurly nod?

'And more than that. Splendid.'

I can'd feed by arms.

'Of course, the effects of the anaesthetic will usually pass after three or four hours. But working so close to a nerve, as we will, in very unusual patients the numbness will pass in three or four …'

It would be tiresome to pause here.

So we won't.

'… months and in some extraordinary cases, you will be like that …

'… for the rest of your life.'

Unf?

'Here we go then.'

It's not that I don't appreciate the chance to feel nothing at all – but this isn't that – this is horror combined with paralysis – only very minutely exaggerated paralysis. I can't see to hit him, I can't fight him off and he's digging and drilling, drilling and digging and the extraction takes forty-five minutes.

Honestly.

That's how long it takes – no exaggeration.

There's blood in his hair.

It's mine.

Finally, I'm released, it's over, the stitches have been stitched, and I ran out of the surgery.

Well, I pay the bill and I run out of the surgery.

Well, I pay the bill and ask them to call me a cab and I run out of the surgery.

Well, I can't really run, but I leave the surgery as best I can and I wait for the cab in what happens to be a colourful urban area, one where relaxed gentlemen stroll the boulevards of an afternoon and possibly sing. Perhaps there may be vomit on a lapel here and there. Perhaps there may be vomit and no lapel. And

I'm standing – just about – and I can hear a relaxed gentleman coming along behind me.

He says something approaching, 'Hhaaaaa.' Which is not much of a story but is true and I know what he means because I can speak alcoholic. I have learned.

He reaches me and he says what might be expected – 'Scuse me cunyou spare twenny pence furra cuppa tea?' And I turn to him with my bleeding mouth and my lazy eye and my dodgy arm and my swollen tongue and I say, 'I don no. Havin a biddofa bad day mysel.'

So he gave me twenty pence.

And a slightly used sweet.

And a kiss.

It's best, if you can, to close up every story with a kiss. If you can.

Story of my life – maybe – going to the dentist.

The story that kept you here with me and that was true. In its essentials it was never anything other than true.

True as going to sleep tonight with the idea of blood beneath my tongue and meeting the old dreams of robbery and tunnels, the ones where I run straight through and beyond myself and on. And sometimes I wake up sore and wanting to set out nice fingers of bread and runny egg and avoiding the issue is always attractive, but I am tired of speaking languages that no one understands and I have only these words and no others and this makes my stories weak, impossible – impossible as the Christmas cards – *with love from all of us* – the night hugs and pyjamas, the tantrums and the lost shoes and the hoarding of eccentric objects: figurines, sea glass, washers: which are the kind of details that should not be discussed. They are impossible as hiding the so many ways that my insides leak out, show in my hands, my face.

Impossible as telling you a story of a new arrival – a small person, turning expansive – someone growing and beautiful, but not perfect, the story of their first trip to the dentist, their first real fear I'd want to drive away. My duty would be to ensure that we would conquer, because every pain is survivable, although it may leave us different, more densely ourselves. The child and I, we would be unafraid and we'd have stories and every one of them would. Start with

In this story you are not like me.

All of my life I'll take care we are never the same.

THE MAN ACROSS THE RIVER

Polly Samson

Polly Samson (b. 1962) is a British author, journalist and songwriter. As well as contributing stories to many anthologies, Samson has published two collections of short stories, *Lying in Bed*, and *Perfect Lives,* and a novel, *Out of the Picture*. She has also co-written lyrics with her husband David Gilmour for his band Pink Floyd.

'Fear grips me from behind, with a knife to my throat. Fear wears a dark cloak. He mourns, the loss of his wife. He's on drugs ...'

My mother laughs a little cruelly as she reads from the stapled sugar-paper book. It's a childhood dirge, yes, one of mine that she's just found in an old biscuit tin.

'They were always so full of terror.' She chuckles, turning the page with an air of confusion, and I try to raise my eyebrows at Simon in a *See what I have to put up with?* sort of a way without her noticing.

She has taken to wearing kaftans of Demis Roussos proportions of late and her hair hangs down her back in a single long grey plait: a bell-pull that secretly I long to tug. I silently thank Simon for ignoring Tim, his twin brother, when he advised him to take a long hard look at the mother before considering the daughter as a wife.

She reaches into the Peak Freans tin and unfolds another effort, clears her throat, ready to mock. It's about a dead jackdaw.

'What do you think of Mummy's poem?' she asks when the jackdaw is duly buried, possibly still alive, in the cruel black earth of my childhood imagination, but Angus and Ivan are more interested in picking the combination lock on her sweets and treasures box than listening to any poem.

'Do you know Mummy won a prize?'

'I had my name in the newspaper,' I tell the boys, who look at me blankly.

'It was for the poem that you wrote about cruise missiles,' my mother remembers. Simon snorts loudly into his mug of tea and she gives him that teacher's look of hers, only these days it rarely works as a corrective, it's just funny.

'Do you think the boys want to watch Cee-bee-bees?' she asks, clapping her hands together, and I almost grind my teeth as the boys jump down, crying: 'Cee-bee-bees! Cee-bee-bees!'

'It's really quite educational.' She leads them off, plait swinging, and as usual I wonder if she's playing an elaborate game.

'It's ridiculous,' I moan to Simon. 'I was never allowed to watch television.' Now she seems to revel in turning my children into couch potatoes. She even bought a DVD of an American television show purporting to be child-friendly science that, when they all watched it, turned out to be nothing but overgrown boys demonstrating massive ejaculations using the explosive properties of Mentos and Diet Cola. Bombs and sweets and America, all at the flick of a switch. What fun. And she buys them sweeties, or even *candy*, to cram into their mouths while they watch this stuff, though she draws the line at Haribo, which she tells them are made from boiled-down bones and will give them cancer. Then she has to explain to them about cancer.

'What sort of child writes poems about cruise missiles?' Simon asks, picking it out of the tin and holding it up. There's an illustration of a wire fence with a rabbit hanging from it, done in felt-tips, and I'm surprised to see how my writing used to slope backwards as though my letters were all trying to jam on the brakes.

Simon goes to her pantry for a loaf of bread so that we can all have toast. White sliced bread, I notice.

'Funnily enough,' I say, 'I can remember writing it.'

It had been fine and dusty that day, the ground hard beneath my flip-flops, the grass just beginning to get scorched, bright sun I could feel against my skin. I was pleased with my tan, I liked the tickle of the grass on my bare brown arms and legs and I had a small white dog at my heels, a rather bouncy and optimistic terrier that my mother had taken pity on.

Up at the cottage she was busy plotting the next revolution with her friend Suzanne. Their uniform was pretty standard dangly earrings and CND T-shirts, their brigade the militant wing of Primary School Teachers for Peace, against Coca-Cola, fur coats, fighting, whatever.

Suzanne had been my class teacher, as well as being my mother's first lieutenant and partner in placards, and was still in the habit of demanding that I write poetry. In those days I couldn't ask her to pass the salt without her thinking I should write about passing salt, though it was usually current affairs that my self-appointed muse felt should inspire me: starving Africans, homelessness, the sort of things that eleven-year-old girls are keen not to think about too much.

'You should write a poem about the cruise missiles,' she said to me that sunny afternoon. 'It would be interesting to have a child's-eye view of the danger.'

She and my mother had already scared me witless with stories of nuclear attack: it was all coming to Britain, they said, while gloomily sipping their rosehip tea. 'Bloody Americans again.'

Suzanne and my mother were considering going to Greenham Common for the holidays. 'We have to do our bit to stop them storing their missiles here,' they said. 'Sitting ducks we'll be. We have to go for the sake of our children,' and they looked at me cramming my mouth with peanut butter from a spoon and nodded.

I had seen Greenham Common on the news: the high fences and the righteous feral women, in the mud, arms linked, singing protest songs and shouting: 'Whose side are you on?' at the dead-eyed troops.

'I don't think I could live with myself another moment if I didn't do my bit to keep the missiles out.' My mother was emphatic and I didn't think I could live for another moment full stop if I had to stay and listen to another word. I slipped from my chair and headed for the door.

'It might be fun to live in a bender, take the kids,' Suzanne was saying and I thought how much more fun it would be if they all dropped dead. Suzanne's own children were much younger than me. One of each, with permanently encrusted nostrils. They looked like trolls with their fuzzy hair and the girl, whose name was Coriander, had a habit of following me around.

I knew from a home-educated girl with a lisp at Woodcraft Folk that a bender was an unglamorous tent made out of bent-over saplings and tarpaulin. She had already been to Greenham Common and the news from the front wasn't good: lavatories that were holes in the ground, 'everyone stinks like wet dogs'. I wondered why I couldn't just spend the summer on a beach somewhere with my dad.

I rolled up my vest in the way that my mother hated me to do and trudged along for a bit on the dirt track past the hazel woods, whipping the heads from weeds and long grass with a swishy branch I'd pulled from a sapling. The white terrier was doing its best to lighten me up, springing back and forth, bringing me the black corpse of a tennis ball that it'd found in the long grass.

Cruise was such a wind-in-the-hair carefree word, I thought, whipping the dry grass, sending little darts of grass-seed flying. Cruise. I choose. To amuse. There were rusty-brown butterflies at every footfall and birds singing, an endless sky that matched the faded denim of my cutoffs. I threw the ball and the dog jumped for it. I swung my arms, enjoying their length and slenderness and the near-burn of the sun on my shoulders.

Heading towards the river I decided that cruise missiles were probably bad in the way that sweets were bad for the teeth, and television, particularly American television, was bad for the soul.

I knew these fields well from walking with my mother. The farmer would be topping the grass for hay soon so I should try not to make tracks and opted for the well-trodden path along the riverbank. Until all this stuff about Greenham Common had arisen the long summer had stretched before me as blissfully as empty golden sands. I was dying for school to end. There were girls in the third form with spiteful nails. In the loos there were girls who waited for you to thump you, to write your name on the wall, to surround you and bruise you or nuke you with their words. Sign here if you hate so and so.

Cruise. The last thing I needed was another thing to be afraid of. The terrier ran for the ball and startled a duck who shot from the reeds, desperately calling to her ducklings who fell in two by two behind her, leaving chevrons in their wake.

Cruise, cruising by. The river was at its widest, practically a pool and smooth as glass. In the winter it flooded completely and the footpath was submerged in knee-deep water meadow, it even had a current running through it then. In the spring the drowned grass was flattened and feathered, littered with plastic bottles. But in the summer the grass was tall and unswayed with buttercups, and lily pads bloomed on the black river that ran through it, easing itself along the sloping bank from which some people swam, though not me because I never liked the ooze of mud between my toes.

I stopped for a moment on the bank and watched the river slip by, its glossy surface shirred by the breeze and stippled with small circles from darting insects. A pair of damselflies were disco dancers, dressed in blue sequins. The water lily buds looked fit to burst their corsets in the heat.

The bank on the opposite side of the river was in shadow and heavily wooded so I didn't see him at first. A couple of times as I wandered along the sunny side I thought I saw a flash of white in the woods and I later realised that this must have been the white of his T-shirt.

I could only look once. First, I saw his dogs snuffling around and then the man emerged between the trees. The dogs were large, not a breed I recognised, with muscular hind limbs and hacksawed tails. The man was powerfully built too, his white T-shirt looked stretched across his chest and he was holding a stick. His hair stuck up from his head, an army sort of style, so blond it was almost yellow. He didn't look like the sort of person that you normally encountered on a footpath and I was immediately glad that we had a river between us. It was the stick in his hand that spooked me most: it wasn't long and thin like a walking stick, nor was it the sort of rough stick that you might throw for a dog. His stick was squat and thick at the end like a baseball bat and he was holding it in front of his chest like he meant business.

I found myself walking a bit faster and calling to the little terrier, though I wasn't quite sure which way to head. Jumping beans had started in my stomach. I kept walking faster still and wondered if I was crazy to have this reaction to a man out walking his dogs. The spit in my mouth turned to paste as I tried to work out how far I was from the bridge that separated his side of the river from mine. I rounded the bend and the bleached carcass of the lightning oak came into view. The oak, I knew, wasn't far beyond the bridge; if I could see the bleached oak then the iron bridge that crossed the river was maybe five minutes away at a fast pace. I'd frightened myself enough by then to turn heel and started heading back in the direction I'd come, trying not to run at first. When I did run I felt foolish, almost cursing myself, my disbelieving legs disobeying me all the way.

They seemed to have taken on a life of their own: it was as though at each step my ankles and knees had become spongy, cartilage rather than bone. I tripped on a rut, my ankle twisted, and it was as I clambered back up on to my knees that I knew for sure that the man had indeed turned around and was keeping up because I could see his dogs reflected in the river.

I pounded along, not even aware of the pain in my ankle; I saw the dogs running, heard the crack of branches from across the water. Though we had left the lightning oak bridge far behind I knew there was another bridge, a stone one, just ahead. I was going to have to veer off the path and cut across the fields to get back to the cottage quickly; it would only be trespassing a little bit. It seems mad now that my degree of trespass should even have entered my mind. I might have done better to think about the barbed wire fences and hedges I would have to fight my way through. As I started to run up the field I heard a splash and turned to look back at the river. The two dogs were crouched over the bank, barking. The man's head appeared, breaking the surface like a seal; the sunlight hit the rivulets running off his shoulders as his arms parted the river around him in a muscular vee. He was shouting to me but I couldn't hear what as my heart hammered in my ears. It just sounded like, 'Oi oi oi.'

Fear gripped me. I ripped my thigh on the barbed wire of the first fence. I raced on, barely aware of the blood running down the inside of my leg and having to rid myself of my flip-flops which were getting tangled between the toes with grass, as if trying to run wasn't hard enough anyway. I fell over twice, expecting to see the man looming over me as I scrambled to my feet. I could hear his dogs bark and as I hurtled past the hazel copse I almost imagined I could see the shadow of his club, their breath at my heels.

I didn't go back to the river all summer long. It was restful to be in the company of the women and the girls at the camp, gathering firewood on the Common, singing songs, becoming gently smoked by the fire. I became skilled at fence rattling and chanting: 'Take the toys from the boys!' I wore tie-dye and rainbow braids in my hair. I enjoyed the singing but grew to hate the underwater sounds of the ululating at the fence.

We ate loads of apples and cheese instead of meals and I pretended not to mind when someone shouted 'Lesbians!' out of the car window while my mother and I were walking up the hot tarmac to find a standpipe.

When we packed up our stuff at the end of the summer I tied my floppy stuffed rabbit to the perimeter fence. The part of the fence where we camped was festooned with other people's toys and bras and babies' booties and bits and pieces that were supposed to remind everyone of peace. Suzanne's children tied their teddy bears to it. My mother handed me a shoelace and I fixed the small silky-eared rabbit to a higher part of the fence where it immediately hung its head like any other tatty thing. It seemed a pity then because I had slept with my nose pressed to its silky ears for every night I could remember.

I never told my mother about the man across the river because I couldn't be sure about what I had seen. It only happened a couple of weeks before we left for Greenham Common and my shame had grown by the day. I was first to switch on the local news every night and I scoured the county gazette. After a while I doubted myself more and more and the face of a drowning man started to surface in my dreams and I would wake with the sheets wound around my legs like weeds. When we moved later that year, though I had loved the cottage and my bedroom in the eaves, I was relieved that I would never have to go anywhere near the river again.

Simon puts the cruise missiles poem down. 'You poor little thing,' he says, ruffling my hair, and I nearly cry. From the other room we can hear the blare of Cee-bee-bees and Angus's throaty laugh. 'Daddy,' he calls.

I refold the poem and fix the lid back on the tin.

'Your mother wants to know if we're bringing the kids to the climate change demo on Sunday.' Simon's her messenger, returning to the kitchen with an article she's clipped from the *Guardian*. 'She said she thought we ought to.'

'Did you tell her that last week Angus had nightmares every night about the sun exploding?' I say.

Unlike my mother, I don't want Angus and Ivan to have to worry about cancer or have images of people jumping from burning tower blocks scorched into their retinas. I don't want the terror to live in the marrow of my children's growing bones.

Simon shrugs. 'It's climate change,' he says. 'It's all about them—'

I interrupt. 'They don't like crowds,' I say, and gesturing with my thumb towards the noise of canned laughter: 'And I'm not like her.'

Simon shushes me.

'Remember when Angus was a baby and we took him to the Iraq War demonstration in Hyde Park?' My mother has come back into the kitchen though she'd kicked her shoes off in the other room and I didn't hear her approach. 'You and Simon didn't dress properly,' she says.

'What?' I say.

'You were both freezing.' She says it as though somehow even in protesting we were deficient and I wonder if she overheard me telling Simon that I was different from her, telling him as though being different from her was something to boast about.

Remembering the demonstration makes me shiver. As it happens my clothing had been perfectly adequate against the clear cold day, as was Simon's: thick padded jackets, pashminas and hats. My mother worried that people taking photographs were from M15. 'Look at that man,' she kept saying when we'd finally come to a standstill with the crowds in the park. 'Dressed in tawny colours, big camera. He's not part of the protest. He's here to keep a record of the people.'

'Don't be so paranoid,' I said, laughing.

'Look, he's systematically moving along the lines. He doesn't look right.'

There were two million people in Hyde Park that day and not a single arrest. Having Angus in his pushchair made me feel historic, like Demeter charged with a flaming torch. It was his future we were all shouting about, my fists were aloft with the rest of them. Ken Livingstone called for peace, and I looked at Angus sleeping, wrapped safe and warm in his cocoon, just his palely beautiful face appearing from the folds like a Russian doll.

My mother was carrying a banner that said NOT IN MY NAME, and wearing a colourful Peruvian knitted hat with little woollen plaits that made her look like a rather incongruous schoolgirl. She met a woman in the crowd and they embraced. 'Yes, here we are again,' she said, shaking her woolly plaits. 'Nothing changes.'

It was during a lull in the speeches that she told me what she'd read in that morning's newspaper. Something grisly about a missing girl and a man who drove a butcher's van.

'Remember the one?' she asked. I shook my head. 'It was a green van. When we lived at Riversdale,' she prompted, raising her arm in a fist as high as her shoulder would allow her. 'Impeach Bush, Impeach Blair!'

'I thought you were vegetarians,' Simon said, blowing into his hands and putting them back into his pockets.

'We were vegetarians,' said my mother, as wistfully as a woman remembering her miniskirt days, 'but it didn't stop him calling. No matter how often I told him we didn't eat meat, he still called in the van every Friday.'

'Impeach Bush, Impeach Blair! It *stank* of meat,' she said.

'Sometimes, I think, he hunted deer with his dogs, and butchered them himself. Oh, what a horrible thought. It's been in all the newspapers, you know.'

Something small but monstrous was hatching in my memory.

'That's what the smell was,' she said, 'the venison. In the end I had to ring up the butcher and complain but I think he still came even after that.'

I thought I could picture the green van parked outside our cottage, the blond man hulked at the wheel. The thing that was hatching grew tentacles that slithered down the back of my neck.

'It's horrible to think of myself talking to him now,' she continued.

There was something glinting in my mother's eyes that made me think of a cat bringing a mouse to the door. 'It must have been around the same time that he did it,' she said, shuddering. 'Around the time he used to park outside our place. They only caught him because of his DNA on a completely separate charge.'

Just then Angus started to whimper. My breast tingled, filling with milk. It was as though it was a separate entity, beating to a different tune, with a different conductor from the other parts of my body. A man from the United Nations had just taken to the podium and a cheer went up from the crowd. The rest of me was running with ice but my only thought was that I would have to find a bench to sit down and produce warm milk to comfort my crying son.

AHEAD OF THE PACK

Helen Simpson

Helen Simpson (b. 1959) is a British novelist and short story writer. She worked at *Vogue* for five years before becoming a writer full-time. Her first collection, *Four Bare Legs in a Bed and Other Stories*, won The Sunday Times Young Writer of the Year award, and her second, *Hey Yeah Right Get A Life*, won the Hawthornden Prize. In 1993 she was selected as one of *Granta*'s top twenty novelists under the age of forty.

Thank you for making the time to see me. I do appreciate how busy you are; so, I'll talk fast! I'd like you to think of this presentation as a hundred metre dash.

Yes, you're right, it can be difficult to find finance for a new idea. But not in this case. I'm far more concerned about someone stealing this idea than turning it down, to be honest; which is why I want to tie up a joint venture agreement as soon as possible. By the end of the week, preferably.

So. A little bit about where I'm coming from first. My original background was in TEFL, then in PR for various NGOs – I've had something of a portfolio career – but in the last decade I have concentrated on developing my motivational skills in the areas of personal training and weight loss. I'm a zeitgeisty sort of person and I've found I have this unerring instinct for homing in on what the next big thing will be. You could say I was like a canary in a mineshaft – but more positive, I hope!

The next big thing? Carbon dioxide is the next big thing! Yes, I am talking global warming, but please don't glaze over quite yet. Yes, I do know how boring it is, how much of a downer it can be but bear with me for the next seven minutes and I promise you'll be glad you did so.

I know, I know, there are still some people who say it isn't really happening, but they're like my weight-loss clients who say, 'It's glandular' or 'I've got big bones'. What they're really saying is, they're not ready to change. Whereas the client who *is* ready to change is very often the one who's had a nasty scare. My prize slimmer is a man who'd been living high for years and then a routine scan revealed completely furred-up carotid arteries. He had a great sense of humour, he used to wear a T-shirt with 'I Ate All the Pies' on it, but underneath his heart was breaking. Literally. At twenty stone he was threatened with the very real prospect of a triple bypass, not to mention a double knee replacement, early-onset diabetes and gout.

Now, another client in a similar situation might have chosen to ignore the warning; opted to dig his grave with his own teeth, basically. I've seen that happen, I've been to the funeral. Fair enough, their choice. This man, though – a well-known local entrepreneur as it happens (no, I'm sorry, client confidentiality, I'm sure you'll understand) – this man directed his considerable drive towards losing seven stone over ten months, and as a matter of fact he finished in the first thirty-five thousand in this year's London Marathon.

And my point is? My point is: either we can carry on stuffing our faces and piling it on; or we can decide to lose weight. We've suddenly acquired this huge communal spare tyre of greenhouse gases; our bingeing has made the planet morbidly obese and breathless. Food, fuel; same difference. See where I'm coming from? And that was my eureka moment, when I realised that what's needed is a global slimming club.

I thought of calling it *Team Hundred*, because we in the motivational world have a belief that it takes a hundred days to change a habit; plus, there are only a hundred months left in which to save the world, apparently. Then I tried *Enough's Enough*, but *that* was too strict, and possibly a teensy bit judgemental. Finally I came up with *Ahead of the Pack*, which I think you'll agree sounds both positive and urgent plus it has the necessary lean competitive edge. Perfect!

It's simply a matter of time before it's compulsory for everyone, but those who've managed to adapt by choice, in advance, will be at a huge advantage. Ahead of the Pack! I mean, think of the difference between someone who's achieved gradual weight loss by adjusting their portion size and refusing second helpings, and someone else who's wolfed down everything but the kitchen sink for years and years and then wonders why he needs gastric banding. I know which one I'd rather be.

Yes, you're right, that is exactly what I'm proposing – to set up as a personal Carbon Coach! In fact, I think you'll find that very soon it'll he mandatory for every company to employ an in-house Emissions Expert, so you might well find me useful here too in the not-too-distant future, if we're counting our chickens. The thing is, I have this programme tailor-made and ready to rock. I've already test-driven it for free on several of my clients, and it's been fantastic.

First off I take their measurements, calculate the size of their carbon footprint – very like the BMI test, obviously, as carbon dioxide is measured in kilos too – and work out how far outside the healthy range they've strayed. We talk about why shortcuts don't work. Carbon capture and control pants, for example, squash the bad stuff out of sight rather than make it disappear. And, somehow, magic solutions like fat-busting drugs and air-scrubbers always seem to bring a nasty rash of side-effects with them.

Anyway, we visit the fridge next, discuss the long-distance Braeburn apples and the Antipodean leg of lamb, calculate their atmospheric calorie content. My clients generally pride themselves on their healthy eating habits and they're amazed when I tell them that a flight from New Zealand is the equivalent of scoffing down two whole chocolate fudge cakes and an entire wheel of Brie. We move on, room by room, talking weight loss as we go, how to organise loft insulation, where to find a local organic-box scheme; I give advice on fitting a Hippo in the loo, and practical help with editing photo albums.

Photo albums? Oh yes. Very important.

In ten years' time we'll be casting around for scapegoats. Children will be accusing parents, and wise parents will have disappeared all visual evidence of Dad's gap year in South America and Mum on Ayers Rock and the whole gang over in Florida waiting in line to shake Mickey's hand. Junk your fatso habits now, I advise them, get ahead of the pack, or you'll find yourself exposed – as hypocritical as a Victorian adjusting his antimacassars while the sweep's boy chokes to death up the chimney. Nobody will be able to plead ignorance, either. We can all see what's happening, on a daily basis, on television.

And if they have a second home I advise them to sell it immediately – sooner, if the second home is abroad. Of course! Instant coronary time! Talk about a hot potato.

Really? Oh. Oh.

I hear what you're saying. You think I'm going directly against my target client base with that advice. Yes. Well, maybe I do need to do some tweaking, some fine-tuning.

Basically though, and I'm aware that I've had my ten minutes, and I'd like to take this opportunity to thank you for your time – basically, is it your feeling that you're prepared to invest in *Ahead of the Pack*?

You'll get back to me on that one. I see. I see.

So, you happen to have a house near Perpignan, do you? Yes, it certainly is your hard-earned money. A bit of a wreck but if you can get there for twentynine pounds, why shouldn't you? No reason, no reason. O reason not the need, as Shakespeare says! As long as you know of course it means that, globally speaking, in terms of your planetary profile, you've got an absolutely vast arse.

TO BRIXTON BEACH

Stella Duffy

Stella Duffy (b. 1963) is a writer and performer, born in London and raised in New Zealand. She has written thirteen novels, ten plays and fifty short stories. Duffy has twice been longlisted for the Orange Prize, for her novels, *State of Happiness* and *The Room of Lost Things*. She is a member of the comedy improvisation company, Spontaneous Combustion.

There are images in the water. The pool holds them, has held them, since it was built in the thirties and before. And before that too, when there were ponds here, in the park, ponds the locals used to bathe in. Men at first, then men and women, separate bathing times, of course. A pond before the pool, a house with gardens before the park, perhaps a common before that, a field, a forest. We can go back for ever. And on, and on.

6 a.m. The first swimmers arrive, absurd to the gym-goers, the yoga-bunnies, those impatient, imperfect bodies readying for the cold, clear, cool.

When Charlie was a boy he and his brother Sid used to run all the way up from Kennington to swim, skipping out in the middle of the night, long hot summer nights, too sweaty in their little room, no mother there to watch over them anyway, sneaking off on their mate Bill's bike, to where the air was fresher, the trees greener, the sky and stars deeper, wider. And the pond so clean, green. Charlie hadn't been to the sea or to the mountains then, but the air in Brockwell Park felt cool enough.

8 a.m., the pre-office rush, pushing at the entrance desk, swimmers to the right, gym-ers to the left, one half to fast breath, hot body, pumping music, the other to cold, cool, clear.

Mid-morning and the local kids begin to arrive. Jayneen lives in the Barrier Block, in summer she and her friend Elise and Elise's cousin Monique go to the lido every day. They walk along streets named for poets, poets Monique has read too, poets she knows, smart girl, smart mouth an all, they walk in tiny shorts and tinier tops and they know what they do, and they laugh as they do it, as those boys slow down on the foolish too-small bikes they ride, slow down and look them up, look them lower, look them over. They three are all young woman skin and flesh showing and body ripe. And they know it, love it. The girls walk along and make their way to the lido that is Brixton Beach and they don't bother getting changed, they are not here to swim, Elise spent five hours last weekend getting her hair made fine in rows, tight and fine, she doesn't want to risk chlorine on that, they come to the lido to sit and soak up the sun and the admiring glances. Jayneen looks around, smoothing soft cocoa butter on her skin, as she does twice a day, every day, as she knows to do, and sucks her teeth at the skinny white girl over there by the café, all freckles and burned red, burned dry, silly sitting in the sun. Jayneen's skin is smooth and soft, she's taught Monique too, white girls need to oil their skin too. Maybe white girls need black mothers to teach them how to take care of themselves.

Charlie is in the water. He is already always in the water. Strong powerful strokes pulling him through. He slips past the young men who are running and cartwheeling into the pool, trying to get the girls' attention, trying not to get the lifeguard's attention, paying no attention to the long low deco lines. The young men look only at the curving lines on young women's bodies. Charlie finds himself thinking of young women and turns his attention back to water, to swimming hard and remembering how to breathe in water. He swims fast and strong up to the shallow end, avoids the squealing, screeching little ones, babes in arms, and turns back, to power on down, alone.

Lunchtime, the place is full. Midday office escapees, retired schoolteachers and half of Brixton market, rolled up Railton Road to get to the green, the water, the blue. One end of the café's outdoor tables over-taken with towels and baby bottles and children's soft toys, floating girls and boys in the water with the yummy mummies, wet mummies, hold me mummy, hold me.

Two babies hanging on to each arm. Helen can't believe it. This is not what she'd planned when she booked that first maternity leave, four years ago. Can it really be so long? She looks at her left hand where Sophia and her play-date Cassandra jump up and down, pumping her arm for dear life (dear god, who calls their daughter Cassandra? Foretelling the doom of the south London middle classes), while in her right arm she rocks the little rubber ring that Gideon and Katsuki hang on to. Helen shakes her head. Back in the day. Back in the office, loving those days in the office, she wondered what it would feel like, to be one of them, the East Dulwich mummies clogging cafés and footpaths with their designer buggies. She looks up as a shadow crosses her, it is Imogen, Cassandra's mother. Imogen is pointing to the table, surrounded by buggies. Their friends wave, lunch has arrived, Helen passes the children out one by one and immediately they start whirling, wanting this, wanting that, she can feel the looks, the disapproval from the swimmers who have come here for quiet and peace. Helen has become that mother. The one with the designer buggy. And she hates the lookers for making her feel it, and hates that she feels it. And she wouldn't give up her babies for anything. And they do need a buggy, and a big one at that, they're twins. (At least she didn't call them Castor and Pollux;) Helen can't win and she knows it. Sits down to her veggie burger. Orders a glass of wine anyway. After all.

Charlie swims, back and forth, back and forth. He lurches into the next lane to avoid the young men dive-bombing to impress the girls and irritate the life guards, makes his perfect turns between two young women squealing at the cold water. He swerves around slower swimmers, through groups of chattering children, he does not stop. Charlie is held in the water, only in the water.

3 p.m., a mid-afternoon lull. Margaret and Esther sit against the far wall, in direct sunlight, they have been here for five hours, moving to follow the sun. From inside the yoga studio they can hear the slow in and out breaths, the sounds of

bodies pulled and pushed into perfection. At seventy-six and eighty-one Marga-ret and Esther do not worry about perfection, though Margaret still has good legs and Esther is proud of her full head of perfectly white hair. Margaret looks down at her body, the sagging and whole right breast, the missing left. She had the mastectomy fifteen years ago, they spoke to her about reconstruction, but she wasn't much interested, nor in the prosthesis. Margaret likes her body as it is, scars, white hair, wrinkles, lived. She and Esther have been coming to the pool every summer, three times a week for fifty years, bar that bad patch when the council closed it in the 80s. They swim twenty lengths together, heads above the water, a slow breaststroke side by side because Esther likes to chat and keep her lovely hair dry. Then Esther gets out and Margaret swims another twenty herself, head down this time, breathing out in the water, screaming out in the water sometimes, back then, when it was harder, screaming in the water because it was the only time Esther couldn't hear her cry. It's better now, she is alive and delighted to be here, glad to be sharing another summer with the love of her life. Esther passes her a slice of ginger cake, buttered, and they sit back to watch the water. Two old ladies, holding age-spotted hands.

Charlie swims on.

5.30 p.m., just before the after-office rush. In the changing rooms, Ameena takes a deep breath as she unwraps her swimming costume from her towel. She sent away for it a week ago, when she knew she could no longer deny herself the water. It arrived yesterday. It is a beautiful, deep blue. It makes her think of water even to touch it, the texture is soft, silky. She has been hot for days, wants to give herself over to the water, to the pool. She slowly takes off her own clothes and replaces them as she does with the deep blue costume. When she has dressed in the two main pieces – swim pants and tunic – she goes to the mirror to pull on the hood, fully covering her hair. Three little girls stand and stare unashamedly. She smiles at them and takes the bravery of their stare for herself, holds her covered head high, walks through the now-quiet changing room, eyes glancing her way, conversations lowered, walks out to the pool in her deep blue burkini. Ameena loved swimming at school, has been denying herself the water since she decided to dress in full hijab. She does not want to deny herself any more. The burkini is her choice, the water her desire. She can have both, and will brave the stares to do so. In the water, Ameena looks like any other woman in a wetsuit, swims better than most, and gives herself over to the repetitive mantra that are her arms and legs, heart and lungs, working in unison. It is almost prayer and she is grateful.

Charlie swims two, three, four lengths in time with Ameena, and then their rhythm changes, one is out of sync with the other, they are separate again.

8 p.m., the café is almost full, the pool almost empty, a last few swimmers, defying the imploring calls of the lifeguards. Time to close up, time to get out. Diners clink wine glasses and look through fairy lights past the lightly stirring water to the gym, people on treadmills, on step machines, in ballet and spinning classes. Martin and Ayo order another beer each and shake their heads. They chose food and beer tonight. And will probably do so again tomorrow evening, they are well matched, well met.

It is quiet and dark night. Charlie swims on, unnoticed. Eventually the café is closed, the gym lights turned off, the cleaners have been and gone, the pool and the park are silent but for the foxes telling the night, tolling the hours with their screams. And a cat, watching.

Charlie climbs from the water now, his body his own again, reassembled from the wishing and the tears and the could be, might be, would be, from hope breathed out into water, from the grins of young men and the laughter of old women and the helpless, rolling giggles of toddlers on soft towels. Remade through summer laughter spilling over the poolside. He dresses. White shirt, long pants, baggy trousers falling over his toes, a waistcoat, tie just-spotted, just-knotted below the turned-up collar, then the too-tight jacket, his big shoes. Without the cane and the moustache and the bowler hat he was just another man, moving at his own pace, quietly through the water. With them, he is himself again. The Little Tramp walking away, back to Kennington, retracing the path he and Sid ran through summer nights to the welcome ponds of Brockwell Park.

Behind him the water holds the memory of a man moving through it in cool midnight, a celluloid pool which he flickers to life, and is gone.

EXTENDED COPYRIGHT